THE HELLFIRE CLUB

ALSO BY PETER STRAUB

NOVELS

Marriages
Under Venus
Julia
If You Could See Me Now
Ghost Story
Shadowland
Floating Dragon
The Talisman (with Stephen King)
Koko
Mystery
Mrs. God
The Throat

POETRY

Open Air
Leeson Park & Belsize Square

COLLECTIONS

Wild Animals
Houses Without Doors
Peter Straub's Ghosts (editor)

THE HELLFIRE CLUB

PETER STRAUB

HarperCollins*Publishers*

HarperCollins*Publishers*
77–85 Fulham Palace Road,
Hammersmith, London W6 8JB

Published by HarperCollins*Publishers* 1996
1 3 5 7 9 8 6 4 2

This edition published by arrangement
with Random House, New York

A catalogue record for this book is
available from the British Library

ISBN 0 00 225454 9

Set in Sabon

Printed and bound in
Great Britain by Caledonian International
Book Manufacturing Ltd, Glasgow

FOR

Benjamin and Emma

Hallucinations are also facts.

LOUIS ALTHUSSER, *The Future Lasts Forever*

CONTENTS

SHORELANDS, JULY 1938

An uncertain Agnes Brotherhood brought her mop, bucket, and carpet sweeper to the door of Gingerbread at nine-thirty in the morning, by which hour its only resident, the poet Katherine Mannheim, should have been dispatching a breakfast of dry toast and strong tea in the ground-floor kitchen. Agnes selected a key from the thick bunch looped to her waist, pushed it into the door, and the unlocked door swung open by itself. More uncertain than ever, Agnes bit her tongue and braved the interior.

She put her hands on her hips and bawled out the poet's name. No response came from anywhere in the cottage. Agnes went into the kitchen and was dismayed to find on the floor an enormous coffee stain which had dried during the night to a tough brown skin. She attacked the stain with mop and bucket. When she had worked her way upstairs, she aired out the unused bedrooms and changed the linen on the poet's rumpled but unoccupied bed.

On her way to Rapunzel and its two terrible occupants, one a penniless ferret, the other a pitted bull toad with wandering hands, Agnes ignored a Shorelands commandment and left Gingerbread's door unlocked.

An hour after lunch, the novelist Mr. Austryn Fain carried a chilled bottle of Shorelands' best Puligny Montrachet to the same door, knocked, tried the knob, slipped in, and peered into every room before taking the bottle back home to Pepper Pot. There he swigged half of the wine and hid the remainder in his closet to protect it from his more successful fellow novelist Mr. Merrick Favor, Pepper Pot's other inhabitant.

After dinner the following night, the Shorelands hostess, Georgina Weatherall, led a deputation of anxious guests across the lawn from Main House and up the path to Gingerbread. Georgina trained her flashlight on the keyhole and declared the door unlocked. Directly behind her, Mr. Fain wondered how she could tell this from a merely visual inspection. Georgina banged the door open, stamped into Gingerbread, and threw on all the lights.

The search party found some of Miss Mannheim's clothes in her closet, her toothbrush and other intimate things in the bathroom on the landing, a photograph of two small girls, pens, nibs, and ink bottle on the bedroom table, a few books stacked beside the bed Agnes had made up the previous morning. Over the coverlet lay a slate-gray silk robe, ripped about the arms. Georgina lifted the robe with two fingers, pursed her mouth, and let it drift back down onto the bed. "I am sorry to say," she announced, not at all sorry, "that Miss Mannheim appears to have jumped the wall."

No manuscript complete or incomplete was ever found, nor were any notes. Agnes Brotherhood never spoke of her misgivings until the early 1990s, when a murderer and a kidnapped woman were escorted into her invalid's room on the second floor of Main House.

BOOK I

BEFORE DAWN

In a time just before this time, a lost boy named Pippin Little awoke to deep night.

1

AT THREE O'CLOCK in the morning, a woman named Nora Chancel, soon to be lost, woke up from the usual nightmares with the usual shudder and began for the thousandth time to check her perimeter. Darkness; an unknown room in which she dimly made out two objects which could have been chairs, a long table mounted with a mirror, invisible pictures in frames, a spindly, inexplicable machine out of Rube Goldberg, and a low couch covered in striped fabric. Not only was none of this familiar, all of it was wrong. Wherever she was, she was *not safe*.

Nora propped herself up on an elbow and groped for an illicit handgun on permanent loan from a neurosurgeon named Harwich, who had rotated back to a world neither one of them could actually remember. She missed Dan Harwich, but of that one did not think. (Good old Dan Harwich had once said, *A bullet in the brain is better than a bullet in the belly.*) Nora's fingers slid across the sheet and rifled beneath pillow after pillow until bumping against the mattress seam at the other end of the bed. She rolled over and sat up, having just heard the sound of distant music.

Music?

Her own dark shape stared back from the mirror, and the present returned in a series of almost instantaneous recognitions. At home with her chairs, pictures, striped couch, and her husband's unused NordicTrack, Nora Chancel had again murdered the demons of the past by scrambling out of sleep in her bedroom on Crooked Mile Road in Westerholm, Connecticut, a fine little community, according to itself a completely *dandy* community, thank you, except for one particular present demon who had murdered a number of women. Someday, she hoped someday soon, this would end. Her husband had spent hours reassuring her that it would end. As soon as the FBI and the Westerholm police did their job, life would go back to normal, whatever that was. The demon would turn out to be an ordinary-looking man who sold bug zappers at the hardware store, who trimmed hedges and skimmed pools on Mount Avenue, who came to your house on Christmas morning and waved away a tip after fixing your gas burner. He lived with his mother and worked on his car in his spare time. At block parties, he was swell behind the grill. As far as Nora was concerned, half a dozen oversized policemen were welcome to take turns jumping up and down on his ribs until he drowned in his own blood. A woman with a wide, necessarily secret knowledge of demons, she had no illusions about how they should be treated.

The music downstairs sounded like a string quartet.

Davey was up, trying to fix things by making endless notes on a yellow pad. He would not or could not take the single action which would fix those things that could be fixed: he refused to confront his father. Or maybe he was lying down on the family room sofa, listening to Beethoven and drinking kümmel, his favorite author's favorite drink. Kümmel smelled like caraway seeds, and Hugo Driver must have reeked of caraway, a fact unmentioned in the biographies.

Davey often reeked of caraway on the nights when he climbed late into bed. Last night, it had been two when he made it upstairs; the night before, three-thirty. Nora knew the hours because both nights the familiar nightmares had sent her galloping out of sleep in search of an automatic pistol she had dropped into a latrine one blazing June day twenty-three years before.

The pistol lay rusting at the bottom of what was by now probably a Vietnamese field. Dan Harwich had divorced and remarried, events for which Nora considered herself partially responsible, without ever having stirred from Springfield, Massachusetts. He might as well have been rusting beneath a field, too. You couldn't fall in love that way twice; you couldn't do anything the same way twice, except in dreams. Dreams never gave up. Like tigers, they simply lay in wait until fresh meat came along.

2

DAVEY HAD KNOWN Natalie Weil, too. Half of Westerholm had known Natalie Weil. Two years ago, when she had sold them the three-bedroom raised ranch with downstairs "family room" on Crooked Mile Road, Natalie Weil had been a small, athletic-looking blonde perhaps ten years younger than Nora, a woman with a wide white smile, nice crinkles at the corners of her eyes, and a former husband named Norm. She smoked too much and drew spirals in the air with her hands when she talked. During the time when Nora and Davey were living in the guest wing of the Poplars on Mount Avenue with Alden and Daisy, the older Chancels, Natalie Weil had intuited the emotional atmosphere within the big house and invited her grateful charges for dinner at her own raised ranch house on Redcoat Road. There Nora and Davey had eaten chili and guacamole, drunk Mexican beer, and half-attended to wrestling matches on cable while Natalie anatomized, to their delight, the town where Nora's new husband had grown up. "See, you're from Mount Avenue, Davey, you see this town the way it was about fifty years ago, when everybody dressed for dinner and everybody stayed married forever and nobody knew any Jews. Forget it! These days they're all divorced or getting divorced, they move in and out of town when their company tells them to, they don't think about anything except money—oh my God, there's Ric Flair, one day I am going to humiliate myself and write him a really lurid fan letter. And we have three synagogues, all booming. Ric sweetie, could you be true to me?"

After selling them the house on Crooked Mile Road—a house paid for by Alden and Daisy Chancel—Natalie took them for lunch at the General Sherman Inn, advised them to fill the family room with babies as soon as possible, and disappeared from their lives. From time to time, Nora had seen her spiraling one hand in the air as she steered two new prospects up the Post Road in her boatlike red Lincoln. Six months ago, she had come across Natalie dumping frozen pizzas into a shopping cart already piled with six-packs of Mexican beer and Diet Coke, and for ten minutes they caught up with each other. Natalie had said yes, she was seeing someone, but, no, it wouldn't amount to anything, the guy was a prune. She would call Nora, you bet, it would be great to get away from the Prune.

Two nights before, Natalie Weil had disappeared from a blood-soaked bedroom. Her body had not been left behind, like those of the other four women, but Natalie was almost certainly as dead as they. Like Natalie, they were divorced businesswomen of one kind or another, and they lived alone. Sophie Brewer was an independent broker, Annabelle Austin a literary agent, Taylor Humphrey the owner of a driver-service company, Sally Michaelman the owner-operator of a lighting-supplies company. All these women were in their mid- to late forties. The younger Chancels had installed a security system soon after they moved into their new house, and after the first two deaths, on nights Davey came home late Nora punched in the code that turned it on before she went to bed. She kept all the doors locked when she was in the house. After Taylor Humphrey's murder, she began hitting the buttons as soon as it got dark.

Nora had heard about Sally Michaelman from an immaculate twenty-something two places in front of her at a checkout counter in Waldbaum's, the supermarket where she had last come across Natalie Weil. Nora first noticed the young woman because she had put on drop-dead makeup and a loose but perfectly fitted linen outfit to visit a supermarket at ten in the morning. She might have been drifting past fluted columns in an advertisement for a perfume named something like Arsenic. In the baggy shorts and old blue shirt she had changed into after her morning run, Nora leaned over her cart to see what the twenty-something had put on the belt: thirty cans of gourmet cat food and two bottles of Swedish water, now joined by a third.

"Her cleaning woman called my cleaning woman," she was saying to the woman behind her, also an armored twenty-something. "Can you believe this crap? It's that woman from Michaelman's, and I was in there last *week,* looking for a, you know—"

"That thing in your entry, that thing just inside the door."

"For something like *you* have. Her cleaning woman couldn't get in, and with all the, you know—"

She took in Nora, glared, and swooped into her cart to drop a bag of plums on the moving belt. "We might as well be living in the South *Bronx.*"

Nora remembered that woman from Michaelman's; she didn't know her name, but the woman had persuaded her to go ahead and buy the halogen lamp she wanted for the family room. She had been down-to-earth and handsome and comradely, the kind of person Nora instinctively thought of as a fellow traveler. Her first impulse was to defend this terrific woman to the two self-centered idiots in front of her, but what had they done besides call her that woman from Michaelman's? Her second impulse, almost simultaneous with the first, was to panic about whether or not she had locked the back door on her way to the car.

Then Nora had seen the bloody corpse of the terrific woman from the lamp store. This figure instantly mutated into that of a boy soldier on a gurney, his belly blown open and his life slipping out through his astonished eyes. Her knees turned to water, and she dropped her head, breathing hard until the twenty-somethings had moved away from the register.

The dying young man and others like him inhabited her better nightmares. The worse ones were much worse.

3

NORA DISMISSED THE nightmare, decidedly of the worse variety, and got out of bed. Because she wanted to look more in control of herself than Davey was likely to be, she rubbed her hands over her forehead and wiped her palms on her nightgown. Out in the hallway, the music no longer sounded like a string quartet. It had a wilder, more chaotic edge; Davey had put on one of the Mahler symphonies he had taught her to enjoy.

Nobody who did not enjoy classical music could stay married to Davey Chancel, who fled into music when troubled. Nora, the pride of the Curlews, had decided to marry Davey during his second proposal, six months after they met, one year after Springfield and her never-to-be-thought-of reunion with Dan Harwich.

Nora padded past a case filled with Chancel House books and reached the stairs to the front door. Beside it, the red light glowed reassuringly above the keypad of the security system. Nora went quietly down the stairs and checked that the door was still locked. When she started down the second set of stairs to the family room, the music came into focus. Indistinct voices sounded. She had been hearing a soundtrack. Davey, who never watched anything except the news, had turned on the television. She went down the last of the stairs, her sympathy hardening into anger. Again, Alden had again publicly humiliated his son.

She opened the family room door and leaned in. Startled but in no obvious distress, wide-eyed Davey stared at her, wearing a lightweight robe of Thai silk over his pajamas and holding a pencil upright over an open notebook. The surprise in his face echoed her own. "Oh, honey," he said, "did I wake you up?"

"Are you all right?" Nora padded into the room and glanced at the screen. A ragged old man waved a staff in front of a cave. *Pippin! Remember to be brave! You must be brave!*

Davey aimed the remote control at the set, and the soundtrack disappeared. "I didn't think you'd hear, I'm sorry." As neat as a cat in the even light of the halogen lamp, he placed the remote on top of the notebook and looked at her with what seemed like real remorse. "Today we ran into a problem, some nuisance Dad asked me to handle, and I thought I should watch this thing."

"It wasn't the TV. I woke up."

He tilted his head. "Like last night?" The question may not have been perfectly sympathetic.

"This business about Natalie—you know . . ." Nora cut herself off with a wave of a hand. "All the hags in Westerholm have trouble sleeping these days." She turned back to the television. A bedraggled boy of eight or nine shouldered a sack through a dripping swamp. Twisted, monstrous trees led into gleaming haze.

"And most of them have no more to worry about than you do."

Last night Davey had listed the reasons why Nora should not worry: she did not live alone or run a business; she did not open the door to strangers. If anyone suspicious turned up, she could push the panic button above the keypad. And, though this remained tactfully unstated, wasn't she overreacting, letting the old problems get to her all over again?

"I wondered where you were," she said.

"Well, now you know." He tapped his pencil against the notebook and managed to smile. Faced with a choice, he chose kindness. "You could watch this with me."

She sat beside him on the sofa. Davey patted her knee and focused on the movie.

"What is this?"

"*Night Journey.* You were making so much noise I got out of bed, and when I looked at the paper, I saw it was on. I have to see the thing anyhow, so I might as well do it now."

"You have to take notes on *Night Journey*?"

"We're having some trouble with the Driver estate." He pointed the remote at the screen and raised the volume. Distant in the hazy swamp, wolves howled. More peeved than she wished to be, Nora watched the boy make his way beneath the monstrous trees. "It'll be okay," Davey said. For an instant he took her hand. She squeezed it and tucked up her legs and rested her head on his shoulder. Davey twitched, signaling that she was not to lean on him.

Nora slid away and propped her head on the back of the sofa. "What kind of trouble?"

"Shh." He leaned forward and picked up the pencil.

So she was not to speak. So she was a distraction. For some reason Davey had to get out of bed in the middle of the night to take notes on the film version of *Night Journey,* Hugo Driver's wildly successful first novel and the cornerstone of Chancel House, founded by Lincoln Chancel, Davey's grandfather and Hugo Driver's friend. Davey, who took enormous pride in the association, had read *Night Journey* at least once a year since he was fifteen years old. Anyone less charitable than Nora might have said that he was obsessed with the book.

4

MANY WERE OBSESSED with Hugo Driver's first novel. One of Davey's occupations at Chancel House was answering the requests for photographs, assistance with term papers and theses, and other mail concerning the writer that flowed into the offices. These missives came from high school students, stockbrokers, truck drivers, social workers, secretaries, hairdressers, short-order cooks, ambulance drivers, people who signed their letters with the names of characters in the novel, also famous crazies and sociopaths. Leonard Gimmell, who had murdered the fourteen children in his second-grade class during an outing to the Smoky Mountains, wrote once a week from a state prison in Tennessee, and Teddy Brunhoven, who had appeared in front of a recording studio on West Fifty-fifth Street and assassinated the lead singer of a prominent rock and roll band, communicated almost daily from a cell in upper New York State. Both men continued to justify their crimes with complex, laborious references to the novel. Davey enjoyed responding to Hugo Driver's fan mail much more than the other duties, matters like crossword puzzles and paper plates, wished on him by his father.

Twice Nora had begun *Night Journey,* but she never made it past the chapter in which the boy hero succumbed to an illness and awakened to a landscape meant to represent death. Bored by fantasy novels, she could smell the approach of trolls and talking trees.

Davey also revered *Twilight Journey* and *Journey into Light,* the less successful sequels, but had opposed the decision to sell the film rights to *Night Journey.* On the movie's release a year ago, he had refused to see it. Any movie of the novel would be a failure, a betrayal. You could make good movies of second-rate books; movies based on great books left an embarrassing stink. Whether or not this rule was generally true, it had applied to *Night Journey.* Despite forty million dollars' worth of special effects and a cast of famous actors, the movie had been greeted by hostile reviews and empty theaters. It disappeared after two weeks, leaving behind the stink Davey had predicted.

5

FORBIDDEN TO SPEAK, Nora slumped back and watched the disaster unfurl. All that money had bought unconvincing trees, tattered clothes, and a great deal of fog. The boy came through the last of the trees and found himself on a desolate plain. Here and there, plaster boulders floated up out of silver mist. Distant wolves howled.

Bent over his notebook, Davey frowned like an earnest student taking notes in a class he didn't like. Seriousness and concentration increased the accidental likeness between them. At forty, he still had the large, clear eyes and almost translucent skin that had both attracted and repelled her when they had first met. Her first coherent thought about him, after she had adjusted to the unexpected resemblance between them, had been that his version of her face was *too* pretty. Any man who looked like that had to be impossibly vain. A lifetime of being indulged, petted, and admired would have made him selfish and shallow. Added to these insurmountable failings was his age. Men about ten years younger than herself were still blind, ambitious babies with everything to learn. Most damning of all, an envelope of ease and carelessness surrounded Davey Chancel. Her father, a foundry worker and lifelong union man, had known that such people were the enemy, and nothing she had seen or experienced had taught her otherwise.

Eventually Nora had learned that only the last of her first impressions had been correct. It was true that he had been born into a wealthy family, but Davey was too insecure to be vain. He had been mercilessly criticized, not coddled, all his life. Oddly vulnerable, he was thoughtful; his ambitions had to do with pleasing others and publishing good books. He had one quality that might have been considered a flaw, even a serious flaw, but Nora had decided that this was a *trait* rather than a serious problem. He was imaginative, and imagination, everyone agreed, was an exceedingly Good Thing. And he needed her. It had been seductive, being needed.

"It's like they set out to trash the book. Every single thing is wrong." He gave her an exasperated glance. "Whenever they come to a big moment, they squash it flat. Pay attention, you'll see what I mean."

Nora watched the boy trudge through the fog.

"The pace is all wrong, so is the *tone*. This should seem almost *exalted*. Everything should be filled with a kind of *radiance*. Instead of experiencing profound emotions, the kid looks like he's going out for a sandwich. I bet it's five minutes before we see Lord Night."

Nora had no idea who Lord Night was and in fact thought that Davey had said Lord Knight.

"He's going to plod along forever, and in the meantime, the Stones of Toon look totally fake." He made another note. "You saw Gentle Friend, didn't you? When you first came in?"

Nora supposed that the old man in rags must have been Gentle Friend. "I think so."

"That proves my point. *Driver's* Gentle Friend is a heroic aristocrat who has renounced the world, and this one's a dirty hermit. When he tells Pippin to be brave, you don't have the feeling that he knows any more about bravery than anyone else. But in the book . . . well, you know."

"Sure." Without ever telling an actual lie, Nora had allowed Davey to imagine that on her second attempt she had read the novel and seen that it was a masterpiece.

"Gentle Friend is passing on the central message of his life—that bravery has to be re-created daily. Because he knows it, Pippin can know it, too. In this travesty, the scene is pure cardboard. Okay, here comes Lord Night, completely wrong, of course."

A big, brindled animal that could have been either a dog or a wolf leaped onto the boulder in front of the boy. In pairs, dogs or wolves appeared on the other boulders. The boy looked up at the animals with an absence of expression which might have been intended to represent determination.

"Duh, and who, I wonder, might you be? See, you don't have any idea that *this* is why Pippin had to really *get it* about bravery. He has to prove himself to Lord Night, and he's scared out of his wits. Would that mutt scare you?"

"Probably," Nora said.

"Lord Night is scary, his teeth are like razors, he's magic. He's the reason for all the emotion that should have been, but *wasn't,* present at the start of this scene. We know we're supposed to meet this dangerous creature, and who shows up instead? Rin Tin Tin."

To Nora, the animal staring down from the rock looked exactly like a wolf. It had been fed before the scene, but just in case, its trainer had been standing immediately off camera with a tranquilizer gun. The wolf was the best thing in the movie. Utterly real, it was a lot more impressive than what it was supposed to be impersonating. The boy had so little expression on his face because he was too scared to act. He was a sensible boy.

Then Nora saw that Davey was right; the movie wolf was only a dog. She had turned him into the Wolf of Westerholm, the unknown man who had stolen away the corpse of funny, desperate, appealing Natalie Weil and murdered four other women. And the boy playing Pippin Little wasn't scared or sensible, he was just a lousy actor. Looking at him, she had seen her own fear.

"Of course they screw up the dialogue," Davey said. "Lord Night doesn't say, 'How are you called, child?' He *knows* his name. What he *says* is 'Pippin Little, do you travel with us tonight?' "

Some renegade part of Nora had overlooked the savagery of the unknown man to remark on his reality. The unknown man strolled here and there on Westerholm's pretty, tree-lined streets, delivering reminders. He was like war.

The animal in the movie opened his long mouth and said, "Will you come with us tonight, Pippin Little?"

Davey slapped his forehead. "I suppose they think that's an improvement."

Nora supposed that when she caught herself finding valuable moral lessons in murder it was time to get out. Year after year, Westerholm proved that Natalie Weil had been charitable about its pretensions. Leo Morris, their lawyer by virtue of being Alden and Daisy's lawyer, had chartered the *QE2*, all of it, for his daughter's sweet-sixteen party. One of their neighbors had installed a bathtub made of gold in the bathroom off the master bedroom and regularly invited his guests to step in and check it out.

For at least a year, an idea had been growing within Nora, retreating in the face of all the objections to be made against it, also in the face of Davey's certain rejection, and now this idea returned as a conviction. They had no business living here. They should sell the house and leave Westerholm. Alden and Daisy would bluster and rant, but Davey made enough money to buy an apartment in New York.

Yes, Nora said to herself, it is time to wake up. It was simple, it was true, it was overwhelming. The move would be difficult, a risk, a test, but if she could retain this sense of necessity, in the end their lives would improve.

She glanced over at Davey, almost fearful that he had heard her thoughts. Davey was giving her a look of shocked disbelief. "Isn't that incredible?"

"What's incredible?"

He stared. "You have to read the book again. They cut all of Paddy's tale and went straight to the Field of Steam. Which means that the first whole set of questions and answers is out, and so are the rats. It's crazy."

"Imagine it without the rats."

"It's like *The Wizard of Oz* without the flying monkeys. It's like *The Lord of the Rings* without Sauron."

"Like *Huckleberry Finn* without Pap."

"Exactly," Davey said. "You can't change these things, you can't do it."

We'll see about that, Nora said to herself.

6

SOMETIME LATER SHE came groggily awake with her head in Davey's lap. A wide-shouldered man with crinkly eyes and a heroic beard was carrying the boy through an enormous wooden door. The soundtrack, all shining violins and hallooing trombones, applauded. This stage of events was coming to an end. Nora remembered a sense of resolve, but could not remember what she had resolved to do. With the memory of her own determination came the return of renewed strength. She had resolved to act. *Time to wake up.* She and Davey would turn their backs on Westerholm and move the forty crucial miles into New York City. It was time to be a nurse again.

Or if not that, she immediately thought, something else. Nora's last experiences of nursing were a radioactive substance too hot to touch. Until the final month, the radioactivity had expressed itself privately, in nightmares, stomach problems, sudden explosions of temper, depressions. The gleeful demons had put in occasional appearances. Neither Nora nor Davey had connected this stream of disorder to her work at Norwalk Hospital until her last month, when Nora herself had become radioactive. An improperly considered but nonetheless necessary action had for a time brought her into the orbit of the police. Of course she had not committed a crime. She had behaved morally, not immorally, but recklessly. After she had agreed, naturally to the regret of all, to "take a sabbatical," she had signed half a dozen papers and left the hospital too unhappy to pick up her final paycheck.

Nora's reckless but moral action had at first resembled kidnapping. The year-old son of a prominent man had been brought in with a broken leg and bruising around the chest. A fall downstairs, the mother said.

She had not seen it, but her husband had. Sure did, said the husband, a sleek item in a Wall Street suit. His skin had an oily shine, and his smile was amazingly white. Took my eye off the kid for a second, and when I looked back, bam, almost had a heart attack. Half an hour after the child was admitted, both parents left. Three hours later, stuffed bunny under his pin-striped arm, back came smiling Dad. Into the private room he went, came out fifteen minutes later, even oilier, smiling hard. Nora checked on the child and found him all but unconscious.

When she reported what she had seen, she was told that the father could not be responsible for any injuries to the child. The father was a wizard, a financial genius, too noble to beat his own child. The next day Mom and Dad came in at eight. Dad left after half an hour, Mom went home at noon. At six, just as Nora was leaving, Dad returned alone. When Nora checked in on the child the next day, she learned that he had suffered a mysterious "failure" the previous evening but was now recovering. Once again she reported her suspicions to her superiors, once again she was rebuked. By this time, two or three other nurses silently agreed with her. The parents had been in again at eight, and these nurses had observed that the wizard seemed to be merely *acting* the role of a worried parent.

When the father returned that evening, Nora, after an hour railing in vain at administrators, planted herself in the child's room until Dad asked to be left alone with his baby, at which point she left long enough to make three telephone calls—one to an acquaintance who ran the Jack and Jill Nursery School on the South Post Road in Westerholm, another to the chief of pediatrics, the third to Leo Morris, her lawyer. She said, *I am saving this child's life*. Then she reported back to the room. The irritated wizard said that he was going to file a complaint and bustled out. Nora wrapped up the child and walked out of the hospital. She drove to the Jack and Jill Nursery, delivered the child into her friend's care, and returned to face the storm she had created. Four months after the turmoil had subsided, the wizard's wife issued a statement to the press saying that she was seeking a divorce on the grounds that her husband regularly beat both herself and their son.

"At least they got one thing right," Davey said. "The Green Knight really *does* look like a grown-up Pippin. But you can't tell that *Pippin* realizes it."

On the screen, electronic manipulation was transforming the bearded man's face, stripping away years by smoothing wrinkles, shortening his hair, drawing in the planes of his cheeks, leaving the beard as only a penumbra around a face almost identical to the boy's.

"You need the words. *His own salvation lay within himself. Pippin had come to the great truth behind his journey through vast darkness.*

Life and death stirred beneath his own hands, and his hands commanded them." Davey recited the words unemotionally but without hesitation.

"Oh, of course," Nora said. "Absolutely."

For less than a second, the boy's face shone out from within the shadow of the man's, and then the wild hair, frothing beard, and hard planes of the forehead and cheekbones locked back into place. The man carried the boy down a grassy slope. Sunlight gilded his hair and the tops of his arms. On the hill behind the man and the boy stood a huge door in a dark frame, like a mirage. Before them in the fold of a valley at the bottom of the hillside, oaks the size of matches half-hid a white farmhouse.

She turned her head to Davey and found him looking not at the screen but down at her with a suggestion of concern in his eyes.

"Kind of pretty," she said.

"So it's completely wrong." His eyes darkened. "That's not Mountain Glade. Does it look like there's a secret in that place? Mountain Glade isn't pretty, but it contains the great secret."

"Oh, sure."

"It's the whole point," Davey said. His eyes had moved backward into his head.

"I better go back to bed." Nora pushed herself upright without any assistance from Davey. "Isn't it almost over, anyhow?"

"If it *is* over," he said.

Onscreen, the bearded man faded toward transparency. When she stood up and took an undecided step away from the sofa, he vanished altogether. The boy sprinted toward the farmhouse, and then the cast list obliterated his image.

Nora took another step toward the door, and Davey gave her a quick, unreadable glance. "I'll be there in a little while," he said.

Nora climbed the stairs, again reflexively checking that the front door was locked and the security system armed. She slid back into bed, felt the night sweat soak through her nightgown, and realized that she had to convince Davey that her desire to leave Westerholm had nothing to do with Natalie Weil or the human wolf.

Half an hour later, he entered the bedroom and felt his way along the wall until he found the bathroom. Without really being aware that she had fallen asleep, Nora opened her eyes from a dream in which Dan Harwich had been looking at her with colossal, undimmed tenderness. She rolled over and pushed her head deep into the pillow. For a long time Davey brushed his teeth while the water ran. He washed his face and yanked a towel off the rack. He spoke a few reproachful words she could not make out. Like his mother, when alone or unobserved he often conducted one-sided conversations with some person not present, a habit which Nora thought could not technically be described as talking to yourself. The bathroom light clicked off, and the door opened. Davey groped toward the bed, found the bottom of the mattress in the dark, and felt his way up his side to pull back the duvet. He got in and stretched out along his edge of the bed, as far from her as he could get without falling off. She asked if he was all right.

"Don't forget about lunch tomorrow," he answered.

Once during her period of radioactivity, Nora had forgotten that they were due at the Poplars for a meal. Usually, Davey's reminders of this distant error struck her as unnecessarily provocative. Tonight, however, his remark suggested a way to put her resolution into effect.

"I won't," Nora said.

She could help them by drawing nearer to Daisy Chancel; she could soften the blow before it fell.

7

A FEW MINUTES after they had wandered out onto the Poplars' terrace early the next afternoon, Nora left Davey and Alden holding Bloody Marys as they looked out at the sun-dazzled Sound. The announcement that she was going upstairs to see Daisy had met only a token resistance, although Davey had seemed disgruntled to be left alone with his father so soon after their arrival. Davey's father had seemed pleased and even gratified by Nora's words. Alden Chancel had grown into a handsome, unruffled old age by getting everything he had ever wanted, and while he had certainly wanted his son to get married, he had never imagined that Davey would marry someone like Nora Curlew.

Nora quickly traversed the downstairs living room, came out into the marbled entrance, and turned to mount the wide staircase. On the landing she paused in front of the huge mirror. Instead of changing into her usual jeans and top after her morning run, Nora had dressed in white trousers and a loose, dark blue silk blouse. In the mirror these clothes looked nearly as appropriate for lunch on the Poplars' terrace as they had at home.

She pushed at her hair without significantly rearranging it and started up the remaining steps to the second floor. A door closed, and the Italian girl, Maria, the short gray-haired woman who decades ago had replaced the famous Helen Day, called the Cup Bearer, at other times referred to more mysteriously as O'Dotto, came out of Daisy's studio carrying an empty tray. The Cup Bearer, whom Davey had loved, had made legendary desserts, seven-layer cake and floating island; Maria was serviceable, not legendary, and in Nora's experience prepared excellent French and Italian meals.

Maria smiled at her and gave the tray a short, emphatic slap against the air, as if to say, *So! Here we are!*

"Hello, Maria, how's Mrs. Chancel today?"

"Very fine, Mrs. Nora."

"How are you?"

"Exactly the same."

"Would she mind company?"

Maria shook her head, still smiling. Nora knocked twice, then pushed open the door.

Seated at the far end of a long, cream-colored couch facing a glass coffee table and a brick fireplace, Daisy raised her head from the paperback in her hands and gave Nora a bright look of welcome. The white oak desk at her shoulder, placed at the top of the couch like the crossbar of a capital T, was bare except for an electric typewriter and a jar of yellow pencils; the glass table held a tall vase crowded with fleshy-looking, white Casablanca lilies, a pack of low-tar cigarettes, a gold lighter, a stone ashtray brimming with butts, books in stacks, and a tumbler filled with ice and pale red liquid. Mint green in their own shadows, white aluminum blinds were canted against the sun.

"Nora, oh goody, what a treat, come in and join me, where's your drink?"

"I must have left it on the terrace." Nora stepped into Daisy's atmosphere of flowers and cigarette smoke.

"Oh no, mustn't do that, let's have the Italian girl fetch it." She slid a postcard into the book.

"No, no, I don't—"

Daisy had already leaned forward and taken a little bell off the table. It uttered an absurdly soft, tinkling ring. "Maria," she said in a conversational voice.

As if summoned out of the air, Maria opened the door and stepped inside. "Mrs. Chancel?"

"Will you be a sweetie and bring up Nora's drink? It's on the terrace."

Maria nodded and left, closing the door behind her.

Daisy patted the creamy couch and set the paperback, *Journey into Light,* Hugo Driver's second posthumous book, on the glass table.

"I'm not interrupting anything?"

In the mid-fifties, newly married, forty pounds lighter, Daisy Chancel had published two novels, not with Chancel House, and ever since she had supposedly been writing another.

Nora had nearly, but not quite, ceased to believe in this book, of which she had never seen any evidence on her infrequent visits to the studio. Davey had long ago refused to talk about it, and Alden referred to it only euphemistically. Daisy's manner at evening meals, rigid and vague, suggested that instead of working she had been drinking martinis supplied by the Italian girl. Yet once there must have been a book, and that Daisy maintained the pretense of work meant that it was still important to her.

"Not at all," Daisy said. "I thought I'd read Driver again. Such an inspiring writer, you know. He always inspires *me,* anyhow. I don't know why people never took to *Journey into Light.*" She gave Nora a mystical smile and leaned forward to tap the book approvingly with her thick fingers. Her hand drifted sideways to capture the tumbler and carry it to her mouth. She took a good swallow, then another. "You're not one of those people who think *Journey into Light* is a terrible falling off, are you?" Daisy set down the drink and snatched up the cigarettes and lighter.

"I never thought of it that way."

Daisy lit a cigarette, inhaled, and as she expelled smoke waved it away. "No, of course not." She tossed the pack onto the table. "You couldn't, not with Davey around. I remember when *he* read it for the first time."

Someone knocked at the door. "Your potion. Come in, Maria."

The maid brought in the Bloody Mary, and when she proffered it to Nora her eyes sparkled. She was pleased to see Daisy enjoying herself.

"When will things be ready?"

"Half an hour. I make fresh mayonnaise for the lobster salad."

"Make lots, Davey likes your mayonnaise."

"Mr. Chancel, too."

"Mr. Chancel likes everything," Daisy said, "unless it interferes with sleep or business." She hesitated for a moment. "Could you bring us fresh drinks in about fifteen minutes? Nora's looks so *watery.* And have Jeffrey open the wine just before we come down."

Nora waited for Maria to leave the room, then turned to find Daisy half-smiling, half-scrutinizing her through a murk of cigarette smoke. "Speaking of Hugo Driver, is there some kind of trouble with his estate?"

Daisy raised her eyebrows.

"Davey got up in the middle of the night to watch the movie of *Night Journey.* He said that Alden wanted him to take care of some kind of problem."

"A problem?"

"Maybe he said it was a nuisance."

At these words Daisy lowered her eyebrows, lodged the cigarette in her mouth, and picked up her glass. She nodded slowly several times before withdrawing the cigarette, blowing out smoke, and taking another mouthful of the drink. She licked her lips. "I always enjoy your visits to my little cell."

"Did you ever meet Hugo Driver?"

"Oh no, he was dead before Alden and I were married. Alden met him two or three times, I believe, when he came here for visits. In fact, Hugo Driver slept in this room."

"Is that why you use it?" Nora glanced around the long, narrow room, trying to imagine it as it had been in the thirties.

"Could be." Daisy shrugged.

"But is your own work like Driver's—is that the kind of thing you've been working on?"

"I hardly know anymore," Daisy said.

"I guess I'm a little curious."

"I guess I am, too!"

"Has anybody ever read what you've been writing?"

Daisy sat up straight and glanced at the bookshelves next to the fireplace, giving Nora a view of soft, flat white hair and the outline of a bulging cheek. Then she turned to look at her in a way unreadable but not at all vague. "A long time ago, my agent read a couple of chapters. But over the years, we . . . *drifted* . . . away from each other. And it's changed a lot since then. Several times. You'd have to say it changed completely, several times."

"Your agent wasn't very helpful."

Daisy's cheeks widened in a brief, cheerless smile. "I forgave him when he died. It was the least both of us could do." She finished off her drink, dragged on the cigarette, and blew out a thin shaft of smoke that bounced like a traveling cloud off the vase.

"And since then?"

Daisy tilted her head. "Are you asking to read my manuscript, Nora? Excuse me. I should say, are you offering to read it?"

"I just thought . . ." Nora did her best to look placating. Her mother-in-law continued to examine her out of eyes that seemed to have become half their normal size. "I just wondered if . . . if a reader might be helpful to you. I'm hardly a critic."

"I hardly want a *critic.*" Daisy leaned forward over her stomach and stubbed out the cigarette. "It might be interesting. Fresh pair of eyes and all that. I'll think about it."

A rap sounded at the door, and Maria came in with two tall drinks on a tray. She removed Daisy's empty glass and placed Nora's second beside her nearly untouched first. "I give you extra jar mayonnaise to take home, Mrs. Nora."

Nora thanked her.

"Are the boys doing all right down there, Maria?"

"Doing beautiful."

"No shouts? No threats?" Nora had rarely seen this side of Daisy.

Maria smiled and shook her head.

"Are they talking about anything interesting?"

Maria's smile went rigid.

"Oh, I see. Well, if they ask, which they won't, you can tell them that *everything* we're talking about is interesting."

It struck Nora that the closest relationship Daisy had was with Maria.

Daisy surprised her again by winking at her. "Isn't that right, dear?" This bright, lively Daisy had appeared immediately after Nora had suggested looking at her manuscript.

Nora said yes, it was interesting, and Maria beamed at her before leaving.

"What do you think they're talking about downstairs?"

"Want to make a publisher's heart go *trip trap, trip trap,* like the baby goat walking over the bridge? Show him a nice, juicy crime, what he would call a 'true crime.' " Daisy smiled another mirthless smile and took a swallow of the fresh drink. "Don't you love that term? I think I'll commit a true crime. Right after I commit a nonfiction novel. *Trip trap, trip trap, trip trap.*" She opened her mouth, rolled up her eyes, and patted her heart in mock ecstasy. "I know, I'll commit a true crime by writing a nonfiction novel about Hugo Driver!" Daisy giggled. "Maybe that's what I've been doing all these years! Maybe Alden will give me a million dollars and I'll go away to Tahiti!"

"Maybe I'll come with you," Nora said. It would be fun going to Tahiti with this Daisy Chancel.

Daisy wagged a fat forefinger. "No, you won't. No, you won't. You can't go away and leave Davey all alone."

"I suppose not," Nora said.

"No, no, no," Daisy said. "Nope."

"Of course not," Nora said. "Are you really writing a nonfiction novel?"

The older woman was nearly gloating, as if she knew secrets so outlandish that she could hint eternally without ever divulging them. Nora took in her shining, slightly filmy eyes and understood that Daisy was going to let her read her manuscript.

8

"SURE, EVERY WOMAN in Westerholm is frightened," Alden said. "They're supposed to be."

"What do you mean, supposed to be?" Nora asked.

"You think I'm defending murder."

"No, I just want to know what you meant."

He surveyed the table. "When Nora looks at me, she sees the devil."

"A *nonfiction* devil," said Daisy.

"Dad, I don't think I understand, either."

"Alden wants people to think he's the nonfiction . . . true crime . . . devil." Daisy had reached the stage of speaking with exaggerated care.

"The devil does, too," Nora said, irritated.

"Exactly," Alden said. "Wherever this fellow goes, he's hot stuff. He gets his weekly copy of the *Westerholm News,* and he's on the front page."

He helped himself to another portion of lobster salad and signaled Jeffrey, generally referred to as "the Italian girl's nephew," to pour more wine. Jeffrey took the bottle from the ice bucket, wiped it on a white towel, and went to the end of the table to refill Daisy's glass. He moved up the table, and Nora put her hand over the top of her glass. Jeffrey gave her a comic scowl before he went to the head of the table.

Nora had never known what to make of Jeffrey. Tall, of an age somewhere between forty-five and fifty-five, his speech without accent, his fair brown hair thinning evenly across his crown, Jeffrey was an unlikely relative of Maria. Nora gathered that she had produced him some ten years before when Alden had begun to talk about hiring someone to answer phones, open doors, run errands. Jeffrey had clever eyes and a graceful, guarded manner that did not preclude playfulness. Some days he looked like a thug. Nora watched him offer the wine to Davey, turn away to twist the bottle into the ice, and return to his post at the edge of the terrace. In a close-fitting dark suit and black shirt, Jeffrey was having one of his thug days. Daisy reminded her of her private theory about Jeffrey by saying, "You're usually more . . . original . . . than *that,*" and tapping her fork on the table in rhythm with her words.

Jeffrey had been hired to cover for Daisy.

"I'm not finished, my dear."

"Then please, please enlighten us."

Alden smiled universally at the table. His perfect teeth gleamed, his white hair shone, a flush darkened the smoothly tanned broad face. In a blazer and snowy shirt, the top button opened over a paisley ascot, with bright, expressionless eyes and deep indentations like divots around his mouth, Alden looked just like the kind of person who hired someone like Jeffrey. Nora realized how much she disliked him.

"Think of how many copies the *Westerholm News* is selling. People who never looked at it in their lives are buying it now. And this isn't true just of our rinky-dink little paper. The tabloids in New York jump up and salute every time another lady is slaughtered in her bed. And do you think the security system business in Fairfield County is having the usual August lull? What about the handgun business? Not to mention fencing, yard lights, and locksmiths? How about television reporters, the photographers from *People*?"

"Don't forget publishers," Nora said.

"Absolutely. What's your best guess on how many books are being written about Westerholm at this minute? Four? Five? Think of the paper that will go into those books. The ink, the foil for the covers. Think of the computer disks, the laptops, the notebooks, the fax machines. The *fax paper.* The *pencils.*"

"It's an industry," Davey said. "Okay."

"A darn bloody industry, if you ask me," said Daisy. Nora silently applauded.

"So was World War Two," said Alden. "And so was Vietnam, Nora, if you'll forgive me."

Nora didn't think she would.

"Ah, if looks could kill—but did or did not unit commanders have a certain amount of shells they were supposed to fire on a daily basis—not officially, I mean, but pretty specific anyhow? Didn't we use up a tremendous amount of uniforms and vehicles over there, didn't we build bases and sell beer and buy tons of food? Wasn't somebody manufacturing body bags? Nora, I know I'm flirting with danger, but I love it when your eyes flash."

He was flirting with her, not danger. She looked across the table at her husband and found him gazing at the napkin in his lap.

"Gee, I love it when your eyes flash, too, Alden," she said. "It makes you look so young."

"Actually, Nora, you're the oldest person at this table."

For both her husband's sake and Daisy's, Nora forced herself to relax.

"You were tempered in ways the rest of us were not, and that's why you're so beautiful! I've admired beautiful women all my life, beautiful women are the saviors of mankind. Just being able to see your face must have pulled a lot of guys through over there."

She opened her mouth, closed it, and looked back at Alden. "Aren't you sweet."

"You must have had a great effect on the young men that passed through your hands."

"I think your viewpoint cheapens everything," Nora said. "Sorry. It's disgusting."

"If I could snap my fingers and make it so that you'd never gone to Vietnam, would you let me do it?"

"That would make me as young as you are, Alden."

"Benefits come in all shapes and sizes." He distributed a smile around the table. "Is there anything else I can clear up for you?"

For a moment nobody spoke. Then Daisy said, "Time for me to return to my cell. I'm feeling a little tired. Wonderful to see you, Davey. Nora, I'll be in touch."

Alden glanced at Nora before pushing back his chair and getting up. Davey stood up a second later.

Daisy grasped the top of her chair and turned toward the door. "Jeffrey, please thank Maria. *Lovely* lobster salad."

Jeffrey's courtly smile made him look more than ever like a dapper second-story man disguised as a valet. He drifted sideways and opened the door for Daisy.

9

ALDEN AND DAVEY took their chairs again. "Your mother'll be right as rain after her nap," Alden said. "Whatever goes on in her studio is her business, but I have the feeling she's been working harder than usual lately."

Davey nodded slowly, as if trying to decide if he agreed with his father.

Alden fixed Nora with a glance and took a sip of wine. "Planning something with Daisy?"

"Why do you ask?"

Davey flicked his hair out of his eyes and looked from Nora to his father and back again.

"Call it an impression."

"I'd like to spend more time with her. Go shopping, have lunch someday, things like that." Alden's gaze made her feel as though she were lying to a superior.

"Terrific," Alden said, and Davey relaxed back into his chair. "I mean it. Nice thought, my two girls having fun together."

"Mom's been working hard?"

"Well, if you ask me, something's going on up there." He looked at Nora in an almost conspiratorial fashion. "Was that your impression, Nora?"

"I didn't see her working, if that's what you mean."

"Ah, Daisy's like Jane Austen; she hides all the evidence. When she was writing her first two books, I never even saw her at the typewriter. To tell you the truth, sometimes this voice in my head would whisper, *What if she's just making it all up?* Then one day a box came from one of my competitors, and she whisked it away into her studio and came back out and handed me a book! Year after that, the same thing happened all over again. So I just let her do her thing. Hell, Davey, you know. You grew up in this crazy system."

Davey nodded and looked across the table as if he, too, wondered whether Nora possessed secret information.

"All my life, I've dealt with writers, and they're great—some writers anyhow—but I never understood what they do or how they do it. Hell, I don't think even they know how they do it. Writers are like babies. They scream and cry and bug the hell out of you, and then they produce this great big crap and you tell them how great it is." He laughed, delighted with himself.

"Does that go for Hugo Driver, too? Was he one of the screaming babies?"

Davey said, "Nora—"

"Sure he was. The difference with Driver was, everybody thought his dumps smelled better than the other brats'." Alden no longer seemed so delighted with his metaphor.

"Daisy said you met him a couple of times. What was he like?"

"How should I know? I was a kid."

"But you must have had some impression. He was your father's most important author. He even stayed in this house."

"Well, at least now I know what you and Daisy were talking about up there."

She ignored this remark. "In fact, Driver was responsible for—"

"Driver wrote a book. Thousands of people write books every year. His happened to be successful. If it hadn't been Driver, it would have been someone else." He struggled for an air of neutral authority. "You have a lot to learn about publishing. I say that respectfully, Nora."

"Really."

Davey was combing his hair off his forehead with his fingers. "What you say is true, but—"

His father froze him with a look.

"But it was a classic collaboration," Davey continued. "The synergy was unbelievable."

"I'm too old for synergy," Alden said.

"You never told me what you thought of him personally."

"Personally I thought he was an acquaintance of my father's."

"That's all?"

Alden shook his head. "He was this unimpressive little guy in a loud tweed jacket. He thought he looked like the Prince of Wales, but actually he looked like a pickpocket."

Davey seemed too shocked to speak, and Alden went on. "Hey, I always thought the Prince of Wales looked like a pickpocket, too. Driver was a very talented writer. What I thought of him when I was a little boy doesn't matter. What kind of guy he was doesn't matter either."

"Hugo Driver was a great writer." Davey uttered this sentence to his plate.

"No argument here."

"He was."

Alden smiled meaninglessly, inserted another section of lobster into his mouth, and followed it with a swallow of wine. Davey vibrated with suppressed resentment. Alden said, "You know my rule: a great publisher never reads his own books. Gets in the way of your judgment. While we're on this subject, do we have anything for our friend Leland Dart?"

This was the most exalted of their lawyers, the partner of Leo Morris in the firm of Dart, Morris.

Davey said he was working on it.

"To be truthful, I wonder if our friend Leland might be playing both ends against the middle."

"Does this have something to do with the Driver estate?" Nora asked.

"Please, Nora," Davey said. "Don't."

"Don't what? Did I just become invisible?"

"You know what's interesting about Leland Dart?" Alden asked, clearly feeling the obligation to rescue the conversation. "Apart from his utter magnificence, and all that? His relationship with his son. I don't get it. Do you get it? I mean Dick—I sort of understood what happened with the older one, Petey, but Dick just baffles me. Does that guy actually do anything?"

Davey was laughing now. "I don't think he does, no. We met him a month or two ago, remember, Nora? At Gilhoolie's, right after it opened."

Nora did remember, and the memory of the appalling person named Dick Dart could now amuse her, too. Dart had been two years behind Davey at the Academy. She had been introduced to him at the bar of a restaurant which had replaced a mediocre pizza parlor in the Waldbaum's shopping center. Men and women in their twenties and thirties had crowded the long bar separating the door from the dining room, and the menus in plastic cases on the red-checked tables advertised drinks like Mudslides and Long Island Iced Teas. As she and Davey had passed through the crowd, a tall, rather fey-looking man had turned to Davey, dropped a hand on his arm, and addressed him with an odd mixture of arrogance and diffidence. He wore a nice, slightly rumpled suit, his tie had been yanked down, and his fair hair drooped over his forehead. He appeared to have consumed more than a sufficient number of Mudslides. He had said something like *I suppose you're going to pretend that you don't remember our old nighttime journeys anymore.*

During Davey's denial, the man had tilted back his head and peered from one Chancel to the other in a way that suggested they made an amusing spectacle. Nora had endured ironic compliments to her "valiant" face and "lovely" hair. After telling Davey that he should come around by himself some night to talk about the wild rides they'd enjoyed together, Dart had released them, but not before adding that he *adored* Nora's scent. Nora had not been wearing a scent. Once they reached their table, Nora had said that she'd make Davey sleep in the garage if he ever had anything to do with that languid jerk. Give me a break, Davey had said, Dart's trying to get in your pants. He gets it all from old Peter O'Toole movies. More like old George Sanders movies, Nora answered, wondering if anyone ever got laid by pretending to despise the person he wanted to seduce.

Midway through the tasteless meal, Nora had looked up at the bar and seen Dart wink at her. She had asked Davey what his old pal did for a living, and Davey had offered the surprising information that Dick was an attorney in his father's firm.

Now Davey said to his father what he had explained to Nora at Gilhoolie's, that Dick Dart lived off the crumbs that fell from the tables of Dart, Morris's wealthier clients; he took elderly widows to lunch in slow-moving French restaurants and assured them that Leland Dart was preserving their estates from the depredations of a socialist federal government.

"Why does he stay on?"

"He probably likes the lunches," Davey said. "And I suppose he expects to inherit the firm."

"Don't put any money on it," Alden said. Nora felt a chill wind so clearly that it might have blown in off the Sound. "Old Leland is too smart for that. He's been the back-room boy in Republican politics in this state since the days of Ernest Forrest Ernest, and he's not going to let that kid anywhere near the rudder of Dart, Morris. You watch. When Leland steps down, he'll tell Dick he needs more seasoning and pull in a distinguished old fraud just like himself."

"Why do you want Davey to know that?" asked Nora.

"So he'll understand our esteemed legal firm," Alden said.

"Maybe Leland's wife will have her own ideas about what happens to Dick," Nora said.

Alden grinned luxuriantly. "Leland's wife, well. I wonder what that lady makes of her son going around romancing the same women her husband seduced forty years ago. Leland took them to bed to get their legal business, and Dick sweet-talks them to keep it. Do you suppose our boy Dick climbs into bed with them, the same way his daddy used to do? It'd be a strange boy who did that, wouldn't you think?"

Davey stared out at the Sound without speaking.

"I suppose you think the women are grateful," said Nora.

"Maybe the first time," Alden said. "I don't imagine Dick gives them much to be grateful for."

"We'll never know," Davey said, smiling strangely toward the Sound.

Alden checked the empty places as if for leftover bits of lobster. "Are we all finished?"

Davey nodded, and Alden glanced up at Jeffrey, who drifted sideways and opened the door. Nora thanked him as she walked past, but Jeffrey pretended not to hear. A few minutes later, Nora sat in Davey's little red Audi, holding a Mason jar of homemade mayonnaise as he drove from Mount Avenue into Westerholm's newer, less elegant interior.

10

"ARE YOU UPSET?" she asked. Davey had traveled the entire mile and a half of Churchill Lane without speaking.

It was a question she asked often during their marriage, and the answers she received, while not evasive, were never straightforward. As with many men, Davey's feelings frequently came without labels.

"I don't know," he said, which was better than a denial.

"Were you surprised by what your father said?"

He looked at her warily for about a quarter of a second. "If I was surprised by anybody, it was you."

"Why?"

"My father gets a kick out of exaggerating his point of view. That doesn't mean he should be attacked."

"You think I attacked him?"

"Didn't you say he was disgusting? That he cheapened everything?"

"I was criticizing his ideas, not him. Besides, he enjoyed it. Alden gets a kick out of verbal brawls."

"The man is about to be seventy-five. I think he deserves more respect, especially from someone who doesn't know the first thing about the publishing business. Not to mention the fact that he's my father."

The light at the Post Road turned green, and Davey pulled away from the oaks beside the stone bridge at the end of Churchill Lane. Either because no traffic came toward them or because he had forgotten to do it, he did not signal the turn that would take them down the Post Road and home. Then she realized that he had not signaled a turn because he did not intend to take the Post Road.

"Where are you going?"

"I want to see something," he said. Evidently he did not intend to tell her what it was.

"This might come as a surprise to you, but I thought your father was attacking me."

"Nothing he said was personal. You're the one who was personal."

Nora silently cataloged the ways in which she had felt attacked by Alden Chancel and selected the safest. "He loves talking about my age. Alden always thought I was too old for you."

"He never said anything about your age."

"He said I was the oldest person at the table."

"For God's sake, Nora, he was being playful. And right then, he was giving you a compliment, if you didn't notice. In fact, he complimented you about a hundred times."

"He was flirting with me, and I hate it. He uses it as a way to put people down."

"That's crazy. People in his generation all give out these heavy-handed compliments. They think it's like offering a woman a bouquet of flowers."

"I know," Nora said, "but that's what's crazy."

Davey shook his head. Nora leaned back in the seat and watched the splendid houses go by. Alden had been right about one thing: in front of every estate stood a metal plaque bearing the name of a security company. Many promised an ARMED RESPONSE.

He gave her a brief, flat glare. "One more thing. I shouldn't have to say this to you, but apparently I do."

She waited.

"What my mother does up in her studio is her business. It doesn't have anything to do with you, Nora." Another angry glare. "Just in case you didn't get what Dad was telling you. Pretty damn tactfully, too, I thought."

More dismayed than she wished to appear, Nora inhaled and slowly released her breath as she worked out a response. "First of all, Davey, I wasn't interfering with her. She was happy to see me, and I enjoyed being with her." In Davey's answering glance she saw that he wanted to believe this. "In fact, it was like being with a completely different person than who she was at lunch. She was having a good time. She was funny."

"Okay, that's nice. But I really don't want you to wind up making her feel worse than she already does."

For a moment, Nora looked at him without speaking. "You don't think she does any work up there, do you? Neither does your father. Both of you think she's been faking it for years, and you go along because you want to protect her, or something like that."

"Or something like that." Some of his earlier bitterness put an edge on his voice. "Ever hear the expression 'Don't rock the boat'?" He glanced over at her with an unhappy mockery in his eyes. "You believe she goes up there to work? Is that what you're saying?"

"I think she's writing *something*, yes."

He groaned. "I'm sure that's nice for both of you."

"Wouldn't you like your mother and me to be, maybe not friends, but more like friends than we are now?"

"She never had friends." Davey thought for a second. "I suppose she was friends, as close to it as she could get, with the Cup Bearer. Then she quit, and that was that. I was devastated. I didn't think she'd ever leave. I probably thought Helen Day was my real mother. The other one certainly didn't spend much time with me."

"I wish you could have seen the way she was with me. Sort of . . . lighthearted."

"Sort of drunk," Davey said. "Surprise, surprise." He sighed, so sadly that Nora wanted to put her arms around him. "For which, of course, she has a very good reason."

Alden, Nora thought, but Davey would never blame the great publisher for his mother's condition. She tilted her head and quizzed him with her eyes.

"The other one. The one before me, the one who died. It's obvious."

"Oh, yes." Nora nodded, suddenly seeing Davey, as she had a hundred times, seated in the living room under a lamp from Michaelman's with *Night Journey* in his hands, staring into pages he read and reread because, no less than the killers Leonard Gimmel and Teddy Brunhoven, in them he found the code to his own life.

"You think about that a lot, don't you?"

"I don't know. Maybe." He checked to see if she was criticizing him. "Kind of—thinking about it without thinking about it, I guess."

She nodded but did not speak. For a moment Davey seemed on the verge of saying more. Then his mouth closed, his eyes changed, and the moment was over.

The Audi pulled up at a stop sign before a cluster of trees overgrown with vines that all but obscured the street sign. Then across the street a gray Mercedes sedan rolled toward the intersection, and as Davey flicked on the turn signal before pressing the accelerator and cranking the wheel to the left, the name of the street chimed in her head. He had taken them to Redcoat Road, and what he wanted to see was the house in which the wolf had taken Natalie Weil's life and caused her body to disappear.

11

Beside Natalie's drive was a metal post supporting a bright blue plaque bearing the name of a local security firm more expensive than the one the Chancels had chosen. Natalie had taken account of the similarities between herself and the first victims and spent a lot of money for state-of-the-art protection.

Davey left the car and walked up along the grassy verge of Redcoat Road toward the driveway. Nora got out and followed him. She regretted the Bloody Mary and the single glass of wine she'd taken at lunch. The August light stung her eyes. Davey stood facing Natalie's house from the end of the driveway, his trousers almost brushing the security system plaque.

Set far back from the road, the house looked out over a front yard darkened by the shadows of oaks and maples standing between grassy humps and granite boulders. Yellow crime scene tape looped through the trees and sealed the front door. A black-and-white Westerholm police car and an anonymous-looking blue sedan were parked near the garage doors.

"Is there some reason you wanted to come here?" she asked.

"Yes." He glanced down at her, then looked back toward the house. Twenty years ago it had been painted the peculiar depthless red-brown of information booths in national parks. Their own house was the same shade of brown, though its paint had not yet begun to flake. In design also Natalie's house replicated theirs, with its blunt facade and row of windows marching beneath the roof.

A white face above a dark uniform leaned toward a window in the bedroom over the garage.

"That cop's in the room where she was killed," Davey said. He started walking up the driveway.

The face retreated from the window. Davey came to the point where the yellow tape wound around a maple beside the drive, and continued in a straight line toward the house and garage. He put out his hand and leaned against the maple.

"Why are you doing this?"

"I'm trying to help you." The policeman came up to the living room window and stared out at them. He put his hands on his hips and then swung away from the window.

"Maybe this is crazy, but do you think that you wanted to come here because of what you were talking about in the car?"

He gave her an uncertain look.

"About the other one. The other Davey."

"Don't," he said.

Again the Chancel tendency to protect Chancel secrets. The policeman opened the front door and began moving toward them through the shadows on Natalie Weil's lawn.

12

NORA WAS CERTAIN that Davey's fascination with *Night Journey*, a novel about a child rescued from death by a figure called the Green Knight, was rooted in his childhood. Once there had been another David Chancel, the first son of Alden and Daisy. Suddenly the infant Davey had died in his crib. He had not been ill, weak, or at risk in any way. He had simply, terribly, died. Lincoln Chancel had saved them by suggesting, perhaps even demanding, an adoption. Lincoln's insistence on a grandson was a crucial element of the legend Davey had passed on to Nora. An adoptable baby had been found in New Hampshire; Alden and Daisy traveled there, won the child for their own, named him after the first infant, and raised him in the dead boy's place.

Davey had worn the dead Davey's baby clothes, slept in his crib, drooled on his bib, mouthed his rattle, taken formula from his bottle. When he grew old enough, he played with the toys set aside for the ghost baby. As if Lincoln Chancel had foreseen that he would not live to see the child turn four, he had purchased blocks, balls, stuffed bunnies and cats, rocking horses, electric trains, baseball gloves, bicycles in graduated sizes, dozens of board games, and much else besides; on the appropriate birthdays these gifts had been removed from boxes marked DAVEY and ceremoniously presented. Eventually Davey had understood that they were gifts from a dead grandfather to a dead grandson.

Ever since the night drunken Davey had careered around the living room while declaiming this history, Nora had begun to see him in a way only at first surprising or unsettling. He had always imagined himself under the pitiless scrutiny of a shadow self—imagined that the rightful David Chancel called to him for recognition or rescue.

13

THE DETECTIVE SKIRTED a dolphin-colored boulder and came forward, regarding Nora with a combination of official reserve and private concern. She could not imagine how she could have mistaken his blue suit and ornate red necktie for a police uniform. He had a heavy, square head, a disillusioned face, and a thick brown mustache that curved past the ends of his mouth. When he came close enough for her to notice the gray in the Tartar mustache, she could also see that his dark brown eyes were at once serious, annoyed, solicitous, and far down, at bottom, utterly detached, in a way that Nora assumed was reserved for policemen. Some portion of this man reminded her of Dan Harwich, which led her to expect a measure of sympathetic understanding. Physically he was not much like Harwich, being blocky and wide, heavy in the shoulders and gut, a Clydesdale instead of a greyhound.

"Are you okay?" he asked, which corresponded to her unconscious expectations, and when she nodded, he turned to Davey, saying, "Sir, if you're just being curious, I'd appreciate your getting this lady and yourself away from here," which did not.

"I wanted to see Natalie's house again," Davey said. "My name is Davey Chancel, and this is my wife, Nora."

Nora waited for the detective to say, *I thought you were brother and sister,* as some did. Instead he said, "You're related to the family on Mount Avenue? What's that place? The Poplars?"

"I'm their son," Davey said.

The man stepped closer and held out a large hand, which Davey took. "Holly Fenn. Chief of Detectives. You knew Mrs. Weil?"

"She sold us our house."

"And you've been here before?"

"Natalie had us over a couple of times," Nora said, for the sake of including herself in the conversation with Holly Fenn. He was a hod carrier, a peat stomper, as Irish as Matt Curlew. One look at this guy, you knew he was real. He leveled his complicated gaze at her. She cleared her throat.

"Five times," Davey said. "Maybe six. Have you found her body yet?"

Davey's *trait,* that which had caused Nora second and third thoughts about the man she had intended to marry, was that he stretched the truth. Davey did not lie in the ordinary sense, for advantage, but as she had eventually seen, for an aesthetic end, to improve reality.

Davey was still nodding, as if he had gone over their visits and added them up. When Nora added them up for herself, they came out to three. Once for drinks, a week after they started looking at houses; the second time for dinner; the third time when they had dropped in to pick up the keys to the house on Crooked Mile Road.

"Which is it?" Fenn asked. "A couple of times, or six?"

"Six," Davey said. "Don't you remember, Nora?"

Nora wondered if Davey had visited Natalie Weil by himself, and then dismissed the thought. "Oh, sure," she said.

"When was the last time you were here, Mr. Chancel?"

"About two weeks ago. We had Mexican food and watched wrestling on TV—right, Nora?"

"Um." To avoid looking at the detective, she turned her head toward the house and found that she had not been mistaken after all. The uniformed policeman she had seen earlier stood in the bedroom window, looking out.

"You were friends of Mrs. Weil's."

"You could say that."

"She doesn't seem to have had a lot of friends."

"I think she liked being alone."

"Not enough she didn't. No offense." Fenn shoved his hands in his pockets and reared back, as if he needed distance to see them clearly. "Mrs. Weil kept good records as far as her job went, made entries of all her appointments and that, but we're not having much luck with her personal life. Maybe you two can help us out."

"Sure, anything," Davey said.

"How?" Nora asked.

"What's in the jar?"

Nora looked down at the jar she had forgotten she carried. "Oh!" She laughed. "Mayonnaise. A present."

Davey gave her an annoyed look.

"Can I smell it?"

Mystified, Nora unscrewed the top and held up the jar. Fenn bent forward, took his hands from his pockets, placed them around the jar, and sniffed. "Yeah, the real thing. Hard to make, mayonnaise. Always wants to separate. Who's it for?"

"Us," she said.

His hands left the jar. "I wonder if you folks ever met any other friends of Mrs. Weil's here."

He was still looking at Nora, and she shook her head. After a second in which she was tempted to smell the mayonnaise herself, she screwed the top back onto the jar.

"No, never," Davey said.

"Know of any boyfriends? Anyone she went out with?"

"We don't know anything about that," Davey said.

"Mrs. Chancel? Sometimes women will tell a female friend things they won't say to her husband."

"She used to talk about her ex-husband sometimes. Norm. But he didn't sound like the kind of guy—"

"Mr. Weil was with his new wife in their Malibu beach house when your friend was killed. These days he's a movie producer. We don't think he had anything to do with this thing."

A movie producer in a Malibu beach house was nothing like the man Natalie had described. Nor was Holly Fenn's manner anything like what Nora thought of as normal police procedure.

"I guess you don't have any ideas about what might have happened to your friend." He was still looking at Nora.

"Nora doesn't think she's dead," Davey said, pulling another ornament out of the air.

Nora glanced at Davey, who did not look back. "Well. I don't know, obviously. Someone got into the house, right?" she said.

"That's for sure. She probably knew the guy." He turned toward the house. "This security system is pretty new. Notice it the last time you were here?"

"No," Davey said.

Nora looked down at the jar in her hands. What was inside it resembled some nauseating bodily fluid.

"Hard to miss that sign."

"You'd think so," Davey said.

"The system was installed a little more than two months ago."

Nora looked up from the jar to find his eyes on hers. She jerked her gaze back to the house and heard herself saying, "Was it really just two weeks ago we were here, Davey?"

"Maybe a little more."

Fenn looked away, and Nora hoped that he would let them go. He must have known that they had not been telling him the truth. "Do you think you could come inside? This isn't something we normally do, but this time I'll take all the help I can get."

"No problem," Davey said.

The detective stepped back and extended an arm in the direction of the front door. "Just duck under the tape." Davey bent forward. Fenn smiled at Nora, and his eyes crinkled. He looked like a courteous frontier sheriff dressed up in a modern suit—like Wyatt Earp. He even sounded like Wyatt Earp.

"Where are you from, Chief Fenn?" she asked.

"I'm a Bridgeport boy," he said. "Call me Holly, everybody else does. You don't have to go in there, you know. It's pretty bloody."

Nora tried to look as hard-bitten as she could while holding a quart jar filled with mayonnaise. "I was a nurse in Vietnam. I've probably seen more blood than you have."

"And you rescue children in peril," he said.

"That's more or less what I was doing in Vietnam," she said, blushing.

He smiled again and held up the tape as Davey frowned at them from beside a bank of overgrown hydrangeas.

14

ONE OF THOSE men who expand when observed close-up, Holly Fenn filled nearly the entire space of the stairwell. His shoulders, his arms, even his head seemed twice the normal size. Energy strained the fabric of his suit jacket, curled the dark brown hair at the back of his head. The air inside Natalie's house smelled of dust, dead flowers, unwashed dishes, the breath and bodies of many men, the reek of cigarettes dumped into wastebaskets. Davey uttered a soft sound of disgust.

"These places stink pretty good," Fenn said.

A poster of a whitewashed harbor village hung on the wall matching the one covered by their Chancel House bookshelves. In the living room, three men turned toward them. The uniformed policeman for whom Nora had mistaken Holly Fenn came into the hall. The other two wore identical gray suits, white button-down shirts, and dark ties. They had narrow, disdainful faces and stood side by side, like chessmen. Nora caught the faint, corrupt odor of old blood.

Davey came up the last step. Abnormally vivid in the dim light, his dark eyes and dark, definite brows made his face look white and unformed.

Fenn introduced them to Officer Michael LeDonne, and Mr. Hashim and Mr. Shull, who were with the FBI. Hashim and Shull actually resembled each other very little, Mr. Hashim being younger, heavier, in body more like one of Natalie's wrestlers than Mr. Shull, who was taller and fairer than his partner. Their posture and expressions created the effect of a resemblance, along with their shared air of otherworldly authority.

"Mr. and Mrs. Chancel were friends of the deceased, and I asked them if they'd be willing to do a walk through here, see if maybe they notice anything helpful."

"A walk through," said Mr. Shull.

Mr. Hashim said, "A walk through," and bent over to examine his highly polished black wing tips. "Cool."

"I'm glad we're all in agreement. Mike, maybe you could hold that jar for Mrs. Chancel."

Officer LeDonne took the jar and held it close to his face.

"These people were here recently?" asked Mr. Shull, also staring at the jar.

"Recently enough," said Fenn. "Take a good look around, folks, but make sure not to touch anything."

"Make like you're in a museum," said Mr. Shull.

"Do that," said Mr. Hashim.

Nora stepped past them into the living room. Mr. Shull and Mr. Hashim made her feel like touching everything in sight. Cigarette ash streaked the tan carpet, and a hole had been burned in the wheat-colored sofa. Magazines and a stack of newspapers covered the coffee table. Two Dean Koontz paperbacks had been lined up on the brick ledge above the fireplace. On the walls hung the iron weathervanes and bits of driftwood Natalie had not so much collected as gathered. The FBI men followed Nora with blank eyes. She glared at Mr. Shull. He blinked. Without altering her expression, Nora turned around and took in the room. It seemed at once charged with the presence of Natalie Weil and utterly empty of her. Mr. Shull and Mr. Hashim had been right: they were standing in a museum.

"Natalie make any phone calls that night?" Davey asked.

Fenn said, "Nope."

It occurred to Nora as she tagged along into the kitchen that she did not, she most emphatically did not, wish to see this house, thanks anyhow. Yet here she was, in Natalie's kitchen. Davey mooned along in front of the cabinets, shook his head at the sink, and paused before the photographs pinned to a corkboard next to the refrigerator. For Natalie's sake, Nora forced herself to look at what was around her and recognized almost instantly that no matter what she did or did not want, a change had occurred. In the living room, a blindfold of habit and discomfort had been anchored over her eyes.

Now, blindfold off, traces of Natalie Weil's decisions and preferences showed wherever she looked. Wooden counters had been scarred where Natalie had sliced the sourdough bread she liked toasted for breakfast; jammed into the garbage bin along with crumpled cigarette packets were plastic wrappers from Waldbaum's. Half-empty jam jars crowded the toaster. Smudgy glasses smelling faintly of beer stood beside the sink, piled with plates to which clung dried jam, flecks of toast, and granules of ground beef. A bag of rotting grapes lay on the counter beside three upright bottles of wine. Whatever Norman Weil and his new wife were drinking on the deck of their beach house in Malibu probably wasn't Firehouse Golden Mountain Jug Red, $9.99 a liter.

Blue recycling bins beside the back door held wine and Corona empties and a dead bottle of Stolichnaya Cristall. Tied up with twine in another blue bin were stacks of the New York and Westerholm newspapers along with bundles of *Time, Newsweek, Fangoria,* and *Wrestlemania.*

"I wish my men looked at crime scenes the way you do."

Startled, Nora straightened up to see Holly Fenn leaning against the open door to the hallway.

"Notice anything?"

"She ate toast and jam for breakfast. She was a little sloppy. She lived cheap, and she had kind of down-home tastes. You wouldn't know that by looking at her."

"Anything else?"

Nora thought back over what she had seen. "She was interested in horror movies, and that kind of surprises me, but I couldn't really say why."

Fenn gave her a twitch of a smile. "Wait till you see the bedroom." Nora waited for him to say something about murder victims and horror movies, but he did not. "What else?"

"She drank cheap wine, but every now and then she splurged on expensive vodka. All we ever saw her drink was beer."

Fenn nodded. "Keep on looking."

She walked to the refrigerator and saw the half-dozen magnets she remembered from two years before. A leering Dracula and a Frankenstein's monster with outstretched arms clung to the freezer cabinet; a half-peeled banana, a hippie in granny glasses and bell bottoms dragging on a joint half his size, an elongated spoon heaped with white powder, and a miniature Hulk Hogan decorated the larger door beneath.

Holly Fenn was twinkling at her from the doorway. "These have been here for years," she said.

"Real different," said Fenn. "Your husband says you don't think Mrs. Weil is dead."

"I hope she isn't." Nora moved impatiently to the corkboard bristling with photographs. She could still feel the blood heating her face and wished that the detective would leave her alone.

"Ever think Natalie was involved in drugs?"

"Oh, sure," Nora said, facing him. "Davey and I used to come over and snort coke all the time. After that we'd smoke some joints while cheering on our favorite *wrestlers*. We knew we could get away with it because the Westerholm police can't even catch the kids who bash in our mailboxes."

He was backing away before she realized that she had taken a couple of steps toward him.

Fenn held up his hands, palms out. They looked like catcher's mitts. "You having trouble with your mailbox?"

She whirled away from him and posted herself in front of the photographs. Natalie Weil's face, sometimes alone, sometimes not, grinned out at her. She had experimented with her hair, letting it grow to her shoulders, cropping it, streaking it, bleaching it to a brighter blond. A longer-haired Natalie smiled out from a deck chair, leaned against the rail of a cruise ship, at the center of a group of grinning, white-haired former teachers and salesclerks in shorts and T-shirts.

Some drug addict, Nora thought. She moved on to a series of photographs of Natalie in a peach-colored bathing suit lined up, some of them separated by wide gaps, at the bottom of the corkboard. They had been taken in the master bedroom, and Natalie was perched on the bed with her hands behind her back. Uncomfortably aware of Holly Fenn looming in the doorway, she saw what Natalie was wearing. The bathing suit was one of those undergarments which women never bought for themselves and could be worn only in a bedroom. Nora did not even know what they were called. Natalie's clutched her breasts, squeezed her waist, and flared at her hips. A profusion of straps and buttons made her look like a lecher's Christmas present. Nora looked more closely at the glint of a bracelet behind Natalie's back and saw the unmistakable steel curve of handcuffs.

She suppressed her dismay and stepped toward Fenn. "Probably this looks wildly degenerate to you," he said.

"What does it look like to you?"

"Harmless fun and games." He moved aside, and she walked out into the hall.

"Harmless?"

Nora turned toward the bedroom, thinking that maybe the Chancels had a point after all, and secrets should stay secret. Murder stripped you bare, exposed you to pitiless judgment. What you thought you shared with one other person was . . . She stopped walking.

"Think of something?"

She turned around. "A man took those pictures."

"Kind of a waste if her sister took them."

"But there aren't any pictures of him."

"That's right."

"Do you think there ever were?"

"You mean, do I think that at some point he was on the bed and she was holding the camera? I think something like that probably happened, sure. I took your picture, now you take mine. What happened to the pictures of the man?"

"Oh," she said, remembering the wide gaps on that section of the board.

"Ah. I love these little moments of enlightenment."

This little moment of enlightenment made her feel sick to her stomach.

"I'm kind of curious to hear what you know about her boyfriends."

"I wish I did know something."

"Guess you didn't notice the pictures, last time you were here."

"I didn't go into the kitchen."

"How about the time before that?"

"I don't remember if I went into the kitchen. If I did, I certainly didn't see those pictures."

"Now comes the time when I have to ask about this," Fenn said. "Did you and your husband ever join in your friend's games? If you say yes, I won't tell Slim and Slam in there. Got any pictures at home with Mrs. Weil in them?"

"No. Of course not."

"Your husband's a good-looking guy. Little younger than you, isn't he?"

"Actually," she said, "we were born on the same day. Just in different decades."

He grinned. "You probably know where the bedroom is."

15

THROUGH THE OPEN door Nora saw a rising arc of brown spots sprayed across an ivory wall. Beneath the spray, the visible corner of the bed looked as if rust-colored paint had been poured over the sheets.

Fenn spoke behind her. "You don't have to go in there if you don't feel like it. But you might want to reconsider the idea that she isn't dead."

"Maybe it isn't her blood," she said, and fumed at Davey for having made her say such a thing.

"Oh?"

She made herself walk into the room. Dried blood lay across the bed, and stripes and splashes of blood blotted the carpet beside it. The sheets and pillows had been slashed. Stiff flaps of cotton folded back over clumps of rigid foam that looked like the entrails of small animals. It all looked sordid and sad. The sadness was not a surprise, but the sense of wretchedness gripped her heart.

Slumped in the far corner beside Officer LeDonne, Davey glanced up at her and shook his head.

She turned to Fenn, who raised his eyebrows. "Did you find a camera? Did Natalie have a camera?"

"We didn't find one, but Slim and Slam say all the pictures in there were taken with the same camera. One of those little Ph.D. jobs."

"Ph.D.?"

"Push here, dummy. An auto-focus. Like a little Olympus or a Canon. With a zoom feature."

In other words, Natalie's camera was exactly like theirs, not to mention most of the other cameras in Westerholm. The bedroom felt airless, hot, despairing. A lunatic who liked to dress women up like sex toys had finally taken his fantasies to their logical conclusion and used Natalie Weil's bed as an operating table. Nora wondered if he had been seeing all five women at the same time.

She was glad she wasn't a cop. There was too much to think about, and half of what you had to think about made no sense. But the worst part of standing here was standing *here.*

She had to say something. What came out of her mouth was "Were there pictures in the other houses? Like the ones in the kitchen?" She barely heard the detective's negative answer; she had barely heard her own question. Somehow she had walked across several yards of unspattered tan carpet to stand in front of four long bookshelves. Two feet away, Davey gave her the look of an animal in a cage. Nora fled into the safety of book titles, but she found no safety. In the living room Fenn had said something about Natalie's affection for horror novels, and here was the proof, in alphabetical order by author's name. These books had titles like *The Rats* and *Vampire Junction* and *The Silver Skull.* Here were *They Thirst, Hell House, The Books of Blood,* and *The Brains of Rats.* Natalie had owned more Dean Koontz novels than Nora had known existed, she had every Stephen King novel from *Carrie* to *Dolores Claiborne,* all of Anne Rice and Clive Barker and Whitley Strieber.

Nora moved along the shelves as if in a trance. Here was a Natalie Weil who entertained herself with stories of vampires, dismemberment, monsters with tentacles and bad breath, cannibalism, psychotic killers, degrading random death. This person wanted fear, but creepy, safe fear. She had been like a roller coaster aficionado for whom tame county fair roller coasters were as good as the ones that spun you upside down and dropped you so fast your eyes turned red. It was all just a ride.

At the end of the bottom shelf her eyes met the names Marletta Teatime and Clyde Morning above a sullen-looking crow, the familiar logo of Blackbird Books, Chancel House's small, soon-to-be-discontinued horror line. Alden had expected steady, automatic profits from these writers, but they had failed him. Gaudy with severed heads and mutilated dolls, the covers of their books came back from the distributors within days of publication. Davey had argued to keep the line, which managed to make a small amount of money every season, in part because Teatime and Morning never got more than two thousand dollars per book. (Davey sometimes frivolously suggested that they were actually the same person.) Alden dismissed Davey's argument that he had condemned the books by refusing to promote or publicize them; the beauty of horror was that it sold itself. Davey said that his father treated the books like orphaned children, and Alden said damn right, like orphaned children, they had to pull their own weight.

"Mrs. Chancel?" said Holly Fenn.

Another title shouted at her from the bottom shelf. *Night Journey* protruded at a hasty, awkward angle from between two Stephen King encyclopedias as if Natalie had crammed it in anywhere before running to the door.

"Mr. Chancel?"

She looked at the *D*'s, but Natalie had owned no other Driver novels.

"Sorry I wasn't more helpful." Davey's voice sounded as if it came from the bottom of a well.

"No harm in trying." Fenn stepped out of the doorway.

Davey shot Nora another anguished glance and moved toward the door. Nora followed, and LeDonne came along behind. The four of them moved in single file toward the living room, where Slim and Slam faced forward, automatically shedding any signs of individuality. Davey said, "Excuse me, I have to go back."

Fenn flattened his bulk against the wall to let Davey get by. Nora and the two policemen watched him go down the corridor and swerve into the bedroom. LeDonne quizzed Fenn with a look, and Fenn shook his head. After a couple of seconds, Davey emerged, more distressed than ever.

"Forget something?" Fenn asked.

"I thought I saw something—couldn't even tell you what it was. But—" He spread his hands, shaking his head.

"That happens," Fenn said. "If it comes back to you, don't be shy about giving me a call."

When they turned to go down the stairs, the two FBI men split apart and looked away.

16

"WHAT DID YOU think you saw?"

"Nothing."

"You went back in the bedroom. You had something on your mind. What was it?"

"Nothing." He looked sideways at her, so shaken he was white. "It was a dumb idea. I should have just gone home."

"Why didn't you?"

"I wanted to see that house." He paused. "And I wanted you to see it."

"Why?"

He waited a second before answering. "I thought if you looked at it, you might stop having nightmares."

"Pretty strange idea," Nora said.

"Okay, it was a rotten idea." His voice grew louder. "It was the worst idea in the history of the world. In fact, every single idea I've ever had in my life was really terrible. Are we in agreement now? Good. Then we can forget about it."

"Davey."

"*What?*"

"Do you remember when I asked if you were upset?"

"No." He hesitated, then sighed again, and his glance suggested the arrival of a confession. "Why would I be upset?"

Nora gathered herself. "You must have been surprised by what your father said about Hugo Driver."

He looked at her as if trying to recall Alden's words. "He said he was a great writer."

"You said he was a great writer." After a second of silence she said, "What I mean is his attitude."

"Yeah," Davey said. "You're right. That was a surprise. He sort of jolted me, I guess."

For Nora the next few seconds filled with a hopeful tension.

"I've got something on my mind, I guess I was worked up. . . . I don't want to fight, Nora."

"So you're not mad at me anymore."

"I wasn't mad at you. I just feel confused."

Two hours with his parents had turned him back into Pippin Little. If he needed a Green Knight, she volunteered on the spot. She had asked for a job, and here one was sitting next to her. She could help Davey become his successful adult self. She would help him get the position he deserved at Chancel House. Her other plans, befriending Daisy and moving to New York, were merely elements of this larger, truer occupation. *Start,* she commanded herself. *Now.*

"Davey," she said, "what would you like to be doing at Chancel House?"

Again, he seemed to force himself to think. "Editorial work."

"Then that's what you should be doing."

"Well, yeah, but you know, Dad . . ." He gave her a resigned look.

"You're not like that disgusting guy who takes old ladies to lunch, you're not Dick Dart. What job do you want most?"

He bit the lining of his cheek before deciding to declare what she already suspected. "I'd like to edit Blackbird Books. I think I could build Blackbird into something good, but Dad is canceling the line."

"Not if you make him keep it."

"How do I do that?"

"I don't know, exactly. But for sure you have to come at him with a plan." She thought for a moment. "Get all the figures on the Blackbird Books. Give him projections, give him graphs. Have lists of writers you want to sign up. Print up a presentation. Tell him you'll do it on top of your other work."

He turned his head to gape at her.

"I'll help. We'll put something together that he won't be able to refuse."

He looked away, looked back, and filled his lungs with air. "Well, okay. Let's give it a try."

"Blackbird Books, here we come," she said, and remembered seeing the row of titles by Clyde Morning and Marletta Teatime in Natalie's bedroom. Unlike Natalie's other books, these had not been filed alphabetically, but separated, at the end of the bottom shelf.

"You know, it might work," Davey said.

Nora wondered if putting the books together meant they were significantly better or worse than other horror novels. Maybe what was crucial about them was that they were published by Blackbird—Chancel House.

"I was thinking once that we could do a series of classics, books in the public domain."

"Good idea," Nora said. Looking back, she thought that the Blackbird Books on Natalie's shelf seemed uniformly new and unmarked, as if they had been bought at the same time and never read.

"If we can put together a serious presentation, he'll have to pay attention."

"Davey . . ." A sense of hope and expectancy filled Nora, and the question escaped her before she could call it back. "Do you ever think of moving out of Westerholm?"

He lifted his chin. "To tell you the truth, I think about getting out of this hole just about every day. But look, I know how much living here means to you."

Her laughter amazed him.

BOOK II

PADDY'S TAIL

THE FIRST THING PIPPIN SAW WAS THE TIP OF A LITTLE TAIL, NO WIDER THAN FOUR HORSEHAIRS BOUND TOGETHER, BUT IN SEARCH OF THE REST OF THE ANIMAL, HE FOLLOWED THE TAIL AROUND ROCKS, THROUGH TALL WEEDS, IN GREAT CIRCLES, UP AND DOWN GREAT LOOPS ON THE GRASS, AND WHEN AT LAST HE REACHED THE END OF THE LONG, LONG TAIL, HE FOUND ATTACHED TO IT A TINY MOUSE. THE MOUSE APPEARED TO BE DEAD.

17

ALTHOUGH DAVEY SEEMED moody and distracted, the following five days were nearly as happy as any Nora could remember. One other period—several weeks in Vietnam, in memory the happiest of her life—had come at a time when she had been too busy to think of anything but work. Looking back, she had said to herself, *So that was happiness.*

Her first month in the Evacuation Hospital had jolted her so thoroughly that by its end she was no longer certain what she would need to get her through. Pot, okay. Alcohol, you bet. Emotional calluses, even better. At the rate of twenty to thirty surgical cases a day, she had learned about debridement and irrigation—clearing away dead skin and cleaning the wound against infection—worms in the chest cavity, amputations, crispy critters, and pseudomonas. She particularly hated pseudomonas, a bacterial infection that coated burn patients with green slime. During that month, she had junked most of what she had been taught in nursing school and learned to assist at high-speed operations, clamping blood vessels and cutting where the neurosurgeon told her to cut. At night her boots left bloody trails across the floor. She was in a flesh factory, not a hospital. The old, idealistic Nora Curlew was being unceremoniously peeled away like a layer of outgrown clothes, and what she saw of the new was a spiritless automaton.

Then a temporary miracle occurred. As many patients died during or after operations, the wounded continued to scream from their cots, and Nora was always exhausted, but not *as* exhausted, and the patients separated into individuals. To these people she did rapid, precise, necessary things that often permitted them to live. At times, she cradled the head of a dying young man and felt that particles of her own being passed into him, easing and steadying. She had won a focused concentration out of the chaos around her, and every operation became a drama in which she and the surgeon performed necessary, inventive actions which banished or at least contained disorder. Some of these actions were elegant; sometimes the entire drama took on a rigorous, shattering elegance. She learned the differences between the surgeons, some of them fullbacks, some concert pianists, and she treasured the compliments they gave her. At nights, too alert with exhaustion to sleep, she smoked Montagnard grass with the others and played whatever they were playing that day—cards, volleyball, or insults.

At the end of her fifth week in Vietnam, a neurosurgeon named Chris Cross had been reassigned and a new surgeon, Daniel Harwich, had rotated in. Cross, a cheerful blond mesomorph with thousands of awful jokes and a bottomless appetite for beer, had been a fullback surgeon, but a great fullback. He worked athletically, with flashes of astounding grace, and Nora had decided that, all in all, she would probably never see a better surgeon. Their entire unit mourned his going, and when his replacement turned out to be a stringy, lint-haired geek with Coke-bottle glasses and no visible traces of humor, they circled their wagons around Captain Cross's memory and politely froze out the intruder. A tough little nurse named Rita Glow said she'd work with the clown, what the hell, it was all slice 'n' dice anyhow, and while Nora continued her education in the miraculous under the unit's other two surgeons, one a bang-smash fullback, one a pianist who had learned some bang-smash tendencies from Chris Cross, she noticed that not only did geeky Dan Harwich put in his twelve-hour days with the rest of them but he got through more patients with fewer complaints and less drama.

One day Rita Glow said she had to see this guy work, he was righteous, he was a fucking *tap dancer* in there, and the next morning she swapped assignments to put Nora across the table from Harwich. Between them was a paralyzed young soldier whose back looked like raw meat. Harwich told her she was going to have to help him while he cut shell fragments from the boy's vertebrae. He was both a fullback and a pianist, and his hands were astonishingly fast and sure. After three hours, he closed the boy's back with the quickest, neatest stitches she had ever seen, looked over at Nora, and said, "Now that I'm warmed up, let's do something hard, okay?"

Within three weeks she was sleeping with Harwich, and within four she was in love. Then the skies opened. Tortured, mangled bodies packed the

OR, and they worked seventy-eight hours straight through. She and Harwich crawled into bed covered with the blood of other people, made love, slept for a second, and got up and did the whole thing all over again. They were shelled in the middle of operations and in the middle of the night, sometimes the same thing, and as the clarity of the earlier period shredded, details of individual soldiers burned themselves into her mind. No longer quite sane, she thrust the terror and panic into a locked inner closet.

After three months she was raped by two dumbbell grunts who caught her as she came outside on a break. One of them hit her in the side of the head, pushed her down, and fell on her. The other kneeled on her arms. At first she thought they had mistaken her for a Vietcong, but almost instantly she realized that what they had mistaken her for was a living woman. The rape was a flurry of thumps and blows and enormous, reeking hands over her mouth; it was having the breath mashed out of her while grunting animals dug at her privates. While it went on, Nora was punched through the bottom of the world. This was entirely literal. The column of the world went from bottom to top, and now she had been smashed through the bottom of the column along with the rest of the shit. Demons leaned chattering out of the darkness.

The second grunt rolled off, the first grunt let go of her arms, and they sprinted away. She heard their footsteps and realized that now she was on the other side, with the gibbering demons; then she gathered the demons into her psychic hands and stuffed them into an inner container just large enough to hold them.

Nora did not tell Harwich what had happened until hours later, when she looked down at the blood soaking through her clothes, thought it was hers, and fainted. A grim Harwich accepted her refusal to report the incident but followed her out of the OR on a break to pass from his hands to hers a dead officer's handgun. This she kept as close as possible until her last morning in Vietnam, when she dropped it into the nurses' latrine. Even after Dan Harwich left Vietnam, vowing that he would write (he did) and that they had a future together (they didn't), she used her awareness of the gun beneath her pillow to fend off nightmares of the incident until she could almost think that she had forgotten it. And for years after Vietnam it was as if she really had forgotten all about it—until she had reached a kind of provisional, static happiness in Westerholm, Connecticut. In Westerholm, the ordinary, terrible nightmares of dead and dying soldiers had begun to be supplanted by the other, worse nightmares—about being pushed through the hole at the bottom of the world.

Long after, Nora sometimes looked back at that exalted period before the war slammed down on her and thought: *Happiness comes when you are looking elsewhere, it is a by-product, of no importance in itself.*

18

EVERY NIGHT THAT week, Nora and Davey delved into Blackbird Books, playing with figures and trying to work out a presentation that would convince Alden. Davey remained moody and remote but seemed grateful for Nora's help. To see what Blackbird Books were like, Nora read *The Waiting Grave* by Marletta Teatime and *Blood Bond* by Clyde Morning. Davey sounded out agents; he and Nora drew up lists of writers who might sign up with a revitalized Blackbird Books. They learned that Blackbird's greatest appeal was its connection to Chancel House, but that Chancel House had done even less with the line than Davey had imagined.

In 1977, its first year, Blackbird had published twelve paperback originals by writers then unknown. By 1979, half of the ten original writers had left in search of more promotion, higher advances, and better editing. In those days an assistant editor named Merle Marvell had handled the line. Marvell's secretary, shared with two other assistant editors, copyedited Blackbird novels for fifteen dollars a book. (Alden would not waste money on a professional copy editor.) Blackbird stubbornly refused to lay golden eggs, and by 1981 all of its original writers had moved on, leaving behind only Teatime and Morning, who had produced their first books. No longer an assistant editor, Merle Marvell bought one first novel that won an important prize and another that made the best-seller list and thereafter had no more time for Blackbird. Since then, Blackbird's two stalwarts sent in their manuscripts and took their money. Neither had an agent. Instead of addresses, they had post office boxes—Teatime's in Norwalk, Connecticut, Morning's in midtown Manhattan. Their telephone numbers had never been divulged. They never demanded higher advances, lunches, or ad budgets. Clyde Morning had won the British Fantasy Award in 1983, and Marletta Teatime had been nominated for a World Fantasy Award in 1985. They went on producing a book a year until 1989, when each of them stopped writing.

"Chancel House has been publishing these people for more than ten years, and you don't even know their telephone numbers?"

"That's not the weird part," Davey said. They were devouring a sausage and mushroom pizza delivered by a gnome in a space helmet who on closer inspection had become a sixteen-year-old girl wearing a motorcycle helmet. Room had been made on the table for a bottle of Robert Mondavi Private Reserve Cabernet Sauvignon and two glasses by shoving papers, printouts, and sheets torn from legal pads into piles. "The weird part is what I found on a shelf in the conference room today."

Like the old Davey, he raised his eyebrows and smiled, teasing her. Nora thought he looked wonderful. She liked the way he ate pizza, with a knife and fork. Nora picked up a slice and chomped, pulling away long strings of mozzarella, but Davey addressed a pizza as though it were filet mignon. "Okay," she said, "what did you find on this shelf?"

"Remember I told you that every new manuscript gets written down in a kind of a ledger? Now all this is on a computer. Whatever happens to the submission gets entered beside the title—rejected and returned, or accepted, with the date. I was wondering if we might have rejected books by Morning or Teatime, so I went back to '89, the first year we used computers, and there was Clyde Morning. He submitted a book called *Spectre* in June '89, and the manuscript never left the house. It wasn't rejected, but it was never accepted, either. He didn't even have an editor, so no one was actually responsible for the manuscript."

"What happened to it?"

"Precisely. I went down to the production department. Of course nobody could remember. Most of the scripts they work on are kept for a year or two after publication, why I don't know, and then get returned to the editor, who sends them back to the author. I looked at all of them, but I couldn't find *Spectre.* A production assistant finally reminded me that they sometimes squirrel things away on the shelves in the conference room. It's like the dead letter office." Davey was grinning.

"And you went to the conference room"—he was nodding his head and grinning even more wildly—"and you . . . you found the book?"

"Right there! And not only that . . ."

She looked at him in astonishment. "You read it?"

"I skimmed it, anyhow. It's kind of sloppy, but I think it's publishable. I have to see if it's still available—I suppose I have to find out if Morning is still *alive*—but it could be the leadoff in our new line."

She liked the *our.* "So we're almost ready."

"I want to go in on Monday." He did not have to be more specific. "He's still in a pretty good mood on Monday afternoons." This was Friday evening. "I got a call back from an agent this morning, sounding me out about a couple of writers I'm sure we could get without breaking the bank."

"You devil," she said. "You've been sitting on this ever since you came home."

"Just waiting for the right moment." He finished the last of his pizza. "Do you want to play around with the presentation some more, or is there something else we could do?"

"Like celebrate?"

"If you're in the mood," Davey said.

"I definitely feel a mood coming on," Nora said.

"Well, then." He looked at her almost uncertainly.

"Come on, big boy," she said. "We'll take care of the dishes later."

Twenty minutes later, Davey lay with his hands folded on his stomach, staring up at the ceiling. "Sweetie," she said, "I didn't say it hurt, I just said it was uncomfortable. I felt dry, but I'm sure that's just temporary. I have an appointment with my doctor next week to talk about hormone replacement. Look at it this way—we probably don't have to worry about getting pregnant anymore."

"I have condoms. You have your . . . thing. Of course we don't have to worry about that."

"Davey, I'm forty-nine. My body is changing. There has to be this period of adjustment."

"Period of adjustment."

"That's all. My doctor says everything will be fine as long as I eat right and exercise, and probably I'll have to start taking estrogen. It happens to every woman, and now it's my turn."

He turned his head to her. "Were you dry last time?"

"No." She tried not to sigh. "I wasn't."

"So why are you this time?"

"Because this is the time it happened."

"But you're not an old woman." He rolled over and half-buried his face in the pillow. "I know what's wrong. I got too excited or something, and now you're turned off."

"Davey, I'm starting to go through menopause. Of course I'm not turned off. I love you. We've always had wonderful sex."

"You can't have wonderful sex with someone who wakes up moaning and groaning almost every night."

"It isn't . . ." This was not going to be a fruitful remark. Neither would it be fruitful to remark that you couldn't have sex with a man who would not come to your bed, or who left your bed to worry about work or Hugo Driver or whatever it was Davey worried about late at night.

"Well, a lot of nights, anyhow," he said, taking up her unspoken comment. "Maybe you need therapy or something. You're too young for menopause. When my mother went through it, she had a lot of white hair, she was over fifty, and she turned into a total bitch. She was impossible, she was like in a rage for at least a year."

"People have different reactions. It's nothing to be afraid of."

"People in menopause don't have periods. You had one a little while ago."

"I had a period that lasted more than two weeks. Then I didn't have one for about six weeks."

"I don't have to hear all the gory details."

"The gory details are my department, right. But everything's going to be all right. This is *temporary.*"

"God, I hope so."

What did Davey hope was temporary? Menopause? Aging? She moved across the sheet and put an arm over his shoulder. He turned his face away. Nora kissed the back of his head and slid her other arm beneath him. When he did not attempt to shrug her off or push her away, she pulled him into her. He resisted only a second or two before turning his head to her and slipping his arms around her. His cheek felt wet against hers. "Oh, honey," she said, and moved her head back to see the tears leaking from his eyes. Davey wiped his face, then held her close.

"This is no good."

"It'll get better."

"I don't know what to *do.*"

"Try talking about it," Nora said, swallowing the words *for a change.*

"I sort of think I have to."

"Good."

Now he had a grudging, almost furtive look. "You know how I've been kind of worried lately? It's because of this thing that happened about ten years before I met you." He looked up at the ceiling, and she braced herself, with a familiar despair, for a story which would owe as much to Hugo Driver as to Davey's real history. "I was having a rough time because Amy Randolph finally broke up with me."

Nora had heard all about Amy Randolph, a beautiful and destructive poet-photographer-screenwriter-painter whom Davey had met in college. He had lost his virginity to her, and she had lost hers to her father. (Unless this was another colorful embellishment.) After graduation they had traveled through North Africa. Amy had flirted with every attractive man she met and threw tyrannical fits when the men responded. Finally the two of them had been deported from Algeria and shared an apartment in the Village. Amy went in and out of hospitals, twice for suicide attempts. She photographed corpses and drug addicts. She had no interest in sex. Davey once said to Nora that Amy was so brilliant he hadn't been able to leave her for fear of missing her conversation. In the end, she had deprived him of her conversation by moving in with an older woman, a Romanian émigrée who edited an intellectual journal. He had never explained to Nora how he had felt about losing Amy, or spoken of what he had done between the breakup and their own meeting.

"Well," Nora said, "whatever this is, it couldn't have been much stranger than life with Amy."

"That's what you think," Davey said.

19

"IT WAS ABOUT a month after Amy left. You know, I think I was actually kind of happy for her. Some people acted like they thought I should be disturbed by what she did, but I didn't know why. Amy never liked sex anyhow, so it was more like getting worked up about who she *wasn't* doing it with than who she was, and that's ridiculous. Anyhow, after about a month, I repainted my apartment and put new posters on the walls, and then I got a really good stereo system and a lot of new records. Whenever I found anything that reminded me of her, I threw it out. A couple of times when she called up, I hung up on her. Because it was all over, right?"

"You were pretty angry," Nora said.

Davey shook his head. "I don't remember being angry. I just didn't see the point of talking to her."

"Okay." Nora reached over the side of the bed and picked her bra and blouse off the floor. She tossed the bra into the clothing bin and put on the blouse.

"I wasn't angry with Amy," he said. "Everybody kept telling me that I had to be, but I wasn't. You can't get angry at crazy people."

Nora gave up and nodded.

"Anyhow, I was in a funny mood. After my apartment was all redone, I reread Hugo Driver—all three books—after I came home from work. Then I read *Night Journey* all over again. I felt like Pippin."

In other words, Nora thought, he felt as though Amy had killed him.

"I couldn't stand being in the apartment by myself, but I hardly had any friends because Amy, you know, made that difficult. I didn't want to spend time with my parents because they hated Amy, and they *loved* telling me how lucky I was. I went through this weird period. Sometimes

I'd spend the whole night staring at the tube. I'd listen to one piece of music over and over, all weekend."

"I guess you got into drugs," Nora said.

"Well, yeah. Amy always hated drugs, so now that I was free . . . you know? A guy in the mailroom named Bang Bang sold stuff, which Dad didn't know about. So one day I saw this guy coming out of the mailroom on a break, and I looked at him, and he looked at me, and I followed him outside. I got some coke and some pot, and I pretty much did those for about a year. At work I stayed pretty straight, but when I got back to my apartment, boy, I poured myself a glass of Bombay gin on the rocks, did two big, fat lines, rolled a joint, and had a little party until I went to bed. Or didn't. I was thirty, thirty-one. I didn't need a lot of sleep. Just take a shower, shave, drop in some Murine, couple lines, fresh clothes, off to work."

"And one day you met this Girl Scout," Nora said.

"You sure you want to hear about this?"

"Why don't you just say, 'Nora, once when I was fooling around with drugs I had this messed-up girlfriend, and we got crazy together'?"

"Because it's not that simple. You have to understand where I was mentally in order to understand what happened. Otherwise it won't make any sense."

It occurred to Nora that whatever he had to say, strictly factual or not, would be instructive. Maybe Davey had been a weekend punk!

"This isn't just about a girl, is it?"

"Actually it's about Natalie Weil." He pushed himself upright and pulled the sheets above his navel. "Look, Nora, I didn't tell you the truth the other day. This is the real reason I wanted to get into Natalie's house."

She tucked up her legs, leaned forward, and waited.

20

"I WAS IN a stall in the men's room one morning, feeling lousy because I'd stayed up all night. I snorted some coke, and my nose started to bleed. I had to sit on the toilet with my head back, holding toilet paper against my nose. Finally the bleeding stopped, and I decided to try to get through the day.

"I came out of the stall. Some little guy was going toward the sinks. I grabbed some towels and dried my hands, and this guy was messing with his hair, and I looked at his face in the mirror, and I almost had a heart attack."

"The little guy was a girl."

"How did you know that?"

"Because you almost had a heart attack."

"She was in the art department. She had short hair and she wore men's clothes. That's all I knew. I didn't even know her last name. Her first name was Paddi." He looked at her as if this were of enormous significance.

"Patty?"

"Paddi. Two *d*'s and an *i*. Okay, my nose started bleeding again. I grabbed another towel and held it up against my nose. Paddi was dumping two piles of coke on the sink in front of her. 'Try this,' she said. We're right in the middle of the men's room! I leaned over and snorted the stuff right off the sink, and bingo! I felt a thousand percent better. 'Get it?' she said. 'Always use good stuff.'

" 'What planet are you from?' I asked her.

"She smiled at me and said, '*I was born in a village at the foot of a great mountain. My father is a blacksmith.*'

"I almost passed out. She was quoting *Night Journey.* I said, '*I wander far and sometimes get lost. I own a purpose greater than myself, the saving of children from the darkness.*'

"And she chimed in, '*I conquer my own fear.*'

"We grinned at each other for a second, and I shooed her outside before someone came in. She was waiting for me across the hall. 'I'm Paddi Mann,' she said. 'And you're Davey Chancel, of the famous Chancel House Chancels. Want to buy me a drink tonight?'

"Normally, assertive women put me off, and we're not supposed to go out with women from the office, but she could quote Hugo Driver! I told her to meet me at six-thirty at Hannigan's, a bar a couple of blocks away, and she said no, we should go to the Hellfire Club down on Second Avenue, great place, and let's meet at seven-thirty so she could take care of some things she had to do. Fine, I said, and she came right up in front of me and tilted up her head and whispered, '*His own salvation lay within himself.*' "

Nora had heard these words before, but she could not remember when.

"You know what? I thought I could learn things from her. It was like she had secrets, and they were the secrets I needed to know."

"Sure," Nora said. "You needed to know the secret of how to score coke better than Bang Bang's."

Davey had gone home and changed into jeans, a black sweater, and a black leather jacket before walking to Second Avenue. The Hellfire Club was between Eighth and Ninth, on the East Side. He reached the corner of Ninth and Second only a minute or two past seven-thirty and walked down the east side of the avenue, passing a fast-food restaurant, a Mexican restaurant, and saw a bar farther down the block. He picked up his pace and went past a window that showed a few men huddled over a long, dark bar, put his hand on the door, and just below his hand saw the name MORLEY'S.

He had managed to miss the club. He went back up the east side of the avenue, checking the names on buildings, and missed it again.

A rank of three telephones stood only a few feet away. The first had a severed cord instead of a receiver, the second did not provide a dial tone, and the third permitted six-sevenths of Davey's quarter into its slot and then froze.

Disgusted, Davey stepped away from the telephones and went to the corner to wait for the light to change. He glanced down the block and this time noticed a narrow stone staircase with wrought-iron handrails between Morley's bar and a lighting-goods shop. The stairs led to a dark wooden door, which looked too elegant for its surroundings. Centered in the door's top panel was a brass plate slightly larger than an index card.

The light changed, but instead of crossing the street, Davey walked to the foot of the stairs and looked up at a five-story brownstone wedged between two apartment buildings. On either side of the door were two curtained windows. The lettering on the plaque was not quite legible from the bottom of the stairs. He climbed two steps and saw that the plate read HELLFIRE CLUB and, beneath that, MEMBERS ONLY. He went up the stairs and opened the door. Across a tiny entry stood another door, glossy black. Three commands had been painted on a white wooden plaque fixed just beneath the level of his eyes:

DO NOT QUESTION.
DO NOT JUDGE.
DO NOT HESITATE.

Davey opened the black door. Before him was a hallway with a floral carpet which continued up a flight of stairs. To his left an elderly woman stood behind a checkroom counter beside the opening into a dim barroom. Past the bar, a wide leather armchair stood beside an ambitious potted fern. A white-haired concierge at a glossy black desk turned to him with a diplomatic half smile. To eliminate the preliminaries, Davey peered into the barroom and saw only prosperous-looking men in suits seated around tables or standing in clusters of three or four. He noticed a few women in the room, none of them Paddi. In the instant before the man at the desk spoke to him, he saw—thought he saw—a naked man covered to wrists and neck with elaborate tattoos beside a naked woman, her back to Davey, who had shaved her head and powdered or otherwise colored her body a flat, dead white.

"May I assist you, sir?"

Startled, Davey looked at the concierge. He cleared his throat. "Thank you. I'm here to meet a woman named Paddi Mann." He glanced back into the bar and had the sense that the other people in the room had shifted their positions to conceal the surreal couple.

"Sir."

Davey looked back at the concierge.

"That was Miss Mann?"

When Davey said yes, the concierge told him to be seated, please, and watched him proceed to the leather chair, which provided a view of nothing more provocative than the wide mahogany doors and a row of hunting prints on the opposite wall. The concierge opened a drawer and drew out a ribbon microphone at least fifty years old, positioned it squarely in front of him, and said, "Guest for Miss Mann." The words reverberated from the barroom, from rooms upstairs, and from behind the mahogany doors.

One of the mahogany doors opened, and a Paddi Mann who looked less raffish and more sophisticated than her office persona stepped smiling into the hallway. The dark suit into which she had changed looked more expensive than most of Davey's own suits. Her shining hair fell softly over her forehead and ears.

She asked why he was dressed that way.

He explained that he thought he was going to meet her at a bar.

Bars were disgusting. Why did he think she had invited him to her club?

He hadn't understood, he said. If she liked, he could go home and put on a suit.

She told him not to bother and suggested they swap jackets.

He took off his leather jacket and held it out. Paddi slipped off her suit jacket and twirled herself into his jacket so smoothly that he barely had time to notice that she was wearing suspenders.

"Your turn," she said.

He was afraid he'd rip the shoulder seams, but the jacket met his back and shoulders with only a suggestion of tightness.

"You're lucky I like big jackets."

Paddi opened the mahogany door to a lounge in which groups of chairs and couches were arranged before a window. He saw the backs of several male heads, a white gesticulating arm, newspapers and magazines on a long wooden rack. A waiter with a black bow tie, a black vest, and a shaven head held an empty tray and an order pad.

Paddi directed him to a pair of library chairs before a wall of books at the right of the room. Between the chairs stood a round table on top of which lay a portfolio-sized envelope with the Chancel House logo. The waiter materialized beside Paddi. She asked for the usual, and Davey ordered a double martini on the rocks.

He asked what the usual was, and she said, "A Top-and-Bottom: half port and half gin." It was an outsider drink, she told him.

While he pondered this category, Davey took in that the owner of the naked arm he had glimpsed from the hallway was a middle-aged man seated in a leather chair near the center of the room. The arms of the chair cut his midsection from view, but there were no clothes on his flabby upper body, and none on the thick white legs crossed ankle to knee in front of the chair. A leather strap circled his neck. From the front of the strap, a chain, an actual chain, said Davey to Nora, like you'd use on a dog if the dog weighed two hundred pounds and liked to munch babies, hung between him and the bearded guy in a three-piece suit holding the other end. The man wearing the chain swiveled his head to give Davey a do-you-mind? glare. Davey looked away and saw that while most of the people in the room were dressed conventionally, one man reading a newspaper wore black leather trousers, motorcycle boots, and an open black leather vest that revealed an intricate pattern of scars on his chest.

He wondered how Paddi could have objected to his clothing when at least one person in the club wore no clothing at all.

"In here," she said, "people wear whatever is right for them. What's right for you is a suit."

"Some of these people must have a lot of trouble when they leave the club," he said.

"Some of these people never leave the club," she said.

"Is this stuff real?" Nora asked. "Or are you making it all up?"

"As real as what happened to Natalie," Davey said.

Paddi worked at Chancel House because it had published *Night Journey.* Her job gave her a unique connection to the book she loved above all others. And since she was on the subject, she drew out of the big Chancel House envelope a stiff, glossy sheet that Davey recognized as the reverse side of a jacket rendering.

"An idea of mine," Paddi said, turning the sheet over to display a drawing it took Davey a moment to understand; when he did, he wondered why the idea had never occurred to him. Paddi had drawn the jacket for an annotated scholarly edition of *Night Journey.* (Her design was based on the famous "GI edition" of the novel.) Every one of the hundred thousand Driver fanatics in America would have to buy it. Scholars would be able to trace the growth of the book over successive variations and discuss the meanings of the changes in the text. It was a great idea.

"But there was one problem," Davey told Nora. "In order to do it right, we needed the manuscript."

"What's the problem with that?" asked Nora.

The problem, Paddi said, was that the manuscript seemed to have disappeared. Hugo Driver had died in 1950, his wife in 1952, and their only child, a retired high school English teacher, had said in an interview on the twentieth anniversary of the book's publication that he had never seen any manuscripts of his father's books. As far as he knew, they had never come back from Chancel House.

Davey said he would try to find out what had happened to the manuscript. Lincoln Chancel had probably installed it in a bank vault somewhere. It certainly couldn't be lost. Nothing so important could have slipped through the cracks—it was the manuscript of the first Chancel House book, for heaven's sake!

"That would be unfortunate in light of the rumors," Paddi said.

"What rumors?"

"That Hugo Driver didn't really write the book," Paddi said.

Where did this stuff come from? She knew what it was, didn't she? It was what happened whenever somebody great appeared, a bunch of weasels started trying to shoot holes in him. Davey ranted on in this fashion until he ran out of breath, at which point he inhaled hugely and declared that after all it all made perfect sense; *Night Journey* was such a brilliant book that the weasels couldn't cope with it. It happened all the time. Somewhere, someone was saying that Zelda Fitzgerald was the real author of *Tender Is the Night.*

"Zelda *was* the real author of *Tender Is the Night,*" Paddi said. "Sorry. Just kidding."

Davey asked her if she believed this crap.

"No, not at all," she said. "I agree with you. Hugo Driver should be on stamps. I think his picture should be on *money.* One of the reasons I like this club is that it seems such a Hugo Driver–ish sort of place, doesn't it?"

Davey guessed that it did.
Would he like to see more of it?

"I wondered when we were going to get to this part," Nora said.

21

AT THE LANDING above the curved staircase, Paddi did not take him down the dark corridor but led him up another flight of stairs. An even narrower version of the staircase continued upward, but Paddi took him into a corridor identical to the one below. Davey felt as if he were following Paddi through a forest at night.

Then she vanished, and he realized that she had slipped through an open door. The shade had been pulled down, and the room was darker than the corridor. After they undressed she led him to a futon. Davey stretched out against her, his body as hot as an oven-warmed brick, hers as cool as a stone drawn from a river. He hugged her close, and her cool hands ran up and down his back. When his orgasm came, he yelled with pleasure. They lay quiet for a time, then talked, and when they had established that neither of them was seeing anyone else, Davey fell asleep.

He woke up an hour later, hungry, light-headed, uncertain of his surroundings. He remembered that he was lying on a floor in the East Village. He was suddenly, shamefully certain that Paddi had stolen his money. He sat upright, and his hand touched a girlish shoulder. He looked down and made out the shape of her head on the pillow. Pillow? He did not remember a pillow. A sheet covered both of them.

"We should get something to eat," he said.

"I'll take care of that. Isn't there something else you'd like to do first?"

He stretched out beside her and once more felt that he was as hot as a potbellied stove and she as cool as a substance just extracted from a river. Davey surrendered to sensation.

Unimaginably later, they lay side by side, staring up. Davey had forgotten where he was. A slight, high-pitched buzzing sounded in his ears. The woman beside him seemed completely beautiful. Paddi rolled over, picked up an instrument like the mouthpiece of an old-fashioned telephone, and ordered oysters and caviar and other things he didn't quite catch and what sounded like a lot of wine.

Soon two young women entered the room carrying circular trays, from which they distributed around the futon a number of covered dishes. Two open bottles and four glasses appeared beside Davey's left shoulder. The women smiled at Paddi, who was sprawled on top of the sheet, but did not look at Davey. When they had put in place the last dish, they stood and turned to the door, where one of them said, "Shall I?"

"Yes," Paddi said. A low, rosy light spread through the room, and the women backed smiling through the door.

Plovers' eggs, dumplings, steaming sautéed mushrooms, eel, whitebait, rich finger-sized segments of duck, similar sections of roast pork, little steaming things like pizzas covered with fresh basil and glistening shreds of tomato, in a crisp transparent seal, round, pungent objects that must have been meatballs and tasted like single malt scotch, grapes, clementines; an excellent white burgundy and a better red bordeaux. Taking almost nothing herself, Paddi brought plate after plate before him. Davey sampled everything, and together they emptied half of each bottle. Paddi kept him amused with tales of the art department and gossip about people who worked at Chancel House; she quoted Hugo Driver and wondered at the friendship between the author and Lincoln Chancel. Did Davey know where this unlikely pair had met?

"Sure, at Shorelands," Davey said, "this estate in Massachusetts. They were put up in the same cottage." He thought that the owner of the place, Georgina Weatherall, who knew that Davey's grandfather was on the verge of starting a publishing company, had put them together in the hope that Lincoln Chancel would help Driver in some way. And exactly that had happened. Driver must have shown Chancel the manuscript of *Night Journey,* and Chancel had used it to make Driver's fortune and increase his own.

"Is that really how they met?" Nora asked Davey. "In a sort of literary colony?"

"Shorelands was a private estate where the hostess liked to feel that she was encouraging works of genius, but yeah, that's more or less right. And whether Georgina Weatherall had anything in mind or not, she did put Driver together with my grandfather, and things fell into place. Neither one of them had been at Shorelands before, so they probably spent a lot of time together, like the new guys at school."

A millionaire businessman and a penniless writer? Nora doubted that Lincoln Chancel, a ruthless acquirer of companies, had ever felt like a new boy in school. "Who else was at Shorelands at the same time? I bet, afterward, they all wished that they'd been put together with your grandfather. Did he ever go back?"

"God, no," Davey said. "Haven't you ever seen that *picture*?"

Davey began to laugh.

"What's funny?"

"I just remembered something. There's a picture from when my grandfather was at Shorelands—a photograph of all these guys sitting on the lawn. Georgina Weatherall's in it, and Hugo Driver, and all the people who were there that summer. My grandfather's squeezed into this rickety lawn chair, and he looks like he's about to strangle someone."

The rest of that night Davey lay with Paddi, sipping from a variety of drinks brought in by women he sometimes saw and sometimes did not, occasionally hearing music from the floors below, now and then catching a sob or a shout of laughter from rooms throughout the building.

And then, immediately it seemed, he was locking the door of his apartment, having showered, shaved, and changed clothes without any memory of returning home or performing these tasks. His watch said it was eight o'clock. He felt rested, sober, clearheaded. But how had he gotten home?

22

HE HAD PUSHED through the front doors of the Chancel Building with two appointments in mind, one still to be made, the other already fixed. At some time before he left the building today, he had to see his father to talk about Hugo Driver's manuscripts and doing a definitive edition of the novel, and this evening he was going back to the Hellfire Club. He was ready for both encounters. His father would welcome an idea sure to bring more prestige to the firm, and to his meeting with Paddi he could bring the good news from his father. If Alden Chancel had taken charge of the manuscript of *Night Journey,* Davey intended to take charge of its rebirth.

His ordinary duties devoured the morning until eleven, when he had to go to a meeting. After the meeting, he went up two floors to his father's office, where the secretary told him that Alden had left for lunch and would not be free until three-thirty.

At three twenty-five, Davey went back to see his father.

At first impatient, Alden grew interested in the project Davey described. Yes, it might be possible to publish such an edition as a paperback intended for classroom use. Yes, let's think about using the cover of the GI edition, we got a lot of mileage out of that. As for the manuscript, hadn't that gone back to Driver?

Davey said that an assistant in the art department, the person who had come to him with the idea, had already told him that Driver's son thought it was still with Chancel House. When he named the assistant, his father said, "Paddi Mann, interesting, the meeting I just came from was about an idea of hers, using two different covers on the new paperback of *Night Journey.* Bright girl, this Paddi Mann." But as for the manuscript, if the sole remaining Driver didn't know where it was, maybe it was lost.

For the next two hours, Davey searched the wrapped manuscripts on the conference room shelves and looked in broom closets and the windowless cubicles where copy editors toiled. He stopped only when he noticed that it was twenty minutes before he was to meet Paddi.

A low conversational buzz came from the bar, and Davey glanced through the arched opening as automatically as he had read the admonitions on the inner door. For a moment he thought he saw Dick Dart, but the man vanished behind the crowd. Dick Dart? Could he be in the Hellfire Club? Was *Leland*?

The voice of the concierge forced him to turn away from the bar. "May I assist you, sir?"

Davey placed himself in the chair beside the fern, the concierge opened the drawer, removed the heavy microphone, positioned it with excruciating exactness, and uttered his sentence. Paddi came through the mahogany door. She had her "Hellfire Club look," even though she seemed to be wearing exactly what she had worn to work. They ordered the same drinks from the same waiter. Davey described his searches, and Paddi told him it was important, crucial, to find the manuscript. Wasn't there a record somewhere of everything that came in and went out?

"Yes," Davey said, "but it didn't start until a month or two after the founding of the house. Before that, things were less formal."

"We'll think of something," Paddi said. "Think—what did you forget?"

"The storage area in the basement," Davey said. "I don't think anybody knows what's down there. My grandfather never threw anything out."

"Okay. What would you like to do tonight?"

There were some new movies, how about a movie?

"Or we could go upstairs. Would you like that?"

"Yes," he said. "Yes, I would."

23

AFTER THEY DRESSED and left the room, their arms around each other's waists, Davey felt that his life had undergone a fundamental change. His days and nights had been reversed, and his daytime self, which did boring things at Chancel House, was merely the dream of the more adventurous night-self, which bloomed under the ministrations of Paddi Mann.

They unclasped at the staircase, too narrow to permit them to walk down side by side. Paddi went before him, and he placed his hands on her shoulders. His shirt rode up on his wrist, uncovering his square gold watch. It was a few minutes past six. He wondered what they would do when they reached the street—it was scarcely believable that an outer world existed.

Davey followed her down the last of the stairs, past the empty desk, and outside into a world far too bright. Noises clashed and jangled in the air. Taxis the color of brushfire charged along Second Avenue. A drunken teenage boy in jeans and a denim shirt three times his size lolled against a parking meter; poisonous fumes of sweat, beer, and cigarette smoke came boiling through his skin and floated into Davey's nostrils.

"Davey—"

"Yes?"

"Keep looking for that manuscript. Maybe it's in the Westerholm house."

A bus the size of an airplane whooshed up to the curb, displacing thousands of cubic feet of air and pulverizing a layer of rubble. Davey clapped his hands over his ears, and Paddi waved and glided away.

Alden must have looked into the unused office and seen him leafing through a stack of forgotten manuscripts, some so old they were carbons, because when Davey looked over his shoulder his father loomed behind him. Where the hell had he been the last two nights? His mother had been trying to get him out to Connecticut for the weekend, but the kid never answered his phone. What happened, had he found a new girlfriend or was he turning into a barfly?

Davey said he had been feeling antisocial. It had never occurred to him that it might be his parents who were calling. After all, he saw his father every day.

He was expected at the Poplars for the weekend, beginning Friday night. Alden turned and marched out of the little office, which had the dreariness of all empty spaces meant to be occupied by busy and productive people.

Paddi's trophy did not appear among the papers in the empty office. Davey took the elevator to the basement.

At two twenty-five, he emerged from the storage enclosure with blackened hands and smears of dust on his suit and his face. He had found boxes of letters from deceased authors to deceased editors, group photos of unknown men in square double-breasted suits and Adolphe Menjou mustaches, a meerschaum pipe, a badly tarnished silver cocktail shaker with a silver swizzle stick, but he had not found his trophy.

Two hours before he was to meet Paddi at an address she had printed on a slip of paper now in his jacket pocket, he returned to the basement and again attacked the boxes. He unearthed a carton of Artie Shaw seventy-eights and a deerstalker hat once likely paired with the meerschaum. In a jumble of old catalogs he came across copies of his mother's two early novels, which he set aside. A fabric envelope tied with a ribbon yielded a copy of the photograph he had described to Paddi, and this, too, he set aside. *Night Journey*'s precious manuscript declined to reveal itself. Paddi's final words came back to him, and he promised himself to have a good look through the closets and attic of the Poplars before coming back to town on Sunday.

24

AN ELEMENT OF disaster, however muted, was built into all of Davey's weekends at his parents' house. Daisy might appear for dinner too drunk to sit upright, or a lesser degree of intoxication might bring on a bout of weeping before the end of the soup course. Accusations, some so veiled Davey could not understand exactly who was being accused of what, might fly across the table. Even the uneventful weekends were tainted with the air of oppression, of mysterious but essential things left unsaid. This weekend, however, was an outright calamity.

The Italian girl's nephew, Jeffrey, had recently joined the Poplars household. At this point, his presence seemed an unnecessary affectation on Alden's part. Until Davey arrived in Westerholm on Friday evening, he had expected a younger male version of Maria, a cheerful, smiling person with the stout physique of a tenor hurrying forward to snatch away his weekend bag. But once Davey and Alden came in through the front door, Jeffrey was revealed to be a tall, middle-aged man in a perfectly fitted gray suit who showed no signs of hurrying forward, snatching bags, or doing anything but nodding at them and continuing to pass through the rear of the hall, presumably on his way to the kitchen. His face seemed to suggest a quantity of thoughts and judgments held in check, and his eyes were hooded. Davey thought he must have been some foreign publisher his father had enticed into his web. Then Alden had introduced them, and the two had exchanged a look, Davey imagined, of mutual suspicion.

Friday's dinner had not been unusual. Alden had dominated the conversation, Daisy had agreed with everything he said, and Davey had been silent. When he mentioned the new edition of Driver's book, his father changed the subject. After dinner, Alden said that he hoped Davey would get some rest, he wasn't looking very good, to be frank. By ten, despite the coffee, he was asleep in his old bed.

To his surprise, Davey did not wake up until eleven on Saturday morning. By the time he left his room, it was eleven-thirty. The irregular tap of typewriter keys and the smell of cigarette smoke, along with the faint drone of a radio, came through the door of his mother's studio. For a moment he considered going back for the books he had brought along from the Chancel House basement, but he decided to surprise his mother with them at brunch on Sunday, as he had originally planned.

Maria poured steaming coffee into a mug, uncovered golden toast in a silver rack, and asked if he would like a small omelette. Davey said that toast and jam would be fine and asked if she knew where Mr. Chancel was. Mr. Chancel had gone out shopping. Then, because she seemed to be preparing to leave, he asked her about Jeffrey.

Jeffrey was the son of her sister-in-law. Yes, he did enjoy very much to work for the Chancels. Before he come here? Well, before he come here, he do many things. College student. Soldier. Yes, officer in Vietnam.

Where college?

Maria struggled to remember. Harterford? Haverford? Davey supplied, aghast. In Massachusetts, said Maria, badly mangling the name. A terrible possibility occurred to Davey. *Harvard?* Maybe, could be, Maria offered. She untied her apron, and left him to wonder.

With at least an hour to squander before either parent appeared, Davey searched the basement without any luck. When he came back upstairs, he found his father removing groceries of various kinds, including scotch and vodka, from bags bearing the names of Waldbaum's and Good Grape Harvest.

"Doesn't Jeffrey do that sort of thing?" he asked.

"Jeffrey has the weekend off," his father announced. "Like you. What were you up to down there, that you got so dirty?"

"Trying to find some old books," Davey said.

During lunch, Alden abandoned the usual monologue to question his son about Frank Neary and Frank Tidball, their longtime crossword-puzzle makers. For decades Neary and Tidball had dealt with the company through Davey's predecessor, an amiable old alcoholic named Charlie Westerberg. Soon after Charlie had staggered cheerfully off into retirement, Neary and Tidball hired an agent, with the result that they were now paid a slightly higher fee for their puzzles. Most of the increase went in the agent's commission, but Alden had never ceased to blame Davey for the insurrection. For half an hour, he was forced to defend the two old puzzle makers against his father's implications that they were past their prime and should be replaced. Alden's real but unadmitted objections lay in the discovery, made soon after Westerberg's departure, that the two men shared an address in Rhinebeck. Neary and Tidball would be more difficult to replace than his father understood. There were only a few young crossword-puzzle makers, most of whom had adopted innovations undesirable to Chancel House customers, who did not long for clues about Moody Blues lyrics or the films of Cheech and Chong.

During this discussion, Daisy toyed with her food, at random intervals smiling to indicate that she was paying attention. As soon as Maria began clearing the plates, she excused herself in a little-girl voice and went back upstairs. Alden asked Davey a few questions about Leonard Gimmel and Teddy Brunhoven—he was always interested in the murderers—then wandered off to watch a baseball game on television. Within fifteen minutes, he would be dozing in his easy chair. Davey thanked Maria for the lunch and climbed the stairs to the attic.

The Poplars' attic was divided into three unequal areas. The old maid's rooms, the smallest of these, were a series of three chambers situated around a common bathroom and a narrow staircase at the north end of the house. These wretched rooms had been empty since early in the reign of Helen Day. (Davey's parents had ordered the construction of two large apartments over the garage, one for the Cup Bearer, the other for any overflow guests, and these apartments now housed Maria and her nephew.) The second, central portion of the attic, roughly the size of a hotel ballroom, had been floored and finished but otherwise unchanged.

It was here that Lincoln Chancel's gifts to the first David Chancel had been preserved for the second, and for this reason the central section of the attic had always inflicted an oppressive, uncanny feeling of fraudulence upon Davey. The third section, reached by a door from the middle attic, had been floored but not otherwise finished.

Metaphorically holding his breath against the psychic atmosphere in the central portion of the attic, Davey walked through the jumble of old chairs, broken lamps, boxes upon boxes, and ratty couches to make sure that the old maid's rooms were as empty as he remembered.

The three little rooms contained nothing but spiderwebs, white walls blossoming with mildew, and dust-gray floors. Then he made another quick pass through the center of the attic to inspect the unfinished section. At last he could no longer postpone moving into the main area of the attic, jammed with Victorian furniture.

The old oppression came back to him in various forms as he lifted padded cushions and bent down to see far back into wardrobe closets. Davey experienced resentment. Why should he waste his time like this? Who was Paddi, anyhow, to set him prowling thieflike through his parents' house?

Davey's thoughts had reached this unhappy point when he heard footsteps on the stairs leading to the maid's quarters. He froze. His mind went empty, as though he were a burglar about to be discovered. He half-padded, half-ran to the light switch beside the main attic stairs, flicked it down, and crouched behind a Chinese screen in a heavy wooden frame.

The footsteps on the stairs reached the maid's rooms a few seconds after Davey had found shelter. Footsteps rang on the wooden floor. Peering around the side of the screen, Davey saw a line of light appear beneath the door separating the maid's quarters from the rest of the attic. He drew back. The footsteps advanced toward the door. He flattened his upper body over his knees and covered his head with his hands. The door swung open, and a shaft of light hurtled toward him. Then the entire room flared with light.

A voice he did not know called out, "Who's here?"

Footsteps came toward him. Davey found himself on his feet, fists raised against the shadow whirling to meet him. The shadow grunted in shock and surprise and struck out. The blow drove Davey's right hand into the bridge of his nose. Blood spurted out onto his clothes, and a bright, clear wave of pain made the world go dark. The side of his head crashed into the frame of the screen.

A hand caught his hair and pulled sharply, painfully, upward. "What the hell did you do that for?"

Puckered with consternation, Jeffrey's face stared down at him.

"I thought you were someone else," Davey said.

"You attacked me," Jeffrey said. "You jumped up like a—"

"Wraith," Davey said. "I'm sorry."

"So'm I," said Jeffrey.

Davey clutched the standard of a tall lamp and tilted back his head. Sluggish blood ran down his throat. He said, "I guess I got scared. How did you know someone was up here? I thought you had the weekends off."

"I saw the lights go on from my windows."

Davey groped in his pocket for his handkerchief and swabbed his face before holding it to his nose. "Say, Jeffrey."

"Yes?"

"Did you go to Harvard?"

"If I did, I hope nobody finds out," Jeffrey said.

Davey swallowed. His entire face hurt.

He spent half an hour cleaning bloodstains from the attic floor, then went to his bathroom, washed his face and hands, and fell asleep stretched out on his covers with a cold cloth on the bruised parts of his face. He woke up in time to shower and put on fresh clothes for dinner. His nose was swollen, and a purple lump had risen on his right temple. When he explained at dinner that he had hit himself in the face with the bedroom door, his father said, "Funny, when you have kids nobody ever tells you how many lies you're going to have to listen to over the next thirty or forty years."

Daisy murmured, "Oh, Alden."

"If he hit himself in the face with his door, then he took a practice swing."

"Did someone hit you in the head, darling?" asked his mother.

"Since you ask, yes. Jeffrey and I had a little misunderstanding."

Alden laughed and said, "If Jeffrey ever hit you in the head, you'd be in the hospital for a week."

At twelve-thirty the next day, Davey brought down to the dining room the rescued copies of his mother's two novels and placed them under his chair. His father raised an eyebrow, but Daisy seemed not to notice. Unasked, Maria brought Bloody Marys to all three of them.

After the Bloody Marys came a bottle of Barolo and a soup in which streamers of egg, flecks of parsley, pesto sauce, and pasta circulated through a chicken broth. Davey took half a glass of the wine and nervously devoured the soup. A homemade mushroom and Gorgonzola ravioli followed the soup, and tender little filets of beef and potato croquettes followed the ravioli. Maria announced that in honor of Mr.

Davey she had made a zabaglione, which would be served in a few minutes. Did they have these stupendous meals every weekend, did they eat this way every night? It was no wonder that Daisy was looking puffier than ever, although Alden seemed utterly unchanged. Davey said that he didn't remember the Italian girl's being such a great cook and Alden said, "*Vin ordinaire,* my boy."

The brief silence that followed his father's remark seemed the perfect time to produce his gift.

"Mom, I've got something for you."

"Goody, goody."

Unwilling to tell Alden that he had been prospecting in the Chancel House basement, Davey said that he had found two books in the Strand one day last week, and he hoped she would be pleased to see them again. He rose from his chair to bring the humble package down the table.

Daisy grasped the bag, tore out the books, smiled at their jackets, and opened them. Her eyes retreated into a band of red that appeared over her face like a mask. She set the books on the edge of the table and turned her face away. Still thinking that she was pleased by his gift, Davey said, "They're in such good shape." Daisy drew in a breath and let out a frightening sound that soon resolved into a wail. She shoved back her chair and ran from the room as the Italian girl entered with cups of zabaglione on a silver tray. Baffled, Davey looked inside the first of the two books and saw written in a hand more confident and decisive than his mother's, *For my heart's darling, Alden, from his dazzled Daisy.*

25

AT EIGHT O'CLOCK on the previous Thursday night, a flat package clamped under his left arm, Davey had stood uncertainly in front of a restaurant called Dragon Seed on Elizabeth Street, looking back and forth from the restaurant's front door to a slip of paper in his hand. A row of leathery ducks the color of molasses hung across the restaurant window. The black numerals beside the menu taped to the door matched the number, 67, Paddi had written on the piece of paper.

A delicious odor of roast duck and frying noodles met him when he opened the door. Davey stepped inside, stood at the end of the counter for a moment to look over the room, then went to the only empty table and sat down.

All the men in the room ignored him. Davey looked around for the door that would lead to a staircase and saw two set into opposite ends of the rear wall, one of them marked RESTROOMS, the other PRIVATE. Then he was on his feet.

Two waiters in black vests and white shirts watched him from across the room, and a third set a platter of noodles before four stolid men in suits and began cutting toward him through the tables.

Davey tried to wave him off, and said, "I know it says Private, but it's all right."

"Not all right."

Davey put his hand on the knob, and the waiter's hand came down on his before he could open the door. "You sit."

The waiter pulled him away to his table and pushed him down. Davey placed his package on his lap and considered making a break for the door. He looked around and found that everybody in the restaurant was eyeing him.

The waiter came back through the tables carrying a tray with a teapot and a cup the size of a thimble. He set these before Davey and spun away, revealing a small man in a zippered jacket behind him who rotated a chair and straddled it, and gave Davey a horrible smile. "You funny," the man said.

"I was invited." Davey withdrew from his pocket the paper on which Paddi had written her address and showed it to the man.

The man squinted at the paper. He looked straight into Davey's eyes, then back at the paper. Without any transition, he started laughing. "Come," the man said, and got on his feet. He led Davey to the front door, stepped outside, and motioned Davey to follow him. Davey came out. The man moved one step to his left and pointed at Dragon Seed's door. He pointed again, and this time Davey saw it.

Set back into the building between the entrance to Dragon Seed and a shop filled with souvenirs of Chinatown, at an angle that concealed it if you did not know it was there, was a plywood door with the number 67 spray-painted on it in black.

Grinning, the man prodded Davey's chest with his forefinger. "Dey go in, but dey don't come out." Davey settled the package under his elbow and knocked on the spray-painted door, and a faint voice told him to come in.

He found himself at the foot of a tenement staircase. "Lock the door behind you," the voice called down.

He came upstairs and passed through another door into a vast, darkened loft created by the removal of most of the tenement's walls. A few dim lights illuminated crude murals it took him a moment to see were illustrations of passages in *Night Journey.* Thick, dark curtains covered the windows. In the distance a high-backed sofa and two chairs stood in front of an ornate wooden fireplace frame and mantel affixed to a wall without a fireplace. Long bookshelves took up the wall at the front of the building. Rough partitions marked off two rooms, and one of these opened as Davey came deeper into the murk. Completely at ease, Paddi Mann emerged naked through the door.

"What is this place?"

"Where I live," Paddi said, not naked after all, but wearing a flesh-colored leotard. She gave him a smile and moved toward the sofa, swept up from a cushion a man's wing-collar formal shirt, slipped it on, and buttoned the last few buttons so that it covered her like a short white frock.

"What's that under your arm?"

"I had some trouble finding you." Davey's legs finally unlocked and permitted him to move toward her through the darkness.

"Looks like you had trouble finding the manuscript, too. Unless *that's* it."

"No."

Paddi shifted her position, drawing her legs up beside her and tucking them in. She gave three smart pats to the seat of the sofa.

He found that he was standing directly in front of her and sat down as ordered. Her feet insinuated themselves against his thigh as if for warmth. "Here," she said, and turned sideways to take from a tray and press into his hand a glass filled with ice cubes and a cloudy red liquid.

He drank, then jerked back his head at the pungent, unpleasantly sweet shock of the taste. "What's this?"

"A Top-and-Bottom. Good for you."

Davey let his eyes wander around the dark, jumbled spaces of Paddi's loft. Arches and openings led into invisible chambers from which came inaudible voices. "Are you going to show me what's in that package?"

Davey said, "Oh," because he had forgotten the package, and handed it to her. In seconds her fingers had undone the knots. In another second the wrapping lay in her lap like a frame around the frame and Paddi was gazing down at the long photograph with her mouth softly opened.

"Shorelands, July 1938."

"And here is your grandfather."

Warts and carbuncles jutting from nose and cheek, jowls bulging over his collar, eyebrows nearly meeting in a ferocious scowl above blazing eyes, hands locked on the arms of his chair, rage straining at the buttons, seams, and eyelets of his handmade suit, Lincoln Chancel appeared to have breakfasted on railroads and coal mines.

Davey regarded the phenomenon with the mixture of wonder, respect, and terror his grandsire invariably aroused in him. For the fifty years of his adult life, he had bullied his way south from Bridgeport, Connecticut, to New York and Washington, D.C., north to Boston and Providence, swallowing human lives. Before a massive stroke had felled him in a private dining room in the Ritz-Carlton Hotel, indictments and lawsuits had buzzed around the great man's head. After his death nearly all of the intricately pyramidal structure Lincoln had constructed had tumbled. What remained was a transient hotel in Rhode Island, a struggling woolen mill in Lowell, Massachusetts, both of which had soon folded into bankruptcy, and his last bauble, Chancel House.

"He looks so unhappy."

"He's the only one looking at the camera," Davey said, having noticed this for the first time. "See? Everybody else is looking at another person in the group."

"Except for her." Paddi delicately tapped the glass over the face of a small, strikingly pretty young woman in a loose white shirt, a half-mast necktie, and trousers. Seated on the ground beside Lincoln Chancel, she was gazing down at the grass, lost in thought.

"Yes," Davey said. "I wish I knew her name."

"Whose names *do* you know?"

"Apart from Driver and my grandfather, only her." He indicated a tall woman with a bulldog chin and a fleshy nose who sat upright staring at Lincoln Chancel from a wicker chair. "Georgina Weatherall. She and Hugo Driver are both staring at my grandfather."

"Probably wondering what they can get out of him," Paddi said.

"Oh?"

"There have been a couple of books about Shorelands," Paddi said. "Georgina wanted to be the center of attention. Everybody made fun of her behind her back."

"Georgina couldn't have been too pleased about that girl."

Now Davey indicated an elongated, bearded gentleman in sagging tweeds gazing down at the young woman, his lips stretched so tightly that they looked like wires. "That's not a very friendly smile," Davey said. "I wonder who this guy was?"

"Austryn Fain," said Paddi. "In 1938 he had just published a novel called *The Twisted Hedge*. It was supposed to be wonderful and all that, but from what I gather people forgot about it in a hurry. He killed himself in 1939. January. Cut his wrists in a bathtub."

"Georgina wouldn't help him?"

"Georgina dropped him flat. But, Davey, look at this man. Merrick Favor was his name. He was murdered about six months after this photo was taken."

Paddi was pointing at the broad, handsome face of a man in an unbuttoned double-breasted blue blazer and white trousers who stood immediately behind Georgina. Like Austryn Fain, he was smiling at the girl seated on the grass.

"Murdered?"

"Merrick Favor was supposed to be a rising star. His first novel, *Burning Bushes,* got great reviews when Scribner's published it in 1937, and he was supposed to be working on something even better. One day his girlfriend showed up after trying to call him for a couple of days, and when she couldn't get him to come to the door, she climbed in a window, took a look around, and almost passed out."

"She found his body?"

"His house was torn up, and there were bloodstains everywhere. Favor had been stabbed to death, and his body was in his bathtub. They never found who killed him. The book he was working on was torn to scraps."

"Shorelands didn't bring much luck to these people," Davey said. "What happened to this guy?"

He was pointing at a long-haired young man with horn-rim glasses, a floppy bow tie, velvet jacket, soft eyes, short nose, and a witty mouth. This person seemed to be concentrating all of his thoughts on handsome Merrick Favor.

"Oh, Creeley *Monk*. Another sad story. A poet. His second book was called *The Field Unknown,* and the only reason anybody remembers it is that a lot of third-graders used to have to memorize the title poem."

"Oh," said Davey, "we had to recite that at the Academy. *The field unknown, the unknown field I thought I knew / In childhood days, my ways return me now to you.*"

"Creeley Monk killed himself, too. Shotgunned himself in the head. Right around the time Merrick Favor was killed."

Davey stared at her. "This guy blew off his head a few months after he left Shorelands?"

Paddi nodded.

Davey was staring at her. "Two of the guests at Shorelands that summer killed themselves?"

"It's even better than that. Three of them killed themselves. This man here, the one who looks like a bricklayer, he did, too." Paddi's finger was tapping the chest of a wide, sturdy man in a lumpy blue turtleneck sweater who was trying to smile at the camera and Lincoln Chancel at the same time.

"His name was Bill Tidy, and he'd published one book, called *Our Skillets*. It was a memoir of his childhood in the South End of Boston. Must have been the only really working-class guest Georgina ever had at Shorelands. *Our Skillets* is a beautiful book, but it went out of print right away and only came back into print in the late sixties. I don't know about this for sure, but I think Tidy had a lot of trouble getting to work on a new book after he got back to Boston. Anyhow, he jumped out of his fifth-floor window. In January 1939."

"When . . ."

"Right between Merrick Favor's murder and Monk's suicide, which happened a few days apart, and two days before Fain killed himself. It's like a curse or something, isn't it?"

"God, it's like they paid for Hugo Driver's success."

"You should write a book about all this," Paddi said.

"I thought you already read a book about all this."

"I read a lot of books about Shorelands because I'm interested in Hugo Driver, but this information is scattered all over the place. Actually, hardly anybody cares about what was going on at Shorelands after the early thirties. By the start of the war, it was all over. Georgina was drinking a lot and taking laudanum and her stories began smelling like fish. She told people that Marcel Proust used to stink up Honey House with his asthma powders, which is a nice story, but Proust never left France. Georgina finally retreated into her bedroom, and she died around 1950. The house rotted away until a preservation group bought it."

"What happened to the girl sitting on the ground next to my grandfather?"

"She was supposed to have disappeared during her stay, but even that isn't really clear."

The characters in the photograph on his lap, his grandfather and the great author, Austryn Fain and Merrick Favor and Creeley Monk, Georgina Weatherall and Bill Tidy and the abstracted young woman, seemed as familiar, as *known,* as his old schoolmates at the Academy. He saw into them so clearly that he could not understand why until now he had not seen the clearest thing in the picture. All he had really seen before was his grandfather's comic fury. What was clearest in the photograph was the reason for the universal discomfort.

As if the picture came equipped with a soundtrack and a flashback, it all but shouted that Lincoln Chancel had uttered a crude flirtatiousness to the attractive young woman at his feet, and that the young woman had swiftly, woundingly rebuffed him. While she looked inward and Chancel erupted, everyone else in the photograph took sides.

Davey said, "You know what? I don't know anything about you. I don't know where you were born, or who your parents are, or what college you went to, if you have brothers and sisters, anything like that. It's like you stepped out of a cloud. Where did you live before you walked into our offices?"

"Lots of places."

"Where were you born?"

"You really want to do this, don't you? Okay. I was born in Amherst, Massachusetts. My parents' names are Charles Roland and Sabina. Sabina teaches German in a high school in Amherst, and Charles Roland was an English professor at Amherst College. I went to the Rhode Island School of Design. After I got out of RISD, I went to Europe and traveled here and there, but mainly lived in London, painting and taking art courses, and after a couple of years I came back and lived in L.A. and did some design work for a couple of small presses and read everything I could about Hugo Driver, which is when I learned about Shorelands, and after a while I came to New York so I could get a job at Chancel. I just walked in, showed my work to Rod Clampett, and he hired me."

"I should have guessed the RISD part," Davey said. Rod Clampett, Chancel's art director, had gone to RISD and liked hiring its graduates.

Paddi said, "Don't you think all this Shorelands business is like some huge plot that you can't quite see?"

Davey began to laugh. "Well, if you're looking for a sinister plot, Lincoln Chancel is your man. He was a tremendous crook, I'm sure. It's like the big secret in my family—the thing we don't talk about. On the way up, my dad's dad obviously stabbed everybody he met in the back, he must have stolen with both hands whenever he had the chance, he raped his way into a huge fortune . . ."

Davey stopped talking for a moment, a meaningless smile stuck to his face, as the crowded darkness in the center of the room seemed to thicken. He glanced down, and his eye found propped on the sofa the photograph from Shorelands. Lincoln Chancel was suddenly before him, beaming undimmed fury, rage, and frustration into his soul.

Paddi stroked his cheek with a cool finger and then stood up, held out her hand, and stepped back to lead him across the room.

"She insulted my grandfather, didn't she? That girl who disappeared."

"Maybe your grandfather insulted her."

Moving backwards, she drew him toward a mural in which Lord Night stood guard at the black opening of a cave, came up to the wall, and instead of bumping into it, slipped into the cave. Davey followed her through the opening.

And that, Davey said, was the end of his story.

26

"HOW CAN THAT be the end?" Nora was trying not to yell. "What happened?"

"This is the part that's hard to talk about."

Davey had not finished talking about Paddi Mann. He had merely finished talking in that way.

"You remember what we saw today? Where we went?"

Nora nodded, almost dreading whatever he would say next.

He gave her no help. "That's the point."

"Did you ever find the manuscript? What happened to her? Oh no, you're not going to tell me she was killed, are you?"

"I never did find the manuscript. Anyhow, my father told me that he'd decided against doing a scholarly edition of *Night Journey.*"

"That must have upset Paddi."

Davey went back to smoothing out the bedcover, and Nora tried again. "She was so committed to that project."

Davey nodded, looking down and pushing his lips forward in the way he did when forced into an uncomfortable situation.

"Just tell me what happened."

"We had that Thursday night, when I gave her the picture. On Monday, I never saw her at all, and when I got back to my apartment all the coke caught up with me and I slept for two straight days. I just conked out. Woke up barely in time to shower and put on new clothes before I went back to the office."

"Where Alden told you he wasn't going through with your pet project. And you had to break the news to Paddi."

"She was hanging around in the hallway when I got up to the fifteenth floor, like someone had told her what was going to happen. We didn't really have time to talk before I went in, and she said, 'Seven-thirty?' or something like that, and I nodded, and then I went in and saw Dad. She was still there when I came out, and I gave her the bad news. She didn't say a word. Just turned around and left. So at seven-thirty, I went to her place.

"When I got up to the loft, she wasn't there, so I walked around for a little bit. I thought she might have been asleep or in the bathroom or something. I looked at her books. You know what they were? Nothing but editions of Driver novels. Hardbacks, paperbacks, foreign languages, illustrated editions."

"That's not too surprising," Nora said.

"Wait. Then, of course, I had to go through the opening in the mural and look at the only other place in the whole loft I'd ever seen. So I walk into the cave. And my eyes bug out and my heart just about stops and I'm stuck. And after about a hundred years go by, I'm unstuck, I realize I'm not going to faint after all."

He looked at Nora, who did nothing but look back at him. This, too, had the tone of one of Davey's inventions.

"It was like a slaughterhouse. There was blood everywhere. I was so *scared.* I was pretty sure you couldn't lose that much blood and still be alive, and I was gritting my teeth until I saw her body. I got to the other side of the bed, where this big smear of blood went all the way across the floor and halfway up the wall. And that almost made me puke, because I'd been sure I was going to see her there. I even looked under the bed."

"Why didn't you call the police?" *And why do I want to believe this? He's describing Natalie's room.*

"I didn't know where the phone was! I don't even know if there was a phone!" Davey looked wildly around the bedroom and opened and closed his mouth several times, as if trying to swallow this remark.

"Weren't you afraid that whoever did it was still there?"

"Nora, if I'd even *thought* of that, I would have had a heart attack on the spot."

"Where did you find her body?"

"I didn't."

"Well, where was it? It must have been somewhere."

"Nora, that's what I'm saying. Nobody found it. It wasn't there."

"Somebody took it?"

"*I don't know!*" Davey yelled. He pressed both hands to his face, then let them drop.

"Oh. It was like Natalie, you mean. The body was gone, like Natalie."

He nodded. "Like Natalie."

Nora struggled to regain a sense of control, of a world in which things made sense. "But there can't really be any connection, can there?"

"You think I know?"

She tried again. "I don't suppose Natalie Weil quoted Hugo Driver at you and had you rummaging around for lost manuscripts . . ." In the midst of this, Nora remembered the books in Natalie Weil's bedroom, and the sentence trailed off.

"No, I don't suppose," Davey said, still not looking up.

The moment of silence which followed seemed extraordinarily crowded to Nora.

"What did you do when you realized that she wasn't there?"

Davey inhaled deeply and looked over her shoulder. "I was too scared to go home, so I walked all the way to midtown and took a hotel room under a phony name. Around noon the next day, I called Rod Clampett and asked if Paddi had turned up yet. He said he hadn't seen her all day, but he'd tell her to give me a call when she showed up. Of course, she never did."

"I guess you couldn't exactly look for her," Nora said. "But, Davey, excuse me, what's the point of all this?"

"I have to get up and move around a little. Could you make some coffee or something?"

"I could make decaf," she said, looking at the digital clock on the bedside radio. It was 2:00 A.M. She took from the couch a pale yellow robe, slipped it on, and tied its sash. Davey was sitting up in bed and staring at nothing. For a second, he looked like someone Nora had never seen before, an ineffectual man who would always be puzzled by life. Then he glanced up at Nora and was again her husband, Davey Chancel, trying to seem less distressed than he was.

"Nora," he said, "do you know where that blue silk bathrobe is, the one from Thailand?"

"On the hook in the bathroom," she said, and padded out to make coffee.

27

DAVEY SIPPED HIS decaffeinated French Roast and winced at the heat. "A little kümmel would go nicely with this mocha java, don't you think?"

Nora shook her head, then changed her mind. "What the hey."

Davey went to the cupboard and took out a bottle of Hiram Walker kümmel, all Nora had been able to find on her last visit to the liquor store. He frowned at the label to remind her that she should have gone to another liquor store, if not to Germany, to find decent kümmel, and filled his cup to the brim. Then he moved behind Nora and tipped perhaps half an inch of the liquid into her cup. A smell of caraway and drunken flowers filled the kitchen.

"Well?" she asked.

"Yes."

"Yes, what?" She sipped what tasted like a poison antidote with an accidental similarity to coffee.

"Yes, there is more. Yes, I'm kind of leery of telling you about it."

She found herself taking another sip of the mixture, which seemed less ghastly than before.

"I left out one thing about the last time I was in Paddi's loft."

"Oh, no."

"It wasn't anything I *did,* Nora. I'm not *guilty* of anything."

Then why do you look so guilty? she wondered.

"Okay, I did something." He drank again and tilted back his head as if, like a bird, he had to do that to swallow. Then he lowered his head and folded his hands around his cup. "I told you about looking under her bed."

Nora suddenly felt that whatever Davey said next would forever change the way she felt about him. Then she thought that his story about Paddi Mann had already changed the way she thought about Davey.

"I saw something under there."

"You saw something," she said.

"A book."

Is that all? Nora thought. *No severed head, no million dollars in a paper bag?*

"After I fished it out, I thought she might even have left it for me. What do you think it was?"

"The Egyptian Book of the Dead? The, uh, that Lovecraft thing, the *Necronomicon*?"

"*Night Journey.* A paperback."

"Forgive me," she said, "but that doesn't actually seem too startling."

Davey held her eyes with his own and took another swig of his doctored coffee. "Uh huh. I opened it up. You know, maybe there was a note or something in it for me. But there wasn't anything in it except what was supposed to be there. And her name."

"Her name," Nora said, feeling like an echo.

"Written on the flyleaf. At the top. Paddi Mann."

"She wrote her name in it."

"That's right. I shoved the book in my pocket and took it away with me. A few days later I tried to find it, but the damn thing was lost."

"It fell out of your pocket."

"Here we go," he said, and set his cup down. "Hold on. I'll be right back." Davey stood up and walked out of the kitchen, nervously straightening his blue robe.

Nora heard him return to the bedroom. A closet door opened and closed. In a moment, he reappeared holding a familiar black paperback. As if reluctant to surrender it, he sat down and held it up before him in both hands before offering it to Nora.

"Well, I don't suppose this is . . ." Nora noticed that she was as reluctant to take the book as he was to let go of it. She stopped talking and accepted it. Printed on the flyleaf, which had become slightly discolored, in small clear letters with a ballpoint pen, was PADDI MANN. Beneath her name, Davey had signed his own.

"So it turned up," Nora said.

"Where, do you suppose?"

"How should I know?" She took her hands off the book, thinking that she did not actually care where the book had surfaced, and for some reason hoping that she would not have to find out. She braced herself for another of Davey's inventions.

"Natalie Weil's bedroom."

"But—" Nora closed, then opened her mouth. No longer able to bear the expression in Davey's eyes, she looked down at her fingers spread on the edge of the table as if she were about to play the piano. "This book, the same book."

"This same book. I saw it when we went in, and after that big cop took us out, I went back, remember? I opened it up and just about passed out. Then I shoved it in my pocket."

"What made you go back in? Did you suspect that it might be—?"

"Of course not. I wanted to take a closer look at it." He shrugged his shoulders.

"You don't know how it got there."

"I didn't put it there, if that's what you mean."

"You never gave Natalie a copy of *Night Journey.*"

He looked at her in real exasperation. "Do I have to spell it out for you?"

Nora guessed he did.

"Someone took it from me. He killed Paddi and left the book for me to find. Later that week he stole it from me. And the same person killed Natalie and left it in her bedroom."

"The wolf killed Paddi Mann?" Nora asked, too confused to speak clearly.

"Lord Night? What does he have to do with it?"

"No, sorry, I mean *our* wolf—the Westerholm Wolf." She waved her hands in front of her, as if she were erasing a blackboard. "That's what I call the . . . the guy. The man who murdered Natalie and the others."

"*Our* wolf." Davey seemed disturbed, and Nora feared that his disturbance was caused by her appropriation of an animal sacred to Hugo Driver. "Yeah. It was the same guy. Okay. It has to be. He's not much like Lord Night, though."

"Davey," she said, "not everything is related to Hugo Driver."

"*Night Journey* is. Paddi Mann was certainly interested in Driver."

She had made him defensive. "Davey, all I meant is that he couldn't have left Paddi Mann's copy of *Night Journey* in Sally Michaelman's bedroom, or in Annabelle Austin's, or any of the others. And maybe he didn't steal yours. He probably found it."

Davey was vigorously shaking his head. "I bet there's some correspondence between the women he killed and certain parts of the book. In fact, that's obvious."

"Why is it obvious?"

"Because of Paddi," he said. "Paddi was obviously Paddy, don't you think?"

"Paddi was Paddi," she said. "I don't get it."

"In the book. The mouse. The mouse named Paddy, who tells Pippin Little about the Field of Steam. Jesus, don't you remember *anything*? Paddy is . . . Sometimes I wonder if you ever even read *Night Journey.*"

"I read parts of it."

"You lied." He was looking at her in absolute astonishment. "You told me you finished it, and you were lying to me."

"I skipped around," she said. "I apologize. I realize that this is important to you—"

"*Important.*"

"—but aren't you maybe a little upset that a man who killed five women is—"

"Is what?"

"—somehow connected to you? I don't know how to say it, because I don't really understand it." A flash of pain exploded behind the right half of Nora's forehead and sent a hot tendril down into her pupil. She leaned back in her chair and placed her hand over her eye.

"I'll never be able to get to sleep. I think I'll go down to the family room and put on some music."

Nora waited to be invited into the family room, so that she could refuse. She heard him push back his chair and stand up.

He told her that she could try lying down. He advised aspirin.

Nora removed her hand from her face. Davey tilted the square brown bottle over his cup and poured out several inches of amber liquid that reeked of caraway seed.

"You said you had that manuscript you found in the conference room, the Clyde Morning book? Would you mind if I took a look at it?"

"You want to read Clyde *Morning*?"

"I want to see the first new Blackbird Book," Nora said, but Davey acknowledged this conciliatory sally only with a frown and a shrug of his shoulders. "Would you get it for me?"

Davey tilted his head and rolled his eyes. "If that's what you want." He went into his "office." Nora could hear him talking to himself as he worked the catches on his briefcase. He came back into the kitchen, awkwardly holding a surprisingly slim stack of typing paper held together with rubber bands. "Here you are." He set the typescript on the table. "Tell me if you think it's any good."

She said, "You doubt the great Clyde Morning?"

Already at the kitchen door, Davey turned to give her a look that pretended to offer her sympathy for being left alone, and escaped.

She removed the rubber bands and tapped the bottom edge of the manuscript on the table. Then she folded over the last page and looked at the number in the top right-hand corner. Whatever miracles of the narrative art the hope of Blackbird Books had performed in *Spectre,* he had contained them within 183 pages.

From downstairs floated the eerie sound of Peter Pears singing words from a Britten opera Nora had heard many times but could not place. The voice seemed to come from an inhuman realm located between earth and heaven. *Death in Venice,* that was what Davey was listening to. She picked up the slim manuscript, carried it into the living room, switched on a lamp Sally Michaelman had sold her, and stretched out on a sofa to read.

BOOK III

AT THE DEEP OF NIGHT

At last the child lost all hope and admitted to himself that this dark land was death, from which no release could be had. For a time he lost all strength and reason, and wept in panic and despair.

28

EARLY THE NEXT morning, Nora turned her back on Long Island Sound, ran over the arched wooden bridge at Trap Line Road, and came into the twelve acres of wooded marsh known as the Pierce A. Gordon Nature Conservancy. The air was cool and fresh, and behind her seagulls hopped along the long, seaweed-strewn beach. She had reached the midpoint of her run, and what lay before her were the pleasures of the "Bird Shelter," as Westerholm natives called the Conservancy, where for just under fifteen minutes she enjoyed the illusion of passing through a landscape like that of the Michigan wilds to which Matt Curlew had taken her on weekend fishing trips during her childhood. These fifteen minutes were the secret heart of her morning run, and on the morning after her first literally sleepless night in years, Nora wished no more than to stop thinking, or worrying, or whatever it was that she had been doing for the past four hours, and enjoy them. Familiar trees filled with cardinals and noisy jays surrounded her. She looked at her watch and saw that she was already nearly five minutes behind her usual time.

Davey's crazy story had affected her more than she liked to admit. In the past, Davey's embellishments, when not clearly self-serving, had been in the service of either color or humor. Though nothing if not highly colored, the tale of Paddi Mann had seemed to conceal more than it gave away. Even if he had been trying to emphasize the extent to which he had been seduced, he had overdone his effects.

Other things, too, had distressed her. Nora had read the first twenty-odd pages of *Spectre* in such a swirl of doubt and anger that the sentences had instantly disappeared from her memory.

What right did Davey have to demand that she be interested in a second-rate author? For his benefit, Nora had absorbed a lot of information about classical music. She knew the difference between Maria Callas and Renata Tebaldi, she could identify fifty operas from their opening bars, she could tell when it was Horowitz playing a Chopin nocturne and when it was Ashkenazy. Why did she have to bow down to Hugo Driver?

At this point, Nora's conscience forced her to acknowledge that she had, after all, lied to Davey about reading Driver's book. She had closed the manuscript, gone downstairs, and paused outside the family room door. *Death in Venice* poured from the speakers. She slowly pushed open the door, hoping to see Davey sitting up and making notes or staring at the wall or doing anything at all that would prove he was at least as awake as she was. Covered to the throat by a plaid throw rug, eyes closed and mouth fluttering, Davey was lying on the couch. Exactly as she had foreseen, Mr. Sensitivity had loaded the two Britten CDs into the player, stretched out with the rug wrapped around him like a baby blanket, and trusted that she would be asleep before he was.

That was it, that *did it*. Nora took herself back to the living room and turned on the radio. She dialed until she reached a station pounding out James Cotton, blues with *wheels,* blues with *guts,* cranked up the volume, and sat down to start reading *Spectre* all over again.

Spectre was the second topic she wished to put out of her mind during the favorite part of her run. After about an hour's reading, a certain possibility concerning Clyde Morning had occurred to her. This possibility, if true, might mean something to herself and Davey, or it might not. Then there was a problem with the book itself. As she had feared, *Spectre* was a slight book. It read like a fictional skeleton barely fleshed out by a writer too tired or lazy to keep his characters' names straight. George Carmichael, the main character, had become George Carstairs by page 15, and by page 35 he had changed back to Carmichael. For the rest of the book, he switched back and forth, depending, Nora thought, on which name surfaced first in Clyde Morning's mind when he reported to his typewriter.

Even worse was the exhaustion which weighed down the writing. Three different characters said, "Too true." Far too many sentences began with the word "Indeed" followed by a comma. George Carmichael/Carstairs's eyes were invariably a "deep, soulful brown," and his shoes were always "crosshatched with scuff marks." Neither sense nor grammar was safe. As he ran down the stairs, the sun struck George in his eyes of deep, soulful brown. When he "gazed longingly" at his beloved, Lily Clark, his eyes adhered to her dress. Or they flew across the room to meet her "tigress' lips." Half a dozen times, George and other people "wore out shoe leather" by "pounding the pavement" or "double-jumping the stairs." After she had begun to notice these repetitions, Nora got up, found a pencil, and made faint check marks in the margin whenever one of them appeared.

When she had finished reading, pale light came slanting in through the windows at the front of the house. She returned to the kitchen for more coffee and discovered that she had ground beans from the package of French Roast that was not decaffeinated. Her radio station had pumped out blues all during the night and switched over to jazz while she read the manuscript's last pages. A tenor saxophone was playing some ballad so tenderly that individual notes seemed to float through her skin. "Scott Hamilton," said the announcer, "with 'Chelsea Bridge.' "

Scott Hamilton . . . wasn't that the name of an ice skater?

Nora had looked up from the manuscript, dazed and uncertain. It was as if along with the sound of the saxophone, some secret thought, one not to be admitted during normal hours, had swum into her mind, taken form, and floated out. Carmichael/Carstairs and Paddi Mann had been part of this thought, but it was gone. The experience had made her feel oddly like a visitor in her own life. She stood up, put her hands on her hips, and twisted her back twice sharply to the right, then twice to the left.

Davey had not left the family room during the night, but her irritation with him had passed. After nearly a week of keeping his fears inside him, he had finally blurted out his confession. Even if only a tenth of it was true, it was still a confession.

Nora went downstairs and peeked in on her husband. Above the rug, his face was tight with an anxious dream. She switched off the light and turned off the CD player. Upstairs, she put *Spectre* back in its rubber bands. She felt at once utterly tired and completely awake. Why not now, in the gift of these extra hours, take her run, and then make breakfast for them both before Davey left for New York? Inspired, she put on her shorts and running shoes, slipped into a tank top and a cotton sweater, pulled a long-billed cap on her head, and left the house. After a few minutes of stretching in the dew-soaked grass on a front lawn that looked exotic in the unfamiliar gray-blue light of dawn, Nora was loping past the sleeping houses on Fairytale Lane.

Tendrils of doubt and worry continued to prod at her concentration as she ran through the almost hallucinatory landscape of the Bird Shelter. Paddi Mann was not a problem; nor, really, was whatever Davey had been hiding. Davey's secrets invariably turned out to be less significant than he imagined. The problem was whether or not to tell him what she had inadvertently discovered about Clyde Morning.

29

NORA PICKED UP *The New York Times* from her doorstep, unlocked her front door, and automatically checked the signal on the security keypad. The green light burned; no one had touched the system since she had left the house. She carried the paper downstairs and opened the door to the family room. There, lost in untroubled sleep, was Davey, throw rug twisted around his hips, eyes closed, mouth open just wide enough for him to lick his lips.

She knelt in front of Davey and drew her hand down his cheek. His eyes fluttered open. "What time is it?"

She looked at the digital clock next to the CD player. "Seven-seventeen. You have to get up."

"Why? Jeez, did you forget it was Saturday?"

"It's *Saturday*? Good God," she said. "I'm sorry. I'm so mixed up, I guess I thought it was Monday."

He noticed what she was wearing. "You already did your run? It's so *early*." He sat up and took a closer look at her face. "Did you get any sleep?" He sat up and swung his feet to the floor. A faint smell of used alcohol clung to his skin. He drooped back against the wall and looked at her. "You really have this completely *wired* look. I didn't think *Spectre* was that exciting. In fact, from what I saw, it was kind of sucky."

This did not seem the time to risk telling him her theory about Clyde Morning. "Well, I had an idea or two, but I should take another look at the manuscript before I talk about them."

"Oh?" He tilted his head and looked wary.

"I just want to make sure of a few things. Do you want to go back to sleep?"

He rubbed his cheek. "Might as well get up. Maybe I can get in some golf before lunch. Would that be okay with you?"

"Good idea." Nora kissed his whiskery, slightly stale cheek and stood up. In the living room, she realized that she was still carrying the newspaper and tossed it onto a chair.

After a hurried shower, Nora turned off the water and left the compartment just as naked Davey entered the bathroom. When she reached for a towel, he grabbed one of her buttocks. She bunched the towel in front of his chest and pushed him toward the shower.

She toweled herself dry, wrapped the towel around her trunk, and came out into the bedroom to get dressed. Naked, pink, and rubbing his hair with a towel, Davey came out of the bathroom and said, "The only problem with going to the club so early is that you have to play with these old jock-type guys, and they all treat me like somebody's retarded grandson. They never pay attention to anything I say."

The telephone next to the bed rang. Both of them stared at it. "Must be a wrong number," Davey said. "Get rid of them."

Nora picked up the telephone and said, "Hello?"

A male voice she had heard before but did not recognize pronounced her name.

"Yes."

"This is Holly Fenn, Mrs. Chancel. I'm sorry to bother you so early, but in the midst of all the excitement down here, something came up that you might be able to help us with."

Davey appeared before her in a pale green polo shirt, boxer shorts, and blue knee-high socks. "So who is this idiot?"

She put her hand over the mouthpiece. "Holly Fenn."

"I don't know anybody named Holly Fenn."

"That cop. The detective."

"Oh, *that* guy. Swell."

Fenn said, "Hello?"

"Yes, I'm here."

"If you wouldn't mind performing a little public service for your local police, I wonder if you and your husband could come down here to the station. As friends of Mrs. Weil's."

Davey removed a pair of khaki pants from the dry cleaner's plastic bag and tossed the bag, now entangled with the hanger, toward the wastebasket, missing by a yard.

"I don't quite understand," she said. "You want to talk to us about Natalie?" Davey muttered something and thrust one leg into the trousers.

"I might have some good news for you," Fenn said. "It seems your friend may not be dead after all. LeDonne found her, or someone who claims to be Mrs. Weil, down on the South Post Road just a little while ago. Can you be in soon? I'd appreciate your help."

"Well, sure," she said. "That would be great news. But what do you need us for, to identify her?"

"I'll fill you in when you get here, but that's about it. You might want to come around to the back of the station. Everything's crazy around here."

"See you in about ten minutes," she said.

"In the midst of the pandemonium, I'm grateful to you," Fenn said. "Thanks." He hung up.

Still holding the receiver, Nora looked at Davey, who was now at his shoe rack, deliberating. "I still don't get it," she said. Davey glanced at her, made an interrogatory noise in his throat, and bent down to select penny loafers. "He wants us to come down to the station because that policeman who was at Natalie's house—LeDonne?—because he says LeDonne found a woman who said she was Natalie down on the South Post Road."

Davey slowly straightened up and frowned at her. "So why do they need us?"

"I'm not really sure."

"It's stupid. All they have to do is look at her driver's license. What's the point of dragging us in?"

"I don't know. He said he'd explain when we got there."

"It can't be Natalie. You saw her bedroom. People don't get up and walk away from a bloodbath like that."

"According to you, Paddi Mann did," she said.

His face turned a bright, smooth red, and he moved away to slip on the loafers. "I didn't say that. I said she disappeared. Natalie was murdered."

"Why are you blushing?"

"I'm not *blushing,*" he said. "I'm pissed off. You expect cops to be kind of dim and incompetent, but this is a new low. They pick up some screwball who says she's Natalie, and we have to waste the morning doing their job for them." He paced to the door, shoved his hands in his pockets, and gave her a guarded look. "I hope you know enough not to blurt out anything I told you last night."

Nora noticed that the receiver was still in her hand and replaced it. "Why would I?"

"I wish we had time to get something to eat," Davey said. "Let's get this over with, shall we?"

A few minutes later, the Audi was zipping beneath the trees that lined Old Pottery Road as Davey wondered aloud if he should tell the police about finding Paddi Mann's copy of *Night Journey* in Natalie Weil's bedroom. "The problem is, I took it. I bet I could get into trouble for that."

For Nora, the question represented another instance of Hugo Driver's amazing ability to go on making trouble long after his death. "There's no reason to bring it up."

Davey gave her an injured look. "This *is* serious, Nora. Maybe I shouldn't go in with you. This woman can't be Natalie, but what if she is?"

"If she can't be, she isn't. And if somehow she is Natalie, she'll have a lot more to talk about than a copy of *Night Journey.*"

"I guess so." He sighed. "You said you had some idea about *Spectre.*"

"Oh!" she said. "When I was running into the Bird Shelter, something about the writing occurred to me. But I could be wrong."

Davey accelerated downhill toward the green light on the Post Road, signaled for a turn, and swung north into the fast lane.

"You know how you used to joke about Clyde Morning and Marletta Teatime being the same person? I think they really could be."

He gave her an incredulous glance.

"Last month, I read a Marletta Teatime novel, remember? *The Grave Is Waiting?*"

"*The Waiting Grave,*" Davey said.

"Right. Some things in the style struck me as funny. Marletta had people say 'too true' a couple of times when they agreed with something. Who says 'too true'? English people, maybe, or Australians, but Americans don't say it. In *Spectre,* people say 'too true' over and over."

"Obviously Clyde reads her books."

"But there's more. Marletta started half a dozen sentences with the word 'indeed.' The same thing happens in *Spectre.* And there's something about shoes. In the Marletta book, the gardener character, the one who kills the little boy, his shoes are crosshatched with scuff marks. That's how you find out later that he was impersonating a minister in the other town. Well, in *Spectre,* Morning keeps saying that George Whatshisname's shoes are crosshatched with scuff marks. It's not even a very good description."

"Oh great, now you're an editor."

Nora said nothing.

"You know what I mean. I don't think it's a bad description, that's all."

"Okay, look at their joke names," Nora said. "Morning and Teatime, it's like being called six o'clock and four o'clock."

"Hah," Davey said. "You know, maybe Morning invented Teatime as a pseudonym. It's not actually impossible."

"Thank you."

"If he had two names, he could unload twice as many books. God knows, he must have needed the money. All he had to do was set up Marletta's post office box and a separate bank account. Nobody ever saw either one of them, anyhow."

"So if they were the same person, it wouldn't cause any problems?"

"Not if we don't tell anybody," Davey said. "When *Spectre* is edited, we take out all the 'indeeds' and 'too trues' and the crosshatches, that's all."

"You could get a little publicity out of it," Nora said.

"And make us look like fools. No thanks. The best thing is to keep quiet and let the problem go away by itself. Which is what I wish we could do with this stupid Driver business."

"What Driver business?"

"It's so ridiculous I don't even want to talk about it."

"This is the problem your father told you about."

"The reason I had to watch that travesty. Okay, here goes."

Davey turned off the Post Road and drove toward the stone building of the Westerholm police station. The adjacent parking lot seemed unusually full to Nora.

"How can that movie be a nuisance for Chancel House?"

"It can't be," Davey said, sounding weary, "not in itself. What happened was, these two screwball women in Massachusetts went out to see that dumb movie right after they were going through some family papers in their basement." Davey came out of the main lot and turned into the police department lot, which was as crowded as the one they had just left. Cars and vans were parked in front of the station.

Nora said, "Look at those vans." She pointed at two long vans bearing the logos and call letters of network news programs in New York.

"Just what we need."

"These women found old family papers?"

"They thought they found a way to scare a lot of money out of my old man. Their greasy lawyer did everything but admit it."

Davey had now driven to the far end of the police lot without finding an opening, and he circled around toward the parking places reserved for police vehicles.

"I don't get it," Nora said.

"They found notes a sister of theirs was supposed to have made. Like *three pages*. In a suitcase." He pulled into an empty spot between two police cars.

"They're claiming that their sister wrote *Night Journey*?"

Whatever the women in Massachusetts were claiming was apparently not to be discussed, because Davey immediately got out of the car. Nora opened her door, stood up, and saw Officer LeDonne approaching. He looked like a man under a great deal of pressure.

"I'm not moving this car," Davey said. "You asked us to come down here."

"Will you follow me into the station, please? Mr. Chancel? Mrs. Chancel? I'll have to ask you to move pretty quickly, and not to talk to anyone until we're with Chief Fenn." He came toward them as he spoke and halted about two feet away from Davey. "Stick as close to me as you can." He looked at them both, turned around, and set off toward the front of the building.

When they came around the side of the station, Nora noticed something she had not taken in earlier. Unlike the cars in the main lot, these were occupied. The men and women waiting in their cars watched LeDonne lead the Chancels toward the steps of the police station.

"Why, half the town is out here," she said.

"Been here since dawn," LeDonne said.

They hurried up the three long steps. Nora felt hundreds of avid eyes watching them from behind windshields and then was distracted by the commotion on the other side of the door. LeDonne sighed. "Up to me? We'd put 'em all in the holding pen and let 'em out one at a time." He faced the door, motioned them nearer, and lunged inside. Davey moved in behind Nora, put his hands on her hips, and pushed.

As Nora knew from her misadventure with the millionaire's child, the tall desk manned by a sergeant dominated one side of the space beyond the entrance, and on the other stood two long rows of wooden benches. A few steps ahead of her, LeDonne was pushing his way through a crowd surging forward from the benches. Two uniformed men behind the desk shouted for order. Davey's hands propelled her past an outheld microphone into a babble of questions and a sudden wave of bodies. Voices battered at her. Davey seemed to lift her off the ground and speed her along into the narrow vacancy behind LeDonne. From behind her right ear, Nora heard a reporter asking something about the Chancel family, but the question vanished as they turned into a wide hallway, where, abruptly, they found themselves alone.

"Chief Fenn's office is up ahead," LeDonne told them, seeming to promise that everything would be answered there, and started off again, leading them past a series of doors with pebbled glass windows. On the far side of a wide metal staircase he opened a door with the words CHIEF OF DETECTIVES written on the opaque window.

In the office stood a rolltop desk, a long, green metal desk facing two wooden chairs, and a gray metal table pushed up against a pale green cinder-block wall. Both the metal desk and the table were covered with papers, and more papers bristled from the open rolltop. A narrow window behind the green desk looked out on the police parking lot, where the Audi stood like a trespasser in the rows of black-and-white cars.

"Holly Fenn is a slob," Davey said, surveying the room with his arms crossed over his chest. "Are we surprised? No, we are not."

Nora sat on a wobbly wooden chair, and Holly Fenn charged through the door, carrying a thick, battered notebook before him like a weapon. "I suppose the press sort of closed in on you out there."

"They did," she said, and laughed. "What are they doing here, anyhow?"

Fenn stood up. "Our chief thought we could manage them a little better inside the station." He held his hand out toward Davey, who shook it. "Thanks for showing up like this, Mr. Chancel."

"I meant, what are they doing *here*?" Nora said. "I don't understand how they found out so fast about this woman who says she's Natalie."

Fenn paused halfway to his desk and turned to look at her. "You mean you really don't know?"

"Guess not," she said.

"Didn't you see the papers this morning?"

She saw herself tossing the newspaper toward a chair.

"Oh, my God." Davey put his hands on the top of his head. "You did it? You got him?"

"Looks like it." For a moment Fenn looked almost pleased with himself.

"Did what?" Nora asked.

"Brought in our murderer," Fenn said. "Been in custody since about ten last night. I think Popsie Jennings must have called the *Times* herself. You know Popsie, don't you?"

Both Chancels knew the notorious Popsie Jennings, who owned a women's clothing store on Main Street called The Unfettered Woman and lived in the guesthouse of her third husband's estate on the good side of Mount Avenue, about a quarter of a mile from the Poplars. A short, solid, blond woman in her mid-fifties with a Gitane voice and a fondness for profanity, Popsie looked as though she had been born on a sailboat and raised on a golf course, but she had lived unconventionally, even raucously, and was supposed to have named her dress shop after her conception of herself. She was rumored to have in her bedroom two paintings of horses by George Stubbs given her by her first husband, and to declare that all three were well hung—the paintings, the horses, and the first husband.

"He broke into *Popsie's* house?" Davey said. "He's lucky he didn't wind up tied naked to a bed and force-fed vodka."

"He almost was," said Fenn. "He came over to her house around nine last night. She got suspicious, nailed him with an andiron, taped his hands and feet together while he was out, and then got a cleaver and said she'd castrate him if he didn't confess."

"Wow," Nora said. "Popsie was pretty sure of herself."

"Pretty damn mad, too."

"So who was the guy?" asked Davey.

"I suppose you know him, too. Richard Dart."

"Dick *Dart*?" Davey sat down clumsily on the chair next to Nora's and gave her a look of utterly empty astonishment. "I went to school with him. His brother, Petey, was in my class, and Dick was in the sophomore class when I graduated. We were never friends or anything like that, but I see him around town now and then. I introduced him to Nora a couple of months ago—remember, Nora?"

She shook her head, wondering why they were not talking about Natalie Weil and still not quite capable of taking in that she had actually met the man she had called the Wolf of Westerholm. "Where?"

"Gilhoolie's. Right after it opened."

And then she remembered the languid, drawling man in the awful bar, the man who had complimented her scent when she had not been wearing one. So she had spoken to, had looked into the eyes of, had been lightly touched by, the man she called the Wolf, who turned out to be a creepy, aging preppy with a drinking problem. The reason he acted as though he hated women turned out to be that he really did hate women. Still, Dick Dart did not at all match the vague mental images she had formed of Westerholm's murderer. He was too ordinary in the wrong ways, and not at all ordinary in other wrong ways. But maybe she should have guessed that the Wolf would have an ill-concealed sense of his own superiority.

"I still can't believe it," Davey said now. "You remember him, don't you, Nora?"

"He was awful, but I wouldn't have imagined he was *that* awful."

"His father is having a little trouble with that one, too." Fenn proceeded around to the front of his desk, thumped down the notebook, and sat to face them. "Leland sent over Leo Morris as soon as he heard what happened, and Leo has been in our face since two A.M. He's still back in the holding cell with your friend."

Though Leo Morris, the Chancel family lawyer who had hired the *QE2* for his daughter's sweet-sixteen party, was one of the most powerful attorneys in Connecticut, he was not usually thought of as a criminal lawyer, and Davey expressed his surprise at this choice.

"Leo won't argue the case in court, they have a sharp young guy for that, but he'll stage-manage the defense. We'll have a fight on our hands."

"You're sure he's the guy," Davey said.

"He is the guy," said Fenn. "When we booked him, he had a silver cigarette case of Sally Michaelman's in his jacket pocket. She stopped smoking ten, twelve years ago, but her husband gave her the case a couple of years before they divorced. And when we searched Dart's apartment, we found lots of goodies. Jewelry, watches, little things that belonged to the victims. Some of this stuff was engraved, and we're checking the rest, but I'd bet you anything you could name we'll find that most of it came from the women's houses. Hell, he even took a book about Ted Bundy from Annabelle Austin's house—she wrote her name in it. Guess he wanted to pick up some pointers. Besides that, Dart had a scrapbook of articles about the killings, clippings from every newspaper for fifty miles around. And on top of *that,* while Popsie was threatening his manhood, he coughed up a detail we never told the press."

Davey, who had looked a little alarmed at the mention of the book, asked, "What detail?"

"I can't tell you that," said Fenn.

"What made Popsie suspicious in the first place?" asked Nora.

"Dart had no real reason for showing up at her house. He called to say he had to discuss something, but once he got there he just rattled off some gobbledygook about the inventory at the dress shop—stuff he didn't have anything to do with. Then he says it would be useful to have a look at the paintings in her bedroom, maybe she could will them to a museum for a tax deduction. He wants to look over the paintings before they go any further. Popsie tells him he's full of it, no tours of the bedroom tonight, junior, go home, but really what she thinks is, *This guy is lonely, he just wants to talk*. Popsie has been around enough men to understand that this guy isn't on the normal wavelength, it isn't about sex after all, so she figures she'll give him one more drink and throw him out. So she gets up, walks around him, and realizes that he's not just making her nervous, he's making her *really* nervous. She's standing next to the fireplace. And then she realized something that made her pick up the andiron and clout him in the head."

"What was that?" Nora asked.

"All the murdered women were Dart, Morris clients. Popsie referred Brewer, Austin, and Humphrey to Dart herself, and Sally Michaelman had referred *her*. They weren't on Dick's luncheon list, but they all knew him. She had what you could call a brainstorm, and because she's Popsie, instead of falling apart she got mad and brained him."

"Was Natalie a client of Dart's?" Nora asked.

Fenn tilted his head back and contemplated the ceiling for a couple of seconds. When he looked back at them he seemed almost embarrassed. "Thank you, thank you, thank you, Mrs. Chancel. I must be getting too old for this screwball job. Got so caught up in the excitement around here, I forgot the reason you came in." He slid the thick notebook closer to him and opened it to read the last page. From the other side of the desk, Nora saw that instead of the scrawl she might have expected, Fenn's notes were written in a small, almost calligraphic hand. He looked up at Nora, then back down at the page. "Let me tell you about this woman. Officer LeDonne was reporting to the station early, at my request. He was coming up the South Post Road when he noticed a woman behaving oddly on the sidewalk in front of the empty building that used to house the Jack and Jill Nursery, in the 1300 block there, just south of the old furniture factory?" He looked up at her.

"Yes." She felt a faint stirring of alarm.

"Officer LeDonne pulled over and approached the woman. She appeared to be in considerable distress."

"Did she look like Natalie?" Nora asked.

Fenn ignored the question. "The woman more or less begged to be taken to the police station. She was insistent on getting away from the old nursery. When LeDonne helped her into the patrol car, he saw a resemblance to the photographs he had seen of Mrs. Weil, and asked her if she was Natalie Weil. The woman responded that she was. He brought her here, and she was taken to the station commander's office, where she almost instantly fell asleep. We called her doctor, but all we got was his service, which said that he'd call us back. We'll take her to the hospital this morning, but in the meantime she's still asleep on the station commander's couch."

"She didn't explain anything about what happened to her? She just passed out?"

"She was asleep on her feet from the second she came into the station. I should mention this. LeDonne never met Mrs. Weil. I never met Mrs. Weil. Neither did the station commander. None of us knows what she looks like in person. So it seems as if the two of you can help us out again, if you don't mind."

"I hope it is Natalie," Nora said. "Can we see her?"

Holly Fenn came around the side of his desk with a half smile visible beneath his mustache. "Let's take a little walk."

"Hey, when Dick Dart was spilling his guts to Popsie and the policemen at her house, what did *he* say about Natalie?" Davey followed Nora and the detective toward the door.

"Said he never went near her."

"He never went near her?" Nora still had not quite separated Natalie's bloody disappearance from the fate of the other women.

"You believe him?" Davey stopped moving and let Fenn walk past him to get to the door.

"Sure." Fenn opened the door and turned toward them. "Dart admitted everything else to Popsie. Why would he lie about one more victim? But the real reason I believe him is that Natalie Weil didn't use Dart, Morris."

"He only killed his father's clients," said Davey, with a fresh recognition of this fact.

"Makes you think, doesn't it?" Fenn motioned them through the door.

Out in the hall he led them past dull green walls, bulletin boards, doors open upon rooms crowded with desks. They were approaching a metal door which stood open behind a uniformed policeman. Through the door a row of barred cells was visible. It struck Nora that the cells looked exactly the way they did in movies, but until you actually saw them you would not guess that they were frightening. "Your friend Dart is back there," said Fenn. "He'll stay until we move him to the county lockup. Leo Morris is with him, so it might be a while. We still have to take his picture and print him."

Nora imagined the languid, smirking man from the bar at Gilhoolie's penned up in one of these horrors. The image filled her with dread. Then she took another step, and the entire row of cells came into view. In the last of them, one man sat bowed over on the end of the cot and another, his face obscured by a row of bars, stood. They were not speaking. Nora could not look away.

Davey and Holly Fenn moved past the open door. Nora looked at the man hunched at the end of the cot, then took in his curly gray hair and realized that he was Leo Morris. Involuntarily she glanced at the man standing beside the lawyer, and at that second the man moved sideways and became Dick Dart, his face brightening with recognition. She felt an electric shock in the pit of her stomach. Dick Dart *remembered* her.

Dart looked relaxed and utterly unworried. His eyes locked on hers. He derived some unimaginable pleasure from the sight of her. He winked, and she pushed herself forward, telling herself that it was ridiculous to be frightened by a wink.

Farther down the hallway was a door marked STATION COMMANDER. Nora forced herself to stop seeing the mental picture of Dick Dart winking at her and took a long, deep breath.

"Let's see what's happening." Fenn cracked open the door and peered in. A wide young woman in a police uniform immediately slipped out. Fenn said, "Folks, this is Barbara Widdoes. She's our station commander, and a good one, too. Barbara, these are the Chancels, friends of Mrs. Weil's."

"Holly gave me this job." Barbara Widdoes held out her hand and gave them each a firm shake. "He has to say I'm good at it. How do you do?" She was attractive in a hearty, well-scrubbed way, with friendly brown eyes and short, dark hair as fine as a baby's. Nora had misjudged her age by at least five years. The woman before her was in her late thirties but looked younger because her face was almost completely unlined. "Actually, all I do is keep everybody else out of this old bear's way. And rent my couch out to exhausted strays."

"Can we look in on her?" Fenn asked.

Barbara Widdoes glanced inside. She nodded and allowed Nora, Davey, and Holly Fenn to enter her office.

Covered to her neck by a blanket, a small old woman lay on a short, functional couch against the side wall of the dark office. Her eyes were deep in their sockets, and her cheeks were sunken. Nora turned to Holly Fenn and shook her head. "I'm sorry. It's someone else."

"Move a little closer," Fenn whispered.

When Davey and Nora took two steps nearer the woman on the couch, her face came into sharper focus. Now Nora could see why LeDonne had mistaken her for Natalie. There was a slight resemblance in the shape of the forehead, the cut of the nose, even the set of the mouth. Nora shook her head again. "Too bad."

Davey said, "It's Natalie."

Nora shook her head. He was blind.

"*Look,*" Davey said, and instantly the woman opened her eyes and sat up, as if she had trained herself to spring out of sleep. She wore a filthy blue suit, and her bare feet were black with grime. Nora saw that this old woman was Natalie Weil after all, staring directly at her, her eyes wide with terror.

"*No!*" Natalie shrieked. "*Get her away!*"

Appalled, Nora stepped back.

Natalie screeched, and Nora turned openmouthed to Holly Fenn. Davey was already backing toward the door. Natalie pulled up her legs, wrapped her arms around them, and lowered her head, as if trying to roll herself up into a ball.

Fenn said, "Barbara?"

"I'll deal with her," said the policewoman, and moved across the room to put her arms around Natalie. Nora followed Fenn through the door.

"Sorry you had to go through that," said Fenn. "Do you both agree that she's Natalie Weil?"

"That's Natalie, but what happened to her?" Nora said. "She's so—"

"Why would Natalie react to you like that?" Davey asked.

"You think I know?"

"We'll get Mrs. Weil to the hospital," said Fenn, "and I'll be in touch with you as soon as I can make some sense out of all this. Can you think of any reason Mrs. Weil might be afraid of you?"

"No, none at all. We were friends."

Looking as perplexed as Nora felt, Fenn took them down the corridor, not back toward the entrance but in the same direction they had been going. "Can I ask you to stay home most of the afternoon? I might want to chew the fat later."

"Sure," Davey said.

Fenn opened a door at the back of the station, and the Chancels stepped outside into bright, hot light.

Davey said nothing on the way to the car and did not speak as he got in and turned on the ignition. "Davey?" she said.

He sped behind the station and into the little road that curved away from the empty field and the river. It would take them longer to get home this way, but Nora supposed that he wanted to avoid the crowds and reporters at the front of the station. "Davey, come on."

"What?"

Something unexpected leaped into her mind, and she heard herself ask, "Don't you ever wonder what happened to all those people from Shorelands? Merrick Favor and the others, the ones that girl told you about?"

He shook his head, almost too angry to speak, but too contemptuous to be silent. "Do you think I care about what happened in 1938? I don't think you should start bugging me or anybody else about stupid *Shorelands* in stupid *1938*. In fact, I don't think you should have done anything you did. Whatever you did."

"Whatever I did?" This was really beyond her.

But Davey refused to say anything more on the ride home, and when they returned to Crooked Mile Road, he jumped out of the car, hurried into the house, disappeared into the family room, and slammed the door.

30

AT TIMES LIKE this, Nora wished that her father were still alive to give her advice about the male mind. Men were capable of behavior explicable only to other men. Most conventional wisdom on the subject was not only wrong but backwards, at least in Nora's experience. Would Matt Curlew tell her to confront her husband, or would he advise her to give him the temporary privacy he wanted? Some furious part of herself suggested that Matt Curlew would remind her that these days even

Catholics were known to get out of bad marriages. Certainly Matt Curlew would not have regarded Davey Chancel as a suitable son-in-law. In any case, she could hear him advocating both courses with equal clarity: *Get in there and make him open his yap* and *Back off and give the moody bastard a little time.*

Nora turned away from the door, remembering that her father had sometimes retreated to his basement workshop in a manner which indicated that he was to be disturbed only in case of emergencies on the order of fire or death. Davey was doing pretty much the same thing.

Nora went back upstairs to read about Richard Dart in the *Times.* On the bottom half of the front page, the headline SOCIALITE ALLEGED FAIRFIELD COUNTY SERIAL KILLER stood above a face-forward photograph of a barely recognizable grinning boy with shadowy eyes. Nora thought it must have been his law school graduation photo. According to the article, Dart was thirty-seven, a graduate of the Mount Avenue Academy of Westerholm, Connecticut, Yale University, and the University of Connecticut Law School. Since graduation, Dart had worked for the firm of Dart, Morris, founded by his father, Leland Dart, a significant figure in Republican politics in the state of Connecticut and a failed candidate for state governor in 1962. Richard Dart's specialty within the firm was estate planning. He had been brought in for questioning after Mrs. Ophelia Jennings, 62, widow of the yachtsman and racehorse owner Sterling "Breezy" Jennings, had rendered the suspect unconscious after becoming convinced of his guilt during a late-night legal consultation. Westerholm's chief of police expressed confidence in the identification of Richard Dart as the murderer of four local women, saying, "We have our man, and are fully prepared to offer conclusive evidence at the appropriate time." Did policemen ever really talk like that, or did reporters just pretend they did?

Leland Dart declined to speak to the press but said through a spokesman that the charges made against his son were completely without foundation.

Two long columns on page 21 gave the limited information the *Times* reporters had been able to unearth during the night. Mr. Dart's brother, Peter, a lawyer with a Madison Avenue firm, expressed conviction in his brother's innocence, as did several neighbors of the accused's parents. Roger Struggles, a currently unemployed boatmaker and close friend of the accused, told a reporter, "Dick Dart is a loose, witty kind of guy with a great sense of humor. He couldn't do anything like this in a million years." A bartender named Thomas Lowe described him as "laid-back and real charming, a sophisticated type." Mr. Saxe Coburg, his retired former English teacher, remembered a boy who "seemed remarkably comfortable with the idea of completing every assignment with the least possible effort." In his yearbook entry, Dart had expressed the surprising desire to become a doctor and chosen as his motto *As for living, our servants do that for us.*

At Yale, which both his grandfather and his father had attended before him, Dart was suspended during the second semester of his freshman year for causes undisclosed, but he managed to graduate with a C average. Out of the two hundred and twenty-four graduates in his law school class, Dart placed one hundred and sixty-first. He had passed his bar examinations on the second try and immediately joined Dart, Morris. The firm's spokesman described him as "a unique and invaluable member of our team whose special gifts have contributed to our effort to provide outstanding legal service to all of our clients."

The uniquely gifted lawyer lived in a three-room apartment in the Harbor Arms, Westerholm's only apartment building, located beside the Westerholm Yacht Club on Sequonset Bay in the Blue Hill area. His neighbors in the building described him as a loner who played loud music on the frequent nights when he returned home at 2:00 or 3:00 A.M.

This lazy, self-important pig had managed to slide through life, not to mention three good schools, on the basis of his father's connections. He had chosen to live in three rooms in the Harbor Arms. Blue Hill was one of the best sections of Westerholm, and the Yacht Club admitted only people like Alden Chancel and Leland Dart. But the Harbor Arms, which had been built in the twenties as a casino, was an ugly brick eyesore tolerated only because it provided convenient housing for the bartenders, waitresses, and other lower-level staff of the Yacht Club. What was Dick Dart doing in this dump? Maybe he lived there in order to irritate his father. Dick Dart's relationship with his father, it came to her, was even worse than Davey's with his.

She had a vivid, instantaneous flash of Dick Dart stepping sideways in his cell to freeze her with a gleaming wink. Nora folded the newspaper, sorry that she had met Dart even once and happy that she would never have to see him again. When the stories got worse, when the trial produced the torrent of ink and paper which Alden had cheerfully predicted, she promised herself to pay as little attention as possible.

Then she wondered what it would be like to have actually known Dick Dart. How could you reconcile your memories with the knowledge of what he had done? Shuddering, she recognized the reason for Davey's distress. He had been given a moral shock. Someone he had seen every day for two years had been exposed as a fiend. Now sensible Matt Curlew could speak to her: *Let him think about it by himself for as long as he likes, then make him a good breakfast and get him to talk.*

Nora dropped the paper on the kitchen table and went into the kitchen to toast bagels, get out the vegetable cream cheese, and crack four eggs into a glass bowl for scrambling. This was no day to fret about cholesterol. She ground French Roast beans and began boiling water in a kettle. After that she set the table and placed the newspaper beside Davey's plate. She was setting in place the toasted bagels and the cream cheese when the music went off downstairs. The family room door opened and closed. She turned back to the stove, gave the eggs another whisk, and poured them into a pan as she heard him mount the stairs and come toward the kitchen. With a pretty good idea of what she was about to see, she forced herself to smile when she turned around. Davey glanced expressionlessly at her, then looked at the table and nodded. "I wondered if we were ever going to have breakfast."

"I'm scrambling some eggs, too," she said.

Davey entered the kitchen in a way that seemed almost reluctant. "That's the paper?"

"Page one," Nora said. "There's another long article inside."

He grunted and began reading while smearing cream cheese on a bagel. Nora ground some pepper into the eggs and swirled them around in the pan.

When she set the plates on the table, Davey looked up and said, "Popsie's real name is *Ophelia*?"

"Live and learn."

"Just what I was thinking," Davey said, concentrating on his plate. "You know, not that we have them that much, but you always made good scrambled eggs. Just the right consistency."

"Made?"

"Whatever. The only other person who got them just the way I like them was O'Dotto."

She sat down. "If her name was Day, why did you call her O'Dotto?"

"I don't know. It was what we did."

"And why did you call her the Cup Bearer?"

At last he looked at her, with the same irritated reluctance with which he had joined her in the kitchen. "Can I read this?"

"Sorry," she said. "I know it must be upsetting for you."

"Lots of things are upsetting for me."

"Go on," she said. "Read."

He placed the newspaper on his far side, so that he could glance from plate to print and back again without risking whatever he thought he would risk by looking at her. Behind Nora, the kettle began to sing, and she stood up to decant ground beans into the beaker and fill it with boiling water. Then she clamped on the top and carried the machine back to the table. Davey was leaning over the paper with a bagel in his hand. Nora put a forkful of scrambled egg in her mouth and found that she was not very hungry. She watched the liquid darken in the beaker as flecks of pulverized bean floated toward the bottom. After a while she tried the eggs again and was pleased to find that they were still warm.

Davey grunted at something he had read in the paper. "Geez, they got a statement from that cynical old fart Saxe Coburg. He must be about a hundred years old by now. I asked him once if he had ever considered putting *Night Journey* in the syllabus, and he said, 'I can trust my students to read drivel in their spare time.' Can you believe that? Coburg wore the same tweed jacket every day, and bow ties, like Merle Marvell. He even looked a little bit like Merle Marvell." Marvell, who had begun by editing the Blackbird Books, had been the most respected editor at Chancel House for a decade, and Nora knew that Davey's admiration of him was undermined by jealousy. From remarks he had let drop, she also knew that he feared that Marvell thought little of his abilities. The few times they had met at publishing parties and dinners at the Poplars, she had found him invariably charming, though she had kept this opinion from Davey.

She touched his hand, and he tolerated the contact for a second before moving the hand away from hers.

"This must be very strange for you. A kid you knew in school committed all these murders."

Davey pushed his plate away and pressed his hands to his face. When he lowered them, he stared across the room and sighed. "You want to talk about what's upsetting me? Is that what you're trying to get at?"

"I thought we were getting at it," she said.

"I could care less about Dick Dart." He closed his eyes and screwed up his face. Then he put his hands on the edge of the table and interlaced his fingers and stared across the room again before turning back to her. The alarm in the center of her chest intensified. "Nora, if you really want to know what I find upsetting, it's you. I don't know if this marriage is working. I don't even know if it *can* work. Something really bizarre is happening to you. I'm afraid you're going off the rails."

"Going off the rails?" The thrilling of alarm within her had abruptly dropped into a coma.

"Like before," he said. "I can see it happening all over again, and I don't think I can take it. I knew you had some problems when I married you, but I didn't think you were going to go crazy."

"I didn't go crazy. I saved a little boy's life."

"Sure, but the way you did it was crazy. You stole the kid out of the hospital and put us all through a nightmare. You had to quit your job. Do you remember any of this? For about a month, actually more like two months before you capped things off by abducting that kid instead of going through channels, you got into fights with the doctors, you almost never slept, you cried at nothing at all, and when you weren't crying you were in a rage. Do you remember smashing the television? Do you remember seeing *ghosts*? How about *demons*?"

Davey continued to evoke certain excesses committed during her period of radioactivity. She reminded him that she had gone into therapy, and they had both agreed it had worked.

"You saw Dr. Julian twice a week for two months. That's sixteen times altogether. Maybe you should have kept going longer. All I know is, you're even worse now, and it's getting to be too much for me."

Nora looked for signs that he was exaggerating or joking or doing anything at all but speaking what he imagined was the truth. No such signs revealed themselves. Davey was leaning forward with his hands on the table, his jaw set, his eyes determined and unafraid. He had finally come to the point of saying aloud everything he had been saying to himself while listening to Chopin in the family room.

"I wish you'd never been in Vietnam," he said. "Or that you could just have put all that behind you."

"Swell. Now I'm talking to Alden Chancel. I thought you understood more than that. It's so dumb, the whole idea of putting things behind you."

"Going nuts isn't too smart, either," he said. "Are you ready to listen to the truth?"

"I guess I can hardly wait," she said.

31

"LET'S START WITH the small stuff," he said. "Are you aware of what you're like in the middle of the night?"

"How would you know what I'm like in the middle of the night? You're always downstairs drinking kümmel."

"Did you ever try to sleep next to someone who jerks around so much the whole bed moves? Sometimes you sweat so much the sheets get soaked."

"You're talking about a couple of nights last week."

"This is what I mean," he said. "You don't have any idea of what you really *do.*"

She nodded. "So I've been having more bad nights than I thought, and that's been disturbing for you. Okay, I get that, but I'll sleep better now that Dick Dart is behind bars."

He bit his lower lip and leaned back in his chair. "When you're having one of these bad nights, do you sometimes look around under the pillows for a gun?"

For a moment Nora was too startled to speak. "Well, yes. Sometimes, after a really bad nightmare, I guess I do that."

"You used to sleep with a gun under your pillow."

"At the Evac Hospital. How did you ever figure out what I was looking for?"

"It came to me one night while you were sweating like crazy and rummaging under every pillow on the bed. You were hardly looking for a teddy bear. I'm just wondering, what would you do with a gun if you found one?"

"How should I know?" He was waiting for the rest of it. *Go on,* she told herself, *give him the rest of it.* "One night two guys raped me, and a surgeon gave me a gun so I'd feel more protected."

"You were raped and you never told me?"

"It was a long time ago. You never wanted to hear any more than about a tenth of what used to go on. Nobody does." Feeling that she had explained either too little or too much, Nora assessed Davey's response and saw equal quantities of injury and shock.

"You didn't think that this was something I ought to know about?"

"For God's sake, I wasn't deliberately keeping a big, dark secret from you. You weren't exactly in a hurry to tell me all about Paddi Mann and the Hellfire Club either, were you?"

"That's different," he said. "Don't look at me that way, Nora, it just is different." His eyes narrowed. "I suppose some of these nightmares of yours are about the rape?"

"The bad ones."

He shook his head, baffled. "I can't believe you never told me."

"Really, Davey, apart from not wanting to think about it all that much, I guess I didn't want to upset you."

He looked up at the ceiling again, drew in a huge breath, and pushed it out of his lungs. "Let's get to the next point. This Blackbird Books stuff is just a delusion. You had me going for a while, I'll grant you that, but the whole thing is ridiculous."

It was as if he had slapped her. "How can you say that? You can finally—"

"Stop right there. There's no way in the world my father would agree to it. If I went in there the way we planned, he'd bust me down to the mailroom. The whole thing was just a hysterical daydream. What got into me?" For a time he rubbed his forehead, eyes clamped shut. "Next point. You are not—I repeat, not—under any circumstances, to badger my mother into giving you her so-called manuscript. That is *out.*"

"I already told you I wasn't," she said. "Why don't you move on to the next point, if there is one."

"Oh, there are several. And we're still dealing with the little stuff, remember."

She leaned back and looked at him, inwardly reeling from the irony of the situation. When he finally displayed the confidence she had been trying to encourage in him, he used it to complain about her.

"I want you to show my father the respect he deserves. I'm sick and tired of this constant rudeness."

"You want me to keep quiet when he insults me."

"If that's how you hear what I just said, yes. Now, about moving out of Westerholm. That's crazy. All you want to do is run away from your problems, and on top of that you want to destroy my relationship with my parents, which I won't let happen."

"Davey, Westerholm doesn't suit us at all. New York is a lot more interesting, it's more diverse, more exciting, more—"

"More dangerous, more expensive. We hardly need any more excitement in our lives. I go to New York every day, remember? You want to deal with homeless people lying all over the streets and muggers around every corner? You'd go crazier than you already are."

"You actually think I'm crazy?"

He shook his head and held up his hands. "Forget about it. We're getting into the serious stuff now. Let's consider the way Natalie Weil reacted to you in the police station. She went nuts. And it wasn't because of me. It wasn't because of that cop. It was because she saw you."

"Something happened to her. That's why she acted like that."

"Something happened to her, all right. And where it happened was in the same nursery where you took that kid when you decided to play God. Do you want me to believe that's a coincidence?"

"You think *I* took her there?" The sheer unreasonableness of this idea made her momentarily forget to breathe.

"There's no other way to explain things. You locked her up in that empty building and kept her there until she managed to get out. Now

I'm wondering whether or not you remember doing all this. Because you really did seem startled when Natalie started screaming, and I don't think you're that good an actress, Nora. I think you must have had some kind of psychotic break."

"I kept her locked up in an empty building. I guess I must have thrown all that blood around her bedroom, too. What else did I do? Torture her? Did I let her starve?"

"You tell me," Davey said. "But from the way she acted—the way she *looked*—I'd say both."

"You astound me."

"The feeling is mutual."

Nora regarded him during the silence which followed this exchange, thinking that he had somehow managed to become a person she did not at all know. "Would you mind telling me why I would do all this to Natalie Weil, whom I like? And whom I haven't seen, in spite of what you told Holly Fenn, for almost two years?"

For the first time during this confrontation, Davey began to look uncomfortable. He turned some thought over in his mind, and the discomfort moved visibly into anger. "Dear me, what in the world could it be? Wow, I wonder."

"Well, I do," Nora said. "Apparently it's staring me in the face, but I can't see it."

"Is this really necessary? At this point, I mean?"

"You bastard," she said. "You want me to guess?"

"You don't have to guess, Nora. You just want me to say it."

"So say it."

He rolled his head back and looked at her as if she had just asked him to eat a handful of dirt. "You know about me and Natalie. Satisfied now?"

"You and Natalie Weil?"

Wearily, he nodded.

"You were having an affair with *Natalie Weil*?"

"Our sex life was hardly wonderful, was it? When we did have sex, you were turned off, Nora. The reason for that is, you started going into the Twilight Zone. *I* don't know where you went, but wherever it was, there wasn't much room in there for me."

"No," she said, battling to contain the waves of rage, nausea, and disbelief rolling through her. "You cut *me* out. You were anxious about work, or so I thought, you had all this anxiety, and it began to affect you when we went to bed, and then you started getting even more anxious because of that, which affected you even more."

"It was all my fault."

"It was nobody's fault!" Nora shouted. "You're blaming me because you were sleeping with Natalie, damn her, and you know what that is? Babyish. I didn't tell you to stick your dick into her. You thought that one up all by yourself."

"You're right," he said. "You're not responsible. You hardly know what reality is anymore."

"I'm beginning to find out. When did this start? Did you drive up to her house one day and say, Gee, Natalie, old Nora and I aren't getting it on very well anymore, how about a tumble?"

"If you want to know how it started, I met her in the Main Street Delicatessen one day, and we started talking, and I invited her to lunch. It just sort of took off from there."

"How long ago was this wonderful lunch?"

"About two months ago. I'm just wondering how you found out about it, and when you started to hatch your crazy plan."

"I found out about two seconds ago!" she yelled.

"It's going to be interesting to hear what Natalie says when she's able to talk. Because from what I saw, you scare the shit out of her."

"I should," Nora said. "But because of what she did to me, not the other way around."

At an impasse, they stared at each other for a moment. Then a recognition came to Nora. "This is why you wanted to go to her house that day. You wanted to see if you left anything behind. All that stuff you told me last night was just another Davey Chancel fairy tale."

"Okay, I was afraid I might have left something at her house. If I saw something, I could say I left it behind the last time we visited her."

"And tell me some lie about how it got there."

He shrugged.

"How did Paddi Mann's book get into Natalie's house?"

He smiled. "Dick Dart didn't give it to her, that's for sure."

Nora felt like throwing every dish in the kitchen at the wall. Then, in a shivering bolt of clarity, she remembered Alden's talking to Davey on the terrace about Dick Dart, saying something like *I wonder what Leland's wife thinks about her son romancing the same women her husband seduced forty years ago.* Alden had said, *It'd be a strange boy who did that, wouldn't you think?* Alden had been the man Natalie called "the Prune." Alden had probably taken the photographs in Natalie's kitchen. No longer smiling, Davey gave her an uncertain, guilty glance, and she knew she was right. "Natalie had an affair with your father, didn't she?"

Davey blinked and looked guiltier than ever. "Ah. Well. She did." He bit his lower lip and considered her. "Funny you should know about that."

"I didn't know. It just sort of hit me."

"I suppose she could have told you when it was going on. Didn't you meet Natalie in the supermarket a while ago?"

"Alden gave her those Blackbird Books," she said, having come to another recognition. "I wondered why they were separate like that on the shelf. They were a gift from a lover, and she kept them together."

"She never got around to them," Davey said.

"No wonder, given her active life. Did she cut him off when you turned up? Was it like a trade-in deal, a newer model, like that?"

"Their thing was over by then. It was no big deal in the first place."

"Unlike your grand passion. Stealing your old man's slut away from him must have perked the old ego right up. Kind of a primal victory."

"I didn't know about her and my father until later." Davey's left leg began to jitter, and he chewed on his lip some more.

"Did you get any comparisons? Length? Endurance? The sort of thing you boys worry about so much?"

"Shut up," he said. "Of course not. It was no big deal."

"Nothing is a big deal to you, is it? You have no idea what your feelings are. You just push them aside and hope they'll go away."

"Nora, I had a fling. People all over the world do the same thing. But if I'm as emotionally stupid as you say I am, why are we having this conversation? I'm worried about you, I know that much. The only way *I* know to explain these things is what I just said. And if you're going off the rails, I don't know what to do with you."

"But I didn't do it! You had this sneaky little affair, you *betrayed* me, and then you took your guilt and handed it over to me. If I'm crazy, your adultery is justified."

"Okay," he said. "Maybe there is some other explanation. I hope there is, because I really can't say I like this one very much."

"Oh, I love it," she said. "It shows so much trust and compassion."

"So I guess we'll wait and see."

"I can't stand this anymore," Nora said, electric with rage. "I can't stand *you* anymore. I'm furious with you for sleeping with Natalie, yet if you can show me that you might begin to understand who I am, I could probably get over that eventually, but this garbage is so much worse that I . . ." She ran out of words.

"If I'm wrong, I'll crawl over broken glass to apologize."

"Gee, it makes me so happy to hear that," she said.

He stood up and hurried from the room without looking at her.

32

After the door to the family room had opened and closed, Nora unclenched her hands and tried to force her body to relax. The beginning of *Manon Lescaut* drifted up the stairs. He was going to hide, presumably until a squad of policemen showed up to drag her away in shackles to the lunatic asylum.

He had *reduced* her, *dwindled* her. In his version of their marriage, a criminally irrational wife tormented a caring, beleaguered husband. Nora was not too angry to admit that their sex life had been imperfect, and she knew that many marriages, perhaps even most, had repaired themselves after an unfaithfulness. She could acknowledge that her night terrors, apparently far worse than she had imagined, might have played a role in what Davey had done. She found herself ready to take on her share of guilt. What she could not forgive was that Davey had *written her off*.

As soon as the difference in their ages had become a *difference*—Davey had started to panic. A woman's forty-nine lay several crucial steps beyond a man's forty. Menopause, not nightmares and irrational behavior, was spooking Davey Chancel.

This was really bleak, and Nora pushed herself away from the table. She piled their dishes and gathered the silverware, resisting the impulse to hurl it all to the floor. She put the plates, cups, and silver into the dishwasher, the pans into the sink. If Davey left her, where would she go? Would he move into the Poplars while she stayed in this house? The idea of living alone on Crooked Mile Road made her feel almost dizzy with nausea.

She could remember what she had done every day since Natalie's disappearance. She had shopped, made the bed, cleaned the house, read, exercised. She had phoned agents on behalf of Blackbird Books. The afternoon of the day after Natalie's disappearance, when Davey would have had her tormenting the missing woman on the South Post Road, Nora had run into Arturo Landrigan's wife, Beth, in a Main Street café called Alice's Adventure. In spite of being married to a man so crass that he felt he should bathe in a golden tub ("Makes you feel like a great wine in a golden goblet," Arturo had confided), Beth Landrigan was an unpretentious, smart, sympathetic woman in her mid-fifties, one of the few women in Westerholm who seemed to offer Nora the promise of friendship, the chief obstacle to which was their husbands' mild mutual antipathy. Davey thought that Arturo Landrigan was a philistine, and Nora could imagine what Landrigan made of Davey. The two women had taken advantage of their chance meeting to share an unplanned hour at Alice's Adventure, and at least half of that time had been spent talking about Natalie Weil.

Maybe I really am crazy, she said to herself twenty minutes later as she drove her car aimlessly down Westerholm's tree-lined streets. Nora took another turn, went up a curving ramp, and found herself surrounded by many more cars than she had noticed before. Then she realized that she was driving down the Merritt Parkway in the direction of New York. Some part of her had decided to run away, and this part was taking the rest of her with it. They had covered about fifteen miles; New York was only twenty-five more away. In half an hour she could be ditching the car in a garage off the FDR Drive. She had a couple of hundred dollars in her bag and could get more from an automatic teller. She could check into a hotel under a false name, stay there for a couple of days, and see what happened. *If you're going to change your life, Nora,* she said to herself, *all you have to do is keep driving.*

So there were presently two Noras seated behind the wheel of her Volvo. One of them was going to continue down the Merritt Parkway, and the other was going to get off at the next exit and drive back to Westerholm. Both of these actions seemed equally possible. The first had a definite edge in appeal, and the second corresponded far more with her own idea of her character. But why should she be condemned always to follow her idea of what was right? And why should she automatically assume that turning back was the only right course of action? If what she wanted was to flee to New York, then New York was the right choice.

Nora decided not to decide: she would see what she did and add up the cost later. For a few minutes she sped down the parkway in a state of pleasantly suspended moral freedom. An exit sign appeared and slipped past, followed by the exit itself. The two separate Noras enjoyed their peaceful habitation of a single body. Ten minutes later another exit sign floated toward her, and she remained in the left-hand lane and thought, *So now we know.* Several seconds later, when the exit itself appeared before her, she flicked her turn indicator and nipped across just in time to get off the parkway.

33

NORA PULLED HER Volvo into the empty garage. That she would not have to explain herself to Davey came as a relief mixed with curiosity about what he was doing. At first she thought that he must be visiting his parents, but as she moved to the back door, she realized that Holly Fenn might have called with news of Natalie. A vision of her husband murmuring endearments to Natalie Weil made her feel like getting back into the Volvo and lighting out for some distant place like Canada or New Mexico. Or home, her lost home, the Upper Peninsula. She had friends back in Traverse City, people who would put her up and protect her. The notion of protection automatically evoked the image of Dan Harwich, but this false comfort she pushed away. Dan Harwich was married to his second wife, and neither groom nor bride would be likely to welcome Nora Chancel into their handsome stone house on Longfellow Lane, Springfield, Massachusetts.

She glanced into the family room and continued on upstairs. She wondered if Davey had gone out to look for her. The most likely explanation for his absence was that he had been summoned to the police station, in which case he would have left a note. She went to the usual location of their notes to each other, the section of the kitchen counter next to the telephone, where a thick pad stood beside a jar of ballpoint pens. Written on the top sheet of the pad were the words "mushrooms" and "K-Y," the beginning of a shopping list. Nora went to the second most likely place, the living room table, which held nothing except a stack of magazines. Then she returned to the kitchen to inspect the table and the rest of the counter, found nothing, and went finally to the fourth and least likely message drop, the bedroom, where she found only the morning's rumpled sheets and covers.

Feeling as if she should have become the irresponsible Nora who had disappeared into New York, she was moving toward the living room when the telephone rang.

She lifted the receiver, hoping in spite of herself to hear Davey's voice. A woman said, "I made up my mind, and I want you to do it."

"You have the wrong number."

"Don't be silly," said the woman, whom Nora now recognized as her mother-in-law. "I want to go ahead with it."

"Is Davey there?"

"Nobody's here. I can shoot right over and give it to you. I've been alone with the thing so long, I think it's *crucial* that you read it. I won't be able to sit still until I hear from you."

"You want to bring your book over here?" Nora asked.

"I want to get out and around," Daisy said, misunderstanding Nora's emphasis. "I haven't been out of this house in I don't know how long! I want to see the streets, I want to see everything! Ever since I made up my mind about this, I've been absolutely *exalted.*"

"You're sure," Nora said.

"I bless you for offering, I bless you twice over. You can bring it back to me Tuesday or Wednesday, when the men are at work."

"You're going to drive?" Daisy had not undertaken to pilot a car as far as the end of the driveway in several decades.

Daisy laughed. "Of course not. Jeffrey will drive me. Don't worry, Jeffrey is *completely* dependable. He's like the *Kremlin.*"

Nora gave up. "You'd better do it fast. I don't know when Davey's coming home."

"This so *exciting,*" Daisy said. She hung up.

Nora released a moan and slumped against the wall. Davey could never know that she had seen his mother's book. The entire transaction would have to be conducted as if under a blanket in deepest night. Daisy would give her the manuscript, and after a few days, she would give it back. She did not have to read it. All she had to do was give Daisy the encouragement she needed.

Nora straightened up and went to the living room window, not at all comfortable with the idea of treating Daisy so shabbily.

When she thought that Daisy's car would soon be turning into Crooked Mile Road, she left the house and walked down to the end of the drive. A Mercedes came rolling toward her. Daisy began to open the door before the car came to a stop, and Nora stepped back. Daisy leaped out and embraced her. "You darling genius! My salvation!"

Daisy leaned back to beam wildly at Nora. Her eyes were wet and glassy, and her hair stood out in white clumps. "Isn't this wonderful, isn't this wicked?" She gave Nora another wild grin and then turned around to wrestle from before her seat a fat leather suitcase bound with straps. "Here. I place it in your wonderful hands."

She held it out like a trophy, and Nora gripped the handle. When Daisy released her hands from the sides, the suitcase, which must have weighed twenty or thirty pounds, dropped several feet. "Heavy, isn't it?" she said.

"Is it finished?"

"You tell me," Daisy said. "But it's close, it's close, it's close, and that's why this is such a brilliant idea. I can't wait to hear what you have to say about it. My God!" Her eyes widened. "Do you know what?"

Nora thought that Daisy had read about Dick Dart in the morning paper.

"They've gone and put up this hideous *fortress* on the Post Road, right where that lovely little clam house used to be!"

"Oh," said Nora. Daisy was talking about a cement-slab discount department store which had occupied two blocks of the Post Road for about a decade.

"I think I should write a letter of complaint. In the meantime, Jeffrey is going to expand my horizons by driving me hither and yon, as you are going to do, also, my dear, by talking to me about my book. While I'm taking in the sights, you'll be peering into my *cauldron.*"

"Enjoy yourself, Daisy," Nora said.

"You must enjoy yourself, too," Daisy said. "Now I think Jeffrey and I had better make our getaway. I will be calling you this evening for your first impressions. We need a code word, to announce that the coast is clear." She closed her eyes and then opened them and beamed. "I know, we'll use what you said when I called you. If Davey's in the room, you say 'wrong number.' That's perfect, I think. I do have a gift for this sort of thing. Perhaps I should have been a spy." She climbed back into the car and whispered through the open window, "*I can't wait.*"

Nora bent down to see what Jeffrey made of all this. His face was rigidly immobile, and his eyes were dark, shining slits. He leaned forward and said slowly, "Mrs. Chancel, I don't mean to be presumptuous, but if I can ever do anything for you, call me. My last name is Deodato, and I have my own line."

Nora stepped back, and the car moved forward. Daisy had turned around in her seat, and Nora tried to return her smile until Daisy's face was only a pale, exulting balloon floating away down the street.

34

NORA HOISTED THE case onto the sofa and undid the straps. Scuffed and battered, variously darkened by stains, the suitcase appeared to be forty or fifty years old. When Nora finally yanked the zipper home, the top yawned upward several inches, the mass of pages beneath it expanding as if taking a deep breath.

Thousands of pages of different sizes, colors, and styles rose up. Most of these were standard sheets of white typing paper, some of them yellow with age; some of the remainder were standard pages shaded ivory, gray, ocher, baby blue, and pink. The rest, amounting to about a third, consisted of sheets torn from notebooks, hotel stationery, Chancel House invoice and order forms used on their blank sides, and the sort of notepaper that is decorated with drawings of dogs and horses.

Where could she hide this monstrosity? It would probably fit under the bed. She knelt to get her arms under the bottom of the case, lifted it off the sofa, and staggered backwards, barely able to see over the top. A faint odor of dust and mothballs hung about the weight of paper and leather in her arms.

The first sheet floated along in front of her and resolved itself into a title page which had never managed to make up its mind. Over the years Daisy had considered an ever-growing number of titles, adding new inspirations without rejecting the old ones.

In the bedroom Nora cautiously made her way toward the couch, then bent down to lower the case onto an outflung leg of a pair of jeans and a blouse she had been intending to iron. Holding her breath, she put one hand on top of the suitcase while with the other she tugged the jeans to one side, the blouse to the other. Then she sat beside it. She looked at it for a moment, regretting that she had ever offered to read this unwieldy epic, then grasped it front and back and lowered it to the floor. Yes, it might just, it probably would, fit under the bed.

Nora regarded the bright double window in the wall to her left. She stood up to raise the bottom panes as far as they would go and returned to the couch. She looked down at the untidy stack of pages at her feet, sighed, picked up sixty or seventy pages, turned over the title, or non-title, page, and read the dedication. Typed on a yellowing sheet with the letterhead of the Sahara Hotel, Las Vegas, complete with an idealized front elevation of the building, it read: *For the only person who has ever given me the encouragement necessary to any writer, she who alone has been my companion and without whose support I would long ago have abandoned this endeavor, myself.*

On the next page, also liberated from the Sahara Hotel, Las Vegas, was an epigraph attributed to Wolf J. Flywheel. *The world is populated by ingrates, morons, assholes, and those beneath them.*

Nora began to enjoy herself.

PART ONE: How the Bastards Took Over.

She began reading the first chapter. Through a maze of crossed-out lines, arrows to phrases in the margins, and word substitutions, she followed the murky actions of Clementine and Adelbert Poison, who lived in a decrepit gothic mansion called The Ivy in the town of Westfall. A painter whose former beauty still shone through the weight she had put on during the course of an unhappy marriage, Clementine drank a bit, wept a bit, pondered suicide, and had a peculiarly ironic, distant relationship with her son, Egbert. Adelbert made and lost millions playing with the greater millions left him by his tyrannical father, Archibald Poison, and seduced waitresses, secretaries, cleaning women, and the Avon Lady. When he was home, Adelbert liked to sit on his rotting terrace scanning Long Island Sound through a telescope for sinking sailboats and drowning swimmers. Egbert was a boneless noodle who spent most of his time in bed. Some vague but nasty secret, possibly several vague but nasty secrets, fouled the air.

When she reached the end of the first chapter, Nora looked up and realized that she had been reading for half an hour. Davey had still not returned. She looked back at the page, the last line of which was *"You know very well that I never wished to reclaim Egbert," said Adelbert.* Reclaim him? Egbert did resemble something reclaimed, like a lost dog.

The telephone rang. Hoping to hear her husband's voice, Nora picked it up and said, "Hello?"

"Goody goody, you didn't say 'Wrong number,' so you can talk." Daisy's voice, slightly slurred. "What do you think?"

"I think it's interesting," Nora said.

"Poop. You have to say more than that."

"I'm enjoying it, really I am. I like Adelbert and his telescope."

"Alden used to spend hours looking for topless girls on sailboats. How far are you?"

"The end of chapter one."

"Umph." Daisy sounded disappointed. "What did you like best?"

"Well, the tone, I suppose. That sort of black humor. It's like Charles Addams, in words."

"That's because you've only read the first *chapter,*" Daisy said. "After that it goes through all kinds of changes. You'll see, you're in for a real treat. At least I *hope* you are. Go on, go back to reading. But you really like it so far?"

"A lot," Nora said.

"Whoop-de-do!" Daisy said. "Stop wasting time talking to me and *surge ahead.*" She hung up.

Nora went back to the couch and began the second chapter. Adelbert stood beside a tall, bony, blond woman and signed a hotel register under a false name. In their room Adelbert ordered the woman to undress. *Honey, can't we have a drink first?* He said, *Do what I say.* The woman undressed and embraced him. Adelbert pushed her away. The woman said she thought they were friends. Adelbert took a revolver from his jacket pocket and shot her in the forehead.

Nora read the line again. *Adelbert raised the revolver, squeezed the trigger, and put a bullet through her stupid forehead.* This was a new side of Adelbert. Nora smiled at the idea of Daisy's turning Alden into a murderer. She was killing off her husband's conquests.

The telephone rang again. Groaning, Nora got up and answered it by saying, "Daisy, please, you have to give me more time."

A male voice asked, "Who's Daisy?"

"I'm sorry," Nora said. "I thought you were someone else."

"Obviously. I hope she gives you all the time you need, whoever she is."

"Holly," Nora said. "Chief Fenn, I mean. How embarrassing. I'm glad you called, actually. You must have some news."

"It's Holly, and the reason I'm calling is that we don't have any news yet. We finally got Mrs. Weil's doctor off the golf course, and he shot her full of sedatives and put her in Norwalk Hospital. According to him, the earliest we can get a straight story out of her is probably Monday morning. I thought I'd pass that along, so you can relax for one night, anyhow."

She thanked him and said, "I guess if I'm going to call you Holly, you ought to start calling me Nora."

"I already do," he said. "I'll be in touch Monday morning around nine, ten at the latest."

A wave of relief loosened the muscles in Nora's back. Holly Fenn assumed her innocent of whatever had happened to Natalie, that sow. Holly Fenn wanted to *clear things up*.

She returned to Daisy's epic. Adelbert parked in front of his crumbling mansion and went inside to pull Egbert out of bed. Egbert got off the floor, crawled back into bed, and pulled the covers over his head. Adelbert went downstairs to order a cringing servant to bring a six-to-one martini to the library. By the time the servant appeared with his drink, Adelbert was deep into a volume called *The History of the Poison Family in America.*

A new chapter, apparently from a much older version of the novel, began. On yellowed pages, the letters rose above and sank beneath the level of the lines, every *e* tilting leftwards, every *o* a bullet hole. After a battle with the style, far more congested than that of the first two chapters, Nora saw that Adelbert was reading about the history of his father during the period immediately after the birth of Egbert. A secret Nazi sympathizer, Archibald had made millions by investing in German armament concerns and was presently diverted from his covert attempts to consolidate a group of right-wing millionaires into a Fascist movement by a maddening personal problem. After rereading several pages three times over, Nora gathered that Adelbert and Clementine had perhaps produced the grandson Archibald passionately desired. Either the child had died or they had put him up for adoption. Archibald's tirades, lengthily represented, had not convinced them to repair the loss. When his orders and ultimatums came to nothing, Archibald informed his son that he would be cut out of his will if he did not provide an heir.

All of this lay half hidden beneath a furious explosion of exclamation points, tangled grammar, and backwards sentences. Archibald's fantasies about American Fascism clouded whole pages with descriptions of Nazi uniforms and other regalia. Hitler appeared, confusingly. She could not be certain if the new child had been reclaimed, adopted, or even resurrected.

Nora turned to a page typed on a sheet of Ritz-Carlton stationery and skimmed through three paragraphs before the first two sentences chimed in her head. She went back and reread them and then reread the sentences again. *Adelbert's shoes were crosshatched with scuff marks. Indeed, Adelbert's were not the shoes of a fastidious man, and such secret stains and stinks permeated his entire character.*

"Oh, my God," Nora said. "It was Daisy."

35

SHE LOOKED UP in astonishment. Not only were Clyde Morning and Marletta Teatime the same person, but both were Daisy Chancel. After Blackbird's initial authors had deserted Chancel House, Alden had replaced them with his wife, who had churned out piecework horror novels while she labored on her grim monstrosity. Blackbird's two stalwarts had never been seen or heard from because they were phantoms. *Spectre* had been hidden on a conference room shelf because Daisy had lost interest and written it when tired, drunk, or both. Alden would never revive Blackbird. Davey had been right about that, though he did not know why.

She wondered how he would react if she presented him with her discovery, then realized that she could not. Nora knew exactly how Davey would respond, by frothing at the mouth for twenty minutes before disappearing downstairs to hide behind Puccini. A more urgent question was whether or not to tell Daisy what she had discovered. Once again, for a time two separate Noras inhabited a single body, which stood up to move into the kitchen and make a ham sandwich. Daisy's instability made it equally possible that she would be enraged or delighted to have her pseudonyms known. Nora carried the sandwich back into the bedroom and realized that Davey had been gone for hours. At least he was not in Norwalk Hospital cooing over Natalie Weil. She decided to do precisely what she had done on the parkway, postpone any decision until it made itself. Daisy's manner would dictate her choice.

Nora bit into her sandwich and began skipping through the pages, trying to learn where this story was going.

After another hour, she decided that if this story was going anywhere, it was in some Daisyish direction unknown to the normal world. Scenes concluded, and then, as if an earlier draft had not been removed, repeated themselves with slight variations. The tone swung from dry to hysterical and back. At times Daisy had broken up a straightforward scene to interpolate handwritten passages of disjointed words and phrases. Some scenes broke off unfinished in midsentence, as if Daisy had intended but forgotten to return to them later. There was nothing faintly like a conventional plot. One chapter read in its entirety: *The author wants to have another drink and go to bed. You idiots should do the same.*

After following these confusions through a maze of arrows and crossings-out, Nora began to feel sick to her stomach. She decided to see what happened at the end and dug the last thirty pages out of the pile. Cleanly typed on fresh white bond, they were free from alterations, insertions, or marks of any kind. Nora leaned back, resumed reading, and soon found herself once more entangled in barbed wire.

The ending of Daisy's book described an argument between Clementine and Adelbert ranging over the whole of their marriage. At various moments, they were in their twenties, their forties, fifties, and sixties. The site of the argument shifted from different rooms in their house to train compartments, hotel dining rooms, and terraces in European cities. They lounged on the grass in a London park and propped up the bar of a Third Avenue gin mill at two in the morning. The ending was a compilation of the occasions of their dispute. What Nora did not understand was the nature of the dispute itself.

Clementine spewed accusations, and Adelbert responded with irrelevancies, most of them about music. *I have kept your business going, you bastard, but instead of thanking me you kicked me in the teeth.*

(Adelbert: *I never liked Hank Williams all that much.*) *Your entire existence is based on a lie, and so is our son's.* (Adelbert: *Cheap music sounds good on car radios.*) *You're not merely a fraud, but a fraud soaked in blood.* (Adelbert: *Most people would rather go to a ball game than a symphony, and they're correct.*) Bile soaked the paragraphs, a bitterness evoked by a subject as familiar to Clementine and Adelbert as it was opaque to Nora.

The last paragraph drew away from the protagonists to describe the terrace of a restaurant in the Italian Alps. Glasses sparkled beside white plates and shining silverware arrayed on pink tablecloths. Snow gleamed on the peaks beyond the terrace. A distant bird sang, and a diner answered with an imitation as exact as an echo. A white cloud of cigar smoke arose from a far table and dissolved into the air.

"Fraud," Clementine said, and the moron sun, having no choice, shone down upon the Poisoned world.

Nora placed the last page atop the others and heard the sound she had most been dreading, the ringing of the telephone.

36

"THANKS BE TO God, I did not hear the most hateful phrase on the face of the earth, 'Wrong number.' Haven't I been good? Haven't I been the most restrained little thing on the face of the earth? I am proud of myself, unto the utmost utmost. I have been circling this phone, picking it up and putting it down, I have several times dialed the first three numerals of your phone number only to put the blasted thing down again, I promised you hours of peace and quiet untroubled by little me, and by my count three hours and what's more twenty-two minutes have passed, and so what did you think? Tell me, speak, discourse, dearest Nora, please say something."

"Hello, Daisy," Nora said.

"I know, I'm too nervous to shut up and let you speak, listen to me babble! How far are you? What do you think? You like it, don't you?"

"It's really something," Nora said.

"Isn't it ever! Go on."

"I've never read anything like it."

"You got through the whole thing? You couldn't have, you must have *skimmed.*"

"No, I didn't," Nora said. "It isn't the kind of book you can skim, is it."

"What do you mean by that?"

"For one thing, it's so intense." Daisy uttered a satisfied grunt, and Nora went on. "You have to pay attention when you're reading."

"I should hope so. Go on, Nora, *talk* to me."

"It's a real experience."

"What kind of experience? Be more specific."

Confusing? Irritating? "An intense experience."

"Ah. I think you already said that, though. What *kind* of intense experience?"

Nora groped. "Well, intellectual."

"Intellectual?"

"You have to think when you're reading it."

"Okay. But you keep saying the same things over and over. A little while ago, when you were talking about how it wasn't the kind of book you could skim, you said, 'for one thing,' so you must have another reason in mind, too. What was it?"

Nora struggled to remember. "I guess I meant the condition of the manuscript."

An ominous silence greeted these words.

"You know what I mean, all those changes and deletions."

"For God's sake, the whole thing has to be retyped, but you asked to see it, remember, so I gave it to you as is, this is so obvious, but anybody can read a book after it's published, that's hardly the point, I want to hear what you have to say, and you're talking about something completely irrelevant."

"I'm sorry. All I meant was that you have to read it more slowly this way."

"Yes, you have been abundantly clear on the subject, trivial though it is, and now that we have that out of the way I wish to sit back and soak up your observations."

Nora could hear Daisy's impatience compounding itself several times over. "Some of it is very funny," she said.

"Goody goody. I meant for parts to be *ecstatically* funny. Not all of it, though."

"Of course not. There's a lot of anger in it."

"You bet. Anger upon anger. Grrr."

"And you took a lot of chances."

"You wonderful girl, you saw that? Blessings on your head. Tell me more."

"So it seemed very experimental to me."

"Experimental? What could possibly seem *experimental* to you?"

"The way you repeat certain scenes? Or how you end some sections before they're finished?"

"You're talking about the times when the same things happen all over again after they happened the first time, but differently, so the real meaning comes out. And the other thing you're talking about is when anyone with half a brain can see what's going to happen, so there's no point in writing it all down. My God, it's a novel, not journalism."

"No, you're right. It's a wonderful novel, Daisy."

"Then tell me why it's wonderful."

Nora groped for the safest comment that could be made about the book. "It's bold. It's daring."

"But why do you think so?" Daisy shouted.

"Well, a lot of books start in one place and tell you a story, and that's that. I guess what I mean is, you're willing not to be linear."

"It's as linear as a clothesline. If you don't see that, you don't see anything at all."

"Daisy, please don't be so defensive. I'm telling you what I like about your book."

"But you're *making* me be defensive! You're saying these stupid things! I spent most of my life laboring over this book, and you sashay up to me and tell me it doesn't even have a story."

"Daisy," Nora said, "I'm trying to tell you that it's much richer than the books that only tell you a story."

Slightly mollified, Daisy asked, "What's your favorite part so far?"

Nora tried to remember something she had liked. "I have lots of favorite parts. Adelbert killing the women. The way you present Egbert. Your descriptions of Adelbert's clothes."

Daisy chuckled. "How far are you? What's happening now?"

Nora tried to remember what had been going on at the point she had skipped ahead. "I'm at the part where Archibald is carrying on about Nazi uniforms and talking to Hitler while he's making Clementine and his son give him a grandson."

"The fantasia? You're only as far as the fantasia? Then you can't possibly see the pattern, you're not entitled to speak about it at all. I trusted you with my soul and you're walking all over it with your big dirty feet, I give you a masterpiece and you spit on it."

Nora, who had been uttering Daisy's name at intervals during this tirade, made a desperate effort to placate her. "Daisy, you can't twist everything around this way, I am not lying to you, I understand what you have put into your book, and I know how special it is because I know you wrote those Clyde Morning and Marletta Teatime novels, and this is so much more adventurous and complex."

During the long silence which followed she thought that she might have reversed the trend of this conversation, but Daisy had been gathering herself to scream. *"Traitor! Judas!"*

The line went dead.

Nora dropped the receiver in its cradle and blindly circled the bedroom, hugging herself. When she reached the telephone again, she sat on the bed and dialed the Poplars' number. She heard the phone ring three times, four times, five. At the tenth ring, she hung up, fell back on the bed, and groaned. Then she sat up and dialed the Poplars' number again.

After the second ring, Maria picked up and spoke a cautious "Hello?"

"Maria, this is Nora," she said. "I know Mrs. Chancel doesn't want to talk to me, but could you please tell her I have important things to say to her?"

"Mrs. Chancel doesn't want," Maria said.

"Say whatever you have to, but get her to talk to me."

Nora heard the telephone clunk down, then a few nearly inaudible words from Maria followed by a series of howls.

"Mrs. Chancel say you not family, her son family, not you. No good. Not talk." She hung up.

Nora fell back onto the bed and contemplated the ceiling. After an indeterminate time, one small consolation offered itself. Daisy would never speak to Alden of what had occurred. From this certainty grew a larger consolation. Because Daisy would not trouble Alden, Alden would not trouble Davey. Over time, the issue of Daisy's novel would vanish into the established pattern. In a week or two she and Nora could work out a reconciliation.

She got off the bed to reassemble the manuscript and stuff it back into the suitcase.

37

STILL ANXIOUS, NORA wandered into the kitchen and wiped down the counter. The problem was that if something could go wrong, it usually did. For Daisy, the manuscript was in enemy territory as long as it remained with Nora. She thought about dragging the suitcase from under the bed and driving it to Mount Avenue, but this prospect immediately induced exhaustion and despair.

Without considering what she was doing, Nora went to the sink, turned on the hot water, squirted soap into the palm of her hand, and began washing her hands. Then she washed her face. When she was done, she washed her face and hands again. The fourth time she scrubbed soap into her cheekbones and the flanges of her nose, Nora became conscious of these actions. Hot water stung her skin. She turned on the cold tap, rinsed herself, and reached for a dry dish towel. Her face stung as if she had sandpapered it. Blotting herself dry, Nora realized that she still felt appallingly dirty—no, not *still,* but rather as though someday very soon she *would* be appallingly dirty. Fighting the urge to turn the water back on and scrub herself all over again, she drifted into the living room, lay down on the sofa, and closed her eyes until the sound of Davey's car turning into the driveway awakened her. She wondered where he had been for the previous nine or ten hours and decided she didn't care. The Audi pulled into the garage.

Here was an interesting problem: would he slip into the family room and pretend she was not there, or would he come upstairs to confront her? Davey opened and closed the back door. His footsteps brought him toward the stairs. However slowly, he was moving in her direction.

Davey reached the top of the stairs and glanced into the kitchen before turning to the living room. He was looking for her, definitely a good sign. Was this what was called grasping at straws? *Go on,* she thought, *grasp away.* He came into the living room. His eyes locked with hers and slid away. He dropped into the chair most distant from Nora, leaned back, let his arms fall, and closed his eyes.

Nora said, "Welcome back."

"Did the police call?"

"Natalie's under sedation."

He was still collapsed into the chair as if thrown into it, and his eyes were closed.

"It might be nice if you said something."

Davey opened his eyes and leaned forward, catching her eyes yet again and then quickly looking down. "When I heard you leave, I bounced around the house like a Ping-Pong ball. Finally I went for a drive, got on the expressway and headed north. No idea where I was going. I had to think. That's what I've been doing all this time, driving and thinking. When I got to New Haven, I got off the highway, went to the campus, and walked around for about an hour."

"Eli, Eli," Nora said. She wondered if Davey had ever associated with Dick Dart in New Haven.

"Don't be sarcastic, all right? Nora, I was thinking about you. This morning everything seemed so clear. About ten minutes after you left, I began to wonder. Did that sound like you? You can do some rash things, but I thought you'd draw the line a long way short of kidnapping and torture."

"What do you know?" Nora said.

"I thought about what you said—that I was putting my guilt on you. But all the pieces fit together so perfectly, the whole pattern was so convincing, that it seemed like it had to be the truth. It was like one of those crossword puzzles Frank Neary and Frank Tidball do! The only part that didn't fit was you."

"You debated with yourself."

He nodded. "The more I thought, the idea that you kidnapped Natalie got more and more ridiculous. I got back in my car and drove around New Haven. New Haven is a crummy town, once you get away from Yale." Here he looked up at Nora, as if the irrelevance of the sentence had released him.

"I got completely lost, if you can believe that. I spent four years in New Haven, and it isn't that big. You know what happened? I got scared. I thought I'd never find my way out. I kept driving past the same little diner and the same little bar, and it was like I was under a curse. I almost had a *breakdown.*" He wiped his forehead. "After about an hour I finally drove past this pizza joint I used to go to, and I knew where I was. No kidding, I almost cried from relief. I got back on I-95. My hands were still shaking. It felt like my whole life was up in the air."

"Good thinking," Nora said.

He nodded. "I was so *tired* and so *hungry.* When I got to Cousin Lenny's, I drove in. I grabbed a booth and ordered meat loaf and mashed potatoes. When it came, I dumped ketchup all over the meat loaf like a little kid, and when I was eating, this idea opened up in my head like a giant scroll: If I could get so lost in New Haven, you could be telling the truth. Who says all the pieces have to fit, anyway? One thing I knew for sure. Even if you did find out about me and Natalie, you could never kidnap her. That's not you."

"Thank you."

"You really didn't, did you?"

"I said that three or four times this morning."

"I was just so *convinced.* I . . ." He shook his head and looked down again, then back up. Complicated feelings, all painful, filled his eyes. "Will it do any good if I apologize?"

"Try it and see."

"I apologize for everything I said. I wish with all my heart for you to forgive me. I'm sorry that I let myself get into that thing with Natalie Weil."

"That thing is commonly called a bed," Nora said.

"You're mad at me, you must despise me and detest Natalie."

"That's about right."

"This morning, didn't you say that we could eventually work things out? I want to do that, Nora. I hope you'll forgive me. Will you take me back?"

"Did you leave?"

"God bless you," said Davey, uncomfortably reminding Nora of his mother. He pushed himself out of the chair and came forward. Nora wondered if he intended to kneel in front of her. Instead, he kissed her hand. "Tomorrow we start over again." He placed her hand on her lap and began caressing her leg. "What did you do all day?"

"I almost drove to New York." She moved her thigh away from his hand. "I was thinking about not coming back. Then I turned around and came back."

"I would have gone crazy if you hadn't been here when I got back."

"Here I am."

He kissed the top of her head. "I have to lie down and get some sleep. I can barely stand up. Do you mind?"

"Of course not."

He went toward the hallway, turned to give her a grateful look and a sketchy wave, and was gone.

Nora leaned back against the sofa. If she had any feelings, they were like the little, black, shriveled husks left behind by a fire. She supposed that someday they would turn back into feelings.

38

HUNGER EVENTUALLY FORCED Nora off the sofa. Her watch said it was ten minutes to eight. Davey slept on. Nora thought he would probably wake up around midnight, fumble his way out of his clothes, and climb right back into bed to finish digesting his meat loaf and mashed potatoes, another example of Davey's habit, when under stress, of regressing to the age of training wheels. A search of the kitchen shelves yielded a can of mushroom soup, hot diggity. She plopped the congealed gray-brown cylinder into a pot, turned on the heat, and waited for it to melt while she toasted two slices of whole-wheat bread.

As soon as she began to spoon soup into her mouth an inner rheostat dialed itself upward, and a sense of well-being came to life within her. She'd return Daisy's book, and that would be that. She could get over Natalie Weil, though she would never trust her again. Nora didn't have to trust her; she never had to see or speak to the platinum cockroach again. If they met over the dairy counter at Waldbaum's, in a nanosecond Natalie's frisky little cockroach heels would skitter her away behind a mountain of toilet paper until Nora was in the parking lot. Pleased by this image, Nora took the last spoonful of soup, crunched the final inch of toast, and stood up to rinse the dishes.

The telephone went off. Nora abandoned the dishes and hastened to pick it up before it awakened Davey. She said "Hello?" What followed froze her stomach before it reached her mind. A man ice cold with rage said something about an unimaginable breach of trust, something about an unspeakable intrusion, something else about devastation. At last she recognized the ranting voice as Alden Chancel's.

"And what I will never understand," he was saying now, "besides the unbelievable pretension of imagining that you could offer advice about writing, is your persistence in following a course you knew to be dangerous. Didn't it ever occur to you that your recklessness might have *consequences*?"

"Alden, stop yelling at me," Nora said.

"You refuse to listen to people who know better than you, you pick up an axe and start swinging. You burrow in like a termite and eat away at other people's lives. You are an outrage."

"Alden, I know you're upset, but—"

"I am not *upset*! I am *furious*! The person who is going to be upset is *you*!"

"Alden, Daisy wanted me to read her manuscript. She insisted on bringing it here, she wouldn't have let me say no."

"She has been laboring over this god-awful thing for decades, but until you came sidling up to her, did it ever occur to her to show it to anyone else? Daisy doesn't solicit comments on unfinished work. You weaseled into her like you weaseled into this family, and you planted a virus inside her. You might as well have killed her outright."

"Alden, I was trying to help her."

"Help? You picked up a knife and stuck it in her heart."

"Alden!" Nora shouted. "None of that is true. When Daisy called me to see how I was getting on with her book, I said it was a wonderful book. She kept twisting everything I said into an insult."

"This surprised you? You must be feebleminded. Daisy knows her book is a chaotic mess. It can't be anything else."

"I don't know if it's a chaotic mess or not, and neither do you, Alden."

"You're a destructive jackass, and you should be horsewhipped."

"Alden!" she shouted again. "Unless you calm down and try to understand what really happened, you're going to—"

Hair flattened on one side, clothes crisscrossed with wrinkles, Davey came into the kitchen and stared at her openmouthed.

"That's Dad? You're talking to my father?"

Nora held the telephone away from her ear. "I have to explain this to you," she said to Davey. "Your mother misunderstood something, and now your father's going crazy."

"Misunderstood what?"

Alden's voice bellowed from the receiver.

"You have to stick with me on this," Nora said. "They're both flipping out."

Alden tinnily bawled Nora's name.

She put the receiver to her ear again. "Alden, I'm going to say one thing, and then I'm going to hang up."

"Let me talk to him," Davey said.

"No!" Nora told him. "Alden, I want you to calm down and think about what I said to you. I would never deliberately hurt Daisy. Let things quiet down, please. I'm not going to talk to you until you're willing to listen to my side of the story."

"Nora, I want to talk to him."

"I hear my son's voice," Alden said. "Put him on."

Davey put his hand on the receiver, and Nora reluctantly surrendered it.

"He called me a termite. He called me a jackass."

Davey waved for silence. "What?" He clutched his hair and fell against the counter. His fingers burrowed further into his hair, and he gave Nora an agonized look of disbelief. "I *know* that, how couldn't I know that?" He closed his eyes. Though he had clamped the receiver to his ear, Nora could still hear the clamor of Alden's voice. "Well, she says she wanted to help Mom . . . I know, I know . . . Well, sure, but . . . Yeah. Okay, fifteen minutes." He hung up the receiver. "Oh, God."

He looked around the kitchen as if to reassure himself that the cabinets, refrigerator, and sink were all still in place. "We're going over there. I have to wash my face and brush my teeth. I can't show up like I am now."

"Call him back and tell him we'll come tomorrow night. We can't go over there now."

"If we don't show up in fifteen minutes, he'll come over here."

"That'd be better," Nora said.

"If you want to piss him off even more." Davey came across the kitchen and glowered at her. "Where is that blasted manuscript, anyhow?"

"Under the bed."

"Oh, God." Davey hurried into the hallway.

39

By the time they reached the Post Road, Nora had described the conversations she had had with Daisy before and during her reading of the book, and by the time the barred iron fence in front of the Poplars came into view, she had finished telling him about the telephone call which had led to the present difficulty. What she had not described was the book itself. She also left out one other detail. Emitting noxious fumes, the suitcase sat in the trunk.

"She forced it on you," Davey said.

"If I hadn't agreed, she would have started screaming at me then."

"It doesn't sound like she gave you any way to say no."

"She didn't."

Davey turned into his parents' drive. Looking at the gray stone facade of the house, Nora experienced even more tension than the sight of the Poplars usually aroused in her.

"We ought to be able to make Dad understand that," Davey said.

"You're going to have to do most of the talking."

When they got out of the car, Davey looked up at the house and rubbed his hands on his trousers. For a couple of seconds, neither of them moved.

"Was the book any good, anyhow?"

"I have no idea," Nora said. "It's mostly a furious attack on Alden. His name in the book is Adelbert Poison."

Davey closed his eyes. "What's her name in the book?"

"Clementine."

"Clementine Poison? Am I in there, too?"

"Afraid so."

"What's my name?"

"Egbert. You almost never get out of bed."

"I want to get this over with and go home." He went to the back of the car and, grunting, lifted out the suitcase. "It must be one elephant of a manuscript."

"You have no idea," Nora said. "Davey, I was serious about what I said before. You're going to have to speak up, because if I say anything, Alden is going to yell at me."

"He'll yell at me, too." Davey closed the trunk and lugged the case toward the steps. "No matter what you think you want, Nora, you can't stay out here."

She and Davey slowly ascended the steps. He pushed the brass-mounted button beside the huge walnut door.

Maria opened the door before Davey's hand left the button. Evidently she had been posted at the entry. "Mr. Davey, Mrs. Nora, Mr. Chancel say you go to library." She gave the suitcase an uneasy glance.

"Is my mother in there, too?"

"Oh no, oh no, your poor mother she can't leave her room." Maria stepped back and held the door.

"When I was a little kid, he always chewed me out in the library." In the living room, a water stain twice the size of the suitcase darkened the carpet at the foot of an empty pedestal intended for a Venetian vase. A second large stain dripped down the wall beside the fireplace.

At the far end of the living room, the door to the library was closed. "Here goes nothing," Davey said, and opened it.

Wearing a blue pin-striped suit he had put on for the occasion, Alden stood up from a red leather chair at the far end of an Oriental rug bursting with violent blues and reds. "I think the first order of business is the surrender of the manuscript."

Davey walked toward his father as a man armed with a Swiss Army knife approaches a hungry tiger. Alden accepted the suitcase and put it down. He pointed at a tufted leather couch behind a leather-topped coffee table. "Sit."

"Dad—"

"Sit."

They moved around the table and sat. Alden placed himself on the chair and moved his foot to press a raised button set into the floor amid the fringes of the rug.

"Dad, none of this is—"

"Not now."

The door opened to admit Jeffrey.

"The object is now returned," Alden said. "Take it upstairs to Mrs. Chancel and place it in her hands."

Jeffrey bent to pick up the suitcase and turned around to carry it off as if he were disposing of a dead animal. On his way out, he gave Nora a dark, unreadable glance. The door closed behind him.

"You have nothing to say in this matter," Alden told his son. "Unless, that is, you encouraged either your wife or your mother in their actions."

"Of course I didn't," Davey protested. "I told Nora to stay away from Mom's work. I knew something terrible would happen."

"As it did. Now we must deal with the fallout. Your mother is in great emotional extremity. When I came home this evening, I found her weeping and hoarse from screaming. The living room was littered with broken glass. Maria was too frightened to cope, and Jeffrey, who must have understood that his role in this unhappy matter would rebound on him, was cowering in his apartment."

"Jeffrey?" Davey said. "What role did Jeffrey have?"

Alden ignored him. "Of course Jeffrey was responding to a request on the part of his employer. I have spoken to him, and we can all be sure that Jeffrey will never again be involved in any transaction of this kind. But nothing like this is ever going to happen again."

"What did he do?" Davey asked.

"He drove her," Nora said.

"Yes. He drove Daisy to the house you share with this viper."

"Please, Dad, don't call her names. I want you to understand what really happened. Mom called Nora and insisted that she read the book. She didn't give her a chance to say no."

"Really." Radiating contempt, Alden turned to Nora. "You have no free will? You don't have the excuse of being on our payroll, except indirectly, and you cannot be said to be a friend of Daisy's. Daisy doesn't have friends. Were you being a dutiful little daughter-in-law?"

"In a way, that's right," Nora said. "I did think I might be able to help her in some way."

"So you suggested that you read what she had written in order to offer editorial advice."

"No, just to give her someone to talk with about her book. Give her support."

"We see how well that worked. But you don't deny that this evil suggestion came from you?"

"I wanted to be helpful."

"I repeat. The suggestion was yours?"

"Yes, but Davey and I talked about it, and I agreed not to pursue it. Today Daisy called me and said it was crucial that I read her book and she was coming over right away."

"At which point you could have told her that you were too busy, or any one of a hundred other things."

"She wouldn't have accepted any excuses. If I had tried to back out, she would have been terribly insulted."

"You encouraged her mania instead of dampening it. But that wickedness is nothing beside the unspeakable obscenity of claiming that my wife is the author of Clyde Morning's and Marletta Teatime's novels."

"What?" Davey whirled to stare at Nora.

"She is," Nora told him. "In her book, there are those crosshatched scuff marks and sentences starting with 'Indeed.' "

"Why didn't you tell me before this?"

"I forgot," she said, which was the truth. "There was so much else, it just slipped my mind."

Alden said, "Are you starting to see the kind of woman you married? Is a bit of light beginning to dawn?"

"He doesn't want you to know," Nora said. "He doesn't want anyone to know."

"Shut your vile mouth," Alden shouted, pointing at Nora. "Not only does this lie insult my wife, who considers herself an artist and has never even *read* one of our horror novels, it throws mud at my firm and myself. You are endangering our reputation and mine. It's scandalous, and I won't stand for it."

"Oh, God," Davey said.

"Davey, stop moaning and pay attention to me." Alden inhaled. "Your marriage was a mistake. This creature has brought discord into our family from the moment she appeared. She has injured you in ways you can't even begin to comprehend." Alden, who had begun to shout again, brought himself under control. "Maybe we share a taste for erratic women."

"I'm leaving," Nora said, and stood up.

"You generally run away when you hear the truth, don't you?"

"I don't take orders from you, Alden. Davey, let's go."

Looking only half awake, Davey began to stand up.

"Sit down," Alden said.

Davey sat down.

"I am going to make this very simple for you, Davey. I am presenting you with a choice. If you divorce this woman and get your life in order, you stay on at Chancel House and remain in my will. If you refuse to see reality and stay in your marriage, you're out of both your job and my estate. You'll have to find a way to support yourself—if you can, which I'm sorry to say I doubt."

"That's not a choice, it's an ultimatum," Nora said.

"As far as I'm concerned, you are no longer in this room. Davey, I want you to think about your decision. Think hard. Do you want to stay with the madwoman you married, or do you want the life you deserve? We would be more than delighted to have you back with us."

"Do you really mean all this?" Davey asked.

"You have a week to think things over. I want you to do the right thing, and I think you will see that I am acting in your best interests."

Nora said, "You're using your money like a club. If you stick to this sadistic plan, you'll wind up losing your son. Do you want that to happen?"

Alden stood up. "Davey, you may leave. I have to go upstairs and deal with your mother."

Davey obediently stood up. Alden marched to the door and held it open.

"Dad," Davey said.

"I'll speak to you next Sunday."

Davey moved toward the door. "Boy, are you going to be sorry," Nora said. Pretending that he could not see or hear her, Alden patted Davey on the back as he went through the door. Nora suppressed the impulse to slap away his hand.

Clutching a white cloth in a distant corner of the living room, Maria quivered and began to move toward the entry. Alden said, "My son can let himself out of the house." She froze in midstep.

"Good-bye, Maria," Nora said, but Maria was too terrified to speak.

40

THEY CAME OUT of the house into abrupt night. Davey went down a step and looked back at the door. "Maybe we should go back in."

"What for? He gave his speech."

"I guess you're right. He's too angry."

"Phooey. He's happier than he has been in years. He thinks he's got you right where he wants you."

Davey shook his head and went down the rest of the stairs, fumbling in his pocket. "Would you drive? I feel kind of scrambled."

Nora took the keys. By the time she got into the driver's seat and moved it forward, he was leaning back with his eyes closed, his body so limp it seemed lifeless. "Come on," she said. "He'll never go through with it. All you have to do is call his bluff."

"He doesn't bluff."

Nora started the car and drove toward the distant gate in a cocoon of darkness. After a moment she turned on the headlights. "Do you think he's really willing to cut you out of his life forever?"

"I don't *know,*" Davey moaned.

"Of course he isn't," Nora said. "He's trying to bully you. This time, you can't let him get away with it." She turned onto Mount Avenue, accelerated, and the car shot forward like a nervous horse.

"What are you talking about?"

Usually an excellent, even a bold driver, Nora made a small adjustment to the wheel, and the Audi twitched sideways over the broken yellow line. She steered back into the proper lane and deliberately relaxed her hands. "The last thing in the world he wants is to lose you. That's what this is all about."

Davey moaned again, whether at his plight or her handling of his car she could not tell. "He's going to do everything he said."

"So what? After a couple of weeks he'll come nosing around to see how you're doing. If you don't have a new job, he'll give you your old one back. If you accept, he'll offer you a higher salary or a better position."

"Suppose he doesn't. Suppose it isn't a strategy."

An odd sense of familiarity as strong as déjà vu took possession of Nora. Hadn't she been reading a book in which a character presented an ultimatum much like Alden's? What scene, what book? Then it came to her: Alden had reminded her of Archibald Poison forcing Adelbert and Clementine to provide him with a grandson.

"Don't have an answer, do you?"

"What?"

"What happens if he really means it?"

"Every publishing house in New York would take you on. Some of them would hire you just to spite Alden. In fact . . ." She grinned sideways at Davey, who had flattened both hands on top of his head. "Screw the week. Call the people you know at other houses. Take the best offer you get, then go into your father's office and resign. He'll go nuts."

"No, he won't," Davey said. "Why would anybody give me a job? I edit crossword puzzle books. I send out form letters on behalf of the Hugo Driver Society. Besides, you don't know what's going on in publishing. Nobody quits anymore. It's not like the eighties, when people hopped around all over the place."

"Davey, you don't need this crap. Make some calls and see what happens."

They drove the rest of the way home in silence.

In the dark, Nora felt her way to the light switch and realized that Davey was still in the Audi. She spoke his name. He slowly left the car. When Nora opened the back door, he began moving zombielike to the front of the garage.

"It's going to be all right," she said, struggling to maintain her optimism. She closed the door behind them and saw him glance at the family room. "Come on upstairs," she said.

He dragged himself toward the stairs. Nora followed him into the kitchen, turning on lights as Davey advanced before her. "Let me make something for you," she said.

"Who can eat?"

Nora watched him take the bottle of kümmel from the shelf, select a lowball glass, and fill it to within an inch of the rim. He sat down opposite her and began revolving the glass on the table. At last he looked up at her.

"You're letting this get to you too much."

"There's one big difference between us, Nora. He's not your father."

"Thank God," Nora said, perhaps unwisely. "My father would never have treated you like that."

"I forgot, the great Matt Curlew was perfect. According to you, my father is the scum of the earth."

"I never said that," Nora protested. "I hate the way he treats you, and this ultimatum is the perfect example. He's using Daisy's tantrum to drive us apart."

"Gee, thanks. In case I don't understand what my father is doing, you have to explain it three or four times." He took a gulp of his drink, and a delicate shade of pink rose into his cheeks.

"Oh, Davey, maybe I've been talking too much, but he made me incredibly angry. And you were so silent."

"You keep forgetting he's my *father.* This guy you say has mistreated me all my life sent me to the best schools in America—something the sacred Matt Curlew never did for you—he gave me a job and pays me a lot more money than I deserve, he runs an important company—another thing Matt Curlew didn't do—and in case you forgot, see this table? He paid for it. He paid for everything in this house, including the lightbulbs and the toilet paper. I think he deserves some gratitude, not to mention respect."

"In other words, he owns you."

"He doesn't own me, he loves me. Even though I don't like some of the stuff he does, you can't order me to hate him."

"I don't want you to hate him," Nora lied. "But I love you, too, and I'd like you to get out from under his thumb." Davey lifted his glass and drank. "In a way he was right. You have to decide which one you want more, him or me. But if you choose him, you lose me for good, and if you choose me, you'll get him back in about a second."

"I'm married to you, not my father," he said.

"Thank God, I was beginning to get worried."

"But I don't want to lose either one of you. I think you're nuts to imagine that he'll change his mind."

"He won't change his mind, he'll just wait for another chance."

"How can you be so sure? If he cans me and I can't find another job, we're going to run out of money in about three months. Then what? Welfare? A cardboard box?"

"He'd never let that happen. You know he'd—"

"If I do get a job with another publisher, do you know what my salary would be? About a third of what I'm making now. We move out of here, okay, but all we could afford would be some dinky rathole of an apartment."

"Who says you have to work in publishing? The world is full of jobs."

"Don't you read the newspapers? Okay, maybe I could get a job as a clerk, but then we'd get half of a rathole."

"I can get a job," Nora said. "That way we get the whole rathole."

"God, it's like being married to Pollyanna."

"But you will make the calls, won't you?"

Davey pursed his lips and gave the refrigerator a considering glance. "Actually, there might be another way."

"What other way?"

"I could tell him that I'll move back into the house if he lets you stay here as long as you want. I think he'd go for it."

"We'd have lawyers all over us before you stopped talking. Good old Dart, Morris would build a wall between us six feet thick. How does that help us?"

"Once I'm there, I can talk to him, and if I can talk to him, I can soften him up. Sooner or later, he'll listen to reason."

"Davey, the Trojan horse."

"That's right."

Nora leaned back in her chair and looked at him steadily for what seemed a long time.

"I knew you wouldn't like it," he said. "But he has to calm down sooner or later."

"Davey, your father is doing his damnedest to turn you back into a child, and you want to give him a helping hand. Once he has you locked up in there, he's going to keep hammering away. By the time he's finished, you'll be wearing diapers and eating pureed carrots, and we'll be divorced."

"What a high opinion you have of me." His face had turned a brighter shade of pink.

"I know what happens when you're around your father. You turn mute, and you do everything he says."

"Not this time." He frowned at his glass, then looked back up at Nora in a way that seemed almost challenging. "Where did you find that garbage about my mother writing the Morning and Teatime books, in the astrology column?"

"It's true," Nora said. Davey grimaced. "I was reading along, and there they were, the crosshatch scuff marks and a sentence starting with 'Indeed.' I was flabbergasted."

"Not as flabbergasted as my mother. She's never even read novels like that. You heard my dad. Why would she do it in the first place?"

"Because Alden talked her into it. He thought he could make a lot of quick money out of horror novels."

He put on a disgusted expression and gazed at his drink. "Nora, even if this crazy idea came to you, why did you decide to tell her about it? Didn't you realize what would happen? I don't get how . . ." He threw up his hands.

"She was already ranting at me about spitting on her masterpiece, and I tried to rescue myself by telling her that it was so much better than those books. I guess I thought she'd be flattered."

"Smart," he said. "You throw a bomb into the living room and expect her to take it as a compliment."

Nora pushed herself away from the table. "I have to go to bed. Will you come, too?"

"I'm going to stay up. I won't be able to get to sleep for hours."

"But you will make those calls?"

"I don't need another bully in my life."

"I'm sorry, I won't say any more about it, I promise." Nora backed toward the door. "I'll see you later, then."

"I suppose."

She forced herself to smile as she left the room.

41

ABOUT HALF AN hour after Davey had left for work on Monday morning, Nora cried out aloud and woke herself up. Sweat covered her body and dampened the sheets. A small, trembling pool lay between her breasts. She groaned and wiped her face with her hands, then grabbed a dry portion of the top sheet on Davey's side of the bed and blotted her chest. "Holy cow," she said, an expression inherited from Matt Curlew. As soon as she wiped away the moisture, more of it rolled from her pores. Her body radiated heat. "Oh, hell," she said. "A hot flash." She had not known that you could get a hot flash while sleeping. An insect of some kind began crawling up her right thigh, and she raised her head to look at it. Nothing was on her thigh, but the sensation continued. Nora tried to rub it away. The invisible bug moved another two inches up her leg and ceased to be. She lay back on the damp sheets, wondering if phantom insects were common occurrences during hot flashes, or if this were some little treat all her own. A few seconds later the moisture on her body turned cold, and it was over.

After she had showered and out of habit put on a dark blue T-shirt, white shorts, and her Nikes, Nora realized that she had dressed for a run. She padded into the kitchen for a glass of orange juice and realized that she knew at least one person sufficiently down-to-earth not to mind being asked what some would consider an intrusive question. She pulled the telephone directory toward her and looked up Beth Landrigan's number. Only when she heard the telephone ringing did she wonder if she might be calling too early.

Beth's untroubled greeting dispatched this worry. "Nora, how nice, I was just thinking about you. Our lunch last week was so much fun that we should do it again. Just us, no noisy husbands. Let's cut loose and go to the Chateau."

"Great," Nora said. "I love the Chateau, and Davey never wants to go there."

"Arturo practically lives at the Chateau, but he never goes there for lunch, so we'd be safe. Wednesday?"

"You're on. Twelve-thirty?"

"Could you wait until one? I have a Japanese lesson at eleven-thirty on Wednesdays, and it lasts an hour."

"Sure," Nora said. "Wow, Japanese lessons. I'm impressed."

"So am I. I'm getting to speak it like a native . . . of Germany, unfortunately. Anyhow, you didn't call me to talk about my language difficulties. What's on your mind?"

"I wanted to ask you a question, and I hope it won't offend you."

"Fire away."

"It has to do with menopause."

"Offended, are you kidding? Everybody I know is menopausal, including me. It's all the rage. What's the question?"

"I had my first hot flash this morning."

"Welcome aboard."

"This strange thing happened. In the middle of it, I felt a bug crawling up my leg, but there wasn't any bug. I could really *feel* it. Did that ever happen to you?"

Beth was laughing. "Oh God, the first time that happened I almost jumped out of my skin. They tell you about the flashes, they tell you about night sweats and lots of other unpleasant things, but they never get around to telling you about the bug."

"I'm glad it's not just me."

"There's even a name for it. I can't remember the word, but it's something like masturbation. Maybe I'll ask my tutor what it's called in Japanese. On second thought, I'd better not. He'd probably run out of the house. He's an intellectual lad, but he probably doesn't know a thing about menopause."

"Probably knows a lot more about masturbation," Nora said, and the two women laughed and talked another few minutes before saying good-bye.

Cheered by this conversation and delighted by the promise of a friendship with funny, smart, levelheaded Beth Landrigan, Nora settled her long-billed blue cap on what she hoped was her own level head and left the house.

Forty-five minutes later, Nora heard the telephone ringing as she opened her front door, and she rushed up the stairs to answer it. Sweat darkened the blue T-shirt and shone on her legs. She snatched up the receiver and said, "Hello."

"Nora, this is Holly. I'd like you to get down to the station right away. Can you do that?"

"Did Natalie say something?"

"We have a lot of things to talk about, and that's one of them. If you don't have a car, I can send a man for you."

"I came in from my run just this second, and I'm dripping. Let me take a quick shower and change clothes, and I'll be right in."

He hesitated. "Okay, but some folks here are going to get nervous if you don't show up soon, so make it as quick as you can."

"Holly, you sound so . . . kind of abrupt. Should I be worried about anything? My life has gone so haywire lately, I wouldn't be surprised."

"It isn't quite that simple," he said. "Do what you have to do and get here as fast as you can."

"I'll see you in twenty, twenty-five minutes."

"Come around to the back. This place is a zoo."

Nora said, "Okay, good-bye," and Fenn hung up without speaking.

42

Nora parked in the slot Davey had taken behind Fenn's office, and saw through his window the back of his head and shoulders as he talked to Barbara Widdoes, who was wandering back and forth in front of his desk. Several other people, dark shapes in the back of the room, also seemed to be present. Through the humid air, Nora rushed past the row of police cars. She had put on a blue chambray shirt, jeans, and brown loafers. Wet hair clung to her ears. Her heart pounded.

It isn't quite that simple. What did that mean?

The back door swung open as she hurried up the concrete path. A red-haired, acne-pitted fullback in a tight uniform shirt stepped out. He looked from side to side before turning his corrugated face to her.

"Mrs. Chancel, okay? I'm going to take you down the hall to Chief Fenn's office, and we're going to have to do this fast. Things are real complicated here today."

"They're real complicated here, too," she said. The policeman gave her a neutral look. She moved through the door into relative coolness. A chaos of voices came from the front of the building. "This way," the policeman said, moving past her to walk briskly down the cement-block corridor. It occurred to Nora that she spent a great deal of time following men. They passed the door marked STATION COMMANDER and approached the metal door to the double row of cells. A vivid memory of Dick Dart's winking at her reminded Nora to look straight ahead, and she took in no more than that men in the tribal uniforms of police officers and lawyers crowded the passage between the cells. An intense, quiet conversation was going on among the lawyers, but she could not, and did not wish to, make out their words. The babble from the front of the station increased as she double-timed behind the officer. At last they came to Fenn's office.

The policeman knocked on the door and leaned in. He said, "Mrs. Chancel." Several people moved into different positions. A chair scraped. Fenn said, "Show her in."

Behind his desk Fenn was standing with his arms at his sides, looking at her in a distinctly unsmiling fashion echoed by Barbara Widdoes, who stood at attention at the far corner of his desk. Nora felt panic's icicle jab her stomach. Two men in dark suits and white shirts, one wearing black-framed sunglasses, stepped forward from the adjacent wall: Slim and Slam, the FBI men who had been in Natalie Weil's house.

"Hello, Mrs. Chancel," said Fenn. So Nora was no longer Nora. "I think you've met all the people in this room. Barbara Widdoes, our station commander, and the federal agents assigned to this case, Mr. Shull and Mr. Hashim." Mr. Shull, the taller of the two, wore the sunglasses. They gave him a vaguely hipsterish air which suddenly struck Nora as hilarious.

"Nice to see you again," she said, and a second of silence greeted her remark.

"I guess we can get this thing straight," Fenn said, and became Holly once again. "Let's try to figure out what we have here."

"About time," said Mr. Shull, speaking either to himself or to Mr. Hashim, who crossed his arms and watched Nora take one of the chairs. Holly sat down, and Barbara Widdoes perched herself on the edge of the chair next to Nora's and put her fat knees and calves together. The two federal agents stayed on their feet.

Mr. Shull folded the sunglasses into the top pocket of his suit jacket.

"Well now, Nora," Holly said, and smiled at her. "The people in this room have differing opinions on various matters, one of them being what to do with you, but with your help we might work out a consensus. It's going to be important for you to be completely frank and open with me. Can you do that?"

"What did Natalie say?" Nora asked. Behind her, one of the FBI men made a little popping sound with his lips.

"Mrs. Weil said a lot of things, which we'll get to in a minute. I want you to go back to the time we met on her front lawn. We had a little discussion there that made me think you and your husband might be able to help us. Do you remember that?"

"I remember," Nora said. "We said we'd been there a couple of times."

"Six, if I recall. The last time being two weeks before her disappearance."

Nora nodded, silently condemning Davey for his self-serving lie.

"Do you want to stand by that statement, or have you had second thoughts about it?"

"Well, the truth is, I hadn't been in that house in over two years."

Barbara Widdoes clasped her hands on top of her knees, and Mr. Hashim and Mr. Shull slowly moved to the other side of Holly's desk.

"That agrees with what Mrs. Weil told us. If there was some point to misleading me as to the nature of your relationship with Mrs. Weil, I'd certainly like to hear it."

Nora sighed. "Actually, it was Davey, my husband, who said we'd been there all those times, and that we had dinner at her place two weeks before. Remember? He said we had Mexican food and watched wrestling on TV, but that was what we did about a month before we bought our house, the time we did go there."

"Do you have any idea why he'd say all that?"

She sighed again. "He has this, I don't know, habit of stretching the truth. Almost always, it isn't anything more than exaggerating—like decorating the facts."

"As I remember, you went along with this particular decoration."

"We'd just had a quarrel, and I didn't want to irritate him, especially by contradicting him in front of you. Now that I'm thinking about this, I thought you knew he was lying right away."

"Didn't take Sherlock Holmes," Holly said. "From our point of view, this made the two of you kind of interesting. So I decided to let you into the house and see if any other interesting things might come up."

"Are we getting to it now?" asked Mr. Shull. "Can we skip the cracker-barrel stuff?"

"It?" Nora looked at Mr. Shull, who smiled at her.

"There's something all of us find puzzling," Holly said. "It has to do with the physical evidence at the crime scene, and also a couple of remarks made by you and your husband. Do you recall your husband telling me that you didn't think Mrs. Weil was dead?"

"I don't know where he got that from. I was sure she was dead."

"Your husband's comment showed considerable foresight, wouldn't you say?"

"To tell you the truth, I think he was just trying to make me look foolish."

"Because of your quarrel?"

"I suppose."

"What was your quarrel about?"

"He thinks I don't show his father enough respect, and I think his father's a bully. We go round and round."

"The argument isn't important," said Mr. Shull. "If you don't get to it right now, I'm taking over."

"We're there," Holly said. He smiled at Nora again, but not vindictively, as Mr. Shull had done. "Let's get to when we were standing outside Mrs. Weil's bedroom. Do you remember the condition of the room?"

Nora nodded.

"Do you remember what I said to you?"

"I didn't have to go in if I didn't want to."

"Do you remember what I said right after that?"

"No, I don't. I'm sorry."

"I suggested that you might want to reconsider the idea that Mrs. Weil was not dead."

"I don't remember that," Nora said.

"You don't remember your response? It concerned the blood in the room."

"It did?"

"You said, 'Maybe it isn't her blood.' Do you remember now?"

"Oh, you're right, I did, I remember. But that just popped into my mind because of Davey, what he told you outside." She glanced up at Mr. Shull, who, smiling, looked back. "Of course it was her blood, it couldn't have been anything else." She turned to Holly Fenn. "It wasn't her blood? It was some kind of blood."

"Yes, it was some kind of blood."

"What kind?"

"Animal blood," Holly said. "Pig, most likely. You see why we're interested in your remark."

"I guess I do," Nora said. "But it was just this dumb thing I said."

"We're in sort of a quandary here, Nora."

"You're in a quandary," said Mr. Shull.

"So you weren't speaking with any real knowledge when you told me that the stains in that room might not have been Mrs. Weil's blood."

"None at all. But everything connected to Natalie's disappearance is strange."

"Yes, let's turn to Mrs. Weil at this point. Mrs. Weil said a lot of contradictory things, but she did give us one new bit of information."

Barbara Widdoes spoke for the first time. "You were aware that your husband and Mrs. Weil were having an affair, weren't you?"

"I only found out on Saturday afternoon."

"How did that happen?"

"Davey told me. He was very distressed about what had happened to her, and he blurted it out."

"You deny any involvement in Mrs. Weil's abduction and mistreatment?"

"It still isn't clear that abduction occurred," Holly said.

"Holly, you were in my office Saturday morning," said Barbara Widdoes. "You saw the woman go into hysterics when she saw Mrs. Chancel and stay that way until she was sedated. What occurred is pretty clear to me, and it ought to be clear to you, too. Mrs. Chancel learned about her husband's affair, removed the victim from her bedroom, and kept her prisoner in her old stamping grounds, the former nursery. I'm sure you remember the incident. She detained her there until the victim managed to escape. I don't like all these coincidences. We have a pattern here, and I don't think Mrs. Chancel should be permitted to leave this station until she is read her rights and booked on a variety of charges."

"Somebody finally came out with it," said Mr. Shull.

"You want to arrest me?" Nora asked. "I didn't do anything to Natalie. I wouldn't treat my worst enemy that way." She looked across the desk at Holly Fenn. "Didn't you say Natalie contradicted herself? About me?"

"Didn't she, Barbara?" Holly said. "You think about this, too, Mr. Shull. We have a victim one step away from saying she was abducted by little green people from outer space. She says Mrs. Chancel forced her out of her house and locked her up in the old nursery, but is there anything in all that about the animal blood in the bedroom?"

He focused on Nora again. "Here's the situation with Mrs. Weil. The first thing she said when we went in there this morning was that you went to her house, threatened her with a knife, drove her to that building, and chained her up. Two minutes later we want her to repeat her story so we can take a statement, and she says she has no idea what happened to her. She looks back at the past week, and it's all a fog. She thinks she found her own way to the South Post Road but couldn't say how or why. So we write that down all over again and read it back to her and we say, Is that what happened? and she says, I don't remember. Then she lies there for a while, and after that she can respond to questions again, and we ask her about you, and she cries and says you took her to the building, and the whole thing starts all over again." He looked over at Barbara Widdoes. "Is that accurate? Have I exaggerated anything?"

"Holly, our victim is considerably disordered. But she keeps returning to the accusation, and that's enough for me. Give her another day or two, she'll be able to connect the dots."

"Barbara, Mrs. Weil keeps returning to the kidnapping story, yes, but she also keeps returning to wandering away by herself. Unless Mrs. Chancel gives us a confession and pleads guilty, we'll have to put our victim on the stand. Do you think we really have a case here?"

Barbara Widdoes glanced at Mr. Shull. "We have the grandmother of all motives, she had nothing but opportunity, and we'll come up with physical evidence in about ten seconds. In the old nursery where Mrs. Chancel took a child the first time she experimented with kidnapping."

Nora and Holly Fenn both began to protest, but Barbara Widdoes stood up and said, "I want to move on to the next phase. As soon as we process Mrs. Chancel, she can get in touch with her lawyer." She looked down at Nora. "In fact, your lawyer is probably here. Aren't you a Dart, Morris client? Leo Morris is waiting for charges to be filed against Mr. Dart, and we'll be doing that after we finish with you. If you like, I could advise him of your situation and tell him you have asked to see him."

Nora swiveled in her chair to look at Holly. "This is really happening? I'm going to be arrested for something I didn't do?"

"Barbara's our station commander. This is her call. Get your lawyer on it."

The entirety of her situation burst upon her, and its sheer, improbable hopelessness caused her to slump against the back of the chair and laugh out loud. Everybody in the room stared at her, exhibiting emotions from concern to contempt.

"Mrs. Chancel, are you all right?" asked Barbara Widdoes.

"I wish you knew what else is going on in my life."

Holly looked at his watch as he came around the side of his desk. "I'd let you use my phone to call your husband, but we're running out of time. I want to get you through our procedures before the Dick Dart circus gets out of hand. When we're done, I'll take you around to one of the interview rooms. You can use the phone there while you wait for Leo Morris."

She stood up.

"We need a little time with Mrs. Chancel, too," said Mr. Shull.

"How could I forget?" Holly placed his hand between her shoulder blades and urged her forward. "If we don't get this done fast, it'll take hours. Everything's going to go crazy around here in about ten minutes."

"Everything already has gone crazy," Nora said.

Holly opened the door with one hand while keeping the other on her back, moved her into the corridor, and followed immediately behind. Voices and the tramp of feet came from the front of the station, and before Barbara Widdoes and the FBI men were out of the office, a crowd of men burst around the corner and came hurrying toward them. At the front of the crowd, Officer LeDonne was a few paces in front of Leo Morris, who gave Nora a look of intense, unfriendly curiosity. Next to the lawyer, Dick Dart, in a gray suit and a white shirt but without a necktie, caught sight of Nora and grinned.

"What's this?" said Holly. "Cripes, they're taking him around the back to keep him away from the reporters. I'll send them back to the cells so we can take care of you first."

Officer LeDonne slowed down at the sight of Holly Fenn, and the other two men bumped into him.

"LeDonne, take this man back to the holding cell. I want my other business out of the way before we deal with him. Is that okay with you, Counselor?"

Leo Morris gloomily inspected Nora with his dark-rimmed eyes.

Nora tried to back through the door so that Dick Dart would stop grinning at her, but Barbara Widdoes pressed against her and gripped her arms.

"Davey Chancel's lovely spouse," Dart said. Nora closed her eyes.

Holly turned to LeDonne. "Take them back and keep the reporters away."

Before LeDonne could respond, a second group burst around the corner and filled the corridor, bawling out questions. Two or three men with video cameras on their shoulders forced their way to the front of the crowd.

"Everybody stop!" Holly shouted. "People, stop moving. LeDonne, wait a second before you lead the prisoner around the back. I want our station commander to take these men into her office. Mrs. Chancel and I will wait here."

Barbara Widdoes released her grip on Nora and squeezed out of the office, followed by the FBI men. They escaped down the corridor.

Holly raised his voice. "Media people, go back to the front of the station, this is not permissible, am I understood?"

"Nora-pie," said Dick Dart, and she looked up at the eyes sparkling in his grinning face.

Leo Morris and Holly Fenn suggested in their various fashions that Dart refrain from speaking, but he held Nora's eyes with his own and said, "What an interesting day." Then he wrapped his left arm around Officer LeDonne's neck and snatched his revolver from its holster so quickly that LeDonne was straining against the arm clamped over his throat, and the revolver was aimed at his temple before Nora was aware that Dart had moved at all.

LeDonne stopped struggling, and Holly stepped forward. The reporters fell silent. Dart tightened his finger on the trigger. "Now, now," he said. "Be a good boy."

Holly held up his hands. "Mr. Dart, you are in a police station. Release the officer and surrender his weapon."

"Do what he says," said Leo Morris. The lawyer's voice came out in a high-pitched squeak.

"Leo, isn't it obvious that I am in charge here?"

"Not for long," Holly said.

"Move against the wall."

Holly slowly began going to the other side of the hall, and Nora followed.

"No, Nora, you go back into the doorway." Dart pushed the gun barrel into LeDonne's head and walked the policeman toward her like a doll. LeDonne's face was mottled scarlet, and rage and panic filled his eyes. Nora glanced at Holly Fenn, who frowned and nodded. She stepped backwards.

"What do you think you're doing?" Holly asked.

"Simple exchange of prisoners," said Dart. "Followed by a daring escape and a successful flight, that kind of thing."

Holly opened his mouth, but before he spoke, Dart sent LeDonne reeling toward him and immediately materialized beside Nora. LeDonne collided with Holly, and Dart circled Nora's neck with his arm and pressed the barrel of LeDonne's revolver to her temple. The metal felt cold and brutal, and Dart's arm cut off her breath. "Ready?" he asked. "Bags packed? Passport in order?" He pulled her into Holly's office and slammed the door with his foot.

BOOK IV

GENTLE FRIEND

THE OLD MAN TURNED TO THE TREMBLING BOY AND SAID, "YOU HAVE ENTERED MY CAVE FOR A PURPOSE. IN THIS DARKNESS SHALL YOU LEARN ABOUT FEAR."

43

DICK DART BENT Nora back over his knee to turn the lock on the office door. "You and I are going out that window. If you give me any trouble I'll kill you on the spot. Do you understand?" She nodded, and he propelled her across the room. "Where's your car?" She pointed through the window at the Volvo. Holly Fenn shouted from the other side of the door, and the knob rattled. "I lead a charmed life," Dart said. "Open the window. Now. Jump out and get into the driver's seat. I'll be right behind you."

Nora's hands moved to the bottom of the window, efficient little hands, and pushed it up. She thrust her left leg through the frame and saw it outlined against the grass below, her slim leg encased in blue denim, her ankle, her narrow, sockless foot in a brown basket-weave loafer. Her leg seemed entirely surreal, suspended above the grass. What would it do next, this entertaining leg?

The entertaining leg strained toward the strip of green between the building and the concrete path, and, when she pushed her bottom over the windowsill, abruptly landed on the grass. Awkwardly, she pulled her right leg through the window. As soon as she hopped backwards, Dick Dart flew face first through the empty space, the revolver clutched to his chest. He got his feet under him in midair, landed so close to her that she felt the shock in the earth, spun her around, and jabbed the gun into her back.

"Keys," Dart said. She reached in her pocket and pulled them out as she trotted toward the car. "Get in and drive. *Go!*" He was already sliding into the passenger seat.

Sweating, Nora backed out of the parking space. "You want me to take that little road?"

"What a piece of shit you drive. We're going to have to trade up. Faster, faster. When you get to the end of this street, turn left and get to I-95."

Nora slowed down for the stop sign at the end of the road, and Dart swore and held the gun to her head. Nora pressed the accelerator, rocketed past the stop sign, and turned left. Holding the gun to her head, Dart checked the rear window and whooped. "They're not behind us! Those dummies are still talking to the door!" He lowered the gun and slapped his knee. "Hah! They couldn't get through the reporters. Shows you how shitty the press in this country is." He grinned at her. A stench of sweat, oil, bad breath, and secret dirt floated out of him. "Brighten up, you're on the road with Dick Dart, it's an adventure."

Traveling at sixty miles an hour down a tree-lined, completely foreign street she knew she had seen dozens of times, Nora barely took in his words. Her hands had clamped to the wheel, her teeth were gritted, and her eyes felt peeled. She ran two more stop signs. Where *was* I-95?

"I knew we were connected the first time I saw you. I'm protected, I'm guided, and nothing bad is ever going to happen to me. What the fuck are you *doing*?" He rammed the revolver's barrel into her ear. "Stop, damn you."

Nora slammed her foot on the brake. Her hands shook, and her throat had constricted.

"Where are you going? Hardly the time for the scenic route." Metal ground into her ear.

"I don't remember how to get there," she said.

"Cool under fire, are we?" He glanced at the rear window, then removed the gun. "Back up past the stop sign, turn right. Go to Station Road, turn left. We want north, toward New Haven."

She backed up and made the turn toward Station Road. In the distance, sirens wailed.

"Step on it, bitch, you cost us about thirty seconds. Move it!"

Nora hit the accelerator, and the Volvo jolted forward. At the next stop sign, she nipped past a Dodge van just entering the intersection. The driver hit the horn and held it down. "Asshole," said Dart. "Blow these guys off, run around them."

Two cars proceeded down the road ahead of them. The sirens seemed to get nearer. A man in cycling shorts and a helmet rode a bicycle toward them in the center of the opposite lane. "What about—"

"Go through the dumb fuck."

Nora accelerated into the cyclist's lane. The man driving the car in front of them turned his head to stare, the surprise on his face nothing compared with the astonishment on the cyclist's. Nora honked. The man, who had something like five seconds in which to decide what he wanted to do, wasted two of them on wagging his index finger and shouting. Nora locked her elbows, stretched her mouth taut, and uttered a high-pitched, panicked whine.

"Bye-*byeee,*" Dart sang.

The cyclist wrenched himself sideways and disappeared from the windshield a moment before being struck by the Volvo. Nora twisted her head. She had a momentary glimpse of man and bicycle entangled at the bottom of a shallow, grassy ditch, then blew past the second car at seventy miles an hour.

"Hope he broke his dumb neck," Dart said. "Good work, kiddo. But if you stop for the Station Road light, I'll shoot off your right nipple, am I understood?"

Nora blasted up a little rise, and at the top felt the car leave the road for a second before thumping back down. Dick Dart yipped and waved the revolver. Two blocks away, at the end of the empty road, the traffic light burned red. Cars streamed in both directions through the intersection.

"I can't do this."

"Poor baby, you'll miss that nipple. Gonna smart, too. But you know what?" He patted her on the top of her head. "I bet it turns green before we get there. If I win, you have to tell me everything you did to Natalie Weil."

"If you lose, we get turned into tomato soup." She roared through an intersection, and one block separated them from the traffic light.

"C'est la vie."

Making a low sound in her throat, Nora straightened her arms and locked her elbows.

"Slow down a little for the turn." Dart sounded completely calm.

Nora slammed her foot on the brake, and her chest bumped the wheel. Dick Dart, who had been lounging back in his seat, slipped forward and down until his knees hit the dashboard. The car slewed halfway around and shot out into the intersection just as the light turned green. Dart pushed himself back into his seat and grabbed the door handle. Nora hauled on the wheel and brought the car into line.

"Hooray! Nora keeps her nipple," Dart shouted. "Personally, I'm very happy about that."

He's happy about that? Nora thought. She said, "I have to slow down—look at all these cars." A line of automobiles was strung out in packs of two and three on the long four-lane straightaway of Station Road.

"Pass 'em, crank it up and pass 'em, I'm not kidding. We get on the expressway, we're outta here. Then you can tell me about Natalie Weil."

The next four minutes were a blur of honking horns, startled faces, waving fists, and accidents averted only by the last-second recognition on the part of other drivers that, yes, the woman driving the Volvo wagon in the oncoming lane really did intend to keep moving. Several times, Nora's insistence on forward progress caused some minor fender damage to the vehicles of the drivers who had to accommodate the drivers who had to accommodate her. Finally, she crossed laterally over the right lanes in another outraged din and twirled onto the ramp to the northbound lanes of the expressway. What seemed to be four solid lanes of cars and trucks racing in the direction of Hartford and New Haven appeared before her. Nora closed her eyes and kept her foot down on the accelerator. When she opened them three long seconds later, she found herself about to smash into the rear end of a sixteen-wheeler with huge BACK OFF, DUMMY mud flaps. She backed off.

A state police car with a flashing light bar screamed toward them on the other side of the divider and flew past.

"You want to continue your criminal career, you could always get a job as a getaway driver. Now we want to move along a little less conspicuously before we turn into Cousin Lenny's."

This was the restaurant where Davey had convinced himself of her innocence while eating meat loaf submerged under ketchup.

"Why there?"

"Every cop in the state—fuck, every cop in the Northeast—is looking for this Swedish piece of shit. Nora, sweetie, if you're going to be a getaway artist, you have to learn how to think like one."

I'm not your sweetie, she thought.

"Okay, tell me what you did to Natalie Weil."

He was leaning against the passenger door, smirking.

"How do you know about her? You were in a cell for two days."

"When I wasn't discussing my *hobbies* with nauseating Leo Morris, that dishonest squirrel-eyed fart, I spent a lot of time talking with Westerholm's fine young officers. They told me about the *other* interesting matter taking place in the station. I heard that the station commander thought you kidnapped Ms. Weil and the chief of detectives thought you were innocent."

"They told you that?" asked Nora, aghast.

"If I happened to be the murderer of several of Westerholm's most notable bitches, a matter I strenuously denied, though not to you, of course, *if* I happened to be the celebrity in question, I would undoubtedly be interested in learning that I had inspired a copycat. Not just any old copycat, no no, but the delightful Nora Chancel, wife to pretty but ineffectual Davey Chancel. Needless to say, I was honored. Leo Morris, on the other hand, did not take the news as happily as I did."

"Leo Morris knew?"

"I told him. He was not delighted by the prospect of mounting your defense. In fact, he dislikes you, your husband, and the entire Chancel clan."

"Leo Morris?"

"Let us not wander from the point. You did it, didn't you? You beat the crap out of that little asshole. You locked her up and did nasty stuff to her."

Nora did not respond for a second, and then said, "Yes. I beat the crap out of her, and then I dragged her into a filthy room and did nasty stuff to her."

"What did she do to *you*?"

"She slept with my husband."

"Were you going to kill her?" Dart had become less offhand.

"I could hardly let her go, could I?"

"What an event! My opposite number, my female self! It doesn't mean I won't kill you, but I'm thrilled."

"Why break me out of jail if you're going to kill me?"

"If you're a good girl I might keep you around."

"You could travel faster on your own."

"What would you do if I let you go?"

"Get some money from a cash machine, I guess, and go to New York. Figure out a way to get in touch with Davey."

"You wouldn't last a day. You'd be standing in a phone booth a block away from the cash machine, trying to sweet-talk nebbishy Davey Chancel into sending you your favorite Ann Taylor dress, and all of a sudden a hundred cops would be aiming guns at you. Listen, you have to learn to think in a whole new way. In the meantime, I can keep you out of trouble."

"This is your idea of staying out of trouble?"

"This is my idea of staying out of prison," he said. "There's one other reason I want to keep you around for a while."

The skin on the nape of her neck contracted. She glanced sideways to see him leaning against the door, his hands folded on one knee and his mouth in a twist of a smile. "What would that be?"

"Unlike you, I have a plan. You have this quality—what to call it?—a sort of a peasant forthrightness, which I see opening necessary doors."

"Which doors?"

He placed his index finger to his smiling lips.

"What's this plan?"

"I suppose I can give you the broad outlines. We are going to go to Massachusetts and kill a couple of old farts. Here comes that disgusting restaurant. Turn into the lot."

Nora flicked the turn indicator and changed lanes. The huge sign, COUSIN LENNY'S FOOD GAS, floated toward them.

"Can I ask you another question?"

"Ask."

"How did you know I wear Ann Taylor dresses?"

"Nora, my love, I spend my entire life doing nothing but talking to women. I know everything."

"Can I ask you another one?"

"As long as it isn't tedious."

Nora turned onto the access road into Cousin Lenny's parking lot. "Holly Fenn said one detail about those murders was never released to the press. What was it?"

"Ah, my little signature. I cut them open and took out most of their internal organs. Let me tell you, you learn a lot more doing that than you do from anatomy books. Okay, go over there to the far side, and we'll wait for the right donor to come along."

Nora advanced down a row of parked cars to the far end of the lot. Concrete barriers stood before a line of green Dumpsters. Behind the Dumpsters a weedy field extended toward a distant windbreak of gaunt trees.

"Back in," Dart said. "We want to be able to see our prospective benefactors. Weigh their advantages and disadvantages."

"You know how to do that thing with the wires?"

"If I knew how to hot-wire a car, we'd already be *in* a car on our way to Fairfield. But we're not, are we, dearest Nora? No no, no no. We desire the keys to our new vehicle, and therefore we must take them from the hands of the temporary owner. We prefer an elderly person who trembles at the prospect of violence." He leaned forward, put his hands on the dash, and looked from side to side. His right hand held the revolver, index finger inside the trigger guard. "The constables are bound to show up soon. We need our benefactor, and we need him now."

"Don't kill anybody," Nora said. "Please."

"Little Miss Failed Executioner. Excuse me." He scanned the lot again. "Hello, hello. What do we have here? A definite possibility." A long, black Lincoln driven by an elderly man with a round, bald head moved toward them through the sunlight. Beside the driver sat a young woman with shoulder-length dark hair. "Daddy Warbucks and his trophy bimbo," said Dart. "Two-for-one sale."

"Everybody in the restaurant would hear the shots."

"And pretend they didn't."

The Lincoln backed carefully into the second of three empty spaces. "The man loves his vehicle," said Dart. He fastened his hand around Nora's wrist. "My side." He pulled her toward him and slid the hand holding the revolver into his jacket pocket.

"You're hurting me."

"Diddums widdums hurtum booboo?" He kept his hand around her wrist as Nora squirmed out of the car, and pulled her along behind him toward the Lincoln. "I start to run, you start to run, got it?"

She nodded.

Dart dragged her another two yards, then stopped moving. "What the hell?"

The bald man was gazing at the young woman with an expression of absolute innocence. The woman gestured; the man smiled. Pulling Nora behind him, Dart walked slowly toward the Lincoln. The woman smacked her palm against her forehead, opened her door, got out, and resolved into a fourteen-year-old girl in a tight white jersey, cutoff jeans, and platform espadrilles. Without bothering to close her door, she loped toward the entrance to the restaurant. In a seersucker suit, a starched white shirt, and a navy blue necktie, the old man sat peacefully behind the wheel of his car.

"Allah is good, praise be to Allah." Dart jerked Nora across the asphalt to the open door. He bent down and said, "Greetings."

The old man blinked his shining blue eyes at Dick Dart. "Greetings to you, sir. Can you help me?"

"I intend to do just that," Dart said. His hand hung suspended within his pocket, the revolver bulging the fabric.

"I do not remember who I am. Also, I have no idea where I am or how I got here. Do you know if this is my car?"

"No, old buddy, this one's mine," Dart said. The hand came out of his jacket pocket, and the bottom half of his suit jacket swung forward. "But I saw you come in, and I can tell you where yours is."

"Goodness, I do apologize. I can't imagine how I came to . . . I hope you didn't imagine that I intended to steal your car." The old man got out and stood blinking benignly in the sun. "I have a granddaughter, I know that much, and I seem to have the impression that she was with me just now."

"She went into the restaurant," Nora said.

"Goodness. I had better go in and look for her. Where did you say my car was?"

"Other end of the lot." Dart glared at Nora. "Can't miss it. Bright red Cadillac."

"Oh, my. A Cadillac. Imagine that."

Dart took Nora's hand and pulled her toward the open door. "Miles to go before we sleep. Better find your car before you look for your granddaughter."

"Yes." The old man marched a few paces across the lot, then turned around, smiling. "Miles to go before I sleep. That's Robert Frost."

Dart got into the Lincoln. For a moment, the old man looked disappointed, but the smile returned, and he waved at them before resuming his march toward a nonexistent red Cadillac.

Dart spun the car toward the expressway. "God, it's even full of gas." Then he snarled at Nora. "Why did you tell the old zombie about his granddaughter?"

"I—"

"Don't bother, I already know. You felt sorry for him. We're the two most wanted people on earth, and you take time off to do social work."

He moved smoothly out into the traffic. Cool air streamed from vents on the dashboard. "That was so beautiful I can't stay mad. *'Can you help me?'* I almost fainted. He asked me if this was his car!" Dart tilted back his head and released a series of laughs abrupt as gunfire. "He gave it to me!" More laughter. "See that big goofy face? Old fuck looked like a blank tape."

"You're right," Nora said.

"Check the glove compartment and find out his name from the no-fault slip."

Nora opened the glove compartment and stared at what was within. A fat, shiny, black leather wallet sat beside a tall stack of bills held together by a rubber band. "You're about to get a lot happier."

"Why?" Nora removed the wallet and the money from the glove compartment. "Oh. My. God. Look at that. How much is it?"

A wad of bills distended the wallet's money compartment. She riffled them, hundreds and fifties and twenties. Then she pulled the rubber band off the stack. "An amazing amount."

Dart yelled at her to count it. Nora began adding up denominations—twenty thousand in hundreds, a thousand in fifties, and five hundred in twenties.

"Twenty-one thousand, five hundred dollars? Who the hell was this guy?"

Nora raised a leather flap and looked at the driver's license. "His name is Ernest Forrest Ernest. He lives in Hamden."

Dick Dart started laughing as soon as he heard the name. "That was the great Ernest Forrest Ernest?" He gave a whoop of joyful disbelief. "This day is right up there with the greatest, most supremo, days of my entire life. You don't know who he is?" Ticking and rumbling with suppressed laughter, he slanted his head to look at her. "No, you're too out of it to know about him. Alden would know him, though. In the great man's presence, Alden Chancel would stain his Polo trousers."

"Who is he?"

"Twenty years ago he was the lieutenant governor of Connecticut, and now he's like the grand old man of the Republican party in this state. The distinguished pile of shit I'm proud to call my father worships him. What can I say? The man is a god."

At first faintly, then gaining in volume, the sound of a police siren came to them. Dart checked the rearview mirror, gave Nora a warning look, took the revolver out of his pocket, and held it in his right hand. "They can't know about this car already."

Nora clenched her fists and forced herself not to scream. Disgust, hatred, and fear washed through her body. She looked back, saw that the flashing light bar was still a quarter of a mile behind them, and turned to inspect Dick Dart, for the first time really to examine him with the intensity of her loathing. Two years younger than Davey, he appeared to be at least five years older. His skin had a gray pallor. Many shallow wrinkles creased his forehead. Two small, vertical lines, now barely visible beneath dark stubble, ran down his cheek. Above the stubble fine red veins rode on his cheekbones, and larger red and blue veins had surfaced at the base of his long, fleshy nose. Dick's liver had been putting in a good deal of overtime. His long, oval face would have had an unremarkable handsomeness except for the sneering self-regard which permeated its every inch. His eyebrows were permanently arched above his light, alert eyes, and his lashes were a row of pegs. An untrustworthiness, a sly disregard for rules and orders came like an odor from his face. If his hair had been recently washed, it would have been perfect prep hair, slightly too long, falling in soft, natural curves on the sides of his head, and flopping boyishly over his forehead. His wide, blunt hands had enjoyed a manicure a few days earlier. The tired-looking gray suit had clearly cost a lot of money, and he wore a gold Rolex watch. His old ladies had one and all found him delightful.

"What are you doing, taking a fucking inventory?"

"No," Nora said hastily. "I was thinking about something."

"Give me that wallet and the rest of the money."

The wallet lay forgotten in her lap, and she was still holding the bills. She stuffed as much as she could into the money compartment and handed it all to him, and he shoved it into various jacket pockets. "Thinking about what, exactly?"

"I was wondering how you got suspended during your freshman year at Yale."

"How did you—oh, the newspaper. Well, what I did, I beat up this pig of a townie. Lucky for me, she really was a pig, and all that ever came out of it was the suspension." He glanced at the rearview mirror. "Here he comes. He's gotta be looking for your crappy Volvo wagon."

Nora braced herself.

The screech of the siren grew louder and louder. If Dart started shooting, she would crouch in the well before her seat. Could she grab the gun away from him? Nora remembered how he had jumped through the window and discarded the notion of trying to snatch the gun. For a person in lousy shape, Dick Dart was amazingly strong. She was in excellent shape, and she knew she could not have made that catlike leap.

The patrol car slipped into the next lane and sped past. Neither of the policemen in the car glanced at them. In seconds, the flashing lights and the noise were five cars away, and Dart applauded himself with yips and hoots.

"Did I call it, or what?" He held the barrel of the pistol up to his mouth. "I want to thank the members of the Academy, my mother and father, all my colleagues at the office, you guys know who you are, Leo, Bert, Henry, Manny, I couldn't have done it without your support, and I must not fail to mention those lovely ladies, my special clients, Martha, Joan, Leslie, Agatha—love those eyes, Agatha!—dear JoAnne, who never fails to order the best Margaux on the Château's wine list, Marjorie, Phyllis, sparkly little Edna of the pudgy ankles, and last but not least, the enchantress Olivia, who makes liver spots look like beauty marks. I wish to thank the Creator for the gifts He has lavished upon this unworthy being, and the Westerholm police force for all their assistance. But above all, I wish to thank my good-luck charm, my rabbit's foot, my four-leaf clover, my shining star, my hostage and partner in crime, the delectable Mrs. Nora Chancel. Couldn't have done it without you, babe, you make the magic, you are the wind beneath my wings." He blew her a kiss with the revolver.

"You're even crazier than I thought you were," Nora said.

"Most people can never be their real selves, they could never let themselves do what you did to Natalie Weil. The difference between you and me is that when you call someone crazy you think it's an insult, and I understand that it's a compliment."

"I don't think I have a real self anymore," Nora said.

"I'll show you your real self," Dart told her. "Remember, you make the magic."

Nora groaned, but only inwardly, with her real self, and Dick Dart smiled his mockery of a human smile as he drifted onto the off ramp for the Fairfield exit.

44

DART STEERED THROUGH a series of narrow streets lined with two-story houses on small lots sprouting lawn furniture, plastic pools, and brightly colored children's toys. A dancing gleam kindled in his eyes. "Dear Nora, to me has fallen the serious responsibility of freeing you from your illusions." He rolled up to a stop sign and turned right onto nearly empty Main Street toward Fairfield's small business district.

"You'll see what I see, see through my eyes. I sense—I sense . . ." He turned into an angled parking spot in front of the hardware store and leaned toward Nora, his right hand three or four inches from her face, thumb and index finger nearly touching. "You're *this* close."

His odor coated her like a mist. Dart lowered his hand and leaned back, eyes gleaming and mouth compressed. Nora tried not to show the nausea she felt.

"I'm going into the hardware store," he said. An incandescent sliver of hope sparked into life within her.

"You're coming with me, Nora. Any appeal for help, any attempt to get away from me, will be dealt with very seriously." He was still gleaming, as if saying these words in this way amused him enormously. "I have to make some purchases, and as yet I cannot leave you alone in the car. This is a test, and if you fail it you'll certainly never have to face another one."

"You could leave me in the car," Nora said. "I won't go anywhere. How could I? I'm one of the two most wanted people on earth."

"Bad girl." Dart patted her lightly on the knee. "There will come a time when you are allowed various freedoms, but we have to know you will not abuse them."

He got out and walked around the front of the car to open her door. She said, "Aren't you afraid of being recognized?"

"I've been in this store maybe once. Besides, nobody has a good photograph of me." He leaned down smiling and whispered, "And should some unfortunate happen to recognize me, I have Officer LeDonne's mighty thirty-eight."

Dart wrapped a hand around her elbow and propelled her into the hardware shop.

The dim, cool interior instantly reminded Nora of the hardware stores of her childhood. At the far end a man in shirtsleeves stood between a wooden counter and a wall covered with battery displays, coiled hoses, ranks of scissors, rolls of tape, and a hundred other things. On the soft wooden floor between the counter and the front door stood rows of shelves and bins, each as chaotic as the rear wall. Matt Curlew had drifted entranced through such places. Unlike Matt Curlew, Dick Dart moved quickly through the aisles, snatching up ropes, two differently sized screwdrivers, a roll of duct tape, pliers, a hammer. He had released Nora's elbow as soon as they entered the store, and she trailed after him, noting his purchases with increasing alarm.

"You could set all that on the counter and let me begin totaling it up," said the clerk. When he glanced at Nora, whatever he saw in her eyes caused him to step back from the counter.

"Great idea," said Dart, and moved to the counter. "Need some items from your knife case. Open it for me?"

"Sure thing." The owner glanced again at Nora but now apparently saw nothing to alarm him. Pulling a fat key ring from his pocket, he led Dart toward the glass case. He unlocked the metal ratchet at the front of the case, slid back one of the panels, and said, "Anything in particular?"

"Just a good knife or two."

"We're no fancy knife shop, but I got some good German stag handles, that kind of thing."

"I like a nice knife," Dart said.

The man stepped back, and Dart slid the panel farther along and reached in to pick up a brutal-looking, foot-long knife with a curved blade and a thick black handle.

"You got one serious knife there," said the owner.

Dart scuttled along the case to select an eight-inch knife which folded into a handle carved from an antler.

"That's the one I told you about, that one there's a real collectible."

"Pop for one more." Dart stood up to inspect the smaller knives at the top of the case. Humming to himself, he danced his fingers over the glass without actually touching it. After a few bars, Nora recognized the song he was humming, "Someone to Watch Over Me." "Here we go." He bent down to remove a short, double-edged knife with a utilitarian black handle. "Got a sheath for this?"

"A belt sheath? Yep."

The owner placed the knives and a black leather case beside the other purchases, looked up the tax on a chart, and added the column of numbers. "Well, sir, that comes to two hundred twenty-eight, eighty-nine. Cash or charge?"

"Hey, I'm an old-fashioned American, cash on the barrelhead." Dart took the bulging wallet from his jacket pocket and put two hundred and forty dollars on the counter.

The owner grunted and began bagging the items on the counter.

"Separate bags for the knives," Dart said.

"Didn't do too badly, Nora baby." Dart was driving up a side street toward the Fairfield railroad station, the smallest of the knives concealed under his jacket in the leather sheath, which he had clipped to his belt. The other two knives were in a bag on the backseat, the rest of the purchases in the trunk. "You gave that old dodo one hell of a look, though. Have to watch out for that, have to control yourself."

"I did control myself," Nora said. "What are you doing? I don't suppose we're going to take the train."

"Daddy is looking for something, and, wonder of wonders, I believe he has just found it. You're a fucking rabbit's foot." He slid past a dark blue sports car with tinted windows and swerved into the curb next to an empty lot. "Get out of the car and stand next to me."

She joined him at the back of the Lincoln. While Dart leaned into the trunk and removed a screwdriver from the bag, Nora glanced up and down the street, praying for the arrival of a police car. Before them, on the other side of a long, narrow parking lot, lay the railroad station; back toward Main Street, beyond the empty lot, stood the flowered walkway and green-striped canopy of a restaurant called Euphemia's Diner.

Dart closed the trunk without latching it. "Stand between me and the street. Don't let anybody see what I'm doing." He grinned at her, and with his right hand reached around to the small of his back.

"What are you going to do?"

"Buy a little time." He led her toward the rear of the little blue car. "You're not going to take a stupid pill, are you?"

"No," she said. A small, bright blade projected from his palm.

He knelt beside the rear bumper and jabbed the blade into the tire. The blade slipped out, and the tire hissed and softened. "If anybody happens along, we're inspecting our flat. Don't look at me, watch the street and tell me if anybody comes along." He slipped the little knife back into its sheath.

Nora moved to shield him from the sidewalk. "I don't get what you're doing."

"Swapping plates. It's not as easy as it used to be. All these idiots treat their plates like oil paintings. This was the first one that didn't have a *frame* around it." The screwdriver clicked against metal. Dart grunted, then began humming "Someone to Watch Over Me" again. Heat poured down on them. The police car for which Nora continued to pray neglected to appear.

"Now the front." She followed him and stood in the road as metal rubbed against metal. "Want to hear a little-known fact about our old pal Ernest Forrest Ernest? This great man fancied the Nazis during the Second World War, though it was of course a deep dark secret, and afterward he was part of a splendid little group of ultrawealthy men who tried to promote Fascism right here in our good old cradle of liberty. . . . All right!"

He went two paces to the rear of the Lincoln and started to remove the screws in its license plate. "They didn't use the nasty F-word, of course. They called it the Americanism Movement, which lasted about five minutes until Joe McCarthy came along and put them in his pocket and they had to pretend they liked it. But the point of this"—he slapped the other car's plate into position and fit the screws into place—"is that little Davey's grandfather was behind the whole show."

Nora remembered the passages about Fascism in the chapter of Daisy's book she called "the fantasia."

"Lincoln Chancel was the badass's badass."

"So I gather."

Dick Dart looked up at her in amused surprise. "I don't think Davey knows a quarter of the stuff the old man did."

"He knows he wasn't a saint."

Dart stood up, went to the front of the Lincoln, and knelt down while Nora posted herself to shield him from the empty street. She had been in Fairfield perhaps thirty times during the two years of her marriage, she had shopped on Main Street for her jeans and Ann Taylor dresses, she had bought veal chops and crown roasts from the excellent butcher, enjoyed lunches and dinners at three different restaurants, and in all that time, it came to her now, she had never seen a single policeman.

"We behold an unhappy degeneration in the Chancel line," Dart said. "Lincoln Chancel wouldn't have used Davey for a toothpick. Lincoln was one dangerous son of a bitch, and Davey doesn't have the guts of a teddy bear. Alden is sort of halfway between them, a thug and a bully, but not a *real* thug or a *real* bully."

"He has his moments," Nora said.

"You never met the real thing. Alden thinks he's a big shot and he prances around talking tough, but I think his old man cut his nuts."

He stood up and motioned for Nora to follow him to the rear of the sports car.

They were walking side by side down the street like any ordinary couple. The man beside her looked like a stockbroker or lawyer after a rough night, and she probably looked like his wife.

The old plate came off, the new one went up. "If Alden Chancel hadn't inherited Chancel House, what would he be doing? He has one great editor, Merle Marvell, and a lot of blockheads. One dead writer, Hugo Driver, keeps the company solvent. His royalties bring in about forty percent of the company's total revenue, and almost all of that is generated by one book, *Night Journey.* Alden's a disaster. Right now he's negotiating a deal to sell the company to a German publisher—to get a lot of money out of the business before he runs it into the ground. The only reason the German publisher is interested is *Night Journey.*"

"Alden's trying to sell the company? How do you know about this?"

"We're the lawyers, baby. Remember? As we go along putting dents in dear old Dart, Morris, I am going to give you an education. Before I begin, I have to *do* something, but after that, tutorials in the real world are in session. Okay, let's wrap up this tedious bullshit."

He stood up and shook out his arms, then produced a wrinkled, distinctly unclean handkerchief from a trouser pocket and swabbed his forehead.

"He's selling the company?"

"Trying to." Dart pulled her up the street and knelt in front of the Lincoln. "I'm going to tell you something little Davey never heard about his grandfather. The guy wasn't born rich, you know, he got there by himself. Did many, many nasty deeds. Even murdered someone once."

"I don't believe that," she said, although what she knew of Lincoln Chancel nearly made it possible.

"Old Lincoln was a brute, baby. My sainted daddy, who has been privy to the real history of the Chancels for the last forty years, told me in a moment of imperfect sobriety that Lincoln Chancel once tore a man to pieces—turned him into hamburger with his bare hands. Lincoln was caught short playing too many ends against the middle, threat of scandal, and the only way out was the removal of one man. He arranged a confidential appointment with the guy, canceled it on the morning of the day they were supposed to meet, and showed up unannounced around the time of the meeting he canceled. Nobody knew he was supposed to be there, and the guy was all alone. Got away scot-free."

Dart said, "Good for another day, anyhow. Let's go to Main Street and pick up a couple of bottles."

45

Police cars swept past them, most of them silently, several flashing and wailing. Dart amused himself by pointing the revolver at drivers and passengers in other cars and pretending to shoot them. Hartford loomed up alongside the expressway, and Nora sped upward to fly through the office towers at seagull height. Dart lolled, half in his seat, half against the door, and sneered his smile at her.

"Why do you have your window down? What happened to air conditioning? Save-the-planet kind of thing?"

"I don't want to pass out from your stink."

"My stink?" He opened his jacket and sniffed his armpits. "You're probably having some feminine disorder."

"You hate women, don't you?"

"No, I hate my father, women I actually adore. They're physically weaker than men, so they had to work out a million ways to manipulate them. Some of these stratagems are fantastically ornate. Guys who don't understand that women are incapable of psychological straightforwardness don't stand a chance. One morning they wake up beside some cash register who has a big fat diamond ring and a gold band on her finger, and she controls the pussy. If he wants any, he has to hand over the credit cards. If he complains, she makes him feel so small and selfish he makes her breakfast for a week. But is he allowed to say no? Uh uh, baby. And think about this. She can hit him, that's fine. Brute like him deserves to be hit. But can a man hit a woman? If he does, she whips his ass in divorce court and takes all his money without even having to give him sex. He's completely under the control of a capricious, amoral being with a tremendous capacity for making trouble. Remember the Garden of Eden? Great place until this woman came along, whispering, *Come on, take a bite, the Big Guy isn't paying any attention.* Been the same way ever since. If the woman's really good, this poor sucker with a noose around his neck, a perpetual hard-on, and someone else's hand in his pocket is convinced that he's running the show. He's so tangled up he thinks his wife is this sweet little thing who isn't very good at practical matters but sure is great, damn it, a goddamned pearl for putting up with him. Once a year she gives him a blow job, and he's so grateful he races out to buy her a fur coat. Those fur coats in a restaurant, where women don't want to put them in the checkroom? Every single one of those coats? A blow job, and every woman in the place knows it. And here's something else—the older the woman, the better the coat."

"And you claim to adore women," said Nora.

"I didn't make this stuff up. Spent the last fifteen years of my life taking my Marthas and Ednas and Agathas to the Château and listening to them talk. I hear the things they're telling me and I also hear what they're *really* saying. And sometimes, Nora, more often than you would imagine, they are the same thing. An eighty-five-year-old woman who has had three face-lifts, two husbands, at least one of them seriously rich, both currently dead, also a couple of glasses of wine with a rakish, good-looking young lawyer, is likely to let down her guard and tell you how she got through a long and pampered life without ever working a single day. Once they see that I already know how it works, they can start having a good time. These ladies are generally pissed off, they used to be fascinating, the whole male world used to stand in line to get into their pussies, and all of it went away when they turned into old ladies. Husbands are dead. Nobody on earth is interested in listening to them. Except me. I could listen to them all day long. Love those soft, elegant, smoky voices full of hidden razor blades, but even more I love their stories. They're so corrupt. They don't even begin to know how corrupt they are, can't, don't have the moral machinery for it. The only thing they regret is that the good part didn't last another ten years, so they could have gotten their hooks into one more rich sucker who got off on hearing about his great big cock. I love the way they look—hair all stiff but made to look fluffy and soft, makeup put on so well you can hardly see their wrinkles, their hands covered with rings so you won't notice the brown spots and the veins and lumpy knuckles. Nobody can tell me I don't like women."

"Did you sleep with your old ladies?"

"Haven't had sex with a woman under sixty-five in at least nine or ten years. No, sixty-two, I forgot about Gladys."

"But you *killed* women," Nora said.

"Wasn't personal."

"It was to them," Nora said.

"I was killing clients, understand? Every time I murdered someone, another chunk fell off the old man's business. Along about the time I did Annabelle Austin, that book agent, he spent two days saying, Couldn't somebody else's clients get killed? If I could have done another ten, he'd be tearing his hair out."

"But you always chose women clients, and always a certain kind of woman."

Dart's eyes went flat and two-dimensional.

"Oh. You didn't like the way they lived."

"Could put it that way," Dart said. "Those people went around acting like men."

His tone gave her an insight. "Did they behave well around you?"

"The times they came into the office, when I came up them and said something flattering, they could barely bring themselves to speak to me."

"Unlike your old ladies."

"I would never have murdered my old sweethearts . . . unless they were the only clients left."

"What about me?"

He smiled, slowly. "Do you mean, am I going to kill you?"

Nora said nothing.

"Dear Nora-pie. We'll know more after our reality lesson."

"Reality lesson?"

He patted her knee. "Lots of motels in Massachusetts. We want one with a nice big parking lot."

46

ON THE FAR side of Springfield, Dart pointed at a three-story, sand-colored building with white balconies outside the windows. "Bingo!" It stood at the far end of a half-filled parking lot the size of a football field. A vast blue-and-yellow sign stretching across the roof said CHICOPEE INN. A Swiss ski lodge called Home Cooking faced the lot from the left. "Get over, we don't want to miss the exit."

Nora crossed two lanes and left the highway. "Forgot I was talking to Emerson Fittipaldi," Dart said.

She drove a short distance down the street and turned into the lot.

"Darling, we'll always have Chicopee. And home cooking, too! Don't you love home cooking? Mom's famous razor blade soup, that sort of thing?"

"Should I park in any particular place?" Nora was weary with dread.

"Right in the goddamned middle. Do you have some favorite alias, my dear?"

"Some what?" She drew the Lincoln into an empty space approximately in the center of the lot.

"Need new names. Have any suggestions, or shall I choose?"

"Mr. and Mrs. Hugo Driver." She closed her eyes and slumped back against the seat. "The Drivers."

"Love the concept, tremendously appropriate, but using the names of well-known people is usually an error." He turned sideways and tried to reach the bags on the backseat. "Hell." Dart knelt on his seat and leaned over, almost touching the top of the car with his buttocks. Nora opened her eyes and saw the pocket containing the gun hanging a foot away from her face. She considered the energy and speed necessary to snatch it out of his pocket. She wondered if she knew how to fire a revolver. Dan Harwich had instructed her in the operation of the safety on the pistol he had given her, but did revolvers have safeties, and if so, where were they? By the time this baffling question had occurred to her, Dart was pulling himself and two brown paper bags back over the top of the seat. He pushed the bag containing the bottles into her lap. "You carry this one and the one in the trunk. One more thing: please refrain from giving people these bone-chilling looks of anguish, okay? World loves a happy face. Come to think of it, I don't think I've ever seen you smile, and I smile at you all the time."

"You're having a better time than I am."

"Smile, Nora. Brighten up my day."

"I don't think I can."

"Rehearsal for the wonderful smile you're going to give the moron behind the desk."

Nora faced Dart, pulled back her lips, and exposed her teeth.

He gave her a long, considering look. "Call on some of the old fire, Nora-pie. Let's see the blazing figure who beat the shit out of Natalie Weil."

"Too scared to come out."

He gave an exasperated sigh. "This is a *project.*" He made the sign of the cross over his heart.

"A project?"

"Inside." He took the keys and got out. She waited for him to pull her across the seat, but instead he walked to the front of the car and looked back at her, eyebrows raised. Nora left the car and looked around at a vibrant blur. She blotted her eyes on her sleeve and moved toward Dart.

A young man with shoulder-length blond hair lowered a half-liter Evian bottle to an invisible shelf in front of him, smiled across the desk as they came into the chill of the lobby, and stood up. His lightweight blue blazer was several sizes too large for him, and the bottoms of the sleeves were rolled. A silver tag on his lapel said that his name was Clark. "Welcome to the Chicopee Inn. Can I help you?"

"Need a room for the night," Dart said. "Sure hope you got one for us. Been driving two days straight."

"Should be no problem." His eyes moved to the bags they were carrying, then from Dart to Nora and back again. His smile vanished. He sat down in his chair again, pulled a keyboard toward him, and depressed random-seeming keys. "One night? Let me set you up, and then we'll take some information." He brushed his hair back with one hand, exposing a circular gold ring in his ear. Keys clicked. "Three twenty-six, third floor, double bed. Is that okay?" Dart agreed. Nora slumped against the counter and regarded the bright, unreal green of the carpet. "Name and address, please?"

"Mr. and Mrs. John Donne, Five eighty-six Flamingo Drive, Orlando, Florida."

At the boy's request, he spelled out Donne. Then Dart spelled Orlando for him. He supplied a zip code and a telephone number.

"Orlando's where they have Disney World, right?"

"No need to leave America, you want to see exotic places."

"Uh, right. Method of payment?"

"Cash."

Clark paused with his hands on the keyboard and looked up. He flicked back his hair again. "Sir, our policy in that case is to request payment in advance. The rate for your room is sixty-seven dollars, forty-five cents, tax included. Is that all right?"

"Policy is policy," Dart said.

Clark returned to the keyboard. The tip of his tongue slipped between his lips. A young woman in a blazer identical to his came through a door behind him to his right and gave Dart a double take as she walked past the desk to another door in the wall to his left.

"I'll get your keys and take the payment." He opened a drawer to remove two round-headed metal keys. He put them into a small brown folder and wrote 326 in a white space at the top of the folder. The boy stood up and slid the folder across the desk. Dart placed a hundred-dollar bill beside it. "You can swing your car right up in front here to bring in your bags," the boy said, his eyes on the bill.

"Everything we need in the world is right here."

The boy picked up the bill and said, "One minute, sir." He went through the door from which the young woman had emerged.

Dart began humming "I Found a Million-Dollar Baby."

A few seconds later, the boy reappeared, smiled nervously at Dart, unlocked a cash drawer, and counted out change.

"Good business demands vigilance," said Dart, shoving the bills and coins into a trouser pocket.

"Yeah. I should explain, we don't have a restaurant or room service, but we serve a complimentary continental breakfast from seven to ten in the Chicopee Lounge just down to your right, and Home Cooking—right outside in our lot—they give you good food there. And checkout is at twelve noon."

"Point me toward the elevators," Dart said. "You behold a pair of weary travelers."

"Past the lounge, on your left. Enjoy your stay."

Nora jerked herself upright, and Dart took a step back from the desk, opening a path to the elevators. She plodded past him, trying not to hear the cajoling voices in her head. The bottles took on weight with every step. She barely noticed the small, open room outfitted with couches, chairs, and tables into which Dart slipped to extract a folded newspaper from a rack. He placed a hand in the small of her back and urged her toward the elevators, where he punched a button. "Every little bird must find its branch."

Upstairs in a hazy corridor, Dart fit one of the keys into the lock of room 326. "Nora, look." It took her a moment to notice the three round holes, puttied in and clumsily retouched with paint, in the brown door. "Bullet holes," Dart said.

Nora walked in. Every little bird must find its branch. You didn't have to leave America to see exotic places. As she moved past the bathroom and the sliding panel of a closet, she heard Dart close the door and slide a lock into place. A window leading onto a narrow white balcony overlooked the parking lot. She put her bags on the table. Dart brushed past her, clicked the lock on the window, and moved a metal rod to draw a filmy curtain. He shrugged off his jacket, hung it over the back of a chair, and took his knives from their bag. "Lookee, lookee." He was pointing at discolored blotches on the lampshade. "Bloodstains. *Our* kind of place."

Nora glanced at the queen-sized bed jutting out into the room.

Dart unpacked the purchases from the hardware store and arrayed them in a straight line on the table. He moved the coils of rope from first place to second, after the roll of duct tape, and made sure everything was straight, bottom ends lined up. "Forgot scissors," he said. "We'll survive." He laid the two larger knives at the end of the row, then fussed with the alignment. "Shall we begin?"

She said nothing.

He picked up a vodka bottle, untwisted the cap, and swished vodka around in his mouth before swallowing, then recapped the bottle and set it gently on the table. "Take your clothes off, Nora-pie."

"I don't feel like doing that."

"If you can't do it yourself, I'll have to cut them off."

"Please," she said. "Don't do this."

"Don't do what, Nora-pie?"

"Don't rape me." Soundlessly she began to cry.

"Did I say something about rape? What I said was, take off your clothes."

She hesitated, and through her tears saw him pick up the larger of the two knives, the one Matt Curlew would have called an Arkansas pig-sticker. He stepped toward her, and she began unbuttoning her shirt. A small, separate part of her mind marveled at the quantity of tears spurting from her eyes. She placed the blue shirt uncertainly on the chair and glanced at the blurry figure of Dick Dart. The blurry figure nodded. Nora undid her belt, unbuttoned her jeans, pulled down the zip, and stepped out of the brown loafers. Hatred and disgust penetrated the cloud wrapped around her emotions. She made a small, high-pitched noise of outrage, pushed down her jeans, and, one leg after the other, stepped out of them. She draped the jeans over the arm of the chair and waited.

"Not really *into* underwear, are you? Dear me, look at that bra. Your basic no-frills Maidenform Sweet Nothings, isn't it? A thirty-four B? You should try one of those new uplift bras, not just an underwire, but the new kind, do wonders for you, give you a nice contour on top. Well? Let's unhitch Nora's pretty mammaries, shall we?"

Nora closed her eyes and reached up to unhook the bra, which was, as Dart had said, a Maidenform Sweet Nothings, size 34 B. She let the straps slip backward over her shoulders, exposing her breasts, pulled it away from her body, and dropped it onto the chair.

"Don't really hang up our clothes at home, do we? You've got, ummm, you've got an overstuffed chair with layers of T-shirts and blouses draped over the back and jeans folded on the seat. No, I take it back. For you I see a nice long couch, hardly visible under all those clothes. What you do is grub around in these clothes, wear them a few times, and then dump them into the hamper and start all over again."

This was, in fact, exactly what Nora did, except that she did it less consistently than Dart had suggested.

"Oh my, look at that. Hanes Her Way undies—purple, what's more, to go with your tired white Maidenform. Nora, you shouldn't buy your dainties at the drugstore. At the very least, your bra and undies should match. With your body, you'd look good in Gitano. They make pretty matching bras and underpants, and they're cheap. You want to spend more money, try Bamboo or Betty Wear. Myself, I'm crazy about Betty Wear, it's nice stuff. Listen, do yourself a favor and stop throwing out those Victoria's Secret catalogs. I know you think they're cheesy, but if you'd just *look* at them at least as thoroughly as Davey undoubtedly does, you'd see that they're very useful. Above all, you owe it to yourself to look at *Vogue* now and then. Great magazine, I never miss an issue. I bet you've never even bought one."

"I bought one once."

"When? In 1975?"

"Around then," she said, her arms folded over her chest and her hands on her shoulders.

"Written all over you, especially those Hanes Her Way spanky-pants. Should take better care of yourself. Take the dumb things off."

She pushed down the waistband on her underpants, shoved them to her knees, and stepped out.

"Nora's got a great big bush! God, Nora, you've got this *clump*, get out the Weedwacker!"

She had gradually been convincing herself that no man who spoke in this way to a woman would rape her—a rapist would never advise the purchase of Betty Wear, much less be able to identify a Maidenform Sweet Nothings bra and Hanes Her Way underpants—but his next words undermined her shaky hope that Dart wished to do no more than inspect her body.

"Sit on the bed," he said.

She walked to the end of the bed as if over broken glass and sat down with her hands on her shoulders and her legs clamped together. A sudden mental flash of Barbara Widdoes's plump knees and fat calves above her heavy shoes brought with it the surprising thought that Barbara Widdoes was probably a lesbian.

"Have to restrain you for a while," Dart said, and picked up one of the coils of rope to slice off two sections, each about four feet long. These he carried toward Nora, along with the knife and the roll of duct tape. "Might be a little uncomfortable, but it won't actually hurt." He knelt in front of her, looked up into her eyes, winked, and wound one of the sections of rope around her ankles. "You have a nice body," he said. "Maybe just the teeniest bit stringy, and your skin could use a moisturizer." The rope bit into her skin, and she said, "Ouch."

"Doesn't pinch, isn't tight enough," Dart said, tying the ends of the rope into an elaborate knot. He put his hands on her knees and looked directly at her breasts. "Small, and they kind of sag, but still pretty, if you want my opinion." He reached for the tape, unpeeled a strip three feet long, tore it off the roll, and wound it over the rope around Nora's ankles. Then he stood up, touched her chin with the tips of his fingers, and tilted her face toward his. "You're the kind of person who thinks she's above makeup, apart from a little lipstick now and then, but you're wrong. You ought to try Cover Girl Clean Make-up, or maybe Maybelline Shine Free. That's all you need, a little blush. Plus one of those nice new mascaras, like Cover Girl Long 'N Lush. And you really do need a good scent. You have a teeny-tiny little bottle of Chanel No. 5 on your dresser, right, and you put on a dab or two when Davey takes you out somewhere fancy. Right?"

She nodded.

"You're not really the Chanel No. 5 type, but nobody ever knew enough to tell you. You should wear Chanel Coco, if you want Chanel, or L'Air du Temps, if you're feeling a little more feminine. You ought to wear a good scent every day, *all* day, no matter what you're doing."

He took his fingers from her chin and moved behind her. The bed sank under his weight. "Hands," he said. She put her hands behind her back, and he grasped her wrists and lashed them together. "This is a disgrace. You need a manicure more than anyone I've ever met. Pedicure, too. And you have to start using some really good nail polish, I don't care what kind. We're going to have to shop for some essentials, and after we get toothpaste and stuff like that, I'll get you some female equipment. It'll help our project."

She heard him rip off a length of tape and felt him coil it around her joined wrists. "Why are you doing this? Are you going somewhere?"

"Don't want you to run away while I wash the Westerholm slammer off me. Want to come in with me?"

"No, thanks."

He cackled. "You can have one after."

"After what?"

He patted her shoulder and hitched himself off the bed to carry the tape and the knife to the table, where he placed them in their old positions and made sure they were properly aligned.

"Are the two of us going to sleep in this bed?"

He looked over his shoulder in mock surprise. Slowly, as if pondering the question, he revolved to face her. "Since there's only one bed, I suppose I presumed . . . And twin beds are so Ozzie and Harriet . . . But if you have strong objections, I guess I could sleep on the floor." His drawl ridiculed his own words. "All right?"

She nodded.

"All right, then." Dick Dart stripped off his shirt, dropped it on the floor, and undid the top of his trousers. His tasseled black loafers came off, and he bent down and skipped out of his trousers. His arms and shoulders were flabby, and a crust of black hair covered his chest. The shapeless slab of his stomach pushed out the waistband of boxer shorts decorated with a fly-fishing pattern. "But I don't expect to have that problem." He pushed down the shorts, exposing a nest of brown curly hair and a long, thick cucumber penis ridged with prominent veins. He tossed the shorts onto the chair and unselfconsciously walked to the table to pick up the roll of tape. His buttocks were flat, almost absent, and his heavy thighs and calves ended in wide, oddly primitive-looking feet, like those of dinosaurs. Tufts of black hair grew alongside his spine at the small of his back.

He ripped a four-inch section off the tape and came toward Nora, penis swinging before him like a pendulum. "We'll work things out." Then he was standing in front of her, the ridged gray cucumber at the level of her eyes radiating stinks like a swamp. She began to shake. Tears slipped from her eyes. He pushed up her chin, smiled down over the bulge of his belly, and flattened the tape over her mouth. "Breathe through your nose. Don't panic."

He pushed her shoulders and sent her flopping backwards onto the bed. Dart disappeared. She tried to gasp, and coarse tape clamped against her lips. Her body demanded oxygen, immediately. Pain blazed in her shoulders, and the rope chewed her wrists and ankles. She rolled from side to side, choking on tape, and finally remembered to breathe through her nose. Dimly she heard a chuckle, then the closing of the bathroom door. The shower hissed and rattled against the tub. Dart's unmelodious voice began singing "Them There Eyes." Nora rotated her hands and wrists the quarter inch permitted by the rope handcuffs. She lay collapsed against the bedspread, too terrified to cry.

Nora had a sudden vision of herself as seen from above: naked, bent across the bed, trussed like a roaster for the oven. She looked like a corpse in a crime-scene photograph. The woman in the photograph was nothing, an emptiness, less than pathetic. Some deaths might be preferable to the madness waiting within her, but not that one.

Dart came out of the bathroom, hair plastered to his head, water shaping the hairs on his legs into vertical lines. "What a picture you make." He unfurled a towel and systematically began rubbing it over his arms, chest, gut, genitals, legs.

"Back in a second." He vanished into the bathroom and reappeared with a fresh towel. Instead of returning to the bedside, he closed the bathroom door and stepped back toward the closet. Nora watched his reflection in the mirror on the bathroom door. He scrubbed his hair until it floated about his head, and then lightly ran the towel over his neck, his chest, his penis. He clutched himself with the towel, pulled himself roughly several times, and manipulated his testicles. After reaching a satisfactory stage of self-arousal, he stood sideways, held in his belly, gave himself an encouraging pat, as much a slap as a caress, and twitched upward another half inch. Dart had forgotten all about her. His beloved, the cucumber, jutted out before him. Dart clutched it in his fist and jerked up and down, causing the entire structure to darken to purple, bloat out another half inch, and raise itself in an upward curve. This accomplished, Dart turned to face himself head-on. Excited by the sight of itself, the thing in front of him stiffened into a curved rigidity ending in a red-blue knob the size of a small apple. Dart's eyes were glazed, and his mouth was open. Nora thought he was about to ejaculate. He hefted his testicles and groaned. *Go on,* she said to herself, *spurt all over the mirror.*

The eyes in the mirror met hers.

47

DART STRODE BACK into the room. "Hope you appreciate my consideration in showering. Did it for me more than for you, but wouldn't want any unseemly body odors distracting you from what most women find a deeply enjoyable experience." He straddled her legs, bent over her, pushed the head of his penis into her stomach, and rubbed it back and forth across her stomach. "Like that?" He stroked one of her breasts with his free hand. Nora closed her eyes, and he pinched her nipple. She uttered a sharp sound of protest into the tape over her mouth. "Pay at-*ten*-tion," he sang, twirling the nipple painfully between his thumb and index finger. "We are going to perform an introduction, and it isn't polite to close your eyes." Smiling, he hitched himself up onto the bed and settled his knees on either side of her rib cage. "Nora's titties, meet the Big Guy." He leaned forward and ran the Big Guy along first one nipple, then the other. He lowered himself between her breasts, squeezed them around himself, and pumped back and forth. Dart released her breasts and hitched himself forward to thrust his beloved before her eyes. "Don't call me Dick for nothing, right? Never saw one like that before, did you?"

The object four inches from Nora's eyes looked like something pried out of calcified mud at an archaeological dig, something offered for half price at an Arabian bazaar, something carved from an enormous root. Granddad had brought it home from his travels and shown it to Grandma, and after she stopped shouting at him he had taken it upstairs to the attic and buried it in a steamer trunk. Varied in texture from corrugation to a dangerous, slick smoothness, lumpy with veins, a goiter stuffed with rocks—was this what most men wanted to have? Would Davey wish to swap his nice, willing member for this? She knew the answer. He would, absolutely.

She shook her head, *No.*

"Going to go places hubby could never take you, Nora-pie."

He moved off the bed, went to the table, and picked up the largest knife. Then he knelt in front of Nora and peeled the tape off her legs. Instead of cutting the rope, he laboriously untied the knot. Her legs loosened and sagged. Nora instantly closed them, and Dart chuckled and stood up. "Move up on the bed," he said.

She hesitated, and Dart brought the point of the knife into contact with her left thigh.

She got her feet on the bed and levered herself up to the pillows. Her arms and shoulders ached, and her wrists burned. Dart walked up beside her on his knees. When he reached her groin, he slapped the knife on the pillow, thrust his hand between her legs, and rummaged around until he inserted a blunt fingertip. Nora's body shuddered and went cold.

Humming to himself, Dart withdrew his finger and slid on top of her. He pushed her legs apart, planted his knees between them, and moved down to take aim. Nora made a high-pitched sound muffled by the tape. Her face was covered with tears.

Dart maneuvered a portion of himself into her and grunted. He shoved forward. Nora felt as though she were being torn apart. She screamed and heard only a thin, weightless wail. Smiling, Dick Dart propped himself on his elbows and held the knife to her throat. "What we have here is a reality lesson. All sex is rape, pure and simple. I am going to put my cock into your pussy. This act has been known to send women out of their minds, even then it was rape . . ." He pushed himself another quarter inch forward.

". . . and do you know why? Because when it was all over, I owned them. That's the secret." He hoisted himself up, withdrew a tiny bit, and then rammed himself into her. Nora screamed again and rolled to one side.

Dart shoved her back down.

"Better relax, or there's going to be a lot of blood. Have to stretch you out, and you'll get there as long as you loosen up." He withdrew and plunged ahead again, invading her. "Do you know the secret?" Nora had been hiding within herself with her eyes closed, her body clamped in revulsion, and when Dart slapped her cheek she realized that he was talking to her. "Didn't think so." He shoved forward again. "Women, who run rings around men all the time, who can outthink any man ever born, have one weakness. They love being fucked more than anything else on earth." His voice seemed to come from a distant professorial source completely unrelated to what he was doing.

"Money, cars, fur coats, jewelry, houses, they're smart enough to know those things are just toys. Give them all away for a guy with a johnson big enough to turn them inside out. Trouble is, most women never find that guy. But if they do, they're *his*. Every guy is trying to do this, because deep down every guy knows how it's supposed to be, and every woman is secretly hoping he'll turn her inside out, because deep down she knows that's the way it's supposed to be. So it's always a rape."

Nora opened her eyes to a curious sight. Dick Dart's upper portion hung over her. His mottled face had hardened around his concentration, and another face, a secret face, seemed to surface beneath the public one. His lips had drawn back from his yellow teeth. His nose had sharpened, and a suggestion of hair darkened his cheeks. She closed her eyes and heard distant artillery fire.

Eternities later, a quickening in her torture returned Nora to the world. Dick Dart's sweat plopped on her in great tears. He groaned; his hands locked on her shoulders. His body froze, his legs turned to iron bars. Her mind seemed to burst into flame. He arched his back and slammed into her twice, three times, four, five, so forcefully her head banged the headboard.

Dart collapsed on top of her. She felt extraordinarily defiled, so dirty that she could never again be clean. When he rolled off, she felt as though he had broken each of her bones systematically. She would never open her eyes, never again. A hand crawled over her thigh.

"Was it good for you, darling?"

He left the bed and padded into the bathroom. Everything hurt everywhere. She was afraid to open her eyes.

Little voices hissed and chattered. Her demons had found her again. The demons were fond of room 326, and presently they were fond of Nora also, because once more she had been pushed through the bottom of the world into the devastation where they flourished. Nora hated and feared the demons, but she was much more fearful of what she would see if she opened her eyes; therefore she had to endure them. She remembered from her last exposure that although demons did not wish to be seen, you occasionally caught sight of those who crept up to impart a morsel of demon knowledge. Some of them were tiny red devils with toothpick pitchforks, some looked like animals created by mad scientists: long-toothed badgers with rat's tails, hairy balls with darting eyes and heavy claws. Some demons looked like moving smudges.

An indistinct, winged thing flapped past her head whispering, *"He isn't a wolf."*

Nora wondered if she would have the demons if she had been raised in some sensible religion, like Buddhism.

The thing circled around and flew past again. *"He's a hyena."*

"You belong to a hyena," giggled something invisible but near. A tinny ripple of demon laughter greeted this remark.

"Wasn't it fun, wasn't it fun?" sang another. *"And now you're back with us again!"*

Most of the information imparted by demons was true, for if they told lies they would be lunatic annoyances, not demons.

She heard them rattling up to her, whispering to each other in their rapid-fire voices, and drew into herself as tightly as possible, though she knew that the elated demons would never touch her. If they touched her, her mind would shatter, and then she would be too crazy to be interesting.

A demon who looked like a rat with small blue wings and granny glasses whispered, *You can't get out of this one, is that clear? You passed through and now you're on the other side, is that clear?*

When she nodded, the ratlike demon said, *Welcome to the Hellfire Club.*

"It's not as bad as it looks," said Dick Dart. Nora opened her eyes, and the demons scattered under the bed, behind chairs, into drawers. Her pain bounded back into her body and stretched like a big cat. Naked, smiling, his hair combed, Dart stood beside the bed, idly tugging at himself. His free hand held a damp white towel. The secret face moved toward the surface of his public face. Nora saw that it was true; he was a hyena. "Take a gander. You have to sit up anyhow, so I can get the rope off your wrists."

She shook her head.

Dart told her in an equable, good-humored fashion that like it or not she was going to sit up, grasped an upper arm, and jerked her forward. The room swung before and beneath her. Grimacing, she looked down and nearly fainted.

"Okay, let's get this off." Dart reached across the pillow for the knife and expertly nicked the tape around her wrists. He ripped off the tape and worked on the knot until the rope released her wrists. "Now the gag. I'm going to do this fast. Make any noise louder than a peep, I'll ram this knife in you, understand?" She closed her eyes. The chattering demons crowded around. Her lips and a good deal of skin seemed to rip away with the tape, but she managed not to whimper.

He tossed the damp towel onto her legs. "Wipe yourself off. Have to strip the bed. I don't want to sleep in this mess."

Nora obediently passed the towel down the tops of her thighs and realized that if he was going to strip the bed, she would have to get off. She moved her right leg half an inch to the side, and her various pains held steady. Gritting her teeth, Nora swung both legs off the bed and forced herself to stand up. Her head swayed, and a bolt of pain shot upward in her groin.

"Girl's a trouper," said Dart, reclaiming the knife. "To prove I'm not completely evil, I did you a favor. Try to guess what it is."

"Can't," she muttered.

He smiled at her and tugged out the bedclothes. "Ran you a bath, Nora-pie. Aren't you grateful?"

"Yes." At that moment she wanted a bath more than she wanted freedom.

"Pop yourself in that tub." In a single gesture, he jerked the bloody cover and sheets off the bed, balled them up, and threw them into the corner.

She walked, knees trembling, to the bathroom. The casket-sized tub was three-fourths filled with water. The soap dish held a tiny plastic bottle of shampoo and a cake of soap the size of a commemorative stamp. Two curling black hairs adhered to the soap.

Nora's stomach contracted, and she turned to the toilet in time to vomit pinkish drool into the bowl. She wrenched a tissue out of the dispenser, tottered over to the tub, picked up the soap as she would have a dead spider, then dropped the wrapped obscenity in the toilet and flushed it away. From a shell-shaped dish beside the sink she took another minuscule bar of soap and, stepping as gingerly as a stork, at last got into the tub.

Ah, yes. She never wanted to be anywhere at all except the inside of the tub. A pink cloud swam into the water from the center of her body. Delicately Nora explored herself. She was still bleeding, not seriously, and she had a lot of sore tissue. Various little fires continued to burn along the path of Dart's invasion. She soaped her arms and legs and realized that she would have to wash again under the shower to remove the film of blood deposited by the water in the tub. She was bending forward to open the drain when Dick Dart sauntered into the bathroom. She leaned back and sank up to her neck in the cloudy water, and her knees rose like islands.

"Comfy?" Dart grinned down at her, then inspected his face in the mirror. "I hate the way your teeth feel when you haven't brushed. Being unshaven doesn't exactly fill me with joy, either. On our way to lunch, we can see if this place has a gift shop."

Dart moved forward and peered into his eyes in the mirror, twirled around, and sat on the toilet, regarding her almost paternally. "Couldn't help but notice you experienced some discomfort during our encounter." He put a sarcastic stress on the last word. "To facilitate matters I'm going to do what I do with my old dears and buy some K-Y. Lubrication will eliminate about half of your problem, but if you don't relax, you're going to keep on getting hurt."

Nora closed her eyes. A demon flapped up and hissed, *"You're going to get hurt!"*

She opened her eyes.

"Embarking on the great adventure of menopause, aren't we?"

"Yes," she said, startled.

"Irregular periods, vaginal dryness?"

"Yes."

"Irritability?"

"I suppose."

"Hot flashes?"

"Just started."

"Formication?"

"What's that?"

"Sensation of an insect crawling on your skin."

She astounded herself by smiling.

"Doing any hormone replacement therapy? You should, but you have to experiment with the dosage levels before you get it right."

She closed her eyes.

"I suggest a shower and a shampoo before we visit Home Cooking. Time for the next step in your education."

He bestowed another hyena smile upon her and walked out. Moving as if in a trance, Nora dialed a disk at the end of the tub, and the bathwater gurgled into the drain. She pulled herself to her feet, waded through the froth, and twisted both dials at once. Water shot from the faucet. She flipped the lever directing the water to the showerhead, and freezing water shattered against her body.

BOOK V

LORD NIGHT

THE HUGE BLACK ANIMAL MIGHT HAVE BEEN GRINNING AT HIM. "WHY, NOW THAT YOU HAVE LEARNED ABOUT YOUR FEAR, YOU MUST LEARN TO TRUST IT, OF COURSE."

48

"OF COURSE IT'S about money." Dart put down his fork and grinned. He had taken her to the hotel's gift shop, where he bought toothbrushes and toothpaste, a pack of disposable razors and shaving cream, two combs, mouthwash, a deodorant stick, a black polo shirt with MASSACHUSETTS stitched across the left breast in small red letters, and a copy of *Vogue*. His teeth were no longer so yellow, and without the stubble his cheeks were almost pink. Nora had heard only something like half of what Dart said, and half of that had disappeared into the demonic buzz filling her head. "Hey, this is America! Bid'ness is bid'ness. When you see the other side is likely to rake in a hell of a lot more money than you are, what do you do? Switch sides. Here, what we have on the table adds up to four or five million smackers. Put that against a pissy billing of maybe ten thousand tops, you've got what the boys call a no-brainer."

"From *Night Journey*." This, along with the name of the young woman who had mysteriously disappeared from Shorelands, was most of what she had been able to retain from Dick Dart's explanation.

"Absolutely. You prove that Hugo Driver stole the manuscript, fifty-four years' worth of royalties, not to mention all future royalties, go to the real heirs. And if you can prove that the publishing house cooperated in this fraud, all of their profits from the book, plus a whopping payment in damages, go into the pot. On top of that, there's all the money from foreign editions."

Nora's legs felt like rubber, and the center of her body sent out steady waves of pain. She looked at her plate. Beside a nest of french fries glistening with grease, a rectangle of processed cheese drooped over a mound of whitish paste on a slice of toast.

"So the old man cut a deal with this Fred Constantine, the old ladies' lawyer. Constantine knows he's in over his head, little practice in Plainfield, does a few penny-ante divorces and real estate closings, sixty-five years old, hasn't seen the inside of a courtroom since he got out of law school. Imagine his relief when after making him piss blood for a couple of weeks the great Leland Dart suggests—suggests, mind you—that an accommodation might be arranged. Whoopee! If Mr. Constantine could settle for a payment of something on the order of a hundred thousand dollars, Dart, Morris might be willing to render some assistance to his poor defrauded clients, who would no doubt be delighted to receive fifty percent of the ultimate proceeds. Mr. Constantine, who has no idea how much money is at stake, thinks he's getting a great deal!"

A bitten-off portion of a french fry lay on Nora's tongue like a mealworm. She spat it into her hand and dropped it on her plate. "How can they do something like that?"

"Very carefully." His eyes glowing, he pushed the remains of his first cheeseburger into his mouth and wiped his fingers with his napkin. "Operative word? Buffers. By the time you're done, you're in a fortified castle a thousand miles away, and, baby, the drawbridge is up."

"I mean, how can they *do* it?"

Holding his second cheeseburger a few inches from his mouth, Dart looked away and giggled. "Nora-pie, you're so touching. I mean that sincerely. Bid'ness is bid'ness, I told you. What's the name of our economic system? Isn't it still called capitalism?" He shook his head in mock incredulity and took an enormous bite out of the cheeseburger. Frilly lettuce bulged from the back of the bun, and pink juice drooled onto his plate.

Nora closed her eyes against a wave of nausea. Alden Chancel and Dick Dart thought alike. This discovery would be amusing, had she the capacity to be amused. Leland Dart, who shared Alden's moral philosophy, used it to justify betraying his own client. Presumably this moral philosophy reached its fulfillment in the lunatic cheerfully demolishing a cheeseburger across the table.

Nora remembered a detail from the Poplars terrace. "I heard Alden tell Davey that your father might be playing both ends against the middle."

Dart swallowed. "Do the Chancel boys talk about this in front of you?"

"Davey was taking notes on the movie of *Night Journey,* and when I asked him why, he said there was some problem with the Driver estate."

The night in the family room seemed to have taken place on the other side of an enormous hole in time. "A little while later, he told me something about two old ladies in Massachusetts who found some notes in their basement."

She realized that she was having a civil conversation in a restaurant with Dick Dart as if such occasions were absolutely normal.

"Notes on the movie. What a schlump. Katherine Mannheim's sisters never read the book, of course, they remembered the movie when they found the notes, but I mean really . . ."

"I suppose you want to kill the sisters." Nora poked her fork into the white paste and transported a portion the size of a pencil eraser to her mouth. It seemed that she had ordered a tuna melt.

"Absolutely not. The people I want to kill might help the case against Chancel House. We'll be protecting Hugo Driver's name, something I am pleased to do because I always liked Hugo Driver. Not the last two, you know, only the good one."

"You like *Night Journey*?" That Dick Dart had enjoyed any book surprised her.

"Favorite book, bar none," he said. "Only novel I ever really liked. To keep up with some of my old ladies, I had to pretend to swoon over Danielle Steel, but that was just work. Agatha had a pash for Jane Austen, so I plowed through *Pride and Prejudice*. What a waste. Literally about nothing at all. But I reread *Night Journey* every couple of years."

"Amazing." Nora ate another forkful of her tuna. If you peeled off the plastic cheese and avoided the bread, it was edible after all.

"Amazing? *Night Journey* is one twisted motherfucker of a book. Whole thing takes place in darkness. Almost everything happens in caves, underground. All the vivid characters are monsters."

It was like a warped echo of Davey; for the thousandth time she was listening to a man rave about the book. In asking him to research the case against Chancel House, Leland Dart had exploited his son's one conventional passion. The recognition that Alden Chancel had done the same thing with Davey brought with it an upwelling of her nausea.

"I never read it," she said.

"Davey Chancel's wife never read *Night Journey*? You lied to him, didn't you? You told him you'd read it, but you were lying."

Nora turned her head to stare at the two elderly couples at separate tables in front of the window. The big reversed letters on the window arched over them like a red rainbow.

"You did, you lied to him." Another dirty explosion of laughter. He went back to work on the second cheeseburger. "Don't suppose you ever heard of a place called Shorelands."

"Hugo Driver was there. And Lincoln Chancel. In 1938."

"Bravo. Do you remember who else was there that summer?"

"A lot of people with funny names."

"Austryn Fain, Bill Tidy, Creeley Monk, Merrick Favor, Georgina Weatherall. The maids. A lot of gardeners. And Katherine Mannheim. Did Davey tell you anything about her?"

Nora thought for a moment. "She was good-looking. And she ran away."

"Upped and vanished."

"What do you think happened to her?"

"Her sisters say she had a 'weak heart,' whatever that means. Supposed to avoid exertion, but she refused to be an invalid. Rode bikes, went on trips. If she'd lived like Emily Dickinson, she might still be alive."

"You read Emily Dickinson?"

He made a sour face. "Florence. One of my ladies. Besotted with Emily Dickinson. Had to put up with reams of that stuff. Even had to read a *biography.* Bitch makes Jane Austen look like Mickey Spillane." He closed his eyes and recited.

> *"There's a certain Slant of light,*
> *Winter Afternoons—*
> *That oppresses, like the Heft*
> *Of Cathedral Tunes—*
>
> *Heavenly Hurt, it gives us—*
> *We can find no scar,*
> *But internal difference,*
> *Where the Meanings, are—"*

He opened his eyes. "It's not even actual English, it's this gibberish language she made up. Read page after page of that vapor for Florence, and now it's stuck in my mind, along with everything else I ever read."

The lines had swept into Nora like an inexorable series of waves. "That's too bad," she said.

"You have no idea. Anyhow, I guess the Mannheim girl croaked, and in the confusion Driver swiped her manuscript. *Night Journey* was published the next year, and what do you know, pretty soon every other person in the world was reading it."

"I saw soldiers carrying it in Vietnam," Nora said.

"You were in Nam? Excuse me, *the* Nam. No wonder you have this wild streak. Why were you there?"

"I was a nurse."

"Oh, yes, I recall a certain adventure involving a child, yes, yes."

She looked down at her plate.

"Nora fails to demonstrate excitement. Very well, let us return to our subject. Most, I repeat, most unusually, Mr. Driver makes over the copyright to his book to his publisher in exchange for an agreement that he shall be paid all royalties due during the course of his and his wife's lifetime, all rights thereafter to revert to said publisher, who agrees to remit a smaller portion to Driver child or children for the course of their lives. This was supposed to be a gesture of gratitude, but doesn't it seem a bit excessive?"

"You've been doing a lot of work." Acting on its own instructions, her hand detached another wad of tuna and brought it to her mouth.

"Made stacks and stacks of notes, none of them currently available, due to the interference of our local fuzz. Fortunately, I retain all of the essentials. I'd like to visit a library during our busy afternoon, continue my research, but let me distill our mission for you." He looked sideways to ensure that the waitress was still seated at the counter. "You know three of these scribblers offed themselves."

She nodded.

"Austryn Fain. No wife, no little Fains. Creeley Monk was a perv, so of course he left behind no weeping widow or starving children. But luck is with us, for in the summer of 1938 Mr. Monk was sharing his life with a gentleman still with us, a doctor in fact, named Mark Foil. Dr. Foil, bless him, still lives in Springfield, the very same city in which he dwelt with our poet. I very much want to think that he occupies the same house, along with lots and lots of Monk memorabilia. Unfortunately, I couldn't find an address for him, but once we get to Springfield, I'm sure we will be able to unearth it."

"Then what?" Nora asked.

"We telephone the gentleman. You explain that you are doing research for a book on the events at Shorelands in 1938. You feel that the other guests, Creeley Monk in particular, have been unfairly overshadowed by Hugo Driver. Since you happen to be in Springfield, you would be extremely grateful if Dr. Foil could give you an hour of his time to discuss whatever he remembers of that summer—anything Monk might have said to him, written to him, or put in a diary."

Even in her present condition, encased within a tough, resistant envelope which at the cost of prohibiting any sort of action protected her from feeling, Nora remarked upon the oddity of this creature's obsessions so closely resembling Davey's. What Dart was asking her to do seemed as abstract as the crossword puzzles concocted by Davey's two old men in Rhinebeck. She filled in a square with a question. "What if Monk never even mentioned Hugo Driver?"

"Very unlikely, but it doesn't matter. After we get inside I have to kill the old boy."

The hyena within Dick Dart displayed its teeth. "He'll see us, baby. If we get lucky down the line, the old guy is going to put things together. Next stop is Everett Tidy, son of Bill. Everett lives in Amherst, he's an English professor. Don't you think the name Tidy in a headline will catch Foil's eye? Gots to cover our tracks."

The smell of cigarette smoke floated toward them, and Nora turned to see the waitress approaching their table.

Dart said, "Let's shop and do the library while we can still use the Lincoln."

49

MAIN STREET, OF what town? Dart pulled her into women's clothing stores, shooed away the clerks, and hand in hand drew her up and down the aisles, flicking through dresses, blouses, skirts. Here a sand-colored linen suit, skirt knee-length, jacket without lapels ("Your interview suit," Dart said), in the next shop brown pumps and a cream silk jersey, short sleeves, collarless. No, she did not have to try them on, they would fit perfectly. And they would; without asking, he knew her sizes. Into a barn where summer-school students with lumpy backpacks prowled the long aisles and Dart heaped up jeans, hers and his, T-shirts, ditto, a dark blue cotton sweater, hers. A minimalist boutique, a conference with another charmed clerk, the production of six Gitano bras, white, six pairs of Gitano underpants, white, six pairs of Gitano pantyhose. Around the corner, his and hers low-cut black Reeboks.

Two wheeled carry-on black fabric suitcases. Into Main Street Pharmacy for quick selections under the eye of a blond-gray mustache with granny glasses: L'Oréal Performing Preference hair color, Jet Black and Starlight Blonde; LaCoup sculpting spritz; Always ultra plus maxi with wings, her brand, though Dart had not asked; Cover Girl Clean Make-up, Creamy Natural; Cover Girl Lip Advance, Poppy; Maybelline Shine Free Sunset Pink eye shadow ("Glimmer, don't glitter," said Dart); K-Y; Cover Girl Long 'N Lush mascara; Vidal Sassoon Ultra Care shampoo and conditioner; Neutrogena bath bars; Perlier Honey Bath and Shower Cream; Revlon emery boards and cuticle sticks; OPI Nail Lacquer, a smooth, quiet blush she could not catch before he tossed it into the basket; a dram of Coco by Chanel; a jug of Icy Cool Peppermint Scope mouthwash; Hoffritz finger- and toenail clippers, styling scissors, tweezers, nail cleaner. From behind the digital register where the numbers mounted past one hundred dollars, the mustache declared, "Mister, I've seen savvy husbands before, but you take the cake."

Back to the car. Dart angled in before a bowfront shop, Farnsworth & Clamm, and drew Nora into an air-conditioned club room where another mustache marched smiling toward them through glowing casements hung with suits. Yes, Dart murmured, 46 extra long—this one, this one, a double-breasted blue blazer, four blue shirts, four white shirts, cotton broadcloth, spread collars, 17 neck, 36 sleeves, eight boxer shorts, 38 waist, eight pairs calf-length black socks, a dozen handkerchiefs, pick out some ties too, please. Alterations immediately, if poss. Nora deposited in a stiff leather chair near the tall mirror, a stooping man with a tape measure around his neck summoned from the depths, Dart disappeared into the changing room for an eye blink before emerging in the first of his new suits. Another stooping figure materialized to whisk away the suit while Dart twinkled into number two. Dart and his reflection preened. The fittings completed, Dart inhabited another club chair and the mustache presented a bottle of Finnish vodka, two glasses, a bucket of ice. While you wait, sir. The presentation of the bill. Nora looked over and saw that Dart had purchased six thousand dollars' worth of clothes.

"Nearest really good library?" Dart asked.

He swung the Lincoln into the exit near the Basketball Hall of Fame, and Nora realized that, wherever they had been before, now they were in Springfield, where Dr. and Mrs. Daniel Harwich lorded it over Longfellow Lane. If she could escape from Dick Dart, would the doctor and his wife give her shelter in their basement? Answer cloudy, ask again. Three years before, a semi-radioactive Nora had whirled into Springfield on what she imagined was a sentimental visit, wound up in a bar, then a motel, with a strange, embittered Dan Harwich, who afterward talked her into coming home with him. Ten-thirty at night. The Mrs. Harwich of the time, Helen, who had microwaved her half of dinner an hour earlier and dispatched it with several vodka tonics, started shouting as soon as they came through the door. Nora had attempted an exit, but Harwich had settled her in a chair, presumably as a witness. What she had witnessed had been an old-time marital title bout. Helen

Harwich ordered them both out, Dan to return the next morning to pick up some clothes and depart for good. Back to the motel, Harwich uttering evil chuckles. The next morning, he promised to call her soon. Soon meant two days later, another call a week later, a third after another two weeks. After that, intermittent calls, intermittently. Two years later, a wedding announcement accompanied by a card reading, *In case you wondered.* The new Mrs. Dr. Harwich was named Lark, née Pettigrew.

"I have to use the bathroom when we get to the library," Nora said.

Dandy, he'd go with her, fact was, he had to bleed the lizard.

Dart parked across the street from a long stone building resembling the Supreme Court, complete with Supreme Court steps. In a wide marble hall on the second floor, the ladies' room, like the reading room downstairs, was empty. Dick Dart lounged in behind her. Nora took one stall, he another. They left together, startling a pop-eyed, quavery woman whose mouth opened and closed like a molly's until they had passed out of sight on the stairs.

Dart pushed Nora not ungently into a chair before a long wooden table, sat beside her, and opened a fat volume entitled *Shorelands, Home to Genius.* She sat beside him, now and then hearing tiny, metallic voices like the voices of insects. She was within the envelope, the envelope excluded feeling, she was fine. Dart grinned at his book. She pulled toward her *Muses in Massachusetts* by Quinn W. S. Dogbery, opened it, and read a random paragraph.

> Due to the erratic nature of the artistic personality, any community like Shorelands will produce scandal. On the whole, Georgina Weatherall's colony of gifted personages ticked peacefully along, producing decade after decade of significant work. Yet problems did arise. There are those who would list the "strange" disappearance of the minor poet Katherine Mannheim among these, though the present writer is not of their number. This young woman had alienated both staff and fellow guests during her brief residence. There can be no doubt that her hostess was resolved to issue her walking papers. Miss Mannheim, who did not wish to face an humiliating expulsion, departed in a fashion calculated to cause a maximum of confusion.
>
> Shorelands' true scandals, as we might expect, are very different in nature.

Dart thumped two telephone directories on the table and patted her on the back.

> Perhaps most distressing to Georgina Weatherall was the disappearance, not of a troublesome young malcontent, but of a favorite work of art from the dining room, a drawing by the Symbolist Odilon Redon of a strapping female nude with the head of a hawk upon her shoulders. There can be no doubt that Georgina's desire for the Redon drawing had its origin in its title, identical to that of a central Shorelands tradition. The works in the dining room were typically of a more traditional nature. The Redon drawing, measuring some eight by ten inches, hung far up on a wall filled with more notable works. A guest with a particular interest in Redon first noted its absence in 1939. An immediate search of the rooms and cottages yielded no result. Georgina Weatherall remarked several times to guests during the succeeding years that it would not surprise her to discover that Miss Mannheim had absconded with it during her "midnight flit," and while the matter may never be resolved, it may be not uncharitable to acknowledge that the drawing did then and does now possess considerable monetary value.

Dart said, "Out of here," gripped Nora's arm, and pulled her outside into the heat and light.

They made three trips to get all the bags and packages into the hotel.

"Clark, my old friend, could you spare a moment to help us convey these essentials up to our charming room?"

Clark licked his lips. "Whatever." He leaned into the office behind him and said something inaudible to whoever was in there. Then he emerged through the lobby door, glanced at Dart, and moved toward the suitcases. He was shorter than he had seemed behind the counter, four or five inches over five feet.

"I'll get the suitcases," Dart said. "Help my wife."

"Whatever." Clark picked up as many bags as he could. Nora took up three others, leaving one on the floor. Clark looked up at Dart, who smiled, opened his mouth, and chopped his teeth together. The boy glanced at Nora, and bent over, bit down on the twine handles of the remaining bag, and jerked it upward.

The three of them crowded into the elevator.

"I'm interested in your use of the word 'whatever,' " Dart said. "Mean something, or merely verbal static?"

The boy grunted and clutched his armful of bags. Sweat ran down his forehead.

"Is it as rude as it sounds? Sort of a hint that the person who says 'Whatever' feels a mild disdain for the other party. Is that accurate, or am I being paranoid?"

Clark shook his head.

"A great relief, Clark."

The elevator reached the third floor, and Dart led them down the hall. "Clark, old dear, deposit those shopping bags in front of the closet and hang the suit bags."

Dart motioned Nora through the door. Clark bent over to deposit on the floor the bag he held with his teeth, exhaled a shaking breath, and lowered the shopping bags. He succeeded in getting the hanger wires over the rail in the closet and backed out into the corridor.

Dart locked the door and came into the room to stand smiling in front of her. Nora drew up her knees and hunched her back. He moved away, and she looked up. He was selecting a length of rope. "Do I have to tell you everything?"

She kicked off her shoes. Her fingers, which did not have to be told what to do, began unbuttoning her shirt. Dart went to the bathroom for the pharmacy bag and carried it to the table as she undressed. One by one, he took the items out of the bag and arranged them on the table. When everything had been satisfactorily aligned, he took the scissors from their plastic case and beckoned Nora into the bathroom.

"Straddle the toilet," he said. Quivering, Nora positioned herself over the bowl, and Dick Dart hummed to himself as he cut off most of her pubic hair and flushed it away.

"Okay," he said, moved her backwards like a mannequin, turned her around, planted a hand between her shoulder blades, and urged her back into the bedroom, where he tied her hands behind her back and taped her mouth shut.

She looked up at the flat white ceiling. Dart hiked himself up onto the bed. "It's not going to be as bad this time, see?" She turned her head to see him brandishing a tube of K-Y.

It was slightly less painful than before, but every bit as bad.

50

"KEEP YOUR HEAD upright. You have to cooperate with me, or you'll end up looking like a ragamuffin." Bath cream scented the air in the bathroom, and her hair, still wet, hung straight and flat. Dart lowered his head alongside hers so that the mirror framed their faces. "Tell me what you see."

Nora saw a terrorized version of herself with shocked eyes, parchment skin, and wet hair, posing with a hyena. "Us."

"I see a couple of fine desperadoes," said the hyena in the mirror. "You needed me to open your eyes, and along I came. Wasn't any accident, was it?"

"I don't know what it was, but—"

Before she could add *I wish it had never happened,* the eyes in the mirror charged with an illumination. "Used to do this with hubby dear, didn't you? Put your heads together and looked at yourselves in the mirror. I know why, too."

She did not have to tell him he was right; he already knew that. "Why?"

"Until now, I hadn't seen how much you and Davey resemble each other. Bet there's a nice little erotic charge in that—probably helped Davey get it up. Like making it with who you'd be if you were the opposite sex. But Davey isn't your male self. The biggest risk Davey-poo ever took was getting into bed with Natalie Weil, and the only reason he did that was his old man made him so insecure about his manhood that he had to prove he could use it."

Nora clamped her mouth against agreeing, but agree she did.

"I'm your real male self. Only difference is, I'm more evolved. Which means that eventually we are going to have tremendous sex."

The hyena surged into his face once more. "In fact, Nora-boo, didn't you have a bit of an orgasm that time?"

"Maybe," she said, thinking it was what he wanted to hear.

He slapped her hard enough to snap her head back. A broad, hand-shaped red mark emerged on her cheek. "I know you didn't come, and so do you. Goddamn it, when I make you come, they'll hear you howling in the next county. Shit."

He slammed his fist against the bathroom door, then turned around and pointed at her face in the mirror. "I bust you out of jail, I buy you clothes, I'm going to give you the best haircut you ever had in your life, after that I'm going to do what your mother should have done and teach you about makeup, and you *lie* to me?"

She trembled.

"I have to keep remembering what women are like. No matter how much a man does for them, they stab you in the back first chance they get."

"I shouldn't have lied," she said.

"Forget it. Just don't do it again unless you want to hold your guts in your hands." He wiped his face with a towel, then draped it over her shoulders. "Stop shaking."

Nora's eyes were closed, and in some world where the demons did not exist she felt a comb running through her hair. "This is going to be an inch or two shorter all over, but it'll look completely different. For one thing, I cut hair a lot better than the last guy who did this. Also, I know how you ought to look, and you don't have the faintest idea. It's too bad we have to turn you into a blonde, but that'll be okay too, believe me. You'll look ten years younger."

He positioned her head and started cutting with small, precise movements of the scissors. Dark hair fell onto the towel and drifted down to her breasts. He said, "Hold still. I'll get the hair off you later." Wisps of hair landed on her forearms, her stomach, her back. Dart was humming "There'll Be Some Changes Made." "Good hair," he said. "Nice full texture, good body."

She opened her eyes and beheld exactly what he had promised, the best cut of her life. It was too bad that she should be given such a cut when she was a corpse being prepared for the coffin. His hands flew about her head, fluffing, cutting.

"Pretty good, if I do say so myself." He snapped the towel away from her shoulders and brushed hair from her body. "Well?"

Nora snatched the towel and wrapped it around her chest. Dart grinned at her in the mirror. She ran her fingers through her short, lively hair and watched it fall perfectly back into place. Apart from the fading red mark on her cheek, the only problem with the woman in the mirror was that beneath the cap of beautifully cut hair her face was dead.

Dart opened the box of hair coloring and removed a white plastic bottle with a nozzle and a cylinder of amber liquid. He snipped off the tip of the nozzle. "You won't be as blond as the picture, but you'll be blond, anyhow." He wiggled his hands into the transparent plastic gloves from the inner side of the instruction sheet. After pouring in the amber liquid, Dart shook the bottle.

"Bend forward." She leaned over the sink, and Dart squeezed golden liquid into her hair and worked it in with his fingers. "That's it for twenty-five minutes." He looked at his watch. "Sit here so I can use the mirror." She dragged her chair in front of her as she backed toward the toilet.

Dart leaned forward and began cutting his own hair. He did a better job with the back of his head than Nora had expected, missing only a few sections where long hair fanned over the rest. "How's it look?"

"Fine."

"In the back?"

"Fine."

He snorted. "Guess that means close enough for jazz." He opened the box of black hair color and mixed the ingredients. "I'm going to have to close my eyes, so I want you to put your hand on me. If you take it off, I'll smash your head open on the bathtub."

"Put my hand where?"

"Grab anything you like."

She hitched herself forward and, shivering with revulsion, placed her hand on his hip.

Dart squeezed the fluid into his hair. "I wish I were a woman, so I could have me do this for myself. Without doing it like this, I mean."

"You wish you were a woman," Nora said.

He stopped massaging the lather into his hair. "I didn't say that."

Goose bumps rose on Nora's arms.

"I didn't say I wanted to be a woman. That's not what I said."

"No."

Violence congealed about Dart's heavy body and sparkled in the air. He lowered his hands and faced her.

"I mean, I would enjoy having these things done to me by me. The women who get my special treatment are *extremely* lucky people. I think it would be nice to be pampered, like I pamper you. Anything strange about that?"

"No," she said.

He turned back to the sink and shot her a simmering glance. She settled her hand on his hip. "You're tied down by the crappy little conventions that inhibit melon-heads like your husband. The truth is, there are two kinds of people, sheep and wolves. If anyone should understand this, it's you."

He peeled off the smeary gloves. "That's that." She lowered her hand and looked at the door. "Nope, we're staying in here. Sit on the side of the tub."

Nora moved. Dart frowned, tossed the gloves into the basket, checked himself in the mirror, and sat on the toilet. "We have some time to kill. Ask me something, and try not to make it too stupid."

She tried to think of a question that would not infuriate him. "I was wondering why you live in the Harbor Arms."

He held up his finger like an exclamation point. "Very good! First of all, my parents will never come there—the place gives them hives. Secondly, nobody gives a shit what you do." For fifteen minutes, he described the advantages of living in a place where the fellow residents willingly supplied drugs, sex, and gossip—the members of the Yacht Club universally assumed that their waiters and busboys, Dart's confidants, chose not to overhear their private conversations.

If she were alive, Nora thought, most of what she would feel about this vain, destructive, self-important man would be contempt. Then she realized that what she was now feeling actually was contempt. Maybe she was not entirely dead after all.

"Anyhow," Dart said, "time to wash that gunk out of your hair and do the conditioner."

"I'd like to do it by myself."

He held up his hands. "Fine. Use a little warm water, lather up, and rinse. Then take that tube on the side of the sink and massage the whole thing into your hair. After two minutes we'll rinse it out."

Nora worked her fingers through her hair until a cap of white foam appeared, then lowered her head beneath the tap and washed it away.

"Amazing," Dart said.

Nora looked up.

A drowned sixteen-year-old blonde stared at her from the other side of the mirror. Short, wet hair only slightly darker than Natalie Weil's lay flat against her head.

"I didn't think it'd be *that* good," Dart said. "Don't forget the conditioner."

Nora took her eyes from the drowned girl's and unscrewed the cap, then faced the strange girl again and squeezed the contents of the tube over the top of her head in a long, looping line. Together she and the girl worked their fingers through their hair.

"My turn." Soon a black-haired Dick Dart was grinning at his image in the mirror. "Should have done this years ago. Don't you think I look great?"

A greasy crow's wing flattened over his head. Stray feathers adhered to his temples and forehead.

"Great," she said.

He pointed at the sink, and she came forward to rinse out the conditioner.

"Okay, next step." Dart pulled her toward the bedroom and sat her at the table. "Watch what I'm doing so you'll be able to do it for yourself, later." He flipped open a mirrored case and handed it to her. He smoothed a dab of makeup across her cheekbones and feathered it down her cheeks, stroked mascara into her eyelashes, brushed lipstick onto her mouth. "When we're all done, I want you to clean up your nails and cuticles and put on that polish. I suppose you *have* done that before?"

"Of course." She could not remember the last time she had applied nail polish.

"One last touch," Dart said, putting a dime-sized dab of the sculpting spritz on his palm. Behind her, he began massaging her scalp. He combed, patted, combed, tugged at her hair. "Impress myself. Go in the bathroom and take a look."

Nora slipped into her blue shirt.

"You won't believe it."

Nora stood in front of the mirror and lifted her eyes. A woman just beginning her real maturity, the second one, a woman who should have been selling expensive shampoo in television commercials, looked back at her. Her glowing gamine's hair had been teased into artful ridges and peaks. She had perfect skin, a handsome mouth, and long, striking eyes. She was what the lacquered twenty-somethings who lived on mineral water from Waldbaum's wanted to be when they grew up. For some reason, this woman wore Nora's favorite blue shirt.

Nora moved her face to within three inches of the mirror. There, lurking beneath the blond woman's mask, she saw herself. Then she pulled back and disappeared beneath the mask. A howl of rage came from the bedroom.

Dick Dart was seated at the table with the newspaper he had taken from the lounge. The bottle of Cover Girl Clean stood open on the bottom half of the paper, and he was jabbing the brush at a story, spattering the paper with tan flecks. "Know what these idiots are saying?" He turned toward her a face from a trick photograph, its left half smoothed into a younger, unlined version of the right. "I should sue the bastards."

Nora went past the row of shopping bags outside the closets. "What's wrong?"

"The *Times,* that's what. They got everything wrong, they fouled up in every possible way."

She sat on the bed.

"Know what you are, according to this rag? A socialite. If you're a socialite, I'm the Queen of Sheba. 'To abet his escape, Dart seized a hostage, Westerholm socialite Nora Chancel, 49, wife of David Chancel, executive editor at Chancel House, and son of the current president and CEO of the prestigious publishing company, Alden Chancel. Neither David nor Alden Chancel could be reached for comment.'" He read this in a mincing, sarcastic drawl which made every word seem a preposterous lie.

She said nothing.

"If you go by this article, the only criminal in Westerholm is me, and can you guess what they say I am? Go on, take a stab at it."

"A murderer?"

"A *serial killer*! Are they so brain-dead they can't tell the difference between me and some psycho who goes around killing people at random?" Indignation brought a flush to the side of his face he had not made up. "They're insulting me in print!"

"I don't really—"

Dart pointed the makeup applicator at her like a knife. "Serial killers are scum. Even Ted Bundy was a nothing from a completely insignificant family of nowhere Seattle nobodies."

He was breathing hard.

"I see," Nora said.

"What's the point of doing anything if they're going to twist it around? What about credit where credit is due?"

She nodded.

"Here's another lie. They say I'm an *accused* serial killer. Excuse me, but when did that happen? I was brought into the station because of the allegations of a drunken whore, I spent about twelve hours with Leo Morris, but when during all that time was I accused? This is libel."

She kept her eyes on his.

"Work like mad, put yourself in constant danger, accomplish things the ordinary jerk couldn't even dream of, and they go out and peddle these *lies* about you. It makes me so *mad*!"

"Do they have any idea of where we are? What about the car?"

"For what it's worth, it says here that the fugitive and his hostage—hostage, that's a good one—fled in the hostage's car, which was later discovered in the parking lot of a restaurant stop on I-95. Probably they do know about that old asshole's Lincoln. I was going to get a new car tonight anyhow." He picked up the makeup bottle and threw the newspaper at her. *"Serial killer."*

She sat back on her haunches. "What are you going to do?"

He dipped the applicator back into the jar of makeup, positioned the mirror in front of him, and started working on the right side of his face. "We're going to change into new clothes and pack up. Early tomorrow, we're going to await the arrival of a weary traveler, kill him, and steal his car. Move to another motel. Sometime before noon tomorrow, we'll locate Dr. Foil. After that, we'll journey on to Northampton and pay a call on Everett Tidy, son of poor Bill."

He replaced the cap on the bottle and offered his face for inspection. "What do you think?"

From the neck up, he was a different, younger man who might have been a doctor. Nurses would have flirted with him, gossiped about him. "Remarkable," she said.

He reached across the table for the rope and the duct tape.

51

NORA RETURNED TO her body. Perhaps her body returned to her. The process was unclear. From an indefinite realm, she had fallen into a damp bed already occupied by a large male body sweating alcoholic fumes. Her body was sweating, too. She raised a tingling hand to wipe her forehead, and the hand jerked to a halt before it reached her face, restrained by a tight pressure encircling her wrist. On examination this proved to be a rope. The rope extended beneath the inert body of the man, whom Nora could remember linking them wrist to wrist as she passed through the interior of cloud after cloud. She was back with Dick Dart, and she was having the second hot flash of her life. A nice mixture of demons in high good humor squatted around the bed, sniggering and muttering in their rat-tat-tat voices.

A man half visible in the darkness crossed his legs ankle to knee in a chair near the window. She looked more closely at the man and saw that her father had found a way to join her in this netherworld.

Daddy, she said.

This is a pretty pickle you're in, said her father. *Seems to me you could use a little good advice from your old man right about now.*

Don't wake him up. You're talking too loud.

Hey, this clown can't hear me. He drank most of that bottle of vodka, remember? That guy's out cold. But even stone-cold sober, he wouldn't be able to hear either one of us.

I miss you.

That's why I'm here.

Nora began to cry. *I need you.*

Honey, the person you need is Nora. You got lost, and now you have to find yourself again.

I don't even have a self anymore. I'm dead.

Listen to me, sweetie. That pile of horse manure did the worst thing to you he could think of because he wants to break you down, but it didn't work, not all the way. Forget this dead business. If you were dead, you wouldn't be talking to me.

Why not? You're dead, too.

You're not as easy to kill as Dick Dart thinks you are. You're going to get through it, but to do that you have to go through it. It's hard, and I wish it didn't have to be this way, but sometimes you have to take an awful bitter pill.

The form facing her in the chair, one ankle on the opposite knee, had been gradually coming clearer in the darkness, and now she could make out his plaid shirt open over the flash of a white T-shirt, the vertical red stripes of his suspenders, his work boots. His close-cropped white hair glimmered. She fastened on his beloved, familiar face, the clear eyes fanned with deep wrinkles and the heavily lined forehead. Here was Matt Curlew, her strong capable steady father, looking back at her with a mixture of tenderness and authority which pierced her heart.

It's too much, she said.

You can come through. You have to.

I can't.

He folded his hands together on top of his raised leg and leaned forward.

Okay, maybe I can. But I don't want to.

Of course not. Nobody wants to go all the way through. Some people, they're never even asked to do it. You might say those are pretty lucky people, but the truth is, they never had the chance to stop being ignorant. You know what a soul is, Nora? A real soul? A real soul is something you make by walking through fire. By keeping on walking, and by remembering how it felt.

I'm not strong enough.

This time, you get to do it right. Last time you got hurt as bad as this, you closed your eyes and pretended it didn't happen. Inside you, there are a lot of doors you shut a long time ago. What you have to do is open those doors.

I don't understand.

Just let yourself remember. Start with this. Remember one summer when you were nine or ten and I taught you all those knots? Remember doing the half hitch? The slipknot?

Tying knots when she was ten years old? The present Nora had never been ten years old.

You were sitting on that stump in the backyard, the one from the oak that fell down during that hellacious storm.

Then she did remember: the smooth white surface of the stump, her tomboy self fooling with a length of rope she had unearthed in the garage, her father wandering up to ask if she wanted to learn some fancy knots. Then the pleasure of discovering how a random-seeming series of loops magically resolved into a pattern. She had badgered him for weeks, showed off at the kitchen table, impressed various boys, absorbed by one of those childish fascinations which last a season and then disappear for good.

I remember.

What was the best one? You used it to tie up Lobo.

The witch's curse?

The guy who taught it to me called it the witch's headache. Probably has a dozen names. If you tie it right, nobody who doesn't know the trick can ever undo it. From what I can see, your friend Dick Dart tried to put a witch's headache on your wrist, but he doesn't know as much about knots as he does about cosmetics.

Nora looked down at the complication on her wrist, as solid as a bracelet and intricate as a maze. Something about the pattern was misshapen.

You can get out of that contraption in a couple of seconds. You see how?

Nora tugged here and there with her free hand, gently loosening the web, then slowly drew the end of the rope from under a strand, unwound it from around her wrist, and passed it beneath another strand. The knot sagged into a series of loops from which she could easily slide her hand.

Now tie it all back up again with that stupid mistake where he missed the choke.

But I can get away!

You're not done yet, honey. You have to stick with this animal for a while, then you'll be able go through with what you have to do.

I don't know what you're talking about!

I wish I could guarantee you it'll all turn out the way it should, but can anybody ever promise that? Don't worry about the knot—it'll tie itself, and miss the choke, too.

I suppose you think this is easy.

Nothing about this is easy. Go all the way through it, honey. This time go all the way through.

Nora watched the rope slither twice around her wrist, create a loop, wind around, slip beneath a strand and through the loop, miss the essential hitch, and tuck itself into the web. When she looked up, her father said, *I love you, Sunshine. You're one hell of a girl.*

Help me, she said, but the chair was empty.

52

FAINT GRAY LIGHT touched the edge of the curtains. The last time she had looked at them, she had seen darkness, so she had slept. Dart had planned a busy day, and she was supposed to stop him. She could not stop Dick Dart. A thick membrane made of transparent rubber surrounded her, stealing her will, robbing her of the power to act. Within the membrane, she could do no more than follow orders and utter occasional remarks. Matt Curlew had come to her in a dream and shown her that Dart couldn't tie the witch's headache, but he knew nothing about the membrane.

Dart lay on his side, turned away from her. Experimentally, she put her hand on his shoulder. He rolled over to face her, his bloodshot eyes gleaming. "Need an early start today. Get any sleep?" His breath smelled like burning tires.

"A little, I guess."

He sat up and pulled her wrist onto his broad thigh. "Don't suppose you made any little efforts to untie that knot while I was out."

"I touched it, that's all."

"Ooh, Nora, you excite me." He giggled. "This knot, you try to get out of it, it tightens up on you. Called the devil's conundrum. Watch this." He tugged at a strand, passed it beneath another, and the knot dissolved. "Need two hands to make it work. If you try it, you'll cut off most of the circulation to your hand."

If you tied it right, that is, she thought. Inside the bubble, she made a ghostly smile.

He looked at his watch. "The first thing I want you to do is pack everything in your suitcase, leaving out one of the new T-shirts and jeans. I have to fix your face and hair. Then we're going to keep our eyes on the parking lot." He patted her face. "If I say so myself, I improved your looks about a thousand percent. Don't you agree? Don't you have to admit that your rescuer from Durance Vile is a genius?"

"You're a genius," Nora said.

Dart jumped out of bed and spun around. "I'm a genius, I was born a genius, I always will be a genius, and I have never done anything wrong!

Ladies and gentlemen, please put your hands together for a man who can truly be said to be one of a kind, the great one, the maestro, Mr. RIIICH-ARD *DART!*"

He flapped a hand at Nora, and she clapped twice.

"Hustle your fine little buns into the bathroom and brush your teeth. Void your bowels. Enjoy a lengthy urination. While I do the same, get your shit packed. Time's a-wasting."

Nora had folded all the new clothes into the suitcase, slid the unopened packets of soap and bath cream down the sides, jammed in the mouthwash, and begun placing all the makeup and beauty-care equipment on top of the pile. After packing his own clothes twice as well as she in half the time, Dart stopped admiring himself in the mirror to check her progress. "Didn't your mother teach you *anything*? You can't put that stuff in your suitcase, for God's sake."

"Where do you want me to put it?"

He winked at her. "Little surprise." He opened the closet door, took from the shelf a black leather handbag with a golden snap, and danced toward her. "Gucci, you will observe. Testimonial to your invaluable assistance."

"I didn't see you buy this."

"Took advantage of the trusting inattention of the salesladies at our second stop. Fit neatly into the bag from the first emporium."

Nora scooped the bottles, cases, and containers into the bag and snapped it shut.

"Let's find our victim," Dart said.

53

"A LOT OF people think traveling salesmen died out with Willy Loman, but the world is full of guys with their backseats full of sample cases and catalogs. Travel these huge territories, two or three states, the whole Northeast. Drive high-end Detroit iron and pull into joints like this too tired to fight."

Standing on the balcony a few feet from Dart, Nora rubbed her bare arms. Condensation shone on the empty cars beneath them, and the windows of Home Cooking were dark. The headlights of a dark green sedan on the side of the lot shone on a cement planter in which geraniums wilted in a carpet of cigarette butts.

"Idiot's battery is going to die before he gets his ass out of bed," Dart said. "Some people shouldn't be allowed to drive."

"You're sure someone's going to come in?"

"Dick Dart's word is his bond," he said in a booming voice. "If Dick Dart tells you something, you can take that motherfucker to the motherfucking bank."

A car veered into the exit. "What did I tell you?" Dart pulled her into the room and looked back at the car, which drove past the entrance to the lot. "Cheapskate's looking for a place costs five bucks less a night." He dropped Nora's arm and stepped back out onto the balcony. "Let's see some action here, people. Haven't got all day."

He shoved his hands in his pockets and rose onto the balls of his feet. He patted the top of the balcony rail with his fingertips. "Still can't get over that serial killer thing." For a minute or two, he paced up and down on the narrow balcony. "Let's take our bags downstairs."

Nora carried her suitcase in one hand, and with her other arm clutched to her chest the bags from the hardware store and liquor store. Draped over these was Dart's bulging suit bag.

They carried their things past an empty desk. "No conception of service left in this country. We're turning into *Nigeria.*" He crammed himself into the revolving door, swore, swung it around, and disappeared from view, leaving Nora to solve the problem of the revolving door by herself. She had to struggle around twice to move everything outside. Once, she would have fled through the hotel and escaped, but the person she was now could not do that; she had been punished too much, and the transparent membrane protected her from further punishment.

Dart was standing beneath the marquee. "Get over here in case one of those morons actually *deigns* to work the desk." He pulled keys from his jacket pocket and displayed them on his palm. "These things cost something, but hey, they just work here, it's not their money." He tossed them into the cement planter. "That thing is supposed to add some beauty to the place, and what do people do? Turn it into an ashtray. First of all, they *smoke,* as if nobody ever told them they're begging for lung cancer, and then they throw their butts into a planter. Anybody can stop smoking. Used to smoke four packs a day, and I stopped. What happened to self-control? Fuck self-control—what happened to simple consideration for others?"

Nora watched dark outlines speed down the highway against the brightening sky.

"Isn't there any work ethic left in this country?"

Nora looked at the car with its lights burning and made out a shape behind the wheel.

"Come on, Nora. Can't do everything by myself. Wind it up, cross your fingers, turn the key, do whatever the hell you do."

"I don't do anything."

"Do you . . ." He stopped talking and looked at her, blinking rapidly. "If that dodo left his lights on, maybe he left his keys in his car."

He walked out from under the canopy, bent to look into the car, and ran toward it, pulling the revolver from his jacket pocket.

Nora pressed the heavy suit bag to her eyes and waited for the explosion. Dart's shoes thudded on the asphalt and came to a stop. She heard his dirty bow-wow-wow laugh.

She lowered the bags. Dart was blowing her a kiss from beside the open car door. "Goddamn it, Nora, you deserve a bonus."

She moved toward him.

"Ta da!" Dart stepped aside to reveal an obese male body slumped behind the wheel. A yellow tie had been yanked sideways, and the first four buttons of the shirt had been torn off.

"Heart attack, wouldn't you say?"

"Looks that way," Nora said.

"Butterball here's about fifty pounds overweight, and the inside of his car reeks of cigarettes." He touched the corpse's flabby cheek. "This bag of shit drove in about a minute before we went out onto the balcony, turned off his car, and dropped dead before he could switch off his lights. He's been here all along! Put down that stuff and give me a hand."

Dart kneeled on the passenger seat, wrapped his arms around the dead man's chest, and yanked him sideways. Nora bent down and pushed. Her hands sank into the soft body.

"Jesus, Nora, you've handled dead bodies before. You can't wimp out on me now."

Nora put her shoulder into the dead man's side. "Push!"

The body tumbled into the passenger seat.

Dart tossed the keys over the top of the car. "Put the bags in the trunk."

Obedient Nora opened the trunk and laid the suit bag across cartons and boxes. Then she got in the backseat and Dart accelerated backwards, braked, and shot toward the front of the hotel. The dead man's head rolled sideways. They jammed the rest of the bags into the trunk and backseat. The knives between his feet, Dart rolled chuckling toward the exit. Then he braked and leaned toward the corpse.

He tugged a wallet from the dead man's jacket. "Check out these business cards. Playtime Enterprises, Boston. Gumbo's Goodies, Boston. Satisfaction Guaranteed, Waltham. What are these places? Hot Stuff, Providence. The Adults Only Parlor." Dart started laughing. "Jumbo sells sex toys! What a gem! Let's find out his name."

He held up a license displaying a photograph of a pudgy face with distended cheeks and close-set eyes. "We have the pleasure of being in the company of Mr. Sheldon Dolkis. Mr. Dolkis is, let's see, forty-four years of age, weight two hundred twenty-five pounds, height five feet, eight inches. He claims to have hazel eyes, and he has declined to be an organ donor. We shall see about that, I believe." Dart grasped the corpse's right hand. "A treat to make your acquaintance, Shelley. We'll paint the town red."

He drove into the southbound lanes of the highway. "We want a Mom and Pop motel redolent of the two quintessential Normans, Rockwell and Bates. A shabby little office and a string of depressing cabins."

"Why is that what we want?"

"Can't leave our new friend in the car, now, can we? Shelley is part of our family."

"You're going to *keep* him?"

"I'm going to do a lot more than that," Dart said.

54

"DELIGHTFUL PLACE, SPRINGFIELD," Dart said. "Pay attention now, Shelley. Even a lowlife like you must have heard of the Springfield rifle, but did your education cover the Garand? Wonderful weapon for its time. For two hundred years, both of these rifles were manufactured in Springfield. It may be the only city in America with a weapons museum. Now, *there's* a museum worth visiting. Of course it also has that Basketball Hall of Fame, if you can believe that. Have to throw the yokels a crumb now and then.

"Basketball was okay when white people still played it, but look what happened. Overgrown glandular cases took over, and now it's all exhibitionism. Sportsmanship? Forget it, there's no sportsmanship in the ghetto, and basketball is only the ghetto with big paychecks. All part of the decline in public morality. My father—you think he cares who really wrote *Night Journey*? His idea of good literature is a copy of *American Lawyer* with his picture on the cover. You should see what goes on at Dart, Morris—the bill padding, the Concorde flights we charge to the client. What gets me, they don't see the humor in this stuff, they chug down two bottles of Dom Pérignon and stuff themselves with caviar at what they call a conference, bill the client five hundred bucks for the dinner, and don't even think it's funny! No wonder people hate lawyers. Compared to the other guys, I'm a paragon. I take care of my old ladies. If I bill them for lunch, it's because during that lunch, we talked about business. It isn't all Danielle Steel and Emily Dickinson, you know."

They had been driving aimlessly through the outskirts of Springfield, Dart scanning both sides of the streets for a motel as he talked.

"Take Shelley Dolkis here. Delivered dildos and inflatable dolls to guys too feeble to have sex with other people. Even the sex industry has a hierarchy, and Shelley was on the bottom end—the jerk-off end. But if he could talk, he'd tell you he provided a necessary service. If people didn't have access to his products, why, they'd go out and commit rape!"

"I suppose you're right," Nora said.

"Whole thing comes down to having the balls to be completely straight about being crooked. The guy who runs for the Senate and says he wants the job so he can screw the aides, stuff his pockets with payoff money, take a lot of drugs, and swim naked with a couple of strippers, that's the guy who gets my vote. This country founded on fairness? A bunch of other guys owned it, and we *took* it. Wasn't there a little thing called the Boston Tea Party? Suppose you came to Connecticut in 1750 and happened to see a nice plot of land on the Sound with half a dozen Pequot Indians living on it. Did you say, too bad, guess I'll move inland? You killed the Indians and got your land. You lived in Westerholm a couple of years. Ever see any Pequots? The same things happen over and over. History books lie about it, teachers lie about it, and for sure politicians lie about it. Last thing they want is an educated public."

"Yes."

"This is a happy time for me. I'm a lot more sensitive than most people think I am, and you're beginning to see that side of me."

"That's true," Nora said.

"And here's a place that will suit our little family just fine."

A shabby row of cabins stood at the top of a rise. Numbered doors lined a platform walkway. A neon sign at the entrance to the parking lot said HILLSIDE MOTEL.

"Hillside, like the strangler," Dart said. He pulled up in front of the last unit and patted the corpse's cheek. "Relax for a moment, Shelley, while Nora and I secure our accommodations."

An ancient Sikh accepted twenty-five dollars and shoved a key across the counter without leaving his chair or taking his eyes off the Indian musical blaring from the television set on his desk.

"Nora, Nora," Dart said as they w000alked on creaking boards back toward their car and Sheldon Dolkis. "As they say in beer commercials, does it get any better than this?"

"How could it?" Nora said.

"You and me and a big fat dead man." He slid the key into the door of the last room. "Let's have a look at our bower."

An overhead light in a rice-paper bubble feebly illuminated a bed covered with a yellow blanket, a battered wooden dresser, and two green plastic chairs at a card table. Worn matting covered the floor. "Nora, if this room could talk, what tales it would tell."

"Suicides and adulteries," Nora said, and felt a dim flicker of terror. This was not the kind of thing the person inside the bubble was supposed to say.

But she had not displeased Dick Dart. "You get more interesting with every word you say. When you were in Vietnam, were you raped?"

She collapsed against the wall. *Davey couldn't figure it out in two years of marriage, and Dick Dart saw it in about twenty-four hours.*

He glanced outside. "After we escort Shelley into this lovely room, I have a story to tell you."

Back outside, Dart opened the passenger door and put his hand on Dolkis's shoulder. The dead man was regarding the roof of his car as if it were showing a porn movie. "Shelley, old boy, time for a short stroll. Nora-sweetie, what I am going to do is pull him toward me, and I want you to get up behind him and catch him under the other arm."

Dart leaned into the car and pulled the dead man's head and shoulders into the sunlight. "Get set, don't want to drop him." Nora wedged herself next to the car and bent down. The dead man's suit was the oily green of a Greek olive and stank of cigarette smoke. "Here we go," Dart said. The suit jerked sideways. She lifted the arm and edged in close to the body. "Good hard pull," said Dart. The body lifted off the car seat, and its feet snagged. A soft noise came from the open mouth. "Don't complain, Shelley," Dart said. He reared back, and Dolkis's feet slid over the flange. One of his shoes came off. "Walky walky," Dart said.

They dragged him inside. At the far end of the bed, Dart lowered his side of the body and let go. The weight on Nora's back slipped away, and the body's forehead smacked against the rattan carpet. Dart rolled the corpse over and patted the bulging gut. "Good boy." He untied the twisted necktie and threw it aside, then unbuttoned the shirt and pulled it out of the trousers. A thin line of dark hair ran up the mound beneath the sternum and down into the dimple of the navel. Dart unbuckled the belt and undid the trouser button.

"What are you doing?" Nora asked.

"Undressing him." He yanked down the zipper, moved to the lower end of the body, pulled off the remaining shoe, and peeled the socks off the plump feet. He yanked at the trouser cuffs. The body slid a couple of inches toward him before the trousers came away, exposing white shorts with old stains on the crotch. Dart reached into the left front trouser pocket and extracted a crumpled handkerchief and a key ring, both of which he threw under the table. From the right pocket he withdrew a brass money clip and a small brown vial with a plastic spoon attached to the top.

"Shelley took coke! Do you suppose he actually *tried* to get a heart attack?" He unscrewed the cap and peered into the bottle. "Selfish bastard used it all up." The bottle hit the floor and rolled beneath Nora's chair. "I have to get some things out of the car."

Dart strode out into the dazzling light. Grateful to be powerless, to feel nothing, Nora heard the trunk of the car open, the rustle of bags, a lengthy silence. A blue jay screamed. The trunk slammed down. A dignified, doctorly man carried a lot of bags into the room and became Dick Dart.

He hitched up his trousers, knelt beside the body, and arranged the bags in a row beside him. From the first he dumped out his knives. From the second he removed a pair of scissors. He took the half-empty vodka bottle from the third, removed the cap, winked at Nora, and took a long pull, which he swished around in his mouth before swallowing. He shuddered, took a second drink, and replaced the cap. "Anesthesia. Want some?"

She shook her head.

Dart walked up the body and levered the trunk upright. "Give me a hand."

When the body was naked except for underpants, Dart rummaged through the suit pockets: a ballpoint pen, a pocket comb gray with scum, a black address book. He threw these toward the wastebasket, then noticed the money clip on the floor beside him. "My God, I forgot to count the money." He pulled out the bills. "Twenty, forty, sixty, eighty, ninety, a hundred, a hundred and ten, four singles. Why don't you take it?"

"Me?"

"A woman's incomplete without money." He folded the bills into the clip, scooped coins from the floor, and dropped it all into her palm. "Nora-pie, would you be so kind as to go into the bathroom and tear down the shower curtain?"

She went into the bathroom and groped for the switch. Glaring light bounced from the walls, white floor, and mirror. A translucent curtain hung down over the side of the white porcelain tub. Nora reached up and tore at the curtain. One by one, plastic rings popped off the rail.

When she carried the sheet into the bedroom, the light from the bathroom fell across the floor. "Perfect." Dart cut away the dead man's underpants and spread the shower curtain next to the body. A flap of underwear lay across Sheldon Dolkis's groin. "Let's see how our boy was hung." He ripped away the cloth. "Had to jerk off with tweezers."

Dart draped his suit jacket over the back of a chair. He rolled his sleeves halfway up his biceps and tucked his necktie in between the third and fourth buttons of his shirt. Kneeling beside the body, he slid his arms under the back, grunted, and rolled it onto the shower curtain. He moved up and rolled it over again, so that the body faced upward. He fussed with it, centering it on the plastic sheet. "All righty." He rubbed his hands together and looked fondly down at the corpse. "Do you know what I wanted to be when I grew up?"

"A doctor," Nora said.

"A *surgeon.* Loved cutting things up. *Loved* it. What did the great Leland Dart say? 'I'm not wasting my money on some medical school that'll flunk you out in a year.' Thanks a bunch, Dad. Lucky me, I found a way to be a surgeon despite him."

He lowered himself to his knees and picked up the stag-handled knife. "You've seen a million operations, right? Watch this. Tell me if I'm any good." She watched him slide the knife beneath the breastbone and draw it down the mound of the belly, bisecting the line of hair. Yellow fat oozed from the wound. "I don't suppose, when reminiscing about his dear old Yale days, your husband ever mentioned an organization called the Hellfire Club?"

55

SHE GAVE A start of surprise and said, "You did that very well."

"Of course," he said, annoyed. "I'm a born surgeon. What's the essential quality of a born surgeon? A passion for cutting people up. Used to practice on animals when I was a kid, but I didn't want to be a *vet,* for God's sake." He cut away wide semicircles of flesh on either side of the incision, then carved off soft yellow fat and dropped it onto the shower curtain. In a few seconds, he had exposed the lower part of the rib cage and the peritoneum. "Want to take a look at Shelley's liver—a real beauty, I bet—and his pancreas, check him for gallstones and anything else that might turn up, but I have to get this huge, ugly membrane, the greater omentum, out of the way. Look at that fat. This guy could keep a soap factory running for a month."

"You've been doing your homework."

"Medical books are much more enjoyable than the nonsense I read for my old darlings." He sliced through the thick, fatty membrane and peeled it back, then began probing the abdominal cavity.

"The Hellfire Club?" Nora asked.

"You know about the secret societies at Yale, don't you? The *secret* secret societies are a lot more interesting. The Hellfire Club is one of the oldest. Used to be you could only get in through heredity, but during the forties they started taking in outsiders. Lincoln Chancel was buddy-buddy with some old sharks who were members, and they bent the rules to get Alden in, so Davey was eligible, and he joined. I came in when I was a sophomore, so we were there together for a year. Jesus Christ, look at this."

He sliced the peritoneal attachments and pulled the liver out of the body. "Right lobe is about half the size it's supposed to be. See all this discoloration? A decent liver is red. Here, around the vena cava, this big vessel, it's turning black. The texture is all wrong. I don't know what the hell old Shelley had, but his bad habits were killing him." Dart placed the severed liver on the plastic sheet and cut it in half. "What a mess. Hepatic artery looks like a toothpick. . . . I don't know why Davey stayed in the club. Probably his old man thought it would toughen him up. He was all wrong for the place. It was about cutting loose, getting down and dirty. Sex, drugs, and rock 'n' roll."

This was interesting, even within the comforting membrane. Most of what Davey had said to her had been a lie. "Where did you meet?"

"Used to rent a couple of floors in the North End. When the neighbors got suspicious, we'd move into another building. Point was, once you got inside the club, you could do whatever you liked. Nobody was allowed to criticize anything another member chose to do. Don't question, don't hesitate, don't judge. Naturally, we had a few ODs. No problem, dump the body in a vacant lot. People in your generation think they invented drugs. Compared to us, you were pussies. Hash, LSD, angel dust, speed, heroin, bennies, lots and lots of coke. Now, that's one area where little Davey felt right at home. He'd go three and four nights without sleeping, shoving blow up his nose with both hands, babble about Hugo Driver until he finally passed out."

Nora watched his hands working inside the gaping body.

"Hate the smell of bile. If people think shit smells bad, they ought to take a whiff of the stuff that goes through their gallbladder." Dart brought a roll of toilet paper from the bathroom to mop up a dark brown stain spreading across the sheet. He sliced the pear-shaped sac of Dolkis's gallbladder in half and crowed. "What did I tell you? Gallstones. At least ten of 'em. If his liver didn't kill him first, Shelley was in line for some painful surgery." He wrapped the mutilated gallbladder in toilet paper and set it aside, but the wet, dead stench still hung in the air.

"I want to check out this guy's pancreas and look at his spleen. The spleen is a gorgeous organ."

"Did you bring girls to the Hellfire Club?" asked Nora.

"Any woman who walked into that place was fair game. Even Davey's crazy girlfriend, Amy something or other, came there once. Made her even crazier than she was before. Then Davey started turning up with this chick. If Amy was strange, this babe was *completely* weird. Men's clothes. Short hair." Dart was severing connective tissue and ducts with quick, accurate movements of his knife. "You'd see this cute little thing sitting alongside Davey and think *Yeah, I'll jump her bones,* and then for some reason you realized no, no way. Also, every word she said about herself was a lie. *Hello.*"

Dart held up a dripping, foot-long pancreas with a gray-brown growth the size of a golf ball drooping from its head. "I've seen tumors before, but this baby is something special. Shelley, your body should be on display in a glass case. I can't wait to see what his heart looks like."

"She was a liar?"

"Have you noticed your hubby has a tendency to expand upon the truth? This girl was even worse. I guess little Davey had a propensity for crazy ladies." He put down the diseased pancreas and gave her a twist of a smile.

"What was her name?"

"Who knows? She even lied about that. As you may have noticed, I can tell when people are lying. She was about the best liar I ever met, but she was a liar, all right. According to Davey, she went to New Haven College, and came from some little town up around here, I forget which. Chester, something like that. Granville, maybe. I checked her out. She wasn't registered at New Haven College, and no family with her last name lived in that town."

"Could it have been Amherst?"

"Amherst? No. Why?"

"Davey once told me a story about an old girlfriend of his who said she came from Amherst. I thought it might be the same girl."

He gave her a long, straight look. "The lad probably reeled in wacko ladies by the hundreds. He's very pretty, after all. Anyhow, he spent almost all his free time with this one. I don't suppose they spent the whole time talking about Hugo Driver, but whenever *I* saw them together she was after him to get his father to do something or other with *Night Journey.* She was totally focused on that book. The girl was after him to let her see the manuscript—something like that. I know he tried, but it didn't work."

Dart manipulated the knife and held up a purple, fist-shaped organ. "Looks surprisingly okay, considering the company it kept."

"What happened to the girl?"

He placed the spleen beside the oozing liver. "One night I happened to walk into our favorite pizza place, and who should I see in the back of the room but Davey and his friend. Your husband-to-be was polluted. I was hardly sober myself, but I wasn't nearly as bad as Davey. He waved me over to their table, pointed at me, and said, 'There's your answer.' The girl said no. It had to be the two of them, no one else. I was the answer. No, I wasn't. The girl was stone-cold sober. Finally I figured out that until he got loaded, she'd wanted him to drive the two of them someplace, and he still wanted to do it. She kept saying they could wait until the next day. That fool you married was insisting on going that night—to Shorelands. She wanted to see the place, so tonight was the night. I could drive. All this without asking me if I had the slightest interest in driving across Massachusetts at night.

"The girl refused to have me drive them, so naturally I decided to do it. Along the way I planned to inform Davey of his girlfriend's inventions. *Then* we'd have an entertaining scene, wouldn't we?

"Davey was too drunk to see that the girl was furious. He couldn't drive, and she didn't have a license. I solved their problem. 'It's no good anymore,' the girl kept saying, but he wouldn't listen to her. Well, off we go. Davey passed out in the backseat. The girl sat up front with me, but she wouldn't say any more than it took to give me directions. We got about a hundred miles down the highway, and Davey woke up and started quoting from *Night Journey*. I wish I had whatever you're supposed to use to cut through ribs, because this knife isn't making it. I got through the cartilage and stripped away a lot of the intercostal muscle, but I'm going to have to break 'em off with my hands."

Dart grasped a rib and pulled, swearing to himself. The curved bone gradually moved upward and then snapped in half. "Good enough, I guess." He sliced through more cartilage.

"I tried to drown him out with the radio, but all I could find was disco shit, which I *hate*. Know what I like? Real music. Kind of singers you never hear anymore. Give me a good wop baritone and I'm a happy camper. Ah, getting a good view of the heart now.

"There we are, a hundred miles into the middle of nowhere, Davey spouting Hugo Driver, the girl sitting like a marble statue. All of a sudden she has to pee. Which makes me see red, because we just *passed* a rest stop, why didn't she pipe up then? Like a peek into this girl's mind?

'Whenever possible,' she says, 'I like to pee in the woods like Pippin Little, because I *am* Pippin Little.' This seemed like the moment to tell Davey what I know about the bitch, so I do. I have to repeat it two or three times, but he does finally get it. She may be Pippin Little, but she sure as hell isn't who she told him she was. In fact, it hits him, drunk as he is, that what she was calling herself was a hell of a lot like the name of *another* character in *Night Journey.* The girl doesn't turn a fucking hair. She says, 'Turn off at the next exit. I can get out there.'

" 'If you won't tell me who you really are, you can get out and stay out,' Davey yells.

"We're so far in the country it's like a coal mine. I get off the highway, and we're at the edge of these woods. Davey makes a grab for the girl, but she zips out and runs into the trees. Davey starts swearing at me—now it's *my* fault she's a liar. After ten delightful minutes, I finally suggest that his friend is taking an extremely long time to finish her business. He piles out and charges around in the woods for about half an hour. The hell with this, he says, let's go back to New Haven and this time I'm driving. He gets behind the wheel and guns the car around. All of a sudden the bitch is right in front of the car, and then she disappears. Our hero starts crying. Then he whips a gram out of his pocket, snorts about half of it, and drives away."

"He left her there?"

"Drove away. Eighty miles an hour all the way back to dear old Yale, that maker of men, not to mention hit-and-run drivers."

"What happened after that?"

"Crazy Amy got out of the locked ward, and Davey went straight back to mooning over her. Never came back to the Hellfire Club. Boo hoo, we all sure missed him."

"Is there a Hellfire Club in New York?"

Dart looked up at her, eyes narrowed. "As a matter of fact, yes. In the twenties, a group of alums decided there was no reason the fun should stop on graduation day. More formal than the New Haven thing—servants, a concierge, great food. The dues are high enough to keep out the riffraff, but the essential spirit remains the same. Why do you ask?"

"I was wondering if Davey ever went there."

His eyes shone. "Might have spotted that gutless hit-and-run artist within the hallowed halls a time or two. Avoided him like the plague, of course."

"Of course."

"Darling heart, would you do me a favor? The hammer I bought in Fairfield is in a bag on the backseat. If I'm going to break these ribs, I might as well do it a little more efficiently."

Entirely amused, Dart stood up and watched her move toward the door. Nora went outside, where the air was of an astonishing sweetness. She looked back and saw Dart just inside the door, holding his arms, stained red to the elbows like a butcher's, out from his sides. Amusement radiated from his eyes and face. "You should smell the air out here," she said.

"I prefer the air in here," Dart said. "Funny old me."

Heat shimmered off the top of the car. Nora leaned into the oven of the interior and opened a bag on the laden backseat. The long wooden shaft of the hammer met the palm of her hand. Her heart leaped in her chest, and her face grew hot beneath the makeup. She became aware that the thick balloon filled with emotional exhaust fumes was no longer about her. She had not noticed its departure, but it had departed all the same. Dart beckoned her back into the room with a courtly wave.

"Close the door, my dear. Only a tiny test, but you passed it beautifully."

"You're a fun guy."

"I am!" He pointed a red finger at Sheldon Dolkis. "I want you right beside me. You're a nurse, you can assist. Kneel on a pillow, so as not to hurt your knees. Considerate me. Take one off that scabby bed."

Nora knelt on the pillow and set the hammer down next to her right thigh. Dart squatted and pointed into the body cavity. "That aortic arch looks more like a slump, and the old pulmonary trunk is like a worn-out inner tube. I want to see his superior vena cavity. Bet it's a terrible mess." He leaned forward to peer between the ribs on the far side of the chest, clearly expecting her to do the same.

Nora's heart jumped like a fish. She picked up the hammer, still wondering if she could actually go through with it. Then she planted her left hand in the middle of his back as if for support and smashed the hammer into the side of his head.

Dart exhaled sharply and almost fell into the open body. He caught himself by sinking his hands into the cavity and tried to get to his feet. Nora leaped up and battered the back of his head. Dart sagged to his knees. She cocked back her arm and whacked him again. He toppled sideways and struck the floor.

Nora crouched over him, the hammer raised. Her heart beat wildly, and her breath came in quick, short pants. Dart's mouth hung open, and a sliver of drool wobbled from his lower lip.

She dropped to one knee and thrust her hand into his pocket for the car keys. A second later, she was running through the sunlight. She started the car and backed away from the motel. Through the open door, she saw Dick Dart rising to his knees. She jolted to a stop and tried to shift into drive but in her panic moved the indicator to neutral. When she hit the accelerator, the engine raced, but the car slid downhill. She pressed the brake pedal and looked back at the room. Dart was staggering toward the door.

Her hand fluttered over the shift lever and moved the car into drive. Waving his red arms, Dick Dart was racing toward her.

The car shot forward. She twisted the wheel, and the right front fender struck him with an audible thump. Like the girl in the story, he disappeared. Nora fastened her shaking hands on the wheel and sped downhill.

BOOK VI

FAMILIAR MONSTERS

Pippin understood the nature of his task. That was not the problem. The problem was that the task was impossible.

56

Streets, buildings, stoplights flew past her, other drivers honked and jolted to standstills. Pedestrians shouted, waved. For a lengthy period Nora drove the wrong way down a one-way street. She had escaped, she was escaping, but where? She drove aimlessly through a foreign city, now and then startled by the stranger's face reflected in the rearview mirror. She supposed that this stranger was looking for the expressway but had no idea of where to go once she got there.

She pulled to the side of the road. The world outside the car consisted of large, handsome houses squatting, like enormous dogs and cats, on spacious lawns. It came to her that she had seen this place before, and that something unpleasant had happened to her here. Yet the neighborhood was not unpleasant, not at all, because it contained . . .

Sprinklers threw arcs of water across the long lawns. She was in a cul-de-sac ending in a circle before the most imposing house on the street, a three-story red-brick mansion with a bow window, a dark green front door, and a border of bright flowers. She had arrived at Longfellow Lane, and the house with the bow window belonged to Dr. Daniel Harwich.

Her panic melted into relief. She had reached the end of the street before she realized that Mrs. Lark Pettigrew Harwich might not welcome the sudden appearance of one of her husband's old girlfriends, however desperate that old girlfriend might be. At that moment, coffee mug in one hand, Dan Harwich emerged from the depths of the room and stood at the bow window to survey his realm. A fist struck her heart.

Harwich gave Nora's car a mildly curious glance before taking a sip of coffee and raising his head to look at the sky. He had changed little since she had last seen him. The same weary, witty competence inhabited his face and gestures. He turned and disappeared into the room. Somewhere behind him, pouring coffee for herself in a redesigned kitchen, very likely lurked wife number two.

Nora cramped the wheel and sped out of the circle, wondering how on earth she was going to find a telephone. She turned left onto Longfellow Street, another treeless length of demi-mansions old and new, all but identical to Longfellow Lane except for being a real street instead of a cul-de-sac and the absence from any of its numerous bay windows of Dr. Daniel Harwich. At the next corner, she turned left onto Bryant Street, another stretch of wide green lawns and sturdy houses, and began to feel that she would spend the rest of her life moving down these identical streets past these identical houses.

At the next corner she turned left again, this time into Whittier Street, then into Whitman Street, another replica of Longfellow Lane, the chief difference being that instead of an asphalt circle at the end of the block there was a stop sign at an intersection, and directly beside the stop sign stood the metal hood and black rectangle of a public telephone.

57

THREE FEET FROM a chintz sofa piled with cushions, Nora felt herself slip into a collapse. She sank a quarter of an inch, then another quarter of an inch, taking Dan Harwich's unresisting hand with her. Then an arm wrapped around her waist, a hand gripped her shoulder, and she stopped moving.

Harwich pulled her upright. "I could carry you the rest of the way."

"I'll make it."

He loosened his grip, and Nora stepped around the side of a wooden coffee table and let him guide her to the sofa.

"Do you want to lie down?"

"I'll be okay. It's letting go of all that tension, I guess." She slumped back against the cushions. Harwich was kneeling in front of her, holding both her hands and staring up at her face.

He stood up, still staring at her face. "How did you get away from this Dart?"

"I hit him with a hammer, then I ran into him with the car."

"Where?"

"Outside some motel, I don't remember. Don't call the police. Please."

He looked down at her, chewing his lower lip. "Back in a sec."

Nora put an arm behind her back and pulled out a stiff round cushion embroidered with sunflowers on one side and a farmhouse on the other. There was still an uncomfortable number of cushions back there. She did not remember the chintz sofa or this profusion of cushions from her earlier visit to Longfellow Lane. Helen Harwich's living room had been sober and dark, with big square leather furniture on a huge white rug.

Now, apart from the mess, the room was like a decorator's idea of an English country house. Dirty shirts lay over the back of a rocking chair. One running shoe lay on its side near the entrance to the front hall. The table on which she had nearly cracked her head was littered with old newspapers, dirty glasses, and an empty Pizza Hut carton.

Harwich came back with a tumbler so full that a trail of shining dots lay behind him. "Drink some water before it slops all over the place, sorry." He handed her the wet tumbler and knelt in front of her. Nora swallowed and looked around for a place to put the glass. Harwich took it and set it on the table.

"You're going to leave a ring," she said.

"I don't give a shit." He grasped her right hand in both of his. "Why don't you want me to call the police?"

"Right before I got abducted by Dick Dart, I was about to be charged with about half a dozen crimes. It sounds a little funny, given what happened, but I'm pretty sure that kidnapping was one of them. That's why I was in the police station."

Harwich stopped kneading her hand. "You mean if you go to the police you'll get arrested?"

"Think so."

"What did you do?"

She pulled her hand away from his. "Do you want to hear what happened, or do you just want to call the FBI and have me hauled away?"

"The FBI?"

"Couple of real charming guys," she said. "They had no trouble at all assuming I was guilty."

Harwich stood up and moved to the other end of the sofa.

"If this is too much for you, I'll get out of here," Nora said. "I have to find this doctor. If I can remember his name."

"You're not going anywhere," Harwich said. "I want to hear the whole story, but before that, let's see if we can take care of Dick Dart."

He stood up and took a cellular phone from the mantel. Nora started to protest. "Don't worry, I won't say anything about you. Try to remember the name of that motel." He went across the room and pulled a telephone book from beneath a stack of magazines and newspapers.

"I can't."

"Did it have a sign?" He held his finger over a number.

"Sure, but . . ." She saw the sign. "It was called the Hillside. 'Like the strangler,' Dart said."

"Like the strangler?"

"The Hillside Strangler."

"Jesus." Harwich punched numbers. "Listen to me. I'm only going to say this once. The escaped murderer Dick Dart checked into the Hillside Motel in Springfield this morning. He may be injured." He turned off the phone and replaced it on the mantel. "I suppose you'll feel safer once Dart is off the streets."

"You have no idea."

"So talk," Harwich said.

She told him about Natalie Weil and Holly Fenn and Slim and Slam, she told him about Daisy's book and Alden's ultimatum, she described the scene in the police station, Natalie's accusation, her abduction, Ernest Forrest Ernest, the Chicopee Inn. She told Harwich that Dart had raped her. She told him about the library and the shopping spree and being made up; she told him about Sheldon Dolkis.

While she spoke, Harwich scratched his head, squinted, circled the room, flopped into a chair, bounced up again, interjected sympathetic, astounded, essentially noncommittal remarks, and finally urged her into the kitchen. After gathering up the dirty glasses and utensils and stashing them in or around the sink, he made an omelette for them both. He leaned forward, his chin on his elbow. "How do you get yourself into these situations?"

She put down her fork, her appetite gone. "What I want to know is, how do I get out of it?"

Harwich tilted his head, raised his eyebrows, and spread his hands in a pantomime of uncertainty. "Do you want me to take a look at you? You should have an examination."

"On your kitchen table?"

"I was thinking that we could use one of the beds, but if you prefer, I could take you to my office. I have an operation this afternoon, but I'm free until then."

"There's no need for that," Nora said.

"No serious bleeding?"

"I bled a little, but it stopped. Dan, what should I *do*?"

He sighed. "I'll tell you what baffles me about all this. This woman, this Natalie Weil, accuses you of beating her, starving her, God knows what, and the FBI and most of your local police force believe her. Why would she lie about it?"

"Screw you, Dan."

"Don't get mad, I'm just asking. Does she have anything to gain from having you put away?"

"Can we turn on the radio?" Nora asked. "Or the TV? Maybe there'll be something about Dart."

Harwich jumped up and switched on a radio beside the silver toaster at the end of a counter. "I guess I don't have the fugitive mind-set." He moved the dial to an all-news station, where a man in a helicopter was describing a traffic slowdown on a highway.

"The fugitive mind-set," Nora said.

"I'm only a jaded old neurosurgeon. I lost all my old wartime instincts a long time ago. But I'd better hide your car."

"Why?"

"Because about a minute after they show up at the motel, they're going to be looking for an old green Ford with a certain license plate. And it's in my driveway."

"Oh!"

The telephone rang. Harwich glanced at the wall phone in the kitchen and then back at Nora before pushing himself away from the table. "I'll take this in the other room."

No longer certain of what she made of Dan Harwich or he of her, Nora turned back to the radio. An announcer was telling Hampshire and Hampden counties that the temperatures were going to stay in the high eighties for the next two or three days, after which severe thundershowers were expected. In the next room Harwich raised his voice to say, "Of course I know! Do you think I'd forget?"

She stood up and carried her cup to the coffeemaker. Dishes and glasses filled the sink, and stains of various kinds and colors lay on the counter. Then she heard the words "Richard Dart" come from the radio.

". . . this vicinity. Police in Springfield discovered a mutilated male corpse and signs of struggle in a room at the Hillside Motel on Tilton Street. Springfield police have indicated the possibility that the fugitive serial killer has been injured, and are conducting a thorough search of the Tilton Street area. Residents are warned that Dart is armed and extremely dangerous. He is thirty-eight years old, six feet, two inches tall, weighs two hundred pounds, has fair hair and brown eyes, and was last seen wearing a gray suit and a white shirt. The fate and whereabouts of his hostage, Mrs. Nora Chancel, are likewise unknown."

Smiling an utterly mirthless smile, Dan Harwich came back into the kitchen and stopped moving at the sound of Nora's name.

"Mrs. Chancel is described as being forty-nine years of age, five-six in height, slender, weighing approximately one hundred and ten pounds, with short, dark brown hair and brown eyes, last seen wearing blue jeans and a long-sleeved dark blue shirt. Anyone seeing Mrs. Chancel or any person who appears to be Mrs. Chancel should immediately contact the police or the local office of the FBI.

"Police have not yet been able to identify Dart's latest victim.

"In other local news, State Senator Mitchell Kramer resolutely denies recent charges of mishandling of . . ."

Harwich switched off the radio. "Give me the keys." Nora handed them over.

"Your life is a lot more adventurous than mine." He smiled almost apologetically.

"I'm making you uncomfortable, so I'll go," she said. "You don't have to keep me around out of charity because we used to be friends."

"We were a lot more than that. Maybe I ought to be uncomfortable now and then." He grinned at her, and his eyes flickered, and for a second the old Dan Harwich shone through the surface of this warier, more cynical version. "Back in a flash."

"In the meantime, try to think about what I ought to do, will you? Can you?"

"I'm thinking about it already," Harwich said.

58

WHEN HARWICH CAME back, Nora said, "I get the feeling your wife isn't expected anytime soon."

"Don't worry about her." Harwich arched his back. "Lark's not in the picture anymore."

"I'm sorry. When did that happen?"

"The disaster took place on the day we got married. I think I got involved with her to get away from Helen. You remember Helen, I suppose?"

"How could I forget Helen?"

"Probably the only time you were thrown out of somebody's house." Harwich laughed. "In the end, she didn't want to live here and I did, so

I bought her out. *Bought* is the word, believe me. Two million in alimony, plus ten thousand a month in support payments. Thank God, last year she suckered some other poor bastard into marrying her. At least I covered my ass when I married Lark. She signed a prenuptial—two hundred fifty thousand, all her clothes and jewelry and her car, that's it. On the whole, I should have been smarter than to marry someone named Lark Pettigrew. I let her redo the whole place, and now I'm living in this dollhouse." He gave Nora a rueful, affectionate look. "The woman I should have married was you, but I was too stupid to know it. There you were, right in front of me."

"I would have married you," Nora said.

"That last time? You turned up here like Vietnam all over again, I mean, you were *wild*. And I was already seeing Lark, anyhow. What I'm saying is, I should have married you instead of that miserable witch Helen."

"Why didn't you?"

"I don't know. Do you know? It's probably better we didn't. I don't seem to be very good at marriage." He made a wide gesture with one arm and laughed. "Lark took off about three weeks ago, and the week after that I fired the cleaning woman. I don't mind the mess. Damn woman used to rearrange all my books and papers. Excuse me, but I never understood why I should have to learn my *cleaning woman's* filing system."

She smiled.

"Christ, what's the matter with me?" He clamped his eyes shut. "All this stuff happening to you, and I'm talking about bullshit instead of helping you."

"You're already helping me," Nora said. "You don't know how often I think about you."

He leaned over the top of his chair and closed one hand around one of hers, squeezed, and released it. "I think you should stay here at least a day or two, maybe more. I have that operation this afternoon, but I'll come back around four or five, get some food, we can see if they picked up Dart, talk things out. Let me pamper you."

"That sounds wonderful," Nora said. "You'd really let me stay?"

Harwich leaned forward and took her hand again. "If you even try to get away, I'll lock you in the attic."

Her pulse seemed to stop.

"I can't believe I said that." He gripped her hand, which wanted to shrink to a stone. "Nora, you're like a godsend, you remind me of real life, can you understand that?"

"I remind you of real life."

"Yeah, whatever that is. You do." Harwich let go of her hand and wiped his eyes, which had suddenly filled with tears. "Sorry. I'm supposed to be helping you, and instead I come unglued." He tried to smile.

"It's okay," Nora said. "My life is a lot messier than yours."

He rubbed his finger beneath his nose and withdrew into himself for a moment, gazing unseeing at the plates stacked at the edge of the table. "Let's make up your bed." He stood up, and she did too, returning his smile. "Do you want to bring in your bags, or anything?"

"Right now, all I want to do is rest."

"Sounds good to me," Harwich said.

59

AFTER STOPPING AT the linen closet for paisley sheets and matching pillowcases so new they were still in the package, they went into a front bedroom with flowered blue wallpaper and knotty pine furniture disposed around the edges of a pink-and-blue hooked rug. A rocker made of lacquered twigs sat in front of the window. Harwich ripped the sheets from their wrappers before flipping the dark blue duvet off the bed.

"The bed's comfortable, but stay out of that chair." Harwich nodded at the rocker. "One of Lark's inspirations—a two-thousand-dollar chair that tears holes in your sweaters."

He snapped a fitted sheet across the bed. Nora slid the top corner over the mattress as Harwich did the same on his side. They moved down the bed to fit the sheet over the bottom corners. Together they straightened and smoothed the top sheet and tucked it under the foot of the bed.

"Hospital corners," Harwich said. "Be still, my heart." They began stuffing pillows into the cases.

"Dan, what am I going to do?"

He shoved his hands in his pockets and stepped toward her, the playfully ironic manner instantly discarded. "First of all, we have to see if the police pick up Dart, or, even better, find his body. Then we want to find out if the FBI is still after you." He put his right hand on her shoulder.

"You don't think I should try to see this doctor?"

"Aren't I good enough for you?" He tried to look wounded.

"The one Dick Dart wanted to kill."

"The only thing you should do, if you still care about Davey, is tell him the Chancel House lawyers are selling them down the river. That might straighten out your problems with the old man."

Dan Harwich seemed to have admitted fresh air and sunlight into a dank chamber where Nora had been spinning in darkness.

"If I were you," Harwich said, "I'd take his father for everything I could get. That tough old number from up the road in Northampton, Calvin Coolidge, wasn't wrong: the business of America is business."

Nora closed her eyes against a wave of nausea and heard the shufflings of a gathering of demons. "Don't do this to me," she said. "Please."

Harwich put an arm around her waist and guided her to the side of the bed. "Sorry. You need rest, and I'm talking your ear off."

"I'll be okay." She clasped her hand on his wrist, feeling completely divided: one part of her wanted Harwich to stay with her, and another, equal part wanted him to leave the room. "I should apologize, not you."

"Stretch out."

She obeyed. He went to the foot of the bed, untied her shoes, and pulled them off. "Thanks."

"You remember this doctor's name?"

She shook her head. "Something Irish."

"That narrows the field. How about O'Hara? Michael O'Hara?"

She shook her head again.

"The man you want is gay, isn't he?" He began kneading the sole of her right foot with his thumbs. "I can't think of more than three gay doctors in the whole town, and they're all younger than I am." What he was doing to her foot set off reverberations and echoes throughout her body. "Did you hear his first name?"

She nodded.

"What letter did it start with?"

Without any hesitation at all, Nora said, "M."

"Michael. Morris. Montague. Max. Miles. Manny. Mark. What else? Monroe."

"Mark."

"Mark?" He dug his thumbs into her left foot, and a tingle wound all the way up her backbone. "Mark. With an Irish last name, and gay to boot. Let's see. Conlon, Conboy, Congdon, Condon, Mulroy, Murphy, Morphy, Brophy, O'Malley, Joyce, Tierney, Kiernan, Boyce, Mulligan, this isn't easy. Burke. Brannigan. Sullivan. Boyle."

"Hold on. That was close. Sounds like Boyle." She held her breath and closed her eyes, and a name floated toward her out of the darkness. "Foyle. His name was Mark Foyle."

"Mark Foil?"

"That's the name."

He laughed. "Yes, but you were thinking F-o-y-l-e, which is why you thought it was an Irish name. Mark Foil is about as Irish as the queen of England, and his name is Foil as in *tinfoil.* Or as I heard him say once, Foil as in *fencing.*" He spoke the last phrase in a mincing, affected voice.

"You know him."

"Foiled again," Harwich said, using the same swishy voice.

"Is he like that?"

"He couldn't afford to be. The man was a GP for upwards of forty years, and this isn't the most liberated place on the face of the earth."

"Where does he live?"

"The good part of town," Harwich said. "Unlike we lesser mortals, Dr. Foil can behold a great many trees when he glances out of his leaded windows." He patted her foot. "Look, if you want to see the guy, I'll take you over there. But the guy's one of those patrician queers."

The word *queers* chilled Nora. It sounded ugly and wrong, especially coming from Dan Harwich, but she pushed aside her distaste. "You think he wouldn't have time for me?"

"Foil never had time for *me,* if that's any indication. God, you should see his boyfriend."

The telephone down the corridor began ringing. "You could probably use a nap," Harwich said.

"I could try."

Released, he gave her foot a last pat, went smiling toward the door, and closed it behind him. Nora heard his footsteps racing toward the telephone, which must have been in his bedroom. A moment later, in a voice loud enough to be overheard through the door, he said, "Okay, I know, I know I did."

She thought she might as well take a bath. On the marble shelf beside the antique sink in the bathroom lay three new toothbrushes still in their transparent pastel coffins and a pump dispensing baking soda and peroxide toothpaste. Nora struggled with one of the toothbrush containers until she managed to splinter one side. Above the tub, modern fittings protruded from the pink-tiled wall. Checking for the necessary supplies, Nora saw a tall, half-filled bottle of shampoo and a matching bottle of conditioner, both for dry or damaged hair, surrounded by a great number of hotel giveaway containers. A used shower cap lay over the showerhead like a felt mute over the bell of a trombone.

Lark had moved out of Harwich's bed before she had moved out of his house. On a shelf above the towels Nora saw a deodorant stick, a half-empty bottle of mouthwash, a Murine bottle, a nearly empty aspirin bottle, an emery board worn white in a line down the middle, a couple of kinds of moisturizer and skin cream, and a tall spray bottle of Je Reviens, almost full. She began pulling the T-shirt out of her jeans.

Someone behind her said, "Hold it," and she uttered a squeak and jumped half an inch off the ground.

"Sorry, I didn't mean to . . ."

She turned around, her hand at the pulse beating in her throat, to find an apologetic-looking Dan Harwich inside the bathroom door.

"I thought you heard me."

"I was getting ready to take a bath."

"Actually," Harwich said, "maybe we ought to get in touch with Mark Foil. In case Dart did get away, as unlikely as that is, we have to make sure Mark is protected."

"Well, fine," Nora said, unsure what to make of this sudden reversal.

"We might be able to go over there this morning." His whole tempo had sped up, like Nora's pulse. Smiling in an almost insistent way, he went sideways through the bathroom door, silently asking her to come with him.

"You changed your mind in a hurry."

"You know my whole problem? I can't get out of my stupid patterns. I think Mark Foil looks down on me, and I resent that. An egotistical voice in my head says I'm a hotshot and he's only a retired GP, who does he think he is, screw him. I shouldn't let that kind of crap keep me from doing what's right."

Nora followed him into a huge bedroom with a four-poster bed and a big-screen television set. Clothes lay scattered across the floor. "What was Dart going to say to these people? How was he going to get into their houses?"

"I was supposed to be writing something about that summer at Shorelands—the summer of 1938. Everybody knows about Hugo Driver, but the other guests have never been given their due. Something like that."

"Sounds good," Harwich said. "If I have a talent for anything besides surgery, it's for bullshit. Who do you want to be?" He kicked aside a pile of old socks and sweat clothes on his way to a bookcase.

"Gosh, I don't know," Nora said.

"What's a lady-writer kind of name? Emily Eliot. You're my old friend Emily Eliot, we went to Brown together, and now you're writing a piece about whatsit, Shorelands. Let's see, you got a Ph.D. from Harvard, you taught for a while, but quit to be a freelance writer." He was paging through a fat directory. "We have to make you a respectable citizen or Mark Foil won't give you the time of day. You published one book five years ago. It was about . . . hmm . . . Robert Frost? Was he ever at Shorelands?"

"Probably."

"Published by, who? Chancel House, I guess."

"And I was edited by Merle Marvell."

"Who? Oh, I get it, he's the big gun there."

"The biggest," said Nora, smiling.

"The whole point about lying is to be as specific as possible." He flipped a page and ran his finger down a list of names. "Here we go. Since this is Mark Foil we're talking about, he might be spending the summer on a Greek island, but let's give it a try. What was his boyfriend's name, Somebody Monk, like Thelonious?"

"Creeley," she said.

Harwich dialed the number and held up crossed fingers while it rang.

"Hello, I wonder if I could speak to Mark, please. . . . This is Dan Harwich. . . . Yes, of course, hello, Andrew, how are you? . . . Oh, are you? Wonderful. . . . Provincetown, how nice for you. . . . Well, if you think you could. . . . Thanks."

He put his hand over the receiver. "His boyfriend says they're going to Provincetown for the rest of the summer. Doesn't sound too good." He attended to the telephone again. "Mark, hello, this is Dan Harwich. . . . An old friend of mine from Brown, a writer, showed up here in the course of doing research for a book, and it turns out that she wants to get in touch with you. . . . That's right. Her name is Emily Eliot, and she's completely house-trained, Harvard Ph.D. . . . A poet named Creeley Monk? . . . Yes, that's right. She's interested in the people who were at a place called Shorelands with him, and it seems she came across your name somewhere. . . ."

He looked at her. "He wants to know where you saw his name."

Dart had not explained how he had heard of Mark Foil. "Doing research on Creeley Monk."

He repeated the phrase into the telephone. "No, she did a book before this. Robert Frost. . . . Yes, she's right here."

He held out the receiver. "Emily? Dr. Foil wants to talk to you." When she took it from him, he pretended he was working a shovel.

A clipped, incisive voice nothing like Harwich's effeminate parody said, "What is going on, Miss Eliot? Dan Harwich doesn't have any serious friends."

"I was a youthful mistake," Nora said.

"You can't be writing a book about Creeley Monk. Nobody remembers Creeley anymore."

"As Dan said, I'm working on a book about what happened at Shorelands during the summer of 1938. I think Hugo Driver's success unfairly eclipsed the other writers who were there."

"Do you have a publisher?"

"Chancel House."

A long silence. "Why don't you come over and let me take a look at you? We're going out of town this morning, but we still have some time."

60

A SLENDER, SMILING young man in a lightweight gray suit and black silk shirt opened the door of the stone house amid the oak trees and greeted them. Harwich introduced his friend Emily Eliot to the young man, Andrew Martindale, who looked straight into Nora's eyes, widened his smile, and instantly changed from a diplomatic male model into a real person filled with curiosity, humor, and goodwill. "It's wonderful that you're here," he said to Nora. "Mark is tremendously interested in your project. I wonder if you know what you're in for!"

Nora said, "I'm just grateful that he's willing to talk to me."

"Willing is hardly the word." Martindale let them pass into the house and then stepped backwards onto a riotous Persian rug. A broad staircase with shining wooden treads stood at the end of a row of white columns. "I'll take you into the library."

At the end of the row of columns, he opened a door into a book-lined room twice the size of Alden Chancel's library. In a dazzle of sunlight streaming through a window, a white-haired man in a crisp dark suit who looked unexpectedly familiar to Nora was standing beside an open file box on a gleaming table. He grinned at them over the top of his black half-glasses and held up a fat volume bound in red cloth.

"Andrew, you said I'd find it, and I did!"

Martindale said, "Nothing ever gets lost in this house, it just goes into hiding until you need it. And here, just in time to share your triumph, are Dan and Ms. Eliot. Would you like some coffee? Tea, maybe?"

This was addressed to Nora, who said, "If you have coffee ready, I'd love some."

The white-haired man tucked the red book under his arm, twinkled the half-glasses off his nose and folded them into his top pocket, and came loping across the room with his right hand extended. He was as smooth as mercury, and though he must have been in his mid-seventies, he looked as if he had undergone no essential physical changes since the age of fifty. He shook Harwich's hand, then turned, all alertness, interest, and curiosity, to Nora, who felt that with one probing glance Mark Foil instantly had comprehended all that was important within her, including a great deal of which she herself was unaware.

Harwich introduced them.

"Why don't we sit down so that you can tell me about yourself?" Foil indicated a plump sofa and two matching chairs near the bright window. A glass table with a neat stack of magazines stood within reach of the furniture. Nora took one end of the sofa, and Mark Foil slid into the other. As if he were cutting her loose, Harwich moved around the glass table, sat down in the chair beside the far end of the sofa, and lounged back.

"You haven't been sleeping very well, have you?" Foil asked.

"Not as much as I'd like," she said, surprised by the question.

"And you've been under a good deal of stress. If you don't mind my asking, why is that?"

She looked across at Harwich, who looked blandly back.

"The past few days have been kind of strange," she said.

"In what way?"

Looking at the kind, intelligent face beneath the white hair, Nora came close to admitting she was here under false pretenses. Mark Foil took in her hesitation and leaned forward without altering his expression.

Nora looked up from Foil to Harwich, who was staring at her in unhappy alarm.

"To tell you the truth," she said, "I've just become menopausal, and my body seems to have turned against me."

Foil leaned back, nodding, and behind him, unseen, Harwich flopped back into his chair. "Apart from your looking much too young, it makes a lot of sense," Foil said. "You're seeing your gynecologist, keeping a watch on what's going on?"

"Yes, thanks."

"I'm sorry if I seemed to pry. I'm like an old firehorse. My reflexes are stronger than my common sense. You and Dan were friends at Brown?"

"That's right."

"What was our eminent neurosurgeon like in those days?"

Nora looked across at our eminent neurosurgeon and tried to guess what he had been like at Brown. "Ferocious and shy," she said. "Always angry. He improved once he got into medical school."

Foil laughed. "Wonderful thing, the memory of an old friend. Keeps us from forgetting the cocoons from which we emerged."

"Some old friends remember more than you imagine possible," Harwich said.

"When I was that age, I read Browning and Tennyson until they came out of my ears. Not very up to date, I'm afraid. I suppose part of what I liked about Creeley's work was that although he was much better than I ever would have been, he wasn't very up to date, either. In medicine you have to be up to the minute to be any good at all, but I don't think that's true in the arts, do you?"

Andrew Martindale backed through the door holding a wide silver tray with three cups and a silver coffeepot in time to hear Foil's last sentence. He turned around to carry the tray toward the glass table. "Not again."

"But this time we have a Harvard Ph.D. and professional writer to consult. Emily, what do you think? Andrew and I have an ongoing argument about tradition versus the avant-garde, and he's completely pig-headed."

Martindale slid the tray onto the table, almost clipping the stack of magazines. Nora looked at them and knew she was lost, out of her depth, about to be exposed as a fraud. *Avec, Lingo,* and *Conjunctions,* which almost certainly represented Martindale's taste in literature, might as well have been written in Urdu, for all she knew of their contents.

"Settle our argument," Foil said.

Harwich said, "You shouldn't—"

"No, it's all right," Nora said. "I don't think you can settle it, and I don't think you want to, because you get too much fun out of it. Speaking for myself, I like both Benjamin Britten and Morton Feldman, and they probably hated each other's music." She looked around at the three men. Two of them were gazing at her with undisguised friendly approval, the third with undisguised astonishment.

Martindale smiled at them all and vanished.

As if following stage directions, the three of them picked up their cups and sipped the excellent coffee.

"You're right, we enjoy our ongoing argument, and part of what I like in Andrew is that he keeps trying to bring me up to date. And although Creeley's work is not the sort of thing he generally likes, he's been supportive of my efforts to publish a Collected Poems." Foil smiled at her. "It would be nice if your work finally permitted me to do him justice."

Nora felt like crawling out of the house.

"Merle must be your editor."

"Excuse me?"

"Merle Marvell. At Chancel House. Isn't he your editor?"

"Oh, yes, of course. I didn't realize you knew him."

"We've met him a half dozen times, but I don't really know him except by reputation. As far as I know, Merle is the only person at Chancel who'd have enough courage to take on a project which might turn out less than flattering to Lincoln. In fact, I have the idea that Merle is the *only* real editor at Chancel House."

Nora smiled at him, but this conversation was making her increasingly uncomfortable.

"Do you think Chancel House would be willing to publish something which puts Driver in a different light? Creeley didn't think much of him to begin with, and by the end of the summer, he positively detested the man."

"I think they're willing to present a balanced viewpoint," Nora said.

"Well, then." Foil placed his cup in its saucer. "I don't see why I shouldn't share this with you." He picked up the thick red book. "This is the journal Creeley kept during the last year of his life. I read it when I went through his papers after his death. Read it? I *studied* it. Like every suicide's survivor, I was looking for an explanation."

"Did you find one?"

"Does anyone? He had been disappointed the day before he killed himself, but I wouldn't have thought . . ." He shook his head, the memory of defeat clear in his eyes. "It still isn't easy. Anyhow, if you're interested in bringing the celebrated Hugo Driver down a peg or two, this will be useful to you. The man was a weakling. He was worse than that. It took a while for Creeley to convince anybody of the fact, but he was a thief."

61

NORA'S BLOOD SEEMED to slow. "Are you saying that he stole other writers' work?"

"Oh, they all do that, starting with Shakespeare. I'm talking about *real* theft. Unless you're saying that Driver actually plagiarized *Night Journey.* But if that was your story, I hardly suppose Chancel would be backing you." He grinned. "Instead of giving you a contract, they'd be more likely to put one out on you, Merle Marvell or no Merle Marvell."

Harwich chuckled, and Nora silenced him with a murderous glance. "Are you saying that Creeley Monk saw him steal things from the other guests?"

"Not just Creeley, thank goodness. You're interested in all of them, aren't you? In everything that went on that summer?"

She nodded.

"This is what I'm prepared to do." He gestured with the book. "I'll describe some of the contents of this journal. You continue your research while Andrew and I are on Cape Cod. When I get back, I'll talk to Merle Marvell and hear what he has to say about you and your project. I'd do that now, but we have limited time this morning. You have the most—ah, colorful—neurosurgeon in the state vouching for you, so I'm willing to go farther than I normally would, but I want to be as cautious as is reasonably possible. You have no objections, I assume?"

She thought hard for a moment while both men looked at her, Harwich shooting sparks of wrath and indignation, Foil calmly. "Why don't I send you the chapters after they're written? If you let me borrow the journal, I could have more time to sort through all the information, and I can get it back to you at the end of the summer."

He was already shaking his head. "I hold Creeley's papers in trust." Seeing that Nora was about to object, he raised an index finger. "However! When Merle tells me that you are indeed what you say you are, as I'm sure he will, I'll give you a copy of all the relevant pages from this diary. Do we have an agreement?"

Harwich gave her a grim, unhappy glance. Nora said, "I think that will be fine."

"Okay, then." A suppressed vitality came into his features, and Nora saw how eager he had been all along to do justice to his dead lover. "Let me tell you something about his background, so you'll be able to appreciate what sort of person Creeley was." He paused to gather his thoughts. "He was a year behind me at the Garand Academy, on a scholarship. We were all alike—except Creeley. Creeley was as conspicuous as a peacock in a field of geese.

"Creeley's father was a bartender, and his mother was an Irish immigrant. They lived in a little apartment above the bar, and he had to take two buses to get to school. Creeley turned up wearing big black work shoes, a hideous striped suit far too big for him, and a Buster Brown collar with a *velvet* bow tie. Of course, the older boys beat him up, and that was that for the Buster Brown collars, but he kept the velvet bow tie. That had been *his* idea. He'd read that poets wore velvet bow ties, and Creeley already knew he was a poet. He also knew, at the advanced age of fourteen, that he was sexually attracted to other males, although he pretended otherwise. In order to survive, he had to. But he didn't see any point in pretending about anything else.

"By his second year he resembled the rest of us. Because he was absolutely fearless, because he was such a *character,* he already had a place in the school. Everybody cherished him. It was remarkable. Here was this utterly philistine school, and Creeley Monk single-handedly made them—us—respect a literary vocation. In his junior year, he published a few poems in national magazines.

"I went to Harvard, and he came on a full scholarship a year later. It didn't take us long to become close. Creeley and I lived together while I was at medical school, and he moved to Boston when I had my internship and residency there. He got a job writing catalogue copy for a publishing house, and we had separate apartments in the same building, which was his choice. He didn't want to do anything that might compromise my career. But in every other way we were an established couple, and when I moved back here, he did, too. Again, we had separate apartments, and I went into practice with two older men. During this time, Creeley and I were like people in an open marriage. He was devoted to me, and God knows I was devoted to him, but he was promiscuous by nature, and he was commuting to Boston almost every day, so that was how it was.

"He began publishing in all kinds of journals and magazines, gave readings, won a few prizes. In 1937 *The Field Unknown* came out, and I'm happy to say it was nominated for a Pulitzer Prize. Georgina Weatherall invited him to Shorelands for the following July, and we both saw this as a great sign.

"In the end, he was disappointed. None of the writers he most admired were present, and two people there had not even published books—Hugo Driver and Katherine Mannheim. He had seen one story by Katherine Mannheim in a literary magazine, and rather liked it, but she had published a fair amount of poetry, which he liked a lot more. In person, she turned out be a very pleasant surprise. He had imagined her as a kind of a lost, waiflike little thing, and her sharpness and toughmindedness came as a surprise. There was something else he liked about her, too. I'll read you some of that from the diary. Hugo Driver was another matter. Creeley had read some of his stories in little magazines and thought they were weak tea. Even before Creeley became aware of his thieving, Driver made him uncomfortable. In his first letter back to me, he said Driver was 'dank and desperate,' which turned into a running joke. After a while, he was referring to Driver as 'D&D' in the diary, and then that became 'DD,' which became 'DeDe,' like the girl's name.

"The others were a mixed bag. Austryn Fain struck him as a clever nonentity, a sort of literary hustler who spent most of his time trying to charm Lincoln Chancel into giving him a lot of money for his next book. Then there was Bill Tidy. Creeley respected Tidy, and he loved his book, *Our Skillets*. They had a lot in common. So he went to Shorelands anticipating a kind of meeting of minds, but Tidy put up a rough-spoken, workingman front and refused to talk to him.

"And then there was the rising star of the gathering, Merrick Favor. Creeley was instantly attracted to him, but it was hopeless. I could see what was coming when he wrote that the first time he went to dinner in

Main House and saw Favor talking to Katherine Mannheim in a corner, he thought he was seeing me!"

Suddenly Nora realized that the reason Mark Foil had seemed like a known quantity to her was that he was an older version of the handsome young writer in the famous photograph. She managed to say, "Yes."

"I suppose he really did look like me, but that was all we had in common. Favor was straight as a die and a compulsive womanizer to boot. He and Austryn Fain both flirted with Katherine Mannheim, but she wouldn't have either one of them. She made fun of them. Even Lincoln Chancel made some kind of crude pass at her, and she demolished him with a joke. But you know the lure of what you can't get. Creeley developed a hopeless crush on Favor. It drove him crazy, and he enjoyed every frustrating second of it."

"You didn't mind?" Nora asked.

"If I'd minded that sort of thing, I couldn't have put up with Creeley for a week, much less all those years. He wasn't designed to be celibate. Do you know how the place was set up, how they lived, what their days were like?"

"Not in much detail," Nora said. "They lived in different houses, didn't they, and they had dinner together every night?"

Foil nodded. "Georgina Weatherall lived in Main House, and the guests were assigned to cottages scattered through the woods around the gardens. These were one- and two-story affairs originally built for the staff, back when the family who owned the place had an army of servants. Creeley was in Honey House, one of the smallest cottages, all by itself on the far side of the pond. He had only two tiny rooms and a saggy single bed, which made him very grumpy. As the only woman guest, Katherine Mannheim was put by herself in the next-largest guest house, Gingerbread, stuck back in the woods past the gardens. Austryn Fain and Merrick Favor shared Pepper Pot, and Lincoln Chancel and Dank and Desperate were installed in the biggest cottage, Rapunzel, which had a stone tower on one side and was halfway between Gingerbread and Main House. Chancel had the tower for himself. I suppose he commandeered it."

"I still don't really understand why Lincoln Chancel wanted to go there in the first place," Nora said, having just realized this. "He had his businesses to take care of, and he hardly had to spend a month in a kind of literary colony for the sake of Chancel House."

Foil started to answer and checked himself. "I always took his being there for granted, but he didn't have to subject himself to Georgina's selection of writers, did he? He wasn't there for the entire month, though, he showed up only for the last two weeks."

"The answer's obvious," Harwich said. The other two waited. "Money."

"Money?" Nora said.

"What else? The Weatheralls owned half of Boston. Lincoln Chancel was supposed to be richer than God, but didn't his whole empire turn belly-up pretty soon after all this? He was looking for cash to start up his publishing company."

"Anyhow," Foil said, "to get back to Shorelands, even the normal guests had no formal daily schedule. During the day they could do as they pleased as long as they stayed on the estate. If they wanted to work, the maids carried box lunches to the cottages. If they wanted to socialize, Georgina held court on the terrace. You could swim in the pond or play tennis on the courts. The gardens were famous. Guests wandered around the different areas, or sat on the benches and read. At six everyone gathered in Main House for drinks, and at seven, they went into the dining room. Let me read you something. This is what Creeley wrote when he got back to Honey House on his first night."

He opened the red book and flipped through pages until he found the entry he wanted.

> "The gods in charge of railways having seen to my arriving at this longed-for destination five hours late, thereby postponing the death of my illusions, I was escorted in haste by the alarming Miss W., an apparition in blazing, ill-assorted colors (purple, red, orange, and pastel blue) distributed among layers of scarves, shawls, gown, stockings, and shoes, also in a not-to-be-ignored profusion of monstrous jewels, also in ditto face paint, down a narrow path through the gardens—all splendid so far—to a narrower path leading at weary length to my abode, Honey House, a name which had implied rustic charm to susceptible me. In reality, rustic Hovel House is charmless. Miss W. pointed with a ring-encrusted finger to a tiny prison bedroom, a squalid kitchen alcove, a clunky desk where I am to Create! Create! Cawing, she 'left me to my devices.'
>
> "Whom do I see upon first entering the Baghdad of the Main House lounge but, sensibly engaged with a pretty boy, my life's ever-sensible companion? Salvation! He had arrived to rescue me from the Hovel! Down flaps Milady, attired in even gaudier rags, face a-glow with fresh paint, to screech introductions to

my own, yet not my own MF but his virtual doppelgänger, MF2, who in fact is last year's literary darling, Merrick Favor, and the boy, an actually not-terribly-androgynous young woman revealed to be Katherine Mannheim, whose work appeals to me. As does Katherine herself, due to her prickly unsentimental good nature, her stylish unstylishness, her caustic wit, and, not least, her readiness to admit dismay at our hostess and her realm. And also, alas, to the Favored one, due no doubt to all of the above save the last, Well-Favored being too polite for words, but more than these to her physical attractions. MF2 tolerates my intrusion, and we three discuss our current projects, I already in thrall to 2, he eyeing the girl. 2 at work on a novel, of course, at which KM declares herself 'unwriting' a novel. I ask about unwriting, and she replies, 'Just like writing, only in reverse.' We murmur admirations of Georgina, which 2 sweetly takes at face value. Among the others I recognize Bill Tidy from publicity photos—awkward, shy, and out of sorts, I must make common cause with him soon—and a bearded string bean who must be Austryn Fain. (At dinner I will be across from him, and yep, he is, fain would I lament he is a talentless lunkhead intent on buttering up Milady, even unto exclaiming over her tacky collection of 'art,' which consists of a jumbled crowd of earnest daubs all but obliterating her prize, a fine Mary Cassatt, and her only other decent piece, a moody Redon vastly preferred by me.) 2 shares lodgings with Lunkhead and pretends not to be displeased, and Lunkhead, as misguided as his roommate, shares 2's yearnings for KM. In a corner lurks a bedraggled soul later revealed to be one Hugo Driver, of whom the better must remain less said. Invited to drink, I strike a blow for the proletariat by requesting an un-posh Wine Spo-dee-o-dee, half red wine, half gin, oft served at the paternal inn, and KM delights by putting down her bubbly and asking for a lethal Top-and-Bottom, equal parts port and gin. These are wincingly delivered.

"Dinner likewise consists of sweet and raw in equal portions, for while KM coruscates and gorgeous 2 is resolutely amiable, our hostess utters dila-

> tions upon the Germanic Soul. I deflect attention to the paintings. Mary Cassatt receives her due, and the earnest daubers are praised to the skies, creepy Fain chiming in. I remark upon the little Redon, which displeased Milady screeches she installed only because of its name. What does Miss Mannheim think of the wondrous Lockesly portrait of yon peasant before his sheepfold? enquires Georgina, seeking to restore the proper moral tone. 'I think,' said KM, 'of Aristotle Contemplating the Home of Buster.' 'Oh my dear,' smirks Georgina, 'you mean, you surely intend to say . . .' 'That bellwether is a Buster if I ever saw one,' said KM, and sharply we returned to the magnificence of all things Teutonic."

Mark Foil looked up from the diary and gave Nora an almost apologetic glance. "Creeley fell into this tone when he was rattled or insecure, and alcohol always encouraged his showy side. He mentions only one Wine Spo-dee-o-dee, something he only drank when he wanted to offend people he thought were being pretentious, but I'm pretty sure he had at least three of them. Of course he loved the girl's ordering a Top-and-Bottom, it proved they were two of a mind. They used to talk about their 'outsider drinks.' "

"Outsider drinks," Nora said, jolted by another reference to Paddi Mann.

"Creeley learned about them from the musicians who used to come to the family bar. But he also meant that the two of them were outsiders at Shorelands. The joke about Aristotle Contemplating the Bust of Homer took care of *her,* and Georgina wasn't completely obtuse, she at least *sensed* that Creeley thought she was absurd, so he was on the outs, too. Which meant we have this little situation here."

"What did Driver steal?" Nora asked.

Two loud thumps came from the other side of the door. Andrew Martindale walked in, tapping the face of his watch with a satisfied expression on his face. "Thirty-three minutes, a world record. How are we doing?"

"As usual, I've been talking too much," said Foil. He pulled up his sleeve to glance at his own wristwatch. "We still have plenty of time if we don't dawdle on the way."

Martindale went to a wing chair on the far side of the room, where he crossed his legs and composed himself.

"Where were we?" Foil asked.

"Stealing," Nora said.

"We were stealing something?" said Martindale.

"Hugo Driver was stealing something." Foil opened the red diary and turned pages. "This was a few days before Lincoln Chancel's arrival, and all sorts of trunks and boxes, even furniture, had been delivered to Rapunzel and set up in the tower. Chancel insisted on his own bed, so it came on a truck and was carried up into the tower, and the old one went into the Main House basement. He had a ticker tape machine put in, so he could keep up with the stock market. A big carton of cigars arrived from Dunhill. A catering company installed a mahogany bar in one room and stocked it with bottles."

Foil examined a page. "Here we are, the day before Chancel's arrival. Like good outsiders, Creeley and Katherine Mannheim had been indulging in Top-and-Bottoms, and in the middle of dinner he had to leave the table to visit the bathroom. Who should he spot acting fishy in the lounge but good old D&D, Hugo Driver, who had left the dining room without anyone's noticing.

> "I did not even see him at first, and I might not have seen him at all if he hadn't sucked in enough air to fill a balloon and followed that by kicking one of the legs of the sofa. When I looked toward the source of these noises, I observed KM's embroidered bag sliding down the back of the sofa and coming to rest on the seat with a distinct rattle. D&D, whom I had thought wrapped in his usual nervous gloom back at the table, emerged around the side of the sofa and slid something into the right pocket of his shabby hounds-tooth jacket. He twitched the flap over the pocket and tried to face me down. What a pathetic creature it is. I stopped moving and smiled at it and in a very quiet voice asked it what it was doing. I believe it all but fainted. I said that if it replaced the stolen object at once, I would keep silent. The nasty sneak bared its teeth and informed me that Miss Mannheim had requested that it bring her a pillbox from an inner compartment of the bag, and that had I not been fixated on Rick Favor, I would have overheard the exchange. I had observed KM whispering to D&D, and its dank desperate glee at having been so favored, but that had been all. It produced the proof of its innocence, a small silver pillbox. Soon after my return

> from the bathroom, another laborious dinner and its hymns to Nietzsche and Wagner happily in the past, I inserted myself into the scented region between 'Rick' (!!) and KM and described what I had seen and said. KM brandished the pillbox, and 2 unsubtly implied I had imagined the theft. I implored her to look through the bag, and when she complied I saw, though 2 did not, an amused expression cross her features. 'Who steals my purse steals trash,' she said. Excited now, dear 2 prepared himself to assault D&D, but was stayed by KM's saying that no, nothing was missing, certainly nothing of value, and he had after all produced the invaluable box, from which she then extracted a minute ivory pill and lodged it like a sweet beneath her pointed tongue.

"But two weeks later," Foil said, "while everyone else paid court to Lincoln Chancel, Driver slipped a pair of Georgina's silver sugar tongs into his pocket, and Creeley saw him do it. The first person he told was Merrick Favor, and Favor called him a degenerate and said that if he didn't stop slandering Hugo Driver, he'd punch him in the face."

"Speaking of degenerates," Andrew Martindale said from his distant chair, "the lunatic who escaped from jail in Connecticut is on the loose in Springfield, what about that? Dick Dirt?"

"Dart," Nora croaked, and cleared her throat. "Dick Dart."

"He was in a motel on the other side of town. When the police got there, all they found was a corpse cut to pieces in one of the rooms. No sign of Dart. The reporter said the body looked like an anatomy lesson."

Nora's face felt hot.

Foil was watching her. "Are you all right, Ms. Eliot?"

"You have to drive to Provincetown, and we're keeping you."

"Let me worry about getting us to Cape Cod in time. Are you sure you're all right?"

"Yes. It's just . . ." She tried to invent a reasonable-sounding explanation for her distress. "I live in Connecticut, in Westerholm, actually, and I knew some of Dick Dart's victims."

Andrew Martindale looked sympathetic, Mark Foil concerned. "How terrible for you. Did you ever meet this Dart person?"

"Briefly," she said, and tried to smile.

"Would you like to break for a couple of minutes?"

"No, thank you. I'd like to hear the rest."

Foil looked down again at the book open in his hands. "Let's see if I can boil this down. Lincoln Chancel arrived on schedule and almost immediately turned Hugo Driver into a kind of servant, sending him on errands, generally exploiting him in every way. Driver seems to have gloried in the role, as if he expected to keep the job when the month was over. Poor Creeley was left out in the cold. I gather that Merrick Favor mentioned his accusations to one or two people, and after that both he and Katherine Mannheim were out of favor with their hostess. She more than Creeley, actually, because she quickly became absorbed with her 'unwriting,' whatever that meant, and even skipped a few dinners to work on it. This put her in such disfavor that everybody began to feel that it was only a matter of time before Georgina booted her out, as she'd been known to do when a guest seriously disappointed her.

"One night they all took part in a ceremony called 'the Ultimate,' which took place in an area called Monty's Glen. I don't know any more about it, except that it was boring. All Creeley said in his diary was *'the Ultimate, yawn, glad that's over.'* But the next day all the excitement began. After lunch, Creeley was out walking through the gardens. Merrick Favor came up behind him and tapped him on the shoulder, and Creeley all but passed out. For a second, he thought Favor had boiled over and wanted to hit him, but instead he apologized to Creeley. Hugo Driver really *was* a thief, or so he strongly suspected. Then he explained himself.

"Favor had been trailing after Katherine Mannheim through the gardens, hoping to have a word alone with her, but every time she sat down for a moment, one of the other men popped through an opening in a hedge and sat down beside her. The last one had been Driver, and Favor had watched them say a few words to each other until Miss Mannheim got up and walked away through a gap in the hedges. Favor had started to go toward her when he saw Driver notice that she had left her bag lying half open on the bench, and he stopped to watch what would happen. Driver glanced around"—Foil imitated the quick movements of a man who wishes not to be observed—"and moved closer to the bag. From where he was standing, Favor couldn't see Driver dip into the bag, and Driver was clever enough not to look at his hands. Favor was pretty sure what was going on, anyhow, and he was almost certain that he *did* see Driver slide some kind of object into his jacket pocket, so he came out of hiding and confronted the little weasel. Driver denied everything. He even said he'd had enough of these accusations and intended to complain to Georgina. Off he went. Favor took the bag to Miss Mannheim and told her what he'd seen. When she looked in the bag, she laughed and said, 'Who steals my trash steals trash.' That night she disappeared."

"After Favor thought he saw Driver stealing something from her bag," Nora said.

"Right. She didn't show up for dinner. Georgina was irritated and foul to everyone, even Lincoln Chancel. Late at night, Creeley went out for a walk and came across Chancel and Driver near Bill Tidy's cottage, and Chancel was extraordinarily rude to him. He told him to stop sneaking around. The next night, again no Katherine Mannheim, and after dinner, Georgina led the entire party to Gingerbread on the pretext of seeing whether Miss Mannheim was ill. Everybody could sense that unless they found Katherine Mannheim in a high fever and too weak to get out of bed, Georgina was going to throw her out on the spot. Instead, she was gone. She'd taken off sometime between the previous afternoon and that night. Georgina didn't even seem surprised, Creeley wrote. She behaved as though she expected to find an unlocked door and empty cottage. 'I am sorry to say,' she said, 'that Miss Mannheim appears to have jumped the wall.' And that was that. She had a number for one of Miss Mannheim's sisters and called her to ask her to remove the few things left behind in the bungalow, and the next day the sister arrived. She had no idea where Miss Mannheim could have gone. She wasn't in her apartment in New York, and she hadn't spoken to anyone in her family. She was unpredictable, and she'd previously disappeared from places where she'd felt uncomfortable. But her sister did have one huge worry."

"That she was dead," Nora said.

"You've heard about her weak heart. The sister was afraid that she might have wandered into the woods and suffered heart failure, so she insisted on calling in the police. Georgina was furious but gave in. For a couple of days, the Lenox police questioned the guests and staff at Shorelands. They searched the grounds and the woods. In the end, it seemed pretty clear that she had run off, and a week later, the summer was over."

"And then all these deaths," Nora said.

"Like a plague. Georgina must have felt some sort of renewal was called for, because she immediately paid for a lot of extensive renovations, but all those deaths cast a long shadow over the place."

"There's going to be a long shadow over *us,*" Andrew Martindale said.

"One more minute." Foil consulted his watch and skipped over a thick wad of pages. "I want you to hear something from the end, so you'll know as much as I do about Creeley's death." He looked up again. "If you learn anything at all that might shed light on this, I'd appreciate being let in on it. I know it isn't likely, but I do want to ask."

"I'll tell you about anything I find," Nora said.

"It's so enigmatic. Here's what Creeley wrote in his journal three days before he killed himself.

> "All at once, a beam of light pierces the depression I've been in since leaving Shorelands. It seems there is hope after all, and from a most Unexpected Quarter. Interest in high places! What a blessed turn, if all goes as it should.

"Then this, the next day.

> "Nothing, nothing, nothing, nothing, nothing. Done. Finished. I should have known. At least I did not babble to MF. How cruel, to be written only to be unwritten.

"And that's it, that's all, that's the last entry. I didn't hear from him on either of those days. When I tried to call, the operator told me his phone was off the hook, and I assumed he was working. I knew he'd been unhappy for a long time, so it was good to think he was working hard. But he never let three days go by without at least talking to me, and the next day, when I still couldn't get through to him, I drove to his apartment after my last patient."

Foil paused for a moment. "It was a dark, miserable day. Freezing. We'd had a terrible winter. I don't think we'd seen sunlight for a month. I got to his building. Creeley had the top floor of a duplex, with a separate entrance to his part of the house. After I got out of the car, I climbed over a snowbank and looked up at his windows. All his lights were on. I went up the steps to the porch and rang his bell. His downstairs neighbors, the owners, were both out, and I could hear their dog barking. They had a collie named Lady—high-strung, like all collies. That's a desolate sound, you know, a dog barking in an empty house. Creeley didn't answer. I thought he'd turned up his radio to drown out the sound of the dog, which he had to do off and on during the day. He didn't mind, Creeley played music all the time when he was writing, and the only problem with turning it up was that sometimes he couldn't hear the bell. I rang it a few more times. When I still didn't hear him coming down the stairs, I took out my key and let myself in, just like a hundred times before.

"As soon as I got in, I heard his radio going full blast. 'Let's Dance,' Benny Goodman's theme song. It was one of the remote broadcasts they used to do in those days. I went up the stairs calling out his name. Lady was going crazy. Before I got to the top of the stairs, I started smelling something. I should have recognized the smell right away. I opened his living room door, but he wasn't there. I hollered his name and turned the radio down. That blasted collie got even louder. I knocked on the bathroom door and looked in the kitchen. Then I tried the bedroom.

"Creeley was lying on his bed. Blood everywhere. Everywhere. He'd used the shotgun his father had given him for his sixteenth birthday, when he still had hopes of normal male hobbies for his son. I went into shock. I just *shut down.* It seemed like I stood there for a long time, but it could only have been a couple of minutes. After a little while, I called the police and waited like a robot until they came. And that was that. Try as I might—and I tried, all right—I never understood why he did it."

62

"WELL, I UNDERSTAND why he did it." Harwich turned out of the driveway onto Oak Street and rotated his shoulders several times, as if trying to shake off the atmosphere of the past thirty minutes. He leaned sideways to see himself in the rearview mirror and ruffled the tight gray curls on the side of his head. "Mark is an okay guy, but he doesn't want to see the truth."

Nora pointed at a driveway a little way ahead of them on the other side of the street. "Pull in there."

He stared at her. "What?"

"I want to see them leave."

"You want— Oh, I get it." He pulled up slightly ahead of the driveway between two wings of a stone wall, and backed in. "See? You think I don't know what this is about, but I do."

"Good," Nora said.

"You want to make sure they get away safely."

"I'm glad you don't mind."

"I didn't say I didn't mind. I'm just a very agreeable person."

"So tell me why Creeley Monk killed himself."

"It's obvious. This guy reached the end of his rope. First of all, he was a working-class kid who pretended to be high society. From the second he got into that school, his whole life was an act. On top of that, he couldn't sustain his initial success. Shorelands was supposed to raise him to a new level, but no one wanted to publish his next book. One flutter of interest sends him into ecstasies, and when it doesn't pan out, he's devastated. He takes the shotgun out of his closet and ends it all. Simple."

This clever, rapid-fire dissection, as of a corpse under a scalpel, irritated Nora unreasonably; Harwich had reduced Mark Foil's account to the empty diagram of a case history.

"Anyhow, you did a good job in there," Harwich told her. "But there is this little issue about that editor who turns out to be part of the Homintern. Did you get that? *We've* met him a couple of times? Pretty soon Mark is going to know this book is just a smoke screen, and then he's going to have a lot of questions for me."

"It's no big deal. I said I had a book contract, and it turns out I don't. I'm writing the book before I take it to a publisher."

"I'm still in a tricky position. Anyhow, there they are, safe and sound." He nodded toward a long, graceful-looking gray car moving down Oak Street in front of them. "Not a care in the world, as usual."

"You don't like them, do you?"

"What's to like?" he burst out. "These two guys live in a world where everything's taken care of for them. They're so smug, so lovey-dovey, so pleased with themselves, tooling off to Cape Cod in Martindale's new Jaguar while his patients climb the walls."

"I thought he was retired."

"*Mark's* retired, except from all the important stuff, the state boards and the national committees. Andrew has about six jobs, as far as I can make out. Head of psychiatry here, professor of psychiatry there, chief of this and that, a great private practice full of famous painters and writers, plus his books. *The Borderland of the Borderline Patient. The Text of Psychoanalysis. William James, Religious Experience, and Freud.* I forget the others." He pulled out of the drive, enjoying her amazement.

"I thought . . ." Nora did not want to admit what she had thought. "How can he take a month off? Oh, I forgot. It's August, when all the shrinks go to Cape Cod."

"That's right, but Andrew spends *his* month off running a clinic in Falmouth. And writing. He's a busy lad." He gave her a sidelong, appraising look. "Hey, why don't you take some time off yourself? You shouldn't run around on your own while your madman is on the loose. And there's no point in trying to find this Tidy character."

"What do you think happened to Katherine Mannheim?"

"Easy. Everybody thought either she ran away or died in the woods, so they couldn't see that both things were true. She's carrying her suitcase through the woods at night, the weight is too much for her, an owl scares her, blooey. A couple of nitwit cops pretend to search the woods, and surprise, surprise, they don't find her. I've never been inside Shorelands, but I've seen it, and even now we're talking about two square miles of wilderness. An army couldn't have found her."

"You're probably right," she said, idly watching suburban houses grow closer together as the lots shrank and sprouted the swing sets, wading pools, and bicycles in the driveway she had seen while Dick Dart drove them into Fairfield in Ernest Forrest Ernest's car. "Oh, my God."

Harwich gave her a look of concern.

"I know why Lincoln Chancel went to Shorelands."

"Money, I told you."

"Not for the reason you think. He was trying to recruit Georgina Weatherall for his Fascist cause, the Americanism Movement. Lincoln Chancel secretly supported the Nazis. He got together a bunch of sympathetic millionaires, but they had to keep quiet during the war. In the fifties, Joe McCarthy roped them into anti-Communism, I guess, and they had to go along."

He looked at her suspiciously. "I have to say, you do liven things up. Let me take you out for dinner tonight, I know a great French place out near Amherst—a little bit of a drive, but it's worth it. Amazing food, candlelight, the best wines. Nobody'll see us, and we'll be able to have a good long talk."

"Are you worried about somebody seeing us?"

"We have to keep you under wraps. In the meantime, I'll order a pizza. There's not much food in the house. You can get a nap, and I'll go to the hospital. Don't answer the phones or open the door for anyone, okay? We'll keep the world at arm's length for a while and get reacquainted all over again."

Nora leaned back against the seat and closed her eyes. Instantly, she was standing in a forest clearing ringed by tall standing stones. Counting money into neat stacks at a carved mahogany desk placed between two upright stones, Lincoln Chancel glanced up and glared at her. Misery and sorrow overflowed from this scene, and Nora stirred and awakened without at first recognizing that she had fallen asleep. Longfellow Lane rolled past the windows like a painted screen.

"Right now you need to be taken care of," Harwich said.

He pressed a button clipped to his visor to swing up the garage door and drove inside to park beside Sheldon Dolkis's green Ford. As soon as he got out of the car, he moved to the wall and flipped a switch to bring the heavy door rattling down. A bare overhead light automatically turned off, and the door clanked against the concrete. Nora felt almost too tired to move. Harwich's dim form moved past the front of the car toward the right side of the garage. "You okay?" he said, and opened an interior door. A panel of gray light erased the front of his body and turned his hair to silver fuzz.

"Guess I didn't know how tired I was." She dragged herself out of the remarkably comfortable seat and noticed that a small figure like a white sparrow had perched atop the car's hood. No, not a bird, a winged woman, poised for flight. This had a meaning, but what meaning? Oh yes, what do you know, Dan Harwich numbered among his possessions a Rolls-Royce. How odd; the deeper into the world she descended, the further up she went. The car door closed with a bank vault's serious thunk, and Nora went past the waiting Harwich into the house.

"Everything caught up with you," he said from behind her. He put a sympathetic hand on her shoulder and squeezed past in the narrow space of the rear entry, lightly kissed her, and took her with him through the kitchen to the living room, where she stood embarrassed in the midst of a yawn while he darted forward and drew down on a cord which advanced dark curtains across the bow window. "Let's get you settled," he said, and ushered her gently up the stairs, past the linen closet, and into the guest room, where he conducted her toward the bed and removed her shoes once she had stretched out. She yawned again, hugely.

"You fell asleep in the car for about ten minutes."

"I did not." The protest sounded childish.

"You did," Harwich said in an amused echo of her tone. "Not very peacefully, though. You made a lot of unhappy noises." He began massaging the sole of her right foot.

"That feels wonderful."

"Why don't you take off that T-shirt and unbutton your jeans? I'll help you slide them off."

"No." She shook her head back and forth on the pillow.

"You'll be more comfortable. Then you can slide under the covers. Hey, I'm a doctor, I know what's best for you."

Obediently she sat up and yanked off the white V-necked shirt, turning it inside out in the process, and flipped it toward him.

"Cute bra," he said. "Do the top of those jeans."

Protesting, she flattened out and undid the button, pulled down the zip, and wiggled the jeans over her hips. Harwich yanked them down, and in one quick movement they whispered over her thighs, knees, feet. "Matching panties! You're a fashion plate." He raised the sheet and the cover so that she could wriggle under and then lowered them over her, not without a little tucking and patting. "There you are, sweetie."

"What a guy," she heard herself say, and roused herself to add, "Give me about an hour, okay?" The words sounded distant in her ears, and soft, slow-moving bands of color began to spill from the few objects visible through the slits of her eyes, one of them being Dan Harwich as he drifted toward the door.

The broad circle of grass within the tall stones looked like a stage. Nora moved forward as Lincoln Chancel wrapped bands around the stacks of bills before him and one by one placed them in a satchel as carefully as if they were raw eggs. He gave Nora a sharp, disgruntled look and returned to his task. "You don't belong here," he said, seeming to address the satchel.

His ugliness outdid the famous photograph, in which it had seemed a by-product of rage. It was an entire ugliness, domineering in its force.

"No sand in your craw. A few setbacks and you're on your knees, whimpering *Daddy, help me, I can't do it on my own.* Pathetic. When people talk to you, all you hear is what you already know."

"I understood why you went to Shorelands," she said, doing her best to mask the fear and impotence she felt.

"Consider yourself fired." He sent her a cold, ferocious glance of triumph and pulled a thick cigar from his top pocket, bit off the end, and lit it with a match which had appeared between his fingers. "Go home. It's not a job for a little girl."

"Screw you," Nora said.

"Gladly." He grinned at her like a dragon through a flag of smoke. "Even though you're too scrawny for my taste. In my day we liked our women ample—womanly, we used to say. Tits like bolsters, buttocks you could sink your hands into. Women to make your pole stand up and beg for it. One other kind I liked, too—small ones. Every big man wants to roger a little thing. Get on top, you feel like you'll either snap their bones or split 'em in half. But you're not that type, either."

"The Katherine Mannheim type."

He drew on the cigar and blew out a quivering ring of smoke that smelled like rotting leaves. "The runaway." Instead of losing its shape and drifting upward, the trembling smoke ring widened and began shuddering toward Nora. "Little bitch didn't have the manners of a whore."

The smoke ring floated into the middle of the grassy circle, paused, and twisted into nothingness. Pretending that she had already followed orders and left, Chancel snapped the lock of the satchel over the last wad of bills, and her question spoke itself in her head. *What did she say . . .*

"What did she say to you while the photograph was being taken?"

He looked over at her and mouthed the cigar. "Who?"

"Katherine Mannheim."

"I graciously invited her to sit on my lap, and she said, 'I've already seen your warts, I don't have to feel one, too.' Tidy and that blockhead Favor both laughed. Even the pansy smiled, and so did that poser with the funny name. Austryn Fain. What kind of a handle is Austryn Fain?" He aimed the astonishing nose at her like a gun. "You don't know anything. You don't even read the right books. Get out of here. Lose yourself in the woods."

She cried out and found Harwich's shadowy, reassuring face inclining toward her. "Ow, that hurt," he said, maintaining his smile. "You walloped me!"

"Sorry. Bad dream." A long leg brushed hers, and she squinted at his face.

"Do you always make so much noise in your sleep?"

"Get out of this bed. What are you *doing* here?"

"I'm trying to calm you down. Come on. There's nobody here but me."

Nora dropped her head back on the pillow.

"Nobody's going to hurt you. Dr. Dan is right here to make sure of that." He slid closer to her and inserted an arm between her head and the pillow. A smooth cotton shirt encased the arm. "In my medical opinion, you need a hug."

"Yeah." She was grateful for this simple kindness.

"Close your eyes. I'll get out of here when you fall asleep again."

She turned into his arms and tugged a corner of the pillow between her head and his shoulder. He caressed the side of her head and began stroking her bare arm. "Your operation," she murmured.

"Long way off."

"I never sleep during the day," Nora said, and in seconds proved herself a liar.

When she opened her eyes again, Harwich passed a warm hand up her arm and tugged the sheet over her shoulder. Various, not entirely subjective internal dials and gauges informed her that she had spent a significant time asleep. What time was it? Then she wondered if Dick Dart had been arrested since they had left Mark Foil's house. Harwich circled her waist with an arm.

"Don't you have an operation pretty soon?" she asked.

"Took less time than I thought it would."

"It went all right?"

"Except for the demise of the patient."

She whirled around to face him and found him propping his head on one hand, smiling down. "Joke. Barney Hodge will live to tear another thousand divots from the country club greens."

"How long have I been asleep?"

"Most of the day. It's about five-thirty."

"Five-thirty?"

"When I got back, I checked on you, and there you were, out cold, even quiet. I was getting the feeling that you refought the war every time you fell asleep."

"I just about do, according to Davey."

"Not in my house." He leaned forward and brushed his lips against her forehead. "My house is good for you."

"So are you," she said.

"I like to think so." He raised her chin with his hand and kissed her gently on the lips.

"The perfect host."

"The perfect guest." He kissed her again, for a longer time and far more seriously.

"I'd better get out of bed before we do something foolish," she said, relieved that he was in his clothes, and then noticed his bare shoulder visible above the sheet. "You took your shirt off."

"More comfortable. Fewer wrinkles. Besides, a shirt seemed so unfriendly." He circled her waist and pulled her toward him to whisper, "Pants did, too." She stiffened, and he said, "We're alone here. We don't have to answer the phone or open the door. Why don't we spend a little time together? I want us to be nice to each other. You're this spectacular person, and we really care for each other."

"Whoa, hold on," she said. "What are you doing?"

He smiled at her. "Nora, one of the best things about this lovely relationship of ours is that we always wind up in bed. You go out and raise hell all over the place while I stay here in my hole, marrying the wrong people out of boredom, I guess, but sooner or later you always explode back into my life and we charge our batteries all over again. Isn't that right?"

"Jesus," Nora said.

"It's always the same, and this time you show up more gorgeous than ever! You're out of your mind with worry . . ."

"Hardly just worry."

". . . and come right here because you knew you belonged with me. We're in this little bubble of time made just for us. Inside that bubble we help each other, we heal each other. When we're healed, we go on and tackle all the other crappy parts of life."

"I'm not so sure about that," Nora said. "Hold it, I have to tackle the bathroom before I make any decisions here."

"All the decisions were made a long time ago," Harwich said. "This is the follow-through."

Some fierce emotion she could not begin to identify gripped her, lifted her out of bed, and carried her toward the bathroom. Harwich said, "I'll be here when you get back," but she hardly heard him. She locked the door and sat on the toilet, her face blazing. The enormous feeling within her refused to speak its name even as it sent tears brimming in her eyes. He wanted to take care of her, she needed his care. This had seemed to be true. "But I don't need to get *laid,*" she whispered to herself. "I don't *need* him to *fuck* me." She flushed the toilet and looked around at the objects on the bathroom shelves, the dangling shower cap, the lush hotel bathrobe, the shampoo and conditioner, the perfume. "Oh, my God," she said to herself, "I'm an idiot."

She stood up, washed her hands, and wrapped the thick robe around herself, all the while watching her feelings align themselves into new positions. The largest of these feelings—not humiliation, chagrin, regret, not even the ghost of her old attachment to Dan Harwich, but simple anger—sent her back into the bedroom to face him.

"What's that for?" he asked, referring to the robe.

"My self-respect," she said. "Battered as it is."

"Uh oh. Come on, Nora, sit down and talk to me. I want to help you."

"You did help me," she said, moving toward the chair where he had deposited her clothes. His own jeans lay folded over the top of the chair, his shirt unfurled like a jacket across the back. "You took me in, you fed me, you let me see Mark Foil. I'm grateful, so thanks, Dan."

"You're not grateful, you're upset. I understand, Nora. You went through a terrible experience, and it's still affecting you. You don't think you can trust anybody, and when I try to comfort you, all the bells go off. You suddenly think you can't trust even me. Part of the fault is mine, I can see that."

Halfway to the chair, she turned around and faced him, wrapping her arms around her chest. "What part is that, Dan?"

"I take too much for granted."

"Christ, you said it."

"I mean, I didn't think you could misunderstand me that much. I promise you, Nora, I had no intention of doing anything you didn't want to do."

"And one of the best things about our relationship is that we always wind up in bed, so after I felt good and safe, you'd really help me out and have sex with me."

"Let's face it, Nora, we do go to bed together, and we do feel better afterwards."

"You feel so much better afterwards you go out and get married. You always have girlfriends, don't you, Dan? When one wife finally figures you out and gets fed up, you have her replacement lined up to put her name on the prenuptial agreement. The first time I turned up here, you brought me home from the motel to meet Helen and give her a really good reason to get out quick so you could marry Lark. You couldn't marry me, I'm too crazy."

"Nora, you don't want my life. There isn't enough excitement here for you."

She turned away, went to the chair, and stepped into her jeans with her back to him.

"I'm crazy about you. I think you're an amazing woman."

"You don't have any idea who I am. I'm your shipboard romance." She fastened the jeans and threw the robe aside, let him gape. "You're tantalized by the chaos I bring to your tedious, self-important existence, but you want to keep it at bay. It's whoopee time with the emotional bag lady, and when party time is over, back to the girl in the on-deck circle, right?" She had been wrestling the T-shirt, trying to pull it right side out but in her agitation only bundling the body of the shirt into one of the sleeves. She pulled fabric out of the sleeve and tugged the shirt on inside out. "The girl whose things are all over the bathroom, the one who called you twice this morning, the girl who swipes little mementos from the hotels the two of you stay in when you go away together."

"All the fiction in the world isn't in novels," he said, marveling.

"This is the same girl who told you she was coming over here this morning, when you suddenly changed your mind and decided to whisk me off to Mark Foil's house. You figured you could fend off the third Mrs. Harwich for a day or two. I'm too much of a risk to keep around longer than that, aren't I?"

Harwich was sitting up in bed with his arms around his raised knees, watching her with an expression of mild, half-amused perplexity. He hesitated for a conspicuous beat before speaking, as if assuring himself that she had finished at last. "Would you like to stop fantasizing and listen to the truth?"

"The only thing I don't understand," she said, "is why she doesn't sleep in your bedroom. I really don't get that part. Does she snore like a pig, or are the two of you saving a whole night together in the master's bedroom for after the wedding, like a reward kind of deal?"

Harwich inhaled deeply, leaned forward, and opened his hands, palm up, the image of beleaguered reason. "This whole picture you're describing is *all made up*. It isn't *real*. Dick Dart knocked you for a loop, remember? As long as you can keep in mind who I am, the real me and not this monster you just invented, I'll be as patient and supportive as I know how. Maybe you can't accept that right now, but it's the God's truth."

This spoke to all of her old feelings about Dan Harwich, and his reasonableness, his steady, kind, affectionate regard, filled her with doubts. This was *Harwich,* she reminded herself. Three years ago she had thrown herself at him. Could she blame him for catching her? It was true. She had willingly helped him speed up the wreckage of his first marriage. "Say more," she said.

"I don't blame you for feeling strange about Lark. But I was honest about her. I told you I was already seeing her when you came here last time. I can't pretend I've ever been a faithful husband, because I haven't. Okay? I confess. I mess around. I get bored. I need what you have, that . . . spirit. But honest, this is the truth, I don't have a new bride waiting in the wings."

"Then whose stuff is that in the bathroom?"

He looked sideways for a moment, considering, then again met her eyes. "Okay. But bear in mind that I don't really have any reason to explain this or anything else. You see that, don't you?"

"So explain." Her angry certainty was ebbing away.

"What the hell, Nora, I'm not a monk. During the course of my tedious, self-important life, it has now and then come to my attention that some women really do prefer having their own separate bathroom. So I put some toothbrushes and other stuff in there just in case."

"You didn't change your mind about taking me to see Mark Foil because your new girlfriend said she was coming over?"

"I don't blame you for letting the past few days make you suspicious of men. And I know it looks bad, my getting into bed with you, but cross my heart, I had no intention of coercing you into having sex. I hope you believe me."

She sighed. "Honest to God, Dan, I almost—" The telephone in the bedroom down the hall rang once, twice, and Harwich's face modulated from earnest entreaty to a spasm of irritation and back to a close approximation of innocent indifference before it rang a third time. "Don't you want to get that?"

"This is more important."

"It might be the hospital."

"Trust me, it's just some pest."

The distant telephone continued to ring: a fifth time, a sixth, a ninth time, a tenth.

"Don't you have an answering machine?"

He held her eyes expressionlessly for a moment or two. "I turned off the machine on that line."

"Why would you do that?" Nora watched calculation, annoyance, and something alert and wary appear in his face. "Why, Dan?"

The telephone stopped ringing.

"I guess it wasn't such a good idea," he said. "But hell, nobody's perfect."

"You bastard." She felt as though she had been punched in the stomach. "You slimy, self-serving, lying creep." The feeling in her stomach intensified. "You almost had me talked into getting back into bed with you."

"Do it anyhow. What's the difference? This is about you and me. To hell with anybody else."

"You still think you have a chance, don't you?"

"Consider this. I was protecting your feelings. Okay, I have a woman friend, I've known her for a couple of months, and she stays here from time to time. *I* don't know if I'm going to marry her. If I'm not willing to let her destroy our relationship, why should you?"

She looked at him in outright amazement. "You really are an absolute bastard. Boy, I wonder what you . . . No, I already know."

"You know what I think of you? I doubt that very much. But don't waste time brooding about it, just get in your car and go. At this point, I don't see much point in prolonging the situation. Take off. Nice to know you, kind of."

She considered throwing some heavy object at him but then realized with a sad, final thump of defeat that he was not worth the effort. "Answer one question for me, will you?"

"If you insist."

"Why does this woman sleep in here instead of your bedroom? I don't get it."

"Because of the pillows," Harwich said. "If you really want to know."

"The pillows?"

"She's allergic to down pillows, and they're the only kind I can stand to sleep on. These are foam. I think sleeping on a foam pillow is like having sex with a condom."

She found she could smile. "Dan, I don't see much of a future for your third marriage."

His eyes hardened, and his mouth thinned like a lizard's. "The truth is, Nora, you were always a little nuts. Being nuts was okay in Vietnam—it probably helped you make it through—but it sure as hell doesn't work anymore."

"I'm beginning to understand that you have a lot in common with Dick Dart." She walked down the side of the bed toward the door. Harwich slid an inch or two away, trying to pretend that he was merely finding a more comfortable position. "On the whole, I prefer Dick Dart. He's a lot more upfront than you are."

"See what I mean?" he said, smirking, now that he was out of reach.

She opened the door and looked at him as calmly as she could. "Aren't you a little worried?"

"Why don't you just leave? Do I have to tell you never to come back, or have you figured that out for yourself?"

"That old Ford is parked *really* close to your car," she said, and closed the door behind her. She could hear his shouts as she went down the stairs, and they followed her through the kitchen. By the time she had raised the garage door and started the car, he was standing naked in the back door, no more than an absurd figure with a potbelly, stork legs, and graying pubic hair, yelling but too afraid of being seen by his neighbors to come any closer. She backed out without touching the Rolls.

63

"D-E-O-D-A-T-O," NORA SPELLED.

During the seconds while the telephone reported a dense silence, she regretted the impulse to call the Chancels' manservant. Why had she imagined that Jeffrey would not go immediately to Daisy, or Alden if Alden was home, or even the police? When the need to talk to someone in Westerholm had seized her, enigmatic Jeffrey had seemed the most likely candidate, although for an irrational moment she had imagined consulting Holly Fenn. She *still* wished she could talk to Fenn, absolute proof, if after Harwich she needed proof, of her rotten taste in protective men. A telephone began to ring, and she realized that she had not considered what she would do if an answering machine picked up. Nora moved the receiver away from her head and heard a metallic voice say "Hello." Was this voice Jeffrey's? Nora envisioned a room full of cops in headphones leaning over a tape recorder. She moved the receiver back to her ear, more uncertain than ever.

A male voice, Jeffrey's, repeated the greeting as a question.

She spoke his name.

Silence. Then, "Nora." She had never before heard him speak her name without calling her "Mrs." Most often, he had never called her anything but "you." "Where are you?"

"In Massachusetts."

He paused for a moment. "Would you prefer me to keep quiet about this? Or would you like me to speak privately to anyone in particular?"

"I don't know yet," she confessed, understanding that "anyone in particular" meant Davey. Jeffrey's tact extended to his private life.

He weighed this. "Are you all right?"

"I think that remains to be seen. I guess I'm trying to decide what to do. Everything's so *complicated.*" She fought the desire to break down into tears. "Jeffrey, I'm sorry to do this to you, but I don't exactly feel safe right now."

"No wonder," he said. "All sorts of people are trying to find you."

"Don't make me ask a lot of questions. Please, Jeffrey."

Nora could all but hear him thinking. "I'll try to tell you what I know, but don't hang up and disappear on me, okay? Nobody's listening, I'm alone in my room, and you're fine as long as you stay where you are, at least for now. You're at a pay phone?"

"Yes." Her anxieties ebbed.

"All right. It's a good thing you called on this line. The other ones are all tapped."

"Oh, God," she said. "They still think I kidnapped Natalie Weil."

"They're acting that way." An ambiguity hung in the air while he hesitated. "From what I overhear, Mrs. Weil isn't making a lot of sense." There was another brief silence. "For what it's worth, I don't think you went near her."

"What about Davey?"

"Davey's under a lot of pressure."

"He's staying with his parents?"

"Yes. Pretty soon he'll be right *here*."

"With you?"

"In my apartment. In what used to be my apartment. Until yesterday he was staying in your house, at least at night, but with all the excitement, Mr. Chancel persuaded him to move back here. He put his foot down about staying in his old bedroom, but after Mr. Chancel . . . um, temporarily changed the conditions of my employment, he agreed to take over my place."

"Alden fired you?"

"Mr. Chancel called it a provisional suspension. He was very sorry about it. Our salaries will be paid through the end of the month, and if conditions are right, we can return. If not, he'll give us two months' severance pay and sterling recommendations."

"Us?"

"My aunt and me. I'm packed up, and when she finishes we'll be leaving."

Nora discovered that she could be shocked. "But Jeffrey, where will you go?"

"My aunt is going to stay with some cousins on Long Island. I'd drive her out there, but she won't let me, so I'm dropping her at the train station, and I'll stay with my mother for a while."

Nora had never considered that Jeffrey might have a mother. He seemed to have arrived on the planet fully formed, without the customary mediation of parents. "He ordered you and Maria out so that Davey could stay in your apartment?"

"Mr. Chancel told us that his business was not doing as well as it should, and that for the time being he had to make certain sacrifices."

It sounded to Nora as though the German deal Dick Dart had mentioned had fallen through. Good. She hoped that Chancel House would dwindle and starve. For a time, her attention wandered from whatever Jeffrey was saying.

". . . but still. Here's Merle Marvell asking about that time, that place, and right away we get suspended, or fired, or whatever it is."

"I'm sorry, Jeffrey, I faded out for a little bit. What happened?"

"Merle Marvell asked Mr. Chancel if the firm had signed up a woman to do a book about . . . a certain subject. A few writers. Someone had just called *him* asking about it, and he thought it sounded funny because he'd never heard of it."

"Hold on, hold, on." Nora tried to grasp what he had said. "Merle Marvell told Alden someone was asking about a woman who claimed to be writing a book?"

"I'm sorry for bringing it up. I wondered . . . sorry. Forget it."

"Jeffrey—"

"My aunt would jump down my throat if she knew I brought this up. The Chancels have always been very generous to us. Look, is there anything I can do for you? Do you need money? I'm coming up to Massachusetts anyhow, so I could bring you whatever you need."

"Jeffrey," Nora said, and then thought that she probably would be in need of money before long. But that was not Jeffrey's problem; his problem sounded closer to home. "Did this woman's book have to do with a place called Shorelands? And what went on there in 1938?"

Jeffrey did not respond for a moment, and then said, "That's an interesting question."

"I'm right, aren't I?"

Again he considered his words. "How do you know?"

"Well, I hope you'll keep this to yourself," she said, "but I'm the woman."

Jeffrey managed a partial recovery. "The woman pretending to be writing the book about Shorelands in 1938 was you."

"Why does it matter to you?"

"Why does it matter to *you*?"

"That's a long story. I think I'll get off now, Jeffrey. I'm getting nervous."

"Don't hang up," he said. "This might be straight out of left field, but have you ever heard of a woman named Katherine Mannheim?"

"She was at Shorelands that summer," said Nora, more baffled than ever.

"Were you looking for information about her? Was Katherine Mannheim why you cooked up this story about a book?"

"What's all this to you, Jeffrey?" Nora asked.

"We have to talk. I'm going to pick you up and take you somewhere. Tell me where you are and I'll find you."

"I'm in Holyoke. At a pay phone on a corner."

"*Where?*"

"Ah, this is the corner of Northampton and Hampden."

"I know exactly where you are. Go to a diner or something, go to a bookstore, there's one down the street, but wait for me. Don't run away. This is important."

The line went dead. Nora stared at the receiver for a second and then dropped it on its hook. No longer quite aware of her surroundings, she stepped away from the telephone and tried to make sense of what she had just learned. Jeffrey had overheard Alden's half of a conversation with Merle Marvell. Mark Foil, no fool, had called Marvell to check on "Emily Eliot," and the puzzled editor had immediately telephoned his boss at home. Why was Alden at home? Because the president of Chancel House had to face the unpleasant task of firing two long-standing employees? Or because Daisy had not recovered from her fit, and the great publisher had to deal with the consequences of dismissing her caretakers? Nora could not imagine Alden fetching drinks and bowls of soup to his stricken wife . . . Ah, of course: tricky Alden, getting, as usual, exactly what he wanted. Daisy's weakness had forced Davey back to the Poplars. Alden had put him under his thumb by linking his concern for his mother to the hypothetical independence of separate living quarters over the garage. Getting what you wanted was easy if you had the morals of a wolverine.

Nora's satisfaction at having worked out this much evaporated before the remaining mystery, that of Jeffrey. Why should he care about an obscure, long-dead poet?

64

NORA WALKED SLOWLY to the edge of the pavement. There, side by side in the next block, stood the plate-glass window of Unicorn Books and a dark blue awning bearing the words Dinah's Silver Slipper Café. As if on cue, her stomach told her that she was ravenous.

Into the bookstore she sailed, for the moment holding her hunger at bay. She moved along toward *Night Journey* and its less celebrated siblings, pulled all three paperbacks from the shelf, and carried them to the counter.

"Driver, Driver, Driver," the man said. "Dark, darker, darkest."

"I gather you don't approve," Nora said.

He rang up the total, and she gave him twenty of Sheldon Dolkis's dollars.

"I have a few doubts about *Night Journey.*"

"What kind of doubts?"

"Not my cup of tea," he said, and handed her the bag.

"I want to know more about your doubts," she said, fending off her hunger. "People keep telling me I have to read it."

"The Driver people are like Moonies. They're worse than authors, worse even than authors' *wives.*"

"I know two people who read it once a year," Nora said.

"All kinds of people get the bug. A lot of them never read anything else. They love it so much that they want to read it all over again. Then they think they've missed something, and they read it a third time. By now they're making notes. Then they compare discoveries with other Driver-ites. If they're tied into computer discussion groups, that's it; they're gone. The really sick ones give up on everything else and move into those crazy houses where everybody pretends to be a different Driver character." He sighed and looked away. "But I don't want to spoil the book for you."

Within the pastel interior of Dinah's Silver Slipper, an efficient young woman led Nora to a table by the window, handed her a three-foot-high menu, and announced that her waitress would be right with her.

Nora lined the books up in front of her. The later two were each several hundred pages longer than *Night Journey.* Nora turned them over and read the back jackets. *Night Journey* was the classic, world-famous, much-beloved, et cetera, et cetera. Readers everywhere had blah blah blah. The manuscripts of *Twilight Journey* and *Journey into Light* had been discovered among the author's papers many years after his death, and Chancel House and the Driver family were pleased to grant his millions of admirers the opportunity to blah blah blah.

"Hold on," Nora said. "Author's papers? What papers?"

An alarmed female voice said, "Excuse me?"

A college-aged girl in a blue button-down shirt and black trousers stood beside her. "I'll have the seared tuna and iced coffee, please."

She opened *Night Journey,* leafed past the title page, arrived at Part One, entitled "Before Dawn," and began grimly to read. The waitress placed a basket of bread sticks at the far end of the table, and Nora ate every one before her meal appeared before her. She fed herself with one hand while propping up the book with the other. The landscapes were cardboard, the characters flat, the dialogue stilted, but this time she wanted to keep reading. Against her will she found that she was *interested.* The hateful book had enough narrative power to draw her in. Once she had been drawn in, the characters and the landscape of caverns and stunted trees through which they wandered no longer seemed artificial.

She knew the reason for her anger, and it had nothing to do with *Night Journey* or Hugo Driver's unfortunate influence on susceptible readers. Jeffrey had told her that Davey was moving back to his parents' house. He had succumbed to Alden's gravitational pull.

More than an hour had passed while she consumed the seared tuna and nearly a third of *Night Journey.* Jeffrey was close to the Massachusetts border, speeding toward Holyoke to pick her up and take her somewhere.

BOOK VII

THE GOLDEN KEY

"You shall find it, Pippin," said the old man. His beard rustled along the ground. "I promise you that. But will you recognize it when you find it? And do you imagine that if you succeed in claiming it, it will make you happy?"

65

NORA WENT BACK down the sidewalk and sat facing Northampton Street on a wrought-iron bench in the shade of an awning. Shelley Dolkis's Ford stood at a parking meter on the far side of the pay telephone, some ten or fifteen feet away. A few cars drove past, none containing Jeffrey. At five-thirty on an August afternoon in Holyoke, most people had already reached the places they were going.

Nora had forgotten to put another set of quarters in the meter, which now displayed a red violation band. She had no desire to get back into that car. Then she remembered the suitcase on the backseat and darted over to it. She leaned into the airless oven of the interior, grabbed the handle of her suitcase, and tossed the keys onto the front seat.

At first she placed the carry-on bag on the bench beside her, then tucked it under the bench and gave herself a gold star for criminal cunning. Jeffrey failed to appear. Two or three minutes later, a dark blue vehicle with the sobriety of a hearse drew near. Nora straightened up and waited for it to pull to the curb behind the Ford, but at a steady fifteen miles an hour it proceeded toward the corner of Northampton and Hampden. The driver, a gaunt old party in sunglasses and a fishing hat, stared straight ahead as the car crept past her.

Now the only two cars on the street were a block away to the north, the wrong direction. Nora leaned back into the bench and closed her eyes. She counted to sixty and opened them. A muddy pickup with a Red Sox pennant dangling from the antenna chugged in from the south. She sighed, opened her bag, and took out *Night Journey.* Pippin was hiding in a crumbling old house where an evil crone dragged herself from room to room searching for him. The door creaked, and Pippin heard the crone's hairy feet whispering on the rotting floorboards. She looked up. The old man in the fishing hat had pulled into a parking spot in front of Dinah's Silver Slipper and was now stepping cautiously toward the restaurant's entrance. Behind him, like an ocean liner following a tug, came an old woman in a bright print dress. Nora looked the other way, and a police car with HOLYOKE P.D. on its door was swinging out around the mud-splashed truck.

Nora dove back into the book. *"Where, oh, where can my pretty be? I want to stroke my pretty boy."*

The police car drove past, and the tingling in her scalp receded. She kept her head tilted toward the book, watching the car move toward the end of the block. It veered left and made a wide U-turn in front of the pickup. She moved the book closer to her face. The police car cruised to a stop in front of the blue hearse. She peeked at the policemen. The officer in the passenger seat got out, walked across the sidewalk, and went into the Silver Slipper.

The police were looking for Nora Chancel, a woman with dark brown hair who never wore makeup. She opened her bag, found the Cover Girl Clean, and snapped it open to examine herself in the mirror. Far too much of Nora Chancel had surfaced through her disguise. She smoothed on a layer of makeup and erased the more prominent lines, applied mascara and lip gloss, tweaked and ruffled her hair into an approximation of what Dick Dart had accomplished. She risked another glance at the policemen and felt half the tension leave her body. They were leaning against the car and drinking coffee.

Far off to the south, a siren rose into the air, at first barely audible, gradually growing more insistent, finally becoming the distant explosions of red and yellow from the lights across the top of a state police car. Nora rammed the bag under her arm, stood up, and took a step forward. One of the Holyoke cops looked at her. She stretched her arms, twisted right and left, and went back to the bench. Where's the book, get the book, it's in here somewhere. She pulled a book from the jumble in the bag, opened it, and pretended to read.

The two cops gulped the last of their coffee, strolled to the corner, and dropped their cups into a wire basket. Fiddling with their shirts and ties, they moved off the sidewalk to walk down the street toward the Ford. When they passed Nora, the officer who had looked at her turned his head and made a flapping, downward gesture with his hand. Stay put.

She nudged the suitcase farther back under the bench and watched the flamboyant arrival of the state police.

The car wailed to the front of the Ford and turned off its lights and siren a second before another highway patrol car came screaming into Northampton Street. Two big men in flat-brim hats left their car angled in front of the Ford. One of them began questioning the two policemen while the other walked past the green car and waited for the second state vehicle. The clamor of the siren shut off in mid-whoop, but the light bar stayed on. One of the big troopers consulted with the driver of the second car, who got out along with his partner and matched the plate with a number in his notebook. Both men from the second car walked crouching around the Ford to peer through the windows. They pulled gloves from their belts and opened the front and rear doors on the driver's side. One of them leaned in and brandished the keys. He gestured to the local cops. The younger of the two jogged back toward his police car while the trooper opened the trunk and began poking through bags and boxes.

His partner walked back to their vehicle and rapped on a rear window. The window rolled down, and the state policeman put his hands on the sill and leaned forward to talk to two men in the backseat. The troopers who had arrived first were talking to the remaining Holyoke cop, who pointed across the street, then at the Ford, and finally at his own car. Nora bent forward and groped for the handle at the top of her suitcase.

One state policeman looked up, grinning, from the trunk. The rear doors of the second state car opened, and two men in dark suits, white shirts, and dark ties, one of them taller and fairer than the other, got out. The taller man wore heavy black sunglasses. Nora froze, her case halfway out from under the bench. Mr. Shull and Mr. Hashim, Slim and Slam, idled up to the trunk and inspected a box proffered by the grinning trooper. Nora pushed her suitcase back under the bench and tried to vanish into the shadow of the awning.

Slim looked inside the box, and the corners of his mouth jerked down. He displayed its contents to Slam, who nodded. Slim handed the box back to the trooper, and the trooper allowed himself a final smirk before returning it to the trunk. Mr. Hashim began rooting through the Ford's glove compartment. Mr. Shull wandered away, thrust his hands in his pockets, and regarded the surface of Northampton Street through his hipster sunglasses.

The trooper who had shown Mr. Shull the box came up beside him, attended to a few words, and then signaled to one of the big troopers from the first car. After another brief exchange, he waved at the local cop, who bounced forward and answered a few questions. He nodded, shrugged, nodded again, then turned to point at Nora.

The trooper glanced at her, asked a question, got another nod in return, and planted his hands on his hips as the policeman began walking toward Nora. Mr. Shull lifted his head and looked at Nora, then at the cop, then back at Nora. He drifted to the passenger door and said something to Mr. Hashim. Mr. Hashim leaned forward and gave her a skeptical glance through the windshield of the Ford.

The policeman coming toward her had concerned brown eyes and a wispy mustache, and his belly was beginning to roll over his belt. Nora swallowed to loosen her throat and sat up straight. She found that she was still holding the book open somewhere in the middle, and inserted a finger to look as if she had been interrupted while reading. "Hi," she said.

The policeman moved into the shade. He took off his hat. "Hot out there." He wiped his forehead with a hand and wiped the hand on his trousers. "I'd like to ask you a few questions."

"I don't know what I can tell you."

"Let me ask the questions and we'll find that out." He put his hat back on his head and took a notebook and ballpoint from his shirt pocket. "How long have you been out here, ma'am?"

"I'm not too sure."

The policeman put his foot on the bench and flattened the notebook on his knee. "Could you give me a rough estimate?"

"Maybe half an hour."

He made a note. "Did you observe any activity taking place in or around the vehicle under investigation? Did you observe anyone in contact with the vehicle?"

She pretended to consider the question. "Gee, I don't think so."

"Would you give me your name and address, please?"

"Oh, sure. No problem. My name is . . ." Her mind refused to supply any name but Mrs. Hugo Driver. "Dinah," she said. Shorelands? "Dinah Shore." As soon as the words were out of her mouth, she felt like holding out her hands for the cuffs.

The policeman looked up from his notebook. "That's your name, Dinah Shore?"

"I got teased about it all the time in school. For a long time I had to listen to all these Burt Reynolds jokes, but that stopped a couple years ago. Thank God." She forced herself to stop babbling.

"I can imagine," said the policeman. "Address?"

Where did Dinah Shore live? "Boston." She groped for a Boston street name. "Commonwealth Avenue. Four hundred Commonwealth Avenue. I just moved there about a week ago. Half my stuff is still in storage."

"I see." Another note. "What brings you to Holyoke, Dinah?"

"I'm waiting for a friend. He's picking me up."

"You don't have a car, Dinah?"

Of course she had a car. Every American had a car. "I have a Volvo station wagon, but it's in the garage." The policeman stared down at her, waiting for Dinah Shore, a resident of Boston, to explain her presence on a bench in Holyoke. "A friend gave me a ride this far, and my other friend is coming along to pick me up. He should be here soon."

"And you've been here how long, Dinah?"

What had she said earlier? "I'm not too sure. Maybe forty-five minutes?"

"You bought your book in the Unicorn?"

How did he know that? The policeman nodded down at the brown paper bag printed with a picture of a unicorn and the name of the bookstore beside her bag. "Oh, yes. I knew I'd have to wait for a while. So I went into the bookstore, and then I had something to eat at that restaurant next to it."

"Dinah's?"

"Is it called Dinah's? What a coincidence."

He stared at her for a moment. "So you went into the Unicorn, you looked around, you bought a book—"

"Three books," she said. She looked away from the policeman's troubled gaze. A red MG convertible driven by a man in a blue Eton cap was cruising past the patrol cars and officers taking up most of the southbound lanes in the region of Sheldon Dolkis's Ford. Another Holyoke squad car had joined them, and two burly men in sports jackets were talking to the troopers. A tow truck turned the corner of Hampden Street and came to a halt. The man in the Eton cap pulled to the curb across the street from Nora. Her heart gave a thump of alarm; the face under the blunt visor of the cap was Jeffrey's. He looked back at the crowd of policemen and their vehicles. One of the highway patrol cars was moving out of the way, and the tow truck was making beeping sounds as it backed up toward the Ford.

"You bought three books, and you went into Dinah's. You had something to eat. You did all that in forty-five minutes?"

"It was probably more like an hour. My friend just showed up."

The policeman twisted his body to look across the street. "That's him in the MG?"

She raised her arm and waved. Jeffrey was looking at the corner where she had said she would meet him. "Jeffrey!" He snapped his head in her direction and took in the spectacle of an unknown blond woman waving at him from a bench while a policeman glanced back and forth between them. It was dawning on him that the unknown blond woman had called him Jeffrey. He bent over the top of the door and peered at her. Nora prayed he would not utter her name.

The cop said, "That guy doesn't look like he knows you."

"Jeffrey's a little nearsighted." She spread her arms and shrugged, miming her good-humored inability to leave the bench.

"Oh, *there* you are," Jeffrey said. He opened the door and put one leg out of the car, but she waved him back.

The policeman faced her again and hitched himself back into position. "Where did your friend from Boston drop you off?"

"On the corner. Where all the people are."

"Did you happen to notice if the vehicle was parked there at the time?"

"Yes. I saw it parked right there."

"How long were you in the bookstore?"

"Maybe five minutes."

"And then you go into Dinah's. They give you a table, you look at the menu, right? Somebody takes your order, right? How long did that take?"

"About another five, ten minutes."

"So we have forty to forty-five minutes in Dinah's. And in that time, you ate lunch and managed to read half of that book?"

"Oh." Nora held up the book. Her finger was still inserted between the pages.

"Dinah, we have a big problem here." He adjusted his cap. He put his hands on his hips. Nora prepared herself for imminent arrest. The cop sighed. "Do you have any idea at all of what time it was when your friend dropped you off on the corner?"

She looked up at his cynical young face. "Around four-thirty," she said.

"So you've been in this vicinity for more like two hours, isn't that about right, Dinah?"

"I guess it must be."

"We don't have much of a sense of time, do we?"

"Apparently not."

"Apparently not. But that's how long you have been wandering around this part of Holyoke. In all that time, did you happen to see a woman who would be, say, about ten years older than you are, about your height and weight, with chestnut-brown hair down to just below her ears?"

"Are you looking for her?"

"She might have been wearing a long-sleeved, dark blue silk blouse and blue jeans. Five six. A hundred and ten pounds. Brown eyes. She probably came here in that car that was towed away."

"What did she do?" Nora asked.

"Let me try one more time. Have you seen the woman I described to you?"

"No. I haven't seen anyone like that."

He took his foot off the bench and flipped the notebook shut. "Thank you for your cooperation, Dinah. You can go."

She stood up. "Thank you." She went across the curb, and Jeffrey got out of the MG. When she stepped down into the street, the policeman said, "One more thing, Dinah."

She turned around, half-expecting him to handcuff her. He shook his head, then bent down to pull her case from beneath the bench. "Good luck in all your endeavors, Dinah."

66

JEFFREY DID NOT speak until they were out of Holyoke and accelerating onto I-91. With her legs stretched out before her and the rest of her body tilted back at a surprisingly relaxed angle, Nora felt as if she were being carried along on a conveyance more like a flying carpet than an ordinary car.

"I was worried about you back there." Jeffrey shifted gears to overtake a moving van bulling along at a mere ten miles over the limit, and the magic carpet lengthened out and sailed into the wind.

"Me, too."

"I didn't recognize you. This . . . transformation. It's quite a surprise."

"There have been a lot of surprises lately."

"I must say, if you're anything to go on, more women ought to be—"

"Don't. Please? Just don't." Jeffrey looked abashed, and to mollify him she said, "I'm glad you didn't yell my name."

"All I really meant was, it's a relief to see you like this. You know, apart from the . . ." He drew a circle around his face with an index finger.

"The transformation."

"Better disguise than a hat and a pair of dark glasses."

"Dick Dart has strong feelings on the subject of cosmetics." Saying his name out loud made her chest feel tight. "He's still out there somewhere."

"You're sure of that?"

"Pretty sure. The cop who was questioning me while you were being so sensible said they were looking for an old dame with brown hair. No, he didn't, don't look dismayed. But Dart couldn't have told them about the new me, or right now the FBI would be dragging me away in leg irons."

Jeffrey nodded while levitating into a new lane. "I noticed Hashim and Shull, those two human andirons. Charming couple."

"They were at Mount Avenue?"

"For a couple of hours yesterday and this morning, while they were setting up the phone equipment and talking to Mr. and Mrs. Chancel—and your husband." He glanced at her with the consciousness of introducing a new and difficult subject. "The old manse has been a little chaotic the past few days."

For the moment, she avoided the topic of her husband. "Weren't you afraid they'd see you?"

"I would have been if they'd ever seen *me*. Mr. Chancel had me bring him lunch in the library because he had to do a lot of business over the phone. The andirons were in the kitchen, so I just got a glimpse of them as I went past the door."

"Tell me about Davey. Is he moving back to the Poplars because the FBI wanted him there?"

"Or was it his father's idea, you mean? A little of both. The agents did want to keep an eye on him, and Mr. Chancel was after him to help take care of his mother. To tell you the truth, I did wonder if Mr. Chancel was getting rid of us in order to pressure Davey back into the Poplars." Jeffrey looked over at Nora to see if this had been too critical of his employer.

"Could you put your radio on, Jeffrey?"

"Sorry." He reached for the dial. "I should have thought of that earlier."

With another smooth change of gears, the magic carpet flew around a brace of plodding cars. An announcer with a buttery voice said it was a glorious evening in Hampden, Hampshire, and Berkshire counties, and proceeded to go into details.

"How bad is Daisy?" Nora asked.

"She discovered *All My Children,* and it seems to have cheered her up. Someone named Edmund kidnapped someone named Erica in Budapest and kept her in a wine cellar, but then the Erica person decided she wanted to stay kidnapped in order to get back at someone named Dmitri. My aunt told me all about it. I gather that Mrs. Chancel feels that your story is similar to the Erica person's. You're a romantic heroine."

"Lovely."

"She's reconsidered whatever you said to her about her book. My aunt has been bringing her sections, and she rewrites them, propped up in bed."

"Before and after *All My Children.*"

"During, too. It's inspirational."

"Is Alden helping her?"

"Mr. Chancel isn't allowed in her room." Jeffrey paused; apparently he had said all he wished to say about the Chancels. "Could you tell me why you claimed to be writing a book about Shorelands?"

"Dick Dart has this mission. He wants to keep anybody from proving that Hugo Driver didn't write *Night Journey,* so he wants to eliminate people connected to writers who were at Shorelands that summer. The man I talked to left for Cape Cod right after he called Merle Marvell, so he's safe, but that still leaves one. A professor in Amherst. I'd better get in touch with him soon. Dart has his address."

"You said two men. The writers they had connections to were . . . ?"
"Creeley Monk and Bill Tidy. Why?"
"Not Katherine Mannheim."
"No, but her sisters started all the trouble, I guess."
Jeffrey nodded. "Would you fill me in on this mission of Dart's, and tell me whatever you know about Shorelands and *Night Journey*?"
"Jeffrey, who *are* you? Why do you care?"
"I'm taking you to someone who'll be able to answer most of your questions, and I don't want to say anything first. I can tell you about me, though, if you're interested, but I'm not very important."
"Who are you taking me to?" An entirely unforeseen possibility occurred to her. "Katherine Mannheim?"
He smiled. "No, not Katherine Mannheim."
"Did she write *Night Journey*?"
"To tell you the truth, I hope she didn't. I'm one of the few who can resist that book."
"I never even gave it a serious try until a couple of hours ago."
"And?"
"Jeffrey, I'm not going to say any more until you tell me about yourself. You've always been such an *enigma*. How can someone like you be happy working for Alden and Daisy? Did you really go to Harvard? What's your *story*?"
"My story, well." He looked more self-conscious than she had ever seen him. "It's a lot less interesting than you make out. My mother wasn't prepared to raise a child after my father died, so I was raised by my father's relatives, all those Deodatos on Long Island. For a couple of years, I was moved around a lot—Hempstead, Babylon, Rockville Centre, Valley Stream, Bay Shore. I saw my real mother on her holidays, but I had plenty of other mothers, and they all doted on me. Went to Uniondale High School. Got a scholarship to Harvard, which was a big deal, majored in Asian studies, got halfway proficient in Chinese and Japanese, graduated magna cum laude. Instead of going to graduate school, I disappointed everybody and enlisted in the army. After I got through officers' training and the Vietnamese course in Texas, I pulled a lot of strings and got into the military police in Saigon. I did some good there, and the work was interesting. Continued the karate lessons I started in Cambridge.
"When I came back, I took the test for the Long Beach police and got in despite being ridiculously overqualified. One of my uncles was a detective in Suffolk County, and that helped. For three years I did that, took more Japanese at Hofstra, private calligraphy lessons, got my black belt, took a lot of cooking classes, and then I sort of fell apart. Quit the force. Did nothing but kill time on the boardwalk and sit in my apartment. After six or seven months, I took all my money out of the bank and went

to Japan to polish up my Japanese and live in a Zen monastery. It took two years, but I was accepted into a monastery—long story—and stayed there about eighteen months. Very satisfying, but I had this problem: I wasn't Japanese and never would be. I came back so broke that I had to teach karate on a cruise liner for my passage. No idea what I was going to do. I decided to take the first job anyone offered me and devote myself to it as selflessly as possible. When my aunt told me the Chancels wanted to hire a male housekeeper, I moved to Connecticut and tried to do the best job I could."

Nora was gaping at him in unambiguous astonishment. "And you say that's not *interesting*? My God, Jeffrey."

"It's just a series of anecdotes. Spiritually I never got anywhere until I moved in with the Chancels. I have no actual ambitions, obviously, apart from that, and helping the Chancels was a lot more satisfying than a lot of other things I could have done."

Nora, who had been marveling at the disparity between her fantasies about Jeffrey and his reality, suddenly heard what the announcer was talking about and turned up the volume on the radio. "I have to hear this."

Jeffrey seemed startled but not at all offended. "Certainly."

What had snagged in her ear was an account of a fire in Springfield. ". . . as we have been informed, no fatalities have been reported as yet, though according to our most recent reports, the blaze has spread to several other houses in the exclusive Oak Street residential area."

"It's him," Nora said.

"Him?"

"Shh."

"To repeat, arson is now assumed to be the cause of the fire in Springfield's Oak Street region first reported shortly after five o'clock this evening by neighbors of Dr. Mark Foil, in whose residence the blaze originated. Area residents are advised to keep in touch with the Fire Department's emergency hotline, which is providing minute-by-minute—"

Nora turned off the radio. "Do you know who Mark Foil is?"

"I'm completely in the dark."

"Mark Foil is the man who called Merle Marvell." Jeffrey still did not quite seem to take it all in. "Which was why Marvell called Alden." The appalled expression on Jeffrey's face made it clear that he understood what had happened.

"You're convinced it was Dart who torched that house."

"Of course it was him."

Jeffrey looked at his watch, made some rapid mental calculations, then hauled down on the steering wheel and without bothering to signal rocketed across two lanes of moderately heavy traffic. Horns blared. He spun the car into Exit 18 at the last possible second. The MG squealed down the ramp and blasted through a stop sign to turn right on King Street in Northampton.

Nora unclenched her hands from the door handle. "What the hell was *that* all about?"

Jeffrey pulled over to the side of the road and stopped the car. "I want you to explain why Dick Dart is willing to murder people and burn down houses in order to protect Hugo Driver's reputation. Start at the beginning and end at the end."

"Yes, sir," Nora said.

67

ONCE NORA BEGAN, she found that talking to Jeffrey Deodato was very different from telling the same story to Harwich. Jeffrey was *listening* to her. By the time she finished, she felt as if her story, initially as confused as Daisy's novel, had in the act of telling reshaped itself into a coherent pattern, at least within Jeffrey.

"I see," he said, with the sense of having seen more than she had. "So now that Dick Dart has done what he could to hurt Dr. Foil, he'll move on to Everett Tidy. And he probably has a car."

"Cars sort of give themselves to him."

"We'd better see Professor Tidy. All I need is a telephone."

"You're going to call him?"

Jeffrey pulled away from the curb. "I'm going to call a friend of his."

"You know him?"

"I've known him forever." Jeffrey turned right at the end of the block and rolled up to a telephone. "I'll just be a minute," he said, and jumped out of the car, fishing in his pocket for change.

Nora watched him dial a number and speak a few sentences into the receiver. He turned his back on her and spoke another few inaudible sentences. He hung up and came back.

"Who was that?" Nora asked, and Jeffrey smiled but did not answer. He spun the MG around in a tight circle and zipped back out onto King Street. "How do you know Bill Tidy's son?"

"I met him a long time ago."

"*Now* where are we going?"

"Amherst, where else?" Jeffrey turned right into a parking lot and continued straight through it into another parking lot, from which he emerged onto Bridge Street and accelerated back toward the distant parade of cars and trucks on the highway. "Just out of curiosity," he said, "do you remember if Davey told you the name of that girl who was so interested in Hugo Driver? The one who did or did not work for Chancel House, and was or was not a member of something called the Hellfire Club?"

"Paddi Mann."

"I was afraid of that."

It took her a moment to gather herself. "You know Paddi Mann, too?"

"Paddi's dead now, but I used to know her. Her real name was Patricia, but she turned into Paddi after she fell in love with Hugo Driver. The person we're going to see in Amherst, the one who knows Everett Tidy, is Sabina Mann, her mother."

"How do you know Sabina Mann? *Why* do you know Sabina Mann?" Nora wailed. "What is *going on?*"

Jeffrey would not answer.

Davey had not made up the whole story. It had really happened, but five years earlier, in New Haven. Or it had happened twice.

"Don't tie yourself into knots," Jeffrey said.

"And you won't tell me how you know them."

"First we'll take care of Everett Tidy."

"Then tell me who you were taking me to in Northampton. I'm going to be meeting him anyhow when we leave Amherst."

"Not him," he said. "Her."

"Who is it?"

"It's about time you met my mother," Jeffrey said.

68

ON THE WAY into Amherst, Nora idly inspected a bronze sign and saw that the comfortable-looking two-story brick house on a little rise had been the residence of Emily Dickinson. She heard Dick Dart saying, "*We can find no scar, But internal difference, Where the Meanings, are—*" and her mouth went dry and goose pimples rose on her arms.

Uphill into a commercial section with bookstores and restaurants, left past a pretty commons like a green pool, uphill again past Amherst College's weathered brown and red buildings.

Jeffrey turned into a side street lined with handsome old houses, some of them surrounded by white fences, others nearly hidden by gardens of vibrant, nodding lilies and lush hydrangeas. He pulled up in front of a house barely visible behind its front garden.

Nora followed him up a path through waving pink and yellow lilies as high as her head. Three brick steps led up to a gleaming wooden door with a brass bell. The perfume of the lilies surrounded her and drifted off in a breeze she could barely feel. When the door swung open, a tall, gray-haired woman in half-moon glasses and a loose, long-sleeved smock the yellow of daffodils gave her a spine-stiffening glance and pulled Jeffrey into an embrace.

"Jeffrey, you horrible beast, sometime I hope you'll give me more than fifteen minutes' warning before you decide to favor me with a visit. I suppose you're staying with your mother, that's the only reason I ever get to see you!"

"Hello, Sabina, now let go of me before you break something."

She stepped back and grasped his upper arms. "You look very dashing in that *cap*."

"You look wonderful yourself, but you always do."

"I trust your mother's fine? She's so busy all the time, I never get to talk to her. I know she did the Trustees' Banquet at the start of the summer, and of course the reception at the President's House, but that's nothing to her, food for two hundred, is it?"

"Piece of cake. Lots of pieces of lots of cakes."

"And how are things with you?" She had kept her grip on his arms. "Still happy working for your inferiors?"

"I'm fine. Sabina, this is my friend Nora."

She released him and extended a hand to Nora. "You're the mysterious person who had to see Ev Tidy?"

Nora took Sabina Mann's hand and met her intelligent, commanding eyes, a few shades bluer than glacier water. "Yes, thank you, I hope I didn't put you to any trouble."

"No trouble, Ev came right over. Jeffrey knows he can get anything he wants. The only problem is he doesn't want enough." Sabina Mann was making rapid assessments of Nora's age, marital status, social position, and role in Jeffrey's life. "I'm sworn to silence and secrecy, Jeffrey won't tell me why, but I suppose I might be allowed to ask if you have known him long?"

Nora thought that she had been given a passing grade on the first test. "I've known Jeffrey for a couple of years, but actually I hardly know him at all."

Sabina Mann continued her silent assessment. She was far more annoyed than she would let Jeffrey see. "Let's explore what our mutual friend has told you. I suppose you know about that ridiculous job he's so pleased with, but has he told you about—"

"Now, now, Sabina."

"Indulge me, dear. Has our friend mentioned his wonderful success at Harvard?"

"He has."

"Good. Do you know about the Silver Star and Bronze Star he got in Vietnam, or his tenure in a monastery in Japan?"

"No to the first, yes to the second," Nora said with a glance at Jeffrey.

"Since you have been so *favored*, you must know that he's fluent in Mandarin, Cantonese, and Japanese, but I wonder if he's told you—"

"Please, Sabina, be fair."

"Has Jeffrey ever told you, my dear, that he has written two plays which were produced off Broadway?"

Nora turned to stare at him.

"Pseudonymously," he said. "Weren't nothin'."

"Now I know something about you, Nora."

"Don't, Sabina."

"Be quiet, Jeffrey. You're using my house for your own private reasons, so I'm entitled to all the information I can unearth. And what I have unearthed is that this lovely young woman is an employee at Chancel House, because that awful Mr. Chancel is the person from whom you most wanted to keep that particular secret. I'm sure she shares my distaste for your employer and his entire family, including his peculiar wife, his useless son, and the son's unsuitable wife, sufficiently to keep it safe. Isn't that right, my dear?"

"I didn't know the son's wife was as bad as the rest of them," Nora said.

"She isn't, that's why she's unsuitable. The only thing wrong with her is that she was foolish enough to marry into that family. But you're under Alden Chancel's thumb just like Jeffrey, so you can't be expected to comprehend the trail of destruction left behind by the Chancels."

"Are you finished, Sabina?" Jeffrey asked.

"I'd better be. Everett never enjoyed being kept waiting."

69

A STOCKY MAN with a steel-gray Vandyke beard and short, silver gray hair abruptly closed the book in his hands and looked up frowning. "Twenty minutes, Sabina. Twenty *full* minutes."

"It was only fifteen minutes, Ev. As I am to be excluded from this gathering, I needed a little time by myself with Jeffrey and his companion."

One side of Everett Tidy's frown tucked itself into his cheek in what might have been amusement.

"Would you like some coffee or tea, Jeffrey? Nora?"

"No, thank you," Jeffrey said, and Everett Tidy said, "Tea. Gunpowder."

"Gunpowder tea, then." She closed the door behind her.

Nora glanced back at Tidy and caught him looking at her. Unembarrassed, he held her eyes for a moment before turning to Jeffrey. "Hello, Jeffrey."

"Thank you for coming on such short notice."

Tidy nodded, turning over the book in his hands as if puzzled to be still holding it. He moved toward a high-backed velveteen sofa, placed the book on an end table, and looked up at Nora again. A cold, brisk wind, as much a part of him as the crease in his khaki trousers and the brutal little brush of his beard, seemed to snap toward her.

"Sabina thinks I'm impatient," he said. "The reason for this misperception is that my awareness of the many tasks which immediate obligations keep me from fulfilling makes me testy." The temperature of his private breeze dropped by several degrees.

"Until my retirement, I lived in college housing, which means that for twenty-two years I had an extremely pleasant house with plenty of room for my family and my library. I could have *remained* in my extremely pleasant house, but my wife is dead and my children are gone, and other faculty members had much more need of the space than myself. Therefore I bought an apartment, and when I am not writing two books, one about Henry Adams, the other about my father, I am weeding out books so that I can fit the remainder of my library into three rooms. Half an hour ago Sabina told me that an acquaintance of Jeffrey's wished to speak to me on a matter of the gravest importance. This matter concerned my safety." He inhaled, and his chest expanded. "Well, here I am, and I must insist that you tell me what the ragtag *hell* is going on here."

Jeffrey said, "Ev, you should know that—"

"I am talking to your companion."

The abyss between this man's experience and hers momentarily silenced Nora. She would never be able to convince Everett Tidy that someone wanted to kill him.

Tidy conspicuously looked at his watch, and Nora at last registered why he had to sort through his books. "How long ago did you move into your apartment?"

He lowered his arm with exaggerated slowness, as if he thought sudden movement might startle her. "Six weeks. Is there some point to your question?"

"If someone came looking for you at your old house, would the new people tell him where you are? Do they know your new address?"

He turned to Jeffrey. "Are we to go on in this fashion?"

"Please answer her question, Ev."

"Fine." He swung back to Nora. "Does Professor Hackett know the street address of my apartment building? No, he does not. In any case, the Hacketts are spending the month in the upper valley of the Arno—the Casentino. Who are you, and what are you after?"

"Her name is Nora Chancel," Jeffrey said.

Tidy blinked rapidly several times. "I know that name."

"Have you been watching the news the past few days?"

"I don't own a television set. I listen to the radio." He was talking to Jeffrey but keeping his eyes on Nora. His entire body seemed to lose its stiffness. "My God. Nora Chancel. The woman who was . . . Heavens. Until now I didn't connect the name to . . . Good Lord, and to think . . . So that's you."

"That's me."

Sabina Mann backed through the door carrying a tray and stopped moving as soon as she turned around. "I seem to be interrupting you." She looked at each of them in turn. "It must be an extraordinary conversation." She put the tray on the end table and fled.

Tidy had not taken his eyes from Nora. "Are you all right? You don't appear to have been injured, but I can't even begin to imagine the psychic trauma of such a thing. How are you doing?"

"I can't really answer that."

"No, of course not. What a thoughtless question. At any rate, you escaped that fellow and had the good sense to summon Jeffrey. If I were in trouble, I'd want Jeffrey's help, too. Please, let's sit down."

He patted the sofa, and Nora sat on the worn plush. He added milk to a cup of tea and gave it to her. She felt slightly dizzied by the reversal of his manner. Jeffrey slid into an overstuffed chair on the other side of the fireplace. Tidy remained on his feet, fingering his beard. There was no trace of the arctic wind.

"I apologize for blustering. I got in the habit when I discovered that it was useful for intimidating my students."

Nora said, "I'm glad that you're willing to hear me out."

He perched on the edge of the sofa. "I can only suppose that what you want to say to me concerns the man who abducted you. Please remind me of his name."

"Dart," she said. "Dick Dart. You wouldn't ever have heard of him."

He considered the notion for a few seconds. "No. On the other hand, I gather that he has heard of me. I'm right in saying he is a murderer, aren't I? There is no doubt about that?"

"No."

"And he wishes me ill."

"Dick Dart wants to kill you."

He straightened his back and gave her the benefit of his fine blue eyes. "What an extraordinary thing, to hear such a sentence. I find myself at a loss."

"Everett," Jeffrey said, "would you please shut up and let her talk?"

"Let me ask one more question, and then you can fill in the details, if there are any. Is there a motive, or did this man pick my name out of a hat?"

Nora looked at Everett Tidy, visibly restraining himself, all but biting his tongue. "He wants to kill you because you're Bill Tidy's son."

Tidy brought his hand to his cheek as if he had been slapped. Making a monumental effort to remain silent, he nodded for her to continue.

When she had finished, Tidy said, "So Dart assumes my father kept journals, which he did, that they deal with his stay at Shorelands, which they do, and that I am in possession of these journals, which I am. Tell me, do I have the honor of being first on Dart's list? I suppose I must."

"You're the second. This afternoon he started in Springfield with a doctor named Mark Foil. Foil was the longtime companion of Creeley Monk, and now he's his literary executor. I saw Foil just before he went out of town. Dart got there a little while later."

"Dart set the fire in Springfield?"

"He isn't very subtle," Nora said.

Tidy sat perfectly still for a moment. "Might I ask why you and Jeffrey did not go to the police before arranging to see me?"

"I can't talk to the police."

Tidy faced Jeffrey. "Is that so? She cannot?"

"Leave it alone, Ev," Jeffrey said.

"I don't imagine this fellow will have any luck finding my apartment, but I cannot allow him to destroy Professor Hackett's house under the impression that I still live there. I do not have to give my name or mention you in any way. All I have to say is that I saw a man resembling Mr. Dart in the area, and they will do the rest. Then I have some things to tell you, if you have the time."

"Good," she said.

Tidy stood up and gazed at her for a moment, biting his lower lip. "I won't let Sabina overhear my call." He bustled out of the room.

"Oh, I brought you some money." Jeffrey stood up, digging his wallet from his back pocket as he came toward her. "Three hundred dollars. Pay me back anytime, but take it. You're going to need money." He offered her what seemed a large number of bills.

Here she was, Nora Chancel, about to accept the offer of Jeffrey's money. She did not want to take it, but she supposed she had to. She was the object of other people's whims, some of them kindly, others malign. "Thank you," she said, a little stiffly, and accepted the money. "I'm grateful." She bent down for her bag and snapped it open. "I'll pay you back as soon as I can."

"There's no rush." He glanced at the door. "I hope Ev isn't saying too much."

The door opened just as he finished speaking, and Tidy walked in, frowned at him, and closed the door with theatrical care. "I had to persuade Sabina to go upstairs before I placed the call. She isn't very happy with us, I'm afraid." He watched Nora fasten her bag, then looked back up at her face. "Would you mind going somewhere with me? You too, of course, Jeffrey."

"Another trip," Nora said. "Where this time?"

"Amherst College Library, where I deposited my father's papers. It's closed, but I have all the keys we'll need. Jeffrey, it might help if you picked up that tray."

Sabina Mann was stationed on her bottom stair as the three of them came out of the living room. Everett Tidy did not see her until he was almost directly front of her, and then he stopped short. Nora, right behind, almost bumped into him. Jeffrey fell into place beside her, and an awkward moment passed.

"Sabina," Tidy began, but she interrupted him.

"They come, they confer, they make clandestine telephone calls, and then, en masse, they depart. It's like a play."

Jeffrey held out the tray, and she reluctantly stepped down to accept it. "I promise to explain everything as soon as I can."

"The Lord knows what that means. Everett, may I ask where you are going, unless that is another state secret?"

"Sabina," he said, "I understand that all of this must be very puzzling to you, and I regret the necessity of rushing out without an explanation. However, I—"

"Why don't you try telling me, in simple words, where you are taking them?"

He tilted his head. "How do you know that I'm taking them somewhere?"

"You're holding your car keys," she said.

With all the dignity he could summon, Tidy said, "We have to go to the college library, Sabina. I'll come back in half an hour or so, shall I?"

"Don't bother. Call me tomorrow, if you have anything to say. Jeffrey, will you be returning?"

"I'm sorry, but I'll have to get to Northampton. I'll see you soon, I promise."

"You are the most maddening person." She gave Nora a look in which outright disapproval threatened to appear. "I'll see you to the door."

70

THERE WAS SO much space in front of the long backseat that the two men seemed to be twice the normal distance from her. "That woman isn't happy with me."

"It isn't just you," Jeffrey said. "Sabina's used to being unhappy with *me*."

"Your aunt hasn't been happy with me since I dropped out of the Emily Dickinson Society," Tidy said.

"Your aunt? Sabina Mann is your aunt?"

"You really do talk too much, Ev."

Tidy swung his head sideways to stare at him, then looked forward again. "Excuse me, Jeffrey, but I naturally assumed that your friend knew who you are. Why would she get in touch with you if—"

"That's enough."

"Damn you, Jeffrey, let him talk," Nora said. "I tell you everything, and all you do is move me around like a puppet. I don't care if you won the Congressional Medal of Honor and the *Nobel Prize*, you hear me? You're not my golden boy. I'm really, really sick of this."

What she really wanted to do, what every cell in her body *told* her to do, was open the door and jump out. If she didn't get out of the car soon, she would have to flail out, scratch their faces, bite whatever she could bite, because if she didn't something worse would happen to her.

"I don't blame you for being annoyed with me, Nora."

"Stop the car."

"I want you to think about two things."

"I don't care what *you* want, Jeffrey. Let me out."

"Calm down and listen. If you still want to get out afterwards, fine, do it."

"To hell with you." She gripped the door handle.

"You were fed up back at the house, too, weren't you? That was when this started—when we were alone in the living room."

Nora opened the door, but before she could jump out, Jeffrey had scrambled over the seat and was lunging toward her. Tidy shouted something from the front. As Nora leaned out of the door, Jeffrey caught her around the waist and pulled her back in. Holding her tight while she fought to get free, he slammed the door and locked it. She hit him in the arm, but he fastened his hands around her elbows and pushed her down into the seat.

"Let *go* of me!"

His face was a few inches from hers. She kicked at his ankle, missed, and tried again. Her foot banged against his leg. "Ow," he said, and his face came closer. "Tell me why you're mad. It isn't because of me."

She kicked out again, but he had shifted his leg and her foot shot into empty air. She tried with the other foot and missed again. He pressed her arms against her body and pinned her to the seat. "Come on, tell me why you're mad."

She yelled, "Let go of me!"

"I'm letting go." Little by little, his grip loosened as his face drew back, until finally he was no longer holding her at all. She raised her right hand, but it was too late to hit him. Her mind was already working. She lowered her hand and glared at him. Jeffrey fumbled with something beneath him which floated upward and became a jump seat.

"What kind of car is this, anyhow?" she said, collapsing back into the seat. "A taxi?"

"A Checker," said Everett Tidy. He had pulled over to the side of the road and was staring back at them with one arm over the top of his seat. "My father used to drive one, and they're all I've ever owned. Had this one since 1972. Are you all right?"

"How could I be all right?" Nora said. "People keep grabbing me and moving me from one place to another without ever telling me the truth. Even before the FBI showed up, my life turned into a catastrophe, and then horrible things happened to me and I just about lost my mind. People lie to me, they just want to use me, and I'm sick of all these secrets and all these plots."

She stopped ranting and drew in a large breath. Jeffrey was right. She was not angry with him. It had come to her that she was still furious at Dan Harwich, or if not at the real Dan Harwich, the loss of the man she had imagined him to be. This loss felt like an enormous wound, and part of her fury was caused by the knowledge that the wound had been self-inflicted.

"Excuse me," Tidy said.

"Wait a second," Jeffrey told him. "It's Dick Dart, isn't it? Plus Davey moving out of your house. You *have* been mistreated, of *course* you feel like you have no control over your life. Anybody would."

"I suppose." Another recognition moved within her: that her real resentment had to do with an almost impersonal aspect of her predicament. From the beginning, she had been forced to concentrate on a matter far more important to everyone else around her than to herself. A cyclone had smashed her life and whirled her away. The cyclone was named Hugo Driver, or Katherine Mannheim, or Shorelands, or *Night Journey,* or all of these together, and even though Dick Dart, Davey Chancel, Mark Foil, and the two men in the Checker cared enough about the cyclone to open their houses, ransack papers, battle lawsuits, drive hundreds of miles, risk arrest in its name, it had been she, who cared not at all, who had been taken over.

Tidy said, "Jeffrey, I must—"

"Please, Ev. Nora, I didn't feel I could speak for my mother, so I had to postpone certain things until she could meet you. What would you like to do? It's up to you."

She leaned back against the seat. "I'm sorry I got wild. Why don't we just forget about it and go back to what we were doing?"

"I'm sorry," Tidy said, "but I can't do that until somebody tells me what you meant about the FBI."

Jeffrey said, "You heard her say she couldn't go to the police. You took that in stride, I remember."

"I want to know why the FBI is involved. I'm not going anywhere until I do."

"Nora?" Jeffrey said, and put a hand, one of the hands which had recently held her down, on her knee.

She jerked the knee from under his hand. "No problem. I don't have any secrets, do I? You want to hear the story, Professor? Fine, I understand, you want to know if you'll be morally compromised by associating with me."

"Nora," Jeffrey said, "Ev is only—"

"A neighbor of mine was kidnapped. We thought she was murdered, but she wasn't. When she turned up, she claimed that I kidnapped her. At least that's one of the things she says. She isn't very rational. Because it turned out my husband was sleeping with her, which was news to me, the FBI took her seriously. Is there anything else you'd care to know?"

Tidy scratched his beard. "I think that will do. Are we still going to the college library, then?"

"I wouldn't dream of going anywhere else," Nora said.

71

Nora told Everett Tidy what she had learned about Creeley Monk in a monastic room on the top floor of the Amherst library. Beside her at a long wooden table, Tidy had listened with a gathering excitement which finally had seemed to freeze him into the inability to look at anything but the old upright typewriter at the end of the table and the photograph on the wall of his father seated before the same typewriter.

After Nora had finished, Tidy slid a file box forward and said, "I'm grateful to you for sharing your information with me."

"You're welcome," she said, waiting to hear what the story had meant to him.

"My father did distrust Creeley Monk, and I should explain that first. He simply did not believe Monk's story of being a working-class boy from Springfield, the son of a barkeep, and so on. Monk had attended Harvard and wore expensive clothes, and my father, who was almost completely self-taught, thought he was being laughed at. Almost everything about Shorelands made him uncomfortable. He would not have accepted Georgina's invitation at all if he had not seen it as a way through his difficulties with his second book. He knew he'd made a mistake almost as soon as he got there, but he thought he had no choice but to stick it out. He was not a person at ease with the notion of giving up."

"I understand," Nora said.

"He was depending on the book to earn enough so that he would never have to drive a cab again. And within a day, he knew that Lincoln Chancel was coming, presumably to scout out writers for his new publishing house."

Nora wanted to steer the conversation toward whatever had aroused the enormous quantity of feeling beating away within this disciplined man, a matter presumably related to Katherine Mannheim, but one question about the admirable Bill Tidy troubled her. "Didn't he more or less abandon your mother and you when he went to Shorelands?"

Tidy shook his head vehemently. "There was no question of abandonment. We had a standing invitation to Key West, where an old friend of my father's named Boogie Ammons owned a small hotel. When the invitation to Shorelands came, my father arranged for my mother and me to stay there. That entire month, we lived better than we would have at home. We missed him, of course, but he wrote two or three times a week, so we had some idea of what he was doing."

"Did you keep the letters?"

"I have most of them. They tend to be noncommittal about his stay there. It wasn't until years after his death that I could face reading his journals, and then I learned how much he had hated Shorelands."

Tidy opened the file box and took out a dark green, clothbound volume. "I also saw how uncomfortable he was with himself. Do you understand? He was on a kind of high wire, gambling that he wouldn't fall."

"I don't think I do understand," Nora said.

Tidy nodded. "Think of his situation. My father was really struggling with a new book. If everything worked, he would finally be set free to do nothing but write. Lincoln Chancel was a crude, grasping monster, but he represented a way out. My father was so desperate that he could not keep himself from playing up to the man. Against his own moral sense. Unfortunately for him, another guest was even more desperate. Hugo Driver capitalized on the accident of being in the same house as Chancel by turning himself into a human barnacle."

"So he must have envied Driver," Nora said.

"Which made him feel even worse about himself. He couldn't trust his own instinctive dislike of the man. Therefore, my father never joined the group on the terrace, where Chancel appeared almost every afternoon, because Hugo Driver would be there. And, because he questioned his antipathy toward Driver, he forced himself to suspend judgment when he heard gossip, all the more so since he distrusted the source."

"He already thought Creeley Monk was a liar," Nora said.

"Monk struck him as exactly the sort of person who made up stories about other people. Especially if it might help his own cause. In this instance, with Merrick Favor."

Here at last was a chance to move into the center of his concerns. "What did your father think of Katherine Mannheim?"

Everett Tidy puzzled her by looking across the table at Jeffrey, who shrugged. He ran his fingers across the top of the book in front of him, clearly considering his words.

"Mostly for the reasons I've explained, my father actually had little contact with the other guests. The other part of his isolation was physical. Georgina put him in Clover House, off in the woods behind Monty's Glen, so far away from Main House that poachers sometimes wandered through in the middle of the night. He heard poachers even on the night Miss Mannheim vanished."

Tidy fell silent, and Nora waited for him to work out a way to speak of whatever had ignited him.

"There's nothing in my father's journals to suggest that Driver stole a manuscript from Miss Mannheim."

"I see," Nora said, feeling that she did not at all see.

"But you ask me what my father made of Miss Mannheim, and this information might still be useful to you—and through you, to me. My entire life, I can say, has been haunted by whatever happened at Shorelands that summer." His mysterious excitement seemed to intensify. "There is still one great matter to discuss, and it may be as critical to you as it is to me. If it's at all possible, will you let me know whatever you manage to discover?"

"Of course."

"Thank you. Now to Katherine Mannheim." He said this with the air of deliberately postponing his "great matter." "Clearly she was an attractive, interesting presence, utterly self-reliant. She could be intentionally rude, I gather, but what really struck my father, apart from her independence, was what he called her serenity."

"Serenity?"

"That surprises you, doesn't it? He meant a combination of self-confidence, instinctive goodness, courage, and compassion. Initially her prickliness, her willingness to be indifferent to conventional manners, misled him, but after the first week, he began to see these other qualities."

Tidy opened the journal. "Listen to this.

> "I have been thinking about this curious person, Katherine Mannheim. She has never had any money and lives simply and without complaint. Where she seems bohemian and reckless, she is utterly focused. She writes slowly, with great care, publishing little, but what is published shines. To her, recognition, acclaim, every sort of public reward, mean nothing. I wonder if I would be as foolish as Merrick and Austryn if I were not so gladly married to my darling Min."

"Min and Bill?" asked Nora. "Wasn't there a movie—"

"Family joke," said Tidy. "My mother's real name was Leonie.

> "Even the monstrous Lincoln Chancel, thirty years older than Katherine, and who wears his gluttony on his face, desires her. Merrick and Austryn are attracted to her inner being but imagine they want her body, so do not see that Katherine is chaste. It is not warm, this chastity; it is icy and determined.

"Katherine Mannheim never expected to live to old age. All her life she was aware of her weak heart, but she refused to live like an invalid except in this one regard. What I've always imagined is that where she considered activities like bicycle riding, drinking wine, and taking long walks potentially dangerous, she was certain that sex could kill her. And in any case, her instincts led her to a modest way of life."

"Did your father know what she was working on?" asked Nora.

"Not at all. What Georgina called the Ultimate, a kind of end-of-term tradition, should have explained it, but she didn't play along."

"What was the Ultimate?"

"At the end of the third week of their stay, all the writers met at dusk for a kind of round-robin in Monty's Glen, inside the ring of standing stones known as the Song Pillars. The gardener who had created the clearing, Monty Chandler, had noticed that a number of boulders dug out of a nearby field were all roughly twelve feet high, flat on both ends, and he had gone to a lot of trouble to upend them in the clearing. The guests sat in a circle inside the pillars. Georgina delivered some set pieces about Shorelands' history. When she finished, the guests described what they were working on, how it was developing, and so on. Of course, they were expected to pay tribute to Georgina's hospitality and describe the ways in which Shorelands had inspired them. They were also supposed to be amusing. Georgina Weatherall expected to be entertained as well as praised. As you might expect, Katherine Mannheim refused to play the game."

He turned over a few more pages. "Here it is.

> "After Merrick's song of praise to Miss Weatherall's hospitality, the wonders of Shorelands, and his own talents, it was Katherine Mannheim's turn to speak. She smiled. She was sure, she said, that we would understand her decision to obey her usual practice of choosing not to speak of work in progress. Those who had preceded her were braver and less superstitious than she, qualities for which she admired them greatly. As for Shorelands, its magnificence was so great as to defy description, but she was pleased to mention the services of Agnes Brotherhood, the maid who every morning cleaned her kitchen and made her bed. Upon leaving Shorelands, she would sorely miss the domestic assistance of Miss Brotherhood."

"She refused to talk about her work and thanked the maid," Nora said. "Sounds like she knew she was going to be asked to leave."

"Or wanted to be," said Tidy. "Georgina was outraged. Here's what my father says:

> "Miss Weatherall tugged her layers of purple and crimson around her shoulders. Her face turned bright red beneath her makeup. She muttered that she would convey Miss Mannheim's compliments to the maid. Hugo Driver, next in line, began by praising Miss Weatherall's generosity and went on to speak at such length of the meals, the gardens, the conversations, that by the time he finished with a panegyric to our hostess, a genius whose greatness lay in this, that, and the other, no one noticed that he had never bothered to mention his writing.

"As a result," Tidy concluded, "we don't actually know what either one of them was working on during that summer."

"Driver saw a chance to hide behind a smoke screen," Nora said.

"Maybe because he wasn't making much progress, which would mean that he was more and more dependent on Lincoln Chancel. Anyhow, when it was my father's turn, he spoke as much to Chancel as to Georgina Weatherall. My father continued to hold out hope even after he came back home."

"Did he ever finish his book?" Nora asked.

Tidy inhaled sharply, then swiveled his chair to face her with all of his suppressed intensity visible in his eyes. "Let me ask you this. Have you been told what happened to the novel Merrick Favor was working on?"

"It was torn to pieces."

"As was my father's book. Shredded, carbon and all."

Jeffrey spoke for the first time since they had come into the library. "What are you saying, Ev?"

With what seemed to Nora a deliberate and momentary relaxation of his iron self-control, Tidy looked up at his father's photograph. "So here we are, at the serious matter."

"Don't keep us in suspense," Jeffrey said.

"I'll try not to." Tidy glanced at Nora, then back up at the photograph. "The winter after he came back from Shorelands, my father told my mother that he was pretty sure he could finish his book in two or three weeks if he could work without interruptions. The upshot was that we were invited back to Key West—when my father was done, he was invited down, too, to celebrate. Boogie Ammons said, 'It's worth a few hamburgers to finally get that book out of you.' A little more than two weeks later, a policeman came to the hotel and told my mother that my father had killed himself.

"I couldn't read anything he wrote until I was teaching here and had a family of my own. His journals were in a trunk in my basement. One night when everyone else was in bed, I drove to this library, took out *Our Skillets,* brought it home, opened a bottle of cognac, and stayed up until I finished the book. It was an incredibly emotional experience. Then I had to read his journals. When I finally felt strong enough to face the last one, I found something completely unexpected. A week before we went to Florida, his agent had written to tell him that he'd been approached by Lincoln Chancel, who was interested in making a confidential exploration of my father's situation. Chancel had liked what he'd heard of the new book, wondered how close the book was to completion and whether my father might be willing to consider his publishing it. My father wrote back, saying that he was close to finishing the book and wanted to show it to Chancel. He didn't mention any of this to my mother.

"About a week later, he got some exciting news. Since he was writing for himself, he wasn't very specific about this in his journal. See what you make of this.

> "I left my typewriter to answer the telephone. I spoke my name. What a great change came then. There is to be a royal visit. The Royal Being will come alone. I am to tell no one, and if I violate this condition by so much as hinting about this matter, even to my wife, all is off. Only He and I are to be present. The great event is to take place in three days. I don't know what I expected, but THIS, well, THIS beats all."

He looked over at Nora. "Well?"

"It's like Creeley Monk," she said. "Was the visit called off?"

"Here's the last thing my father wrote.

> "Cancellation. No explanation. I can hardly pick myself up off the floor. Can I continue? Do I have a choice? I have no choice, but how can I continue when I feel like this?

"It's exactly what happened to Creeley Monk a few days later. Do you think it can be a coincidence?"

"I guess not," Nora said, "but that would mean . . ."

"That Monk got the same kind of call as my father. Doesn't it seem likely that Merrick Favor and Austryn Fain were approached in the same way? And doesn't it seem even likelier that the person who arranged a private meeting and then canceled it was Lincoln Chancel?"

"Good God," Jeffrey said. "You think it was a setup."

"It would have taken more than rejection from Lincoln Chancel to make my father throw in the towel."

Nora stared at him. Then she gave a wild look across the table at Jeffrey, who had evidently seen where all this was going sometime before. "You think Lincoln Chancel murdered your father and Creeley Monk. And Merrick Favor and Austryn Fain, too."

"I think Chancel pushed him out of the window and tore his manuscript to bits, just like Favor's."

"Maybe this is obvious, but why would he do it?"

"I suppose he had something to hide," said Tidy.

"The real authorship of *Night Journey.*"

"Of course," said Jeffrey. "Monk knew that Driver was a thief. He told Merrick Favor, and both your father and Fain overheard, but nobody believed him. Later Favor told them both that Monk was right. He was convinced he'd seen Driver steal something from Katherine Mannheim. Everybody knew that Driver was having trouble with whatever he was writing, but six months later he produces this stupendous book, and gives the copyright to Chancel House."

"There you are," Tidy said. "Chancel was as ruthless with Driver as with everyone else. All he had to take care of was the possibility that Katherine Mannheim had spoken about her work to one of the other guests."

"He made these confidential appointments," Nora said, "and canceled them. Then he showed up on their doorsteps and waited for them to turn their backs."

For a second, the three people in the room at the top of the library said nothing.

"Now what?" Nora asked.

"It seems the rest is up to you," said Tidy.

72

"WHAT AM I supposed to do?" Nora asked. "I can't prove that Davey's grandfather murdered four people fifty-five years ago. It makes sense to Everett Tidy and you and me, but who else is going to believe all this?"

"I think Ev meant that you should continue what you're already doing." The sky was still bright, and vibrant green fields lay on either side of the long, straight road to Northampton. Warm wind streamed into Nora's face and ruffled her short hair while seeming to slip past Jeffrey without touching him.

"What am I doing?"

"Taking one step after another."

"Brilliant. After all that, do you think that Katherine Mannheim wrote *Night Journey*?"

"I think it's more likely than I did this morning."

"Why is it so important for me to meet your mother?"

"I always forget how pretty this part of Massachusetts is."

He would not be drawn. "All right. Let's try another subject. What did your father do?"

"He was a cook, or maybe I should say chef. My whole family, on that side anyhow, were all great cooks. My great-grandfather was the head chef at the Grand Palazzo della Fonte in Rome. His brother was the head chef at the Excelsior. Despite the handicap of not being Italian, my mother was as good as all the rest of them. Before my father died, they were going to open a restaurant. She still loves it, in fact."

"And now she keeps herself busy cooking for the Trustees' Banquet and the President's Reception."

Jeffrey gave her a sidelong look.

"Your aunt Sabina said something about it."

"You have a good memory."

"Is Sabina your mother's sister?"

Jeffrey tugged the Eton cap an eighth of an inch lower on his forehead. For the first time, the breeze buffeting Nora seemed also to touch him.

"I see. That's the end of the line. Can you at least tell me about Paddi?"

"I can tell you part of it, but the rest will have to wait. You remember how Sabina feels about the Chancels. She blames them for a lot of things, but the main one is what happened to her daughter. She was a nice girl before she went off the tracks. Maybe she was a little like me, and that was why I liked her. Patty, which was her name then, was a lot younger than I, but I always enjoyed her company. Of course, I was gone a lot, so I wasn't around when she discovered *Night Journey.* The book took over her life. She changed the spelling of her name. Sometimes she pretended to be other characters in the book. I guess Patty got deeper and deeper into her obsession, to the point where she would disappear from home to visit other Driver people. There was a lot of drug abuse, fights at home, her entire personality changed, she wouldn't spend time with anyone who wasn't capable of spending day after day talking about nothing but Driver and the book, and when she was sixteen she ran away.

"One Driver person told her about another, and she floated through this seedy underworld devoted to Pippin Little, living in Driver houses. These people spend their lives acting out scenes in the book. Nobody knew where she was. A couple of years later, she managed to fake her way into the Rhode Island School of Design, I can't imagine how, and Sabina sent her money, but Patty refused to see her. She was there maybe a year, then she vanished again. Sabina got one postcard from London. She was in another art school and living in another Driver house. Lots of drugs. Then she moved to California—same situation—and wound up in New York, moving back and forth between the East Village and Chinatown, completely submerged in this crazy Driver world. That must have been when she zeroed in on Davey. Anyhow, she took off again, and nobody knew where she was until she died of a heroin overdose in Amsterdam and the police got in touch with Sabina."

There had been less decoration in Davey's story than Nora had thought. "Thanks for telling me," she said. "But I still don't understand why she was so fixated on the manuscript and Katherine Mannheim."

"Stop asking questions, and tell me about your childhood or how you met Davey. Tell me what you think of Westerholm." He would go no further.

"I can't stand Westerholm, I met Davey in a Village bar called Chumley's, and my father used to take me on fishing trips. Jeffrey, where am I going to sleep tonight?"

"There's a nice old hotel in Northampton. You can stay there as long as you like."

A few minutes later they passed beneath the highway and came into Northampton from the east. Rows of shops and grocery stores lined the street. At the bottom of a hill, the buildings became taller and more substantial, and the MG moved slowly amid a lot of other cars. They passed beneath a railway bridge, and young people moved along the broad sidewalks and stood in clusters at the immense intersections. Jeffrey pointed down a wide, curving street at the Northampton Hotel, an imposing brown pile with a flowery terrace before a glassy new addition.

"When we're all through at my mother's place, I'll bring you back, get you a room. Over the next couple of days we can talk about what you ought to do. We can probably have lunch and dinner together most of the time, if you like."

"This great cook doesn't feed you?"

"My mother isn't very domestic."

Nora looked out at pleasant, pretty Main Street with its lampposts and restaurants advertising wood-fired brick oven pizzas, tandoori chicken, and cold cherry soup; at galleries filled with Indian art and imported beads; at the pretty throngs and gatherings of the attractive young, mostly women, strapped into backpacks in their sawed-off jeans and halter tops or T-shirts; and said to herself: *What am I doing here?*

"Almost there," Jeffrey said, and followed a flock of young women on bicycles out of the traffic into a quieter street running alongside a tract like a parkland where dignified oaks grew alongside well-seasoned brick buildings connected by a network of paths. The young women on bicycles swooped down a drive with a Smith College plaque. Jeffrey executed a smooth U-turn in front of a large, two-story, brown clapboard building with a roofed porch wide enough for dances on the front and left side. It looked like a small resort hotel in the Adirondacks. A sign set back from the sidewalk said HEAVENLY FOOD & CATERING.

Jeffrey turned to her with an apologetic smile. "Just let me go in and prepare her, will you? I'll be back in a couple of minutes?"

"She doesn't know I'm coming?"

"It's better that way." He opened his door and put one leg out of the car. "Five minutes."

"Fine."

Jeffrey got out, closed the door, and leaned on it for a moment, looking down at her. If he had been tempted to say something, he decided not to.

"I won't run away," she said. "Go on, Jeffrey."

He nodded. "Be right back." He went up the long brick walkway, jumped up the steps, and glanced back at Nora. Then he walked across the porch and opened the front door. Before he went inside, he took off his cap.

Nora leaned back, stretched her legs out before her, and waited. An insect whirred in the grass beneath the sign. Across the street a dog woofed three times, harshly, as if issuing a warning, then fell silent. The air had begun faintly to darken.

After five minutes, Nora looked up at the porch, expecting Jeffrey to come through the door. A few minutes later, she looked up again, but the door remained closed. Suddenly she thought of Davey, at this moment doing something like arranging his compact discs on Jeffrey's shelves. Poor Davey, locked inside that jail, the Poplars. She got out of the MG and paced up and down the sidewalk. Could she call him? No, of course she couldn't call him, that was a terrible idea. She looked up at the porch again and felt an electric shock in the pit of her stomach. An extraordinarily beautiful young black woman with a white scarf over her hair was looking back at her from the big window. The young woman turned away from the window and disappeared. A moment later, the door finally opened and Jeffrey emerged onto the porch.

"Is there a problem?" Nora asked.

"Everything's all right, it's just sort of hard to get her *attention.*"

"I saw a girl in the window."

He looked over his shoulder. "I'm surprised you didn't see a dozen."

She preceded him up the slightly springy wooden steps and walked across the breadth of the porch to the front door. Jeffrey said, "Here, let me," and leaned in front of her to pull it open.

Nora walked into a big open space with a computer in front of an enormous calendar on the wall to her right, and a projection-screen television and two worn corduroy sofas on its other side. At the far end a wide arch led into an even larger space where young women in jeans bent over counters and other young women carried pots and brimming colanders to destinations farther within. One of the pot carriers was the striking black woman she had seen in the window. A slender blonde in her mid-twenties who had been watching a cartoon looked up at Nora and said, "Hi!"

"Hello," Nora said.

"You're the first woman Jeffrey ever brought here," the blonde said. "We think that's cute."

On the other side of the arch, ten or twelve young women chopped vegetables and folded dumplings on both sides of two butcher-block counters. Copper pots and pans hung from overhead beams. In front of two restaurant ranges, more women, most of them in white jackets and head scarves, attended to simmering pans and bubbling vats. One briskly stirred the contents of a wok. A stainless-steel refrigerator the size of a Mercedes stood beside a table at which two young women were packing containers into an insulated carton. Beyond them, a long window looked out onto an extensive garden where a woman in a blue apron was stripping peas. All the women in the kitchen looked to Nora like graduate students—the way graduate students would look if they were all about twenty-five, slim, and exceptionally attractive. Some of the women at the counters glanced up as Jeffrey led her toward the cluster in front of the nearest range.

Slowly, like the unfolding of a great flower, they parted to reveal at their center a stocky woman in a loose black dress and a mass of necklaces and pendants stirring a thick red sauce with a wooden spoon. Her thick, iron-gray hair had been gathered into a tight bun, and her face was unlined and imposing. She looked at Jeffrey, gave Nora an appraising, black-eyed glance, and turned to the woman Nora had seen at the window. "Maya, you know what to do next, don't you?"

"Hannah's mushrooms, *then* the other ones, and then it all goes into the pot with Robin's veal, five minutes, and bang, out the door."

"Good." She slapped her hands together and took two steps away from the range. "Let's get Sophie doing something useful. How's the packing going?"

"Almost done with this one," said one of the girls at the table.

"Maribel, get Sophie to help you carry them out to the van." A tall, red-haired girl with round horn-rim glasses moved toward the arch. The older woman looked at her watch. "Jeffrey picked a busy day to drop in. We're doing the Asia Society at nine, and a dinner party in Chesterfield just before that, but I *think* everything is running on schedule." She made another quick inspection of her troops and turned to Nora. "So here you are, the woman we've all been reading about. Jeffrey says you want to talk to me about Katherine Mannheim."

"Yes," Nora said. "If you can spare me some of your time."

"Of course. We'll get out of here and sit in the front room." She held out her hand and Nora took it. "Welcome. I gather that you may have to conceal yourself for a time. If you like, you could pitch in here. I can't give you a room, but you could sleep on a sofa until we find something nicer for you. I can always use another hand, and the company's enjoyable for the most part."

"I think I'll get her a room at the Northampton Hotel," Jeffrey said.

Jeffrey's mother had not taken her eyes off Nora. "Do whatever you please, of course, but if you're at loose ends, you can always pitch in here."

"Thank you. I'll remember that."

"I'd be happy to help the woman who married Davey Chancel."

Nora looked in surprise at Jeffrey, and his mother said, "I take it that my son left the explanations to me."

"Would I dare do anything else?" Jeffrey asked.

Sophie and Maribel had paused on their way to the table to help themselves to Swedish meatballs from a steaming platter, and the older woman said, "Pack the van, my little elves." Chewing, they hurried across the kitchen. "Let's go to the front room and sit down. I've been on my feet all day."

She gestured toward the sofa where Sophie had sprawled in front of the television. Nora sat, and Jeffrey put his hands in his pockets and watched his mother switch off the set. She placed herself at the end of Nora's sofa and rested her hands on her knees. "Jeffrey didn't introduce us, and I gather that you have no idea of who I am, apart from being this person's mother."

"I'm sorry, but I don't," Nora said. "You knew Katherine Mannheim? And you know the Chancels, too?"

"Naturally," she said. "Katherine was my older sister. I met Lincoln Chancel at Shorelands, and before I knew what was what, he hired me to work for him. I was still there when your husband was just a little boy."

Nora looked from the older woman to Jeffrey.

Jeffrey cleared his throat. "Mr. Chancel disliked the sound of Italian names."

"When Mr. Chancel hired me, I was Helen Deodato, but you may have heard of me as Helen Day," his mother said. "I got so used to it that I still call myself Helen Day. When Alden Chancel and his wife took over the house, they used to call me the Cup Bearer."

BOOK VIII

THE CUP BEARER

For a long time, Pippin sat in the warmth and the flickering light of the fire without speaking. He gazed into the old woman's face. After all she had told him, the white whiskers sprouting from her upper lip and pointed chin no longer frightened him. Not even the skull from which she drank her foul brown potion, nor the heap of skulls behind her, frightened him now. He was too interested in her story to be afraid.

"I don't understand," he said. "You are his mother, but he is not your son?"

73

For what seemed to her an endless succession of seconds, Nora could not speak. She could not even move. The decisive old woman before her, her necklaces of antique coins, of heavy gold links, of pottery beads, silver birds, silver feathers, and shining red and green stones motionless on her chest, her broad hands planted on her knees, sat tilted slightly forward, taking in the effect of her announcement as Nora stared at the firm black eyebrows, clever black eyes, prominent nose, full, well-shaped lips, and rounded chin of Helen Day. The Cup Bearer, O'Dotto—Day and O'Dotto, the two halves of her last name—unknown to Davey because his grandfather had thought Italian names too proletarian to be used in his house.

The woman said, "Jeffrey, you should have told her *something,* at least. Springing all this on her at once isn't fair."

"I was thinking about being fair to you," Jeffrey said.

"I'll be all right," Nora said.

"Of course you will."

"It's a lot to take in all at once. I've heard so much about you from Davey. You're legendary. They still talk about your desserts."

"Whole family has a sweet tooth. Old Mr. Chancel could eat an entire seven-layer cake by himself. Sometimes I had to make two, one for him and one for everyone else. Little Davey was the same way. I used to worry about his getting fat when he grew up. Did he? No, I suppose not.

You wouldn't have married him if he'd been a great lumbering bag of guts like his grandfather."

"No, I wouldn't have, and he isn't."

"Who am I to talk, anyhow?" Helen Day seemed almost wistful. "Davey must have missed me after his parents got rid of me. Poor little fellow, he'd have had to, with those two for parents."

Nora said, "He once told me he thought you were his real mother."

"His real mother hardly spent much time with him. Hardly knew he was in the house, most of the time."

"And of course even *she* wasn't his real mother," Nora said. "You must have been at the Poplars when the first child died."

Helen Day put a forefinger to her lips and gave Nora a long, thoughtful look. She nodded. "Yes, I was there during the uproar."

"Daisy and Alden didn't even want a child, did they? Not really. It was Lincoln who made them adopt Davey."

Another considering pause. "The old man let them know he wanted an heir, I'll say that. There weren't too many quiet nights on Mount Avenue during that time." She looked away, and her handsome face hardened like cement. "According to Jeffrey, you wanted to talk to me about my sister."

"I do, very much, but can I ask you a few questions about other people in your family first?"

She raised her eyebrows. "Other people in my family?"

"Is Sabina Mann your sister?"

The old woman flicked her glance toward Jeffrey.

"We had to see Ev Tidy," Jeffrey said. "His number is unlisted, so I called Sabina and asked her to invite him to her house."

"Which she was delighted to do, I'm sure. I bet she bustled in and out with lots of cheap cookies and cups of Earl Grey."

"It was Gunpowder, and she only bustled in once. I have to admit that she was peeved with me."

"Gunpowder," said Helen Day. "Dear me. She'll get over it. You wanted to talk to Everett about Shorelands because of his father, I suppose."

"That's right," Nora said.

"And was he helpful?"

"He had some ideas," Jeffrey said, with a warning glance at Nora which did not escape his mother's notice.

"I won't pry. It isn't my business, except for what concerns my sister. But from what I remember of Everett's father, he couldn't have had much to say about Katherine. It was my impression that he'd scarcely talked to her. Couldn't be much there to excite poor old Effie and Grace." When Nora looked confused, Helen Day added, "My sisters. They're the fools who saw that movie and hired a lawyer."

"You're right," Jeffrey said. "Bill Tidy had no idea what Katherine was writing."

"Hardly a surprise. The whole idea is mad. Now I am informed that this madness has infected the wretched man who stole you out of a police station." She shook her head in disgust. "Let me answer your question. No, Sabina Mann is not my sister, thank the Lord. She was Sabina Kraft when she married my brother Charles. Thereby completing the severing of relations between my brother and myself which began when he changed his name."

"Why did he change his name?"

"Charles hated my father. Changing his name was no more than a way to cause him pain. He did it as soon as he turned twenty-one. The disgrace nearly cost Effie and Grace what little minds they have. Katherine didn't care, of course. It didn't mean anything to *her.* Katherine was like a separate country all her life."

Nora was thinking that Helen Day, who had apparently not protested Lincoln Chancel's desire to change her own last name, was no less idiosyncratic than her sister.

"You weren't close to Charles or your two other sisters?"

"I got along with the Deodatos a lot better than my own family, if that's what you're after. Good, sensible, warmhearted people, and they were delighted to take Jeffrey in when it became obvious that I couldn't cope with being a single mother. I certainly wasn't going to subject my little boy to *Charles,* never mind Sabina, and Effie and Grace could scarcely take care of themselves. But here was this glorious clan, full of cooks and policemen and high school teachers. I was so fond of them all, and they had no problems with my way of life, so there was never any difficulty about my seeing Jeffrey whenever I could. When I left the Chancels, I knew I had to come back to this part of Massachusetts. This was my home, and it was where my husband died. It's the one place in the world I've ever really loved. Jeffrey understood."

"I did," Jeffrey said. "I still do."

"I know you do. I just don't want Nora to judge me harshly. Anyhow, between us all, we did a pretty good job with Jeffrey, didn't we? He's done a lot of interesting things, even though his Mannheim half meant that other people had a lot of trouble understanding them. There's a lot of me in Jeffrey, and a lot of Katherine, too. But Jeffrey is much nicer than Katherine ever was. Or me either, come to that."

"Katherine wasn't nice?"

"Am I? You tell me."

"You're beyond niceness," Nora said. "I think you're too good to be nice."

Tiny pinpoints of light kindled far back in the old woman's eyes. "You just described my sister Katherine. I'd like you to remember my offer. If you ever find yourself in need of a safe place, you'd be welcome here. You would learn to cook every sort of cuisine, and you'd be able to put away some money. We operate on a communal basis, and everybody shares equally."

"Thank you," said Nora. "I'm tempted to sign up on the spot."

"I should have known," Jeffrey said. "The famous Helen Day Half-way House, Cooking School, Intellectual Salon, and Women's Shelter strikes again."

"Nonsense," the old woman said. "Nora understands what I mean. Now we are going to talk about my sister Katherine, so you can stop fretting."

"Halleluiah." Jeffrey went to the other sofa and sat down facing them.

"Did Katherine ever talk to you about her writing?" Nora asked.

"I can remember her reading some poems to me when she was twelve or thirteen and I was about nine. It was an occasion, because Katherine was always very private about her writing. Not her opinions, mind you. If she thought something was absurd, she let you know. Anyhow, as I was saying, I used to see her writing her poems all the time, and once I asked her if I could read them. No, she said, but I'll read some of them to you—and she did, two or three short poems, I forget. I didn't understand a word, and I never asked again."

"But later on? When you were both grown up?"

"By that time, we didn't talk to each other more than once every couple of months, and all she said about her writing was that she was doing it. She did call to tell me she was going to Shorelands. She was pleased about that, and she was going to stay with me for a couple of nights when she left. I was up here, and Katherine lived in New York—by herself, of course, in Greenwich Village, a tiny apartment on Patchin Place. I went there two weeks after I came back home from Shorelands. I knew she was dead, I hope you take my word for that."

"What did you think had happened to her?" Nora asked.

"Years later, that silly old windbag Georgina Weatherall pretended to think Katherine had run away with some drawing of hers and changed her name to keep out of sight. What a story! Katherine never stole anything in her life. Why should she, she never wanted anything. It just made Georgina look better than having one of her guests die so far off in the woods that you could never find her body."

"You're positive that's what happened."

"I knew it the second I saw that ridiculous woman. Katherine would have known just how to ruffle her feathers, and the last thing that kind of woman can stand is the thought that someone is laughing at her. It was exactly like my sister to provoke a fool like that, and then decamp a split second before she was ordered off the premises. It was just her bad luck to die in the midst of this particular jaunt, so that we could never give her a burial. Her heart caught up with her at the wrong time, that's all."

"How did Georgina know to call you after she disappeared?"

"Katherine gave her my number. Who else's? She wouldn't have given her Charles's number, or Grace and Effie's, heaven knows. Katherine always liked me more than any of the rest of them. I want to show you some things."

She stood up with a rattle and rustle of the necklaces and went through the arch. Nora and Jeffrey heard her giving orders in the kitchen, then the slow march of her footsteps up a staircase.

"What do you think she wants to show me?" Nora asked.

"Do you think I ever know what my mother is going to do?"

"What's wrong with Grace and Effie?"

"They're too normal for her. Besides, they were scandalized that she went off and worked for Lincoln Chancel. They thought it wasn't good enough for her. My aunts don't much like what she's doing now, either. They don't think it's very ladylike."

"Hard to see how it could be any more ladylike," Nora said.

He smiled. "You haven't met Grace and Effie."

"How did they wind up with this notebook, or whatever it was, the one that caused all the trouble?"

"My mother used to keep her sister's papers in the basement here, but after she had a couple of bedrooms put in downstairs, she didn't have much room left. Grace and Effie agreed to take them—four cardboard boxes, mostly drafts of stories and poems. I looked through them a long time ago."

"No novel."

"No." He looked back toward the arch and the kitchen full of women. "By the way, despite the way she talks about Lincoln Chancel, or even Alden and Daisy, my mother's still loyal to them. Don't mention what we were talking about with Ev Tidy, okay? She'd just get angry."

"I saw the look you gave me."

"Remember, when she stopped working for them, she recommended Maria, who was about eighteen and just off the boat. Maria hardly even spoke English then, but they hired her anyhow. They hired me, too. She thinks the Chancels have done a lot for our family."

"I never did understand why Alden and Daisy fired her," Nora said. "She was like a member of the family."

"I don't think they did. She quit when she had enough money saved up to start this business."

The treads of the staircase creaked.

"I'm sure Davey told me that they fired her. Losing her was very painful for him."

"How old was he, four? He didn't know what was really going on." He gave her a tight little smile as his mother's footsteps came down the stairs. "Too bad they didn't send him out to Long Island. It might have done him some good."

"Might have done him a lot of good," Nora said, and turned toward the kitchen to see Helen Day, flanked by three of her assistants, leaning over a copper vat. She inhaled deeply, considered, and spoke to an anxious-looking girl who flashed away and returned with a cup of brown powder, a trickle of which she poured into the vat.

The long day caught up with Nora, and she felt an enormous yawn take possession of her. "How rude," she said. "I'm sorry."

Helen Day marched back through the arch, apologizing for the delay. She sat a few feet away from Nora and lowered two objects onto the length of brown corduroy between them. Nora looked down at a framed photograph on top of a spring binder so old that its pebbled black surface had faded to an uneven shade of gray. "Now. Look at that picture."

Nora picked it up. Two little girls in frocks, one of them about three years old and the other perhaps eight, stood smiling up at the photographer in a sunny garden. The smaller girl held a doll-sized china teacup on a matching saucer. Both girls, clearly sisters, had bobbed dark hair and endearing faces. The older one was smiling only with her mouth.

"Can you guess who they are?" asked Helen Day.

"You and Katherine," Nora said.

"I was playing tea party in the garden, and wonder of wonders, Katherine happened along and indulged me. My father came outside to memorialize the moment, no doubt to prove to Katherine at some later date that she was once a child after all. And she *knows* what he's doing, you can see it in her face. She can see right through him."

Nora looked down at the intense self-sufficiency in the eight-year-old girl's eyes. This child would be able to see right through most people. "Did you find this picture in her apartment?"

"No, that's where I found the manuscript. This picture was on her desk in Gingerbread, and it was the first thing I saw when I went there. *Good heavens,* I said to myself, *look at that.* You know what it means, don't you?"

Nora had no idea what it meant, but Helen Day's eyes and voice made clear what it meant to her. "Your sister felt close to you," she said.

The old woman reared back with a rustle of necklaces and pointed a wide pink forefinger at Nora's throat. "Grand-slam home run. She felt closer to me than anyone else in our whole, all-balled-up family. Whose address and telephone number did she give in case of emergency? Mine. Whose picture did she bring to Shorelands and put right in the place of honor on her desk? Mine. It wasn't a picture with stuffy Charles, was it?"

Because the finger was still aimed at her throat, Nora shook her head.

"No. And it wasn't a picture of those two idiots who never read a book in their lives, Effie and Grace, not on your life. She never felt any closer to those three than she did to strangers on the street. At first, I couldn't understand Katherine going off and leaving our picture behind, but when I noticed she had left her silk robe and a bunch of books, too, I saw what she was doing. She knew I'd be coming to get everything for her. She left those things behind for me, because she knew I'd take care of them for her. And I bet you can guess why."

Again Nora gave the answer Helen Day waited to hear. "Because you understood her better than the others."

"Of course I did. She never made any sense to them her whole life long. It was like Jeffrey with the Deodatos. I love them, and they're wonderful people, but they never could figure out some of the things Jeffrey did. People like Jeffrey and my sister always color outside the lines, isn't that right, Jeffrey?"

"If you say so, Mom," Jeffrey said. "But you've colored outside the lines a few times yourself."

"That's what I'm saying! A couple of times in my life people said I was crazy. *Charles* told me I was crazy. Going with Lincoln Chancel! Giving up my son, and not even to him, but to people he thought were inferior! You must be as crazy as Katherine was, he said. Well, I said, in that case I'm not doing too badly. You can bet he changed his tune when Jeffrey got his scholarship to Harvard and did so well there. When people don't have a prayer of understanding you, the first thing they do is call you crazy. Grace and Effie *still* think I'm crazy, but I'm doing a lot better than they are. They thought Katherine was crazy, too. She embarrassed them, just like I did when I went to work for the Chancels."

She folded her arms over her chest in a clatter of coins and beads and gave Nora a flat black glare. "My sisters actually thought Katherine ran away with that drawing, changed her name, and lived off the money she got for it. Know what they told me? They said Katherine never had a bad heart in the first place. Dr. Montross made a mistake when she was a little girl, and she's had special treatment ever since. Stole that drawing and took off, changed her name, now she's laughing at us all. They said

Charles changed his name, didn't he? Didn't you? they said. Wasn't Mr. Day you married, was it? I said I never changed my name, man I worked for did that, and when he spoke, you *listened*. All I did was get used to it, and it was only my married name anyway. All that writing, they said, that was crazy, too, but it wasn't, was it, Jeffrey?"

"Not at all," Jeffrey said.

"She was invited to Shorelands. Nobody says those other people were crazy. And Dr. Montross wasn't a fraud. Katherine had rheumatic fever when she was two, and her heart could have given out at any time. We all knew that. She *died*. Grace and Effie said, You never found her, did you, and neither did all those policemen, but they didn't see what it was like. You could have sent twenty men into those woods for a month, and they wouldn't find everything."

"If she wanted to get out, why go through the woods instead of taking some easier way?"

"Didn't want to go past Main House," said Helen Day. "Katherine didn't want anyone to see her. And you know, maybe she did get to the road. Maybe she even got a ride and a room for the night, or took the train somewhere, but her heart stopped and she died. Because she never got in touch with me about her things. I waited two weeks, but neither Katherine nor anyone else called me, and I *knew*."

"But your brother and your two older sisters didn't agree? They thought she might still be alive?"

"Charles didn't. He was sure Katherine had died, just like me. Dr. Montross told our parents that it would be a miracle if Katherine lived to be thirty, and she was twenty-nine that year."

"And Grace and Effie?"

"They knew it, too, but they changed their minds when that book came out, almost saying in black and white that Katherine took that picture from the dining room. Katherine couldn't do anything right, as far as they were concerned. They never had a good word to say for her until they started going through her papers before throwing them out—papers I gave them for safekeeping—and saw some scribbles on a few pieces of paper that reminded them of a movie they didn't even like! They still thought she was crazy, but they didn't mind the idea of making some money off of her. Old fools. Katherine didn't write that book, Hugo Driver did. If you want to know what my sister was writing, look in that folder."

74

WITH A RUSH of expectant excitement, Nora opened the spring binder. Jeffrey stood up to get a better look.

UNWRITTEN WORDS
by
Katherine Mannheim
15 Patchin Place, #3
New York, New York
(copy 2)

She turned over the title page to find a poem titled "Dialogue of the Latter Days," heavily edited in green ink. Her heart sank. *This* was what Katherine Mannheim had been writing? The poem continued on to the second page. She flipped ahead and saw that it took up twenty-three pages. "Second Dialogue," also heavily edited, ran for twenty-six pages. Two more "dialogues" of thirty to forty pages apiece filled out the book.

"It's one long poem, or so I've decided, divided up into those dialogues. She had two copies, and made changes to both of them. She must have taken the first copy to Shorelands to spend the month revising it there, and I think she was planning to type up a third and final copy with all the revisions when she got back."

She had been "unwriting" the *Unwritten Words* through a lengthy, painstaking series of revisions. "This was on her desk?"

"In her apartment, right next to her typewriter, along with a big folder full of earlier versions. The one she took to Shorelands was lost along with everything else she put into her suitcase."

"You never showed it to me," Jeffrey said.

"You weren't here all that often, and I wasn't done looking at it. I always had trouble understanding the things Katherine wrote, and this was harder than anything else, especially with all those scribbles. After a couple of years, I began to find my way. I saw—I think I saw—that she was writing about her death. About living with her death, the way she did for so long. If you had asked me, I would have said that she never thought about it because she didn't seem to. Katherine wasn't a brooding sort of person at all, but of course she thought about it all the time.

That's why she wrote the way she did, and why she lived the way she did. What I think is, my sister Katherine was a saint. A real-life saint."

Startled, Nora looked up from the book. "A saint?"

Helen Day smiled and glanced down at the photograph. "Katherine was the most sensitive, most intelligent, most dedicated person I've ever known, and deep down inside herself the *purest.* What most people call religion didn't affect her at all, even though we were raised Catholic. You'll find more spiritual people outside churches than in them. Katherine couldn't be bothered with the unimportant things most people spend their whole lives worrying about. She knew how to have a good time, she sometimes shocked ordinary-thinking people, but she had *focus.* When I take on new girls here, I look to see if they have at least a little bit of what Katherine had, and if they do, welcome aboard. You do, you have some of it."

"Well, a lot of ordinary-thinking people might think I'm a little bit crazy," Nora said, thinking of her gleeful demons.

"Don't you believe it. You've been *hurt.* I can see that. No wonder, considering what happened to you. Here you are, chasing around Massachusetts instead of going back home, if you still have a home to go back to." She looked over at her son. "Alden Chancel might not think you're the right wife for his son, but you're hardly crazy. In fact, what *I* think, you're one of those people who take in more than most of us."

"You're giving me too much credit," Nora said.

"You're a person who wants to know what's true. When I look back, it seems to me that most of what I learned when I was little was all wrong. Lies were stuffed down our throats day and night. Lies about men and women, about the proper way to live, about our own feelings, and I don't believe too much has changed. It's still important to find out what's really true, and if you didn't think that was important, you wouldn't be here right now."

Yes, Nora thought, *I do think that it's important to find out what is really true.*

Helen Day checked her watch. "I have to make sure everything's all right before I put in an appearance at the Asia Society. I hope you'll think about everything I said."

"Thank you for talking to me."

All three stood up. "You'll be at the Northampton Hotel?"

"Yes," Jeffrey said.

Helen Day had not taken her eyes off Nora. "If you're still up around ten, would you give me a call? I want to talk about something with you, but I have to think it over first."

"Something to do with your sister?"

The old woman slowly shook her head. "While I'm thinking about my question, you should think about your husband. You're stronger than Davey, and he needs your help."

"What's this 'question' of yours?" Jeffrey asked.

She turned to him and took his hand. "Jeffrey, you'll come here tomorrow, won't you? We'll have time for a real conversation. If you turn up around eight, you can help with the driving, too. We have to pick up a lot of fresh vegetables."

"You want me to drive one of the vans while Maya and Sophie sit in the back and make fun of me."

"You enjoy it. Come over tomorrow."

"Should I bring Nora?"

Helen Day had been moving them slowly toward the front door, and at this question she met Nora's eyes with a look as significant as a touch. "That's up to her." She let them out into the warm night.

75

"You liked her, didn't you?"

"Who wouldn't like her?" Nora asked. "She's extraordinary."

Jeffrey was driving them down Main Street, where restaurant windows glowed and gatherings of three and four drifted in and out of pools of light cast by the streetlamps.

"I know, but she drives a lot of people up the wall. She makes up her mind about you as soon as she meets you, and if she takes to you, you're invited in. If not, you get the big freeze. I was almost certain she'd warm to you right away, but . . ." He glanced at her. "I guess you see why I couldn't say much about her beforehand."

"I suppose I do," she said.

"What would you like to do?"

"Go to bed," she said. "After that, maybe I'll spend the rest of my life chopping celery for your mother. I'd have to change my name, but that's all right, everybody else already has. After a couple of years maybe I'd get to be as perceptive as your mother thinks I am."

Jeffrey gave her one of his sidelong looks. "I thought you seemed unhappy back there. Disappointed, I guess."

"Well, you're already perceptive enough for both of us. Yes. I guess I was expecting too much. I thought that even if everything was falling apart around me, at least I could help prove that your aunt was the real writer of *Night Journey*. Instead, all I managed to find out was that Hugo Driver was a nasty little creep who stole things. But if he didn't steal *Night Journey*, then everything we thought we knew was all wrong. What did your aunts see in those pages, anyhow? What excited them so much?"

"Phrases. Descriptions of landscapes, fields and fog and mountains. Most of them were sort of like Driver, but not close enough to justify calling a lawyer. There was something about death and childhood—how a child could see death as a journey."

"That makes a lot of sense for Katherine Mannheim, but it hardly proves anything about the book."

"Two other phrases got them excited, mainly. One was about a black wolf."

"That doesn't mean anything."

"The other was 'the Cup Bearer.' They did get excited about that." The front of the hotel floated past them. A guitarist played bossa nova music on the terrace.

"I don't get it. That's what Davey used to call your mother."

"You saw that picture of the two of them as little girls, where my mother is holding a cup. After that, Katherine started calling her the Cup Bearer." He rolled the MG down into the lot. His smile flashed. "I forgot, you never read *Night Journey*."

"I still don't get it."

"Book Eight of *Night Journey* is called 'The Cup Bearer.' That's what really got Grace and Effie going, that and the wolf." He pulled into an empty spot and switched off the engine.

"But Davey was calling your mother the Cup Bearer before he could even read. How did he ever hear about it?"

"He must have seen the photograph in her room," Jeffrey said. "He went there looking for her sometimes, when Alden and Daisy left him alone. If he'd asked her about it, she would have told him about the nickname. That would have been another reason why the book meant so much to him later on. It reminded him of my mother."

Now she knew why Davey had been irritated with her when she had asked him about the origin of the nickname. Jeffrey was waiting patiently for her to finish asking questions so that they could leave the car. "Is the Cup Bearer in the book anything like your mother?"

"Well, let's see." He propped his chin in his hand. "She makes this foul-smelling brew. She had no children of her own, but she raised someone else's child. On the whole, she's pretty fearsome. I'd have to say she's a lot like my mother."

"Hugo Driver never saw that picture. Where did he get the phrase from?"

"You got me."

In the warm evening air they moved toward the concrete steps, washed shining white by the lights, leading to the hotel's back door. Half his face in shadow, the Eton cap tilted over his forehead, Jeffrey more than ever resembled a jewel thief from twenties novels. "Maybe this is none of my business," he said. "But if she leans on you to call Davey, think hard before you do it. And if you do decide to call him, don't tell him where you are."

He turned away and led her up the gleaming steps.

76

WITHIN A SMALL, wary portion of her mind, Nora had been awaiting the news that the hotel had only a single unoccupied room, but Jeffrey had not turned into Dan Harwich. He had returned from the desk with two keys, hers for the fifth-floor room overlooking the terrace and the top of King Street where she had taken a long bath and now, wrapped in a white robe, occupied a grandmotherly easy chair, the radio playing Brahms's Alto Rhapsody and the air conditioner humming, reading her husband's favorite novel as an escape from thinking about what to do next.

Pippin Little wandered from character to character, hearing stories. Some of these characters were human and some were monsters, but they were fine storytellers one and all. Their tales were colorful and involved, full of danger, heroism, and betrayal. Some told the truth and others lied. Some wanted to help Pippin Little, but even they were not always truthful. Some of the others wanted to cut him up into pieces and turn him into tasty meat loaf, but these characters did not always lie. The truth Pippin required was a mosaic to be assembled over time and at great risk. Nearly everybody in *Night Journey* was related to everybody else; they made up a single enormous, contentious family, and as in any family, its members had varying memories and interpretations of crucial events. There were factions, secrets, hatreds. Pippin had to risk entering the Field of Steam to learn its lessons, or he had to avoid its contagion; if he stood among the Stones of Toon, he would acquire a golden key vital to his search, or he would be set upon by the fiends who pretended to possess a golden key.

It was just past nine-thirty, half an hour before she had been invited to call Helen Day. Did she want to call Helen Day? Not if Jeffrey's mother was going to do no more than try to make her feel sorry for Davey. She already felt sorry for Davey. Then she remembered that Helen Day had spoken of having to think about some matter before she could discuss it. Probably the old woman was considering telling her something she had already guessed, that the Chancels had never wanted their son.

She might as well get as far as she could with *Night Journey.* If she skipped here and there, she could just about finish the hundred pages remaining. Or she could go straight to the last twenty-five pages and see if Pippin ever made it to Mountain Glade. On the night her life had started to go wrong, she had come awake in time to see Pippin racing downhill toward a white farmhouse, which she had made the mistake of calling "pretty." *Pretty, so what if it's pretty,* Davey had said, or something close; *it's all wrong, Mountain Glade isn't supposed to be pretty. Does that place look like it contains the great secret?*

So what *did* this all-important place look like? Lord Night said it was "an unhallowed haunt of baleful spirits revealed by the Stones of Toon"; the Cup Bearer described it as "a soul-thieving devastation you must never see"; even less satisfactorily, Gentle Friend called it "the locked prison cell wherein you have interred your greatest fear." Nora turned over most of the pages remaining before the end of the book and skimmed down the lines before finding this paragraph:

> The great door yielded to the golden key and revealed what he had most feared, yet most desired to see, the true face of Mountain Glade. Far down the stony, snow-encrusted mountain, he beheld a misshapen cottage, a bleak habitation of lives as comfortless as itself.

Pippin had come back home.

A few minutes before the appointed time, Nora found the Northampton telephone directory in a drawer and sat on the bed to use the telephone.

"Heavenly," said a female voice.

Nora asked for Helen Day, and the phone rapped down on a counter. She heard a buzz of cheerful female voices.

"Hello, this is Helen Day."

Nora gave her name and added, "Sounds like you're having a party over there."

"Some of the elves got home early from the Asia Society. I have to change phones." Nora held the dead receiver while time ticked on. She moved the telephone closer to the side of the bed, stretched out, yawning, and closed her eyes.

"Are you there? Nora? Are you all right?"

The ceiling of a strange room hung above her head. She lay on an unfamiliar bed slightly too soft for her taste.

"Nora?"

The strangeness around her again became the room at the top of the Northampton Hotel. "I think I fell asleep for a second."

"I have at least half an hour before anybody's going to need me again. Can you talk for a bit, or do you want to forget about it and go back to sleep?"

"I'm fine." She yawned as quietly as possible.

"I often think about Davey. He was such a darling little fellow. I want to hear whatever you can tell me about him. What is he like now? How would you describe him?"

"He's still a darling little fellow," Nora said.

"Is that good?"

Nora did not know how honest she should be, nor how harsh an honest description of Davey would be. "I have to admit that being a darling little fellow at the age of forty has its drawbacks."

"Is he kind? Is he good to people?"

Now Nora understood what Helen Day was asking. "He isn't anything like his father, I have to say that. The problem is, he's insecure, and he worries a lot, and he's frustrated all the time."

"I suppose he's working for his father."

"Alden keeps him under his thumb," Nora said. "He pays Davey a lot of money to do these menial jobs, so Davey is convinced he can't do anything else. As soon as his father raises his voice, Davey gives up and rolls over like a puppy."

Helen Day said nothing for a moment. "Do you and Davey go to the Poplars often?"

"At least once a week. Usually on Sundays."

"How are relations between Alden and you?"

"Strained? Rocky? He put up a good front for about six months, but then he started to show how he really felt."

"Is he civil, at least?"

"Not anymore. He despises me. I did this stupid thing and Daisy went out of her mind, so Alden called Davey on the carpet and said that unless he left me, he'd fire him from Chancel House and cut him out of his will."

Helen Day was silent. "I had the feeling that you had something else in mind when you asked me to call," Nora said.

"Alden is blackmailing Davey into leaving you."

"That's the general idea. I tried to convince him that we didn't need Alden's money, but I don't think I did a very good job."

"What was this thing that gave Alden his excuse?"

"Daisy talked me into reading her book. When she called me up to talk about it, she went on a kind of rampage. Alden blamed me."

"He's a terrible bully. I respect the man no end, but that's what he is."

"I don't respect him. He never wanted Davey, but he can't let him go. All Davey's life he's suffered from the feeling that he's not the real Davey Chancel, so he'll never be good enough."

"I was afraid of this," Helen Day said. "Alden's making him *pay.*"

"Lincoln did the same thing, didn't he? He forced Alden and Daisy to adopt a grandson, and they went along for the sake of the money. Isn't that what you were thinking about telling me? You didn't want to say it in front of Jeffrey."

Again Helen Day waited a long time to speak. "I wish I could discuss that subject, but I can't."

"I already know. There was something just like it in Daisy's book."

"Daisy was furious with both of them."

"She didn't want him, either. I'm surprised they ever had a child in the first place."

Helen Day said, "I suppose they were surprised, too."

"You were at the Poplars when the first one was born. You saw them go through all that."

"I did."

" 'The uproar,' you called it."

"That's exactly the right word. Noise day and night, shouting and yelling."

"And you think Davey ought to know why his parents have always treated him the way they do. That he was only a way for Alden to stay in his father's will."

Silence.

"Alden made you promise, didn't he? He made you promise never to tell Davey about this." Another recognition came to her. "He made you leave, and he gave you enough money to start up your own business."

"He gave me the chance I needed."

"You've been grateful ever since, but you've never felt right about it."

After a pause, the old woman said, "He shouldn't be playing the same dirty trick on his son that his father played on him. That makes me very unhappy."

"Did they even want the *first* child? They must have had it because of Lincoln."

"If you guess, I'm not telling you. Do you understand? Keep guessing. You're doing an excellent job so far."

"So they didn't. How did the first one die?"

"I thought you said that Daisy wrote about this in her book."

"She did, but she changed everything." An amazing thought flared in Nora's mind. "Did Daisy kill the baby? It's a terrible thing to say, but she's almost crazy enough to have done it, and Lincoln and Alden wouldn't have had any trouble hushing it up."

"The only thing Daisy Chancel ever killed was a bottle," said Helen Day. "What would you do with an unwanted baby?"

"You gave yours to your relatives."

"But what would most people do?"

"Give it up for adoption," Nora said.

"That's right."

"But then why make up a story about it dying? It doesn't make sense."

"Keep guessing."

"You give up one child and then adopt another one? I don't even know if that's possible. No agency would give a child to a couple that had given their own away."

"Sounds right to me," said Helen Day.

"So the first one died. It must have been a crib death. Unless Alden murdered it."

"What did Daisy put in her book?"

"It was all mixed up. There was a child, and then it was gone. The Lincoln character rages around, but half the time he's in a Nazi uniform. Lincoln Chancel didn't wear Nazi uniforms, did he?"

"Mr. Chancel collected Nazi flags, uniforms, sashes, armbands, things like that. After he died, Alden asked me to burn them. You have to *guess,* Nora. Do you guess the baby died?"

"I guess it didn't die," Nora said. "I guess it was adopted."

"That's a good guess."

"But . . ." A moment from Daisy's book played itself out in her mind: Adelbert Poison squabbling with Clementine on his rotting terrace. Nora tried to remember what he had said about Egbert—some word Daisy had written. What had actually happened to Davey, the only sequence of actions which made sense out of these uproars, came to her an instant before she recalled the word, which was *reclaim*. It felt as though a bomb had gone off in her chest.

"Oh, no," she said. "They couldn't have."

After she said what was in her mind, she had no doubt that she was right. "They had Davey adopted, and then Lincoln made them take him back. There was no first Davey. *Davey* was the first Davey."

"Sounds like a pretty good guess to me," said Helen Day. "The Chancels have grand imaginations. Everyday truth doesn't stand a chance."

Nora let her idea of their crime speak for itself. "Neither one of them ever wanted him. They had to take him back for the sake of the money. They would have been happier if he *had* died."

"And Alden's been making him pay ever since."

"He's been making him pay ever since," Nora echoed.

"I was right about you. You do see more than most other people."

"They lied to him all through his life. How old was he when they got him back?"

"About six months. The other family didn't want to lose him, but Lincoln made Alden and Daisy go up to New Hampshire, and they said all the right things and got him back."

"Everybody believed that their child had died. The only person who knew what had happened was you. When Davey got older, they were afraid you'd tell him the truth, so they made you leave."

Helen Day sighed. "One of the hardest things I ever did in my life. I could *see* Jeffrey whenever I wanted, and I knew he was with people who loved him. But Davey was all alone. When Mr. Chancel died, they just ignored him. They're fine people, but they didn't want to be parents."

Nora was still reeling. "How can you say they're fine people when you know what they did?"

"It isn't so easy to judge people when you understand them. Alden has a cold heart and he's a bully, but I know why. His father. That's the pure and simple truth."

"I bet that's right," said Nora.

"You never knew Lincoln Chancel. Mr. Chancel had more energy, brains, and drive than any other six men put together. He was a *fighter.* Some of the things he fought for were wrong and bad, and he didn't give a hoot about the law unless it happened to be on his side, but he didn't pussyfoot through life—he *roared.* There were times when I was angrier at him than I've ever been at anyone, but there was something magnificent about him. I always thought Mr. Chancel was a lot like my sister, with everything turned inside out. Neither one of them was very nice, but if they'd been nice people they wouldn't have been so impressive."

"But he was a monster."

"You have to have a saint inside you to be a monster. Mr. Chancel caused a lot of damage, but his heart wasn't cold, not at all. When I went to Shorelands, who do you suppose tried hardest to find my sister? Who talked Georgina into letting me stay four days? Mr. Chancel. Who went out into the woods with me and the policemen? He had his businesses to run, he had his ticker tape and his telephone calls, but he did more to help find Katherine than any of those writers."

"I see," said Nora.

"I hope you do. And he saw what kind of shape I was in, with my husband dead and my son gone and my heart broken over poor Katherine, and he offered me a job at twice what I was getting, plus room and board."

"You feel strongly about him."

"Some things you don't forget. If Mr. Chancel had lived, he would have told Davey the truth, I know that."

"Should I?" Nora asked.

"You do whatever you think is best, but that's the kind of person you are anyhow. I just want you to remember that *I* didn't tell you, because I do what I think is best, too, and I don't go back on my promises."

"Look, didn't they have to have some kind of burial? There was supposed to be a *body.*"

"Private burial. In the graveyard behind St. Anselm's. Just Alden, Mr. Chancel, and the rector. Short and sweet, and the only man crying at the funeral was Mr. Chancel, because Alden knew damn well that what they were burying was a couple bricks packed in a shroud so they wouldn't slide around in the coffin."

"God, what a devil," Nora said.

"His father said a lot worse than that when he found out." Helen Day surprised Nora by laughing out loud.

77

DAVEY WAS IN Jeffrey's apartment, where the telephone line was untapped. If she called him, she was under no obligation to reveal his father's treachery. He would believe her in time, she knew, but if she troubled him with Helen Day's revelation while he was still under Alden's spell, he would accuse her of lying. Once he accepted the truth, he would have to burst out of the Poplars, out of Chancel House, out of Alden's life forever.

Nora reached out and touched the receiver. The plastic seemed warm and alive. She pulled back her hand, then reached out again. The bell went off like an alarm, and she jumped. *Davey.*

She picked up the receiver and said hello.

"Nora, is that you?" The man at the other end was not Davey.

"It's me," she said.

"This is Everett Tidy. I tried to call you before, but you were on the phone. It's not too late to talk, is it?"

"No."

"I thought you ought to know about something. I don't mean to worry you, but it's got me a little disturbed."

She asked him what had happened.

"I got two calls. The first was from a lawyer named Leland Dart. He's the father, isn't he?"

Nora asked what Leland Dart had wanted.

"He apologized for taking my time and all of that. He explained that he was the counsel for Chancel House and asked if I was aware that there had been some recent discussion about the authorship of one of their properties. I told him I knew nothing about it. Then he told me the property was *Night Journey*, and that, as I undoubtedly knew, my father had once had some contact with its author, Hugo Driver. He wanted to know if I was in possession of any papers of my father's which could demonstrate Driver's authorship. If I didn't have the time, he'd be happy to send one of his staff up to Amherst to go through everything for me."

"What did you say?"

"That nothing my father had written could prove anything about *Night Journey* one way or the other. Had I examined everything? Yes, I said, and he'd have to take my word for it, there wasn't anything he could use. Then he asked how many journals or diaries my father had left, and where I kept them. Were they on deposit in a library somewhere, or were they in my house? The Amherst College Library, I told him. If he sent a young fellow up to Amherst, would I agree to let him inspect the papers? Not on your life, I said. Then he said that he might need to be in correspondence with me, and he wanted to verify my address. He read out the address of my old house. Was that right? I said that as far as I was concerned, we had no more to talk about."

"Good," Nora said.

"Then he asked if I had been discussing this matter recently with any other parties. I told him that was none of his business, either. Had I heard of a woman named Nora Chancel, he asked. Had Nora Chancel come around making inquiries related to Hugo Driver?"

"He asked about *me*?"

"Right. I said no, I hadn't had any contact at all with you, and if he wanted to have a sensible business discussion, why didn't he call at a sensible hour? Well, he as good as called me a liar, and said you were a fugitive from justice, I should refuse to have anything to do with you, and there would be serious consequences if I ignored his advice."

"Why would Leland Dart—"

"The next thing he said was that he had a young lawyer already in the Amherst area, and wouldn't I agree at least to meet with the man? No. I would not. He argued with me a little while, and then I heard it."

"It?"

"The background. People talking. Voices. This strange ringing noise. Then I recognized it, that bell sound a cash register makes when a total is rung up."

"A cash register?"

"So I said, 'Are you calling me from a bar?' and he hung up."

"Oh, no."

"Are you thinking what I'm thinking?"

"That it was Dick pretending to be his father?"

"I thought about all the stress the man is under. If your son is Dick Dart, maybe you'd be tempted to do some of your business in bars. But after the next call, it occurred to me that it might have been Dick."

No more than twenty minutes after the man calling himself Leland Dart had hung up on him, Tidy had heard from a Captain Liam Monoghan of the Massachusetts State Police. Everett Tidy was on the verge of being taken in for questioning, perhaps even charged with various crimes, and if he had one hope in the world of escaping these humiliations, that hope was in Captain Monoghan. Monoghan said, *I don't think you were aware that this woman was a fugitive from the FBI,* and, *We have information that Mrs. Chancel has altered her appearance. We also have information that she may be in the Northampton area. Is that correct?*

"If he'd named any other town, I wouldn't have said anything at all, Nora. I would have thought he was bluffing. But you have to appreciate my position. I want to help you in any way I can, but I am not willing to go to jail. That man *promised* that I'd spend at least one night in jail if I didn't come across, and if that happened, I was afraid I'd involve Jeffrey and his mother."

"Professor Tidy, Dick Dart cut and dyed my hair, but the police don't know that. The only way they *could* know it is if Dick Dart told them."

There came a silence nearly as long as one of Helen Day's. "I don't think the man I talked to was a policeman," he finally said.

"What did you tell him?"

"He said he'd be satisfied that I was acting out of innocent motives if I could confirm or deny the information that you were in Northampton. If I continued to obstruct the police, there were people down at State Police headquarters who wanted to bring me in for the night. It seemed to me that the way to do as little damage as possible was to confirm what they already knew, so I told him that I did have the feeling that you had intended to go to Northampton, but I didn't know any more than that. He thanked me for my cooperation and said an officer would be coming over soon to take a statement. I called you as soon as I got off the phone."

"No officer turned up at your apartment."

"No. I suppose one could still show up. What do you think?"

"It was Dick Dart both times," Nora said. "When he was pretending to be his father, he learned enough to be pretty certain that I'd visited you, so he made the second call to see if he could bluff more information out of you."

"I'm so sorry." He groaned. "Nora, I had no idea I was putting you in danger. How did he figure out where you were?"

"He didn't," Nora said. "Northampton was just an educated guess. If he guessed wrong, he'd just have to keep naming towns until he got it right."

"Do you think I should call the police—the real police?"

"No, don't do that."

"Get out of there," Tidy said. "Go to Boston and hide out until you can be sure you're safe. If you can get there tonight, call me and I'll wire you enough money to hold you for a while. Get Jeffrey to take you."

"I want to find out if I'm still in trouble, but if I am, I might take you up on that."

"I have a little house up in Vermont which is looking very attractive right about now. Do you think Dart might still be trying to find out where I live? I hate to think of him being in Northampton, but I have to say that I don't like the thought of him in Amherst, either."

There was a silence Nora chose not to fill.

"I've been learning a very unhappy truth, the past hour or so."

"What's that?"

"It is extremely unpleasant to be afraid," Tidy said.

78

"DAVEY?"

The shocked silence, which rode atop a swell of violins and horns, continued until Nora filled it herself. "Davey, it's me."

"Nora?"

"Can you talk to me?"

"Where are you?" His voice sounded a little slower than usual.

"Is it safe to talk?"

"How did you know I was here?"

"That's not important. Is this line tapped?"

"How should I know? No, I don't think it is. My father got rid of Jeffrey and the Italian girl, so that's why I'm in Jeffrey's apartment." A blast of music obliterated his next few words.

"Davey, please turn down the music. I can't hear you."

He must have waved a remote control, because the music instantly subsided. "So how are you? Are you okay? You *sound* okay."

"It's a little complicated. How are you?"

"Lousy," Davey said. "I've been worried sick ever since Dart grabbed you out of the police station. I thought he was going to kill you. You know how I found out? The receptionist saw it on television on her break! She called me, and I ran downstairs. There were about twenty people around her desk. For half an hour they were showing stuff about you and Dick Dart, and then Dad took me back to Westerholm. Ever since, all we do is watch the news channel and talk to cops. And Mr. Hashim and Mr. Shull, boy, do we ever talk to those guys. Mr. Shull is sort of cool in a dumb kind of way. They both really hate Holly Fenn. They'd like to skin him alive."

Nora heard the sound of ice cubes chiming against glass. "Holly Fenn should get canned, he messed up big-time on this one. Hey, Nora, are you really all right?"

"In some ways, Davey."

"When Mr. Shull told us you got away, I was really glad."

"Glad."

"I was relieved. Don't you think I was relieved?"

"Davey, can I come home?"

"What do you mean?"

Her heart sank at the suspicion in his voice. "Is Natalie still accusing me of kidnapping her?"

"From what I hear, Natalie still isn't saying anything at all. Mr. Hashim and Mr. Shull still think you're guilty." He hesitated. "Natalie took a lot of drugs, did you know that?"

"No."

"One of those cops found a coke stash taped to the back of a drawer in her bedroom. Remember her refrigerator magnets? I guess they should have told us something." Again she heard ice cubes rattling in a glass. "Were you in Holyoke?"

"Yes," Nora said.

"You drove to Holyoke and ditched that dead man's car?"

"I didn't intend to. I went into a restaurant and had something to eat, and when I came out the police were all over the place."

"You went into a *restaurant*? You *had something to eat*? What is this, a field trip?"

"I have to eat now and then," Nora said.

"But you could have come home. It makes you look so guilty when you hide out like this."

"Come home where—to the Poplars?" Nora asked. "I suppose Alden would greet me with shouts of joy."

"Come home and face the music, I mean. My father doesn't have anything to do with that. He didn't do anything wrong."

"Neither did I," Nora said. "But I bet your father is trying his damnedest to make you think I did." Another chink of ice cubes. "What are you drinking, Davey?"

"Vodka. Did you know that Jeffrey supposedly wrote plays that were put on at the Public Theater? I asked him about these posters he has up in his living room, and he claimed he wrote these plays, under the name Jeffrey Mannheim. I don't think he did, do you? They got awfully good reviews."

"Jeffrey has hidden depths," Nora said.

"He's the Italian girl's nephew, for God's sake! What kind of hidden depths could *he* have?" He took another chiming mouthful of the drink. "Yeah, forget Dad. Of course my father is running you down all over the place. Mom is even worse. She thinks you *arranged* to be kidnapped by Dick Dart. She wishes she'd thought of it. I think Mr. Hashim almost sort of believes her."

"Wonderful."

"I tell you, Nora, I've been really worried about you, but I have no idea what you think you're doing."

This had the ring of an accusation. "Mainly, Davey, I've been trying to stay away from Dick Dart and avoid the police until it's safe to come back home."

"The cops found a lot of new clothes from a fancy men's store in that car, and when they went to the shop, the salesman remembered the two of you very well. Dick Dart tried on a bunch of new suits, and you just sat there and watched him. Then the cops went up and down the street, and they find out that the two of you have been in half the shops in town. *Everybody* remembers this nice lovey-dovey couple."

"Dick Dart is a lunatic, Davey. Do you think I cooperated with him because I *like* him? I hate him, he makes my skin crawl. If I had done anything to call attention to myself, he would have killed me."

"Not if he couldn't see you," Davey said. "Like if he was in a changing room."

"I wasn't feeling all that confident, Davey. Just before we went on our shopping expedition, he raped me. I wasn't actually thinking too clearly. I felt like I'd been broken in half, and I wasn't up for any heroics."

"Oh God, oh no, I'm so sorry, Nora."

"I didn't cooperate with him, in case you're wondering. I was trying too hard not to pass out. Besides, my hands were tied behind my back and my mouth was taped shut."

"You must have been scared to death."

"It was even worse than that, Davey, but I'll spare your feelings."

"Why didn't you tell me before?"

"Because you didn't ask me any real questions. You went on and on about Jeffrey and watching the receptionist's television. Also because you didn't sound too sympathetic, and now I know why. You imagined that I was having all that fun with Dick Dart. You want to know how I got away from him? I hit him on the head with a hammer. I thought I'd killed him. I got outside and started the car, but what do you know, I didn't kill him after all, because he came charging out of the motel room, and I steered toward him and hit him with the car."

"My God. That's terrific."

"It would have been terrific if I'd killed him, but I didn't. He's still wandering around trying to find people who might help prove that your beloved Hugo Driver didn't write *Night Journey.*"

Davey made a strangled sound of protest and outrage, but Nora ignored it. "He just found out where I am, and now he's probably sharpening his knives so he can do a really good job on me."

"Where are you?"

"If I tell you, you can't tell anyone else. You can't even tell them we had this conversation."

"Sure."

"I'm serious, Davey. You can't tell anyone."

"I *won't.* I just want to know where you are."

"I'm in Northampton, in a room in the Northampton Hotel."

"Hold on a sec."

She heard him put down the receiver. A refrigerator door opened, and ice cubes chinked into a glass. Liquid gurgled from a bottle. He came back to the telephone. "What are you doing in Northampton?"

"I'm *hiding,* what do you think I'm doing?"

"Hold on, does this have anything to do with Jeffrey? Did he tell you I was staying in his apartment? Are you with Jeffrey? What the hell are you doing with Jeffrey?"

"I needed help and I called him."

"You called *Jeffrey*? That's crazy."

"I couldn't call you, could I? All the lines are tapped. And once Jeffrey realized that I'd been asking questions about Katherine Mannheim, he insisted on picking me up."

"I'm lost. Jeffrey is a servant, he's Maria's goddamned nephew, what can he possibly have to do with Katherine Mannheim?" A slosh, a chinking of ice cubes. "I'm beginning to hate the sound of that woman's name. I hope she died a horrible death. Why are you asking questions about her?"

"Dick Dart is doing more than buying new clothes." For a little while she explained Dart's mission, and Davey responded with moans of disbelief. "I don't care if you don't believe it, that's what's going on, Davey. As for Jeffrey, he's Katherine Mannheim's nephew because his mother, Helen Day, was her sister."

"His mother? Helen Day?"

"She met your grandfather at Shorelands when she went there to see if she could find Katherine. Her husband had died, and she wasn't happy in her work, and he hired her." She went on to explain the connections between Helen Day, Jeffrey, and Maria.

"Do these people think Katherine Mannheim wrote *Night Journey*? That could ruin us!"

"But Chancel House is in plenty of trouble even without a scandal about Hugo Driver. According to Dick Dart—"

"That expert on the publishing industry."

"He knows a lot about Chancel House. Your father is running it into the ground, and he's been trying to sell it to a German firm. This Katherine Mannheim business is driving him crazy, because it could wreck the German deal."

"There is no German deal. Dick Dart made it all up."

"He passed along another interesting story, too. About the Hellfire Club."

"Oh," Davey said. "Well, okay."

" 'Well, okay'? What does that mean?"

"Okay, I didn't exactly tell you the truth."

"You belonged to the Hellfire Club."

"There was no Hellfire Club, not really. That was just what we called it."

"But there's a branch in New York, isn't there? And you're a member."

"It isn't *like* that. You keep making it sound like a real club, when it's just these guys who get together to mess around. They do hire a good chef now and then, or they used to, and they did have a concierge and a coat-check woman. There was a bar, and you could take girls to the rooms upstairs. I only went a couple of times after Amy and I broke up."

"Who was the girl you took to the Hellfire Club in New Haven?"

"The same little menace who turned up in the art department. At Yale she called herself Lena Ware. Every time I saw her, she was reading *Night Journey*. I think she came to New Haven *looking* for me."

"Why didn't you tell me you'd met her twice?"

"It would have sounded so strange. And I didn't want to tell you about . . . you know . . . about what Dart probably told you."

"About hitting her with the car."

"I *didn't* hit her. Well, I *thought* I did, but I didn't. When I met her at Chancel House a couple of years later, and she was calling herself Paddi Mann, she said she was so mad at me that she wanted to scare me. Nora, she was nuts. I love Hugo Driver, but she never thought about anything else. You should have seen her friends! There are Driver houses, did you know that? I went to one with her. It was in a tenement over a restaurant on Elizabeth Street. It was really bizarre. Everybody was high all the time, and they had cave rooms, and people who dressed up like wolves, and all this stuff."

"That was what you described to me, wasn't it?"

"Uh huh. Anyhow, she kept trying to get me to go to Shorelands because she had this screwball theory that Shorelands was in *Night Journey*."

"How?"

"She said she thought you couldn't understand the book unless you went to Shorelands, because Shorelands was in it. Something about the places, but that's all she said. The whole idea was goofy. I got a book about Shorelands by a guy with a funny name, and it didn't say anything new about *Night Journey*."

"Just out of curiosity, what really happened the last time you went to her place?"

"I found the book under her bed, and I really did think that something bad had happened to her, because she just disappeared. Her room was completely empty. The other Driver people who lived there didn't know where she had gone, and they didn't care. She wasn't a girl to them, she was Paddi Mann, the real one, the one in the book. When I left, I felt so depressed that I couldn't stand the thought of going home, so I did check into a hotel for a couple of nights. When we moved into our house, the book turned up in a carton I took out of the Poplars."

"It was in our house?"

"I remember opening it up and seeing her name. For a second, Nora, I almost fainted. Every time that girl turned up, my life went haywire. I put it in the Chancel House bookcase in the hallway. The day I met Natalie in the Main Street Delicatessen, she mentioned that she'd never read *Night Journey.* She liked horror novels, but Driver always seemed too much like fantasy to her, so she'd never tried him. The next day I pulled one of the *Night Journeys* out of the bookcase and gave it to her, and it turned out to be that one."

"Oh, Davey," she said. He took another swallow of his drink. "So you wanted to get it before the cops saw it."

"I told you that. It had my name in it, too."

"So to cover up your affair, you told me this story instead of saying, 'Well, Nora, after we bought the house I gave this book to Natalie.' "

"I know." He groaned. "I was afraid you'd figure out that I was seeing her. Anyhow, why are you asking me all this stuff? You don't care about Hugo Driver."

"I bought all three of his books today."

"No kidding. After you finish the first one, you have to read *Twilight Journey.* It's really great. God, it would be wonderful to talk to you about it. Want to know what it's about?"

"I have the feeling you want to tell me," Nora said.

As ever, Davey instantly became more confident when given the opportunity to talk about Hugo Driver. "Like in the first book, he has to go around talking to all these people and piece together what really happened out of their stories. He learns that his father killed a bunch of people, and almost killed *him* because he was afraid he'd find out. Anyhow, early in the book he hears that his parents aren't his real parents, they just found him in the forest one day, which in some ways is a tremendous relief, so off he goes in search of his real parents, and a Nellad, which is a monster that owns a gold mine and looks like a man but isn't, slices him with its claws, and the old woman who dresses his wounds tells him that his mother really is his mother. His parents left him in the forest when he was a baby, but she went out that same night and brought him back. He says, '*My mother is my mother.*' "

79

FOR THE SECOND time that night, an enormous recognition seemed to gather in the air around Nora's body, cloudy, opaque, awaiting the moment to reveal itself. "Incredible," she said.

"It's a fantasy novel—what do you want, realism?" The ice cubes rang in the glass, and music rustled in the background. "It's so strange. You've been through all this terrible shit, and we're talking about Hugo Driver. I'm pathetic. I'm a joke."

"No, what you're saying is interesting. Tell me what happens in the third one."

"*Journey into Light*? Pippin learns that the real reason they're living way out in the forest at the foot of the mountains is that his grandfather was even worse than his father. He tried to betray his country, but the plot failed, and they escaped into the woods before their part in it was discovered. The Nellads are some other descendants of his grandfather's, and they have all his evil traits. They're so bad they turned into monsters. Pippin's grandfather killed a whole lot of people to gain control of a gold mine, but that was a secret, too. The gold mine has to be taken back from the Nellads, and Pippin has to reveal the truth, and then everything is all right."

It was not merely incredible; it was stupefying: Hugo Driver had structured his last two novels around the best-kept secrets of his publisher's family. *No wonder they were published posthumously,* Nora thought, and then wondered why they had been published at all. She marveled at the grandeur of Alden Chancel's cynicism; certain that no one but himself and his wife would understand the code, he had cashed in on Driver's popularity. Probably his audacity had amused him.

"Your father published these books," she said, as much to herself as to Davey.

"They don't sound like his kind of thing, do they? But you know how proud he is of never reading the books he publishes. He always says he wouldn't be able to publish them half as well if he actually had to read them."

Davey was right. Alden took an ostentatious pride in never reading Chancel House books. He had not known the contents of Hugo Driver's posthumous novels.

"Why are we talking about this?" Davey asked. "Nora, come home. Please. Come here, and we'll settle everything." With these words, he had produced his own golden key. He wanted her back; he would not abandon her during the ordeal of Slim and Slam. "I'll drive up there and bring you back. You could stay the night in the house, and I'd come over in the morning to take you to the station. Everybody's going to be pissed as hell at me, but I don't care."

He wanted her to stay in the house while he returned to the Poplars. He wanted her back, but only so that he wouldn't have to worry about her. "You can't drive, Davey," she said. "You've been drinking."

"Not that much. Two drinks, maybe."

"Four, maybe."

"I can drive."

"No, don't do it. I don't want to come back until I know I'm not going to be arrested."

"What about not getting killed? Isn't that a little more important?"

"Davey, I'll be fine." Nora promised herself to leave Northampton early the next morning. "Listen, I was looking at those books I bought today, and there's something I can't figure out. On the paperbacks of the last two, the copy on the back cover says that the manuscripts were discovered among the author's papers."

"Where else do you find manuscripts?"

"Hugo Driver's haven't exactly been easy to find, have they? Hugo Driver is about the only writer in history who didn't leave any papers behind when he died."

"Well, they didn't just drop down out of the sky."

The recognition hovering about Nora streamed into her in a series of images: a baby left in a forest, then reclaimed by his mother; an old man, the baby's grandfather, wearing a Nazi uniform; Daisy Chancel exhaling smoke as she fondled a copy of Driver's last book. *You're not one of those people who think* Journey into Light *is a terrible falling off, are you?*

The last two Driver novels had not fallen from the sky; they had flowed from the busy typewriter just off the landing of the Poplars' front staircase. Twenty years before he had turned to Daisy to produce the Blackbird Books, Alden had cajoled her into giving him two imitation Hugo Driver novels. He had needed money, and sly Daisy, knowing he would never read the books, had vented her outrage while she saved his company. Alden—Adelbert—was a fraud in more than one way. This was the real reason for her hysteria and his rage at Nora's discovery that Daisy had written the Blackbird books.

"What's going on?" Davey asked. "I don't like this. I know you, you have something up your sleeve. You could have come home this afternoon, and instead you get *Jeffrey* to drive you around the Berkshires so you can meet the Cup Bearer and ask a lot of questions about Hugo Driver. Are you trying to help these Mannheim people destroy my father?"

"No, Davey—"

"Jeffrey is like a spy, he came here to burrow around for proof his aunt wrote *Night Journey,* Helen Day was probably doing the same thing, they both wanted the money, only my father figured out what the Cup Bearer was up to and he fired her, but he's such a good guy he hired half her family anyhow."

"That's wrong. Neither one of them wants anything from you. Helen Day is convinced that her sister didn't write *Night Journey.*"

"They're using you. Can't you see that? God, this is horrible. I used to love the Cup Bearer, and she lied to my parents, she lied to me, and she lied to you. Her whole goddamned life is a lie, and so is Jeffrey's. I'm coming up there tonight and taking you away from these people."

"No, you're not," she said. "Helen Day is not a liar, and you're not coming up here just to drive me back to the police."

"Hold on, I'll be right back." The clunk of the telephone against the desk, the opening of the refrigerator. The rattle of ice cubes, the gurgle of vodka. "Okay. Now. Helen Day, damn her to hell. Can't you see that if she was Katherine Mannheim's sister, she's also the sister of these two old bats who are suing us?"

"She never even liked her other sisters. She won't have anything to do with them."

"Sure, that's what she told you, and you're so naive you believed her. What's this 'Day' business, anyhow? That can't be her name. She came here under an alias. I suppose that isn't suspicious."

Nora explained how and why his grandfather had shortened her name.

"But she's still a liar."

"Helen Day isn't the liar in this story, Davey." She immediately regretted having been provoked into making this statement.

"Oh, it's me, isn't it? Thank you so much, Nora."

"I didn't mean you, Davey."

"Who's left? I was right the first time, you have something up your sleeve. Oh God, what else? You hate my father and you'd like to ruin him, just like these Mannheims or Deodatos or whatever their real names are. I should hang up and tell the cops where you are."

"Don't, Davey, please." She drew in a large breath. "You're right. There is something I'm not saying, but it doesn't have anything to do with *Night Journey.*"

"Uh huh."

"I found out something about you tonight, but I'm not sure I should tell you now because you won't believe me."

"Swell. Good-bye, Nora."

"I'm telling you the truth. Helen Day knows this *thing,* this *fact* about you. She kept it secret all her life, but now she thinks you ought to know it."

Davey abused and insulted Helen Day for the space of several sentences, and then asked, "If this information is so important, why didn't she tell it to me?"

"She promised not to."

"Then why did she tell you? I hear the faint sound of tap dancing, Nora."

"She didn't tell me. She made me guess until I got it right."

He gave a weary chuckle.

"Why do you think Helen Day left the Poplars?"

After another couple of abusive sentences, he said, "At the time, what my parents told me was that she decided to go away and open her own business. Which I guess is what she did, right?"

"On her savings? Do you think she could have saved up that much money?"

"I see. The story is that my father paid her to keep quiet, right? This secret must be right up there with the key to the Rosetta stone."

"For you it *is* the Rosetta stone," Nora said.

"I know, *I'm* the real author of *Night Journey.* No, too bad, it was published before I was born. Nora, unless you spit out this so-called secret right now, I'm going to hang up on you."

"Fine," she said. "I just have to work out a way to say it." She thought for a moment. "Do you remember what your mother did all during your childhood?"

"I do believe we're about to go to Miami by way of Seattle here. Fine. I'll play along. Yes, I remember. She sat up there in her office and she drank."

"No, when you were a child, she wrote all day long. Your mother got a lot of work done in those days, and not all of it was put into the book she asked me to read."

"Okay, she wrote the Morning and Teatime books. You're right about that. I went through four or five of them, and all those things you mentioned were there. It's kind of funny, because I also found some expressions I must have heard her say a thousand times. They just never registered before. Like 'sadder than a tabby in a downpour'—stuff like that. 'We wore out a lot of shoe leather.' That's one reason the old man came down on you so hard. He overreacted, but he doesn't want anybody to know. I can see why. It wouldn't make him look very good."

"Thank you."

"But she wrote those books in the eighties, and we're talking about the sixties."

"Do you have copies of the last two Driver novels with you?"

"No way, you hear me? If you're trying to tell me my mother wrote the later Drivers, you belong in a loony bin."

"Of course I'm not," she lied. "The whole point is in the difference between the two styles."

"I am really not following you."

"I'm going to Miami by way of Seattle, remember? Unless I do it this way, you'll never believe me. So humor me and get the books."

"This is nuts," Davey said, but he put down the receiver and came back in a few seconds. "Boy, I haven't read these in probably fifteen years. Okay, now what?"

Nora had pulled the two books from her bag, and now she opened *Twilight Journey,* looking for she knew not what, with no assurance of finding it. She turned over some thirty pages and scanned down the paragraphs without finding anything useful.

"What do you want to show me?"

Some lines on page 42 rose up to meet her eye. *"Too true," said the wrinkled creature squatting on the branch. "Too true, indeed, dear boy."* She had to get Davey to notice these Daisyish sentences without seeming to point them out. "Turn to page forty-two," she said. "About ten lines down from the top. See that?"

"See what? *'He looked up and scratched his head.'* There?"

"A few lines down."

Davey read, " *'Pippin turned slowly in a circle, wishing that the path were not so dark, nor the woods so deep.'* That?" This was the sentence immediately below those with Daisy's trademarks.

"Read that paragraph out loud, and then read the whole page to yourself."

"Fine by me." He began reading, and Nora frantically searched through random pages.

"Now I should read the page to myself?"

"Yes." She scanned another page and saw a second *indeed.*

"All right, what about it?"

"That didn't sound a lot like your mother's writing, did it?"

"No, not really," Davey said, sounding uneasy. "Of course not. How could it? What's your point, Nora?"

"Look on page eighty-four, right below the middle of the page."

"Huh," Davey said. "That long paragraph, beginning with '*All the trees seemed to have moved*'?"

She told him to read it aloud, then read the whole of the page to himself, as before.

"I'm getting a funny feeling about this."

"Please, just do it."

He began reading, and Nora turned to the back of the book and found, just above the final paragraph, the proof she needed. *'With a shock, Pippin remembered that only a day before he had felt as bereft as a long-haired cat in a rainstorm.'* She waited for Davey to finish reading page 84.

"Are you being cute or something?" he asked. "You told me you weren't trying to tell me that my mother wrote this. A few piddly coincidences don't prove anything. I'm starting to get highly ticked off all over again."

"What coincidences? Did you see something in those paragraphs you didn't mention?"

"I'm getting fed up with your games, Nora."

Time to raise the ante: she had to give him part of the truth. "I don't think Hugo Driver wrote this book," she said. "It really did appear out of nowhere, didn't it? There were no papers. You would have seen them long ago, if they existed."

"Are you ever on thin ice. What's next? Hugo Driver was my mother in male drag?"

Nora seized on a desperate improvisation. "I think Alden wrote these books."

"Oh, come on. I never heard anything more ridiculous."

"Just consider the possibility. Alden knew he could make a whopping amount of money in a hurry if he brought out posthumous Driver novels. Because there weren't any real ones, he had to provide them." Nora continued improvising. "No one could know that they weren't real, so he couldn't farm them out. He couldn't even trust Daisy. Haven't you always thought these were different from the first one?"

"You know I have. They're good, but not like *Night Journey.* A lot of writers never come up to their first successes."

"The same person wrote these two, isn't that right?"

"And the same person wrote *Night Journey.* Who sure as hell wasn't my father."

"What's the name of that monster who cuts Pippin with his claws?"

"He doesn't have a name. He's a Nellad."

"Nellad. Remind you of anything?"

"No." He considered it for a moment. "It does sort of sound like Alden, if that's what you mean." He laughed. "You're telling me he put his own name in the book?"

"Wouldn't it be just like him to thumb his nose at everybody that way?"

"I have to give you credit for ingenuity. All these other people are trying to show that Driver didn't write *Night Journey,* and you're saying, yes, he did write that one, but not the other two. Which is almost possible, Nora. I'll grant you that much. If you weren't all wrong you could actually be right."

"Some of this really does sound like Alden to me. Look at the last page."

"All right." He read in silence for a time. "Come on. You mean that cat?"

Nora said that she meant the entire page. "I think Alden wrote this. I didn't even notice about the wet cat until you mentioned it."

"Well, it sounds more like my mother than my father, because my father never wrote anything except business letters."

"I don't think it sounds like your mother's writing," Nora said.

"God damn, you haven't been *listening* to me. I told you, someone's as sad as a wet cat in a couple of those Blackbird Books, and she used that phrase all the time when I was a kid. She still does sometimes."

"I had no idea."

"It still can't be true. My *mother*?"

"Alden used some of her favorite phrases. He wouldn't trust her that much."

"She's about the only person he would trust. I have to look at more of this." She heard him turning pages, breathing loudly, now and then taking a sip of his drink. "It can't be, can it? There are a million different ways to explain . . ." He let out a noise halfway between a wail and a bellow. *"NO!"*

"What?"

"One of the villagers, right here, page one fifty-three, says, '*You may ask me twenty-seven times, and the answer will never change.*' Twenty-seven times! My mother used to say that all the time. It was her expression for infinity. Holy shit."

"Your mother wrote it?"

"Holy shit, I think she did," Davey said. "Holy shit. She really did. Holy shit. It's no wonder they were so freaked when you accused her of writing the horror novels. This could absolutely finish us off."

"I don't see why," Nora said. "Doesn't it put your mother in a good light? If she did write those books, that is."

"God, you're naive. If this gets out, my father gets accused of fraud, and *Night Journey* immediately becomes suspect. There'll be lawyers all over the place."

"If it gets out."

"It better not. This has to stay secret, Nora."

"I'm sure it does," she said.

"At least we finally got to Miami. If the Cup Bearer knew my mother wrote those books, I guess I'm not surprised that they had to buy her off and get rid of her. Wow."

"Hold on to your hat," Nora said.

80

AS SHE TOLD Jeffrey early the next morning in the restaurant off the terrace, the rest of their long conversation had lasted half an hour, and in the course of it Nora had felt Davey's universe spin and wobble. His past had been yanked inside out; Nora had questioned the central theme of his life. He ridiculed, protested, denied. He had hung up after ten minutes and picked up the telephone again only after it had rung a dozen times. "Think about what she *wrote,*" Nora had said, and listening to her account while spreading damson preserves on a croissant, Jeffrey shook his head. He, too, at first had been suspicious of the night's discoveries. "Think about what your grandfather was like and what your father did to us, but first of all, think about what Daisy put in that book. That's your story, Davey. It's a message to you." No, no, no. Helen Day had lied. Nora had brought him back again and again to the child abandoned in and rescued from the forest, to *My mother is my mother.* "If it's true, I'm Pippin," Davey had said, sounding the first note of the awe which follows all great revelations. Nora had told him, "You've always been Pippin," and she had not added what she told herself: *Me, too.* "I feel like Leonard Gimmel or Teddy Brunhoven," he had said. "There is a code, and I can read it."

"Yes. There is a code, and it's about you."

"She wanted me to know. Even though she couldn't tell me."

"She wanted you to know."

"Should I confront him? Should I go over there and tell him I know?"

For the first time in their marriage, Nora advised Davey not to confront his father. "You'd have to tell him how you found out, and I don't want anybody to know where I am."

"That's right. I'll wait until whenever. Until I can."

This had left unspoken more than Nora liked. "You believe me, anyhow, don't you?"

"It took me a while, but, yeah, I do. I guess I really ought to thank you. I know that sounds funny, but I am grateful, Nora."

Fine, but gratitude isn't enough is what she had said to herself when the conversation had limped to an inconclusive end.

She tore a flaky section off a croissant and put it in her mouth. Less than a quarter of the pastry, her second, now remained on her plate, and she was still hungry. Three tables away, a pair of heavyset men in windbreakers stoked in enormous breakfasts of scrambled eggs, bacon, and fried potatoes. Nora felt as though she could have eaten both of their meals.

On the other side of the window wall to her right, a tall boy in a blue shirt was washing the terrace flagstones with a bucket, a long broom, and a hose. Rivulets sparkled and gleamed between the shining stones. Another boy was flapping pink tablecloths over the tables like sails and smoothing them out with his hands. It was as humble as the two men and their breakfasts, but to Nora this scene suddenly seemed to overflow with significance. Then she remembered a photograph Dick Dart had shown her in the Springfield library. *The golden key.*

"To change the subject, you think Dart called Ev Tidy," Jeffrey said.

She nodded and reached for another section of croissant, but she had eaten it all.

"Let me get you some more of those." In a few seconds, Jeffrey returned carrying a plate heaped with sweet rolls, croissants, and thick slices of honeydew. Nora attacked the melon with her knife and fork.

"Do you think Ev is safe?"

"He said he was going to a house he owns in Vermont." Nora finished the melon and began on the Danish. She felt as energetic as if she'd had a full night's sleep, and she had an idea of how to fill the next few days.

"You can't be as casual as you seem about Dart being in town," said Jeffrey.

"I'm not casual about it at all. I want to leave Northampton this morning."

"I was thinking about a nice little inn not far from Alford. If you like, we could see my mother for a bit, and then I could run you over there. It's charming, and the people who own the place were friends of my parents. Besides, the food is great."

For a secular monk, Jeffrey placed a sybaritic degree of importance on meals. "I do want to see your mother, but I'd like to go somewhere else after that, if you don't mind."

"You want to stay with Ev in Vermont?"

"That's not quite what I had in mind. Don't they rent out the old cottages at Shorelands?"

He gave a doubtful nod. "You want to go to Shorelands?"

Nora groped for an explanation that would make sense to him. "I've spent days listening to people talk about that place, and I'd like to see what it looks like."

Jeffrey folded his arms over his chest and waited.

She glanced outside at the boys, one of them sluicing away the last of the soapy water, the other arranging chairs around the tables, and moved a step nearer the truth. "I'm in a unique position. I've talked to Mark Foil and Ev Tidy, but they've never talked to each other. Foil knows what Creeley Monk wrote in his journal, and Tidy knows what his father wrote, but the only person who really knows what's in both journals is me, and I have the feeling that there's a missing piece. Nobody ever tried to put everything together. I'm not saying I can, but last night and this morning, when I was thinking about all these conversations I've been having, it seemed to me that I at least had to look at the place. Half of me has no idea what's going on or what to do, but the other half is saying, *Go to Shorelands, or you'll miss everything.*"

" 'Miss everything,' " Jeffrey said. " 'A missing piece.' Is it just me, or are you talking about Katherine Mannheim?"

"She's at the center of it. I don't know why, but I almost feel responsible for her." Jeffrey jerked up his head. "All these people had conflicting views of her. She was rude, she was impatient, she was a saint, she was a tease, she was truthful, evasive, dedicated, frivolous, completely crazy, completely sane. . . . She goes to Shorelands, she gets everybody worked up in a different way, and she never comes out. What comes out instead? What's the only thing that really comes out of that summer? *Night Journey.*"

Jeffrey regarded her with what looked like mingled interest and doubt. "The way you put it, you make it sound like the book is a kind of substitute for her." He thought for a second. "Or like she's in it."

"Not directly, nothing like that. But a phrase of hers is: the Cup Bearer." Jeffrey opened his mouth, and Nora rushed to say, "I know we've talked about this before, but it still seems like an enormous coincidence. Davey saw that photograph of the sisters in your mother's apartment at the Poplars, but Hugo Driver couldn't have seen it. It's part of the missing piece."

"If you want to play detective, I'll cooperate. It is possible to stay there. Five or six years ago, a French publisher, a great Driver admirer who wanted to stay there for a night, had some trouble getting accommodations. Alden asked me to take care of it for him. Which I did. The Shorelands Trust runs the estate, and some of the old staff is put up in Main House, but Pepper Pot and Rapunzel have rooms for people who want to stay the night. I got the French guy a room in Rapunzel, and he was delighted. So was Alden."

"Will you call them?"

"While you pack, but first I want to ask you a question."

"Go ahead." She braced herself, but Jeffrey's question was milder than any she had expected.

"Why did you want to tell me the family secrets? I came to the Poplars so late that I didn't even know Davey was supposed to have been adopted."

"I didn't want to be the only other person who knew." She stopped short of adding, *In case anything happened to me.*

"I'm sorry to hear that," he said, and signaled the waitress for their check.

81

WHEN THE TELEPHONE rang, she was in the bathroom, considering the question of makeup. On the fourth ring she picked it up and heard Jeffrey answer her question.

"I hope you don't mind waiting about half an hour," he said. "I called my mother to tell her we were coming over, and she's in a high old state. Apparently I agreed to drive some of the girls over to a market this morning, and I'm already late. It'll take forty minutes at the most, and I'll swing by to pick you up as soon as we're back."

"Perfect," she said. "I was just thinking that I'd be safer if I put my disguise back on."

"Your . . . ? Oh, the war paint. Good idea. You're checked out of the hotel, and I booked you into Pepper Pot as Mrs. Norma Desmond. I thought you were probably tired of being Dinah Shore."

They agreed to meet in the lobby in forty minutes. Jeffrey would call up to her room if he returned before that. "Do me a favor," he said. "Wait for me in the lobby, okay? I don't want to be responsible for all the skeletons in the Chancel closets."

Half an hour later the young woman at the desk glanced at Nora as she came out of the elevator and then returned to explaining the hotel's charges to a flustered old couple complaining about their bill. A soft pinkish light suffused the otherwise empty lobby. Nora wheeled her case to an armchair next to a table stacked with brochures and sat down to read "The 100 Most Popular Tourist Sites in Our Lovely Area." The white-haired couple were still wrangling over their room charges, but now it was the clerk who was flustered. The husband, a pipestem with a natty blazer, ascot, and shining wings of white hair, was loudly explaining that the telephone charges *had* to be mistaken because neither his wife nor himself ever used the telephones in hotel rooms. Why pay a surcharge when you could come down to the lobby and use the pay phone?

The clerk spoke a few words.

"Nonsense!" the old man bellowed. "I've just explained to you that my wife and I don't *use* telephones in hotel rooms!"

His wife backed away from him, and the young woman behind the desk spoke again.

"But this is an error!" the man shouted. The clerk disappeared, and the old man whirled on his wife. "You've done it again, haven't you? Too lazy to take the elevator, and what happens? *Two dollars* wasted, and here I am, making a scene, and it's all your fault."

His wife had begun to cry, but she was too frightened to raise her hands and wipe her eyes.

Nora saw an echo of Alden Chancel in the domineering little dandy and could not bear to be in the same room with him. She left the suitcase beside the chair and went down the hallway to the exit onto the terrace. Through the windows, she saw half a dozen cars, none of them Jeffrey's, driving down King Street. Sunlight glittered on the washed flagstones, and yellow lilies nodded beside the steps down to the pavement. She pushed through the door into fresh, brilliant morning.

When she reached the top of the steps, she looked up King Street for the MG, wishing that she could have taken a run that morning. Her muscles yearned for exercise; her breakfast seemed to have vaporized into a need for work and motion. She looked back at the hotel and through the glass wall saw the elderly husband spitting invective as he put down his suitcase to open the door for his wife. He was a gentleman of the old school, complete with all the tyrannical courtesies, and he had parked on the street because he thought he might be charged for using the hotel lot. Gripping the strap of her handbag, Nora marched down and walked five or six feet up the block, looking for Jeffrey.

The MG did not appear. Nora glanced over her shoulder and saw the couple coming down the steps onto the sidewalk. The man's face was pink with rage. She put them out of her mind and concentrated on the pleasures of walking briskly through the air of a beautiful August morning, still nicely cool and scented with lilies.

When she reached Main Street she looked left toward the row of shops extending toward the Smith campus and Helen Day's house, by now expecting to see Jeffrey tooling along in the sparse traffic. Half the shops on both sides of Main had not yet opened, and none of the few cars was Jeffrey's. With the blunt abruptness of a heart attack, a police car appeared from behind a bread truck and came rolling toward Nora. She forced herself to stand still. For a long moment the police car seemed aimed directly at her. She swallowed. Then it straightened out and came with no great urgency toward the intersection. Nora pretended to search for something in her bag. The car drew up before her, rolled past, and turned into King Street. She watched it move, still in no apparent haste, in the direction of the hotel. She decided to forget about exercise and wait for Jeffrey in the lobby.

Down the block, the dandy was standing beside an antique touring car with sweeping curves, a running board, and a massive grille decorated with metal badges. He opened the passenger door and extended his hand to his wife. Quivering, she hoisted herself onto the running board. The police car slid past them. The old man strutted around to the driver's side, giving the hood a pat. Down the street, the police car pulled up in front of the hotel, and two officers began moving up the steps.

King Street remained empty. When Nora turned back, the policemen were striding across the terrace toward the glass doors. Telling herself that they were probably after nothing more than coffee and apple turnovers in the café, she stepped into the street and began walking toward the shelter of a movie theater. The old man started up his extravagant car and pulled away from the curb. Standing near the middle of the street, Nora waited for him to go past. The car came to a halt before her, and the window cranked down. The old woman sat staring at her lap, and her husband leaned forward to speak. "The crosswalks are designed for use by pedestrians," he said in a pleasant voice. "Are you too good for them, young lady?"

"I've been watching you, you brutal jerk," she said, "and I hope your wife kills you in your sleep one night."

His wife snapped up her head and stared at Nora. The old man jolted away with a grinding of gears. Either a laugh or a scream came through the open window. Nora hurried to the other side of the street and moved beneath the theater marquee to the concealment of an angled wall next to the ticket booth. She looked at the hotel without seeing the policemen, then back at the antique car, which sat waiting for the light to change at the top of the street. A red car, not Jeffrey's but familiar all the same, swung around the antique vehicle into King Street, followed by an inconspicuous blue sedan. *It isn't, it can't be,* Nora said to herself, but the Audi moved steadily toward her, and it was. She saw Davey's dark hair and pale face as he hunched over the wheel to stare at the Northampton Hotel.

She stepped out of the angle in the wall, then moved back. Davey drove by. The blue sedan followed him to the hotel. Both cars pulled into the lot and disappeared.

Nora hovered in the shelter of the wall, praying for the policemen to leave the hotel. If Jeffrey came by, she'd wave him down and explain that her plans had changed, she was going to go back to Westerholm after all. Shorelands represented someone else's past, and she had to tend to her present. The policemen stayed inside the hotel, and she hugged herself, watching the glass doors at the edge of the terrace.

Children ran back and forth on the flagstones, weaving around the waiters. The glass door swung open, and a waiter with a tray balanced on his shoulder and a folding stand in his hand came outside. Before the door could swing shut, Davey rushed out and looked over the tables. When he did not see Nora, he walked across the terrace and came to the steps to the sidewalk.

Nora moved forward. Another police car turned into King Street. Davey scanned the sidewalk in front of him. The police car approached. Nora left the angle of the wall and began walking back up toward Main. The patrol car went past without stopping. She turned around on the sidewalk to see Davey making his way back through the tables. When the car reached the front of the hotel, it made a U-turn and pulled up behind the first one. Two officers got out and jogged up the steps, and a third patrol car came up from the bottom of King Street and turned into the hotel parking lot.

Her only hope was that Davey would return to the terrace alone. She moved a little farther up the street and watched him go back into the hotel. The two policemen were pushing through the tables under the curious gazes of most of the people eating breakfast. Davey disappeared, and the policemen reached the door a few seconds after it closed.

Come back out, she said to herself. *Get out of there and walk up the street.*

Two hefty parents and three even larger teenagers crowded toward the door. Davey came out just as they reached it, moved to one side, and held the door. Nora began walking toward the hotel. When the last of the family had waddled through, Davey held it open for two men in business suits. One of them wore black sunglasses. Davey shrugged and put his hands in his pockets. Nora's breath caught in her throat, and she took a step backwards. The men in suits were Mr. Hashim and Mr. Shull.

Conversing like old friends, Davey and the FBI men were walking around the street side of the tables, going toward the steps.

Too shocked to process what she had just seen, Nora began moving up the street. About twenty feet away was a parking lot for shops fronting on the lower end of Main. If she could get into the lot without being seen, she could walk through one of the shops and work her way to Helen Day's house.

She looked over her shoulder. Mr. Shull was jabbing his thumb toward the hotel and talking to Mr. Hashim, who glanced at Nora. Her heart struck her ribs, and her knees seemed loose. She marched past faded posters of handsome old buildings and trees in their fall colors in the windows of an empty information booth. A big black-and-white CLOSED sign, spotted brown by the sun, had been taped to the inside of its door. Nora turned into the lot and risked another glance over her shoulder.

Davey and Mr. Shull were moving toward Main Street. Mr. Shull was ticking off points on his fingers, and Davey was nodding.

You worm, you weasel, how could you do this to me?

An arm wrapped itself around her neck. Shock and terror locked her heart, and the arm tightening around her throat turned her scream into a croak. The man bent her backwards and dragged her into the lot.

82

"LOVE THESE REUNIONS of ours," said Dick Dart. "So important to keep up with old friends, don't you agree?" Nora pulled at the arm cutting off her breath, and her feet scrabbled on the dirty asphalt. "Especially those who have reached out and touched you." She tried to kick him, and then her balance was gone. Dart circled her waist with his free arm, lifted her off the ground, and carried her deeper into the lot.

"You'll love the car," he said. "As soon as I saw it, I knew that the time had come to gather in my little Nora-pie, and if you don't stop thrashing around I'll slit your throat right here, you stupid piece of shit." He let go of her waist, and her body sagged against his chest. Beneath his forearm, a sharp point jabbed into her neck. "Don't want that, do we?"

She shook her head the eighth of an inch his grip would allow. A dry rattle came from her throat.

"I'm a forgiving person," Dart announced into the rush of blood filling her ears. "Understand your distress, your confusion. Gosh golly gee, you're a human being, aren't you? I bet you'd love to take a breath right about now."

She did her best to nod.

"Let me get us out of sight, and we'll take care of that."

He carried her between two vans and pulled her to the wall. His arm loosened. A single breath of burning air rushed into her lungs, then he tightened his grip again. "There, now. Like another one?"

Braced against the wall, Dart held her back over his knee. If she struggled she would drop to the ground. Her feet dangled on either side of his bent leg. She nodded, and the arm relented for the length of another gasping inhalation.

She twisted her head and looked at him out of the side of her right eye. He was grinning, his eyes alight with pleasure below the brim of a black poplin cap which revealed a strip of white bandage above his ear. She could just see the shining edge of the knife where it met the hilt.

"I've missed you, too," he said. "To prove it, I'm going to let you breathe again." His arm dropped. "We'll be nice and quiet now, won't we?" Gulping air, she nodded. "Darling Davey turned you in, didn't he? Thrill for the boy, hanging out with the big, bad FBI. Think he's bonded with the one in sunglasses." He yanked her farther up his leg and closed his arm around her throat a little less tightly than before. "Over the initial shock of joy? Adjusted to the delightful reappearance of an old friend? Do we understand that any outburst will result in a little rough-and-tumble throat surgery?"

Nora came as close as she could to saying yes.

"I'm going to prove something to you." He stood up and deposited her on the ground. She was standing with her back to Dick Dart in the three feet of space between a battered brown van and an even more battered blue one painted with the words MACMEL PLUMBING & HEATING. At the end of the tunnel formed by the vans lay an asphalt parking lot scattered with crumpled candy wrappers and cigarette butts. Amazed to be alive, she turned around.

Dart was leaning against the side of the tourist center, one leg bent under him and his arms crossed over his chest. The black cap came down to just above his glittering eyes. A faint stubble covered his cheeks and chin, and in his right hand was the stag-handled German knife he had bought in Fairfield.

"Do you see?"

"See what?" Her hands trembled, and something in her stomach trembled, too.

"You're not running away."

"You'd kill me if I did."

"There is that. But I'm your best bet for getting out of this mess. You're afraid of me, but you're beginning to believe that I'm too interested in you to kill you out of a simpleminded motive like revenge, and you're furious with Davey. As long as I seem reasonable and calm, you'd rather take your chances with me than let that weak sister see you get arrested."

She stared at him—this was almost right.

"The difference between Davey and me is that I respect you. Am I going to lose my mind because you acted like a woman when I let my guard down? Not at all. You hurt me, but not that much. I have a truly hard head, after all. I'll have to take more precautions with you, but don't we still have things to do together? Let's do them."

"Okay," Nora said, thinking fast and hard. "Whatever you say."

"I suppose you did your best to make yourself up, but that's ridiculous. You smeared it on with a trowel."

"Are you going to get me out of here or not?"

Dart uncoiled from the wall, gripped her arm, and led her out between the vans. Two uniformed policemen ambled past the entrance. "You're responsible for my acquiring this wonderful work of art." She turned from the policemen to see the antique car owned by the tyrant in the ascot and blazer. "We'll even be able to keep it for a while."

He led her to the driver's door and helped lever her up onto the running board. "Know how to drive stick shift?"

"Yes."

"The perfect woman." Dart sighed. He trotted around the back of the car to get in on the passenger side. Nora looked at the seats and floor carpeting and was relieved not to see bloodstains.

BOOK IX

MOUNTAIN GLADE

. . . THE HEART'S GLADE, WHERE THE GREAT SECRET LAY BURIED.

83

"NICE AND EASY, now. This is an actual Duesie, treat it with respect."
"A doozy?"
Dart rolled his eyes, and Nora backed smoothly out of the parking spot, shifted into first, and drove toward the King Street exit. "A Duesie. A Duesenberg, one of the greatest cars ever made. An aristocrat. It's really delicious, the way these plums fall into my hands when you're around."
Davey and the two FBI agents stood at the center of a group of uniformed policemen in front of the hotel. Some of the men looked at the Duesenberg as Nora turned toward Main Street.
"People are so busy looking at the car that they don't pay any attention to who's driving it."
Out of habit, she turned right on Main. Two college-aged young women crossing Gothic Street watched them go by with smiles on their faces. Dart was right, people stared at the car, not the people in it.
"You've had time to consider things, see what the world is like without me, so all you need is some consistent supervision and we'll be back on the right track. How'd you learn to work a gearshift, anyhow? Most women don't have a clue."
"I learned to drive in an old pickup." Dart was leaning against a walnut-paneled door, smirking at her and fondling the pistol he had taken from Officer LeDonne. "How did you get this car?"
"Nora magic. If not for this evidence of your ability to smooth my passage, I might have treated your moment of rebellion a good deal

more harshly. But here *you* are, and instantly, here's the *Duesie*. Kismet. Though I did have my eye on your friend's MG. Is he an ex-cop?"

"He's an ex–lots of things." She glanced again at his twist of a smirk, unwilling to let him see her dismay. "Including a cop. He was the housekeeper at the Poplars."

"Devoted manservant," Dart said. "Deeply attached to the young lord's beloved. A romantic dalliance, perhaps?"

"No."

He raised his eyebrows and grinned. A stream of pedestrians moved staring past the front of the car.

"Last night, I asked some questions of the local citizens. An MG fancier who had observed the two of you pointed me toward the hotel, and there I came upon the vehicle in question. I thought I'd collect your friend when he came back for you this morning, but you came out and had your encounter with the previous owners of the Duesie. The old black magic has them in its spell, I says to myself, I says. Give me a little peek into the workshop, Nora-pie, tell me what you said to them."

"I said I hoped his wife would kill him in bed one night."

Dart barked out his ugly laugh and patted his fingertips against the barrel of the gun in applause. "Struck a nerve, magic one, struck a nerve. By the time they got to the corner, the old waffle was screeching at him. When you ducked into the front of the theater, I hustled across the street and followed them, acting on faith, always the proper thing to do, and before they went ten feet, Douglas Fairbanks pulled over to chastise her. The waffle got out and walked away. Doug took after her, so angry he forgot his keys. He trotted along, screaming at her, collapsed, bang—the old boy's flat out on the sidewalk. Another victim of an unwise marriage. I got in the Duesie and drove it right past the commotion, and do you know what? I think the waffle saw me. Bet she experienced one of the great moments of her life. When Douglas Fairbanks wakes up in the hospital, he'll take one look at the monitors at his bedside, the tubes coming from his every orifice, and he'll say—*What happened to my car?* And the waffle will say, *Dear, I was too worried about you to think about the Duesie*. This is the most important thing in his life, but can he criticize her for letting it get stolen? He wants to tear her heart out and fry it over an open fire, but instead he has to be grateful to her!"

Dart smiled to himself. "Sometimes I doubt myself. Sometimes I stop and wonder if I'm wrong and everybody else is right. And then something like this happens, and I know I can relax. Men are just dogs, but women are lions."

He reached over what seemed a much greater distance than would have been the case in any other car and patted her knee.

"You, Nora, are still a baby lion, but you're a *great* baby lion, and you've grown by leaps and bounds. When we started on our odyssey, you didn't know enough to last five minutes. But after twenty-four hours at the feet of the great Dick Dart, you're able to figure out a way to see Dr. Foil and Everett Tidy."

Nora pulled up at the stop sign before the Smith campus at State Street, and the usual backpacks and blue jeans gave the car the usual appreciative stares.

"Thought we'd get out of Massachusetts for a couple of nights, find a nice motel somewhere up in Maine. Safest place in America. Half of Maine hasn't even heard of television yet. They're still waiting to see if that moon-landing thing worked out." He opened the glove compartment. "Must be some maps here. Assholes with medals on their cars always have a million maps. Right again, Dick, we knew we could count on you."

Smith College rolled past the side of Dart's head. Nora glanced up Green Street and saw Jeffrey sprinting across the sidewalk to his car. "Would you consider another possibility?"

He tilted his face toward her as he sorted through the maps. "Maine sound a little primitive? I have a better idea. Canada. Don't need passports, they just wave you in and out. Our charming cousins to the north. Most self-effacing people on earth. You know what a Canadian says when you're about to kill him? 'May I floss first?' "

"I have a reservation in one of the cottages at Shorelands."

"Shorelands?" He fell back against the leather seat. "Idea has a decided sparkle. Continuation of our original quest. I trust this reservation is in some suitably neutral name."

"Mrs. Norma Desmond."

"Lovely. I can be Norman Desmond. My character takes shape about me even as we speak. Norm, husband of Norm. Lawyer by day, devotee of the written word by night. All my talks with my old dears very useful. Every now and then I could reel off some verse to impress the shit out of the guardians of culture. Wouldn't have to be Emily, I can quote lots of other idiots, too. Keats, Shelley, Gray—all the greats."

"Can you?"

"I told you, as soon as I read something, it's in there for good. Let me win a couple of bets in bars, but after a while, I couldn't get anybody to wager that I wasn't able to recite all of 'To a Sky-Lark.' Want to hear it?"

"Not really."

"Good. It's terrible. Now, were you going there by yourself?"

"Jeffrey was going to drive me there and drop me off."

He nodded. "Pull over to the side, so I can look at one of these maps and figure out how to get there."

She coasted to a stop. Dart removed a folded map from the pile. "Okay, here's Lenox and here's us. No problem. We go back into town, take 9 all the way to Pittsfield, and go south on 7. On the way, you can tell me what you got out of Mark Foil and Everett Tidy. But before that, do explain why you decided to go to this broken-down literary colony. Documents hidden under the floorboards? Katherine Mannheim's draft of *Night Journey* salted away in the bole of a tree?"

"I want to see where they all met each other."

"And?"

"Get a better idea of the layout."

"Piece together their comings and goings, that sort of thing? What else?"

She remembered the boys arranging the terrace in the lemon light of the morning; she remembered Helen Day. "I thought I might be able to talk to some of the maids."

"You mystify me."

"Some of the old staff is still around. The other night I realized that servants know everything. Like those boys you told me about, the ones who work at the Yacht Club."

"Deeply flattered, but the hag who changed Hugo Driver's sheets fifty-five years ago isn't likely to know what he wrote or didn't write, even if she's still alive."

"Katherine Mannheim didn't write *Night Journey.* That isn't the issue anymore."

He took it in. "Then why didn't Alden Chancel tell the old ladies to cram their lawsuit up the old rectal valve? He could have told their lawyer to go to hell at the beginning, but he put Dart, Morris on the case. If he's in the clear, why fork out money to his law firm?"

Nora remembered how she had felt when she had seen Davey on the hotel terrace with his new pals, Mr. Hashim and Mr. Shull. Dart was going to love what she was about to tell him. "Alden doesn't want anybody to question Driver's authorship of his books. That's a sensitive point."

He became instantly attentive. "Do tell. I mean, do. Tell."

"The horror novels weren't the first books Daisy wrote for Alden under a phony name. The other name she used was Hugo Driver."

Dart blinked, then laughed. "That boozy old pillowcase wrote *Night Journey*?" For a second he was the nice-looking man he would have been if he were not Dick Dart, and he laughed again. "No wonder Alden got rid of the manuscript! No, it can't be. She's too young. You're riding the wrong horse, babycakes."

"She didn't write the good one," Nora said. "She wrote the other two."

Dart opened his mouth as if to make a point. Then he regarded her in pure appreciative amazement. "Bravo. They came out in the sixties. How'd you find out?"

"You'd never see it unless you compared the Driver books with her horror novels, but once you do it's obvious. Daisy has certain trademark expressions she uses over and over. There was never any reason for anyone to read her horror books side by side with the last two Drivers, so no one ever noticed."

Dart grinned. "Hate poetry, love poetic justice. Once you start questioning Hugo Driver, everything he owns is up for grabs. *That's* why he called my old man." He tapped the gun barrel against his lips. "If Driver wrote *Night Journey,* why did he give the copyright to Lincoln Chancel?"

"I think something went on at Shorelands that nobody but the two of them knew about. After they came back, they were partners. Chancel even had Driver stay overnight at the Poplars a couple of times. Ordinarily, he wouldn't have bothered to spit on a weasel like Hugo Driver, even one who made a lot of money for him."

"So Driver had something on him."

"Or he had something on Driver, and he wanted to make sure that Driver didn't forget it."

"Could only be one thing," Dart said. "Tell me what it is. Get it right, I'll do you a big favor."

"Hugo Driver killed Katherine Mannheim. Maybe he didn't mean to, but he killed her anyhow, and Lincoln Chancel knew it. Chancel helped him hide the body in the woods, and Driver was in his power ever after."

Dart nodded. "Desperate man, desperate act. Why? What happened?"

"One day Bill Tidy spotted Driver doing something fishy with her bag. Maybe he stole a notebook and found enough to realize that all he needed to pull himself out of his hole was a little more of the story. Driver was a thief; he did what came naturally to him, he stole her ideas. Maybe he broke into Gingerbread looking for more material, and Katherine surprised him. She said something cutting to him—she was good at that, you wouldn't have liked her at all. Maybe he hit her. Whatever he did, she died. Driver wasn't ruthless enough to be a killer, like Lincoln Chancel."

Another thought came to her. "It almost has to have been something like that. She would never have invited Driver into Gingerbread, but he was inside it because in the book he used a photograph she kept on her desk."

Dart smiled up at the roof of the car and hummed a few bars of "Too Marvelous for Words." His smile broadened. "Turn this buggy around and pick up 9. I've just had a particularly lovely idea."

"Didn't you say something about a favor?"

"I believe I did. This is going to mean a lot to you."

She glanced at his gleeful face.

"The time ever comes I have no choice but to kill you, I'll do it quickly. Goes against the grain, making a sacrifice here, but I guarantee you won't suffer."

"You're quite a guy, aren't you, Dick?"

"Go to the wall for my friends," he said.

84

WHEN THEY GOT to Pittsfield, Dart manacled a hand to her elbow and guided her through shops for shaving supplies, a toothbrush, a glossy silk tie, boxer shorts, and over-the-calf socks. Outside of town, he asked her to drive into a gas station and pulled her into the men's room. Nora looked away as he filled the tiled cubicle with a fine sea-spray. "If cars could run on piss, I'd be a national resource." Dart removed his cap and leaned over the sink to inspect the bandage wound around the sides of his head. "Cut this off me." Nora found the scissors and worked the tip of one blade under the topmost layer of cloth. Soon she was unwinding a long white strip from around his head.

"Who did this for you?"

He gave her a glance of weary irony.

When the last of the bandage came away, Dart tilted his head and probed his hair with his fingers while scrutinizing himself in the mirror. "What's a couple of lumps to an adventurous soul, eh? Hurt pretty good at the time, though. Distinct memory of pain. Flashes of light behind my eyes. Second biggest headache of my life."

"What was the biggest?"

Dart lowered his hand and his suddenly expressionless eyes met hers in the mirror. In the hot little box of the bathroom, Nora went cold. "Popsie Jennings. Old whore landed a solid one with her andiron. Still hurts worse than either of yours." He looked away and fingered a spot on the back of his head. "I have to shave, brush my teeth, make myself pretty for Shorelands. What's my name again?"

It took her a moment to understand what he meant. "Norm. Norm Desmond."

He smiled at her and took the razor and shaving cream from a paper bag. "Tonight Mrs. Desmond is going to bestow upon Mr. Desmond a particularly deep marital pleasure. At least twice. You have to work off your debt." He squirted shaving cream onto his fingers and began working it into his stubble.

"I want to tell you about the fun we're going to have at Shorelands. Going to be a great pleasure for both of us." He rinsed his fingers and began drawing the razor down the right side of his face. "You want to talk to the old ladies, right? Win them over, pump them for information?"

"That's right."

"Let's do it the stand-up way. Scare the shit out of some old dame, she'll spill everything she knows. You did it to Natalie Weil, so do it to one of them."

Nora watched him shave. Unlike any other man she had known, Dart cleared an area of foam and whiskers, then ran the razor back over the same patch of skin in the opposite direction, in effect shaving himself twice. "You want me to kidnap one of the maids."

"Tie her up, beat the crap out of her, whatever. Get her out of the house and into the car. She says whatever she says, and then I kill her. Be interesting. Lot of entertainment in an old lady." He threw out his arms, splattering foam on the tiles. "I award myself the Dick Dart Prize for Superior Achievement in Twisted Thinking. I'll be your support group, give you all the help you need to do your thing." He finished shaving his face, ran water over the head of the razor, and began on his neck. "Afterwards, we have to trust each other. It'll be you and me, babe, the Dream Team. After the first one, cops don't care how many murders you commit. In death-penalty states they don't bring you back to execute you all over again. Shows how fucked up they are, the low value they put on life." He ran the razor over a few patches of foam, reversed direction and shaved the same places again, then rinsed his face with cold water and reached for a handful of paper towels.

"How do you see us ending up? If you don't mind my asking."

Dart blotted his face, threw the wadded towels on the floor, and looked meditative for a moment before taking the new toothbrush from the bag. He snapped the case in half and tossed it aside. "Toothpaste."

Nora rooted in her bag and brought out her toothpaste. "Well?"

"Roadblock. A million cops and us. Hey, if we get to Canada, we might have a whole year. Essential point is, we do not under any circumstances allow ourselves to be arrested. We broke out of one jail, we're not going to wind up in another one. Live free or die." He bent forward and attended to his teeth.

85

AT THE BRONZE SHORELANDS TRUST sign, they drove between overgrown stone pillars into a tangle of green. "The drums, the beastly drums," Dart intoned, "will they nevah cease, Carruthers?"

Crowded on both sides by trees, the path angled right and disappeared. Nora reached the curve and saw the path divide at a wooden signpost standing on a grass border. One branch veered left, the other right, into a muddy field. As they approached the sign, the words grew legible. MAIN HOUSE. GINGERBREAD. HONEY HOUSE. PEPPER POT. RAPUNZEL. CLOVER. MONTY'S GLEN & THE SONG PILLARS. MIST FIELD. All of these lay somewhere up the left-hand path. VISITOR PARKING pointed to the field.

Nora drove out of the woods and turned right. A man in khaki work clothes pushed himself out of a lawn chair next to a trailer on a cement apron and came forward, admiring the car.

"What a beauty," he said. "Godalmighty." He had furrowed cheeks and small, shining eyes. Dart snickered.

"We like it," Nora said, giving Dart a sharp look.

The man stepped back and licked his lips. "Don't make them like this baby anymore."

"By gum, they shore don't, Pops," Dart said.

The man glanced at Dart and decided to pretend he wasn't there. "Ma'am, if you're here on a day visit, there's a ten-dollar entrance fee. If you're an overnight guest, pull right into the lot there and check in at Main House after I find your name on the list."

"We're staying overnight. Mr. and Mrs. Desmond."

"Back in a jiffy." After another lingering look at the car, he went into the trailer.

"Did a little prison time, but not for anything interesting," Dart said.

"You don't know that."

"Wait."

The man came out of his trailer holding a clipboard with a pen dangling from a string. He thrust it through the window and pointed at a blank space on a form. "Sign right there, Mrs. Desmond. Hope you enjoy your stay."

Dart leaned forward with a wicked smile. "What did they put you in for, old-timer?"

"Pardon?"

"Knife a guy in a bar, or was it more like stealing bricks off a construction site?"

Nora handed him the clipboard. "I apologize for my husband. He thinks he's a comedian."

"Not all comedians is funny." The man's face had gone rigid, and the light had disappeared from his eyes. He grabbed the clipboard, stamped across the cement, climbed into his trailer, and slammed the door.

"This may come as a surprise to you," Nora said, "but you have an unpleasant streak."

"Now you want to bet that I can't quote all of 'To a Sky-Lark'?"

The field squished under the Duesenberg's oversized tires. "No."

"How about every third word? Slightly adjusted for effect?"

"No." She put the car in a spot at the far right end of the field.

"Too bad. It's a lot better my way.

Thee, bird wert—
Heaven it full profuse unpremeditated
still from thou a fire.
Deep and still and singest.

There are a lot of ways to be a genius. I'm going to feel right at home here."

Nora picked her way across the field, stepping over the muddy patches. "I'm not sure it's an act of genius to hang on to that car."

Dart moved along behind her. "After you perform your kidnapping stunt, we'll liberate another one. In the meantime there isn't a safer place in the whole state for the Duesie than right here. This was a *brilliant* idea."

Nora circled a mudhole and realized with a sinking of her heart that she had brought this madman into a private playpen. After the trust had decided to rent out cottages, they must have put in telephones. Dart could not watch her every minute; by now, he didn't even feel that he had to. They were partners. As soon as possible, she would call the local police and escape into the woods.

The path leading into the center of Shorelands held long, slender pockets of water, and the raised sections gleamed with moisture. Sometime during the night it had rained. While the sidewalks and highways had dried in the sun, open land had not. She looked up. Heavy clouds scudded across a mottled sky.

"Going to be good for both of us," Dart said.

"Imagine how I feel," Nora said.

Her short heels sank into the earth, and she moved onto a wet, stony ridge. The trees on either side seemed to close in. Dart began humming "Mountain Greenery." They came out of the trees and moved toward a gravel court surrounded by a low stone wall topped with cement slabs. The wall opened onto a white path between two narrow lawns, and the path led up four wide stone steps to the centerpiece of this landscape, a long stone building with three rows of windows in cement embrasures, some dripping water stains like beards. At every second window the facade stepped forward, so that the structure seemed to spread its wings and fold out from the entrance. Near the far end, a workman halfway up a tall ladder was scraping away a section of damaged paint, and another was repairing a cracked sill on the ground floor. Dick Dart linked his arm in hers and led her up the path to Main House.

86

WHITE-HAIRED MEN AND WOMEN lingered inside a gift shop across from a black door marked PRIVATE STAFF ONLY. Beyond, marble steps ascended to a wide corridor with high peach walls broken by glossy plaster half columns. In the big lounge across the corridor, a group of about twenty people, most of them women, listened to an invisible guide. French doors opened onto a terrace. Dart pulled Nora up the steps. At the left end of the hallway, a knot of tourists emerged from a room at the front of Main House and pursued a small, white-haired woman into another across the corridor. To their right, a curved staircase led past a gallery of paintings to the second floor. Nora thought of screaming for help, and words thrust up into her throat until she realized that if she released them, Dart would yank the revolver from his pocket and murder as many of these people as he could. The group in the lounge began shuffling after their guide through an interior arch on the far side of the fireplace.

Dart tilted his head to admire the plaster palmettes and arabesques spread across the barrel-vaulted ceiling. "Hell with the roadblock and the violent demise. We lie low for a while, then I touch my old man for a couple million dollars. We go to Canada, buy a place like this. I put in a couple hidden staircases, state-of-the-art operating theater, big gas furnace in the basement. Have a ball."

The short, white-haired guide led her party into the big room across the corridor and spread her arms. "Here we have the famous lounge, where Miss Weatherall's guests gathered for cocktails and conversation before their evening meal. If you're wishing you could listen in, I can tell you one thing that was said in this room. T. S. Eliot turned to Miss Weatherall and whispered, 'My dear, I must tell you . . .' "

In a carrying voice, Dart announced, "That stuffed shirt Eliot stayed here exactly two days, and all he did was complain about indigestion."

Most of the tourists who had been listening to the guide turned to look at Dart.

" *'The breeding of land and dull spring, us, earth, snow, life, tubers.'* Every third word of the beginning of 'The Waste Land,' with certain adjustments for poetic effect, *'Us, the shower; we went sunlight. Hofgarten coffee.'* Heck of a lot punchier, don't you think? My 'Prufrock' is even better."

The guide was trying to shepherd her charges into the next room.

"Can you do that with everything?" Nora asked.

"Everything. *'Go, and the spread, the patient upon; Let through muttering, restless hotels, restaurants, shells insidious. Lead an . . . Oh, ask it.'* "

A voice behind them asked, "Are you a poet?"

A tall woman in her late twenties, her face strewn with freckles and her strawberry-blond hair hanging straight to her shoulders, stood behind them, one foot on the top of the stairs. She wore a simple off-white suit, and she looked charming.

Dart smiled at her. "How embarrassing. Yes, I hope I may claim that honor."

The young woman came toward them, holding out a deeply freckled hand. "Mr. and Mrs. Desmond?"

Dart enfolded her hand in both of his. "I'll tell, if you will."

"Marian Cullinan. One of my jobs here is being in charge of Guest Services. Tony let me know you were coming, and I'm sorry to be late, but I had to take care of a few things at my desk." Dart released her. "You had no trouble finding us, I hope?"

"None at all," Dart purred.

"Good. And please, don't be embarrassed that we inspired you to think about your work. We hope we have that effect on all the writers who visit us. Are you published, Mr. Desmond?"

"A fair bit, I'm happy to say."

"Wonderful," said Marian. "Where? I should know your name. I do my best to keep up with people like you for our reading series."

Dart glanced at Nora and presented Marian with a shy, modest face. "Here and there."

"You can't get out of it that way. I'm interested in contemporary poetry. I bet your wife will tell me where you've placed your work."

Nora struggled to remember the magazines on Mark Foil's coffee table. "Let's see. He's published quite a bit in *Avec* and *Conjunctions*. And *Lingo*."

"Well!" She looked up at Dick Dart with a quick increase of interest and respect. "I'm impressed. I thought you must be a Language poet. I'd love to ask you about a thousand questions, but I don't want to be rude."

"Might be enjoyable," Dart said. "Poets don't get a great deal of attention, all in all."

"Around here they do. We'll have to make sure you get our VIP treatment. When good writers do us the honor of visiting, we like to extend our hospitality a little further than we can with the usual guest."

"Isn't that sweet as all get out?" Dart looked at Nora with dancing eyes.

"This is *wonderful*. I can show you Miss Weatherall's photo archive, her private papers—really anything you might care to see—and tonight you must have dinner with Mrs. Nolan, Margaret Nolan, the director of the trust, and me in the dining room. It would be such a treat for us. We'll have a splendid dinner, we do that for our literary guests, something off the original Shorelands menu. Margaret and I love the opportunity to re-create the old atmosphere. Does that sound like something you'd like to do?"

"Honored," Dart said.

"Margaret will be thrilled." Marian looked as if she wanted to give Dart a hug. "We'd better take care of the paperwork so I can start organizing matters. Would you come into my office?"

"Putty in your freckled little hands," Dart said.

She gave him an uncertain glance before deciding that what he had said was hilarious. "My freckles used to make me feel self-conscious, but I don't think about them anymore. Sometimes, I confess, I'd still like to cover them up, if I could find a cosmetic that worked."

"I could help you with that," Dart said. "No problem at all."

"Do you mean that?"

Dart shrugged and nodded. The young woman looked at Nora.

"He means it," Nora said.

"Artists are so . . . *extraordinary*. So . . . *unexpected*."

"I'm a little more in touch with my feminine side than the average guy," Dart said.

Marian brought them through the door marked PRIVATE, down a functional hallway to an unmarked door, and into a tiny office with a window on the entrance. A photograph of a young soldier in uniform had been pinned to the bulletin board. She moved behind the desk, took a form from the top drawer, and smiled at Dart. "Mr. Desmond, since I suppose you will be filling this out, perhaps you should take the chair? I wish I had two, but as you can see, there's no room."

Dart examined the form. Grinning, he took a pen from her desk and began writing.

Marian looked brightly up at Nora. "Now that I know who you are, I'm so glad we're putting you and Mr. Desmond in Pepper Pot. Pepper Pot is where Robert Frost stayed when he was Miss Weatherall's guest in 1932."

"And where Merrick Favor and Austryn Fain stayed in 1938."

Marian tilted her chin, and her hair swung to the back of her neck. If the poetic Mr. Desmond appreciated freckles, she intended give him a good view. "I don't think I know those names."

"My wife has a special interest in the summer of 1938." He smiled as if to suggest that wives must be expected to have their foibles, and Marian smiled back in indulgent understanding.

"We'll have to see what we can do to help you." She read what Dart had written on the form. "Oh, isn't that cute. Your names are Norma and Norman."

"Language poetry strikes again."

She smiled and gave her head a flirtatious shake. Norman Desmond was a hoot. "There's a tour beginning in forty minutes, which would give you more than enough time to settle in. Afterwards, I'll take you into the parts of the house normally off-limits. We're not really a hotel, so we can't provide valet or room service, but if you have any special needs, I'll do my best."

Dart turned a rueful smile to Nora. "We're gonna have to tell her, Norm."

Nora had no idea what he thought they had to tell Marian Cullinan. "I guess so."

"Truth is, we don't have our bags. Stolen out of our car at a rest stop this morning. All we have is in Norma's handbag and what we're wearing."

Marian looked stricken. "Why, that's terrible!" She ripped a sheet off a yellow pad. "I'll have Tony pick up some toothbrushes and toothpaste in town, and whatever else you need. A razor? Shaving soap? Tell me what you need."

"Thankfully, we have all the toiletries we need, but there are some other items I'd be grateful for."

"Fire away," Marian said.

"We enjoy a nightcap in the evenings. Could your lad pick up a liter of Absolut vodka? And we'd like an ice bucket to go with that."

"Sounds sensible to me." She wrote. "Anything else?"

"I'd like two more items, but I don't want you to think they're strange."

She positioned her pen.

"A twelve-foot length of clothesline and a roll of duct tape."

She looked up to see if this was another of his little jokes.

"Doesn't have to be clothesline," Dart said. "Any smooth rope about a quarter inch in diameter is dandy."

"We aim to please." She wrote down his requests. "We do have a lot of rope coiled up in the bathroom down the hall. The workmen store it there, even though I've asked and asked . . ."

"Too rough," Dart said.

"Would you mind if I asked . . . ?"

"Medical supplies," Dart said. "Repair work."

"I don't quite . . ."

He tapped his right knee. "Not the leg I was born with, alas."

"*Excuse* me. It should all be in your room by the time you're finished with the tour." She looked stricken again. "Unless you need something right away."

"No hurry. The old joint's had a bit of a workout, little loose, little floppy, and I want to stiffen it up later."

"Our pleasure. And you, Mrs. Desmond? Is there anything I can do for you? I hope I might call you Norma." She gave Nora a closer look. "Are you all right?"

"Are some of the people who were at Shorelands at the end of the thirties still here? If so, I'd like to speak to them."

Brilliant smile. "Lily Melville is a fixture here, and she was a maid in those days. When the trust came into being, Lily was so helpful that we put her on the staff. You might have seen her leading a group through the lounge."

"White hair? Five two?" Dart asked. "Pink Geoffrey Beene knockoff, cultured pearls?"

"Why, yes." She was delighted with him. "Norman, you are an amazing man."

"Sweet old darling," Dart said.

"Well, she's going to get a kick out you, but don't let on you know it isn't a real Geoffrey Beene."

Dart held up his hand as if taking a vow. Nora broke in on their rapport. "Is Lily Melville the only person left from that time?"

"Another former maid, Agnes Brotherhood, is still with us. She's been under the weather lately, but it might be possible for you to talk to her."

"I'd like that," Nora said.

"Hugo Driver," Marian said, pointing at Nora. "I *knew* there was something about 1938. So you are a Hugo Driver person." She smiled in a way which may not have been entirely pleasant. "We don't see as many Driver people as you might expect. As a rule, they tend not to be much like ordinary readers."

"I'm not only a Driver person," Nora said. "I'm a Bill Tidy, Creeley Monk, and Katherine Mannheim person, too."

Marian gave her a doubtful look.

"Fascinating group," Dart said. "Class of '38. Tremendous interest of Norma's."

"You're involved in a research project."

"According to Norma," Dart said, "*Night Journey* wouldn't exist without the Shorelands experience. Essential to the book."

"That is incredibly interesting." Marian pushed herself back from the desk and folded her hands in front of her chin. "Given Driver's popularity, we ought to be doing more with him anyhow. And if we can claim that Shorelands and these people you mention are central to *Night Journey*, that's the way to do it." She stroked her perfect jawline and gazed out of the window, thinking. "I can see a piece in the Sunday *Times* magazine. I can certainly see a piece in the book review. If we got that, we could put on Hugo Driver weekends. How about an annual Driver conference? It could work. I'll have to run this past Margaret, but I'm sure she'll see the potential in it. To tell you the truth, attendance has been suffering lately, and this could turn things around for us."

"I'm sure Leonard Gimmel and Teddy Brunhoven would be delighted to participate," Nora said.

Marian swung toward her and raised her eyebrows.

"Driver scholars," Nora said.

"With luck, we could have everything in place by next spring. Let's discuss these matters with Margaret during dinner, shall we? Now, the rate for your accommodations is ninety-six twenty with the tax, and if you give me a card, you can be on your way to Pepper Pot."

"Always use cash," Dart said. "Pay as you go."

"*That's* refreshing." She watched Dart take his wallet from his trousers and marveled at the number of bills.

Marian made change from a cash box and handed him two keys attached to wooden tabs reading PEPPER POT. "You'll meet Lily outside the lounge, and I'll be waiting for you when the tour ends. I think we'll all have a lot of fun during your stay."

"My plans exactly," Dart said.

87

"SHOULD HAVE BECOME a poet a long time ago. If the spouse hadn't been present, I could have planked our new friend right there in her office."

"You made a big impression on her," Nora said.

"I bet Maid Marian has freckles in her armpits. For sure she has freckles on the tops of her udders, but do you think she has them on the undersides, too?"

"She probably has freckles on the soles of her feet."

They had left Main House by the front door and taken the path angling into the woods on the far side of the walled court. Tall oaks interspersed with birches and maples grew on either side of the path. A signpost at a break in the wall pointed to GINGERBREAD, PEPPER POT, RAPUNZEL.

"Isn't it wonderful how everything falls into place when we're together? We show up as ordinary slobs, and two minutes later we're VIPs. We have the run of the place, and on top of that, they're giving us one of the historic old-time Shorelands dinners. Do you understand why?"

"Marian thinks you're hot stuff."

"That's not the reason. Here's this big place, four or five people in it full-time, tops. Night after night, they have soup and sandwiches in the kitchen, complaining to one another about how business is falling off. Rope in someone they can pretend is a VIP, they have a pretext for a decent meal. These people are starved for a little excitement. In the meantime, we get to see how many people are in the house, find out where their rooms are, check the place out. Couldn't be better."

Another wooden signpost came into view on the left side of the path. A brown arrow pointed down a narrow lane toward GINGERBREAD.

She looked over her shoulder. "I wish you hadn't asked for the rope and the duct tape. There's no need for those things."

"On the contrary. I'll need them twice."

They reached the sign. Nora looked to her left and saw the faint suggestion of a gray wooden building hidden in the trees. A window glinted in the gray light.

"Twice?"

His mouth twitched. "In your case, we can probably dispense with the tape. But our old darling is another matter. Physical restraint adds a great deal to the effect. Which one do you fancy, Lily or Agnes?"

She did not reply.

"Like the sound of Agnes. Touch of invalidism, less of a fight. Thinking of your best interests, sweetie."

"Very kind of you."

"Let's press on to dear old Salt Shaker or Pepper Grinder or whatever the place is called."

Wordlessly Nora turned away from Gingerbread, where Katherine Mannheim had probably died in a struggle with Hugo Driver, and began moving up the side of the path. Dart patted her shoulder, and she fought the impulse to pull away from his touch. "You're going to do fine." He ruffled the hair at the back of her head.

The path curved around an elephant-sized boulder with a rug of moss on its rounded hips. On the other side of the path a double signpost at the edge of the trees indicated that RAPUNZEL lay beyond a wooden bridge arching over a narrow stream, and PEPPER POT at the end of a narrow trail leading into the woods to their right.

Dart hopped neatly over four feet of glistening mud onto a flat rock, from there onto the grassy verge. He rattled the heavy keys in the air. "Home, sweet home!"

Nora moved a few feet along her side of the path and found a series of stones and dry spots which took her across.

The trail slanted upward through Douglas firs with shining needles. A small hewn-timber cottage gradually came into view at the end of a clearing. Extending from a shingle roof, a canopy hung over a flat porch. A brick fireplace rose along the side of the cottage, and big windows divided into four panes broke the straight lines of the timbers on both sides of the front door. An addition had been built onto the back by workmen who had attempted to match the timbers with machine-milled planks. No telephone lines came into the house.

"Hear the banjo music?" Dart said. "The Pinto put me in a shit-kicker's cabin."

"Two or three people made this place by hand," Nora said. "And they did a good job."

Dart drew her up two hewn-timber steps onto the porch. "Your simple midwestern values make me feel so decadent. In you go."

They entered a dark room with double beds and pine desks against the walls at either end. In the center of the room a brown sofa and easy chair flanked a coffee table. Along the far wall were a counter, kitchen cabinets, a sink beneath a square window, and an electric range. Heavy clothespresses occupied the far corners of the room, and the apron of the stone fireplace jutted into the wooden floor. Dart locked the door behind them and flipped up a switch, turning on a shaded overhead light and the lamps on the bedside tables.

"Fucking Dogpatch." He wandered into the kitchen and opened and closed cabinets. "No minibar, of course."

"Aren't you getting a bottle?"

"If you don't have choices, you might as well live in Russia. How much time do we have? Twenty-five minutes?"

"Just about," said Nora, grateful that it was not enough for Dick Dart's idea of an enjoyable sexual experience.

"Do you suppose this dump has an actual bathroom?"

She pointed at a door in the rear wall. "Through there."

"Let's go. Take your bag."

Nora questioned him with a look.

"Want to repair your makeup. I can't stand the sight of that mess you made of my work."

88

THE SHORT, WHITE-HAIRED guide trotted up the steps and bustled forward. She was energetic and cheerful, and she seemed to know several of the people in the group.

"Hello, hello!" Two men in their sixties, like Dick Dart in jackets and ties, one with a gray crew cut, the other bald, greeted her by name. Her smile congealed for a moment when she noticed Dart.

"Here we are," she said. "I don't usually lead groups back to back, but I was told that we have a promising young poet with us, and that he specifically asked for me, so I'm delighted to be with you." She turned her smile to a dark-haired young man who looked like an actor in a soap opera, one of Daisy's Edmunds and Dmitris. "Are you Mr. Desmond?"

Edmund/Dmitri looked startled and said, "No!"

"I'm afraid that's me," Dart said.

"Oh, now I understand," she said. "You have strong opinions, that's only natural. From time to time, Mr. Desmond, please feel free to share your insights with the rest of us."

"Be honored," Dart said.

She smiled at the group in general. "Mr. Norman Desmond, the poet, will be giving us his special point of view as we go along. I'm sure we'll all find him very interesting, but I warn you, Mr. Desmond's ideas can be controversial."

"Little me?" Dart said, pressing a hand to his chest. Some members of the group chuckled.

"I also want to inform you that two other creative people, old friends of ours, are with us today. Frank Neary and Frank Tidball. We call them the two Franks, and it's always a pleasure when they join us."

The two older men murmured their thanks, mildly embarrassed to have been identified. Their names sounded familiar to Nora. Frank Neary and Frank Tidball, the two creative Franks? She didn't think that she had ever seen them before.

"You might be interested in how this old lady in front of you learned so much about Shorelands. My name is Lily Melville, and I've spent most of my life in this beautiful place. Lucky me!"

One of those people capable of saying something for the thousandth time as though it were the first, Lily Melville told them that Georgina Weatherall had hired her as a maid of all work way back in 1931, when she was still really just a child. It was the Depression, her family's financial situation meant she had to leave school, but Shorelands had given her a wonderful education. For two years she had helped cook and serve meals, which gave her the opportunity to overhear the table talk of some of the most famous and distinguished writers in the world. After that, she took care of the cottages, which put her into even closer contact with the guests. Regrettably, in the late forties Miss Weatherall had suffered a decline in her powers and could no longer entertain her guests. During the years following her departure from Shorelands, Miss Melville frequently had been sought out by writers, scholars, and community groups for her memories. Soon after the trust had acquired the estate in 1980, she had been hired as a resident staff member.

"We'll begin our tour with two of my favorite places, Miss Weatherall's salon and private library, and proceed from there. Are there any questions before we begin?"

Dick Dart raised his hand.

"So soon, Mr. Desmond?"

"Isn't that very attractive suit you're wearing a Geoffrey Beene?"

"Aren't you sweet! Yes, it is."

"And am I wrong in thinking that I caught a trace of that delightful scent Mitsouko as you introduced yourself so eloquently?"

"Mr. Desmond, would you join me as we take our group into the salon?"

Dart skipped around the side of the group and took her arm, and the two of them set off down the hallway ahead of Nora and the others.

They had visited the salon, library, lounge, and famous dining room, where a highly polished table stood beneath reproductions of paintings either owned by Georgina or similar to those in her collection. Like her library, her paintings had been sold off long ago. They had strolled along the terrace and descended the steps to admire the view of Main House from the west lawn. Lily spoke with the ease of long practice of her former employer's many peculiarities, representing them as the charming eccentricities of a patron of the arts; she invited the remarks, variously startling, irreverent, respectful, and comic, of the poet Norman Desmond, who now accompanied her down the long length of the west lawn toward the ruins of the famous gardens, restoration of which had been beyond the powers of the trust.

Nora fell in step with the two Franks and wondered again why their names seemed familiar. Certainly their faces were not. Without quite seeming to be academics, both Franks had the bookish reserve of old scholars and the intimate, unintentionally exclusive manner of long-standing collaborators or married couples. They had been amused by some of Dick Dart's comments, and the Frank with the gray crew cut clearly intended to say something about Mrs. Desmond's interesting husband.

Here are your telephones, Nora told herself. *You can get these guys to go to the police. But how to convince them?*

"Your husband is an unusual man," said Gray Crew Cut. "You must be very proud of him."

"Can I talk to you for a second?" she asked. "I have to tell you something."

"I'm Frank Neary, by the way, and this is Frank Tidball." Both men extended their hands, and Nora shook them impatiently. "We've taken Lily's tour many times, and she always comes up with something new."

Tidball smiled. "She never came up with anything like your husband before."

Dart and Lily had paused at the edge of a series of overgrown scars, the remains of one section of the old gardens. Past them, an empty pedestal stood at the center of a pond. Lily was laughing at something Dart was saying.

"You can hardly be a poet if you don't have an independent mind," said Neary. "Where we live, in Rhinebeck, up on the Hudson River, we're surrounded by artists and poets."

Nora took an agonized look across the lawn. Dart spoke to Lily and began walking quickly toward the group moving in his direction, Nora and the two Franks a little apart from the others.

"Wasn't there something you wanted to say?" Neary asked.

"I need some help." Dart advanced across the grass, smiling dangerously. "Would you please take my arm? I have a stone in my shoe."

"Certainly." Frank Neary stepped smartly up beside her and held her elbow.

Nora raised her right leg, slipped off her shoe, and upended it. "There," Nora said, and the two men politely watched the fall of a nonexistent stone. "Thank you." As Neary released her arm, she watched Dart striding toward her with his dangerous smile and remembered where she had heard their names. "You must be the Neary and Tidball who write the Chancel House crossword puzzles."

"My goodness," Neary said. "Frank, Mrs. Desmond knows our puzzles."

"Isn't this *lovely*, Frank?"

Nora turned to smile at Dart, who had noticed the tone of her conversation with the Franks and slowed his pace.

"You know our work?"

"You two guys are great," Nora said. "I should have recognized your names as soon as I heard them."

Dart had come within hearing distance, and Nora said, "I love your puzzles, they're so clever." Something Davey had once said came back to her. "You use themes in such a subtle way."

"Good God, someone understands us," Neary said. "Here is a person who understands that a puzzle is more than a puzzle."

Dart settled a hand on Nora's shoulder. "Puzzles?"

"Norman," she said, looking up with what she hoped was wifely regard, "Mr. Neary and Mr. Tidball write those wonderful Chancel House crossword puzzles."

"No," said Dart, instantly falling into his role, "not the ones that keep you up late at night, trying to think of an eight-letter word for smokehouse flavoring?"

"Isn't that great?"

"I'm sure you three have a lot to discuss, but we should catch up." Dart smiled at the two Franks. "I *wondered* what you were talking about. Do you have an editor over there at Chancel House?"

"Yes, but our work doesn't need any real editing. Davey makes a suggestion now and then. He's a sweet boy."

The four of them came up beside the rest of the group, and Lily said that after viewing the pond, they would be going on to Honey House, at which point the official tour would conclude. Anyone who wished to see the Mist Field, the Song Pillars, and Rapunzel was free to do so.

"You gentlemen come here often?" Dart asked.

Together, swapping sentences, Neary and Tidball told their new friends that they tried to visit Shorelands once a year. "Five years ago, we stayed overnight in Rapunzel, mainly so we could walk through Main when it wasn't filled with tourists. It was tremendously enjoyable. Agnes Brotherhood was full of tales."

"What kind of tales?"

Neary looked at Tidball, and both men smiled. Neary said, "There's a big difference between Lily and Agnes. Agnes never liked Georgina very much, and back then she was willing to gossip. Frank and I heard stories that will never be in the history books."

Lily had begun to speak from the raised flagstone ledge surrounding the pond. Frank Neary raised a finger to his lips.

After telling two mildly prurient anecdotes about the accidental unclothed encounters of writers of opposite sexes, Lily hopped off the ledge and declared that their final stop, Honey House, the only cottage restored to its original condition, was the perfect conclusion to their tour.

An overgrown stone path curved away from the pond and led into the trees. At the rear of the group, Nora and Dart walked along just behind the puzzle makers, and the others strung out in pairs behind Lily's pink suit. The air had darkened.

"Might rain," Dart said.

"It will," Tidball said. "It's getting here a little ahead of schedule, which is good for them. Rain cuts into attendance quite a bit. Shorelands gets muddy when it rains. If it's going to happen, they'd rather have it now instead of on the weekend."

"Cuts into attendance?" Neary asked. "I should *say.* Rain has the same effect on attendance that the fellow in the papers, Dart, had on his victims."

Lily and the couple behind her stepped onto a bridge over the stream which wandered through the northern end of the estate. Their shoes rang on the bridge, *trip trap, trip trap,* like the three billy goats gruff in the fairy tale.

"Heard anything new about good old Dart?" Dart asked. "What a story! We couldn't make much sense out of it. Fellow was accused of murder but never charged. What was the woman doing in the police station? More there than meets the eye. Still on the loose, this odd couple?"

"Oh, yes," said Neary. "According to the radio, Dart is supposed to be in Northampton, and that's not far from here." His eyes had become large and serious. "I agree that more is going on than meets the eye. Frank and I have a connection with the woman." He leaned in front of Nora to look into Dart's face. "You asked about our editor, Davey Chancel. Well, she's his wife. If you ask me, Nora Chancel had something going with this Dart."

"I should say that's a definite possibility," Dart said. "What do you know about this woman, your editor's wife?"

The others had crossed over the bridge, and now the two Franks, followed closely by Nora and Dick Dart, stepped onto it. *Trip trap, trip trap.*

"We've heard rumors," Tidball said.

"Go on," said Dart. "I'm absolutely riveted."

"Apparently the woman is an unstable personality. We think they were in cahoots. When he got arrested, she went to the police station and staged her own 'kidnapping,' quote unquote, to get him out. She's probably more dangerous than he is."

Neary laughed, and a second later Nora laughed, too.

They followed the others toward a cabin tucked away at the base of the trees. Lily stood at the front door facing them.

"Quite a saga, isn't it?" Dart asked.

"I can hardly wait for the movie," Nora said.

Lily held up a hand as if taking an oath. "We here at Shorelands are very proud of what you are about to see. The planning began four years ago, when our director, Margaret Nolan, said to us at dinner, 'Why don't we make it possible for our guests to walk into one of our cottages and experience the world created by Georgina Weatherall? Why not recreate the past we celebrate here?' We all fell in love with Margaret Nolan's vision, and for a year we assembled records and documents in order to reassemble a picture of a typical cottage interior from approximately 1920 to approximately 1935. We vowed to cut no corners. Let me tell you, when you begin a project like this, you find out how much you don't know in a hurry!"

Polite laughter came from everyone but Nora and Dart.

"You are wondering how we chose Honey House. I'll be frank about that. Expense had to be a consideration, and this is one of the smallest cottages. Our last great general renovation was in 1939, and the task before us was enormous. With the help of Georgina Weatherall's records, we covered the walls with a special fabric obtained from the original manufacturer. It had been out of production since 1948, but several rolls had been preserved at the back of the warehouse, and we bought all of them. We learned that the original paint came from a company which had gone out of business in 1935, and nearly lost hope, but then we got word that a paint supplier in Boston had fifteen gallons of the exact brand and color in his basement. Donations poured in. About a year and a half ago, it all came together.

"This should go without saying, but I must insist that you touch none of the objects or fabrics inside. Honey House is a living museum. Please show it the respect it deserves, and allow others to enjoy this restoration for many years to come. Am I understood?"

Dart's cry of "Absolutely!" rang out over the mutter of assent from the group.

Lily smiled, turned to the door, took a massive key from a pocket of the pink suit, and looked over her shoulder. "I love this moment." She swung the door open and told the young couple directly in front of her to switch on the lights.

The boy led the first of the group through the door. Soft sounds of appreciation came to those still outside.

"They all do that," Lily said. "As soon as the lights go on, it's always *Ooh! Aah!* Go on, Norman, get in there. It'll knock your eyes out."

Dart patted her shoulder and followed Nora through the door.

89

EVERY POSSIBLE SURFACE had been covered with porcelain figurines, snuffboxes, antique vases, candles in ornate holders, and lots of other things Nora instinctively thought of as gewgaws. Paintings in gilt frames and mirrors engulfed in scrollwork hung helter-skelter on the aubergine-colored walls.

Lily addressed the group. "I will leave you to feast upon this splendid re-creation. Feel free to ask me about anything that strikes your eye." The couples separated into different portions of the interior, and she came up to the Franks with a proprietary swagger. "Isn't it wonderful?"

Nora said, "I had no idea the guests lived in this kind of splendor."

"Nothing was too good for the people who came here," said Lily. "To Miss Weatherall, they were the cultural aristocracy. Mr. Yeats, for example." She pointed across the room at a photograph of a man with a pince-nez on the bridge of his nose. "He was a great gentleman. Miss Weatherall loved his conversation."

"A writer named Creeley Monk stayed here, too," Nora said.

"Creeley *Monk*? I don't seem to recall . . ."

"In 1938."

Lily's eyes went flat with distaste. "We like to dwell on our triumphs. And here we have one example, standing right next to you! Frank and Frank are published by Chancel House, which was born that very summer, when Mr. Driver met Mr. Lincoln Chancel. Now, *he* was a great gentleman."

"I guess it wasn't such a bad summer after all," Nora said.

Lily gave a ladylike shudder.

"Is this a reconstruction of what would have been here during the thirties?"

"No, not at all," Lily said, untroubled by the contradiction of her earlier remarks. "We wanted to represent the estate as a whole, not just a single cottage. When you put it together like this, you get a real feel of the times." A man who apparently wanted to question her about a collection of paperweights waved to her, and she scampered away.

"Nineteen thirty-eight isn't their favorite year," said Tidball.

"I wonder if you know anything about a poet named Katherine Mannheim," Nora asked.

Tidball rolled his eyes upward and clasped his hands in front of him.

"It seems you do," Nora said. Dart looked on, indulgent, pleased to sense the presence of trouble ahead.

The Franks exchanged a brief glance. "Let's wait until the tour is over," Neary said. "Were you going to look at the Mist Field and the Song Pillars?"

"You haven't seen the Song Pillars, you haven't seen Shorelands," said Dart.

Half an hour later, the four of them lagged behind the others on the path threading north through the woods. Dart was walking so close behind Nora that he seemed almost to engulf her.

"Where did these airy-fairy names come from?" he boomed out.

"Georgina," Neary said, striding along at the head of their column of four. "When her father owned the estate, the only cottage that had a name was Honey House, after an old butler who lived there, Mr. Honey. After her father turned it over to her, all of a sudden everything had a new name." He looked back, grinning at the others. "Georgina's romantic conception of herself extended to her domain. These people tend to be dictatorial."

Frank Neary was a clever man. Dart could not keep his eye on her all afternoon, and she needed only a few seconds.

"That's where your poet went wrong," Neary said. "We got all this from Agnes Brotherhood, so you have to take into account that she never really cared for Georgina. Lily, on the other hand, worshiped her. Lily detested Katherine Mannheim because she didn't give Georgina the proper respect. Agnes told us that Katherine Mannheim saw right through Georgina the first time she met her, and Georgina hated her for it."

Tidball said, "According to Agnes, Georgina was jealous. But the entire subject still seemed to make her nervous."

The path curved around the left side of a meadow and disappeared into the trees on its far side, where several large, upright gray stones were dimly visible. "Here it is, the famous Mist Field."

"Mist Field," Nora said. "Why does that sound familiar?"

"Mr. Desmond, do you write every day?" Tidball asked.

"Only way to get anything done. Get up at six, scribble an ode before going to the office. Nights, I'm back at it from nine to eleven. By the way, please call me Norman."

They began moving up the path again.

"Are you part of a community of poets?"

"We Language poets like to get together at a nice little saloon called Gilhoolie's."

"How would you define Language poetry?"

"Exactly what it sounds like," Dart said. "Language, as much of it as possible."

"Have you ever read Katherine Mannheim's poetry?" asked Neary.

"Never touch the stuff."

Neary gave him a puzzled look.

"Why did Agnes think Georgina was jealous of Katherine Mannheim?" Nora asked.

"Georgina was used to being the center of attention. Especially with men. Instead, they were drooling over this pretty young thing. Being the kind of person she was, it took her a couple of weeks to understand what was going on. Lily Melville set her straight."

"Should have thrown the bitch out right then," Dart said.

Neary seemed startled by his choice of words. "Eventually she decided to do that, but she didn't want to act in any way that might injure her reputation. She was worried about finances, and sending away a guest could look like a distress signal. Here are the Song Pillars and Monty's Glen. Impressive, aren't they?"

A short distance from the path, six tall boulders with flat ends had been placed in a circle around a natural clearing. The other members of Lily Melville's group were already drifting back to the path, and a sixtyish woman in a turquoise exercise suit came up to them and introduced herself as Dorothea Bach, a retired high school teacher. She wanted to know all about Mr. Desmond's poetry.

"My odes and elegies were originally inspired by my own high school English teacher." He began spouting nonsense which thrilled Dorothea down to her bright blue running shoes. Fascinated, Tidball moved a step nearer.

Nora hurried up beside Neary, who was moving toward the boulder. He turned to her with a conciliatory smile, apologizing in advance for what he had to say. "To hear your husband talk, you'd think he didn't know anything about poetry at all."

"I need your help."

"Another imaginary stone?" He held out his arm.

"No, I—"

Dart stroked the back of her neck. "Don't let me break up this private moment, but I couldn't bear that woman a second longer."

Neary turned to Nora with a questioning look. She shook her head.

They passed through the Pillars and walked to the center of the clearing. "Every single time I come here, I think about going back in time to one of the great summers and listening to the conversation here. I get goose bumps. Right here, great writers sat down and talked about what they were working on. Wouldn't you like to have heard that?"

"Must have been a stitch," Dart said.

"You're a piece of work, Norman," Neary said.

"Humble laborer in the vineyards," Dart said.

"All in all, Norman, I wouldn't say that humility is your strong suit."

"Maybe you boys should leave us alone," Dart said. "After a while, little old swishes start to get on my nerves."

Frank Tidball looked as if he had been struck on the back of his head with a brick, and Frank Neary was enraged and weary in a manner to which he had clearly grown accustomed long ago. "That's it. This man is a lunatic, and he frightens me."

"I *should* frighten you," Dart said, glimmering with pleasure.

Neary held his ground. "Good-bye, Mrs. Desmond. I wish you luck."

Dart laughed at him—every word he said was ridiculous.

"Frank, I know my husband has offended you, but what were you saying about Georgina's money troubles? It might be very important to me." Nora had seen the money problem like the hint of a clue to an answer, and it was too important to be allowed to escape.

"I have no problem with you, Mrs. Desmond." He gave a contemptuous glance at Dart, who briskly stepped forward and grinned down at him.

Neary refused to be intimidated. "Georgina's trust fund wasn't large enough to pay for all the servants and upkeep or the food and drink for the guests. Her father indulged her for a long time, but in 1938 he lost patience. He cut her off, or seriously cut her back, I'm not sure which. Georgina was almost hysterical."

"Lily Melville told us that she had the whole place renovated the next year," Nora said.

"He must have relented. I'm sure that he was used to giving her whatever she wanted."

"Tale of Two Bitches," Dart said.

"I've spent enough time with this madman," Neary said. "Let's go." Tidball was staring at Dick Dart. Neary touched his elbow as if to awaken him, and Tidball spun away and marched toward the edge of the clearing. Neary followed him without looking back. They passed through the Pillars and moved toward the path with a suggestion of flight.

"Let's amble back to the house and meet the dear little Pinto. Something has occurred to me. Can you guess what?"

Before Nora could tell Dart that she could not read his mind, she read his mind. "You want Marian Cullinan."

He patted her head and grinned. "Probably time for me to bid farewell to older women. And Maid Marian has two great advantages."

She began to walk over the matted grass toward the boulders. "Which are?"

"One, you don't like her. She's fair Natalie all over again, wants to steal your man. Let's punish the cow—hey, it's what you want to do anyhow."

"And the second advantage?"

"Marian undoubtedly owns a nice car."

Heads down, moving a little faster than was necessary, Neary and Tidball were already most of the way across the meadow. Dart indulgently watched them wade through the long grass. "Lots of fun in store for us tonight, sweetie-pie."

90

MARIAN CULLINAN'S EAGER face appeared at her window as they approached the front of Main House, and when they came inside she was waiting for them, taking in Dart with theatrical awe. "Norman, you made Lily's day. She wants to take you on all of her tours."

"Entirely reciprocated. Reminds me of some of my dearest friends."

"Isn't he off the scale when it comes to charm, Mrs. Desmond?"

"Completely," said Nora. This dopey woman, so bored that she made passes at married male guests, probably represented her last hope of getting the police to Shorelands. "But please, call me Norma."

"Why, *thank* you!"

"Maybe you could join us for a nightcap up at good old Salt Shaker after dinner," Dart said. "So much to talk about, so many avenues to explore."

Marian's freckles slid sideways with a knowing twitch of the mouth. "That depends on how much paperwork I can get done. I used to have an assistant, but the Honey House restoration ate up most of our budget." Most of her bright, spurious eagerness reappeared. "And of course we're very proud of the result. Didn't you just love it?"

"Who wouldn't?" Dart said. "Can we get you up there tonight, Marian, or are we going to have to abduct you?"

"You'd be doing me a favor." She sighed and pantomimed exhaustion. "Would you like to see the rooms upstairs?"

Nora asked if they could talk to Agnes Brotherhood.

Marian closed her eyes and pressed a hand to her forehead. "I forgot to check on that. I'd have to look in to see how she's doing. Why don't we go upstairs?"

"Does this VIP treatment extend to a sandwich before we start laying our hands on history?"

"A sandwich? Now?"

"Circumstances deprived me of my usual healthy breakfast. Could gobble up the Girl Scouts along with their cookies."

Marian laughed. "In that case, we'd better take care of you. How about you, Norma?"

Nora said she could wait for dinner.

Dart grasped her wrist, killing her hopes of getting to a telephone while he gobbled up any nearby Girl Scouts. "When it comes to appetite, Norm Desmond has never been found wanting."

"I wouldn't think so," Marian said. "Let's see what damage you can do to our kitchen." An unmarked door at the right side of the marble stairs opened onto a steep flight of iron steps. "You'll be all right on these, with your . . . ?" She touched her knee.

"All is well."

Marian started down the staircase. "Would you mind if I asked how . . . ?"

"'Nam. Pesky land mine. Your brother was there, wasn't he?"

She looked back up at him. "How did you know about my brother?"

"Handsome picture on your bulletin board. I gather he was killed in action. Hope you will accept my condolences, even after all this time. As a former officer, I regret the loss of every single man in that tragic conflict."

"Thank you. You seem so young to have been an officer in Vietnam."

He barked out a laugh. "I'm told I was one of the youngest officers to serve in Vietnam, if not the youngest." He sighed. "Truth is, we were all boys, every one of us."

Nora felt like pushing him down the stairs.

"I'm going to make you the best sandwich you ever had in your life," Marian said.

"I have the distinct impression that you went to a Catholic girls' school. Please don't tell me I'm mistaken."

"How can you tell?" Marian began to descend the clanging stairs again, looking up at him with the smile of a woman who had never heard a compliment she didn't like.

"Two kinds of women hatch out of Catholic girls' schools. One is sincere, hardworking, witty, and polite. Best manners in the world. The other is unconventional, intellectual, bohemian. They're witty, too. Tend to be a bit rebellious."

At the bottom of the stairs Marian waited for Dart and Nora to come down into a good-sized kitchen with a red-tiled floor, a long wooden chopping block, glass-fronted cabinets, and a gas range. There was a teasing half smile on her face. "Which kind am I?"

"You fall into the best category of all. Combination of the other two."

"No wonder Lily enjoyed your tour." Smiling, Marian opened a cabinet, took down a plate and a glass, and opened the refrigerator. "Dinner is going to be one of our specials, so I'd better let that remain a surprise, but here's some roast beef. I could make you a sandwich with this whole-wheat bread. Sound good?"

"Yum yum. You got some mustard, mayo, maybe a couple slices of Swiss cheese to go with that?"

"I think so." She bent down to root around on a lower shelf, giving Dart a good view of her bottom.

"Any soup?"

She laughed and looked at Nora. "This man knows what he wants. Minestrone or gazpacho?"

"Minestrone. Gazpacho isn't soup."

Marian began pulling things out of the refrigerator.

Dart was wandering around and inspecting the kitchen. "Norma can give you a hand."

"Once an officer . . ." Nora said.

Marian told her where to find the can opener. Nora picked up a saucepan and poured the soup into it. After she had set the pan on the stove, she looked up to find Dart staring into her eyes. He glanced at her bag, which she had dropped on the counter, back at her, and then at a spot above the counter behind Marian's back. The handles of at least a dozen knives protruded from a wooden holder fastened to the wall. Dart smiled at her.

Marian took a bag of leftover lettuce from the refrigerator and dropped it on the counter. "Men are amazing," she said. "Where do they put it all?"

"Norman puts it in his hollow leg," Nora said. Standing behind the other woman, she looked at the knife holder and shrugged. She could not steal a knife without Marian's noticing.

Nearly undressing Marian with a smile, Dart said, "Might some beer have found its way into the refrigerator?"

"That's a distinct possibility."

"Don't like invading strange refrigerators. Let's hunker down, survey the vintages."

Marian glanced at Nora, who was stirring the soup. She set down her knife and moved toward the refrigerator, where Dart beamed at her, rubbing his hands.

" *'Open thy vault most massy, most fearsome, Madame Ware,'* " Dart said, quoting something Nora did not recognize.

"I know that!" Marian cried. "It's from *Night Journey,* the part near the end where Pippin meets Madame Lyno-Wyno Ware. He has to talk that way because, um . . ."

"Because the Cup Bearer told him he had to, or she wouldn't tell the truth."

"Yes! And the vault disappoints him because it's only a metal box, but when she opens it up he sees that inside it's the size of his old house, and Madame Ware says . . . something about a book, the mind . . ." She snapped her fingers twice. "They're bigger on the inside."

" *'My vault, like a woman's heart or reticule, is larger within than without. Even a little pippin was once held within a seed.'* "

Nora had been backing away from the stove and was now nearly within reaching distance of the knife rack.

"Right! That's it!" Marian spun around and pointed a shapely, freckled finger at Nora. "See? I'm not completely ignorant about Hugo Driver. We can work together."

"Marian," Dart said, an impatient edge in his voice, "open the massy vault, will you?"

She turned her back on Nora and made an elaborate business of opening the refrigerator.

"Hunker, Marian. Can you hunker?"

"With the best of them." She squatted down before the crowded shelves knee to knee with Dart. "Behold the beer."

"I don't see any beer."

She leaned over to point, in the process brushing a breast against Dart's arm. "Are you a Corona kind of guy?" Marian asked.

Dart glanced at Nora over the top of the other woman's head, and she stepped back and lifted the first knife out of the holder.

"In weak moments." Dart looked at the hefty, workmanlike carving knife in Nora's hand, nodded minutely, and glanced again at the holder.

"What are your feelings about Budweiser?" She leaned into him more firmly.

"I think I like the looks of the one beside it."

Nora pulled a cleaver from the rack, and Dart's eyes crinkled. "Yes, that's a lovely shape. Pull it out, so I can get a good look at it."

Marian reached into the refrigerator, bringing herself into closer contact with Dart. "Grolsch does have a nice shape, doesn't it?"

Nora carried the knife and the cleaver to the counter. While Dart and Marian Cullinan admired different sorts of vessels, she opened her bag and slipped them inside. She moved over to stir the soup, and the other two stood up. Marian gave her an uncertain smile. Her face seemed a little flushed along the tops of her cheekbones.

Nora poured the soup into a bowl, and Marian found a soupspoon and a bottle opener in a drawer.

Dart raised the Grolsch bottle and took a long swallow.

Nora slid her bag off the counter and took it to a chair beneath a wall-mounted telephone.

"Don't hang back, darling spouse. Join the party."

Nora considered her bag. Dart still had his back to her. "Are you abandoning us?" Marian asked, smiling at Nora as she assembled beef, Swiss cheese, and lettuce on top of a slice of toast. Dart waved her forward, and she walked away from the fantasy of ramming a carving knife into his back.

Nora patted a spot beneath his left shoulder blade. "Are you happy now?"

Dart sang the first phrase of "Sometimes I'm Happy" and pushed away the empty bowl. "Bring on the meat."

"I didn't imagine you could actually quote Hugo Driver," Marian said to him.

Dart said something unintelligible through a mouthful of food, apparently quoting more of *Night Journey.*

"Don't get him started," Nora said.

"Could we get him to recite some of his poetry during dinner?"

Dart uttered a gleeful *"Ungk!"* around the sandwich. His eyes sparkled.

Forced to deal directly with Nora, Marian fell back on cliché. "What was your favorite part of the tour?"

"Can I ask you about the restorations?"

"That's practically an obsession with us. Lily must have told you about how hard we worked to put Honey House together. I could tell you lots of horror stories."

"I wasn't thinking so much of Honey House."

"Main House is a more interesting problem, I agree. As great as Georgina Weatherall was, she had been going downhill for some time before her death, and toward the end she pretty much retired into one room on the second floor. Which meant that the roof leaked in a hundred places, and there was water damage just about everywhere. As you probably saw when you came in, we're still having work done. The next big project is restoring the gardens, and that's a *huge* job."

"Are any of the former gardeners still around?"

"No. Georgina had to let everyone but Monty Chandler, the head gardener, go. You saw the Song Pillars and Monty's Glen?"

"We did."

"When you were up there, did you hear the stones singing?"

"They sing?" Nora asked.

"When there's any kind of a wind, you can hear them make this *music*. Eerie."

"I suppose Monty Chandler is dead."

"He passed away a couple of years before Georgina, which was another reason things got out of hand. Monty Chandler kept things in line by being a sort of handyman–carpenter–security force. There used to be problems with poachers and people breaking into the cottages, but Monty scared them all off. And when he wasn't overseeing the gardens, he was patching roofs and doing other repairs. That's why Georgina could get by for so long without bringing in workmen. I know she spent a lot of money fixing the place up when her father gave it to her, but she didn't have to do that again until the late thirties!"

"I understand she was having some money troubles then," said Nora.

Footsteps sounded on the metal staircase.

"Margaret and Lily are coming down to start dinner. We'd better do the second floor."

Heavy lace-up brown shoes topped with swollen ankles appeared on the stairs, followed by a long, capacious navy blue cotton dress buttoned up the front, then a wide arm, and finally an executive face, broad in the cheeks and forehead, and gray hair clamped into place with a tightly wound scarf, also navy blue. Margaret Nolan reached the bottom of the stairs and stopped, her hand on the railing, taking them in with an alert curiosity which did not completely disguise her mild irritation. Lily Melville smiled at Dart from over her shoulder.

"Our special guests have an interest in the kitchen, Marian?"

"One of them had a special interest in a snack," Marian said.

Margaret inspected Dart with a level glance. "Looking at Mr. Desmond, I don't suppose it will affect his performance at dinner." She pushed herself away from the stairs and came puffing toward them.

"Margaret Nolan." She extended a wide, firm hand to Dart. "I run this madhouse. We are delighted to have your company, Mr. Desmond, though I must confess that I've never read your work. Marian tells me that it's very exciting."

Dart said, "We do what we can, we can do no more."

Margaret turned to Nora with the air of having chosen to ignore this remark. Her handshake was quick and dry. "Mrs. Desmond. Welcome to Shorelands. Are you happy with Pepper Pot?"

"It's great," Nora said.

"I'm pleased to hear it. But now, if we are to meet our schedule, we must begin. You'll forgive us, I hope?"

"Certainly," Nora said. Here before her, five feet, eight inches tall, weighing one hundred and eighty pounds, chronically short of breath, radiating decisiveness, common sense, and strength of character, was her answer. This woman would take in Nora's situation and figure out a way to resolve it in three seconds flat. She would need half as much explanation as Frank Neary, and a tenth as much as Marian Cullinan. But when could she get her aside? After dinner she would volunteer to carry the plates down to the kitchen—something, anything—to be alone with Margaret Nolan and whisper, *He's Dick Dart. Call the police.*

"All right, then." Margaret smiled as briskly as she had shaken Nora's hand. "Lily?"

Lily trotted to the side of the kitchen to take two white aprons from a hook on the far side of the wall telephone, and paused at the chair on the way back. "Isn't this your bag, Mrs. Desmond?"

"Oh, it is, I'm sorry." Nora took a step toward Lily and the chair, but Margaret stopped her with a touch. "Bring it to her, Lily."

Lily picked up the bag. "What do you have in here, brass knuckles?"

"I never go anywhere without my weapons collection," Nora said.

Marian said, "We should go upstairs and let them work their wonders."

"Where *is* that carving knife?" Margaret asked. "It couldn't have just walked away."

"I'm so curious," Dart said. "What treat are you two wonderful ladies going to whip up?"

Looking at Dart as if she were a second-grade teacher faced with an impertinent student, Margaret turned from the rack and put on her apron. "We are going to prepare one of Ezra Pound's favorite meals."

"Georgina liked Ezra, didn't she?"

"She did."

"Real-world politics," Dart said. "None of that guff about equality our leaders spout while they plunder the till. I'm on their side. Let's call a jackboot a jackboot, okay?"

Both Lily and Margaret were staring at him. Dart held up a hand. "Hey. What was good enough for Ez is good enough for me." Smiling at the two women frozen behind the chopping block, he pulled Nora toward the stairs.

91

MARIAN CLOSED THE door with a bang. "Norman, don't you understand that I could lose my *job*?"

"Solemn promise," Dart said. "By the time we finish dessert, they'll be begging me to come back."

"But you practically called Georgina Weatherall a Nazi!"

"Wasn't the old girl a tad gone on the majesty of the Fatherland? Doesn't make her a bad person."

Marian shook her head and checked to make sure that no one could overhear their conversation. "Norman, you can't go around saying these things in front of Margaret."

"Try to stop him," Nora said.

"I understand," Dart said. "Divine handmaiden to the diviner arts. Natural aristocrat. *My* problem is, I can't stand women like that."

Marian calmed down enough to say, "We don't admit it very often, but I'm sure Georgina Weatherall could be hard to deal with."

"Not her, Madame Director," Dart said. "Women like that might as well grow beards and smoke cigars. Nonetheless, I promise you a tremendously entertaining evening." He touched a finger to her chin. "I want you to have a glorious time. Still depending on you to drop in for that nightcap."

"This man," Marian said. "You can't stay angry with him."

* * *

Portraits lined the broad staircase. "This one used to hang in Georgina's bedroom." Marian was pointing at an oil painting of an elderly man in a business suit coiled in a leather chair. He had a tight, fanatical face dominated by a heavy nose and a protruding chin. "George Weatherall."

"'My Heart Belongs to Daddy.'"

Marian smiled at him from the top of the stairs, then conducted them down a hallway darker and narrower than the one below. Despite the framed book jackets and photographs of Main House in various stages of restoration on the walls, the second floor was more utilitarian and domestic than the first. They had moved from the public life into the private.

Nora asked, "Why don't you let people into her bedroom?"

"Wait'll you see it. That's not the way we want people to remember Shorelands."

"I thought you were after historical accuracy."

"*Accurate* accuracy is too raw for the public. The longer I stay in this job, the more I wonder if there is any such thing as historical accuracy. But I can't say that's very helpful when you have a painting contractor standing in front of you who wants to know right now what exact shade of purple to put on the wall."

"I thought Lily said that you were given a lot of the original paint. How could there be a problem with the shade?" Nora asked.

"We did have the original paint, but only about half the amount we needed, and it had turned into glue. The whole thing was a nightmare. In the end, we mixed whatever we could salvage in with new paint."

"How did you know what shade it was supposed to be?"

"From Georgina's room."

"The paint you got for Honey House was actually the kind used in Main House?"

"Nobody really knows what kind of paint was used in the cottages." Marian gestured at the doors lining the hallway. "The two rooms on the left are Margaret's bedroom and office, and she'd rather not have us go in there. In the old days, Georgina Weatherall kept this entire floor for her personal use. Emma Brotherhood, Agnes's sister, her personal maid, lived in this first room. The second was a wardrobe and changing room, and it's connected to the bathroom, the third door along, directly across from Georgina's bedroom. Next to that was the morning room, where Georgina wrote her letters and planned the menus. These days, that's where we store all the donations we can't use."

Marian smiled at Dart. "Anyhow, behind the door on the other side of the stairs is the staircase to the third floor. I have the two rooms immediately across the hall at the top of the stairs, and Lily has the two rooms next to me. Margaret's secretary, who's on her vacation this week, has the room next to Lily's. All the other rooms up there are empty. This room on the right, which we use for meetings, was where Georgina met special guests." She opened the door to a small, efficient chamber dominated by a boardroom table. "This was where Miss Weatherall would complain, gossip, get recommendations about new writers. And in here, people like Lily and Agnes could pass along anything she ought to know."

"KGB," Dart said. "Ears at the keyhole."

"We had a thief here once, you know."

"You surprise me," Nora said.

"A young woman took off with a valuable drawing just before she was to be asked to leave. Can you imagine? It was worth a fortune. By Rembrandt, or maybe Rubens, I don't remember."

"Neither one," Nora said. "It was by an artist named Redon."

"Somebody with an R name, anyhow," Marian said. "Georgina's bedroom is next. During the last two years of her life, she almost never left it. It's cleaned and dusted twice a week, but we never go in there ourselves. Personally, I think it's a little creepy."

She ushered them into a dark space where dull glints of glass and metal and a sense of hovering presences suggested a spectacular jumble of objects. "Georgina never opened her curtains, so we keep them closed. I always have a little trouble finding the light, because the switch is in back of . . . Here we go."

Layer after layer, the room emerged into view. In delirious profusion, silks, faded tapestries, worn Oriental rugs, and swags of lace dripped from the top of the canopied bed and over the backs of chairs, and hung on the crowded walls, folding behind and draping over a riot of ornate clocks, mirrors, framed drawings, and photographs of a woman whose face, a replica of her father's, had been softened by enthusiastic makeup and a surround of shapeless dark hair. An impressively ugly Victorian desk lay buried beneath a drift of papers lapping against porcelain animals and glass inkwells. A gramophone with a bell-like horn stood on an ormolu table. Other small tables draped with lace held stacks of books, silver-backed hairbrushes, and much else.

The room reminded Nora of a more chaotic Honey House. A second later, she realized that she had it backwards: Honey House was a more presentable version of this room. As her eyes adjusted to the clutter, she began to take in the real condition of Georgina's bedroom. Ancient water stains had leached the purple to blotchy pink. The fabrics strewn over the furniture were ripped and discolored, and the lace canopy hung in tatters. Stains mottled the white ceiling. Beside the bed, in front of an anachronistic metal safe with a revolving dial, brown threads showed through the pattern of the rug.

"I'd better see if Agnes is up to company," Marian said, and disappeared.

Here was the real Shorelands, the one room in all of the estate where real history was still visible. Concealed at the center of the house, it was a shameful secret too important to erase. Georgina Weatherall, whose greatest advantages had been wealth, vanity, and illusion, had risen day after day to admire herself in her mirrors, brushed her hair without ever managing to push it into shape, painted on layers of makeup until the mirrors told her that she was as commanding as a queen in a fairy tale. If she noticed a flaw, she submerged it beneath rouge and kohl, just as she buried the stains on her walls and the rents in her lace beneath layers of fabric.

Monty Chandler had never entered this room to repair the water damage: no one but Georgina and her maid had been allowed here. The maid had loved Georgina, who had so demanded love that she had seen it in people who mocked her. This monolithic ruthlessness was what was meant by a romantic conception of oneself.

Nora could almost respect Georgina Weatherall. Georgina had been sick with self-importance, and if Nora had met her at a party, she would have fled from the airless closet such people always create around themselves. But Georgina Weatherall had worked heroically in the service of her illusions. In her, perhaps for the first time in his life, Lincoln Chancel had met his match.

Marian opened the door and said, "Wonder of wonders, you could have a word with Agnes now, if you like."

92

"SHE REALLY IS SICK, I know, but boredom makes her cranky, and when Agnes gets cranky she lays it on a little too thick. I can't promise you more than a couple of minutes." Marian paused. "A couple of minutes will probably be enough."

An irritated voice came through the door. *"Are you talking about me?"*

"Why don't you let us see her alone?" Nora said. "I know you have work to do."

"I shouldn't." Marian looked up and down the hallway. "You might need help getting away."

"We'll manage."

"Maybe just this once. Margaret doesn't . . ." She bit her lower lip.

Margaret doesn't want strangers left alone with Agnes? "Margaret doesn't have to know."

"All right. If I can get my work done, I'll be able to come up for that nightcap." She knocked once and opened the door. "Here they are, Agnes. I'll look in on you later."

"Bring me some magazines. You know what I like."

Marian moved back, and Nora and Dart stepped into the doorway.

The old woman lying in the bed was about as thick around as a kitchen match. The straight hair, dyed black, falling from a center part on either side of her shrunken face, looked like a doll's wig. Her eyes were bright, lively, and suspicious. She had inserted one twiglike finger into the book in her lap, as if she had to see who these people were before deciding how much time to give them.

Marian introduced them and left.

"Come in, close the door."

They walked up to the bed.

"I'm surprised she left. You'd think I was a mad dog, the way they carry on." She examined Dart. "You're this fellow who's supposed to be a poet? Norman Desmond?"

"And you're the historical monument, Agnes Brotherhood."

She gave him a close inspection. "You don't look much like a poet."

"What *do* I look like?"

"Like a lawyer who spends a lot of time in bars. Should I know your name?"

"I wouldn't go that far," Dart said. He was enjoying himself.

"Don't pretend to be modest. You don't have a modest bone in your body." Agnes turned her eyes on Nora. "Does he?"

"Not a one," Nora said.

"Marian wouldn't be wasting her time on you if you were a nobody. Have you published a lot of books?"

"Alas, no."

"Who's your publisher?"

"Chancel House."

Agnes Brotherhood waved a hand in front of her face as if to banish a bad smell. "You'd leave them in a hurry if you'd ever had the misfortune of meeting the founder."

"In a class by himself," Dart said. "Villainy personified."

"You might as well stay awhile. Move those chairs up to the bed." She nodded at two folding chairs against the wall and slipped a card into her book, the Modern Library edition of Thoreau.

Agnes noticed Nora's interest. "I reread *Walden* once a year. Do you like *Walden,* Mr. Desmond?"

Dart lifted his chin and recited, " '*When I wrote the following pages, or rather the bulk of them, I lived alone, in the woods, a mile from any neighbor, in a house which I had built myself,*' so on and so forth. Does that answer your question?"

"Let's hear the rest of the sentence."

". . . '*on the shore of Walden Pond, in Concord, Massachusetts, and earned my living by the labor of my hands only.*' "

"Not quite the truth, I believe, but lovely all the same. Now what would you like me to talk about? The great hostess and her noble guests? What D. H. Lawrence ate for breakfast? That kind of thing?"

Dart glanced at Nora. "You're not as reverent about the great hostess as Lily Melville, are you?"

"I knew her too well," Agnes snapped. "I had a job, and I did it. Lily had a *cause,* the adoration of Georgina Weatherall. I used to laugh at her sometimes, and she didn't like it one bit."

"You used to laugh at Georgina?"

"At Lily. Nobody laughed at Georgina Weatherall. She had her qualities, but a sense of humor wasn't one of them. If you were going to make fun of Miss Weatherall, you had to do it behind her back, and a lot of them did, but that isn't something you're going to hear about these days. Were you on Lily's tour?"

Nora said they had been.

"Tour of the shrine, that's what you get with Lily. When the mistress got sick and she was let go, she went around being the Shorelands expert in front of all these groups." She laughed. "It's a lot more fun meeting people without Freckle Face listening in. She used to interrogate people from my groups to see if I'd said anything I shouldn't. Hah! As if I didn't know my job. I know more than they like, that's what bothers them. I know things they don't know."

"Reason they keep you around," Dart said.

Agnes frowned at him. "I devoted my life to Shorelands. They know that much." She nodded at a pitcher and a glass on the window ledge. "Could you get me a glass of water? I keep asking them to get me a table on wheels, like in hospitals, but do I get one? Not yet, and it's been days."

"Would you mind if I asked what's wrong with you?" Dart said. "Do you have an illness?"

"My illness is called old age," Agnes said. "Plus a few other disorders."

Dart peered into the pitcher. "Empty."

"Take it into the bathroom and fill it up, please?"

"Well . . . ," Dart drawled. "Can I do that, honey? Dare I leave you alone? Hate to miss anything."

"I'll fill you in," Nora said.

Dart shook a warning finger at Nora and carried the pitcher from the room.

Agnes fixed Nora with bright, suspicious eyes. When Dart's footsteps had crossed the hall, Nora leaned toward her. "Do you have a telephone?"

Agnes shook her head.

"Have you ever heard of a man named Dick Dart?"

Agnes shook her head again. Across the hall, water splashed noisily into a container.

"Can you get to a phone?"

"There's three or four in the director's office."

"As soon as we leave, go to the office and call the police." The water cut off. "Say that Dick Dart is having dinner at Shorelands. Agnes, this is extremely important, it's life and death." Footsteps left the bathroom. "Please."

Dart surged into the room, and water splashed out of the pitcher. "Filled to overflowing. What have we been talking about, my dears?"

"My health," Agnes said. "Present and future." She turned her puzzled, now decidedly alarmed, gaze to him.

"What *are* your health problems, sweetheart?" He poured several inches of water into her glass. "Dehydration?" She reached for the glass and he pulled it back, laughed, and allowed her to take it. "Little joke."

"Arrhythmia. Sounds worse than it is." She took two swallows and handed him the glass. "Put it on the floor beside my bed. I'm going to be back on my feet in a couple of days. I can still lead a tour as well as Lily Melville."

"Of course you can, lots better than that old fool," Dart said. He sat down, crossed his legs, and patted Nora on the back. "Did you miss me, my sweetie?"

"Horribly," Nora said.

Agnes was staring at him as if she were trying to memorize his face. "What are the names of your books, Mr. Desmond?"

He looked, smiling, toward the ceiling. "The first one was called *Counting the Bodies. Surgical Notes* was the name of the second."

Her hands twitched. "What are you especially interested in, Mrs. Desmond? You don't want to waste time listening to me complain."

"The summer of 1938." Agnes held herself utterly still. "I'm interested in whatever happened that summer, but especially in a poet named Katherine Mannheim."

The old woman was staring at her with even more concentration than she had given Dart. Nora could not tell what she was thinking or feeling.

"I'm also interested in the renovation that happened the year after that."

"Who are you? What do you want?" Her voice trembled.

"I'm just an interested party."

"What is this about?" Agnes looked back and forth between Dart and Nora.

"History," Dart said. "Flashlight into the past. What Honey House is supposed to be." He grinned. "'Fess up now, did it ever look like that antique shop we saw today?"

Agnes was silent for a time. "I went in and out of the cottages every day of my life, and the only one that ever had what you could call a lot of *stuff* in it was Mr. Lincoln Chancel's Rapunzel, and he put all of it in there himself. If our guesthouses had been like that, some of these noble individuals would have waltzed off with whatever they could stuff into their suitcases. The trust people, they don't care, as long as it looks pretty."

She turned her gaze to Nora. "By and large, this was a fine, decent place. I won't say otherwise. And the things I think, I'm not going to say to any policeman, that's for sure."

"We mentioned policemen?" Dart asked.

"Not at all." Nora tried to communicate silently with Agnes and saw only anxiety in her eyes.

"I don't understand what's going on," Agnes wailed.

Nora leaned forward. "All I want to talk to you about is that summer. That's all. Okay?" She saw a looming panic. "Whatever you have to do afterwards is fine. You can do whatever you want." She waited a beat, and Dart turned his entire body in her direction. "Call down and talk to Margaret. Call anyone you like. Do you understand?"

The dark eyes seemed to lose some of their confusion. "Yes. But I don't know what to say."

Nora remembered her conversation with Helen Day. "I know this is difficult for you. Let me tell you what I think. I think you don't want to be disloyal, but at the same time you've been keeping something secret. It isn't pretty, and people like Marian Cullinan and Margaret Nolan wouldn't want it to come out. But they don't even know about it, do they?"

"They're too new," Agnes said, looking at her in mingled wonder and suspicion.

"Lily knows part of it, but not as much as you do, isn't that right?"

Agnes nodded.

"And here come two people you never saw before. I think part of you wants to get this thing off your chest, but you don't see why you should tell it to *us*. I'd feel the same way. But I'm interested in what happened that year, and almost no one else is. I'm not a cop or a reporter, and I'm not writing a book."

Agnes glared at Dart.

"He doesn't care what happened to Katherine Mannheim," Nora said.

To indicate his indifference to the disappearances of female poets, Dart faked a yawn.

"I might be the only person you'll ever meet interested enough in this to talk to people who knew Bill Tidy and Creeley Monk."

"Those poor men," Agnes said. "Mr. Tidy was a good, honest soul, and Mr. Monk, I liked him, too, because he could make you laugh like anything. Didn't matter to me if he was a . . ."

"A wagtail?" Dart said. "A prancer? A tiptoe boy?"

Agnes gave him a disdainful glance. "There's a lot of ways to be a good person." She returned to Nora. "Those two didn't know anything. They were here, that's all. Even if they heard anything, they wouldn't have thought twice about it."

Nora remembered something Everett Tidy had told her. "On the night Katherine Mannheim disappeared, Bill Tidy thought he heard poachers."

Agnes shook her head. "Wasn't a poacher in a hundred miles who'd risk his hide at Shorelands, not in those days. Monty Chandler gave one a load of bird shot and caught another in a mantrap, let him starve for two days, and that was it for poachers."

"So he heard something else."

Agnes pulled her robe closer to her neck. "Guess he did."

Almost against her will, Nora pushed forward. "I have some ideas. What if I tell you about them, and you tell me if I'm right?"

Agnes squinted at her and nodded once. "I could do that." She took in a great breath and pushed it out. "After all this time . . ." She began again. "That girl had a little sister. Kept her picture on her desk. The sister came here. Fine young lady. If she's still alive, she deserves to know the truth." She gave a flickering, almost frightened glance at Nora.

Nora tried to look as if she knew what she was doing. "I don't think Katherine Mannheim ran away from Shorelands. I think she died. Is that right?"

"Yes." Agnes's upper lip began to tremble.

"I think Hugo Driver had something to do with her death. Am I right?"

"What do you mean?"

"Didn't she come into Gingerbread and find Driver looking through her papers? Wasn't there a struggle?"

"No! That's all *wrong.*" Agnes's chin began to tremble.

Nora's impersonation of confident authority began to evaporate. Her favorite theory had just been destroyed. "She died that night. Her body had to be hidden."

A tear slipped from Agnes's right eye.

"She's buried somewhere on the estate."

Agnes nodded.

"And you know where."

"No, I don't. I'm *glad* I don't." She glanced at Nora. "I have to do tours, you see. Couldn't go where they put her."

"Hugo Driver and Lincoln Chancel."

"Did everything together, those two."

"That's why you still hate Lincoln Chancel."

Agnes shook her head with surprising vehemence. "I hated Mr. Chancel from the beginning. That man thought he had a right to touch you. Thought he could do anything he wanted and then make it all right with money."

"He offered you money?"

"I told him he was trying his dirty tricks with the wrong girl. He laughed at me, but he kept his hands to himself after that."

As interesting as this digression was, Nora wanted to get back to the main subject. She tried another approach. "Georgina knew that Katherine Mannheim hadn't just disappeared, didn't she? When she led everyone up to Gingerbread after dinner the next night, she already knew that the girl was dead."

"I hate to say it, but she did."

"She knew the door was unlocked even before she opened it."

"I wasn't there," Agnes said miserably. "But Miss Weatherall knew."

"How did you know her door was unlocked? Did you tend to Gingerbread?"

She nodded. "When I went to do the cleaning that morning, the door was unlocked and she wasn't inside. I hoped she was probably out in the gardens. At noon I put her box lunch in front of her door, because that was what we did, and it was still there the next morning."

"You didn't know that she was never going to come back."

"How could I? The mistress told me she'd run away. 'Climbed the wall,' she said. Made me feel funny. Especially after . . . after what happened."

A hint of understanding came to Nora. The reason that Georgina Weatherall had known her troublesome guest was gone before she opened the door to Gingerbread was directly in front of her, becoming more troubled with every second. "Did you say something to her, Agnes? Did you see something that disturbed you and tell Georgina about it?"

"I wish I never had." She held herself stiffly for a moment, and then another bolt of emotion went through her, and she began to cry.

Perfectly at ease, Dart twisted his mouth into a smile.

Nora tried to work out what Agnes had seen and remembered that Creeley Monk had seen Driver and Lincoln Chancel on the grounds late that night. "Tell me if I'm right. Did you take walks at night?" Agnes glanced fearfully at her, then nodded. "The night Katherine Mannheim died, you took one of your walks. You went up the path toward Gingerbread." Agnes lifted her head and gave her another frightened glance. "Were they carrying her body? Is that what you saw?"

"No! No!" She covered her eyes with her hands. "Then I would have known right away, don't you see? I saw . . . you have to tell *me.*"

"You saw them."

Agnes shook her head.

"You saw Hugo Driver."

Agnes looked at her in furious disappointment. "No!"

"Lincoln Chancel," Nora said. A great deal of what was as yet unspoken fell into place. "You saw Lincoln Chancel leaving Gingerbread. My God, Lincoln Chancel killed her."

Dick Dart took his hands from behind his head and leaned forward, malicious delight alive in his face.

Nora said, "He was going back to Rapunzel to get Driver. I'm right, aren't I, Agnes? You saw him going through the woods, but you didn't know why."

Agnes forced herself to take a deep breath. "He was *running.* I couldn't tell what the noise was. I thought it was some animal. I was by the big boulder up on the path. We used to have bears in our woods back then, and sometimes we still do. I hid behind the boulder, and the noise got closer and closer. Then I heard a man swearing. I knew it was Mr. Chancel. I peeked out. Here he comes out of the path, racing like a crazy man up toward Rapunzel. He went over the bridge, *bang! bang! bang!* I was so *afraid.* I wished it was a bear! I should have . . ." She drew up her knees and buried her face in the covers.

Nora moved onto the bed and embraced her.

"Female bonding," Dart said.

"You thought you should have gone to the cottage," Nora said. Agnes sighed in her arms. "But you were afraid. You were right to be afraid. They might have caught you."

"I *know.*" Agnes leaned into Nora's chest and took another deep breath. "I started back to Main House, and then I decided I had to look in on Miss Mannheim after all, but I heard Mr. Chancel and Mr. Driver coming down from Rapunzel, so I stayed behind the boulder. They came over the bridge, clump clump clump, and went up the Gingerbread path."

She pulled away from Nora and patted her face with the bedcovers. "You can sit down again."

"Are you sure?" Agnes shrank from another attempt at an embrace, and as Nora got off the bed, she collapsed onto her pillow. "I went flying back to Main House. I got upstairs, and the mistress was standing in the hallway. What's going on, Agnes, she says, why are you running around in the middle of the night, I demand an explanation. I told her. She says, Agnes Brotherhood, you leave this to me. She slapped on her big red hat and out she went. The mistress loved that big red hat, but it was the silliest thing you ever saw." Agnes glowered at the ceiling.

"You waited for her to come back," Nora said.

"Waited and waited. After a long time she looks around my door and says, Agnes, Miss Mannheim is one of those women who require male companionship when their spirits are low. Mr. Chancel chose to protect himself from scandal. Put the entire matter out of your mind, she says."

"And you tried to do that."

Agnes gave an unhappy nod. "I asked if Miss Mannheim was all right, and she said to me, Women like that are always all right." Dart grunted in approval. Agnes scowled at him. "I'm not saying there aren't women like that, but Miss Mannheim was a fine person."

"The next day you must have thought that she'd run away."

"I thought she *left*. There's a big difference between running away and leaving. Miss Mannheim wouldn't have run away from anything."

Agnes tugged her robe around her and looked at Nora with frustrated defiance. She had told her story, but at the center of the story was a vacuum.

A knock at the door cut off whatever she might have said next. Marian Cullinan peeked in. "We must be having a wonderful time, you've been in here so long."

"High point of the tour," Dart said. "Fantastic tales of the good old days."

"*Wonderful.*" She approached the bed.

Nora looked at Agnes to see if she remembered what she had been asked to do, and the old woman dipped her head a fraction of an inch.

Marian stepped between them. "Agnes, you know the rules. I bet your blood pressure is through the roof."

"I want to say something to Mrs. Desmond, Marian."

"One little teeny-tiny thing, and then I have to take these nice people away."

Agnes reached for Nora's hand. "You have to hear the rest."

Marian laughed. "You want to tell these people your life story, Agnes? Mrs. Desmond will stop in again, I'm sure."

"Tonight," Agnes said, clutching Nora's hand.

Marian displayed a trace of impatience. "That won't be possible, Agnes. We have to protect your health."

Agnes dropped Nora's hand. "You're not my doctor."

"Well, on that note." Marian smiled at Nora. "Shall we?"

She bustled them out with a complicitous glance at Dart and a pained smile for Nora. "I hope that wasn't too awful."

"You kidding?" Dart said. "That was better than *Psycho*."

Shaking her head, she took them toward the staircase. "I don't know how we're going to tell her that she can't lead any more tours. I mean, look at her, would you want to follow Agnes around the estate?"

A door clicked open behind them.

"Now what?" Marian said.

Clutching her bathrobe about her, Agnes hobbled out of her bedroom.

Marian put her hands on her hips. "I see it, but I don't believe it."

"Last roundup," Dart said.

Marian hurried up to the old woman and whispered to her. Agnes tottered forward another step. Roughly, Marian turned her around and marched her back to her room. Agnes shot Nora a look of bleak humiliation. A few seconds later, Marian came out and locked the door.

"Honestly. I've had my difficulties with Agnes, but I never had to lock her in her room before. She said she had to go to the office, can you imagine?"

"It can't really be necessary to lock her up," Nora said. "What if she has to go to the bathroom?"

"She can hold it until she gets her dinner. Margaret's already in a fine old state, thanks to Norman and his jackboots. By the time dinner is over, I'm going to need that nightcap." Marian took them to the staircase. "I'm not sure what to suggest. Ordinarily you'd want to go back to Pepper Pot or walk around Lenox, but it looks like we're building up to a rainstorm, and when that happens our paths turn into mudslides. Let's go down and see what it's doing outside."

A gust of wind slammed against the building. Somewhere beneath them, windows rattled in their frames. "As we speak," Marian said. Rain struck the front of the house like buckshot, fell away for a second, and then came back in a stronger, continuous wave.

The lights had been turned on in the lounge. The windows showed a dark sky sheeting down rain onto a sodden lawn. "At least the last tour ended before we had a lot of would-be lawyers demanding their money back." In the distance, trees bent before the wind. "It's a wild one." She turned to Dart. "What do you want to do? We have umbrellas, but they wouldn't last a second out there. You could make a run for Pepper Pot if it dies down, but you'd be covered with mud by the time you got there."

"Screw that," Dart said. "I hate getting wet. Mud drives me up the wall."

Beyond the splashing lawn, the trees threw up their arms. "It looks like you're stuck here until the end of dinner. We might be able to scrounge some boots for you, Norma, but Norman, what do we do about you?" Marian rubbed her forehead. "I'll get Tony to bring up a slicker and a pair of boots after dinner. Norma can use a raincoat of mine. And don't worry if the lights go out. We have lots of candles. Besides, our power company may be run by a bunch of hicks, but they always get the lights back on about an hour after the storms end. I promised you a special dinner, and that's what you're going to get."

"Goody."

"What would you like to do? I have to get some more work done in my office, and then I have to help in the kitchen, so you'll be more or less on your own."

"I'd like to talk to Agnes some more," Nora said.

"We'll have to save that for another day." Three short dashes bracketed by outturned parentheses appeared in the middle of Marian's forehead, then melted away. "Weren't you interested in Georgina's papers?"

"I'd love to see them." The records were bound to be in the office on the second floor, and Dart had to go to the bathroom sometime.

"Can a thirsty man get a drink around here?" Dart asked.

"Absolutely," Marian said. "Come with me and I'll set you both up."

Tossing back her hair, she took them into the main corridor, went down the marble steps, and looked back up at Nora. "Don't you want to see the records?"

"Aren't they upstairs?" Nora asked.

"They were, but after a couple of writers invaded Margaret's office, we moved everything into the little room my secretary used to have, when I *had* a secretary."

Marian led them to a windowless cubicle fitted with a desk, a schoolroom chair, and metal shelves half-filled with bound ledgers, files of correspondence, and boxes marked PHOTOGRAPHS. "Norman, I'll be right back with your drink. Vodka, is that right? On the rocks?"

"Drink to build a dream on."

If there had ever been a telephone in the cubicle, it had vanished along with Marian's secretary.

93

TEN MINUTES LATER, Dart repeated the first thing he had said after Marian had left them. He was leaning back in the chair with his feet up on a shelf, stirring the ice cubes in what was left of his drink with a finger. "That story was even worse than Jane Austen's garbage."

Nora closed one ledger and took another from the pile in front of her. Throughout the twenties and early thirties Georgina had spent a great deal of money on champagne acquired through a bootlegger named Selden, who after the repeal of the Volstead Act in 1933 had apparently opened a liquor store. Models of order in one regard, the ledgers were chaotic in most others. In a hand which degenerated over the years from a Gothic upright to a barbed-wire scribble, Georgina had recorded every dollar which had entered and left Shorelands, but she'd made no distinctions between personal expenses and those of the estate. A five-dollar outlay for a new fountain pen appeared beneath one for three hundred dollars' worth of Dutch tulip bulbs. Nor had she been rigid as to dates.

"Maybe Agnes saw Chancel running down the path. Maybe she made the whole thing up one night after nipping too much amontillado, but *we'll* never know. You know why? Shorelands is the Roach Motel for reality. The truth goes in, but it never comes out, and the reason for that is Georgina. Do you think Georgina Weatherall was ever capable, even way back in the days before she swapped sherry for liquid morphine, of giving you an accurate account of what took place on any given day?"

"Judging by the state of her records, not really."

"Those novelists must have felt right at home. This whole place is fiction." He laughed out loud, delighted by his own cleverness. "Even the name is a lie. It's called Shorelands, but it isn't on any shore. Old George thought she was beautiful and grand and universally adored, but the truth is, she was a horse-faced joke in circus clothes who got people to show up by giving them free room and board. Having famous writers suck up to her made her feel important. She couldn't stand reality, so she went around pretending the run-down shacks her servants used to live in were 'cottages.' She handed out these fancy names. 'I dub thee Gingerbread, I dub thee Rapunzel, and while I'm at it, I think I'll dub that mangy swamp up there the Mist Field.' What does that tell you? Pretty soon a little girl with an apron is going to show up trotting after a rabbit on its way to a tea party."

"I think I'm the little girl," Nora said.

"There you are. Why should Agnes be any different? She spent her whole life in this illusion factory. She has no idea what really happened to that girl."

"I think she does," Nora said, "and something you said a little while ago gave me an idea."

Dart looked pleased with himself again. "I don't believe it for a second, but how did she find out?"

"Georgina told her what happened to Katherine."

"That makes a lot of sense. The great lady tells a servant that she helped conceal a murder? If it *was* a murder, which I also doubt."

"You heard Agnes."

"Agnes is stuck in bed while her archrival, Lily Melville, is bouncing around handing out lies to tourists. She's alone up in that room with Henry David Thoreau, and she thinks he's a liar, too."

"They do need a little more reality around here," Nora said.

"About eleven or twelve tonight, they'll get more than they can handle. In the meantime, find anything in those books?"

"Not yet." She took another ledger from the pile. The entries began in June of an unspecified year with the receipt of a five-hundred-dollar check from G.W., presumably Georgina's father, and the expenditure of $45.80 for gardening supplies. The next entry was *18 June, $75—, Selden Liq., Veuve Clicquot,* so the ledger had been filled sometime after 1933. The handwriting had only just begun its deterioration.

"What a diligent little person you are, Nora-pie." He lounged over to the shelves and pulled down a box marked PHOTOGRAPHS. Nora flipped pages of the ledger, and Dart began sifting through the box.

She worked her way through another three or four pages without finding mention of any sum larger than a few thousand dollars. "Agnes wasn't bad-looking way back then," Dart said. "No wonder Chancel groped her."

He handed her a small black-and-white photograph, and she looked at the pleasant face of the young Agnes Brotherhood, whose prominent breasts plumped out the front of her black uniform. Undoubtedly the maid had been forced to swat away any number of male paws. She passed the photograph back to Dart, and the instant he took it from her, she knew how Katherine Mannheim had died. She had known all along without knowing: her own life gave her the answer.

Shaken, she turned a few pages at random, scarcely taking in the cryptic entries. A case of gin and two bottles of vermouth from the liquor store owned by Georgina's former bootlegger. *Meds., $28.95. Disc, $55.65. Whl.Mt., $2.00. Mann & Ware, phtgrs., $65.*

"Hold on," Nora said. "Did professional photographers take any of those pictures?"

"Sure. The big group photos."

Dart rooted through the box and handed her an eight-by-twelve photograph of the usual group of men in suits and neckties surrounding a regal Georgina. Stamped on the back was the legend "*Patrick Mann & Lyman Ware, Fine Portraiture, Mann-Ware Studios, 26 Main St., Lenox, Massachusetts.*"

Patrick Mann, Paddy Mann, Paddi Mann.

Lyman Ware, Madame Lyno-Wyno Ware, Lena Ware.

Shorelands, *Night Journey,* Davey Chancel.

Two photographers who took the group portrait every year, two fictional characters, a troubled Driver fanatic who had pursued Davey.

"A little bee is buzzing around up there."

She handed the photograph back to him. A girl named Patricia Mann, Patty Mann, had immersed herself in the Driver world and become first Lena Ware, then Paddi Mann. Part of her entry into the world of lunatic Driver fans had been the coincidence of her name resembling that of a Lenox photographer.

Then it came home to Nora that Paddi Mann had been Katherine Mannheim's niece: family rumor had pushed her even deeper into the Driver world. She had been convinced that her father's unconventional sister had written her sacred book and had twice tried to rescue her aunt from oblivion. She had even dressed like Katherine Mannheim.

Nora riffled the pages of the ledger, and a name and a number seemed to leap up toward her. *Rec'vd L. Chancel: $50,000.* "Lincoln Chancel gave her fifty thousand dollars."

Dart ambled over to look at the entry. "Isn't even a date there. It sure as hell doesn't prove she blackmailed him. Nobody could blackmail that old bastard."

Nora turned another few pages. "Here are the renovations. Look, five hundred dollars to a roofer, two hundred to a painter. About a week later, the same painter gets another two hundred. Fifteen hundred to a building contractor. Six hundred to B. Smithson, electrician. The painter again. Then down here at the bottom of the page, the contractor is getting another thousand. It goes on and on."

"The old scorpion guzzled a lot of the widow, didn't she?"

"The widow?"

"The widow Clicquot, you ignoramus. All right, he gave her a lot of money, and she used it to spruce up the place. Chancel was greedy, but he sure as hell wasn't a miser. Made a lot of money and threw half of it away. 'Georgina, you old ratbag, here's fifty thou, whip those hovels into shape, and get yourself a couple cases of the widow while you're at it.' That's what happened."

"Lincoln Chancel voluntarily gave fifty thousand dollars to a woman he probably despised? At a time when fifty thousand was about three or four hundred thousand in today's money?"

"The man was hardly petty. Besides, he had two other reasons for being generous to Georgina. He wanted to enlist her in his movement, and he met Driver because of her. I bet he had some idea of how much he was going to make out of *Night Journey.* Fifty thousand was chump change."

Nora smiled at him. "You don't want to think that your hero could have been blackmailed."

"The man *was* a hero," Dart said. "The more you learn about the guy, the better he gets. Anyone tried to blackmail him, he'd start up the chain saw. Trust me."

Dart adored monsters because he was one himself, but about this he was right: it would not have been easy to extort money out of Lincoln Chancel. Someone knocked at the door.

"Refill," Dart said. "Love that woman."

Marian Cullinan peeped inside. "Sorry to interrupt, Norma, but you have a phone call. A Mr. Deodato?"

Dart looked lazily down at her.

"I'll wait in here until you're done," Marian said.

94

DART CLOSED MARIAN'S door and whispered, "Be a smart girl, now." Smiling, he waved her to the telephone. When Nora picked up the receiver, he came up beside her and pressed his head next to hers.

Nora said, "Jeffrey? It's nice of you to call."

"That's one way to put it," Jeffrey said. "I called before, but some woman told me you were on a tour. Why didn't you phone me?"

"There are hardly any telephones in this place, and I've been pretty busy. I'm sorry you were worried, Jeffrey."

"What did you think I'd be? Anyhow, I made it most of the way there before the rain stopped me. How did you manage to get to Shorelands?"

"It's not important. Once I saw all those policemen at the hotel, I went out by a side door and ran into a friend who gave me a ride. I'm sorry I couldn't get in touch with you. Where are you now?"

"A gas station outside Lenox. It looks like I'll have to stay here a couple of hours. Look, Nora, I have some important things to tell you."

"You must have walked into all those cops."

"Did I ever. I spent most of the day at the police station. I was sure I was going to be arrested, but they finally let me go."

"I saw Davey just before I left. Did he meet your mother?"

"That's one of the things I want to tell you. He came to her house with a couple of FBI agents. It was quite a scene. Davey broke down and cried. Even my mother was touched. From what she told me, all hell broke loose in Westerholm this morning. Davey went to his father with what you told him last night, and Alden threw him out of the Poplars. Davey's falling apart. He wants you back. I didn't know how you'd feel about that, so instead of calling him after I talked to my mother, I wanted to get in touch with you. I'd prefer to be doing it in person, but from here on the road is under water."

"Instead of calling him? Why would you call Davey?"

"To tell him you might have gone to Shorelands. Or, what I was afraid of, that Dick Dart had managed to get ahold of you again."

"I don't understand."

"That's because you don't know the rest of my news. After I get to Shorelands, you'll probably want to come back to Northampton with me. Or I could drive you back to Connecticut, if that's what you want to do."

Dart pulled the knife from his belt sheath and held it in front of her face.

"Jeffrey, slow down. I have to stay here tonight, and I don't want you to come until tomorrow. I'm sorry, but that's how it is. How could I go back to Connecticut, anyhow?"

"Well, it's kind of strange, but everything's cleared up," he said. "You're not wanted anymore."

Dart's eyes flicked toward her.

"What happened? How do you know, anyhow?"

"My mother. Nobody really understands this yet, but one of the FBI men said that Natalie Weil has completely recanted. She told the police that you didn't kidnap her after all."

"I'm in the clear?"

"As far as I know. The whole thing seems very confused, but I guess Natalie did say that she was wrong or mistaken or something, and she's sorry she ever involved you."

Dart's gaze had become flat and suspicious. Nora said, "I don't understand that."

"I get the impression that Natalie has everybody a bit baffled, but it's certainly good news as far as you're concerned. The only thing the police want to talk to you about now is Dick Dart. He got out of Northampton by stealing an antique Duesenberg, if you can believe that."

"Did he really?" Nora asked.

"Why don't I pick you up as soon as I can and take you wherever you want to go?"

"I know it's a tremendous inconvenience, but I want to stay here and wrap up the work I'm doing."

"You want me to wait at this gas station until the rain stops and then drive back to Northampton?" He seemed almost dumbfounded.

"I wish there were a way to do this that would be easier on you."

"So do I. Can you call me tomorrow? After about eight in the morning, I'll probably be at my mother's house." His voice was flat.

"I'll call you."

"You want me to call Davey and tell him you're okay?"

"Please, no."

"You must be on to something pretty interesting, to want to stay there."

"I know you deserve better than this, Jeffrey. You're a good friend."

"Have I earned the right to give you some advice?"

"More than that."

"Leave him. He'll never be anything but what he is right now, and that isn't good enough for someone like you."

"So long, Jeffrey."

Dart set down the telephone. "I think you broke his heart. Jeffrey wanted to spend the night with my own Nora-pie. But let's consider a more crucial matter. Little Natalie has recanted. You never kidnapped the whore after all." He waved his hands in circles at the sides of his head. "The curse of Shorelands strikes again; we're wading through lies." Dart put the point of the knife under her chin and brushed it against her skin. "Help me out here."

"I can't explain it." Nora raised her chin, and Dart jabbed her lightly, indenting her skin without breaking it. "You heard him. Nobody understands what Natalie's doing."

"Give it your best shot."

"Natalie's been medicated for days. I don't think she can even remember what happened. And she takes drugs. Davey told me the cops found a bag of cocaine somewhere in her house."

"Adventurous Natalie."

"Maybe she can't remember what I did. Maybe she has some other reason for lying. I don't know, and I don't care. I was going to kill her."

He stroked her cheek. "These threats of unexpected visitors make me uncomfortable. Let me tell you what I want to do tonight. Everything is going to work out fine. Daddy has a new plan."

95

AT A LITTLE past six, Marian returned to say that dinner would be ready in a few minutes. She had applied a pale pink lipstick and a faint eyeliner and put on a necklace of thin gold links which drooped over her clavicles like a pet snake. "I hope you're hungry again," she said to Dart, who was bored and grumpy because he had not been offered a second drink.

"I'm always hungry. I tend to be on the thirsty side, too."

"Could that be a hint? Margaret opened a bottle of wine, and I think you'll enjoy her selection."

"Only one?" Dart held out his glass. "Why don't you do your best to guarantee high spirits by arranging at least one more bottle to go with our feast?"

Her smile slightly strained, Marian took the glass and stepped behind Nora. "Find anything useful?"

Nora had seen two more entries of payments from Lincoln Chancel, one for thirty thousand dollars, the other for twenty thousand. Each had been followed by outlays to dressmakers, milliners, fabric shops, and the ubiquitous Selden. After spending most of the first fifty thousand on the estate, Georgina had devoted the second to herself.

"I'm getting there," she said.

"You could come back here after dinner, if you like."

This suggestion dovetailed with Dart's new plans for the night, and Nora forced herself to say, "Thank you, I might want to do that."

"I'd better tend to your thirsty husband or he won't be in a good mood."

"Damn right," Dart said. "Speaking of moods, how's Lady Margaret's? Has she bounced back?"

"Margaret doesn't bounce," Marian said. "But I'd say there's still hope for a civilized evening."

"Boring. Let's get down and dirty."

"I'd better hurry up with that drink."

The chandelier had not been turned on, and all the light in the room came from sconces on the walls and candles in tall silver holders. Five places had been set with ornate blue-and-gold china. Reflected candle flames shone in the silver covers of the chafing dishes and the dark windows. Invisible rain hissed onto the lawn. Margaret Nolan and Lily Melville turned to Dart and Nora, one with an expression of neutral welcome, the other with an expectant smile. Lily danced up with her hands folded before her.

"Isn't this storm *terrible*? Aren't you happy this didn't happen when we were on our tour?"

"Rain was invented by the devil's minions."

"Big storms always scare me, especially the ones with thunder and lightning. I'm always sure something awful is going to happen."

"Nothing awful is going to happen tonight." Margaret came toward them. "Except for the usual power failure, and we're well equipped to deal with that. We're going to have a lovely evening, aren't we, Mr. Desmond?"

"Are we ever."

She turned to Nora. "Marian says that you've been roaming through our old ledgers in aid of a project related to Hugo Driver. I hope you'll share your thoughts with us."

Margaret was willing to overlook Dart's provocations for the sake of the business to be brought in by Hugo Driver conferences. Nora wondered what she could say to her about the importance of Shorelands to Driver's novel.

"What became of Marian? We expected her to come in with you."

"Arranging a libation," Dart said.

Margaret raised her eyebrows. "We have a good Châteauneuf for the first course, and something I think is rather special, a 1970 Château Talbot, for the second. What did you ask Marian to bring you?"

"A double," Dart said. "To make up for the one she forgot."

"You are a poet of the old school, Mr. Desmond. Mrs. Desmond? A glass of this nice white?"

"Mineral water, please," said Nora.

She went to the bottles as Marian hurried in with the refilled glass. "Margaret, I hope you won't mind," she said, handing off the drink, "but Norman felt that one bottle of the Talbot might not be enough, so I looked around and opened a bottle of Beaujolais. It's down on the kitchen counter."

Margaret Nolan considered this statement, which included the unspoken information that the second bottle was perhaps a tenth the price of the first, and cast a measuring glance at Dart. He put on an expression of seraphic innocence and swallowed half his vodka. "Very intelligent, Marian. Whatever our guest does not drink, we can save for vinegar. Please, help yourself."

Marian poured herself a glass of white wine. "I called Tony and asked him to bring up rain clothes for Norman and leave them inside the front door. The telephone lines might go down, and the poor man has to get back to Pepper Pot. I can loan Norma some things of my own."

"Another intelligent decision," said Margaret Nolan. "Since you are on a first-name basis with our guests, all of us should be. Is that agreeable?"

"Completely, Maggie." Dart raised his glass to his mouth and gulped the rest of the vodka.

With elaborate ceremoniousness, Margaret indicated their seats: Norman to the right of the head of the table, Nora across from him, Marian next to Norman, Lily beside Nora. "Please go the sideboard and help yourselves to the first course. Once we are seated, I will describe our meal, as well as some aspects of this wonderful room not covered during the normal tours. Lily, will you start us off?"

Lily skipped to the sideboard, where she lifted the cover from an oval platter next to a basket of baguettes. On either side of a mound of pale cheese strips lay broiled peppers, sliced and peeled, red to the left, green to the right, flanked with black olives and topped with anchovies. Quarters of hard-boiled eggs had been arranged at either end of the platter. An odor of garlic and oil rose from the peppers. Lily took a salad plate from the stack next to the platter and held it up before Dart. "This is Georgina's own china. Wedgwood."

" 'Florentine,' " Dart said. "One of my personal faves."

"Norman, you know everything!"

"Even beasts can learn," Dart said.

Lily gave herself minute portions of both kinds of peppers, a few olives, and a single section of hard-boiled egg. Dart took half the red peppers, none of the green, most of the olives, half of the eggs and cheese, and all but three of the anchovy slices. Atop it all he placed a six-inch section ripped from the French bread. The others followed, choosing from what was left.

Dart sat down, winked at Lily, and filled his wineglass with white wine from the bucket.

Margaret took her seat and gave his plate a lengthy examination. "This is what Miss Weatherall called her 'Mediterranean Platter.' Monty Chandler grew the peppers, along with a great many other things, in a separate garden north of Main House."

While she spoke, Dart had been shoveling peppers into his mouth, demolishing the hard-boiled eggs, loading strips of cheese onto chunks of bread and chomping them down. As she finished, he bit into the bread and tilted in wine to moisten it all. His lips smacked. "Weird cheese."

"Syrian." Margaret gravely watched him eat. "We get it from a gourmet market, but Miss Weatherall ordered it from an importer in New York. Nothing was too good for her guests."

Dart waggled the bottle at her. "Yes, please." He gave her half a glass and then filled Marian's.

A blast of wind like a giant's hand struck the house. Lily crushed her napkin in her hands. "Lily, you've lived through thousands of our storms," Margaret said. "It can't be as bad as it sounds, anyhow, because the power's still on."

At that moment the wall sconces died. The reflections of the candle flames wavered in the black windows, and again the wind battered the windows.

"Spoke too soon," Margaret said. "No matter. Lily, stop *quivering*. You know the lights will come on soon."

"I know." Lily thrust her hands between her thighs and stared at her lap.

"Eat."

Lily managed to get an olive to her mouth.

"Marian, perhaps you'd better take a candle up to Agnes. She has eaten, hasn't she?"

"If you can call it eating," Marian said. "Don't worry, I'll take care of it. And I'll bring back more candles, so we can see our plates."

"And will you check the phones?" She turned to Dart. "One of the few drawbacks of living in a place like this is that when the lights go out, fifty percent of the time the phones do, too. They're too miserly to put in underground phone lines."

"Curse of democracy," Dart said. "All the wrong people are in charge."

Margaret gave him a look of glittering indulgence. "That's right, you share Georgina Weatherall's taste for strong leaders, don't you?"

Lily looked up, for the moment distracted from her terror. "I've been thinking about that. It's true, the mistress did say that powerful nations should be led by powerful men. That's why she liked Mr. Chancel. *He* was a powerful man, she said, and someone like that should be running the country."

Dart beamed at her. "Good girl, Lily, you've rejoined the living. I agree with the mistress completely. Lincoln Chancel would have made a splendid president. We need a man who knows how to seize the reins. I could do a pretty good job myself, I venture to say."

"Is that right," Margaret said.

Dart took the last of the white wine. "Death penalty for anyone stupid enough to be caught committing a crime. Right there, give the gene pool a shot in the arm. Public executions, televised in front of a live audience. Televise trials, don't we? Let's show 'em what happens after the trial is over. Abolish income tax so that people with ability stop carrying the rabble on their backs. Put schools on a commercial basis. Instead of grades, give cash rewards funded by the corporate owners. So on and so forth. Now that the salad part of the meal has been taken care of, why don't we dig into whatever's under those lids?"

Margaret said, "It occurs to me that a playful conversation like this, with wild flights of fancy, must be similar to those held here during Miss Weatherall's life. Would you agree, Lily?"

"Oh, yes," Lily said. "To hear some of those people talk, you'd think they'd gone right out of their heads."

"One of the paintings in this room was actually here in those days. Along with the portrait of Miss Weatherall's father on the staircase, it's all that survives from her art collection. Can you tell which one it is?"

"That one." Nora pointed to a portrait of a woman whose familiar face looked out from beneath a red hat the size and shape of a prize-winning pumpkin.

"Correct. Miss Weatherall, of course. I believe that portrait brings out all of her strength of character." Marian came back into the room with a candlestick in each hand and two others clamped to her sides.

"I think you might remove the hors d'oeuvres plates, Marian, and give me the others so that I can serve up the main course. How is poor Agnes?"

"Overexcited, but I couldn't say why." Marian began collecting the plates. "The phones are out. I suppose they'll be working again by morning."

"I'd love to see Agnes once more," Nora said.

Margaret lifted a silver cover off what appeared to be a large, round loaf of bread. Flecks of green dotted the crust. "Norma, I'm sure that Lily and I can be at least as helpful as Agnes Brotherhood. What is this project of yours? A book?"

"Someday, maybe. I'm interested in a certain period of Shorelands life."

Margaret cut into the crust. With two deft motions of the knife, she ladled a small section of the dish onto the topmost plate. Thin brown slices of meat encased in a rich gravy slid out from beneath the thick crust. To this she added glistening snow peas from the other serving dish. "There are buttermilk biscuits in the basket. Norma, would you please pass this to Lily?"

Dart watched the mixture ooze from beneath crust. "What is that stuff?"

"Leek and rabbit pie, and snow peas tossed in butter. The rabbit is in a *beurre manié* sauce, and I'm pretty sure I got all the bay leaves out."

"We're eating a rabbit?"

"A good big one, too. We were lucky to find it." She filled another plate. "In the old days, Monty Chandler caught three or four rabbits a month, isn't that what you said, Lily?"

"That's right." Lily leaned over and inhaled the aroma.

"Marian, would you bring us the Talbot?" She arranged the remaining plates, and Marian poured four glasses of wine.

As soon as she sat down, Dart dug into his pie and chewed suspiciously for a moment. "Pretty tasty for vermin."

Margaret turned to Nora. "Norma, I gather that the research you speak of concentrates on Hugo Driver."

Nora wished that she were able to enjoy one of the better meals of her life. "Yes, but I'm also interested in the other people who were here that summer. Merrick Favor, Creeley Monk, Bill Tidy, and Katherine Mannheim."

Lily Melville frowned at her plate.

"Rather an obscure bunch. Lily, do you remember any of them?"

"Do I ever," Lily said. "Mr. Monk was an awful man. Mr. Favor was handsome as a movie star. Mr. Tidy felt like a fish out of water and kept to himself. He didn't like the mistress, but at least he pretended he did. Unlike *her. She* couldn't be bothered, sashaying all around the place." She glared at Nora. "Fooled the mistress and fooled Agnes, but she didn't fool me. Whatever happened to that one, it was better than she deserved."

The hatred in her voice, loyally preserved for decades, was Georgina's. This too was the real Shorelands.

Margaret had also heard it, but she had no knowledge of its background. "Lily, I've never heard you speak that way about anyone before. What did this person do?"

"Insulted the mistress. Then she ran off, and she stole something, too."

A partial recognition shone in Margaret's face. "Oh, this was the guest who staged a mysterious disappearance. Didn't she steal a Rembrandt drawing?"

"Redon," Nora said.

"Made you sick to look at. It was a woman with a bird's head, all dark and *dirty.* It showed her private bits. Reminded me of *her,* and that's the truth."

"Norma, perhaps we should forget this unfortunate person and concentrate on our Driver business. According to Marian, you feel that Shorelands may have inspired *Night Journey.* Could you help me to understand how?"

Nora was grateful that she had just taken a mouthful of the rabbit pie, for it gave her a moment's grace. She would have to invent something. Lord Night was a caricature of Monty Chandler? Gingerbread was the model for the Cup Bearer's hovel?

A gust of wind howled past the windows.

Sometime earlier, following Lily on the tour, she had sensed . . . had half-sensed . . . had been reminded of . . .

"We should visit the Song Pillars," Marian said. "Can you imagine how they sound now?"

Lily shuddered.

A door opened in Nora's mind, and she understood exactly what Paddi Mann had meant. "The Song Pillars are a good example of the way Driver used Shorelands," she said.

Dart put down his fork and grinned.

"He borrowed certain locations on the estate for his book. The reason more people haven't noticed is that most Driver fanatics live in a very insular world. On the other side, Driver has never attracted much academic attention, and the people who know Shorelands best, like yourselves, don't spend a lot of time thinking about him."

"I never think about him," Margaret said, "but I think I am about to make up for the lapse. What is it you say we haven't noticed?"

"The names," Nora said. "Marian just mentioned the Song Pillars. Driver put them into *Night Journey* and called them the Stones of Toon. Toon, song? He changed the Mist Field into the Field of Steam. Mountain Glade is—"

Margaret was staring at her. "Mountain Glade, Monty's Glen. My Lord. It's true. Why, this is wonderful. *Think* of all the people devoted to that book. Norman, help yourself to more of that wine. Your wife has earned it for you. Marian, get the bottle of Beaujolais you opened before dinner, and bring it up with the champagne in the refrigerator. We were going to have a Georgina Weatherall celebration, and by God, we shall."

Marian stood up. "You see what I mean about the Driver conference?"

"I see more than that. I see a Driver *week*. I see Hugo Driver T-shirts flying out of the gift shop. What cottage did that noble man stay in when he was here?"

"Rapunzel."

Lily mumbled something Nora could not catch.

"Give me three weeks, and I can turn Rapunzel into a shrine to Hugo Driver. We'll make Rapunzel the Driver center of the universe."

"He wasn't noble," Lily muttered.

"He is now. Lily, this is a great opportunity. Here you are, one of the few people living actually to have known the great Hugo Driver. Every single thing you can remember about him is worth its weight in gold. Was he untidy? We can drop some socks and balled-up typing paper around the room. Did he drink too much? We put a bottle of bourbon on the desk." Lily took a sullen gulp of wine. "Come on, tell me. What was wrong with him?"

"Everything."

"That can't be true."

"You weren't here." She looked at Margaret with a touch of defiance. "He was sneaky. He was nasty to the staff, and he stole things."

Marian appeared, laden with bottles and a second ice bucket. "Who stole things?"

"We may have to rehabilitate Mr. Driver a bit more than our usual luminaries," Margaret said.

"You knew he was a thief," Nora said.

"Of course I knew. Stole silver from this room. Stole a marble ashtray from the lounge. Stole two pillowcases and a pair of sheets from Rapunzel. Books from the library. Stole from the other guests, too. Mr. Favor lost a brand-new fountain pen. The man was a plague, that's what he was."

The cork came out of the Veuve Clicquot with a soft, satisfying pop. "Maybe we should rethink our position on Mr. Driver," Marian said.

"Are you serious? We're going to polish this fellow up until he shines like gold, and if you're not willing to try, Lily, we'll let Agnes do it."

"She won't." Lily drank the rest of her wine. "Agnes was the one who told me half of what I just said. I want some champagne, too, Marian."

"What else did he steal, Lily?" Nora asked.

The old woman looked at a spot on the wall above Nora's head, then pushed her champagne flute toward Marian.

"He stole that drawing, didn't he? The missing Redon. The one you never liked."

Lily glanced unhappily at Nora. "I didn't tell you. I wasn't supposed to, and I didn't."

Margaret took a sip of champagne and looked back and forth from Nora to Lily in great perplexity. "Lily, two minutes ago you said that the Mannheim girl stole the drawing."

"That's what I was supposed to say."

"Who told you to say that?"

Lily swallowed more champagne and closed her mouth.

"The mistress, of course," said Nora.

Dart chuckled happily and helped himself to rabbit pie.

Lily was gazing almost fearfully at Nora.

"She knew because she saw the drawing in Rapunzel the night Miss Mannheim disappeared," Nora said.

Lily nodded.

"When did she tell you about this? And why? You must have asked the mistress if it was really Hugo Driver and not Miss Mannheim who had stolen the drawing," Nora said.

Lily nodded again. "It was when she was sick."

"When there were no more guests, and she almost never left her room. Agnes Brotherhood spent a lot of time with her."

"It was *unfair,*" Lily said. "Agnes never loved her the way I did. Agnes's sister Emma used to be her maid, and then Emma died, and the mistress wanted Agnes next to her. She didn't know the *real* Agnes, it was only that the sisters looked alike. I would have taken better care of her. I tried to watch out for her, but by that time it was Agnes, Agnes, Agnes."

"So it was Agnes who told you about the drawing first."

Margaret put her chin on her hand and followed the questions and answers like a spectator at a tennis match.

"She came out of the mistress's bedroom, and I looked at her face, and I said, 'What's wrong, Agnes?' because anyone could see she was upset, and she told me to go away, but I asked was something wrong with the mistress, and Agnes said, 'Nothing we can fix,' and I kept after her and after her, and finally she put her hand over her eyes and she said, 'I was right about Miss Mannheim. All this time, and I was right.' That trampy little thing, I said, she made fun of the mistress, and besides she stole that picture. 'No, she didn't,' Agnes says, 'it was Mr. Hugo Driver who did that.' She started laughing, but it wasn't like real laughing, and she said I should go upstairs and ask the mistress if I didn't believe her."

"So you did," Nora said.

Lily finished her glass and shuddered. "I went in and sat down beside her and touched her hair. 'I suppose Agnes couldn't keep quiet,' she said, and it was like before she got sick, with her eyes alive. I said, 'Agnes lied to me,' and I told her what she said, and she calmed right down and said,

'No, Agnes told you the truth. Mr. Driver took that picture,' and she knew because she saw it in his room at Rapunzel. 'Why would you go to his room?' I asked, and she said, 'I was being my father's daughter. You could even say I was being Lincoln Chancel.' So I said, 'You shouldn't have let him take it,' and she told me, 'Mr. Chancel paid for that ugly drawing a hundred times over. Send Agnes back to me.' So I sent Agnes back to her room. The next day, the mistress told me that she couldn't afford my wages anymore, and she would have to let me go, but I was never to tell anyone about who stole that picture, and I never did, not even now."

"You didn't tell," Nora said. "I guessed."

"My goodness," said Margaret. "What a strange tale. But I don't see anything that should trouble us, do you, Marian?"

"Mr. Chancel bought the drawing," Marian said. "Hugo Driver borrowed it before payment had been arranged, that's all."

"Love it," Dart said.

"If we could arrange for the loan of the drawing from the Driver estate, we could hang it in Rapunzel and weave it into the whole *Night Journey* story." Margaret sent a look of steely kindness toward Lily. "I know you didn't like the man, Lily, but we've dealt with this problem before. Together, you, Marian, and I can work up any number of sympathetic stories about Mr. Driver. This is going to be a windfall for the Shorelands Trust. More champagne, Norman? And we do have, as a special treat, some *petits vacherins*. Delicious little meringues filled with ice cream and topped with fruit sauces. Mr. Baxter, our baker in Lenox, had some fresh meringue cases today, wonder of wonders, and Miss Weatherall loved *vacherins*."

"Count me in," Dart said.

"Marian, would you be so kind?"

Marian once again left the room, this time patting Dart on the back as she went past him. As soon as she had closed the door, Lily said, "I don't feel well."

"It's been a long day," Margaret said. "We'll save you some dessert."

Lily got unsteadily to her feet, and Dart leaped out of his chair to open the door and kiss her cheek as she left the room. When he took his chair again, Margaret smiled at him. "Lily had some difficulties tonight, but she'll do her usual splendid job during our Driver celebrations. I see no hindrances, do you?"

"Only acts of God," Dart said, and refilled his wineglass.

Marian returned with a tray of *petits vacherins* and another bottle of champagne. "Despite Lily's qualms, I thought we had something to celebrate, so I hope you don't mind, Margaret."

"I won't have any, but the rest of you help yourselves," Margaret replied. Yet, when the desserts had been given out and Marian danced around the table pouring more champagne, she allowed her glass to be filled once more. "Mr. Desmond," she said, "I've been wondering if you would be so kind as to recite one of your poems. It would be an honor to hear something you have written."

Dart gulped champagne, took a forkful of ice cream and meringue, another swallow of champagne, and jumped to his feet. "I composed this poem in the car on the way to this haven of the literary arts. I hope it will touch you all in some small way. It's called 'In Of.' "

"Farewell, bliss—world is, are,
lustful death them but none
his can I, sick, must—
Lord, mercy us!

"Men, not wealth, cannot
you physic, must all to are
the full goes I sick must—
Lord, mercy us!

"Beauty but flower
wrinkles devour falls the Queens
died and dust closed eye;
am I die?
Have on!

"Strength unto grave feed Hector swords,
not with earth holds her
Come!
the do, I,
sick, must—
Lord, mercy us!"

He surveyed the table. "What do you think?"

"I've never heard anything quite like it," Margaret said. "The syntax is garbled, but the meaning is perfectly clear. It's a plea for mercy from a man who expects none. What I find really remarkable is that even though this is the first time I've heard the poem, it seems oddly familiar."

"Norman's work often has that effect," Nora said.

"It's like something reduced to its essence," Margaret said. "Have you spoken to Norman about our poetry series, Marian?"

"Not yet, but this is the perfect time. Norman, can we talk about your coming back to do a reading?"

Once again Marian had unknowingly assisted Dart's plans for the night. He pretended to think it over. "We should take care of that tonight. The only problem is that I'm going to need my appointment book, and it's in the room. But if you decide you want that nightcap, you could come up later."

"And let my appointment book talk to your appointment book? Yes, why don't I do that?"

"You young people," Margaret said. "You're going to have hours of enjoyment talking about all sorts of things, and I'm going to fall asleep as soon as I fall into bed. But before that, Marian, you and I have to see to the kitchen."

"Let me help," Nora said. "It's the least I can do."

"Nonsense," Margaret said. "Marian and I can whip through everything in half an hour. Anyone else would just get in our way."

"Margaret, dear," Dart said. "It's only seven-thirty. You can't mean you're really going to go to bed as soon as the dishes are done."

"I wish I could, but I have an hour or so of work to get through in the office. Marian, let's take the dishes down and attack the kitchen."

Dart glanced at Nora, who said, "Marian, I'd like to spend more time with the records and photographs, but I want to rest for a little bit first. So that you won't have to jump up and down answering the door, do you think you could give me a key?"

"Why don't we just leave the door unlocked?" Margaret said. "We're completely safe here. When were you planning on coming back?"

"Nine, maybe? The storm should be over by then. I could get some work done while Norman and Marian match their schedules."

"Oh?" Marian glanced at Dart. "That works for me. I'll leave the downstairs lights on and come over to Pepper Pot about nine. Does that sound all right to you?"

"Perfect," Dart said. "Did I hear a promise of rain gear?"

"Let's take care of that right now." Marian left the room, and Nora helped Margaret stack the dishes. Soon Marian returned with green Wellingtons, a shiny red raincoat with snaps, and a wide-brimmed matching hat. "My fireman outfit. Don't worry, I have lots of other stuff to get me over there dry. And Norman, Tony's gear is just inside the door."

Nora removed her shoes and pulled on the high boots. Marian had big feet. She put on the shiny coat and snapped it up, and Dart put down his empty glass. "Very fetching."

The sound of the rain was stronger at the front of the building. Dart examined Tony's dirty yellow slicker with revulsion, and he wiped his handkerchief around the interior of the hat before entrusting his head to it. His shoes would not go into the boots, so he too took off his shoes and jammed them into the slicker's pockets. "Almost rather get wet," he muttered.

"Wait! Don't go yet!" Marian called from behind them, and appeared at the top of the marble steps with Nora's bag and four new candles. "You'll find matches on the mantelpiece. Good luck!"

96

THE WORLD PAST the front door was a streaming darkness. Chill water slipped through Nora's collar and dripped down her back. Water rang like gunfire on the stiff hat. Dart grasped her wrist and began running toward the gravel court. When they reached the path, she nearly went down in the mud, but Dart wrenched her upright and tugged her forward. Water licked into her sleeves. The trees on either side groaned and thrashed, and hallucinatory voices filled the air.

Nothing had worked; she had been unable to speak to any of her possible saviors, and Dart was going to kill Marian Cullinan and spend a happy two hours dissecting her body while waiting for the older women to sink into sleep. Then he would pull her back through the deluge to Main House, where he looked forward to watching her murder Agnes Brotherhood. As he had said to her, genius was the capacity to adapt to change without losing sight of your goal. "Let's face it," he had said, "we're stuck here for the night, so the kidnapping is out. We have to take care of them all—those three old Pop-Tarts, too. They're calling me a serial killer, I might as well have a little fun and act like one. First of all, we convince everybody that you'll be coming back here by yourself. When we're through with the Pinto, we trot back here and visit the bedrooms so kindly pointed out to us. No alarms or telephones. Safety, ease, and comfort. When we're done, we enjoy a champion's breakfast of steak and eggs in the kitchen, and depart in the Pinto's car."

Trying to match her pace to Dart's, Nora bent over and ran, able to see no more than the rain sheeting off the brim of the red hat and the mud rising to her ankles. Dart yanked at her hand, and she lost her grip on the bag, which dropped into the mud. The cleaver, the carving knife, and much else tumbled out. Dart yelled something inaudible but unmistakable in tone, dragged her back, and bent down to scoop what had fallen out into the bag. Off to the right, a branch splintered away from a tree and crashed to the ground. Dart rammed the bag into her chest, whirled her around, and pushed her through the mud to the PEPPER POT sign and the ascending path. Her feet slipped, and she slid backwards into him. He pushed her again. Rain struck her face like a stream of needles. Nora tried to walk forward, and her right foot slipped out of the lower part of the boot. Dart circled her waist and lifted her off the ground. Her foot came out of the boot. Dart kicked it aside and carried her up the path.

He set her down on the porch and unfastened the clasps of the slicker to pull the key from his jacket pocket. Rain drummed down onto the roof. An unearthly moaning came from the woods. *Hell again,* Nora thought. *No matter how many times you go there, it's always new.* Dark puddles formed around them. A film of water covered her face, and her ribs ached from Dart's grip. He opened the door and pointed inside.

His hat and slicker landed on the floor. Nora put down the bag and fished the candles from the pockets of Marian's coat. Dart took the candles, locked the door, and made shooing motions with his hands. Nora hung Marian's things on a hook beside the door and lifted her foot out of the remaining boot. "Hang up that garbage I had to wear and find the matches. Then put your bag in the bathtub and get back here to help me pull off these disgusting boots."

"Put my bag in the tub?"

"You want to destroy a Gucci bag? I have to clean it off and try to dry it."

Nora carried the dripping bag across the lightless room into the bathroom. Was there a window in the bathroom, a back door? A gleaming black rectangle hung in the far wall. She moved forward until her legs met the bathtub, stepped inside, dropped the bag, and ran her hands along the top of the window. Her fingers found a brass catch. The slide refused to move. "What are you doing?" Dart shouted.

"Putting down the bag." She pulled at the slide, but it was frozen into place.

"Get back in here."

A column of darkness against a background of lighter darkness ordered her to the fireplace on the far side of the room. Holding her hands before her, Nora put one foot in front of another and made her way across the room.

Apparently able to see in the dark, Dart directed her to the fireplace and matches, then told her to walk fifteen paces forward, turn left, and keep walking until she ran into him.

Dart grabbed the matches out of her hands, lit a candle, and walked away. She could see nothing but the flame. He jammed the candle into a holder from the windowsill, lit the other two, and put them into the candlesticks on the table in the center of the room. The rope and duct tape lay beside an ice bucket and a liter of Absolut. Dart took two gulps of vodka and drew in a sharp breath. Muddy bootprints wandered across the floor like dance instructions. "Sounds like the inside of a bass drum." He dropped into a chair and stuck out one leg. "Do it."

Nora put her hands on the slimy boot. "Pull." Her hands slipped off. "Take your clothes off."

"Take my clothes off?"

"So you can prop my legs against your hip and push. Don't want to wreck that suit."

While she was undressing, Dart sent her to the kitchen for a glass. He blew into it, held it up to the flame for inspection, and pulled a dripping handful of slivers from the bucket. Before drinking, he drew a circle in the air with the glass, and Nora walked back to the bed and removed the rest of her clothes. "Hang up your things. Have to look good until we can get new clothes." He followed her with his eyes. "Okay, get over here, and put your back into it this time."

She pulled his outthrust leg into her side. His trousers were sodden, and an odor of wet wool came from him. She held her breath, gripped his leg with her left hand, pushed at the heel, and the boot came away. "Let my people be!" Dart swallowed vodka. "One down, one to go."

When the second boot surrendered, Nora staggered forward and felt an all too familiar surge of warmth throughout her body. Dizziness, a sudden sweatiness of the face, a hot necessity to sit down. "Oh, no," she said.

"Mud washes off," Dart said. Then he bothered to look at her. "Oh Christ, a hot flash. God, that's ugly. Wipe off the mud and lie down."

She got to the bathroom and splashed water on her face before erasing the clumps and streaks from her body.

When she came out, Dart pointed to the bed. "Women. Slaves to their bodies, every one." She was vaguely aware of his giving her another disgusted look. "Seven-hundred-dollar Gucci bag, covered with mud. Here I go, doing your work for you again."

He poured more vodka. "And wouldn't you know it, the ice is all gone." Nora watched the ceiling darken as he carried a candle into the bathroom.

Her body blazed. Water ran. Dart spoke to himself in tones of complaining self-pity. Nora wiped her forehead. She could feel her temperature floating up. Bug, where are you, little bug? A hot flash is hardly complete without a touch of formication. Shall we formicate? Come on, let's try for the brass ring. Dick Dart is repulsed by female biology, let's have the whole menopausal circus. Give me an F, give me an O, give me an R. Formication, of thee I sing. The riot in her body swung the bed gently up and back. A rustle of leathery wings and a buzz of glee came from beyond the fireplace. Begone, fiends, I don't want you now. She wiped her face with a corner of the sheet, and it came away slick with moisture.

Dart poked his head through the bathroom door and announced that if she wasn't ready by the time the Pinto came, she'd be sorry. *I'm plenty sorry right now, thank you very much.*

Having enjoyed itself for some three or four minutes, the hot flash subsided, leaving behind the usual sense of depletion. From the bathroom came swishing sounds accompanied by Dartish grumbles. Nora remembered that he had put the gun in his desk drawer. Surprise, surprise! She wiped her body with her hands and swung her legs off the bed. The sounds of running water and exclamations of woe testified to the absorption of Mr. Dart in his task. Despite her ignorance of revolvers and their operation, surely she could work out how to fire the thing once she got her hands on it. She moved silently toward the middle of the room and observed that the desk drawer appeared to have been pulled open. Another six tiptoe steps brought her to the desk. She lowered her hand into the drawer and touched bare wood. What's the matter, Dick? Don't you trust me?

She moved to the door, put on the slicker, and snapped it shut. In the bathroom, Dart was bent over the tub, his sleeves pushed up past his elbows. A candle stood at the bottom of the tub, and flickering shadows swarmed over the walls. Dye dripping from Dart's hair had stained the top of his shirt collar black. A thick line of grit ran from the middle of the tub to the drain, and limp bills had been hung over the side to dry. The cleaver and the carving knife lay encased in mud beside the bag. Various bottles and brushes and other cosmetic devices had already been washed and placed atop the toilet.

He took in the slicker with contempt. "Grab a towel. One of the little ones."

She gave him a hand towel, and he passed it under the running tap. "Wipe up the mud out there before it dries."

"Aye, aye, sir." Nora took the towel into the room to swab muddy footprints. By the time she returned, Dart was holding the bag out before him.

"This thing might survive after all." He handed her the wet bag. "Get it as dry as you can. Tear the pages out of one those books, wad a towel into the center of the bag, and cram the pages between the towel and the inside of the bag. Don't forget the corners. Do it in here, so I can make sure you do it right."

She brought the paperbacks into the bathroom and placed them on the floor beside the toilet to buff the handbag with the towel.

"Blot up as much water as you can. Ram it into the bottom corners."

Nora pushed the towel around the inside of the bag, and Dart bent over the tub to rinse the towel she had used on the floor under hot water, rub soap into it, and begin washing the cleaver.

"You memorize everything you read, and you never forget it?"

He sighed and leaned against the tub. "I told you. I don't *memorize* anything. Once I read a page, it stays in there all by itself. If I want to see it, I just *look at* it, like a photograph. All those books I had to read for my old ladies, I could recite backwards if I wanted to. Let me feel that."

He swiped his fingers on her towel and ran them across the lining of the bag. "Wad toilet paper down in there. Would you like to hear the complete backwards *Pride and Prejudice*? Austen Jane by? Almost as bad as the forward version."

Nora stuffed toilet paper into the corners of the bag and began ripping pages out of *Night Journey.*

Dart ran the cleaver under hot water and soaped it again. "How do you think I got through law school? Name a case, I could quote the whole damn thing. If that was all you had to do, I'd have made straight A's."

"That's amazing." She plastered the first pages against the sodden silk lining.

"You'll never know how relieved I was when I got assigned someone like Marjorie West. Seventy-two years old, rich as the queen of England, never read a book in her life. Four dead husbands and never happier than when talking about sex. Ideal woman."

Nora had met Marjorie West, whose Mount Avenue house was even grander than the Poplars. She was herself a structure on the grand scale, though much reconstructed, especially about the face. Nora found that she did not wish to think about Marjorie West's relationship with Dick Dart. These days, Marjorie West probably did not want to think too much about it, either. Nora tore another twenty pages out of *Night Journey.* "So you could quote from this book, too."

"You heard me quote from that book." He placed the cleaver on the rug and addressed the carving knife.

"Tell me about that massy vault, the one that's bigger on the inside than on the outside."

"You have the book right in front of you."

"I can't read in this light. What does the vault look like?"

Dart grimaced at the amount of mud still clinging to the knife. "What does it look like on the outside? I'll have to give you the whole sentence so you get the atmosphere. '*With many a fearsome and ferocious glance, many a painful jab about the ribs, many an adjustment of her enormous hat, Madame Lyno-Wyno Ware led Pippin through the corridors of her spider-haunted mansion to a portal bearing the words*

MOST PRIVATE, *thence into a chamber of gloomy aspect and to another such door marked* MOST MOST PRIVATE, *into a far gloomier chamber and a door marked* MOST MOST MOST PRIVATELY PRIVATE, *which creaked open upon the gloomiest of all the chambers, and therein extended her gaudy arm to signify, concealed beneath a tattered sofa, a homely leaden strongbox no more than a foot high.'* That's all, 'homely leaden strongbox no more than a foot high.' From there on, it's about Pippin's disappointment, that little thing can't be the famous massy vault, but the boy bites the bullet and forges ahead, says the right words, and it all turns out all right, kind of."

He rinsed the carving knife, brought it near his eyes for inspection, and rubbed the soapy cloth into the crevices around the hilt.

"The golden key brings him to Madame Lyno-Wyno Ware?"

"Lie? No. Why, nowhere." Dart picked up his glass with a dripping hand and finished the vodka. "The truth is all-important, can't lie to Mrs. Lyno-Wyno Ware, nope." Twitching with impatience, he watched her stuff paper into the bag. "That'll do. Scamper into the kitchen and get me a refill."

When she returned, Dart took a mouthful, set down the glass, and meticulously dried the knives. A hard red flush darkened his cheekbones. "Clean the mess out of the tub. Work fast, I have a lot to do, must prepare for the arrival of sweet Marian."

Nora knelt in front of the bathtub. A few dimes and quarters glinted in the slow-moving brown liquid. The thunder of rainfall on the roof suddenly doubled. The window over the tub bulged inward for a second, and the entire cottage quivered.

Nora came out of the bathroom. Dart was staring at the ceiling. "Thought the whole thing was going to come down. Put the bag on the table and bring me the rope. Hardly need the tape, wouldn't you agree?"

She placed the bag on the table. "Coat." Dart removed his tie and draped it over a shoulder of the suit. Nora unsnapped the red slicker, put it on the hook, and, her heart beating in time to the drumfire on the roof, carried the rope toward him. "Slight possibility I may have overdone the vodka, but all is well." He concentrated on arranging his shirt on a hanger.

Aligned with Dart's usual care, the knives had been placed beneath the pillow on the left side of the bed. "Rope." She came close enough to hand him the coil of clothesline. He yanked off his boxer shorts. "Sit."

Dart drew the carving knife from beneath the pillow, cut off two four-foot lengths of rope, and stumbled around to the side of the bed. "Hands." Eventually he succeeded in lashing her hands and feet. "Little sleep. Party isn't over yet."

Nora worked herself up the bed and watched Dart fussing to align the knife under his pillow. He stretched out on the bed and closed his eyes. Then he rolled his head sideways on the pillow and seemed to consider some troubling point. The rope bit into her ankles and wrists. "What the fuck you care about the massy vault, anyhow?" Wind and rain thrashed against the kitchen windows.

"I like hearing you quote," Nora said.

"Right. Worry not, I'll wake up in time." He was asleep in seconds.

97

CANDLELIGHT FELL TO the floor in a shifting, liquid pool. On the other side of the table, paler light filtered through the bathroom door. All else was formless darkness. Dick Dart began sending up soft, fluffy snores barely audible under the drumming on the roof. Her hands were falling asleep. Drunk and hurried, Dart had made the knots tighter than before, and the rope was cutting off her circulation. She made fists, flexed her fingers, slid her wrists up and down. A dangerous tingling began in her feet. With her eyes on the pool of light wavering across the smooth floor, Nora explored the knot with her fingers.

Dart's failure to include what her dream-father called "the choke" meant that Nora could fight the rope without immobilizing her hands. If she could locate the end of the rope, slide it under the nearest strand, unwind it once around, and pass it beneath the next strand, the entire mechanism would collapse. But every time her fingers traced a strand, it disappeared back into the web. The first time she had escaped this knot, Dart had tied a single hand in front of her; with both hands tied behind her back, she would have to find the end of the rope with her fingers.

The shoulder beneath her ached, and her wrists were already complaining. Her feet continued their painful descent into oblivion. She rolled her eyes upward in concentration and found the darkness obliterated by the yellow afterimage of the candlelight. If she wanted to see anything at all, she would have to look away from the light.

Groaning, she swung up her knees and flipped onto her back. A flaring red circle blotted out the ceiling. Another shift of her body rolled her over to face Dart. His breath caught in his throat before erupting in a thunderous snore. Nora tried to force her wrists apart, and increased the pain. Again she closed her hands into fists, extended and stretched her fingers, slid her wrists from side to side. There was some give, after all. The tingling in her hands began to subside.

How much time did she have? Not even Maid Marian was desperate enough to run through a deluge to sleep with Norman Desmond, but Dart's vanity ignored storms. He expected eager Marian in something like twenty minutes. Even drunk, he was probably capable of waking up in time.

Nora folded her hands, rubbed the tips of her fingers over the web of rope, and felt only interlocking strands. She maneuvered herself back onto her other side and shifted toward the end of the bed. She swung her legs out and lowered her feet to the floor. They registered only a profound, painful tingling. Her fingers probed the knot without success. She had to increase the amount of rope she could reach, and the only way to do that was by sliding the whole structure closer to her hands.

If she could put it between her wrists and pull her hands up, the doorknob might work. She stamped her feet on the floor, and a red track burned all the way from her soles to her knees.

Time's running out, girl.

The first two fingers of her right hand plucked at a thread. The thread moved. Her heart surged, and her breathing accelerated. Something flapped above her head. She urged the thread up from the knot, and mingled terror and hope flared white hot in the center of her body. The thread jittered out of her fingers and slipped away. Another nonexistent being chattered from the kitchen counter. She fumbled for the thread and met only interlocking strands.

Move!

She planted her burning feet on the floor and stood up, biting her tongue against the pain. Her ankles dissolved, and she fell like a tower of blocks, in sections, her hips going one way, her knees another. A hip struck the floor, then a shoulder. Dart belched, coughed, resumed snoring. Nora adjusted to her new pains. A pair of happy red eyes gleamed at her from the bathroom door. *Screw you.* She considered sitting up and noticed that roughly three inches above and behind her, a brace ran from the bottom of the bed to its head. A brace was probably as good as a doorknob.

She curled her knees before her, grunted, and jerked herself up. Flattened under her legs, her feet continued to burn. She inched backwards until her forearms met the brace, twitched herself a few inches farther back, and settled the rope against the edge of the wood. Then she pushed down and groped for the loose thread. Nothing. Gasping, she pushed again. The knot slipped an eighth of an inch, and her fingers met the raised line of the thread. Sweat poured down her forehead. A soft, high-pitched sound seemed to leave her throat by itself. The thread crawled out and came free.

She closed her eyes and worked it around and under. The braided handcuffs went limp. She shook her wrists, and the knot fell away. Her feet slid from beneath her thighs. Panting, she bent over and sent her fingers prowling through the rope around her ankles. A push, a pull, an unthreading, and the rope tumbled to her feet.

She moved away from the bed on hands and knees, then got one foot beneath her. The foot didn't want to be there, but it was not in charge of this operation; it would do what it was told. She levered herself upright, took an experimental step forward, and managed not to fall. The storm, suspended since she had noticed the wooden brace, exploded back into life.

Where had Dart put the gun? She could not remember his putting it anywhere, so it was still in his jacket. She limped toward the closet. Feeling returned to her feet in stabs and surges, but her ankles held. She stretched out her hands, moved forward until she felt the fabric of Dart's suit, ran her fingers down to a pocket, and thrust in her hand to discover the keys. She took them out and reached into the empty pocket on the other side.

Gripping the keys in her left hand, she inched up alongside the bed. Dart had put the knives under his pillow; why not the gun, too? He smacked his lips. She extended a shaking hand, touched the edge of the pillowcase, and found a wooden handle. Beside it was another. Millimeter by millimeter her trembling hand slid them from beneath the pillow. Dart sighed and rolled away. She groped for the revolver and touched metal.

"What?" Dart said, and reached into the space where she should have been. Too frightened to think, Nora snatched up the carving knife and jabbed it into his back. For an instant, his skin resisted, and then the blade broke through and traveled in. He jerked forward, carrying the knife with him. Nora scrabbled beneath the pillow, and her hand closed on a metal cylinder. Dart twisted around and lunged toward her. The revolver in her hand, she pulled away and ran to the other side of the room.

He was staggering past the end of the bed. She yelled, "Stop! I have the gun!" and tried to find the safety Dan Harwich had mentioned, but could hardly see the gun. "I'll shoot you right now!"

"You stabbed me!" he yelled.

Nora ducked behind the second bed and moved her thumb over the plate behind the cylinder. Wasn't that where the damned thing was supposed to be? The pistol Harwich had given her had no cylinder; did that make a difference?

Dart stopped moving when he reached the table. Astoundingly to Nora, he laughed, shook his head, then laughed again. Although she could be only a vague suggestion in the darkness, he found her eyes with his.

"I have to say this hurts."

He twisted his neck to look at the knife sagging from his back. "I thought we were past this kind of bullshit." He looked, sighed, and reached back. "I may require the services of a nurse." He closed his eyes as he pulled out the knife. "Don't think I can overlook this matter. Serious breach of conduct."

"Shut up and sit down," Nora said. "I'm going to tie you up. If you're still alive in the morning, I'll get you to a hospital. With a police escort."

"Sweet. But since you already tried to kill me once, twice if we count Springfield, I tend to think Nora-pie doesn't actually have the big bad gun. If you did, you'd shoot me now." He clamped a hand over his wound, tossed the knife into the darkness, and took a step past the table.

"Stop!" Nora shouted.

"Why don't I hear any noise?" He took another step.

Because she had not found the safety, Nora pulled the trigger in despair and panic, certain that nothing would happen. The explosion jerked her hand three feet off the bed and released a lick of flame and an enormous roar. Her ears closed.

Dart vanished into the darkness. She aimed where she thought he had gone and pulled the trigger again. The gun jumped, carrying her hand with it. She fired again, causing another explosion which yanked her hand toward the ceiling. Nora gripped the wrist of her right hand with her left and trained the revolver back and forth against the rear of the cottage. A vivid mental picture of Dick Dart crawling across the floor sent her backwards until her shoulder struck the wall.

With nowhere else to go, she crawled under the bed. An unimaginable distance away, candles she could not see burned on a table she could not see. She crawled forward and realized that she had left the keys on the floor. When she reached the other side of the bed, she slid out and sat up.

A huge shadow rose up in the middle distance and charged toward her. Nora clenched her teeth, clamped her left hand over her right wrist, and aimed without taking aim. She squeezed, not jerked, the trigger, this also being a lesson Dan Harwich had given her. Dirty-looking fire blew out of the barrel, and the gun jumped in her hands. The charging shadow disappeared. She felt but did not hear a body strike the floor.

Nora crawled back under the bed and waited for the floorboards to vibrate, a hand to snake toward her. Nothing happened. She moved forward, and her hand touched warm liquid. She slithered out and moved to the foot of the bed. A dark shape lay a few feet away.

With the gun straight out in front of her, Nora moved around the body in a wide circle. It did not move. She came closer. A ribbon of blood curled away from Dart's head and trailed glistening across the floor. She jabbed the barrel into his forehead and for what seemed a long time applied pressure to the trigger, released it, pressed it again. The idea of touching him made her stomach cramp.

She tottered to her feet, remembered to get the keys, and pulled on Marian Cullinan's coat, surprised to feel nothing but a dull acceptance. The demons had fled, and only numbness was left. The rest, whatever the rest was to be, would come later.

Her ears ringing, she rammed the revolver into the pocket of the red coat and thrust her feet into Tony's rubber boots. She unlocked the door. When she pushed it open, the storm wrenched it out of her hands and threw it back against the front of the cottage. All of Shorelands, maybe all of western Massachusetts, was like the center of a waterfall. For a moment she thought of staying inside until the storm ended; then she imagined the candles burning down and the two of them, she and Dart, waiting for the night to end.

She slapped Marian's hat on her head and heard a wheezy cough. Her heart froze. A vague shape pushed itself up on its knees, collapsed, hauled itself an inch forward. She fumbled the gun out of the pocket. The shape gathered into itself and surged ahead like a grub. The gun in her hand released another flare of light. The explosion yanked her hand three feet into the air, and something smacked into the kitchen cabinets. The grub stopped moving.

Then she was on the porch and moving toward the waterfall with no memory of having gone through the door. She thrust the gun into her pocket and ran off the porch.

98

HER FEET SLITHERED away, and a fist of wind smacked her into the muck. Cold ooze embraced her legs and flowed into the coat. She scrambled to get up, but the ground slipped away beneath her hands, and for an eternity she crawled through gouting mud. At last grass which was half mud but still half grass met her hands. She struggled upright, and another endless wave of wind-driven rain sent her reeling.

Miraculously, in another few minutes she was no longer blind and deaf. The trunks of massive oaks framed her view. A few feet away the deluge continued to assault the sluggish river which had once been a path. The wind had thrown her into the woods, where the canopy of leaves and branches broke the rainfall. Her breath came in ragged gasps, and her heart banged. Behind her, the trees groaned. She turned toward Main House and took a step. Wasn't Main House off to her right, not her left? She took a step in what seemed the wrong direction as soon as she had taken it. An enormous branch cracked away above her and crashed to the ground ten feet in front of her. Deeper in the woods, another limb broke off and tumbled to earth. When she looked back she saw that she had managed to get only a little way beyond the cottage.

Dim light flickered in the doorway; a second later, the silhouette of a large male body filled the opening. Reflected yellow light glinted off a flat blade. She backed into a tree and yelped. The man jumped off the porch and vanished into the darkness. Nora plunged into the woods in what she hoped was the direction of Main House.

She stumbled over fallen branches and walked into invisible trees. Waist-high boulders jumped up at her; streaming deadfalls towered over her, branches smacked her forehead and thumped her ribs. She moved with her hands in front of her face; now and then, she set a foot on empty air and went skidding downhill until she could grasp a branch. She fell over rocks, over roots. The weapon in her pocket bruised her thigh, and the rocks and branches she struck in her falls bruised everything else. She had no idea how far she had gone, nor in what direction. The worst thing she knew was that Dick Dart, who should have been but was not dead, followed close behind, tracking her by sound.

She knew this because she could hear him, too. A minute or two after she had run from the sight of him leaping off the porch, she had heard him curse when a branch struck him. When she had taken a tumble over a boulder and landed in a thicket, she had heard the harsh bow-wow-wow of his laughter, faintly but distinctly, coming it seemed from all about her. He had not seen her, but out of the thousands of noises surrounding him, he had heard the sounds of her fall and struggle with the thicket and understood what they meant. He could probably hear her boots slogging through the mush. She ran with upraised arms, hearing behind her the phantom sound of Dart picking his way through the woods.

A few minutes later this ghostly sound still came to her through a renewal of the waterfall's booming; Nora pushed her way past nearly invisible obstacles and came to the reason for the noise. On the other side of a veil of trees, a curtain of water crashed down onto a black river. She had come to another path, which made it certain that she had run in the wrong direction: paths led to cottages, and there were no cottages in a direct line from Pepper Pot to Main House. Dart's ghost steps advanced steadily toward her.

Nora came up to the trees bordering the path, bent her head, and moved out into the deluge. Fighting for balance, she trudged forward, the boots sticking, slipping. At length the tide began to solidify underneath her feet, and she peered ahead at another wall of trees. The barrage diminished to heavy rainfall.

Nora looked back and thought she saw a pale form flickering through the woods on the other side of the path. She dodged into a gathering of oaks and began to work down a slight grade. The ground softened, then dropped away, and her feet went into a sliding skid. Instinctively, she crouched forward to keep her center of gravity in place and slipped down past the oak trees, skimming around rocks, tilting from side to side to stay upright. She stayed on her feet until a low branch struck her right ankle and sent her tumbling into a tree trunk. Sparks flared in front of her eyes, and her body slipped into a slow downhill cruise. When she came to rest, Marian's hat was gone, her head was pounding, and the lower half of her right leg seemed to be underwater. Her leg came out of the water when she crawled to her knees.

She was on open ground, and the storm had begun to slacken. At some point during the trip downhill, the wind had lessened. Dizzy and exhausted, she raised her right leg to pour water out of the boot. Her muscles ached and her head throbbed. The sky had grown lighter. More quickly than it had come, the storm was ending.

Before her a five-foot sheet of water moved swiftly from right to left. Rain dimpled and pocked the surface of the water. A river? Nora wondered how far she had come. Then she realized that fattened with rainwater and overflowing its banks, this was the little stream running through the estate. Behind her, some enormous object creaked, sighed, and surrendered to gravity. Dart was gaining on her. She had to hide from him until she could get to Main House.

Why didn't he just bleed to death like normal people?

She strode forward into the quickly moving water, and slick stones met the soles of the boots. The rain dwindled to a pattering of drops. Wind ruffled the surface of the water and flattened the coat against her body. Overhead, a solid mass of great woolen clouds glided along. With a shock, she realized that it was now a little past nine on an August night. Above the storm, the sun had only recently gone down. She climbed over the opposite bank of the stream and waded through the overflow into the fresh woods to conceal herself.

She heard laughter in the pattering rain and the hissing leaves.

Through the massed trunks Nora saw what looked like gray fog. She moved forward, and the fog became an overgrown meadow where grasses bent before the cool wind. On the other side of the meadow, high-pitched voices swooped and skirled, climbing through chromatic intervals, introducing dissonances, ascending into resolution, shattering apart, uniting into harmony again, dividing and joining in an endless song without pauses or repeats.

Singing?

For a second larger without than within, like the massy vault, Nora dropped through time and awakened to unearthly music in a bedroom on Crooked Mile Road in Westerholm, Connecticut, scrambling for a long-vanished pistol. Then she realized where she was. Instead of going south, she had run almost directly west. The meadow in front of her was the Mist Field, and the voices came from Monty Chandler's Song Pillars. Unable to hide, she pulled the gun from her pocket and whirled around to look for Dart. She ranged in front of the woods, jerking the gun back and forth. Dart did not show himself. She moved right, then left, then right again, waiting for him.

Then she understood what he had done. Dick Dart had half-followed, half-chased her across the stream and toward the Mist Field. He wanted her to cower in a hidey-hole and wait for him to move past. In the meantime, he was on his way to Main House.

"Oh, my God," Nora said. She began to run along the edge of the meadow toward a point in the woods where she could wade back across the stream, cut past Honey House, and approach Main House from the west lawn. She stopped to pull off the clumsy boots. Bare-legged, the ground squashing beneath her feet, she started running again.

A pale figure emerged from the woods at the far corner of the Mist Field. Nora froze. The revolver wanted to slip out of her muddy hand. Maybe it was empty, maybe not. If not, maybe it would fire, maybe not. The figure moved toward her. She raised the gun, and the man before her called out her name and became a drenched Jeffrey Deodato.

99

NORA LET HER arm fall. Jeffrey had lost his Eton cap. Covered with muddy streaks and smears, his raincoat clung to him like a wet rag. Other streaks adhered to his face. Because he was Jeffrey, his bearing suggested that he had deliberately camouflaged himself. He got close enough for her to see the expression in his eyes. Clearly she looked a good deal worse than he did.

"You came after all," she said.

"It seemed like a good idea." He looked down at the gun. "Thanks for not shooting. Where's Dart?"

Apparently Jeffrey had learned a good deal since their telephone conversation. "I killed him," she said. "But it didn't work." She lifted the revolver and looked at it. "I don't think there are any bullets left in this thing, anyhow."

Jeffrey delicately took the gun from her. "So you got away from him."

"It started out that way. But I think after a while he was chasing me away. He wanted me out of his hair so he could enjoy himself with the women at Main House. Then he could come back and have all the fun of hunting me down. We can't stand around and talk, Jeffrey, we have to get moving."

He snapped open the cylinder. "You have one bullet left, but it's not in a very safe place, unless you want to shoot yourself in the leg." He moved the cylinder, clicked it back into place, and handed her the revolver, grip first. "Let's get out of here and find a phone."

Frantic with impatience, Nora rammed the revolver back into her pocket. "The phones don't work." She looked around wildly. "We have to get to Main House." Jeffrey was still examining her. The spectacle she presented obviously did not inspire much confidence in her ability to deal with Dick Dart. Nora glanced down at the ruined coat and her streaky legs. She looked like an urchin pulled from a swamp.

"Main House?" Jeffrey asked.

She grabbed the sleeve of his coat and pulled him back toward the woods. "If we don't, he'll murder everybody. Come on, if you're coming. Otherwise I'm going by myself."

She saw him decide to humor her. "We'll make better time if we stick to the edges of the path." She started to say something, but he cut her off. "I'll show you. All I need to know is where Main House is from here."

"*There.*" She pointed into the woods.

Maddeningly, Jeffrey began jogging back in the direction from which he had come. She ran after him. "We're going the wrong way!"

"No, we're not," he said, unruffled.

"Jeffrey, you're lost."

"Not anymore, I'm not."

At the end of the meadow Jeffrey pointed to the strip of wet but solid ground directly in front of the trees. He was right. The path had turned into soup, but they could move along beside it without falling down. The faint light was fading, and Nora remembered what it was like to move through the woods in the dark. "Okay?"

"*Go,*" she said.

So close to the trees that Nora could feel roots under her bare feet, they began to move at a steady trot. "Too fast for you?" Jeffrey asked.

"I can run as well as you," Nora said. "What did you do after we talked?"

Waiting out the storm in the gas station, Jeffrey had grown increasingly uneasy. Nora's explanation of how she had come to Shorelands and her reasons for sending him back to Northampton seemed flimsy, her attitude unnatural. He had managed to coax the MG over the drowned roads to Shorelands and seen the Duesenberg in the parking lot. Just getting into his truck, Tony had ordered him off. *Where is Mrs. Desmond?* Jeffrey had asked. Tony said, *If you're a friend of that asshole Desmond's, you can go to hell.* His roof leaked; he could make it to his sister's house in Lenox; he didn't care what happened to Jeffrey. Jeffrey had pleaded with him to call the police, and Tony said that he couldn't call the police even if he wanted to because the phones were out. *Where is Pepper Pot?* Tony had sworn at him and driven away. Jeffrey set off on foot through the storm. He passed Main House, moved up the path, found Pepper Pot empty, and entered the woods again. He realized that he had no idea where he was going. Then the storm relented, and he found himself at the edge of a field. Far off to his right he saw a muddy scarecrow, and the scarecrow pointed a gun at him.

"I guess Tony doesn't care much for Dick Dart," he said. "Tell me about what's going on in Main House."

Before them, the bridge in front of Honey House arched up out of a flat, moving sheet of water. Nora walked out from under the dripping trees and waded into the flooded stream while Jeffrey kept pace beside her, the bottom of his coat floating behind him.

"I wish I knew. There are four women in there. Marian Cullinan, who works for the trust, Margaret Nolan, who runs the place, and two guides who used to work here in the old days." On the opposite side of the streambed, they began trotting beneath the oaks again. "He wants to kill them, I know that much. A normal psychopath would sneak into their bedrooms and take them one by one, but Dart wants to have a party. He's been chortling all afternoon."

"A party?"

At the end of the avenue between the rows of oaks, Nora could make out the edge of the pond. "He loves to talk, and he loves an audience. He'll want to get them all together and give himself some entertainment. He'd love the idea of making them watch while he kills them one by one."

"I hate to say this, but wouldn't he want to get it over with as soon as possible so he can get away?"

"Dart feels *protected.* He assumes he'll be able to walk away, no matter how long he takes."

Jeffrey considered this while they moved toward the pond and open ground. "How much time has he had already?"

"My sense of time went south with my sense of direction." She tried to work out how long she had flown through the woods. "He really was chasing me at the start. He was in a rage. I stabbed him, and then I shot him."

"You shot him? Where?"

"He was lying on his front, so all I could see was blood coming out of his head. He sure looked dead to me, but I couldn't see the wound. I would have checked his life signs, but I couldn't stand the idea of touching him. I guess I just grazed him, damn it. Anyway, I ran out, and about a minute later, he somehow got up and came after me. Hold on, Jeffrey, I want to do something."

She trotted up to the lip of the pond, plunged her muddy hands into the water, and scrubbed them clean before running back to him. "I don't want that blasted gun to slip out of my hands."

He began gliding up the sodden lawn. "Could he have had half an hour?"

Nora stopped moving. She stared at her wet hands, realizing that Dart had given them more time than they thought.

"Not that long. He probably spent at least ten minutes coming after me before he changed his mind. He made sure I knew he was close behind me, and then he started toward the house. That might have been twenty minutes ago. It would take him ten or fifteen minutes to get to the house, but he wouldn't start right away."

Jeffrey scratched his forehead, leaving a muddy smear which increased the camouflage effect. "Why not?"

She held up the hands she had washed in the pond. "This guy is one of the most fastidious men on earth. The first thing he'd do when he got inside would be to clean himself up. There's a bathroom in a little office corridor downstairs. He may even have taken a *shower.* Everybody was upstairs, and he had plenty of time to clean himself up for his party."

"This isn't a joke?"

"Jeffrey, this is a guy who goes crazy if he has to go a day without brushing his teeth. If he isn't presentable, he won't have half the fun he wants."

Jeffrey clearly decided to believe her. "I hope he doesn't have another gun."

"No. But the last time I saw him, he was holding a cleaver, and the kitchen is full of knives."

They looked up over the lawn to Main House. Real night had arrived, and the curving stone steps rose indistinctly to the terrace. Beyond the terrace, the big windows of the lounge blazed with light. As Marian had predicted, the power had been restored with astonishing speed.

Nora looked upward. All the second-floor windows were dark, but at the top left-hand corner of the house, the windows of Lily's and Marian's rooms showed light. "Dart likes knives," she said.

Jeffrey pointed at the windows of the lounge. "Is that where you think he'd take these women?"

"He's in a mood to strut his stuff. He wants to use the best room in the house, and that's it."

"If that's true, we'll be able to see what's going on." Jeffrey unbuttoned his raincoat, yanked his arms out of the sleeves, and dropped the coat onto the grass. He broke into a businesslike jog across the lawn. When they had gone half the distance, they began moving in a quiet crouch.

Together they glided up to the terrace stairs and squatted in front of the bottom step. They glanced at each other, came to a wordless agreement, and went up side by side, bent low to stay out of sight. Four steps from the top, they peered across the terrace floor to the bottom of the lounge window. Nora saw only the white fringe of a carpet, the wooden floor, and the polished cylindrical legs of a table. She put her head closer to Jeffrey's and saw only a little more of the carpet.

Jeffrey crept up another two steps and leaned out onto the terrace. He looked back at Nora and shook his head, telling her to wait for him, then flattened out and began crawling slantwise across the terrace. Nora came up behind him and watched the soles of his shoes work across the wet tiles. When they were about six feet away, she lowered the top of her body to the floor and crawled after him, grating her knees and toes on the stone. The coat's metal clasps made a high-pitched sound of complaint against the terrace floor, and she scrabbled ahead on forearms and knees. Jeffrey slithered on before her with surprising speed and reached the window at the far end. Rain dripped steadily from the gutters.

For the first time Nora became conscious of the deep silence encasing the sound of raindrops pattering against the ground, the delicious freshness of every odor carried by the air. Even the rough tiles beneath her face sent up a vibrant smell, sharp and alive.

Jeffrey lengthened himself beneath the window, and she flattened out with her face next to his head, raised her neck, and looked into the lounge.

In a blue nightgown, Lily Melville sat lashed into a chair near the middle of the room. Another length of rope stretched from her ankles to her wrists, which had been pulled behind the back of the chair. Her head was bent nearly to her chest, and her shoulders were trembling. Facing the window, Margaret Nolan, still in the dress she had worn to dinner and similarly bound, was speaking to her, but Lily did not seem to hear what she was saying.

Margaret glanced over her shoulder, and Nora slid away from Jeffrey to be able to see the opening into the front hallway. Just appearing in the entrance was a hysterical Marian Cullinan, propelled from behind by Dick Dart. She looked as if she were trying to do pull-ups on the arm clamped around her neck. Dart held a long knife against her side with his other hand, and his face was alight with joy.

100

MARIAN HAD PUT on a low-cut, black, sleeveless dress for her poetic encounter. Dart was naked and completely clean. Only slightly mussed, his freshly washed hair fell over a bloody strip of gauze taped to the side of his head. He dropped Marian into a chair facing Lily Melville, shifted to her side, and bent down. She bolted forward. Without even bothering to look at her, Dart thrust out his left hand, closed it around her throat, and pulled her to the floor. Marian's scream penetrated the window. Nora felt her body clench.

Dart put down the knife and reached for something out of sight. Marian shot forward and flailed at him, and Dart pulled her off the floor by the neck, as if she were a kitten.

"What are we going to do?" Nora whispered to Jeffrey.

"I'm thinking about it," he whispered back.

Shaking his head, Dart raised Marian until her feet were off the floor. Then he dropped her, caught her around the waist, and pinioned her arms. While she thrashed against him, he brought a hand holding a rope back into view. He carried Marian back to the chair and slammed her down.

She screeched again.

Margaret turned her head toward Dart and said something surprisingly measured. Ignoring her, he knelt behind Marian, passed the rope twice around her, and released his hold. She jumped up and tried to sprint away with the chair on her back. He pulled her back and passed the rope over her shoulder, down, under the seat of the chair, then duck-walked to the front of the chair. She kicked at him, and he snatched her ankles, looped the rope around them, and worked it back beneath the chair. He sliced through the rope and knotted it behind her back. Margaret spoke to him again. Whatever he said caused her face to quiver.

"Strong son of a bitch," Jeffrey whispered.

Marian bucked in her chair, bucked again, then sagged back.

Dart jerked her chair into place and moved frowning past the three women, rubbing his chin. On either side of Margaret and a few feet in front of her, Marian and Lily sat facing each other. Dart came to a halt in front of them and stepped backwards toward the terrace. Considering the women, he gently fingered the gauze pad he had succeeded in taping over the wound in his back. His body winced, and a blotch of red at the center of the pad darkened and grew.

Jeffrey tilted his head toward Nora. "Isn't there another woman?"

She pointed upward. "Sick in bed."

Dart wandered around the women, measuring the effect he had created. They watched him, Marian sullenly and Margaret in thoughtful concentration like Dart's own. Even the back of Lily's head expressed stunned terror. Marian flipped her hair and moved her lips in a sentence Nora could read: *You hurt me.* Dart went behind Lily, shifted her a little way toward the window, and patted her head. Margaret clamped her mouth shut as Dart tugged her chair a few inches backwards. Marian spoke again: *Norman, why are you doing this?*

Margaret uttered a brief sentence. Marian's body went rigid, and all emotion left her face.

Dart, whose real name had just been uttered, held out his arms and twisted from side to side, acknowledging imaginary applause.

"What are we waiting for?" Nora whispered.

"For him to tell us what to do."

Dart swayed up to Marian and kissed her cheek. Talking, he went behind her chair and shook her hand. He stroked her arms, her hair, drew a finger along the line of her chin. Margaret watched this procedure without any demonstration of emotion. Marian closed her eyes and trembled. The freckles blazed on her face. Still talking, Dart went around the chair and kissed her. She jerked her head back, and Dart slapped her hard enough for the sound to carry through the window, then kissed her again. When he pulled away, the red mark on Marian's cheek obliterated her freckles.

Raising his hands as if to say, *I'm a reasonable guy,* Dart backed away from Marian and addressed all three women. He smiled and pointed at Marian. He put a question to the two older women. Margaret gave him an impassive stare, and Lily shook her head. Dart put his hand on his heart, he looked hurt. He bounced up to Lily and lifted her chin. Nora saw his mouth utter the words *Lily, my darling, I love you.* Then he sauntered over to Margaret and spoke to her. Margaret clearly said, *No.* He staggered back in mock disbelief. He was having the time of his life. For a time he wandered back and forth, engaged in some hypothetically puzzled debate. He waggled his head sadly. He walked over to the knife on the floor, pretended to be surprised to see it, and in glad astonishment picked it up.

Nora looked at Jeffrey. Jeffrey shook his head.

Dart strolled toward them across the carpet. First his head, then all of his body above his knees, disappeared behind the table. Jeffrey touched her hand: *Don't move.* She jerked her head toward her side: *The gun?* Jeffrey barely moved his head, telling her, *Not now.* Dart's legs spun around, and his feet padded away. When the rest of his body came into view, he was no longer holding the knife. He snapped his fingers and disappeared. Margaret's eyes moved, and Marian twisted her neck to watch him go. The women's faces registered Dart's reappearance, and when he sauntered into view he held the cleaver. He displayed it to the women, chopped the air, and padded toward the table.

Jeffrey somehow managed to flatten himself nearly to the lip of the sill below the French doors. Nora folded her arms over her head and held her breath. When she risked peeking at the window, Dart's hairy legs still bulged out below the table. He was aligning his tools. One of his feet slid sideways as he turned to look back at the women in the chairs. One of them must have asked him a question. "The little woman?" he said, close enough to the window to be heard through it. "When last seen, my former companion was charging in full flight through the forest primeval. At the moment, she cowers in a thicket waiting for me to give up the hunt." He came up to the window. "*Nor-ma! Nor-ma!* Come home, honey, the fun's just beginning! Can you hear me, sweetie?" He turned to the women and lowered his voice. "Maybe she's hiding right outside! Let's see!"

Nora's heart stopped, and her body went cold. She sensed Jeffrey gathering himself to leap.

If Dart came through this window, his foot would land about three inches from Nora's elbow. She lifted her chin, peered in, and her heart started back into life with a massive thump. He was moving away from the table toward the other windows. In seconds, he passed out of view. Down the terrace a handle rattled, and the French door opened. It was all part of the performance, a show for the ladies. In high good humor, Dart was demonstrating their helplessness. He leaned out and bellowed her name. "*Norma! Norma! Mrs. Desmond!*"

He must have looked back into the room. "Hear anything, Marian?"

Softly, Marian said, "No."

He was still leaning out through the French door. "You know who she is, don't you?"

"The woman you kidnapped," Marian said.

Margaret Nolan said, "Nora Chancel."

Dart sighed lightly, mockingly, as if lamenting Nora's treachery.

"You made a serious mistake, Mr. Dart," Margaret said. "You let her go. Please understand what I'm telling you. Mrs. Chancel isn't cowering in the woods. She's on her way to find help. You should get away now. You can go back to Pepper Pot, put on your clothes, and take a car. If you waste a lot of time with us, you will certainly be captured by the police. You see that, don't you?"

"Captured?" Dart said. "Wonderful word. Suggestion of the jungle beast."

"We aren't asking to be untied. But if you want to keep your freedom, you have to leave Shorelands now. Mrs. Chancel is probably already talking to Tony."

After a long moment of silence, an owl hooted from the other side of the pond. Drops pattered down onto the tiles. Dart snickered. She glanced sideways. He was smiling up at the sky.

"What a worry. If Nora-pie does talk to your charity case, he'll come up here to check out her story. I can take care of Tony. But do you know what's really going to happen? In a little while, Nora is going to sneak into this house. Written in stone. The girl knows my little ways. Won't be able to help herself. Never abandon you, not possible."

"That's stupid," Marian said. "Save yourself. Leave now. You don't even have time for clothes."

"Like me naked, don't you, Marian? I like me naked, too. Love standing here, the fresh air drifting around my body. Arouses me. I do especially enjoy being aroused, as you will discover. Do you have freckles on the soles of your feet, Marian?"

For several seconds, she said nothing. Dart waited her out.

"No."

"What a pity. Shall we see if Nora's already here? Promised her a treat, and I dearly wish to keep my promise." Dart shouted her name, cupped a hand to his ear, shouted it again. "No answer, girls. Must carry on by ourselves. Never fear, Nora's arrival won't spoil our fun." He pulled himself back in, and the French door grated shut.

Jeffrey jerked his head toward the front of the terrace and was instantly slithering over the tiles, making no sound at all. With a superhuman effort, Nora pushed herself up onto her hands and knees and followed him.

Jeffrey slipped around the edge of the pillar at the top of the steps and waited. When she reached him, he led her down the stairs to the grass, moved sideways to the wall beneath the terrace, leaned his head back against the stone, and stared out at the dark lawn.

"Is he always like that?"

"Pretty much," Nora said. "What are we going to do?"

"We have plenty of time. He's still winding himself up." He smiled. "You know, as long as you didn't care too much about who he killed, Dick Dart could have been a terrific combat soldier. He's incredibly strong and quick, he can absorb a tremendous amount of pain and keep going, he thinks ahead, and adverse situations bring out the best in him. So to speak."

"You're asking me to admire Dick Dart?"

"Not at all," Jeffrey said. "I'm describing him. If I don't take him into account, I don't have a prayer of defeating him. I don't suppose he was always like what we saw just now?"

"Being brought in for murder liberated him. He didn't have to hide what he was like anymore."

Jeffrey smiled again. "*Escaping* liberated him. After that, all the normal rules were suspended. He's a brand-new person in a brand-new world, stretching his wings, discovering himself."

This was so accurate that Nora set aside her impatience.

"He's not going to get around to doing any damage to those women for at least half an hour. He's having too much fun. In the meantime, he'll be waiting for you to show up. Is the front door locked or unlocked, do you know?"

"Unlocked," Nora said.

"Okay." Jeffrey looked up at nothing and wiped his face. "Does he know that *you* know it's unlocked?"

"Yes."

"That's where he expects you to come in." He walked out onto the lawn and looked up at the house. "Let's cook up a little surprise for Mr. Dart." He ran his eyes along the rear of the building. "The French doors weren't locked, either. Farther down from where we were, there was another set at the back of the room he went into to get the cleaver."

"The dining room."

"I bet every window in the building is unlocked. They rely on their isolation and Tony to keep them safe. They've probably never had a break-in. You say there's another woman in the house, some kind of invalid?"

"Agnes Brotherhood."

"What floor is she on?"

"The second."

"All right. When I was trying to find you, I saw a ladder next to the wall in the court. Some workmen must have left it behind. I'll go in through an upstairs window. Once I'm up there, I'll make some kind of noise, and Dart will think Agnes is about to join the party. He'll be delighted. You go back up there and stand at this end of the lounge. When you see him leave the room, go into the dining room and *stay* there."

"All right."

"We have to play this by ear, but hide in the dining room until you know you can take Dart by surprise. He won't expect you to come in that way. He won't be expecting me, either. If I can take care of him, I will. If I can't, he's going to bring me into the lounge, and that's when you come out."

"You should take the gun," she said.

"No, you keep it." Jeffrey raised one leg, untied his shoe, wiggled it off, and set it beside the wall. He did the same with the other shoe. "You have one bullet left. Don't waste it." He tapped the center of her forehead with his index finger. "Put it right here. This guy is made of iron."

"I know," Nora said, but Jeffrey was already slipping away through the dark.

101

MARIAN'S COAT FELT like a ridiculous encumbrance. Nora took the revolver from the pocket, ripped open the snaps, hitched her shoulders, and lowered her arms. The coat slid off and landed heavily on the grass. Except for the parts of her legs washed by the stream, the entire front of her body was dark with mud. She settled the revolver in her hand and moved up the stairs to the terrace. Quietly, she slipped across the tiles and flattened herself against the building beside the second set of French doors. She tilted her head and looked in to see three-fourths of the bright lounge. Marian Cullinan's back obscured half of Lily Melville. Margaret

Nolan, fully visible, faced the all too visible Dick Dart. He was holding a champagne bottle in one hand, his half-erect penis in the other, and talking to Margaret, no doubt on the subject of the many delights he had given elderly women. She looked at him unblinkingly.

For the first time Nora began to doubt her assumptions about why Agnes was not with the others. Dart would not have left her in her room simply because she was too weak to get out of bed. Maybe he had tied her up and stashed her in a part of the room they could not see, saving her as a spider leaves extra meals in its web. If he had brought Agnes downstairs, he would know something was wrong the instant he heard a noise inside the house, and Jeffrey would be in even greater danger.

Dart swigged champagne and offered the bottle to Lily. When she did not respond, he moved in front of her. Nora thought he was putting the bottle to her lips. He made a sideways comment to Margaret. Of course. She was the one he hated most; he was performing for her benefit. He carried the bottle to Marian, tilted it like a waiter to display the label, and put the bottle to her mouth. Whatever Marian did or said evoked an expression of unhappy disbelief. Dart backed away, pouting, and walked across the room to pick the knife off the table. He explained what he would be forced to do if she did not join him in a drink and tried again. She must have allowed him to pour some of the liquid into her mouth, because he gave her a happy smile. He went to Margaret, who grimly opened up and let him tip in champagne.

Dart gulped from the bottle and turned to Marian. He tilted his hips, offering the cucumber. No? He put the bottle on the floor and said something which involved pointing to both the knife and the cucumber. Still talking, he tugged at himself, and the obedient cucumber plumped forward. Pleased, he displayed it to the other two women. Lily's eyes were closed, and Margaret barely glanced at his prize. Returning to Marian, Dart again indicated the knife and the cucumber. The back of Marian's head gave no clue to her response. Dart moved up beside her and rubbed the cucumber across her cheek. He glanced at Margaret, whose face settled into bleak immobility. Lily dared to take a peek at him and instantly squeezed her eyes shut again.

What was Jeffrey doing, admiring Georgina Weatherall's bedroom?

Dart backed away, raised the knife, and fingered the loops of rope binding Marian to her chair. After selecting one, he slipped the knife underneath it, severed the rope, and knotted it in a new place. Marian's right arm was freed to the elbow. It was an exchange of favors. Be nice to me, I'll be nice to you.

Stroking himself, Dart moved in front of Margaret. He waved himself at her and went through the same grinning pantomime he had with Marian. For Margaret's benefit, he manipulated himself into another inch of bloat. Pulling and stroking, a dreamy expression gathering in his eyes, he extended himself in front of her face, demanding admiration. He stroked her hair with his free hand. Then his head snapped sideways.

The muscles in Nora's arms and legs went tense. Dart said something to Marian. Marian shook her head. He whirled away from Margaret, bounded to the side of the entrance, and pressed his back to the wall. Marian turned her head, and Margaret quizzed her with a look. They had all heard something, and no one in the room thought it was the sound of Agnes Brotherhood wandering down to the main floor. Nora stared at the empty opening. Dart put a finger to his lips. A few seconds ticked by. The women strained in their chairs.

Dart licked his lips and stared at the entrance, ready to leap.

Nora's body decided for her. Before she had time to think, she moved across the window and pushed down the handle. Dart jerked his head sideways and stared at her in shock, surprise, and rage. He took a step forward, baring his teeth. Nora yanked open the French door, put a foot inside the lounge, and turned to stone as Jeffrey flew into the room. He somersaulted over, bounced to his feet behind Marian, and instantly began circling toward Dart, his body bent forward and his arms slightly extended.

Dart shifted his eyes to Nora, then back to Jeffrey. "Who are you supposed to be, Action Man?" He sidled away from the wall. "Ladies, say hello to Jeffrey, the manservant. You'd be dead already, Jeffrey, if the mudpie hadn't distracted me."

"*Norma!*" Marian shrieked. "Shoot him, shoot him!"

"Shut up," Nora said. She moved alongside Lily, who was gazing at her in pure terror.

"*Shoot him, Norma!*" Marian yelled.

"Baby, she's a lousy shot, and the gun's already empty," Dart said. Already wholly adjusted to this turn of events, he was once again in confident good humor. All he had to deal with was an unarmed man and Nora-pie, who was a lousy shot, especially when the gun was empty. He loved his odds. Jeffrey was still circling toward him. "Come on, manservant," Dart said.

Jeffrey had not glanced at Nora since he had rocketed into the room. So focused on Dart that he seemed not to have heard Marian's outbursts, he advanced with one slow, deliberate crab-step after another. Dart rolled his eyes in amusement. Jeffrey was not a serious threat. He threw out his arms and shrugged at Nora. "Should tell you the bitter truth, sweetie. I lied to you. The tits aren't pretty. Too small and too flat." He glanced at Jeffrey, and his smile widened.

Nora said, "Do you ever wear women's clothes, Dick?"

He lost his smile, then began to move toward Jeffrey with the air of one having to conduct a necessary but tedious bit of business.

Lily looked up fearfully at Nora. "Is that you, Mrs. Desmond?"

"It's me, Lily." Nora touched her shoulder. The men drew closer. Nora was aiming the revolver at Dart, but she had no confidence in her ability to hit him. She said, "I can see your closet, Dick. There are two dresses inside it, and nobody's ever seen them but you."

Dart growled and sprang, and Jeffrey seemed to flow backwards. Dart sailed four feet through the air and thudded down onto his stomach. In a second he pulled himself upright and went into a crouch. "So we know you're fast," he said, and bunched himself to charge.

Jeffrey jumped right, then left, so quickly he seemed not to have done it at all. He moved directly behind Margaret, who, unlike Lily and Marian, was looking at Nora. Her eyes moved to something near the windows, then back to Nora. Nora looked behind her and understood. She ran to the table and picked up the cleaver. "Are you crazy?" Marian yelled. "You have a gun!"

Dart twitched right, Jeffrey twitched left, a mirror image.

Marian screamed at her to shoot.

Dart ripped his knife through the empty air where Jeffrey had been, then pivoted and charged forward. Instead of floating back, Jeffrey ducked sideways, gripped Dart's arm, rolled his body over his hip, and spun him wheeling to the carpet a few feet past Marian. Nora remembered that Jeffrey had once been, among a dozen other unlikely things, a karate instructor.

Wincing, Dart picked himself up nearly as quickly as he had the first time. "Cool," he said. "Faggy martial arts. Way you fight when you can't really fight." He jumped forward, jabbing, and Jeffrey faded back. Six feet from Dart, Jeffrey glanced at her over Marian's head and spoke with his eyes. Nora switched the cleaver into her right hand and chopped at the ropes running across the back of Margaret's chair.

"Now me!" Marian yelled.

Margaret pulled herself forward. The ropes fell away from her chest, but her hands were still tethered. "*Me!*" Marian screamed. Nora put down the gun and knelt to saw the cleaver between Margaret's wrists. Lily cried out, and a body hit the floor. Dart was getting up on his knees, holding a bloody knife. Jeffrey dodged toward the hallway. An oozing, foot-long slash ran up the side of his chest, and his face looked as though he were listening to music. He filtered through the air, caught Dart's arm, and slammed him back down on the carpet. Instead of waiting for Dart to twitch himself upright and charge again, Jeffrey followed him over in one smooth, continuous movement. With the electric immediacy of a bolt of lightning, Dart twisted to one side and thrust the knife into Jeffrey's ribs.

During an endless few seconds in which Nora tried to convince herself that she was mistaken, that she had seen something else entirely, the two men hung locked into position. A red stain blossomed on Jeffrey's wet shirt, and then he sagged down onto Dart's body. Nora wavered to her feet.

Marian shrilled to be set free.

Dart released a sigh of triumph and pushed Jeffrey off his chest. Jeffrey pressed a hand over his wound and lay still.

Sitting up, Dart was sliding backwards to disentangle his legs from Jeffrey's. Nora took a step toward him. Jeffrey looked up at Dart and grunted, the first sound he had made since he had come hurtling into the room. The stillness of intense concentration had not left his face. Marian sent up insistent waves of sound. Frantic, Nora cocked the cleaver over her shoulder and walked toward the men.

Dart pulled himself easily to his feet and spun to face her. "Really, Nora."

Playful, taunting, the knife punched out at her. It was impossible, she could not do it, he was too fast for her. The knife jumped forward in another parody of a thrust, and Dart came smiling forward. Nora backed away, holding up the cleaver, knowing she could not hit him before he stabbed her. Superior, silvery amusement ran through him. "I expected a little more of you," he said, and then his eyes enlarged and his body dropped away in front of her with amazing, surreal speed.

She looked down. His arms around Dart's ankles, Dart's heels pressed against his chest, Jeffrey pulled him back another inch.

In the second of grace Jeffrey had given her, Nora sprinted forward, raised the cleaver high over her shoulder, and slammed it down into one of the tufts of hair on Dart's back. The fat blade sank two or three inches into his skin, and blood welled up around it. She tugged at the handle, intent on smashing the cleaver into his head. Dart shook himself like a horse and twitched the handle away from her grasp. "Hey, I thought we were friends," he wheezed. He kicked himself free from Jeffrey's grip and dragged himself forward. He wheezed again, got his elbows under him, and pulled himself toward her. She stepped back. He looked up at her, eyes alight with ironic pleasure. "I don't understand this constant rejection."

Nora's heel came down on the barrel of the revolver.

Marian's screams floated to the ceiling. Nora wrapped her hands around the grip of the revolver and took two steps forward, her mind a white emptiness. She squatted on the soles of her feet and pressed the barrel against Dart's forehead.

"Cute," Dart said. "Pull the trigger, show our studio audience the show must go on."

Nora pulled the trigger. The hammer came down with a flat, metallic click. Dart gave out a breathy chuckle and clamped a hand around her wrist. "On we go." He pulled down her hand, and she squeezed her index finger again. The revolver rode upward on the force of the explosion, and the last bullet burned a hole through Dart's laughing eye, sped into his brain, and tore off the back of his skull. A red-gray mist flew up and out and spattered the wall far behind him. *A bullet in the brain is better than a bullet in the belly.* Even Dan Harwich was right sometimes. Dart's fingers trembled on her wrist. Faintly, as from a distant room, Nora heard Marian Cullinan screaming.

102

HALF AN HOUR later the larger world invaded Nora's life, at first in the form of the many policemen who supplied her with coffee, bombarded her with questions, and wrote down everything she said, thereafter as represented by the far more numerous and invasive press and television reporters who for a brief but intensely uncomfortable period pursued her wherever she went, publishing their various inventions as fact, broadcasting simplifications, distortions, and straightforward untruths, a process which led, as always, to more of the same. If she had agreed, Nora could have appeared on a dozen television programs of the talk-show or tabloid kind, sold the rights to her story to a television production company, and seen her photograph on the covers of the many magazines devoted to trivializing what is already trivial. She did none of these things, considering them no more seriously than she considered accepting any of the sixteen marriage proposals which came to her in the mail. When the public world embraced her, its exaggerations and reductions of her tale made her so unrecognizable to herself that even the photographs in the newspapers seemed to be of someone else. Jeffrey Deodato, who endured a lesser version of Nora's temporary celebrity, also declined to assist in the public falsification of his life.

Once Nora had satisfied her laborious obligations to the law enforcement officers of several cities, what she wanted was enough space and time to reorder her life. She also wanted to do three specific things, and these she did, each one.

But this long, instructive process did not begin until forty minutes after she put Dick Dart to death, when the world rushed in and snatched her up. In the interim, Nora freed the other two women and let Margaret Nolan comfort Lily Melville while she held Jeffrey's hand and tried to assess his injury. Clearly in pain but bleeding less severely than she had feared, Jeffrey said, "I'll live, unless I die of embarrassment." Marian Cullinan retreated to her room, but sensible Margaret volunteered to drive Jeffrey to the hospital and used the imposing force of her personality to dissuade Nora from coming along. She would try to call the Lenox police from the hospital; if the telephones did not work, she would go to the police station after leaving the hospital. She ran to the lot and returned with her car. Staggering, supported by Margaret and Nora, Jeffrey was capable of getting to the door and down the walk. While easing him into the car, Nora remembered to ask Margaret what had happened to Agnes Brotherhood.

"Oh, my Lord," Margaret said. "Agnes is locked in her room. She must be frantic." She told Nora where in her office to find the key and suggested that she might want to clean herself up and put on some clothes before the police came.

Nora had forgotten that she'd been naked ever since she had taken off Marian's coat beneath the terrace.

Margaret raced off toward Lenox, and Nora walked back toward Main House and Agnes, who had escaped the attentions of Dick Dart because he had been unable to get into her room.

She walked past the lounge without looking at Dart's body. The keys, each with a label, were in the top left-hand drawer of the desk, just as Margaret had said. Nora pulled on Margaret's big blue raincoat and went down the hall to Agnes's room.

The thin figure in the bed was sleeping, Nora thought, but as she took two steps into the room, Agnes said, "Marian, why did you take so long? I don't like being locked in, and I don't like you, either."

"It's not Marian," Nora said. "I'm the woman who saw you this afternoon. Do you remember? We talked about Katherine Mannheim."

A rustle of excited movement came from the bedclothes, and Nora could make out a dim figure pushing itself upright. "They let you come back! Or did you sneak in? Was that you who tried to get in before?"

Agnes had no idea of what had gone on downstairs. "No, that was someone else."

"Well, you're here now, and I know you're right. I want you to know. I want to tell you."

"Tell me," Nora said. She bumped into a chair and sat down.

"He raped her," Agnes said. "That terrible, ugly man raped her, and she died of a heart attack."

"Lincoln Chancel raped Katherine Mannheim." Nora did not say that she already understood at least that much.

"You don't believe me," Agnes said.

"I believe you absolutely." Nora closed her eyes and sagged against the back of the chair.

"He raped her and she died. He went to get the other one, the other horrible man. That was what I saw."

"Yes," Nora said. Her voice seemed to come from a great distance. "And then you told the mistress, and she went to Gingerbread and saw them with her body. But you didn't know what she did after that for a long time."

"I couldn't have stayed here if I knew. She only told me when she was sick and taking that medicine that didn't do anything but make her sicker."

"Did you ask her about it? You finally wanted to know the truth, didn't you?"

Agnes started to cry with muffled sniffs. "I did, I wanted to know. She *liked* telling me. She *still* hated Miss Mannheim."

"The mistress got money from Mr. Chancel. A lot of money."

"He gave her whatever she wanted. He had to. She could have sent them both to jail. She had proof."

Nora let her head roll back on her shoulders and breathed out the question she had to ask. "What kind of proof did she have, Agnes?"

"The note, the letter, whatever you call it. The one she made Mr. Driver write."

"Tell me about that."

"It was in Gingerbread. The mistress made Mr. Driver write down everything they did and what they were going to do. Mr. Chancel didn't want him to do it, but the mistress said that if he didn't, she would go back to the house and get the police on them. She knew he wouldn't kill her, even though he probably wanted to, because she put herself in with them. Mr. Chancel still wouldn't do it, but Mr. Driver did. One was as good as two, she said. She told them where to bury that poor girl, and she put that in the note herself, in her own writing. That was how she put herself in with them."

She managed to say what she knew. "And she put the note in her safe, the one under her bed, didn't she?"

"It's still there," Agnes said. "I used to want to look at it sometimes, but if I did I'd know where they buried her, and I didn't want to know that."

"You can open her safe?"

"I opened it a thousand times when I was taking care of her. She kept her jewelry in there. I got things out for her when she wanted to wear them. Do you want to see it?"

"Yes, I do," Nora said, opening her eyes and straightening up. "Can you walk that far, Agnes?"

"I can walk from here to the moon if you give me enough time." Agnes reached out and closed her hand around Nora's wrist. "Why is your skin so rough?"

"I'm pretty muddy," Nora said.

"Ought to clean yourself up, young thing like you."

Agnes levered herself out of the bed and shuffled toward the door, gripping Nora's wrist. When they moved into the light, she took in Nora's condition with shocked disapproval. "What happened to you? You look like a savage."

"I fell down," Nora said.

"Why are you wearing Margaret's raincoat?"

"It's a long story."

"Never saw the like," Agnes said, and shuffled out into the hallway.

In Georgina Weatherall's bedroom, the old woman switched on the lights and asked Nora to put a chair in front of the bed. She twirled the dial. "I'll remember this combination after I forget my own name." She opened the safe door, reached in, extracted a long, once creamy envelope yellow with age, and held it out to Nora. "Take that with you. Get it out of this house. I have to go to the bathroom now. Will you please help me?"

Nora waited outside the bathroom until Agnes had finished, then conducted her back to her room. As she helped her get back into bed, she told her that there had been some trouble downstairs. The police were going to come, but everything was all right. Marian and Lily and Margaret were all fine, and the police would want to talk to her, but all she had to do was tell them that she had been locked in her room, and they would go away. "I'd rather you didn't say anything about the letter you gave me," she said, "but of course that's up to you."

"I don't want to talk about that note," Agnes said. "Especially not to any policeman. You better wash yourself off and get into some real clothes, unless you want a lot of men staring at you. Not to mention tracking mud all over the house."

Nora showered as quickly as she could, dried herself off, and trotted, envelope in hand, to Margaret's room. A few minutes later, wearing a loose black garment which concealed a long envelope in one of its side pockets, she went downstairs. Seated at the dining room table, Marian jumped up when Nora came in. She had changed clothes and put on fresh lipstick. "I know I have to thank you," Marian said. "You and that man saved my life. What happened to everybody? What happened to *him*? Are the police on the way?"

"Leave me alone," Nora said. She went to a chair at the far end of the table and sat down, not looking at Marian. A current of emotion too complicated to be identified as relief, shock, anger, grief, or sorrow surged through her, and she began to cry.

"You shouldn't be crying," Marian said, "you were great."

"Marian," Nora said, "you don't know anything at all."

From the front of the building came the sounds of sirens and police cars swinging into the gravel court, bringing with them the loud attentions of the world outside.

ONE DAY AT THE END OF AUGUST

One day at the end of August, a formerly lost woman who asked the people she knew to call her Nora Curlew instead of Nora Chancel drove unannounced through the gates on Mount Avenue and continued up the curving drive to the front of the Poplars. After having been ordered out of the house by his father, Davey had been implored to come back, as Nora had known he would, and was living again in Jeffrey Deodato's former apartment above the garage. Alone in the house on Crooked Mile Road, Nora had spent the past week dealing with endless telephone calls and the frequent arrivals of cameras, sound trucks, and reporters wishing to speak to the woman who had killed Dick Dart. She had also contended with the inevitable upheavals in her private life. Even after she told him that she wanted a divorce, Davey had offered to move back in with her, but Nora had refused. She had also refused his invitation to share the apartment above the garage, where Davey had instantly felt comfortable. *You told the FBI where I was,* she had said, to which Davey replied, *I was trying to help you.* She had told him, *We're finished. I don't need your kind of help.* Not long after this conversation, she had called Jeffrey, who was out of the hospital and convalescing at his mother's house, to tell him that she would see him soon.

Alden Chancel, whose attitude toward Nora had undergone a great change, had tried to encourage a reconciliation by proposing to build a separate house, a mini-Poplars, on the grounds, and she had turned down this offer, too. She had already packed most of the surprisingly few things she wanted to keep, and she wished to go someplace where few people knew who she was or what she had done. Nora was already impatient with her public role; another explosion of reporters and cameramen would soon erupt, and she wanted to be far away when it did. In the meantime, she had three errands to accomplish. Seeing Alden was the first of these.

Maria burst into a smile and said, "Miss Nora! Mr. Davey is in his apartment."

A few days after being suspended, Maria had been rehired. The lawsuit against Chancel House had been withdrawn, and Alden no longer feared revelations connected to Katherine Mannheim.

"I'm not here to see Davey, Maria, so please don't tell him I'm here. I want to talk to Mr. Chancel. Is he in?"

Maria nodded. "Come in. He'll like to see you. I will get him." She went to the staircase, and Nora walked into the living room and sat down on one of the long sofas.

In a few minutes, radiating pleasure, affability, and charm, Alden came striding in. He was wearing one of his Admiral of the Yacht Club ensembles: white trousers, a double-breasted blue blazer, a white shirt, and a snappy ascot. She stood up and smiled at him.

"Nora! I was delighted when Maria told me you were here. I trust this means that we can finally put our difficulties behind us and start pulling together. Davey and I need a woman around this place, and you're the only one who would possibly do." He kissed her cheek.

A week ago, announcing that she had finally had enough of his abuse, fraudulence, and adulteries, Daisy had left the Poplars to move into a suite at the Carlyle Hotel in New York, from which she refused to be budged. She would not see or speak to Alden. She had emerged from her breakdown and subsequent immersion in soap operas with the resolve to escape her imprisonment and revise her book. During one of his pleading telephone calls, Davey said that his mother wanted "to be alive again" and had told him that he had "set her free" by learning the truth about his birth. He was baffled by his mother's revolt, but Nora was not.

"That's nice of you, Alden," she said.

"Should we get Davey in on this talk? Or just hash things out by ourselves for a while? I think that would be useful, though any time you want to bring Davey in, just say the word."

Alden had been impressed by the commercial potential of what she had done at Shorelands, and Nora knew from comments passed along by Davey that he was willing to provide a substantial advance for a first-person account of her travels with Dick Dart, the actual writer to be supplied later. The notion of her "true crime nonfiction novel" made his heart go trip trap, trip trap, exactly as Daisy had described. But the most compelling motive for Alden's new congeniality was what Nora had learned during her night in Northampton. He did not want her to make public the circumstances of the births of either Hugo Driver's posthumous novels or his son.

"Why don't we keep this to ourselves for now?" she said.

"I love dealing with a good negotiator, love it. Believe me, Nora, we're going to come up with an arrangement you are going to find very satisfactory. You and I have had our difficulties, but that's all over. From now on, we know where we stand."

"I agree completely."

Alden brushed a hand down her arm. "I hope you know that I've always considered you a tremendously interesting woman. I'd like to get to know you better, and I want you to understand more about me. We have a lot in common. Would you care for a drink?"

"Not now."

"Let's go into the library and get down to the nitty-gritty. I have to tell you, Nora, I've been looking forward to this."

"Have you?"

He linked his arm into hers. "This is family, Nora, and we're all going to take care of each other." In the library, he gestured to the leather couch on which she and Davey had listened to his ultimatum. He leaned back in the chair he had used that night and folded his hands in his lap. "I like the way you've been handling the press so far. You're building up interest, but this is about when we should do a full-court press. You and I don't need to deal with agents, do we?"

"Of course not."

"I know some of the best architects in the New York area. We'll put together a place so gorgeous it'll make that house on Crooked Mile Road look like a shack. But that's a long-range project. We can have fun with it later. You've been thinking about the advance for the book, haven't you? Give me a number. I might surprise you."

"I'm not going to write a book, Alden, and I don't want a house."

He crossed his legs, put his hand to his chin, and tried to stay civil while he figured out how much money she wanted. "Davey and I both want this situation to work out satisfactorily for all three of us."

"Alden, I didn't come here to negotiate."

He smiled at her. "Why don't you tell me what you want, and let me take it from there?"

"All I want is one thing."

He spread his hands. "As long as it's within my powers, it's yours."

"I want to see the manuscript of *Night Journey.*"

Alden stared at her for about three seconds too long. "Davey asked me about that, hell, ten years ago, and the thing's lost. I wish I did have it."

"You're lying to me," Nora said. "Your father never threw anything away. Just look at the attic of this house and the storeroom at the office. Even if he had, he would have kept that manuscript. It was the basis of his greatest success. All I want to do is take a look at it."

"I'm sorry you think I'm not telling you the truth. But if that's what you came here for, I suppose this conversation is over." He stood up.

"If you don't show it to me, I'm going to say things that you don't want people to hear."

He gave her an exasperated look and sat down again. "I don't understand what you think you can get out of this. Even if I did have it, it couldn't do you a bit of good. What's the point?"

"I want to know the truth."

"That's what you came here for? The truth about *Night Journey*? Hugo Driver wrote it. Everybody knows it, and everybody's right."

"That's part of the truth."

"Apparently your adventures have left you more unsettled than you realize. If you want to come back in the next couple of days to talk business, please do, but for the present, we have nothing more to talk about."

"Listen to me, Alden. I know you have that manuscript somewhere. Davey once came to you with an idea that would have made you even more money from the book, and you never even bothered to look for it. He did, but you didn't. You knew where it was, you just didn't want him to see it. Now I want to look at it. I won't open my mouth to a single human being. I just want to know I'm right."

"Right about what?"

"That Driver stole most of the story from Katherine Mannheim."

Alden stood up and looked at her in pity. Just when she could have turned things around and joined the team, Nora had turned out to be a flake after all, what a shame. "Let me say this to you, Nora. You think you know certain facts which could damage me. I would rather not have these facts come to light, that's true, but while they might stir up some publicity I could do without, I'll survive. Go on, do whatever you think you have to do."

Nora took a folded sheet of paper from her bag. "Look at this, Alden. It's a copy of a statement you probably won't want made public."

Alden sighed. He came across the room to take it from her. He was bored, Nora had thrown away her last chance to be reasonable, but he was a gentleman, so he'd indulge her in one final lunacy. He took his reading glasses from the pocket of the blazer, put them on, and snapped open the paper on his way back across the room. Nora watched this performance with immense pleasure. Alden read a sentence and stopped moving. He read the sentence again. He yanked off his glasses and turned to her.

"Read the whole thing," Nora said. Until this moment, she had wondered if he had already known. The shock and dismay surfacing through his performance made it clear that he had not. She could almost feel sorry for him.

Alden moved behind the leather chair, leaned over it, and read Hugo Driver's confession and Georgina Weatherall's postscript. He read it all the way through, then read it again. He looked up at her from behind the chair.

"Where did you get this?"

"Does it matter?"

"It's a fake."

"No, Alden, it's not. Even if it were, would you want that story to get out? Do you want people to start speculating about your father and Katherine Mannheim and Hugo Driver?"

Alden folded the letter into one pocket, his glasses into another. He was still hiding behind his chair. "Speaking hypothetically, suppose I do have the manuscript of *Night Journey.* Suppose I satisfy your curiosity. If that were to happen, what would you do?"

"I'd go away happy."

"Let's try another scenario. If I were to offer you two hundred thousand dollars for the original of this forgery, solely for the protection of my father's name, would you accept my offer?"

"No."

"Three hundred thousand?"

Nora laughed. "Can't you see that I don't want any money? Show me the manuscript and I'll go away and never see you again."

"You just want to see it."

"I want to see it."

Alden nodded. "Okay. You and I are both honorable people. I want you to know I never had any idea that . . . I never had any idea that Katherine Mannheim didn't just walk away from that place. You gave me a promise, and that's my promise to you." He recovered himself. "I still say that this is a forgery, of course. My father followed his own rules, but he wasn't a rapist."

"Alden, we both know he was, but I don't care. It's ancient history."

He came out from behind his barricade. "It's ancient history whether he was or wasn't." He moved along the bookcase and swung out a hinged section of a shelf at eye level to reveal a wall safe, another massy vault larger within than without. He dialed it open and with more reverence than she would have thought him capable of reached in and took out a green leather box.

Nora came toward him and saw what looked like the bottom of a picture frame on the top shelf of the safe. "What's that?"

"Some drawing my father squirreled away."

Alden pulled the drawing out and showed it to her before sliding it back into the vault. "Don't ask me what it is or why it's there. All I know is that when Daisy and I moved into the Poplars, he showed it to me and told me to keep it in the vault and forget about it. I think it must be stolen. Somebody probably gave it to him to pay off a debt."

"Looks like a Redon," Nora said.

"I wouldn't know. Is that good?"

"Good enough."

She took the box to the couch and looked inside. A small notebook with marbled covers sat on top of a lot of typed pages. She picked up the notebook. Katherine Mannheim's signature was on the inside cover. She had written "*Night Journey, novel?*" on the facing page. Nora turned page after page filled with notes about Pippin Little; this was the embryo of Driver's book, stolen from Katherine Mannheim's bag. *He who steals my trash steals trash.* She put the notebook beside her and took the manuscript from the box. It seemed such a small thing to have affected so many lives. She opened it at random and saw that someone had drawn a line in the margin and written in a violent, aggressive hand, *p. 32, Mannheim notebook.* She turned to another page and saw in the same handwriting, *pp. 40–43, Mannheim.* Lincoln Chancel had demanded the stolen notebook, kept the manuscript, and marked in it everything Driver had stolen from Katherine Mannheim. If Driver ever ruined him, he would ruin Driver.

"Do you see?" Alden said. "Driver wrote the book. These Mannheim people don't have a leg to stand on. He borrowed a few ideas, that's all. Writers do it all the time."

Nora returned the manuscript and notebook to the box. "I'm grateful to you, Alden."

"I still don't see why it was so important."

"I just wanted to see it all the way through," she said. "In a day or two, I'm going to be moving to Massachusetts for a little while. I don't know where I'll be after that, but you won't have to worry about me."

Alden told her he would say good-bye to Davey for her.

"I already did that," Nora said.

The second of Nora's errands took her to the post office, where she withdrew from an unsealed envelope addressed to *The New York Times* a letter describing Hugo Driver's debt to the forgotten poet Katherine Mannheim and an account of the poet's death and her burial a few feet north of the area known as Monty's Glen in the Shorelands woods. To the letter she added, in her hasty hand, this note: "*Katherine Mannheim's original notebook and Hugo Driver's manuscript, with Lincoln Chancel's marginal notes referring to specific passages taken from the notebook, are in a wall safe located in the library of Alden Chancel's house in Westerholm, Connecticut.*" Having kept her promise never to speak of these matters, she refolded the letter, wrapped it around another copy of Hugo Driver's confession, put them back into the envelope, sealed it, and sent it by registered mail to New York.

Nora's third errand brought her to Redcoat Road. Natalie Weil's house was still in need of a fresh paint job, but the crime scene tapes had been removed. She pulled up in front of the garage door, walked up the path to Natalie's front door, and pressed the bell. A friendly female voice called out, and footsteps ran down the stairs to the door. As soon as Natalie saw her, she immediately tried to slam the door, but Nora thrust herself inside and backed Natalie toward the stairs. "I want to talk to you," she said.

"I suppose you do," Natalie said. She seemed aggrieved and reluctant, which did not displease Nora. "I know how you feel, but all of a sudden three new listings showed up, and I have to show my boss I can still do my job, besides which there's a little problem with the police, some crap about drugs, but that won't stick, so what the hell, right? Come upstairs and have a beer."

"You're calmer than I expected," Nora said.

"You win some, you lose some. I'll have a beer, even if you're not going to."

Nora went up the stairs and waited for Natalie. Despite her Westerholm weekend uniform of a faded denim shirt and khaki shorts, she looked wary and defensive, and though not as ancient as she had appeared on Barbara Widdoes's couch, older than Nora remembered her. She pulled her refrigerator open, took out a bottle of Corona, and popped the cap. "Come on in, sit down, we've known each other a long time, what's a little husband fucking between old friends? I can't blame you for being mad at me, but it was hardly a big deal, if you want to know the truth."

"Yes," Nora said. "I do." She came into the kitchen and sat opposite Natalie at her kitchen table. "That's exactly what I want to know."

"Join the crowd." Natalie drank from the beer bottle and gently put it down. Her eyes looked bruised. "Hey, at least for the time being, I'm still in the real estate business. You know what that means? We sell dreams. Truth is what you say it is. Right?"

"A lot of people think so," Nora said. The handcuff photographs had been taken off the corkboard, and the refrigerator magnets had been thrown away.

Natalie took another swallow of Corona. "How do you like being famous? Is it neat? I wouldn't mind being famous."

"It isn't neat."

"But you killed Dick Dart. You wasted the bastard." The beer in front of Natalie was not her first.

"So they say," Nora answered.

Natalie toasted her with the Corona bottle. "You and Davey all right?"

"He moved back in with his father and I'm leaving town. So, yeah, we're probably all right."

"God, he's going back to Alden." Natalie twisted her mouth into a half smile. "I heard Daisy took off. About time. That guy is bad news, and he always was. I mean, you make mistakes, but Alden was about the worst mistake I ever made. Well, let's drop that subject."

"Let's not," Nora said. "After all, you and Alden caused me a lot of trouble. I was about to be arrested when the wonderful Dick Dart abducted me."

"Nobody's perfect. For what it's worth, Nora, I'm sorry." Natalie was having trouble looking at her. "Sometimes you do things for the wrong reasons. It's a lousy deal, you know? You get strapped, you agree to stuff you'd never do otherwise. I never wanted to get you into trouble—shit, I *like* you. I always liked you. The whole thing was Alden's idea in the first place. It was just business."

"Bid'ness is bid'ness," Nora said.

Natalie made a wry face. "Know how many houses sold here last year? Exactly nineteen. And not precisely at my end of the market, no siree, I get the top of the bottom end, like your place, no offense, but the office doesn't give me the two-million-dollar properties." She swallowed more beer and put down the bottle. "Alden's a jerk, but he's willing to put cash on the table, I'll say that for him. And I got you off the hook, didn't I?"

"Yes," Nora said. "But you almost got me arrested for kidnapping."

Natalie took another swallow of Corona. "It was never supposed to get that far, Nora. He just wanted to jerk Davey around, that's all. He was pissed off. We didn't know that whole thing with Dick Dart was going to happen, who could know that?"

"Tell me about the blood in your bedroom."

Natalie smiled at her like a conspirator. "One of Alden's brilliant ideas. He wanted to get everybody worked up, tie my thing into the murders. Stir the pot, you know? He got this pig blood from a butcher and wrecked my bedroom. But you're okay now, aren't you? I went through my act, it's all over, what's the difference?"

"If you don't know, I'll never be able to explain it to you," Nora said.

Natalie turned her head away.

"Natalie," Nora said, and Natalie looked at her again. "You disgust me. Alden *bought* you, and you ruined my life."

"You didn't like your life anyhow. How could you, married to that baby?"

"How much did he pay you?" Nora asked.

"Not nearly enough," Natalie said. "Considering what's probably going to happen to me. I'd like you to leave my house, if you don't mind. I think we're done. If you ask me, I did you a favor. You came out of this deal a lot better than I did."

"I didn't volunteer," Nora said. "I was drafted."

An unfamiliar car was nosed in toward Nora's garage door, and thinking it belonged to yet another reporter or to one of the unknown men who had proposed to her, she nearly drove on to the end of Crooked Mile Road until she saw Holly Fenn get out of the car and walk toward her front door. Nora turned into her driveway, and Fenn waved at her and started moving slowly back to the garage. She pulled in beside his car, got out, and walked toward him. He needed a haircut, he was wearing the ugliest necktie she had ever seen, and there were weary bags under his eyes. He looked great.

"So there you are," he said. "I called a couple of times, but I all I got was your machine."

"I'm not answering my phone all that much."

"I bet. Anyhow, I wanted to see you, so I thought I'd take a chance and come by." He tucked in his chin, stuffed his hands in his pockets, and looked at her from under his eyebrows. A spark of feeling jumped between them. "I have something to tell you, but mainly I just wanted to see how you were."

"How am I?"

"Holding up pretty good, I'd say. I like your new hair. Cute."

"Thanks, but you're lying. You liked it better the old way. I did, too. I'm going to let it grow out."

Fenn nodded slowly, as if agreeing with her on a matter of great importance. "Good. You getting your life back together okay?"

"I'm taking it apart pretty well, so I guess I am, yes. It isn't the same life, that's all. Holly, would you like a cup of coffee or something?"

"Wish I could. I have to be somewhere in five minutes. But I thought you ought to know something I learned about that old nursery school on the South Post Road. It occurred to me that I didn't know who held the lease on that building, so I checked. The lease is made out to a guy in New York named Gerald Ambrose. I called him up, and he told me that a citizen here in Westerholm rented it from him for the rest of the summer."

"Ah," Nora said. "You're a good cop, Holly."

"Yeah, maybe, but I turn out to be a little on the slow side. If I'd checked this out before, I could have saved you a lot of trouble."

She smiled at him. "I don't blame you, Holly. Who rented the building?"

He smiled back. "Do I get the feeling you already know, or am I making that up?"

"I have an idea, but tell me."

"The citizen who rented the building is a big-time publisher who told Ambrose he needed temporary storage for some overstock. Are you on good terms with your father-in-law?"

"My soon-to-be-ex-father-in-law and I have a long history of mutual loathing." She remembered Alden Chancel stroking her arm and saying *I'd like to get to know you better.* "Holly, if you stop in on Natalie Weil, she'll probably tell you an interesting story. I just saw her, and she's sort of killing time until her world caves in."

Fenn wiped his hand over his sturdy mustache and nodded, taking in both the remark and Nora. "Your friend put on a pretty good show."

"She even fooled Slim and Slam."

Fenn's eyes crinkled. "I gather some money changed hands."

"Not enough, according to Natalie."

Fenn grinned at the driveway, marveling at the ingenuity of the human capacity for committing serious error. "And you called me a good cop."

"I think you're pretty good all the way around," Nora said. "You stuck by me."

"Yeah, well, I tried." He gave her a rueful glance which managed to encompass compassion for what she had endured and anger at having been unable to spare her from it. "Anyhow," he said, "I better get going."

"If you must." She walked him to his car.

"Look, maybe this is none of my business, but did you say that you were leaving your husband?"

"I already left."

Fenn looked away. "Are you going to stay in town?"

"I think I'll go to Northampton for a while. I can work with a woman who runs a catering business for a couple of weeks. I want to get away from the telephone and clear my head. After that, who knows?"

Fenn nodded his big, shaggy head, taking this in. "After I'm through with Mrs. Weil and your soon-to-be-ex-father-in-law, do you suppose I could come back here and take you out for coffee or something?"

"Holly, are you asking me for a date?"

"I'm too old for dates," he said.

"Me, too. So come back later and we won't have a date, we'll just knock around together. I want to hear about your encounter with Alden. You can tell me all your favorite war stories."

Fenn smiled at her with every part of his face. "And I promise not to ask to hear yours."

"Or tell me any lies."

"I wouldn't know how to lie to you."

"Then it's a deal," Nora said.

"Well, okay." He lowered himself into his car, winked at her through the windshield, and backed away from the garage. A few seconds later, he was gone.

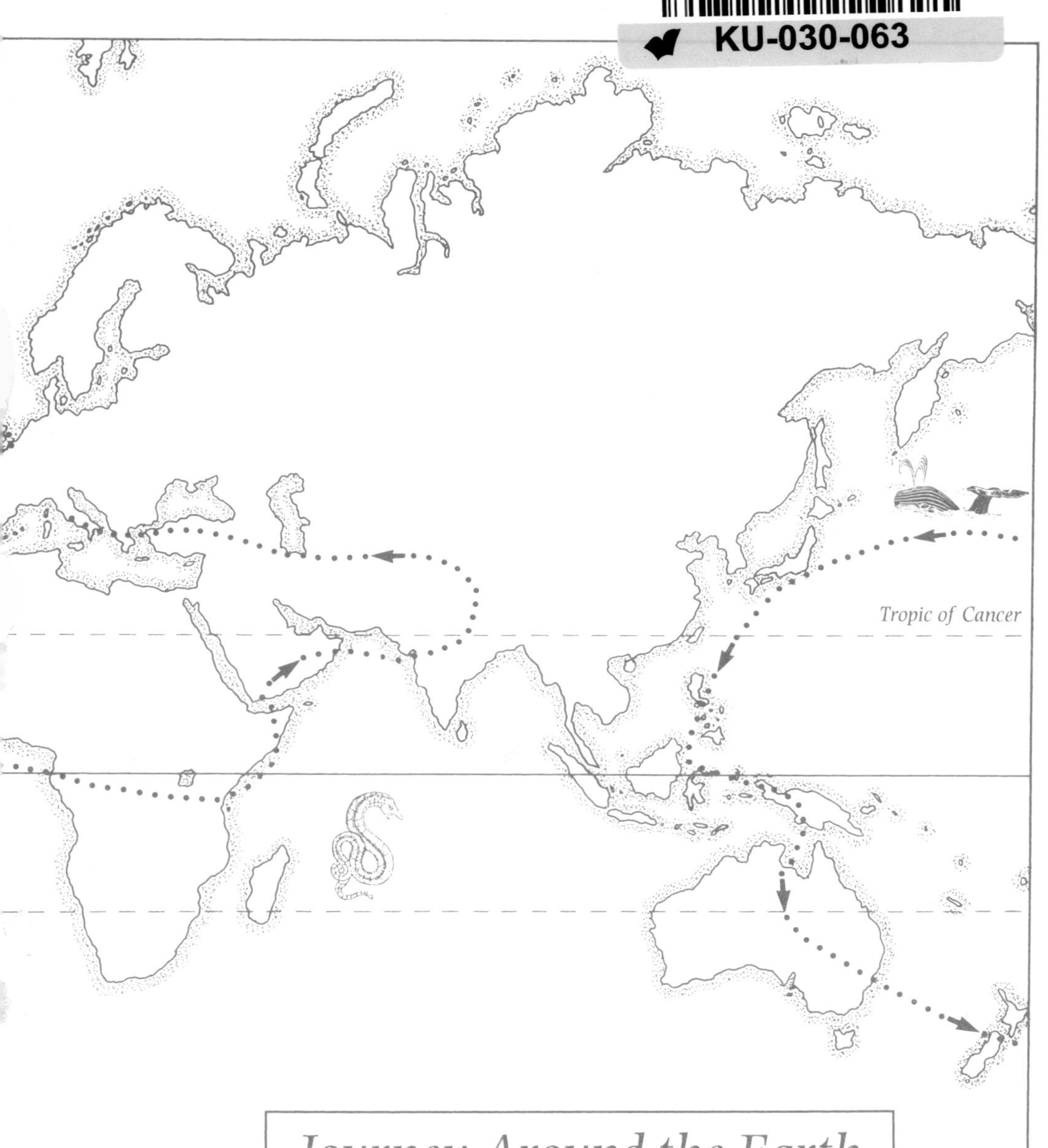

Journey Around the Earth

The Earth

The Earth

AN INTIMATE HISTORY

RICHARD FORTEY

HarperCollins*Publishers*

For Jules, with my love

HarperCollins*Publishers*
77–85 Fulham Palace Road,
Hammersmith, London W6 8JB

www.harpercollins.co.uk

3 5 7 9 10 8 6 4 2

First published in Great Britain by
HarperCollins*Publishers* 2004

A catalogue record for this book
is available from the British Library

ISBN 0-00-257011-4

Set in Postscript Linotype Minion with
Helvetica and Photina display by
Rowland Phototypesetting Ltd, Bury St Edmunds, Suffolk

Printed and bound in Great Britain by
Clays Ltd, St Ives plc

CONTENTS

ACKNOWLEDGEMENTS

It would have been impossible to write this book had I not been awarded the Collier Chair in the Public Understanding of Science and Technology at the University of Bristol for 2002. I am most grateful to the Institute of Advanced Studies, University of Bristol, and particularly Professor Bernard Silverman, for granting me time, and a quiet attic, to escape the hassles of my normal life. Karine Taylor, secretary to the Institute, was helpful in countless small ways which made my stay in Bristol a pleasure. I thank Paul Henderson of The Natural History Museum in London for facilitating my sabbatical leave at Bristol.

While researching the book I was compelled to explore parts of the geological column that are not my usual habitat, and to extend my expertise into new fields. I profited enormously from the generosity of several geologists who guided me over territory well-known to them, but novel to me. Geoff Milnes, and his daughter Ellen, were charming guides around the eastern Alps, and patiently tolerated my naive questions. Graham Park took me around the Northwest Highlands at a time of the year when most sensible people (even Scottish people) are sat round the fire with a hot toddy. Geoff and Graham also revised the appropriate parts of my manuscript, and corrected mistakes and misapprehensions. I need hardly add that any infelicities or inaccuracies that remain are entirely the responsibility of the writer. Several years ago, Dr Ajit Varkar of the University of Pune arranged my trip to the Deccan traps in northwestern India, negotiating with drivers and guides alike. I could not have completed this excursion without his help. Paul and Jodi Moore provided unstinting hospitality in Hawai'i for me and my family, and were the best possible company in the tropical evenings (I hope they got the sand out of the carpet).

I cannot thank them enough. Sam Gon helped me understand aspects of Hawaiian culture. Several colleagues generously gave me advice in return for no more than a free lunch. I may still owe one or two. I particularly thank Claudio Vita-Finzi and David Price of University College, London, for advice on the Bay of Naples, and the middle of the Earth, respectively. Bernard Wood of the University of Bristol spent an afternoon showing me how rock samples can be crushed so hard as to change their character, which was invaluable for my chapter on Deep Things. I also thank John Dewey, Tony Harris, David Gee, Bob Symes, Joe Cann, and my old Newfoundland friends for advice of one kind or another. Adrian Rushton and Derek Siveter provided moral support in the pub at times of crisis.

I am particularly indebted to Robin Cocks, John Cope and Heather Godwin, who read through the first version of the book, and made several suggestions for its improvement. Heather has always had a crucial role in my writing career, as an infallible arbiter of taste, and excisor of bad jokes. Arabella Pike at HarperCollins has proved again an enthusiastic and supportive editor, and her organisational skills ensured that the whole work came together.

I sincerely thank my wife Jackie for once again tolerating the writer at work, and, more specifically, for organising several of the field trips which comprise the core of the book. Jackie and my daughter, Rebecca, did much of the picture research for the colour plates.

Robert Francis provided me with many excellent photographs, which greatly enhanced the attractiveness of my natural history of the earth. I thank Ray Burrows for his skillful drawings. James Secord, Ted Nield, John Cope, David Gee, Jerry Ortner, Graham Park and Geoff Milnes also provided illustrations for which I am much indebted.

PREFACE

For some years I have been thinking about how best to describe the way in which plate tectonics has changed our perception of the Earth. The world is so vast and so various that it is evidently impossible to encompass it all within one book. Yet geology underlies everything: it founds the landscape, dictates the agriculture, determines the character of villages. Geology acts as a kind of collective unconscious for the world, a deep control beneath the oceans and continents. For the general reader, the most compelling part of geological enlightenment is discovering what geology does, how it interacts with natural history, or the story of our own culture. Most of us engage with the landscape at this intimate level. Many scientists, by contrast, are propelled by the search for the inclusive model, a general theory that will change the perception of the workings of the world. In most scientific papers, the intimacies of plants or places are hardly given a second glance. Plate tectonics has transformed the way we understand the landscape, for the world alters at the bidding of the plates, but much of the transformation has been expressed in the cool prose of the scientific treatise. The problem is how we can marry these two contrasting modes of perception – the intelligent naturalist's sensitive view of the details of the land with the geologist's abstract models of its genesis and transformation. My solution has been to visit particular places, to explore their natural and human history in an intimate way, thence to move to the deeper motor of the Earth – to show how the lie of the land responds to a deeper beat, a slow and fundamental pulse. I have chosen my examples with some care, for they are all places that have figured in unscrambling this complex and richly patterned planet of ours. I have visited them all, so that the reader will also have this particular guide's reactions to the sights, sounds, smells and ambience of the critical localities. At the same time, I have endeavoured to show how knowledge of the deeper tectonic reality has changed over the last century or so. Great minds have pondered the shape of the world, and have purveyed 'theories of everything' that have come and gone. Many past theories have been founded on good reasoning for their time and place, and it would be a complacent scientist today who would claim that present knowledge is as far as it goes. Understanding advances by building upon, and criticising the work of those who went before. It is a messy and complicated business, in which the human heart has as much a part to play as human intellect. This, too, is an ingredient in my story. The most difficult decisions I faced were not what to include, but what to leave out. I am acutely aware that there are areas of science that are merely sketched herein, any one of which would merit a book of its own. Geochemical cycles and their role in Earth systems are a case in point. The intercedence of extraterrestrial events in our history is another, fascinating field in which many recent advances have been made. The omission of such things in the interest of a coherent narrative was a painful necessity. What my story lacks in omniscience I hope it makes up for in coherence and accessibility.

1

Up and Down

It should be difficult to lose a mountain, but it happens all the time around the Bay of Naples. Mount Vesuvius slips in and out of view, sometimes looming, at other times barely visible above the lemon groves. In parts of Naples, all you see are lines of washing draped from the balconies of peeling tenements or hastily-constructed apartment blocks: the mountain has apparently vanished. You can understand how it might be possible to live life in that city only half aware of the volcano on whose slopes your home is constructed, and whose whim might control your continued existence.

As you drive eastwards from the centre of the city the packed streets give way to a chaotic patchwork of anonymous buildings, small factories, and ugly housing on three or four floors. The road traffic is relentless. Yet between the buildings there are tended fields, and shaded greenhouses. In early March the almonds are in flower, delicately pink, and there are washes of bright daffodils beneath the orchard trees; you can see women gathering them for market. In the greenhouses exotic flowers such as canna lilies can be glimpsed, or ranks of potted plants destined for the supermarket trade. Oranges and lemons are everywhere. Even the meanest corner will have one or two citrus trees, fenced in and padlocked against thieves. The lemons hang down heavily, as if they were too great a burden for the thin twigs that carry them. The soil is marvellously rich: with enough water, crops would grow and grow.

This was an abundant garden in Roman times, and it still is, even if crammed between scruffy apartments and scrap metal yards.

The Bay of Naples in the early nineteenth century, Vesuvius in the distance an Arcadian prospect. An engraving by E. Bejamin from an original painting by G. Arnald.

Volcanic soil is rich in minerals; it is correspondingly generous to crops. Outside the city, Vesuvius is more of a continuous presence; the ground rises gently towards its brown summit. New buildings cling on to the side of the mountain, even high up among the low trees and broom bushes that clothe its flanks. The buildings are indistinct, however, hidden by a creamy-yellow haze of petrochemical smog spreading outwards from the frantic centre of Naples towards the mountainside. You pass a road sign to Pompeii, but from the road there is little to distinguish this suburb from any other, for all its fame.

When the road rises into the hills that abut the southern margin of the Bay of Naples, the urban sprawl begins to thin out. The orange groves are more orderly, with the trees neatly planted in rows inside cages made of makeshift wooden struts, draped over the top with nets. The slopes become much steeper than on the volcanic flanks –

close terraces piled one upon the other, each banked up with a wall of pale limestone blocks. Medium-sized trees with small, grey-green leaves – which appear almost silvery in the afternoon light – cling to the most precipitous terraces. These are olive trees, the definitive Mediterranean survivors, oil-producers and suppliers of piquant fruit. Their deep roots can seek out the narrowest cracks. They relish limestone soils, however poor they are in comparison with volcanic loam. The villages in this part of the bay are as you would expect of regular, tourist Italy, with piazzas and ristorante-pizzerias and youths with slick hairstyles on the lookout for a fast buck. Even this long before the summer season there is opportunity for a smooth operator. You find yourself agreeing to hire a cab for a day for €200 to hug the congested roads, when you could travel faster on the excellent Circumvesuviana railway for a tiny fraction of the price. Somehow, you, the visitor, have become the rich volcanic soil primed to yield a good harvest.

Near the tip of the southern peninsula, Sorrento commands a wonderful prospect of Mount Vesuvius across the entire Bay of Naples. From this steep-sided town, Vesuvius looks almost the perfect, gentle-sided cone. It could be a domestic version of Mount Fuji, the revered volcanic mountain in Japan. It can appear blue, or grey, or occasionally stand revealed in its true brown colours. On clear days Vesuvius is starkly outlined against a bright sky: a dark, heavy, almost oppressive presence. Or on a misty morning its conical summit can rise above a mere sketch or impression of the lower slopes, which are obscured in vapour, as if it were cut off from the world to make a house for the gods alone. At night, ranks of lights along Neapolitan roads twinkle incessantly. Vesuvius is often no more than a dark shape against a paler, but still Prussian blue sky. The lights might persuade you that the mountain was still in the process of eruption, with points of white illumination tracking lava flows running down the hillsides. From Sorrento, you can make of Vesuvius what you will, for within a day it will have remade itself.

The Bay of Naples is where the science of geology started. The description of the eruption of Vesuvius and the destruction of

Pompeii in AD 79 by Pliny the Younger is probably the first clear and objective description of a geological phenomenon. No dragons were invoked, no clashes between the Titans and the gods. Pliny provided observation, not speculation. Not quite two millennia later, in 1830, Charles Lyell was to use an illustration of columns from the so-called 'Temple of Serapis' at Pozzuoli, north of Naples, as the frontispiece to volume one of the most seminal work in geology – his *Principles of Geology*. This book influenced the young Charles Darwin more than any other source in his formulation of evolutionary theory: so you could say that the Bay of Naples had its part to play, too, in the most important *bio*logical revolution. Everybody who was anybody in the eighteenth and nineteenth centuries visited the bay, and marvelled at its natural and archaeological phenomena. For geology – a latecomer to the pantheon of sciences – the area is the nearest thing to holy ground that there is. If you were going to choose anywhere to retrace the growth in our understanding about how the earth is constructed, what better place to begin? Where else more appropriate to explain first principles? The long intellectual journey that eventually led to plate tectonics started in this bite out of the western shin of Italy's boot-shaped profile. A voyage around this particular bay is a pilgrimage to the foundations of comprehension about our planet.

Everything about Sorrento is rooted in the geology. The town itself is in a broad valley surrounded by limestone ranges, which flash white bluffs on the hillsides and reach the sea in nearly vertical cliffs – an incitement to dizziness for those brave enough to look straight down from the top. Seen from a distance, the roads that wind up the sides of the hills look like folded tagliatelle. Stacked blocks of the same limestone are used in the walls that underpin the terraces supporting the olive groves. In special places there are springs that spurt out fresh, cool water from underground caverns. These sources are often flanked by niches containing the statue of a saint, or of the Virgin: water is not taken for granted in these parts. There are deep ravines through the limestone hills, probably marking where caves have collapsed. The country backing the Bay of Naples is known as Campania, and the same name, Campanian, is applied to a subdivision of geological time belonging to the Cretaceous period. If you look carefully on some of the weathered surfaces of the limestones you will see the remains of sea-shells that were alive in the age of the dinosaurs. I saw some obvious clams and sea urchins, belonging to extinct species, emerging from the cliffs as if they were on a bas-relief. A palaeontologist can identify the individual fossil species, and use them to calibrate the age of the rocks, since the succession of species is a measure of geological time. The implication is clear enough: in Cretaceous times all these hilly regions were beneath a shallow, warm sea. Limy muds accumulated there as sediments, and entombed the remains of the animals living on the sea-floor. Time and burial hardened the muds into the tough limestones we see today. They are sedimentary rocks, subsequently uplifted to become land; earth movements then tilted them – but this is to anticipate. What one can say is that the character of the limestone hills is a product of an ancient sea.

The massive limestones continue westwards on to the island of Capri, which is a twenty-minute ferry ride from Sorrento and bounds the southern edge of the Bay of Naples. The island rises sheer from the sea, circumscribed by steep limestone cliffs, and your first thought is how could it support the smallest village, let alone a town. The town of Capri lies at the top of a vertiginous funicular railway running from the harbour. The buildings are ancient and quaint, and, naturally enough, built of the local stone. The blocks themselves are often concealed under stucco. There is a fine medieval charterhouse where the pale limestone is put to good effect in columns supporting cloisters. Almost everything else is fabricated of limestone – walls, floors, piazzas. In the bright Mediterranean light there is an overwhelming sense of whiteness; some of the villas glimpsed on the hillside have the appearance of frosted cakes tucked under umbrella pines. Only dark basalt must have been imported from Vesuvius to make the surfaces of the streets: this volcanic rock is less liable to shatter than limestone. It is not difficult to imagine the racket that iron-rimmed wheels made as they clattered over these roughly-matched, large blocks. On the inner side of the island there are truly astonishing vertical limestone cliffs dropping hundreds of metres to the sea. The Roman Emperor Tiberius spent his declining years in a palace on the island, the ruins of which endure. According to the prurient accounts of his chronicler Suetonius, he indulged every kind of sexual perversion in a life of epicene self-gratification. Small boys were favoured. Those who displeased him were liable to be thrown off the monstrous cliffs. There is a subtle undercurrent in the Capresi atmosphere that hints at such darker things. Just offshore there are two enormous and forbidding sea-stacks – masses of limestone isolated from the main cliff by the relentless erosion of the sea. According to Norman Douglas, this was the abode of the Sirens, whose alluring and fatal song Odysseus was able to resist only by being strapped to the mast of his vessel, while his muffled crew rowed onwards to safety. Capri makes you wonder whether an idyllic hilltop haven might eventually also deprave and destroy. One of the grandest villas (now a hotel) overlooking the fearsome cliffs was built by the Krupps dynasty, once the armourers of German ambitions. Unexpectedly, the builder apparently immersed himself in studying the growth of lampreys, a primitive and parasitic fish. On this island there is a seamless continuity with the past – with Hellenic myth and Roman decadence and medieval devotion. The island gardens have seen the ages come and go, perched high upon the hardened sediments of a sea far more ancient than human frailty.

There is something different about the cliffs behind the harbour in the middle of Sorrento. From afar they have a greyish cast, a dull uniformity, lacking all the brilliance of limestone. The streets career downwards towards the sea below the central piazza, following a steep-sided valley. Now you can see the rock in the valley sides. It is brownish, like spiced cake, and displays little obvious structure. Look closely and you see that embedded within it, like dates in a home-bake, there are darker patches. Some are little more than wisps, others are larger – angular pieces of another rock, here nearly black, there umber brown, some including little bubbles. Then you notice that the same rock has been recruited by the local builders to construct the high walls that line the steeply sloping path, comprising blocks a few tens of centimetres across, neatly cut and used like bricks. Clearly, this rock is softer than the rough limestones that bolster the hilly vineyards and terraces. Then you notice that the same stone has been used to construct the older buildings. Down by the port there are shops and cafés painted jolly ochre and sienna, but where the stucco has peeled – or where warehouses have simply been left undecorated – the same rock is revealed as having been used for their construction. Much of the town has grown from the identical rock that forms the steep cliffs backing the harbour.

This rock is called the Campanian Ignimbrite. Its origin was a catastrophe that happened 35,000 years ago: a gigantic volcanic explosion threw out at least 100 cubic kilometres of pumice and ash. The evidence still covers an area of more than 30,000 square kilometres around the Bay of Naples, extending from Roccamonfina in the north to Salerno in the south. The violence of this eruption would make the event that buried Pompeii seem like a small afterthought. An explosion of steam and gluey lava blew out a great hole in the earth at the edge of the Tyrrhenian Sea – not so much a bite out of Italy's profile as a huge punch. A vast cloud of incandescent material buoyed up with gas flowed like a fiery tidal wave across the limestone terrain. Lumps of volcanic rock were carried along willy-nilly in the mayhem: destruction of vegetation was complete. When the cloud settled, in many places it was hot enough to fuse solid: the wispy remains of volcanic fragments testify to this welding.* There were almost certainly Palaeolithic human witnesses to this destruction, who must have thought the gods had gone berserk. The legacy of the earth's ferocity is this apparently mundane rock that looks like

* This is what makes an ignimbrite; the general term for this kind of volcaniclastic rock is 'tuff'. This has nothing to do with tufa, which you can see encrusting the rocks around the limestone springs, even obliterating the feet of the saint in his niche, where lime is deposited.

cake. The angular fragments of rock within can now be seen for what they are – pieces of a destroyed volcano. It is ironic that this destruction has now been reversed into constructing buildings that are 'safe as houses'. Naturally, nothing is safe in this uncertain world. Looking down from the limestone hills you can imagine the hot, devastating clouds settling over where limoncello is now brewed and pizzas are spun, dumping down on the low ground as a thick, lethal blanket. These kinds of rocks were deposited from pyroclastic surges. Another eruption about 23,000 years later was marginally less devastating and did not spread so widely – it produced a different deposit known as the Tufo Galliano Napoletano, the Neapolitan yellow tuff. Rather than the colour of cake, it is the colour of Dijon mustard. Once you can recognize it, you spot blocks of it in many walls and buildings around Naples itself – it is almost reminiscent of the 'London stock' bricks that make the Georgian parts of the English capital so appealing. It is there in the walls of Roman remains. Most experts believe that the volcanoes that remain to this day in the Campi Flegrei are aligned around the edge of the massive hole, or caldera, left behind as the legacy of this second huge eruption. The Bay of Naples itself hides most of it. It may yet blow again.

It must be appropriate now to visit Mount Vesuvius. It is 1281 metres high – not a great peak, but grand enough. Strictly speaking, only the cone itself should be called Vesuvius: the wider region, including older volcanic remnants, should be called Somma Vesuvius. To reach the mountain, go to Erculaneo station and catch the bus waiting outside in the bustling suburb. The route climbs upwards through improbably narrow streets, and then out into fields planted with almonds and vines. The mountain produces a wine called Lachrymae Christi – the tears of Christ – as evocative a name as you could wish for an indifferent *rosso*. Now you can see close up the random assortment of houses that were visible only as flashes of light from the other side of the bay. They seem perilously close to the volcanic cone, and unplanned, as if dropped haphazardly from the sky. Higher still, there is dense scrub, and then, looming above you, the cone itself. The bus disgorges its passengers, who must then climb to the summit along a relentless upward trail. You are following in famous footsteps, for the poets Goethe and Shelley were here before you. Nor are you ever alone: the view provides an irresistible photo-opportunity for tourists of all nationalities. The conurbation of Naples stretches away below, as insubstantial as postage stamps pasted on the landscape.

The dominant colour is a warm brown-black. Nobody could pretend that a huge slope of clinker is aesthetically pleasing. The waste of the mountain has a curiously industrial feel, like slag from a smelter; it is easy to understand the classical notion of Vulcan's forges working away in the earth's interior. An excellent guide-book by Drs Kilburn and McGuire of University College, London, reveals that these unpromising pieces of debris are scoria and lithic fragments of the March 1944 eruption. Looking down, you can make out the edges of these latest flows in Vesuvius' long history extending beyond the base of the cone itself, like chocolate sauce sliding off a steamed pudding. By the pathside, there are occasional large boulders that show black crystals the size of a fingernail; these are pyroxene minerals that had time to crystallize out deep within the chamber of liquid rock – or magma – beneath the volcano. Like everything else around, these rocks are igneous in origin: formed in fire, cooled from melt derived from the earth's depths. The crater itself is the kind of gaping hole that induces despair in those suffering from vertigo: it is 500 metres across, and 300 metres deep. From the far side of the rim path you can just make out the amphitheatre at Pompeii, with the misty blue of the Bay of Naples beyond; it seems entirely plausible that destruction could be meted out at a distance by suitably violent explosions. The crater sides are sheer. Wisps of steam still arise from one side, like smoke from a poorly extinguished cigarette. Looking across the crater, you can readily see that it is made of piled layers of lava metres thick. You can also make out where flowing lava was replaced by explosive pyroclastic deposits, which are crumbly and easily eroded. Here is evidence for the origin of the kind of lethal

Inside the cone of Vesuvius, showing the lavas produced by successive eruptions.

clouds that wiped out Roman Herculaneum in the AD 79 eruption. The crater is not stable. Listen: there is a continuous tinkling, like ice in a glass, as pebbles fall from the sides into the interior. The volcano is temporarily quiescent, but there are many descriptions of it while awake. Here is a little of what the philosopher Bishop Berkeley had to say about it in 1717:

> I saw a vast aperture full of smoke, which hindered me from seeing its depth and figure. I heard within that horrid gulph certain extraordinary sounds, which seemed to proceed from the bowels of the mountain; a sort of murmuring, sighing, dashing sound; and between whiles, a noise like that of thunder or cannon, with a clattering like that of tiles falling from the tops of houses into the streets. Sometimes, as the wind changed, the smoke grew thinner, discovering a very ruddy flame and the circumference of the crater streaked with red and several shades of yellow . . .

Nowadays, handwritten labels creak in the wind. On the top of the cone you can make out a solar-powered global positioning system. So often in Italy there is this odd mixture of the improvised with the latest technology.

Vesuvius is an irritable mountain. It has been erupting for 25,000 years or so. It will do so again. It is a classic in geological literature because several of its eruptions have been accurately described over two thousand years. It also demonstrates many kinds of different volcanic activity, from sluggish flows that slowly and inexorably eat up landscape and houses, through ash-falls that suffocate, to pyroclastic flows and surges that run faster than a racing car and engulf the plains in heat and terror. It is a vulcanological case-book. After the AD 79 debacle, which killed two thousand people and buried Herculaneum and Pompeii, there was a great eruption that began in the morning of 16 December 1631. Within a day, ash from Naples had reached Istanbul, more than 1000 kilometres distant. This eruption killed almost twice as many people as had died at the time of the Roman Empire. The rich volcanic soil had once more encouraged the growth of a prosperous people, who had spread over vulnerable areas. Massive pyroclastic flows took their toll. So did the engulfing slurries of mud and ash that flow downhill when heavy rains blend with volcanic outpourings. Ironically, the particles thrown up by a major event serve to 'seed' rainclouds in the atmosphere; thus in this tragedy the four ancient elements – earth, air, fire, and water – conspired towards a common deadly destruction. Naples itself, however, was spared. There were many subsequent minor eruptions, usually about eleven years apart, all of which avoided it. An eruption is now overdue, and might well be a big one. The latest, 1944, eruption was studied in detail: something like thirty-seven million cubic metres of magma were expelled within a few days in March of that year. Much was released in the form of ash and 'bombs', black masses often shaped like horns or twisted loaves. There were several eruptive phases separated by periods of quiescence, when the crater collapsed temporarily to block the throat of the vent. The almond blossoms everywhere shrivelled on the branch. The villages of Massa and San Sebastiano were destroyed by slow-moving lava flows. *The Times* (of London) correspondent eloquently described the process:

> The progress of destruction is almost maddeningly slow. There is nothing about it like the sudden wrath of devastation by bombing. The lava hit the first houses in San Sebastiano at about 2.30 a.m. but by dawn it still had not crossed the main street only 200 yards away, but was nosing its way through the vines and crushing down the small outhouses more slowly than a steam roller . . . For a while it seemed as if it would engulf the houses as they stood but then, as the weight grew, a crack would appear in the wall. As it slowly widened first one wall would fall out and then the whole house would collapse in a cloud of rubble over which the mass would gradually creep, swallowing up the debris with it . . . Masses of steam of slightly darker quality rose as cellars full of casks of wine exploded. Over all one heard a steady cracking as the monster consumed *hors d'oeuvre* of vine stalks, olive trees and piles of faggots stored in backyards . . .

If it had been a pyroclastic surge, the whole thing would have been over in a second.

A geologist amongst the crowds at Pompeii would probably be there to observe the effects of an ash-fall that destroyed a whole city as much as to wonder at the level of luxury enjoyed by the Roman elite. Nonetheless, the city's sheer size comes as a surprise. The discouragingly large crowds at the entrance soon disperse, and you are left to pick around at your leisure. Some of the roads allow a clear view of Vesuvius, and it is not so difficult to envisage the huge shower of hot ash that so effectively entombed this wealthy city for the archaeologists: the warning earthquakes, the great boom of an explosion, the dark cloud shooting into the atmosphere above the looming cone, the sky blotted out, wonderment turning instantly to horror as the fall began. The bodies of the inhabitants were moulded by the ashes that covered them. The most pathetic testimonies to the catastrophe are the casts that have been taken from these moulds, which are now stored at one end of a vineyard – in particular a figure half rising from sleep, hardly stirred from private oblivion before returning to it forever, thereby preserving something of the monumentality of a sculpture, but with a vulnerability that is wholly personal. Even the stones have their own story to tell. The streets were shod with pieces of tough basalt fitted together in a coarse jigsaw. There is something peculiarly eloquent about seeing the grooves that generations of cartwheels wore into these roads. They are imprints of time itself upon what is inevitably described in the tourist blurb as a 'time capsule'. The surfaces of the roads are lower than the sidewalks and the kerbs are marked by courses of large basalt blocks. The walls of the houses and shops and temples were often constructed of alternating courses of large blocks of ignimbrite and small, sienna-coloured Roman bricks. The corners were often entirely of brick, since the larger blocks chip easily. The architects knew their local geology. In the Villa di Misteri there was much use made of the Tufo Galliano Napoletano, often built into a lozenge pattern. Originally, the surfaces along the streets would have been rendered, as they are inside the villas. But since cement was originally discovered by the Romans from grinding up tuffs, so even the dressing of the buildings is geological. In the smarter buildings the walls were painted and ornamented with figures and curlicues. Mosaic floors consisted of patterned tesserae, the common black and white ones being made of marble and basalt. Discovery of pattern books has shown that these floors could be ordered 'by the yard'. There is a section of the hypocaust, or plumbing, on display that shows the use of lead pipes – who knows if some of that lead could not have come from as far away as Britain, where the geological circumstances are just right for lead ores? In short, Pompeii grew from the geology, just as it was eventually consumed by it.

Herculaneum was destroyed by pyroclastic flows. The inhabitants had time to attempt to flee to sea, but no time to succeed in their flight. For a small tip, a guide will let you see the skeletons of the huddled bodies down by the former harbour. The temperature must have been sufficient to kill instantly, but not to calcine the bones. Why should the outlines of the flesh at Pompeii be more affecting than these horrific accumulations of bones? It must be something to do with gesture, with individuality. All skulls smile alike.

Both Pompeii and Herculaneum have geological bones. The fire has done no more than expose them. This is not only true of famous archaeological sites. Whatever the surface decoration, geological truths determine much of the reality and character of cities; the stone that builds them, the height to which towers can rise. This is a subtler connection than that with agriculture. It is more obvious that the dark, rich soils around Summa Vesuvius are the product of the weathering of old flows, and that this explains why men and women have always repopulated the area after the latest disaster ('If San Gennaro [the patron saint of Naples] looks after us, *Deo gratias*, we will prosper'). The geology in turn is often related to tectonic plates: a deeper reality still, arbiter of the shape of the world.

It seemed appropriate to pay our respects to S. Gennaro. There is a chapel dedicated to him in the Duomo in Naples. In the third century the saint was martyred for his Christian beliefs. He was first sentenced to be torn to pieces by animals, but this was commuted to beheading. The decapitation took place at Solfatara north of Naples, where a shrine has been erected. Some of the saint's blood was scooped up after the execution. This is still preserved as a precious relic. It supposedly has the extraordinary property of turning *back* into blood when it is brought out on religious occasions three times a year. Thus is Naples' safety guaranteed, or so the Neapolitans believe. The Duomo is reached by walking through narrow streets where squalor and splendour rub shoulders. Dark alleyways draped with washing lines and oozing suspicious liquids are cheek by jowl with churches and courtyards of decayed magnificence. The silence in the Duomo is all the more impressive for the noise and chaos outside. The saint's chapel is an ebullient confection of columns and gilt, with masses of marble and serpentine, panels of onyx, busts and paintings. The saint is depicted above the right-hand altar emerging unscathed from a fiery furnace – sanctity rises above mere volcanics. The sixteenth-century crypt is an extravaganza of marble. The floor is constructed from marble lozenges and triangles of every imaginable hue: yellow and pink and all manner of mottled and blotched shades, framed in white. The walls have ranks of white marble niches capped by huge marble scallops, and flanked by urns and flowers, drapes and *putti*. The whole is supported by rounded marble columns – white, with gentle streaks of grey – while the ceiling sports square panels painted with the effigies of saints, angels, and bishops. A pearly marble statue of Cardinal Carata kneels on the floor facing towards a locked bay containing S. Gennaro's relic. It is like being inside a palace of spun sugar. More mundanely, the crypt serves as a reminder of the third great class of rocks besides those of sedimentary and igneous origin. These are metamorphic rocks. They may have started out as either of the other two categories, but have been altered – or even completely transformed – by heat, pressure, or by any combination of the two, when caught in the great mill of mountain-building within the depths of the earth. Marble is one kind of metamorphic rock and comes in a thousand shades, although it started out as humble limestone as plain as the cliffs of Capri. Along the Apennine 'spine' of Italy there are many places where heat and pressure have altered limestones in this fashion. Renaissance architects made luscious use of these rocks. They can appear to resemble anything from blue cheese to slices of liver, or they can be pure white, like the Carrara marble favoured by great sculptors such as Michelangelo. Naples was just following the fashion. S. Gennaro's niche is clad in the products of the infernal heat to which he is now impervious.

Early visitors to the Roman antiquities of the Bay of Naples were following the tradition of the Grand Tour, a cultural perambulation around Italy made by young gentlemen with pretensions to enlightenment. Eighteenth-century English aristocrats would have been as familiar with the classics – with the writings of Virgil and Horace – as they would have been with the salty, home-grown vigour of Chaucer, or the sonnets of Shakespeare. They would have known about the hot springs that supplied the baths in which Roman gentry lounged for the good of their health; they would have been familiar with the ambulatoria along which the pampered rich strolled with their favourite philosophers for the good of their minds. The archaeology of the area was the latest sensation. Sir William Hamilton is known now mostly for his marriage to Lord Nelson's mistress, but he was a considerable archaeologist and antiquarian and the purchaser of treasures that still grace the collections of the British Museum. He also appreciated the uniqueness of the Neapolitan landscape, and strove to make known its volcanic features. While he was British Envoy in Naples towards the end of the eighteenth century he published a book about the Phlegraean Fields, *Campi Phlegraei*, which well described the area to which he was devoted. Perhaps it is this for which he should be remembered. Certainly, his work was known to the young Charles Lyell. Lyell had travelled to Italy in 1828 in the company of Sir Roderick Murchison, who was then the most influential British exponent of the young science of geology. If classic areas are made so by the observations of perceptive eyes, and measured by the hard currency of influence on subsequent thought, then there is a claim to be made for this modest Roman site in the middle of the town of Pozzuoli, west of Naples. But no plaque records it, no signs direct you to it. You simply come across it, as you might a standing-stone in England, or a roadside shrine in Italy.

The Phlegraean Fields! The very name sounds like some version of Arcadia (it is in fact derived from Greek for 'burning'). I had seen Sir William Hamilton's portrayals of the scenery: trees giving on to a rustic scene, the odd peasant going about his business, in the distance some interesting volcanic phenomenon in progress. This was the area of Campania described by the second-century historian Florus as 'the most beautiful region not only in Italy, but also in the world. Nothing is sweeter than its climate: to say everything, spring flowers twice there. Nothing is richer than its soil . . . nothing is more hospitable than the sea.' Times do change, of course, and the region has been swamped by undistinguished suburbs. But the Campi Flegrei is still the same collection of craters and calderas, separated by volcanic hills as it was in Florus' time – only the flat bottoms of the former have often been filled in with army barracks or cheap industrial units. The reality of these evocatively named fields are sadly something of a disappointment.

Lake Averno was considered to be one of the entrances to the underworld in classical times. In those days, birds roosting around it were wont to fall dead from the trees. From here, Dante was led by Virgil into the *Purgatorio*. If geology is the true underworld, then Lake Averno seemed to provide a kind of metaphorical entry point to the deep regions that form the subject of this book. Can you imagine anywhere with richer associations? It is an almost perfectly circular crater lake, three-quarters surrounded by steep walls of tuff. When I visited in early spring it had a slightly sinister character: plumes of smoke arose, not from volcanic exhalations, but from burning heaps of rubbish left over from the last summer season. A few mean reeds grew from the lake bottom, and bubbles of gas arose and broke the surface – methane, I suppose, from the de-oxygenated mud. Perhaps, after all, this is a postmodern underworld, with existential gloom presiding.

There is a geological explanation for this lethal lake. After volcanic eruptions have subsided, invisible eruptions of gas may continue. Carbon dioxide is one of them. It is odourless, and heavy – much heavier than air – so it sits around invisibly, or flows into pockets and depressions. It induces suffocation. Until a century ago, a cave with these properties in another crater in the Campi Flegrei, Astroni, was shown to visitors as a tourist attraction. It was called Grotto Del Cane (cave of the dog), for reasons which will become apparent. The playright and jobbing writer Oliver Goldsmith reported in 1774 on this grisly natural phenomenon in *An History of the Earth and Animated Nature*:

> This grotto, which has so much employed the attention of travellers, lies within four miles of Naples, and is situated near a large lake of clear and wholesome water. Nothing can exceed the beauty of the landscape which this lake affords; being surrounded by hills covered with forests of the most beautiful verdure, and the whole bearing a kind of amphitheatrical appearance. However, this region, beautiful as it appears, is almost entirely uninhabited; the few peasants that necessity compels to reside there, looking quite consumptive and ghastly, from the poisonous exhalations that arise from the earth. The famous grotto lies on the side of a hill, near which place a peasant resides, who keeps a number of dogs for the purpose of showing the experiment to the curious. These poor animals always seem perfectly sensible of the approach of a stranger, and endeavour to get out of the way. However, their attempts being perceived, they are taken and brought to the grotto; the noxious effects of which they have so frequently experienced. Upon entering this place, which is a little cave, or hole rather, dug into the hill, about eight feet high and twelve feet long, the observer can see no visible mark of its pestilential vapour; only to about a foot from the bottom, the wall seems to be tinged with a colour resembling that which is given by stagnant waters. When the dog, this poor philosophical martyr, as some have called him, is held above this mark, he does not seem to feel the smallest inconvenience; but when his head is thrust down lower, he struggles to get free for a little; but in the space of four or five minutes he seems to lose all sensation, and is taken out

> seemingly without life. Being plunged into the neighbouring lake he quickly recovers, and is permitted to run home, seemingly without the smallest injury.

It is the recovery of the dogs from their ordeal that identifies the gas as carbon dioxide. Goldsmith goes on to say that the vapour 'is of the humid kind as it extinguishes a torch', an experiment still performed in school laboratories to this day. Had the gas been sulphur dioxide or hydrogen sulphide the poor dogs would have suffered a rapid and painful death.

In 1750, a statue of the god Serapis was excavated from a Roman site at the coastal town of Pozzuoli. Serapis was based ultimately upon the Egyptian god, Osiris, but 'hybridized' with Graeco-Roman gods to become the basis of a widespread cult in the Mediterranean at the time of the Emperor Hadrian. For more than a century and a half the impressive archaeological discoveries in Pozzuoli were known as the Temple of Serapis, or the Serapion, under the belief that the statue indicated a sacred function. This is the name that appears in the caption to the illustration that forms the frontispiece of Charles Lyell's *Principles of Geology*. The image is also engraved on the Lyell Medal of the Geological Society of London, so it clearly mattered to his contemporaries. The current perception is that 'the temple' is nothing of the sort, but was in truth a rather opulent market-place, or *macellum*. But it is still a geological shrine, an emblem for the coming of age of geology as a science. It is something of a disappointment that it had to be de-consecrated; after all, the 'temple' is a holy place for rationalists, if that is not an oxymoron. At first sight, the Serapion is curiously unimpressive. The old town of Pozzuoli lies on a hill, and has been out of bounds since the earthquake crisis of 1982. The site lies near the harbour beyond the hill. A few yards seawards from the ancient mart there is still a market, selling oranges and lemons and local fish. Then you see the old market-place lying beyond a well-shaded square. It lies about six metres below the level of the present Piazza: it is like looking down into a sports field or a football pitch, a resemblance increased at

The 'Temple of Serapis' from the frontispiece of Lyell's *Principles of Geology*, first edition (1830). Some later editions omit the philosophical figure on the left.

night when the area is floodlit. The large rectangle is dominated by three huge columns, which a notice tells us are 12.5 metres high and composed of a single piece of marble. They must have been expensive items even at the time the market was built. In front of them there is a raised circle carrying a series of smaller columns that were probably reconstructed relatively recently, whereas the great columns were 'in place'. The circle is constructed of the familiar tuff, underlain by courses of Roman bricks. There are planted palm trees whose trunks supply a kind of biological equivalent to the marble columns. All around the edge of the market square are remains of the stalls of the traders.

The monument has none of Pompeii's breathtaking qualities, tucked away as it is so matter-of-factly in the middle of Pozzuoli. The casual observer might wonder at its importance. To discover the reason requires closer examination of the great columns: about four metres above their pedestals there are what look from a distance to be zones of blackish discoloration, where the marble appears roughened or eroded. The lower parts of the columns are, as Lyell said, 'smooth and uninjured'. Look more closely at the discoloured parts of the columns. You can now see that the marble has been perforated and pierced. Identical borings are caused by the marine clams that Lyell knew as *Lithodomus*. They can be found around the Bay of Naples today. The great Swedish biologist Linnaeus had originally named the destructive species *Lithophaga lithophaga*, a name that tells you all you need to know; for 'lithophaga' means 'rock-eater' in Greek, which is exactly what these clams do. They bore into rocks at the water-mark, eventually reducing the host limestone to a kind of framework. The implication should be clear, just as it was to Charles Lyell. The columns were – of course – constructed above the sea, but the whole market-place must then have been immersed beneath the sea sufficiently to drown the lower part of the columns. Not only that, the whole market-place must have been raised again for the visiting archaeologist to inspect the borings. It was possible to infer further details. The rock-eaters operate only in clear water, so it seems that the lower parts of the columns must have been buried beneath sediment in order to remain so clean. The borings total almost three metres of the columns; thus, the immersion, and subsequent elevation, must have been greater than six metres, and could well have been more. Lyell was tempted to associate the depression of the 'temple' with an eruption at Solfatara nearby in 1198, and its subsequent elevation with the eruption of Europe's youngest mountain, the small volcano of Monte Nuovo, which appeared almost overnight on the outskirts of Pozzuoli in 1538. I went there: although so juvenile, it is already weathering away to rich soil.

Thus the interpretation of these past events was made – rationally – by reference to what could still be observed at the present time. The clams had not changed their habits. The world had gone up and down, or rather down and up, but this was not catastrophic: the street markets still plied their many trades, the same physics that had operated in past years operated again today. This statement seems almost banal now, but it provides the basis for all modern geological reasoning. There has been much puffy stuff written about whether or not Lyell's uniformitarianism permitted variations in intensity of causes, or whether he applied his logic in a consistent way, and whether he assumed indefinite stretches of geological time. And there is a good case for making the Edinburgh geologist James Hutton (1726–97) the true father of the modern geological method. For most geologists, though, the important fact is that Lyell provided a clear way of thinking about the world. He substituted a rational system of investigation based upon present processes for a belief in a series of catastrophes, the latest of which was the biblical Flood, according to some. A marvellous cartoon by Henry de la Beche, first director of the Geological Survey of Great Britain and Ireland, shows the 'Light of Science Dispelling the Darkness which covered the World'. The light in question that dispels the clouds covering the globe is carried by a female figure who also bears in her right hand a geological hammer, for this was the particular discipline that was seen as attacking reactionary thinking by main force. The Lyellian method still lies

'The Light of Science Dispelling the Darkness which covered the World'. Drawn by Henry de la Beche, first Director of the Geological Survey of Great Britain. The cartoon portrays Lady Murchison in the fashion of the time, and notice that she brandishes a geological hammer in her right hand.

behind everything described in this book: look at volcanoes today to understand volcanoes in the past; do experiments in the laboratory to understand what goes on at depth in the earth; look at what plates do at the present time to understand how the world was made. Steven Jay Gould has pointed out that the 'Temple of Serapis' was a much more appropriate symbol for the Lyellian method than temperamental Mount Vesuvius. Gould remarks in *Lyell's Pillars of Wisdom* (1986) that 'Lyell presented the three pillars of Pozzuoli as a triumphant icon for both key postulates of his uniformitarianism – the efficacy of modern causes, and the relative constancy of their magnitude through time'. Scientists now tend to downplay the second part of this thesis, because they know that the earth has evolved and changed from its origins more than four billion years ago. Not every process has continued at exactly the same pace at all times – there have, on occasion, even been catastrophes; but the principle of reconstructing the past by using present-day analogues has remained at the centre of the process of turning geology from a pastime for dilettantes into a science. I could not have said what I have said about the ignimbrite of Sorrento or the limestones of Capri without Lyell's example. Put simply, Pozzuoli made a difference to science.

Charles Babbage should be mentioned at this point in the story. Born in 1792, Babbage was a brilliant mathematician, known today as the originator of computing and the inventor of the calculating machine. He, too, visited the Serapion in 1828, two years before the publication of the first part of Lyell's *Principles.* He presented a paper on his very detailed computations on the site at the Geological Society of London on 12 March 1834, and it is a model of Lyellian reasoning. It was not published until 1847, as a 'postponed paper' in Volume 3 of the *Quarterly Journal of the Geological Society of London.* The editor included the intriguing note that the paper 'by the request of author was returned to him soon after it was read, and has been in his possession ever since'. One wonders what sort of inhibition caused Babbage to delay nearly twenty years before printing observations that would have placed him at the start of uniformitarian reasoning. By 1847, the scientific *Zeitgeist* had already changed. However, you cannot but admire Babbage's summary:

> In reflecting . . . on the causes which produced the changes of level of the ground in the neighbourhood of Pozzuoli, I was led to consider whether they might not be extended to other instances, and whether there are not other natural causes, constantly exerting their influence, which, concurring with the known properties of matter, must necessarily produce alterations of sea and land, those elevations of continents and mountains, and those vast cycles of which geology gives such incontrovertible proof.

From Pozzuoli to the world! In this brief summary, Babbage encapsulated much of the research programme undertaken by modern geology.

* * *

This book is about explaining the character of the earth. The ultimate controls on the personality of the planet are tectonic plates – they *are* the 'natural causes, constantly exerting their influence' of which Babbage wrote. So my story will inevitably lead to an outline of plate tectonics. But I shall get there through special and particular places – like the Bay of Naples – where geology and history are interwoven. I shall explore the influence of geology on the character of landscape and the character of people. Far from being the driest of the sciences, geology informs almost everything on our planet, and is rich with human entanglements. The rocks beneath us are like an unconscious mind beneath the face of the earth, determining its shifts in mood and physiognomy. The progress of our understanding is also inextricably linked with the virtues and failings of the investigators. Different eyes at different times looked at the same view across the Bay of Naples and saw different things; one perhaps saw the wrath of the gods, another relief of pressure from a magma chamber. Textbooks tend to fillet out the history and scenery in order to give the current scientific consensus, so this is a kind of anti-textbook. In truth, the same classical areas have seen a half-dozen different generations of scientists tapping the rocks or putting their instruments about. But I shall try my best to avoid what the historian James Secord terms the Whiggish view of history, by which you uncover the mistakes of your forbears in the progress towards present enlightenment. Understanding is always a journey, never a destination.

If you try to comprehend how thought has changed over a century or more, there are a few books that can act as useful benchmarks. Since Lyell, there has been a handful of authors who have comprehensively summarized the knowledge of their time – who have tried to write down the world on paper. One of those was the Austrian geologist Eduard Suess (1831–1914), whose *Das Antlitz der Erde*, published in four massive volumes between 1883 and 1904, is probably the most amibitious attempt ever to capture the entirety of everything: you feel that a fact foolish enough to escape Suess' grasp probably was not worth his notice. Suess sat in Vienna like an omnivorous spider with a web spread over the world, tugging in facts. *Das*

Antlitz der Erde was translated into English, as *The Face of the Earth*, by Hertha Sollas, the wife of an eccentric Oxford Professor of Geology, and published 1904–9. If you want a view of what geological knowledge was like at the end of the nineteenth century, when geologists using the scientific method had already scanned much of the world, then Suess is your best guide. He, too, wrote of the Bay of Naples and of the 'Temple of Serapis', noting that on Capri there are *Lithophaga* borings as much as 200 metres above present sea-level. He had insights that are still woven into the fabric of geological thought, and even where we now know he was mistaken it is instructive to try to understand why he thought what he did. Yesterday's cast-iron inference is often today's discarded argument. As Mott Greene has pointed out in *Geology in the Nineteenth Century*, Suess differed fundamentally from Lyell in believing that, far from operating in a kind of steady state, the history of the earth was punctuated by periods of pronounced change – revolutions during which mountain belts were thrown up, for example. We shall see that this tension between continuity and sudden change was resolved only when the plate tectonic view was established.

In 1944, forty years after the last volume of Seuss's magnum opus was published, another widely influential work appeared: *Principles of Physical Geology* by Arthur Holmes. Known to generations of students simply as 'Holmes', it was a tremendously successful textbook from the outset, for two reasons: it was well and clearly written, and it was illustrated thoughout with photographs. Holmes was a professor at the Universities of Durham and Edinburgh, and in some ways a more radical figure than Suess (Cherry Lewis has recently written the first biography of him). Holmes did not try to write out the whole world in longhand like Suess, but sought to illustrate geological principles by selected examples, which could come from anywhere appropriate around the globe. It was a successful formula, and will do well as a record of mid-twentieth-century views of how geology makes the world what it is.

My own intention is much more modest, since I have no pretensions towards the omniscience of Suess, nor to the didactic skills of

Holmes. The few places I describe in detail, many of which I have visited, show what geology *does* – to the landscape and its history, or the kinds of animals and plants that flourish there. The intention is selectively to illuminate rather than to be comprehensive.

Arthur Holmes is relevant for another reason, at the point we have reached in the journey around the Bay of Naples. He was a pioneer in methods of radiometric dating of rocks. This is vital to the narrative of the earth. Lyell may have provided the intellectual tools for understanding geological processes, but he did not provide a time scale. The span of geological time was a mystery, and contemporary estimates of the age of the earth varied wildly, from a few to many millions of years. There were even those who still adhered to the calculations of James Ussher (1581–1656), Archbishop of Armagh, which placed the date of Creation in the year 4004 BC. However, most scientists agreed that the earth had to be old to accommodate all the rocks in their various sequences, all those Lyellian events – but how old? Leading twentieth-century physicists (notably Sir Harold Jeffreys) made estimates based upon good physics but false assumptions, such as the presumptive cooling rate of the earth. Such estimates invariably proved too young, but were vigorously defended for decades. The development of radioactive 'clocks' have served to put an objective date on remote antiquity. The method is based on the natural rate of decay of the radioactive isotopes of certain elements, such as uranium, carbon, and potassium. These rates can be determined experimentally. For example, 235 Uranium decays very slowly over hundreds of millions of years to 207 Lead. Hence, if you measure the amount of decayed product, you have a measure of time elapsed: it's as simple as that, though many complexities arise along with accuracy of measurement. Holmes' working lifetime spanned an era of technical improvements – which continue today – and estimates of the age of the earth steadily increased and became more accurate as methods were refined, and older and older rocks were discovered in the field. After Holmes' death, dating of moon rocks and solar system meteorites finally 'nailed' the time of the origin of the earth at four and a half billion years ago. These refinements of dating techniques allowed for calculation of the rates of change of what Babbage had called the 'vast cycles of geology': the speed at which plates move; the time taken to erode a mountain range; the length of time of an eruptive phase; how long dinosaurs were in charge of the land. Because different radioactive elements decay at varying rates, techniques must be tailored to the problem at hand: thus, 14 carbon decays very fast and can only be used to date comparatively recent events up to about 30,000 years ago. I have a scientific paper before me that uses radiocarbon dates extracted from the same kinds of clams that bored into the Serapion's columns to show that on the island of Ischia there has been seventy metres of uplift in 8500 years. So there are clocks for the world, completing the task that Lyell started.

It has become almost a cliché that we cannot grasp the immensity of geological time – what five, fifty, or five hundred million years actually *means.* But around Pozzuoli the changes we observe have taken place over thousands, rather than millions, of years. Luciano Bagnoli has been compelled to move the mooring of his fishing boat nearly a metre lower since his father's time, such is the rate of uplift in Pozzuoli. You do not have to travel very far if you want to see evidence for the forces that are lifting the whole region from the sea. The Solfatara crater lies just on the edge of town. You smell it before you see it – a result of what Oliver Goldsmith would have called its noxious emanations and pestilential vapours. It is still hissing, furiously. Courses of angular boulders line the rim of the volcano, the remains of its last explosive phase, resulting in a volcanic *breccia*. Half of the crater floor is devoid of vegetation, and as active volcanically as you could wish. There are numerous fumaroles belching forth steam. Holmes calls these active vents *solfataras*, so evidently we are at the type locality for this kind of thing. The Bocca Grande is the largest of them all, a roaring vent that emits steam at a temperature of 160° C. It sounds like a perpetually boiling kettle of enormous size, or the gasping of some great steam engine. It has been carrying on like this for years and years. A vulcanologist called Friedlander built a hut almost adjacent to it, the better to monitor its exhalations:

such is scientific obsession. The ancients called the area around the Bocca Grande the 'Forum Vulcani' and you do feel that the earth is manufacturing or forging something deep beneath your feet. What actually comes out are sulphides. The stink in the air is hydrogen sulphide – the smell of rotten eggs. There are smears of reddish-yellow colour around the lips of the vents. These are condensed patches of rare minerals – compounds of arsenic and mercury with sulphur – with names like realgar, orpiment, and cinnabar that would have been familiar to alchemists five centuries ago. This is indeed where the alchemy of the earth distils precious elements upon the ground. Most of them are also very toxic – they were the preferred materials of nineteenth-century poisoners. In 1700, a high tower was built to collect condensate from the steam, and particularly for alum, which is used as a mordant in the dyeing industry. It no longer stands. This steamy natural cauldron is a place where chemistry happens in the open air. Around some of the hot holes thrive heat-loving bacteria that have probably endured on earth for as much as four billion years.

Elsewhere, the ground is pitted and fuming, as if a bomb had recently been dropped. In the centre of the crater, a mud volcano is still spitting. There is also the famous stufe – two ancient brick-lined grottoes excavated into the side of the mountain. They were once used as sweating rooms (*sudatoria*): since classical times this has been one of the alleged health benefits of the Campi Phlegrei. One room was known as Purgatory (60° C) and the other as Hell (90° C). I sat in the steam inside the entrance to Purgatory for a few seconds, but had to crouch because it was just too hot near the ceiling. Sulphur and alum were crystallizing on the brickwork. Within a few seconds the swelter became insufferable – in a word, purgatory. All these steamy phenomena are the result of a magma chamber hidden beneath the Pozzuoli area. Ground water percolating downwards becomes superheated, and then blasts upwards, carrying with it mineral exhalations from the depths: the volcano is literally 'letting off steam'.

Current estimates are that the magma chamber is two kilometres below the surface, and rising. Some vulcanologists are deeply worried that the Campi Flegrei – rather than Vesuvius, where the magma is at about five kilometres deep – may be about to explode and that the Monte Nuovo eruption of 1538 might have been no more than a preamble. If so, the prospect is terrifying. If there were an eruption rapidly followed by a pyroclastic flow, the effects would be overwhelming. The chaos of the roads is bad enough on a fine spring afternoon, and speedy evacuation of thousands of people would be an impossibility. Hidden forces may yet take vengeance on lax town planners and profiteering builders in a drastic and unpredictable way. It is conceivable that the 'Temple of Serapis' could be interred beneath a pyroclastic tuff, and once more consigned to archaeological oblivion. There were earthquakes in 1982–4 that were sufficiently worrying to prompt the evacuation and abandonment of part of the old town of Pozzuoli. A seismic hazard map published by the Osservatorio Vesuviano shows an area with 'maximum observed values of seismic energy released and intensity' centred on Pozzuoli, and concentric zones of destruction all around. The magmatic masses are moving at shallow depth in the western part of the Gulf of Pozzuoli. The successor to the Neapolitan Yellow Tuff may yet be brewing unseen. You would never guess it from the insouciant joshing of the customers in the bars near the litter-strewn beach in Pozzuoli, even though the evidence of past volcanic fury lies in the rocks exposed all along the shore.

The problem lies in predicting when disaster might happen. It could be many years away, but it might be much sooner. This is the paradoxical nature of risk. Earthquake shocks of a particular kind should provide a signal; but you cannot live every day expecting it to be your last. By now it will be scarcely surprising to learn that attempts at scientific prediction of eruptions also had their origin around the Bay of Naples. The Observatory was founded on Vesuvius in 1841, making it the oldest of its kind in the world. The scientific office has now moved to Erculaneo, where electronic monitoring can be collated at a distance, but the older, more elegant building remains on the flanks of the volcano and houses a museum, including some of the original instruments. The very first seismograph was made by Ascanio Filomarino – and there it is. It is a wonderfully simple contraption, comprising an iron pendulum 2.6 metres long with a suspended weight of 2.5 kilograms, to which is attached a pencil that draws on a scroll of paper below. When the world shook, it moved. Charmingly, there are some little bells attached to the weight, presumably so that the natural philosopher might be awakened from his slumbers if a tremor happened along. But the virtuoso had a very clear idea of what he expected of his instrument. Writing about his invention in 1797, Filomarino observed that 'in the towns and villages near the volcano, use can be made of it together with an atmospheric electrometer, and observing them together with the several signs of the volcano one can sometimes, if not foresee clearly some new eruption, at least conjecture it'. No modern vulcanologist could have put it better. For two hundred years, the business has been trying to predict when a volcano will 'blow'. But even with the most sensitive seismometers, and with the help of computers of great power, it is still possible to be caught unawares by Vulcan in retributive mood.

Ascanio Filomarino would have been delighted by the measurements that are now routinely taken around the Campi Flegrei. At the edge of the Solfatara crater, I spotted another one of the solar-powered instruments that were on Vesuvius. Thanks to refinements in the Global Positioning Satellites, the smallest heaves in the surface of the ground can now be measured. These systems are now so sensitive that it is possible to detect the depression of the surface of the earth produced by heavy snowfalls, as has been demonstrated by experiments in Japan. Far from being stable, the earth seems to pulse irregularly in ways we could never have imagined. For the Bay of Naples, the Argo Project is a network for Italian geochemical and seismic observations: the communications company Telespazio has set up a network to control seismic risk for the Ministry of Civil Defence, enabling seismic and geochemical data to be transmitted to a stationary satellite. Around Solfatara there is a main outpost and two secondary outposts. The latter are powered by solar panels and have electronic sensors to measure any seismic activity, as well as changes in gaseous composition around the crater, that might indicate a change in the magma chamber beneath. The data are transmitted to the main outpost, and thence by way of a parabolic antenna to the stationary satellite. This information is then available to research stations around the world. In theory, it should be possible to recognize the potential for an eruption far sooner than has ever been feasible in the past. A sudden acceleration in the 'inflation' of the ground, changes in gas emitted from fumaroles, or a juddery earthquake of the harmonic type – all might indicate an impending crisis. The most difficult problem will be making the local population take the warning seriously.

The story of geology has been one of letting go of permanence: from a world created just as it should be by God, we now have a world in flux. Volcanic eruptions may have once been considered a punishment for the sins of mankind, but they were not necessarily the symptom of a mutable world. If the 'temple' of Serapis demonstrated up and down movements beyond question, then it was only a beginning. It was evident in Pozzuoli that the land, rather than the sea, had changed level. But as the geological record was investigated elsewhere, it soon became clear that there were other times in other places when the sea was high relative to the land – as when it spilled over on to continents to leave a record of sedimentary rocks deep in their interiors. During the Cretaceous, when the white cliffs of Capri were laid down beneath the sea, there were similar sediments being laid down far and wide across the world – most familiar to the English in the white cliffs of Dover. Suess had recognized these transgressions of the sea. Fossils of a single species could be found in many localities, which enabled timelines to be cast across continents. The distributions of land and sea as they are today are just in passing, moments in the slow march of geological change. Former sediments could be raised high, to provide places where the silky-white villas of the Caprese rich enjoy a temporary vantage point, but destined to be reduced again to sea-level by the slow, inexorable mills of erosion.

How much more extraordinary still to contemplate the earth

wholly in motion. Nothing seems to be at rest. The surface of the earth dilates and collapses; the seas rise and fall; further, the very continents move. Suetonius would have dismissed me as a madman had I pointed out to him that Vesuvius is a consequence, ultimately, of Africa moving bodily northwards. But Africa really is on the move. The floor of the Mediterranean Sea is a collage of tectonic plates. Ultimately, that sea is doomed to obliteration when the main body of Africa ploughs into the European mainland in thirty million years or so. But now the sea exists in an awkward accommodation – as the saying has it, 'between a rock and a hard place'.

The northern edge of the African plate is plunging downwards beneath the southern tip of Italy, which allows the infinitely slow oceanic contraction to continue. Italy is twisted and swivelled in the process; the energy released deforms rocks to marble and uplifts the limestone hills. A whole series of Italian volcanoes are engaged in this congress of plates: Stromboli, with its continuous, grumbling eruptions; Etna, on Sicily, which has erupted recently and dramatically; Vulcano, the home of Vulcan himself, and the eponymous epitome of a volcano; and more than twenty others with less familiar names spanning much of the length of Italy and scattered through the Aeolian waters. The story of how these volcanoes relate to the movement of tectonic plates is a complicated one, and geologists do not agree on the details. However, all specialists seem to concur that the region behind the African collision zone has rotated anticlockwise. Rending of the earth's crust produced the Tyrrhenian basin here eight million years ago. The volcanoes were related to fracture zones that accommodated this convulsion in the skin of the earth; they are like sticky blood oozing from deep wounds where the earth's crust thinned. The jostling of the plates results in fractures in the crust – faults – movement along which caused earthquakes and tremors. The uplift and tilting of strata are the testimony to this activity. Ultimately, the energy needed to produce lava derives from the crunching drive of Africa northwards into Europe. As crust plunged downwards it partly melted, creating the magma which ultimately fed volcanoes. Lavas rich in the element potassium still retain a signature that proves that a proportion of melted continental crust must have been mixed up with oceanic crust. This magma recipe also conditions the fluid properties of the lava during eruption: at some times it flows in an almost docile, if relentless, fashion; at others, mixed with gas and water, it explodes in a series of devastating pyroclastic flows. Everything around the Bay of Naples is controlled by the movements and interactions of tectonic plates kilometres below the surface: the seen is under the control of the unseen; the surface is at the behest of the underworld. Exploring such connections is the theme of this book.

Even the most apparently ephemeral of earth's memorials are a reflection of a deeper reality. What could be more superficial than man's concern with his appearance: with cosmetics – the paint on the surface – that attempt to plaster over his own mortality? What could be more trivial by comparison with geological reality? The town of Baia on the western side of the Bay of Naples was born out of hedonism and beauty treatments. The hot springs there fed Roman baths of unrivalled luxury. There are still ghosts of paintings on the ceilings of the rooms where the rich went to cool off (or heat up) and giggle at the latest gossip, or discuss the hottest scandal of the first century. What modern-day Italians call the *bella figura* was just as important nearly two thousand years ago. The baths were fed from springs that were plumbed down into a tectonic reality that cared nothing for the carnal scandals of a two-legged ape that had only moved out of Africa a few thousand years ago. These springs were the exhalations of the magmatic unconscious. Yet Baia and the Pozzuoli coast invented the concept of the holiday: time out in luxury, to tickle the palate or the fancy. According to contemporary sources, the slopes of the bay were lined with marble palaces, and walkways furnished with columns, and with cool fountains for reflection and dalliances. Eduard Suess was disapproving: 'It was in the flowery fields of Puteoli, Baiae, and Misenum that under the Empire at the expense of a subjugated world the most sumptuous festivals were celebrated.' This area was like Nice on the French Riviera in the days of the English aristocracy, or the Big Sur coast of California in the days of the Hollywood glamocracy – except that it was on a scale altogether more grandiose. You can still get some impression of the vanished splendour and luxury, for Baia remains, although the plaster has mostly fallen off the walls and the paintings have often faded. The hillside where the stylish Romans strolled after their bath is still there, but it now has the atmosphere of a terraced provincial park gone to seed. The view across the Bay of Naples remains splendid, and with a little effort it is possible to imagine a continuous stretch of villas lining the bay. Close up, however, all is decay. Even the diamond pattern of the yellow tuff bricks, the *opus reticulatum* that built the walls, shows mortar standing proud of the weathered bricks it supports, for the rocks produced by a violent eruption do not necessarily make strong building stones. The earth movements in this area have submerged the ancient waterfront, so that it now lies more than 400 metres from the present shoreline. Part of the drowned city is still visible in the clear water. The thermal springs no longer bubble up in the ancient baths, since the tectonic wellsprings have moved on. You can still have a thermal bath on the island of Ischia, which lies off the north-western edge of the Bay of Naples and where the springs are alive and pumping. A doctor there will advise you on which particular elixir you need for your aches and pains; but fashion and geological plumbing have deserted Baia.

The western end of the Bay of Naples is the Capo Miseno. It is now a deserted spot, although it was once a great naval base for the Empire, and housed perhaps ten thousand sailors. Only scattered foundations and remains of columns attest to its former greatness. From here, you can look back across the Bay of Naples towards Vesuvius, with the Sorrento coast beyond, where this chapter began. It is a good place to reflect on historical and geological time, and the forces that have shaped everything in prospect: the bay itself, the craters around the Campi Flegrei, even the distant hills. This was the spot where geology could be said to have begun when Pliny the Younger, as a youth of eighteen in AD 79, observed from a safe distance the eruption of Vesuvius that obliterated Pompeii. His uncle, the elder Pliny, died in the eruption. The latter's *Natural History* was a cornerstone of natural philosophy for more than a thousand years,

Plinian style eruption of Vesuvius in 1822 illustrated by George Scrope (1797–1876)

so it would not be too much of an exaggeration to say that the future of all science was engaged with the magma chamber of one temperamental mountain. The younger Pliny described the cloud that proved his uncle's nemesis as resembling one of the umbrella pines, or Italian stone pines, that still provide welcome shade around the villas dotted about the bay. The volcanic cloud

> shot up to a great height in the form of a very tall trunk, which spread itself out at the top into a manner of branches; occasioned either by a sudden gust of air that impelled it, the force of which decreased as it advanced upwards, or the cloud itself being pressed back again by its own weight, expanded in the manner described; it appeared sometimes bright and sometimes dark, according to whether it was more or less impregnated with earth and cinders.

This type of volcanic event is still known as a Plinian eruption. The ash column can rise to fifty kilometres into the atmosphere, and then the ash can be spread for thousands of kilometres by winds. An eruption can alter weather patterns for months. The force behind the expulsion of the column is the result of gases expanding within the magma as it rises, as the overlying pressure is reduced. A kilometre below the surface the rising mass loses all coherence. The volcano violently boils over.

As for the pyroclastic flow of AD 79, it, too, reached Pliny the Younger. It travelled across the Bay of Naples, shedding its lethal load and losing strength. By the time it reached the young man it was little more than a miasma. It dropped the merest layer of fine ash over his sandals.

2

Island

Hawai'i is evidently paradise. There are Paradise Restaurants, Paradise Realtors, Paradise Tours, Paradise Apartments. The *Hawaii Star Bulletin* modestly describes itself as 'The Pulse of Paradise', thereby grafting paradise on to the qualities of a living being. There is a lot of business hanging on Hawai'i's paradisiac qualities.

When you first approach Waikiki, the resort town on the developed island of O'ahu, paradise is not the first comparison that comes to mind. One traffic jam is much like another, and vast hotels vaguely themed on ersatz Polynesian mementos are no vision of life in the Garden of Eden. To be sure, the lawns in front of the hotels are immaculately trimmed, palm trees lean out to greet you, there are even waterfalls tastefully constructed about the entrances, and there is a smile on the lips of every flunkey. This is paradise designed for the determined shopper: Armani and Gucci and Tommy Hilfiger outlets line up along the sidewalk (doubtless, too, in the Paradise Mall) alongside a hundred other familiar names to nudge the relaxed holidaymaker with bargains that will seduce them from their cash. The goods are mostly the same as can be bought in London or Rome or Tokyo – a kind of global cornucopia, deceptive in its promise of local idiosyncrasy. Most of the Aloha shirts are made in China. Perhaps the visitor should turn elsewhere to discover paradise.

Not far behind Honolulu, mountains rise surprisingly quickly, and they are clothed in forest. There is an easy walk through it to the Manoa Falls north of Waikiki. The little path dodges this way and that through the trees, ever upwards, often muddy. This is more like the paradise of the movies: vast trees soar away above you, and their huge trunks are decked with climbing plants, some of them with enormous leaves, or heart-shaped foliage blotched with yellow patches. These vines seem vaguely familiar from florist's shops, though here they grow on a giant scale. There is an intense and humid odour of prolific growth. You can almost hear the shoots squeezing upwards towards the sun. There are pale yellow spikes of fragrant ginger flowers on either side of the path. Within a few minutes, you are dripping with perspiration, for no breeze disturbs this extravaganza of unfettered growth. Piping noises echo somewhere in the canopy way above. Half-seen birds such as these are obligatory in Eden. When the waterfall is reached at last, some of your fellow-walkers cannot resist the urge to wade out among the rounded boulders to catch a fickle spray that has plunged 200 feet down a lava flow. Bathing in a pool in the midst of a primeval jungle is the dream of paradise on the holiday brochure.

But this, too, is a bogus paradise. Almost none of the plants that climb up the massive trees along the path are a native of O'ahu or the Hawaiian islands. Indeed, neither are the trees themselves. They are interlopers, brought to this remote place by humans. These plants settled in the tropics and thrived, displacing much of the native vegetation. The resemblance of the climbers decking the trees to pot plants is no coincidence: some of them are the same species that can be bought in a supermarket in Norfolk, England, or Plains, Iowa – as commonplace in their way as tomato ketchup. Even the sweet-smelling ginger plant that looks so at home by the pathside is a johnny-come-lately, an aggressive colonizer. This place is not so much Paradise Lost as Paradise Replaced – a paradise of aliens dressed up to look as if they belong. The massive assurance of the trees is play-acting.

The Hawaiian islands were once pristine. As remote from any major continent as anywhere in the world, they were originally colonized by a mere handful of hardy, far-travelled plants and animals – birds, insects, reptiles – that subsequently evolved prolifically in their new Eden. The species that appeared as a consequence were

Honolulu Harbour as it was in 1854. From Manley Hopkins (1862) *Hawaii: the Past and Present and Future of its Island Kingdom.*

endemics; that is, they were found nowhere else in the world. The islands became a natural evolutionary laboratory. There were several hundred fruit-flies found nowhere else, and an array of flightless birds pecked among the underscrub. This is where a caterpillar learned to be a meat eater. The landsnail *Achatinella* evolved a thousand or

more species. The familiar plant *Lobelia*, blue-flowered mainstay of a thousand hanging-baskets, evolved fantastical tubular flowers that could only be pollinated by even more fantastical birds – scarlet or yellow honeycreepers with bills as narrowly curved as precision surgical tweezers. The Bishop Museum displays glorious, ceremonial capes of Hawaiian chiefs fabricated from the feathers of countless honeycreepers. They must once have been abundant. These wonderful birds are now, alas, mostly displaced by interlopers – mynah birds and doves – with more ordinary dietary requirements. They can feed on the crumbs and scraps left by tourists where the honeycreepers dined solely on nectar. Even the flightless birds had their part to play in the original ecosystem: they ate the fruits of the aboriginal trees, whose seeds could only germinate once they had passed through the avian digestive system. But then, the introduction of the mongoose saw to the extermination of the flightless birds.

So why introduce the mongoose? These aggressive little predators were brought in deliberately from India to catch rats, themselves another introduction. The rats escaped from ships, doubtless, as they have all over the world. They threatened the sugar cane crop – which, of course, was yet another introduction, and one which transformed the Polynesian mixed economy of taro cultivation supplemented by fruit and fish into the specialized cosseting of a cash crop. But then, the Polynesians themselves had already introduced the breadfruit, and several useful species of palms. You begin to wonder at what point paradise first became corrupted. Nowadays, mongooses skitter across the road in front of you when you least expect it, cheekily self-confident. They must have made short work of endemic flightless rails and other birds. But the rats are still there. Mongooses are mostly diurnal, whereas rats are nocturnal. The extermination policy that introduced them was as pointless as proposing to introduce bats in order to eliminate wasps. Both mongooses and rats prospered while the birds disappeared. The few trees that remained from archaic times have no method of reproduction. They have outlived their propagators and have become sad remnants enduring from a vanished paradise. They are not entirely doomed because attempts in the Lyon Arboretum to regenerate them from culturing slivers of their living tissue have met with some success. The Arboretum where this work goes on is where you might get a hint of what might have been in the original islands – but carefully cultivated, a kind of Garden of Eden reconstituted. You begin to wonder whether you can go anywhere to see the real thing.

Hawai'i is actually a group of islands, all of them volcanic. The island of O'ahu is the one that people tend to imagine represents the typical Hawai'i: this is where the hotels and surfing beaches of Waikiki promise counterfeit paradise. Most of the islands, however, are completely different from this urban fantasy. The volcanic activity on O'ahu is quiescent. The other main islands are: Molokai, Kaua'i, Nihau, Maui, and the youngest, and by far the largest, known everywhere as the Big Island – strictly speaking, this island *is* Hawai'i, and it is still actively erupting. This is where you can go to see the world being made.

On the rainy side of the Big Island, on one flank of the Volcanoes National Park, there is a remnant of the original forest. This area is several thousand metres above sea-level, and the rain is often heavy. In the mornings a drenching mist can smother the landscape, only to be fried off by the sun before midday. The dominant canopy plant is the Ohi'a, a greyish tree of medium height, often gnarled and dressed with lichens, and carrying small, oval, dark green leaves that shine attractively in a certain light. Early in the day there is a silvery brilliance in the Ohi'a forest that cannot be matched anywhere else in the world. When in flower the Ohi'a is called *Ohi'a lehua*; the flowers look like old-fashioned shaving brushes made of dense red stamens. Several of the remaining honeycreepers earn their living from sipping the nectar of their blossoms, and there always *do* seem to be flowers somewhere in the Ohi'a forest. Around Volcano Village the understory is composed prominently of tree ferns. The commonest species is the hapu'u, *Cibotium*, a majestic and graceful fern with all the elegance of a green fountain. There are so many of them it looks almost as if the earth has sprung a series of verdant, spouting leaks. Other herbs and small trees clamber among the ferns, bewildering botanists who try to place them with their more conventional relatives. In this forest there is at least a chance that the piping you hear is from a native bird. The chirring is almost certainly the native cicada. But along the pathsides there are already plantains that you recall as weeds from Europe, the scourge of every lawn; and the seductive ginger plant pokes out from the undergrowth. There is trouble already in this paradise.

This jungle is simply structured, comprising only a canopy and understory. The Ohi'a trees are not like the dominating and diverse monsters of the Amazonian rain forest, with layer upon layer of tiering beneath them. Yet within these grey woodlands there are hundreds of species unique to the Hawaiian islands. Then we must add the fact that each island has a windward and a leeward side. Most of the rain falls prolifically on the windward side; the other side is in a 'rain shadow': clouds throw down what moisture they carry as they climb the mountains, but the further side remains dry. The animals and plants are different again on the dry flanks, tougher in several ways, survivors in the face of hardship. They comprise an entirely distinct community from that of the rain forest. Growing on nearly bare lava flows, the flora includes small relatives of the familiar cranberry: the ohelo carries a bright red, succulent berry that was once a staple item in the diet of the *nene*, the Hawaiian goose. The *nene* is a handsome bird that almost became extinct in the wild but was reintroduced successfully from ones bred in captivity. Ohelo berries are pleasantly tart, like watery cranberries, but scarcely the forbidden fruit of paradise. Ritual dictates that you must offer a berry or two to Pele, the fierce goddess of fire, before you eat them yourself. Many of the drought-tolerant species like the ohelo are rarities now, too.

Because the volcanic mountains rise to great heights there are some unique species adapted to alpine conditions. The most extraordinary of these is the silversword, a huge bundle of silvery, blade-like leaves looking something like a crouching, bristling porcupine. It lives high on the bare volcanic slopes at an altitude where little else will grow. It flowers and then dies. The flowering spike arises like some huge, columnar firework from the centre of the leaf rosette. Close examination reveals that each flower head is little more than a daisy – there are hundreds of these humble purple flowers on each spike. It takes the silversword twenty years to screw up the energy for its final floral pyrotechnic. This is what Hawaiian isolation has done to one of our most familiar flowers.

The remarkable forests with their remarkable animals, the rain shadow plants, the *nene*, and the hundreds of inconspicuous fruit-flies, all owe their existence to the geology of the Hawaiian islands. This is a place where the geology announces itself in everything you see. Only in Honolulu and Waikiki do the works of mankind obscure the works of nature: save for the star-fruit trees in the backyards, the neat suburban roads lined with well-tended villas surrounding these cities might be in almost any small town in Iowa or Michigan. North-American domestic vernacular architecture has become the *lingua franca* of middle-class habitation. On the remoter shores you may see the open canopy dwellings of the Polynesians (there are very few pure bred Hawaiians). On the windward shore of O'ahu these houses are often backed by steep cliffs of dark volcanic lavas. Scratch around almost anywhere and there will be similar volcanic rock beneath the dirt. The geology dictates the soil. Along the trail to Manoa Falls this rock weathers to something with the colour and consistency of gingerbread. It can be ground to crumbs in your hand. Constant tropical rain makes a mush of hard old lavas. The end product is a brick red soil called laterite. Its colour comes from all the iron (in the oxidized, or ferric, state) it contains, its other important element being aluminium. Laterite soil is not suited to growing many crops, but sugar likes it. The great cane fields of Hawai'i used to occupy much of the lower ground, at least from the nineteenth century onwards. Feral canes are still everywhere: to a European they look like hugely overgrown leeks. The bottom fell out of the market during the Reagan era, and now the great mills stand idle, and some of the fields are reverting to scrub. Others have been taken over by pineapple plantations. In the saddle or valley between the huge extinct volcanoes on O'ahu, the Dole plantations stretch for mile after mile along Route 99. The pineapple was once considered so exotic that it became a symbol of wealth to the aristocracy who alone could afford it; pineapples sculpted in limestone often adorn the gates of stately homes in England. It comes as something of a disappointment to see huge pineapple fields so relentlessly uniform in ranks of green rosettes. You expect to see trees as exotic as the fruit itself.

Isolation created the opportunities for the species to evolve that made the original paradise. The islands all grew as volcanoes from the sea-floor over the last five million years or so; the Big Island is still growing. Twenty miles off the south-east coast of this island there is an active volcano still hidden beneath the sea. The Lo'ihi sea-mount is steadily erupting, and one day it, too, will break above the waves, and a new land will be born. Within a year or two the first pioneer plant species will arrive to colonize the bare lava, their seeds perhaps being carried on the feet of a passing booby. The process of evolution will happen all over again. This insular birth is supposed to occur in fifty thousand years or so, a geological tomorrow.

The Hawaiian islands provide an opportunity to see the birth, maturity, and death of a landscape. Creation is here; so, too, is massive erosion: and it has all happened in a timescale of just a few million years, a span that we can begin to understand. The Polynesian peoples arrived by boat for the first time about AD 500 but a second wave of immigration from Tahiti was more or less contemporaneous with the Norman Conquest of England in 1066. The evolution of the web of interrelated island endemic species took thousands of times longer. Time enough for some species of birds to lose the capacity for flight, and for others to develop long curved bills. Think of what has happened in the thousand years since the Norman Conquest, all the advances and reverses and complexity of history, the technological revolutions, the rise and fall of empires. It then seems less astonishing that a complete and distinct biology should arise in a span of more than fifty thousandfold again.

The Big Island is the most southerly island of the group, and near its southern side you can witness the genesis of new crust. Lava has erupted from Kilauea for hundreds of years. Occasionally it blasts out in major eruptions, hurling volcanic bombs hundreds of feet into the air. Mostly, however, the eruption is comparatively benign, by volcanic standards. The kind of basaltic lava that has built Hawai'i is highly fluid, and charged with gas. It flows rather than explodes. A new lava flow cannot be entirely stopped, but it can be outrun if your house is about to be engulfed. The flow of 1992–7 blocks the coastal road that used to run southwards from the town of Hilo. It

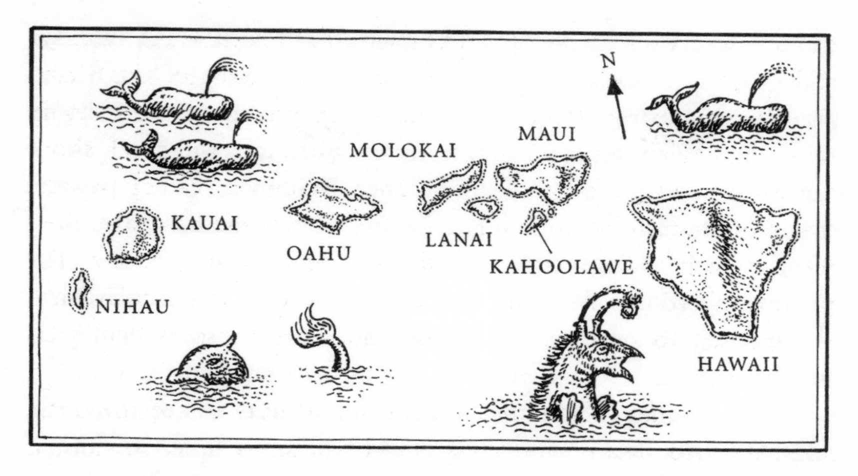

Sketch map of the Hawaiian Chain, the Big Island to the right, and older islands progressively to the left.

simply truncates the paved surface at right angles, abruptly. From one side it looks as if a gigantic load of tar had been dumped by a disgruntled contractor: the road disappears beneath the flow, and sure enough if you walk to the far side of the flow a few miles along the coast the road emerges the other side, apparently unscathed. But the surface of the flow is hard to walk over, being a mass of black and twisted lava. Sometimes it is only too clear that it has cooled from a sticky liquid. Braided curtains or wrinkled sheets of shiny, tarry lava heave and plunge under your feet. The texture of the surface is often described as ropy, and it is an apt description to anyone who has seen tangled masses of ropes on the side of a harbour. On steeper slopes, twisted clots of entrails come to mind. It is astonishing to stand in the midst of a huge lava field with the undulating masses of volcanic material stretching away as far as you can see, for this is a fresh-made world.

You are permitted to inspect the current eruption from a safe distance. Parts of the old road have recently been revived and you can drive very carefully and very slowly over graded parts of recent flows to get near to where the lava still debouches into the sea. Steam plumes, visible from miles away, rise continuously at the meeting between the new crust and the eternal waves, and there is a fierce hiss at the boiling junction. The stench of sulphur is everywhere, sharp in the back of your throat. If this is the breath of the deep earth, then it is poison. You must watch where you step over the recently cooled lava flows, for there are areas where the surfaces have heaved into cracked slabs, as if a vast tarmacadam airfield had been bombed almost to oblivion. It is easy to twist an ankle. On humid days water vapour combines with the sulphurous emanations to produce an acrid mist known as vog. As dusk falls, the brightness of the living lava becomes more evident. The warm red glow at the sea's edge has a brilliant orange heart. Then you witness an explosion where the combination of violent boiling, sudden cooling, and expulsion of gas result in luminous chunks – one might be the size of a pumpkin – rolling up into the miasma of steam; fireworks almost, but more inexorable. For the moment the lava wins against the ocean, but one day the balance will be reversed.

Now it is dark you can see other brilliant lights along the flanks of the landward slope. They form a line. It is easy to deduce that this line marks the current course of the flow. It is not at the surface, but flows in a conduit, a lava tube, a short distance under the inky wasteland. You can trace the lights to the vent itself, at Pu'u O'o on the flanks of the older Kilauea caldera. After the initial eruption from the new vent, the crust on top of the lava flow solidified, but the flow continued unabated beneath the skin covering over the tube. It is like an artery continuously bleeding the red blood of the earth. In places, the roof of the tube has crumbled away, and the lights on the hillside trace these windows giving into the streaming inferno beneath, glowing bright orange. There is a lucrative local trade in lava photography, and many Hawaiian photographers like to crawl close to the windows and record the streams of magma and the fountains of fire that splatter up from time to time. But there are dangers. Where the lava hits the sea it often builds out into an unstable platform. Only a few years ago two over-confident visitors were killed when the platform broke away into the violent and boiling sea. The process of creation is not merely dramatic, it can be lethal.

In the Volcanoes National Park, you can walk inside a lava tube, which has long since voided its last molten load. The Thurston Lava Tube now lies in the rain forest, and tree ferns decorate its entrance. It had a curiously familiar feel to me, and it was some minutes before I realized that this was because it had the exact dimensions of that other Tube – the Piccadilly Line tunnel in London – on which I travel virtually every day. It is indeed almost perfectly tubular. The walls are curiously smooth. There is nothing here to produce the stalagmites that adorn caves in Kentucky or Cheddar. Part of the tube has been illuminated, but you are permitted to go on into the darkness, at your own risk. It is a strange sensation to creep by flashlight into the guts of a former eruption, and just for a moment you might wonder if that rushing sound might be something other than the wind in the Ohi'a trees. But the dimensions of the tube do give you a very good idea of how much lava can be transported in an eruptive phase – by measuring the velocity of a flow it is easy to calculate the volume of an eruption. On the present eruption at Pu'u O'o, flow velocity is measured using radar through the 'skylights': since 1983, 300,000 cubic metres per day have been flowing down towards the sea. Creation can be calibrated.

The eruptions happening now are as nothing compared with those of the recent past. The Kilauea caldera remains as a testament to this activity. It is huge: four miles (6.4 kilometres) across. You come across it almost unawares driving through the lush Ohi'a forest. Suddenly the colossal hole of Kilauea Iki is before you, and you have glimpsed a different world. It is as if some irresistible force had pulled an enormous bung or plug out of the earth. Far below, the congealed lava in the crater still smokes from cracks in its surface. The whole pit is so clear of vegetation and so regular that for a moment you wonder whether such a structure might be man-made. It has been cauterized clean, and surely only human labour could carry out such an efficient scrubbing job? Then you can visualize that beneath the crusty surface there is still liquid rock, lying low. It somehow *looks* as if it had only recently finished cooking. Kilauea Iki erupted as recently as 1959, and there was a major flow from elsewhere on Kilauea in September 1982. The whole place is not exactly sleeping, more pausing for a moment in the middle of a bad dream. When the Volcano House Hotel was opened in the nineteenth century the visitor could look down at boiling magma pools from the balcony while sipping a Scotch and soda. From time to time spectacular lava fountains might create a pause in the conversation, but mostly the Hawaiian lava was benignly spectacular. Mark Twain entertained his readers in California with his graphic account of an eruption on 3 June 1886:

> A colossal column of cloud towered to a great height in the air immediately above the crater, and the outer swell of every one of its vast folds was dyed with a rich crimson luster, which was subdued to a pale rose tint in the depressions between. It glowed like a muffled torch and stretched upward to a dizzy height toward the zenith. I thought it possible that its like had not been seen since the Children of Israel wandered on their long march through the desert so many centuries ago over a path illuminated by the mysterious 'pillar of fire'.

On occasion, eruptions can be much more dangerous, particularly when ground water comes into contact with hot magma. Instantly, vast quantities of steam are generated, which punch out vents with colossal force, carrying rocks, volcanic bombs, and hot steam hundreds of metres into the air. A great roaring and hissing sound accompanies the drama. Such was the origin of Halema'uma'u, now an almost perfectly circular crater within sight of the Hawaiian Volcano Observatory. Its flanks show several former lava flows quite clearly, while stains of yellow smear its sides. The crater's eruption history has been closely studied. When it contained an active lava lake in the early years of the twentieth century, the level of the lake went up and down by many metres. It overflowed on to the floor of the Kilauea caldera in 1919 and 1921. In 1924 the lava withdrew, simply draining away via subterranean fissures. The unsupported sides of Halema'uma'u collapsed and created an obstruction – until groundwater penetrated its underground plumbing. Violent explosions then showered the surrounding lava plains with rocks, which still lie scattered over the surface. During the explosive phase the dimensions of the pit increased from 800 by 500 feet to 3400 by 3000 feet (243 by 152 metres to 1036 by 914 metres). A trail takes you past a series of steam vents from which the last gasps of this volcanic fury are exhaled. Superheated steam issues from inconspicuous holes – fumaroles – which are dotted over the ground. If you get too close you get scalded very quickly. This kind of steam is colourless and undetectable, and only when it cools down does it make a wispy plume. In the early morning, when the humidity in Volcanoes National Park is high, the whole area looks as if a dozen or so kettles were boiling away, each with its own steamy signal. The yellow patches that commonly smear the ground around the fumaroles are composed of raw sulphur, and there are red patches on the flows where the steam has oxidized the iron in the basaltic rock. The bright-coloured sulphur is brimstone – the fuel of hell itself. Brought up from the depths, it crystallizes at the cooler surface. It is easy enough to scrape a few crystals on to a knife. If you examine the crystals under a lens you will see that they form tiny, but perfect prisms. The fumaroles emit a gas which is also linked with sulphur – sulphur dioxide, produced when oxygen and sulphur combine. This is the gas that once made London the perfect place for Jack the Ripper to vanish without trace after his crimes; more than half a century later the smog was abolished by banning open coal fires. You can still get the same hellish whiff in big industrial cities in China and Russia. Sulphur dioxide is distinctly bad for weak chests and is heavily implicated in acid rain, since it is readily transformed into sulphuric acid. But here, on Hawai'i, its occurrence is wholly natural, the exhalation that accompanies the birth of the crust.

Halema'uma'u is the home of the goddess Pele. She is only one of a complex series of gods and goddesses that once influenced almost every aspect of life in Hawai'i. Everything in nature had a god responsible for it, and the gods themselves were capable of embodiment in a variety of natural things. A dolphin or a turtle may be the embodiment of Kana Loa, god of ocean and winds. All natural phenomena are extensions of the gods, who were prolific in their varied ranks and stations. In this pantheon perhaps even rocks had a kind of consciousness. The operation of taboos – or *kapu* – kept society ordered, quite cruelly on occasion. Pele, as you might expect, has a volcanic temperament in keeping with her preferred habitation. She was wont to take a fancy to handsome young men and embodied the dry and fiery leeward side of the island. Pele's lover and opposite, Kama Pua'a, was associated with rain, and with the windward side. One of her tricks was to change herself into an ugly old woman, ready to reward those who offered her charity, or launch an eruption on those who did not. After the hold of the other gods has faded, Madame Pele still seems to excite superstition. In the Volcano House Hotel there are pieces of pumice returned from all over the world. Accompanying letters claim that after taking this or that small piece of Pele's volcanic property the owners have had nothing but bad luck and so have despatched the pieces of purloined rock back to their rightful place in the hope that Pele will lift the curse. The eruption of Halema'uma'u was naturally attributed to Pele's displeasure. Perhaps she would be pleased to know that there is a volcano named in her honour on Jupiter's satellite Io.

If you rootle around among the more recent lava flows, you will find her tears and hair. Pele's tears are shiny, black, drop-shaped stones. They formed when hot lava sputtered or exploded into the air; as the tears fell to earth they cooled suddenly, frozen in shape. Now they can be found preserved in crevices in the top of lava flows. Pele's hair is spun from liquid lava: glassy filaments drawn out as the gases sped from the lava. It has something of the texture of spun sugar, but is rather brittle – the candyfloss of the earth. It has an almost golden sheen, so this conjures up a picture of Pele as flaxen-haired, but with black tears coursing down her cheeks. I also found an extraordinary light material called reticulite, a kind of froth frozen in spun glassy lava. It looks much like foam, such as might be blown

Frozen lava: Pele's tears, and Pele's hair, resting on pumice full of gas holes.

up by a landward breeze on a beach, but then strangely solidified. It is very fragile, and almost as easy to damage as foam itself. Intense frothing of the magma threw up this delicate confection. Eruptions can have a light touch in the right circumstances.

Lava flows can be well over forty kilometres long before they reach the sea, like the great flow of 1859, which runs north-westwards from Mauna Loa. There are two principal types of lava, readily distinguished in the field. The twisty, ropy kind that personifies flow – all congealed motion – is called *pahoehoe*. This is the easy kind to walk over: it is like traversing an irregular road that has been partially melted, heaved, and distorted. The other kind is all blocky and lumpy, a jumble of sharp chunks and clinker, rough and impassable. This is known as *a'a* lava, and it is truly dreadful stuff to walk over. I overheard a geologist say that a good pair of boots can be rasped to bits on *a'a* in a couple of months. The flows are initially as black as a Sunday hat, but as they weather a crusty brown predominates. Looking down on the landscape, from the side of Kilauea, fresh black flows overlie the older brownish ones, as if some giant had carelessly spilled a great pot of black paint down the hillside. Or it might be the shadow of a dark cloud cast upon the ground. Where the road has cut through the flows, you can easily see how one flow lies upon another. Often the surface of an individual flow is weathered, brownish, with an *a'a* topping, so that stacked flows have the appearance of a kind of volcanic club sandwich. The whole island is built of these flows, one on another. Perhaps a better image than a sandwich for the formation of the islands is a giant stack of pancakes: countless, endless sheets of congealed lava piled up, as if cooked for the fattest and most insatiable Polynesian god of gastronomy. My map tells me that the summit of Mauna Kea, the highest volcanic mountain on Hawai'i, is 13,796 feet (4205 metres) high. The other great volcano on the Big Island, Mauna Loa, is hardly less considerable at 13,679 feet (4169 metres). But this is only the part that projects above sea-level. The average depth of the ocean floor in the Hawaiian region is 16,000 feet (4877 metres). A simple calculation reveals that, measured from the sea-floor, their true base, these volcanoes are approaching 30,000 feet, or 9000 metres, high. Taken together, they make up one of the greatest structures on earth, higher than Mount Everest. Mauna Loa is estimated to occupy 19,000 cubic miles.

When submersibles were used to examine submarine eruptions – those unseen events that even now are building up Lo'ihi towards the sea surface – the form of the lava flows discovered was different from anything on land. Cooled rapidly as it belched out under pressure, each lava pulse congealed into gobs and lobes. The globular masses piled up. Volcanic rocks of this kind are known as pillow lavas. Ancient pillow lavas are easily recognizable. I first saw them underneath a lighthouse on the coast near Fishguard in western Wales, where they were nearly 500 million years old, but they did not look so different from some of those listed in Hazlett and Hyndman's *Roadside Geology of Hawai'i*. There are different processes again when the stack of flows rises above sea-level, when sea and lava engage in violent conflict. This is the battle that I had witnessed for myself, in the voggy dusk. Explosive cooling and the sedimentation of glassy fragments results in a rock with a characteristic speckly texture known as hyaloclastite. So you can now envisage the succession of flow types that would follow one another to construct a volcanic island: pillow lavas at first, then a mixture of pillows and hyaloclastites as the island wins the battle for emergence, and then pile upon pile of flowing *pahoehoe* and its crusty companion *a'a*. All these stages are exhibited in one or another of the Hawaiian islands.

The first western visitor to the islands was not slow to appreciate their mode of formation. Captain Cook recorded in 1778: 'The coast of the Kau district presents a prospect of the most horrid and dreary kind: the whole country appearing to have undergone a dreadful convulsion. The ground is covered with cinders and intersected with black streaks which mark the course of lava that has flowed, not many ages back, from the mountain to the sea. The southern promontory looks like the dregs of a volcano.' James Cook was under no illusions about this place as a kind of paradise. To him paradise would have been a much more orderly affair, a garden of organized orchards and well-tended herbs, perhaps with a passing resemblance to his home in Marton, Yorkshire. Cook was killed by the locals on his return to Hawai'i the following year, allegedly in retaliation for a flogging administered to a native thief. If there was a moment that marked an end to the islands' isolation it would be Cook's visit, for afterwards they were located accurately on a map for others to find.

* * *

The missionary William Ellis visited Kilauea in 1823, probably the first westerner to enter Pele's demesne. The perception of the place had changed utterly in forty years. In his *Narrative of a Tour through Hawai'i* (1826) he enthused that 'in appearance the island of Hawai'i is grand and sublime, filling the beholder's mind with wonder and delight'. The poet Samuel Taylor Coleridge read and approved. The modern version of the island as Eden was born.

The best views of the great volcanoes of Mauna Loa and Mauna Kea are from the air. From the ground, it is difficult to appreciate their colossal scale, and they are often obscured by clouds. When the sky clears, they do not tower in quite the way that mountains are supposed to. Rather, they loom. It is only when you realize that all roads directed towards them go relentlessly upwards, apparently for ever, that you begin to understand their height: it takes several days to hike to the cold top of Mauna Loa. The summit of Mauna Kea is considered the ideal place to mount an astronomical observatory, for above the clouds there is only the stars and the skies are ideally transparent. From an aeroplane, you can see why these giant Hawaiian volcanoes are known as shield volcanoes: they do indeed resemble upturned Roman shields, at least until they begin to be dissected by erosion. Their comparatively gentle slopes are no less than the natural angle engendered by the solidification of countless lava flows. The shield analogy fails in detail, for at the centre of Mauna Loa (and Kilauea) lies not a boss, but rather a great depression. Such a caldera marks the collapse of the centre of the cone as the lava, which once buoyed it up, drains away to the underworld.

The ages of the volcanoes on the Big Island of Hawai'i decrease from north to south. The youngest, Kilauea, is the most active and the most southerly. Mauna Loa is the next oldest, then Mauna Kea, then Hualalai near the western Kona coast, and finally the oldest, Kohala, at the north of the island, which last erupted about 100,000 years ago and the main shield of which was probably built by 400,000 years ago. We shall see that this progression is a result of plate movements.

The first phase of igneous development is the great shield volcano. Later, volcanic vents open up wherever a tongue of magma can find an outlet to the surface. Many parts of the Big Island have experienced the sudden expression of Pele's anger, for the early phases are often the fiercest. Around the main volcanoes the eruptive centres are localized along rift zones. These zones are the traces on the ground of planes of weakness marked by faults, along which lava preferentially penetrates. The Chain of Craters road in the Volcanoes National Park follows the eastern rift zone of Kilauea. As its name implies, there are craters all along it. Mauna Ulu erupted in 1969–74 and now its legacy is a vast field of black *pahoehoe* lava glistening in the sunshine, in some places smooth and undulating like massed kidneys, in other places twisted like intestines. A little searching will turn up more of Pele's hair, so this is a truly anatomical landscape. In little crevices in the lava there are ferns growing: it does not take long for life to reclaim the barrenness. Where the lava is broken it is easy to see the bubble-shaped holes from which gas has been released during the eruption. In places, it seems as much bubble as rock – clinker, you might say, or, more correctly, scoria. Further down the Chain of Craters road there is a pagoda at Ke Ala Komo with a wonderful view of the side of Kilauea. The landscape is terraced into a series of grassy hillsides. Each scarp is thirty metres or so high, and is the graphic expression of faults that prove that Kilauea is sliding into the sea. Even as the volcanic pile heaves itself thousands of metres above the sea-floor its edges begin to collapse, like the flanks of an over-ambitious children's sandcastle. The 1969–74 lava flows tip over the terraces like so much spilled treacle, and crawl all the way across the plains below to the sea. The cliffs are already more than thirty metres high, and constant erosion has forged natural arches.

Eruptions are spawned from a magma chamber – a fiery stomach – beneath the main volcano. As pressure builds up in the chamber it is released in the spewing, flaming fountains and vivid showers of lava that spill out from the crater. Tributaries of magma insinuate themselves through cracks in older flows: splits brought on by the relentless pressure from beneath. Once breached, a crack will spill forth lava until the source dries up. Occasionally, in a roadside cut, you will spot vertical feeder dykes that once fed liquid rock to the surface. They sit at odds with the general attitude of the rocks – a perpendicular injection through the layered skin of the volcano. As the magma builds up pressure within the chamber, the ground swells, as if the earth were taking a deep breath prior to strenuous activity. Sense the swelling and we may have a way of anticipating an eruption, and taking precautions against disaster.

At the Volcano Observatory on Kilauea, the eruptive activity has been monitored continuously since 1912. Batteries of instruments scattered over the ground are able to measure even the subtlest changes. Originally, the data were gathered by intrepid and persistent geologists. Nowadays, much of this information can be relayed instantly and electronically back to the Observatory, where computers do their usual job of totting it all up. Tiltmeters on Mauna Loa and Kilauea monitor the heave on the ground – they work like sophisticated spirit-levels – to an accuracy of a tenth of a microradian. That is a very small tilt indeed. Evacuation bottles take samples of the gases issuing from vents and fumaroles; levels of sulphur dioxide and carbon dioxide can be measured precisely back in the laboratory. Elevated concentrations signal hot breath issuing from rising magma. It has been estimated that between a hundred and two hundred tonnes of carbon dioxide are exhaled every day at Kilauea. This is magnified tenfold at an active eruption site: the breath of an eruption is not only choking, but stifling. A network of sixty seismometers records the pulse of the ground. Earthquakes precede eruptions as jitters do a first night. There are Global Positioning Satellites to record precise position – and any changes – by reference to satellite standards passing above in the skies. Even cleverer instruments can measure increase in pressure within the crust itself. A bore-hole dilatometer operates inside a bore-hole driven several hundred metres down into a lava pile. The instrument is essentially a bag of oil that senses changes in the 'squeeze' on the sides of the bore-hole. This meter is so sensitive that one deployed on the flanks of Mauna Loa detected a rise in magma under Kilauea eighty kilometres away and about three kilometres down. The crust must have tightened under the press of the filling subterranean reservoir and squeezed the bag. Other features of the physics of the earth, such as changes in the gravity and the magnetic field, are measured periodically. Taken together, all these different measurements provide a diagnosis of Pele's temper. And when she finally gives vent to her fury, another arsenal of instruments measures the temperature of her choler. Some of them are thermocouple thermometers, which measure heat directly. Others are optical pyrometers, which convert the colour of the erupting lava to a measure of its temperature. At about 1200° C, lava is white hot; at 1100° C it is yellow; then it fades through orange (900° C) to bright red at 700° C, while the dull red reminiscent of glowing embers of the Christmas yule log is about 500° C. Any colour at all would fry you soon enough.

The Observatory was founded by Dr T. A. Jaggar, who initiated the scrupulous series of observations that today still continue to provide the basis of our scientific understanding. He wanted to quantify the Hawaiian volcanic eruptions. At first, they had been more the subject of gasps of admiration or distressed hand-wringing. Then, through the nineteenth century, Hawaiian volcanoes came under the scrutiny of scientists who tried to deduce the role of the underworld in their formation. This was helped by the appearance of scientific journals, like the *American Journal of Science*, in which the results could be published, and the establishment of the US Geological Survey, which could pay an occasional salary. C. E. Dutton published his account of Hawaii in 1884, in which he identified the process of collapse as essential to the formation of calderas. He also recognized the rift zones radiating from the principal shield volcanoes. Of Mauna Loa he wrote: 'So extensive has each and every one [eruption] of them been that the greater portions of them always reach far beyond the limits of vision, and mingling together are lost in the confusion of multitude.' This paints the right picture of the bewildering profusion of vast flows and how they overlap in such a complex and braided way to build a single, great structure. Perhaps the giant stack of pancakes was not an entirely appropriate analogy after all, since the pile is built up from smeared dabs rather than sheets. For many years, the definitive account of Hawai'i was based on field studies that mapped out individual flows and that was based on an understanding of the relative ages of the main volcanoes. It was written by the great American geologist James Dwight Dana, who was seventy-seven when his work was published in 1890. He himself had the stature of a Mauna Loa compared with most of his contemporaries. But the eruptions of 1912 and onwards allowed many more physical measurements around the craters themselves. Curiously, Dr Jaggar, for all his pioneering objectivity, was convinced that changes in volcanic behaviour were related to an 11.1-year sunspot cycle. He looked to the sun rather than to igneous plumbing here on earth. His statistics are not now taken seriously, but the observations on which they were based are still used. There is a pattern, but it has nothing to do with the sun.

Most important, it is clear that the plumbing systems of the great volcanoes are all separate. They do not originate from a single magma chamber. If they had been intimately connected, movements in the lava fields of one should be obviously connected with events in another, just as a domestic heating system requires central equilibrium. This patently was not the case: a drain-out from Mauna Loa was not necessarily accompanied by a reaction from Halema'uma'u. With modern techniques it is possible to distinguish the source magma for each of the volcanoes; each bears a distinctive signature in the elements they contain, and these, especially the very rare ones known as the Rare Earth Elements, can be measured with precision of parts per *billion,* thanks to modern technology. The main volcanoes, then, are separately connected to the deep underworld.

Yet to the casual eye the rock type making up the lavas looks extremely similar almost wherever you are on the Big island: when fresh, it is black and fine-grained, occasionally glinting slightly if you turn it in the light. It frequently contains holes, or vesicles, especially nearer the surface of a flow where gas has escaped. Ultimately, it weathers to the gingerbread rock we saw near the waterfall on O'ahu. It is called basalt,* and is one of the commonest rock types on earth.

* Correctly speaking, Hawaiian basalt is not just basalt, but is a special variety enriched in silica known as *tholeiite.* This variety is typical of basalts extruded in the 'hot spot' situation.

There is nothing with which you can exactly compare its texture: heavy German black bread comes closest, perhaps. The pottery manufacturer Wedgwood went to a lot of trouble to produce a black porcelain called 'Basalte', which is now much sought after – it is certainly easier to collect examples of its natural namesake. You cannot often make much of basalt in the field. However, if you cut a slice from a fresh basalt deposit, and then grind it thin enough to see through, you can examine it under a petrological microscope. You will then see that it is a mass of tiny crystals, many scarcely larger than sandgrains. Basalt is evidently a composite rock. If you turn up the magnification further you will soon recognize that the most obvious of these minerals is transparent, forming tiny, elongate crystals, shaped like the fine chaff you can make if you rub brittle straw stems between your hands. These crystals are of one of the most abundant minerals in nature – feldspar; furthermore, they are of a particular kind of feldspar rich in the element calcium, termed plagioclase. A mineral displaying a pale green colour makes up much of the space between these prismatic crystals. This second important component of basalt is the dark mineral pyroxene, a compound of predominantly silica, iron, and magnesium. Then there is a green mineral called olivine. The olivine crystals in most basalts are imperfect, lacking clear crystal faces. Gem quality olivine is known as peridot, which has a subtle green light all its own. Chemists will recognize that the green is the colour of the element iron in its ferrous state. When you have studied a few rocks in thin section, these minerals become old friends, and much of their chemistry can be identified just by studying their optical properties, such as their refractive index. But some little black grains between the crystals never become transparent, no matter how thin you cut the section: these are metallic sulphides, usually iron pyrites. In many basalts, the memory of flow is retained in the orientation of the longer feldspars: they seem to blow in one direction, pointing all one way, like chaff in the wind. It is easy, then, to imagine this broth of crystals forming as the liquid magma cooled downwards progressively from white-hot, separating out into different minerals, which were then entrained in further flow. Cooling was rapid enough to ensure that the individual crystals had no time to grow large: all was flux. There is an urgency about this rock. When the flow cools even more quickly, there is no time to form visible crystals. A *glass* is the result: Pele's tears and hair are glassy, the product of the most ebullient phases of eruption, when Pele's irate lava was thrown skywards and froze in mid-air.

Hawaiian natives had an eye for the subtlest differences in the rocks. The lavas on the summit of Mauna Kea are glassy and flinty. They make very good stone tools, since their edges can be 'knapped' to keenness. All around the world, native wit has appreciated the technology implied by such stone. One of the craters near Kilauea is called Keanakako'i – literally, the 'cave of the adze', which was another source of superior stone. For pestles and mortars, more massive basalt, *pohaku*, was required. There were also game stones for rolling, a kind of Pacific bowls – *'ulu maika*. And stone has always been the recipient of carvings, or petroglyphs – in Hawai'i's case, often pleasantly rudimentary figures with arms and legs akimbo. The basalt was also piled to outline large squares in the ceremonial centres known as *heiau*s. They are forgotten now, but in the eighteenth century they would have been heavily populated, and cultivated all around. Somewhat forlorn in decline, they are slowly becoming engulfed with scrub and secondary forest. Even the red pigment that results from prolonged weathering of basalt had its use as a dye, a feature that some imaginative entrepreneur has revived, so that you can purchase Red Dirt Shirts from many outlets. The Hawaiian islands were stone-age homelands at one time, and their cultural possibilities were circumscribed by the potential of basalt. Rock ultimately rules.

The story of the volcano is not over when the great shields are complete and the calderas collapse around their summits. The magma reservoirs still have life in them. Late-stage volcanic eruptions are different. First, they are more violent, and they build steep-sided cinder cones, which resemble everyone's first notion of a volcano. Second, they are smaller by far. From high in the air they look like boils or carbuncles on the flanks of their parent volcano. They are built from a different kind of lava, much gummier than that of the free-flowing tholeiitic basalt. This is the result of changes in the magma chamber, where the liquid mixture has had time to evolve and so produce a more viscous alkali-rich lava. Magma evolution proceeds little by little over several thousand years, as heavier minerals crystallize out and drop slowly to the bottom of the chamber, enriching and altering the composition of the magma that remains. It's a kind of underworld fractionation. The type of rock that results is often described as trachyte and contains abundant crystals of a different kind of alkali-rich feldspar, such as sanidine, rather than plagioclase. The spattered cones can maintain a steeper slope than the fluid flows. There are several cinder cones near Honolulu on the island of O'ahu. The Punchbowl Crater standing high above the town is home to a tasteful monument to the war dead of the Pacific war. The crater floor is now all lawns and plantings, and you would scarcely guess that it was born of a violence commensurate with the conflict it memorializes. Diamond Head, which bounds Waikiki's western edge, is wilder, making a feature against the sky, its steep sides supporting rather miserable scrub (this is the drier side of the island), and displaying ranks of rough, brown volcanic rock-beds plunging obliquely towards the sea. Some spectacular surf gets up off Black Point. A few kilometres to the West, Hanauma Bay is a former cone breached by the Pacific. Shaped like a deep bite into the coastline, it is one of the few places where the novice can swim over corals by a close and protected shoreline. It has become a favourite tourist stop as a result, and the corals have not benefited from the abrasion of a thousand flip-flops. But you may still get a glimpse of Hawai'i's famous incarnation of Lono, god of rain, peace, and agriculture, a little bluish fish called Lumuhumunuknukuapua'a. On the way down to the bay you pass much clinker-brown volcanic rock in the cliffs. I thought my eyes were deceiving me when I examined this rock closely because it quite obviously contained chunks of white coral amongst its volcanic matrix. Bleached by time, the coral lumps seemed suspended like figs in a cake. Evidently, the explosive violence had been sufficient to punch a hole through a fossil reef and the smashed coral got caught willy-nilly in the blast.

There are three kinds of sand in Hawai'i: black, white, and green. The commonest kind is white sand, the staple feature of those brochures promising paradise. It creates the beaches on the older islands, always behind the fringing coral reefs. It constitutes the sea-front at Waikiki, and at Kahana on Maui. Coconut palms really do tower over these ivory sands, making little puffs of shade. Visitors like myself are accustomed to white sand being, well, sand – that is, finely-rounded quartz such as you find on the beaches of New England, New South Wales, or Newquay. Hawaiian sand is utterly different: it is comminuted coral and algae, the broken detritus of a hundred thousand storms washed up against the land. It has been churned to fineness in the massive winter breakers upon which surfers perform their improbable feats. It sticks to you. Quartz sand brushes off as you dry, but coral sand seems determined to add itself to your skin. It is light stuff, startlingly white, not rock at all. It is curious to experience its opposite just a day's journey away. On the southern shore of the Big Island, Punalu'u Beach is backed entirely by black sand. The beach seems to suck light in rather than reflect it. Take a handful of this sand and smear it out so that you can examine it under a hand lens, and it is easy to see that the 'sand' is composed of tiny, smoothed-out fragments of glassy basalt, which are quite shiny when they are moist. The grains have something of the lustre of black pearls. This sand is from a geologically young beach, freshly ground from the newest part of the island. There are no coral fragments offshore to dilute its dark purity. On this particular beach, huge Hawaiian green turtles bask. Perhaps they appreciate the warmth that the black sand quickly picks up from the morning sun. The third sand colour is a pale olive green, and it is much rarer. It occurs near Ka Lae on the Big Island, a promontory that has the distinction of being the most southerly point in the United States. This bleak shore is where older flows originating from Mauna Loa confront the full force of the Pacific Ocean. It is a slightly spooky place. An oddly uninterested man in an Information Centre (which contains very little information) offers to guard your vehicle for a small fee. From whom? There is hardly anyone around. The only trees are stunted and pressed downwards, reaching away from the sea. Near the sea's edge little pockets of green sand are tucked among the rocks. If you scoop up some of this material, a hand lens will reveal that each grain is a transparent crystal, rounded, green like bottle glass. These are olivine crystals. They have been concentrated from the eroding lavas in this special place by the particular combination of sea and wind winnowing away all other minerals.

This variety of sand is the most superficial aspect of the ageing of the islands. The greatest and newest island still lives and grows, with the red ichor of lava streaming through its arteries. The other islands are all about erosion and decay, after the death of the volcanoes that gave them substance. Maui lies north-west of the Big Island and is the youngest of the other islands. Maui may – perhaps – be dead, but it feels as if the corpse is hardly cold. Erosion is still in its early stages. Charcoal recovered from soil beds buried by late lavas can be radiocarbon-dated to show that there were large eruptions not much more than a thousand years ago. In 1786 a Frenchman called La Pélouse mapped a bay near the south-western tip of the island, which had already been obscured by fresh lava when the navigator George Vancouver passed the same spot seven years later. This eruption originated from the end of a rift zone, and could conceivably revive once more. Maui is an amalgamation of two volcanoes, West Maui to the north-west, and Haleakala to the south-east, connected by a lowland known as The Isthmus, an area scattered with ancient dunes. The shield of West Maui was complete 1.3 million years ago, while the main shield of Haleakala was built up layer by layer about 700,000 years ago. Later, explosive eruptive phases followed, and pock-marked the landscape with cinder cones. Some of the original form of the volcanoes is preserved. On the wetter eastern side of Haleakala there are thousands of cascades that are eroding deep valleys. But on the summit basin it can seem as if the acrid smoke faded away only yesterday. The scale is vast: the floor of the basin is more than 610 metres (2000 feet) below Kalahaku Overlook, and the highest cinder cone within it is 180 metres (600 feet) high, but by a natural *trompe-l'oeil* contrives to look much smaller. The cinder cones are arrayed in a range of reds – some raw and startling, others like old blood – that were painted on the rocks as the result of alteration of the lavas by steam and volcanic gases after the main eruption. The cone is only the accumulation of the coarsest scraps of lava coughed up during the eruption, built up from tossed volcanic bombs and gobs of lava tumbling down the growing slopes. Larger bombs still lie around on the bluffs: they are often rounded by their passage through the air and, where they are broken, their glassy skins prove how quickly they cooled. Much of the finer stuff would have been carried away by the wind as ash. The last blasts left craters in the top of the cones, like raw carbuncles.

O'ahu is older again: it grew above the sea nearly four million years ago. It, too, is an amalgamation of two volcanoes, but the dual mountainous spines of the island are the wreckage of the shields that once made it. The mountains are only minutes away from the urban anonymity of Honolulu. You can drive into them along the interstate Highway 3, a road that Senator Inouye managed to get built to connect the two strategic bases of Pearl Harbor on the leeward, and Kanehoe on the windward shore of the island: allegedly it was the most expensive road in the world. After emerging from a tunnel you seem to fly alongside the most precipitous cliffs; yet these mountain-sides are carved and grooved with valleys, which are so steep they seem to be draped over the scenery. No matter how sheer the slope, everything is covered with a green blanket of ferns and trees. Within minutes the view is wrapped up in clouds and it begins to pour with rain. Mark Twain perfectly described this eroded volcanic panorama in April 1866: 'It was a novel sort of scenery, those mountain walls . . . Ahead the mountains looked portly – swollen if you please – and were marked all over, up and down, diagonally and crosswise, by sharp ribs that reminded one of the fantastic ridges which the wind builds of the drifting snow on a plain . . . the whole upper part of the mountain looking something like a vast green veil thrown over some object that had a good many edges and corners to it.' Twain was free with references to Eden and to paradise in his letters. But this island, like all the others, is doomed to return to the sea above which it once had the temerity to rise. Is paradise necessarily eternal?

Twain was right to use the analogy of hidden struts propping up the improbably steep mountain slopes. They are actually partly bolstered by the vertical supports of basalt feeder dykes. These once supplied the great lava flows that built a shield volcano, long since ruined and dismantled by time. Just as reinforced concrete pillars sustain a soaring tower, dykes act as struts supporting the beetling precipices. The steepest drop of all is at the Pali Lookout. You can drive there easily enough through forested slopes, but when you reach the top, the prospect westwards into the sheer drop of the Ko'olau caldera is enough to make your legs go peculiar. A thousand tourists try, and fail, to capture the view on film. It was here in 1781 that King Kamehameha I (known as 'the Great') drove three hundred warriors of the King of O'ahu over the cliff to their deaths, thereby uniting most of the islands under his rule. A highway named after him runs around the island.

If you follow King Kamehameha's road close along the windward shore of O'ahu, you see something of the island as it was before the appearance of the first tower block. In spite of the dominance of secondary vegetation, paradisical thoughts come easily. It is a lazy-feeling place, green and lush, with open verandahs dotted along an almost continuous coral-sand beach. There are delicious bananas, and papaya, and fresh coconut milk to drink. I thought of the medieval Earthly Paradise – an alleged island of perfection and immortality located far out to sea. (It is actually marked on the *Mappa Mundi* in Hereford Cathedral, located near India in that eccentric geography.) Perhaps the memory of this ideal place does linger somewhere in our psyche. A remote island with coconut palms fringing it, like hair round a tonsure, and coral reefs' surf delineating a line no more than a swim away from shore, seems to chime with an idea of escape from the worries of life into primordial calm. Hawai'i was made this way, and the causes are wholly geological. Along the shore, cliffs of bedded lava of the Ko'olau caldera sometimes squeeze the road into a narrow belt beside the sea, without room even for a dwelling. At Kualoa a marvellous vertical-sided valley almost reaches the sea; offshore, there is a stack known locally, and appropriately, as the Chinaman's Hat. This side of O'ahu, far from being the product of slow and peaceful weathering of the crust, was the result of a catastrophe. The steep topography was the consequence of an enormous collapse of the eastern half of the original Ko'olau Volcano. It slid off the edge and into the Hawaiian Deep as if it had been amputated, creating a tidal wave of almost inconceivable power. This event is known as the Nu'uanu Slide. Nor is it unique. On the island of Molokai the eastern volcano was virtually bisected when its northern flank collapsed into the Pacific Ocean. The great slide left a scar that now makes the sea cliffs along the northern shore; and they are possibly the most spectacular cliffs in the world: 24 kilometres long and rising vertically to 11,000 metres. Molokai is but a sliver now. When their volcanoes die, islands perched in the midst of an ocean begin to founder.

The most north-westerly, most eroded, and oldest island is Kaua'i. This is where you must go to see the maturity of a volcanic island. It is the gutted remnant of a single, huge volcano, Wai'ale'ale, which still sits at its centre, 1576 metres (5170 feet) high, and almost always veiled in cloud. Although much of the island has been weathered down to soil, and is heavily cultivated, the mountains remain extraordinarily rugged and remote. The Alaka'i Swamp has the reputation of being the wettest place on earth, and it is so isolated that relatively few interloper plants have yet established themselves there. It is one of the last havens for native birds: there are still twittering honeycreepers among the lichen-clad branches of the Ohi'a trees. There were massive slides on Kaua'i, too, the largest of which left as its legacy the greenclad, inaccessible, and mighty cliffs of the Na Pali coast (the movie *Jurassic Park* set its dinosaurs down here). The forbidding cliffs mean that no road can circumscribe the island, and part of it remains inviolate. From the viewpoint at the top of Na Pali you can look down on helicopters taking tourists along the cliffs. From this height these machines look like mosquitoes skimming alongside the hide of a great, wrinkled elephant. It is hard to believe that, in former times, even the most remote valleys on this coast supported native Hawaiian villages.

Kaua'i is dissected by huge, eroded valleys. They are ripping into the volcano's heart and will one day strip out its lava flows and dykes. The island will not be ground down so much as wasted away. You can get some idea of the rate at which this happens at Wailua Falls, where twin, 25-metre waterfalls plunge over a massive lava flow. This resistant flow is underlain by a rubbly looking flow that is clearly more susceptible to erosion than its overlying neighbour, thus becoming continually undermined; pieces of it eventually break off and fall into the waters below, ensuring that the precipice remains sharp. Hence the falls fitfully retreat, and a gorge grows seaward of them. This gorge was excavated through some of the later, stickier lavas that are a couple of million years old. Since the gorge is between three and five kilometres long, very approximately, the lavas retreat in the gorge at 1.6 kilometres per million years. There are all kinds of complications possible – for example, the relative sea-level has not been stable – but this is probably about the right order of magnitude. We can imagine that twenty million years or so would have to elapse for similar erosional processes to traverse the island. When the island finally reaches close to sea-level there will no longer be sufficient elevation to produce the rainfall that drives the erosional machine. The island will be ready to sink slowly beneath the waves.

The most spectacular valley is Waimea Canyon, which has been described as 'The Grand Canyon of the Pacific', a description that is woefully inaccurate as far as the geology is concerned. However, the epithet 'grand' is unquestionably apt. For the Waimea gash has opened up into lavas that reflect only a geological instant compared with the billion years or more of strata that are on display along the Colorado River: but what a display this brief moment of geological history has given us! The Waimea River cuts into two series of lavas and their related volcanic rocks. The Canyon is at least 22 kilometres long, 1.5 kilometres across, and up to 228 metres deep. A road runs up its western side, so that if you stop regularly on the way upwards you are vouchsafed intermittent views across this vast dissection through a volcano; and every view you have is a surprise. The sides of the valley are striped with the flows that give them a spurious resemblance to the strata of Colorado. There are pinnacles and ridges, often wisped in cloud. You wonder that there could be so many shades of red, which change and change again with the angle and intensity of the sun. The slopes are dappled with reflections of the clouds, which enhances the drama of it all. As you get higher, native vegetation takes over, so a prospect might be framed by the dangling leaves of the beautiful *koa* tree, each leaf a gently curved, trembling sickle. The course of the river is shown only by a thin line of green impossibly far away in the base of the valley – how could such an insignificant trickle grind away such a mountain-side? Then you notice isolated buttresses of weathered lavas, some beginning to totter. Where there have been cliff falls and landslides – the evidence of debris lies before you – in your mind's eye the whole process can be imagined. As in a cartoon where the speed absurdly redoubles, you envisage the rise of the shield volcano, catastrophic collapse of its sides, and initiation of the rift zones, then the blasting of late lava cones and the inroads of streams into the caldera, and finally the rotting of its lava by the elements and vegetation and its eventual erosion to a stump of its former mightiness. It is more challenging to imagine the sheer weight of these vast volcanic constructions on the ocean floor. Once they have ceased being built, they start to sink. This is because of the kind of isostatic adjustment that was explained above. Everything is against the survival of the islands: once born, they struggle above the waves, only to be assaulted by the elements, but they are already sinking under their own mass of basalt. If this is paradise, it is a kamikaze paradise.

There are messengers from the underworld preserved among the lavas. Occasionally, geologists have discovered places where the contents of the magma chamber itself survive. Because they cooled more slowly, these rocks are composed of large crystals, which catch the light on a fresh example, but they are similar minerals to those in the basalts: plagioclase feldspar and pyroxene and some olivine. These lend the rock a comparable dark colour: it's heavy and oppressive in a hand-specimen, but lovely and lustrous black-and-grey when polished. It is known as gabbro and is thought to form the lower layer of the oceanic crust at about four kilometres depth and to comprise a layer up to six kilometres thick, making it one of the most abundant, if least recognizable, materials on earth. Then there are small boulders of other kinds of coarse-grained rocks, much rarer than gabbro, brought up from the innards of the earth in the explosive events that accompanied later phases of eruptions. These are envoys from the most alien parts of the underworld. They are collectively known as xenoliths, Greek for 'foreign rocks', and they are indeed out of place on our green planet's surface. Their natural habitat is in the nethermost kingdom of Pluto, from which they have been abducted by the pull of eruption. They look like rocky chips, or triangular to spherical bodies dotted within the main mass of basalt. They often weather to a different colour, a leprous brown, as if distressed by their journey to an alien sphere. They rot readily. Most are varieties of peridotite, and it will be recalled that peridot is the more glamorous name for the green mineral olivine, so coarsely crystalline olivine is an important constituent of this rock type. Varieties of peridotite are distinguished by their mineral composition; for example, dunite is a peridotite which is virtually all olivine, and a dense, dark green in colour. The most important variety is called lherzolite: its list of constituent minerals includes a lot of olivine but also feldspar and pyroxene, and often small quantities of two other minerals: garnet and spinel. These last give a clue to the conditions from which these strange fragments were recruited, for they form at high temperatures and pressures. These superficially unimpressive fragments of rock are incredibly important, for they provide us with just about the only direct evidence of what rocks are like, deep, very deep, *down there*. They have been hijacked from the mantle. The inner earth is green, too, but a rich green such as is seen on the leaves of climbing plants in the rain forest, the green of the forest floor at Manoa Falls. Incredible though it may seem, these little chips are what most of the earth is made of.

The basalt lavas of Hawai'i are derived from the selective melting of such mantle rocks. As a whole, rocks of this type are referred to as mafic, because of the importance of magnesium and iron in their composition. Chemists appreciate the subtleties of differences between their various species, but to us the extraordinary thing is the differences that appear once the breaking and dissolving powers of rain and sun and plants have wrought their metamorphosis. So much variety wrung from a seemingly uniform raw material spewed from the depths is a wonder worthy of an Earthly Paradise.

Putting the facts of the Hawaiian chain of islands together, what can be deduced? First, think about the age of the islands, and the state of their decay. The youngest island is Hawai'i itself, the Big Island, erupting steadily, still building itself from its deep magmatic wells, shields still turned to the sky. Except to the south-east of it, a new island is growing beneath the sea, and will one day take its place. Even *within* the Big Island the younger volcanoes are to the south-east. Alas, the great shields afford no protection from geological inevitabilities. Maui to the north-west of the Big Island is extinct, but hardly cold (it may still have life in it). Its recent history is written all over the landscape. The small island of Lanai was once part of it. Following the same line to the north-west, Molokai and the Oah'u are still older, more worn down, with major slices from their sides collapsed into the deeps, presaging their ultimate ruin. The edges of the old calderas are now fantastically fluted by erosion; a lot of the volcanic rock that was once black and tough is weathered soft as cake, and is much the same colour. Thence north-west again to verdant and rich Kaua'i, the oldest island of all, gouged by chasms of erosion digging towards its very heart. Geologists can see into the deeper layers of volcanoes thanks to this progressive erosion.

As an aside, I should not forget to mention Ni'ihau, west of Kaua'i. This is the island that nobody can visit; it is known locally as 'The Forbidden Island'. Can this be where Forbidden Fruit still grows? Is this the real Garden of Eden? It is easy to see it from the Na Pali heights on Kaua'i. It is a small island, representing just one flank of an ancient and decayed volcano, the rest of which foundered into the ocean. It is privately owned by a family called Robinson, who forbid access to outsiders. Of course, there is nothing like the word 'forbidden' to make you itch to go to it. It is now the last bastion of the Hawaiian language; McDonald's has no franchise there, and it is beyond the dominion of Colonel Sanders. Fish is still farmed in the traditional way. Its total privacy has guaranteed the survival of a culture which has blended with the American way elsewhere to the point where the enquiring visitor begins to wonder what, if anything, is authentic. There is such a thing as an authentic hula dance, but it is not the one you see in the Hilton Hotel; and even grass skirts did not originate on Hawai'i. The Robinsons have taken on the role of the traditional Lord, and thereby kept this island race alive: the honeycreepers of *Homo sapiens.*

The islands age on a line from south-east to north-west, progressively and regularly. Each island was created by lava, but then the source died. One way to encompass these facts might be to propose that the heat source of the volcanoes migrated south-eastwards, one by one. Such was an early explanation. But what if the tables were completely turned, so that the fiery source of magma was fixed, and instead it was the volcanoes that moved? Or, to be more accurate, crust passed over a fixed heat source, so that its volcanic progeny erupted in sequence in harmony with this movement. As long as a favoured volcano lurked above the source of magma, it would grow and grow above the sea, flow by flow, eventually forming a shield, like Mauna Loa. This would be how islands were created. Life would colonize the new land, seeded from the next oldest island. Isolation from the neighbours might then engender another endemic species. Thus, even biological richness might be accounted a geological phenomenon. The effect can be simulated, more in spirit than in truth, by moving a sheet of thickish polystyrene foam a few inches over a lighted candle – carefully, I should add, and outdoors to avoid any toxic fumes. When I tried this experiment at the right speed the sheet did not simply melt in two; rather, it became corrupted with blobby, burned holes in an approximate line – some large, some small. Islands in the negative, you might say.

Then, as the tectonic conveyor moved the plate onwards, away from the heat, the island would begin to founder slowly under the intolerable load of its massed lava layers. The crust would adjust to the weight loaded upon it; unstable slopes would break along faults, and, once in a few dozen millenniums, huge slides would collapse and tumble to the same sea-floor above which the islands so impertinently rose. Another of these catastrophes may happen even now, carrying a slice of paradise to oblivion.

The moving crust is part of one the great tectonic plates of which the earth is composed: the Pacific Plate. Hawai'i is almost in the middle of it. The fixity of the magmatic heat source supplies a wonderful test of the reality of plate movements, because it provides a fixed marker on this peripatetic earth of ours. In a world that shifts, here is an igneous reference whose fidelity has been tested over millions of years. If the theory is right, it will be relatively easy to calculate the rate of movement of the Pacific Plate over the volcanic source. The first direct measurements using modern instruments were made on Maui, at Science City on Haleakala. It seems that the Pacific Plate moves north-westwards at about ten centimetres, or four inches, a year. Hair grows much faster. Cumulatively, this is all that is needed to throw up new crust, make an island, and move it onwards to begin its destruction.

What of the heat source that has been so steadfast while invading species, and belatedly humankind, have settled upon its productions? The lumps of peridotite preserved as xenoliths – those strange rocks so far from home – give evidence that there is more or less direct plumbing down into the depths, way below the crust itself. The persistence of the site suggests a permanent flow of energy coming from far inside the underworld, from which strange emissaries with strange names like lherzolite bring news of alien spheres. They come from a high-pressure world, brought upwards by what has been called a mantle plume. Despite the name, a plume is not liquid; at great depths solid rocks behave in a curious way. A plume is a high energy, hot 'jet' of solid rock that rises through the mantle. Many geologists believe that plumes originate at a depth of nearly 3000 kilometres. Where the plume hits the crust, it is called a hot spot. The paradise of the Hawaiian islands is thus the product of the most direct route to Hades we have on earth. Heat is lost from the interior of our planet by means of these ducts, which maintain the same position for millions and millions of years. Not all the magma that erupts as lava on the surface, however, has streamed directly from unfathomable depths. Much of it is generated by heat melting of peridotite – strictly speaking, its variety lherzolite – at about a hundred kilometres below the surface. The kind of magma that is produced is dependent on the exact conditions of temperature and pressure, which change with depth. This can be simulated by 'melting' experiments carried out inside special pressurized apparatus in the laboratory – a kind of pressure-cooking. The peridotite is partially melted to generate the most stable magma under the ambient conditions of pressure and temperature: basalt magma is the result. The magma then seeks out weaknesses above and, once the ocean floor is breached, the growth of the shield is relentless. A magma reservoir forms within the growing volcano at two kilometres or so below the surface, which is where the density of the magma matches that of the surrounding rock. Magma is delivered into the chamber in 'pulses'. Its upward passage has been monitored by measuring the small earthquakes generated during its movement: a newly-cooked stew of magma can erupt just a month or so after it starts to rise in the mantle. When the new batch arrives in the magma chamber, the ground draws its breath, and the tiltmeters register; then comes the exhalation of lava. Thus goes the respiration of the living earth as it generates new crust.

The detailed structure of Mauna Kea on the Big Island is currently being investigated by means of a deep bore-hole in the old airfield at Hilo, which is scheduled to reach a depth of 6000 metres (the lava at this level should be 700,000 years old). It is hoped that this deep probe will reveal some of the secrets of the mysterious mantle plumes.

The time represented is long enough to record the shift of the volcano from off the centre of the plume. There is a lot of clever science that can be carried out on the fresh, unweathered rocks recovered from the bore-hole. Very precise measurements of abundances of elements like barium show when the later, alkali phases of eruption are reached. Other rare elements, like neodymium, exist in more than one isotopic form, the ratios of which can provide a measure of the depth from which the flow material may ultimately have been derived. These are like xenoliths, but at a molecular level: hidden messages from the underworld that require the most sophisticated tools of modern science for their translation.

So the increasing age of the islands towards the north-west is now readily explicable as the ancient track of the moving Pacific Plate. Modern studies suggest that the Hawaiian hot spots are probably paired: there may well be two of them, side by side. In spite of their common cause, rare earth elements tell us that each volcano is in detail an individual: every version of magmatic plumbing is unique. The logic of the plate tectonic explanation for islands demands that north-west again of Kaua'i there must be further islands, still older expressions of the hot spot(s). So it proves to be. There is a whole chain of islands, their rock outcrops now effectively submerged, aligned along the Hawaiian Ridge; northwards again there is a train of submerged volcanic cones known as the Emperor Sea-mounts that extend all the way to the Aleutian Trench at the edge of Asia. Once deep beneath the waves, sea-mounts are protected from further major erosion. In total, this chain of volcanoes extends across more than thirty degrees of latitude. Drawn upon the sea-floor is a line of geological time, burned into its very fabric. There were still dinosaurs alive at the time the first islands over the hot spot were erupting. It has taken more than seventy million years to build this memorial recording the slow march of plates across the face of the earth. For once the cliché is true: this trace is literally a graphic illustration of the span of geological time. Recall that everything I have described in the Hawaiian chain – from the birth of an island to its erosion – has taken less than 10 per cent of the time recorded by the complete chain of islands related to the same hot spot. Now, multiply the time taken for the formation of the *entire* chain of islands by ten, and this will still be only about one-sixth of the age of the oldest Archaean rocks on earth. To put it another way, imagine a plate spinning about six times around the whole world with a speed not much exceeding the rate at which our fingernails grow. This is a more realistic – more graphic – way of signifying the sheer immensity of time involved in earth history than the twenty-four hour clocks, or running tracks, or the other commonly used analogies that attempt to bring geological time down to a domestic scale. To collapse time by whatever analogy is to misunderstand it. You have to think hard, in order to appreciate the geological scale. As John Keats said:

> Time, that agèd nurse,
> Rocked me to patience.*

The islands of the Hawaiian Chain to the north-west of Kaua'i are mostly atolls – circular reefs surrounding a warm lagoon. The volcanic islands themselves may have sunk below the waves but the corals that are ultimately founded upon them continue to live close to sea-level. Charles Darwin himself when he was naturalist on the voyage of HMS *Beagle* in 1837 made observations that allowed him brilliantly to deduce an explanation for atolls. As in the reefs that form a clear white line along the shore of Oah'u, coral growth begins close to land in the early stages of the life of a volcano. Most reef-forming coral can only grow in shallow water, since the algae that live inside the tissues of massive corals need light – without it they fade and eventually die. And, of course, the shield volcanoes are surrounded by deep water, so corals may only perch on their margins. As the islands sink, as sink they must, the corals grow upwards. They are as vigorous as forest trees. Built on the firm base of their own dead skeletons, the coral animals comprise no more than a skin of living tissue. When the island eventually subsides below the waves the corals keep abreast of sea-level, and they continue to fringe their

* *Endymion: A Poetic Romance* (1818), bk i.

vanished host. Their waste fills the lagoon inside the reef, white sand that reflects the sky so perfectly as to produce the most aquamarine water in the world. It is astonishing how much debris a healthy coral reef can yield, for as much or more as ends up in the lagoon is tipped seawards to buttress the whole structure. Darwin's scenario remains definitive. In 1910, R. A. Daly added further observations about changing sea-levels that would have inevitably been associated with the glacial epoch. During the maximum extent of the glaciers in the northern hemisphere, so much water was locked up in ice that global sea-level was greatly lowered. Then surf would have renewed its onslaught on some of the volcanic islands. So the actual history of the coral reefs on any given island or atoll might prove to be rather complicated, depending on the relative trade-off between sea-level and subsidence rate. There will be places where the sea deepened so rapidly when ice-sheets melted between glacial pulses that reef construction was perforce abandoned, as in the battle that happens on every sandy beach in summer as the tide comes in, when small children vainly pile sand against implacable waves to protect their carefully-constructed castles. In other sites, a coral reef may have grown when sea-level was high, only to be stranded as a bleached fossil when the waters once more withdrew. These reefs are like ghosts of the real thing: wan, skeletal, and retaining no trace of the brilliance of marine life, but the intricate lattices of the corals are still unmistakable, even in petrifaction. There are several of these bleached reefs on the island of Molokai, which has probably stopped sinking. Eventually, however, steady and unstoppable plate motions carry any island beyond the tropics to a place where corals cannot grow. In higher latitudes they are preserved only as fossils on the sea-mounts where they once prospered. Such is the end of paradise.

Plate motions provide a marvellous, yet simple explanation for a range of apparently disparate facts about the earth, several of which have been the subject of speculation for more than 150 years. The march of erosion north-westwards through the Hawaiian islands, and the ever-southerly birth of new volcanoes; the prolific endemic species on those islands; the line of sea-mounts and atolls and volcanoes, of which the Big Island forms the largest and the latest; Pele's fury and her subsequent quiescence; even the colours of the beach sands: they are all explicable by a combination of hot spots* and the movement of the Pacific Plate. Can there be a more gratifying example of how plate tectonics has transformed the way we look at the world?

* Science moves on. As this edition goes to press, a 'counter culture' questioning the reality of mantle plumes has started to surface in the scientific literature. It is early days, but this may prove to be the basis of another paradigm shift in the coming decades.

3

Oceans and Continents

The Hawaiian Islands are remote. It is hard to appreciate quite how far away they are from any continent, when an aeroplane can whisk you there in a few hours from San Francisco. As you look through the cabin windows at endless blue water, time seems to collapse, hours blur . . . yet all the time you pass over the vast and apparently featureless Pacific you are also traversing an incalculable stretch of basalt. Down, down, far below the waves, into the dark abyss where no light reaches except the luminous flashes of deep-sea organisms, the sea-floor is dressed in sediment – but this is only a thin blanket atop five kilometres or so of basalt. If some terrible explosion in the sun were to vaporize the seas and blast clear its sedimentary top-dressing, the Pacific hemisphere would be black – the dark, matt signature of basalt. The area floored by varieties of this igneous rock covers about two-thirds of the earth's surface. It is invisible to a passing satellite because this is an area that coincides exactly with the major oceans. Basalt provides the lining of the basins that cradle the seas. There are 363 million square kilometres of sea-floor; there is a lot of basalt in the world.

The depth of much of the ocean floor lies at about 10,000–16,000 feet (approximately 3000–5000 metres). It has been observed that we know more about the topography of the moon than we do about some parts of the ocean floor. It is an extraordinarily difficult place to reach. Bathyscaphes are designed to withstand the enormous pressures that come with depth. They are like small, riveted coffins of steel, lowered for hours into the dark. Modern successors include the submersible vessel *Alvin* operating off the research ship *Atlantis*. Few people have been privileged to make the journey to the Deeps, and until a few years ago our knowledge of the ocean floor was negligible. Anything could hide there. One of my early cinematic memories is going to see Jules Verne's *20,000 Leagues Under the Sea* with James Mason playing an obviously deranged Captain Nemo (Latin for 'Nobody'). What stays in the mind about this film is not so much the jerkily animated giant squid as the sheer mystery of the depths. When Eduard Suess was writing – not long after Verne, and a little more than a century ago – it was still possible to imagine whole continents foundered upon the ocean floor. The lost land of Atlantis – paradise, even. The dredging of samples was technically difficult. Maps made by soundings were hardly possible. The greatest single advance in the nineteenth century was the voyage of HMS *Challenger*, the first ship equipped for, and dedicated completely to, oceanographic research, which steamed out of Portsmouth in December 1872. *Challenger* made thousands of measurements, and collected an equal number of samples. Most of what was brought up from the ocean floor was just mud. Soft sediment is the easiest thing

HMS *Challenger* at St Thomas in the West Indies during the Challenger Expedition of 1872–6.

to collect from a simple dredge. The chances of picking up a good rock sample are about the same as catching a fish with a pair of tweezers at the end of a long pole. The ubiquity of the basaltic underlay was not at first apparent; but the *Challenger* did discover something of the ocean's extremes. On 23 March 1875, near the island of Guam, more than five miles of sounding line were run out before the bottom was reached. The crew did not know what they had found: we now know that it was the first sounding of an ocean trench, part of the Mariana Trench that forms part of the marginal zone of the Pacific. Not far away is the deepest spot in the ocean, 11,034 metres (36,200 feet) deep – 6.85 miles. In January 1960 the famous Swiss physicist and derring-doer August Piccard descended in a bathyscaphe of his own design, *Trieste,* to the bottom of the appropriately named Challenger Deep. It's worth remembering that it was only nine years later that footprints were first left on the moon. Robert Kunzig in his book *Mapping the Deep* points out that Mount Everest tipped upside down would tuck comfortably into the Challenger Deep, leaving room for a minor alp on top. Nonetheless, it is interesting that the tallest mountain and deepest depth are of the same order of magnitude, with mean sea-level providing the zero calibration. This may not be a coincidence.

Challenger also made the first reliable measurements on one of the other great features of the ocean. Near the middle of the Atlantic the soundings unaccountably diminished. Depths of considerably less than 2000 fathoms (3660 metres) were commonly encountered. The conclusion that there was a mid-oceanic shallowing seemed inescapable, if unexpected. To visualize this as a mountain range was more imaginative. We would now know these measurements were a consequence of peaks aligned along the mid-ocean ridges. But, at first, images of foundered lands came to mind – could these represent land bridges that had once connected the continents? In *Das Antlitz der Erde* Eduard Suess had written:

> This contrast between the outlines of the Ocean basins and the structure of the continents shows in the clearest manner that

> *these Ocean basins are areas of subsidence* reproducing, but on a far larger scale, the subsidence with which we have become familiar in the interior of the continents . . . (his italics)

For Suess, the ocean floors were but foundered continents. He reasoned that the processes that generations of geologists had so meticulously investigated on land should still apply even in the abyss. The realms of Neptune and Jupiter observed the same rules, at least according to one of the greatest geologists at the end of the nineteenth century. At the time that Suess wrote, this uniformity of concept must have seemed what is now termed 'good science'. The fundamentally different geological nature of the ocean basins was only slowly accepted, but it is always easy to be wise after the event. It does Suess and his contemporaries more justice to realize that they were seeking to apply general principles in a general way – a reliable scientific practice in most circumstances. They would no doubt have answered any potential critics that they were observing good Lyellian principles – to infer from the secure basis of processes you understand to ones you wish to investigate. If we can observe subsidence in the Bay of Naples even in historic times, then is it not reasonable to anticipate the same processes elsewhere, even if it is difficult to make the necessary observations to confirm what you surmise? Lost continents were *expected* – and here they were.

As for the composition of the ocean floor beneath its sedimentary covering, direct evidence from dredging was elusive. It was only samples from mid-ocean ridges that were relatively easy to gather, for the simple reason that sedimentary cover is thinner there. Currents sweep away a thin dusting of sediment in many places. What was retrieved, of course, was basalt. On occasion, other rock types were recovered from different ocean-floor sites that served to confuse the issue. More than twenty years ago, when I was a new boy at the Natural History Museum in London, I received a sample dredged, I believe, from the deep Atlantic. The samples were black shale, and on the shales were some ancient fossils called graptolites. They were instantly identifiable as of Ordovician age. Had they been retrieved from the crust of the ocean, they might have caused a major problem for plate tectonic theory (since all the crust should have been much younger than Ordovician). Under the lens, however, the pieces of rock showed the remains of a crust of marine creatures – the blocks must have been lying around on the sea-floor just waiting, as it were, to be dredged up. A little more research work revealed the likely source of the shale as a smallish area of New York State. It is likely that the fragments were ballast, taken on board to weight an empty hold, a common practice in the days of sail. Jettisoning the ballast for whatever reason showered the sea-floor with an alien load. There are other rocky strangers out there: granite boulders rafted by ice floes from the far north, foundered blocks slumped from the edge of the continental slope. It is not surprising that the basalt underlay was not immediately obvious.

The development and application of seismic methods, especially in the 1950s, had an effect upon our knowledge of the earth's anatomy comparable with that of the discovery of X-rays on the diagnosis of disease. Seismics provided a way of peering into regions where eyes were useless. Nature provides seismic information in the form of earthquakes, but these are not focused necessarily in the areas you might want to explore. For the investigation of the structure of the ocean floor, timed artificial explosions (often dynamite) were set off from a 'shooting' ship, and the pulses so released probed the deep layers of the ocean floor. It is necessary to know the water depth fairly precisely for the method to work, but that can be obtained by sonar. Where there are changes in the composition of the rock layers, these seismic waves should be reflected in different ways. A receiving ship some kilometres away from the 'shooting' ship would then pick up all the consequent signals; the timing of returned signals can reveal the thickness and characteristics of the rock layers traversed. Different kinds of rocks are able to transmit waves at diagnostic speeds. The calculations involved are not complicated as calculations go. However, it is important to know what *type* of waves are being recorded. The several kinds of waves are conveniently distinguished by mnemonic capital letters. P-waves are the first to arrive; that is, they travel fastest. These are 'push-pull' waves analogous to sound waves, in which each particle moves back and forth as the waves propagate. Then come S-waves – shear waves. In this kind of wave, every particle moves up and down. If you lay out a longish rope along the ground, holding one end, and then shake that end vigorously up and down, waves of this kind travel along the rope, like shivers. P- and S-waves do different things: P-waves can travel through liquids, for example, which is something that S-waves cannot do. So this is like having more than one kind of X-ray at your disposal, capable of seeing more than one kind of internal organ. Later still, long-period or L-waves arrive at the receiving station. These are surface waves, confined in their movement to the crust. They have different characteristics again, notably that they travel further more strongly than either P- or S-waves.*

The instrument that measures the arriving effects of an earthquake or explosion – natural or artificial – is a seismometer. The measurements are recorded on a seismograph, usually a continuous paper log of the intensity of seismic activity, scratched by a needle (or a light beam) on to a rotating drum. Early instruments often had to be tuned to receive a particular frequency, but modern broadband instruments can measure and record the whole gamut of amplitudes and frequencies within the same black box: they listen to the music of the earth. Amplification of the faintest signals is now routine, including those that have travelled through the innermost core of our planet.

The statement that the main refracting layer beneath the sedimentary cover has the capacity to transmit P-waves at 5 km/sec will now, I hope, make sense. This is the velocity figure appropriate to a dense, iron-rich igneous rock like basalt, and it is almost ubiquitous in the ocean basins. It is underlain by another layer with a velocity of 6.7 km/sec – appropriate for gabbro. The seismic reflection profiles

* This is because their energy dispersal is inversely proportional to the distance they are from the source; whereas for P- and S-waves this figure is the square of the distance. Hence over a distance of three kilometres an L-wave will diminish to one-third, but a P-wave to a mere one-ninth. L-waves also come in more than one variety, named after prominent scientists in wave theory – [John Strutt, 3rd Baron] Rayleigh waves and [Professor Augustus] Love waves.

tell us also that the oceanic crust is thin: no more than ten kilometres thick, and in places half that thickness. By contrast, the crust under the continents is up to forty kilometres thick (around twenty-four miles), and always much thicker than under the ocean basins. This is, quite simply, the most important distinction on the face of the earth. Eduard Suess did not know it; but Arthur Holmes did. The fundamental and invariable distinction between oceans and continents was essential to seeing the physiognomy of the world drawn in plates. The earth can be divided into basalt and the rest. Not that a ubiquitous basalt underlay is the only interesting thing about the ocean floors; as we shall see, its sedimentary cover has provided evidence crucial to several other important scientific advances.

At the time of writing, the ocean floor has been core-sampled at more than a thousand sites by the Ocean Drilling Program. The technical problems and expense of this kind of research mean that it has to be funded internationally. 'Sea time' is always one of the most expensive items on any project budget. Since January 1985, the Ocean Drilling Program has recovered almost 160,000 metres of drill core, much of it sedimentary, from the deep oceans. It is sobering to compare this with the scattered recovery of odd rocks from dredges at the time of the first *Challenger*. The Deep Sea Drilling Program ship was christened, appropriately enough, the *Glomar Challenger* in deference to its pioneering predecessor. The current 'state-of-the-art' ship, the *JOIDES Resolution*, is able to collect samples from below a water depth of more than 8.2 kilometres, and carries an on-board team of about thirty scientists. The technical problems of drilling literally miles away from the mother ship are now almost routine. The most challenging problem is that of maintaining position above the hole while being buffeted by waves and winds, and the ship is generously provided with stabilizers. Acoustic beacons near the drill-site on the ocean floor ensure that the *Resolution* does not drift from where it should be. As for the drill itself, its housing is constructed in sections and extruded through the bottom of the ship. There is hardly any part of the ocean that can escape its probe. Even this paragon of a ship will be updated. A new vessel is under construction

Crusty a'a lava by a roadside on the Big Island, Hawai'i.

The entrance to the Thurston Lava Tube draped with ferns, Volcanoes National Park, the Big Island, Hawai'i.

Dark, recent lava flows on the Big Island, spilling over the verdant landscape.

Beach of black sand almost entirely composed of minute fragments of volcanic rock, with Hawaiian turtles, the Big Island, Hawai'i.

in Okayama, Japan, that will be able to drill holes in the ocean floor as much as seven kilometres deep – three times more than the current ODP fleet. This will penetrate into the gabbro layer that underlies the basalt. There is still much to discover 'down there'.

It is one thing to take samples; it is quite another to make a map. Yet understanding is often rooted in a map. Problems often need to be anatomized first, before they can be tamed by explanation. The circulation of the blood was inferred in part from anatomical charts of veins and arteries. Elucidation of the principles of stratigraphy accompanied the publication of the first geological maps. So it was with the oceans. The map of the ocean floor that often adorns the walls of geography classrooms around the world was prepared by Bruce Heezen and Marie Tharp and first published in *National Geographic* in 1967. It almost glows with reality: here is the ocean drained. The sea-floor is a mass of fissures and mountain ranges, and everything seems to be arranged in lines: the mid-ocean ridges are the most linear features on the earth, one of them bisecting the entire length of the Atlantic Ocean. At its apex is a neatly marked rift. There is the Hawaiian Chain and its extension northwards to the Aleutians. Sea-mounts teeter. In places the ridges are displaced by craggy lines, as for example opposite the Guinea coast. In other places the tip of sediments from the great rivers – Amazon and Mississippi – is patent alongside the steeply-sloping continental edge. It's all so exact. I remember wondering when I saw this map for the first time: how do they *know* that? It was clearly prepared by an artist well trained in the skills of suggesting three dimensions. In fact, much guesswork was involved. Since the days of HMS *Challenger* depth soundings had been developed using sonar equipment – more sophisticated versions of the kind of equipment that is now standard in modern ocean-going yachts. Even so, there were parts of the ocean across which there were remarkably few surveys: there was much need for imaginative extrapolation. Tharp constructed a long stretch of mid-ocean ridge, around 6000 kilometres, between Australia and Antarctica on the basis of one line of soundings; this portrayal, as she said later, 'was of necessity sketched in a very stylised manner'. So it was, but the guesses were masterly. This was the map that made clear to the interested observer that there were natural seams in the oceanic crust. The world began to look like a kind of irregular sports ball, sewn together from disparate patches. The joins were apparently located at the mid-ocean ridges, those most persistent lines at once elevated above and graven into the surface of the ocean floor. Those who knew that the Great Wall of China could be seen from a space satellite orbiting the earth would instinctively know that these basalt walls were more fundamental to the planet than anything humans could construct. The spot depths that the *Challenger* had discovered were now rationalized into ocean trenches – mysterious and profound dark blue arcs skirting the edge of Asia. For all its imperfections, the Heezen/Tharp map made the imaginative leap for the workaday scientist. However, it did exaggerate the vertical scale twentyfold. This had the effect of making the mountains and slopes look imposingly steep. This is a distortion of real nature; for example, the Hawaiian volcanoes do not rise so precipitously: if they had the proportions shown on the map they would founder immediately. It is important to remember that the oceans are full of gentler slopes, generally of a magnitude that would not trouble the submarine version of an all-terrain vehicle.

Modern multi-beam sonar can enormously increase the accuracy of portraying the ocean floor. Beam technology discriminated the giant landslips that had left Molokai looking a mere sliver of an island, whilst some of the 'hills' on the sea-floor proved to be enormous, foundered blocks over 300 metres (1000 feet) high. Much of the island must have collapsed. Modern mapping techniques have discovered entire submarine mountain ranges that were not portrayed on the Heezen/Tharp map. The Foundation Sea-mounts in the South Pacific form a chain of submerged volcanoes 1600 kilometres long and rising 3000 metres above the sea-floor. This is like omitting from the picture of the world a Great Wall of China, but fiftyfold higher. Nor has discovery stopped. In 2001 a paper in the magazine *Nature* reported the occurrence of volcanoes possibly nearly 900 metres high on the Gakkel Ridge under the Arctic Ocean. You can fly over this region a few hours from Heathrow Airport in London. Who would imagine that there were discoveries of such moment still to be made on one of the standard Great Circle routes? The ocean floor has certainly not yet been mapped in enough detail to be certain that there are no other surprises waiting down there. Perhaps it is as well to retain something of the awe once felt for the biblical monster Leviathan; if not giant serpents, there could still be realms in the deep sea of which we have never dreamed.

The standard basalt is known as MORB – Mid-Ocean Ridge Basalt. Its chemistry is the bottom line for oceanic crust. Other kinds of rocks are often compared with MORB as being enriched in this particular element or depleted in another. The mid-ocean ridges are where new crust is added to the Earth, so MORB is the basic building material of our world. The extrusion of submarine basalt flows supplied by feeder dykes at the mid-ocean ridges may be less spectacular than the foaming lava fountains of Hawai'i, but it is more important to the world. For this is how the ocean floor grows. It grows by stealth in the dark. Hidden in the gloom there are pillow lavas such as those that make up the lower flows on the Hawaiian chain. There are tremors accompanying eruptions, for all that they mostly pass unobserved except by the special instruments trained to spot them. World seismic maps show a thin line of weak earthquakes closely following the ridges. The ridge as a whole is buoyed up by the heat that comes from below. The rift at its apex is the seam at the suture of creation. This is where plates are born and part company forever, for all that they are joined at birth. The new volcanic material added at the apex becomes part of one plate or another. In the simplest system to read, the Mid-Atlantic Ridge, the new crust is either destined to move in the direction of the Americas, or of Europe and Africa. One analogy might be with paired conveyor belts, both tuned to run at the same speed and running back to back. The proper term for the process is sea-floor spreading. Even so, the image is too active: the eruptions do not push the system, they are a consequence of it.

The lavas insinuate themselves into the cracks along the rift system as the oceanic plates on either side spread apart. This is nature abhoring a vacuum, rather than nature punching a hole in the crust by main force. The high heat flow is a measure of an upward movement of the convection cell below the ocean ridge, a movement that both drives the system and engenders the magma that in its turn gives rise to new ocean floor. Spreading rates vary. At some mid-ocean ridges they are slow, including the North Atlantic at 2.5 centimetres a year. This has been compared with the speed at which fingernails grow. The fastest rates are 15 centimetres a year, as measured on the East Pacific Rise. The total length of all the ocean ridges added together is something like 60,000 kilometres.

Water from the sea can seep into the spreading system. In some of the more active spreading ridges it becomes superheated and charged with minerals in solution. This water then discharges through hydrothermal vents, the name being no more than classical science-speak for 'hot water'. Sulphur and iron we have met before on Maui and the Big Island, painting the rock rusty or bright yellow. But at depth, iron sulphide – or pyrites – builds fantastical chimneys. There are encrusted dark towers, and crazily teetering tubes. The surrealist painter Max Ernst drew fantasy landscapes uncannily resembling this scenery, as if his untrammelled unconscious mind had had prescient access to another immersed store of weirdness. Or the ridges may remind you of the delirious castles designed by Mad King Ludwig of Bavaria, piled masses of turrets and pinnacles, daring gravity to do its worst. In the depths of the ocean they can grow undisturbed, for no wind will topple their extravagance. Vents discharge iron-rich, superhot water, and the pyrite is deposited where this water meets the sea-water; the chimneys grow progressively around the hot streams. Water does not boil under the pressures at these depths, so temperatures of 300° C are common. The vents belch forth their sulphurous exhalations as dark miasmas. They have come to be called 'black smokers'. This may seem slightly curious: in a world of blackness, how do you recognize a black fog? It was not until they were seen by the lights of the submersible *Alvin* that these factory chimneys of the deeps could be recognized and christened. Among biologists they soon became famous for supporting a whole ecosystem not previously known on earth. The sulphurous tubes supported sulphur bacteria in profusion, and they in turn gave birth to a food chain comprising crustaceans and worms, and then predators upon these animals – virtually all of these species, in the language of the taxonomist, 'new to science'. Some of the tube worms that lived near the sulphurous springs were almost Leviathans.

That there is always something to be discovered in the deeps is proved by the recent recognition of a new kind of hydrothermal vent. In 2001 Deborah Kelley of the Oceanography Department in Seattle reported masses of white pinnacles growing from the sea-floor, building what was romantically called the Lost City. The chimneys can reach sixty metres in height. Fluted and branched, they look like the façade of Gaudi's famous cathedral of La Sagrada Familia in Barcelona, or like vast quantities of candle wax partly melted and piled into columns by some megalomaniac sculptor. They are largely composed of the common mineral calcite and its relative aragonite, both plain old calcium carbonate – the stuff of chalk. Apparently, there are microbes aplenty there, too. Water emanating from the vents from which the columns sprout is much cooler than that associated with the black smokers – 75° C or less. The site, too, is different. The Lost City lies on that part of the Mid-Atlantic ridge opposite north-west Africa, and positioned a little further from the centre of the ridge than in the case of its boiling hot relatives. This is a slow-spreading ridge, while most black smokers have been found on 'fast' ones. The deposition of calcite is the result of warm vent waters high in calcium coming into contact with cold sea water. The ultimate origin of the fluids may relate to processes deep in the underworld, where the seepage of sea-water reaches the top of the mantle. This results in alteration of peridotite rocks to serpentine, and the residual calcium-rich fluids migrate away towards the sea-floor – ultimately to lay down their chemical burden 800 metres down from the surface of the Atlantic Ocean. The research vessel *Atlantis* carries the submersible *Alvin* for this kind of exploration. Photographs of the

Lost City were taken by digital camera mounted in a remotely operated vehicle called *Argoll.* The scientists aboard the *Challenger* certainly set something in motion when they pioneered the technology of undersea exploration. Will the sea-floor ever become the ultimate tourist destination? There seems to be as much interest there as on the moon, and there is always a chance of coming face to face with some new new species of deep-sea creature. For myself, I would prefer this last, inaccessible, wild place to remain in its dark security. The human touch has been so devastating elsewhere. This may be one place where we should satisfy our curiosity and then move on.

The continents comprise only about one-third of the earth, yet they also compose the greater fraction of all dry land. This is a self-evident fact, yet stating the obvious has one useful function: it makes one wonder why the obvious is also true. They make dry land because continents stand up. They extend outwards under the sea, as continental shelves, which may be up to a hundred kilometres wide but are frequently narrower. In geological terms, shelves are no more than drowned portions of the continents. The real division between the continents and the realm of basalt is the continental slope, the steep edge that bounds the shelf so as to appear almost sheer on the Heezen and Tharp maps (but remember that vertical exaggeration). The edge of the shelf frequently parallels the coastlines of continents with which we are familiar, as in Africa; but in places, such as to the west of the British Isles, there is no relation between the shape of adjacent shores and the outline of the European continental margin. The continents are geologically diverse: being stitched-together masses of a myriad rock types, including granites, gneisses, sandstones, and shales. If this book were to list them all it would be a litany of incomparable dullness. In this fundamental respect continental crust contrasts with oceanic crust, which is a hundred variations on a theme of basalt.*

* Basalt rocks also occur on the continents – it is just one of the many ingredients in their complex make-up.

This is the result of the manufacture of oceanic crust at the mid-ocean ridges: there is a hot umbilical cord connecting its birth with the pervasive mantle rocks beneath. Melting inexorably leads to basalt magma. By contrast, each continent has its own biography, its own genesis and evolution. Continents are *complicated*. But on the simplest level, the difference between oceanic crust and continental is one of weight, or rather density.

Continental crust on average is less dense (upper layer 2.7 gm/cc) than oceanic crust (greater than 3 gm/cc). You can just about feel the difference if you hold a piece of black gabbro in one hand and a comparably sized piece of gneiss in the other. Continental crust is also much thicker than oceanic crust, generally something like thirty to forty kilometres, but may be double again underneath the great mountain ranges like the Himalayas. Oceanic crust, by contrast, does not exceed much more than ten kilometres in thickness. Continental crust rides up as a consequence of its thickness of less dense rock. So where the light continents are thickest (e.g. Himalayas, Alps), there also is the greatest tendency for them to rise: prod a chunk of floating wood down with your finger and see how it bobs up. But this is a misleading analogy, for the wood is too buoyant and the motion too fast. The asthenosphere that underlies the surface plates is not liquid in any vernacular sense, although it *is* relatively plastic. This means it deforms by flow rather than by fracture. Nevertheless, the flow is sufficient to accommodate the Himalayas rising, as erosion by ice and torrent continually wears down and removes some of the load from the summit of the range. The mountains are perpetually delivered into the teeth of storms and the vice of ice, and presented again continuously by uplift to the worst that the elements can do. There is an upper limit to such an uplift process, dictated by physical limits related to the thickness of the crust, so that no mountain can rise much higher than Mount Everest. To put it as teleologically as possible, every mountain will eventually be ground down to the point where it wishes to rise no more. The stable, average continental thickness eventually attained in this way can endure for thousands of millions of years above mean sea-level, or at least above the level as it stands today. We will return to mountains in more detail later.

Within the oceans, there are few places where the crust breaks the sea's surface. The abyssal deep is the stable position for cold oceanic crust. Even on the mid-ocean ridges the volcanoes rise towards the surface but rarely disturb it as islands. Had there been no continental crust, there would have been no evolution of land animals, no trees, and assuredly no thinking bipeds. Intelligence may have become the property of the squid, who communicate through colour changes on their skin. In another world this book might have been written in shimmering, swirling modifications of tens of thousands of chromatic cells. Hence the most important, but often unacknowledged, distinction on the face of the earth – between continent and ocean – is a consequence of the properties of basalt. In order to give habitation to penguins and Polynesians, and bring about land, dense basaltic crust needs an extra 'push' of heat. This brings us back to paradise. The 'hot spots' provide such an additional boost. Hawai'i is an exceptional place, as were its geological ancestors that bulged upwards over the same deep feature, and as its descendants will be in their turn. Pushed upwards into the atmosphere beyond their natural height, when they lose touch with their private artery back into the middle of the earth, these islands will sink below the waves to remain as sea-mounts – unless a persistent coral reef grants them a stay of banishment from Neptune's kingdom.

There are oceanic hot spots elsewhere. Most geologists consider that Iceland is one: it sits atop the Mid-Atlantic Ridge. We have seen that the ocean ridges are prominent features, but submarine ones. Iceland alone forms a substantial island, 480 kilometres long, with enough shallow waters around it to ensure that the sensible, conservationist Icelanders still have a deep-sea fishing industry. Like the Hawaiian islanders, they, too, have a respectful, rather than a fearful relationship with their volcanoes. The eruptions are mostly of the comparatively benign, basaltic kind. Like a northern hemisphere Hawai'i, the island has been built up from countless flows piled on top of one another.

However, Iceland is not part of a chain. Since it is situated so closely on top of the Mid-Atlantic Ridge, plates do not drift over the hot spot: instead, Iceland sits almost still at the centre of creation. The apical rift zone is produced by extension where the two plates are prised apart. It is normally accessible only to probing echo sounders far beneath the sea's surface, but in Iceland it runs right across the centre of the island. The American Plate lies on one side of the island, the Eurasian Plate on the other. Uniquely, on Iceland the plates spread apart on land; so there may be a place on Iceland where you can stand with one foot on America and the other in Europe. Iceland is where geologists can go to study the mechanisms of plate birth. No paradisiac luxuriance decorates the lavas here: mosses and grasses and lichens are what ultimately soften the blackness. The volcanic centres are very much alive, and usually clearly related to the fracture zone. Hekla in the south of the island erupted vigorously in 1947–8. Surtsey was a new island born in the sea off the southern coast in 1963. As I write, the Grimsvotn volcano is erupting underneath an ice-sheet: this combination of ice and fire is especially elemental. On 29 September 1996, there was a magnitude 5 earthquake associated with the eruption at Vatnajokull: thus the earth records its birth pangs.

In Iceland you can wash in water heated by the process of creation, making the island a world centre for the use of geothermal energy. Hot water is piped into offices and private houses for central heating. It is used to heat greenhouses, too, so that you can eat fresh tomatoes and smell fresh roses even as glacier ice grows not so many kilometres away. Water percolates towards the hot plume all the time, and there is an endless supply of heat. Iceland is the home of the original geyser, at a place called Geysir. The spout lies at the centre of a bowl of geyserite some twenty-five metres across. Geysers 'blow' when the water that fountains up so spectacularly is released from overlying pressure, often rising in a single gush up to sixty metres in height. The water spouts out at 75° to 90° C. At that temperature it can retain silica in solution, but as it cools the silica is deposited as a white lacquer which builds the geyserite bowl, layer by layer. This siliceous sinter will outlast the geyser itself, and 'fossil' geyser sites can be recognized by the stony remains of the warm ponds to which they once gave birth.

Not far from Reykjavik there is a geothermal lake where you can sit in hot water for the good of your health, or maybe because you like being simmered. The Blue Lagoon at Svartsengi is backed surrealistically by the silvered pipes of a hydrothermal station. When the sun is upon it, the lagoon is genuinely caerulean blue, coloured with something like the intensity of the utterly different lagoons in Hawai'i. The Icelandic bathers dip in the hot draught that rises from the underworld. You cannot help remembering the spring of eternal youth in Rider Haggard's *She*. If anything is going to have the properties of an elixir surely it should be these special waters. Unfortunately, there is no sempiternal paradise here, either – just as there was none in Hawai'i. Islands grow, islands fade. But there is something miraculous about such pinnacles of life in the vastness of the basaltic oceans. Miraculous, and fragile, too. We shall discover that they are all – islands large and small – doomed to obliteration.

4

Alps

Every river in Switzerland has a companion highway, perched precariously above the white water below as it seethes and rushes downstream between giant boulders. In the canton of Glarus the little road that runs to the village of Elm is no exception, closely dogging the course of the River Sernft, and dotting back and forth from it like a persistent beggar. This is comparatively low alpine country, and the steep valley sides are densely clothed with trees. Winter drapes their crowns with brilliant clots of snow, imparting airiness to the landscape; but in summer, when the geologist does his fieldwork, the trees are altogether denser and more serious. Glades of beech and conifers provide deep cover. When I visited the Sernft valley, wisps of low cloud clung to its sides, as if smoke from some bonfire burning slowly deep within the woods had drifted out heavily upon the humid air. There are cleared pastures among the woods, where the ground slopes less steeply; these are richly green and splashed with yellow daisies. Discreet wooden hay stores poke out of the hillsides as if they were entrances to underground tunnels. Larger chalets are scattered apparently almost randomly over the slopes, with white-rendered foundations and dark brown planking above, each with shutters as neat as can be, and no casement without a window box planted out with bright-scarlet geraniums or extravagant petunias. In the summer there are hardly any tourists, so the inhabitants appear to deck out their houses for their own pleasure. It is hard to believe that these primly picturesque dwellings not so long ago housed peasant farmers whose lives were relentlessly hard, irrevocably linked to the rocky terrain and the imperatives of transhumance. You do not have to look hard for evidence of the geology that controlled their lives, for crags break out from verdant surfaces of the fields and, higher up, on the peaks, there is little else but rock all the way up to the glacier's edge.

The Alps – particularly that part that lies within Switzerland – are the type example of a mountain range. Many great geologists have spent their lives trying to unravel the mysteries of Alpine structure. For this region of the earth's crust is where everything is topsy-turvy, where great slabs of rock may be flipped over like badly-tossed pancakes, and where a mountain of a height to challenge the most experienced alpinist may be no more than the tip of a vast geological fold. It is a place where nature has apparently relished stirring up the strata on such a scale as to make wriggling rock conundra to torment the minds of scientists. The Alpine orogeny (Greek *oros*, a mountain, + genesis) took place over more than sixty million years, continuing into the Pliocene period. These highest parts of Europe are also among the most disturbed – as complex in their way as the Hawaiian chain is simple. Hence you cannot just describe the Alps in lifelike detail, for there is no end to their complications. Instead, I shall take one small piece to represent the whole: a selected microcosm to illuminate the macrocosm. I shall start in the Glarus area of the eastern Alps, where some of the secrets of the range were first decoded from the rocks. It is classical terrain. This simplification is rather like taking one of Shakespeare's sonnets to represent his whole *oeuvre* – it will not do justice to it, of course, but it is enough to suggest the outline of greater things.

Lochseiten in the Sernft Valley is one of geology's holy places. It does not look much when you arrive: just a wood by a minor road. To find rock, you have to scrabble up a steep bank covered in leaves derived from the dense canopy above. It is rather dim under the trees on an overcast, damp day, and hard to keep your foothold on the slippery bank. The path is underlain by a rock termed the Flysch, meaning something like 'slippery slope' in the local patois. After a few minutes of scrabbling along a path through the wood you reach an overhanging cliff a few metres high. A projecting rock ledge provides shelter from the rain. This is where a famous contact between rock formations is exposed. The lower part of the rock section over which you have just climbed is the Flysch: dark grey slaty rocks that come out in small shards if you pick at them with your fingers. These rocks were once soft muds beneath the sea, hardened now by time and pressure. The cliff above is made of a completely different type of rock. It is a massive stone, and, if you scrape off bits of moss and lichen, a rich red colour is exposed: the same ripe berry tones can be seen in the Old Red sandstone of the Welsh Borderland. Look closer and you notice that the red rock is a mass of pebbles of various sizes and colours, some as large as your fist – the red is mostly concentrated in the matrix that encloses them. It is a conglomerate – nature's approximation to concrete – such as might be formed from the cobbles on an ancient beach, or from the pebbles accumulated on a lake bed after storms. The pebbles themselves were the product of weathering of still more ancient rocks: limestones here, a lump of sandstone there, perhaps some resistant volcanic rocks – in fact, something of a pot-pourri, all cemented together by the red matrix. We have all had a comparable experience when picking out the differently coloured cobbles on a beach. This distinctive rock is known as the Verrucano. Look closer again, and you notice something else: the pebbles in the conglomerate are all elongated. They have been turned into parallel sausages, telling you that the whole outcrop of rock must have been extended – stretched plastically on some kind of tectonic rack. This is something that only happens at depth in the earth's crust – where pressure makes rocks 'flow' rather than fracture. So now you can tell that there was once a great thickness of rock above you – where only brooding clouds now float thick and grey – which erosion has removed to expose the rocks seen today. You are looking into the interior of the earth, and back in time. So far, so much deduction.

But there is more. At the contact between the Verrucano above and the Flysch below there is a thin interval of limestone – you might call it a 'bed', but it undulates in thickness. Limestone, of course, is

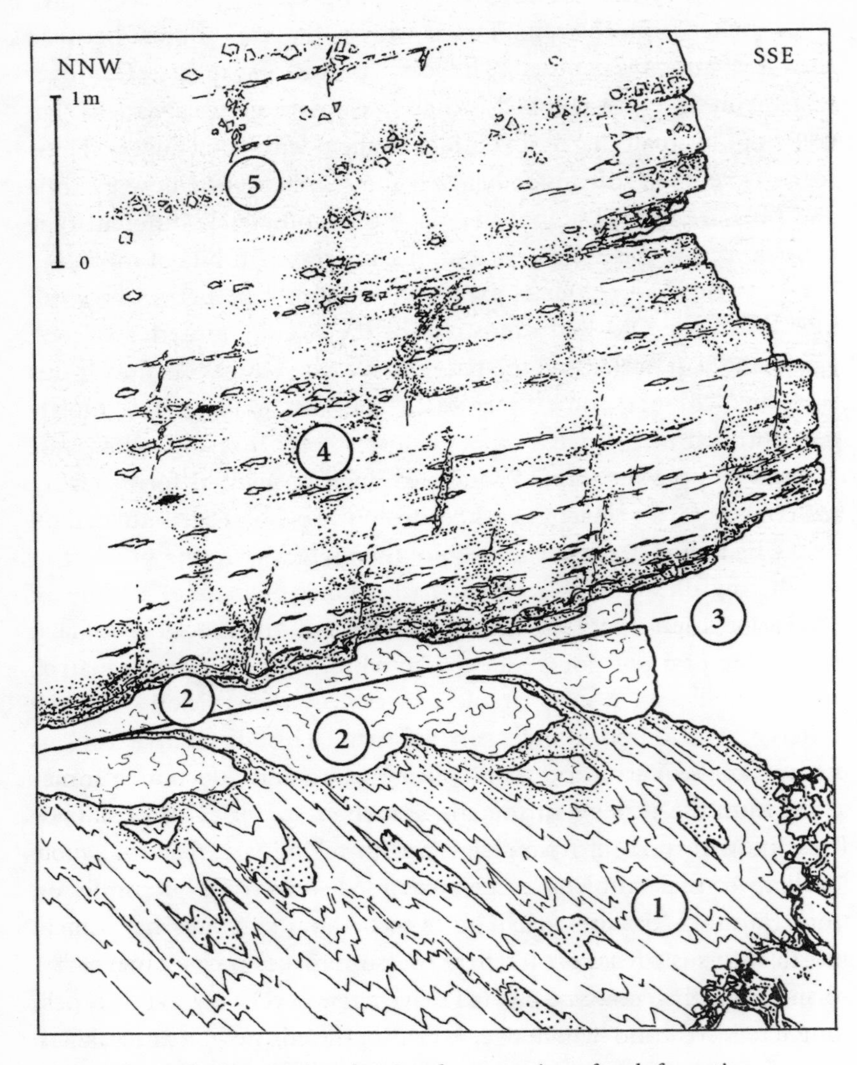

The Lochseiten Section showing the succession of rock formations.
1 – the Tertiary Flysch; 2 – the Lochseiten Limestone (mylonite);
3 – the 'fault gouge'; 4 – deformed Verrucano flattened constituents;
5 – purplish Verrucano (Permian) with undeformed pebbles.

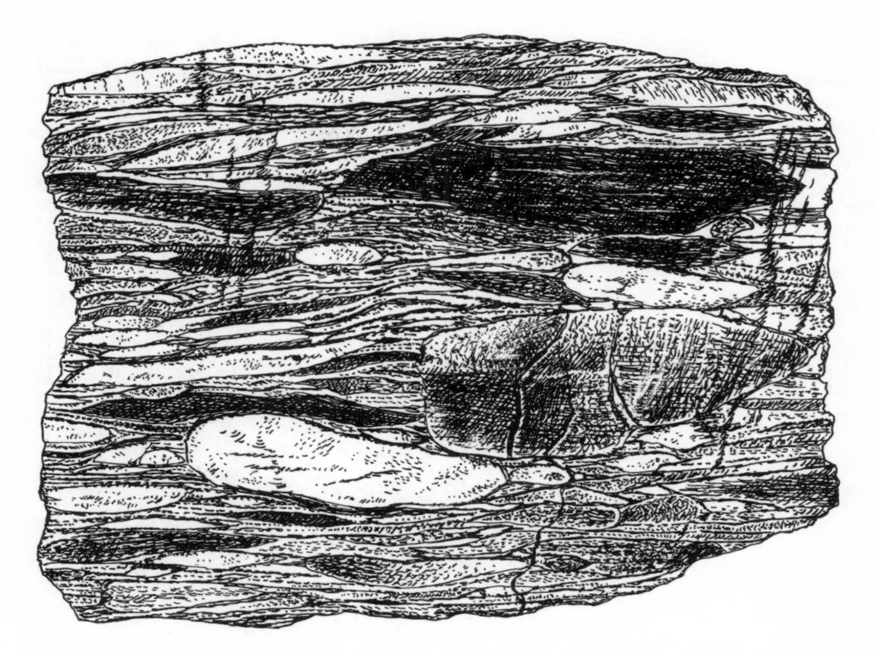

Pebbles elongated by Alpine deformation. Under extreme conditions such pebbles deform plastically.

calcium carbonate, and thus chemically utterly different in composition from the clayey rocks below and the hard, pebbly ones above. It is known as the Lochseiten limestone – named after the type locality. At this spot under the trees it is about thirty centimetres thick (at other localities it can be two metres thick, but never much more); it forms a recessive notch in the cliff's profile – the eaten-away softness of this stratum explains why the overlying, and much tougher, Verrucano forms the overhanging cliff. The limestone is a creamy colour. In several places under the overhang it projects downwards into the Flysch below as a kind of lobe. A closer look reveals that the Lochseiten limestone is all ground up, and contorted; it has been pulverized, mangled, and mashed. In the middle of the limestone there is what appears to be a horizontal crack that extends straight as a die along the length of the outcrop.

At first glance, you might assume that what you were looking at is a normal sedimentary rock succession: oldest rocks below and progressively younger ones above – Flysch, limestone, and Verrucano respectively. This is the kind of sequence you can see in cliffs of undisturbed strata by the seaside all over the world. Rocks that were originally laid down under the sea as sediments and then elevated above sea-level stack up this way: it is as easy to read, as a diary of geological time, as the sequence of basalt lava flows on Oahu. After all, the succession of names for the intervals of geological time shown on the endpapers of this book was worked out by placing one set of strata on top of another in their proper sequence, Jurassic before Cretaceous, Cambrian before Ordovician, and so on, eventually building up the narrative of geological time. Clearly we need to ask what evidence of age is there for the rock sequence in the Sernft valley.

A few kilometres up the river there is an old slate quarry in the Flysch at the hamlet of Engi, today little more than a scattering of houses and a sawmill. The valley is wider here, floored by a few luscious fields in which pretty grey-and-tan Swiss cows munch contentedly. In the nineteenth century it was a bustling place, employing a hundred and fifty people in extracting and dressing the roofing slates. Attractive dark roofs with slates arranged in geometrical patterns can still be seen all up the valley. The inhabitants once built a special barge annually to move the slates downstream to the Rhine, and ultimately to Rotterdam for sale. Today you can walk a steep trail up to the abandoned workings: slabs of steel-grey slate lie about all over the hillside among the wild flowers, and a tap with a hammer will neatly split them into smaller plates. Like the rocks on the cliff face further down the hill, the slaty Flysch has been squeezed in a tectonic vice, which is why it splits so cleanly along its 'cleavage'. The commercial seam is just one part of the hillside and is now marked by a ferny cave where miners once crawled into the belly of the earth. The modern observer cannot but feel a *frisson* of awe when

Evidence from the bones: one of the beautiful fossil fish from the Flysch at Engi described by Louis Agassiz (1807– 1873).

imagining what it was like wriggling into a deep seam to bring out the heavy rock, and all done by hand. But the rocks gave up other treasures, too: fossil fish. The slates yielded exquisite skeletons laid out like bony ghosts on their dark surfaces, some as large as salmon. Their gasping, toothy jaws splayed out flat have something of the grisly intensity of a Francis Bacon painting. They were described in a famous monograph by the great nineteenth-century palaeontologist, Louis Agassiz. His work was lavishly illustrated by four hundred plates (it is said that he kept the lithographic company of Nicolet in Neuchâtel in business and that once the monograph was completed the company went bust). Agassiz named fifty-three species from Engi, but he had reckoned without the distortion that the slates had endured in the grip of the earth. He sometimes described a long and short species, which, in fact, were the same species that had simply been stretched within the rock to differing degrees; after correcting for this, the modern tally of species is twenty-nine. Irrespective of their true number, the fossils told the age of the rocks – for a suite of fossils is as diagnostic of a particular prehistoric time-period as the face of a particular Caesar on a coin is of an historical epoch.

Those spiny-mouthed terrors could not lie: the Flysch rocks were Oligocene in age, laid down on the sea-floor about twenty-eight million years ago.

This is where things get really interesting. For the Verrucano is well known from occurrences outside the Glarus district as being of Permian age – that is, more than 250 million years. Hence in the roadside section, in the cliff under the trees, much older rocks lay *above* Flysch of Oligocene age, with the Lochseiten limestone forming a thin layer in between. Rocks from the age of mammals were overlain by those dating from before the rise of the dinosaurs: the reverse of the normal sedimentary succession. For a while this caused consternation. Could all the edifice of geological time built up so carefully by dozens of palaeontologists around the world be in error? Could geological time itself be as insubstantially founded as a house of cards? Or, if the ages were correct, what convulsions of the earth must have happened to stack the strata in their current order?

Closer inspection of the Lochseiten limestone proved crucial. The contortions within it made sense only if it marked the location of enormous earth movements. Could it have acted as a kind of lubricant as the vast mass of the Verrucano slid over the Flysch beneath? Towards the end of the nineteenth century the crush rock known as mylonite had been recognized, a rocky paste that was ground when one mighty rock mass was pushed bodily – or *thrust* – over another. Very often, younger rock was forced over older. The older Verrucano must have travelled to its present position as it slid and ground its way on the back of the oppressed Lochseiten limestone, which buckled and churned under the superincumbent load. This explained why the limestone fluctuated in thickness according to the local pressure, and, on occasion, pushed its way down into the softer Flysch, but never upwards into the harder Verrucano. If this scenario were true, another inference is now obvious: this mighty earth movement had to have occurred after the *last* sediments of the Flysch were accumulated – that is, in the Oligocene or later. The sliding motion cut short the history of the Flysch like an assassination, providing one way to date the formation of a mountain range. The next question is: how far did this massive horizontal movement extend? And what was the great 'push' that caused the movement?

To answer the first question, one very basic piece of research is required: a geological map. Strata can be plotted out upon the ground – plain or mountain alike – then coloured in on the map to make their distribution clear, so that the extent of the movements that transported Verrucano over Flysch can be traced. Mapping geological strata, or formations as they are usually known, is a skilled business. A good appreciation of subtle changes in rocks, and an accurate grasp of three-dimensional space, are *de rigueur*. In Switzerland, it also requires stamina and persistence. My guide over this ground was Geoff Milnes, formerly at the renowned Technical University in Zürich, who had tramped many kilometres in the area with 'topo map' and notebook in his rucksack, hammer in hand, marking out this boundary or that in order to try and understand how the Alps were put together.

There was an heroic age of rock mapping in Switzerland. In the earlier part of the nineteenth century there were pioneers like Arnold Escher von der Linth. Escher had acquired the last part of his name from his father, an engineer who had built the Linth canal, and drained malarial marshes in the process, so his son had reason to feel proud. Eduard Suess was an admirer of Escher the younger, whom he had met in 1854. In the preface to his own great work, *Das Antlitz der Erde,* he remarked: 'Escher with all his simplicity was a remarkable man. He was one of those possessed of the penetrating eye, which is able to distinguish with precision, amidst all the variety of a mountain landscape, the main lines of its structure.' He went on: 'Escher and Studer's map of Switzerland . . . may serve as monuments of the subject.' Geological insight, thought Suess, was all about *seeing* a deeper geological reality beneath the complex, folded rocks that presented themselves to the observer: a special eye. This remains as true today as it ever was. Albert Heim was Escher's student and intellectual successor, and his *Geologie der Schweiz* in three volumes remains the biggest single-handed contribution to understanding the Alps. Professor Heim did not just make maps – he made mountains.

In his old department in Zürich, they sit in glass cases: models to the life of the peaks he had studied, with the strata painted beautifully and accurately, passing over *arrête* and valley alike. They induce the same feeling of wonder that is experienced on seeing one of those model towns in which a sparrow hardly bigger than a pin-head perches upon the town hall clock. Almost every piece of snow – almost every tree – was modelled on Heim's replication of Saentis on the northern edge of the Alps. No detail was too small to be beneath recording. Heim's modeller, Carl Meili, deserves much of the credit for these marvellous miniaturizations.

Heim used his meticulous scale models as teaching aids for his students – to tame the mountains, to cut them down to size. There was nothing so vast that it could not be conquered by the geologist: see, a whole wild landscape has been caged for your instruction! You could regard Heim's models as embodying in concrete fashion a century's change in attitudes towards great mountains – a change in aesthetics as much as science. Mountainous terrain had once been thought of as terrifying and untameable, a place belonging to wolves and unquiet spirits. An eighteenth-century observer wrote of 'those places where mountains deform the face of nature, where they pour down cataracts, or give fury to tempests'. Rather than exemplifying nature at her most untrammelled, the mountains were a deformity, having little to do with true beauty, which might rather be found in farmed and orderly lowlands, or perhaps in a productive garden. A wise man might well prefer to keep away from them. A grand switch in perception had already happened by the time Ralph Waldo Emerson could write (in *The Conduct of Life*, 1860): 'The influence of fine scenery, the presence of mountains, appeases our irritations and elevates our friendships.' Mountains had become the object of Romantic sensibility, where emotion seemed to be concentrated in direct proportion to the thinning of the air. They became sublime. Mountains were now places for the sensitive soul to visit in order to experience exaltation and grandeur: wild places that revealed deeper truths. Geological elevation was first cousin to spiritual. The hikers that stride off along mountain paths today, equipped with the latest

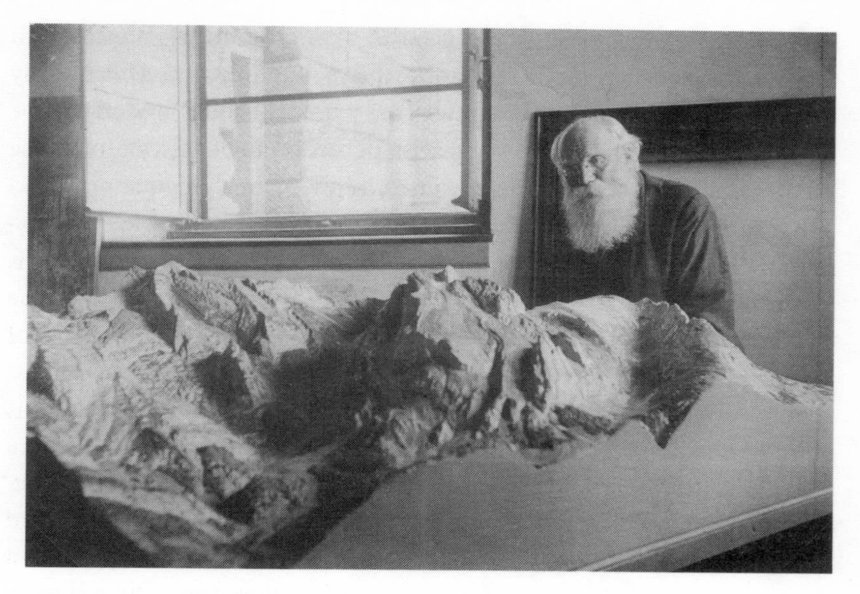

Albert Heim (1849–1937) with one of his superb models of Swiss mountains with their geology laid bare, 1905.

boots and binoculars, probably subscribe to a less passionate version of the same attitudes; but, whether they realize it or not, these modern explorers are following the footsteps of Johann Wolfgang von Goethe and Lord Byron:

> I live not in myself, but I become
> Portion of that around me; and to me
> High mountains are a feeling, but the hum
> Of human cities torture . . .*

Understanding followed upon the removal of terror from the heights. On a mundane level, the heights simply became more accessible as better roads made the mountains negotiable. Spectacular railways followed within a few decades, and are still the arteries of Switzerland. Paradoxically, better engineering helped foster an aesthetic of wildness. Geologists turned their attention to scientific explanations of

* *Childe Harold's Pilgrimage*, III, lxxii.

the action of glaciers and the genesis of high-altitude landforms, the great Louis Agassiz first among them. For other pioneers, the carefully plotted geological map was the primary tool in understanding Alpine structure; Heim's models succeeded the early maps; and then the consideration of deep causes followed in due course, right down to the plate movements we know today. Filleted of fear, even mountains could be encompassed by the powers of deductive reasoning.

We can now return to the structure underlying the Verrucano, mapped by Albert Heim. Geoff Milnes showed me that the notch produced by the erosion of the Lochseiten limestone could be traced quite readily, rising gradually from the top of one peak to the next above the quiet little village of Elm. The 'package' of thin, pale limestone and overlying Verrucano could be seen through good binoculars. The line of contact of the limestone with what lay below seemed to be as straight as a die for several kilometres. Above Elm, far above the tree line, there is a natural hole in that outcrop of Verrucano that forms the jagged crest at the culmination of the mountain. This is called St Martin's Hole (Martinsloch), and it is said that the sun shines through it directly on to the village church every St Martin's Day, 11 November. To get a closer look at this part of the 'Glarus thrust' we need to make a detour, moving slowly southwards, towards Italy.

Just to get round to the other side of the mountain you have to drive for several hours round three sides of a very large rectangle and cross over into another canton. There are no short cuts over the Hausstock (3158 metres) without a helicopter. The town of Flims is much more the classic ski resort town than little Elm, retaining a well-groomed charm in the summer that must be the legacy of the many euros, dollars, and pounds spent when the snow lies crisp upon the *piste*. Even out of season, ski lifts are still available to carry you up the mountain: two chair lifts in succession and a cable car to get you to the very top. The lifts soar above the summer chalets until there is a fine view across the valley of the western branch of the upper Rhine (Vorderrhein) to the mountains to the south. The car continues higher, above the last, stunted conifers, past a magnificent cliff exposure of the Malm, of Jurassic age: a massive, thick-bedded, yellow-creamy limestone that gives rise to features in many parts of the Alps, and which was once laid down under a shallow, warm sea. You feel insignificant measured against the great crags. Upwards and upwards you climb aboard your dangling craft until you debark at the summit of Flimserstein (Cassons). There is a trail leading out over the gentle slope. The close Alpine sward has splashes of the most intense blue in nature: the flowers of the gentian, deeper than cornflower, brighter than human artifice can achieve – except for Raphael's drapery perhaps. D. H. Lawrence described them 'darkening the day-time torch-like with the smoking blueness of Pluto's gloom'. On either side of the path there are other plants to get the botanist excited: creamy milk vetch, rough-leaved lungwort, humble creeping polygonum, delightful little pinks. Here, saxifrages grow so close within cracks that they really do seem to live up to their Latin name for 'rock breaker'. It is a special community of flowers in thrall both to altitude and geology.

A little further along the path, the profile of the reverse side of the mountain tops that towered above Elm is outlined against the sky. There is a line of jagged peaklets, like an array of dog's teeth, called the Tschingelhorner, and beyond them, the Hole of St Martin. On a closer, dumpy peak named Ofen you can see the famous contact very clearly: it is so straight that it looks as if the top of the mountain has been sliced clean through just off the horizontal and then placed back again along the line of severance. The Lochseiten limestone is a pale band, and it undulates in thickness along the length of the outcrop. There is even the same sharp line, or cut, *within* the limestone that was observed in the roadside section. Below the contact, a Flysch (here called Sardona Flysch, South Helvetic Flysch) forms soft-looking, greyish scree slopes. A small glacier creeps down from

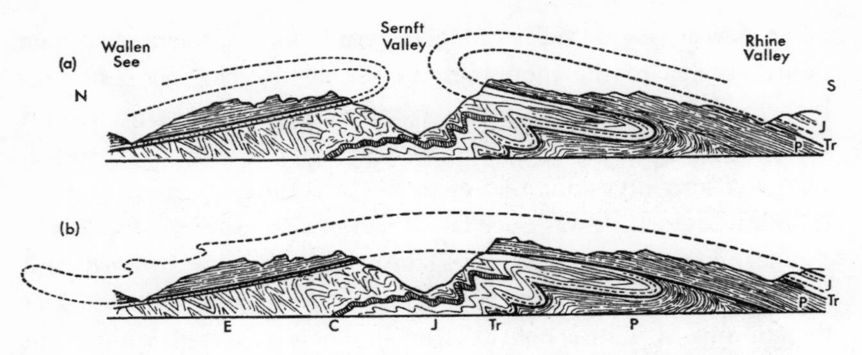

Arthur Holmes' portrayal of the competing hypotheses to explain the Glarus structures. (a) above: the double fold of Escher von der Linth wherein the Verrucano is pushed over the Flysch from opposite sides (b) below: a single nappe pushes the entire Verrucano over the younger Flysch in one mighty slice.

the heights. It is a wonderful view, and one that attracted attention from geologists from the early days. Sir Roderick Murchison's party sketched the same scene in the 1840s. Murchison was an English aristocrat, imperious and brilliant, author of *The Silurian System* (1839), the great attempt to systematize rocks belonging to what we would now call the Lower Palaeozoic Era (545–417 million years ago). Thus the pragmatic geologist followed hard on the heels of the Romantic poets, and the Flimserstein became an obligatory stop for Alpine geotourists. Arnold Escher von der Linth made a painting of St Martin's Hole from near the same spot on which we stood. Famous eyes had taken it all in before us. Looking further afield, the same geological contact could be clearly seen towards the top of several other adjacent peaks: on Piz Dolf (3028 metres) and Piz da Sterls (3114 metres). The temptation to draw a kind of dotted line through the air to connect the separate elements of the contact together was overwhelming: it must, surely, be a single, vast plane.

The story of the development of understanding of the Glarus structure encapsulates that of the Alps. We have traced it from the lower part of the Sernft valley all the way to the Flimserstein and beyond: older rocks above younger. Clearly, there is a vast perturbation of the earth to be considered. There are several ways to bring

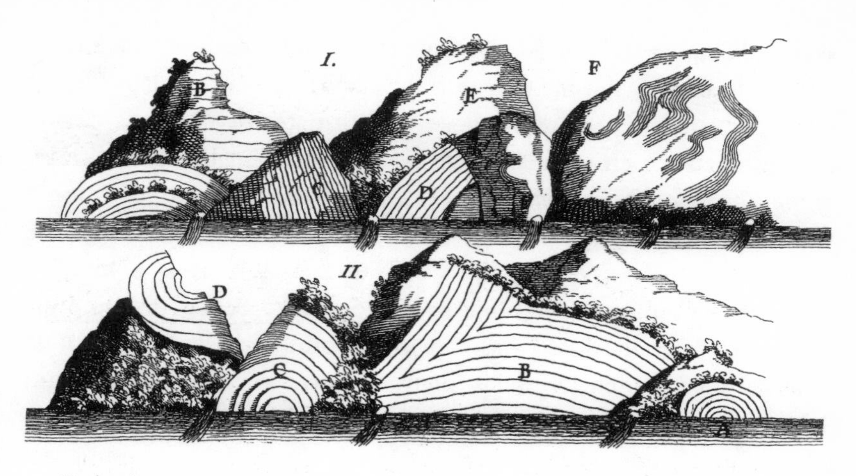

Early views on strata. Drawing of limestones on the shore of the Urnersee by J. J. Scheuchzer (1672–1733) showing little attempt to join up the limbs of the folded strata.

older strata on top of younger: thrusting has been mentioned previously. The other way is to fold and overturn the strata, much as one turns back the underlying sheets and blankets at the head of a bed. It was clear from the early days of geology that parts of the Alps were intensely folded. Whole mountain-sides could evidently be twisted as the heights were built up. There is a drawing dating from the earlier part of the eighteenth century showing one shore of the Urnersee, the easterly lobe of Lake Luzern. It was reproduced in Vallisnieri's *Lezione all'origine delle fontane* in 1715, one of the earliest systematic accounts of mountains. I stood on the very spot from which the drawing had been composed by J. J. Scheuchzer. The same lakeside had other resonances, too, for Tellskapelle was where Wilhelm Tell escaped to freedom from the boat that was to take him to Kussnacht castle and a grim death. Goethe's friend Schiller retold the story in incomparable fashion in 1804; it seems that geological and Romantic locations have a tendency to get tangled together. On the far side of the lake, disturbed Cretaceous limestone strata are splendidly displayed. Scheuchzer clearly portrayed folds in several of the mountains and, overall, made a passably accurate sketch. What he did *not* do was connect any one series of strata from one mountain to the next; each outcrop was its own, self-sufficient story. Scheuchzer is one of those unfortunate men who is chiefly remembered for an error. In 1776 he published, in the *Transactions of the Royal Society of London*, a fossil find from the famous Miocene deposits of Oeningen as proof of the biblical flood. He called the fossil *Homo diluvii testis*, which speaks for itself. It is a kind of spread-eagled object, with obvious legs. Sadly for Scheuchzer, a hundred years later the fossil was shown, beyond dispute, to be that of a large salamander. Diluvial man was but an amphibian, and Scheuchzer joined a select few – like King Alfred – unfairly immortalized for a gaffe. That this was unjust is shown by his competent drawings of strata.

A hundred years later and the strata were joined up. Geological maps showed that one limb of a massive fold might connect the base of one mountain with the top of the next: interconnecting strata had been eroded away. In cross sections, the 'air' became full of dotted lines showing where strata had once passed, only to be removed grain by grain as a result of the operation over millennia of frost and water and wind. Ghosts of vanished mountains could be inferred, faint spectres of topography past imagined. Scheuchzer's outcrops were linked together by the outline of folds. Writing of the same area, Eduard Suess said: 'Those who have seen the cliffs of the Axenberg on the Lake of Lucerne will have viewed with astonishment the inextricable entanglement of the limestone beds.' It became a familiar observation that massive rock-beds might be turned on their sides and crumpled like the bellows of a concertina. Overfolding did indeed turn whole piles of strata upside down. Mapping distinctive rock-beds helped prove this structural suffering of strata beyond doubt. The thin, iron-rich Jurassic rock bed known as the Dogger is but one example. Near the little village of Bristen, Geoff Milnes showed me how its distinctive signature could be traced from one hillside to another, bucking and twisting like some demented fairground roller-coaster. You could see how the earth buckled, and how such complex pleating shortened its crust by folding strata on to themselves. I am reminded of unpicking the bud of a poppy: so much gaudy petal crimped and folded into so small a volume. For many years the careful mappers mapped, and folding became quite the thing to explain virtually all geological problems in the Alps.

Following the *Zeitgeist*, Arnold Escher interpreted the Glarus structure entirely in terms of folding; and Albert Heim, model maker *extraordinaire*, apparently followed suit. Heim was a patriarchal figure: authoritarian and sure of himself. He would not be an easy man to cross. Escher and Heim explained the Glarus structure as a 'double fold' (see p. 110): two mighty overturned and recumbent folds that faced one another across the Sernft Valley. The Verrucano was brought back over the younger Flysch in two folds: imagine turning back *both* the head and foot of the bed, so folding back two swathes of the underlying sheets to oppose one another. One fold came from the north, the other from the south. It was certainly a striking concept, which implied a lateral movement of the Verrucano of at least fifteen kilometres. When Escher first proposed the double fold it seemed a radical, even revolutionary, idea to have so much crustal movement. In his *Tectonic Essays*, Sir Edward Bailey quoted Escher's caution at the time: 'No one would believe me if I published my sections; they would put me in an asylum.' Eduard Suess later summarized the Glarus story as a 'magnificent conception, unheard of in the views of that time, of a double folding of certain parts of the Alps'. Albert Heim defended the idea of the *Dopplefalte* for many years – and who would have dared to disagree to his face? It would be wrong to pooh-pooh these great geologists with the wisdom of hindsight, for what they saw was an honest interpretation of the high ground they knew so well.

The only alternative scheme seemed even more radical: to 'join the dots', as it were: to unite the sole of the structure marked by the thin sliver of Lochisten limestone as one stupendous line of movement, skipping from one summit to the next like a tectonic ibex. I had experienced the temptation to draw such a line atop the Flimserstein. Everything from the Vorderrhein to Glarus would belong to a single structure: you would have to more than double the distance travelled

Albert Heim contemplating spectacular folding in the Verrucano at Mels in St Gallen, Switzerland.

by the great mass of the Verrucano to some thirty-five kilometres. A mighty heave, indeed. Perhaps Escher shrunk from the sheer magnitude of the crustal movements implied. Could the earth shrug its skin so momentously? We know that rocks could crumple and fold, but could huge chunks of crust slither laterally for such great distances? And if they did, what forces could propel them? The proposer of the single Glarus Thrust, the man who attempted to rub out the double fold in 1884 (in a seminal paper published in the *Bulletin de la Societé géologique de France*), was Marcel Bertrand, Professor of Geology at the University of Neuchâtel, in the French-speaking part of Switzerland. What may have galled the meticulous mapper Albert Heim is that fact that Bertrand never actually visited Glarus. Bertrand admitted he had 'utilisé les descriptions de Heim du "double pli"' to draw his new lines and his new conclusions. How dare he be so presumptuous? Even today, there are hardened 'field men' – working geologists on the rough end of a hammer – who feel that the laboratory- or computer-based scientist is something of a softie, a spinner of hypotheses away from the coalface of real observations, and who might have more than a sneaking sympathy for Albert Heim, worsted though he was in the end.

Further geological mapping in the greater Alps – much of it magnificent work by Heim and his colleagues – revealed that nearly all the structures in the rocks faced northwards. Thrusts were directed there; major overfolds bulged outwards towards the north. This was familiar to Eduard Suess, for whom the Alps were home ground. He pointed out that the whole mountain system was bowed outwards in a convex arc to the north. Here the mountains encountered what he termed a rigid 'foreland'. Whatever it was that caused all the rucks and dislocations, it seemed to be 'pushing' from the south. Yet the double fold of Glarus required quite as strong a shove from the north to produce its massive, south-facing overfold, and this force apparently must have operated at exactly the same time as that on the north-facing fold, and exacted the same geological effects; after all, the rock sequences seen in the field in Glarus were similar wherever they occurred. This was all too much to ask; besides, if Bertrand's single thrust were accepted, it was accountable – once again – to movement from the south towards the north, and no need to make an exception for a small area in eastern Switzerland. The double fold, it seemed, was doomed. Albert Heim, with some generosity of spirit, finally acknowledged as much in 1901 in an open letter published in a memoir by Maurice Lugeon (1870–1953) on the structure of the Western Alps.

By now, it was apparent that in mountain belts great masses of the earth could move long distances at low angles. This was the key that unlocked the mystery of the Alps: from Glarus to the world. By a repetition of the same process, mountain chains could be understood as collections of slices piled high on one another; this was how the earth's crust both shortened and thickened. The name given to a slice was *nappe* in French – the word for a table-cloth. It is not clear who first used this word, which has now become the accepted term. Using an analogy appropriate to the name, the historian Mott Greene described the Alpine strata before their elevation as a richly patterned tablecloth on a polished table: 'If you should place your hand flat on the table and push forward, the cloth will begin to rise into folds. Push more and the folds will flop over (forward) and the rearmost fold will progressively override those before it, producing a stack of folds.' The generation of an Alpine mountain range is a matter of piling on the nappes. The early nappes pile up, and are then carried piggy back as a new active zone develops: pile is heaped upon pile. In the Alps, three great 'packages' of nappes moved in succession. Of course, today you very rarely see the whole pile, for erosion has deeply dissected away the landscape, removing some of the uppermost series of nappes. Even at the top of the Flimserstein, we have to imagine several kilometres of rock above our heads. Time has sent it packing. Continuing with Greene's table-cloth analogy: 'Take a pair of scissors and cut away at the stack from various angles, removing whole sections of the pile of folds. Having done so, push the pile again so that the segments become jumbled against each other.' In other words, you add chaos to confusion by adding erosion and later earth movements to the recipe, and that is why you stare at a cliff face in Switzerland and wonder at the spun complexity of its strata. But the recognition of nappes set out the research project: you need not simply throw up your hands in despair at perverse plications and ceaseless crenulations in the Alps. The idea now was to map the nappes, work out their sequence, and identify the rocks of which they were composed. There were many feats of heroic fieldwork: Pierre Termier, Rudolf Staub, Rudolf Trümpy; these geologists will be forever associated with the mountain ranges they unscrambled, as surely as if their names had been etched upon some mighty cliff face. Nappes were named, so that hitherto intractable mountains might now be recognized as comprising several slices stacked one above the other. In science, naming is often taming. The Glarus Nappe it became, and remains, to say nothing of the Saentis Nappe, the Murtschen Nappe, and all the rest – thousands by now – each named for a locality where it was well developed. The deformation of the rocks was often ductile – they were stretched, not broken. Albert Heim himself had collected distorted ammonite fossils that had been deformed along with the rocks that contained them. I examined a few of them in Zürich. They looked somehow hunch-backed, squeezed out of shape, lopsided, their original regular spirals twisted and wonky. In some places, fossils were stretched up to ten times their original length. Mathematical calculations can be made to compute the distortion these rocks have endured. They tell us how the earth behaves *in extremis*. Forget table-cloths for a moment: an image of pasta dough stretched and spun back and forth seems more appropriate. Alpine mountains might be seen as badly-made lasagne, crudely layered and buckled in the cooking.

Perhaps the last of the Alpine heroes is Rudolf Trümpy, scion of the line of 'field men' going back to Arnold Escher von der Linth. I saw him receive the Wollaston Medal (p. 258) of the Geological Society of London in 2002. Wilhelm Tell himself could scarcely be more legendary. In the urbane meeting rooms on Piccadilly, the grand old man seemed somehow as craggy as one of the mountains he had unscrambled. You just knew that his natural habitat was with a party of geologists, bellowing at them through a megaphone on a small cruise ship in the middle of Lake Lucerne. For another important advance, to which Trümpy contributed, was the naming and mapping of the three main 'packages' of nappes. They were emplaced in bundles: tectonic messages on sheets delivered one after another. Each of these packages was the record of a separate mountain-building event. The chronology of the Alps became calibrated by very careful geological mapping, later augmented by radiometric dating. The main events saw the arrival of what were termed Helvetic, Pennine, and Austro–Alpine nappes, respectively; these packages would eventually make sense in the context of plate tectonics. Since nappes preserve chunks of the scrunched-up earth's crust, all out of place, you could find different bits of ancient geography as you moved across Switzerland – you have to imagine taking a map of the past, cutting it up, and then moving chunks around, hither and yon. It was all most confusing. You begin to understand how a scientist might spend a lifetime working on no more than a few mountains. Sometimes the effort entailed in reconstructing the original disposition of the rocks seems like that involved in unscrambling an omelette.

Further south again, we follow the valley of the other branch of the Rhine – the Hinterrhein. All the routes dog the rushing river: the old road alongside the impeccable new autoroute, and the railway to Thusis, all dodging in and out of sight of one another. The modern road misses no excuse to shoot into a tunnel. The Swiss are masters of such engineering, and now the new roads enter and leave tunnels with abandon, apparently ignoring folds and thrusts and nappes in their eagerness to arrive. Older roads tend to wind up precipitous slopes in a series of hairpin bends. Five kilometres south of Thusis the old road takes you into a dreadful chasm – the Via Mala – literally, the Bad Way. It appears to be as much an irregular crack in the earth as a gorge; in places it is only a few metres wide, but as much as 300 metres high. The sun does not reach into it so it is always gloomy, like a grotesquely narrow, unlit passageway. It provokes awe; a small party of schoolgirls we were with even stopped giggling and

The dismal Via Mala, with the bridge of 1739 viewed from below.

jostling as they craned their necks to get a view of the torrent. The river has gathered urgency in its confinement, the white water swishing past and over rounded boulders far below. A few spindly trees cling to the sides of the gorge, but their roothold on the tiny patches of soil gathered in cracks is precarious. It is a place to make you shiver, and pull up your collar even on a warm day. A bad way indeed it must have been in the Middle Ages, when a precarious path allowed for the passage of just one traveller at a time. Traces of the old path can still be made out; in places, chains hammered into the rock helped the traveller retain his foothold. Seventy metres above the river bed there is a remnant of one of the subsequent roads, a single-span stone bridge, built in 1739, crossing from one side to the other. From below, it looks, absurdly, as if it were actually propping the two walls of the chasm apart, like a buttress in a cathedral. The Via Mala owes its eldritch, claustrophobic atmosphere to the geology. The Hinterrhein has cut through the limy schists known as the Bündnerschiefer, which are part of the Pennine nappes. Their remarkably uniform character has ensured the narrowness of the gorge. As the mountains have been uplifted again and again, it is as if the river acted in the manner of a circular saw cutting into a particularly dense log of teak: the gorge maintained its vertiginous integrity as the mountains were delivered into the jaws of erosion. So the character of the rocks determines the character of the land. The Bündnerschiefer are known to be the time equivalents of the massive limestone cliffs of Malm that we passed in the cable car above Flims. They are an utterly different rock type, originally deposited, some geologists believe, as lime-rich muds in a deep-water basin rather like the Gulf of California. Sorted, squeezed, and reshuffled by tectonics, the nappes dictate the lie of the land.

It is something of a relief to emerge on the other side of the Via Mala into the Rheinwald, where the well-wooded valley broadens and comfortable-looking farmhouses reappear. Even so, perched on almost every rocky promontory along the valley there is a castle, or at least the ruins of one. In the latter case you have to look hard to recognize them for what they are, because they are roughly built of local stone and merge naturally into the crags. In the past, they must have protected the important Rhine trade route. The old towns along the route are as solidly built from the gneiss of the region as you might expect. The roofing 'slates' are actually thin slices of gneiss: they must weigh heavily on the massive beams beneath. As so often when natural stones are used for this purpose, these 'slates' have an attractive irregularity, a dappled richness, especially when lichens paint them. The Posthotel Bodenhaus in Splügen, where I stayed overnight, has stone walls as thick as those of a fortress. It was somehow comforting.

When pile upon pile of nappes are superimposed, the earth's crust thickens. Not just the Alps, but virtually all mountain belts are zones of shortening and thickening: the opposite, if you will, of the thinning of the crust over the mid-ocean ridges mentioned previously. When the crust clots together sufficiently, something else happens: the rocks themselves transform. This is because dramatic thickening also entails burial, and burial means that the ambient pressure on the rock increases – as does the temperature. This encourages metamorphism. Minerals change from one to another; the very fabric of the rock is altered. The original rock becomes disguised, and eventually unrecognizable. If the rocks were once sedimentary, any fossils they may have formerly contained become obliterated. Schists and gneisses are the most abundant products of metamorphism in mountain belts. Nature's metamorphism is not like the magical change that happens to Gregor in Franz Kafka's famous tale *Metamorphosis*, who wakes up transformed wholesale into a monstrous insect. Natural metamorphism can only work with the chemistry of the original rock: all the mineral changes that occur are expressible in equations and can be experimented upon in laboratories. These rocks are, to return to the pasta analogy, the result of a kind of cookery – or more correctly, pressure-cookery. The dish is utterly transformed in the oven, which, however, cannot produce anything that is not in the ingredients. This topic will appear several times in this book: for now, I have said sufficient to take us further southwards to the Passo del San Bernadino.

The old pass of San Bernardino (not to be confused with the Great St Bernard Pass), at 2065 metres (6775 feet), forms the watershed between the Italian part of Switzerland and the German part to the north. Nowadays, the main road passes scornfully beneath it through one of those tunnels, but not so long ago all the heavy traffic had to grind up and then down its relentless hairpin bends. Today you can have the summit to yourself. There are wispy clouds below you, and rank upon rank of mountains in the distance; just the place for Emerson's irritations to be appeased and his friendships elevated. The grey rocks emerge from the ground in low hummocks, like a school of whales breaking the water. Some are obviously *roches moutonées*, polished and shaped by the ice-sheet that covered this whole landscape during the last million years of the Pleistocene ice age – a geological yesterday compared with the formation of the Alpine chain itself. Major remnants of this great ice cover remain on parts of the Alps, although the recent retreat of the glaciers is one of the *causes célèbres* in the debate over the effects of global warming. Elevation of the mountain chain to the altitudes at which ice-sheets can grow is itself a consequence of the tectonic thickening of the light crust – as nappe piles on nappe – relative to the dense mantle layer below. As the folding and thrusting doubles the thickness of the light crust, compensation is inevitable, and the mountain chain rises. It is bounce-back. If you look for ultimate causes, then very deep forces sculpted the features of the face of the earth.

The rocks of the San Bernardino are part of the Adula Nappe; to use the geological language unadorned, they comprise coarse gneisses, which have been deeply buried and metamorphosed within the Alpine pile and subsequently exhumed by erosion. Crudely-shaped blocks of similar rocks were employed in the thick walls at the Posthotel at Splügen. They are pallid, banded, with greyish to creamy layers of the minerals feldspar and quartz alternating with dark wisps and stripes composed of several different minerals. Shiny plates that catch the light are black, biotite mica. In some parts of the outcrop the layers are distinctly striped, like the fabric in old-fashioned pyjamas. In other places, the layers undulate and curl in folds that often just peter out: you can almost visualize the squeezing that produced these writhing graffiti. Or there are dark curlicues, resembling Arabic writing. It is all massive, uncompromising, and highly impermeable. As a result, hollows are occupied by mossy little bogs, fringed with cotton grass, looking like so many miniature white sticks of candy floss. Tough, coarse grass and the tiny, creeping dwarf willow grow on the slopes and in wandering cracks and fissures. Animals tend to scream at you up here: alpine swifts screech shrilly; dark crows croak cries of 'quark', and Geoff Milnes assured me that a curious, persistent, piping angry squeak was the call of the marmot, a comical-looking mammal that gets as fat as it can during the short summer season before hunkering down for the long winter. There is a thick vein of milky quartz cutting through the gneiss; it looks as if it might be a precious seam, but it is actually the commonest of minerals. Nonetheless, I could not resist picking up a white morsel of it to take home. The vein must have been a response to some later event when gashes opened up in the obdurate mass; quartz is always ready to fill up cracks created by tension. What struck me was how similar this place was to other gneiss terrains I had visited, no matter what their geological age: bare hills in the Highlands of Scotland, barren boggy wastes in the middle of Newfoundland, ancient areas of Sweden, all obeying the bidding of their geological foundations.

Assiduous field-workers have discovered little pods of a rock called eclogite in the rocks around San Bernardino. This rock has nothing at all to do with Virgil's pastoral verses, the *Eclogues*, good though it would be to imagine an earth scientist taking inspiration from a Roman poet. But it *is* a stone that makes geologists as lyrical as they ever get, because it is composed of special minerals, including one type of garnet, that only form very far down in the crust. Rather like the xenoliths we met in Chapter 2, eclogites tell of deep things. The area now populated by crows and marmots was once buried deeper than we can imagine – 'to exceed 70 miles', thought Arthur Holmes, and modern estimates are not so different. What revolutions of the earth have been played out on this bleak mountain pass, and what work time still has to put in to wear these peaks low again! When I asked Geoff Milnes what age the rocks were *before* they were turned into uncompromising gneisses by the Alpine orogeny he made a rueful face. As with the landscapes they produce, gneisses are much of a muchness and have lost their original personality. Gneisses can start out as shales, or granites, or even another, older gneiss. Heat and pressure is the great leveller; radioactive clocks can be reset. In the case of the San Bernardino rocks, the last option is probably the right one. In the profound tectonic scraping through the crust, older rocks, dating from still earlier revolutions of the earth,* were caught up in the new vice of Alpine mountain-building. Having already endured what the earth could inflict upon them once, they were subjected to it all over again.

But where did all these nappes come from? They have moved northwards, in pick-a-back piles, and, as Eduard Suess noticed even before nappe theory had been fully worked out, 'as a rule the highest lying sheet has been carried furthest'. We have already worked our way steadily southwards into the heated heart of the pile. When the mappers had completed their monumental surveys it became clear that the 'sheets' were tucked downwards towards the south (Maurice Lugeon called such regions root zones). If the nappes were sheets, or recumbent masses, they lie at a low angle, but in the root zones everything is tipped to the vertical. It was as if the mountain belt had been squeezed out progressively from these narrow belts. Cross-sections prepared by modern geologists show the geology arising from these zones like huge cartoon genii whipped up out of the spout of an Aladdin's lamp. A fat series of nappes will taper down to little more than a will-o'-the-wisp at its root zone. It must be time to move further southwards to look at this place where mountains apparently arise in the fashion of gigantic fungi from a small crack in a log. 'Off to Africa!', my guide exclaims. It is impossible not to respond enthusiastically.

The road winds and rewinds upon itself downwards, apparently forever. At some point trees make their reappearance, and there is the plangent dong-dong of cow bells, so the zigzag route must really be shedding altitude. When buildings appear by the roadside you realize that you have crossed into another country. As the bad-tempered crow flies, it is less than twenty kilometres from Splügen, but you have effectively entered Italy (though you're actually in Italian Switzerland). All the signs are in Italian, and the ristorante offers superlative coffee at last. It is easy to understand how effective a cultural barrrier the mountains must have been in the past: geology

* These Hercynian, or Variscan (to use Eduard Suess' term), rocks are the product of tectonics some three hundred million years older. Rock of this aspect surface in the Vosges, the beautiful mountains to the north-west of the Alps and part of Suess' 'foreland'.

separating languages. It is harder for a stranger to comprehend the glue that has retained this canton for so long as part of Switzerland. The road follows the Val Mesolcina towards Bellinzona, downwards all the way, but gently now. All the gneiss roofing slates have vanished, to be replaced by pantiles painting patchworks of all possible orange hues. Broad-leaved trees – chestnuts, limes, beeches – have replaced the conifers. Neat vineyards make green stripes on the south-facing slopes. We are heading for the main root zone of the Alps, which is marked by a major fault, the Insubric Line. It is one of the most important geological lines in Europe. Somehow, you expect to see it drawn out in black on the ground, as it is on geological maps; but of course it is more subtle than that. The San Andreas Fault in California has the same modesty, as we shall see.

We stop in the village of Pianazzo in the Val Morobbia: the river valley follows the famous line here. Streams have a way of seeking out major junctions in the earth's surface, picking out old weaknesses. An ancient and somewhat decayed path leads down to the river. Its walls have been carefully constructed from the local geology, so it must have been important once. It was probably the path that was used by the villagers to conduct their flocks to the summer pastures on the high ground beyond the river, but there is little sign of that ancient peasant life today. It is a pleasant walk downwards underneath the sweet chestnut trees. The ground is moist enough for apricot-coloured chanterelle mushrooms to sprout among the leaf litter, and there is a smell of damp in the air – almost like walking through jungle. When you see the rocks poking out at the sides of the path you are within earshot of the tumbling waters below. You notice at once that the 'grain' of the rock is vertical. Ribs of rock flank the hillside like dense palings. There is a lot of the mineral mica, which glints in the sunlight; every flat little plate of this mineral is also orientated vertically. The 'grain' of the rock is its foliation – the way it splits in response to the massive tectonic forces that have squeezed its every particle. Here, you realize, the rocks have been compressed and mangled in a way that has oppressed their very atoms. Seeking to accommodate unbearable pressure they have realigned themselves at right angles to the lateral forces generated within the earth. A strange-looking lumpy rock is all that remains of a granite, its feldspar crystals reduced to little knobs. Evidently, even the most obdurate of stones has succumbed to relentless pressure. There are creamy-looking rocks, too, which are reminiscent of the Lochseiten limestone: these are mylonites, the paste that results when rock grinds against rock in tectonic torture.

All these highly metamorphosed rocks are the roots of the Austro–Alpine nappes, those that overlie everything else: the roof of the Alps. This is where great sheets of strata come to ground. Here is the aperture that spun out those gobs of tectonic pasta that extend a hundred kilometres to the north. It is a wonder how so much can arise from so little. It is known exactly when it happened, too. The dark, lustrous mica called biotite grew in response to the mighty squeeze; it contains a radioactive 'clock' that was set at the time of the tectonic events, so we know it all happened twenty million years ago. The mountains were made high, and since then the action of eons of erosion has allowed us to see into their guts, as we did at the San Bernardino pass. This story cannot but seem dramatic to the imaginative observer, but the drama, of course, is in our minds: we inevitably anthropomorphize. Even the words we are obliged to use come with our own human baggage: *squeeze*, *pressure*, *grind*. I have tried to avoid using the word *titanic* throughout this book, although it could be strictly applied since the ancient Greek explanation was that mountains were thrown up by the Titans. As science has advanced, the Titans have been sent packing. The rocks are indifferent to humankind; they move to the slow beat of geological time. But our language inevitably still entrains them with our lives. The Scottish poet Hugh McDiarmid put it well (in 'On a Raised Beach'):

We must be humble. We are so easily baffled by appearances
And do not realise that these stones are one with the stars.
It makes no difference to them whether they are high or low,
Mountain peak or ocean floor, palace, or pigsty.
There are plenty of ruined buildings in the world but no ruined
stones.

Onwards – to Africa! Close to the swirling river there is a little rustic bridge that carries the old track across to the other side of the valley, before it snakes upwards again through yet more woods to reach the pastures above. When you lean over the bridge you can see rocks in the river bed. What is immediately obvious is that they are directed at right angles to those we examined by the descending path. They are something quite different. They look completely distinct from the crushed and shiny rocks, too – greenish schists for the most part. On the mountain slopes beyond they are in turn overlain by Triassic age limestones, which have no counterpart in the Alps to the north at all. The conclusion is obvious, yet it is hard to believe: the little bridge spans two worlds. South of the bridge there is a strange continent: it meets the main body of the Alps along the Insubric Line. The fact that the rock sequence to the south is neither squeezed nor deeply metamorphosed like those north of the bridge tells us something else: there must have been something like twenty kilometres of vertical movement along the Line. Squeezed and heated rocks that have been deep inside the earth now lie alongside others that have not. Looking over the bridge at the stream making its way along the ancient junction, you expect to observe something more profound: but no, all that movement has long since sunk into quiescence, and only the waters recognize convulsions that once shook the earth. For this is the place where Europe meets Africa to the south. The bridge spans the two continents. The collision between the masses pushed up the Alps – which is grossly to oversimplify, as you must at first. When we had a closer look we found that Africa actually extended to just the other side of the bridge, so it was possible to take a photograph of my daughter with one leg in Europe and the other in Africa. I can imagine the photograph, by then fading slightly, puzzling one of our descendants – why the legs akimbo on a leafy path somewhere that seems without particular distinction? What would they say if they realized that the curious posture straddled a significant fraction of the world?

Now we come to what, to use a happy pun, is the crunch. For now the confrontation of tectonic plates comes into the argument.

In our mind's eye, we have to draw backwards from the particular spot where my daughter stood on the surface of our kaleidoscopically complex world; or rather upwards, as if we were carried on a rocket into the ionosphere. Distance lends its own clarity. We see that our footpath terminates at one point in the south-eastern part of the Alps. Further upwards and we can see the Mediterranean Sea with its pattern of islands, and the great boot of Italy hanging downwards. We might even make out a plume of smoke from one of the classic volcanoes with which this book began, marking a current engagement of the plates. We can now appreciate the whole sweep of the Alps, and its continuation eastwards into the great arc of the Carpathian Mountains, and beyond that into Turkey, where we know the ground still shakes disastrously when the earth shrugs. We can comprehend that this is all one interconnected system, and that our path through Switzerland was no more than an amble through one tiny piece of a great mountain chain, which in turn links other ranges all the way eastwards to the Himalayas. Then we see Africa: a vast continent, and an ancient one. We can appreciate its presence, its mass, its unyielding solidity. Africa's sheer extent dwarfs that of the Mediterranean Sea. From this height, mountain ranges begin to seem more like wrinkles; nappes might be no more than tics on a spasm of the crust. If Africa is moving northwards – and it is – it suddenly seems plausible that all those monstrous rucks and buckled limestones and squeezed gneisses, over which our insignificant bodies clambered in the Alps, might be no more than the desperate scrambling of the earth away from the encroachment of the inescapable giant. The nappes fled northwards; the whole Carpathian chain curves away from the oppressor. The ancient mass of northern Europe – Eduard Suess' 'foreland' – braced itself against the onslaught, and the effects are felt far beyond the Alps themselves. The basement rocks of Europe shivered, and the rocks that covered them were flexed. Even the shape of south-east England is influenced today by the approach of the distant giant. Everything scales to the great event: the intimate history links with the grander design. You cannot look on too large a scale to help you understand a solitary footstep through the landscape, a single crystal on a cliff.

The mountains grew as ancient oceans vanished. The oceanic lithosphere was consumed until continent collided with continent, Europe with Africa; this whole process was the 'motor' of mountain-building. There were other 'Mediterraneans' before the present one, seas that came and went in the area between Africa and the European foreland. Sediments that accumulated around their continental shelves became the limestones, sandstones, and shales that subsequently fed the nappes. The greatest of these seas was what Eduard Suess called the Tethys (named for a Greek sea-goddess), which largely pre-dated the growth of the mountains. Much of the Tethys was shallow and warm during the Mesozoic, and full of life, a marine paradise of sorts: ammonites and sharks thrived, and are now preserved as fossils that date the rocks. Suess had inferred greater depths in some parts of the Tethys because calcium carbonate shells had apparently dissolved (something which only happens at depth): 'the fact that the calcareous base of the shark's teeth has been dissolved and removed [proves that] the Tethys, where it extended over many places now occupied by the Alps . . . can hardly have been less than 4000 metres depth'. Some scientists may dispute Suess' exact figure now, but nobody doubts that the Tethys spanned everything from the shallows to the deeps. But what of the dark Flysch, over which we had slithered by the roadside where this chapter began? As the mountains rose above the sea in their early stages they were immediately set about by the forces of erosion: the waste derived from the growing chains fed into adjacent marine basins – especially sags lying to the north of the growing chain – as masses of dark sediment. These sediments, the debris of tectonics, comprised the Flysch. As the mountain belt continued to evolve, and the crust shortened further between the opposing jaws of the tectonic vice, the Flysch itself became entrained with the folding and thrusting. In places it became deformed: hence the squashed Flysch fish. The Glarus nappe then slid over it, trapping it forever. By bringing in the movement of plates, the explanation of mountain chains becomes simpler than the recondite geometry of folds and nappes, and all the twisted extravagance of strata, might have suggested to those patient mappers.

Except it isn't so simple: nothing in nature is so obligingly straightforward. The *principle* of the Alps being squeezed out inexorably between the moving mass of Africa and obdurate Europe is correct enough. However, the margins of both 'sides' were not one single piece of continent – like the jaws of a woodworker's vice. Rather, both the African and European edges comprised several smaller pieces that behaved with considerable independence. A better analogy than a vice is to think instead of two huge ice-sheets jostling in the sea, with pieces fragmented from either edge grinding together or free-floating by turn as the gulf between the larger sheets waxes and wanes. The plate that lay on the far side of the bridge in the Val Morobbia should correctly be called Adria – of African origin, surely, but with a tectonic history only loosely tied to its great parent. So it was the collision of Adria – not Africa in the strict sense – with the adjacent part of Europe that was responsible for the heave of the Alpine nappes. By the same token, the margin of 'Europe' actually comprised several blocks – massifs – of old rocks. The field mappers had in fact recognized these masses of ancient (Hercynian) rocks underlying nappe complexes within the Alps. This was a triumph of deduction considering that this 'basement' could look much like some of the baked younger rocks. Most of the massive igneous rocks, like granite, within the Alps actually belong to these ancient massifs, including mighty Mont Blanc itself (15,782 feet, 4810 metres). As we have seen in the San Bernardino pass, the older rocks could also be remobilized in the Alpine movements, just to add perplexity to complexity. These ancient blocks provide an explanation of the separate 'packages' of nappes. A single crunch – Africa (even Adria) on Europe – could not by itself explain the complexity of tectonic events that built the great piles. Instead, there was a long evolution of the mountain chain, event piled on event, which threw one series of nappes above its predecessor. There must have been several closures, block to block, not just the single great one when the opposing continents came into direct confrontation. When one massif collided with its neighbour this produced earlier phases of deformation, the earlier packages of nappes. There was even a pattern to it, a southerly migration of collision events as the African blocks progressively approached the European. There must therefore be more than one root zone – for each of the major events should connect to the line of its own genesis. There was, in short, squeeze following upon squeeze. The last, and arguably the greatest, was the one that left behind the tortured rock along the Insubric Line. So great, in fact, that morsels of 'Africa' were carried bodily northwards over Europe. Each of these events was profoundly important in shaping mountains, and yet, viewed from the high vantage point of a passing comet, none was more than another pulse in the slow and inexorable progress of the plates. Lubrication was important: several of the nappes glided on salt, deposited after one of the ancient seaways dried out during the Triassic. This was the oil that smoothed the passage of mighty segments of the earth.

Such is the moulding of mountains: each one explicable in terms of tectonic principles, yet each stamped with its own individuality. To this extent, mountains are like people, cast from common genetic rules, yet every one having a personality of its own. Mountains are often the personification of strata, and indeed they are often named for their fanciful resemblance to white teeth or a virgin's breasts. Alpinists struggling with difficult peaks always seem to address their adversaries in human terms rather than as examples of tectonics in action. The Matterhorn, on the border between Valais (Switzerland) and Piedmont (Italy), is celebrated for its precipitate sides and for the fact that Colonel Whymper lost four men in its conquest in 1865. Less well known is the – far more astonishing – fact that its upper portion is actually a part of 'Africa' thrust bodily northwards over Europe. The character of the mountain, and the face it presents to the climber, is as surely a product of its geology – and the subsequent effects of weathering – as our own character is a consequence of our genetic make-up acted upon and modified by the vicissitudes of our upbringing.

It is time to leave 'Africa' and head northwards again, back into the Alps to look at one of the ancient massifs. From Bellinzona, this means following the Ticino valley upwards, to the west of our path down from the San Bernadino pass. The climb on the old road to the St Gotthard Pass proved to be a reverse replay of the descent. My visit there was obscured by low cloud: what should have been a splendid panorama was reminiscent of a late Turner painting, a kind of dramatic but milky obscurity. But it was still possible to inspect – up close – the rock of the Gotthard Massif. This is the heaviest kind of grey granitic gneiss, a rock of ancient and implacable solidity, grim and giving no quarter. It is easy to imagine it as one side of a tectonic vice, or as some kind of bulwark against which nappes are no more than pliable mash. The sparse vegetation clearly has a tough time extracting the most meagre rations from its impoverished soil; it is the Scrooge of rocks. Time to move on.

The next massif northwards is the Aar Massif – more grim gneisses forming intimidating cliffs. Sandwiched between the Gotthard and the Aar, like a thin slice of Parma ham between two halves of a loaf, is the root zone of another of the great nappe packages – the Helvetic nappes. At the foot of the Gotthard pass, the town of Andermatt is nearby, one of those places with a kind of story-book Swissness. On the edge of town, near the railway, and in a much less picturesque quarter, is a large, dull grey barracks, behind which the root zone crops out on the hillside. The cliff displays a series of yellowish crushed limestones and – as along the Isubric Line – they are vertical, with a squeezed mien. We have come full circle, for this is also the root zone of the Glarus Nappe, where this journey began. This is the time to envisage the mighty piles above you; how erosion of the higher nappes has opened 'windows' giving on to the earlier tectonic events; how the mountains are still rising, while frost and rivers incessantly seek to render them low; and how all this is accountable to the movement of plates. Modern research is focused particularly on deep processes and structures, in the lower crust and upper mantle, as revealed by seismic reflections. Here you can see how the opposing continental masses really meet. For example, it is likely that a 'wedge' of Adria impinged into the guts of Europe, such was the northward heave of the greater continent to the south. This, the most studied range in the world, still has secrets to reveal.

The waste of a mountain range: the Rigi by Lake Lucerne is composed of molasse derived from erosion of the Alpine chain.

There is one rock-type to mention as a postscript: molasse. The typical locality is the mountain known as the Rigi, west of Lucerne, but the whole area on this shore of the Vierwald is made of it, an old-fashioned-plum-pudding kind of rock, a pebbly pot-pourri, including rounded cobbles of all manner of other rock types. I saw many pale limestone pebbles, some sandstones, even some pieces of what I took to be gneiss, and all dusted with a kind of pinkish skin. It is a massive rock formation, underlying whole mountain-sides. The molasse provides a record of the wearing down of the Alpine range at a late stage; unlike the Flysch, it is largely non-marine. The cobbles and pebbles had their edges knocked off in raging torrents, and they were rounded further in their inexorable progress downhill. Every cobble in the molasse represents a bit broken off a mountain: they were collected together indiscriminately in the deposit. A mountain-side of this conglomerate is a mountain destroyed elsewhere. The rivers of ten million years or so ago drained northwards into a basin that now occupies the Swiss Plain, and so molasse underlies the serious, business side of the country: even commerce bows to geology. By the time they had reached this point, much of the energy of the waters had abated and was insufficient to move pebbles, so sandy and silty rocks predominate under the plain. Around Lake Lucerne, though, there are coarse rocks laid down in ancient channels or spread out by floods. Down by the lake the molasse slopes are gentle, and the soil is a reddish colour that I do not recall seeing elsewhere on our journey. There are old orchards everywhere, but the most profitable crop these days is tourism. Down at Weggis, the Seehof Hotel du Lac is the very picture of luxury, with a waterfront having Venetian pretensions, and wrought-iron balconies and blue shutters. It was fashionable when built a century ago and is now quietly dignified and expensive in maturity; the foreigner's vision of Swiss elegance, perhaps. But I like to think first of the apple orchards on the hillside above, growing on red soil that has been derived from the weathering of peaks long since vanished. The revolution wrought by tectonics has been finally converted into fruit.

We have been on a journey through a small part of a great range, and that range is itself connected to others that extend as far as the Himalayas – and further, through the Malayan Peninsula to Indonesia. Although it is a classic area, it would be foolish to expect the Alps to be a surrogate for all mountain belts everywhere: the world is too rich and complex for that. The Alps are, for example, poor in granites, those most implacable of mountain makers, and most of those that do occur are ancient rocks caught up in the later earth movements.* No matter: we shall meet them elsewhere. Nor are nappes as important in some other mountain belts – the Alps were the product of a particularly hard 'docking' of one continental mass against another. Push invariably came to shove: but it does not have

* There is one important granite associated with the Alpine Orogeny. It cuts through the Pennine nappes and therefore must postdate them. It is thus important for calibrating the timing of the events in the whole range.

to be so violent. And we will encounter in other places fragments of ocean floor caught up in tectonic mayhem. Actually, these *do* occur in the Alps, for the mappers had accurately recorded 'serpentines' in their accounts; it just took a very long time for their significance to be appreciated. According to Rudolf Trümpy, if they had been recognized for what they were, the whole theoretical edifice of plate tectonics might have been deduced from the Alps: but this is to anticipate things to come. What can be said without blushing is that the elements that we met in our journey round Glarus are common to mountain belts through much of geological time and in most orogenic belts. There is 'flysch' and 'molasse' associated with many folded ranges. I have laboured long hours trying to find fossils in flysch nearly 500 million years old: no fishes to gape at me then, just the little 'hack-saw blades' of graptolites. Then, too, the earth's crust has buckled and shortened in every mountain chain, and where it has thickened, metamorphism has produced gneisses not so different from those we saw on the San Bernadino Pass. Strata from ancient seas have been thrust up to cap high peaks (there are fossil shells at the top of Mount Everest). Virtually all ranges, too, are composite like the Alps, with one event following another as the mountains evolved over several tens of millions of years. Convolution and concatenation, folding and refolding, buckling and cracking or heating and bending, squeezing followed by collapse when the pressure is off: it is about as complicated as geology gets. Sometimes rocks are so perturbed and disguised that it is hard to say *what* they once were.

Mountains demand an explanation beyond the fury of the Titans. After all, the thoughtful traveller soon realized that many mountains came in linear ranges: there had to be a *design* to the earth beyond the pettish whims of the gods. The seventeenth-century Jesuit, Athanasius Kirchner saw mountains as an internal skeleton, the bones of the earth. When you view the Alps from a distance, perhaps this does not seem quite so absurd, especially since hard and resistant rocks often take the high ground: rocky bones indeed. Kirchner's *Mundus Subterraneus* of 1664 continued to be quoted until well into the eighteenth century and was, at the least, a stimulant for thinking about mountains in the context of a global explanation. The search for a theory of mountains was to occupy many more able geological minds for the next three hundred years. The Alps were always central to the arguments. With their gift for abstraction, it is perhaps not surprising that the French played a prominent part in the process. Since Descartes had freed the wondering mind from theological baggage, the world had become their philosophical oyster. Léonce Elie de Beaumont (1798–1874) was the director of the *Carte Géologique*, a mighty undertaking to map the rocks of France completely for the first time. He was by training a mathematician, and inclined to view the world as deducable from mathematical principles. He was gifted enough to become the top graduate from the École Polytechnique in Paris, forcing ground for the *élite*, and became a distinguished field geologist. His achievements probably induced in him a certain arrogance; and Elie de Beaumont did indeed become a monolithic authority. For thirty years, between the 1820s and 1850s, he published influential works on the causes of mountain-building. Recall that this period coincided with the acquisition of basic data from the rocks themselves – the heroic efforts of those who climbed the Alps with pencil and paper in their knapsacks as well as a hunk of bread and cheese for lunch. So Elie de Beaumont was theorizing in tandem with new and hard-won discoveries in the field.

The same period also saw the rise to prominence of the scientific methods advocated by Charles Lyell with which this book began. Lyell himself had considered mountain formation in some detail. In line with his uniformitarian notions, he had conceived of grand elevations by the continuous accretion of existing effects, particularly the uplifts in topography that were known to be produced by earthquakes and volcanoes. It was a case of excelsior little by little. By contrast, Elie de Beaumont saw violent revolutions, narrowly confined to zones of weakness in the earth, and limited to special periods of global unease. He was aware of the growing evidence for powerful folding in the Alps: no mere nudging could produce such contortions. He was also attracted to measuring the lie of the mountains, and plotted their linear trends with an eye to their systematization. Elie

An early attempt at global synthesis of tectonics: Elie de Beaumont's (1798–1874) attempt to line up mountain chains into his geometrical system of the *réseau pentagonal*.

de Beaumont was in little doubt that the folding and thrusting he and others had observed in the Alps resulted in an overall piling up of the strata – what we would now recognize as crustal shortening. Some of his results were published in the *Philosophical Magazine* in 1831 as 'Researches on Some of the Revolutions of the Surface of the Globe: Presenting Various Examples of the Coincidence between the Elevations of Beds in Certain Systems of Mountains, and the Sudden

Changes Which Have Produced the Lines of Demaracation Observable in Certain Stages of the Sedimentary Deposits' (*Philosophical Magazine* Volume 10). If an author were to submit such a title today the editor would faint with shock . . . but it does save me the trouble of explaining what it is about. It is tempting to seize upon the 'Revolution' in the title. After all, revolution was likely to figure high in the consciousness of a Frenchman, and Lyell's modest changes, which effect much in small steps, provide the model for accomplishing reform through continuous parliamentary democracy. Lyell's ideas were also crucial to the young Charles Darwin: evolution, not revolution, has been claimed as the mantra of democracy.

The clash of opinion on the origin of the Alps is often presented as a test case for the great nineteenth-century debate on 'uniformitarianism versus catastrophism', but it is not as simple as that. Many geologists of fundamentally Lyellian persuasion were impressed by Elie de Beaumont's results. His political equivalent as the head of the British Geological Survey, Henry de la Beche, was one of them. Other processes might be involved in mountain-building than mere 'up and down' – but what? He viewed with favour Elie de Beaumont's idea that the earth was contracting as a result of its slow cooling, mountains being thrown up as periodic 'adjustments' of the crust to accommodate a diminishing circumference. 'If we suppose with M. Elie de Beaumont,' he wrote in 1834, 'that the state of our globe is such that, in a given time, the temperature of the interior is lowered by much greater quantity than on its surface, the solid crust would break up to accommodate itself to the internal mass; almost imperceptibly, when time and the mass of the earth are taken into account, but by considerable dislocations.' That 'almost imperceptibly', combined with 'considerable dislocations', is suggestive of revolution by stealth; of having his Lyellian cake and eating it, too.

Elie de Beaumont is commemorated by the mountain that carries his name in the Alps – the New Zealand Alps, not the Swiss. By geologists he is remembered – if at all – for the aberrations of his maturity rather than for the brilliance of his youth. Obsessed with finding a mathematical design in the arrangement of mountain belts, he developed what he termed the *réseau pentagonal*. He ascribed the directions of mountain belts to regular pentagons drawn on the surface of the globe – the pentagons themselves being derived from the intersection of fifteen great circles. His lines were 'zones of weakness' along which mountain belts preferentially aligned. This, he believed, was where the subterranean controls on folding were expressed on the ground. It was a total global system, a theory of almost everything. It was also an *idée fixe* for Elie de Beaumont and he defended it to the last, and with his by then considerable authority. When anomalies in his system were discovered he simply made it more complex to cope with them, until his intersecting lines drawn on the earth resembled a spider's web. To historians of science the situation is a classic one: it is reminiscent of the 'epicycles' that had to be introduced to retain an earth-centred astronomy. To account for awkward facts, the system of orbiting planets was tinkered with until it collapsed under the weight of its own modifications. Similarly, the *réseau pentagonal* died with the great geologist. Of course, with the wisdom of hindsight, we might say that Elie de Beaumont was half right. As we shall see, there *are* zones of weakness where tectonics reawaken. He was more accurate in his reading of the Alps than was Lyell. And one day a great earth system would indeed be discovered. His ambitions had exceeded what was known of the earth at the time, and his grand mistake obscured his grander virtues. History sometimes cheats reputations.

Eduard Suess had more of the geology of the Alps at his command than any of his predecessors: after all, it was home territory for him. He was as averse as Elie de Beaumont to the notion of mountains as areas accountable to uplift alone. Everywhere he saw evidence of lateral movement, of rock formations piled on one another. He was familiar with much of the country we have explored, and he read it well. Suess never thought other than globally. Like Marcel Bertrand, he made connections between mountain chains, joining one to another like a cordon drawn across the continents, and he knew that such a global phenomenon required a general explanation. The Andes and the Rockies were all grist to his tectonic mill. By the end of the nineteenth century, it was accepted that there were many ancient mountain belts, and that the history of the planet had been punctuated by mountain-building events, or orogenies. We shall be visiting some of these old scars on the face of the earth later in this book. Whatever the cause of mountain ranges, then, it must be one that could stretch back through geological time. Exactly how much time that involved was far from clear when Suess wrote *Das Antlitz der Erde*, but it was certain that many millions of years were necessary to lay down the rocks of seas long vanished, elevate them into mountain chains, by whatever means, only to have them worn down to contribute to the next cycle of sediments. When Suess compiled his synthesis of the world the geological scale of time periods based upon the succession of stratigraphy and fossils – Cambrian, Cretaceous, and the like – was essentially in its modern form. But much finer subdivisions of geological time had also been introduced. As an example, Suess went to great lengths to show that one small part of the Cretaceous, termed the Cenomanian Stage, was a time when the seas advanced widely over the surface of the globe. What was not known was how many millions of years ago this event happened – the radiometric scale that could measure it was still to be developed. Still, the scientific basis for correlation of rocks was sufficient to make generalizations about when and how the past upheavals of the earth had happened. In Europe, three main mountain-building events – Caledonian, Variscan, and Alpine, respectively – served to divide the history of the continent. They were times when the earth convulsed, when Lyell's slow ticking of the geological clock was speeded up; between times, the earth was calmer. For Suess, summing up folding and thrusting in a dozen mountain chains, orogenic events happened when the earth shrugged violently and pulled itself together. After all, he maintained, the earth was contracting in volume: when the strain became too much, mountain ranges were the planet's way of coping.

* * *

Eduard Suess was a thoroughly political animal. He was a member of the Austrian parliament for twenty years. He knew how to make a case. *Das Antlitz der Erde* is more than a brilliant summary of how the world was made; it is also a disguised polemic for Suess' view of it. He first set out to establish geology's omniscience. An early chapter deals with the biblical Flood. The discovery in Mesopotamia of the clay tablets known today as the Epic of Gilgamesh, and to Suess as the Izdubar Epic, allowed for a new interpretation of the biblical event. The tablets in the Akkadian language described the flood as history, and in some detail. The decipherment of the tablets was a 'state-of-the-art' discovery. Suess took the account on, point by point, to show that the Flood was a geological event: a tidal wave or tsunami approaching from the sea rather than the result of exceptional rainstorms coming from the mountains. It was the first attempt to demystify the Flood.* Geology was a great rationalizing force, and throughout his huge compilation, Suess could not resist providing a rational explanation for legends. Here he is entertainingly slaying a dragon: '*Trionyx aegypticus* lives in the neighbourhood of Beyrut, and it is a remarkable fact that the crocodile of the Nile still exists in the nearby estuary of the Nahr e' Zerka, or crocodile river, three kilometres to the north of Caesarea. Pliny knew of a town – Crocodilion – in this neighbourhood . . . These facts also throw unexpected light on the numerous and circumstantial accounts of the slaughter of a scaly monster by the knight Deodat von Gozon on the island of Rhodes in the first half of the fourteenth century.' Curiously, Schiller, whose Wilhelm Tell was linked above with one of the classical geological sites of Switzerland, also wrote a poem about this 'dragon', based on an account by one J. Bosio published in 1594.

Suess was equally concerned about promoting his view of tectonics. 'A complete revolution of opinion has taken place as regards the formation of mountain chains,' he wrote, and it was his own ideas to which he was referring. When he wished to underscore a

* A recent attempt, by the distinguished oceanographers Drs Ryan and Pitman, makes a good case for the Flood legend originating in a huge marine inundation of the Black Sea. Clearly, geology can yield more than one answer.

point he resorted to italics, so the reader is infallibly guided to the nub of the matter. '*The dislocations visible in the rocky crust of the earth are the result of movements which are produced by a decrease in the volume of our planet.*' Nothing ambiguous about that. The shortening of the earth's crust observed in mountain ranges was inescapable. Since it was also clear that such linear chains had a long history, perhaps extending back in time for hundreds of millions of years, there had to be a way to explain the inevitable telescoping of all those strata. A decrease in the earth's volume would provide it. But Suess regarded ocean basins as areas of subsidence, so there was no opportunity to reduce the area of the earth's surface there. It would take ocean floor spreading to balance an apparently impossible equation, as we shall see. The ancient cores of continents seemed to be inviolable forelands on to which the mountain structures spilled, as would a wad of clay squeezed between two bricks. It had to be the mountain chains that took the strain, and initiated the next geological cycle of erosion and sedimentation in the long, slow dance of the earth. As for the Alps, the details of a single outcrop confirmed the larger scheme. Here is Suess' description of the kind of country we have explored in this chapter:

> The Flysch has been driven like a plastic mass, and the great advancing sheet of Cretaceous limestone rears itself up, creeps upwards over the Flysch, assumes a vertical position and finally turns over backwards. Heim has termed this a turnover klippe . . . it is precisely these ends of the sheets which have directed attention anew to the diminution of the Earth's circumference.

Home territory is always the most persuasive. For 'it is the number of sheets lying upon one another as seen in the Swiss Alps, which most impresses us with the magnitude of the phenomenon [i.e. shortening]'. From Glarus to the world, indeed! The image that was often used to illustrate Suess' idea was a drying, and therefore shrinking, apple, whose wizened countenance and ridges and furrows seemed appropriate for the visage of the earth crossed by mountain ranges. The metaphor was taken so seriously that pictures of old apples actually appeared in textbooks. Perhaps it was secretly hoped that this apple would be to tectonics what Newton's was to physics. As recently as 1952 the Presidential Address to the Geological Society of London was on the topic of a contracting earth.

I like to think of a succession of observers contemplating a mountainside, perhaps the one across the lake from the hotel balcony by the Urnersee where Wilhelm Tell jumped to freedom. Old Kirchner would have seen a kind of girder reaching from the innards of the earth. Charles Lyell might have seen the consequences of ten thousand tremors. Elie de Beaumont might well have seen the same strata as a mere grace note on the *réseau pentagonal*. He might have smiled briefly to himself, recalling the beauty and completeness of his system, then frowned momentarily while recalling some critic or other. And Eduard Suess would have seen folding as yet more incontrovertible evidence of the incessant, slow, shrinking of the earth. The image hitting the retina would be the same for all of them, but what is actually *seen* depends on the secret workings of the brain. Seeing is not believing; rather, it is belief that governs seeing. The modern observer? He might see little squirming strata on the back of the collision of Adria and Europe. No doubt the present-day viewer is closer to the truth than any of his predecessors, and the advances in understanding in the last half century have been enormous and permanent; but it would be foolish to suppose that an observer a century hence will see nothing differently. *Autres temps, autres yeux.*

By the time Arthur Holmes wrote his textbook the structure of nappes was well understood. Heim and his successors' magisterial maps had been published and digested. In the fifty years after Suess, physicists had been to work on the idea of the secular contraction of the earth, which was originally based on the concept that the earth was a cooling body. The discovery of radioactive heating upset all the calculations: it just wouldn't work. We shall soon meet those who thought, on the contrary, that the earth was expanding. The poor old earth could apparently be pumped up and down like a balloon! The global pattern of mountain belts was well known, and Eduard Suess deserved much credit for outlining them; but, as

Holmes remarked, the 'assemblage of mountain systems combines into a world pattern of apparent simplicity which nevertheless masks a variety of details that remain perplexing and unexplained'. There had to be a mechanism for the emplacement of nappes that did not depend on the contraction hypothesis. It must be a force capable of moving large chunks of strata laterally at low angles. Newton's pristine and unshrivelled apple might have its place in the argument after all, for gravity is such a force.

The higher nappes in the Alpine pile might, in this theory, have slid into place, on a lubricated sole of salt, or some other tectonic 'oil'. As they moved, they also folded progressively. You can get some impression of how it works if you lay well-puddled clay in a thin sheet upon a board and tip it upwards: if the consistency of the clay is correct it will eventually slither and fold under the influence of gravity. In the 1950s several serious academics, especially Hans Ramberg of Uppsala University in Sweden, spent a lot of time on clay models, and sometimes produced good simulacra of nature. Analogue models have developed considerably since those days, and are now used extensively in the oil industry. Curiously, the gravity sliding theory was in essence a revival in sophisticated dress of Charles Lyell's notions of uplift as the essential control on mountain-building. For you also need to elevate some region along the growing mountain belt to produce a 'high' from which the nappes could slide. Such a line of elevation became known as a geanticline – an upward swell running along the axis of the mountain chain. As the geanticline rose upwards, nappes glided off like slicks from the back of an emerging whale. This might satisfactorily explain the higher nappes, but then you also need an explanation for the kind of nappes which we saw at the San Bernadino pass – those that involve deeper (and older) rocks, metamorphosed under high temperature and pressure. How do you get them to rise up from the depths? It is a slightly difficult concept to grasp. Arthur Holmes explained it like this. The 'deeper and hotter parts of the infrastructure . . . [were] where these [burial] effects are most intense, as in the core of an orogenic belt, [and hence] the zone rises to higher levels and may pass high into the superstructure'. Deep, hot rocks 'flow' upwards, deforming and creeping like a contrary glacier of the underworld. There was a model for this process in the salt domes of the Middle East. Deeply buried deposits of sea-salt dome upwards and pass through overlying strata, as a kind of intrusive lobe, eventually emerging at the surface – the rising tongue is called a diapir. I examined one of these salt domes in the Oman desert. It makes an improbable hump hundreds of metres across in the middle of a stony, flat wasteland: you can see it from miles away. A partly flowing, partly crusty hilly mass of salt is a curious thing to see in the fiery heat. Even odder is to find all sorts of blocks of rocks lying around that have been carried up with the salt as it cut through strata overlying it, including limestone blocks with fossils. Some of these salt domes have acquired commercial importance as oil traps.

The heyday of gravity tectonics came and went, as the contracting earth had done before it. Once more, detailed field-work provided critical evidence. In the first place, when nappes were very carefully reconstructed back to their original disposition (imagine refolding those sheets back on the bed) the evidence for any kind of downhill slope was very tenuous. It began to seem as if a 'push' were needed after all: gravity alone would not do the work. Secondly, as the history of the various parts of the Alpine chain was unscrambled, it became clear that the emplacement of nappes coincided with the closure of ocean basins – precisely the circumstances when such a 'push' might result from natural causes. The timing of the emplacement of the 'packages' of nappes could be related to the history of the massifs and the sediments that accumulated upon and between them. Further research discovered microcontinents like the Briançonnaise – parts of 'Europe' that, like Adria in relation to Africa, had a semi-detached history. It seemed a logical inference that the Alpine mountains were the consequence of the jugglings of all these major pieces of lithosphere, and not just a question of 'up and down'. That uplift was going on was undeniable – recall the Via Mala, that slit carved steeply into the earth – but this was as much a feature of the present history of the chain as an element in its early evolution. The time was ripe for the Alps to be integrated into the story of the plates, and that of the confrontation of old Africa and old Europe. When that happened, the green serpentinites in the Pennine nappes would suddenly make sense. But this is to anticipate.

We leave Switzerland by way of the Jura Mountains. The name of the mountains is famous in geology, it is the type area for the Jurassic system, 205–137 million years ago, which, as every child now knows, was when Dinosaurs Ruled the Earth. Rocks of this age are beautifully developed in the area, as you would expect of a type locality, although the ones I saw were all sedimentary rocks that had been laid down under the sea, and would therefore yield to the hammer the fossils of humble invertebrates like ammonites, brachiopods, snails, and clams rather than the bones of huge terrestrial monsters. The mountains run in a great swathe north-west of Neuchâtel – where Marcel Bertrand was a professor – following the direction of the Lac de Neuchâtel. All along the northern edge of the lake, the southerly-facing hillsides rise in vineyard after vineyard. Beyond the vineyards a wooded ridge reaches to the skyline. The Jura Mountains comprise a series of great ridges like this one, running in parallel east-south-east–west-north-west. They are like the wrinkles on the forehead of a very old man. The high points of the ridges often exceed 1300 metres, so they are not negligible, even if they are dwarfed by the Alpine peaks south of the Lac de Neuchâtel. Between the ridges there are valleys with the same trend, so the whole countryside is one of densely wooded, rising ridges separated by intensively farmed depressions – corn, beet, and wheat – and this pattern extends well beyond the border into France. Cows have changed from the cute grey Swiss ones to a more everyday red-and-white breed. Most of the rivers faithfully follow the valley floors, but a few of them turn to cut directly through the ridges in steep-sided gorges. We follow one of these north of Neuchâtel, which traverses the Chaumont. Rocks are well exposed in the sides of the gorge. One difference from the Alps is immediately obvious. No longer are the strata thrown into elaborate contortions. They are tipped perhaps thirty degrees from the horizontal, but one stratum succeeds its predecessor in orderly fashion, younger upon older, as well-behaved stratigraphic sections should. An occasional small twitch in the bedding reminds us that these rocks, too, have not escaped tectonic influence, but, clearly, we are beyond the reach of the most violent of the Alpine convulsions.

The little town of Valangin guards the entrance to the gorge. It, too, is a famous name in geology, for the Valanginian is the label attached to the second earliest time division of the Cretaceous, following on from the Jurassic. The strata in the area record the passage of time from one period to another without a break. Old Valangin is built from the local limestones, which yield deliciously creamy-yellow blocks. That the château was defensive in origin is obvious, for its massive walls boast round towers on the corners, and its entrance is heavily fortified. The block-like big house tucked away safely inside is functional first, luxurious second. This place was evidently built to protect the route running through the gorge. In Valangin you are reminded how appropriately villages that have been built from the local geology seem to lie in the landscape. They appear to grow from the hillsides. France, with its abundance of limestones, has hundreds of such towns and villages, from Provence in the south to Caen in the north. No matter if the buildings lack distinction – though they rarely lack individuality – for the harmonious whole is more than the sum of its parts. England, too, has dozens of villages in the Cotswolds with the same charm. Elsewhere, where natural building stone is unavailable, local bricks and tiles still grow out of the land, and add their character to the regional architecture. In Provence, I visited the source of ochre, which is a sandstone formation cutting across the vineyards near Apt. How suitable this colour wash now seems rendering walls in the Midi; like sunflowers – and much the same shade – ochre revels in the rich heat.

The structure of the Jura is comparatively simple. The great waves of hill and vale passing over the landscape reflect similar waves in the strata. The ground undulates in harmony with folding of the Jurassic and Cretaceous limestones. The ridges are anticlines, meaning that the rocks are bowed upwards. The valleys between them are synclines, where the strata are bent downwards in the fashion of a cupped hand. The topography follows the bidding of the underlying structure almost slavishly. Everything else is a consequence of the geological underlay: the cultivated valleys; the wild, wooded hillsides; the courses of the streams; where vines will ripen grapes. Look carefully when crossing over a ridge and you will see the switch in the general dip of the limestone beds as you traverse the axis of the anticline. On the southern side of the ridge most of the limestone beds tilt to the south, northwards they are inclined to the north; a simple scheme only complicated by the inevitable minor undulations. The Jura is a geological switchback, a sine curve graven into the earth.

The form of the ridges was generated as part of the Alpine movements. Looking at the map of Europe it is easy to see the Jura as an outrider to the great weal of the Alps, flanking all that confusing disturbance, that most unruly and stirred-up pile. Imagine scrabbling up a rug into a mass of folds at one end, while at the other the material is thrown into a series of diminishing undulations. The connection between the Alps and the Jura was not always recognized. It was only with the growth of geology as a globally interconnected science that the marriage of the two regions was established. Here is Eduard Suess writing in the second volume of *Das Antlitz der Erde*:

> There was a time when every single anticline of the Jura was regarded as an independent axis of elevation; then it became clear that such a collection of parallel anticlines must have a common origin; next it was seen that there is a certain dependence between the Alps and the Jura; finally, the influence of the obstacle presented by the Black Forest was recognized . . .

Suess saw the Black Forest as part of the 'foreland' against which the Alps were constrained. The Jura Mountains were the relatively minor folds produced as the Alpine movements lost their momentum against the immovable block to the north, a series of shrugs of exhaustion. The modern view is perhaps not so different in outcome, except that the cause is – at the deep root of things – the northward movement of Africa. The Jura is part of the marginal effects of the convergence between the European plate and its great neighbour to the south. The folding is now considered to be the reaction of a thin 'skin' of sedimentary rocks to the kick of continued Alpine movements, lubricated by a detachment in the thick Triassic salt deposits at depth. It is as if the folds in the rug were generated by changing the relief on the especially slippery floor on which it lay rather than by shaking the rug from one side. Seismic profiles made through this part of Europe suggest that the deep detachment extends southwards all the way to the Aar Massif. The vines and forest trees on the flanks of the Jura owe their particular habitat to events that happened several kilometres beneath their roots. Thus it is that the intimate details of natural history link downwards into unseen worlds. Everything connects.

At the top of one of the ridges there is a *Vue des Alpes*. Lying beyond the far shore of the Lac de Neuchâtel, the array of white peaks takes up the horizon, like ranks of shark's teeth. Distance scrambles them together, so it is hard for a foreigner to place them in order. They seem to erect an impenetrable barrier, yet we know that even in the late Stone Age there were skin-clad men who would brave the remote passes; one of them fell into a crevasse and was yielded up from his natural deep-freeze only a few years ago. Forensic palaeontologists have determined that he had ibex for lunch and that he may have been shot in the shoulder by a rival. Can it really be true that the Carthaginian general Hannibal Barca drove elephants over the passes 2200 years ago? We have the word of the Greek historian Polybius that it was indeed so. But before the era of the written word, whether the words we read are true or not, everything has to be established by inference. History envelops the past in uncertainty, like the mist obscuring the beech trees in the valley below me. The deeper the history, the more the outlines blur, the more inferences about the past are subject to change. In this chapter we have seen how different eyes contemplating the Alps each saw their own version of history. We have a vision for our time, but we can be certain that it will not be the last. Modern heroes have followed in Hannibal's tracks, but this time with map and pencil in hand, unscrambling the secrets of the Alps written in a code of writhing rock. We know that it is not faith that moves mountains; it is tectonics. Geophysicists today poke beneath the great pile with their seismic probes. We now know a great deal about the Alps: their structure, the role of plates in their genesis. There has been a revolution in our understanding over the last forty years, and the gains in knowledge are permanent. But we will never know everything, and that is as it should be. From the obscuring mist of the past, science has ensured that some of the mountains have emerged into clear view, but as soon as that happens the misty shadows of further peaks are glimpsed in the distance, rank upon rank: so many other heights to climb, so many mysteries to investigate.

5

Plates

There are lands of the imagination that cannot exist, but seem real; and there are lands that once existed that somehow seem remote and hard to credit. Perhaps their comparative solidity depends on the hand of a skilled writer. Who can doubt the reality of the countries beyond the sea that Jonathan Swift peopled so skilfully for his hero Lemuel Gulliver to visit, not merely to stimulate the imagination, but as a ruse to illustrate human frailties: puffed up and monstrous in Brobdignag, or shrunk in Lilliput to petty proportions to match the triviality of their concerns? Yet to travel back in time to the land of the Gonds – Gondwana – or to try to grasp the reality of Pangaea 250 million years ago seems to require a greater leap of imagination. But these places existed, as solid as Africa is today.

Somewhere in a middling category is Atlantis, a familiar enough name, but one which is either myth, or myth ultimately rooted in reality. Determined researchers strive to place it on the map with the certainty of New York or Vladivostok. Plato described the kingdom in his *Timaeus*, locating it in the Atlantic Ocean – or at least 'beyond the Pillars of Hercules'; but theories abound that prefer to place it within the Mediterranean Sea, near the cradle of the classical world. Whichever the preferred location, its catastrophic elimination as a punishment for the dubious ways of its inhabitants was a tectonic one, for Plato describes earthquakes and floods. A cursory search on the Internet will show the curious observer how many *outré* theories exist about the drowned kingdom. There are claims made for it being in the South China Sea, and, for all I know, on the moon. Probably the most plausible scenario relates the destruction of Atlantis to the eruption of Thera, now known as Santorini, seventy kilometres north of Crete. This was the biggest eruption that *Homo sapiens* has ever witnessed, at least in Europe. It has been estimated that thirty cubic kilometres of material was erupted – that is fifteen times more than in the famous eruption of Vesuvius in AD 79 that eliminated Pompeii. The eruption of 1700 BC also coincided approximately with the decline of Minoan civilization, and is therefore one of the crucial phases of western history. The Bronze Age could have had no better source for its subsequent legends. It must have been a most catastrophic blast, for it left a caldera six kilometres in diameter. It surely generated a vast tsunami, which would have drowned the vibrant coastal towns of Crete. On Thera itself, direct evidence of burial by pumice is preserved in the town of Akrotiri, where colourful frescos and wine jars testify to the good life before the Fall. The sky would have darkened with sheer volume of ash, the grapes would have withered upon the vine; misfortune would have fallen with the inexorability of volcanic tephra upon rich and poor alike. The plain-dwellers would have been punished with the mountain folk. That Thera *was* Atlantis is given some credence by Plato's description of the place (pre-eruption) as comprising several concentric belts of land and lagoons – a rather characteristic volcanic configuration. According to Robert Scandone, a vulcanologist at Rome University, the eruption of Thera may have inspired at least one passage in the story of Jason and the Argonauts. When they returned to Greece with the golden fleece they passed by Rhodes to the eastern part of Crete; here they experienced a pall of darkness – as indeed they would have done if they were under a cloud of volcanic ash. When they fled northwards, a bronze giant called Talos pelted them with fragments of rock (this hardly requires further explanation). The eastern Mediterranean is replete with flood legends, which are not unreasonably linked with tsunamis in the aftermath of major eruptions. Today, what remains of Thera is the precipitous and sun-bleached port of Santorini and its flooded caldera, which shelters a small fishing fleet engaged in satisfying the demand for fresh-grilled sardines in *tavernas* catering for tourist cruise liners. It is a prosaic way for the Argonauts to be shadowed. An observant passenger on one of these liners might spot Nea Kameni, a small island gradually growing from lava extruded out of sight. Who knows if the volcano might once again wreak destruction? For now, we know that all that destruction was caused by Africa moving northwards into and on to Europe; for Santorini lies at the edge of the Aegean plate. What we see at the surface, of course, is all down to the influence of the geological foundations. But how did this understanding arise?

For Eduard Suess the idea of foundered lands was meat and drink. Some Atlantis of the mind enchanted him. Before the fundamental difference between ocean crust and continental crust was appreciated, it was possible – preferable, even – to think of the oceans as places where continents had foundered. It would be wrong to think of that generation of geologists a century ago as reluctant to admit all change. Rather, they would admit the kind of change they wanted and deny other processes. They appreciated some of the evidence for what we would now call plate tectonics. Gondwana* should be taken as the prime example, because it was the acceptance of the existence of this vanished land that set the seal on modern geology. Suess coined the word – the 'Gonds' were an ancient Indian tribe. He saw very well connections between the geology of Africa, South America, and Peninsular India, and appreciated that they were bound together by more than coincidence. Like finding fragments of an old treasure map, he saw that broken lines must connect to make a picture, and that the picture was a key to fundamental truths about the earth.

When I set out to read through Suess' dense prose I had not realized how intelligently he appreciated the evidence of the rocks. Rocks do not lie. They do, however, dissemble as to their true meaning.

* I was once ticked off for using the term 'Gondwanaland' rather than 'Gondwana': my critic pointed out that 'wana' means 'land', making the inclusion of the English equivalent tautological. Both forms can in fact be found in published accounts of the evolution of the continents, and they appear to be interchangeable.

A block of tillite from the Permian strata of South Africa, showing included pebbles of glacial origin. *Natural History Museum.*

The most straightforward example is probably provided by tillites. In the nineteenth century, most geology in remote regions was of no more than reconnaissance standard. Exploring geologists were probing the innards of Africa for the first time, and the dark continent yielded its secrets reluctantly. Reports were sent home to whatever European country had the appropriate colonial interests, there to be published in the journal of the national geological society. Suess hoarded the insights dispatched by these trail-blazers. A rock formation from South Africa was christened the Dwyka Conglomerate, and reported by one pioneer, J. Sutherland, in the *Quarterly Journal of the Geological Society of London* for 1870, under the title: 'Notes of an Ancient Boulder Clay of Natal'. This insouciant title embodies an extraordinary idea. A boulder clay is the deposit left behind as a glacier retreats. You can see deposits broadly of this kind dumped at the foot of Alpine glaciers shuffling backwards in their valleys away from the warm breath of global climate change. The boulder clay is a mucky kind of thing: dumped boulders of various sizes all mixed together and sealed by a sticky brown clayey gum. This is debris dumped unceremoniously by the melting glacier, its dirt alongside its cargo of rocks, unsorted, chaotic. It is like the contents of a badly made, old-fashioned bag pudding. Look closely and you will see characteristic scratches on some of the bigger pebbles where they were scraped along at the base of the glacier. When such a clay becomes hardened and annealed by time it is called a tillite (glacial till is the proper term for the deposits of ice, and the suffix -ite, as usual, designates a rock). But the scratches on the boulders are preserved, and so is the pot-pourri of different kinds of rock types all jumbled up, just as they were picked up and carried promiscuously on the back of the original glacier. So, here in South Africa, in the Great Karroo, was a rock identified as being of glacial origin, in a countryside where succulent plants now abound. It was an original idea, to say the least. Nonetheless, the signature of the fossil action of ice is easily read: there had evidently been an ancient ice age in South Africa. These boulder rocks were followed by what Suess called the 'upper Karroo Sandstone'. When some of these rocks were split they were found to contain fossil leaves having something of the shape of bay leaves but more tongue-like, which is why they were called *Glossopteris* (from the Greek for tongue).

Then, in Peninsular India, very similar conglomerate rocks were discovered in what Suess called the 'Talchir Stage'. Of these beds of boulders he remarks: 'the resemblance to the Dwyka . . . is very striking'. Evidently, the ancient glaciation extended beyond South Africa. As if to confirm this judgement, leaves of the fossil tree *Glossopteris,* and its associate *Gangamopteris,* were found in overlying strata in India, just as they had been in Africa. Suess goes on to describe many Indian basins bounded by fractures in which the 'lower Gondwana coal' derived from these fossil trees can be exploited. *Glossopteris* is unknown in Europe or North America. It was a peculiarly Gondwanan tree. Nowadays, we could enumerate

Leaves of the distinctive Permian Gondwana tree *Glossopteris*, whose remains serve to unite the ancient supercontinent.

dozens of plant and animal fossils with a similar Gondwana signature. We can put a Permian (about 275 million years) age on many of the *Glossopteris* fossils, and we know them well from Australia. Evidence for glaciation is everywhere on Gondwana. I walked along a wadi in Oman in 1995, in the midst of the Arabian Peninsula and in a bone-dry desert, where the sides of the valley were lined with glacial boulder beds as blatant as any I have seen in the Arctic. The floor of the wadi looked as if some gigantic dragon had been sharpening its claws there; the grooves were gouges left in the rock floor by an ice-sheet. Thus evidence is piled on evidence until the signature of Gondwana – its Permian life, its ice age – seems as graphic as the artefacts that define ancient Egypt. But the outline of it all, the facts that lay at the *fons et origo*, were available to Eduard Suess. As he said: 'An undeniable resemblance exists between the structure of South Africa and that of the Indian Peninsula.' He surmised that the former continuity of Gondwana was the appropriate explanation,* the Indian Ocean only subsequently separating the 'fossil tongues' that spoke to him so eloquently: 'Then came collapse. A new ocean was created and the continents assumed other forms . . . Out of the abyss of the ocean arises the great island of Madagascar presenting all the characters of a horst.' As to adducing evidence from other sources, Suess remarks: 'Eminent zoologists have been led to imagine the existence of an ancient continent on the site of the western half of the Indian Ocean to which the name "Lemuria" has been given.' There are indeed similarities between the animals of Africa and India that were accounted for by the existence of a bridge of land joining the two areas, or by a foundered continent. In either case, Africa and India as we know them were, in the past, exactly where we see them today. So the world apparently all makes sense, with the facts tucked away into a neat bag of theory.

But of course the description was all wrong.

It is worth reflecting upon what we would now see as an obvious mistake. Most theories are of their time, and Suess' was no exception. More facts are acquired, and, in the end, a mistaken theory is jettisoned, and then forgotten. The discovery of what made the ocean floors – basalt, and more basalt – is one obvious fact that falsified the subsidence theory: no foundered tillites there, nor *Glossopteris* fossils. However, that the foundering idea was *capable* of such falsification still qualifies it as a scientific theory, at least, if one accepts the criterion of science that Sir Karl Popper has explained in *Conjectures and Refutations*: the scientist has a licence to be wrong. The theories that cause much more trouble are those that can twist and turn in a breeze of new facts without ever fracturing completely. In fact, fixity of continents was already being challenged not long after Suess' *magnum opus* was translated into English. It is one of the famous stories in science how a German meteorologist, Alfred

* The theory of the original continuity of South Africa and India can be found in earlier sources, mostly little acknowledged. See for example an article by Stow in the *Quarterly Journal* of the Geological Society of London (1871).

Wegener,* proposed 'continental drift' many years before it was widely accepted that the continents were neither fixed nor the residues of a swathe of Atlantises. Wegener's first account was published in German in 1915, and was largely dismissed. It was translated into English in 1922, and probably only came to be on the 'serious' scientific agenda by the time of the French edition of 1936, *La genèse des Continents et des Oceans*, although even then it was regarded by most earth scientists as distinctly wacky. Wegener pointed out – and he was not the first – the 'fit' of the continental profiles: the western coast of Africa and South America; Madagascar, far from showing 'all the characters of a horst' seemed instead to wish to snuggle back against the East African coast, into an indentation that closely matched its western outline; and India and Africa were once *joined.* Gondwana was a united entity over which an ice-sheet might move, or a forest might spread. The continents must have moved to their present positions. You could shuffle them back into their original contiguity by solving the jigsaw puzzle of their coastlines. Drift South America back towards Africa and – see! – they lock together in a happy marriage. The ancient glacial deposits made sense if there had been an ice-sheet centred upon this Gondwana; but it must have occupied a different latitude at that time, nearer the pole, to support such frigidity. *Glossopteris* and its allies spread over the cooler parts of this united world, and there were early reptiles that could stroll unencumbered throughout the same ancient glades.

The idea of continent fusion was taken still further by Wegener. Perhaps *all* the continents were once fused together into one 'supercontinent'. At this distant time, all dry land was annealed: terra firma and sea were most perfectly parted one from another, for a single vast ocean counterbalanced one huge continent. North America and Europe/Asia were conjoined in the same way as South America and Africa; the North Atlantic Ocean had yet to appear. According to Wegener, in late Carboniferous times this huge northerly continent

* Tony Hallam has ably summarized Wegener's intellectual prehistory (in his *Great Geological Controversies*, 1989). There were several earlier writers who suggested parts of the continental drift hypothesis. 'New' ideas usually prove to have had progenitors.

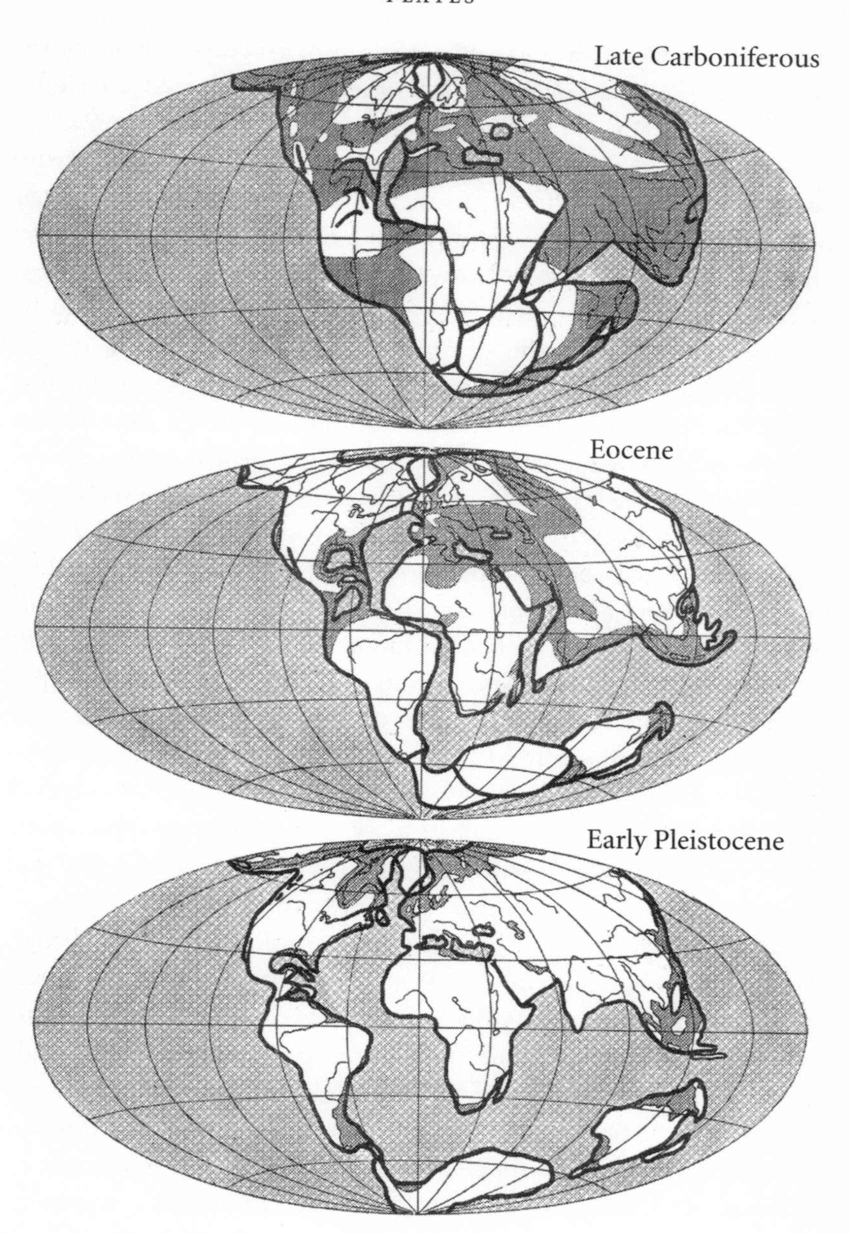

Alfred Wegener's 'pre-drift' map of the supercontinent Pangaea (top), and its subsequent fragmentation.

was bound to Gondwana as well. The current geography of the earth was claimed to be a legacy of a marriage of all continents, consummated more than 250 million years ago. The current continents resulted from the break-up of this continental behemoth. They had moved apart – drifted – to their present positions over many millions of years. This was, by any standards, a profound reorganization of knowledge. Gondwana was the name applied to the united India–South America–Australia–Antarctic portion of the supercontinent; Laurasia usually refers to the northerly part, the marriage across the North Atlantic. The whole is known as Pangaea, from the Greek for 'universal world'. I shall concentrate on the Gondwana portion, if only because the evidence for or against it figured so prominently in the history of the debate about the origin of the shape of the world.

Originality may be the capacity to look at the same facts and see new explanations. Much of the same evidence that Suess had adduced was paraded again by Wegener to draw an utterly different map, and to make predictions as different from drowned continents as could be imagined. And just as Suess' theory died by its predictions, so the notion of Gondwana, and of Pangaea, finally lived by virtue of facts that were still to be uncovered.

The drift hypothesis explained to Wegener the crumpling up of mountain chains. The movement apart of the continents entailed the elevation and folding of ranges at their further edges: the rucked western edge of South America; the huge arc of the Himalayas, pushed upwards as India collided with Asia. To see the world as it should be seen, he implied, the world must be looked at as a totality. The fate of mountains was bound up with the fate of oceans.

Perhaps if Wegener had had the eloquence of Dean Swift, or John Bunyan, then Pangaea, or even 'Gondwanaland', might have rapidly achieved the cultural currency of fictional Lilliput or the Slough of Despond. Instead, the concept lurked on the fringes of respectable science, like some eccentric location for Atlantis. More than forty years elapsed before a version of Wegener's surmise hardened into something like a fact. But there were champions who kept the idea alive. Through the 1920s and 1930s these were primarily field geologists who worked particularly in the southern hemisphere, where the evidence was most striking. The South African Alex du Toit summarized a mass of information in *Our Wandering Continents* (1937). He went far further than Wegener in identifying strong connections between the Gondwana fragments. There were South American rock formations that trended towards the eastern coast of that continent, where they were more or less abruptly truncated at the Atlantic Ocean. He claimed that their natural continuation could be found in southern Africa, and beyond into Australia. Close the Atlantic and Indian oceans, place the continents back together, and the match was perfect. No shattered Minoan urn from Santorini could be repaired with greater confidence. Wegener himself had described the logic behind such observations: 'It is just as if we were to refit the torn pieces of a newspaper by matching their edges and then check whether the lines of print run smoothly across. If they do, there is nothing left but to conclude that the pieces were in fact

The principle of reconstructing continents is not so different from rejoining the headlines from this torn newspaper.

joined this way.' Most geologists today would accept such evidence without demur, but it was still 'fringe' science when du Toit was publishing. Geologists didn't travel as easily then as they do today, so sceptics would not go to the trouble of taking a steamer half way around the world just to disprove some crackpot idea that was bound to crumble under scrutiny. Geologists met at the International

Geological Congress in some capital city every four years or so, as they still do; but not everyone could afford to attend, and the best funded, and therefore the most numerous, attendees were mostly Americans, who included the most convinced anti-drifters. 'What's all this nonsense?' you can almost hear them ask. 'How can a continent motor across an ocean? We all know that the resistant forces of rocks could not accommodate any such motion.'

The opponents included some of the intellectual heavyweights of the day. Harold Jeffreys was a brilliant geophysicist who wrote the standard textbook, published in 1926. He summarized Wegener's theory as an 'impossible hypothesis' and concluded that 'the assumption that the earth can be deformed indefinitely by small forces, provided only that they act long enough, is therefore a very dangerous one, and liable to lead to serious error'. In a word, there was no mechanism for continental movement. That same year, the American Association of Petroleum Geologists' symposium in New York was the first convened to discuss the subject of 'drift': virtually everyone was against it. I wish I could report that those of my own persuasion – palaeontologists – were more positive, but it was not generally so. Charles Schuchert of the Smithsonian Institution in Washington favoured land bridges across the Indian Ocean and elsewhere as the conduits of biological similarity. Where had they gone? Why, they had foundered in Suessian fashion. It may be significant that Schuchert had made his name studying fossil brachiopods (an important group of 'sea-shells' unrelated to molluscs), of an era much older than Pangaea. The world was differently arranged again 500 million years ago, and Schuchert's prejudices may have been forged by an even earlier world in which, indeed, continents were once more separated. The credit of the palaeontologist is somewhat restored by one of my own former colleagues in the Natural History Museum in London, the palaeobotanist A. C. Seward. After he had studied the distinctive flora associated with *Glossopteris*, he found the assumption of the existence of Gondwana more probable than any of the alternatives. He said as much in several papers published in the 1920s and 1930s. Those who studied the fossils of the Indian subcontinent in the field followed suit, notably the remarkable Birbal Sahni, who founded a botanical institute in Delhi that still carries his name. Other palaeontologists on the 'anti' side invoked drifting logs and seeds – the distinguished mammal expert George Gaylor Simpson called them 'sweepstake routes' – to explain far-flung similarities between species. Reports of lizards clinging to floating stumps in the mid-Pacific were eagerly garnered in support. What a lizard could do, *Glossopteris* could do better.

Many tectonicists were on the opposition side, too, and those with thunderous reputations carried their less extrovert colleagues and students with them. Hans Stille was a formidable advocate of the importance of vertical movements in tectonics. Not for him the slithering, sideways movements of drifting continents, where all was push and thrust; no, he was a stabilist. German professors of that time were like God, only more frightening. There were, besides, other things pressing on the German national psyche at the time; perhaps the fate of mountains was low on the agenda. In the USA, there were other stabilists almost as formidable. But they did not have it wholly their own way. Emile Argand's nappe theory of the Alps saw mobility of the crust everywhere, and evidence that rocks could indeed flow was accumulating. But in spite of the efforts of the few, the consensus carried the day. For more than thirty years the idea of mobile continents lurked out of sight of a scientific establishment predominantly certain it was untrue. Continental drift was an appealing distraction, a siren song that needed to be resisted by those grounded in the certainties of physics: if it can't move then it didn't move. To acknowledge the reality of Gondwana would have had the effect of changing just too many things in the geological *status quo*. One is reminded of the lines of Hilaire Belloc on the fate of Jim:

> . . . always keep a-hold of Nurse
> For fear of finding something worse.

But what of Arthur Holmes?

Holmes was, in fact, one of the early pro-drifters. It is clear from his correspondence that he appreciated the explanatory power of the new theory. He was an 'Africa hand' as well: his first geological employment had been on a mineralogical survey there in 1911. This was pioneering exploration in Mozambique, in the most remote country imaginable. His diaries reveal a buoyant enthusiast whose powers of expression did not yet quite match his powers of observation. He was a young geologist in love with his trade, and any scientist will recognize his intemperate zeal to be up and doing, out and discovering. Academic instruction is like fitness training: its point is only revealed when racing over the ground. What Holmes saw in Mozambique was not immediately concerned with the problems of Gondwana, but exposure to field conditions could help but prime his mind to the scale of things. Some years later, Holmes had a position in the University of Durham. He had tenured employment, and his work on the age of the earth had earned him respect in the geological community, even if he had made a few enemies as well as many friends. In December 1927 he read a paper to the Edinburgh Geological Society where he revealed his pro-drift colours. It was an extraordinary presentation and anticipated so much of what was to come. Not only did he accept that 'drift' had occurred, but he also suggested its elusive mechanism. Holmes' work with radioactive elements had made him aware of the possibility that they could be a source of heat. He proposed that the differential effects of such heating created convection currents in a deep 'substratum': solid, yes, but sluggishly flowing over millions of years, in an analogous way to the proverbially slow creep of glaciers. The upward limbs of the convection cells reached the lithosphere and then parted in opposite directions, much as the surface of simmering pea soup develops a pleat between boiling vortices. The drag of the convection cell provided the motor that moved continents. Where the cell arose beneath a continent it could split it and create a new ocean; where a cell turned down again it might pull ocean crust with it to produce an 'ocean deep'. The account is almost clairvoyant in its anticipation of future discoveries. His heat-based scheme was summarized by Holmes as 'a purely hypothetical mechanism for "engineering" continental drift'. This is almost like referring to Darwin's *Origin of Species* as a 'modest proposal possibly germane to the appearance of new forms in nature'. However tentatively couched, it did not go down well with the leading anti-drifters, including Harold Jeffreys, who was obdurate about this force being as inadequate as any other for transporting continental slabs (recall that his own textbook was but a year old). The gap between reading a paper and its publication is one of the running complaints that scientists have, and Holmes suffered very badly with this seminal work – the relevant volume of the *Transactions of the Royal Society of Edinburgh* did not appear until 1931. It is worth remembering that arguments about who made the critical discoveries of the AIDS virus have hinged on matters of days (even hours) in recent years. Priority of discovery has become a crucial passport to scientific glory. This has occasionally led to jiggery pokery, as one research team has attempted to nudge a nose ahead of another, and publication priority is crucial. The leading journals, *Nature* and *Science*, keep discoveries under strict embargo until the very day of publication. Less scrupulous scientists sometimes speak to the press before they speak to their colleagues. Perhaps it was as well that continental drift was so profoundly unfashionable in the 1920s and 1930s. Holmes' paper was seen by his critics as being merely the latest folly in a minority delusion. As one of them wrote: 'I believe that we need to apply elementary physics and mechanics to the continental drift problem to show how impossible drifting would be.' Arthur Holmes would have to wait more than thirty years to establish his priority.

But Holmes did not lose faith in mobile continents. Rather, he was sympathetic to the evidence subsequently accumulated by Alex du Toit and the palaeobotanists – perhaps he appreciated better the hardships under which such evidence had been acquired than did his chair-bound critics. He believed that the rocks, ultimately, would speak the truth, and that appropriate theory would follow. When the first edition of his *Principles of Physical Geology* was published in 1944, continental drift was there in the last chapter. It was a bold move for the times. For the price of thirty shillings, or seven dollars, the reader could find a summary of the evidence for 'Gondwanaland'. Problems in the imperfect 'fit' of the coastlines were aired, too. Critics had been quick to point out that Gondwana was a jigsaw puzzle that had to be fudged to fit. Du Toit's reconstructions had improved on those of Wegener, but neither was perfect. It was realized later that the true edges of the continents lay not where the shorelines happened to be, but at the edges of the continental slabs themselves, below sea-level – the rims of the building blocks of the earth. If the 100-fathom contour was taken to represent the outline of the continent, a much better fit of the pieces of the puzzle was obtained. This was another example of the interplay between sea-level and terrestrial geology with which this book started in the 'Temple of Serapis'. The sea is fickle as to the height it laps on shore: geological reality often operates at a different scale.

Holmes' book sold very well despite its stolid title. The first edition eventually reprinted eighteen times. The reviews were good, but some of the reviewers would have much preferred the last section to have been left out. For them, the mixture of fact beautifully explained with speculation almost smuggled in at the end was disquieting. Some followed the geophysicist's view that what is obviously impossible can never be the case, no matter how the evidence appears to favour it. (I am reminded of those irritating stickers that get posted on office walls: 'Don't confuse me with facts, my mind's made up.') But, as any newspaper proprieter knows, the bottom line is sales. A new generation of students brought up on 'Holmes' (the book became synonymous with the man) would encounter the idea of Gondwana in a less fettered way than their teachers had. The young mind is often a more open one. The post-war years were optimistic and innovative times, a time to jettison received ideas. Technology developed during the Second World War was beginning to make an impact on pure research: ocean depths were there to be read for other reasons than the pursuit of enemy submarines; decoders for intercepting enemy signals were ready to become computers. Thanks to jet engines, air travel to remote lands became commonplace, and so it became easier to organize field trips to establish, test, or clarify geological facts. In the mid twentieth century, mobility of continents began to seem like a theory with a chance of being properly tested. Physicists, who had

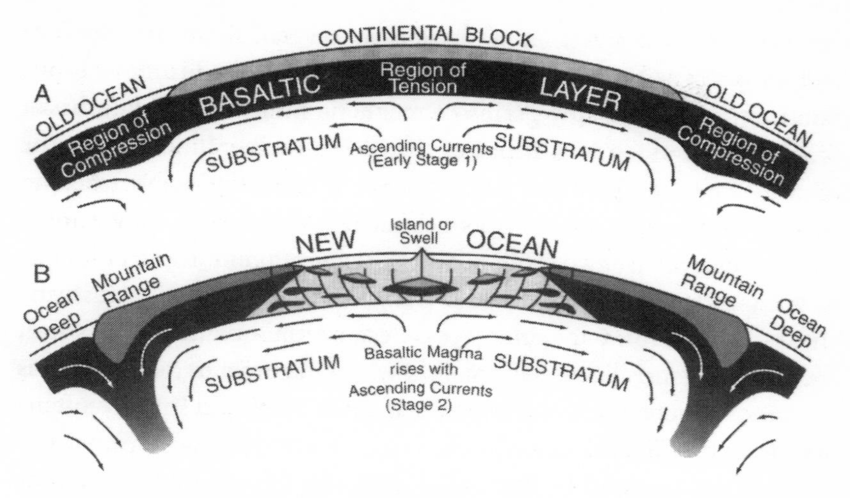

Arthur Holmes' prescient 'purely hypothetical mechanism for "engineering" continental drift' published in the *Journal of the Geological Society of Glasgow*, 1931, redrawn by Cherry Lewis in her biography of Holmes (2000).

been with the sceptics in that war of ideas about continent mobility, were about to become crucial to the campaign on the other side.

It is interesting to follow the change in the respectability of continental movement theory in the later edition of 'Holmes'. Like all such compilations of second thoughts, the revised book got longer (and some would say it lost a little of its punch). The bulky 1965 edition is the one I encountered as a student: twenty years of second thoughts. It is still nothing in bulk compared with the five volumes of Suess, but it is a dozen times more readable. The final chapter on continental mobility is still there, as is the section on 'Gondwanaland'. Of course, there was no mention of plates – that was for the future. But there *was* a section on polar wandering.

The earth behaves like a vast magnet. The magnetic field streams from (magnetic) pole to pole. From time to time the field reverses – north becomes south, and south becomes north. There is a small number of minerals that readily become magnetized. Appropriately enough, the commonest of these, a simple iron oxide, is called magnetite. This is the lodestone, whose interesting properties have been known since antiquity. It is present in several common rocks, of which basalt is the most ubiquitous. There are also plenty of sandstones that contain tiny grains of magnetic minerals. When a basalt cools from molten lava it passes through a threshold known as the Curie Point, at which the magnetite (or a related mineral) takes up magnetization from the earth's field as if it had been freshly minted from a magnet factory. These natural magnets point at the poles like a compass (you have to record the orientation of the rock in the field very carefully, for reference). Because the quantity of the iron mineral is generally rather small, any magnetometer recording this 'fossil' magnetism has to be very sensitive. Technical improvements in these instruments made in the 1950s meant that magnetization of ancient rocks could be examined critically for the first time. This allowed for determination of 'palaeomag', as it is universally known; those who do it are almost as widely known as 'palaeomagicians'. What they did was, after all, a kind of magic. The ancient rocks preserved the signature of where the poles of the time lay. The rocks pointed their time-frozen finger at the pole as it was at the moment of their magnetization. If everything in the world had been fixed forever, then so should the positions of the poles. Fortunately, magnetized rocks could be collected from many sites scattered over former Gondwana where the right kind of basalts and sandstones are common. From these measurements it immediately became apparent that the position of the poles had moved. At first, it seemed possible that the whole crust of the earth might have slewed around relative to the poles, like the 'skin' on a thick broth when you tip the pan. However, soon enough it was clear that the tracks of ancient pole positions from different continents took quite different paths: this would not be expected if the whole crust had behaved coherently; instead, each continent appeared to have a will of its own. And they were indeed paths. The ancient poles did not jump around here and there, hither and yon; instead, progressively older poles in Africa, for example, shifted away from pointing at the present pole along a distinct track, a journey through time towards a different place. There was sense in the signal, and it pointed to Gondwana.

By putting all this evidence together at last, there was a sea change in the respectability of continental movement theory. Precision of physics and delicacy of instrumentation had finally joined cause with the geological hammer. When the apparent polar-wandering curves for the different components of Gondwana were compared, they only made sense if there had once, more than 200 million years ago, been a united supercontinent. Suess' ancient land had finally been explained, and the explanation was accepted by a majority of younger scientists. As Gondwana split up, its component continents embarked on their own tracks, and each 'saw' the poles in a signature fashion as one geological period succeeded another. Lavas erupting on the travelling continents became magnetized, freezing the details of each journey as a diary written in aligned atoms. But all the journeys started in the same place; that was now evident. Then, too, the fossil and ice-age details that had been known for more than half a century fitted logically and convincingly into the same scheme: for 'palaeomag' also indicated that the South Pole in the late Palaeozoic ought to be in the midst of Gondwana – just where an ice-sheet might be expected to grow, and where tillites might be left behind to record the legacy of frigid times. Here was something resembling a vanished Antarctica. And after the ice age had waned, cool forests prospered and spread, with their tongue-shaped leaves sheltering special animals that liked it there. It all added up, and the sum of the facts was more than the parts, as is often the case with momentous scientific shifts.

It is difficult to cite a date, a particular moment in this intellectual drama, when the consensus in the geological community changed. Such transformations are somewhat mysterious; the *Zeitgeist* switches in ways which are not necessarily logical, although the principal players in the drama often like to present it that way. Nor does everyone shift together: the later 'Holmes' pointed out that a Russian textbook published in translation as late as 1962 still berated 'the total vacuousness and sterility of the hypothesis' of moving continents. The crucial work on palaeomagnetism was already under way less than ten years after Holmes' first edition. Keith Runcorn, one of the pioneers of these methods in Britain, was certainly a geophysical convert before 1956. The proceedings of a US symposium published in 1962 in the *International Geophysics Series*, under the explicit title 'Continental Drift', show how far views of the more free-thinking scientists had shifted by then, and there were already inklings of the next phase in the great global tectonic synthesis. On the other side of the newly liberated Atlantic Ocean a symposium at the Royal Society early in 1964 was also overwhelmingly 'pro-drift'. By this time, Americans were among the most radical of the theorists, a position they maintain today. As St Luke's gospel puts it: 'the truth will set you free', and once the continents themselves had been untethered so, too, scientific imaginations were liberated to pursue their dreams. Mountain chains could now be seen as the consequence of continent shifts and collisions; mineral plays might prove to be related to continental movement, too. The truth of the world would be rewritten, and who would be first with the new version? Some scientists were laggards, while others surged forwards. Some geology departments took several years to adapt to the new world. But there was little doubt where the 'cutting edge' of geological discovery now lay: it was in the study of the consequences of continental mobility. What Robert Herrick applied to poetry might apply equally to geology:

> To print our poems, the propulsive cause
> Is fame, the breath of popular applause.

The northern hemisphere equivalent of Gondwana – the marriage of Eurasia and Laurentia – was already familiar in Holmes' second edition. These continents, too, had split apart at the same time as their antipodean counterparts. Evidence for that greater fusion – of Pangaea, the unification of all the continents – followed naturally enough. Both traditional geological and new geophysical facts were employed: it would take a longer book than this to list the detailed evidence, and it would perhaps be nugatory to do so since the arguments are in many ways similar to those rehearsed for Gondwana. There are still differences in detail about the constitution of Pangaea, and for how long it was united at the end of the Palaeozoic. Early computers were used to produce 'best fits' of the continental shelf margins, but the labour required to produce a pre-drift map was still prodigious. In the mid 1960s, the latest equipment was in the Geophysical Laboratory on Madingley Rise, just outside Cambridge, where Sir Edward Bullard presided over the attempt to use the latest technology to solve the fit of the continents. In 1965, the computer fits of the continents around the Atlantic Ocean were published to 'the breath of popular applause'. The originality of Wegener's vision had been successively endorsed, and everyone in 'earth sciences' felt that they were living in exciting times.

But what of the oceans? To concentrate attention on the mobility, or otherwise, of the continents leaves out two-thirds of the world. At the same time as evidence for continental movement was firming up, the distinctiveness of the oceanic crust was being demonstrated by improved sampling of the ocean floor. We have seen how new technology after the Second World War also allowed a clearer picture of the topography of the deep-sea floor. It was possible to look at the whole earth for the first time. We followed the fate of a tiny piece of it – the Hawaiian Chain – in some detail to show how movement of an oceanic plate accounted for so much of the local features. How was the link made between what went on in oceans and what was now accepted as happening to continents? The crucial step was the appreciation of the structure of the mid-ocean ridges as the place where new crust was manufactured. The relevant observations were made by sea-floor sampling and mapping in the 1950s. One of the sea's principle explorers, H. W. Menard, who worked at the Scripps Institute of Oceanography, has described in *The Ocean of Truth* (1986) the kind of discoveries that were made. These were not just details: they were major features, such as the Pacific Fracture Zone. The clearly linear course of the ocean ridges emerged from semi-obscurity; the deepest parts of the ocean, the trenches, were mapped as great lineaments, too. Off south-east Asia, fringing the Philippine Sea, the 'spot depths' already observed by *Challenger* were linked together as the huge Japan–Bonin–Nero trench system – in their own way these trenches are more dramatic than the mid-ocean ridges, somewhat like the Himalayas in reverse. The exploratory process at sea was similar to a version of the child's game of 'join the dots', whereby a picture emerges as more and more numbered dots are joined. You have to be certain that there is a picture to discover in the first place, and, for a while, prejudice about what the finished picture might be can mislead; but eventually a likeness is the outcome, albeit a jerky and disjointed one; and the more dots you join, the better the picture. The image is still being filled in today. Modern methods of surveying, such as multi-beam sonar, simply provide a much more accurate and immediate view of the whole scene.

The breakthrough in understanding can be summarized in one short phrase: 'sea-floor spreading'. The concept grew out of research by two American geologists: the expression was coined by Professor R. S. Dietz, but the pioneer publication was written by Harry H. Hess. This research paper had, like Holmes' thirty-five years before, a publication lag of two years. It had been available in unpublished manuscript in 1960, but did not appear in print until 1962. The earlier typescript is what scientists like to refer to as a pre-print, a kind of moral claim to an idea. If the idea turns out to be a seminal one, a pre-print can be dangerous for the author, to the extent that it tempts others to try to jump the gun. In fact, Hess' ideas spread indecently fast. The 1960s were a time of extraordinarily rapid progress in the understanding of continental mobility. Hess' paper explicitly stated why the most obvious thing about the Mid-Atlantic Ridge was, indeed, so: it was median 'because the continental areas on each side of it have moved away from it at the same rate . . .' This is not exactly the same as continental drift. The continents do not plough through the oceanic crust propelled by unknown forces, rather, they ride passively on mantle material as it comes to the surface at the crest of the ridge and then moves laterally away from it.' Continents are part of processes that entail the oceans, too. Thus, at last, the criticism of the physicist Harold Jeffreys was answered about the impossibility of the continents sailing across the basalt oceans like huge, granitic barques. They didn't. They were at one with the oceans. New oceanic crust was added at the ocean ridges – where it was known that heat flow was high and that there were submarine volcanics. A moving continent and its contiguous ocean crust moved in harmony. Thus South America moved westwards with its associated slab of ocean crust extending as far as the Mid-Atlantic Ridge, while Africa moved eastwards with *its* slab of oceanic crust. The increasing width of the Atlantic Ocean was accommodated by new crust erupted – ultimately derived from melted mantle – and inserted at the Ridge, like caulk in a leaking ship. It was a wonderfully simple way of putting so many disparate observations together: volcanic ridges, which were buoyed up by hot magma, even the rifts at their peaks, were an expression of the urge for separation of plates. Earthquakes below ridges were discovered to be only ten to fifteen kilometres deep; they become deeper outwards – up to a hundred kilometres – just as would be expected. Geologists could go to Iceland and stand astride the Mid-Atlantic Ridge itself to see evidence of the processes on the ground. The irony was that at virtually the same time as the pro-drifters finally triumphed over the stabilists, demonstration of the mechanism of ocean widening rendered the very term 'drift' obsolete. 'Continental drift' had to be expunged from our vocabulary, to be sustituted by 'sea-floor spreading'.

Knowledge and theory move forward together in a kind of uneasy, shuffling collaboration. In an account of the kind I have given above it is easy to forget those who were part of the process but who lurk on the margins of history, because they do not fit into a narrative of brilliant theory anticipation (Wegener, Holmes) or experimental confirmation (Bullard, Hess). They get forgotten; perhaps they had espoused an idea that never had its day. Had you been at a conference in the 1960s, though, these figures might have glittered as brightly as any of the stars that history remembers. In particular, I think of Professor S. Warren Carey, of the University of Tasmania. Carey was one of those 'pro-drifters' who kept the faith through the 1940s and 1950s, when to do so required courage and determination. His ideas were taken seriously, for example, by Arthur Holmes. Carey, though, believed in an expanding earth. His notion was that the increase in diameter of the earth had caused the split-up of Pangaea and was the deep cause behind most of the geological phenomena with which this chapter has been concerned. Continental crust had once almost enwrapped the earth, it was claimed, but with the earth's expansion it split and buckled and parted company, removing the continents to where they are found today, with the ocean basins 'filling' between. No wonder the continents fitted together, just as the pieces of a peeled orange skin fit together! The idea is not so strange. As we have seen, in the nineteenth century, and in the early part of the twentieth, there had been a strong school of geologists who attributed tectonics to a *shrinking* earth. After all (so they supposed) the earth had cooled from its hot 'primeval condition' thus it would shrink, and, as it did so, mountain ranges would result. Suess evidently believed in such a mechanism, when he contemplated the intensely folded rocks of the Swiss Alps. He realized that the recumbent folds there indicated that the surface must have contracted, or shortened: such folds 'have directed attention anew to the diminution of the earth's circumference,' as he wrote. Recall, too, that early estimates of the age of the earth were based on the idea that it was cooling progressively. Discovery of radioactive 'heating' turned the tables. There was now a possibility that the world was actually heating up and expanding, fuelled by radioactive elements in its interior. Carey later turned his attention to changes in the gravitational constant as the cause. For a while, the expanding earth was in with a chance. Serious scientists, like the oceanographer Bruce Heezen, believed it. However, the recognition of sea-floor spreading made sense of continental splitting without having to invoke earth expansion. It seemed to be a more economical explanation. More lethal was the recognition that oceans had existed *before* the assembly of Pangaea; it was only a phase in the history of the planet, after all, and not necessarily its primitive state. If the earth had been smaller still then, how could there be room for such oceans? The expanding earth theory had some trouble accounting for those mountain ranges, like the Andes, that abutted oceans, though it could cope well enough with those marking where continents had collided, as in the Himalayas. Still, Carey gamely defended the theory. I went to a lecture he gave in the early 1970s, and a fine, flamboyant affair it was, a charismatic display of bravado. You could not help admiring his chutzpah, as you might that of a pianist who carries on playing while the ship is sinking. However, he had made a convert in the Natural History Museum in London – my colleague Hugh Owen. Hugh continued to pick holes in the continental reconstructions favoured by computers for the next fifteen years or so, and published an alternative set of maps in which some earth expansion was incorporated. Both Carey and Owen were absolutely convinced of their arguments, and if some twist of knowledge were to prove them right in a hundred years or so, they, too, might gain iconic status. For the moment, this seems improbable.

The proof of sea floor spreading was in the heating. If the theory were correct, hot magma welled up at mid-ocean ridges. When the lavas cooled they would pass through the Curie Point, and their magnetic minerals would become magnetized. If sea-floor spreading theory were correct, such cooled lavas would have the same age symmetrically on either side of the mid-ocean ridge, as their respective pieces of crust migrated away from the line of genesis. So far, so logical. This is where the other property of the earth's magnetic field comes in: its periodic propensity for reversal, for south and north poles to switch. If such a reversal occurred, its record, too, should be symmetrically disposed in the basalts to either side of the centre-line of the mid-ocean ridge. You might expect a strip of oceanic crust on either flank of the ridge that gave a reversed signal, and then, beyond it again, a strip with normal magnetization, and so on. Colour normal white and reversed black and the sea-floor should be painted with symmetrical stripes of black and white running parallel to the ridge. The ocean crust was like a tape recorder spooling away on either side from the mid-ocean ridges, with the narrative recorded in magnetism. A sensitive magnetometer was needed to make these measurements, and the right kind of mid-ocean ridge where a good density of samples might be obtained. Two Cambridge University geophysicists, Drummond Matthews and Fred Vine, got the evidence they needed on the Carlsberg Ridge in the north-western Indian Ocean. The proof was published in the journal *Nature* in 1963. This paper is always referred to in the trade as 'Vine and Matthews', and is one of those rare classics that provides a benchmark in the progress of science, like the determination of the speed of light or Planck's Constant.

My description might give the impression that this was one of those 'Eureka!' discoveries, where prediction met result in a happy consummation. But that is not an accurate portrayal. Fred Vine was far more diffident than one might imagine about the likely acceptance of his paper. He had doubts. He has even recalled saying to his colleagues, 'if they publish that they'll publish anything'. Nor was the discovery as clear cut as the publication date indicated. As so often in science, when the time is ripe for an idea, more than one person has it. Lawrence Morley worked as a palaeomagnetist for the Canadian Geological Survey and had reached similar conclusions to Vine and Matthews, but his letter to *Nature* that same year was rejected. He lowered his sights a little and submitted the paper to the *Journal of Geophysical Research*. In a notorious riposte, it was rejected *again* with the judgement: 'this is the sort of thing you would talk about at a cocktail party'. In other words, it was not to be taken seriously by serious scientists. Morley was thus to be denied 'the breath of popular applause'. The paper was published in modified version a year later by the Royal Society of Canada, but not one in a hundred who read *Nature* would have seen this more obscurely published version, and a year is a long time in science when a subject is 'hot'. Science, like life, is often unfair. Then, too, it has to be admitted that 'Vine and Matthews' was incomplete; they had not really demonstrated the required symmetry of the 'stripes', and there was, as yet, a very imperfect chronology for the magnetic reversals. You need to know just how old a reversal is to approach an estimate of the *rate* of sea-floor spreading, for you require an independent timepiece to calibrate that slow, basaltic conveyor belt. Fred Vine himself was admirably free of hubris, and remained to be convinced by better evidence from better ridges. But, by now, this was 'big science', which meant that the well-funded oceanographic laboratories from the USA provided the next big push. These included the Lamont Geological Observatory, and the United States Geological Survey at Menlo Park, the big boys with big bucks – ocean coring does not come cheap. Within three years of those first, prescient words written in Cambridge, new and more detailed descriptions had been released to the world of the patterns at other ridges that proved to have clearer 'signals', including the Reykjanes Ridge, south of Iceland, and the Juan de Fuca Ridge, off Vancouver Island. When the reversal stripe pattern was proved again on the Pacific Antarctic Ridge it would have taken a sceptic of great pusillanimity to deny that a truly global phenomenon was being recorded. By 1967, it had become material for future textbooks.

The detailed study of ridges revealed one other fact that proved essential to what would soon be known as plate tectonics. As the topography of the ridges was revealed, so it became clear that they were not as straight as was originally believed. In places, the ridges were strikingly displaced, as if they had taken a 'hop' sideways. Something else was going on here that could not be attributed to sea-floor spreading. The geologist Tuzo Wilson realized that the ridges were being moved along faults, but these were faults of a special kind that did not require one or another flank to move up or down. Instead, chunks of ocean floor were slipping past one another. Put two planks side by side on a table and draw a line across them: slide one of the planks, and you will get the idea, as one half of the line is displaced. Tuzo Wilson called them *transform* faults.

The dating of the magnetic reversals required experts in radiometric dating of rocks. As so often in geology, once the need was perceived, the end was achieved by a refinement of technology. The goal was accurately to date the lavas in the reverse magnetic 'stripes'. Did the reversals in different parts of the world coincide, as they should? The short answer is: they did. The longer answer is that a new mass spectrometer was constructed at the University of California at Berkeley that could measure smaller amounts of radiogenic argon than previous instruments, and hence could date the rocks of a given 'stripe' more accurately. Coupled with the new cores derived from recently-explored spreading ridges, the way was open to test the question of the age of magnetic reversals. A prominent reversal interval was discovered in several of the profiles and in 1966 was christened the Jaramillo Event. It has proved to be as identifiable as a fingerprint throughout the world. The rates at which new ocean floor is grown can now be calculated. Even this longer answer is a travesty of a detailed story of discovery that has been related by W. Glen in *The Road to Jaramillo* (1982). In this fashion, knowledge begets questions which beget new technology which provides answers – which in turn beget questions. This is the implacable carousel of research.

Fossils also came to play a part in confirming spreading rates and dating ocean floor. Tiny shells of planktonic animals rain down from the surface waters of the ocean on to the deep-sea floor. Among these are the delicate remains of single-celled organisms, particularly foraminiferans and radiolarians. The former are often tiny spirals, or collections of chambers looking rather like miniscule popcorn, while the latter are glassy silica nets or spheres, delicate as lace. They evolved fast, changing shape in subtle ways; hence their various species can be used as miniature chronometers to measure the passage of geological time. Eocene foraminiferans are very different from Pliocene ones, and even *within* the Eocene there are many fine time divisions that can be recognized using foraminifera. It is actually much quicker to examine a slide of fossils to get a geological age than to go through the technically complex business of extracting isotopes, so the fossils have an advantage. Logically, you would expect the very first shells to fall on newly-minted ocean crust to give a good indication of its age, almost as if it had been date-stamped. By the same reasoning, you would expect the oldest ocean crust to be furthest away from the mid-ocean ridges, the newest, closest. So it proved to be. Of course, old oceanic crust was often covered by progressively younger fossil deposits – it had to await the development of coring on the deep sea-floor to produce good evidence. The results were exhilaratingly consistent with sea-floor spreading theory, and provided concrete evidence that although the ocean floors were of many different ages, none was older than the Jurassic, since when it had spread into existence. The sea-floor was far, far younger than the earth itself.

Some people feel a certain nervousness about mathematics. The world is so wondrously complex that to reduce it to a collection of formulae excites suspicion in many individuals. If the formulae are arcane and impressive it seems to stimulate further anxiety, of the kind that people feel when they are at a party where they know nobody, or where everyone else is talking a foreign language. We all like to feel that we know what is going on, and few are polyglot. At the time Eduard Suess was writing it seemed impossible that the world might be boiled down to numbers. As he wrote: 'It is with extreme distrust that the geologist regards all attempts to apply the exact methods of mathematics to the subject of his studies.' The implication was that the world was too messy to knuckle under to figures. But knuckle under it has. Arthur Holmes was less nervous about quantification, especially since his work on the age of the earth demanded the use of grindingly primitive calculators, but at heart he was still a visionary. In the story I have related it does seem that vision has always preceded calculation, with inspiration preceding measurement. The lesson of Sir Harold Jeffreys and his unyielding (but honest) and careful (but bogus) mathematics impeding the drift hypothesis is one that every gung-ho theoretician has taken to heart. However, there has been a complete change since Suess. Today, the way much geological science is done entails proposing a mathematical model, and then going to the field to see whether it is supported in the rocks, or perhaps conducting an experiment to suggest what we should be looking for in the rocks in the first place. This preamble is necessary to explain the final transformation in the story of moving continents: plate tectonics.

Plate tectonics spliced together all the different aspects of the world we have met within this book into one grand design. What went on in the oceans was linked to what went on in the mountains. The dipping and rising in the Bay of Naples was part and parcel of the fiery trail that led to Hawai'i, and that too could not be disentangled from the heave of the Alpine nappes. Even the genesis of a single crystal in a particular rock might be a response to the bidding of greater forces in the earth's fundamental engine. It was nothing less than a unifying theory of all the world.

And it was once again a visionary who fathered the new ideas. Tuzo Wilson was an unusually imaginative man. We have already met him once, and will do so again. He always seemed to leap ahead to something new, largely because, like Holmes and Suess, he saw the world as a whole. I met him in London when he was a Grand Old Man a few years ago at a lecture at the Royal Geographical Society. There he reviewed his intellectual progress, in a matter-of-fact way. It seemed a little flat, because what he said was now part of the way we all thought. I was reminded of a time when the secret of a magic trick was explained to me: to recapture the sense of wonder you have to stuff the rabbit back into the hat and forget all you know. Tuzo Wilson had invented the trick. He had minted the idea of plates in a paper published in *Nature* in 1965. Within a few years, plates were everywhere.

But first I must add ocean trenches to the plot of the story. As previously noted, these had been recognized since the days of the *Challenger* from spot depths, but their profile had only become known in detail following the surveys of the sea-floor undertaken after the Second World War. The trenches were great gouges in the sea-floor – but not holes; rather, arc-shaped cuts. The greatest series looped off Japan and the Philippines. It is as well to get their profile correct, as trenches are usually portayed with a greatly exaggerated vertical scale on classroom maps: this may add to their drama, but it detracts from the truth. But why were they there at all? The explanation proved to be linked to a series of observations made on earthquakes that happened on the landward side of the trenches. Any seismic map of the world shows that a concentration of earthquakes lies along the length of Japan and southwards through the islands of South-east Asia. This part of the world has the serious shakes. From seismometer readings it is a comparatively simple matter to calculate the epicentre and the depth of origin of any quake, and in Japan there is no shortage of data. What was revealed got into the guts of

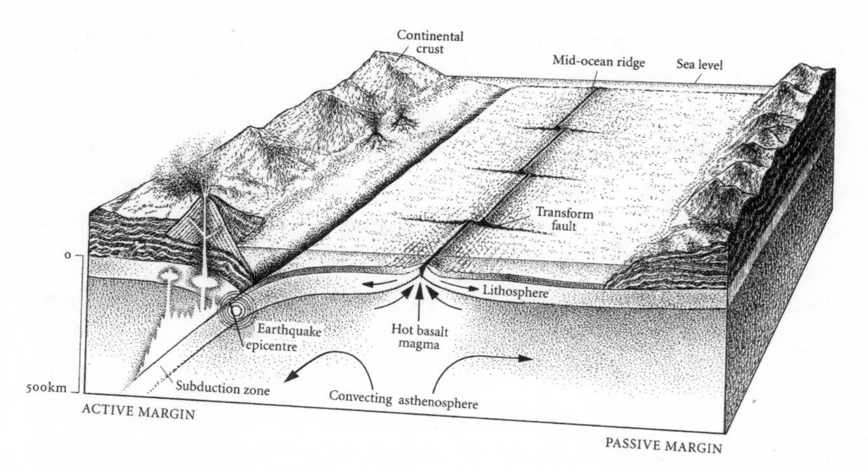

The modern view: a simplified cross-section through the oceans and continents, showing upward limbs of convection and creation of new crust at spreading ridges, consumption of oceanic crust at subduction zones, island arcs, and the generation of magma.

the earth. There was very little activity in the trench and seawards of it; but towards the islands the quakes increased. As more data was gathered it was clear that there was a pattern to the distribution of the quakes. Close to the trench they were shallow, while they increased in depth towards the island. In detail, they lay along an almost straight line, which dipped at an angle away from the ocean and underneath the Japan Sea towards the land. This must, surely, be a major dislocation in the crust of the earth, a line of failure.

Here lay the answer to the obvious question: if new crust was being added at the mid-ocean ridges, where was it being destroyed? The downward-dipping earthquake zones were the burial traces of plunging ocean crust. The trenches were dragged downwards: warped tracts of the ocean floor where the crust dived towards the mantle from which it had once emerged. The 'scrape' of the moving crust against the adjacent buttressed margin engendered earthquakes. Crust was born at ridges and died in deep graves at the edges of continents. Where it plunged downwards it would tend to melt, admixing with partly melted rocks of continental type, perhaps, to feed subterranean chambers of liquid rock. Magma would find its way to the surface in explosive volcanoes: hence the 'ring of fire' that marks the Asiatic margin of the Pacific Ocean. Some of the greatest eruptions of recent years have occurred there: Mount Pinatubo in the Philippines awoke in 1991 after sleeping for four hundred years, sending eruption plumes twenty-five kilometres into the atmosphere.

So the edge of the Asian continent coincided with the line where the rim of the adjacent oceanic plate plunged downwards. The ocean crust is said to be *subducted*, literally 'led under' to oblivion. Even before the topography of the ocean floor was fully known, Eduard Suess had realized that a crucial boundary lay in the deep seas off Japan. Once more, he regarded subsidence as the key to understanding. He remarked that 'all marine abysses which sink below a depth of 7000 meters are foredeeps in a tectonic sense, and indicate the subsidence of the foreland beneath the folded mountains' and also that they 'mark the eastern boundary of the Asiatic system'. He was, as so often, half right. Where Suess saw deep subsidence of continents, a modern observer sees the plunge of basaltic plates. What we see is partly a function of what we believe we see: our truth is constrained by the times in which we live.

The mathematical description of plates required these few assumptions: creation of crust at ridges; its subduction at destructive margins; and transform zones where plates could slip past one another. All were recognizable in the real world. And because that world is not expanding, the overall creation of new crust should be balanced by its destruction elsewhere. It is a matter of reconciling the equation. As we have seen, all the ocean floor today has been manufactured since the Mesozoic began: subduction has removed all that was older. Hence, it became possible to describe the world in terms of a few rigid plates that moved relative to one another over the surface of a sphere. The mathematics involved is a spherical geometry based on Euler's theorem. Leonhard Euler was a brilliant eighteenth-century Swiss mathematician, who became professor in St Petersburg at the time of the Empress Catherine. His ideas came into their own nearly two hundred years after his death.

Imagine! To describe the geometry and structure of the world by the movement of a dozen or so plates: Suess' ineluctable complexity reduced to motion, direction, and spreading rate. How to picture it? I like to think of the different plates as distinctly coloured swathes dividing the earth's surface, growing apart at ocean ridges. Imagine that the oceanic parts of the plates are darker, the continental parts paler. You can visualize the plates jostling one another, like crowded ice floes. In places, two differently coloured 'floes' slide past one another with minimal interaction. But where spreading oceanic crust meets the rim of a stable continent at the edge of an adjacent plate, a subduction zone appears along the join. The darker-coloured oceanic crust will then disappear into the zone of destruction, plunging down to obscurity. Volcanic islands – a Hawaiian chain perhaps – may be plastered on to the neighbouring continent, drawn in willy-nilly by the subduction process. Inexorably, the two continents themselves will begin to approach one another as the oceanic part of the moving plate vanishes into the depths. Thick continents cannot dive under one another; instead they collide, and where this happens the earth suffers, buckles, thickens. A mountain belt arises over millions of years: a Himalayan or an Alpine system. The ocean that once ran before the Indian subcontinent has vanished beneath the Himalayas; now, it is the turn of the continents to meet face to face. The mountain belt grows on a line that marks the demise of the ocean that preceded it. Its linear shape betrays its origin. Forced together, the two continents mark their conjuction by squeezing lathes of land in mutual accommodation; great slabs of crust are folded and ejected, turned over, sliding, slithering, twisting. The light continental crust thickens on collision, then bounces back to rise rapidly. Snows and icefields gather on the jagged peaks. Rivers gouge downwards to reduce the impertinence of altitude. Deep beneath the mountains the isobars, depressed by the squeezed pile, return to heat the roots of the ranges. Rocks melt, but selectively. There are granites, there are gneisses. Deep in the earth there is a cooking extravaganza, a

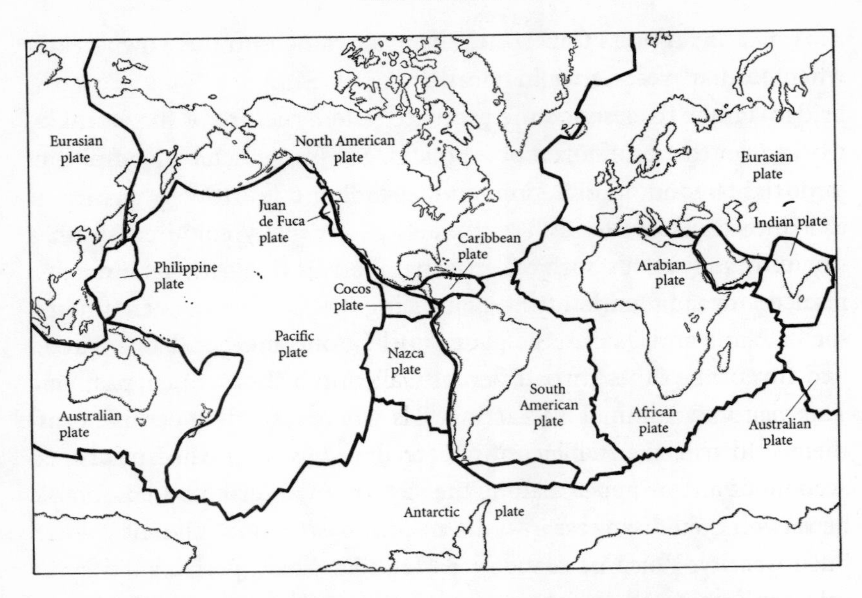

The main tectonic plates as recognized today – with their names.

hundred rock types born of collision. Minerals and metals are squeezed into the interstices of modified country rocks. This marriage of two continents is also a refinement, a distillation of rare elements into ichor that can be infused into secret places. The modern mineralogist sniffs out these places with his instruments; he now knows the knitted continents for what they are. They are the true repositories of the earth's alchemy.

In the original formulation of the theory, a handful of plates encapsulated the rocks of the world, permitting enough permutations to accommodate our apparently inexhaustibly varied planet. This may seem almost an impertinence, in view of Suess' caveat about numbering the world. But this is how the plate tectonic revolution wrought a transformation. At the present time, there are many more plates recognized, but the principles remain valid. 'We shall all be changed, in the twinkling of an eye' – and so we were, at least relative to the fifty years it had taken for the idea of mobile continents to become respectable.

I had the curious privilege of being a bystander during the period when formal plate tectonic models were being developed in Cambridge in the late 1960s. There were two inspired scientists who worked on the mathematical treatment of plates at more or less the same time but on opposite sides of the Atlantic Ocean – Jason Morgan at Princeton, and Dan McKenzie at Cambridge. Cambridge University is organised into colleges, and I belonged to King's College, named after its founder, the devout King Henry VI. King's is famous for its choir and its chapel. The chapel lies on one flank of a quad, and two of the other three sides are walled in by academic buildings. The visitor will notice little stairwells like secret tunnels. Some of them lead to comfortable and cluttered rooms occupied by famous academics and writers. I met E. M. Forster for tea in one such room: he was very old and very polite, and did not say anything memorable, but I was awestruck nonetheless. "Mr E. M. Forster" a painted label said at the base of the staircase, as if he might have been in charge of the plumbing. There were fellows of the college located in other rooms who were solving the problems of the global economy, or the fundamentals of matter, or how to understand the difference between 'ego' and 'I', or things even more important. I was preceded in my college life by Dan McKenzie, while he was solving the problems of the construction of the world. He was a year or two ahead of me, and I was always invisible in the glare generated by his brilliance. After the first degree, came the Ph.D. thesis. Dan McKenzie's on applying Euler to plate motions was instantly famous. At a college function he explained that he had printed *extra* copies to sell on to the leading laboratories in the USA. The usual form in those days was for the student to take a bank loan to pay for the typing of the great work, which would then sit, magnificent but untouched, on a shelf in the University Library. The notion of people queuing up to read your thesis was bizarre. Within a year or two Dan was leading a double life, being flown out to California from Cambridge on a regular basis, like a film star. To the rank and file, all this was impossibly glamorous.

But it was all deserved. There are those who believe that theories have their time, that they arise with a kind of inevitability because of what has gone before, and as a result of new facts added to the store of knowledge. Notwithstanding, it remains true that there are few people who can grasp the historic moment. It always requires boldness, sometimes a certain unscrupulousness, and it is risky. Everything could be wrong, or half-right in the manner of Warren Carey. So credit justly belongs to those who take the first bold leaps. That said, there are usually a few intellectual sprinters who take to the field at the same time, like Morgan and McKenzie. Ideas lie half concealed, awaiting their historic moment for discovery, at which point there could be several gifted people who independently realize what, in retrospect, seems inevitable. By 1970 plate tectonics was not, yet, a 'theory of everything', but there was scarcely any aspect of earth history that plate theory would leave untouched. Plates provided a new way of looking at the world. Most immediately, there was a great boost for the Lyellian method. Geologists could go now into the field and look for analogies with the present-day world in ancient rocks, their search focused through the understanding that plate tectonics brought. In the Himalayas, could this, perhaps, be the remains of an island arc like Japan enmeshed in the mountain-building as two continents collided? In the Alps, might these be the deposits laid down in deep water on a sea-mount? Can we find fossil equivalents of the down-warping crust in front of the Himalayas? Can this particular mineral only grow where the conditions were exactly right during the closure of an ocean? The questions were endless, and answers were often forthcoming.

Take ophiolites first. Eduard Suess had known that there was a characteristic association of rocks that could be found in many mountain belts. These rocks had been studied by an Alpine geologist, G. Steinmann, in the early years of the twentieth century. He had noticed a consistent association of dark, basaltic volcanic rocks, often forming 'pillows', as around Hawai'i, with richly green and speckled serpentinite, topped by beds of the dark, fine-grained siliceous sedimentary rock known as chert. Sometimes the latter included fossil remains of tiny radiolarians, those single-celled oceanic plankton mentioned previously. So common was the association that it came to be known as 'Steinmann's trinity'. For instance, in the eastern Alps, Suess recorded that 'the green rocks (gabbro, serpentine, diabase) are frequently associated with deep sea radiolarian chert of middle to upper Jurassic age'. They were called ophiolites from *ophis*, the Greek for 'serpent', because of their serpentinite component. Fifty years later, Arthur Holmes was to note that ophiolites indicated eruption in deep water in 'geosynclines'. Plate tectonics would show that they were much more significant.

In 1994, I visited the Sultanate of Oman in search of trilobites. To reach my destination in the southerly desert I was obliged to cross the Oman Mountains from Muscat, the capital city. Like many countries in the Middle East, Oman has adopted western styles but has attempted to make them compatible with the region's cultural traditions. This has resulted in some curiosities. The new outskirts of Muscat are cheerily like western suburbs, although the white-walled villas are tiled for coolness rather than lined for warmth. But in the middle of roundabouts, or in public spaces, there are new monuments. I particularly liked an enormous painted coffee pot, complete with matching cups. In another site, a vast dagger in its ornate sheath commanded attention. My assumption was that these were precious items in the tents and caravans that were formerly the common habitat.

You are out of new Muscat soon enough and pass into the foothills of the mountains. There are steep-sided valleys – wadis – with fig trees and almonds in irregular groves wherever there is a little silt on which they can grow. Little brown goats fastidiously pick at spiky bushes. The wadis are dry now, but the large cobbles lying on the dry stream floor tell you that they must be able to turn into torrents when the rains come: how else could such boulders be transported there? Soon, you pass higher into the mountains. The few villages have all grown up around springs and seem to be ancient: uniformly buff or pallid brown, each with a fortress that is all steep walls, punctured with tiny square windows in ranks. There are groves of date palms, making rows of neat canopies. Near the water source are irrigated squares of vegetables looking improbably green against the overwhelming brown. Higher still, and you suddenly pass on to the moon, or so it seems. Here there is nothing and nobody. Even the scrawny acacia bushes seem to have given up the struggle for life. The hillsides, completely barren, are composed of beds of rock, and have an extraordinary heaviness about them, an oppressive blackness crusted with umber brown. It is not just that the rocks are dark: they seem to suck out the very energy from the sunlight, which is brilliant at this height. They absorb everything and give nothing back. They might indeed be from another world. Then you notice that some of the rocks show pillow structures, as if some underworld giant had laid out a whole field of cushions for a hellish party. They are identical to lavas erupted on the ocean floor. Perhaps you might see a few patches of chert, lying in the joints on top of the pillows. Elsewhere, there are black dykes running like ribs over the hills. A coarser crystalline rock glints darkly in the sunshine, and proves to be almost entirely composed of dark green olivine, reminiscent of the green-sand beach in Hawai'i. This rock is called dunite; nearby, there are lumps of dark green and reddish mottled serpentinite scattered about on the ground. No doubt about it, Herr Dr Steinmann would have recognized this part of Oman as an enormous ophiolite complex.

In a sense it is quite appropriate to think of these mountains as being derived from another world. It is the world of the deep sea. As more was learned about the structure of the oceanic crust, it became clear that ophiolites actually *were* slices of the deep sea-floor wrested from the abyss.

In the eastern Mediterranean the island of Cyprus is centred on the Troodos Mountains. The Troodos are another slab of ocean crust that has moved into the sunlight, and the area has become the classic of its kind. Professor Ian Gass and his colleagues showed that rocks recording the whole profile of the ocean crust are preserved in these mountains. Careful mapping revealed a 'fossilized' anatomy of the lithosphere of the sea-floor. Pillow lavas that had been erupted under the ocean depths from liquid magma were merely the top of the pile. Beneath the pillows there was a layer of dykes arranged in steep sheets. These were the 'feeders' that supplied magma to the ocean ridge where sea-floor spreading occurred. These dykes were the very struts of creation. Beneath this layer again there was dark, crystalline, igneous rock – gabbro – which underlies the whole of the ocean. In places, there were black seams of the mineral chromite (source of the element chromium) looking like tarry stripes. No wonder plants eschewed these places, for chromium is poisonous to many of them. Crystals of this heavy mineral must have settled out in the magma chamber, like beans falling to the bottom of a soup tureen. And in places, beneath the gabbro, there were patches of the rocks that lay at the base of the lithosphere, like dunite and lherzolite: we met pebbles of these rocks, as messengers from the deeps, where they had been brought to the surface in some of the lava flows on Hawai'i – dragged up from their natural home at the margin of the mantle. In these ophiolites the same rocks were hijacked wholesale from the depths of Neptune's (or should it be Pluto's?) domain. The whole profile could be more than ten kilometres thick. So this huge pile was out of place, lifted bodily from the ocean to form the backdrop to the traditional home of Aphrodite, goddess of love, whose temples are so numerous in Cyprus. Coins from Paphos show Aphrodite's emblem, a sort of cone, though it would be fanciful to imagine it represented any kind of volcano. But it is not fancy to suppose that Pluto's kingdom had somehow been levitated to the realm of love and sunshine. No wonder those similar mountains in Oman looked so unearthly, darkly glinting in the brilliant light.

Surely, though, this should not be? Ocean crust is destined to be consumed at subduction zones, not displayed layer by layer as in Oman and Cyprus. There was only one possible explanation. In places, slivers of oceanic crust were pushed *upwards*, rather than downwards. They were squeezed out from the tectonic vice, like pips from a crushed orange. In some places, a piece of ocean evidently came to rest on continental crust – as a displaced chunk, a tectonic refugee. This process is called *obduction*, a kind of anti-subduction. Plate tectonics completely altered the perception of these puzzling morsels of the earth, and Holmes' observations of their deep-sea origin were explicable in a different way. Even the little radiolarians made sense, because such plankton drifted on the surface of the seas overlying the depths, and were preserved upon their death in the sediments above the pillow lavas. Later, these little fossils became invaluable in dating the ages of ophiolites and cherts, because they changed with the passage of geological time: a fossil chronometer.

In a nutshell, ophiolites were the pieces of oceanic crust that got away. Steinmann's old 'trinity' proved to be three times as interesting. Within the Alps, too, there must have been other 'pips' squeezed out as ancient oceans closed, when Africa and Europe met. The modern view is that ophiolites are commonly associated with the closure of smaller ocean basins – between an island arc and an adjacent continent, for example. It has become clear that subduction is not entirely destructive. Wedges of sediments may become plastered on to the edge of the continent as subduction proceeds. These form prisms of sedimentary rocks, gummed on, or as we should say *accreted*, to the continental margin. Once more geologists went into the field to decipher plates in action and found evidence of this process on the ground in the Makran desert of Pakistan. But nobody would have heard the message of these rocks without the plate tectonic stimulus.

It could be said that entire cultures are under the influence of the geological underlay. As in Jung's original concept of the Collective Unconscious, we, the surface dwellers, are moved and bound by deeper things. Japan has now, at least superficially, adopted the western capitalist mode. Earthquake-proof technology has allowed for the construction of buildings in Tokyo that are as routinely modern as those in other capitals around the world. However, the classical era of paper-and-wood constructions was entirely appropriate to living on the quaking edge of a great subducting region. Maybe the Shinto religion with its welter of gods provided a way of propitiating the uncertain earth. Iwo-Jima is a small volcanic island 1150 kilometres (715 miles) south of Tokyo. The shore that gave brief haven to the survivors of Captain Cook's fatal voyage of 1779 is now forty metres above sea-level: the height of a church steeple. The island lies in the midst of a caldera hidden beneath the sea that is ten kilometres across and that was formed explosively some 2600 years ago. Magma is evidently rising again and being injected into the crust. There may yet be another cataclysm. Mount Fuji has been stable for hundreds of years, but it is only sleeping. The wonderfully symmetrical cone is a typical stratified volcano, built from successions of pyroclastic flows that would have destroyed everything in their path. The explosive lava type is a particular product of its position where plates meet, so this symbol of everything Japanese is in fact a product of the underworld. Even in these secular times the mountain is dotted with shrines, some of them dedicated to Sengen-Sama, goddess of the mountain. There is no question that its presence in Hokusai's inexhaustibly inventive set of portrayals, *36 Views of Mount Fuji*, is more than merely decorative. The mountain centres the world of his art. In Shinto days everybody made a pilgrimage to the top of the mountain, which at 3776 metres (12388 feet) is the highest in Japan. The sun goddess Amaterasu required it. Today people still feel drawn to watch the sun rise, looking towards Tokyo a hundred kilometres away, or perhaps towards the Pacific Ocean where the unseen plates move. The American journalist and author Lafcadio Hearn, who married a Japanese woman and took her nationality, was one of the first westerners to try to explain the virtues of Japanese culture. A hundred years ago he described his emotions on seeing the sunrise from the summit of Fuji in these terms:

> But the view – the view for 100 leagues and the light of the far faint dreamy world and the fairy vapours of morning – and the marvelous wreathings of cloud: all this, and only this, consoles me for the labour and the pain. Other pilgrims, earlier climbers poised upon the highest crag with faces turned to the tremendous East, are clapping their hands in Shinto prayer saluting the mighty day . . . I knew that the colossal vision before me has already become a memory ineffaceable – a memory of which no luminous detail can fade till the hour when thought itself must fade.

Lush prose, perhaps, but you are left in no doubt as to the importance of the occasion, and the importance of Fuji in Shinto cosmology.

The Shinto religion may not have the grip it once had, but there are still shy little offerings placed in wayside shrines on the way to the summit. Just in case.

Geology dictates the lie of the land, and climate controls how the design of the world accommodates to life. But climate itself is in thrall to geology. A landmass over the poles permits ice-sheets to grow, and this mediates the sea-levels of the world. There have been warm times when much of the land surface has drowned, and such times will come again. Mountain ranges modify weather systems, specify where there shall be deserts, and steal rain. Then, too, oceans are great climatic modifiers. Think how the coast of Europe is so ice free while the icebergs drift off frozen Labrador, at the same latitude. The North Atlantic Drift (Gulf Stream) moves warmth northwards – but only for some. There are climatologists who believe that the warm pump might be turned off in the twinkling of an eye, geologically speaking. Then long, frozen days might turn England's hedge-fringed green fields into birch and conifer scrub. The shape of the ocean basins is the stuff of climate: deep gyres transfer cool water and nutrients about the world. Yet ocean and mountain are no more than a consequence of the geological foundation: the arrangement of plates in this mosaic of our earth. Change the plates, and you will rearrange everything else. Mankind is no more that a parasitic tick gorging himself on temporary plenty while the seas are low and the climate comparatively clement. But the present arrangement of land and sea will change, and with it our brief supremacy.

6

Ancient Ranges

Newfoundland is a curious island. It hangs off the eastern coast of the North American continent as if it doesn't really belong there. The natives call it 'the Rock', and it is an apt name. There is certainly no shortage of geological exposure on the island, although most of it crops out along its rugged and indented shores. The coastline is 10,000 kilometres long if you add in all the numberless bays, where fishermen have established their 'outports'. Inland, Newfoundland is a mass of rambling rivers, and small lakes, called 'ponds'. The cover is a scrubby forest, mostly under-sized conifers, but relieved by shaking aspens, small alders, and birch trees. Many of the conifers have a sickly look, and are crowded together, a working example of the struggle for existence. It is an endless kind of landscape, mile after mile of the same, for hundreds of miles. There are few roads away from St John's, and if you are foolish enough to leave the beaten track and wander into the bush you can become disorientated within seconds.

In spite of the uncompromising terrain, from an early period the island was colonized by Europeans, who displaced the native Micmac Indians. Even the Vikings found their way to L'Anse sur Meadows in the Northern Peninsula, at a time when the climate was more equable than it is now. Hundreds of years later, fishermen from the English West Country and from Ireland followed the first wave of immigration into North America. The coastal villages they settled

Newfoundland, a bleak land. At Bauline, with ice in the bay and a typical outport wooden construction.

were isolated from the world, and from each other. Some of the place names – Trepassey, Tor's Cove – would not be out of place in Cornwall. Others – Blow-me-down Brook, Fogo, Goose Tickle, Heart's Desire – have a unique charm all their own. The extraordinary Newfoundland accent may have preserved something of its original Tudor twang. Certainly, it is most unlike that of the island's Canadian neighbours. To the 'incomer' it sounds Irish at first, but then other harmonics emerge – a hint of Cornish, perhaps. Aitches are dropped and added; and words that are obsolete elsewhere are preserved here in common usage. The island only formally joined Canada in 1949. Before that, it was the oldest British colony, founded in 1583. It remains fiercely proud of its own identity.

The once thriving cod industry has collapsed, ruined by non-indigenous factory ships over-fishing the Grand Banks. Nowadays, the distinctive two-storey wooden houses that line the outports are painted brighter than they have ever been: there is little for a beached fisherman to do other than redecorate the house. The cod 'flakes' along the shoreline on which the fish were once split and dried have all but disappeared. There are still lobsters to be had, and squid some years, but the great days are over. Newfoundlanders annually receive the vilification of animal rights activists because of their participation in seal culling. But to these men it is a tradition, and clubbing is the most humane way of dispatching a proportion of baby harp seals for their skins. The year I was living there I saw the Bishop of St John's bless the fleet before it sailed. This was my first lesson in moral relativism.

Newfoundland is a geological textbook laid open to the skies. The traverse east to west across the island is a pilgrimage that many famous geologists have made. There is something there for everyone: for the palaeontologist, for the tectonician, for the just plain curious. The rocks embrace an appreciable chunk of geological time – several hundred million years – especially spanning the later Precambrian, Cambrian, Ordovician, and Silurian periods, 900–419 million years ago. It is a big slice of earth history spread across a big stretch of land, making it difficult to select just a few places that reveal the secrets of the Rock – many students have spent their whole lives untangling the complex geology of small parts of the island. It becomes necessary, perhaps, to imitate one of the huge seagulls that haunt the Newfoundland shore, alighting briefly on one rocky outcrop before flapping off to another distant cliff.

St John's lies on the eastern edge of the island. It is built on folded, resistant, Precambrian sedimentary and volcanic rocks that form spectacular, sheer cliffs, ribbed and pleated, from the top of which you can watch pilot whales sporting offshore. The old town around the splendid natural harbour is picturesque enough in a scruffy way. Steep terraces of painted wooden houses run down to Water Street, which was once a bustling centre for shopping and shipping before the edge-of-town malls and supertankers took their toll. Grand Victorian houses in their own grounds that belonged to the merchants lie uphill. Those whom Newfoundlanders still call 'marchants' were the beneficiaries of the fishing wealth of the island: it is said that there were more millionaires a century ago in St John's than anywhere else in North America. They kept the fishermen in a state of perpetual debt by an iniquitous system of 'loans' advanced on the year's catch. Older inhabitants still remember running around barefoot through the snow. This is a tribute to their sheer toughness. Because the Gulf Stream passes Newfoundland by, the climate is, to be tactful, frequently inclement. You would never guess it was on the same latitude as Paris. Spring seems to be delayed forever, and a dump of slushy snow down from the north is not unknown even in June. Fog obscures the delightful sea views for what seems half the year; and the mournful lowing of foghorns through the Narrows provides an eerie accompaniment to winter walks. Ice floes brought down on the Labrador Current accompany the brief early days of summer. For geologists, it means that the field season is decidedly limited, and waterproofs are indispensable at all times. When the sun comes out, it is totally delightful, except for the mosquitoes, and the blackflies, and the deerflies.

Bell Island is a small island in Conception Bay, a few miles west of St John's. It is more or less encircled by cliffs comprising dull yellow or brownish sandstones, much less folded than the rocks around St John's. The cliffs are quite accessible in a number of places, and a brisk breeze usually keeps the biting and bloodsucking flies at bay. These sandstones are the kind of rocks that were originally laid down as sediments in quite shallow seas. A very lucky hammer blow might reveal fossils that look like small, black hacksaw blades, laid out on 'leaves' of intercalated shale. These are the remains of extinct, colonial, planktonic animals called graptolites. Every geologist likes to find graptolites because they can be used to date rocks quite precisely. They evolved fast, and spread widely around the ancient oceans in which they floated – making them ideal biological chronometers. The ones on Bell Island are no exception: the local expert, Henry Williams, identified them precisely. They indicated an Ordovician age; more exactly, a part of the early Ordovician called the Arenigian. There were other fossils there as well, including some of my own favourite animals, trilobites. Superficially more complex than the graptolites, trilobites were 'bugs' with jointed legs – arthropods – that swarmed in the seas of the Palaeozoic era. Sadly for all biologists, they are now extinct, but there were once thousands of kinds of trilobites, individual species of which were confined to the seas surrounding different continents of the ancient world. These ones on Bell Island were old friends: I knew their names as well as I know my children's birthdays: *Neseuretus* and *Ogyginus*. Both of them had been yielded up to my questing hammer in strata cropping out along streams and roadsides in Wales. I knew them also from France and Spain; I had even been sent a sample of one of these beasts from the remote deserts of Saudi Arabia. Much more common on Bell Island were scratches and burrows left in the sandy sediments by animals on the Ordovician sea-floor. Some, called *Cruziana*, were probably made by the same trilobites that you could hold in your hand. They look like braided plaits laid on the rocky slab, as distinctive in their way as many more substantial fossils. Exactly the same kinds of *Cruziana* could also be found in France and Spain and North Africa. It is beginning to look as if the sandstones on Bell Island are trying to tell us something.

Move further westwards to Random Island and it is a similar story. More fossils, a little older, just like those from Europe. On the way you pass over a cheerless, bleak, and empty region, where even the hardy conifers have given up trying to take root. These are the 'barrens'. The underlying rock is unforgiving granite, and the soil above it is so poor that little seems to flourish. Little, that is, except a fruit called the partridge-berry that clambers over the ground on inconspicuous vines. It is said to be a good source of Vitamin C and is resistant to frost. Newfoundland families used to keep a stash of these purple-red berries the size of rabbit droppings under water in a jar by the door, and a few would be taken every day over the interminable winter to keep scurvy at bay. In tough places everything seems to have a use. The eastern part of the Rock comprises two broad lobes of land trending north-east–south-west connected to the rest of the island by a narrow link of land that is almost an isthmus.

This eastern part of the island is known as Avalon. As so often in geology, understanding of the area was dependent on making maps of the rocks, and the unscrambling of Newfoundland began in Avalon, with the pioneering geologists Alexander Murray and James Howley publishing the first map of the Avalon Peninsula in 1881. The accounts for 1871 fieldwork submitted to the Geological Survey Office note that 100 lbs of bacon cost five pounds, as did a new tent. Murray was able to hire four men for four months for £120, but his own salary was £490. Those geological maps have been under a continuous process of refinement ever since: no map is ever truly finished, simply because you cannot write down all the truth of the world on a sheet of paper.

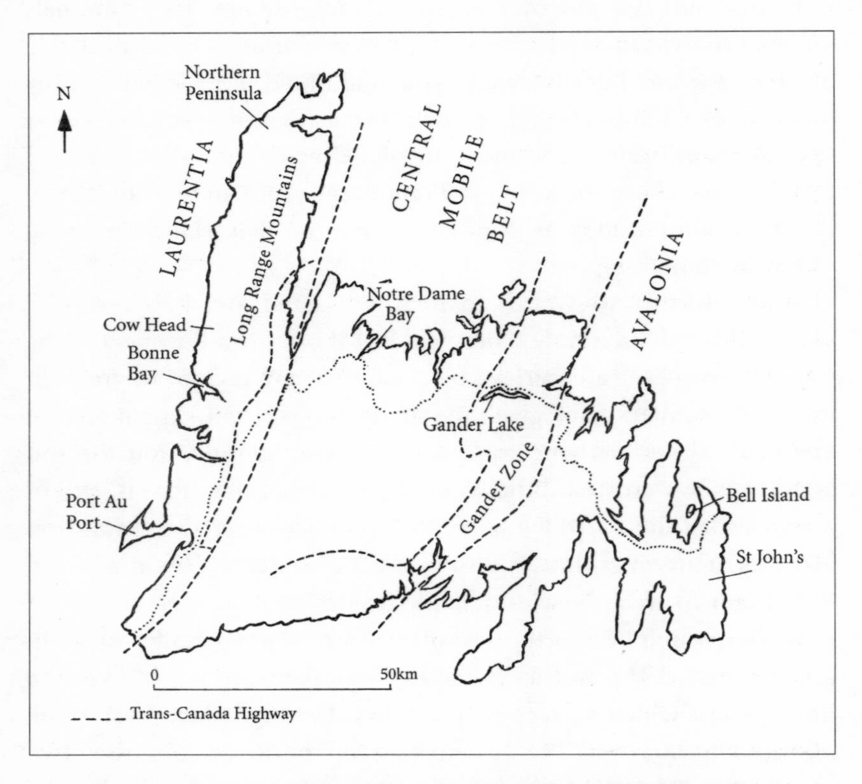

Simplified geology of Newfoundland, showing the Trans-Canada Highway running west from St John's, and locating some of the places visited.

Move westwards again. You will find yourself driving along the Trans-Canada Highway – there is no other way to go. Several hours pass before you get to Gander, a remote settlement with nothing to it except a hotel and an airport. Then, when you reach Gambo and look at the rocks cropping out in cuts along the roadside near the village, you notice that something seems to have changed. Gone are the simple sedimentary and volcanic rocks that we saw around St John's and on Bell Island, which there are laid out in clear layers, even though those layers might have been elevated to the vertical. Instead, the rocks at Gambo present a bewilderingly various appearance: striped and twisted, in places they show a crude layering, though it seems to wander hither and yon. Pinkish layers a foot or so thick can twist and pinch out on a rock face a dozen metres in length. Quite often you see smaller, pale veins that seem to be scribbled on to the rockface like graffiti. If the sun is shining you might notice that many of the rocks glisten and flash briefly as you drive past. If you manage to find a place to get off the road to examine the rocks you will see that the pink ones are mostly composed of creamy-looking feldspar crystals, which impart the dominant colour. Then there are veins of quartz, which sometimes wriggle through the rock like creamy worms, or cut across its grain like petrified flashes of forked lightning. The shine in the sunlight is induced by little crystals of mica, with perfectly flat faces that respond like diminutive mirrors to incident light. Coarse and irregular layering is often picked out by drifts of dark mica crystals. In places, the rocks look as if they had been stirred by a gigantic spoon. They are gneisses. Such rocks have been changed by baking in a terrestrial pressure-cooker. Then they have been disinterred: kilometres of overburden must have been removed. This part of the country is comparable with the pass of San Bernarindo in Switzerland, despite its different geological age. Nowhere near Gander are there marbles, such as those that enclosed S. Gennaro's relics in Naples in such splendour. This is gneiss country, boggy and impenetrable. Just as marbles started life as limestones, many gneisses started out as shales, before they were 'cooked'. More specifically, many of these rocks are described as migmatites, in which the pink veins seem to blend insensibly into a kind of swirling granite. Sometimes it is difficult to be quite sure whether you are looking at gneiss or a banded granite. If you take a diversion off the Trans-Canada Highway, along Bonavista Bay as far north as Deadman's Bay, there are huge masses of wholly unambiguous pinkish granite plunging direct to the sea. Some of the coarse gneisses contain garnets. Jewel-quality garnets are pretty, plum-coloured stones, much beloved by the Victorians for silver settings. Most of the ones you find in metamorphic rocks are a disappointment; the best you can hope for is to find one about the colour, size, and shape of a partridge-berry. They are interesting to find, though, because they only form under particular temperatures and pressures. Almandine, the variety found here, is stable at temperatures of 540° to 900° C at a pressure of 200 GPa. This has been proved by experiment under controlled conditions in the laboratory. So it is possible both to visualize and quantify something of the suffering the rocks in this area endured in the great vice of the earth. No fossils could be expected to survive such treatment.

Between Avalon and Gander, therefore, it is evident that a major geological threshold must have been crossed. The threshold is marked by a great fault cutting through the geology, the Dover Fault, which runs north-east–south-west near the eastern side of Bonavista Bay. The Avalon Platform lies to the east, back to Bell Island and St John's, while to the west lies the Mobile Belt, forming the central part of Newfoundland, a land of complexity and problems. This is where the striped and redoubled gneisses, and many other rocks besides, all run together and are twisted and faulted up. It is mobile, not just in the sense that there must have been movements of strata, faulting, and geological mayhem, but also that whole chunks of the world may have reached where they now lie from some other place.

Past the village of Gambo the road runs along a pond that is big enough to be called a lake – Gander Lake, where there are folded, metamorphosed sandstones (quartzites). The rocks of the apparently impenetrable area north of the lake were mapped in the 1960s by a celebrated Newfoundland geologist, Harold Williams, universally known as 'Hank', a native of the Rock and wise in its ways, with an accent that puzzles those not used to its idiosyncratic inflexions. Hank Williams worked out much of the geology of the Mobile Belt the hard way, by foot and Indian canoe; latterly, helicopters made life easier, if more dangerous. Like Murray and Howley before him, he produced geological maps – but what maps! Unscrambling the Mobile Belt was like solving a cryptic crossword, one in which even the clues were anagrams. The resulting maps are speckled and daubed like a painting by an abstract expressionist, but even through the extravagance of colours you can clearly see how many features have a north-west–south-east trend, governing the shape of the bays and headlands. The design of the country is clearly written in the geology. Hank employed many students, too, and one of his criteria for their selection was the ability to play a musical instrument. There was always a band in the Geology Department at Memorial University in St John's, with Hank on banjo or fiddle, and with assorted bassists and dulcimer players, all making a fine racket with their jigs and reels, of which there seemed to be an endless selection. When the fog was thick on the north shore, I am told that Hank used to sit in the bow of the leading canoe furiously strumming the banjo, to guide the party onwards to the next offshore island. He thought nothing of dumping a student in some remote area until the field season was over, with only a violin and a field assistant for company. But Hank was much more than a decoder of complex geology; he built up a picture of the whole of the Newfoundland central fold belt and extended it far, far beyond the wild shores of the island – finally, it provided an interpretation of the whole eastern side of North America from the Adirondack Mountains to the Appalachians. But here I am getting ahead of my story.

It is clear that there are 'fossil' volcanic islands within the Mobile Belt – around Notre Dame Bay, on the northern coast, for example. Volcanic rocks are easy enough to recognize, even when they have been baked or folded; a number are like those I have already mentioned from Hawai'i, including 'pillow lavas'. A few ancient islands still stick up out of the sea as rock islets today; disinterred, they reproduce their anatomy of 460 million years ago. The detailed chemistry of the lavas can be studied in modern laboratories, and some show the kind of 'trace' elements that are characteristic of oceanic islands at the present day; others are like those from island arcs close to subduction zones. These elemental ratios are like fingerprints that identify the magma source of the ancient lavas. This geochemistry is a wonderful application of Lyellian principles, and a boon to the geological interpretation. Not all the rocks have been as heavily metamorphosed as those near Gander. In places there are beds of rock composed of cobbles (conglomerates) that you can just imagine tumbling off the side of the unstable volcano. Some of the islands had shallow seas around them, and, just once in a while, fossils of some of the shelly animals that lived in those waters have survived all the vicissitudes that nature has thrown at them. These speak of Ordovician dates. It is curious to think of seals now basking where trilobites once crawled. Discovering these critical creatures in these volcanic-derived rocks was an heroic accomplishment; for once the needle and haystack analogy can be used without blushing. So this part of the Mobile Belt is a place where all the branches of geological science meet and converse.

There are ores and minerals in the Mobile Belt, too, and many of them are associated with the volcanic rocks. Every few years there are rumours of gold finds, and indeed in a few localities there are significant amounts of the precious metal – and rather more silver. Sulphide ores have been important enough to give rise to working mines for copper, manganese, and lead-zinc in other parts of the island. For wherever the earth moves, metals are concentrated.

A friend, John Bursnall, was assigned an area around Notre Dame Bay as the ground on which to work up his doctoral thesis. He returned from fieldwork each year with his brow progressively creased, and with thick notebooks full of sketches. The geology was, he remarked from time to time, a real mess. Everything on the ground seemed to be in a state of flux. The rocks he had been assigned are known as the Dunnage Mélange. Poor John was obliged to share an office with me, where I noisily dug out trilobites from their limestone matrix whilst he attempted to put some shape into a hideously complicated piece of Newfoundland. He sometimes had to retire with a headache. A mélange is, I suppose, a polite word for a mixed-up mess. The principal feature of the Dunnage Mélange consists of huge blocks of rock. These now form islands and shoals in the grandly named Bay of Exploits. If you are accustomed to think of rock successions as deposited in a logical order – oldest first, then progressively younger – it is not too difficult to envisage how such successions can get folded, or even, as in the Alps, turned completely upside down. It is not so impossibly hard to conceive of these rocks subsequently becoming metamorphosed by heat and by pressure, and changing their character accordingly, in the grip of the earth's inexorable movements. But in the Dunnage there are places where it is almost impossible to make sense of the relationships between rock units in the field. These enormous blocks – some more than a kilometre in diameter – of oceanic-style volcanic rocks rest on a kind of groundsheet of shales, which must have originally accumulated in the deep sea. Some of the blocks have evidently tumbled or slid downslope until they came to rest in a confusing array. Fortunately, those useful fossils, graptolites, have been found in the shales to tell us that these events happened in the Ordovician. But then the confused mass is itself folded, even overturned, thus superimposing complexity on perplexity. To make matters worse, there are places where igneous rocks, cooled from magma, have been injected into the shales while they were still soft muds, so there are other kinds of rocks swirling around in the mixture. And then the whole area has been cut with steep faults, and pushed bodily north-westwards along thrusts.

Hank Williams and his associates divided Newfoundland into a number of zones, each one with a distinctive geological signature. By now we have moved progressively westwards from the Avalon Zone, through the Gander Zone into the Dunnage Zone. As geology always turns out to be more complicated than was thought at first, the Dunnage is now subdivided in various ways, the details of which would further tax the imagination. Each of the major zones is separated from its neighbour by a major structural line, often a series of faults that cut deep into the crust. The Grub Line separates the Gander Zone from the Dunnage, while the Baie Verte Line separates the Dunnage complexity from what happens further west. Although they wander somewhat, each major fault follows the grain of the land from north-east to south-west. Everything on the surface is in thrall to the deeper order. It is almost a relief that by the time we arrive at the west coast, some of that bewildering complexity is lost.

One important road crosses the Trans-Canada Highway in the west; it runs northwards up the Great Northern Peninsula, a great protuberance that sticks up on the west side of the island like an optimistic thumb. This highway runs to the sea at the Gros Morne National Park. The western part of the Rock retains vestiges of French influence in place names like Port au Port and Port aux Basques – after all, it does face Quebec. But it is still defiantly Newfoundland in spirit, even though the 'mainland' is only a ferry ride away. The Gros Morne Park is spectacularly disposed about Bonne Bay, a 'drowned' valley flanked by relatively lush forests with cliffs comprising mostly Cambrian-age sedimentary rocks plunging steeply to the sea. Down at Norris Point there is a little ferry that will take you across Bonne Bay to Woody Point: on a clear day the crossing is a delight, with the sun flashing the tops of the waves and picking out tree-lined coves up the Bay. Woody Point is protected from the winter weather so it has mature trees, as well as immaculate clapboard houses flanking the hillsides to which some of the more affluent islanders choose to retire.

Following the road upwards from Woody Point towards the outport of Trout River, you suddenly encounter a different world. All the trees have disappeared, as if removed by blight. There is little up here but sphagnum moss and a few hardy plants that seem able to survive on nothing at all on the open, rounded hillsides. The whole landscape has been transformed into a dull brown wilderness. The umber rocks suck out any vigour from the sunshine, while on an overcast and misty day you might easily imagine that you were entering Mordor, J. R. R. Tolkien's blasted and evil kingdom, for so little thrives here. The rocks are clearly of a kind on which terrestrial life is ill at ease. Looking closely, it is clear that there are pillow lavas among them: we have seen those bulbous forms before. Then there are some stratified rocks: their dark and crystalline character shows them to be igneous, and some of them are of the kind associated with mantle material, whilst a few of the dark grains might be the mineral chromite. Elsewhere, there are densely packed dykes – sheeted dykes – that closely resemble the stacked legacy of ocean-floor spreading. Suddenly, it is obvious that the whole desolate area is nothing less than a piece of ancient ocean floor: an ophiolite suite. Its alien bareness is akin to the landscape I encountered under cloudless skies in the Sultanate of Oman. Small wonder that trees cannot flourish on the malnourished hillsides. Rather than becoming obliterated in the plunging mills of subduction, this naked knob of land on the western coast of Newfoundland has been obducted – squeezed upwards rather than downwards, and thereby saved from destruction. Since further westwards lay only the great continent of Laurentia (North America + Greenland), there must have been an oceanic basin to the *east* from which this slice of crustal history was derived. How could it be otherwise? To this we shall return.

The story continues further northwards up the Northern Peninsula. From here you can see the inaccessible Long Range Mountains that form the 'spine' of the Peninsula. These are composed of metamorphic rocks of Precambrian, more particularly Grenville, age, far older than anything in the Mobile Belt: these speak of earlier ages, other dramas. They were annealed before the first rocks around Bonne Bay were laid down under the Cambrian seas. The village of Cow Head is excluded from the park, so it is an agreeably ramshackle kind of place. Youths hang about on the main street, and even the arrival of a geologist is worth a glance. You used to be able to buy a plate of cod's tongues in the Shallow Bay Motel – and surprisingly good they were, too – but the fishing ban probably put paid to that delicacy. I got to stay in a mobile home, and in one of Payne's Cabins. There only seem to be two family names on the coast hereabouts – the Paynes and the Crockers – so I imagine marriages do not cause much taxonomic surprise. Cow Head itself is a prominent headland connected to the settlement by a natural causeway, or 'tickle' as the Newfoundlanders prefer it. The rocks running along the shore are extraordinary. From a distance it looks as if some Titan had emptied out sacks of massive boulders along the cliffs. Closer to, it appears that the rounded boulders are allied to dipping rock-beds, cemented together by smaller pebbles and fine limestone: in fact, everything – boulders, pebbles and all – is made of limestone. These are conglomerates of a very distinctive kind. Then you notice that individual conglomerate beds are separated by something altogether softer that weathers back. This rock comprises thin beds of limestone and shale; you may have to grub with your geological hammer to claw out bits big enough to break. But – wonder of wonders! – the shales are full of useful graptolites. Following one bed of shale to the next above, these fossils show a succession of typical species that prove that the earlier half of the Ordovician period is represented by strata of conglomerates and shales (in fact, similar rocks carry on down into the Cambrian). The shaly rocks were originally laid down under deep water. Then when you bring a bigger and stronger hammer to bear on the limestone boulders themselves you discover that they, too, yield fragments of fossils – trilobites. I spent more hours than I care to remember persuading tough limestones to give up their shelly treasure trove. On clear days, such work was nothing but a pleasure, with gentle breezes bearing the aromatic smell of pinewoods. On wet days it was necessary to keep reminding myself of the nostrum that genius is 99% hard work; this optimistically based on the classical deductive mantra: 'all genius is 99% hard work; this project is 99% hard work: therefore, I am a genius'. However, the labour was worth it, since the kinds of fossil animals recovered showed two things very clearly: they were species that lived in shallow water; and they were utterly different from their near contemporaries on Bell Island, where this journey began. The conclusion is inescapable that the limestone blocks originated in shallow seas, and then slumped or tumbled down to a shale sea-floor in massive flows, carrying with them their cargo of trilobites into the domain of the graptolites. At Lower Head, nearby, some of the blocks are the size of houses.

Journey's end is a little to the south and west: the Port au Port Peninsula. This is a comparatively open part of the island, with many grassy fields, in which a cow or two watches the world go by. It was once very poor, and is still very Catholic. Small square wooden houses sport the longest washing-lines in the world. They are hung with trousers and shirts of various sizes, graded according to age. When there is a wind blowing they look like bunting. As usual, the rocks are exposed along the shore: limestones again, but ones that appear different from the spectacular conglomerates on Cow Head. These are regular limestones, in regular beds of rock. The strata are gently tilted, so you can climb up or down the rock succession much as you might go up and down a staircase, respectively ascending or descending through geological time. This is about as simple as geology gets; it is known as 'layer cake stratigraphy'. Compared with the Mobile Belt, only the gentlest of earth movements has disturbed these rocks. In some places, on the surface of limestones it is easy to see coiled shells of fossil snails, which tell the palaeontologist that – again – the rocks are of early Ordovician age, 470 million years. But on Port au Port there are no deep-water graptolite shales. All the evidence from the limestones points to their accumulation in shallow water environments during the Ordovician. Here and there are beds of oolites, for example, made of little rounded grains – like millet seed – that form only in agitated warm waters, such as you might find off the Bahamas today. Elsewhere, there are fossil algal 'mats' that grew close to the inter-tidal zone: they look like rucked paper tissues in cross-section where the sea has polished them through. Or the limestones have been replaced by dolomite, which is something that happens in hot lagoons. There is no question about it: not only were these limestones laid down in shallow seas, but those seas lay under a tropical sun. There were calcareous lagoons and tidal flats and oolite shoals where now the gulls keen over a choppy Atlantic sea. Similar tropical limestones crop out further north in western Newfoundland, right up to St Antony at the tip of the Northern Peninsula. Further afield, they are widespread over much of North America and Greenland. This was a time when sea-levels were high world-wide, and shallow seas penetrated into the interior of continents. The whole of Laurentia basked under a tropical sun in the Ordovician – a vast area of shallow seas known as a carbonate platform. However we fashion the Ordovician world it is evident that we are obliged to place Laurentia close to the equator of the time. And the trilobites? Some of the species found in the tumbled blocks at Cow Head are found also *in situ* in the contemporary platform limestones. So this where the blocks must have come from: they slumped and tumbled off the edge of the carbonate platform at the rim of the Laurentian continent as it was in the Ordovician. Into the deep sea, and into history.

One final fact: careful geological mapping showed that both the Cow Head conglomerates and the Bay of Islands ophiolites were piled on *top* of the carbonate platform limestones. This happened along a series of thrust faults, a shove of the earth that propelled huge tracts of land towards Laurentia. Unlike the platform rocks on which they lay, the Cow Head rocks and ophiolites were tipped steeply, folded, and faulted; they had suffered as they moved.

How are we to interpret the geology we have seen as we bobbed like a restless seagull from east to west over the Rock? Plate tectonics finally supplied a satisfactory answer, but understanding came piecemeal. It is necessary to avoid thinking of the progress towards what we now know as a kind of moral improvement. It must *always* have felt as if the tectonic truth were just around the corner; but the confident assertion of today is all too often the retraction of tomorrow. To the pioneering geologists making their first maps it must have seemed enough simply to lay out the ground into its constituent rock formations. They would have been delighted to find sufficient fossils to put some dates on the rocks of the Avalon Peninsula, just as on the other side of the island as early as 1865 the Canadian palaeontologist Elkanah Billings was uncovering trilobites from the same limestones I had chopped with my hammer more than a century later. Eduard Suess was certainly aware of the integrity of the ancient continent of which those limestones formed a part: 'That vast region of North America which is formed on ancient rocks overlain by horizontal Cambrian strata has received the name of Laurentia.' This expresses the idea clearly enough. He noted that Cambrian trilobites overlay the older 'schists' of the Northern Peninsula in Newfoundland, making that part of the island a sure component of Laurentia. And he was insistent that Greenland belonged to the same continent, too: '*Greenland is a part of Laurentia*' was an assertion important enough to be worth italicizing. It was also clear that the geology of Newfoundland connected south-eastwards with that of eastern Canada, and beyond into Maine, Vermont, and New York State, and thence to the southern States. The whole grain of the Appalachian mountains followed the same north-west to south-east trend, just like the faults separating the main geological divisions. The Blue Ridge Mountains traced the identical line, as did the Alleghenys. Then there were the metamorphic rocks, those schists and gneisses that gave such clear evidence of having been caught deep in the vice of the earth, but which were now disinterred. They, too, could be followed from Newfoundland through the Appalachians close to the edge of the great Laurentian continent. Surely these rocks proved that a range of mountains more elevated and dramatic than today's scenic remnants had once towered above the Laurentian interior. Hundreds of millions of years of erosion had brought them down, exposing their innards to the snows and rains of the twenty-first century. To be sure, there are places where the mountains are still splendid and wild, especially where granites have bolstered their durability; but there are others where silvery schists crop out along urban roadsides under the sumach trees, or are dug out to make the foundations of superstores. Geological time is enough to wear down the mightiest peaks, and lay low former Everests.

It was appreciated early on that there was a contrast between the successive Cambrian, Ordovician, and Silurian sedimentary rocks that accumulated under the sea on the Laurentian 'platform' and those that were laid down at the same time along the Appalachian line. James Hall was a great geologist who prepared the first official accounts of the fossils and strata of New York State. In 1859 he observed that the sedimentary rocks of the Laurentian platform were ten to twenty times thinner than their time equivalents in the folded mountains – where sedimentary piles could be several kilometres thick. It was evident that linear troughs followed the trace of future mountain chains, which were steadily subsiding over millions of years, simply to accommodate all that sediment. In 1873 James Dana, whom we met earlier, called them 'geosynclinals' – literally, a sag in the earth – and Suess used the same term, though the alternative designation 'geosyncline' is the one that later stuck for more than half a century. For a while, geosynclines were very popular. Forty years ago the crumpled and complex Mobile Belt of Newfoundland would have been considered a typical result of a deformed geosyncline. Many different kinds of geosynclines were recognized in the 1950s, most notably by the 'prince of geosynclines', Marshall Kay of Harvard. He tacked all kinds of prefixes ('taphro-', 'poly-', etc.) on to geosynclines to designate what he considered their distinct geological circumstances. Marshall Kay is principally remembered by those who met him – rather affectionately – as the most garrulous man who ever lived. But he did point to Newfoundland as an ideal place to study the genesis of ancient mountain chains, in which regard he was absolutely correct.

The problem is that the mere fact of a thick pile of Appalachian sediments alone does not explain how they came subsequently to be folded and metamorphosed – in short, having all the features of a mountain belt. A great thickness of comparatively light sedimentary rocks accumulating in a geosyncline would ultimately 'rebound' because of isostasy – like a depressed rubber duck bouncing back upwards in a bath. The lower parts of the sedimentary pile might have been temporarily subjected to sufficient heat and pressure to become metamorphosed, but the effect would not have been adequate to account for the extreme conditions required to produce some of the minerals found in schists and gneisses – nor for the observable tectonic mayhem and thrusting such as forced the ophiolites in western Newfoundland over the 'platform' limestones. Arthur Holmes struggled gamely with applying geosynclinal terminology, but found it inadequate. Clearly, as the detective in 'locked-room' mysteries is wont to say, it was time to consider the facts in a new light.

The acceptance of mobile continents provided more than merely new illumination: it supplied a floodlight. The 1964 edition of 'Holmes' includes a diagram showing what Europe + America looked like when you closed the North Atlantic Ocean, prior to the breakup of Pangaea. An extraordinary convergence happens. The whole Newfoundland–Appalachian mountain chain suddenly joins hands across the (non-)Atlantic with another ancient mountain chain – the Caledonides. Caledonia was, of course, the Roman name for Scotland:

> O Caledonia! stern and wild,
> Meet nurse for a poetic child!
> Land of brown heath and shaggy wood,
> Land of the mountain and the flood

declaimed Sir Walter Scott, who celebrated its romantic embodiment in *The Lay of the Last Minstrel.* The Caledonides, however, do not just include Scotland: the ancient mountains have a compass as generous as that of the Appalachians. Like that range, they comprised a complex of Lower Palaeozoic rocks variously folded, faulted, or metamorphosed: wild country, for the most part, mountains and brown heaths, indeed. The chain ran south-west to north-east through Ireland, embracing hilly Wales and the Lake District, much of rugged Scotland, and thence to include the whole of the Scandinavian coastal mountain chain running through Norway, from Stavanger in the south to Hammerfest in the north – this section alone spans more than ten degrees of latitude. Close the Atlantic Ocean, and the Caledonides run on naturally north of Newfoundland. The whole chain when put together snaked its way through the midst of the ancient supercontinent of Pangaea. Had we been able to peer from a satellite in Permian times, the Appalachian–Caledonian line would have been one of the most easily recognizable signatures written on face of the globe: a seam ancient even then. Clearly, the opening of the Atlantic Ocean had ripped apart two segments of a single geological monument – not neatly so, either, but raggedly, like an incriminating photograph roughly torn in two by a jealous lover.

Eduard Suess had not recognized the northward continuation of the Appalachians for what it was; for him, Newfoundland was the local end of the structure. If anything, he traced the continuation of the Appalachian chain into what he termed the 'Altaides' of Europe and Asia. Marcel Bertrand and, later, Arthur Holmes, had spliced the Caledonides and Appalachians together. By 1964, when the second editon of 'Holmes' was published, the 'drifters' had finally achieved respectability. The recognition of such an extensive ancient range could be viewed as another consequence of the acceptance of Pangaea.

The Caledonides themselves had a tradition of study that was both more historic and more intense than was the case for Newfoundland's geology, largely because these ancient mountains crossed a major part of western Europe, where there were many geologists. After all, Britain was where the rocks of the Cambrian, Ordovician, Silurian, and Devonian periods had first been discriminated one from another during the nineteenth century. The very names still embody country (Cambria: Roman Wales), county (Devon), or ancient tribes (Ordovices, Silures) that were part of the human history of the British Isles. This is where the 'type areas' for rocks of these ages still reside. Pioneer geologists did fieldwork in areas they could reach by train or on horseback, or by foot. Improvements in public transport, particularly expansion of the railway networks, made formerly inaccessible areas readily available for study. And how those pioneers could walk! When Ben Peach and John Horne exquisitely mapped vast areas of the Highlands of Scotland at the end of the nineteenth century, they thought nothing of covering thirty miles a day of 'brown heath and shaggy wood' across some of the most strenuous territory in Britain. As so often, geological maps drawn by heroic foot-sloggers preceded tectonic enlightenment.

Hard on the heels of the first maps were furious geological rows about the interpretation of particular features. In the north-west Highlands there is a geological line running from Durness in the north to the Isle of Skye in the south that marks out the contact between metamorphic rocks – gneisses and schists – to the south-east and what I have called platform carbonate sedimentary rocks, to the north-west. The latter are of Cambrian to Ordovician age, and virtually identical to the rocks that underlay the Port au Port Peninsula in Newfoundland. They even have the same fossils. In a book that records the true density of historical detail accompanying discovery, David Oldroyd has written excellently about the controversy surrounding this single contact, the meaning of which occupied some of the most famous geologists of the nineteenth century. On modern maps the outcome of these intellectual battles is recorded by a mere two words: 'Moine Thrust'. The metamorphic rocks have been bodily pushed north-westwards over the platform sediments in a thrust movement comparable with that around Bonne Bay in Newfoundland, at the western edge of the great mountain range. The rocks under the thrust were ground to paste under the weight of vanished mountains, a paroxysm of the earth now marked by no more than a bluff where a few sheep graze and the wind tickles the cotton-grass. Charles Lapworth, who was as instrumental in working out the truth of the Moine as any geologist, described it thus in 1882:

> Conceive a vast rolling and crushing mill of irresistible power . . . shale, limestone, quartzite, granite, and the most intractable gneisses crumple up like putty in the terrible grip of this earth engine.

It is hardly possible to describe such an historic drama in the dry language of science.

Southwards, the Highlands themselves are a metamorphic geologist's delight and a palaeontologist's despair: even if the rocks were once full of tiny 'bugs', what could survive? Schists, gneisses, and quartzites rule, making for wonderful scenery and no fossils. In fact, most of the rocks were originally deposited in the Precambrian, so you would not find large fossils there anyway. You are obliged to remind yourself that today's steep hills are but a remnant of the grand alps that once towered here. It still seems like hard uphill walking, particularly on wet and windy days (which constitute most of the year). Patient mapping by officers of the Geological Survey of Great Britain has shown that the metamorphosed strata are twisted into great overfolds and nappes, comparable with those of the Alps, that are now concealed beneath bogs or partially exposed along the flanks of the wildest hills. Kilometre-long slabs of the earth have been overturned hereabouts. The crust must have been thickened by the 'earth engine' as one fold piled on another as the mountain range rose up, and then the great pile was subjected to heat and pressure deep within the earth. As the rocks cooked, new minerals grew. Which particular mineral appeared depends on the conditions of temperature and pressure that the buried rocks experienced. There are minerals with simple chemical compositions, like aluminium silicate, which produce different minerals according to how hot and pressurized they became. One of the most famous diagrams in geology is a profoundly simple one that shows the different conditions

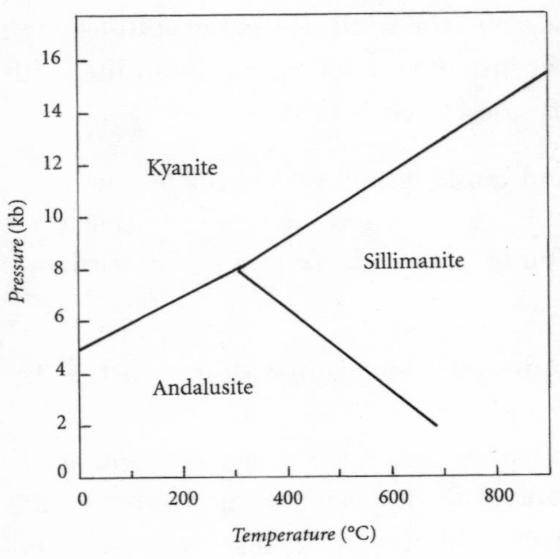

One of the most famous diagrams in determing conditions of metamorphism. Andalusite, Kyanite and Sillimanite have the same aluminium silicate chemical composition, but different crystallography. Experiments determined the pressure (P) and temperature (T) under which each species could exist in nature.

ABOVE View of the Glarus 'Thrust' from Flimserstein, with St Martin's Hole (Martinsloch) on the skyline.

BELOW From the depths of the earth to the heights: highly metamorphosed gneissose rocks on the summit of the old San Bernardino Pass, between Italian and German Switzerland.

OVERLEAF A mountain chain dies away: Lake Geneva, with the highly deformed Bernese Alps to the south and the wrinkled chain of the Jura Mountains to the north.

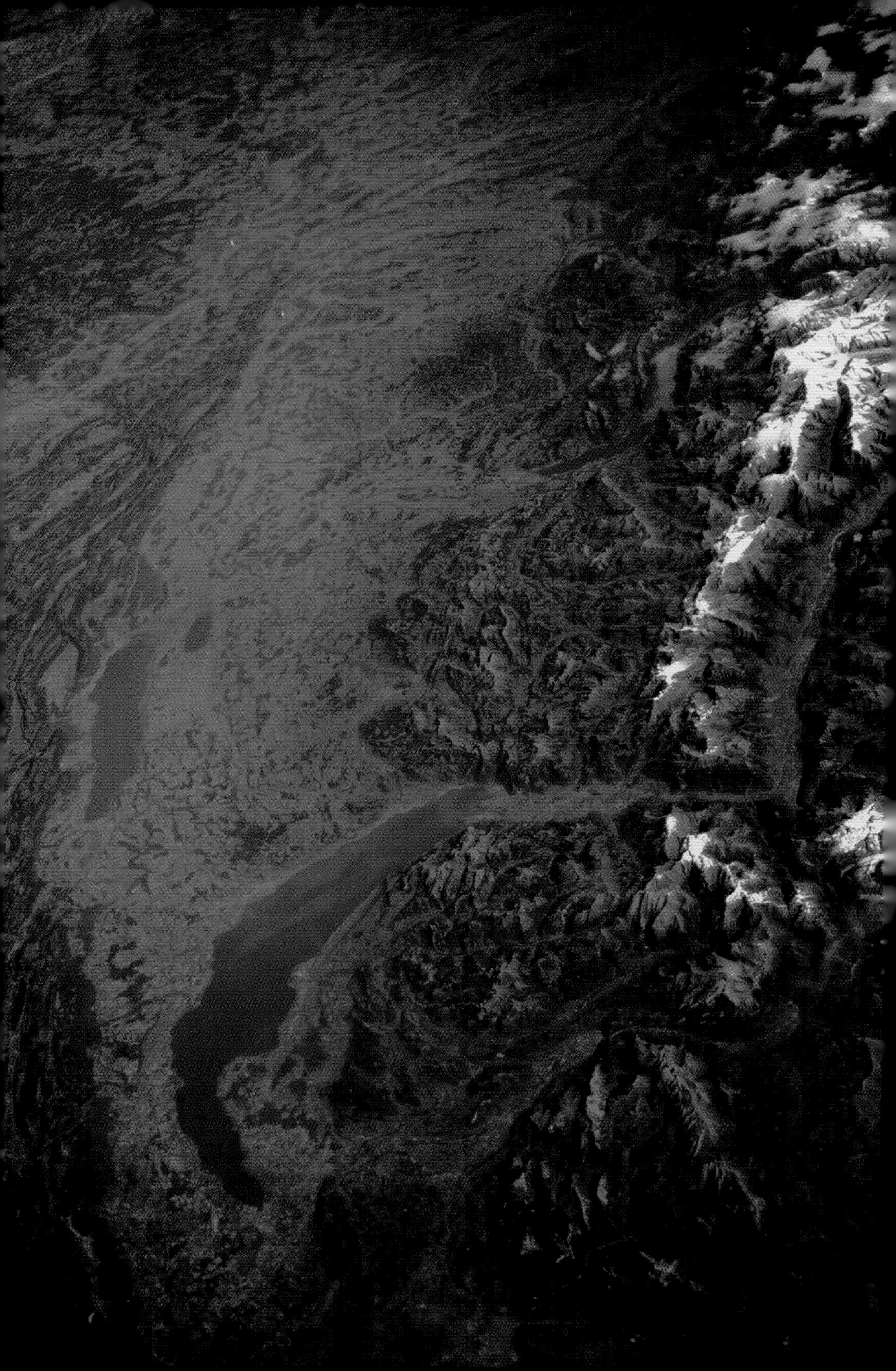

required to grow one of three mineral varieties of aluminium silicate. Enough pressure and you find kyanite; enough heat and you get sillimanite; less of either and you get andalusite. It is almost like whether you get fudge or toffee when you boil sugar. This mineral cookery can stand in for dozens, if not hundreds, of experiments carried out in the laboratory that simulate natural conditions in 'pressure-cookers' to find out which mineral is stable at a particular temperature and pressure. Natural circumstances are often more complicated – for example, the presence of even small quantities of water as an extra component can change the outcome – but the scientists who like these kinds of rocks can now 'map out' the temperatures and pressures in these metamorphic belts much as field geologists map out rock boundaries. It is a way of peering into the intimate thermal history of mountain belts. The Highlands were one of the testing-grounds for this kind of science, where the idea of metamorphic 'grade' was refined: the higher the grade, the more profound the tectonic suffering. It is even possible to plot out the subsequent cooling history of the rocks, as a high temperature mineral 'reverts' to a lower temperature one as it cools, whilst leaving its original signature in the crystal form preserved in the rock. The Highlands have seen it all: heating under pressure, cooling, uplift, and deep erosion. These rocks make for thin soil and poor drainage. Then there are faults. The Great Glen follows one of those profound displacements with a north-west–south-east trend that we have seen in Newfoundland. Long, thin Loch Ness merely fills the gash.

The southern part of Scotland has not been heated so much. Endless bleak, rounded hills composed of shales and ribs of tough 'greywackes' make up the Southern Uplands – all of such rocks were originally deposited under marine conditions. Up on the coast at Ballantrae there are volcanic rocks that compare with the ophiolites in Newfoundland. For the most part, these rocks are folded and thrust, in places furiously concertina'd and rucked. Were it not for the friendly graptolite fossils, this land would have been beyond decoding. As it is, careful mapping has disclosed its secrets. Following stream beds, delicately chipping at the dark shales, the little silvery films of graptolites betray the ages of this mass of similar-looking rocks. It is not merely that Silurian rocks are concentrated towards the south, and Ordovician to the north. The wild, open country is divided into north-east–south-west segments and bounded by thrusts, as if a gargantuan machete had butchered the whole of it into slices; and within each slice the strata rucked and repeated. It is obvious that if all the folds, and all the salami slicing of the crust, were straightened out and restored to their original disposition then this must be a region where everything has been compressed – to use the jargon, there has been 'crustal shortening'. What was once spread out on the ocean floor has been compressed, and stacked and folded in the process. It might seem impossibly complicated, but a plate tectonic explanation made it seem simple at a stroke.

Southwards again – across the Solway Firth into England, and the Lake District. Those who have queued to have a look around Dove Cottage at Grasmere may well have regretted that William Wordsworth and his friends made the 'Lakes' so popular. But you have only to walk up a hill like Skiddaw to get back to wildness. There, the sight of other walkers a few hundred metres away from you serves only to put a scale upon the open landscape and the dark, bald hills in the distance. The rocks themselves frequently resemble the apparently endless marine shales and grits of the Southern Uplands of Scotland, although they are less crumpled. They have been heated enough to impart a delicate blue-green hue, which is because of the abundance of the 'low-grade' metamorphic mineral, chlorite. The geology of the Lake District is still being worked out; only five years ago it was realized that huge Ordovician submarine slumps or slides, like those in Newfoundland, had affected considerable areas. Fossils other than graptolites are very rare. It requires patience and luck to find trilobites in the early Ordovician slates, and, when you do, they are not beautiful – they, too, have suffered with the rocks. But enough have been found to tell us that they are similar to species found from Wales, France, and Morocco. Thus they link also to Bell Island, in eastern Newfoundland, but not to Laurentia.

It grieves me to have to pass over Wales in a few sentences, for I have spent years working there, and have grown fond of its open hills and fern-choked streams. Fossils have helped unscramble its geological complexities, and my work has helped fill in some of the details. In Wales, you always have the feeling of following in the footsteps of great geologists, sometimes revisiting the same quarry as they did, for the same reasons. The rocks are often folded, but there is little of the alteration that has afflicted the Highland strata. To be sure, some of the shales have been changed to hard slates by being squeezed in the inescapable vice of regional compression, particularly in North Wales; but enough has survived to permit the discrimination of strata. Cambrian, Ordovician, and Silurian fossil animals were disinterred in order, even though there were vigorous disagreements among the pioneer collectors in the nineteenth century about exactly how the geological time embracing this succession of 'organic remains' should be divided. By the time of Eduard Suess' global compilation, however, such problems of definition were largely resolved: geological time had labels for the periods on which to pin our understanding; 'Cambrian' described a time interval as well as a region on the map. The classical rock successions of the Principality are usually described as comprising the 'Welsh Basin', which sounds a rather domestic term for a thickness of several kilometres of overwhelmingly shaly rocks. (Of course, this sag in the earth had also been described as a geosyncline in its time.) In the midst of the 'basin' are the deposits left behind by Ordovician volcanoes, forming the untamed heart of the Cambrian Mountains, including Snowdon, where you feel as if the glaciers of the last ice age melted only yesterday. Small wonder that these wild fastnesses preserved the Welsh language from extinction while cultures came and went in the softer countryside of England. The fossils, too, have been sequestered safely. On the western tip of southern Wales there is a tiny blob of land, Ramsey Island, home to many sea-birds and a few sheep. On the top of the windy cliffs on the northern end of the island you can grub out pieces of a rather tough, sandy rock, while far below you the sea boils and seethes against the cliffs. It is the kind of place where you routinely lose your hat. Persist hatless, though, and you will recover specimens of the trilobite *Neseuretus*, the same beast that occurs in the early Ordovician rocks on the far side of the Atlantic Ocean, on Bell Island. Not far from Ramsey Island, on the mainland coast in the pretty little inlet of Abercastle, you can find its companion *Ogyginus*, and the *Cruziana* tracks that are so common in Newfoundland.

Twenty-five years ago I took the coastal steamer along the length of the Norwegian Caledonides. The cruise took more than a week. This is fjord coastline *forma typica*. During the Pleistocene – indeed, until a few thousand years ago – a huge ice-cap on the mountains fed glaciers that nosed their way to the sea along the length of Norway and carved out their paths deep into the country rocks. When the ice age came to an end the glaciers retreated, but left their steep-sided gouges behind. As the polar ice-caps melted, the sea-level rose and flooded the valleys, so that the coastline is today deeply excavated by sinuous marine inlets. Even when the open ocean rages – as it often does at these latitudes – the fjords can be spookily calm. The mountain slopes rise steeply and implacably above the narrow shores. As in Newfoundland, the fishing communities led isolated lives in the coastal villages; different dialects recorded the separation of the populations. You cannot take issue with the tourist blurb: 'spectacular fjord scenery . . . picturesque fishing villages . . . unrivalled vistas . . .' – that kind of thing. I do, however, recall an excess of trolls. In every fjord it seemed that some troll or other had left his mark. 'On your left,' the guide would remark, 'you will see the famous Troll Cave'. In the next fjord a looming lump of rock with vague breasts would be described as the famous Troll Wife; a day later a pinnacle would be the illustrious Troll Castle; and so it went on. When our boat put briefly into harbour at the small towns dotted up the coast it was something of a relief to escape the trolls and look at the rocks. The random samples presented to us were metamorphic, often high-grade gneisses like those in parts of the Highlands. There were also igneous rocks of several kinds. It was clear at a glance that this part of the Caledonides belonged to a most highly deformed part of the great range. It is enormously difficult country to understand geologically, even though the rocks are so well exposed along Trollfjord and on Troll Mountain. Swedish, Norwegian, and more than a handful of British geologists have spent their lives unravelling the structure of the ancient ranges; that they have got so far is a major achievement. It has been shown that the Norwegian Caledonides comprise a series

Which way had the nappes of the Scandinavian Caledonites come from? Professors Törnebohm (left) and Svenonius (right) attempt to push their own points of view. *Carbon originally by E. Erdmann (1896).*

of great nappes, somewhat on the Alpine model. A marvellous cartoon shows two Scandinavian professors of geology fighting over which direction the nappes came from – east or west? Professor Svenonius attempts to push them one way, while Professor Törnebohm tries the other way, both of them puffing like bad-tempered trolls. The answer is now clear: the root zone lay to the west. Eastwards lay folded rocks of the region around Oslo – an area famous for its Cambrian and Ordovician fossils; eastwards again lay the 'platform' rocks of Sweden and the Baltic States. No, the huge overfolds had to come from the seam to the west that was revealed when the present Atlantic Ocean was 'closed'. Not only that, subsequent work has proved that there are four major nappes, piled one on another, like some tectonic pick-a-back on an enormous scale. Imagine! the whole country is like a club sandwich of tectonic slices. Furthermore, they are stacked in order: the highest nappe has travelled the furthest from the west; those lower in the pile have travelled progressively shorter distances. Fossils even helped with this discovery, since there was one corner of the highest nappe that escaped the regional metamorphism, and in one corner of that corner trilobites and brachiopods were discovered. Some of them were like species from the 'platform' limestones of western Newfoundland.

Such is the briefest of sketches of the Appalachian–Caledonide mountain chain. When the Atlantic Ocean opened as Pangaea broke up into pieces it evidently did so approximately following the line of this ancient range. But there is an enormous time gap. The opening of the 'new' ocean happened well over 200 million years *after* those ancient mountains had been elevated to Himalayan proportions. The vast time interval in between had been occupied by the ineffably slow grinding down of the mountain range, for whatever presumes to height will eventually be laid low by erosion. Ice, wind, and rain are inevitably attracted to mountainous regions, and by the same token guarantee their eventual levelling. Many Devonian-age red rocks record the 'waste' (molasse) from the Appalachian–Caledonian chain, and still survive along the flanks of the old mountain system: in Scandinavia, Greenland, Scotland, Wales, and New England. These freshwater sedimentary deposits are of more than passing importance in the history of our planet, because they contain graphic fossil evidence of the transition of life from water to land. This is where four-footed animals began – but that is not our story. From the geological point of view, the salient fact is that the widening Atlantic Ocean followed an ancient seam, an old memory revived, a weakness exploited. But the opening did not follow the old seam *exactly*. Consider that in Scotland, north-west of the Moine Thrust, the trilobites are like those of Laurentia. This is a fragment of earth's crust that really belongs on the other side of the ocean: when the Atlantic Ocean opened, this fragment was, as it were, left behind on the wrong side of the widening seas. Contrariwise, the Avalon Peninsula in Newfoundland truly belongs with Wales, Spain, and North Africa – for that is what those trilobites *Neseuretus* and *Ogyginus* told us – even though it now dangles off the eastern coast of the 'Rock'. You could say that this piece of Newfoundland has been marooned on the Laurentian side: small wonder, perhaps, that it feels so like Cornwall. You cannot trust the permanence of geography in a world on the move.

Now we come to a crucial question. As the Atlantic Ocean slowly widens at the present time – at the pace at which fingernails grow, according to a familiar analogy – no new mountain belt is being generated along the old Appalachian–Caledonian line. This is because both sides of the Atlantic Ocean are passive margins. No subduction happens, no volcanoes, no mountain-building; just slow drifting apart. This leads you to wonder: how did the Appalachian–Caledonian mountain chain get there in the first place? Mountain belts, like the Himalayas, are associated with *active* margins. Surely, then, it follows that at one time there were active margins with subduction zones running along the length of the Appalachian chain. This was the conceptual breakthough that changed our way of understanding how the world works.

Simple to state, perhaps, but hard to conceive of as an idea. The crucial scientific paper was published as a short note to the journal *Nature* in 1968 under the title: 'Did the Atlantic close and then re-open?' The author was Tuzo Wilson, whom we have met previously as one of the crucial players in developing plate tectonic theory. The idea he had was straightforward. Five hundred million years ago there was a great ocean – call it the 'proto-Atlantic' – separating Europe and Laurentia. That oceanic separation accounted for the very different kinds of Ordovician fossils found on either side of it – the differences between what you could collect on Bell Island and the Port au Port peninsula in Newfoundland, for example. The ocean broadly followed the line of the present North Atlantic. That ocean then closed, probably by the late Silurian–Devonian period, involving the usual processes of subduction, and it was this closure that threw up the Appalachian–Caledonide mountains: they were the Alps or Himalayas of their time. This was when Charles Lapworth's great 'earth engine' ground away at its work. By 400 million years ago the process was completed. Several hundred million years later, the present Atlantic opened, passively, along the weakened and eroded line of the ancient mountain chain. Simple as that. The fact that Tuzo Wilson had put a question-mark at the end of the title of his paper signalled that his conclusions were speculative. Top-notch scientific journals do not usually like speculations, but the note survived the editorial review process, no doubt because it came from such a well-known and innovative thinker, and made it into print: a few hundred words that changed the way we look at the world.

Tuzo Wilson's paper revealed a wholly novel way of applying Lyellian methods to very old mountain belts. Plate rules applied in the distant past. You could now look for evidence of the same kinds of tectonic and volcanic processes as happened today – around the Pacific ocean, perhaps – in rocks that had been caught in earth movements hundreds of millions of years ago. A corollary to the methods that had begun in the 'Temple of Serapis' could now be played out on the bleak shores of Newfoundland, or in the Arctic Caledonides. Of course, Wilson's model was far too simple, although right in essence; but it was the changes it wrought in the way geologists *looked* at familiar rocks that was important. The world may have stayed the same, but the perceptual glasses through which it was observed had changed. At such crucial moments, we have already seen that there are those who 'run with the ball' while more cautious souls wait to see who the crowd will follow. So it was on this occasion.

John Dewey was a young lecturer at Cambridge in the 1960s. He was quick to appreciate how the whole Appalachian chain – and particularly the magnificent cross-section seen in Newfoundland – could be viewed in the light of the vanished ocean. He worked at a furious pace to be ahead of the game. He occupied a room adjacent

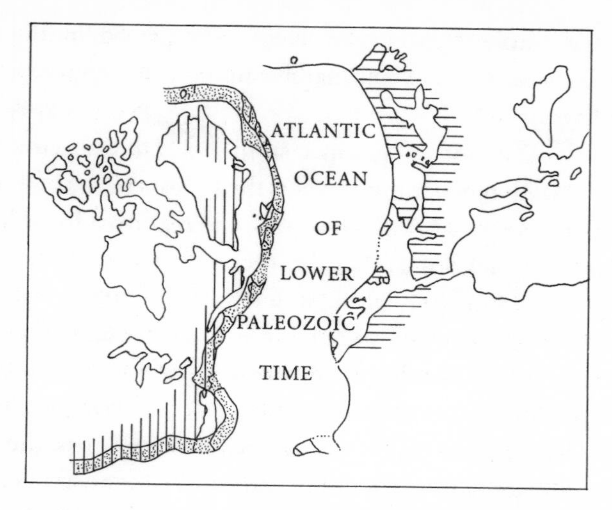

The simple diagram, redrawn from J.T. Wilson's original paper, posing the question: Did the Atlantic close and then re-open?

to mine, and seldom left it during the crucial period, except to go into the field or to conferences. A kind of metabolic speediness makes John Dewey speak at twice the pace of anyone else I know, as if his tongue were struggling to catch up with the pace of his thoughts. He can give the impression that he is not listening to what you have to say, but I have concluded that he actually absorbs it, processes it, and assesses it as uninteresting, all within a couple of seconds. The only truly disconcerting thing about him is, or at least was, a propensity to do handsprings impromptu, and other such athletic feats. As a field geologist he is superb. When his whole concentration is focused on the rocks before him, he has the knack of apparently instantly fitting the detail he has seen not merely into a fold, but into a whole mountain range. To hold the totality of the Appalachians and half the Caledonides in his brain came naturally to him. Dewey had worked in Ireland, and been to Newfoundland with Marshall Kay, and he was primed to make the plate tectonic reinterpretation. Hank Williams was open to the new paradigm, too, and in his case the emphasis was on what he was best at – making maps. From maps of small and difficult areas around Gander, he graduated to maps of the whole Appalachian chain interpreted in the light of plate tectonics, but based, ultimately, upon what could be seen in Newfoundland.

As to complications, Wilson's simple sketch showing the two continents could have implied that their closure was almost like whacking together two blocks of wood. The real world is much more various and complex. In particular, there are volcanic island arcs – perhaps several – that will collide well before the 'main event', which happens when continent–continent collision eventually occurs. They are outriders, if you like. Basins before and behind such arcs collect sediments that become entrained in the whole tectonic process. When one continent *does* eventually engage with its opposite number the relentless pressure and crustal thickening where two thick crustal blocks meet induces the highest grade of metamorphism, making it likely that nappes are then 'squeezed out'. This is the furious centre of orogenesis. But it is also possible to have a much 'softer' approach of continents – for example, if the opposing sides are concave. You can try an experiment to illustrate this that is valid in spirit, if not to the letter. Make a small, book-sized block of modelling clay. If you press it hard between the flats of your hands it will buckle intensely – in some tests part of it will 'mushroom' upwards. But if you use cupped hands instead you will get much more modest crumpling – and more of the original width will be preserved. The latter case is more like Newfoundland, which is why geologists love it. Less has been obliterated: you get a real chance to find out what happened within the vanished ocean. Then there are major faults. It is rather tempting to assume that closure of an ocean was like automatic doors slamming shut. It does not have to have been like this. Some of those faults may have been the site at which huge blocks slid past one another – transcurrent movement – rather than moving 'up and down'. This opens up the possibility that rocks that are neighbours now across faults may have had a very different relationship in the past. Everything, it seems, is capable of being somewhere else.

'Proto-Atlantic' is not a very appealing label – too indefinite –and the vanished ocean soon acquired a better one: Iapetus. It is surprising how the provision of a proper name confers respectability on a concept. In a curious way, naming it makes it *real*. Paradoxically, but appropriately, Iapetus was an entirely mythical name: a Titan, the son of Uranus by Gaea, the Greek earth goddess. Since he also fathered Atlas, which identifies a range of mountains, and Prometheus, provider of fire to mankind, you might say the geological credentials of the name are impeccable and geologists were happy to accept it.

So we can now examine our trip across Newfoundland in the light of Dewey and Williams' reworking of the island's history. It became the story of the life and death of the Iapetus Ocean. Bell Island, and the whole Avalon Peninsula, lay on the eastern* side of a wide Iapetus in the early part of the Ordovician period. The trilobites (like *Neseuretus*) that scuttled over the sandy sea-floors were happy scratching a living in cold water, for at the time Avalonia was at high, even frigid latitudes. This can be confirmed by 'palaeomag'. We have seen already that these particular animals lived over an area that embraced much of Europe and northern Africa, which is where the South Pole lay at the time, and helped map out the former Gondwana continent. If we now jump to contemporary rocks on the other side of the former ocean we arrive at the limestones of the Port au Port peninsula. These rocks were laid down in shallow seas close to what was then the equator. The snails and sponges and trilobites that are found encased within them are all completely different from those on the eastern side of Newfoundland – not just different species, but even different families. Well, of course they are different: they were living in the tropics on a limy sea-floor. We would not expect to find the same seashells living today in the cool waters off the 'Rock' as in the blue lagoons of the Caribbean. In their own way, these tropical fossils were just as distinctive as the cool-water ones on the east of the island. Many of the species are found widely distributed over the Laurentian continent – that much had

* In all accounts of changing global geography 'east' and 'west' orientations will also inevitably change. To simplify matters, I refer to these directions as they are on current maps, whatever orientation they may have had in the past.

been recognized even before Eduard Suess. So, in the early Ordovician, Iapetus was wide enough to have one side in high latitudes and the other in the tropics: a massive ocean, indeed.

Remaining for a while on the western side of the island, the spectacular boulders and their intervening shales around Cow Head can now be seen for what they are: debris that collapsed off the margin of the Laurentian continent, where there was enough of a slope to prompt instability. Once an earthquake set a few, large, tumbling blocks in motion, they would gather force, picking up other fragments on their dramatic slide as the whole slurry rushed down the slope into the deep water beyond. Mud may have lubricated the process. It is no wonder that the boulders look as if they had just been dumped out of a gigantic sack. Then quiet conditions returned for a while, and shales were slowly deposited on top of the boulder beds, and graptolites gently came to rest there to provide us with our yardstick for the passage of time. It must have been a good environment for them. I collected dozens of specimens from thin shales around St Paul's Inlet, laying them out in the sun something like 470 million years after they had first come to rest on the sea-floor.

As for the dark and treeless country above Woody Point, this was a slice from the ancient sea-floor itself. We have seen the evidence that would be needed to prove the existence of an ocean to the east – and these brown hills comprised a piece of it miraculously preserved. Pillow lavas, dykes in sheets, even the deeper layers of mantle-type rocks, like lherzolite – the whole cross-section of oceanic crust was there. Out of the depths of time and the depths of the ocean, history was preserved in this ophiolite by the bleak road to Trout River. Mapping showed that both the Cow Head rocks and the ophiolite were stacked on top of the limestone platform – thrust into place. Furthermore, the ophiolite lay on top of the Cow Head rocks. As in the Norwegian nappes, the highest slice had travelled the furthest distance. We can imagine a massive shove from the east, first slicing up, and then pushing over the Cow Head rocks on to the platform, and then – heave upon heave – a sliver of ocean crust from far away being piled on top again. This small part of marginal Iapetus was pushed upwards and outwards rather than being doomed to destruction, for which redemption all geologists are grateful. It all proves that there was plunging down – subduction – of ocean crust in a westerly direction in the Ordovician. Some part of the floor of Iapetus was diving beneath the rigid mass of Laurentia. It was being consumed, just as the Pacific floor is destined for destruction along the edge of Asia. The ophiolite escaped the general destruction but was propelled in the same direction as the subduction zone. Now, at last, the contrasting rocks that lined the shores of Bonne Bay and the Northern Peninsula made sense. What might seem like baffling complexity when you are standing on a single outcrop of rock, scratching your head at a particular crumple, can be simply explained in a paragraph once you set the ancient plates in motion.

The age of the thrusting event was not, perhaps, what you might expect. It stands to reason that the date of the thrust has to be *after* the youngest platform limestones over which they are driven. Since the latter are of mid-Ordovician age, that sets a lower limit. Nothing in the Cow Head rocks goes any younger than that age either. At the very top of that set of rocks there is a peculiar green sandstone full of the kinds of minerals you would expect to be derived from a volcanic island; but there are no such islands to the west, so these must have been derived from the east, towards the open ocean. These features can be explained if a volcanic island arc was approaching from that direction. The major obduction of the ophiolite occurred in the middle part of the Ordovician when that island arc encountered Laurentia, even as it was being carried relentlessly westwards by the motor of subduction. This event was long recognized southwards in the Appalachians, where the folding associated with it is known as the Taconic orogeny. The implication is that the closure of Iapetus was much more interesting than just the collision of two continents. This crunch was heralded by several other tectonic events as island arcs, and possibly isolated oceanic islands, were all carried alike on the conveyor belt of oceanic destruction. In the Ordovician, Iapetus was still wide, but closing. Folding and destruction at the active margin happened over a long time period before continent–continent collision during the later Silurian. Some of the major faults separating Hank Williams' 'zones' might well mark boundaries between these different events in Iapetus' history of closure.

Now it is even possible to make something of the Mobile Belt. Moving eastwards over the Long Range, it would not be too gross a simplification to describe the Dunnage Zone as the 'squidge' region of Iapetus. This is where residues of the great ocean are crushed together in perplexing ways. In other parts of the Appalachian– Caledonian chain equivalents of this region have been squeezed or subducted out of existence. It is good fortune to have it preserved in Newfoundland because of its 'soft' closure. In places, the chaos seen on the ground is exactly the turmoil you might expect where pieces of ocean floor get mixed up with pieces of volcanic islands, and all blended with sediments that accumulated off their flanks. The latter tend to 'give' more easily, and can be twisted around like so much black lasagne. It is small wonder that some parts of the Dunnage are so difficult to interpret. The zone includes volcanic islands that have survived to the present, and as many places in which blocks of volcanic rocks have slid down into the surrounding sedimentary shale basins to make that perplexing mélange. The detailed geological map of the area shows just about every rock type you can imagine. The fine-grained silica rock known as chert is worth mentioning because it is often associated with volcanic rocks and with what Marshall Kay would have called a 'eugeosyncline'. But there are sandstones, too, some of them the kind that originally rushed downslope as sand in suspension in the kind of slurries that have been termed turbidity currents. There are even blocks of limestone containing fossils: these were probably laid down on the margins of the islands before tumbling into the depths, where they were preserved. A great variety of igneous rocks add to the richness of the geological pot-pourri. Once upon a time, geological observers who pottered in their dories around the northern bays of Newfoundland were as confused as the rocks, but now we can see that the confusion itself is the outcome of explicable processes.

As for the Gander Zone, the heart of mountain-building lay there. It was the site of a thickened pile of sediments and volcanic rocks that experienced the full effects of Gondwana colliding with Laurentia: the crunch zone, if you like. Initially, the rocks between the two great masses accommodated to the pressure by crumpling, and then by sliding and pushing over one another, shortening the crust but also thickening it. Initially, perhaps, the thick pile might have depressed the geothermal gradient deep in the crust. But when the heat gradient recovered, the vast folded pile then heated up at depth, and the minerals composing the rocks became progressively uncomfortable. They needed to change in harmony with the new ambient conditions of heat and pressure surrounding them: metamorphism took over. The mineral legacy of this time is 'frozen' in the rocks today, after tens of millions of years of exhumation from the deep cauldron of the earth. The garnets and the micas speak eloquently of the strata's ordeal. They can be read like fossil thermometers and pressure-gauges. In some places the original strata and folding of the rocks can still be discerned through the transforming prism of metamorphism, like faded snapshots in which a vanished scene can still just be made out. In other places, the rocks have been so transformed that any banding they show is only a reflection of the way minerals grew as they adapted to their clenching by the earth's interior. Those pink rocks I saw not far from the Trans-Canada Highway – migmatites – were so transformed that they began to melt, to sweat out a magmatic juice that was not far from granite in its constitution. Quartz in solution was squeezed out, subsequently to infiltrate surrounding rocks, filling fissures and pods. Finally, granite magma nudged into the centre of everything. And all the while the mountain range grew. For this is how the world bends, with neither a bang nor a whimper. The crust at first winces and buckles, then gives before inexorable tectonic forces; then piles up and dislocates; as mountain-building proceeds it heats up and changes its composition in an attempt to adapt to its profound new circumstances; finally, it may melt. It is hard to avoid dramatic imagery, even in the most sober account of such continental concatenation. There is a shortage of words to embrace all that buckling and thrusting and roasting.

So a journey across Newfoundland is a journey back to the time of Iapetus. Stand on the clifftops at St John's and the early stages of this ocean can be imagined, a time when it was wider than the Atlantic. Pause under the fragrant conifers on Cow Head and you can visualize its subsequent destruction. All the evidence is laid out upon the ground: hardly a pebble on the beach that could not somehow be related to an ocean that vanished hundreds of millions of years in the past. Now another sea washes upon the old ocean floor, or polishes rocks that once were forged anew in the bowels of the earth. You can pick your way over a shoreline that was once the site of massive slides. Barnacles now encrust pieces of foundered volcanic islands where trilobites once hung on to a precarious existence.

Newfoundland provides but one profile of many across the former ocean, and to explore them all would take a book much longer than this. A brief review is all that is possible here. Hank Williams was able to map out his tectonic zones southwards all the way down the Appalachian chain. Avalon continued into eastern Canada, a connection that had been noted as early as 1887 by Marcel Bertrand, 'who, with bold hand, traced the connecting trend lines', as Suess remarked. The other zones expanded or contracted all the way to the Carolinas and beyond. In some parts of New England the metamorphic belt expanded, and fresh mapping revealed huge nappes. Old observations were dusted down and examined in the new light of ancient plates. Eduard Suess himself had recognized lateral movements in the Appalachians and had surmised that they were propelled from the west. He, too, had wrestled with the problem of how to account for such long, linear features as the Blue Mountains. He had to have a global mechanism and opted for a contraction of the earth's interior, which caused the crust above to slide and buckle along zones of weakness. It was ingenious, but ingenuous, and there has never been subsequent evidence for a contraction within. But all those geologists who looked again at the Appalachians found the plate tectonic interpretation to be nothing less than a revelation. Disparate observations all seemed to fall into place: this bed of volcanic rock was arc-related; that piece of chemistry was oceanic. Science proceeds by a thousand small advances when a basis for understanding is in place. Once the big picture is drawn, the colouring-in can begin. And the geosynclines? They simply became expressions of different sites along continental margins. The thickness of strata accumulating off the edge of the Laurentian carbonate platform was not so remarkable on a continent edge. It was to be expected that the more oceanic sites included thick layers of volcanics and shales and cherts, especially in basins related to island arcs. Geosynclines became an 'epiphenomenon' of plate tectonics.

We can move northwards into the Caledonides, where much the same enlightenment took place. There was no shortage of old field data that could be recruited into the new way of seeing: no less than a hundred and fifty years of the tramp of boots and the tapping of hammers. England and Wales were part of Avalonia: the fossils that I had collected in stream bed and quarry told no lies. The limestones of north-west Scotland were a part of the opposing side of the present Atlantic, a stranded fragment of Laurentia. They were just the same as the rocks on Port au Port, down to the identical little snails curled up on the bedding planes. Between Wales and Durness, therefore, lay the wreck of Iapetus. There was an ophiolite in Scotland, too, albeit a much more modest affair than its Newfoundland counterpart. This comprised the pillow lavas and serpentinites and cherts – Steinmann's famous 'trinity' – on the coast at Ballantrae. Delete 'Ballantrae volcanics' from the geological map; substitute 'Ballantrae ophiolite' – such is the mundane end of a great revolution in thought. Then there were the folded and faulted rocks of the Southern Uplands that form such uncompromisingly bare hills, beloved only of sheep and masochistic walkers. They, too, could now be looked at in a different way. That the country was sliced up into north-east–south-west trending 'packages' was already recognized: but could they represent an accretionary prism? When a subduction zone plunges downwards, the sediments lying on top of the oceanic slab may be 'scraped up' against the continent in front rather than destroyed. Jeremy Leggett from Imperial College, London, showed that it was possible to 'read' the Southern Uplands in this fashion. He compared the Scottish rocks with those of the Makran in Pakistan, where more recent oceanic events had accomplished just the same kind of accretion as part of the construction of the Himalayan chain. In Scotland, the slices of graptolite-bearing shales and grits were piled up in slivers in exactly the way that might be expected. This meant, of course, that a subduction zone would have to lie to the *south* of the Southern Uplands, along the present line of the Solway Firth. When deep geophysics investigated this area, the 'shadow' of a northward-dipping line at depth provided just the evidence that was required: a 'fossil' subduction zone. Southwards again, the Lake District had an Avalonian stamp from its Ordovician fossils: the main part of Iapetus thus must have disappeared along the Solway Line that separated the Southern Uplands and the Lakes and followed the familiar Caledonian north-west–south-east trend: a short distance now, but the requiem for an ocean. The sliding and slipping of the Lake District rocks, which have recently been recognized by the officers of the Geological Survey of Great Britain, have echoes of the tumbling blocks on the other side of Iapetus at Cow Head.

The Highlands include the highly metamorphosed belt. Toughened up by gneisses and granites, the geology still allows for respectable mountains, even though they are but shadows of their former greatness. It is clear that the original sediments that were variously baked and squeezed in the Highlands originally lay off Laurentia, since unmistakeable remnants of that continent survive at the edge of the Midland Valley (where younger rocks predominate) and in the Southern Uplands. The whole area divides into two: highly metamorphosed Moine rocks to the north and less maltreated Dalradian rocks to the south and east. Some of the Highland rocks were folded into nappes and have been mapped out by a generation of devoted field geologists. The Tay Nappe and its ilk will be their permanent memorial. The general 'push' of the structures was towards the north-west, just like the Moine Thrust itself. The history of the Highlands is much more complex, and extends over a longer period of time, than that sketched out for the rest of the ancient mountain system. Still earlier phases of history conflate with the Caledonian continental crunch, and whilst radiometric dating has helped unscramble some of this complexity, disentanglement is still in progress.

The Norwegian Caledonides are also generally metamorphosed, as I learned many years ago on that coastal cruise. In the context of plate tectonic history we can now begin to understand its great pile of nappes. They had originated from the west – where Iapetus lay. Squeezed out during orogeny to accommodate closure between opposing continents (rather than 'soft' closure as in Newfoundland), their direction of movement contrasts with the heave towards Laurentia that we have met to the south: instead, the Norwegian nappes were directed eastwards. I have mentioned that there is good evidence from fossils that the furthest travelled – and highest – nappes in the pile had originated from the Laurentian side of Iapetus. This is explicable now that we know the closure story: squeeze upon squeeze propelled masses of rock from the centre to the periphery, one after another, the most distant last. All that remains of the ocean itself are little pods of ophiolites entrained in some of the nappes; they must have been like apple pits squeezed out from a cider mill. This part of the great chain still has an alpine feel to it today, which is appropriate to the geology.

This short *résumé* of the history of a whole mountain chain appears to have the neatness of a 'whodunnit', at the conclusion of which all the loose ends are tied up and the perpetrator is unmasked. It seems almost a pity to introduce further complexity. But nature has a habit of never being quite as simple as you first thought. On reflection, it might seem rather surprising that any mountain system that spans a hemisphere could be simply described as the meeting of two massive slabs. It did, indeed, prove more complicated, though the core of Tuzo Wilson's intuition remained intact.

The first complication concerned the ancient continents themselves. Further work served only to confirm the integrity of Laurentia. But the eastern side of Iapetus was another matter. An area centred on the Baltic Sea comprises a number of countries on the present political map: Norway, Sweden, Finland, the eastern part of Russia, and the old states of Estonia, Latvia, and Lithuania. The ancient geology of this whole area ignored our man-made borders. The Ordovician rock succession is very uniform in character, so much so that it has been claimed that you can trace a single Ordovician stratum throughout much of the region. The whole of it was underlain by very similar and very ancient 'basement' rocks – the Baltic Shield. Not surprisingly, perhaps, the name Baltica has been applied to this area as a whole. In the earlier part of the Ordovician – the same time as the strata on Bell Island were being laid down – much of Baltica was covered by a shallow sea. The legacy of this time is thin limestone beds full of fossils; my own favourites, trilobites, are common, but there are other shells such as brachiopods in equal abundance. The remarkable thing about them is that they resemble neither their contemporaries in Avalonia, nor those in North America. They are their own thing, entirely. The limestones, too, are peculiar, being of a kind typically laid down today in temperate, rather than tropical, latitudes. None of the trilobites (remember *Neseuretus*?) that were found in Avalonia were found in Baltica, yet we have seen that they were common all over central and southern Europe and northern Africa. What can be going on? After all, with Baltica continuing southwards into southern Europe, there seems no reason why the same animals should not have thrived over the entire eastern seaboard of Iapetus.

The answer was that there was a *second* ocean separating Avalonia from Baltica during the early Ordovician (p. 236). Robin Cocks and I christened it Tornquist's Sea in 1982, after a geologist who had recognized a tectonic line running across Europe more or less where we wanted our ocean to be located. The eastern seaboard of Iapetus was divided into two – a simple explanation of the differences between contemporary trilobites in the respective halves. Also, we knew that the Gondwana continent, with Avalon at its edge, was in cool waters, yet Baltica was at temperate latitudes. A physical separation provided a simple way of solving this conundrum. It took a while, but eventually palaeomagnetic evidence came to support the existence of Tornquist's Sea.* A buried mountain belt largely covered by younger rocks runs through Europe along the line of Tornquist's Sea. This line marked the trace of its closure: a closure that happened long before that of Iapetus. In a nutshell, a two-continent closure model had transformed to a three-continent model.

More complexity still: it was soon realized that Avalonia, too, was more interesting than merely being a promontory extending from Gondwana. It broke away from the main Gondwana continent and travelled under its own steam (carried on the back of the appropriate plate) across the ancient oceans, rather in the manner of the volcanic arcs that had preceded it. Both fossils and palaeomagnetic 'fixes' support this interpretation. I have spent a substantial amount of British taxpayer's money – employing expensive computer systems and a post-doctoral assistant, David Lees – in plotting the movement of this chunk of crust – which, to recap, comprised England, Wales, southern Ireland, and a slice of eastern Canada, including eastern Newfoundland. In the early part of the Ordovician, about 480 million years ago, Avalonia was close to Gondwana – hence those similar trilobites on Bell Island and in France and Morocco (our old friend *Neseuretus* included). Later on in the Ordovician the similarity to Gondwana progressively declined, while the similarity to Baltica increased. Thus, Avalonia was moving across Tornquist's Sea towards Baltica: as the Ordovician continued it moved northwards. It may have had a 'soft docking' with Baltica near the end of the Ordovician. Only then did the two, united together, proceed to complete the closing of Iapetus. Avalonia was understood to be a 'fossil' example of what is now termed a microcontinent: a comparatively small piece of continental crust with an independent history. It may have had

* I have told the full story of the battle to get the existence of Tornquist's Sea accepted in more detail in *Trilobite! Eyewitness to Evolution* – it took more than a decade.

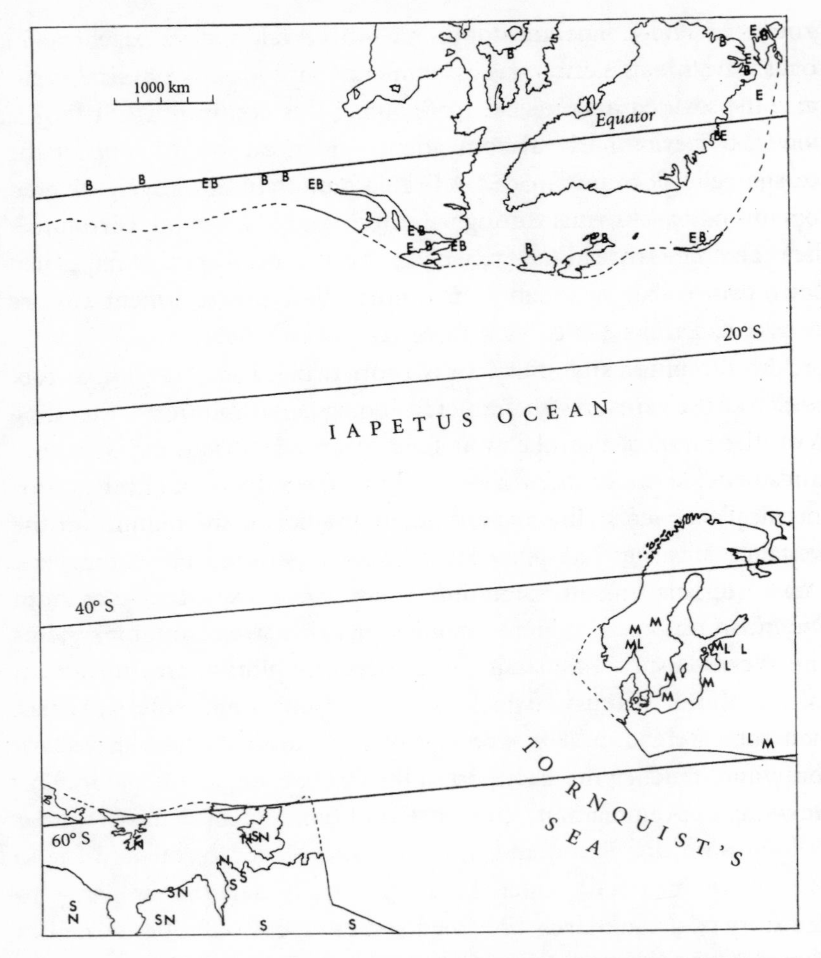

Robin Cocks and myself introduced an early Ordovician Tornquist's Sea between Avalonia and Scandinavia in 1982, and 475 million years ago. The letters (BMLSN) stand for typical fossils on the ancient continents. N, for example, stands for Nereuretus, which we have met in the text. From the original paper in the *Journal of the Geological Society of London*.

something of the proportions of the microcontinental island of Madagascar: if so, it was pretty substantial – after all, 'micro' is only a relative term. It was certainly large enough to push up mountains.

There is much evidence for Avalonia's journey preserved on the ground in Wales. The mountains of Snowdonia are rich in volcanic rocks. Avalonia's grandest peak, and its wild bare landscape, was once the site of eruption after eruption. You can see the ancient ash flows as ribs in the hillside as you climb upwards: rare ferns and ice-age relic flowers cling on to their damp flanks. These are the remains of explosive ashfalls, which prove that violent eruptions once darkened the same skies from which rain now plummets and trickles down your neck. Welsh volcanoes were the subject of classical studies by geologists like O. T. Jones and W. J. Pugh, who mapped their ancient shorelines and identified the sticky rock that had plugged the 'necks' of the vents, in the era before 'continental drift' was accepted. With the hindsight of plate tectonics, it is clear that these were the kinds of explosive eruptions associated with subduction, and modern chemical analyses on the composition of the lavas confirm this. Continental crust was mixed with basaltic magma of oceanic origin to give a characteristic 'mixed' signature. There was, at least for a while, a *southward*-dipping subduction zone under the Cambrian mountains. The Welsh Basin – often called a geosyncline in the past because of its thick fill of sedimentary and volcanic rocks – was nothing more than the 'sag' behind the series of Ordovician volcanoes that now command the heights around Cardigan Bay: deader than dodos, Snowdon supreme among them.

The story of our understanding of the face of the earth has been one of increased freedom of movement. First, there was a fixed world, immutable except for flood, plague, and elemental mayhem intended to demonstrate the power of the Almighty to point moral lessons for craven humanity. Time still had a human scale, for all that we knew our place in nature, and the likelihood of personal obscurity:

O time that cut'st down all!
And scarce leav'st here
Memoriall
Of any men that were.

So the seventeenth-century poet Robert Herrick described our obliteration. Later, the appreciation of the span of geological time rendered much egocentricity on behalf of our own species redundant. There was time enough to free the continents from their moorings. The Atlantic Ocean was allowed to open, to split apart Pangaea. The earth moved. We were free to imagine vanished worlds and vanished lives. It was a romantic vision, but also disconcerting, so to lose our bearings on historical certainty. Next, it was discovered that Pangaea itself was but a phase in earth's history. The supercontinent provided no deeper reality; it, too, was only in passing. Nothing is permanent except change. The Atlantic Ocean opened – but now it was discovered that its predecessor had already closed long before, at the time when Iapetus had been destroyed. Even the continents bordering Iapetus were not those we recognize. Avalonia and Baltica were not obvious from the map of Europe and America. They could only be revealed by understanding the deeper geological reality. That reality still influences what crops can be grown, and what towns can be built from local stone; it has outlasted the present configuration of continents. The geological Unconscious cannot be denied, for it still guides the way we use the land, and rules the plough. We are all in thrall to the underworld.

There is yet one more, final, mechanism of freedom to introduce. Recall the long faults trending south-west to north-east – like the Great Glen Fault in Scotland or those bounding Hank Williams' tectonic zones in Newfoundland. These are great fractures, cutting deep into the crust. They serve to chop the great range into segments. The individual segments often have their own features – unique rock successions not found in their neighbours, for example. It was soon realized that the faults bounding these segments might mark the site of extensive movement: two adjacent segments may have originally been far from where they are found today if they had slid past one another over a long period of time. There is a precedent for this kind of movement on the Pacific coast of the Americas – the most familar example being the San Andreas Fault in California, where one slab of crust is sliding past its neighbours. The units between major faults are known as 'terranes', or, where there is doubt about their original disposition, 'suspect terranes'. The mountain belt came together as an accretion of terranes. Only when terranes were finally docked together would they share rocks with their neighbours, as a single blanket may be spread over sleeping partners. So now there is not only ocean closure to contend with, not to mention microcontinents and oceanic islands, but also a patchwork of shuffling slices as well. Once the moorings had been untied, what a kaleidoscope of moving fragments had been shaken up . . . Forget everything you think you know, and you can remake the world.

There are continuing arguments about the original location of major crustal slices. There are those who believe that Avalonia was originally situated off western Africa in the Ordovician. It was only brought to its present location by a later movement in the Caledonides. For once, the fossils don't help very much because they are similar over the whole of that part of Gondwana. How can we prove Avalonia's previous position one way or the other? What is needed is a kind of geological 'fingerprint' that matches the slice with its nearest neighbour at its 'starting gate'. Current research is trying to identify such critical tests.

One promising line of investigation is provided by zircon crystals. Zircon, zirconium silicate, is a very stable mineral that is a common minor component of granite. It is so tough that when the granite weathers away, the zircon remains behind, to be washed down streams, eventually to reach the sea. Tiny crystals of zircon often finish up as a component of sandstones – one grain of zircon among ten thousand of common quartz. However, methods have been developed to rescue the precious crystals from the common herd. Zircons contain minute amounts of radioactive lead, and thus contain a 'clock' that gives the geological age of the formation of the crystal within its parent granite. Extraordinarily accurate measurements of miniscule amounts of lead isotopes, however, are needed to give reliable results. Sam Bowring's laboratory at the Massachusetts Institute of Technology and Scott Samson's at the University of Syracuse, New York, are the most up-to-date centres of research in this area. I visited the Syracuse laboratory and what most impressed me were the plastic bottles. These have to be cleaned continuously for more than two years to remove every last contaminating atom of lead: everything is purified over and over. At the end of it all they extract dates from within single zircon crystals – so small that they would fit on to the head of a pin – that are accurate to within a million years, a margin of error that applies even with dates of up to a billion years, which is an astounding technical achievement. Of course, this means that geological dates in general have reached a new level of precision. We now know that the base of the Ordovician is 489 million years plus or minus 500, 000 years. But precise dates on zircons also have a use for terrane location. If Avalonia once lay off Africa, then it should have received sediments from that continent – including zircons. Dandruff shaken from the giant came to rest all around. It turns out that there is a close link in age between Avalonian zircons and those of the Precambrian orogenies that affected the African continent. These have a different age spread from those that happened in Brittany or Normandy, off which Avalonia now resides. The new evidence does suggest that Avalonia did indeed travel from off Africa to its present location. Will other evidence confirm its peripatetic history? We shall have to wait and see.

Now let us look again at the whole world. The Appalachian–Caledonian chain is a scar marking an ancient ocean, one that has disappeared. Pangaea evidently *came together* as a supercontinent from a collage of earlier, dispersed continents. The Ordovician world was more like our world than the Permian one of annealed landmasses: it had scattered continents. Plate tectonics did not begin at the time of Pangaea; rather, the slow stroll of continents around the globe has been continuous. The mechanics of the earth have not changed for a far, far longer time than the breakup of the last supercontinent. To be sure, this vision embraces more transformation than Charles Lyell would have ever contemplated. But the application of his principles – to look at 'living' fold belts and subduction zones to interpret fossil ones – has only confirmed the vigour of his scientific method. The reasoning that began in the 'Temple of Serapis' rebuilt the world; and rebuilt it repeatedly.

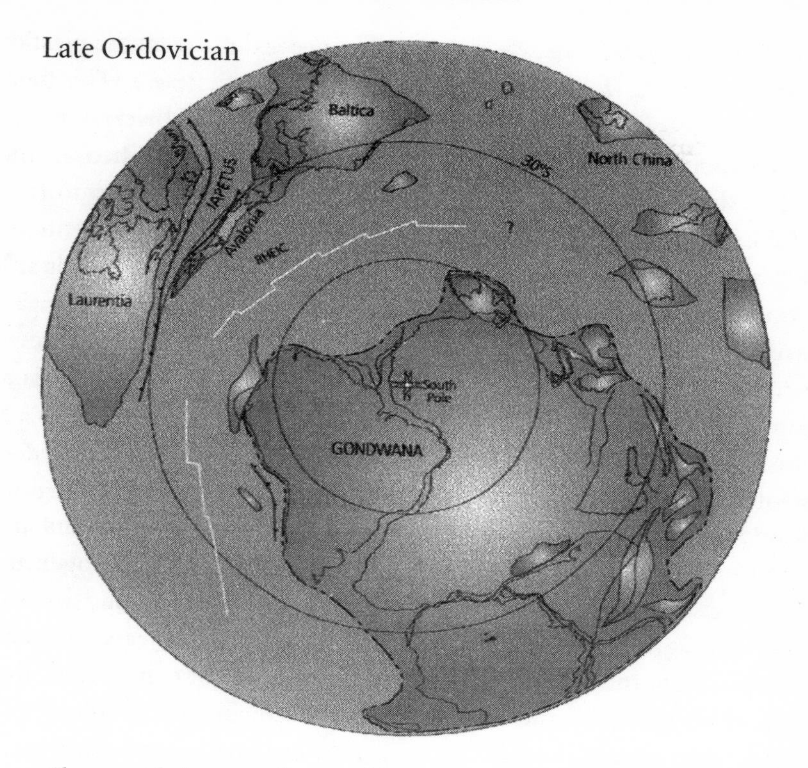

Change and change again: a world map near the end of the Ordovician. Tornquist's Sea has vanished since the earlier Ordovician, and a new, Rheic ocean widened between Gondwana and Baltica.

If we proceed logically, *wherever* there is an ancient scar of a fold-belt running across the surface of the globe, we should expect evidence of a lost ocean, of past subduction. There will be volcanic rocks on the ground, and the thick successions of sedimentary rocks associated with them will be of the type that would once have been termed geosynclines. An assiduous researcher might well discover ophiolites tucked somewhere into the former range. It is what an advertising executive would call a 'package'.

Some of these ancient fold belts are obvious. Any topographic map of Russia shows the Urals almost bisecting it, like a persistent ruck in a carpet. The mountains run from the Arctic Island of Novaya

Zemlya southwards, dividing the endless wastes of the Siberian *taiga* and the steppes from the Russian platform in the west. This line marked the eastern edge of the ancient continent of Baltica, which was separated from its Siberian neighbour by another vanished ocean. When that ocean closed in the Devonian period, another component of the supercontinent Pangaea was assembled. The Siberian continent was already recognized as an important piece of the earth by Eduard Suess: he called it Angara. Some of the largest copper mines in the world are related to ophiolites along the line of closure between Angara and Baltica. Similarly, across the middle of China there is a range called the Tsinling Mountains. Geologists have come to see this line as demonstrating that the most uniform civilization in the world, that of the *han* people, comprises two separate geological foundations: another ocean consumed. Other ancient fold belts are less obvious, although they have been recognized for a long time. The Variscan chain – what Eduard Suess called the Hercynides – we have briefly met before. The fold belt passes west to east through Europe, from the rugged cliffs and intimate coves of Cornwall in the west of England all the way through central Europe north of the Alps. Another vanished ocean: one that had once divided Europe until its closure in the Carboniferous. This one has a name, too – the Rheic Ocean. For each one of these ancient oceans I might have undertaken a geological traverse from one side to the other, as I did for Iapetus in Newfoundland. You have to visualize a thousand geologists crawling over the ground, interpreting these ancient mountain chains in the light of plate tectonics: geophysicists probing ancient sutures with new equipment, trying to read the structure of the depths; geochemists looking at the distribution of rare elements. This is the research programme that continues unabated today, whether pursued in the wooded hills of central Europe, or the treacherous marshes of the Arctic. As with the Appalachian story, every question answered spawns a dozen more that need to be investigated. There are arguments about terranes; there are disputes about timing; there are disagreements about the role of oceanic crust in generating volcanoes. But without the plate tectonic model nobody would have known what questions to ask of the uncomplaining rocks.

The course of some ancient oceans opened upon older lines of weakness, as we have seen in the case of the Atlantic Ocean. Time reopened old wounds. We can now see the earth as a crude mosaic, stitched together in various ways. Scars of past tectonic crises cross continents. Some ranges are shadows of their former grandeur; the Urals, for example, have an average height of only 1000–1300 metres. Other old fold belts still carry glaciers on their heights, although none approach the mighty splendour of the Himalayas, which are the consequence of the latest round of continental movements. But these great mountains, too, will be ground down in millions of years. Where lighter continental crust has been thickened in orogenic piles as continents collide, the whole mass rises inevitably into the fierce realm of the levelling elements, ice and wind. The Himalayas, too, will one day be yet another seam upon the face of the old earth, another wrinkle added to testify to its character.

New York is the quintessential city: glitteringly artificial, Manhattan is a shop-window for capitalism. A city this vibrant and varied is a tribute to what my father would have called 'commerce': the growth of towers from trade, the vindication of the market. It seems as far removed from the geological underlay as it is possible to get. Nature is pushed into few holes in the sidewalks. Tough trees like ginkgos thrive around a few older houses and churches, but then, these trees have survived from the Jurassic and can face out a few fumes.

When you emerge from the ranked stores and offices into Central Park it is always a surprise. What is this undeveloped prime real estate doing here, in the midst of all this money and endeavour? A winding path or two will take you to where you can view through real trees the peaks and pinnacles of the city, as you might a mountain range from the plain. It does not diminish the sense of wonder at human diligence; rather, it lends perspective. Then you notice the rocks. Cropping out in places under the trees are dark mounds of rock, emerging from the ground like some buried architecture of a former race, partly exhumed and then forgotten. New Yorkers might sit on a sloping slab of it to eat a sandwich in the sunshine without giving it a thought. The outcrop is as unremarked as a hot dog stand or a fire hydrant; just part of the scene. But look more closely and you will see it is shiny and slick and layered. The light may pick out the glint of mica. The rock is schist, a metamorphic rock produced in the fold belts that have been the subject of this chapter. That New York can be built so high and mighty is a consequence of its secure foundations on ancient rocks. It pays its dues to the geology. This is just a small part of one of those old seams that cross the earth. But the rocks prove that skyscrapers not of man's making once covered the same ground. These are Grenville rocks. We have met them once before, in Newfoundland, where they formed the core of the Long Range mountains. They are older by far than the Appalachian–Caledonian history. They are the legacy of a still older phase of opening along the line of the Atlantic, another manifestation of the same scar a thousand million years ago, deep within Precambrian time. The Grenville rocks make another belt, broadly following the western edge of the Appalachians. *Autres temps, autres mers.* When these mountains formed where New York now stands, there were no trilobites, no shellfish. The sea hosted algae, and perhaps only the most distant ancestors of animals. Yet it seems that even then, plates still moved, and the earth still carried on its stately dance of splitting apart and reassembling. How far back can we go? Even here, right in the midst of the most artificial habitat on the planet, a place where every second counts, there are relics of a deeper time when millennia counted for nothing.

7

The Dollar

Real Money: a 1922 US silver dollar.

The most ordinary thing in the world, a scrap of paper: a buck, a greenback. The dollar: flimsy fuel for the world's economy. Gross national products are reckoned in it; national debts are totted up in it; currencies fluctuate against it. When I visited Kazakhstan after its separation from the Soviet Union nobody was interested in pounds sterling, or French francs, or German marks, let alone the despised rouble. What people wanted was the mighty dollar. When anything was paid for, the dollars were scrutinized closely. Crumpled ones and dirty ones were unpopular: they were thrown back as if they were contaminated. No, what was acceptable was the pristine dollar bill, the essence of money. I had always been puzzled by the apparent uniformity of US dollar notes, regardless of their denomination – fifty bucks looking so similar to a twenty, or a singleton, and apparently conspiring to aid confusion. Now I realized why this had to be: the dollar bill *is* money: it's what money should look like. Everything else is just numbers.

Yet not long ago there was a silver dollar. When I travelled to the gambling state of Nevada in the late 1970s these coins were still currency. They were a good size, like the largest coins in the sets of gold-clad chocolate money that kids still get for Christmas. Once I received a 1922 silver dollar in change in a small supermarket. Later, in New York, I saw the same coin on sale for twenty-seven dollars, thus making me one of the few people ever to leave Reno with a profit. The old dollar was more than an idealized form of money. The silver in it was, when minted, worth a dollar. Age didn't turn silver dollars into tattered rags: they hung about for years. This kind of money had a durability that feels out of place in the age of the virtual transaction, when money as an entity becomes more and more notional. In the old days, money had substance. The dollars weighed down your pocket. The $ sign itself is considered by some to be a transmutation of '8' and related directly to the Spanish 'pieces of eight'. Once upon a time their exchange values were linked. As for the name – dollar – it has a geological history.

One can find the same word in Danish, *daler*. In due turn, this is a variant of *thaler*. The thaler was the standard silver coinage across Europe in the fifteenth century. Each thaler weighed an ounce. There was a portrait of a bigwig struck on one side, often one of the counts of Slik who profited from their manufacture. At a time when there was much jiggery-pokery and adulterization in coinage the thaler had a reputation for reliability. The reward of virtue in this case was eventually to bequeath its name to the ultimate lingua franca: the dollar that talks to just about everyone. Further, the name thaler was itself a contraction from Joachimsthaler, referring to the mine at Joachimsthal (the valley of Joachim) from which the silver was obtained. This small town in the Czech Republic was once part of old Bohemia, lying on the southern rim of the Krusne Hory Mountains. What remains of the town is quite picturesquely dotted about the wooded hillsides, but it has declined from its great days. In 1530 its population was 18,000, of whom 13,000 were miners. The town will be found on modern maps under the name of Jachymov. So the Joachimsthaler became the thaler, which became the dollar. Thus history covers its tracks.

The rich silver veins were discovered in Jachymov in 1516. A few years later there were eight hundred mines. The first coins were struck by Count Stepan Slik, sometimes Germanized to Schlick, with due permission from the king; the Count had a licence to mint money, and of course he became rich. The relevant document dangling the royal seal is still preserved in the National Archives in Prague. Between 1520 and 1528 more than two million thalers were struck from something like sixty thousand kilograms of fine quality silver. Much of the silver occurred 'native', that is, as the pure metal, and some of the coins could almost be struck on the spot. This kind of silver forms fine strings and sheets rather than nuggets. The silver is laid out in veins that follow lines of weakness in the country rock, often running along faults. Like all mining discoveries in the old days, the initial bonanza occurred on the surface, where some sharp-eyed prospector discovered an outcrop of rock, or weathered material, showing the cherished minerals. Then the vein was chased downwards, as deep into the earth as available technology and profit would allow. In the Svornost Mine at Jachymov, some of the tunnels dug more than 400 years ago are still there, 150 metres below the surface. They are crudely walled with stone slabs knocked in edgewise to help safeguard against rockfalls. A visitor in 1980 found some well-preserved tunnels with rock-lined ceilings that he described as resembling small naves; and there was even an inscription to St Barbara, patron saint of miners.

Where humans have wormed their way into the underworld in pursuit of dollars, the heave of the violated crust often squeezes back again to obliterate their impertinence. In this connection, I discovered that this area of middle Europe is apparently the only part of the world where the cockroach is viewed favourably: their insect senses are peculiarly alert to changes in pressure in the rock – like the pressure-sensitive instruments used in Hawai'i to detect movement in the magma chamber. When a rockfall threatens, the cockroaches head out of their hiding places and scramble away along the conduits and passages in order to escape being crushed. They are the silver miners' friends, like canaries in coal mines, and it is bad luck to crush one. Cockroaches have been around since the Carboniferous period and will doubtless still be here after the last miner has gone.

All mines eventually become exhausted, and the same was true of the silver at Jachymov – but it was not the end of the industry. Different vein minerals are often found nestled together, or at least in close proximity, and when one has been worked out it sometimes happens that another acquires a commercial life. To put it into miner's jargon: today's gangue may be tomorrow's ore. In the mineral underworld of Czechoslovakia there were also plentiful ores of the metallic element cobalt, the heavy element bismuth, and poisonous arsenic. These elements all have medicinal and industrial uses. In their own way they are as precious as silver, even though their route to the dollar is less blatant. Cobalt is what gives a wonderful rich blue glaze to ceramics and enamels, and it can impart the same colour to glass. 'Cobalt Blue' is one of the standard colours of the oil painter's palette. Factories able to exploit these new minerals grew up around Jachymov in the nineteenth century: so there was life after silver. An additional mineral, dark and greasy-looking as pitch, was despised by the silver miners because when it increased in abundance the silver disappeared, like darkness shutting out light. This mineral is called pitchblende and has another peculiarity that belies its ordinary appearance: it is very heavy. This is because it is largely composed of uranium oxide, and uranium is element number 92 in the Periodic Table, almost as heavy as you can go, and heavier than lead. Useless, dark, heavy stuff this pitchblende, to be thrown into the woods, out of the way.

How time changes perceptions of value! In 1852, a chemist called Albert Patera discovered that uranium-based chemical compounds produced unusual and gorgeous colours – greens and yellows especially – when added to glass. There was an immediate vogue for these other-worldly hues, and so mining at Jachymov enjoyed yet another incarnation. At a more recherché level, the mine was a source for beautiful mineral specimens of rare uranium and silver minerals that still adorn great collections. But the major use of pitchblende had to await detection for nearly half a century, when the mines of Jachymov were crucial to a discovery that has changed the course of history. Working in Paris in 1898, Marie and Pierre Curie processed thousands of pounds of pitchblende from the same glass-factory tailings in order to isolate two radioactive elements that had hitherto been unknown: radium and polonium. Uranium's radioactivity had been recognized for a couple of years prior to this, but this pitchblende was *too* active to be accounted for by uranium alone. The Curies deduced that another radioactive element had to be present to make up the balance; they reasoned the existence of highly-active radium before extracting it. But it was present in the tiniest quantities: a gram in seven tons of ore. The labour involved in refining a tiny visible grain from the unforgiving black ore is difficult to imagine. But they convinced the scientific world with sufficient material evidence of the elusive element to be awarded the Nobel Prize in 1903. This was the first international recognition that a woman could have as outstanding a scientific intellect as any man, and Marie Curie's name is still associated with European science funding.

With tragic irony, Marie Curie died of the consequences of the radiation she helped to explain to the world: cancer had yet to be linked with damage to dividing cells. Radiation was to become at once a medical weapon and the agent of mass destruction. Luminous watch-hands painted with radium compounds were formerly the everyday demonstration of radioactive decay: as a child I had an alarm clock on my bedside table that ticked visibly in the dark. Then it was discovered that workers in the USA who decorated these novelty clock faces, and then licked their brushes, had unusually high rates of mouth cancer. The delicacy of the genome proved to be a discovery out of phase with that of glowing radium. However, the

Georgius Agricola (1490–1555), father of mineralogy, and (opposite) one of his practical illustrations of mining practices – taking ore to the shelter.

realization that one element could decay to another at a definite rate also proved central to the endeavour of dating rocks, for this decay provided natural 'clocks' which ticked in sympathy with the antiquity of geological time. This is how the world acquired a birthdate.

Joachimsthal has still other connections to reveal. The town physician at the time of the silver boom of 1527–33 was one Georg Bauer. He is better known under his literary name of Georgius Agricola. He wrote the first books about mining, of which his *De Re Metallica* (1555) is the most famous. Agricola's works became known throughout Europe, where Latin was still the language of instruction. Agricola's writings can claim to be the first widely studied geological texts. I have examined a copy of *De Re Metallica* in the library of the Natural History Museum; carefully leather-bound and stored in an inner sanctum, it seems an improbable handbook. But that is

what it is: an illustrated compendium of practical advice for the miners and metallurgists of the day, with advice on ventilation and smelting and the safe construction of drifts. It also includes the first attempt at the systematic classification of minerals, by their properties and products. This was clearly the work of a good observer, a no-nonsense, pragmatical kind of mind. This probably accounts for its longevity as a reference work for more than two centuries. Agricola was at pains to say that his work was based upon facts he himself had observed. He clearly had little time for hearsay and recycling of mouldering classical sources, and he said as much. In spirit, he was close to his much more famous successor Francis Bacon (born in 1561), who set out the scientific agenda explicitly for the first time. *De Re Metallica* was translated into English in 1912 by Herbert Hoover, surely the only president in US history with sufficient Latin to have undertaken such a task. Agricola had a near contemporary in Jachymov, the Revd Johannes Matthevius, who was sufficiently concerned at the conditions under which the miners laboured to deliver sermons on their rights and safety, and on what would now be called unionization. As was customary among elite clergy, these perorations were eventually published in 1562, under the title *Sarepta oder Bergpostilla*. I would be intrigued to know if there were an earlier example of concern for the rights of the industrial worker. Ever since these early days, mining, above all other commercial activities, has been capitalism laid bare, where grisly toil has been at the service of boom and bust, and where the role of the boss has frequently been tainted with dubious profiteering. Miners have been among the first workers to fight back for their rights. On the side of collective labour, the coal miners have been the most militant trade unionists in the twentieth century, deified by some, vilified by others as communists and trouble-makers. It is sad to reflect that there are parts of the world today where mining conditions are probably worse than they were in Joachimsthal in the sixteenth century, under the brooding eye of the Revd Matthevius. It has to be added that in the Soviet era the Jachymov mines were one of the main sources for uranium concentrates, the basis of bombs and power in the Eastern Bloc, and that the miners were mostly political prisoners. *Tempora mutantur*, as President Hoover might have said.

It is remarkable how all these different historical threads weave together in one mining area on the Czech–German border: the dollar and the first geological textbook; Marie Curie and the dating of the earth; even perhaps industrial justice. Jachymov also embodies much of geology over a few hillsides now strewn with overgrown tailings.

It all has a ground truth in plate tectonics. The mines of Jachymov are just part of a great swathe of mineral riches dotted through central Europe and that run out eventually into the famous tin-mines of Cornwall at the westerly tip of England. All these mines have complex histories, many are played out, and they yield different treasures. But they are all intimately connected with one of the ancient seams that divide the complex European continent – what Suess and Holmes called the Hercynian fold belt, though modern textbooks seem to prefer the term Variscan. There was a range of mountains – real, high mountains – running along this track through Europe, a range that was the consequence of subduction of ocean we have previously encountered, the Rheic Ocean. The silver and the uranium were the last exhalations from the dying seas, a gift from the underworld sealed in cracks since the Carboniferous. In Cornwall that gift was tin, tourmaline, lead, zinc, and silver. The miners in Jachymov had their counterparts elsewhere, speaking Cornish or Old French.

Silver and gold are unusual in occurring in nature as the pure element. Few other elements other than gases occur in such an unadulterated condition. We have already met native sulphur in the yellow-stained exhalations around volcanoes. Copper also occurs in sheets and nuggets, often so distinctively shaped they seem to have been beaten out by an earth sprite with an eye for abstract sculpture. Most elements are prone to combine with one or several others to form a compound – this is a mineral. The 'noblest' metal, gold, is reluctant to become part of a mineral; it will not combine with oxygen in the atmosphere, for example, which is why it does not tarnish, and why gold hoards still glow after years in the ground. Iron, by contrast, is corrupted by water and oxygen and soon becomes crusted and fragile. Like iron, most elements cleave unto others. A mineral has a particular chemical formula, a characteristic combination of elements. An ore is just a mineral, or a set of minerals found together, that is of commercial value. Whether or not a given claim yields a worthwhile ore can change, too, as the market fluctuates, so mining is tied into the flux of capital: there is nothing objective about ores. Minerals carry scientific names that identify them uniquely, 'official names', in the same way as the Latin binomen for animals and plants. Unlike the system developed by Linnaeus for the biological world only one name is required to identify a mineral. Some are ancient names that have a certain romance – sphene, tourmaline, galena, hornblende, topaz, garnet – but the majority are just 'ites'. That is, they have a stem name to which '–ite' is added as a suffix to indicate their mineralogical nature. Many are not very euphonious creations. Leafing through a dictionary that I have in front of me I find bismutotantalite, cuproskodlowskite, fluorapophyllite, guanajuatite, kaemmererite, monteregianite, oosterboschite, shattuckite, vandendriesscheite, yofortierite and, last, the not-to-be-forgotten zinnwaldite. Each mineral name is a label of chemical composition first, but also has a typical crystal structure. As we have seen, atoms can arrange themselves in more than one way even if they have the same chemical formula, and a different arrangement can merit a different mineral name. Each mineral type is termed a 'species', thereby adopting the same language as biology.

It is somewhat confusing to find that some rock types, too, have '-ite' as suffixes. Charnockite is a rock, not a mineral. So are granodiorite and lherzolite. The definition of a rock type is generally looser than that of a species of mineral. In practice, most rocks are recognized from the characteristic assemblage and proportions of their constituent minerals. A rock made of feldspar and quartz will have a different name from one made largely of hornblende. But this system still allows for a lot of variation in appearance of the rock-in-hand specimen, according to how it occurred in nature.

Some minerals have very simple chemical formulae, as easy to remember as those of water and salt, which is a mineral. Many have horribly complicated ones. Some minerals are very common and others are very rare. Some are so rare that they are known from a single locality, the mineralogical equivalent of the Mauritius one-cent postage stamp that haunts the dreams of philatelists. There is a good reason for this. Rare elements combining under rare conditions produce rare minerals. Conversely, common elements make proletarian marriages. The commonest elements, silicon and oxygen, combine to form the remarkably common mineral quartz: the sand on the beach, that rounded cobblestone in the ancient church wall, the grit that gets into your sandwiches in the park – all quartz. This does not mean that a common mineral cannot be uncommonly beautiful. Perfect quartz crystals are much less routine than mere sand and gravel: they are six-sided prisms topped with complex pyramids. Its more massive form, rock crystal, has a kind of vivid transparency that makes most glass look insipid. And then quartz gets tinted by traces of other elements to produce named varieties that are commonly sold in rock shops: amethyst coloured purple by manganese; carnelian made warmly red because of a dash of iron. Such striking colours are not rare in nature: the quartz minerals that produce them are usually described as 'semi-precious', but they are in no sense semi-beautiful.

Gemstones are crystals of greater rarity, and are a more traditional barometer of wealth than mere accumulation of dollars – silver or otherwise. All gemstones are minerals, but not all minerals can yield gems. Often, a common form of the gem mineral exists as a routine ingredient in rocks, but only rarely is it pure-grown, clear and crystalline, in the precious form. The frequent mineral corundum is often matt and uninteresting. Chemically, it is a simple oxide of aluminium. But grown deep in the underworld under special conditions, with the right impurity added by nature to induce colour, it becomes the most regal of all jewels – ruby. It is odd that this stone almost alone is used as a Christian name. If it were a matter of vulgar display, then surely diamond or emerald should be common names, or if exoticism were the important factor 'Opal' should be heard on the streets of London or New York. Some of the best rubies are found near the village of Mogok, in Burma. Benvenuto Cellini (1500–71), greatest of goldsmiths, reckoned that a fine ruby was worth eight times the same weight in diamond. The ultimate rubies are called 'pigeon's-blood rubies', allegedly because their colour resembles that of the blood of a freshly-slaughtered dove: they are a lustrous but absolutely clear red and are the most valuable of all gemstones. They are rarely found in place in their rocky source, a coarsely crystalline marble that cropped out in the wet hills of Burma. Instead, they have to be sifted from ancient gravels into which they were washed and concentrated from their original bed. The largest rubies of all are from what is now Tadjikistan. If another quirk of contamination happens, corundum becomes blue, rather than red, and then you have a sapphire.

Crystals do not usually grow into gem-quality stones. Like most things in life, minerals are commonly compromised with impurities, or grow crushed by others, so cheek by jowl that they do not develop their most beautiful colour and character. The spectacular specimens that are found in museum cabinets are uncommon. More abundant minerals often accompany the rarities, as when a cluster of quartz crystals will form a plinth from which arise elegant columns of green or pink tourmaline. Beautiful gem-quality minerals are particularly found in nature in those geological sites where the crystals were able grow very slowly to achieve their perfection of form. This often happens in profoundly deep fissures in the presence of volatile elements like chlorine and fluorine, and where the crystallizing chamber is bathed in hot, siliceous waters. When miners eventually hollow out tunnels into these underworld crystallization chambers, the crystal seams can be displayed to the visitor as glistening, bejewelled encrustations lining ceiling or walls. There are immediate romantic connotations to such subterranean jewel-boxes. Thus John Keats described Endymion's descent into 'the sparry hollows of the world':

> Dark, nor light,
> The region; nor bright, nor sombre wholly . . .
> A dusky empire and its diadems;
> One faint eternal eventide of gems.

Imitations of such displays were reproduced in the once-fashionable artificial grottos that still adorn the stately parks of Palladian mansions. Unfortunately, their creators often mixed geologically inappropriate materials: geodes of quartz placed alongside calcite stalagmites and stalactites. Their man-made 'dusky empire' was constructed with scant regard to the truths of the real underworld.

Though minerals are named as species they are far fewer in number than the prodigious profusion of species in the biological world. Species of flies alone outrank the number of naturally occurring minerals several times; so do species of mushrooms and daisies. There is a simple reason for this. Life is based upon virtually infinite variations in the organic carbon compounds, of which DNA – the basis of the genetic code – is merely the most well known. The permutations and combinations of these molecules are capable of endless elaboration. Sex and genes are subtler markers of species differences than atoms alone. In the sphere of the rocks, there is a finite number of elements, and a finite number of ways of marrying them: and only those that can crystallize under the conditions pertaining on earth are capable of becoming mineral species. As I write there are about 3,700 different named mineral species. The Amazon rainforest holds many times this total of beetle species still waiting to be discovered. Approximately a hundred new minerals are named each year. Some elements, like aloof gold and platinum, do not readily combine with others under natural conditions, so this reduces the possibilities still further. Other elements, such as mercury, are very particular about their partner, so that cinnabar is one of a very small number of mercury ores. Its rarity is in inverse proportion to its importance, however, because as the source of vermilion it was once king of the painter's palette. Mercury, which is the only metal that is liquid at room temperature, was one of the pivotal elements in the whole philosophy of alchemy; it is still important as an industrial catalyst. So there are severe limits to the possible combinations of the fivescore natural elements. Then there are many elements of such natural rarity that they do not form pure compounds – the rare earth elements are most notable among them. Only eight elements make up ninety per cent of the earth's crust – oxygen, silicon, aluminium, iron, calcium, sodium, potassium, and magnesium, in decreasing abundance. So the real choice of combinations of elements that might make natural mineral species is much more limited than arithmetical permutation alone might suggest. Minerals are families of natural partners born to exist comfortably on this planet. Their cradle is

William Wollaston (1766–1828), chemist, philosopher, mathematician and polymath. The medal struck in palladium (which he discovered) is the senior medal of the Geological Society of London. The mineral Wollastonite is named after him.

often where plates collide, or where the tectonic motor of the earth squeezes out unusual fluxes from the stressed crust.

A new mineral name has to be accompanied by the mineral's chemical formula and an account of its crystal structure. They are sometimes named after the localities in which they were found: thus it is not difficult to deduce from which country brazilianite originates. Others are named after prominent geologists and mineralogists. This is one way to have your name and reputation frozen in stone, in perpetuity. What could be more durable than the stuff of earth itself? Wollastonite is named for William Wollaston (1766–1828), chemist, philosopher, mathematician, and polymath. Among a number of achievements he is probably remembered today for his discovery of the noble element palladium in 1803, named after the great wooden image of Pallas, goddess of wisdom and war, that was supposed to protect the citadel of Troy from mishap. The Wollaston Medal is the highest award of the oldest geological club in the world, the Geological Society of London, and is presented annually to one of the greatest research geologists. It is the only academic medal that is struck in palladium.

Because oxygen forms 46.6 per cent by weight of the elements in the earth's crust, and silicon 27.7 per cent, it is not surprising that silicate minerals that include these two elements are the most abundant materials in the construction of the earth above the core. All the most common igneous rocks are combinations of different silicate minerals. That they have this creative capacity is because of the peculiarities of silica, and to understand the earth it is essential to know something of the chemistry of silica. Silicon and oxygen combine in such a way that the silicon atom sits at the centre of a four-sided pyramid, with an oxygen atom at each apex. You can make the shape of this tetrahedron if you take a small plug of dough and squeeze it between the thumb and index fingers of both hands. Make that finger-and-thumb gesture that French chefs are supposed to use to indicate perfection, then bring together both hands with this gesture at right angles and squeeze the dough between fingertips – a little tetrahedron will result. At the atomic level, these tetrahedra can then link together by their tips as chains, or sheets, or as three-dimensional frameworks. Their apexes may point upwards or downwards. This linkage explains many things about the properties of minerals: their hardness, the way they break, how they behave in the plates of the crust. Quartz is very hard because its pure silica tetrahedra bond in all directions to make a 3-D framework. It does not have natural breakage planes, or cleavage, for the same reason: there is no direction of relative weakness. Its rock-crystal clarity is a way of seeing its atomic purity, the eye appreciating intuitively features that lie beyond even the vision of the electron microscope. By contrast, mica has its silica pyramids bonded into sheets, layer after layer and strongly linked from side to side, but weakly linked in the direction at right angles. It is almost like a stack of leaves of papers.

This is why mica breaks readily into thin sheets: you can pick at, and flake a mica crystal with your finger nail; in theory you could go on splitting it down and down until it is a mere molecule or two in thickness. In practice, it is used as refractory 'glass' windows in boilers and furnaces: it resists temperatures that would melt ordinary window glass.

Almost any configuration of silica tetrahedra that can be devised theoretically can be found in nature. The main mineral 'families' correspond to different designs. The silica tetrahedra can be single, or linked together in pairs, or form rings, chains, sheets, or complex three-dimensional frames. The principal mineral varieties are determined by major differences in construction, much as you might define the main styles of architecture by aspects of proportion and design.

A few examples will illustrate how this works. The frequently beautiful mineral beryl is one of a few minerals that contain the second lightest of all metallic elements, beryllium. It is also one of a number of minerals in which the silica tetrahedra are connected together in rings, six linking one to another to form hexagons. Atoms of beryllium and aluminium make the joins between the silica rings. It is helpful to compare the whole stucture with a honeycomb: the silica hexagons form the cells, which are sealed and bonded together with the metallic elements. The result is a distinctive mineral *species*. Because the structure is so well linked, beryl is hard – it can scratch glass. When beryl crystals grow under special conditions they may be transparent, and then beryl becomes a gemstone called aquamarine. If the colour happens to be yellow it is known as heliodor; if green, it is emerald. These are more romantic names than beryllium aluminium silicate, the scientific description of beryl; but they are are no more than the names of varieties, just as Rhode Island reds and leghorns are all chickens under the feathers. As usual, the colours are associated with 'impurities' of other elements: a trace of chromium is what makes emeralds green.

Crystals of beryl are also often hexagonal in shape; hence the specimen in your hand closely reflects what happens at the atomic scale. The architectural analogy is inappropriate in this respect, for in minerals the finished shape of the construction arises directly from the shape of the bricks – not from the will of the architect. Beryl is a rather easy example to understand because of the distinctiveness of both its atomic and crystal structure – hexagons are familiar enough from close-ups of a fly's eye, or even from grandmother's quilting. Curiously enough, one of the most important structures in organic chemistry is also a six-sided ring: this is the benzene ring, which is a characteristic part of a vast range of naturally occurring carbon compounds. Plants and animals are full of them. It seems that anything silica can do, carbon can do better. It is interesting to speculate, as science fiction has sometimes done, on the possibility of silica-based life, given the similarities between the complexity of silica frameworks and chains and those based on carbon. There is no doubt that silicates are the closest rivals for carbon compounds in their complexity. But there are important differences: for example, carbon–hydrogen bonds are ubiquitous in organic molecules, but do not readily occur with silicon. The relatively tiny number of mineral species compared with carbon-based ones proves that silicon is just not so versatile. At high pressure and temperature, however, silicon bonds are less constrained, more capable of transforming from one shape to another. It is an intriguing thought that silicon life might have to grow deep *within* an alien world to have a chance of reproduction, where heat and pressure free up the rigour of its chemical bonds.

Mineralogy has moved a long way since the time of Agricola. X-rays can spy inside crystals to discover the 'bones' of the atomic structure. Tiny amounts of a mineral can be punched out with a laser beam, and its constituent elements counted almost atom by atom. Electron probes tot up the proportions of the elements within a crystal by their atomic weight as mechanically as a coin sorter might file nickels from dimes, quarters from silver thalers. You sit in front of a computer screen and watch the piles of atoms grow as the analysis proceeds. In a mass spectrometer, the isotopes of single elements are sorted by their different atomic weights. Atoms in 'vaporized' samples are deflected differentially by a magnetic field, like different-sized pigeons lured home to separate roosts, and it is now comparatively easy to measure abundance of elements in parts per billion. The rarest bird can be spotted alongside the pigeon. An atom or two of praseodymium is no problem, nor is it so difficult to sort out your yttrium from your ytterbium.

So the silicate minerals can be investigated in detail, another kind of intimacy in the history of the earth. We have to go back to Hawai'i to see why this matters. Recall the mineral olivine that formed green sand on one of the beaches. Olivine is a simple silicate of iron and/or magnesium. Olivine crystallized out very early in the igneous magma chamber. These first solid crystals would then tend to sink, like lentils settling to the bottom of a stewpot. In so doing they effectively remove magnesium, and other elements, from the remainder of the siliceous melt, which accordingly subtly alters in its composition. Other minerals can then crystallize out in their turn. The magma, in other words, *evolves*. Elements that are reluctant to shuffle into a silicate mineral early on will become commoner and commoner as this natural alchemy proceeds. You can now understand one of the ways in which elements that are very rare in nature can become concentrated. It can happen either by leaving early, or by hanging on late. Heavy minerals will often segregate together precociously. Most of the greatest deposits of ore for chromium were produced by early settling of the weighty mineral chromite within the magma chamber. Black, dense bands of chromite form dull layers of booty; the chromium miner is like the naughty boy scraping all the meatiest bits from the bottom of the stew. In the opposite fashion, after the magma has almost completely crystallized, a fluid residue remains, containing many of the most volatile elements, chlorides and fluorides, and metallic elements in solution. These seek out cracks and fissures in the country rocks surrounding the solidified magma there to lay down their burden of minerals, the source of silver, copper, and zinc, and the wealth of industry. Hence Joachimsthal.

Feldspars are the most important single component of igneous and metamorphic rocks. They can be found almost everywhere: in granites, gneisses, and schists; they are even important in moon rocks.

So it is important to know something about how they are constructed if we are to understand how much of the world is made. Probably the simplest way to see feldspars in the field is to walk to the nearest bank. Financial institutions seem to prefer to face their buildings with polished granite. There is something reassuring about granite – the fact that most modern buildings only have a thin 'skin' of rock as a cosmetic is neither here nor there. The appropriate rock will have an overall pinkish or greyish hue. The feldspars are white or pink blades; they are the largest and most obvious crystals. They are frequently bounded by clearly defined crystal edges, because feldspars crystallize early from magmatic melt and nudge their way ahead of other minerals towards perfection of form. In some ornamental granites the feldspars are huge, making *phenocrysts* – from a distance they look almost as if they had been glued on to the rock surface like small white posters. Some rocks contain more than one kind of feldspar, pink and white together. Because they crystallize early, feldspars in particular are responsible for altering the chemical composition of the siliceous 'stew' that remains behind; they become an important factor in the evolution of magmas. Since the generation of magma in its turn is the outcome of plate tectonic processes, feldspars are woven into the warp and weft of the fabric of the earth. Their chemistry really does matter.

Consider what we have seen on Hawai'i. The lavas there changed from fluid *pahoehoe*, constructing shield volcanoes layer by layer, to a sticky lava building sputtering cones, which still stick to the sides of the huge shields like Mauna Loa as if they were so many tumid pimples. The primitive lava, freshly minted from partially melted oceanic rock, crystallizes out first with calcium-rich feldspar and olivine. The magma held in its deep chamber evolves in composition as these early crystals are removed from the remaining magma. Later lavas are richer in silica, which makes them altogether more gluey; and the feldspars are pushed towards the alkali end of their range as the ingredients of the fecund stew gradually change. The stiff magmas cannot flow as benignly as the *pahoehoe*. Instead, vents build up cones surrounding them composed of pumice and bombs, and occasionally a destructive blast hurls material high into the air. Ultimately, the topography of the Hawaiian Islands is the responsibility of the atomic bonds of minerals.

The individual prospector of popular legend, discovering valuable mineral deposits through a combination of instinct, experience, and luck, is becoming a rare species. Remote sensing equipment can now detect buried minerals from a 'fly past', using the most sensitive gravimeters to detect changes in gravity induced by buried bodies of heavy metallic ores. Rather than laboriously trudging the hills, inch-by-inch, samples can be taken from streams draining a prospect area and precise assays of the elements then taken – a good source will leave traces in the water. It is almost like smelling a potential deposit, with chemical sensors taking the place of the prospector's fabled nose. Large companies operate huge pits with sophisticated methods of recovery – silver, for instance, can be recovered as a by-product of lead and zinc extraction. It is all a matter of profit in a volatile market-place, and the accountant has become as important as the geologist. Still, striking it rich is part of the mythology of geological exploration, and sometimes, rarely, it still happens.

Diamonds, as the saying goes, are forever. Unfortunately, this is not true. They are not really stable under the conditions found in the average jeweller's shop, for their natural home is deep in the underworld. They exist at the surface on sufferance, having been wrested from their profound origins. They are the nearest that carbon comes to imitate the structure of silica, that ubiquitous component of *terra firma*: it is no coincidence that these sparkling jewels are known as 'rocks'. Diamonds are the same material as coal, but transformed wondrously. Under sufficient pressure, the carbon atom is forced to make a three-dimensional framework analogous to that described for silica, except that diamond is pure carbon alone and each atom is strongly bonded to another four in a kind of unbreakable armlock. This is why diamonds are so hard. The largest diamond of all time was the South African Cullinan diamond, 3106 carats, and

Thomas Cullinan was one of the few who did, indeed, strike it rich. This diamond, presented by the Transvaal government to the British King Edward VII, was cut into five huge gems, and ninety-six smaller stones to boot. In 1902 Cullinan had bought the ground on which the Premier Diamond Mining Company operates, since when more than 300 million tons of the country rock known as 'blue ground' have been removed to yield something like ninety million carats of diamonds. Every year, a few stones the size of pigeon's eggs are discovered. In the Kimberley area – and many other places where they occur in situ – diamonds are found in 'pipes'; these are huge tubular structures, punched deep through part of the ancient African shield in Cullinan's claim. Blue ground is the weathered relic of a volcanic rock known as kimberlite. The pipes are believed to be the product of a violent gas-charged magmatic explosion that dragged up diamonds from deep within the earth. It has been estimated that the temperature and pressure needed to turn black carbon to transparent diamond are 1200° Kelvin and 3500,000,000 pascals, respectively. Diamonds can be synthesized by reproducing these conditions. This suggests that natural diamonds originated about 150 kilometres beneath the continents. Most mineralogists now believe that these conditions are satisfied only in the upper mantle. Diamonds are a kind of offering from the gods of the underworld.

So precious minerals can be crystallized from magma, or distilled from its latest breath, or dragged from the depths by volcanic blasts. They will naturally be concentrated where the earth is in transit: where plates have converged along the seams of mountain ranges, or where those ranges once traversed the earth but have now been rendered low by millions of years of weathering and erosion. For where crust has been thickened and heated, there, too, is a crucible in which refinement and concentration can occur. Like almost everything geological on this mutable earth, minerals are genetically related to plate tectonics. The sulphurous breath of igneous activity engenders metal sulphide minerals. Some of these have been the source of riches, but they are usually accompanied by shiny yellow-metallic cubes of common-or-garden pyrites, iron sulphide – 'fool's gold' for the credulous. Tin, copper, zinc, and lead make up the precious cargoes carried by sulphide seams hidden within the greater seams that stitch together the plates of the earth. Lead sulphide is called galena and it, too, forms cubes that are dark as the metal they contain, and as heavy in the hand as you would expect. Where granites are melted in the depths of orogenesis, their subsequent cooling refines the rarer and aristocratic elements, or sequesters those that enter into pacts with volatile elements like chlorine. Vaporous waters carry cargoes of metals and gemstones into the surrounding rocks, fleeing the lumpen mass to hide in cracks and fissures. The silver of Joachimsthal was the product of such a refinement. In the limestone hills of Derbyshire, England, there are buried seams of fluorspar coloured green or mauve, yellow or blue, in which fluorine has married quotidian calcium. Beware testing this with sulphuric acid for, if you do, hydrogen fluoride is generated, a gas that can dissolve glass, and burn holes in flesh, turning black what remains. Fluorine is the most voracious element, eager to combine with others; small quantities are found in many minerals, but fluorspar is its apotheosis.

And then there is gold, the aloof Vanderbilt of the periodic table. Gold is usually found 'native', linked to no other elements. You will have wondered how an element so determinedly celibate can have found its way into veins, let alone gathered into nuggets. In most rocks gold is present in only the minutest traces, as scattered atoms or tiny flecks invisible to a prospector. To become concentrated it somehow needs to congregate. The answers are only just being teased out, particularly by Professor Seward and his colleagues at the Technical Institute in Zürich.* It seems that gold is not so aloof as it appears. Under conditions of high pressure and elevated temperature, and in

* The same team have also shown that other metallic elements, such as lead, cadmium, and thallium, form somewhat comparable partnerships with chlorine in hot hydrothermal situations. This is one of the ways in which the emplacement of metals in mineral veins is becoming understood: they, as it were, hitch a ride on the back of a chloride complex. The study of such processes requires the latest equipment, such as X-ray absorption spectroscopy.

the presence of water, it makes temporary alliances with hydrogen sulphide, to form hydrosulphide complexes that can migrate through the crust. The gold is deposited again in due turn as its temporary partner deserts. Certain other elements, such as arsenic, when in very fine, or colloidal form, can 'scavenge' gold, making it adhere to the surface of the grains. So gold is swept up and captured. When the golden rock is eventually weathered at the surface, heavy and incorruptible gold remains behind and can be concentrated into gravels in river beds. This is where prospectors traditionally 'pan for gold' by swishing away the lighter waste of sand with copious water until the gleaming flakes are concentrated in the bottom of the shallow pan.

Gold was formerly as synonymous with money as the dollar is today. The golden age is still the best of times; the golden rule is still the one that must be observed. Wisdom, like gold, comes in nuggets. Leonardo da Vinci described gold as 'not the meanest of Nature's

Gold sluicing on the Klondike in the summer of 1900 on Number 2 Claim, Anvil Creek, Nome, Alaska

products; but the most excellent . . . which is begotten in the sun, in as much as it has more resemblance to it than to anything else that is, and no created thing is more enduring than gold'. Gold was extracted early in history because its natural purity required no smelting. Its use in artefacts accompanies the appearance of the first civilizations. There were mines in the Sudan from which Pharaonic Egypt obtained plentiful supplies of gold: there is a record of a load which needed a hundred and fifty men to carry it. The inner coffin of Tutankhamun was made of purest gold and weighs over a hundred kilograms. Like Leonardo, the early religions of both Egypt and South America associated gold with the sun, and with their greatest gods. The promise of gold was what led the conquistadors to the New World, and they were not disappointed. Sixteenth-century goldsmiths suddenly had a plentiful supply of the magnificent metal and produced incomparable work, although we might now regret the melting of the Aztec originals that fed it. Gold mingles happily with silver as an alloy and the most durable gold-work is not a hundred per cent pure but has up to a fifth of silver in it. The silver puts some strength into a metal that is definitively malleable and ductile, and which can be beaten into gilding sheets thinner than rice paper. When properly worked, gold has unrivalled delicacy. Only gold is as good as gold.

Gold discoveries have always led to gold rushes, a mad scramble for wealth. The great California Gold Rush of 1849 may have inspired Mark Twain's definition of a mine as 'a hole in the ground owned by a liar'. New and fantastical claims led to hysterical occupation of gold-bearing ground by dreamers: scarcely one in twenty made any money. It was the same in the Klondike fifty years later. Conditions were appalling and the ground worked by the prospectors was permanently frozen. On the other side of the world, it was as hot in Australia as the Klondike was cold. The gold rushes to Bendigo in Victoria in the 1850s, and to Kalgoorlie, Western Australia, in the 1890s were parched affairs. The diggers were often desperate, excavating square miles of holes in favoured areas. Writing in 1852, the sculptor and poet Thomas Woolner described the devastation thus: 'I never saw anything more desolate than the first sight of Mount Alexander was to me: it was what one would suppose the earth would appear after the day of judgement has emptied all the graves.' No matter where you were, you ran the risk of being robbed of your wealth by a highwayman. In California it might be Black Bart, who performed twenty-nine hold-ups disguised by a headgear of floursack with crude eyeholes. After his depradations he left behind verses on morsels of paper:

I've laboured long and hard for bread,
For honour and for riches.
But on my toes too long you've tred,
You fine haired sons of bitches.

Which proves that Black Bart was a more effective robber than he was a poet. He was caught in 1884. In Victoria, the traveller would have had to keep his eyes skinned for Black Douglas, who might have attacked him in the Black Forest. Clearly, the opposite of gold is black.

There are fairy tales which exploit the naive lad who hears that the streets of London are paved with gold. To which he departs with only his cat, or his spotted handkerchief for company. Barnaby Rudge, the simpleton hero of one of Dickens' more esoteric novels, was probably the last literary manifestion of this fantasy. But there *has* been one time when the streets have truly been paved with gold. In the rush of 1893, Kalgoorlie prospectors threw away an excess of a bulky pyritous material as they delved deeper for pure gold, in the same way as the miners at Joachimsthal had once jettisoned pitchblende. They recognized the waste as being rich in yellowish 'fool's gold', iron sulphide, and used it for hardcore, or to fill in ruts, or to bulk up crude sidewalks. Despite what was said above about the nobility of gold, there is, in fact, a stable compound that gold forms in nature with another rare element, tellurium. The resulting mineral is gold telluride, or calaverite, to give it its mineralogical name. The 'waste' material used to pave the roads in Kalgoorlie in fact turned out to be this very uncommon mineral, but nearly three years passed before anyone realized that their streets were paved with the proverbial gold. It was not until 29 May 1896 that the results of an elemental analysis of the strange mineral leaked out to the mining community, resulting in a second gold rush – this time to the dumps where the blocks of waste had been disposed of. Dr Malcolm Maclaren, writing an account of the affair in the *Mining Magazine* in 1912, described how 'blocks of ore, assaying at 500 oz gold per ton, had been utilized to build a rough hearth and chimney in a miner's hut'. Forget the hills. There was gold in them thar bricks.

8

Hot Rocks

Driving in India reinforces your belief in a protective God. The dry and dusty roads north of Pune (formerly Poona) bend this way and that as they climb into the foothills of the Western Ghats. It is the dry season, which lasts for six months or so. The landscape is reduced to a uniform pale tan colour. It is hot enough to make the roadside farmhouses, with their small courtyards draped in leaves, look restful and inviting. The roads are just about wide enough to take two vehicles abreast. Disreputable trucks covered in dents and dust hurtle along the road with no regard for bends or goats or barefoot children. Worse, they overtake other, older trucks even dustier and more dented, whether or not they happen to be climbing up a hill or going round a blind bend at the time. Our own driver is more circumspect, possibly influenced by my drawn face and clenched fists. But it still does no good, because statistical laws beyond the reach of caution inevitably dictated that sooner or later there is an oncoming truck in mid-overtake on our side of the road. I close my eyes. A few milliseconds later there is a tremendous crash as our vehicle veers off the road and into a field. The statistic has been defied, thanks to a lack of roadside fencing, and providence. As we come to a halt our driver exhales between his teeth and says: 'Oh my! We nearly had our chip!' One of the things I like about India is that they still know how to use English understatement.

As we drive northwards changes in the proportions of the landscape become obvious. For a few miles the road runs comparatively straight, then we climb for a while before another level stretch is reached. Any hills has flat tops, and in the distance more terraces rise one after the other, so that the hillsides look like a series of steps stretching away as far as the eye can see. We are in the Deccan Traps, one of the greatest volcanic features on earth, 1.5 million square kilometres of volcanic rock. Each flat level was formed by the top of a single lava flow, which evidently extended for many miles. So as we climb, we ascend through flow after flow. The top of a more resistant flow might make an extensive plain, and then its successor would comprise the next flat area, perhaps half as wide. Each terrace supports a farming population, with many small-holdings carrying humble, single-storey dwellings. There is no corner of the flat area capable of cultivation that had not been dug or tilled. Occasionally, there might be a small square of bright green where some local water source permitted salad plants to prosper, but it is clear that the crops were over for this year. Nothing to do except wait for the next rainy season. We pass only one factory run by the ubiquitous Tata corporation; the dependence on agriculture of this part of Maharastra Province is unlikely to change in the future.

The word 'traps is derived from a Swedish word (*trapp*) meaning stairs or steps, and is certainly an appropriate way to describe the landscape. The Deccan is the apotheosis of the lava flow. The difference from the Hawaiian shield volcanoes is the sheer extent of the flows, which stretch for thousands of square kilometres. Rather than cones, they build up plateaux; for this reason the underlying rocks are sometimes known as plateau basalts. As you drive over the terraces for hour after hour, you begin to appreciate the scale of the traps. Single flows of highly liquid lava must have flooded out on a truly enormous scale, leaving flows the thickness of a house covering more than 100,000 square kilometres. Viewed from the moon at the time of eruption, this area of north-western India would have looked as if a great pot of black paint had been spilled out on the surface of the earth. The other difference with Hawai'i, of course, is that the plateau of the Deccan Traps is built upon continental, rather than oceanic, crust. It makes for an area of the world where dark, oceanic-style rocks have been plastered mightily on top of the continents. This happens on a scale that makes the ophiolites considered in the previous chapters seem insignificant.

Because the lavas are porous, water drains away through them. There are cracks and joints and holes running through the stack of layers, for all that they appear solid and impregnable as you pass them in a road-cut. Water sees the rocks differently: as a mass of tiny channels through which it can pass to lower layers, there to seek out other subtle passages still deeper. It is spirited away further and further from the surface. When the rainy season finally arrives, the landscape bursts into fecund productivity, but it is a time of plenty running against the clock. Even as leaves unfurl into the moist air, water is dribbling away unseen through the flows beneath the ground. I notice empty pits and scrapes all over the Deccan hills. These are temporary reservoirs that try to slow the draining. Roughly caulked, they are a temporary way of making ponds for irrigation. They only stay the inevitable drought for a while. As the sun beats down harder, evaporation takes its share, too. The whole region hunkers down for the mean season. You begin to understand how men are in thrall to geology even though there are many places where it does not blatantly announce itself; it rules unseen.

Native vegetation understands the bidding of climate and rock. Plants have developed all manner of techniques for surviving periods of hardship: leathery leaves, deep roots, deciduous habit. There is not much old woodland left in the parts of Maharastra Province I visited: too many hungry mouths need to be fed. That any remains at all is thanks to 'sacred groves', which are small but inviolate areas associated with gods and legends. They retain a very rich natural flora, with many unique species. They, too, pay homage to the peculiarities of geology. Professor Varkar in Pune maintains a huge personal herbarium for conserving these species that threatens to edge him out of his apartment. Currently, there is concern about keeping some of these endemic species from disappearing altogether, a concern partly fuelled by pragmatic arguments about the loss of uninvestigated plant chemicals that may prove to be useful in areas such as cancer treatment. The case of the critically rare Madagascar rose periwinkle, which has yielded one of the best anti-cancer drugs, is rehearsed again. But the stronger argument is a moral one. Our single species has no right to extirpate what geology and climate has created over millions of years: a whole habitat. Unlike the Hawaiian chain, we cannot even say that these basalts are doomed to immersion. The only sea that swamps these inland terraces is a sea of humankind.

The road climbs more steeply after the town of Aurangabad, named after the last of the Great Moguls, Aurangzheb (1659–1707). Looking down from the hills beyond you can see the magnificent, but now decayed fortress walls that had been built around the town by previous Mogul emperors for its protection. In places, trees now sprout from the battlements. On a cricket pitch, albeit a dusty one, at least three teams of middle sized boys dash about, ignoring the heat. "I am telling you, India is cricket mad!' the driver informs me, unnecessarily. Cricket is the legacy of the British Raj, and possibly one of the few enduring contributions of my own race to India, and certainly the most harmless. The other contribution is our useful and flexible language, which has helped India to take a prominent part in the international communications revolution. The sway of Mogals and British has passed away, but the tumult of the street carries on as it always did, only now enlivened with the cry of "Howzat?"

The Ellora temples and caves lie thirty kilometres on from Aurangabad. The hills in which they lie comprise another stack of horizontal lava flows. The monuments were constructed as rock temples and monasteries between the fifth and ninth centuries: starting more than a thousand years before the British sniffed Indian profits. The Deccan Traps host the most direct link between geology and culture that I know. The work grows from the rock, which provides both inspiration and material. There are three religions celebrated at Ellora; a guide-book tells me that sixteen 'caves' are Hindu, twelve are Buddhist, including the earliest ones, and five are dedicated to that most peaceful of all religions, the Jain faith. The Jains are strictly vegetarian and will not contemplate harm to any living thing. The purist Jain will even sweep the road in front of his advancing feet lest he take the life of an ant. The caves lie in a series running north–south for about two kilometres, and apparently follow the 'seam' of one particular lava flow that is more suited for excavation. Over some parts of the outcrop a more resistant flow overlies the caves; the small lake known as Sita's Bath is fed by a waterfall that plunges over this capping flow. Cave 16 – Kailasa, Shiva's mountain abode – is the one that the tourists flock to first, and you can see exactly why. It is an astonishing construction. I should perhaps rather call it a deconstruction, a piece of architecture in reverse. For this edifice has been fabricated by *taking away* rock, rather than by building up with bricks or blocks. The temple was made by removing masses of lava to leave behind monumental buildings and reliefs. Effectively a gigantic sculpture, hewn from the rock with hammer and chisel, it was made during the eighth and early ninth centuries under the orders of King Krishna I. It is as if the temple lay nascent within the lava flow, until released by a century of chipping and digging by Hindu artisans. Something like three million cubic feet of volcanic rock had to be removed. The main pit dug from the cliff top was approximately 30 metres (100 feet) deep, 84 metres long and 46 metres wide (276 feet by 150 feet); at its centre a huge block was left behind, which was carved over decades into the huge, two-storey temple of Shiva. Inside, rooms were excavated. On the outside, rectangular columns frame sculptures that combine delicacy and extravagance: the richness of decoration is reminiscent of the Victorian embellishments of Pugin, for all that the subject-matter could scarcely be more different. This has something to do with a sense of fecundity, an ebullience of ornament. The friezes of the temple are carved into life-sized elephants, stiff and grand. Standing separately from the temple, there is a victory pillar as splendid as any monolith, resembling a geological outlier, with its lines of detailed carving mimicking a kind of geological stratification, a case of art unwittingly imitating nature.

In several parts of the monument there are sculptures depicting the marriage of Lord Krishna with Parvati. The female figure is voluptuous: she has spherical breasts as plump as small grapefruit and a tiny waist. Krishna is manly, but also tender; his hands reach towards his partner with a decorousness that belies the nudity of the lovers. There is an intimacy between the couple that is affecting and tender. Even their token garments have an understated elegance: they conceal more than they expose. For all that they were gods, these figures were also made in human dimensions. The bodies are different from the Greek archetypes that adorned Pompeii. Here they have more of flesh and blood, even though some may sport extra pairs of arms, or hybridize in interesting ways with animals.

Looking at the rocks close to, it was clear that many of the lavas at Ellora were of the kind described as porphyritic: they show large, flat feldspar crystals 'floating' in a matrix of darker, fine-grained basalt. It was as if bold white brush strokes had been added to the faces of the sculptures. Such prominent, prismatic feldspars had crystallized out at depth, where they had had time enough to grow large, before the main lava eruption spilled out over the ground in the thick flow that would one day give birth to a temple. The crystals were carried along with the fluid lava and then trapped in its solidity like nuts in brownies. The crystals serve to leaven the relentlessness of the black volcanic rock.

An even grander monument lies seventy-five kilometres onwards from Ellora. The Ajanta caves are carved into a vertical scarp along a horseshoe-shaped ravine. They, too, seem to follow a few flows; horizontal 'ribs' above the caves show the boundaries between the flows that were left unworked by human hand. The caves were lost for a thousand years. After Buddhism declined at the end of the seventh century they were simply forgotten, scrub covered their entrances, and bats were left to keep their secrets. A British horseman accidently stumbled upon the site in 1819; it must have been like the moment when the tomb of Tutankhamun was opened. A little road takes you to the base of the cliff, ending at an open space where there are dozens of stalls selling souvenirs. Mineral stores are as numerous as traders selling Thumbs-Up, the subcontinental equivalent of Coca-Cola. When the bus stops, tiny urchins mob you with handfuls of pretty minerals for sale. The minerals are, indeed, beautiful, and they are on sale here for a fraction of the price asked in western 'rock shops'. Pink or green crystals catch the eye; some specimens show gems arranged in delicate rosettes, or there are spiky balls made of elongate prisms. The crystals are another product of the ancient volcanic activity; and some of them belong to rare species, like apophyllite. When the lava cooled there were cavities, or vugs, left within it – many of these were originally air bubbles, part of the 'froth' of eruption. At a late stage, fluids moved through the lava pile and minerals were deposited within the holes. Many of them are of a class called zeolites, which include several rare varieties sought after by mineral collectors. These beautiful crystals appeal to that queasy part of human nature that lies between aesthetics and avarice. I am as vulnerable as anyone to the appeal of rarity dressed up in crystal form. When the Pune–Bombay railway was cut through the Deccan Traps, glittering subterranean galleries lined with crystals were discovered, and these furnished some of the finest specimens now displayed in museums around the world. But even the scruffiest street vendor might have had a lucky day in the hills, and you can make a substantial difference to his family economy by buying an example for a few dollars.

No chance of turning a penny is left unexplored. There is a steep flight of stairs up to the Ajanta Caves. When I finally escaped the mineral vendors, two strapping young men offered to save me the walk by lifting me up the flight on a kind of palanquin. This I huffily refused, although I had second thoughts half way up the stairs. The thirty caves are reached by way of an undulating path that has been scraped along the scarp. Originally, individual caves were reached along steps climbing from the stream below. These have largely collapsed. So now you go from one cave to another as you might from gallery to gallery in the Louvre. The comparison is appropriate, because almost every cave is an artistic treasure-house. Some have entrances supported by round columns of lava, but these were left behind as the excavation of the cave proceeded, rather than built up block by block in the classical fashion, so they are seamless. One cave has a roof made of twisting ropy lava belonging to the overlying flow. In a number of caves, Buddhist wall-paintings have survived in a remarkable state of preservation. They are by turns grand and intimate. Scenes from the life of the Buddha are complemented by episodes from everyday life; some are undoubted masterpieces. The torsos of the figures are unclothed, but all (except, on occasion, the Buddha) wear necklaces and bangles, garters and bejewelled head-gear. It would be an understatement to call the latter 'hats' for they come in every imaginable shape, from sparkling piles to elegant curlicues. The emotions of the figures are easily read by a modern observer; here the same tenderness, there the same sadness, the same humour. The subjects portrayed are those that have always interested artists: mother and child, death and redemption. On the back wall of the ante-chamber in Cave 17 there is a scene depicting the return of the Buddha to his palace as a mendicant, carrying his begging bowl. His son Rahula, whom he has not seen for seven years, in turn begs of the Buddha his recognition as a son. The poet Laurence Binyon (1869–1943), who did much to make the quality of Ajanta's art known to the world, said of this painting: 'No picture anywhere is more profoundly impressive in grandeur and tenderness.' I feel an affinity with this particular visitor to Ajanta because, like me, he spent much of his working life as an employee of the British Museum. There was another detail that moved me for a reason I struggled to understand. In Cave 2 there is a fresco that includes a half-naked girl on a rope swing, set against a rather dark and stylized field of flowers; it is an image of fun, but also curiously solemn. It has an exact counterpart in a painting called *The Swing*, by the pre-Revolutionary French artist Jean-Honoré Fragonard, in which an aristocratic girl, dressed as a notional shepherdess, soars carefree into the sky. Two girls from different millennia and from remote traditions enjoying an identical game, and captured in mid-swing by the hand of an artist. I take this as an emblem of the deep similarity of human responses, and, especially, of the importance of the artist in proving it.

Ajanta, too, was rooted in the geology, and not just because the

ABOVE The Welsh part of the Caledonian chain: a distant view of Snowdon.

RIGHT Ancient rocks come to the surface in the middle of New York City. Belvedere Castle in Central Park is built upon metamorphic rocks.

Real money: a fifteenth century silver thaler. Silver from Joachimsthal provided reliable currency across Europe.

Marie Curie (1867–1934) in her laboratory. Pitchblende from Joachimsthal supplied the ore from which the elment radium was extracted.

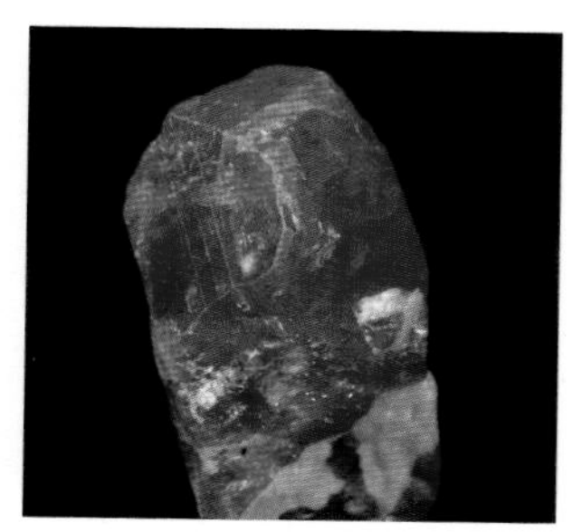

Mineral as gemstone: an uncut ruby from Pakistan – a typical hexagonal prismatic crystal.

A stunning vase made from differently coloured fluorite from Castleton, Derbyshire, UK. Compounds containing fluorine are often associated with hydrothermal deposits at times of mountain-building.

Wollastonite crystals. This mineral, named for William Wollaston is a calcium silicate typical of metamorphosed limestones.

A gold nugget. The Wicklow Nugget, found in Ballin Stream in Co. Wicklow, Ireland, 1795. It was owned by King George III and weighs 682g.

TOP The Deccan Traps, India, a plateau countryside made from basalt flow piled on flow, originally erupted very quickly. A view of the Ajanta outcrop with temples excavated into a single flow.

ABOVE LEFT A temple at Ellora: a case of negative architecture. Massive temples and ornaments carved out of a basalt lava flow.

ABOVE Basalt allows for delicate and erotic sculptures at Ellora.

LEFT Wonderfully delicate painted murals in the hidden caves at Ajanta, in the Deccan Traps.

ABOVE Granite batholith towers above the tropical jungle: Mount Kinabalu, Indonesia.

BELOW An elevated road collapses as a result of the Kobe earthquake of 1995.

OVERLEAF Aerial photograph showing the trace of the San Andreas Fault across the Carrizo Plain.

caves were hollowed out from the appropriate flow. Clay derived from weathered strata was one ingredient of the plaster used to prepare the walls for decoration (the others being cow dung and rice husks), with lime being used as the 'finish'. The pigments were mostly of local origin, like ochre and sienna, the weathered products of iron-rich volcanic rocks. These earthy washes provide a tone to the paintings that makes them feel as if they have grown from the rocks themselves. It is an interesting question where the brilliant colours came from: surely the bright blue used to paint in some of the jewels must have been produced from a cobalt mineral. Other caves are full of sculpture hewn directly from the lava. Rock and man engaging directly via the chisel. Cave 1 has a huge hall nearly twenty metres square, with an aisle flanked by a colonnade. The crude cells for the monks behind would certainly have encouraged a decidedly ascetic life. My favourite sculpted images are the flying couples that adorn the columns: united in ecstasy, these *Gandharvas* loosely embrace as they fly to the heavens, eyes closed. In one cave after another there is a parade of larger-than-life Buddhas that display his various embodiments by means of exquisite hand gestures. Cave 26 is veritably crammed with sculpture, which has a profusion about it that is more organic than the Hindu work at Ellora. A carved tableau tells the tale of how the Enlightened One resisted even the charms of the daughters of his relentless tempter, Mara. At the centre of it all, the giant reclining figure of the Buddha (Mahapari Nirvana), head resting on one hand, exudes peace. Playing about his lips is that distinctive expression that is not quite a smile, but does undoubtedly convey bliss. Basalt, the commonest of rocks, has never been employed for a more rarefied purpose.

I have avoided reflections upon the vastness of geological time in this book. Its extent imbues every page, but I have passed over with hardly a second glance the millions, or even billions, of years that radioactive clocks tell us have elapsed since one geological event or another. If you are not careful, referring again and again to the huge span of time available for earth's evolution becomes something of a mantra, rendered subliminal through its constant repetition.

Familiarity breeds unawareness. But at this point it might be worthwhile to think about what has happened over the historical span of the Deccan caves. Images of three religions have appeared, carved in the rocks; Buddhism faded sufficiently for the Ajanta caves to be lost for a thousand years. Neither Islam nor Christianity left their mark there, as they did elsewhere. The Moguls came and went, as did the British Raj. All this happened within a couple of thousand years, during which time the face of the cliffs altered hardly at all. The changes that mankind has wrought upon the landscape are much more profound: an ecosystem can be destroyed in a couple of human generations. What geology and climate married over millions of years, man can put asunder in a global heartbeat. All our human mess of history hardly registers on the scale of geological processes. It will be clear by now how much the world has changed to this infinitely slower rhythm. Lyell was wrong about the constancy of the earth's processes, but the method he gave us has been crucial to understanding the nature of the fluctuations that have occurred. Nowhere on earth today is a new Deccan erupting. This does not mean that it is beyond study because its peculiarities are readily capable of being interpreted in the light of processes we understand. You cannot describe the world as 'uniform' when such events occur without modern equivalents. However, there will be levels of history that we shall never reach; in 'deep time' there will be millennia beyond recall, simply because the level of dating precision we need to 'see' time is not available to us that far back. Some things are lost forever. Our own species emerged from Africa perhaps 100,000 years ago. This is still nothing, in geological terms. Yet all human biographies are crammed into those few milliseconds of geological time. I wonder if the adherence to the biblical timescale insisted upon by creationists is not partly motivated by a desire to *hang on* to history. Let time go into the millions, and beyond, and the insignificance of our own sector becomes patent.

Time again: the eruption of the Deccan Traps happened over a very short period. The pulse of history quickened. Increased accuracy in radiometric dating techniques has shown that the eruptions were bracketed by an interval as short as 1.5 million years.* It could have been even shorter: longer than the life of our species, to be sure, but still a blink in the gaze of time. Considering the volume of basalt erupted – an estimated 2.5 million cubic kilometres – and the vast area over which it extended, this was an extraordinary outpouring of magmatic floods.

The underworld bubbled over in this part of India. Many of the flows are twenty to thirty metres high and they maintain their thickness over hundreds of kilometres. Charged with gas, and highly fluid, they must have spread at remarkable speed, one after another. The lava emerged from a source that was plumbed into the mantle: the trace elements present in the basalts are consistent with such a deep source. The flows must have discharged from long fissures to account for their wide spread. These would leave their relics today as vertical feeder dykes cutting through the geological underlay, all the way to the depths. It has been estimated that the lava must have gushed out at a rate of hundreds of metres per second, which can be compared with the discharge from some of the world's largest rivers. What a sight it must have been at night! Having resisted the 'rivers of fire' cliché when writing of Hawai'i, this is surely the place to apply it without embarrassment. Floods of flaming fury; a Ganges of geological gaudiness; an Indus of inflagration; it is scarcely possible to go over the top.

Deeper time: the radiometric dates prove that the flood basalts of the Deccan Traps were erupted sixty-six million years ago. This is on the Cretaceous–Tertiary boundary. The same period saw the extinction of the dinosaurs, as well as of other kinds of animals that lived in the sea, such as ammonites. It is one of five mass extinctions that have punctuated the history of life, and probably the second greatest of them all. Not surprisingly, the two events have been linked: eruption and extinction. Quantities of sulphur dioxide and fine dust released into the atmosphere during the plateau basalt eruptions may

* A web report on recent research suggests that different parts of the traps may have erupted over a total of four million years.

have triggered adverse climate changes sufficient to kill vegetation on land and poison the seas. Herbivorous dinosaurs starved, while their predators briefly gorged upon their carcasses, and then followed them to oblivion. The marine plankton was decimated at the same time. Currently, rather more evidence favours the impact of a huge meteorite in the Yucatan Peninsula, Mexico, as the instrument of the dramatic crisis that reset the evolutionary clock. Its direct effects have been detected more widely in sedimentary rock successions around the world than in features that can be definitely attributed to the eruption of the Deccan Traps. Still, it is a remarkable temporal coincidence, and the eruption scenario is a hypothesis waiting in the wings.

It will come as no surprise to discover that the Deccan eruptions are yet another consequence of plate movements. Think back to the northward-'drifting' Indian peninsula and recall that it was not always where it is today. Remember that the world has been re-made, so to understand what happened sixty-six million years ago we have to reset the continental stage and shuffle the props. At the end of the Cretaceous the migrating Indian subcontinent passed over a 'hot spot'. As we saw in the Hawaiian chain, the heat source was stationary. The continent passed over it as a hand might pass over a blow-lamp. When it did so, the mantle plume injected its tholeiitic magma directly on to the continent with redoubled fury. This is one place where ocean and continent meet head on: piled up on the lighter continent, dark flows usually associated with the abyss transformed a part of the face of the earth, like a huge black blister. So much heat was dissipated that it has been suggested that there must have been a 'super-plume' to give birth to the traps, a torch from the mantle bigger by far than the Hawaiian example. But then the Indian plate continued on its way northwards towards its rendezvous with Asia, and left the plume, super or not, behind. The eruptions finished as suddenly as they had begun.

A final twist to the story is that there are some scientists who believe that the huge outpourings of lava, and hence heat energy, in the Deccan could not have been accomplished by normal earth processes alone. They ask: where did the extra energy come from to account for a 'super-plume'? One answer invokes those meteorite impacts. The energy imparted by such an extra-terrestrial interloper may, it is suggested, may have provided just the addition needed to induce the enormous lava outpourings; and since meteorites tend to arrive in clusters, the time equivalence between events in Yucatan and those in north-western India is no coincidence. The earth winced before a double blow. One meteorite left a crater in Mexico; the other provoked floods of basalt that gave the Hindu sculptors their stone and the Buddhist artists their canvas. Perhaps the stars painted on the ceilings of some of the Ajanta caves were strangely prescient.

The Deccan Traps are not unique, although the richness of their human assocations is without parallel. There are comparable massive outpourings of plateau basalts in several other places, forming untamed tracts of country. The Triassic age Siberian Traps are, if anything, even more extensive than those in India, but are remote and inaccessible. They may have erupted over only half a million years. The Columbia River Plateau in the north-western USA was erupted seventeen million years ago and occupies 130,000 square kilometres. The flows filled in an earlier mountainous topography, flooding and levelling former valleys with relentless masses of volcanic darkness. Something like 1500 metres of lava smothered this old landscape, with the effectiveness of a builder pouring in new concrete foundations over an old archaeological site. There may have been as many as a hundred separate flows. Present-day rivers are cutting back into the pile to spectacular effect along deep valleys; one day, the old landscape will once again be exhumed. The Snake River basalts in southern Idaho (50,000 square kilometres) are even younger, of Quaternary age. There are also extensive plateau basalts in Brazil, and even Antarctica. There are ocean floor flood basalts, too, where 'super-plumes' have poured out their effusions far from the eyes of mammal or dinosaur – like the Ontong Java Plateau in the west Pacific, 120 million years old, or those to the south of Madagascar. These rocks are a major feature on the face of the earth.

As to their antiquity, there are indications that these extrusive plateaux may have besmirched the face of the earth as long as there were plates to move. Many researchers are convinced that 'swarms' of basalt dykes dating to about 2.5 billion years ago, at the end of the Archaean, may have been feeders for vast, and now completely eroded flood basalts. In the deep Precambrian there would have been no forest to clothe them, nor any kind of vegetable cosmetic to conceal their darkness. They would have been rawly black, explicit stains from the depths smeared over the landscape. The old earth must have been blackened many times.

Granite is an unforgiving and ungenerous stone, hard to break, slow to decay. Granite does not flinch under the onslaught of the elements. It lends its name to things that are dauntless and immovable. The Granite Redoubt were the grenadiers of the Consular Guard at the Battle of Marengo, 14 June 1800, whose unyielding square formation stopped the Austrian advance and helped win northern Italy for Napoleon Bonaparte. Granite does not give way: granite features belong to the face that reveals no secrets. It lends authority to public buildings. Even those who know nothing about geology can recognize its solidity. It means business. Granite constructions seem to say, 'Here we stand, and here we stay.' It is oddly consoling to know that the bank holding your life savings is made of granite. On the other hand, you do not to expect granite to underlie gentle countryside. Seamus Heaney knew its properties:

> Granite is jagged, salty, punitive
> and exacting. *Come to me*, it says,
> *all you who labour and are burdened, I*
> *will not refresh you*. And it adds, *Seize*
> *the day*, And, *You can take me or leave me.*

Granite is abundant over the surface of the earth: moors and mountains, vast and inaccessible peaks in the Himalayas or the Andes, including some of the ultimate challenges for alpinists, along with monadnocks and inselbergs in Africa, and barrens and tors in Europe and America, all are the surface manifestations of this, the most obdurate geological underlay. After the Deccan Traps, one of the greatest of all basalt bodies, the granites of south-western England, form one of the least spectacular intrusions. Describing them is not perversity on my part. The granites of Devon and Cornwall are, as the tourist brochures relentlessly proclaim, 'steeped in history'. In the West Country you can understand how granite connects with scenery and tectonics – not to mention human character, history, and literature – better than almost anywhere. Dartmoor is often just another destination on the Heritage Trail, a brief stop on an inventory of historic Britain – the kind of tour from which most of the drama has been drained and the history condensed to a handful of brochures. But this does little justice to a wilderness that once struck such fear into the traveller that he would make his will before setting out to cross its dismal wastes. Even today, you have only to walk out of the sight of the nearest road, and hear the wind sweeping through the endless heather, punctuated by the chinking cry of the meadow pipit, while bold clouds scud across an enormous sky, to know that wildness endures here, for all the domestication of the beaten track. The granite moor still says: *You can take me or leave me.*

An ancient granite cross in a churchyard near St Michael's Mount, Cornwall. The roughened surface testifies to the weathering of centuries.

When you approach Dartmoor from the east its appearance is hardly dramatic. Off the new arterial roads there are narrow, beech-lined, sunken lanes, wedged between high banks. These were the ancient tracks into Dartmoor. In the spring, the hedge-banks are miniature botanical reserves, decked with bluebells and red campion, early purple orchids and greater stitchwort. It's like a patriotic flower show: red, white, and blue. Then you catch a view on the skyline of a low swell, with wide and unencumbered contours. This is the moorland, which is higher than it looks, and further away. It seems to take far longer than it should to reach the open skies. The twisting and turning lanes always seem to dodge off in a different direction as if reluctant to confront the bleakness ahead. Then you notice that the walls have changed. They now consist of pale, piled-up blocks: large and rectangular near the base, smaller near the top, and all fitted together in a kind of *ad hoc* jigsaw puzzle. Foxgloves sprout from the interstices, their pink spires always abuzz with bumble-bees when the sun shines; round leaves of pennywort slink in the cracks. These are walls constructed of granite blocks. Some of the walls might be a thousand years old.

After you cross the cattle grid you are on to the open moor. This is where diminutive tousled Dartmoor ponies acquired their hardiness. In the spring, the slopes on the moors can look almost black – even cheerless and oppressive. You could be forgiven for wondering if you were not, after all, looking at some kind of basalt flow, but it is the fine new growth of the ling that lends spurious volcanic heaviness to the moorland. Ling shoots are dark, with tiny leaves packed together against the harsh climate. Later in the year the same plant will wash the hillsides with millions of purple flowers. The heather family has learned the trick of thriving on poor soils almost anywhere in the world: we have already met a relative of ling on the raw volcanoes of Hawai'i, and the thin soil above the granite here is scarcely richer. Sheep pick delicately at fine-leaved grasses among the ling, white puffs of wooliness against the dark hillsides. Granite is used for almost everything out here. As well as the walls, vertical granite slabs are used as gateposts, whilst granite blocks have been employed for constructing dwellings since Neolithic times. Spinster's Rock, not far from Edwin Lutyens' grand granitic house, Castle Drogo, is a chambered tomb dating from about 3000 BC, with three uprights supporting a great horizontal slab. The whole granite intrusion is peppered with several thousand Bronze-Age 'hut circles' that are often marked by stones (there may have been wooden huts, too). In the 1970s the low field boundaries, known as reaves, were recognized for what they were. These unremarkable lines of stones, often capped by gorse bushes, are still used as farm and parish boundaries: a tough farmer at the edge of the moors today might still follow a line laid out by his Bronze-Age predecessor three thousand years ago. The farming habit endures, much like granite.

Stone circles and avenues are numerous over the moor, and isolated standing stones waiting like sentinels in the middle of a field, or by the roadside, are so common that you soon cease to remark on them. Here is a domesticated ancient history, lacking the grandeur of Stonehenge, perhaps, but giving a better sense of the density of occupation of land during the Bronze Age: this was no pioneer community, but a busy, thriving society. The people probably grew oats and beans and scoured the streams for tin. Grimspound is as impressive as Stonehenge in its own way, a stone structure with piled-up walls so thick it has been estimated they would have taken thirty-five man years to build. Dartmoor seems to have been more or less abandoned in Roman times, a process that continued into the Dark Ages. It has been suggested that the eruption of Krakatoa in AD 540 so badly affected the climate that many of the inhabitants of Cornwall emigrated to Brittany in order to avoid starvation. Whatever the cause, the moor was left to itself for almost a millennium. Medieval farmers returned after about AD 950. The long-houses that they built still survive in a few places, for granite walls do not readily tumble down. The population was denser then. Near Hound Tor, there is evidence of an abandoned village, only the low remnants of house walls remaining. In the few surviving long-houses granite slabs make up the lintels and the door jambs, and the walls are thickset against the winter winds. Granite slabs were also used for crossing rivers, which can be intimidating when in full flood. Clapper bridges are simple structures comprising a few piers that support large, flattish granite slabs, over which pedestrians and packhorses could pass. In medieval times there were many tracks across the moor where footpads preyed on lonely travellers. Where these ways crossed one another a stone cross was often erected, and they endure today, even if the tracks have disappeared, so you might come across one standing alone and miles from anywhere, mysterious and somewhat forlorn. More often, you will find one tucked in the corner of a churchyard or on a village green. The cross may be crudely carved, but its import is unmistakeable. Before churches were built, the holy site may just have been an enclosure containing a granite cross. These monuments are peculiarly moving: faith itself, they imply, will endure like granite.

The underlying rock reaches the surface at the high points of the moors: the tors. From afar, tors can look like crumbled castles or ruined pyramids. Close to, you discover extraordinary arrangements of piled-up blocks, sometimes almost teetering on the edge of collapse. It is almost plausible that they were thrown up by some neolithic Henry Moore, for, like good sculptures, tors have the interesting property of looking quite different according to the angle from which they are viewed: from this side an obelisk, perhaps, from the other a medieval keep. You do not have to be very imaginative to see a twelve-metre figure at Bowerman's Nose gazing out over the greener fields below, like a protective god. Combestone Tor rather resembles piled bales or coffins, some tipped over as if they had been dropped from the sky by a careless giant. Vixen's Tor was the legendary home of a witch. All the shapes were the product of natural weathering; they are what remains when the granite around has been removed by hundreds of thousands of years of wind and water. The cracks that define the blocks are joints in the granite, natural cracks. Only the most resistant blocks remain behind. All else is lost to the great cycles of earth history, whittled away by time. The shapes, however fantastical, are no more than the legacy of the whims of the elements.

When you get really close to a tor you realize that you are not seeing the rock at all. The pale grey colour that tints the surface of the granite is a lick of paint. The surface has been decorated with lichens. This poorest of pasture can still support a patina of growth. Lichens grow in patches; they run into one another so that you cannot tell where one patch ends and another begins. The rain that falls so freely in the west of England is all they need to sustain their growth, with a meagre mineral supplement from the rock that provides their home. Many are so tightly bound to the surface that you cannot even scrape them off with your fingernail: they grow partly within the rock. Most are pale in colour, which is why the granite looks white and smooth from a distance. Occasionally, an orange patch reveals a different species. I have seen granites decorated with lichens at eighty degrees north, and I don't doubt that lichens can survive in Antarctica. A symbiotic collaboration between fungus and algae, lichens are tougher than either partner. Look closely and you may see the little pads or cups that are their reproductive structures. Many lichen species grow more slowly than the creep of tectonic plates.

If you want to see the native rock, you must go to a quarry. There are plenty of disused quarries around Dartmoor. Granite makes good road metal, and it underlies the sleepers along many of the great railroads constructed in the nineteenth century. The tough felons locked up in Princetown Gaol were once obliged to break such ungrateful rocks as part of their punishment. The prison is still there, even if the rock-breaking has ceased. It is a steep-sided block looking like an old cotton mill, or a factory from the Industrial Revolution, rather than a gaol – a factory for the manufacture of hardened criminals, perhaps. Merrivale Quarry nearby now lies silent, but the plant that used to lift the granite blocks remains behind, rusting, resembling a collapsed, gargantuan spider. The hole from which blocks were extracted is now full of water, but you can see a cross-section through the granite in the face of the quarry. The whole mass is divided into great slabs by subtle cracks running parallel to the surface of the ground above and by others plunging vertically. The granite was originally a nearly homogeneous mass, with hydrostatic pressure equally distributed in all directions through it. As the aeons of erosion slowly stripped the top of the granite away, the balance was lost and the consequent stresses caused joints to develop. Thus you could say that the shape of the tor was already anticipated deep within the ground. The rusting hulk once moved blocks that had been freed by blasting; then they were cut with diamond saws. To make a facing stone, the cut surface was then mechanically polished to a shine.

Bits and pieces of polished stone lie all over the huge waste tips that surround the quarry. There are other, more exotic granites besides, so the place obviously acted as agent for buffing several types of rock. I recognized the reddish Scandinavian orbicular granite, which is easily identified by its large, circular feldspars, each surrounded by a green rim of altered mineral. The feldspars reacted with magmatic liquor with which they were surrounded to grow these neat fringes of crystals, so now they look like plums in a pudding. The commonest stone on the waste heaps is the local granite, however, mostly whitish and speckled, some blocks pale pinkish. The dominant colour follows that of the orthoclase feldspar that makes up the bulk of the rock. Sections through these big, white prismatic crystals are well displayed on the slabs and show apparently random orientation. It was recognized from the early days of scientific geology that the large crystals proved that the granite magma cooled slowly, at depth within the earth's crust, to allow such a coarse fabric to develop. The largest crystals may be up to seven inches long. There are also crystals of plagioclase feldspar. According to the British Geological Survey, the Dartmoor granite was emplaced as an intrusion, having risen from a depth of 17.5 kilometres (ten or twelve miles). If the plateau basalts were instant scabs on the face of the earth, granites were slow oozings from its deep contusions. The slabs also show clear patches between the feldspars, without clear crystal shape; this is quartz – silica – which fills the gaps between the larger, milky feldspar crystals. As for the black specks, they are probably dark biotite mica. This is a softer mineral than the others in granite's igneous jigsaw; they often pull away at the surface of the polished slabs, making tiny pockmarks in the otherwise flawless complexions of the elegant facing stones that are used as 'skins' to clad buildings constructed of concrete and steel. Even granite can be a cosmetic.

If you want to see how slowly granite succumbs to the elements, look at one of the ancient crosses. It has been standing for a thousand years, yet still retains its shape. Run your fingers over the surfaces, and they are rough – not the crumbly texture of lichen, but something altogether coarser. Irregular lumps protrude from the surface. These are quartz crystals. Centuries of weathering have left these crystals standing proud as the other minerals around them have preferentially worn away. This is the extent of weathering over the time since the medieval serf system faded, the moor was abandoned, and machines that could cut granite to a polish were invented – just a roughening to the touch. Look in the little rills that drain the moors and you will see something similar. Tiny bits of granite, but mostly quartz, form a crunchy stream bed. This is the waste of the moors. The feldspar will rot. The quartz will edge its way seawards over millennia, tumbled downhill during times of flood, but it will endure. The sandy beaches near Padstow, so popular with surfers, will gather the debris. At some time in the future a sedimentary sandstone will incorporate all the silica grains, and then it, too, will be elevated above the sea and eroded. A trillion grains or two might survive again, only to enter into yet another geological cycle. This is endurance. The longevity of quartz is reminiscent of the words of the hymn:

A thousand ages in Thy sight
Are but an evening gone . . .

Dartmoor is part of a still greater batholith. The same granite mass extends westwards to Bodmin Moor and St Austell, and thence to Land's End, where it forms a mighty bulwark against the still mightier Atlantic Ocean. It extends beyond the mainland to the Isles of Scilly, where the early daffodils grow. Radiometric dates tell us this had happened by 290 million years ago. Arthur Holmes portrayed the whole mass as if it were a vast plutonic whale whose back broke the surface in a few places. Its shape is rather longer and thinner than that of a typical whale; but you can, if you wish, view the folded

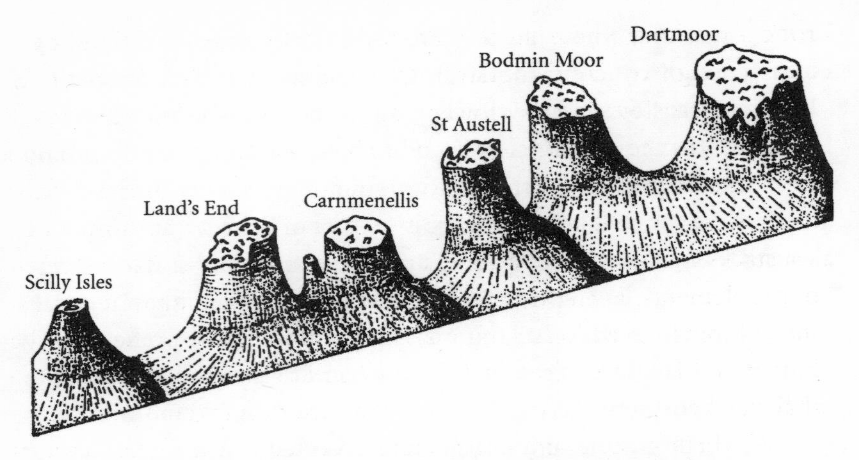

Even bigger than it seems: Arthur Holmes' portrayal of the subterranean continuity of the Variscan batholith in south-west England. The batholith 'breaks the surface' periodically; in another 100 million years it may be exhumed entirely.

sedimentary rocks that surround and overlie the mass as born on the back of a hidden granitic leviathan.

What should have been one of Britain's greatest wild places at Land's End has been turned into a theme park. The drama of land and sea, with waves heaving and sucking at the obdurate cliffs, is played out only a few yards away from a snack bar. Zennor, on the north coast a few miles away, is a much better place to observe the confrontation between erosion and granite. Zennor is a medieval hamlet and has changed little: it still comprises church and farm and few houses. A bowl (granite, of course) is displayed there in which vinegar was placed during the plague years to sterilize money that had to pass between the infected village and the outside world. The pub is called the Tinner's Arms, and there are the relics of mines nearby. The road shies away from the sea along this coast, so you have to walk along an ancient walled path to see it. When I was there the hillsides bore pools of bluebells. The granite plunges sheer to the sea, or else the cliffs are buffered by a zone of huge fallen boulders. Running along the boundary between cliffs and sea there is a blackened zone fifteen metres high – another kind of lichen painting the rock – marking where the winter storms batter the land. The sea is clear enough on a sunny day to see the sandy sea-floor, the long legacy of erosion. Jackdaws and stonechats busy themselves among the gorse that covers the steep slopes. Higher still, the granite emerges from the springy sea-turf and yellow-flowered gorse in pallid or greenish crags. Off the coast, outriders of granite form steep-sided sea stacks that provide a kind of advance guard against the onslaught of the elements. Even on a calm day the waves smash foaming against the columns, greedily seeking out the joints, the weaknesses that lie hidden in the fabric of the rock. The sea seeks to make low everything that has had the temerity to rise above it: it is the great leveller.

Where hot, light granite magma rose deep within the ancient mountain belt that once traversed south-west England, it baked and altered the sedimentary rocks surrounding it. The magma also bodily engulfed chunks of these folded rocks. The zone of thermal alteration around a granite is known as a metamorphic aureole: in Devon and Cornwall this can be as much as four miles wide. You can expect a metamorphic effect upon all the slates of Devonian or Carboniferous age that surround the granite masses. St Michael's Mount is a little boss of granite off the south coast of Cornwall not far from Penzance. It is spectacular when seen from afar: a conical island with a castle perched on its craggy apex. It is almost too romantic to be true. At high tide it is cut off from the mainland and a ferryman takes you across, to disembark in its own granite-walled harbour. At low tide a causeway is exposed, enabling you, rather more prosaically, to walk back to the mainland. The whole island, with its cobbled harbour backed by pretty houses, has been taken over by the National Trust. The dominating granite castle, seat of the St Aubyn family, is everything you expect such a building to be, with thick walls, battlements, an old chapel, and a dizzying view out to sea. It seems to grow out of the rock, and indeed it does, for the building had to accommodate itself to the profile of its granite foundations. Life was much tougher here in the past. Where tended and wooded gardens now flank the heights, a dairy herd formerly provided essential milk and cheese and were pastured on bleak hillsides. The castle started as a Benedictine monastery; after becoming a fortified manor it was sacked and retaken several times. Bleakness can be clothed in trees, but granite cannot be modified so readily. Towards the top of intrusions, however, their cusps may fracture. Just below the castle entrance you can see swarms of parallel veins of quartz cutting through the granite, filling such fractures. They make white stripes running over the surface of the rocky steps, worn smooth by hundreds of years of tramping boots. And a few feet from the granite itself, behind the old dairy, there is an exposure of the metamorphosed country rock, the rock into which the granite was intruded – a brown, crumbly outcrop ('hornfels') that could not contrast more obviously with the granite above you on the hillside. If the tide is low you can examine other altered rocks on either side of the causeway. Similar rocks are better displayed around St Ives, the impossibly picturesque resort and artist's colony on the north-western edge of the Land's End granite. These rocks are spotted with cordierite, a mineral that grew within the slates as they were heated by the granite intrusion, a transformation *in situ*, an alchemy of the underworld. Twisty quartz veins are abundant, writhing through the rock as pale wisps. Pebbles of the same material can be found in rock pools, white as pigeon's eggs.

All around Cornwall there are old chimneys. They arise improbably out of the sides of gorse-clad river valleys or stand alone on the moors. These mark the sites of mines – 'wheals' in Cornish. Many of them were formerly rich in tin, and some were rich in copper as well. Several other metals – silver, tungsten, antimony – have been mined at one time or another. Most scholars believe that the classical Greek name Cassiterides – the 'tin islands' – refers to the Scilly Islands and Cornwall: cassiterite, tin oxide, from the same linguistic root, is the common ore of this vauable metal. The Veneti are said to have bartered for tin and sold it on to the Phoenicians. Bronze, of course, is an alloy of copper and tin. Nearly four thousand years ago the Bronze-Age inhabitants of Dartmoor eagerly extracted the tin ore from the beds of streams that concentrated it. The smelting of tin ore was high technology at the time. Nor did the practice of looking for reworked tin ore in stream beds die out. The eighteenth-century 'streamers' followed the course of former stream beds,* often now buried beneath younger river terraces. But even by Roman times miners had learned to pursue the booty nearer to its source: veins – or lodes – that traversed the country rock surrounding the granite intrusions, or within the upper parts of the intrusion itself. The charmingly named Ding Dong mine in the Land's End Peninsula has been claimed as a Roman survivor. There are dozens of such lodes and many of them follow faults or other fractures in the country rock, which provided preferential passage for the hot fluids that laid down the valuable minerals. The fluids were derived from the latest stages of the intrusion; the lodes within the granite itself are often found along joints, so it must have already solidified. The majority of lodes are described as 'hydrothermal' deposits, a technical term that is unusually self-explanatory ('hot water'). Often they are layered with different mineral products, like a vertical club sandwich. There are almost as many chimney-stacks as there are lodes.

Eighteenth- and early nineteenth-century wheals have a melancholy, romantic feel in ruin that they doubtless lacked when they were working. Wheal Betsy on the western edge of the Dartmoor granite sits on a hillside on one side of a valley, a steeply rectangular building with gaping windows and a chimney adjacent. It marks an ancient tin site that was redeveloped in 1806 and ran successfully for seventy years. It was originally worked by water power, but in 1868 the present building was erected to house the famous Trevithick Cornish beam engine, which did all the necessary pumping and grinding and crushing. Such engines were the work-horses of the Industrial Revolution. The building somehow looks much older. It is built of the local Culm – slabs of slaty material that make up the country rock in those parts. As always, the top of the chimney-stack is finished off with bricks; I imagine the stone could not be trimmed

* These were probably the beds of rivers that received the products of erosion of the granite – and concentrated the tin ore – during the Pleistocene ice age. Dartmoor escaped direct ice cover, but a permafrost climate and exaggerated weathering probably served particularly to enrich these ancient stream beds. A one-ounce gold nugget was once discovered in the Carnon valley.

with sufficient precision. You can still pick up bits of quartz rock containing glinting black ore from the edges of the grassy waste heaps. On the northern Cornish coast, Wheal Coates, near St Agnes, teeters close to the cliff edge, surrounded by gorse and sea-turf. Ridges in the vegetation mark the courses of medieval open-cast workings. It is a challenge to imagine the wheal in 1881, when there were 138 people employed here; the clanking of machinery must have drowned out the sound of the surf breaking against the cliffs far below. The Towanroath pumping station drained a 600-foot shaft – the tin ore was actually chased out under the sea. It is difficult to conceive of worse working conditions: the cramped tunnels, the weight of rock and sea above, looming but unconsidered. There were accidents to contend with, and silicosis. The consolation of religion was of the bleak variety signalled by mean, grey chapels, which can be found on the edges of many villages. The last working tin mine in Cornwall (indeed in Europe), at South Crofty, closed in 1998, so ending a tradition that had endured for two millennia. Who knows if the products of the hot fluids linked with granite will ever be sought again? With the closure of the mines went names that would once have been as familiar to the miners as those of their household pets. Near Basset, there were Theaker's Lode and Paddon's Lode, Doctor's Shaft and Marriot's Shaft, and the Great Flat Lode: all forgotten now, covered by gorse, hardly visible even to the buzzards wheeling above the abandoned workings.

Granite intrusions are found in mountain belts. They, too, follow the bidding of the plates. They appear at the centre of those most dramatic upheavals of the crust where one plate collides with another: they are the sternest legacy of the tectonic cycle on the continents. The Cornish granite is but a ground-down stump from the great Variscan chain that stretched eastwards through Europe at the end of the Palaeozoic Era. From a beginning in the Permian, we know it took nearly 150 million years for the granite to be deeply excavated by erosion. Some of its most characteristic minerals appear in sediments of Cretaceous age lying to the east of Dartmoor. This English pluton is now among the least spectacular of granites, for all its historical resonance. Greater granites lie elsewhere in the British Isles: the mass of the Donegal intrusion in Ireland; or the Cairngorms in the Highlands of Scotland, a granitic heart within the Caledonides. Carved by the glaciers of the Pleistocene ice age, the Cairngorms are still rawly gouged: it will take millions of years to reduce these mountains to domestic proportions. Glaciated granites make fearsome vertical rock faces: Mont Blanc in the Alps, or the sheerest cliffs of El Capitan in the Yosemite National Park, California. Climbers delight in the meagre cracks offered by such rock faces; those who suffer from vertigo can only wince at the mere thought of tackling them. Doubtless, new challenges still await brave or foolhardy alpinists on granite peaks in the Himalayas. There are granites in the heart of the Appalachians, and we have met them already in their northward continuation, the 'barrens' of Newfoundland, whose name so well describes the scenery they produce. The Tatra Mountains of Slovakia are 'barrens' in the heart of Europe. The greatest series of intrusions of them all forms the core of the Andes. Massive granites extend discontinuously along the heights of the mountain chain all the way from Tierra del Fuego almost to Panama; they cover something like 465,000 square kilometres. The batholiths of western North America are hardly less considerable: in Alaska, British Columbia, Idaho, the mighty Sierra Nevada, the Peninsular Ranges of California, granites comprise several millions of cubic kilometres of the most intransigent rock, here of dominantly Cretaceous age. These granite ranges parallel the confrontation of the Pacific plate with the western continental Americas. On the opposite side of South America the Sugarloaf at Rio de Janiero, Brazil, rises like a massive, stuck-up thumb from the eroded gneisses that surround it: the mountain looks almost organic, as if it had grown upwards like a monstrous termite mound, yet it, too, is the product of granite's obstinacy in the face of the elements. Go to the other side of the world, and Mount Kinabalu, on Borneo, is a bald eminence rising from lush and dangerous jungle; it is flanked by cliffs a thousand metres high, broken only by the occasional gulley.

At its summit it carries a few jagged peaks and weird, lobed, weathered protuberances, like malignant growths. Kinabalu is a surreal island of bareness amidst a green sea of tropical profusion. The fiercest, strangest, least tractable features on the face of the earth belong to granite.

But even these proud peaks will be humbled in time. There are ancient granites in the oldest parts of the earth that have been brought low. In central Africa, they form low swells, exfoliated layer by layer as if the granite were the sloughed skin of the earth itself. Tropical weathering peels off the outer layers of granite blocks as if they were onion skins. The granite is reduced to heaps of reddish rounded boulders. These often provide the only feature to relieve the endless savannah, the last remnants of mountains fifty times older than the Alps.

The durability of granite is a gift that has served to preserve the monuments of ancient human cultures. Wherever it has been used as a building stone, the structures survive – whether in the architecture of the Near East, Egypt, and South Africa, or in the pyramids of the Mayan civilization in Mexico, or the temples of Nepal. Steles made of it endure. Granite has outlasted the pomp of despots and recorded the faces of gods whose names have been forgotten. Its hardness and coarseness impose limits on its tractability for sculpture. The 'rose syenite'* of Syene – the Greek name for Aswan – is famous for its use in the sculptures of Pharaonic Egypt at Luxor and was also used in the construction of the obelisks at Karnak. The material itself imposes a certain gentleness of contour and limits the detail that can be portrayed. In some respects this is a virtue, for it obliges the artist to consider essentials of form. The grotesque visages of Mayan deities are the more terrifying because the sculptor has been compelled to simplify and formalize. Thus sculpture is constrained by geology. Much more detail can be imparted to the limestones and sandstones used by medieval sculptors of Romanesque churches and

* There are many varieties of granite, with different names according to the detailed mineralogy of the rock. Syenite is another coarse-grained igneous rock that lacks the abundant free quartz found in the typical granite. Confusingly, the 'rose syenite' is a granite, despite the name.

cathedrals for gargoyles and leaf tracery, but time has served most of them badly. Noses crumble, roses rot. The Sphinx is proof of the same deficiency in the Nile Valley. Marble – metamorphosed limestone – serves the virtuoso chiseller best, especially the white marble of Carrara, which can record every fold of a garment or the delicate swell of the least muscle on a torso. Greek and Roman sculptors sought marble out. How much, one wonders, would Michelangelo have achieved had he been obliged to use only granite?

Abraham Gottlob Werner, Professor at the Mining Academy at Freiberg in Germany at the end of the eighteenth century, taught that granites were part of the *Urgebirge*, the first deposits precipitated from a primeval sea that once covered the earth. Younger rocks, he proclaimed, including all the ones we would now recognize as sedimentary, overlay them. Granites played a part in disproving such theories, not least because they could be seen to *cut through* sedimentary and metamorphic formations – and must, therefore, be younger than the country rock they intruded. Here is how the pioneer experimentalist James Hall of Edinburgh described intrusions in 1790, not many years after James Hutton had outlined his ideas about their fiery origin: 'Wherever the junction of the granite with the schists was visible, veins of the former . . . were to be seen running into the latter and pervading it in all directions, so as to put it beyond all doubt, that the granite in these veins, and consequently of the great body itself . . . must have flowed in a soft or liquid state into its present position.' By the time Charles Lyell made his journey around the Bay of Naples the deep igneous origin of granites was established. But questions remained: why were they associated with mountain belts, ancient and modern? And where did the magma from which they crystallized originate? How did they arrive in their present position?

Eduard Suess appreciated the significance of granites in mountain belts: he had seen splendid examples in Switzerland, where he had learned his geological trade. He recognized that they were not, as it were, bottomless, but were intruded as masses into the deep crust late in the mountain-building cycle. He wrote that 'they lie imbedded

When granite veins merge into gneiss: migmatites on a wave cut a platform in Precambrian rocks on the Baltic Shield.

in older stratified rocks; their form is of large irregular loaves or cakes'. He was right: geophysical evidence can now be used to 'map' the bases of intrusions. Suess also recognized that in places he could see how overlying strata were baked and metamorphosed by the granite, which is 'therefore younger than the overlying strata'. But he also went on to say: 'It is absolutely necessary that the injection of a granitic mass, possessing so high a temperature as to be capable of altering the surrounding rocks, *should be preceded by the formation of a corresponding cavity*.' As usual, Suess' italics indicate that this was a particularly important point and show that he believed strongly that the granite was intruded into a kind of welcoming space that opened up before it.

It is now timely to return briefly to Newfoundland, to recall some of the rocks in the central Mobile Belt. This is part of an ancient mountain belt, the Appalachian chain, stripped down to its innards by millions of years of erosion. There were granites there, as there should be. But there were also rocks – migmatites – in which pods and folded veins of granite intermingled with banded gneisses, which are high-grade metamorphic rocks. It was confusing: some of the rocks cropping out among the stunted conifers seemed more granite than gneiss, with darker wisps alone betraying a kind of gneissic memory, but in other places veins of true granite cut through what was indubitably banded gneiss. There was a transformation happening in front of you. Gneiss seemed to 'dissolve' before your eyes and merge into granite. Then, magma generated by this process in turn squeezed out into adjacent gneisses – or so it seemed. This area of central Newfoundland was evidently exposed to erosion so deep that it penetrated into the tectonic crucible where granite is born. Exactly how this birth happened proved to be controversial.

In both editions of Arthur Holmes' textbook there is reference to a process he termed 'granitisation'. This is the conversion of gneisses and other rocks into granite in the solid state and *in situ* by a kind of wave of transformation. He, too, recognized the importance of deep erosion into the interior of the crust, where 'we can see the granitised rocks of former ages and the crystalline rocks associated with them, all arrested at the particular stages they happened to have reached when the processes of metamorphism and granitization ceased to operate'; or, to put it simply: rocks frozen in time and trauma. The transformation of other rocks into granite had been suggested by J. J. Sederholm, Director of the Geological Survey of Finland, who had studied appropriately ancient Precambrian rocks of the Baltic Shield. He had proposed that the changes happened 'as if by magic', as he said, when a transforming agent he termed *ichor* circulated through the rocks. To invoke the name of the ethereal fluid that flowed like blood through the veins of the gods was a suitable way of signalling the mysterious properties of granite generation. Holmes opted for the less classical though equally insubstantial term 'emanation' to describe what had been modified to 'rock-transforming gaseous solutions' in his textbooks. Moving fronts of these 'emanations' migrated through the rocks deep within mountain belts effecting their wondrous work, transforming gneisses and schists into what would eventually become the substance of unscalable cliffs and bleak uplands. The more extreme granitisers thought that all this could happen without the necessity of invoking magma at all.

Holmes adopted these transubstantiationalist views on the origin of granites because they were also those of his strong-willed second wife, Doris Reynolds. In 1931, while Holmes was Professor of Geology at Durham University, he met Doris on a geological field trip to the Scottish volcanic island of Ardnamurchan. Before two years had elapsed Holmes had secured Doris a job in his own geology department, sitting across from him on the other side of the same large desk. An affair of this kind would scarcely be worth remarking in a modern university department, but in the 1930s it was unusual enough to be something of a scandal, the more remarkable because Arthur Holmes was, by nature, unusually level headed. Holmes and Reynolds were married after his first wife's premature death in 1938. Doris Reynolds had to be a tough-minded and determined woman to prosper in what was in those days an overwhelmingly male profession (which, regrettably, it still is). You disagreed with her at your peril. She became an ardent, even extreme, adherent of granitisation, and Holmes dutifully followed suit.

There was, however, an opposing school, headed by an outspoken Canadian petrologist, Norman Bowen. This group has been labelled the 'magmatists', which is self-explanatory. They claimed that granite had indeed solidified from a liquid magma, and that magma had been generated by the partial melting of gneiss under sufficiently high temperatures at sufficient depth in the crust. Like the granitisers, they could point to field evidence to support their point of view – it was just different evidence. Places like Newfoundland could be used to support both views, depending on which bit of outcrop you examined. The debate between the two schools soon heated up to magmatic temperatures. One of the problems the granitisers had to account for was the loss of certain elements, especially calcium, iron, and magnesium, in the transformation of a typical gneiss into a typical granite. These are the elements characteristic of 'basic' rocks (as opposed to 'acidic' ones, like granite). The granitisers said that these elements migrated away from the freshly transmogrified granite in what they termed a 'basic front' – a kind of fugitive chemical miasma spreading away from the growing granite behind. Bowen described this idea as, on the contrary, 'a basic *af*front to the geologic fraternity' – not a great pun, admittedly, and with a nasty dig, intentional or not, at the sex of his principal opponent. Reynolds returned that Bowen was 'accusing Nature of an intentional break of politeness'. Bowen's friends in the United Kingdom included Professor H. H. Read, who became Reynolds' implacable opponent. He speculated that the 'basic' elements might, after all, remain behind as a kind of residue as granite generation proceeded, and in 1951 he added punning insult to injury by writing, 'I suggest for discussion that some basic fronts may be better interpreted as *Basic Behinds* – a somewhat indelicate term, I admit, but one which expresses the possibility that we may here be dealing with subtraction rocks [i.e. gneiss minus 'basics' = granite].' Doris Reynolds coped with this kind of antagonism in spirited fashion when the Granite Controversy, as it came to be known, was played out in the scientific meeting-rooms of London. As she wrote, she bought herself 'one of those high hats like a witch. I thought that if I kept that on at the meeting I could not be overlooked.' Attitudes had hardened, like granite itself. As Seamus Heaney said, *you can take me or leave me.*

I cannot report that Reynolds triumphed in the battle between miasma and magma. The crucial work in settling the issue was the outcome of improvements in the design of experimental equipment, notably, O. F. Tuttle's cold seal pressure-vessel. The mineral ingredients of rocks could be 'cooked' under pressure; it should then be possible to see under what conditions they melted – became a magma, if you like. Bowen teamed up with Tuttle to study how a 'granitic mixture' of feldspars and quartz behaved under conditions of temperature and pressure like those in the deep crust. Previous experiments under low pressure had only produced a thick, sticky magma at excessively high temperatures. The crucial added ingredient was water. When the mixture was heated with the addition of the aqueous phase, the temperatures and pressures at which a granite melt resulted were lowered considerably, quite consistent with a presumed origin deep within mountain belts. It was shown that natural granite magma should be the first to 'melt out'* under the ambient conditions at depth if there were pore water present. Since water is well-nigh ubiquitous in the crust, this was not an unreasonable assumption. To put it the other way round, if rocks such as gneisses were progressively subjected to higher temperatures and pressures – and this might happen as the crust thickened where two continents collided – the first product that would 'melt out' as magma would have the composition of a granite. Granite magma sweats out in the profound depths of the underworld. The swirling migmatites of Newfoundland, like those that Sederholm had studied in Scandinavia, were granites in the process of their birth, 'frozen' just as Holmes had described it. Like many births, it was a messy business; hence the bewildering arrays of texture and detail – some rocks were already nearly granite, or they were gneisses that had been invaded by granite sweated out elsewhere; other rocks again were neither one thing nor the other. Deep flux flourished.

By 1965, the outlines of the process of granite magma generation were clear. Progressively refined experiments in partially melting rocks continue to this day. As we have seen before in this history of the earth, few issues of geological truth are ever clearly black and white. Doris Reynolds may have been wrong about her mysterious transforming emanations, but much recent research has been focused on the details of how elements move through rocks at the sub-

* The partial melting of the original rock is known as anatexis. There is actually a set of different pressure-temperature conditions under which melting will occur – for example higher pressure might require lower temperature. These stability fields are conventionally plotted on to pressure/temperature (P/T) graphs.

microscopic scale. In a sense, the granitising spirit lives on. As for Arthur Holmes, his association with the discredited theory did his reputation no good at all in the latter phase of his career. This was hardly just, since he was a great geologist with many other achievements to his credit.

It should be added here that granite magma can also be generated from much more basic, oceanic-type lava. This can occur by a continuation of the process of evolution within an oceanic magma chamber, as described previously, whereby the heavier, basic (and darker) minerals progressively crystallize out and 'push' the remaining liquor more and more towards granitic composition. It is rather like making applejack: fermented cider is buried in the freezing ground and as the ice crystallizes out little by little the remaining liquor becomes enriched in alcohol. This process of refinement and magma generation may occur in relation to the subduction of an oceanic slab. The final granite rock may look similar in the hand-specimen to its counterpart generated by the partial melting of gneissose, continental rocks, but its deeper chemistry betrays its origins. The isotope ratios of rare elements (specifically, strontium $^{87}Sr/^{86}Sr$) are not altered by the refinement process and give different signatures for the granites with continental, as opposed to oceanic, origin. This method proved that the large batholiths of California were the product of partial melting of the continental crust – a scientific point that had been in dispute in a place where continent and ocean approach one another so closely. The greatest granites are mostly of this continental kind.

What, now, of Suess' contention that granites must fill in cavities already present for the reception of magma? Clearly, granites like those in Devon and Cornwall had intruded as a mass – and one that was still hot enough to bake surrounding strata in the country rock and give rise to all those lodes filled with hydrothermal ores. The magma also engulfed lumps of the rocks through which they intruded. It seems evident that huge quantities of magma, once it had been sweated out at great depth, moved upwards through the crust. Detailed studies of large batholiths have shown that there were often several pulses of granitic magma. The reason for the upward movement turns out to be rather simple. The hot granitic magma is less dense than the other crustal rocks through which it passes: it rises through heat and sheer lack of weight. Far from entering ready-made cavities, it insinuates itself into the emerging mountain belt. The process resembles what happens when a lava lamp – that iconic 1960s *objet d'art* – is switched on. A heat source at the base of the lamp sufficiently alters the density of an oil layer to make it rise as a weird plume through the overlying liquor; all the materials are rather viscous at this stage, so the process takes some time. For the rise of the granite magma, millions of years must be allowed. Nonetheless, the shapes of such 'diapirs' can be almost as remarkable as those cooked up in the lava lamp. Now you will understand the precipitous oddity of the Sugarloaf at Rio de Janiero.

Like the lava lamp, the generation of granite demands a source of energy. Granites do not rise up from the depths to disrupt the chalklands of England, the Paris Basin, or the Texas plains. These are all areas underlain – at least near the surface – by undisturbed sedimentary rocks. Granite eschews the quiet, uneventful regions of the earth. For the source of heat is subduction: granites are the sweat of earth movements. Whether along the Pacific coast of the Americas, or through the Alpine to Himalayan mountain chains, or in the ancient Caledonides, or in Suess' 'Hercynides', granites rise to dissipate the energy that plates produce by their marginal friction. Particularly where continent collides with continent, the crust is thickened enormously. Nappe piles upon nappe. The concatenation of sediments and volcanic rocks yields a deformed and packed pile sandwiched between approaching continents. The pile may bulge downwards deeply towards the mantle to form what have been termed 'roots' beneath the growing mountain chain, the image perhaps being more appropriate to dentistry than to a tree: mountainous molars have downward extensions into the tissues of the earth. While this happens the temperature gradient can be depressed for a long while, pushed downwards along with the folded sedimentary pile to a region of high pressure at depth. But, given time, the heat flow from the interior of the earth will be restored. The isotherms will bounce back (though 'bounce' is probably too enthusiastic a word for the leisurely progress of geological time). Then, the deep alchemy can proceed further, as additional heat sweats out the granite magma from the already metamorphosed rocks, ready to mass up and rise as plutons through the developing mountain chain. Naturally, this rising body will cut across the earlier folding and distortion that accompanied the thickening of the tectonic pile. Granites are a consequence, a spin-off, a late expression of tectonism and subduction. Given the chemistry of rocks, the physics of their melting, and the temperatures and pressures involved in tectonism at plate boundaries, granites are almost a logical conclusion to a dialectic of the earth. They arise inevitably in mountain belts. Once emplaced, they may themselves be subject to late phases of orogenic activity: sliced or thrust, or even squeezed so hard as to be metamorphosed anew. Nothing, not even this proud rock, is exempt from the mill of the earth.

Both Suess and Holmes realized that the thickened, 'rooted' mass of a mountain chain would ineluctably present itself to the blast of erosion. Such a concentration of light continental rocks as is found in mountain belts would be compelled to rise as a result of isostatic readjustment. As it did so, the resulting mountains have to enter the realm of ice and wind, which diligently do their elemental duty to render the mountains low again. The more the weather slaves away and succeeds in removing rock, the more further isostatic adjustment will successively deliver the depths into the maw of the storm. Deep in the underworld, this flexure of the lithosphere is accommodated by the creeping flow of the underlying plastic rocks of the mantle, which moves as a viscous fluid. I have tried various homely metaphors, like depressing a big crouton on a bowl of pea soup, or plastic ducks in hot baths, to try to make this process more transparent; but the conditions at depth are so different from those in saucepan and bathroom that a bald statement of what goes on will have to suffice. As erosion proceeds, the granite's turn for exposure will eventually arrive, its rounded bulk exhumed from its seat in the

Deeply weathered feldspars in granite is the source of china clay. Cornish clay pit in the early years of the twentieth century.

folded pile. This rock will certainly give erosion something to chew on, but frost is eventually able to shatter it, mercilessly prising it open along its joints. If the granite forms a high redoubt, glaciers will grow upon it. As the ice-sheet creeps downhill it will use boulders of granite entrained within it to scour and gouge the surface beneath it, forcing the rock to conspire in its own destruction. In the end, the forces of erosion will win: they always do. Quartz sand will pass onward into the next cycle of the earth. The ground-down granite will end up as no more than a gentle slope topped by remarkable boulders, standing as witness to their strange journey from deep in the earth's crust.

Where granite has rotted deeply without eroding away, the feldspars may be converted to deposits of the white clay mineral known as kaolinite. This is the china clay used for making fine porcelain. All around the Cornish town of St Austell there are what look like snowy terraces, or perhaps small white volcanoes. They look unnatural; from afar you might think they were made of piled salt. They are in fact the waste heaps from the china-clay pits. The feldspars in the granite of this area have been converted wholesale to white clay. A number of the great chasms from which the clay was extracted remain. One is now the site of the imaginative ecological experiment, the Eden Project, which has reproduced various natural ecosystems inside huge geodesic domes. There is something rather wonderful about growing a tropical jungle in an old clay pit: it is boldly traducing the poverty of granite soils. The clay, though, was always productive in other ways. The very best plates and vases were manufactured from this startlingly white clay. Josiah Spode developed the techniques for making bone china in the mid eighteenth century, but the fine goods were not made on the spot. Instead, the clay was transported all the way to the Potteries, the region around Stoke-on-Trent where the great names in ceramics had their factories. The trade was a stimulus for the construction of canals, which could move great loads, cheaply. Wedgwood, Spode, and the Mintons were enthusiastic experimenters, always coming up with new pottery recipes and new glazes. The delicate blue-and-white ware manufactured by Spode in the early 1800s show rural scenes, or illustrate fables, or reproduce an embellished Orient, with feathery trees and borders of frothy foliage. It is ironic that the exquisite height of refinement in ceramics was grounded ultimately in granite, that coarse and implacable rock, whose natural sculptural expression is the tough stone cross that faces out the centuries in the bleak wastes of the Great Moor.

9

Fault Lines

Some people love Los Angeles. They love its endlessness, the way one conurbation merges with another along freeways that promise more liberation than they ever deliver. They love the sidewalks lined so regularly with teetering palm trees like overgrown fly-whisks. They love the unbridled eclecticism of the prosperous villas, where Spanish haciendas combine with Corinthian columns, and maybe a soupçon of Elizabeth mock-Tudor, all flanked by implausibly verdant, perpetually-irrigated lawns of coarse grass, upon which citrus trees seem always to be either in flower or in fruit. Downtown L.A. may be like any other towering downtown of glass and steel, but away from the commercial centre there are places that are unlike anywhere else. Venice Beach is to narcissism what Rome is to the priesthood. It's a place of impeccable pectorals and toned tans, but it is also a town with one of the best bookshops I have ever visited, where it is possible to sip a leisurely *cappuccino* and discover the meaning of 'chill out'. In older towns like Riverside there are still distinctive hotels, art-deco villas, and orange groves that have escaped redevelopment, that allow you to understand how enticing this part of California must have been before everything became joined together, and the drive-in mall homogenized everyday commerce.

California has a reputation for being laid-back, and the warm climate does indeed produce a kind of dreaminess in the visitor. The smog-filled air backing up on the built-up coastal plain against the San Gabriel Mountains contributes to an unreal, impressionistic haze. A little more experience quickly proves that this is where a

Mediterranean climate mingles with the North American work ethic, and the people that I know in L.A. are every bit as frenetic as New Yorkers, only in Hawaiian shirts. It seems entirely appropriate that the microchip revolution was nurtured here. I was slightly disappointed to find that Häagen-Dazs ice-cream was manufactured in a huge factory in greater L.A. I had naïvely imagined that it was mixed by Flemish maidens in cowsheds. Movies, microchips, and chocolate fudge sundae are all made on a global scale here. When I paid a working visit to UCLA, on its incomparably well-furnished campus, it was humiliating to find that I was always the last person at the desk every morning. I may well have been the first to leave every evening. The art of being Californian, it seems, is to cultivate a loose-limbed insouciance while secretly working away like a frantic ant.

This curious combination of devil-may-care and industry may be a response to living in the shadow of doom. California is one of the least stable parts of the earth. This is the state with the shakes. All that beavering away in the pursuit of fame and the dollar could be regarded as diverting attention from tectonic truth. There is no S. Gennaro to intercede, as there is in Naples. There is only a kind of collective amnesia, produced by keeping your eyes down and your pockets full. Suddenly the ground might start to heave, and the porticoes of the most extravagant villas will come tumbling down, the sprinklers on the lawns will dry up, and automobiles on the freeway will be tossed about like dry beans on a sieve. This will happen when there is an earthquake; and an earthquake will happen when there is sudden movement on a geological fault.

If you had to ask the man in the street to name just one geological structure, he would probably say: the San Andreas Fault. Indeed, in the minds of some people, it is almost synonymous with geology. There are other great faults – like the Anatolian Fault that has wrought periodic havoc in Turkey – but it is the San Andreas that has somehow entered common consciousness as symbol of the power of the earth: the great shaker.

Faults are breaks in the earth's crust. Many of them are brittle fractures, which happen when rocks snap. Most rigid materials break

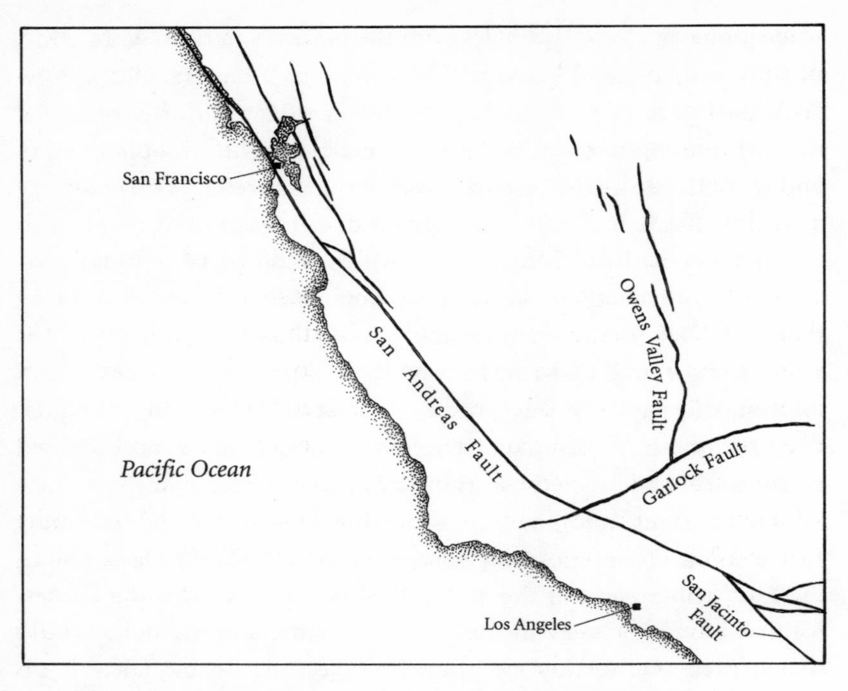

The San Andreas and associated faults running along the western seaboard of North America.

if they are strained beyond endurance. Bones break if they are bent in the 'wrong' direction or if they are forced to carry more than they can bear. Even steel girders will fracture given enough goading, or if some microscopic weakness lurks within them. Why should the earth itself be any exception? For common materials, the strain that has to accumulate before breakage can be measured by experiment: much modern architecture depends on precise knowledge of what a load-bearer can carry without fracturing. When a break occurs, the material is said to have 'failed'. So the language of tectonics has resonance with our own character, our own faults, our own failures. Faults run deep. 'They say best men are moulded out of faults', as Shakespeare put it in *Measure for Measure*: every man his own planet, with weaknesses ingrained. The possibility of failure always lurks when pressure is exerted upon our nature, which is when we may be sure our faults will find us out. Perhaps more than any other geological process in this intimate history of the earth it is faulting that we understand at the most visceral level, for we all know of failure, and most of us acknowledge the flaws that cut through our own thin crust.

The San Andreas Fault is just one of several faults that make up a complex of potential catastrophes, the flagship of a fleet of faults that run close to the western edge of North America. Most of the faults trend more or less parallel to the coast. In places, maps of interweaving faults look more like a braided mesh than the single, deep cut of our imagination. Los Angeles lies off the main fault, but is vulnerable to movement on others. The whole system is 1280 kilometres (800 miles) long – about the same length as the entire British Isles. It is one of the great fractures on our planet. In places, the fault zone is a mile wide. You can see it from space, for many features line up along it. From far above, this scarp lines up with that depression, and the whole picture is gradually revealed. Lakes tend to 'pond back' along the fault zone, both because of its weakness and because different kinds of rocks are brought into juxtaposition on either side of the fracture. Bays and valleys follow it. Rarely is it displayed as an open crack, an explicit fissure, but it can be seen clearly, running straight as a die, as if scribed out by a titanic burin, in arid areas such as the Carrizo Plain in central California. The San Andreas Fault, *sensu stricto*, runs from northern California and San Francisco Bay, southwards to Cajon Pass, near San Bernadino. There, it splits into a number of branches, including the San Jacinto and Banning Faults.* Faults, like football teams, often take their names from towns, although the San Andreas itself is named after a lake of that title in the San Francisco area, along which the main fault runs. New and active side branches are still being discovered, usually when a sudden earthquake reveals what has until then been concealed beneath a cover of rocks or soil, quiet as you like. It is a messy

* The north-easternmost branch is still called the San Andreas in this area.

The aftermath of the 1906 San Francisco earthquake as fire engulfs the town.

business, this slippage of the earth, and liable to spring a surprise in a vulnerable place.

The rocks along the San Andreas move one way. On the seaward side of California they are sliding past the rocks on the coastal

range side and moving northwards. Imagine if you were able to stand and watch the movement from the western side of the fault. You would see the rocks on the far side of the fault slipping away to your right – hence the fault is properly called dextral. If you average out all the movement in the long term it amounts to only about thirty millimetres a year in some segments. You might find it rather boring watching the earth move, if it were continuous. Of course, the segments of crust do not slide past one another in a stately fashion. The reason that there are earthquakes at all is that the crust moves in jerks; it sticks, it judders, it jams, until it is compelled to give way. Faults are not smooth, well-oiled affairs, nor is movement distributed evenly along them all within a system. Strain builds up in a particular segment until failure occurs. Then this one segment may shift dramatically, letting out energy in destructive waves. The longer the period of quiescence on an active fault, the more worrying it is to seismologists. The prelude to seismic cacophony is a silence longer than it ought to be. When the fault finally 'gives', the displacement direction becomes as obvious as if there were a signpost marking it: '⟶Crust This Way'. Streams are diverted. All along the fault those running off the California mountainsides towards the sea show kinks in the course of their little valleys. After the 1906 San Francisco earthquake, a road in Tomales Bay was offset by nearly 6.4 metres (21 feet). The strain of a century or more was dissipated in a dramatic jump. The same event caused destruction in the city on a massive scale. Ironically, the earthquake generated data that helped scientific understanding of the very forces of destruction. It struck at 5.13 a.m. on 18 April. Many of the dignified Victorian houses were not constructed with earthquakes in mind and collapsed. To a geologist briefed in disaster, it is surprising that there are so many of the old houses still standing today. Mature trees were uprooted, and even tossed entirely root-over-crown in places close to the fault line. It has been estimated that some 375,000 square miles were directly affected by the seismicity, half of it on land. Hardly had the dust settled than human faults began to move the tectonics of character. There was plundering. Mayor Schwartz was forced to act. Police and army units enforced order. But the Mayor's problems were just beginning. At 8.14 p.m. there was an aftershock – the rocks were 'settling' after the main event. But the shock was sufficient to bring down buildings already weakened earlier: thousands panicked. Then the real killer started: fire. Conflagration spread through the city. Over the next few days, magnificent hotels crumbled into ashes, and neighbourhoods were destroyed. At one point there was a mass rescue by sea that was probably the greatest such exercise before the evacuation of British troops at Dunkirk in the Second World War. At the final account, the death toll stood at some three thousand souls.

The San Andreas and associated faults will not calm down. The system has been operating at least since the Miocene, for some twenty million years. The fault was already old when the first primates came down from the trees to sample terrestrial life. As I write these words I have checked the US Geological Survey website: it reports that an earthquake of intensity 5.2 on the Richter scale struck Gilroy, California, on 14 May 2002. There were no casualties.

The intensity of earthquakes on the Richter scale is not like temperature measured on the Celsius scale. One degree up is not one degree quakier. It is a logarithmic scale, based upon the energy released during the event, which means that one notch up the scale represents a considerable increase – a magnitude 7 earthquake releases thirty times more energy than a magnitude 6, for example. Charles Richter was a geologist who developed his famous scale in 1935 based on the movements of the San Andreas Fault, so the language of seismology was born along the Pacific Coast. The scale is calibrated precisely with modern instruments, but it has also entered the common vocabulary. The San Francisco event of 1906 has been estimated as 8.3 on the Richter scale.

I have a sneaking regard also for the Mercalli scale, which describes earthquake intensity in terms of what is felt on the ground. Arthur Holmes outlined a twelve-notch scale of this kind (using Roman numerals), which has appealing features. Here are some samples:

> Intensity II. *Feeble*: noticed only by sensitive people . . . Intensity V. *Rather Strong*: felt generally; sleepers are wakened and bells ring . . . Intensity VII. *Very Strong*: general alarm; walls crack; plaster falls . . . Intensity VIII. *Destructive*: car drivers seriously disturbed; masonry fissured; chimneys fall; poorly constructed

> buildings damaged . . . Intensity XII. *Catastrophic*: total destruction; objects thrown into air; ground rises and falls in waves.

Imagine the scene: a Californian ranch-style hacienda with Ionian portico; Myron (a seismologist) vaguely notices something. 'Can it be an earthquake Intensity II?' he muses, ' must call Christabel, she's *so* sensitive . . .' The tingling increases. 'Uh, oh, it's stronger than that . . . in fact, is that a bell I hear ringing? . . . it must be a V!' Almost immediately, an Ionic column collapses: 'Oh my God! I feel generally alarmed and my plaster's falling! We have a VII!' A wild-eyed motorist staggers into the front yard . . .' Heavens to betsy! It's a seriously disturbed car driver! We've moved to an VIII' . . . 'Aargh!' (Myron is thrown into the air . . . it was a XII).

I have seen roadcuts slicing through the fault zone. The rock that is thrown up is hard to characterize – just a tan-coloured mash of little pieces, with an occasional larger fragment. This is the debris of the grind of plate against plate, a kind of tectonic hamburger meat known as fault gouge. Geophysical evidence proves that the San Andreas fault extends at least 16 kilometres (10 miles) down into the crust. It becomes easier to understand how the great fault might 'stick' long enough to build up the kind of strain that would topple the Winchester Hotel in San Francisco when it was suddenly released.

In order to understand what is going on under the sunny coast of the western USA we have to look globally. Plate meets plate at the edge of Asia on the opposite side of the Pacific Ocean, but here it is along oceanic subduction zones. California is very different. To appreciate what is happening, we have to look beyond the hedonistic shores of Venice Beach – out and under the sea, southwards to the Pacific sea-floor adjacent to Central and South America. From quite early days in modern oceanographic exploration, a range-like, relatively shallow region was recognized here rising above the general level of the sea floor. This was named the East Pacific Rise. Later, this structure was identified as a spreading ridge, and was mapped as a more or less linear structure for several thousand kilometres. Its smooth course was offset by transform faults* that shuffle its crest step-wise into a dozen or so chunks. But it is not a typical mid-ocean ridge, not least because it is nowhere near the centre of the Pacific Ocean. Instead, its course heads towards, and under, North America, passing into the continent along that most curious of long, narrow seas, the Gulf of California, which separates the peninsula of Baja California from the Mexican mainland. The conclusion can be drawn that the East Pacific Rise has 'disappeared' beneath the North American continent. A whole chunk of the eastern Pacific has been tucked away beneath the great mass of what is now the United States. To put it another way, the rate of production of new crust at the ridge centre was exceeded by the rate of consumption of oceanic crust at the western edge of the great continent. The result was that the ridge was 'sucked' towards America, and then beneath it. In Oligocene times, thirty million years ago, there was still a continuous East Pacific Rise off the coast of California. Three million years later it had partly disappeared under North America. The subsequent shuffling of the continental and oceanic blocks set up the northward rotation of the western coast that still happens today. The San Andreas was born. Proof of this long-term movement was discovered in fossils of seashells occurring to the west of the San Andreas Fault. If this seaward segment had indeed been shuffling northwards for a sufficiently long time, it should carry with it a cargo of fossil clamshells and snails – the remains of animals that would have originally lived in the subtropics but which were transported tectonically all the way to cold northerly climes. These fossil 'strangers' were indeed discovered by a palaeontologist applying his hammer to ancient marine sedimentary rocks. The beauty of such theories of the earth is that all branches of science have their part to play in unravelling the sequence of movements of the crust. Charles Lyell would have rejoiced in the solution.

* We met this kind of fault in Chapter 4, where blocks of oceanic crust slide past one another during ocean-floor spreading, an altogether gentler process than the kind of transcurrent faulting represented by the San Andreas, where plate grinds against plate.

The next place to go is downwards. The latest methods of analysis of earthquake waves create a three-dimensional picture of 'slices' of the earth's crust in horizontal sections at various levels, much as CAT scans can image the interior of the body. This method is known as seismic tomography. There is an ongoing project in the San Francisco Bay area to understand the deeper connections down to ten kilometres or so into the earth. It carries the happy acronym of BASIX (Bay Area Seismic Imaging Xperiment). The 3-D models developed show the plunging oceanic lithosphere underlying the northward-moving part of the coast. The different faults in the area show up as vertical planes cutting emphatically through the crust. But, more surprisingly, they seem to connect with one another by way of a deep, nearly horizontal zone of weakness – a 'detachment zone' – where the North American plate and Pacific plate interact at depth. When Pacific push comes to American shove, all those diligent Californians are evidently dancing to a deeper tune.

All such advances in knowledge help towards improved prediction of when the next earthquake will strike. This was once regarded as an extraordinarily difficult business, as much art as science. Sudden drops in the level of water in wells might indicate movements along faults at depth, and, as in Mercalli's scale II, some animals might be sufficiently sensitive to notice early signs of which humans might be unaware. Today, early seismic signals that indicate when strain on a particular fault is reaching a critical level can be distinguished from all the other 'noise' produced by our creaking earth. Predictions have improved so remarkably that the Gilroy earthquake of May 2002, briefly mentioned above, was anticipated in an article published in the *Proceedings of the National Academy of Sciences* by John Rundle and Kristy Tiampo, of the University of Colorado's Cooperative Institute for Research in Environmental Sciences (CIRES). The article was published on 19 February – a clear example of being wise *before* the event.

* * *

Similarly, building technology has risen to the challenges of accommodating violent shaking without falling down. Shock absorbers have been designed that rest whole buildings on giant pads of rubber and steel. Webs and struts of steel reinforce concrete slabs to the same effect. Even so, the world was shocked by pictures of collapsed, though reinforced, concrete overpasses after the Kobe earthquake of 17 January 1995, in which over five thousand people died. This devastating event in Japan was exactly one year after an earthquake in Northridge, California, one of the suburbs of greater Los Angeles, lying on a hitherto unremarkable branch of the San Andreas Fault. Roads collapsed there, also; sixty people died. If an earthquake is violent enough, human ingenuity counts for little. Nonetheless, engineers are confident enough to build high towers within earthquake zones. It is impossible to gainsay the confidence of the TransAmerica Pyramid in the middle of downtown San Francisco, an 853-foot needle piercing the skyline, peerless among its towering neighbours; it is earthquake-proof – or so it is said. Sadly, in China, Turkey, and Afghanistan the effects of plate grinding against plate have not been mitigated by the ingenuity of engineers; buildings still collapse like houses made of playing cards when the earth finds the strain too much.

Kobe and Northridge are both symptoms of destruction. Oceanic rocks are being destroyed beneath Japan – and tumbling freeways are a consequence. Equally, oceanic rocks are disappearing on the Californian side of the Pacific Ocean. This, the greatest of the world's oceans, is getting slowly smaller, eaten away at its edges. In fifty million years' time its trans-navigation will not be a challenge.

It must be admitted that the San Andreas Fault is not particularly impressive on the ground. Professor Peter Sadler, of the University of California, Riverside, has been mapping the San Andreas and its splays for years. He smiles somewhat lugubriously when we drive up into the foothills of the San Gabriel Mountains. 'There it is,' he says. 'Where?' I respond. With a little work, you can make out a linear depression in the sparsely-vegetated ground running northwards, and perhaps a modest bank on its eastern edge. It does not seem adequate to account for bucking freeways. Erosion in the soft fault gouge soon modifies the famous fault's discreteness. We pass up into the mountains, leaving behind the slipping margin of the most prosperous nation on earth. The mountains themselves are the legacy of earlier tectonic episodes – phases of terrane 'docking' such as I described in the northern part of the Appalachian chain in Newfoundland. Much of mountainous western North America has been 'plastered on' to the continent. Beyond the mountains lies the Mojave Desert.

There are probably as many mixed feelings about deserts as there are about Los Angeles. Many people drive through it as quickly as they can – usually heading straight for Vegas, where they need never see a saltpan. Most geologists I know are desert lovers. There is nothing like the clarity of light in a desert. There is nowhere better to see geology writ large. Shales that usually weather away to mush can be collected for their fossils. Structures that normally take months to work out are laid out for all to see. Geological maps are written out on the ground, explicit for once. The natural history is intriguing, and no observer capable of detecting an Intensity II earthquake can fail to wonder at the adaptability of organisms in the face of adversity. Some way over the Mojave Desert there is a particular region where Joshua trees grow abundantly on gentle slopes. Their growing tips carry aloft a ball of sharp leaves, like an elephant's trunk bearing a porcupine. Their bare trunks branch sparingly below and are frequently bent fantastically, as if they had sagged once under the burden of hardship and perked up again in times of plenty to point skyward. Then there are yuccas, which may, if you are fortunate, sport a great spike of white, bell-like flowers arising from a spiky rosette of leaves. There are many other varieties of spiny or woody plants – nothing nourishing is given away to grazers in such a hard place. But little footprints impressed on the sand prove that there is plenty of animal life out and about after dusk. The arthropod specialist in me recognizes scorpion tracks.

Turn left at Baker and you can make a visit to Death Valley. Everyone should. Like almost all major features in the far West, the valley trends north-north-west–south-south-east, and is under structural control. Faults define the edges of things: the eastern edge of the mighty Sierra Nevada at the Owens Valley; the western edge of Death Valley. The high country of the Sierra is, to say the least, difficult of access. The snowy peaks are almost intimidating when viewed from the more modest White Inyo Mountains to the east. They are cut off as if by a knife at the edge of the green and domesticated Owens Valley – one of the greatest scenic contrasts in the world. The pioneering conservationist John Muir is said to have burst into tears at the sight. The exploration of the Sierra Nevada, as Eduard Suess said, 'resounds to the lasting honour of Whitney'. Josiah Dwight Whitney first mapped the geology of the area during 1864–70, and has the highest mountain in the Sierra Nevada as his memorial. He it was who recognized the major fault boundaries that are still defined on maps today. These are not faults that shuffle rocks huge distances sideways, in San Andreas fashion. Instead, they are faults that drop chunks of the crust. Gravity alone allows things to sink, so wherever there is crustal tension or extension there are faults of this kind. The rocks relax to a new level, with a fault marking the boundary. There is still movement along the older faults in eastern California – and this is nothing unusual. Like old soldiers, old faults never die, they simply fade away. I once felt a tremor in the agreeable old town of Bishop's Castle in the Welsh Borderland that derived from a fault several hundreds of millions of years old. Death Valley drops to 85 metres below sea-level; this dramatic disparity is a result of movement ('downthrow') on the fault. It is so hot that sweat even drips off the tip of your nose. At Badwater, salty springs evaporate in the sunshine leaving a white crust dusting a saline waste. Astonishingly, there are *things* living in the pools, and scrubby, halophilic plants that seem to eke out a living even on the barest ground. The depth of the valley below sea-level means that it is hotter than you believe possible if you're broken down by the roadside. Air-conditioning systems simply cannot cope with the job of cooling the inside of a vehicle in the fierce heat; engines expire with the effort. The surface of this valley has just been let down too low: it overheats more than it should. It is the fault's fault.

Death Valley is not journey's end. Eastwards again, we cross the border into the state of Nevada, heading for the Great Basin. Unlike geological faults, state borders are arbitrary lines on the map, but sometimes they do flag cultural differences. The contrasts between California and Nevada are the most striking. First, Nevada is so empty. There seems to be nobody there. When you are driving along the paved highways you are often alone with the horizon. After a turn off on to the dirt roads, you soon get used to going for an hour without seeing another vehicle. My colleague Mary Droser and I were accustomed to explore the lesser tracks off the greater tracks in search of fossils. All the *people* are in Las Vegas and Reno, which leaves the rest of this beautiful state to the enthusiasts.

On the slow climb into higher altitudes, you observe that Nevada is sage-brush country. The open valleys in the Great Basin are full of it, dominated by it – a tough little shrub that mostly grows thigh high, bearing thin woody stems and greyish leaves. It takes its name from the aromatic smell of the foliage. This sage-like odour is strongest after rain, when the whole atmosphere is infused with a distinctive fragrance, reminding the European visitor of walking through the Mediterranean *maquis*. Sage-brush has to be tough to endure climatic extremes: the winters are hard in the Great Basin, but the summers are long and dry, and can be very hot. There is little free-standing water in the summer: most of the lakes are salt-pans that shimmer white in the sunlight. This is where the winter waters gather and evaporate, leaving behind another thin layer of salt each year. You can drive as fast as you like across the pans, for they are perfectly flat. Even in summer, there are occasional torrential squalls, and then you had better get out of the pan as fast as you can, for rainwater drains rapidly into it. Mary Droser and I once had to flee such a storm in our all-terrain vehicle, close to the Confusion Range. We saw lightning playing in the hills and felt no more than a hint of anxiety. Within minutes, everything turned dark. Soon it was deluging, and we could see the track over which we had driven washing away in front of our eyes: no choice but to head through the brush. It was startling to discover how quickly the draining flood reached the axles of our vehicle; we could all too easily imagine being carried away to early graves. Observing a semi-desert convert to a shallow sea in half an hour was truly terrifying. Reaching the hard-top was one of those moments that returns to you again in dreams.

The roads across the Great Basin run straight for a while and then climb and loop. This is the Basin and Range Province. Straight courses cross the basins, which are long valleys that run approximately north–south for perhaps a hundred miles. Between successive basins are ranges of comparable length, and up to 3000 metres (10,000 feet) high, one after another. The sage-brush wilderness is used for cattle ranching, but it is poor pasture. You can go for miles without seeing a cow. When you do, it comes as a surprise to see animals that would not seem out of place in a lush European meadow. While you are speeding along the roads across the basins, there is a delicious openness about the world. These roads, you feel, could go on forever. The ranges appear as distant prospects, backed by white clouds, and then quite suddenly are upon you. Each one is a mystery, a surprise. Some are high enough to retain snow late into the year, so as you climb, you cool. The road has to buck and turn back on itself to cross each range. Naturally, the rocks that geologists seek crop out in the ranges, and when the road begins to ascend there are immediately crags and bluffs and roadcuts that reveal the character of the land. The exposures on the flanks of the ranges are superb. You can follow the rock-beds for mile upon mile: the only problem is reaching them, for to get close you rely on rocky old tracks made by hunters and backwoodsmen. The flat tyre becomes an occupational hazard, and walking back to the main road is not an appealing prospect in the heat.

Much of the rain in the Great Basin falls on the ranges. Hence the vegetation is utterly different from that of the valleys, dominated as it is by fragrant sage-brush and almost completely lacking trees. On the ranges, there are large numbers of conifers, often aged and twisted, which line the hillsides without crowding them, so that you can easily amble between the trees in search of rocks. On hot days, the conifers give off an entirely different smell from that of sage-brush, a pleasant whiff of cedarwood and resin. Among the conifers is the piñon pine, the source of pine nuts, which were an important source of protein for indigenous Indian tribes like the Shoshone, whilst the bristle-cone pines are the oldest living things on earth. In the woods, you feel you are alone in the world. You even get to welcome the rare intrusion far overhead of jet aircraft from the Nevada Test Site. From the top of the range the view commands the adjacent basin, and thence to ranges beyond. All the names are evocative: the Monitor Range, Egan, Toquima, Hot Creek, Lost River, the Ruby Mountains.

Towns are small, and a long way apart. Some are ghosts, relics of silver discovered and worked out; others are picturesque in their near abandonment. Carson City used to be the state capital. Now it is an endearingly ramshackle collection of wooden houses scattered over the hillside. Eureka, Nevada, is billed as 'the loneliest town on the loneliest road in North America' on a big hoarding outside the main street. The claim may even be true: Route 50 traverses a lot of sage-brush. There are historic buildings from the days of the great gold boom in the 1870s: a fine old theatre, all painted up, standing opposite the courthouse. I have visited Eureka sporadically over thirty years, and it has changed subtly; smartened up, if anything. It is surprising to hear an enigmatic language spoken in one of the bars: it is Basque. During the boom years, Basque shepherds established themselves in these parts. The miners drifted away when the good times were over, as miners always do, but the farmhands stayed on, as farmhands always do. So here in the loneliest town there is also the strangest tongue. Philologists puzzle over the origins of Basque in the way that geologists puzzle over the deep structure of faults.

Almost everything that I have described in the Basin and Range exists at the behest of the geology: the long mountain chains and the valleys between; the metals sequestered in the hills; the internal drainage that produces the *playas* or saltpans. Faults are the deep control. They chop the landscape into pieces. They direct the ranges north to south. They provide the general control over the most intimate details of the landscape.

The steep scarps of the ranges are defined by huge faults. These let down adjacent chunks of crust that form the basins, so the whole landscape is divided into a series of massive, elongate blocks. The main faults lie on the western sides of the ranges, and they run north–south, albeit with many local complications; hence the direction of the faults determines the grain of the landscape. The downthrow sides of the faults mostly lie to the west: these are cracks in the brittle crust, deep faults, but lacking the transcurrent motion of the San Andreas. The winding roads that require such intense concentration from the driver are, you might say, climbing up the sides of the fault blocks. The level swathes across the basins reflect instead what erosion has done to the mountains. For even as the basins have been let down, so they have filled up. Sediment has flooded in to raise what faults have made low: 1000 to 1500 kilometres (3000 to 5000 feet) of such sediments have filled in the basins. The flood that Mary and I experienced was just one moment in the great levelling, one incident among millions. The sage-brush knows the geology, with the unwavering intelligence of its precise adaptations. Nor would the pine trees lead their slow lives were it not for the gift of the mountains. In the comparatively recent past, when the climate was wetter, many of the basins were united in one vast lake, known as Lake Bonneville. We could see evidence of the ancient shorelines of the lake on the edges of the basins – a kind of bevel in the hillsides. The *playas* were the last remnants of the great lake. Further east, where the basin and range pass into Utah, a more considerable legacy is the Great Salt Lake, a huge expanse of whiteness, testimony to the evaporation of all the salts formerly leached out by rain from the eroding mountains, made solid by evaporation under the fierce sun in drier times. It is a weird place. From a highway passing alongside it you can see mirages, when the horizon suddenly goes liquid. Small buttes arising from the lake appear to float eerily above the ground. Everything shimmers.

The faults that define the edges of the basins dive downwards at a steep angle. Seismic reflections show that the faults actually flatten out at a depth of perhaps twenty kilometres. They are more like a series of scoops than simple vertical cracks dropping chunks of crust to make a step, like a failure in a concrete floor. So now we have what my American friends would call a 'visual': the whole vast Basin and Range area stretching, and the crust accommodating to tension by extending and sliding down faults in parallel chunks; the greater part of several US states shattered and adjusting. The process must, of course, be related to deep things, just as the Californian coast shakes at the bidding of the subterranean engine. Like that area, the evolution of what we see today has a history of thirty million years or so. We have to look far down beneath the sage-brush and the piñon pines to see what guides the character of our journey across the Great Basin.

Arthur Holmes was already familiar with one fact about the deep structure of the Great Basin: the crust is thinner there. It has an average thickness of twenty-five to thirty kilometres – something like fifteen kilometres less than under the Great Plains, which comprise the flat heart of America. At this point we have to recall that the deeper you go into the crust the more the rocks are likely to flow rather than fracture, as pressure and temperature increase; the twisted gneisses in the centre of Newfoundland were an example. Some of the great minds of tectonics, like Dan McKenzie, have pondered the Great Basin, and have used the contrast in behaviour of the brittle upper crust and the ductile lower crust and mantle lithosphere to explain what is seen at the surface, and to infer what happens far beneath it. Deep seismic reflection profiles have revealed that *below* the normal faults that define Basin and Range there is a low-angle 'zone of detachment' flanked by a region of ductile deformation. It is a plane of weakness at great depth where slow slithering happens: one major piece of lithosphere over and past another. In one version of the theory, this shear zone is thought to cut obliquely downwards across the entire lithosphere, providing the deep control of the crustal extension over the Basin and Range – which in turn generates the faults. For example, the crust is thinned where the zone of detachment approaches the surface. Remember that the crust is less dense than the mantle beneath; hence, where it is thinned, this results in subsidence. This is the converse of the situation in mountain ranges that we have considered previously, where *thickening* of crust during continental collision results in its elevation. It is all a matter of checks and balances. Where the crust has to accommodate to such deeper controls it shuffles in blocks in response, brittle-fracturing to obey the bidding from below. At the same time, extension in the crust may induce melting of its lower part, and lavas will erupt at the surface as a consequence. Mary and I saw evidence of these on our traverse across the Great Basin, where piled ashes formed terraces or slaggy piles. Some of them were the product of the kind of explosive aerial eruptions that generate extensive ash flows; these are preserved as ignibrites, like those we met around the Bay of Naples at the start of this book. And faults can be conduits for the hot fluids that distil the bounty of the earth, where minerals and metals escape upwards from the magma chamber. The miner, too, must nod to processes* deeper by far than his shaft can ever penetrate. Pines, sage-brush, salt pans, gold, twisting roads . . . it is a *Gestalt* united by tectonics.

There are other fault lines that traverse the earth. Cutting north–south through eastern Africa there are great valleys: a depression passes southwards from the Gulf of Aden through Ethiopia, then splits into two arms, passing either side of Lake Victoria. The eastern arm strikes southwards across Kenya, its course marked by lakes sitting in the valley base: Lake Turkana, Lake Baringo, Lake Magadi, Lake Natron. The last named is one of the great natural sources of soda, for it is another Great Salt Lake, where evaporation has

* The genesis of the different ore deposits is much more complex than this implies and involves several separate mineralization events, as well as re-activation of older deposits.

concentrated soluble salts. Natron is an old name for hydrated soda and has left its legacy in the chemical symbol for the element sodium (Na). The lake supports a huge population of delicately pink flamingos, which use their extraordinary bills to filter out nutritious micro-organisms from the warm, alkaline lake. For these birds, a soda fountain is a literal description of their source of nourishment – and they derive their colour from their food. The western arm is one of the most blatant lines on the face of the earth, an almost continuous ribbon of water running southwards from Lake Albert to Lake Edward, and thence to Lake Tanganyika and Lake Nyasa (Malawi): the Great Rift Valley. Eduard Suess would have used the term *graben* for this kind of structure. The total length of the system is some 3000 kilometres (1800 miles). The width of the valley is about thirty miles (fifty kilometres) along its entire length. You do not need to be a naturalist to read this line, for political boundaries and, before them, tribal boundaries are drawn along it. The faults to either side of the Great Valley let down the stretch of crust between: slithering cracks delineating a sag. Earthquakes are concentrated along the rift, so much so that a map of earthquake epicentres provides a kind of pointillist map of it. Clearly, the surface of the earth is jittery along these lines. When seen from the air, the faults defining the edges of the rift are clearly visible and can be as straight as a ramrod. They are geological lines graven on the ground. There is often a series of faults at each edge, stepping down, as it were, to the valley floor, rather than a single, mighty fault. Near Lake Turkana the valley is filled with volcanics and sediments to a depth of 8000 metres; since the scarps are up to 2000 metres high, this implies no less than 10,000 metres of movement on the fault. Staggering though this total might seem, when divided by the ten million years over which the movement has been happening, it is slippage averaging just one millimetre a year: lichens grow faster.

Volcanoes follow the rift line less slavishly than earthquakes (the greatest, Kilimanjaro, is outside it), but throughout Ethiopia and Kenya, and further south, there are many active or dormant volcanoes hard by the fault lines. Many of them erupt curious lavas rich in carbonate minerals – which we usually associate with sedimentary rocks – known, rather unsurprisingly, as carbonatites. Ol Doinyo Lengai (2891 metres, 9485 feet high) is a typical volcanic cone that has spewed out lavas that have helped to supply the white crusts of Lake Natron. The crater at the summit of the volcano is one of the most desolate places on earth. A crumpled and petrified sea of carbonatite is dotted with steep-sided conelets, the dark holes in their apexes revealing the volcanic chimneys below. Everything is white. It is a hellish inversion of all we have come to expect from a volcano, a bleached-out counterpart of the realm of Pele. The lava still pours out on to the surface of the crater from time to time, and when it does it is black, like any other lava. But as it cools it changes – first to a chestnut colour, and then, after some hours, it, too, becomes white and crusty. Erupting in the heart of Africa, the lavas have enriched themselves with juices acquired from the continental crust, thereby transformed utterly to a new and strange composition. Black becomes white.

Colourless volcanic gases can be more dangerous than the obvious sulphurous exhalations of more dramatic volcanoes. Carbon dioxide is heavier than air and collects in hollows (as Oliver Goldsmith described so graphically in the 'cave of dogs' near Naples). Investigators in the rift must not be caught unawares in such a pocket. The most lethal carbon dioxide eruption was not in the Great Rift, but in an altogether less impressive volcanic area in the Cameroon Highlands in West Africa. On 26 August 1986, gas bubbled up from Lake Nyos and crept like an invisible stream downhill, a 150-foot thickness of lethal miasma. Twelve hundred people were suffocated in the town below, along with their beasts and the very birds perched on the bushes. Only cattle-herders in the hills escaped to tell the horrible story.

The Rift Valley had another role to play in history. Game has flourished there for millions of years and, in pursuit of it, our distant ancestors and relatives walked upright among the bushes and trees.

If Africa was the cradle of human evolution, it was around the lakes and volcanoes in the great valley that the bones and artefacts of our ancestors stood the best chance of being preserved. Expeditions to Lake Turkana in the Ethiopian Rift discovered fossils which showed that hominid history must now be reckoned in several millions of years. It was here that our history began to reveal its true complexity – that there were many different animals in the family of *Homo sapiens,* from which we, alone, eventually prospered. Just how many species were involved is the subject of endless debate among anthropologists. The details of human evolution are not part of our story, but I am obliged to mention that the flow of new discoveries has not abated – as this was written in 2002, a scientific paper in *Nature* has claimed a new fossil as marking the branch between the human line and that leading to our close relatives, the great apes and chimpanzees. It is no surprise, in such a disputatious area of science, to find that claim already challenged. What is not in dispute is that early hominid evolution involves a cluster of long-extinct species, some of which are not close to our line, and some of which are. Nor that the genesis of the line leading to modern humans was in Africa. The growing richness of fossil evidence is a measure of how much we are learning, but I do not doubt that current textbooks, like their predecessors, will eventually have to be rewritten. That there is such a fossil record, whatever its entanglements, is thanks to the geology. The volcanic rocks that periodically spread, or exploded, over the rift valleys both buried the precious remains and provided the means to date them, for the radioactive clocks which measure time are interred with the bones. And the fact that faults let down the rocks, step by step, preserved their precious cargo of history, which might so easily have been eroded away as if it had never been. What has been dropped down in the rift has survived. We owe our history to our faults.

When Eduard Suess was writing, the structure of the African rift valleys was already partially understood. With his characteristic confidence he extrapolated from what little pioneering geology had been undertaken in this part of Africa. Of Nyasa and Tanganyika he wrote: 'I do not see in what way these two depressions, each of which, although of very trifling breadth, is prolonged through about five degrees of latitude, could have been produced except by trough faults, and in my opinion their origin is very similar to that of the Red Sea, [and] the Dead Sea.' Suess had made a connection that we still observe today – and which we can explain through deep processes. The African rifts ('trough faults') pass northwards to the Horn of Africa. To the west, the Red Sea has rifted margins. So, too, does the great depression running northwards beyond the eastern edge of the Mediterranean Sea. The Dead Sea lies at its lowest point, below sea-level, a sink for all the waters of the Jordan River. One of the first pictures I remember from my children's encyclopedia was of somebody lying on their back in the Dead Sea reading a newspaper. Salt is concentrated by evaporation there to the point where you cannot sink. Faults have let it down deeply: if there was another biblical Flood, the sea would rush in and inundate the whole area in the twinkling of a geological eye.

The Red Sea is a young ocean. Look at the map: it requires little imagination to close it up again. It is like a simple break in a platter. Imagine Africa and the Arabian Peninsula united as a single continent. An irresistible force parts them. First, a rift valley records the tension in the strained crust: it sags and weakens. As Suess noticed, the faults are preserved along the flanks of the Red Sea today. There are associated volcanic eruptions, many related to readier access to the underworld provided by faults along the rift. Then, the true ocean opens out as new, oceanic basalt rocks are emplaced within the nascent basin; a mid-ocean ridge grows. There are two 'arms' to the ocean, one along the Red Sea, the other along the Gulf of Aden, separating the Somalian plate from the Arabian plate, and meeting at Afar, at the end of the Eastern Rift of Africa.* Inexorably, the African and Arabian coasts move apart. In its early phases, the new

* There are thus three diverging systems meeting at Afar: the Red Sea, where the African and Arabian plates separate; the Gulf of Aden, where the Somalian and Arabian plates diverge; and the Eastern Rift, where the Somalian and African plates are pulling apart. Afar is accordingly described as the site of a triple junction.

sea was cut off from the Indian Ocean from time to time and evaporated to dryness, leaving behind thick deposits of salt. Today, there is much active geology within the juvenile ocean: earthquakes are aligned where you would expect them along its mid-line, where oceanic lava can also be sampled; thirteen pools of hot brines have been identified on the ridge in localized 'deeps'. These are places where valuable metals like zinc and copper are concentrated. Originally of volcanic origin, they have been distilled into brines by circulation through the underlying rocks. The young ocean is a kind of chemical brewhouse where the ingredients of continents and mantle can interact and cook up new recipes. Many ancient ore deposits are the fruits of such encounters. In the Red Sea, perhaps, we may obtain a vision of the birth of other, greater oceans. We can imagine the early days of the Atlantic Ocean; it, too, transferred from 'rift to drift', as Pangaea dismembered itself. We can envision how today's familiar continents first shuffled into their separate identities, just one late phase in the slow dance of the plates over the face of the earth.

If the Red Sea shows the birth of an ocean basin, the rift valleys of Africa are thought by many geologists to represent a still earlier phase in continental break-up: a new geography *in statu nascendi*. The Red Sea and Gulf of Aden are but one part of Suess' interconnected system, which extends southwards into the great continent. Given enough time, perhaps the eastern part of Africa will separate from the western, and a new ocean divide the Somalian plate from the mother continent. Another movement of the dance will have begun.

As for the deep cause of the separation of the neighbouring plates, there is much evidence for mantle plumes impinging on the crust beneath the eastern part of Africa. The rising limbs may provide the deep root of the tension that causes the progressive rifting in the valleys: like huge, hot hands parting the brittle skin of the earth. The same volcanoes that buried the remains of early hominids are no more than a consequence of these profound motions, occurring where hot mantle partially melts deep beneath the continent to generate magma. The plume spreads out like a mushroom beneath the lithosphere. This explains why major volcanoes like Kilimanjaro lie beyond the compass of the rift itself. They arise like suppurations from hot sepsis under the skin of the earth. Much evidence from modern measurements along the rift valley testify to the rising of hot mantle material beneath it. For example, the general heat flux is greater within the rift than on the stable continent to either side. Measurements of the minute changes in gravitational anomalies across the region are also consistent with a hot plume beneath the rifts. Current geophysical work seeks to model what is happening at depth. Some geologists believe that the rift system within Africa will develop no further, that it will, in effect, remain forever a 'failed ocean'. Given the slow march of geological change, it is unlikely that mankind will be here to confirm whether this is true or not. Who knows if the fossil remains of the last of our kind will lie entombed beneath some ash-fall within the rift – just one more species among the millions that have already become extinct?

The surface of the earth is criss-crossed by faults like a sheet of crazed glass. How could it be different after thousands of millions of years of the crust being subjected to stress? Uplift produces cracks; loading of the crust often produces the same effect; stretching of the crust again induces faults. Tectonic squeezing may thrust rocks pick-a-back in stacks as the crust shortens, wincing brittlely away from forces greater than it can accommodate. Only in deeply buried rocks will plastic deformation predominate. For the rest, cracking and evidence of movement is everywhere. On average, the longer rocks have endured, the more likely they are to have been affected by faulting at some stage in their history. A walk along almost any beach backed by cliffs of sedimentary rocks will discover places where the strata have been displaced by small faults; sometimes as neat and obvious as cutting a triple-decker sandwich and dropping one side – you can match the layers and tell just how much the fault has displaced the strata. In other places, a greater fault may juxtapose quite different sets of rocks. You may see crushed rock along the fault, or find milky quartz, or the sea may have picked out a cave along the fault plane. In quarries cut into the guts of ancient mountain belts

Portrait of the artist as a young man . . . the author by the Pony Express Route across the Great Basin, Nevada.

you may inspect the polished planes of faults long since sunk into quietude: scratched and gouged in the direction of movement, what once might have rocked the earth is now no more than a passing stop on a geological field trip. The faults of old earth are beyond counting. Green fields may cover them over; or, as in the western USA, they may delimit mountain ranges. Fault lines cut the character into the face of the earth.

10

The Ancient of Days

Dressed in sensible boots and tweeds, in the summer of 1883, the Scottish geologist J. J. H. Teall strode down to the harbour in the little fishing village of Scourie. He looked back on a scattering of cottages, an inn, and a kirk tucked into the back end of a protected bay, not many miles from the far north-western tip of mainland Britain. Teall crossed by Scourie Lodge on his way and passed the time of day with its tenant, the factor of the Duke of Sutherland, Mr Evander MacIver. There were not many educated men in those parts – and Mr MacIver had attended no less than three universities – so he was naturally curious about the presence of a middle-class geologist upon his land. Then, too, as one who had prosecuted the Clearances, he may not have known many among the local population who cared to flatter his erudition. He may well have invited Teall to inspect the wonders of his stone-walled garden, constructed upon one of the few patches of fertile earth in this most barren part of Scotland. The Gulf Stream warmed it to a degree that defied its northerly latitude beyond fifty-eight degrees; in this protected haven the astonished geologist might have seen exotic red-and-blue fuchsias, and even a thriving New Zealand cabbage-palm that had been grown from seed sent by one of the factor's relatives on the other side of the world. But the geologist had other interests today, and, with the factor's blessing, took off along the walled track behind the boat-house that led up over the hillside above the Lodge. He approached the sea along the northern shore of the Bay of Scourie, where the coast was indented by a dozen small inlets backed by modest but rugged cliffs. The rock forming the underlay of the country announced itself everywhere: in lichen-covered crags, in stones lying about the grassy fields, in the crude but durable patchwork of the stone walls, in rounded boulders on the narrow beaches. The rock was gneiss, grey and heavy-looking, finely banded and speckled – mile upon mile of it, apparently. When Teall tramped onwards towards the small headland of Creag a'Mhail his eye caught something different: a steep, dark seam of rock running towards the headland. The sea had eaten through part of the seam, but now he could see that it continued to the east and struck inland. As a good Lyellian geologist he recognized the seam for what it was – a dyke of igneous rock, cutting through the gneisses. It must, therefore, be younger than the rocks it violated. He clambered down to collect a piece of the 'trap' (he probably thought it to be the volcanic rock called dolerite). A few weeks later, back home in the laboratory, he recognized something else: the igneous rock of the dyke had itself been metamorphosed, like the gneisses it intruded. Teall published his results in Volume 41 of the *Quarterly Journal of the Geological Society of London*: 'On the Metamorphosis of Dolerite into Horneblende Schist'. The Scourie Dyke had been introduced to the world.

It has since become one of geology's holy places. Dozens of famous geologists have followed Teall's trail, and you somehow feel there ought to be a plaque somewhere about. There have been structural geologists, geochronologists, geochemists, and palaeomagneticists – the whole tribe of specialists spawned in the century since Eduard Suess wrote *Der Antlitz der Erde*. When I visited the site late in 2002, Mr MacIver's cabbage-palm was still thriving inside its walled garden, a hundred and fifty years old and perhaps fifteen feet high, with many heads that had been sprouted over the years. It was, I was told, the most northerly palm tree in the world, and as I dodged the hailstones I could well believe it. The track behind the boat-house was now boggy and clogged with rushes, and higher up was overgrown with prickly gorse bushes; but the tough gneisses were of course unchanged. It could have been these rocks that Henry M. Cadell of Grange, Bo'ness, had in mind when he wrote in *The Geology and Scenery of Sutherland* in 1896: 'A hand specimen of gneiss resembles a closed book with chapters of varying lengths, each chapter consisting of pages of a different tint'; in other words, striped, but irregularly so. To the geologist, these rocks are known as the Lewisian gneiss. I brought back a beach cobble of the stuff: it was satisfying when clasped in the fist, like a goose's egg. I also found a smaller pebble derived from a dyke: black with subtle lighter speckling, like a piece of the map of deep space. Since Teall's discovery, the area around Scourie had been logged in detail by Dr Clough of the Geological Survey, who had found not one, but many dykes, all with a trend west-north-west–east-south-east. Dykes, like angry wasps, tend to occur in swarms; they are intruded in response to extension over a great area, a crustal cracking filled with magma. Their direction clearly had absolutely nothing to do with the familiar Caledonian trend running from north-east to south-west across Scotland – indeed, they lie almost at right angles to it. Looking at the map, the course indicated by the dykes seems to be rather common in the north-west Highlands, guiding the shape of lochs and the flow of rivers running towards the irregular coastline. What now controls the lie of the land is a legacy of something far, far older than the Caledonides, an antecedent world, a scrap of immemorial crust: the ancient of days.

What with the covering of lichens, the wind and the rain, and the sea splashing up, it is not as easy to distinguish gneiss from dyke as it should be. When a cold wind is stinging your eyes, one dark rock looks much like another; but eventually the famous dyke was identified. My mentor, Graham Park, who has spent much of his life on these rocks, recommended that we went to another dyke locality at Achmelvich Beach, a few miles to the south, where it was easier to clamber over the outcrop. This proved to be good advice. The single-track coast road to Achmelvich follows the contours of the land with precision; it is as if somebody had simply stuck a very narrow strip of tarmac over the switchback terrain. When a vehicle comes the other way, etiquette dictates that you must scuttle into a marked passing-place, while waving at the oncoming vehicle in comradely fashion. The coastline is wonderfully varied, indented with little sea lochs, and strung with half-hidden offshore islands of every size and shape, at low tide all marked out with a bright fringe of yellow bladder-wrack plastered to the shore-rock. The Lewisian gneiss emerges from the ground in numerous grey, rounded hillocks, rank upon rank of them. They look almost like cumulus clouds, and towards dusk they can merge uncannily with the sky. The soil produced from the weathering of old gneiss is thin and poor, as if the passage of billions of years had somehow leached all the goodness out of it. There are boggy pools to either side of the road, each with a meagre fringe of rushes and cotton-grass, and hollows filled with *sphagnum* moss and carnivorous plants, equipped with sticky glands, that supplement their hard rations with what insects they can trap. The late autumnal bracken and dry grasses paint the slopes with a shade that falls somewhere between rust and russet, laid warm against the pallid outcrop. Somehow, the landscape *feels* ancient, worn down, as if it had seen it all before, and could only now manage a hilly shudder when once it might have drawn itself up into great mountains.

Crofters' cottages dot the tiny road to Achmelvich; each one has a few trees of downy birch on the hillside behind it, which is just now carrying lemon-coloured autumn foliage, and perhaps a mountain ash by the garden wall, heavy with orange berries. The older croft cottages are stone built, with one end of the building reserved for winter quarters for animals. Rough lumps of gneiss make for solid but unrefined buildings: they seem almost to grow out of the land. I saw several examples of plain, but comfortable-looking newer houses alongside the original croft buildings, which in some cases had become tumbledown. The tenancy of a croft is rigidly administered by the Crofter's Commission, and crofters enjoy a security of tenure, and of inheritance of that tenure, that many lessees might envy. Each croft has an inviolable parcel of land assigned to it, and rights to run perhaps a dozen sheep and cut peat, all designed to keep a family above subsistence level – the Commission was partly set up to ensure that the commotion of the Clearances did not recur. A modest rent is paid to the landlord, in this part of Scotland usually a landowner like the Duke of Sutherland. There is simply no opportunity for speculative development in such remote communities, but you *can* replace your old croft house with a spanking new bungalow. Of course, modern materials imported from outside are quicker to build with, and cheaper to maintain, so that the umbilical connection to the local geology is lost in most of the newer erections. Something – a little character, a morsel of regional idiosyncrasy – is lost with the transformation; it is a small step towards Sutherland becoming like everywhere else. Graham Park told me that there is a waiting list in the prettier areas to get a croft, so the appeal of life close to the elements in the least populous part of Great Britain evidently endures, although only a minority now follow the farming option.

Achmelvich proved to be a perfect little bay backed by white sands – shell sands, surprisingly, like something you might find on Hawai'i. The shells have been washed in from the Atlantic Ocean, smashed to pieces in storms and blown into marram-covered drifts. On the north side of the bay the old gneiss runs into the sea. You can get a more comfortable look at the geology here than at Scourie. The speckled appearance of the gneiss is more apparent where the sea has washed it clean. These are rocks that have, to borrow a phrase from Cadell of Grange, been 'crumpled by the long-continued ill usage to which they have been subjected'. They have, in fact, been subjected to almost the greatest extremes of pressure and temperature that rocks can endure without completely melting – 'ill usage', with a vengeance. The even-sized grains look almost like some kind of granite: it is as if they had been squeezed so hard that their every component was forced into having similar dimensions. Geologists refer to this high pressure and temperature regime as the 'granulite facies' in recognition of the distinctive texture of the rocks. The strong banding, or foliation, betrays the fact that deformation was the *fons et origo* of the rock's characteristic fabric. Laboratory experiments have shown that the minerals typical of these rocks only co-exist under conditions close to those that pertain near the base of the crust. The gneisses that are now just a few feet away from white, shell sands blown from the Atlantic Ocean have been on a journey deep into the earth, from which they have re-emerged to become encrusted with lichens and moistened by sea spray.

I once went in search of the type locality of another granulite facies rock, known as charnockite. The locality was the gravestone of Job Charnock, founder of Calcutta (d. 1693). It was originally recognized from the great man's memorial, and so, naturally enough, took his name: ancient rocks with origins as deep as the Lewisian gneiss evidently also occur on peninsular India. I struggled through the fug of Calcutta to get to the Anglican Cathedral. Were it not for the presence of that irrepressible city on every side, and the relentless heat, the building might have been in Tunbridge Wells or Ashby de la Zouch; it seemed so *frightfully* English. Inside there were various elaborate memorials to army officers and civil servants; But I never found Job Charnock, nor his charnockite gravestone. Some day I may return to try and find the correct church.

The chemical composition of the Lewisian gneiss on the foreshore at Achmelvich indicates that it was originally an igneous rock known as tonalite. Metamorphism at depth changed it to gneiss. The dingy colour of the feldspars imparts greyness to the whole region; I am used to clear pink or white feldspars, like those in Cornwall. Under powerful modern probes, the Lewisian feldspars can be shown to contain myriads of minute inclusions – comprising elements such as titanium that are 'soluble' in the feldspars at very high pressures – and these, like the chemical smog that fuzzes up the streets of Calcutta, impart a kind of smokiness to the commonest mineral in the gneiss. The world, after all, is painted at the molecular level. On closer inspection, the gneisses can also be seen to contain irregular balls of very black rock – some larger than a football – that look as if they had been caught up in the original igneous intrusion. They are reminiscent of the xenoliths, those messengers from the underworld we first met in the lavas of Hawai'i. They are believed to represent fragments of the original ocean floor from which the tonalites were derived by partial melting when this ancient crust was first formed. The mere fact that we can use such comparisons shows that the processes that operated so long ago can still be interpreted in the light of processes we know today. And then there are the dykes, much more visible than in Scourie: dark walls decked with contrasting white lichen patches like paint splashes, each dyke bounded by narrow sheared edges. If you look hard you can see remnants of the original igneous texture, mere ghosts of crystals of feldspar long since changed into a granular mosaic by transfiguration in the deep earth. We are looking so far back in time that ghosts and chemistry are our best informants.

But how far back in time, and how do we know?

To unravel the argument we have to follow the footsteps of the early investigators a few miles to the east – to the Moine Thrust. Recall that the north-western margin of Scotland is, in its deeper geological reality, part of the old Laurentian continent. Scourie and its environs are but a piece of the old heart of North America, stranded by the subsequent opening of the present Atlantic Ocean on the 'wrong' side of the water. Mr Evander MacIver would no doubt have had to light a second cheroot to take it all in, but the idea is familiar to us by now. To the east of Scourie, forming the highest of the Highlands today, lies the eroded remnant of the great Caledonian mountain chain. The Lewisian territory forms part of what Eduard Suess would have called its foreland – and we have to imagine that foreland stretching far westwards over into what is now the core of Canada. The final heave of the Caledonides towards the foreland happened along the Moine Thrust. The geology is shown at its simplest at the famous locality at Knockan Cliff, a few miles north of Ullapool, close to the A835, the main road northwards. The interpretation of the geology of this unremarkable grassy slope topped by a small crag sparked one of the great rows in the history of science.

When I first visited Knockan Cliff more than twenty years ago there was not much to mark out the place – a small monument, no more. Nowadays, it has a fully-fledged visitor centre topped by a turf roof, and a marked trail, set with plaques, leading upwards to the cliff. I noticed that the construction of the centre had been sponsored by no less than eight different organizations, which reflects how difficult it is adequately to mark sites of scientific pilgrimage. The marked trail was excellent. You are led up through a succession of rocks of Cambrian (about 540 million years) age piled one on top of the other. Near the base is the 'Pipe Rock', riddled with the tubes made by worms in the sands of an ancient sea-shore: from the top, the exit holes of the tubes look as if someone had stubbed out a whole series of cigarettes in the sand; then comes a rock bed including small fossils of the mysterious tube *Salterella*; above again lie shales yielding the beautiful early trilobite *Olenellus*, the size of a crab, which proves as clearly as if the outcrop had been date-stamped that these rocks are not merely Cambrian in age, but *Lower* Cambrian. This was the time-period when marine animal life carrying shells apparently suddenly burst into variety and complexity. A Lower Cambrian sedimentary pile, then, and above it, along the outcrop, a thickness of early Ordovician limestones. Then you are led onwards and upwards to the famous thrust. A dribbling waterfall marks the spot. At the top, forming the little cliff, are some completely different looking rocks. For a start, they have been strongly metamorphosed, whereas the Cambrian rocks beneath them on the slope show no such alteration. These uppermost rocks are known as the Moine schists, a dreary formation that covers a huge area of mountains and heather-clad moors to the east. At the base of the cliff is a rock bed – perhaps two – of a creamy-yellow colour, forming a kind of boundary layer between the Moines above and what lies below.

The nineteenth-century argument centred on the interpretation of the rock succession I have just described: was it a normal sequence, in which case the Moine rocks would have been younger than the rocks that evidently lay below them? Or had the upper part of the sequence been thrust bodily over the underlying sedimentary rocks, and might therefore be much older than the rocks on which it came to rest? In many respects, it is the same problem already examined in detail in the Glarus Nappe in Switzerland, and the arguments do not need to be rehearsed again. It is sufficient to say that reputations were made and lost in defending one view or the other. The name that is in use today embodies the eventual solution to the problem – it was, indeed, a thrust. The yellowish rocks beneath the Moines were mylonites, the ground-up rock paste upon which the huge mass above rode. Look at them closely and you can see evidence of the intense deformation to which they have been subjected: dense pleating and banding. Because it squeezed *over* early Ordovician rocks, the thrust event must have happened after that time, which marks it out as part of the Caledonian deformation. Elsewhere along the long outcrop of the Moine Thrust, which runs from Durness in the north to the Isle of Skye in the south, there are true nappes interposed along the boundary, so the Swiss analogy becomes even closer. The Highlands Controversy, as it came to be known, took more than thirty years to play itself out, during which time tempers inflated to almost orogenic proportions. The visitor centre portrays the heroes of the controversy as the two Geological Survey geologists, Ben Peach and John Horne. Peach and Horne's 1907 *Memoir* is certainly one of the great works of geology, and it mapped out the Moine Thrust in incomparable detail. But the intellectual leap towards the thrust solution was made more than a decade earlier by the great geologist Charles Lapworth, in *opposition* to the then Director of the Geological Survey, one of the most famous scientists of his day. Lapworth himself suffered a nervous collapse as a result of his 'anti-establishment' role in the Highlands Controversy. He dreamed of being crushed beneath the mighty thrust. Peach and Horne were, in a sense, righting a wrong that had once been sustained by their own paymasters. It is all done and dusted now, a controversy subsided, and as I stand in the cold sleet on this bleak slope it is hard to believe that the rocks before me once generated so much heat. In the visitor centre an animation shows how this part of Scotland – in early days a piece of Laurentia – has changed its latitude over the last billion years, playing its part in the stately progress of the drifting continents. It began near the South Pole; by the time that the *Olenellus* trilobites were grovelling around in the Cambrian mud it had reached the equator; thence it moved at an irregular pace towards its current position at high latitudes. This is another lesson in how we must unmake the world as we go back in time – lose all familiar geographical outlines, rearrange everything. The deeper we go, the stranger everything is, the less recognizable.

As we look westwards from Knockan Cliff, we are also looking further back into geological time, to the ages before the Cambrian. Before us lies the mountain of Cul Mor, 981 metres high, presenting a curiously rounded, rather than jagged, outline, and rising with almost improbable steepness from the surrounding undulating plain. A dusting of snow has picked out the higher strata. It is as if white, parallel, horizontal lines had been drawn upon it, lending it the appearance of a layered cake, sprinkled with icing sugar. These are bedded, sedimentary strata, neither folded nor sheared. Yet they are also the rocks that lie *below* the Cambrian succession – there are several sites nearby where you can see the sandstones that form the base of the Cambrian rock succession lying upon this earlier 'package' of sediments. There is also evidence that there was a break in time, an unconformity, below the base of the Cambrian rocks, which records the invasion of the sea over a rocky surface that had previously been weathered down to close to sea-level. So the rocks that make up Cul Mor were, by definition, deposited before the Cambrian began – they are Precambrian in age. All along this part of the west coast of Scotland there are wonderful mountains composed of the same sedimentary rocks: Suilven, Stac Pollaidh, Canisp, Quinaig. Almost wherever you are along the coast on the Lewisian gneiss, one of these mountains seems to peek down at you from beyond one of the low hills in your immediate vicinity. None of them belongs to the select group of Scotland's 'Munros' – the 284 mountains catalogued by Sir Hugh Munro that rise to more than 914 metres (3000 feet) high. But they seem higher than they really are because of their sheer sides – in some cases there is only one way up for the climber without pitons. Uncountable years of erosion have left these peaks standing proud, and their intractable, uniform hardness has resulted in their curious, monument-like topography. You feel an urge to bound to the top, to feel that you have conquered your own piece of deep time. The rocks take their name from Loch Torridon, thirty miles to the south-west – they are Torridonian in age. Careful mapping in the last thirty years has shown that there is an older and a younger series of rocks within the Torridonian as a whole: a further division of Precambrian time. Perhaps we should take a closer look.

It has to be said that this wonderful countryside has one drawback: rain. On my previous visit during the summer twenty years ago, I concluded that I might just as well jump into a lochan early in the morning to save myself the trouble of trying to keep dry later in the day. There was scarcely such an option in late October, with snow on the hills, and even the sheep looking a little depressed. My visit coincided with the heaviest rain in eastern Scotland for years. and so I inspected the Torridonian through a haze of water. Graham Park optimistically insisted that, in western Scotland, the weather is always liable to take a turn for the better. 'It's getting lighter in the west!' he would exclaim, pointing towards a slightly less dense bit of strato-cumulus. We examined the Torridonian along the roadside between squalls. Here was a place where you could see that the rocks were mostly reddish sandstones. Years of rain had weathered out the sedimentary bedding into a kind of naturally sculpted mural, which preserved the traces of the kinds of channels that are produced by vigorous flash floods today. In a broken rockface, crystals of feldspar, still quite fresh and pink, indicated that these ancient deposits were laid down under arid conditions: in moister environments feldspar soon decays to clay. So the Torridonian was indeed torrid – a curious, but entirely coincidental marriage of name and historical fact. A few miles to the south, by Loch Maree, the Torridonian makes an impressive waterfall, the Victoria Falls (Queen Victoria herself had inspected them when staying at the Loch Maree Hotel). The falls are reached by walking up through a majestic conifer forest, underlain by moss and ferns, and no scrub at all. In sheltered places, fir trees make stately specimens in western Scotland, and their branches whisper and sigh. The falls plunge over a rock bed made of massive sandstone. The rock beds underlying it are much shalier, and very much softer, so that the falling water has excavated an impressive overhang, like a miniature Niagara. Little by little, the Torridonian rocks are being worn away, even after having survived for so long. Later that day, Graham Park was proved right: the sun came out. We were in the very eye of the storm.

From the southern shore of Loch Maree we can see the whole story of the rocks laid out on the cliffs on the opposite side. Loch Maree is one of the most beautiful lochs in Scotland. In the seventh century, an Irish monk lived on one of its islands, and converted the local people; his holy well was credited with curative properties, though no one I spoke to could tell me its location. On the flanks of the loch, patches of the old Caledonian forest linger on, with groves of Scots pines with branches that make such interesting crooked-elbow shapes compared with other conifers. Scraps of wild forest also survive on islets in the loch, where seedlings are protected from the depradations of nibbling sheep. The long loch follows the old grain of the land from north-west to south-east, tracing out a fault more than a billion years old. The northern shore is so straight that it might have been ruled out upon the ground. Fundamental faults never entirely go to sleep, and there is evidence that antique faults like the one underlying Loch Maree came alive again when the Atlantic Ocean opened, in the latest of the many tectonic cycles to affect the Highlands. Sir Walter Scott, who virtually invented the Romantic view of Scotland, supplied us with an unexpectedly accurate description of the durability of faults (in *The Lord of the Isles*, 1815, canto iii):

> Seems that primeval earthquake's sway
> Hath rent a strange and shatter'd way
> Through the rude bosom of the hill,
> And that each naked precipice,
> Sable ravine, and dark abyss,
> Tells of the outrage still.

The original lakeside track ran along the straight northern shore, but now the main road runs from Kinlochewe – where Peach and Horne lodged – to Gairloch along the southern shore. From this road, under the shadow of Ben Eighe, we can see the structures written out in the cliffs on the far side of the loch. It is golden eagle country, with open crags and mountainsides. To the east, the Moine Thrust is repeated, but here complicated by one of the nappes, the Kinlochewe Nappe, which actually turns the whole sequence upside down. But we can clearly see the Cambrian sandstones underlying the Thrust forming a steep slope, and beneath them again the thick-bedded, pinkish Torridonian rocks, of which we had already seen so much on the hillsides around the Victoria Falls. But here there is something else displayed: the relationship between the Torridonian rocks and the Lewisian, with which this chapter began. Above the shore opposite to us, around Glen Bianasdail, the low, greyish, mound-like hills have a familiar cast. They recall the low hills around Scourie – and they are, indeed, made of Lewisian rocks. We can now see that the Torridonian sedimentary rocks lie on top of the Lewisian. Canisp, Suilven, and the rest of the western mountains rise above, and lie upon, an undulating basement of Lewisian gneiss; as Cadell of Grange put it in his colourful way: 'These mountains stand like giant sentinels round the margin of a heaving sea of gneiss.' Not only that, on Loch Maree we observe that the Torridonian beds fill in valleys in the original Lewisian surface; they are spread over an older landscape, as a builder might level irregular ground before commencing construction. The ancient surface is being exhumed as erosion slowly, very slowly, strips away the Torridonian rocks above. It reveals a hidden landscape. When we look over the Lewisian terrain we are, literally, looking back nearly a billion years into the past. Strip off the thin veneer of vegetation – it is no more than a flimsy film – and you can imagine walking through late Precambrian territory, while the rocks you are strolling upon provide an inkling of still earlier times. The Torridonian rocks have *not* been metamorphosed; equally, we know that the Lewisian rocks have been altered deep within the earth's crust. So it follows that the Lewisian had already been through its entire 'life cycle' of formation, deep burial, metamorphism, uplift, and profound erosion, before the Torridonian rocks were even laid upon it. And the massive thickness of Torridonian must itself have been derived from the erosion of yet another mountain range* lying to the west on the ancient Laurentian continent – a range now banished to the far side of the Atlantic Ocean. An awesome vista of geological time suddenly opens up before us, a vision of age after age of mountain-building, of continents remaking themselves, stretching far back into the distant reaches of the Precambrian. It should provoke a sense of our own insignificance, but it also stimulates a sense of wonder that we, alone among organisms, have been privileged to see these vanished worlds, and challenged to understand the immensity of time. A sudden squall makes us shiver, and turn up our collars.

The Precambrian is divided into two huge sections: the Archaean, greater than 2500 million years; and the Proterozoic, 2500–542 million years ago, underlying Cambrian and younger strata. Since the earth was formed 4550 million years ago, any rocks that might be discovered dating between then and 2500 million years will be Archaean, by definition. The oldest history of the Lewisian gneiss is Archaean; the Torridonian belongs with the later part of the Proterozoic. Our intimations on the shores of Loch Maree concerning the vastness of geological time were indeed correct: more than two billion years was laid out before us there. Most of earth's history lies in the time before shelly fossils of animals became common in Cambrian and overlying rocks. However, life was present on earth during most of Precambrian time, but it did not include large organisms with shells. Small fossils – thin threads and rods for the most part – miraculously survive from these distant eons. They endure because not all early rocks have been ground through the mill of metamorphism. In a few places, special rocks, mostly cherts, survive that are privileged time capsules carrying traces of these pioneering organisms. The earliest fossils of bacteria date to about 3500 million years ago, deep within the Archaean. The authenticity of these remains has recently been debated, but even if the earliest ones are chimeras, there is geochemical evidence that life has been present on earth for at least 3600 million

* This is proved, for example, by the selection of pebbles found in the conglomerates in the Torridonian, including volcanic rocks, most of which cannot be matched by anything in the Lewisian gneiss.

years. The names used to divide the Precambrian are therefore inappropriate in the light of modern knowledge: there was proto-life before the Proterozoic, and the Archaean was not as barren as was once thought. The story of life is not my story here, but it cannot be excluded from the story of the plates because life and earth are meshed together, as we shall discover. Living organisms have been more than mere passengers on the shifting tectonic jigsaw.

There are many places in the world where Precambrian rocks are more extensively exposed than they are in north-west Scotland, and other places where there are rocks older than the Lewisian. However, the Highlands have a pivotal role in unscrambling Precambrian time. Although the Lewisian takes its name from the Isle of Lewis in the Outer Hebrides, where high-grade gneisses are abundant, it was on mainland Scotland that the main intellectual battles were fought. We have focused our attention there for this reason. When Eduard Suess wrote *Das Antlitz der Erde* little progress had been made in subdividing Precambrian time. The earliest rocks tended to be lumped together as 'basement', or described as 'fundamental', and then swept under the conceptual carpet. 'Basement' still seems rather appropriate for something underlying the whole edifice of geological time. Even in Suess' day, although most serious scientists knew that the world was very old, the calculations designed to find out exactly *how* old all proved to be gross underestimates. They were based on false assumptions – for example, assuming an erroneous rate of cooling of the earth. More objective methods were to change everything. Arthur Holmes was a crucial figure in the development of radiometric dating techniques, especially Uranium–Lead methods, which improved upon the earlier estimates. He spent hour upon hour hand-cranking calculators, performing tasks that a modern computer would take a millisecond or two to complete. No matter, he and his colleagues established – admittedly with huge margins of error – that the earth had to be several billions, rather than hundreds of millions, years old. The Precambrian consequently grew both in extent and importance. Between the two editions of 'Holmes' (1944 and 1964) the earth roughly doubled in age. To understand more about the

Precambrian became a research priority. Could you still invoke the same tectonic processes for deep time that were applicable to the last few hundred million years? And could such apparently intractable rocks as 'fundamental' gneisses be further divided in the field? This is where the Scourie Dykes come back into the story.

We must return to the coast from our tour along Loch Maree. The little seaside town of Gairloch nearby is strung out along a broad bay. Every cottage is rendered for protection against the winter blast, and then whitewashed; the overall effect is pleasantly harmonious. The rain was still coming down in torrents when we arrived, and the place was empty, except for some bewildered but game Dutch tourists. The ground behind the town displayed what had by now become a familiar topography, the grey rounded hills of Lewisian country. The main road heads eastwards out of town through a stretch of boggy terrain, and after a couple of miles passes a small freshwater lake, Loch Tollaidh (Tollie), which, in the curious brooding light of a stormy day, manages to look both silvery and leaden at the same time. Like many lochs, it has a fish farm located within it, the long-term ecological consequences of which are coming under increasing scrutiny. The gneiss in the region, is, if anything, more strongly striped than it was at Scourie, blobby pink and grey seams picking out the strong foliation. Graham Park pointed out to me the outline of the Scourie Dykes intruding the gneiss on the hillside across the far side of the loch. A century ago the skilful Geological Survey geologist C. T. Clough mapped out the course of these dykes across country. It became clear that the dykes could be used to trace out broad 'folds'* and similar structures within the Lewisian confusion: they provided a key to unlocking another phase of the remote past.

It may be helpful to recap the sequence of events. First, the Archaean crust was formed from tonalite; then this crust was buried

* Folding of foliation in metamorphic rocks is not the same as simple folding in sedimentary formations. Because metamorphic rocks are so altered and contorted, it is sometimes not possible to tell their original orientation. So structural geologists call a downfold a synform rather than syncline, and an upfold an antiform, not an anticline.

and deeply metamorphosed to the granulite facies, implying temperatures of 1000° C and pressures of 10 kilobars. This tectonic trauma generated the banded gneiss we saw exposed in undulating, grey masses along the Scourie coast. Then came the intrusion of the dykes, which cut through the earlier rocks. All this history is laid out in the strata around Scourie Lodge, not far from the most northerly palm tree in the world. The ancient events are therefore referred to as Scourian, the oldest rocks in the British Isles. But, in the vicinity of Gairloch, later events have remoulded the earlier Scourian rocks. Insult has been added to injury, Pelion has been heaped upon Ossa. To the uninitiated, one gneiss, to be frank, looks rather like another. But that careful mapping around Loch Tollie proved that earlier structures, *including* the dykes, had been *re*folded by a subsequent tectonic event. This later event was termed Laxfordian.

Structural geologists love such things. They read the flexures in the rocks with the certainty of a blind man reading braille. They can easily imagine what it is for a fold system to be caught up in another, subsequent phase of contortion, fold imposed on fold. I admire this capacity to think in three dimensions – four, if you include time – more than I can say. In 1951, midway between the two editions of 'Holmes', a paper by Janet Watson and her husband-colleague John Sutton outlined the history of the Lewisian in essentially its modern form. All the rocks in the Gairloch area had been re-metamorphosed – heated and baked again – and reset to a lower metamorphic degree than the granulites, known as the amphibolite facies. Less deep, less extreme. A mineralogist reads this change by logging transformations that have occurred to the minerals within the gneisses – technically, the minerals are said to retrogress. Minerals never lie. They tell us exactly the conditions of temperature and pressure to which rocks have been subjected, betraying another phase in their 'long continued ill usage'. This is still a form of cookery. It is just that, in metamorphic geology, cookery can go backwards as well as forwards.

Now we just have to add dates. This is not quite as simple as it sounds. It is not like looking up a date on an old calendar. Dating relies on setting the radioactive 'clock'. This might happen when a mineral crystallizes out from magma; year zero in this case is truly a birth, followed by its own trajectory of ageing as the radioactive clock winds down. But the clock can also be 'reset' by a subsequent metamorphic event. Even the same zircon crystal can respond to one event after another – the inner part of a single crystal can be much older than the outer shell. Zircon is a kind of Methuselah among natural substances and seems to survive five times longer than almost any other mineral, which is why it contains such a useful 'clock'. Modern techniques can obtain separate dates even from within that single zircon crystal. Even the most enthusiastic geochronologist will tell you that all dates still require intelligent interpretation, but radiometric ages have transformed our understanding of the Precambrian, and they are getting better all the time. So here are the dates for north-west Scotland. The crust-forming event at Scourie (the oldest Lewisian if you like) happened at 2960 million years ago – within the Archaean. The main metamorphism to granulites happened almost on the boundary between the Archaean and the Proterozoic, around 2500 million years ago. Graham Park and his colleagues have recognized a third phase, termed Inverian, following the Scourian, but predating the Laxfordian, which produces extensive shearing of the Scourie gneisses in several regions. As for the Scourie Dykes themselves, a sample from Teall's original locality has provided what is currently the best date for their intrusion at 2400 million years ago. Mr MacIver would doubtless have raised both his eyebrows in astonishment had he realized the antiquity of the ground on which the Lodge was built.

Then there is the subsequent phase in the long history of the Lewisian, when the dykes were folded – as traced out in the hills around Gairloch – and when the Laxfordian metamorphism remodelled the ancient gneiss to a whiter shade of grey. The best date at the moment from the Laxford area is 1740 million years ago. To put it in perspective: the events frozen in these ancient gneisses span more than twice the time that lies between the human race and the first trilobite.

As for the Torridon sandstones overlying the Lewisian, those pink rocks that we saw by the Victoria Falls, as rainwater dribbled down our necks, prove to be some 800 million years old; the oldest sandstone group around the village of Stoer may be as much as 990 million years old. So, for a billion years or more, the area occupied by Lewisian gneiss was eroded, ground down grain by grain, until time had breached a window deep into the ancient crust. Then it was blanketed by the sediments that now form Suilven and Stac Pollaidh. The undulating grey Lewisian landscape that we admire today would have looked much the same long before the first trilobite scurried in the mud, or the first snail crawled upon the sea-floor. And it will endure long after our species has vanished from the world. 'Time, that agèd nurse/Rock'd me to patience.'

This is not yet the end of the story. Around Gairloch, and extending inland towards Loch Maree, there is another group of rocks that Graham Park has been studying for many years. They are deeply entrained within the Lewisian gneiss, and have been affected by the same, Laxfordian, metamorphism. But they are rocks that originally lay on *top* of the gneisses. Graham's careful mapping, published by the Geological Society of London, shows that they occupy two synforms within the Lewisian, one of which is now followed on the ground by a little stream running along the charmingly-named Flowerdale. On the other side of the valley, volcanic rocks and sediments, now transformed by metamorphism, provide yet another window opening on to the ancient of days, for these rocks are almost as old as the gneisses they cover, though they embrace a different range of geology. They tell us about what was going on under the sea.

The Old Inn at Gairloch looked singularly welcoming in the rain, but we had to forgo the comfort of a pint of bitter by the fire to look at the rocks. Just behind the pub there are some heavy-looking, greenish-black rocks, which are densely foliated. These are amphibolites, which started out life as lavas with a basalt composition. They were erupted on the sea-floor about two billion years ago and have been compared with oceanic plateau basalts. A little way up the road the rocks take on a kind of brownish cast – a little subtle for my palaeontologist's eye. Graham assured me that these were once sedimentary rocks lying atop the basalts: their chemistry is just what would be expected from sediments associated with an island arc. The alchemy of metamorphism has transformed them into different minerals, to be sure, but they have retained their identity at the most fundamental level of atoms and molecules. To follow the story further we had to walk along a muddy path up the river valley. On a good day it would be a delightful stroll; in the drizzle, the bracken-covered hills fading into distant mistiness retained a flavour of Celtic mystery that Sir Walter Scott would have relished. Even the crude stone walls were made from 'fundamental' rocks. What better way to be led back to the beginnings of things?

After about half a mile we paused to examine some rocks in a slippery bank. The dark amphibolite was still with us, but interleaved with it was something different. To one raised on younger rocks, the black chunks of hard rock we levered out from these layers looked a little like chert, a form of silica, but in the hand they seemed much too heavy for this common material. Examined close up, fine banding was faintly displayed within the rock. These apparently humble pieces of stone proved to be one of the defining rock types of the Precambrian: the banded iron formation, commonly known as BIFs. Their characteristic heaviness is because of their high iron content – in some localities they could be even used as ore. BIFs are another sedimentary rock, but one that is unique to the early earth and that tells us much about its peculiarities. On the far side of the bank, we scraped out some pieces of lighter-coloured stone, which, if I had happened to have a bottle of dilute acid on my person, would have fizzed merrily on being doused. This was a marble, and would have been a limestone before its transformation by heat and pressure – the calcium carbonate of which it is made reacts with acid. No sculptor would have wished to expend his skill on these mean little pieces, but their significance is not aesthetic. Limestones are one of the commonest marine sedimentary rocks through the geological record, and evidently were still being formed two billion years ago. And just underneath the limestone there were other dark rocks with a familiar look that split into thin sheets. At first glance they resembled the marine shales they once were, but they, too, have been transformed – into chlorite schists. Among them are bands that chemical analysis shows have a high content of carbon, and the principal source of carbon in shales is organic, for carbon is the element most basic to biology. Is there a hint here of the presence of oceanic life?

Just on cue, the sun came out, as if to cast light on the mysteries of deep time. The yellowing leaves of the birch trees almost glowed. We stood discussing how to fit together rationally all the features that we had seen along Flowerdale. The rocks exposed in the flank of the valley seem originally to have been a piece of the sea-floor: volcanic rocks at the base, with various kinds of sedimentary rocks accumulating on top. Limestones and shales are familiar enough today, so evidently the sedimentary processes happening two billion years ago were not different in some respects from those operating now. One striking fact is that the metamorphosed sedimentary rocks have patently been incorporated into the Lewisian 'basement'. Once tempered by deep cooking, they became one with the realm of old gneisses. So rocks derived from ancient oceans subsequently became *part* of the Archaean and early Proterozoic shields, which are the oldest and now most stable parts of the earth's crust. Cratons were created. Shields were sealed. Continental crust grew by a process of 'plastering on' – by marginal accretion of bits of ocean crust and sediments. The places such 'additions' occur lie along subduction zones. After all, younger zones of subduction still leave their legacy in great tracts of rock added to the edges of older continents, just as the fold belt of the Appalachian–Caledonian chain was soldered on to edge of the Canadian Shield. The igneous tonalites that comprise the oldest Lewisian rocks may be explained by a process of partial melting not so different in kind from that operating today at depth on active continental margins. It seems that plate explanations can, indeed, be applied to the Methuselahs of rock, the ancient of days. Thus the apparently endless and uniform gneiss begins to reveal its secrets. Those grey hills are not, after all, unreadable, although the script may be distorted. To understand processes that happened billions of years ago, the present is still – at least, up to a point – the key to the past.

Now we can create a vision of the Archaean world. Heat flow from the young earth was greater than it is now. What Charles Lapworth called the 'great earth engine' cranked over faster. There may have been more numerous convection cells within the mantle. Recall how thick soup over a high flame breaks into bubbling fury, while a simmering broth swirls over in a few dignified turns. The nascent masses of continental crust had not yet congealed to their present size. Instead, smaller rafts of lighter rocks formed the nuclei of what would become more stable continental areas. The cycles of the earth – the generation and destruction of plates – probably happened *andante cantabile* rather than *largo*. The sea – and there was certainly an ocean – was whipped up by storms, reducing all land newly elevated by tectonics to sedimentary waste. Slabs of oceanic rock were covered with sediments derived from the rapid weathering of the proto-continents. Unprotected by any cloak of plants, the wind and rain worked fast upon the naked rocks. This was a world of tempests and flash floods, of jagged crags and dunes. Clays and grits, the mucky progeny of erosion, slumped down into deep water. Volcanic rocks were erupted over the sea-floor – many of them associated with a multitude of 'hot spots' that pocked the early earth like a plague of boils. Then sediments and volcanics alike were plastered on to proto-continents at the subduction zone* – or perhaps were sandwiched between two proto-continents that collided. It has been claimed that massive, marine plateau basalts were added to the *base* of proto-continents, because they were reluctant to subduct, like sticky toffee that adheres to the gullet. Gradually, continental nuclei grew, accreted. Buoyed up by their less dense composition,

* It has recently been suggested that subduction zones in the early earth dipped downwards at a lower angle than at present, producing the tonalite magmas, which have distinctive signals in their geochemistry (especially the element Neodymium).

the growing continents bobbed onwards, as would rafts of cork on a mill-pool, while heavy oceanic crust was created and then destroyed in the early cycles of plate tectonics. Smaller continents merged one with another. Thus cratons were born, which were to drift hither and yon for the rest of earth's history, the stablest partners in the dance of the plates. With further erosion, sedimentary rocks were laid down upon the cratons. A few portions of such sediments were to escape all the subsequent vicissitudes of continental collisions, to carry forward to our own era a fossil record of the earliest life. So the world acquired the first of its many faces.

Ancient Precambrian proto-continents often preserve tracts of volcanic and sedimentary deposits – now, of course, metamorphosed – along their edges. They may represent the line along which two proto-continents collided, like a Ural range of the earliest days – seams so ancient that they are often no more than suggestions sketched in pointed minerals, or linear bandages interposed between round masses of granulite. In these 'greenstone belts', the rocks are green because of the abundance of the metamorphic mineral, chlorite, as well as epidote and hornblende, more greens. The belts are often kilometres wide, as they are in the ancient shield regions of Canada, southern Africa, and western Australia. The rocks along Flowerdale exhibited features on the small scale that apply to greenstone belts on the large scale, except that they are often less metamorphosed and the geology is even more complicated. The belts are frequently rich in precious metals, distilled and refined from the early and turbulent earth: gold, silver, copper, nickel. South of Hudson Bay, a swathe of greenstone belts passes east to west across Manitoba, northern Ontario, and western Quebec. The Red Lake Greenstone belt in Ontario is rich in gold, while the Abitibi Belt to the east not only boasts famous gold mines around the town of Timmins, but also has deposits of silver, copper, and tin elsewhere – gifts from the early Precambrian.

But it was a different world, this early one, for all that the same engines drove it. Most important, the atmosphere was initially almost without oxygen, while gaseous hydrogen sulphide and methane were

A fossil stromatolite from Precambrian (early Proterozoic) rocks of eastern Siberia. The fine layers are typical of the rock type.

abundant. Breathing this poisoned air would have killed us very quickly. At Solfatara, on the Bay of Naples, we had the merest hint of such a vile-smelling miasma, which would have been like a thickly-suffocating blanket. Most of the oxygen in the atmosphere today is a by-product of life. Three billion years of photosynthesis, much of it achieved by very simple organisms like blue-green bacteria, added oxygen molecule by molecule to the air. The minute rod- or thread-like remains of the bacteria that changed the world have been found among the earliest fossils. They formed sticky mats, which left their record in finely layered, crimped, or cushion-like fossils called stromatolites, looking like piles of petrified flaky pastry. These survived to the present where they were formed on top of continental fragments that acheived early stability. A well-known example is the Fig Tree chert of southern Africa. Still earlier bacteria could thrive in the *absence* of oxygen – in fact oxygen is a poison to them. These most primitive forms of life survive, indeed prosper, in hot, sulphurous springs and in stinking mud. If we want to know how life started, it is these oddly tough organisms we should consult. Subsequently, life changed the air of the world – scrubbed out the early poisons – and in the process even modified the way rocks decayed, since oxygen is crucial to all sorts of chemical weathering.

Banded iron formations (BIFs), a few dark pieces of which we collected in the drizzle in Flowerdale, were typical of a period 2600 to 1800 million years ago. When these rocks are polished and examined through a microscope they are seen to be composed of alternating layers a few millimetres thick. Dark layers are iron-rich, often made of the mineral magnetite, Fe_3O_4, an iron oxide, alternating with lighter bands of common silica; stripes of a different colour. The fact that the iron is oxidized in this curious sediment indicates that there must have been oxygen around to do it. But the peculiar banding, and the occurrence of magnetite, demands a special explanation – and one of general applicability, too, because BIFs are found on virtually every Precambrian shield. Iron is very greedy to combine with oxygen. Iron artefacts quickly become horrid lumps of rust when buried in the ground. One explanation for the existence of BIFs that has found favour derives the oxygen from microscopic photosynthesizing bacteria (or algae) within the ocean. Iron is weathered from continental rocks, but there is not yet enough free atmospheric oxygen to gobble it all up, so it enters the sea in solution as positively-charged ions. These combine with oxygen derived from the photosynthesizing scum, and at once heavy, insoluble magnetite is formed, which falls to the ocean floor as a gentle rain of minute black specks. Magnetite is the form of iron oxide that has both the most iron and the least oxygen – which implies that the latter was at a premium and had to be scavenged by the greedy iron ions. But biological productivity soon outstripped the available iron, and, so the theory goes, the burgeoning multitude of organisms became a victim of their own success, undergoing a 'bloom' that became lethal. Similar plankton blooms still happen in the sea today. They might even have been poisoned by 'excess' oxygen. During the quiescent phase that followed, only silica accumulated on the sea-floor, until the whole boom–bust cycle started again. It is much more complex than I have described, for several different kinds of BIF have now been recognized, with hematite (Fe_2O_3), or siderite, iron carbonate ($FeCO_3$), as important components. Nonetheless, the theory does conjure up a picture of a simple ecosystem, a lurching, fluctuating one, without the checks and balances that many millions of years of organic evolution have since imparted to the marine realm. However, some plausible explanations of BIFs have been advanced that do not require the intercession of life. For example, it has been claimed that they can be explained by fluctuations in sea-level, combined with a high supply of iron from hot fluids derived the early crust and a low supply of atmospheric oxygen. The definitive explanation still eludes us. The earlier Precambrian was a strange place, with hints of what we know, but much more that is unfamiliar. The past, as L. P. Hartley said, is another country. They do things differently there.

However different they are from anything we know today, BIFs continued to be laid down for 800 or 900 hundred million years – much more time than has elapsed since the beginning of the Cambrian and which embraces the entire proliferation of animal life – five times as long as the 'Age of Dinosaurs'. BIFs can be hundreds of metres thick and extend for a thousand kilometres. Our specimen from Flowerdale was the least impressive example. Just try to imagine how much iron is locked up inside them. The earth was remoulding itself throughout this long period, following the bidding of plate movements, and the atmosphere was changing at the same time. The whole planet was evolving. Life and earth are forever intertwined. The critic John Ruskin wrote in praise of rust, how it paints and dapples; but without oxygen there could *be* no rust. Iron meteorites, whose composition resembles that of the earth's core, arrive from space metallic black and pristine: it is only contact with earth's corrupting atmosphere that paints them rusty brown. Without the free oxygen generated by bacteria and plants there would have been no breathing, no animal life, no trilobites, no dinosaurs, no writer of this book, no reader. And no rust.

There are other rocks that help reveal the early earth. Komatiites are peculiar glassy lavas that are typically found in Archaean terranes. They cooled rapidly from magmas with compositions like that of the mantle. Inside these black rocks there are curious little bunches of olivine crystals that are said to display spinifex texture. The crystals radiate from a common centre into three dimensions, a little like the dark traces produced as mines explode. The name of the texture has a peculiar resonance for those of us who have worked in the outback of Australia. Spinifex is a ghastly, glaucous prickly grass that covers great tracts in the middle of nowhere. It, too, radiates from a common base. Each of its shoots, modified leaves, is tipped with a barb of silica that breaks off into your foot if you are foolish enough to stand upon it. If you light a match anywhere near it, spinifex bursts into flames and seeks to turn you into a crisp. But it does look exactly like the crystals within komatiites. Lavas with komatiite composition are proof of the higher heat flow in those primeval times; the peculiar olivine crystals grew downwards like stalactites from the cooled 'roofs' of the lavas.

Archaean and early Proterozoic shields comprise the middle of continents – the Hebridean area that we examined is unusual in being close to the edge of an ocean. They are the old hearts, the obstinate cores, the unchanging and persistent bulwarks against which subsequent history has piled its afterthoughts. After all, in a world that is 4550 million years old, the last 1000 million years are less than Act Three in the drama of creation. Archaean and earlier Proterozoic rocks and greenstone belts make up the old Baltic shield, underlying the territory where Lapps follow reindeer through lichen-covered and boggy wastes. They underlie the centre of Canada – the Canadian Shield, all stunted fir and endless lakes – and they extend southwards beneath the United States. The ground-down, acacia-sprinkled central veld of southern Africa, including the famous rocks of Barberton in the Transvaal; the dusty plains of much of the Indian peninsula; the rain-sodden northern parts of Brazil; many of the gold-rich regions of Australia, those plains carrying a few low knobs and ridges of fretted rock amidst the stony wastes, or rugged Pilbara in Western Australia – all these terrains are older than we can readily imagine. They display a similar pattern, though with many local variations: old igneous masses – often granulites – form nuclei, around the edges of which greenstone belts have been wrapped or plastered on. They show us the baked and exhumed remnants of splitting and clinching of former micro-continents from a time so long ago. When you are talking about three billion years, you could be forgiven for wondering what difference the odd ten million years or so really makes. Yet it is likely that the earth in those distant days was as rich in events as it has always been, but that the detail has been fogged by metamorphism, or scrubbed away by erosion. Geologists interested in such remote eras have a task comparable to reconstructing a vanished civilization from a thumb and forefinger broken off a sculpture and a few shards of pottery; indeed, for many years geologically incredibly old areas seemed beyond the reach of ratiocination. Largely as a result of being thought about in terms of tectonics and geochemistry, and then being able to date them, such rocky Methuselahs are now capable of being understood, even though all our perceptions are inevitably blurred through the mists of time. As D. H. Lawrence wrote:

> mists
> of mistiness complicated into knots and clots that barge
>   about
> and bump on one another and explode into more mist,
>   or don't
> mist of energy most scientific

Plate tectonic processes evidently carried on from Precambrian into Cambrian times, and thence to the present day. By reversing time's arrow, the movements of continents can be tracked ever further back into the past. There is probably no harder exercise for the imagination within the pages of this book. We have already traced the wandering continents to the time before the assembly of Pangaea. We have seen how 'palaeomag' can be combined with field geology to reveal another, still older world in which the continents were again scattered, as they are today, but with all the pieces in different places and arranged in a different way, as if the earth's surface were a collage reassembled by an amnesiac. To reach this stage, we have gone back perhaps 500 million years, only about one-eighth of the history of the rocks on the planet. There is so much further to go. We must travel backwards, much further backwards in time, following the bidding of the plates, if we are to attempt to find out how the 'knots and clots that barge/about/and bump on one another' were laid out in the eons before the Palaeozoic. We have to let go of even the most rudimentary outlines of the continents we know, some of which accompanied us back as far as Cambrian days. We have to go to worlds without familiar signposts, lost worlds, uncertain worlds.

There is, though, a certain logic to it. If Pangaea split apart a couple of hundred million years ago, but was itself assembled from dispersed continents, then is it not likely that there might be a still older 'Pangaea' when the continents were married on a previous occasion? There is time enough, and more. Perhaps there have even been a number of phases when supercontinents dominated the earth, so that the progress of the continents was like one of those eighteenth-century dances in which the participants move apart at one stage, only to repeatedly find one another again in the centre of the ballroom on an appropriate prompt from the music. There is now evidence for no less than four Precambrian supercontinents: at 2500 million years ago – that is, on the boundary between the Archaean and Proterozoic; then at about 1500 million years; again at approximately one billion years; and once more at about eighty million years before the beginning of the Cambrian period, approximately 625 million years ago, in the late Proterozoic. I say 'approximately' advisedly, because it is very difficult to be precise. The assembly of a supercontinent is a time when most subduction has stopped, and hence most of the activity that might lead to a radiometric date has also become quiescent. It is a kind of 'hole' in history.

Imagine being in the middle of the latest Archaean supercontinent, the first one on the face of the earth. Prior to this time, the continents had mostly been mere fragments, furiously jostling. But now, a crudely rugged landscape, unsoftened by any green vegetation, would extend to the horizon for thousands of kilometres in all directions. You would have to be alert to the possibility of being carried away by a flash flood emanating from the granulite hills thirty kilometres or so away. The ground around you is littered with angular boulders carried by the furious waters; feldspars glisten in the relentless sun. A hot spring bubbling and hissing at your feet is surrounded by brilliant orange and livid purple stains. They feel slick to the touch. The colours are painted by bacterial life that forms a slimy film; the lively hues are pigments that shield the tiny cells from harmful rays in the harsh sunlight. From here, you cannot see the tacky, green mats in the sea that are slowly transforming the earth's atmosphere; the ocean is a kinder place, a womb for the future. But here in the wilderness, you don't know which organisms are going to inherit the earth. The photosynthesis bug is no racing cert; it could equally well be a bacterium that gorges on sulphur and relishes boiling hot conditions.

The early supercontinents juxtaposed parts of the present earth in ways that we would find most surprising. Just think about our small patch of Scotland. It was, of course, part of ancient North America (Laurentia). But in the Late Proterozoic supercontinent, Laurentia lay alongside, of all places, South America. The little patch with the Scourie dykes was not so far from the South Pole. Evidence from matching geological ages and structures turns the world topsy-turvy. What, you wonder, would Professor Suess have made of it all, this world so stripped of fixity? Even those of us who have had a whole working life to get used to the idea of mobile continents have a struggle to remake the world so completely. But what we can accept is that continents cannot jump from one place to another. They have to move in a logical procession in order to make kinematic sense. So we know about the slow march of the polar wandering path for north-west Scotland, from near the South Pole to the northern hemisphere over a billion years, and it is a pattern that has to fit in with other evidence from separate continents and geology. The ancient supercontinents, once so speculative, have started to achieve the respectability that comes with a name. The continental mass at around a billion years ago has been called Rodinia, and now scientists are starting to bandy that name about with the familiarity that Pangaea attained forty years ago. There are other names that have yet

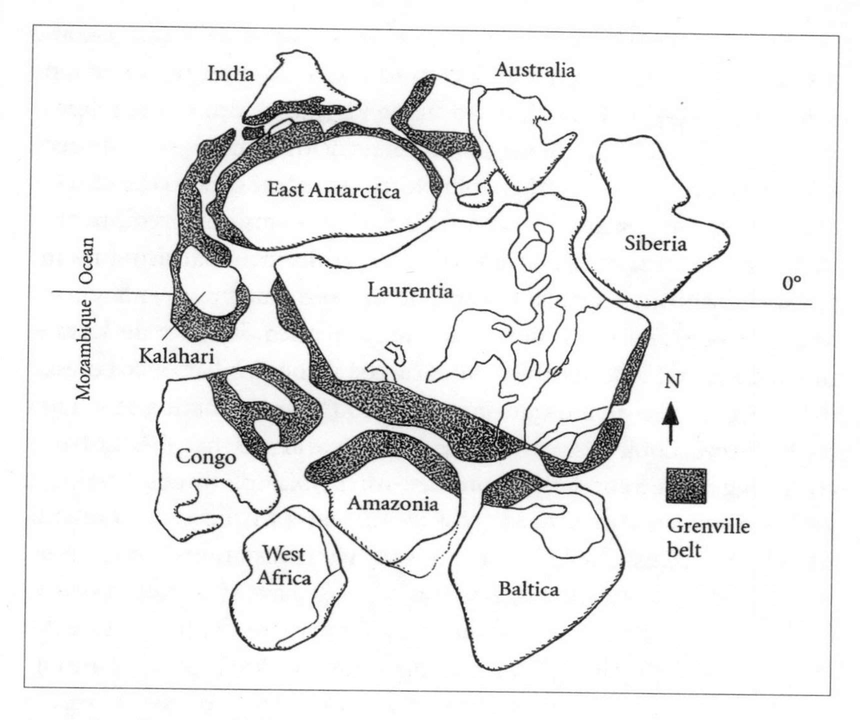

An ancient Pangaea: the late Precambrian supercontinent of Rodinia. Laurentia as its core is easily recognizable. The ancient mountain belt shaded marks the line of 'stitching together' of the supercontinent from the two still earlier separated continents which collided. *Toujours la même chose.*

to achieve widespread currency – 'Kenorland' in the late Archaean is one – but who knows whether they will be part of scientific consciousness in fifty years? It is extraordinary how quickly names useful in scientific discourse become incorporated into the language. Soon, nearly everyone forgets who coined the name, or – more importantly – who first understood the concept that the name embodies. The first supercontinent to be named was Gondwana, but who now remembers that Eduard Suess was present at its christening? Yet without the story of Gondwana and Pangaea there would have been no vision of Rodinia, nor of any of the other continents united together deep into Precambrian times.

A mid-Proterozoic, 1500-million-year supercontinent is also becoming widely accepted as a fact, although at the time of writing it does not have a generally-used name (if it were up to me, I would call it Seussia). It was remarkable for including masses of igneous intrusions, now mostly situated in North America, which do not seem to be related to orogeny in the usual way. Precambrian geologists, if they may be so termed, have had much amusement devising model systems to account for them. The igneous rocks include a widely-used ornamental stone – the rapakivi granite, named for its type locality in Scandinavia. The polished stone can be recognized at once because it looks as if it is made out of sawn-through eggs floating in a dark background. Look more carefully and you will see that the centre of each 'egg' is a very large, rounded-off crystal of pinkish feldspar which has been surrounded by a thin 'shell' of a different mineral, usually a greenish-looking rim of another feldspar. It is quite easy to 'read' this rock. The large feldspars must have crystallized out of the magma first, but then the surrounding magma changed. The early crystals reacted with the liquor to brew up the 'shell' of surrounding (oligoclase) feldspars as the rest of the rock completed its cooling. A later event modified an earlier one: it is not so different in logic from the story of the Scourie Dykes. A rapakivi granite forms the counter of a bar at Paddington Station in London. I come through this station most days. Although Paddington is one of Isambard Kingdom Brunel's finest engineering achievements, the bar is a recent addition. If you have just missed your train, you can at least lean on a bar that is 1500 million years old and reflect that perhaps half an hour is not that serious a delay.

Your fellow commuters might be suprised to learn that the shiny surface of the bar was in fact a piece of a continent more ancient than Pangaea, but one that broke up in the same way as India did from Africa; and that when the pieces came together again, 500 million years later, it marked the formation of the *next* supercontinent, Rodinia, a billion years ago. The Grenville mountain chain was thrown up as a consequence of this *rapprochement*, which towered all along the eastern edge of the old Laurentian shield and made it possible eventually to build skyscrapers in New York on solid foundations.

Those parts of the rough mosaic of plates that were composed of continental crust moved, now together, now apart, in cycle after cycle. Gradually, these lighter continental slabs grew larger, as the squeezing and melting connected with subduction added material to their edges. The days, too, were getting longer as the Precambrian progressed, because the earth slowed on its spinning axis, just as oxygen trickled molecule by molecule into the atmosphere. All these changes, while not exactly pure Charles Lyell, are explicable in terms of modern processes, a transformation rather than a revolution. But there have also been events in the Precambrian that have been claimed as utterly unlike any that followed.

Of these, one that has achieved most notoriety is the 'Snowball Earth' hypothesis, not least because it has such a memorable label. It joins the Big Bang, Black Hole, and Selfish Gene in the pantheon of memorable titles for scientific concepts. The idea is simple enough: that there was a time, or times, when the earth froze from end to end. We have already encountered the ice age of the Carboniferous, and there was another at the end of the Ordovician period; but no ice age after the Cambrian refrigerated the whole world. If this really happened, it would have had an obvious effect on the progress of life, though it is even more superfluous to note that life survived. The rocks produced during an ice age are rather distinctive, so that the evidence required of a global event is that such rocks should cover the whole world at the time. One of the chief proponents of the theory is Paul Hoffman at Harvard, one of those American academics who seem to have twice their fair share of energy. If expertise is defined as knowing more and more about less and less, I am at a loss to describe what it is to know more and more about more and more – but that is the Hoffman condition.

Along the bleak shores of the northern peninsula of Spitsbergen known as Ny Friesland there is little in the way of creature comfort but much to interest another brilliant obsessive – Brian Harland, from the Geology Department at Cambridge. Brian is the authority on the Arctic islands of Svalbard, of which Spitsbergen is the major island, and for many years he ran Cambridge University expeditions there. As befits a Quaker, Brian's expeditions were marvellously organized, but trimmed of all frills. I did my doctoral work in Ny Friesland on Ordovician fossils, so I know the area well. Thirty-five years ago we travelled by small boat towards the rocks that I was about to map, passing by a succession of late Proterozoic strata laid out like a spread deck of cards along the shore. We ascended, rock bed by rock bed, through geological time as we moved southwards, while screaming Arctic terns berated us from the air, urging us ever onwards. The rocks here were younger than the red sandstones of Loch Torridon and Canisp, and very different in character. They were carbonate sedimentary rocks – dolomites and limestones. We knew that they were laid down under the warmth of a tropical sun and that provided an indication of how much the latitude of Spitsbergen had changed over hundreds of millions of years. Rare fossils of marine algae had been discovered in the same rock formations. I knew, too, that the Cambrian and Ordovician strata that lay ahead were also limestones of the same general type, with the important difference that they contained myriads of fossil shells of extinct kinds of animals, including the trilobites that I was to study for several years. The sequence of rocks in Ny Friesland evidently spanned that (literally) vital time in the history of the earth between the later part of the Precambrian and the 'explosion' of animal life that happened at the base of the Cambrian period. However, between the two 'packages' of warm-water carbonate sedimentary rocks something very curious happened, something which Brian Harland had pointed out years before the 'Snowball Earth' theory was proposed. For a brief interval the carbonates disappeared, and in their stead some utterly different rocks took the ground. Prominent among them was a reddish rock that might be best described as a kind of pudding, full of boulders and blocks of various kinds and sizes, all suspended in a pink mud. To a student of glacial phenomena this rock would seem quite familiar. When icebergs have 'calved' from major glaciers to drift out to sea, they deposit just such a heterogeneous dog's dinner as they melt, dropping out the collection of stones they carried, along with the ground-up waste derived from the terrain they scoured. Now we look at an individual pebble we can see it even carries scratches acquired during its sojourn in the ice-sheet. So here is the paradox: a glacial event extending so far into low latitudes as to drop its debris where, not long before, tropical algae and bacteria has flourished on a limy sea-floor. There was no denying the facts: rocks do not lie.

Hoffman vigorously extended these pioneering researches to demonstrate that similar changes could be recognized globally in strata deposited at about 590 million years ago. 'Snowball Earth' had been born. There was a vision of the whole planet engulfed in a shimmering ice-sheet, from pole to pole. Since ice reflects light and heat, from space the earth would then have resembled nothing so much as a giant pearl. Furthermore, since the Cambrian 'Big Bang' in the history of life occurred, geologically speaking, not so very long after the alleged great freeze had relented, it was tempting to link the two as cause and effect. The survivors, released from the grip of global refrigeration, evolved into new ecosystems, reset the evolutionary clock, were stimulated into unparalleled innovation, and so on. The shells that I collected from the hard limestones on the frigid shores of Spitsbergen were ultimately a consequence of an even chillier past. The explanation does, it must be said, have a compelling narrative drive. Of course, there had to be places for life to hang on through the icy crisis, and deep-sea hot vents and similar unfreezable but feasible refuges were cited. Algae that needed light might have hung out on the edges of hot springs. The 'snowball' showed plenty of evidence of unfreezing rapidly: the speedy reappearance of tropical limestones in the Cambrian age rocks in Spitsbergen was one example. Hoffman's idea was that during the 'snowball' phase, volcanic gases like carbon dioxide (for eruptions would not have been affected by the freezing of all that water) accumulated in the atmosphere, building up the greenhouse effect, until a critical level of global warming was reached. Then the ice-sheets would have melted dramatically – even over a few decades – and seas would have flooded back over the continents, and marine life could get on with the job in the nutritious shallow shelf seas that followed.

As with many big ideas, the theory is not without its critics. They point to the fact that more than two-thirds of the earth's surface was covered with ocean, then as now, and since all 590-million-year-old ocean crust has long since been subducted to oblivion, there will never be proof that every part of that vast hinterland became deeply frozen. Others dispute the evidence of complete coverage by ice, and there are indeed places where the evidence is less convincing than in Spitsbergen. Then again, a few fossils of complex animals that antedate the big freeze have been recognized in a few localities, though these, too, are controversial. Some, but by no means all, molecular biologists claim that you need much more time in the Precambrian than 590–542 million years to acccount for the evolution of all the different designs of animals that appeared, apparently suddenly, close to the base of the Cambrian period. Currently, the debate is at that interesting stage where we don't know how the chips will fall: the next decade will probably decide. The intellectual brew has been enriched by Professor Hoffman's imaginative younger colleague, Joe Kirshvink, from the California Institute of Technology, who has recognized up to four 'Snowball Earths' between 900 and 590 million years ago. All these have deposits of glacial origin associated with them. Recently, Joe has upped the stakes still further by adding another, far older one – almost as old as the grey gneisses of Laxford and Scourie – at about two billion years. Glacial rocks that had miraculously survived from this distant era almost unscathed were discovered among the termite mounds and stunted trees in what is now the Kalahari Desert in southern Africa. What is amazing is that the 'palaeomag' in the ancient boulder beds also seems to have survived the passage of billions of years. The readings indicated that the glacial beds were laid down near to the equator of the time: hence Joe's conviction that this was another global event, ice from pole to equator. Far from being a unique event, a frozen earth was allegedly a repeated risk during the Precambrian. I do find it remarkable that life weathered these frigid crises – if they really happened. We know that life existed before the earliest one, and traces of bacteria and algal mats appeared between the times when frigid conditions are supposed to have reigned. To adapt Oscar Wilde's famous line, to survive one snowball is fortunate, but to survive several looks like miraculousness.

We have moved back to earlier and earlier times, but we have yet to answer the question: where are the oldest rocks on earth? Finding the definitive answer is not straightforward. With regard to dates, a record is always liable to be broken by a whisker when a different zircon crystal from the right ancient locality is analysed. Then there is the question of the accuracy of measurement, which is serious if the 'ruler' happens to be a radiometric date because different methods can give different results. The really important fact is that older and older dates are rarer and rarer. You would expect to have trouble finding ancient crust because, as we have seen, it is likely to have been remobilized by younger tectonic events as the old earth cranks over and over. Hence younger dates will be imprinted over older ones as the radioactive clocks are 'reset'. It has proved extremely difficult to discover rocks that are any older than about 3800–3900 million years. There are just a few places where the planet's plates have left small fragments of this antiquity relatively unscathed, scraps from early phases in the earth's history. Endurance may be a matter of luck, perhaps, of survival against the odds, like the grizzled old warrior who emerges from the battlefield with scarcely a scratch while his companions at arms are felled around him. This is the earliest time made tangible. We can put our hands upon the rock, stroke it, examine it with lenses or attack it with sophisticated analytical probes. It may look at first glance like yet more gneiss, but it is precious stuff.

A still more distant period lies prior to the oldest rocks. Dates from meteoritic material surviving from the early days of the solar system reveal that the earth formed at about 4550 million years ago. Hence it follows that there is a 'missing' piece of history, an eon suited only for speculation and conjecture. Something like 600 million years is almost unrepresented by rocks. This period has come to be known as the Hadean, and perhaps appropriately so, for conditions during at least part of it were as furiously inhospitable as hell-fire itself. As the earth gained mass by accretion of planetismals, its increasing gravity attracted massive meteorite bombardments. The energy imparted by massive and relentless impacts eventually caused the melting of the planet. It became a sea of lava, but still the impacts continued. Most planetary scientists believe that the moon was the product of a massive impact. It spun off as a gob of debris. It continues to edge its way slowly further from the parent planet billions of years later, but still blatantly retains the legacy of the time in the meteorite impacts it received upon its surface so long ago. It is likely that both the moon and the earth continued to be bombarded by meteorites until about 3800 million years ago. The iron core of the earth formed while the planet was near molten, and at that point the elements were parcelled out according to their chemical fancies. This was a period when the ground itself was constructed, the dance floor set, before the slow dance of the plates could even begin. It remains a time of mystery, a morass of unanswered questions. However, hints towards some answers are preserved in the oldest rocks.

These great-grandfathers of all gneisses have attracted much attention from geologists, particularly those concerned with the early history of life. There are a handful of places from which rocks yielding ages up to a maximum of 3900 million years have been collected; and there are hints of still deeper time. These sites include the southern edge of the Churchill Province of the Canadian Shield in Montana; the most ancient part of the shield areas of Western Australia; and the Isua rocks of Greenland. The centre of Greenland is covered by a vast ice-cap, but rocks poke out around the edges of the island, forming a rocky fringe, a kind of lithic tonsure around the bald centre. About 150 kilometres north of the capital Nuuk on the west coast, the oldest greenstone belt on earth at Isua takes up a narrow strip of barren outcrop about thirty kilometres long. It is a primeval sliver, underlying everything else. The belt was recognized more than thirty years ago, largely because it included the earliest banded iron formation, which gave a distinct signal to a gravity survey. The whole belt had been heated, of course – perhaps to some 600° C – but there were little pockets here and there that seemed to have escaped the punishment due to them after so long a sojourn on the planet. Even some of the 'pillow' structures of the submarine basalts have been preserved. Like other greenstone belts, the Isua rocks also include metamorphosed sediments. They prove that there was already enough water on the planet when the rocks were originally laid down to erode still earlier formations; though old, they were not yet the beginning. A vision of still deeper time opens up, time beyond time. You can almost hear the sea breaking on some of the first shores, just as in summer it still tumbles against the margins of Greenland, and then you understand that of all things on earth the sea is most nearly immortal. Through all the reconfigurations of the face of the earth, the sea has endured. Beneath the frozen ice-caps that may have once covered the earth, the sea still cradled life. It may be the sea that is the ancient of days.

Yet the sea itself originated, or was gathered together, during the Hadean. An ocean could not have survived during early, molten, violent days. Only when water could condense from hissing, steaming volcanoes – when the cooking-pot of the earth cooled sufficiently – only then could pools and basins survive. The impact on earth of many comets made of dirty ice may have contributed more water – quite how much is still debated. But one fact is certain: without water, there could have been no life. The origin of life on earth and the early history of the crust intersect on the barren, glaciated wastes of Greenland. Enough is now known about the most primitive living bacteria to suggest that all living organisms lying at the base of the tree of life relished high temperatures. A nearly boiling habitat was their land flowing with milk and honey. Recall that these hyperthermophiles do not need oxygen to grow – indeed, for many of them it is a poison. In short, they suited the early earth: hot and anoxic. But were they there? In 1996, a study was carried out upon minute graphite (metamorphosed carbon) specks within crystals of the mineral apatite preserved in some ancient Greenland rocks that have been compared with those at Isua. The negative values of the isotope of carbon (13C) obtained from this sample are typical of the carbon compounds produced by living organisms. Cooked though it was, the stamp of life was there – or so it was claimed. To look at one of the biggest questions about our planet, the scientist rootles around inside a single crystal with an ion microprobe. If life was there 3.8 million years ago, it would have experienced a day only five hours long, as a result of the earth spinning faster, and the moon would have hung large and close in the sky.*

As I write, still older dates from zircon crystals are starting to fill in the mysterious Hadean. The oldest of all is 4400 million years from the middle of a crystal recovered from the Jack Hills of Western Australia. It is within a whisker of the earliest days. The ion microprobe has dug into this token from the aftermath of Hades. If the oxygen isotopes recovered from inside the tiny time capsule are to be believed, there was free water already present on earth even at this extraordinarily early time. The timetables for Hades might have to be rescheduled. There is still so much to learn. The intimate history of the early earth can only be recovered from hints and whispers buried inside crystals. We are only just beginning to translate the story they have to tell.

The eternal sea breaks heavily over the Lewisian gneiss and the dykes of Scourie. The wind whistles through the gorse bushes, but even in October there are a few bright yellow pea flowers hidden among the spines. Looking across the bay, the greyness of the undulating ancient rocks continues onwards to the dense, tossing ocean. The horizon is obscured in mist, and the distant islets fade progressively. Scanning the distance is like trying to penetrate Precambrian time. The furthest objects are hard to see, and so much detail is lost. Generations of geologists have sat in much the same place and contemplated the

* The moon is moving away from the earth at 2.5 inches (6 cm) a year.

same panorama, but what they have seen and understood, their very perception of land and sea, has changed with the knowledge and prejudices of the times. The fundamental rocks that were once so incomprehensible have been picked apart and placed in their proper place in the history of the earth. Supercontinents have come and gone, but the speckled gneisses endure. Now gulls shriek from a rocky promontory that once burned under a Proterozoic sun, before the Torridon sediments buried the Lewisian again beneath a red blanket. These gneisses have seen it all, achieved a kind of repose. The assault by the sea today is no more than a postscript to a history that has seen these rocks glide around the world, roast in a deep furnace, witness silently the transformation of the atmosphere, and the rise of those presumptuous newcomers, animals. The rocks will still be here when the last organism has vanished from a parched earth.

11

Cover Story

The mule has its eyes set in such a position that it can see all four legs at the same time. This is just as well if the track it is traversing is only a a metre or so wide and there is a sheer drop of 150 metres to one side. When it approaches a hairpin bend on the outside of a precipitous trail, the mule prefers to poke its head out into nothingness before jerking sharply round to follow the animal in front. I think it does it on purpose. 'If you don't like it, close your eyes,' says Ken the guide, 'after all, that's what the mule does . . .' I find myself clinging to the pommel on the saddle with terrible determination.

The descent into the Grand Canyon in Arizona is one of the great geological journeys. It is more than a mile down (vertically speaking) from the rim of the Canyon to the Colorado River: a journey through half the earth's history, rock formation by rock formation. As the mule treads delicately but relentlessly onwards, you are carried downwards upon its back through the geological column; you become a time traveller, borne step by lurching step back first through tens, and then through hundreds of millions of years.

You come across the Grand Canyon unexpectedly. In the approach to the south rim across the Coconino Plateau the road hardly undulates. You pass from a dry, flat plain into an endless open forest of piñon and ponderosa pines, mixed with feathery juniper trees. There is a sparse underscrub of spiny *Opuntia* cacti, and *Agave* bushes like green punk haircuts. You cannot see very far. It is all pleasant enough, and rather unremarkable. Then the forest suddenly comes to an end. Something has been slashed into the earth. The

Grand Canyon opens up without any kind of scenic preamble – not even a gentle incline. It is at once familiar and alien: familiar, because you have already seen pictures of it many times – it is one of those universal icons, like the Mona Lisa or the Empire State Building. For an instant you wonder if this apparent chasm might be another, particularly clever, three-dimensional representation. Then, too, it is astonishing and strange, because no image conveys its sheer scale. The far side of the north rim is 16 kilometres away or more; yet in the morning light you might imagine it much nearer – or maybe, in some other lights, much further away. Sometimes, indeed, the distant creeks and buttes look as if they were painted backdrops designed to present the illusion of distance, as in a theatre; wing after wing of cunningly crafted canvas: shades of cream, orange, rich-red, and umber stripes in broad swathes parallel to the horizon. All that scooped and fretted bare rock seems to have been carved, dug away, leaving massive turrets and castles and dark dungeons: architectural similes are irresistible. The appropriate comparison is with the Hindu temples of Ellora in the Deccan Traps, where the hand of man has created architecture by virtue of all the rock that has been removed, a kind of anti-architecture. In Arizona, the carver is the Colorado River, so deeply sunk in its dark ravine that it is usually invisible from the rim. The prime cause of all the erosion is hidden, hinted at only in a black-purple gash that dogs the bottom of the canyon. The dark Inner Canyon is often obscured by features developed higher on the slopes. When you do catch a glimpse of the river it may be no more than a little silvery flash, and it seems absurd to suppose that what looks like a mere trickle could sculpt so vast an array of amphitheatres and promontories of rock.

In the winter, the crowds of tourists keep away. It is too cold for them at the top. You have the canyon almost to yourself. A trail follows the rim, dodging back and forth from the edge as it leads you from one viewpoint to the next. There is a light dusting of snow among the short pine trees. This is a dry climate, and the well spaced and rather stunted conifers take many years to reach maturity. It is quiet, for there are very few birds. Occasionally, a huge, black raven wings past on an inspection flight, faintly sinister. Just past dawn, the shadows are profound in the depths of the canyon, and as the sun rises higher, the shadows are lifted one by one. It feels more like an unveiling, a removal of a series of black opaque sheets from the sculptured forms below, than a progressive illumination. While the light is still at a low angle, the colours of the rock formations are at their most intense. The strata appear unwaveringly horizontal, like an infinity of stacked plywood worked with a giant fretsaw. There is a clear contrast between the cream-coloured layers and those that are richly russet, the colour of mature Italian sausage. From the rim, it is impossible to guess how thick these layers are, for depth and distance confuse your perceptions. You must go down through the great pile of rocks if you wish to reach the Colorado River, and then you will discover their true dimensions for yourself.

The Grand Canyon was not always perceived as one of the 'seven natural wonders of the world', as the postcards put it. The first western visitor to reach it was the Spaniard Garcia Lopez de Cardenas in 1540. He was in search of the legendary Seven Cities of Cibola and, in the spirit of the times, a fortune in gold. He was unable to cross the great chasm, and, horrified by its impassableness, returned to Mexico with no treasure for his pains. Three hundred years later the great gash in the earth was still viewed with as little enthusiasm. In 1858, the surveyor Lieutenant Joseph Ives was to report to his superiors that the 'region is altogether valueless. Ours has been the first, and will doubtless be the last, party of whites to visit this profitless locality.' Exploration of the canyon had to wait for a one-armed Civil War veteran, John Wesley Powell, in 1869. What is now a ten-day 'white-water adventure' along 446 kilometres (277 miles) of the Colorado River was a dangerous ordeal for the first explorers, blindly tumbling into what Powell termed 'the great unknown'. While shooting one of the rapids, one of their four boats was lost, along with much of their food. The party had to cope with meagre, damp rations, on top of the heat and danger. Three of the men never returned. Through it all, Powell continued to survey, and to collect rock samples and fossils. As was to be the case with the moon, it seems that the first way to establish the veracity of the experience was to bring home a piece of rock. Powell's account of the adventure, *Exploration of the Colorado River and its Gorges*, established him as the pioneer's pioneer. The journals of one of his companions cast him in a slightly less heroic light, but no one disputed his bravery. Powell went on to found the US Geological Survey. His memorial is on a promontory on the south rim commanding a panoramic view of the canyon, erected, it says, by order of Congress. A bronze bas-relief of the great man, bearded and splendid, somehow contrives to look like Charles Darwin.

The change in attitude to the grandeur of the Grand Canyon came about quickly. A transformation in appreciation of what made for beauty soon became pervasive: American painters like Thomas Moran began to respond to the aesthetic of the wilderness, creating emotionally charged landscapes of the untamed scene. Pristine acquired cachet. By the 1890s, a few enterprising souls were offering guidance and hospitality to the intrepid visitor to the south rim. Buckey O'Neill's cabin still survives, having been incorporated into the Bright Angel Hotel in 1898. It is a homely enough affair, lined with split logs. There is an appropriately laconic picture of him posted outside, lounging with his gun tucked in his holster, and a candle stuffed into a bottle behind him. He led Teddy Roosevelt down the Canyon on mule-back in 1912. I doubt whether the President would have passed the weight limit of 200 lb. currently imposed on riders down the trail, but this visit doubtless had a part to play in the designation of the Grand Canyon as a national park in 1919. The Santa Fe Railway Company had reached the south rim as early as 1901, bringing those jaded with big-city life to seek a novel form of spiritual refreshment. A humming locomotive was still waiting in the station when I arrived just over a century later. All that was needed was the comfort of a good hotel to cushion the wilderness experience.

The Fred Harvey Company soon provided one. The El Tovar Hotel built in 1904 is still rather stylish, in a knowingly rustic fashion. It settles down unobtrusively into the landscape, which is just as it should be. It helped to set a tone for North American national park architecture that you can identify from New Mexico to Newfoundland: it says, 'harmonize with the natural environment'. During the earlier part of the twentieth century you would have been attended to assiduously by Harvey Girls, neat and spruce and ever-so respectable in their nice little uniforms. There were oysters on the menu, which might be served off monogrammed crockery. The splendour outside was still there, of course, but the middle-class visitors did not now have to suffer hardship to appreciate it. The essence of modern tourism had been defined.

All among the pine trees on the south rim a bedded rock the colour of rich cream crops out in blocky benches. This is a limestone, the Kaibab Formation. You do not have to search for a long time before you notice fossils weathering out on the upper surfaces of the slabs: the skeletons of corals and shells of several kinds. Evidently, this sedimentary rock was originally deposited under the sea, where such animals thrived: you may see the stem of a sea-lily, or crinoid, which would once have waved back and forth in the current. The waters must have been warm and shallow, too, because that is where calcium carbonate precipitates out of solution in sufficient quantities to form limestones. An inland sea evidently invaded this part of the early North American continent. Successive sea-floors are laid out one on top of the other around the rim, as one rock-bed succeeds another; here is a catalogue of the passage of geological time. Looking gingerly over the edge into the Canyon, you can see similar, creamy limestones forming the steep cliff all around the top of the Canyon: the former seaway must have extended for many kilometres. The fossils also tell us the geological age, for they are representatives of species long extinct: these limestones were deposited in the Permian Period, some 260 million years ago. Dinosaurs had yet to achieve their hegemony when the warm sea engulfed this part of Laurentia.

Now that you can recognize the Kaibab, you know that it forms the uppermost layer for as far as you can see. Below it, other rock formations take their turn. So you look back further into the remote past as you look downwards. The Kaibab is only the beginning. The journey down to the Colorado River is a chance to see the ebb and flow of vanished seas over millions of years, to feel the slow pulse of the earth.

Journeying down by mule is remarkably safe these days, but still exhilarating. Going over the edge is something of a shock – like jumping into space. The trail winds steeply downwards for 100 metres from step one. Since winter reigns at the top, the narrow route is coated with ice. You cannot help but glance downwards and visualize a dramatic plummet into space. My mule is called Buttermilk. Soon, I realize that her step is sure and the quaking feeling in my innards subsides, though she lurches and stumbles and I keep my fingers tightly gripped on the saddle. My notebook remains unopened in my coat-pocket.

The personality of the trail precisely reflects the geology. Hard and resistant formations make the steep cliffs and narrow trails, which are sometimes cut dramatically into the bare rock face. There is little vegetation clinging on to such formations, so you can trace them by eye as unscalable walls all around the Canyon. Softer rocks produce gentler trails on gentler slopes, with less scary drops, but they also wash away more readily, so that the way is irregular and dotted with fallen boulders. The mules must pick their way very carefully.

The Kaibab Formation is one of the steeper ones. I tried to remember the names of the succession of rock formations that I would encounter on the way down. In this endeavour, I was helped by a slightly risqué mnemonic told me by a receptionist at the White Angel Lodge (*K*issing *T*akes *C*oncentration. *H*owever, *S*ex *R*equires *M*anoeuvring *B*etween *T*empting *V*ariables: *K*aibab, *T*oroweap, *C*oconino, *H*ermit, *S*upai, *R*edwall, *M*uav, *B*right Angel, *T*apeats, and *V*ishnu, in that order). The list isn't quite complete, but perhaps that was to spare my blushes. That there was a trail at all was the result of a fault that has fractured the whole pile of sediments, a weakness along which erosion had preferentially worked its slow depredations. We are following the side of an enormous Vee-shaped gulley. I did not manage to scrutinize every detail of every formation as we descended: I was far too preoccupied with making sure that Buttermilk kept sniffing the tail in front. But I did notice that the Toroweap Formation marked a pleasant break in the downward zig-zags for a couple of hundred vertical metres and that there were reassuringly solid pine trees alongside the trail: these rocks must be softer as well as somewhat older than the tough Kaibab Formation overlying them. I sit back in the saddle and relax.

This proves premature. For the trail next turns vertiginously along the sheerest cliff I could imagine: it hangs on by its lithological fingernails. This is the Coconino Formation, an almost pure sandstone, shining pale yellow. My geologist's eye takes in the sweep of the vertical cliff it makes all around the amphitheatre; surely, it must be at least 100 metres high. How improbable that anyone could ever have climbed such a barrier . . . it makes a rampart as far as could be seen. Then, the structures embedded in the sandstones catch my eye. There are billowing swathes of cross-bedding several metres high. The outer surfaces of the rock show etched faces scored with lines that sit at an angle to the horizontal lie of the strata above. I do not have to consult the geological guide to recognize this feature: we are traversing desert sands. Wind-blown dunes leave this distinctive cross-section. While the Coconino Formation was accumulating, the sea had abandoned this part of the world: another, arid, sea of sand-dunes stretched from horizon to horizon; no fossils are here but the petrified tracks of scorpions, and the fingered traces of reptiles scampering across the ancient dunes seeking prey. They show as lines of little dimples on the sandstone surface, the kind of thing you might pass by without a second thought. This was a hard world, an ancient Sahara in the earlier part of the Permian period, when the earth was as dry as it has ever been. It seems curiously appropriate that clinging on through this part of the rock section was something of an ordeal.

Then, the rocks turn red. Immediately, the slope of the trail slackens off: gentler rocks, gentler gradients. The colour change marks our downward passage into the Hermit Formation, soft, bright red shales that are easily eroded back to make a sloping bench on the canyon's profile. This abrupt transformation from cream to red is one of the striking lines I traced out as I looked down from the rim, and when I flew in a Cessna from Las Vegas over the canyon I could follow it from the air for many kilometres. The mules now have to cope with an apparently endless switchback of slippery ruts: the problem here is that when it rains, the trail washes out. But the more dignified descent gives me an opportunity to look around at the richer vegetation that is able to grow on the lesser incline. There is no longer any snow. As we descend, the temperature rises so that we move into different climatic zones. A few of the conifers that lined the rim still grow here, but there are now also numerous small oak trees. The redness continues for a long, long time as we descend still further. At one point the track steepens again and there are tracts of sandstones making for a series of steep cliffs and exciting riding. We have passed downwards into the Supai Group, which is itself subdivided into a number of thick, resistant sandstones alternating with softer rocks like mudstones. This variation produces a series of steps down the canyon side as the trail winds ever onwards, now plunging steeply and weaving from side to side, now sloping gently downwards for a longer, shaly stretch during which you can allow yourself to slouch down into the saddle like an old cowpoke. Before you know it, you have gone down another 300 metres. The red colour of these rocks, which lend the Grand Canyon so much of its drama, is just iron. The weathering of iron minerals in the presence of abundant oxygen assures that iron is in its ferric form, which paints russet, rouge, and rust. One of the most abundant elements in the crust is also the most versatile at decorating scenery. Such red rocks often indicate deposition under terrestrial conditions: the influence of wind was still important. Had we been able to scramble off our mules and tap at the rocks with geological hammers (strictly forbidden) we might have found the fossils of horsetails or the tracks of amphibians. There was life in this place between 270 and 320 million years ago, while the varied Supai rocks were accumulating; the strata take us all the way back to a coastal plain of the Carboniferous Period.* The ancient

* US readers will know this as Mississippian and Pennsylvanian.

landscape has been compared with the Gulf Coast today. There were occasional little groves of primitive plants, streams with their own levees, and, elsewhere, more sand dunes. All these have left a legacy in one rock-bed or another. Thus was one more vanished landscape built into the walls of the Grand Canyon, another blanket of sediment covering up the still earlier histories that lie beneath it. Another cover story.

Any such musings are abruptly brought to a halt by a sudden lurch downwards. It is the Redwall Formation. The name is entirely appropriate for what it does: it makes a red wall – an implacable vertical barrier 150 metres high. John Wesley Powell christened it, and feared it. Nothing grows on the bare rock face. The trail winds over the cliff face thrillingly downwards, with the random inflections of a bolt of lightning. The trajectory demands total concentration. As I round one switchback I notice from a broken surface that the rock constructing this geological Jericho is not red at all, it is pale grey, almost white. It is, in fact, a massive limestone, like the Kaibab where we began. The red colour is a superficial stain derived from the Supai immediately above, a kind of iron colour-wash that renders the mighty rampart pink. In the early morning light it seems to glow. There are caves excavated within the upper part of the Redwall limestone that show up black and inaccessible high on the wall. Like almost all limestones, this one was marine, laid down under a warm sea. It contains numerous fossils that betray its origin: shells of brachiopods and nautiloids, skeletons of corals and bryozoans. They also tell us that the limestone was deposited in early Carboniferous (Mississippian) times, when a shallow sea flooded over a large part of the early North American continent. This segment of history makes my legs stiff, and poor Buttermilk comes out all in a lather.

Our guide Ken, however, does not allow us to dismount just yet. He whistles for Buttermilk to catch up and she breaks into a trot. I scarcely notice the Temple Butte Formation, a thin marine formation of Devonian age, but I do notice getting down to the Cambrian rocks below it, for the trail eases up more than a little and the strata are finer-bedded and softer. This is almost like coming home for me, because the Cambrian was the time when trilobites were most abundant and I have been studying trilobites for most of my life: 520 million years ago is my kind of time. Trilobites only lived in the sea, so when the Bright Angel Shale was accumulating the Grand Canyon area was again immersed beneath the waves. It is a time so remote that no creatures had yet ventured on land, and neither the corals nor the nautiloids we saw in the rocks at the beginning of our journey had yet evolved. We are getting back towards the beginnings of animal life. I feel a pang, because there is something missing. There are no rocks of Ordovician or Silurian age in the Canyon, and I have always been an Ordovician man. Nobody has discovered a rock record in this locality representing nearly a hundred million years of geological time. The sea withdrew to somewhere else. Between the Devonian Temple Butte Formation and the Cambrian Muav limestone below there is an unconformity. We shall never know what happened in the Grand Canyon during this great period. Without a rock record, there is no way of reading the book of time. It is lost to us more definitively than the secrets of the Aztecs, or the rituals of the Easter Islanders. We pass downwards through the Cambrian, passing the Muav Formation, and on to the outcrop of the Bright Angel Shale. This is the softest of all the rocks in the Canyon; as a result, it underlies the large bench interrupting the cascading series of cliffs. This is called the Tonto Platform, which can be seen very clearly from the top of the Grand Canyon. It stretches out far below as a kind of dark plain, its sombre colours contrasting noticeably with the warm hues of the steep Redwall limestone above it. It provides a landing upon the relentless stratigraphical staircase, and in the old days it also permitted the principal route to run along the length of the Canyon. A trail still winds along it. From the top, the Tonto Platform also obscures what lies beyond it and below it. As my mule ambles on more comfortably, I have a chance to see that the endemic vegetation is black scrub, a kind of prickly bush, devoid of leaves in the winter. At this depth in the canyon, all the trees have disappeared:

we are effectively in a semi-desert. The layers of clothes we donned on the frigid rim should be discarded soon.

Here, at last, is a chance to restore our legs to their proper shape. We arrive at a little glen known as Indian Gardens – a few trees, and reeds, and a couple of low buildings – where a spring emerges from the ground. Suddenly, the scale of everything is rather domestic. There is a hitching post ahead. Ken kindly helps us off our steeds, and we stagger around for a few minutes, bow-legged. The Pueblo Indians who once lived here would have grown corn, beans, and a couple of varieties of squash. Water gushes out because the Bright Angel Fault throws rocks of different permeability together. The water for all the buildings on the south rim is pumped from this resource. It seems curious that in a mighty landscape eroded by water it should be necessary to pump upwards for a thousand metres to get a decent drink. Evidently, what little precipitation falls upon the Coconino Plateau drains quickly down into the underlying porous rocks, until emerging again deep down at the spring line.

With more reluctance than elegance, I remount Buttermilk. The little stream that emerges at Indian Gardens has carved a charming little canyon of its own a few metres high, with the mule track running along one side. The clunk-clunk of hooves on stone is accompanied by the splashing of the brook. This trail cuts through the outcrop of the Tapeats Formation. I ask Ken whether it is safe to drink the clear water but he warns me that even here there are unpleasant micro-organisms and it is as well not to taste. The trail is gentle now, almost a rustic footpath, and it is pleasantly sunny and warm. The sandstones through which we are passing are yellow and slabby, lining both sides of the little gorge as if we were passing through a sunken passage leading to some antique temple; for once, I have time to look at the rocks properly. Like those making up the Coconino sandstone, they show cross-bedding, but of a steeper and more delicate kind. These are the kind of sands that were swept along by strong marine currents close to the Cambrian sea-shore. For a moment the sun is shining under an ancient sky upon a seascape of the primeval earth. Trilobites scuttle over the sandy sea-floor. There is no bird in the air, nor any tree upon the distant landscape. Now I notice a braided track made by the archaic animals as they plough their way through the substrate. There is the feeling of getting back to the beginning of things.

Which, indeed, we do with some dispatch. Once again, the trail begins to plunge downwards. There is the kind of sinking feeling inside brought on by one of those fairground attractions that does something dramatic just when you think the ride is over. We have entered the Inner Gorge, and all the rules have changed. How accustomed we have become to horizontal sedimentary rocks – that great staircase of strata that we descended level by level. The pink rock now by the trackside is quite different; for a start, it shows no signs of stratification. The little stream cascades over a hard mass into a tumbling waterfall, where the rock has been polished by years of erosion. Why, it is obviously a granite! Before there is a chance to take in the implications of this discovery, the trail starts upon its most contorted descent so far; turn after turn descends implacably. Ken tells us that this is called 'the Devil's Corkscrew', and I reflect briefly that the Devil is always attached to geology's more sinister works: there are any number of Devil's Punchbowls, Devil's Canyons, Devil's Towers, and Devil's Staircases around the world.

The Inner Canyon is a darker world. The rocks have changed tone: some of the strata are almost black. Gone are the horizontal rulings that scored out the upper part of the canyon: the layered strata, the tiered amphitheatre. Now the rocks are all on-end and twisted: they have been squeezed into convolutions and tempered into contortions. The deeper, inner gorge is narrow and steep-sided. It makes a narrow Vee at the bottom of what we now see to be the massively wider cradle of the upper part of the Canyon. It is so deep down that in the winter the sun slinks in there furtively for a short while, like an archaeologist shining a torch inside a burial chamber. When we get a chance to dismount and hobble around at the bottom of the steep descent, I pick up some pieces of the dark rock that makes up much of this inner sanctum. It is a flaky, rich-green stone, streaked with black, and shiny on its flat, broken surface, unlike anything we have seen up above. This is the Vishnu schist. The shine is produced by one of the mica minerals, probably chlorite. The Inner Canyon is made of metamorphic rocks, which have been baked and turned vertically in some ancient paroxysm of the earth. It is another Newfoundland, another alp – but far older. We have taken a further excursion to the ancient of days. In the cliffs, I can see that the schists are intertwined and interwoven with pink veins, which sometimes produce blobby masses, and in other places are crimped like tresses of hair in a turbulent current. It is all so complex that it seems difficult to make any sense of it. The pink rock lying around in lumps is mostly feldspar. It is evidently an igneous rock, injected in magmatic veins into the metamorphic rocks that surround it. The granite that we crossed earlier must also have intruded into the metamorphic mass during an ancient mountain-building episode. I recall the similar rocks seen in the mobile belt of Newfoundland. Further up the Grand Canyon the granite makes a terrifyingly narrow gorge.

Looking upwards from the bottom of the Canyon, what we have seen makes a little more sense. We can see the corkscrew trail winding its way up towards the younger rocks. The Tapeats Formation lies on top of the dark, twisted rocks of the Vishnu schist as if it were a laid blanket. It is the oldest of the many horizontal, undisturbed formations that we crossed on the way down from the Kaibab limestone. The profound events that heated the Vishnu rocks and intruded the granites into them must have been over and done with long before that first Cambrian sandstone was deposited. Everything thereafter was part of the cover story. An ancient tectonic belt had already been worn down, the mountains had been laid low and the rough places had been made plain, before the Cambrian sea crept over its ground-down remnant. Beneath the Cambrian sandstones of the Tapeats Formation there lies what has been described as the Great Unconformity, a great hole in the rock record. In fact, the radiometric 'clock' tells us that the Vishnu metamorphic rocks were squeezed in the earth's vice some 1700 million years ago, in the early Proterozoic, an age not far different from that of the ancient rocks of north-western Scotland. Elsewhere in the Grand Canyon a series of later Proterozoic rocks intervenes between the Vishnu schist and the Tapeats sandstone, rather as the Torridonian rocks filled in the gap between the Lewisian gneiss and Cambrian rocks in Scotland. They serve to 'fill in' some of the missing time but they were tilted and worn down before the Cambrian was deposited, testifying to yet another phase of earth movements. Era after era is laid out before us in this greatest of canyons. When we remember that a thousand years of erosion has been calculated to wear back the walls by no more than a metre, and that a huge fallen stone before us has probably not moved for centuries, we begin to get a feeling for the vastness of geological time; for the ages required to lay down and then uplift the cover rocks; for the still more ancient cycles that were dead and gone even before the first trilobite scurried on its way to extinction over the first Cambrian sandstone; and for the slow procession of the plates that underpinned it all.

Then, suddenly, our trail turns out upon the Colorado River: it is powerfully rushing and swirling with eddies, with a few rollicking masses of waves. Can this be the same river that made such a thin streak when viewed from the rim? It must be the same river that Powell described, fed by water after the spring melt that 'tumbles down the mountain-sides in millions of cascades. Ten million cascade brooks unite to form ten thousand torrent creeks; ten thousand torrent creeks unite to form a hundred rivers beset with cataracts; a hundred roaring rivers unite to form the Colorado, which rolls, a mad, turbid stream into the Gulf of California.' Today, the 'red river' lives up to its name, its water thickly pink-buff from the load of sediment it carries. So, this is the motor of erosion, the only begetter of the Inner Canyon. The Vishnu cliffs plunge giddily several hundred feet towards the water. At this point the river seems almost stately in spite of its strong and relentless flow. But we know its course is punctuated with dangerous rapids where rockfalls have impeded its smooth running, where boulders can smash wooden boats into matchsticks, and where whirlpools can suck you to your death. The admonitory names of the rapids speak for themselves: I particularly like Sockdolager Rapid – in the mid nineteenth century, 'sockdolager' was slang for a knockout punch. It was one of the last words Abraham Lincoln heard, in the play he was attending at the time of his assassination.

The Colorado River has not so much carved out the Canyon as carried it away. Its waters have flooded or gently flowed according to its different moods, moving weathered rock from higher ground to lower, carrying particles, rolling cobbles. The whole Colorado Plateau has been uplifted around the river, allowing it no peace from grind and toil. The river has merely tried to maintain its position while the world has risen around it. It is now trapped within its own canyon like a donkey strapped to a wheel. If you watch a little runnel draining over a sandy beach you might see a micro-canyon form in the sand; soon, it will recruit small side-streams, and these in turn smaller tributaries; in an hour or two the beach will roughly replicate the design of six million years of uplift. The rise of the Colorado Plateau was in its turn a further consequence of the Pacific plate impinging on the North American plate. There are few places in the world where the tectonic circumstances conspire to make a Grand Canyon.

There is no rest for a while. The trail turns to the right and runs parallel to the river. We pass a footbridge. Mules will not cross this one because they can see the river beneath, and this spooks them badly. Instead, a new track takes us along to a more robust bridge at the South Kaibab trail. Much of this track has been blasted out with dynamite, and it hangs on by its fingernails in the middle of a cliff of Vishnu schist, with the Colorado River swirling far below. The trail might be scary, but by now there is no anxiety that the mule will fail to carry you safely through. A few cactus plants cling to the rock walls, apparently subsisting on nothing. If I were here after rain, brilliant scarlet flowers would burst out of their spiny columns. A few skinny mesquite bushes poke out of the gentler slopes, scraggy proof of the near-desert climate at the bottom of the

Canyon. We have come so far down that it is almost warm, even in January; in the summer it must be like a furnace. We pass a disused mine-shaft in the cliff. Further along the Canyon another abandoned mine was formerly the major source for uranium in the US. Its rusting pulleys still stand on the south rim.

Before the first bridge was constructed across the Colorado, visitors to the Phantom Ranch were hauled across the river in a small cable car, completed in 1906. Mules went the same way, reluctantly, one at a time, and it is easy to imagine the discomfiture of these animals dangling above the torrent. Even today, they scarcely approach the crossing with enthusiasm, and mules and riders alike reach the north cliff with gratitude. There is something of a bank on the north side of the river, where the Bright Angel Creek joins the Colorado. The creek has found out the geological fault, exploiting the natural weakness in the strata to produce its own side canyon, and thereby furnishing a natural trail from the north rim. For once, a little soil can accumulate in the valley bottom. We pass the ruins of an Indian hamlet, no more than a cluster of dwellings crudely built from the boulders that litter the narrow shore. There is evidence that people lived here for more than a thousand years, gardening and hunting in due season. Is there no corner of the earth where a seed will sprout that has not been found out by our opportunistic species?

We approach the Phantom Ranch, tucked into the valley of the Bright Angel Creek, where we will finish our downward journey. The mules amble easily now; our legs are promised relief. We dismount at a small corral, and a young woman greets us with a glass of lemonade. The ranch is an oasis in the umber-coloured, dry landscape of the inner canyon. Cottonwood trees planted here in the early years of the twentieth century now make a grove that rustles in the breeze; in the summer, the shade they provide must be a blessing. Cabins are dotted unobtrusively among the trees. The one alloted to us is a single-storey, rectangular building, with walls partly constructed from the same kinds of boulders that were used by the Pueblo Indians; the rest is green-painted wood. Wood also lines the interior, and

In the early days, passage across the Colorado River to the Phantom Ranch was an exciting adventure on Rust's cableway, built in 1907.

One of the huts designed by Mary Colter at the Phantom Ranch makes good use of geological materials to hand.

frames the windows. There are bunk beds, and a kind of wicker-work chair and table: all very simple and functionally effective. The ranch was designed in the 1920s by Mary Colter, who worked for the Santa Fe Railroad – a rare woman in John Wayne territory. She evolved her own style based on natural materials and designs, and inspired by the region's traditions, part Indian, with a touch of Spanish. She was also responsible for some of the memorable buildings on the south rim. The Phantom Ranch works very well. Using morsels of the geology in the buildings helps them settle gently into the landscape, and nurtures the ambient calm.

In the morning, I examine some of the boulders and pebbles down at the streamside, the kind of materials that Mary Colter recruited. There is a selection of cobbles from the formations through which we had passed the previous day, many of them well-rounded. Any rough corners have been knocked off in their passage down the side canyon during stormy crises, when a wall of water might sweep everything before it, rolling and tumbling stones downhill. Buff-coloured sandstone pebbles are probably the commonest ones (Coconino perhaps), and I select one that fits comfortably in my grasp, reminding me of Seamus Heaney's 'Sandstone Keepsake':

> . . . sedimentary
> and so reliably dense and bricky
> I often clasp it and throw it from hand to hand

It might also serve as a reminder of the perpetual state of change of the world: for this ancient pebble is made of grains of sand derived from still earlier cycles of the earth, and now it is halfway towards being worn down again into its constituents – sandgrains that will, eventually, find their way to the sea. Once there, the grains will be incorporated into another sandstone, which will in turn be elevated to form another cliff, another butte. And thus, turn upon turn, until the world ends.

The mule journey back to the rim is along a different trail, and the tape of geological time is wound in again, upwards through history. There is a little more to see of the Late Proterozoic formations in the top of the inner gorge. Above the hidden, steep-sided Inner 'Canyon within a canyon', the familiar rock formations jog past in reverse order: the steep slopes repeat one after the other in due course. Buttermilk needs more frequent rests on the steep return climb, and a lather of sweat soon congeals on her flanks. On the South Kaibab trail, the ascent of the Redwall limestone takes a narrow turn out beside a precipice called Skeleton Point. Eighty years ago, ladies had to be revived with smelling-salts at this prospect. (Ken remarks that if you fall from here, you would have time to roll a cigarette and repent all your sins on the way down.)

From this height, you have a clear view of the sculpted rock masses that flank the Canyon. We are just about to pass around O'Neill's Butte, named for Buckey O'Neill, which is a small platform held aloft on a stunningly steep natural pedestal, a remnant left behind when all the strata surrounding it were eroded away. O'Neill is unusual in having a butte (pronounced 'beaut') named in his honour. Most of the erosional features that you can see from the rim of the canyon are dubbed 'temples', 'shrines', 'thrones', and the like. Then they have something borrowed from classical, Scandinavian, or eastern culture further to identify them. The Cheops Pyramid looks towards the Isis Temple and Shiva Temple. Wotan's Throne, adjacent to Freya Castle, contemplates Krishna Shrine and Sheba Temple. Solomon, Venus, and Zoroaster are all somewhere in the Canyon. The architectural monumentality of the mesas and buttes is indicated by their association with gods, or at least with other famous monuments from the Old World – an ecumenical lucky dip. This lavish mythography was the responsibility of the geologist Clarence Dutton, whom we have already met in Hawai'i. Dutton's *Tertiary History of the Grand Canyon District*, published in 1882, is regarded as a classic account. Dutton did not stint on drama either, as when reporting the prospect from Point Sublime on the north rim: 'The earth suddenly sinks at our feet to illimitable depths,' he wrote. 'In an instant, in the twinkling of an eye, the awful scene is before us.' Indeed it is. His antiquarian eclecticism inspired the choice of names for the amazing features he remarked in the 'awful scene', as if by piling together the great names of the Old World he might validate a claim for the Grand Canyon as the wonder of wonders in the New.

I soon realized where I had seen the same grandiloquent multiculturalism before: Las Vegas, in the adjacent state of Nevada. In downtown Vegas, Luxor (thrill to the ancient Egyptian experience!) rubs shoulders with Excalibur (jousting knightly!), while a stroll away Caesar's Palace (the glory that was Rome!) competes with Paris (Mais Oui – Paree!) or New York! New York! Each gigantic hotel has a kind of symbolic approximation to the source – columns and porticos for ancient Rome, lots of shields for Arthurian romance. Otherwise, the casinos seem much the same wherever you are. It is all most absurd and endearingly exuberant, and entirely inappropriate to the Mojave Desert in which Las Vegas lies, soaking up water. Yet five times as many people visit Las Vegas every year as visit the Grand Canyon.

The peculiar geological circumstances surrounding the Grand Canyon afford us a chance to see deep down into history. However, there are numerous parts of the world where a cut down into the earth – a slice through the upper part of the crust – would reveal a similar succession of cover rocks laid over deep basement that dated from when the world was young. Although these buried strata are concealed beneath younger rocks overlying them they are accessible to boreholes probing for oil, or seeking sources of geothermal energy. A diamond-tipped drill makes our journey for us. The rock cores retrieved from such boreholes are stored as vast lines of stratified poles, laid out on shelves in the archives of surveys and oil companies. These cores may seem rather dull to the eyes of the casual observer, yet if the strata they represent had been exposed to the forces of weather and time they, too, might have made another Grand Canyon. If we could wave a tectonic magic wand and gently elevate southern England, the River Thames would excavate a canyon of its own, another magnificent thing – and, deep enough, there would be the equivalent of the Vishnu schist. If we could do the same in northern France, the Seine would carve through a sequence of hard and soft layers back to a deep and ancient metamorphic foundation. The same goes for Texas, or the Pirana Basin, or the Arabian Peninsula, or western Africa, or much of Siberia. In China, the Yangtze Gorges are perhaps the oriental equivalent to the Grand Canyon, displaying mile after mile of nearly horizontal strata, though never creating a canyon quite on the scale of the Grand. Sadly, much of it will soon be flooded when a new dam is completed. Geologists are now collecting what they can before the rocks become inaccessible.

Stratigraphers love places where the rocks are laid out horizontally, as in the upper part of the Grand Canyon. As Eduard Suess observed of Dutton's exegesis of the Canyon's rocks: 'So Nature writes her own chronology, and we may well envy the observers who are called upon to read this history in the original.' There is no mistaking geological order, as you might among the scrambled and confusing folded rocks in a mountain belt. The strata are laid out for all to see. They are usually referred to as showing 'layer-cake' stratigraphy – lasagne stratification might be another way of putting it. Yet there may be 'holes' in the time actually represented by strata – periods when no rocks at all accumulated, or if they once had, when they were subsequently stripped away by erosion. Caution about dating rocks in any one place is therefore essential. Reading down the rock succession is like turning back the pages in the diary of the earth. The geologist observes when seas flooded continents, or when they retreated, leaving the world to migrating sands and howling winds. He knows from the features of the rocks and fossils when fresh-water lakes and rivers made an environment hospitable for horsetails, thriving alongside cockroaches, fish, and millipedes. He discovers when the climate was tropical, and when it was frigid. He knows from studying sediments when violent storms once raged, or whether the sea-floor was so calm as to leave the carapace of a moulted trilobite undisturbed, the feathery arms of a sea-lily unbroken.

All these cycles of change relate to plate tectonics. Once the continents had formed, parts of them stabilized and were ready to receive a cover of sediments. Whether or not sediments were preserved there depended on the delicate balance between land- and sea-level. It is now quite certain that there were times when the global sea-level was relatively high, flooding the continental interiors, and others when the oceans tended to drain off the continents back into the ocean basins. Times of particularly active ocean-floor spreading seem to coincide with times when the oceanic waters invaded the continents. If global sea-level were to rise now – as it may when the polar ice-sheets melt away – it is easy to imagine waters drowning the plains of Australia, creeping over the Nullarbor Plain and leaving Ayers Rock's standing out as no more than an island above a glittering inland sea, the Blue Mountains an archipelago. Parts of India and most of Bangladesh, the Netherlands, the Mississippi Basin . . . all drowned. In the Grand Canyon, the Tapeats sandstone represents a series of shore sands early in the Cambrian when the sea flooded over an ancient, planed-down, Precambrian landscape. I have stood on similar Cambrian sandstones on the Arctic island of Spitsbergen, with the cold wind whistling through my parka. I have described them already under rain in northern Scotland. I have seen them in Sweden, in Newfoundland, and in Australia. Nobody could doubt that the early Cambrian was a period when the earth was inundated. Contrariwise, that other sandstone, the terrifyingly beetling Coconino, provides testimony to a time of aridity, when prevailing winds drove dunes in shoals across a parched landscape, when hardy animals scuttled across the wastes as fast as they could. Similar sandstones are common around the town of Penrith in the English Lake District. The Permian was the time when the continents assembled together in Pangaea. Deserts spread far and wide. The shape of the world made the climate, and seas were all but banished from the interior of the united supercontinent. What we see in one canyon is but a sample of a hundred places where similar aeolian rocks were accumulating under a fierce sun. The history of plate movements provided the plot-line for the intimate narrative of the rocks.

So much for the story of two sandstones. The same arguments could be rehearsed for all the rock formations encountered in our descent of the Grand Canyon. Any episode recorded on the stratal staircase of the Canyon has to take its place in the narrative of the whole earth. As the continents are carried around the world, so the kinds of sediments that can accumulate upon them are constrained; after all, climate changes profoundly as the plates move from one end of the earth to the other over a billion years or so. All the pulses and retractions of the sea are under their deep instruction. Everything connects.

Everything we have seen falls under the control of forces still deeper, geology more profound, which no canyon will ever reach even if the workings of erosion carry on till the crack of doom. To see further inside the earth we need experiment and intuition. There is an end to intimate exploration, to what can be felt from the back of a mule or tapped with a hammer. That is what we must now investigate.

I say goodbye to Buttermilk with a certain regret. The flight back from the Grand Canyon takes us over other gorges along the Colorado River, where the distinctive markers of the rock formations with which we are now familiar can be traced along the cliffs: cream to red painted up in the evening light. Streams are still seeking out weaknesses in a hundred little valleys, still eroding away what deep time has constructed, essaying to lay low what geological forces once made high. Thousands of years count for nothing, for this is a process with a pace not to be measured against any human chronometer. Now there is Lake Mead below, a giant blue amoeba fingering out into the desert. The Hoover Dam that created it seems little more than a temporary impertinence from this height, although it is doubtless an engineering marvel. I am reminded again of playing on the beach, of temporarily backing a trickle in the sand with a little clay, in order to pond up a transient pool for the amusement of my children. Dusk is falling. The little aeroplane heads towards Las Vegas. Now there are temples and castles, the whole world dressed up in lights. A laser beam shoots vertically upwards from the apex of the pyramid of the Luxor Hotel, routinely dissipating its energy upon the firmament.

12

Deep Things

It would be wonderful to take a trip to the interior of the earth, to see for ourselves the engine-room of plate tectonics. In practice, it is easier to go to Mars or Venus than venture down to the Mohorovičíc Discontinuity, let alone cruise to the mantle. Earthquake waves can reach there, and it is as well that they do – for they send messages back from places we will never see or touch. We have already encountered a few situations where rocks from the depths have been brought to the surface. This may be by wholesale obduction of slices of oceanic crust, preserved in the 'lunar' ophiolites of Oman and Newfoundland. Or else the millstone of geological time, grinding away over many, many millions of years, has exhumed deep layers inside ancient mountain belts, such as those surviving in Archaean shields. Rarely, small boulders from the depths – xenoliths – have been brought to the surface, entrained in vigorous mantle plumes, and torn from their natural home kilometres beneath our feet. *De profundis*, these rocks speak directly of places we can never visit, where no subterranean bathyscaphe can ever cruise; they give us glimpses of the deep underworld.

The endless voyage of the earth's plates is controlled from beneath, by processes operating in profound regions that lie beyond our direct apprehension. In this respect, modern geology comes to resemble chemistry or physics more than its image as a vigorous, field-based, 'hands-on' science might suggest. The properties of matter are in thrall to what is happening at the sub-atomic level, which sometimes seems to resemble a series of Chinese boxes: for every

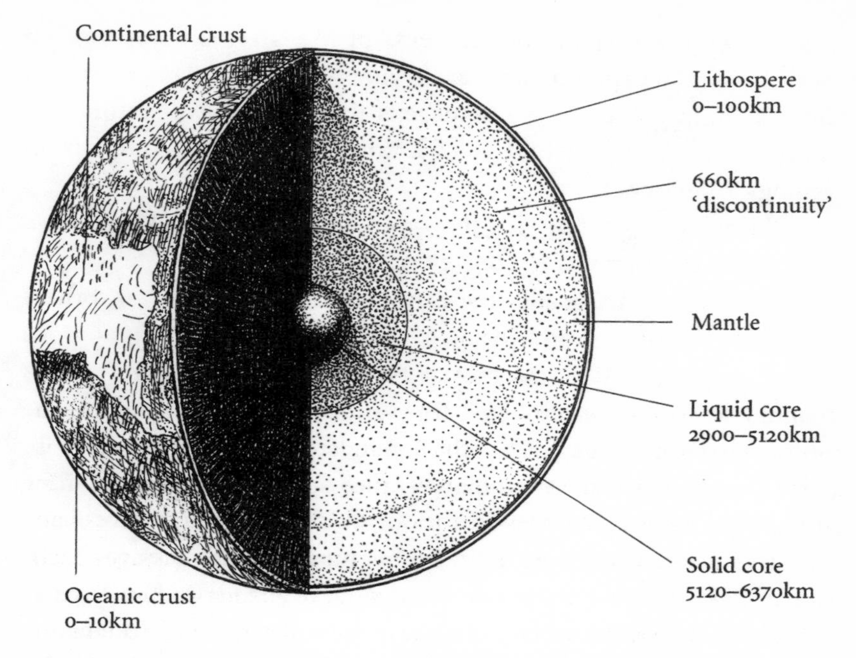

The planetary onion: an outline of the deep structure of the Earth. The 660 km discontinuity within the mantle is indicated.

particle discovered, another is mooted. So we progress from what is observable and solid to what is elusive and quantum mechanical – but also more fundamental. This book has been a portrait of the surface of the earth, where the all-too-solid flesh of the land has proved to be the physical expression of a deeper geological physiology. I have emphasized processes observable in the earth's crust, but they in turn lie atop a deeper motor; to try to understand it, we are forced to move further and further from things directly observable; from the surface, deeper and still deeper into the interior of the earth. As we do so, certainties fade, and mathematical models of what might lie below become progressively important. What are these equations, but a way of writing out dreams in feasible numbers? Experiments in the laboratory take the place of journeys across mountains, or descents into deep mine-shafts. Such tests are not so different in kind from those in nuclear physics conducted in particle accelerators purpose-built to explore the contents of the latest Chinese box. In both cases, the experimenters are trying to reach a place where no one has been before. The difference is that atomic accelerators cost more than the export budget of a small country; in comparison, geology comes cheap.

Although we cannot visit the depths, what we *can* do is observe one of the experiments for ourselves.

In the West of England, the Earth Science Department of Bristol University is to be found inside a very large and slightly pompous edifice called the Wills Memorial Building, which towers over its neighbours like a cathedral. W. D. & H. O. Wills built their fortune on tobacco – and like others who made large amounts of money in ways fraught with moral ambiguity, they spent a lot of it founding one of the best universities in the world. In the basement of Earth Sciences there is much experimental equipment that tries to reproduce what happens deep inside the mantle of the earth, hundreds of kilometres below the surface. This is beyond the roots of the deepest mountain range, and it is a strange world where nothing is as it is under sunshine and rain at the surface. Pressure and temperature increase enormously and progressively deep into the earth. All the properties of materials change utterly under these conditions. The very atoms arrange themselves in different ways, in the manner described previously concerning the structure of diamond. The effects are pervasive; everything is squeezed together in a common regime governed by the 'equation of state'. If we want to know how the earth is made it is important to know what happens to minerals in this strange world – but how to simulate the conditions?

The guru of squeeze at Bristol is Professor Bernard Wood. He is interested in reproducing the deep earth in the laboratory – I should say in a very, very small part of the laboratory, because the amounts of material that can be used as subjects are tiny indeed – a few milligrams at most. I had to put on my extra-strong glasses to see the mounted specimens encased in their ceramic beds. There are different intensities of temperature and pressure as you go deeper through the lithosphere and into the mantle; hence different equipment is appropriate to examining various depths. One problem is that the sample has to be heated, even as it is simultaneously squeezed. Another is that you do not want the sample to explode. All the apparatus looks robust, with thick steel frames, solidly screwed to the floor.

For less extreme conditions a piston cylinder apparatus is suitable. It copes with pressures of up to 40 kilobars and temperatures to about 1500–2000° C, the kind of conditions appropriate to the upper part of the mantle and base of the lithosphere. The equipment is quite simple in principle: it simply squeezes a small sample, encased in a cylinder, with a piston using a hydraulic pump. The sample is surrounded by a graphite 'sleeve', which is turned into a furnace by passing current through it. A thermocouple attached to the sample measures the temperature reached in the test. Thus the experimenter can control both the pressure and temperature (P–T) of the sample under investigation. Then, when it has been tortured sufficiently, the sample is quenched very rapidly. This serves to 'freeze' the mineralogy in the form it took up under high P–T.

So now there is a tiny sample of a mineral preserved under particular deep-earth conditions. The next thing to do is analyse its structure and chemistry. These days, the classical approaches of petrology using thin sections have been superseded by automated methods: years of experience have been replaced by the twiddling of knobs and the flickering monitor in a darkened room. Modern instruments can measure the elemental components of a mineral more or less directly, and they can do so using a minute sample. The principal chemical elements in a sample are measured by an 'electron probe'. A sensitive detector measures the different energies of the X-rays generated from a specimen under examination when it is bombarded by electrons. These energies are characteristic of the various chemical elements that go to make up a given mineral. They are displayed on screen as a spectrum of X-ray lines. Sitting down in comfort in the darkened laboratory, you can watch the various elements under analysis sort themselves out into different 'piles', the heights of which are more or less in proportion to the quantities of the elements present in each sample. Various correction factors have to be incorporated to allow for the absorption and fluorescence within the machine itself, but the analysis is essentially automated.

Although it is indispensable for identifying mineral species, an electron probe is not sensitive enough to measure very minute quantities of the rare trace elements that are more and more important in understanding deep processes. There are other machines that can do this. The current state-of–the-art technology is the Laser Ablation Mass Spectrometer. This can work on exceedingly small quantities of sample with extraordinary accuracy: an interesting speck *within* a small crystal is all grist to its high-tech mill. The laser punches out a tiny sample, which is then analysed by an advanced kind of mass spectrometer that 'sorts' individual atoms by weight. This method is also suited to identifying and counting isotopes of the same elements, which differ in atomic weight, rather than in their chemistry. The accuracy of these instruments makes the mind reel, since there are calibrations approaching picograms – that is, one million millionth of a gram. We are talking about identifying and weighing one grain of sand in a desert. These machines have transformed the scale of study of earth's chemistry and the thermodynamics of rocks at depth.

To take temperature and pressure experiments to a higher level – and deeper into the earth – a multi-anvil apparatus is brought into play. Anvils, of course, were those notoriously heavy pieces of steel upon which blacksmiths beat out horseshoes. The multi-anvil device in the Bristol laboratory is a massive and serious piece of 'kit' weighing 18 tonnes. Despite its size, the sample used is less than 0.1 of a millilitre, a tiny scrap on which to concentrate the fury of the massive press. The sample is embedded into an eight-sided ceramic sample-holder, which is then fitted inside a battery of eight cubes – each the size of a child's building brick – made of tungsten carbide, one of the toughest substances known. Each cube has one corner cut off to accommodate one face of the octagonal sample-holder, so that the sample is held in the middle of the eight cubes as they are pressed

ABOVE Lowest of the low: Death Valley, California.

RIGHT 'The loneliest town on the loneliest road in North America.' Eureka, Nevada: a gold town.

BELOW Fault-controlled scenery: a road across the Basin and Range, Nevada.

RIGHT One side of the Great Rift Valley in Kenya, the ocean that never was.

BELOW Flamingos on Lake Natron, in the African Rift Valley.

Northwest Scotland. Ancient rock relationships: dark Scourie Dyke cutting through even older pale gneiss on the north shore of Loch Torridon.

The view across the alluvial flats at the south-eastern end of Loch Maree. The Kinlochewe Thrust forms the prominent line on the right slicing through Cambrian quartzites, which in turn overlies Torridonian rocks. The Kinlochewe Thrust is part and parcel of the earth movements that produced the Moine Thrust, but is not so historically celebrated.

BELOW Liathach, northwest Scotland: pale-coloured Cambrian sandstones on the hill-tops overlie pinkish Torridonian rocks.

The Inner Canyon is a different world from the higher horizontal strata: Precambrian Vishnu schists make precipitous cliffs plunging into the Colorado River, here living up to its name.

Winter at the Phantom Ranch at the bottom of the Grand Canyon. The Bright Angel Creek has cut out a valley providing a trail to the north rim. Notice the rounded boulders to the right, proof of slow erosion.

The Gulf of Bothnia has 'rebounded' since the last Ice Age at a measurable rate, allowing for calculations on the viscosity of the asthenosphere. On the High Coast World Heritage Site the cultivated fields often lie upon raised beaches as in the middle of the picture.

ABOVE A sulphur miner on Kawah Ijen volcano, Java – the toughest trade on earth?

ABOVE RIGHT Blue Mountains of eastern Australia: an escarpment without equal – and valleys beyond choked with eucalypts.

RIGHT Antipodean Alps where plates collide: Mount Cook in New Zealand.

BELOW One of the driest places in the world: the Atacama Desert, Chile. Its aridity is a product of the Andes, and the Andes are a consequence of the meeting of plates on the Pacific margin.

together to form one larger cube. This in turn is placed inside six massive steel 'squeezers', which press upon the six faces of the large cube. The sample heater has to be immune to the temperatures of the experiment, which rules out any materials familiar to us in the home. Lanthanum chromate ($LaCrO_3$) has just the right properties, when encased within a zirconia (ZrO_2) sleeve. Tungsten carbide's atomic structure has something of the three-dimensional fortitude of diamond; a trace of added cobalt improves the toughness. The equipment takes three or four hours to reach pressures of about 250 kilobars – a long, slow squeeze. It takes even longer – fifteen hours – to decompress. It is worthwhile reciting all these technical details for once, if only to point up that there have been places in this book when I have leapt from idea to conclusion without properly doffing my cap to those with the patience and skill to design equipment. Advances in understanding of how the earth works have tracked the means of measurement almost step for step.

The multi-anvil system is very useful for experiments relating to the mid or deep mantle, below 660 kilometres. Current experiments in Japanese laboratories are trying to push the specification beyond 400 kilobars to 1000 kilobars, approximating to conditions at the core/mantle boundary. With single minerals as the 'squeezee', it is possible to determine their atomic structure at variably high pressures and temperatures. This models what happens to real minerals at great depths beneath the earth's crust. By heating and pressurizing 'mixtures' appropriate for mantle composition it is possible to show under what P–T conditions melting begins, and what kinds of products are produced. An obvious limitation is the minute quantities of material that can be used at any one time. But it does seem likely that conditions 'down there' are much more uniform than they are nearer the surface. The microcosm of the sample might reflect the macrocosm of the world at depth far more faithfully than it would in the crust. Once you predict properties you can look for their expression in nature – how they will transmit S-waves from earthquakes, for example. So the fidelity of your model can be double-checked.

It is possible to push up the pressure even further, by using diamond anvils to press up to 2000 kilobars. Diamond anvils have been used in research programmes based in the University of Mainz, Germany, by Professor Böhler and his group, and in the Geophysical Laboratory, Washington, DC. Diamonds do not crack under pressure, but the sample that can be squeezed by them is extremely small – only a microgram. This is rammed between two diamond anvils and contained within a gasket. The sample is heated by a high-powered laser beam and the temperature attained measured by a ruby fluorescence spectrometer. The whole process can be viewed through transparent diamond windows. Hence the progress of the tiny sample through its transmogrifications under pressure can be monitored directly using a suitable microscope, or by placing the machine within an X-ray diffractometer. The X-rays reveal how the stacking and arrangement of atoms change under the conditions found deep within the earth. Everything – matter itself – alters under pressure. Increase in temperature takes a metallic element towards its melting point, but simultaneous increase in pressure serves to raise the melting point still higher. At high temperatures, natural alloys can also alter the melting properties: a small percentage of another element changes the temperature at which melting occurs. It is exactly this ambiguous and inaccessible world that the high pressure/high temperature experiments in laboratories around the world are designed to investigate. The latest machines employ shock waves rather than 'squeezers' to blast a specimen to extinction, literally shooting at it with a projectile. During the last nanoseconds of its existence, the properties of the sample are captured at P–T conditions close to those pertaining at the centre of the earth. High technology takes us to the innermost regions of the underworld.

It is surprising to discover that experiments on melting rocks were carried out from the earliest days of scientific geology. The Scottish scientist Sir James Hall (1761–1832), (not to be confused with the North American James Hall we met in Chapter 5) was a friend of James Hutton, whose *Theory of the Earth* (1788) is considered the bedrock upon which all subsequent work, including Lyell's, has been constructed. Hutton had adduced good evidence for the formation of igneous rocks from hot magma, and thereby eventually disproved the earlier ideas of the so-called Neptunists, like Professor Abraham Gottlob Werner, who favoured precipitation of such rocks from solution. In the spirit of the muscular scepticism that ruled in Scotland at that time, Hutton wrote: 'The volcano was not created to scare superstitious minds and plunge them into fits of piety and devotion. It should be considered as the vent of a furnace.' James Hall set out to test Hutton's ideas by experiment. Hall was dissuaded by his senior Hutton from experimenting during the latter's lifetime; possibly, Hutton was nervous that the experiments might not come out quite as he would have wished, or perhaps he thought that the differences of scale between nature and laboratory were too important. Hutton warned of 'those who judge of the great operations of the mineral kingdom from having kindled a fire, and looked into the bottom of a little crucible'. What would he have thought about using a fraction of a milligram of material? After Hutton's death Hall did, indeed, melt rocks that had been collected from active volcanoes and showed that when they cooled they yielded products identical to ancient volcanic rocks. Even more remarkably, he used sealed gun barrels as pressure-vessels, which could then be heated to give the first simulation experiments of deep-earth conditions. (In the Grant Institute of Geology, in the University of Edinburgh, Hall's broken barrels are still kept in a display case at the top of the main staircase.) Hall showed that marble was produced by heating limestones under pressure, a persuasive reproduction of the processes of metamorphism.

So how to describe a journey through the deep earth? Perhaps the best way is to move upwards from the middle of things, from the 'still centre of the turning world', and travel towards the surface – from the unfamiliar towards the more familiar. We will take the opposite journey to Jules Verne's entirely fabulous *Journey to the Centre of the Earth* (published in French in 1864), equipped with a modicum of facts and a modest map based on reasonable speculations. Facts first. The centre of the earth is some 6370 kilometres from mean sea-level. The earth's core extends to 2900 kilometres and takes up somewhat less than 20 per cent of the total volume of the planet. From the study of seismic waves reflected back after major earthquakes it has long been recognized that the outer part of the core does not transmit shear (S-) waves, and is therefore liquid. Only solids will transmit such waves.

The inner part of the core begins at 5120 kilometres below the surface and is in a 'solid' condition, but at the enormous pressures at those depths it has a special kind of squeezed solidity. The velocity of pressure (P) waves through the inner core suggests a density appropriate to iron, but with a proportion of some lighter element. This is where high-pressure experiments come into play, because it is possible to investigate the solubility of various elements in iron under core conditions. It is equally possible to make theoretical predictions of the properties of these alloys using quantum mechanical calculations, and thus attempt, in the spirit of Sir James Hall, to match prediction to observation. High-pressure experiments have suggested that a small percentage of sulphur might be the appropriate addition to the inner core. Silica – so important in the outer shell of the earth – is not significant in the core. The outer part of the core, too, is mostly iron, but the reduced pressure, compared with the inner core, and an appropriate temperature (greater than 3000° C), enables it to exist in liquid form. We all sit atop a melted metal sphere. It, too, is lighter than it would be if it were pure iron, and there has been much speculation about what element serves to 'dilute' the liquid metal. Again, ambient conditions at great depth are so different from those we are used to at the surface that we have to forget our everyday ideas of common physical properties conditioned by kettles boiling at 100° C and sugar dissolving in water. Instead, we have to conceive of substances 'dissolving' in liquid iron, to produce strange solutions. High-pressure experiments can play around with sulphur, or carbon, or oxygen to find out their solubility in iron under core conditions. This weird world is not altogether beyond our grasp. Most experiments have suggested that oxygen must be present – probably in the form of iron oxide dissolved in molten iron. It is also apparent that some elements are 'attracted' to the iron in the core because of their solubility in its molten phase. These include tungsten, platinum, gold, and lead: together, they are known as siderophile elements. The result is that these same elements are relatively depleted in the mantle above the core. They were stolen away in the early days of the earth's formation, and sequestered in the very depths of Pluto's kingdom. A further consequence is that such valuable metals require special geological circumstances if they are to occur in commercial quantities near to the surface of the earth. They have to be doubly refined to find their way into veins and skarns. This is one entirely practical reason why we should care about what goes on so far down beneath our human ken.

Another reason is that the outer core is the source of the earth's magnetic field, the result of its behaving as a geodynamo. Without this magnetization there would have been no 'palaeomag', and tracing the history of plate movements would have been much more difficult: no polar wandering if no pole. So the earth's magnetic field is essential to the tale told in this book. If the magnetic field were turned off, compasses would immediately be useless, and some species of migrating birds would wing around in circles, hopelessly disorientated. The magnetic field is an invisible map drawn over the face of the earth: many organisms have sought it out to read their route. It is worth remembering that the magnetic field is also very weak – more than a hundred times weaker than the field between the poles of a toy horseshoe magnet. The development of accurate instruments to measure natural magnetism is another example of technique and theory advancing cheek by jowl. Such scientific progress can be a slow business – after all, the first suggestion that the world *did* behave like a magnet was made by William Gilbert before 1600; it took nearly four centuries for science to investigate Gilbert's insight in detail.

Much still remains mysterious about the geodynamo. It is clear that it has been around for more than 3500 million years because remnants of ancient magnetism have been measured in rocks of this enormous antiquity. Nor does it seem to have altered in strength over that time. So it seems likely that magnetism is an innate property of the liquid outer core. The metallic core is, of course, a very good conductor of electricity, and also a fluid capable of movement; a magnetic field presumably must be generated by the interaction of these two properties. Nonetheless, its mathematical modelling has proved very difficult. Since the dynamo has to be driven by energy, much depends on the nature of the energy source – which must also have been rather constant for a long time. Thermal convection in the outer core is one possibility: a kind of deep, simmering turnover of the molten layer providing a motor of magnetism. Another possibility is harder to understand from our perspective as surface animals – that the inner core grows by liquid iron 'freezing' on to it at its outer boundary (can you imagine freezing at thousands of degrees?). When this happens, it leaves behind a 'light fraction' in the outer core that then rises, leading to another, but compositionally-driven, form of convection. Nor is the magnetic field as simple as that generated by an ordinary bar magnet; in detail, it is very complex indeed, and varies over historical time. A geophysicist at Leeds University, David Gubbins, has mapped variations in the magnetic flux, not at the surface, but at the core–mantle boundary, using mathematical manipulation of historical records of field observations dating back several centuries. It is surprising how the patterns of magnetic flux have changed over this geologically short timescale. Although some 'bundles' of flux are stable and intense (e.g. under Arctic Canada and the Persian Gulf), others drift westwards. Gubbins relates these to columns of liquid within the inner core. Fluid spiralling down through the column creates a dynamo process that concentrates flux at the sites of the columns. It seems that there is a swirling activity 'down there' that is almost indecently fast in comparison with the stately movement of plates at the surface. It is astonishing to be able to peer into such inaccessible regions in intimate detail. However, everything we know is based upon inference, and we have seen already that changes in perception have happened more than once in the story of our understanding of the earth. New thoughts may well change how the moving innards of the earth are modelled.

Then there are the magnetic reversals – those times when north and south poles 'flip over'. This was first suggested in 1906 for some volcanic rocks in the Massif Central in France, a region of classically conical extinct volcanoes known as *puys*. Today, nobody seriously questions the reality of such reversals, since magnetizations have been precisely dated, using evidence provided by the signature of characteristic fossils and confirmed by radiometric dates all over the world. Recall that recognition of compatibly magnetized 'stripes' to either side of the mid-ocean ridges was one of the crucial discoveries that hoisted the flag of plate tectonics over the bodies of its rivals. It proved that new ocean crust – appropriately magnetized at birth – was moving away from the creative centre of the ridges. Hence reversals are another property of the deep earth that constrain the narrative of this history. It is clear that they are by no means as regular as clockwork. There may be a million years or more of one 'north', followed by a short lived reversal – north to south – of perhaps a few tens of thousands. Certain time-periods are characterized by more reversed than normal fields – and vice versa. The Cretaceous was a long period of normal magnetism, though nobody knows whether lumbering dinosaurs used it to negotiate paths through their reptilian world. The periodic switch is like that shown by one of those cheap battery torches that blink on and off, apparently with a maddening will of its own. The short-lived 'reversal events' within a longer period of opposite magnetization are distinctive time markers in geological history – so distinctive, indeed, that they have been given names. As we have seen, the Jaramillo Event is a short period of normal polarity about 900,000 years ago within a long period of reversed magnetism. It can be used as a precise geological tie-line between events on the sea-floor and lava extrusions on the continents, a signal of great prehistoric utility, as might be the issue of a particular coin during the historical era. The 'switchover' from one polarity to another is completed within four thousand years – a mere blip in geological time. Detailed studies on rocks that preserve a record of the 'flip' show a decrease in the intensity of the field for a thousand years or so before the switch, and then short-lived, irregular swings of the magnetic vector, before the opposite polarity is established, weakly at first. It is a subtle thing; no animal species felt it as it might the jolt of an earthquake. In fact, switching poles is a comparatively easy thing for a dynamo to do, and the 'flip' may be controlled by relatively small changes of the fluid motions in the core. It is intriguing that our notions of direction are at the whim of a swirl of liquid iron thousands of metres beneath our feet.

Upwards: to the mantle. If the earth is likened to one of those rounded avocado pears, the mantle is the edible flesh above the core: the crust might be the skin of the fruit. The motor of the earth churns over in the mantle; it is where mountains are born and plates die. It is the deep unconscious of our planet, the hidden body whose bidding the continents obey. The expanding oceans ride upon it. The mantle is the well-spring of tectonics. The remodelling of the face of the world that happens when plates move is ultimately a consequence of the power residing in the mantle.

The possible causes for the shape of the earth have been reflected upon for millennia. Creation myths often invoke the distillation of order from chaos – the ancient Greek word for primeval confusion, according to Hesiod's *Theogony*. The separation of the heavens from the earth and of land from the sea in the biblical account could almost be an historical scenario, if you interpret it generously, and without regard to the time involved. The Kono people of Guinea believe that *Sa* (Death) created endless mud, from which God refined the solid earth, in a kind of sedimentary genesis. The Egyptians described the world as originating from the endless and formless 'sea' known as *Nun*; out of *Nun* an egg was formed from which light emerged. In turn, the sun-god *Atum* arose from *Nun* to form the dry land. On Easter Island, a bird-god laid the egg from which the world hatched. Cosmic eggs figure in many creation myths in cultures stretching from China to South America. In general proportions, the egg – with yolk, white, and a thin outer skin – is a reasonable model for the structure of the earth (especially if you allow it to be a reptilian sphere); for the relative dimensions of core, mantle, and crust, respectively, are not so different from the layers of an egg. To extend the comparison further than it ought, you could say that that shell of the global egg has been repeatedly broken and annealed by tectonics. As for the underworld, in ancient China it was, according to one mythology, the realm of the Emperor of dragons: not exactly a tectonic model, but one at least associated with the vigorous heat of a fire-breather.

The mantle extends from the outer part of the core to the base of the earth's crust, which is at about eleven kilometres below the ocean floor, and, on average, about three times as thick beneath the continents. The mantle thus comprises the bulk of the earth. If our planet were observed by means of a clever instrument from a distant galaxy, an alien astronomer would probably report to his superior a planet composed of the elements silicon, iron, magnesium, aluminium, and oxygen: the elements of core and mantle. He might, if his instruments were sensitive enough, notice traces of carbon from the living gloss on the surface, and detect the components of the atmosphere. Such is the lightest brush of life on the exterior. The uppermost part of the mantle is incorporated, with the crust, into the lithosphere – literally, the 'sphere of rock'. The lithosphere is the part of the earth that comprises the rigid, tectonic plates – hence the most important part for the natural history of the visage of the planet, and the part of which almost all this book has treated. The lithosphere is *not* just the crust, although such is a common misconception. We should add to the catalogue of useful names the layer underlying the lithosphere, which is known as the asthenosphere – and which, of course, lies entirely within the mantle. *Astheno* means weak, or feeble, in Greek, so this is a weak sphere underlying a rocky one. It is hardly surprising that the junction between the two is where the surface of the earth goes a-wandering. This is the layer of weakness that allows the physiognomy of the planet's surface to change with the slow pulse of ocean floor spreading. You will see by now that crude analogies with avocado pears or eggs have already been surpassed: in detail; there are just too many layers in the mantle. There was an egg I bought in St Petersburg in which several eggs were cleverly tucked one inside another, which is a more accurate analogy. The mantle layers are nested within one another like the skins of an onion. Some layers are much thicker than others. To understand the interior of the earth it has to be exposed layer by layer.

You may wonder why the mantle is described as a single unit at all. The answer is that it has a generally comparable composition: iron magnesium silicates are the dominant materials. At least the upper 160 kilometres of the mantle has the composition of the rock type known as peridotite. We have already met this rock in Hawai'i as rare lumps in the lavas, brought up from deep in the earth by the ascending mantle plume. It is a dully lustrous green-black rock, coarse in texture, and heavy – its density is obvious in the hand. The crystals of the minerals olivine (peridot) and pyroxene that make it up can usually be discerned with the naked eye. Because *ma*gnesium and iron (*Fe*) are so dominant, rocks of this kind are known as ultramafic. There is evidence that the deeper layers of the mantle may be somewhat different in composition. One line of research looked at the heat lost at the surface of the earth: to return to the egg analogy, imagine a freshly boiled example cooling in the palm of your hand. Those who work in deep mines experience this heat flux at uncomfortably close quarters. Oliver Goldsmith described the phenomenon in *A History of the Earth* in 1774: 'Upon our descent into mines of considerable depth . . . we begin by degrees to come into warmer air, which sensibly grows hotter as we go deeper, till, at last, the labourers can scarce bear any covering as they continue working.' At the present time, the heat flux at the surface of the earth has been estimated at 44×10^{12} W, derived from within the body of the earth. Unlike the egg, this is heat that replenishes itself. Most of it is derived from the decay of radioactive elements – a kind of internal bonfire that smoulders away in the manner of a fermenting compost heap. The decay of uranium isotopes is the most familiar – they are, of course, one of the sources of the radioactive 'clock' – but potassium and thorium are implicated, too. You have to imagine heat generated by countless, scattered atomic 'sparks' in the subtle bonfire of the earth's interior. However, the content of the radioactive elements in the upper mantle is not sufficient to account for the known heat flux. Recall that the lavas at the mid-ocean ridges are generated by partial melting of higher mantle rocks, so they provide a standard for the precise measurement of isotopes in that part of the mantle. There are not enough of them – only about one-eighth of the total required for the observed heat flow. It is likely, therefore, that the deficiency is made up by a radioactively 'hot' lower mantle enriched, at least at some time in the past, in uranium and its sizzling fellows. So the lower part of the mantle may be subtly different compositionally from the higher.

I can now describe the several layers within the mantle. Because it is so thick, the mantle spans a range of pressures and temperatures that increase with depth. These constraints force its constituent minerals to change their atomic structure, goaded beyond endurance as they lie progressively deeper. The mineral olivine undergoes more than one transformation in its journey towards the centre of the earth. Deeper, and its atoms are forced closer together, jostling for accommodation like crowded passengers on a rush-hour subway train performing subtle readjustments as more and more of their fellows join them. At about 410 kilometres depth olivine changes into wadsleyite, and at about 520 kilometres wadsleyite transforms into ringwoodite. The corresponding temperature is approximately 1600° C. These minerals both have the same composition as common olivine, but different structures: like those subway passengers, pressure has forced them into a new accommodation with the conditions in the underworld.

This is where the experiments with which this chapter began come into the argument. Olivine can, indeed, be squeezed in the apparatus until its atomic pips squeak. When the pressure is piled on, and if it is also sufficiently hot, olivine can be persuaded to change its personality. In the technical jargon, it undergoes a phase change. I have seen artificially made ringwoodite, and it has a blueish hue: only Pluto would be able to admire its colour deep within the earth. Ringwoodite has a distinctive atomic configuration known as the 'spinel structure'. Spinel itself is an attractive gemstone (chemically, magnesium aluminium oxide) that has been employed as fake ruby – even finding a place in crown jewels. Ringwoodite shares its atomic design, despite its different chemical composition. Wadsleyite is a different variant on the spinel structure, one which has 'room' for some water within its atomic lattice. The mineralogist J. R. Smyth calculated that there could be more water locked up within the wadsleyite in the mantle than in all the world's oceans: a sea beyond seeing. Neither ringwoodite nor wadsleyite are stable at the surface of the earth, in the realm where olivine is normal; but, like diamond, once made, these minerals endure for a long time. Wadsleyite *has* been discovered on earth – or, I should say, off earth. It occurs in the Peace River meteorite, which fell in Canada during the 1860s, possibly a piece of a shattered planet that preserved this deep mineral for posterity. So in the laboratory you can look under an eye-glass at a minute piece of earth's interior, forcibly brought to birth in an alien place between carbide jaws of man's invention.

Nor is this the end of the story. Deeper still in the earth, at a depth of about 660 kilometres, ringwoodite comes to pieces. Its atomic framework cannot hang together under the increasing pressure and it splits into component parts. 'Things fall apart; the centre cannot hold,' as W. B. Yeats wrote. This results in two mineral phases coexisting together: one with perovskite structure, the other a magnesium/iron oxide (magnesiowustite).* If you were on a game-show and were asked the question, 'What is the most abundant

* For those who like details, the equation for the transformation is not complicated:
$(Mg, Fe)_2SiO_4 = (Mg, Fe)SiO_3 + (Mg, Fe)O$
Ringwoodite Perovskite Magnesiowustite
Magnesium and iron can replace one another in olivine molecules in a continuous way. This is signified by the brackets (). Ringwoodite was named as recently as 1969. At the molecular level, the stacked octahedra of perovskite are quite different from the 'pseudocubic' structure of spinel. A. E. Ringwood and A. D. Wadsley were notable mineralogists.

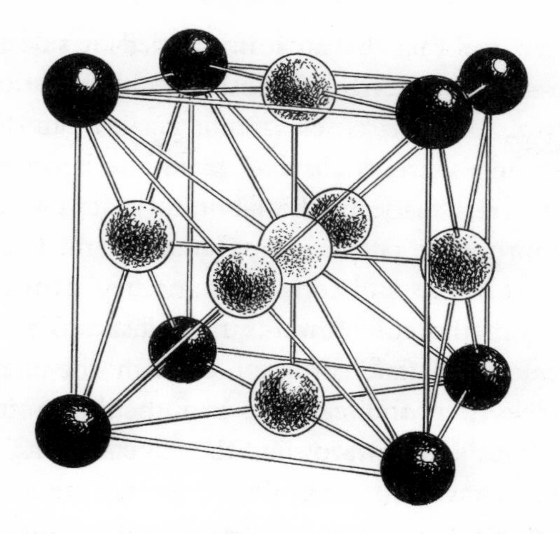

Diagram of atomic structure of perovskite type which is dominant below the 660 kilometre-deep boundary layer.

material on earth?' the answer would be: 'the perovskite phase of the lower mantle'. The applause should be resounding. A simple calculation tells you why your answer is true. The layer of earth's 'onion' containing perovskite stretches from 660 kilometres to the boundary layer at the outer edge of the earth's core, 2900 kilometres below the desk on which this is being written. It is a vast slice of the earth. Since the perovskite phase comprises something like 70 per cent (perhaps more) of this layer, it is an easy calculation to show that this unseen, unheralded, and, some would say, obscure mineral phase is the bed upon which the whole of our multifarious biosphere ultimately lies.

What, it reasonably might be asked, has this deeper reality got to do with us? After all, it is a long, long way down and far removed from the sunshine and clouds under which we live our brief lives. We cannot see into the earth with our light-bound eyes, and who wants to travel to this realm of crushed molecules and phantom phases? But other probes *do* reach there. Earthquake waves respond to the profoundly-concealed mineral phase changes by altering their velocity in 'steps' as they pass from one layer to another deep within the earth. They 'see' that the earth is mantled by successive mineral layers, which are themselves subdivisions within the larger mantle. In a wonderful example of congruent science, it transpires that the seismic changes are *predictable* from the properties of those deep-earth minerals made in the laboratory: it is just a matter of making the appropriate calculations. Hence one field of investigation independently confirms and constrains another. At the end of it all, the journey from the core towards the crust can be recited zone by zone like a travelogue: proceed through the perovskite layer upwards to the ringwoodite layer, and thence to the wadsleyite layer, and onwards and upwards into the olivine layer. Through these layers pass the convection cells that drive the plates that in turn sculpt the face of the world. In this way the depths intercede in our superficial lives: there are unseen and unbidden forces, as indifferent to the fate of the sentient organisms living above them as the distant stars.

The glass in a medieval church plays tricks on you. The world seen through it is a distorted one: swirling, refracted, blurred. Its original transparency has been compromised by some transforming agent. That agent is flow. It operates so slowly that its progress would be hard to see in a century. Over hundreds of years the surface of the pane distorts from the true, crinkles and falls into lobes under the force of gravity, until we see but through a glass, weirdly. Yet we know, too, that glass is a brittle solid. It seems that glass can be simultaneously both solid and flow like a viscous liquid. It is possible to see the same phenomenon over a shorter time scale with a block of asphalt. Follow the smell to where a road is being resurfaced and you may see a dark block of crude asphalt lying in the roadway. It has a fractured edge, so it must have broken like a solid. Yet you will probably notice a side bellying outwards, as if it sagged under its own weight, viscidly flowing. Again, glaciers creep slowly down mountain-sides, yet an ice-block taken from the freezer often cracks and splits when dropped in a glass of whisky at room temperature.

Glass, tar, ice: these are all 'solids' that also show long-term fluid behaviour. They creep, they flow. They help us visualize what happens within the mantle, for this is how the inner earth moves.

The Swedish scientist Anders Celsius was a professor in the earlier half of the eighteenth century at the University of Uppsala, the most ancient establishment of learning in Sweden. It is a place of austere, four-square and solid academic buildings, with a fine cathedral. Celsius is immortalized for having given us the scale that interposed a hundred degrees between freezing and boiling water. He also noticed that around the Gulf of Bothnia on the Baltic Sea there were strand lines – former sea-shores – that were now marooned above the present sea-level. These observations were published as early as 1744. As Eduard Suess described it 150 years later: 'At Tornea, [Celsius] had been shown to his astonishment that the harbour constructed in 1620 was already useless.' The implication must be either that the land was rising, or that the sea was retreating. From a boat on the Gulf you can observe the raised beaches as if they were drawn against the land with a ruler. Celsius himself had concluded that the seas might be shrinking on a global scale, draining away to leave their old shores high and dry. Charles Lyell observed in 1834 that the elevation of the old shores in the north of the Gulf of Bothnia was greater than that in the south, and carefully argued that the former strand lines should be attributed rather to a rise in the land's surface. Curiously, Eduard Suess did not follow Lyell but instead went to some lengths to diminish the rather strong evidence for elevation of the land that had accumulated by the end of the nineteenth century. This may have been because Suess preferred to think of land movements as periodic convulsions, as in his beloved Alps, rather than the steady tinkerings of Lyell's classic explanation. He thought that the Gulf of Bothnia was draining out by '*an emptying out of the water, not a rise of the land*' (his italics, as usual when he signalled what he regarded as a crucial point). All the more curiously, at the time Suess wrote, it had been accepted universally in scientific circles that a huge ice-sheet had covered Scandinavia in the last great ice age, disappearing less than 10,000 years ago. It seemed a reasonable inference that the massive burden imposed by 'loading' of the ice had depressed the land, which had rebounded in a regular fashion after the ice had melted, thereby carrying upwards former shore-lines beyond the reach of the sea. Even with the evidence to hand, Suess was determined to reject the flexibility of the earth's response that this implied, and recruited the ice to his own purposes. Referring to strand lines in Norway that were similar to those in the Baltic he wrote: 'The great majority of terraces in the fjords of western Norway, must be regarded as monuments of the retreating ice, and not as evidence of oscillation of the sea level, and still less of oscillation of the solid land.' You could not wish for a clearer statement of his priorities.

It was not often that Eduard Suess was so in error. The rise of the glaciated country of Finland and Scandinavia is now an established fact: half a century after Suess, Arthur Holmes reported that in the northern part of the Gulf of Bothnia an uplift of about 270 metres (900 feet) has occurred and that it was continuing at a rate of about a thirty centimetre (foot) every twenty-eight years. The degree of uplift is in proportion to the thickness of the ice overburden that is removed: the more ice there was, the more uplift there will be. The uplift has even been mapped in contours. Modern laser techniques can measure the rebound with considerable accuracy. The elastic recovery of the land is produced by compensation in the mantle: it flows in to 'fill the space'. Imagine the world as a balloon filled with honey: the skin of the balloon might be an appropriate surrogate for the earth's lithosphere. Prod the balloon with your finger, and a dent remains. The honey slowly flows in to compensate the depression, which rebounds at a fixed rate in an elastic response. It becomes a comparatively easy calculation to determine the viscosity of the honey from the rate at which this happens. So it is with the mantle. It can be understood as a liquid which is 10^{23} times more viscous than water – trillions of millions times as sticky, but a liquid nonetheless: think, rather, of that asphalt. The exquisite sensitivity of today's instruments shows just how responsive the lithosphere can be to loading: even the weight of a building can produce a detectable downward deflection. Is it possible that even a heavy footfall produces a twitch in the mantle? We live on an elastic, quivering earth, buoyed up on the responsive layer beneath the lithosphere.

The mechanism of convection currents within the mantle will now be understandable. It is flow on a dignified scale. The mantle includes a few huge convection cells that transfer heat from the core-mantle boundary to the base of the lithosphere. A slowly simmering cauldron of porridge, roiling and rolling, is both useful as an image of convection but also misleading as a metaphor for the nature of the flow. In the boiling porridge, the oatflakes are merely carried by the convecting water between them; in the mantle, it is the rock itself that flows. The hot, rising limbs of the convection cell part beneath the mid-ocean ridges, providing the energy source for the lavas that create the surface of the world anew. The lavas are developed from partial melting of deeper peridotites. We have seen that occasionally a lump of peridotite is entrained in an erupting lava: it always contains olivine, and never wadsleyite, showing that it must have originated from the outer mantle layer. The work of the rock-crushing theoretician and the geologist finally meet on the rocks. What mantle convection has created, it also destroys at the subduction zones at the edges of oceans, where the downward-plunging limbs accompany slabs of comparatively cold oceanic lithosphere back towards the foundations of the earth. Described thus, the great convective cycle seems devoid of turmoil: yet it is the destroyer of cities and the generator of mountain ranges. When viewed on the scale of the whole world, however, an alpine system is the merest surface puckering, whilst an earthquake that might destroy a civilization is no more than a momentary shudder. The intimate earth history I have described in this book is like the adventure of a flea on the back of an elephant.

It is difficult to conceive of structures so vast as the convection cells that turn the underworld. One school of earth scientists is persuaded that there are *two* sets of such cells within the mantle, one above the other, turning in tune like linked cogs in a clockwork mechanism. They envisage that the boundary between upper and lower cells is the profound, and profoundly important, 660-kilometre discontinuity, below which the perovskite structure predominates. Recent reviewers have preferred the model that convection operates through the whole mantle, which would make it the greatest single phenomenon on our planet, turning and turning in tune with the slow beat of geological time. The properties of shear waves (S-) show that the lower mantle is not differentiated elastically from the upper mantle, so that convection cells are able to pass through the layers of mineralogical phase changes. They change personality, if you like, but they do not change their purpose. Recall also that there are mantle plumes, like the one underlying the Hawaiian chain, that pass through much of the mantle to form 'hot spots' below the lithosphere. Furthermore, the slabs of oceanic crust that are carried down by the *descending* limb of the convection cell can be detected as heterogeneities in the mantle: they plunge down into its lower part. The downward plunge of the slabs is measured by an earthly equivalent of the CAT (computerized axial tomography) scans that are now routinely used as a more precise alternative to conventional X-rays for 'seeing inside' the human body. Seismic waves provide the data needed to nose into the deep innards of the earth. The method is known as seismic tomography: the earth itself is the patient. Where a subducted slab, which is relatively cold, is pulled downwards into the mantle, it subtly alters the 'speed' of the seismic waves – up to plus 2 per cent. The effects can be mapped with remarkable precision, as, for example, beneath the Tonga-Kermadec Trench in the Pacific. The fast velocities produced by the descending slab can be mapped down to depths of perhaps 1600 kilometres – deeper by far than the epicentres of earthquakes caused by the movement of the slab itself. Under Japan, the 660 layer is depressed by about thirty kilometres where the cold slab plunges downwards. It seems that even when the convected slab is beginning to merge back into the mantle from which it was ultimately born its history is retained as a kind of 'ghost' that the earthquake waves alone can see. The same methods also reveal that the mantle is less homogeneous than was once believed: it includes 'blobs' of different composition on the scale of a few kilometres, which may be the last remnants of subducted lithosphere slabs.

What moves the lithosphere plates above the mantle convection cells? Are they pushed up at the mid-ocean ridges, or are they dragged by the subducting oceanic crust, which is denser than the mantle through which it sinks? The two theories are known as 'ridge push' versus 'slab pull' respectively. Either way, the effect is the same. The mid-ocean ridges are elevated above the sea-floor, where the heat flux is greatest on the upwelling limbs of the convection cells. Do the plates slide away from the ridges towards the trenches? Or do the subducting slabs of 'cold' crust – which, as we have seen, go down deep – tug at the slabs somewhat as one might pull a table-cloth from one side? Intuition would perhaps suggest the former, if only because there seems to be something inherently vigorous about the creation of new crust at the mid-ocean ridges, as if the earth were heaving itself up by its own bootstraps. In detail, however, the volcanic eruptions at the ridges are found to be rather gentle, whatever the impression given by lines of fiery chasms along fault zones. The new crust almost insinuates itself into the spaces generated by adjacent plates moving apart. Furthermore, when different plates are compared, it seems that the velocities* at which they travel are related to the length of trench-edge that they possess: the longer the subducting margin, the faster the plate moves. This supports the notion that slab pull is more important than ridge push. Plunging plates turn the engine of the earth.

The turnover of the oceanic crust also means that much of the earth above the core is recycled. The current rate of subduction down trenches is about three square kilometres per year – the area of a large village, perhaps. This implies that at least 18 cubic kilometres of oceanic crust and something like 140 cubic kilometres of the peridotite layer beneath it are sucked downwards into the maw of Pluto's realm every year. Then, too, there is a quantity of sediment

* This absolute motion can be deduced from the rate of movement of plates above 'hotspots' like Hawai'i, as described in Chapter 2.

that is scraped off and directed Hades-wards along with the oceanic plate. The mantle begins to look more like a thick and varied soup rather than a bowl of porridge. One set of published calculations indicates that almost the entire mantle has been through the recycling process over the course of geological time. The different subducted sources also retain their chemical element signatures, which can be precisely measured to parts per billion with modern mass spectrometers. Isotopes of rarer elements such as uranium and thorium are particularly useful in identifying sources of subsequently erupted lavas. Some oceanic island 'basalts' stand revealed as having originated from recycled ancient ocean crust.

The crust of the continents tends to stand apart from much of the activity at subduction zones. Eduard Suess long ago commented that the continents were of 'trifling density (2.7 grammes per cc) compared with the density of the Earth as a whole (5.6 grammes per cc)'. The continents are composed predominantly of what both Suess and Arthur Holmes would have termed *sial*, light rocks with alumina an important component compared with the dense, basic rocks of ocean floor and mantle: sial included all granites and gneisses, and many sedimentary rocks. A long catalogue can now be added of minor elements also sequestered into the continental crust. The light, thick continents rise above the troublesome subduction zones. They have not been continually recirculated like the ocean basins: they rise above things, which is why they include the ancient survivors, the Methuselahs of rocks. But wherever subduction zones plunge downwards against a continental area, the rocks of continents and oceans interact and fuse. Lavas generated by frictional heating include the gummy magmas that make the catastrophic volcanoes of the 'ring of fire' through Japan, Indonesia and adjacent islands, and the Philippines. They dog the downward-dipping subduction zones around the Pacific, like boils around an infected wound. The trace elements recovered from their volcanic rocks reveal the proportions of the mixture between magmas derived from ocean and continent, respectively, almost in the manner of a genetic marker revealing human ancestry. The volcanoes burst to the surface landwards of the ocean trench, rising as they do from the depths of the subduction zone. Suess had recognized this fact with characteristic clarity. 'The volcanoes which accompany the folded festoons *never* stand in the foredeep,' he wrote, 'but belong entirely to the folded cordillera.' He attributed this to subsidence of crust in the trenches. Would that he had known that the area beyond the trench was where a forced marriage between the kingdoms of Pluto and Zeus had been enacted deep in a subduction zone, and where hybrid magma is the result of their union. These offspring generate splenetic eruptions, spawning pyroclastic surges that wreak destruction indiscriminately on man and beast. The hollow mummies of Pompeii were the tragic consequence of such a magmatic marriage. The same wrathful issue engenders volcanoes along the length of the western rim of the Americas, where the oceanic plates of the Pacific impinge against the unyielding continents to the east. From Popocatépetl to Mount St Helens, destructive volcanoes are the consequence of ocean meeting continent and the furious fulminations that follow.

The boundary between the lithosphere and the asthenosphere beneath it is the top of the Low Velocity Zone. This is a region where both kinds of earthquake waves are slowed down. It lies within the upper mantle, some 40–160 kilometres below the surface. Experimental work suggests that the change in seismic behaviour happens because some small part of the mantle melts – the result of the release of pressure at these particular depths, at the appropriate temperature. The partial melting of mantle rocks is sufficient to reduce the coherence of this layer in the earth: it is where 'slippage' occurs between rigid lithosphere and weak asthenosphere. We have arrived at the base of the shell of earth's egg.

Upwards, ever upwards. The name 'crust' has a nice, homely feel to it, carrying images of pies fresh from the oven. Compared with the alien interior from which we have travelled, it *is* almost like coming home. The rocks of the crust are those familiar to us; they comprise the stage upon which my intimate history has unfolded. We have seen that everything turns upon a deeper geological reality, powered by leisurely rotations and passing through strange mineral phases that cannot exist on the surface. This deep world, accessible only through experiment, or probing earthquake waves, is overlain by one that can be understood by geological mapping and geological tapping. This is our home, our rich and complex habitat, laid out upon a geology as various as human culture, and as challenging to understand; where the history of more than three billion years of life is recorded in ancient sedimentary rocks; where life and the earth have evolved together in an intimate collaboration that is a marvel in the galaxy. Welcome back to the surface, almost.

The base of the earth's crust is drawn at the highest of the seismic lines that I shall mention: the Moho. This is a somewhat anonymous abbreviation for Mohorovičíc Discontinuity, a name that justly commemorates its discoverer, the pioneer Yugoslav geophysicist, A. Mohorovičíc. In 1909, he demonstrated that earthquake (P) waves 'jumped' in velocity from about 7.2 to 8.1 kilometres per second along a discrete surface. Evidence for this boundary was not known to Eduard Suess, but familiar to Arthur Holmes. In the upper part of the crust, rocks fracture brittlely: this is the realm of earthquakes, whose shudders have done so much to help decode the rest of the earth. The junction between crust and mantle is where the dense peridotite layer of the upper mantle circumscribes the earth. This heavy rock speeds earthquake waves. The crust is thinnest under the oceans, especially towards the mid-ocean ridges. We have already met sections through such crust in the obducted ophiolites of Oman and Newfoundland, eight kilometres or so thick, each with their own, distinctive layering. Beneath the lighter continents, crustal thickness is thirty to forty kilometres in the quiescent, ancient, stable parts of the earth, where, all passion spent, the surface of the earth lies calmly on its deeper foundations. Contrariwise, the continental crust is thickened – often doubled again – along mountain belts, especially where continent has collided with continent in ranges like the Alps or the Himalayas. In some places one continent has even underplated its neighbour – pushed bodily underneath – in the ultimate heave. The consequence of earthly engagement is elevation of icy peaks above deep tectonic roots. We have seen how granites are sweated out deep in mountain belts; and how continental rocks are changed by heat and pressure. And then the forces of air and rain and ice seek at once to wear down the elevated peaks, just as the Book of Isaiah describes it: 'every mountain and hill shall be made low: and the crooked shall be made straight, and the rough places plain'.

The face of the earth has its character scoured upon it by the elements, but they can only work on what has been set upon the surface by forces operating in the hidden depths.

The journey from the centre of the earth may seem a more theoretical enterprise than the rest of this book, yet deep forces that we can infer from surface observations and experiments move the plates that make up the world. To the extent that human history has always been in thrall to geography and climate – both of which depend on geology – our very character could be described as geological. We may all ultimately be the children of convection. Mountain ranges – gross thickenings of continental crustal rocks – have divided one race from another, and have helped generate the diversity that is one of the chief glories of humankind; they have even provided refuges for peoples extinguished elsewhere. The great peninsula of India south of the Himalayas displays common cultural roots that dig deeper than modern religious divisions; the same area was the home to some of the earliest civilizations. Greater China to the north of the same range comprises one of the largest areas of cultural idiosyncrasy, abode of the *Han* people, whose sculptures of lions and dragons show cultural persistence over more than four millennia. On a smaller scale, the Pyrenees both guarantee the character of Iberia and maintain a refuge for Basques. The Alps seal in Italy on its northern side – a barrier famously pierced by Hannibal across the Little St Bernard pass in 218 BC. My Scottish friends attribute their Celtic hardiness to that bare country being underlain by gneisses and schists of the ancient Caledonian range. My Norwegian friends show how the northward continuation of the same range has generated a variety of distinctive dialects in isolated communities along their coast. Even today, modern culture retains an inheritance of character and language from these ancient limits: it may even survive the onslaught of global capitalism, for it has already survived centuries of trading. Low sea-levels associated with the last ice age allowed humans to penetrate into North America, perhaps 13,000 years ago, and into Australia before that. Some of those people dispersed into jungles lying along the passive margin of South America, into Amazonia, where the South American continent gently sagged alongside the widening Atlantic Ocean, and a huge river system parted tribe from tribe. In western Africa, the Congo Basin provided a mirror image on the corresponding eastern, passive margin. Cultural diversity was bred by separation at all levels. On the other hand, it is an uncomfortable fact that some of the areas of greatest human conflict, such as central Europe, are those where there are no such natural barriers, where one group after another has pushed for, and achieved, temporary dominance. Hungarians, Romanians, Russians, Poles, Slavs, Austro-Germans, Danes, and so on, have fought viciously over gentle European hills and plains. The sad litany of a hundred wars and skirmishes attests to the grim underbelly of diversity: intolerance.

All the intimate details of landscape and culture that I have described in this book are rooted in geology. Many of the older gods were related directly to landscape and their propitiation was often a way of rationalizing natural phenomena, whether invoking Madame Pele's uncertain temper in Hawai'i, or Vulcan's smoky workshops on Mount Etna. Time was tamed in myth, for humans have always wondered about their beginnings, inventing scenarios spanning primal eggs and sculpted mud. Geology provided a rational timescale, but one so incomprehensibly expanded that our own species might seem no more than an afterthought, a conscious postscript, rather than lying close to the essence of things. There are those who still regret the loss of gods who might intercede on our behalf. The true measure of the earth could be that slow overturning of the mantle that calibrates the march of the tectonic plates. James Hutton's famous statement in 1788 about the earth, that he found 'no vestige of a beginning, no prospect of an end', is now at least constrained by a figure for the former: 4.5 billion years. The record of rocks on earth is consistent with plate activity over some four billion years of that span. During that time the planet has changed from barren to prolific. The photosynthetic activity of 'blue-green' cyanobacteria and plants transformed the atmosphere to an oxygenated one that animals could breathe. Life moved from sea to the land, and thence into the air. All the while, oxygen altered the way the rocks themselves weathered, just as vegetation altered the rules of erosion thanks to their obstinate webs of roots that cling to, and process soil. Earth and life became progressively interlinked: the 'greenhouse' effect that worries us today is just the latest illustration of this obligatory wedding. And during all this slow transformation the motor of the earth reshuffled the continents and oceans, now spreading the continents apart, as at present, now locking them together, a leisurely procession to which life had no choice but to respond.

There are two possible reactions to the tectonic history of the world. Either you might despair at the apparent randomness of it all, at our insignificance in the face of gigantic forces that are as indifferent to our species as is a torrent to the fate of a mayfly that rides upon it; or you might wonder at the extraordinary richness of history, and feel privileged to be able to understand some part of it. Were it not for a thousand connections made through the web of time, the outcome might have been different, and there may have been no observer to marvel and understand. We are all blessed with minds that can find beauty in explanation, yet revel in the richness of our irreducibly complex world, geology and all.

With his own nod towards Indian mythology, Eduard Suess completed volume 2 of *Das Antlitz der Erde* thus:

> As Rama looks out upon the Ocean, its limits mingling and uniting with heaven on the horizon, and as he ponders whether a path might not be built into the Immeasurable, so we look over the Ocean of time, but nowhere do we see signs of a shore.

13

World View

. . . let him not say that he knows better than his master, for he only holds a candle in sunshine.

William Blake, *The Marriage of Heaven and Hell*

The marvellous thing about the face of the earth is that it is such a mess. It is an impossibly complex jigsaw puzzle of different rocks. Like Gilbert and Sullivan's wandering minstrel, it is 'a thing of shreds and patches'. More than three and a half billion years of history have stitched it together. It has been modelled and remodelled, split asunder and rejoined in tune with the waxing and waning of oceans. Here, continents have been inundated by shallow seas which have then drained away, leaving a legacy of sandstones or limestones, shales or gravels. The Painted Desert was painted long ago. Elsewhere, erosion has exhumed baked rocks that once lay deep within the crust. The multifarious world wears geological motley. Mediated by climate, the underlying rocks influence the form of the landscape, the vegetation, the crops that can be grown – even the particular stones and bricks for making cities before steel-and-glass became universal. We have all grown out of the geological landscape, and perhaps unconsciously we still relate to it. Human beings seem to be programmed to love their home territory. Russians pine for the open steppes; Aborigines for the endless Australian interior; shepherds for rolling country dotted with sheep; Shropshire lads for blue remembered hills. Most of us appreciate the world in this intimate way, rocks and all. Our patch is our home. Few shepherds, perhaps, pay much heed to the strata over which their charges scramble, although the rocky underlay is ultimately in control of their livelihood: other rocks, other livings. We respond more affectionately to landscape at the local scale, just as we register tragedies most acutely within our own family; broader issues of society do not tug at our sleeve in quite the same way, although we are reluctant to admit it. Whether we acknowledge it or not, geology is important in the most visceral way.

I have tried to explore the influence of geology on the ground – its intimate ramifications, its pervasiveness. I have let the particular place speak for the general case. I have no doubt that there are a hundred other locations as suitable to make the point as any I have chosen, and any selection will inevitably miss out important things. But then, there was never any intention to write out the whole world in the fashion of Professor Suess. Always in this story – far beneath us and largely unacknowledged – there is the bidding of the plates. The tectonic unconscious may provide a rationale of the earth, but perhaps it seems too remote to interest the shepherd lad with one eye on a lame ewe and the other on the girl from the next village. Nonetheless, an understanding of the deep tectonic driver has unified the world. Our patch is actually linked to every other patch. Perhaps realizing that we are all small creatures riding pick-a-back atop our own tectonic plates located within the irregular chequerboard of the earth might enforce a proper sense of humility upon our arrogant little species. Somehow, I doubt it.

Knowledge advances and old ideas are shed, sometimes with reluctance. Enough has been said already to convey a picture of what has happened to geological thought over the century since Suess' masterly global survey. There is no question that we are now close to a unified theory of the earth. It seems unlikely that many of the recent fundamental advances in understanding of the deep structure of the earth – the lithosphere, the mantle, the movement of plates – will be undermined in the future. Equally, it would be astonishing if there were not new discoveries that will render my account an antique within a few decades. We have seen enough of cherished ideas in the previous hundred years foundering against a new thought or a critical observation to make further enlightenment a sure bet.

However we try to retain a proper modesty in deference to the past, it is difficult to record the growth in comprehension of the earth in the light of plate tectonics without occasionally sounding smug. 'Aren't we the clever ones?' we seem to imply. Nothing could be more unjust to those who went before. The pioneer geologists who provided intellectual ammunition for Suess and his successors were nothing short of heroes: they trekked across remote areas with little more than a hammer and a notebook. There was nobody to airlift them to safety; they had few maps to follow. The information they provided was seminal. Suess gave them the recognition they deserved. He praised W. T. Blanford, pioneer in the mapping of much of India and the Himalaya, and 'Przewalsky's adventurous travels [which] have opened up a large part of Tibet'; and then there was Bell, who mapped the ancient shield areas of Canada (1877) at a time when they were unexplored, mysterious, and dangerous. These were courageous men of rare intelligence. Przewalsky is familiar to some because the wild horse that he discovered still bears his name – *Equus przewalskyii*. But many of these pioneers gave their lives to explore places that can now be reached in a helicopter in an afternoon, and their names are forgotten except to a few *aficionados*. They made their contributions, which are now woven as obscure threads into the tapestry of science. Most of us will have lesser memorials.

J. Tuzo Wilson is the exception. His name is built into the very fabric of the earth. He has been mentioned several times in this book, as a kind of seer for geological processes. He it was who recognized Iapetus. The slow progress of the plates, with initial continental splitting and formation of a new ocean, eventually followed by its closing again with the generation of an orogenic belt, is known as the Wilson, or Wilsonian, cycle. It is just about the biggest generalization that can be made about the world. As we have seen, the whole process may take more than 200 million years to complete. Of the many historical cycles expressed upon the earth – whether of chemical elements, sea-level, or temperature – the Wilson is both the most stately and the most transforming. We have visited just a few of the mountain belts generated by the end of these cycles: the youthful Alps, the old Appalachian–Caledonian chain, the ancient scars of the Precambrian. The face of the world can be seen as the consequence of a succession of Wilsonian events – dominated, naturally enough, by the present cycle – but with the memory of previous cycles preserved as streaks and blotches like old wounds. The traces of ancient cycles far back in the Archaean are sometimes difficult to detect, but they are still there if you search hard enough. And the further back in time, the more the rocks betray the processes that occurred deep in the lithosphere, for these most ancient rocks have been scrubbed clean by erosion of all their overburden, it might be for thousands of millions of years. The motley of the world could well be explicable after all: there is time enough to patch it all together.

After earth was formed some 4550 million years ago, a pattern of plate movements can account for much of what is preserved on its surface – only the first few hundred million years have left little record. As for the end, it is predictable that the present Wilson cycle will continue, so that the Pacific Ocean will be subducted away in a hundred million years or so producing a new Pangaea, another supercontinent when Asia and America finally conjoin. Beyond that? It is impossible to say exactly where it will happen, but it is certain that this future supercontinent will itself fragment again, and once more the continental blocks will be on the move: our world will be forever in transit, forever re-inventing itself, until the internal motor of the earth finally turns no more.

Eduard Suess began his great work by inviting his readers to part the clouds and take a view of the earth from the vantage point of a visitor from another planet. It was a gesture of omniscience on his part. You are reminded of the Temptation of Christ, when the Devil laid out all the kingdoms of the world from the prospect of a high mountain. Geology will master the world – Suess supposed – and bring it to heel. This lofty panorama might have been a bold thing to attempt at the end of the nineteenth century, but we are now thoroughly familiar with the satellite viewpoint. That NASA photograph of earth from space might prove to be the definitive image of the twentieth century, the moment when the finite bounds of our planet entered common consciousness, so fragile it appeared, so blue and dappled – more soap bubble than mountain and mineral. As Suess began, so I shall end. After exploring intimate geological details in just a few places on our cobbled-together planet, it is time to change the focus briefly to look at the whole. We have seen how even a single crystal links to profound circulations of the earth; pull away upwards from that crystal until the granite holding it is just a tumid blemish on the greater landscape; and higher again until the granite is lost within the wrinkles of a mountain belt; from this altitude you can see the oceans and continents together. We will turn our narrative upside-down: from the details of a stone wall, or one lava flow named for a half-forgotten god, we will move to the outlines of oceans and ranges, pausing only fleetingly. Like Puck, we will 'put a girdle round about the earth/In forty minutes'.

Start in my office in the Natural History Museum in South Kensington in the West End of London, on a site where there have been geologists working for more than a century. Imagine flying higher and higher, until we can see that all the fine hotels and monuments and endless suburbs of London lie in a bowl of strata of Tertiary age. The River Thames is now no more than a silvery line following the centre of the bowl. Beneath these strata – mostly soft sands and clays – there are older rocks again; the white Cretaceous limestone known as the Chalk reaches the surface north and south of London on open downs, where sheep were once universal. From his parsonage built upon this rock the incomparable naturalist Gilbert White recorded his intimate history of just one village, Selborne. White's book has sold nearly as many copies as the plays of Shakespeare, and part of its charm is its dedication to the particular place, the particular geology. South of the London Basin, the Chalk frames the Weald, which was the major source of iron in medieval times and now is thick with groves of sweet chestnut burying ancient hammer ponds. From high up, most of what you see is forested. Climb higher still and we can see that the Chalk, again, forms the white cliffs of Dover

– to many English people perhaps the most sentimentally significant piece of geology there is. From this height we can see that the Dover cliffs are of a piece with facing cliffs in France on the other side of the English Channel, which is nothing more than a geological afterthought, breached by the eroding sea just a few thousand years ago. Geology knows no national boundaries and from here we can even make out the Chalk extending far across France, to underlie the endless plains in the north, where the grain that goes into making a hundred million *baguettes* is grown in fields that have neither hedgerows nor apparently any end. And could we but follow the Chalk around the world we would find similar white limestones stretching from the Canadian Shield 'all the way through to Texas and Mexico', as Suess said, to the Black Sea and well beyond in the Middle East. Chalk rock records one of the great transgressions of the sea on to the continents, one which happened close to a hundred million years ago, and which painted great slabs of the world white for eternity with the sediment it left behind. Chalk once extended northwards over much of the British Isles, though erosion has removed nearly all of it; for below us now we see areas underlain by older rocks – Jurassic, Triassic, Permian – north of the affluent south of Britain; and then the blatant spine of the Pennines bisects the north of England along its length. In the south-west, the bare reaches of Dartmoor show where granite comes to the surface, wild still in an island so long tamed and settled. The Cornubian Peninsula is the legacy of an old Wilson cycle, the Variscan orogeny, that cut through Europe more than 200 million years before the Alpine convulsions. Much of the mineral wealth of Europe, like the old mine in Joachim's Valley, is the legacy of this earlier episode, which was as momentous in its day as that which threw up the Matterhorn. Carboniferous coal basins that developed on either side of the Pennines powered the Industrial Revolution and fed the steam-engines of empire. Now virtually all the shafts are flooded and disused, and where you see an old piece of pit tackle it is rusted and useless, like a skeleton of an organism we can barely recognize; human cycles are unconscionably short, after all, compared with the revolutions of the earth.

Cretaceous Chalk at very high magnification is seen to be made up of myriads of coccoliths a few thousandths of a millimetre across. Chalk seas spread widely over the world 95 million years ago.

Now we see the Cambrian Mountains, comprising the rocks that gave their names to the divisions of the Lower Palaeozoic era: Cambrian, Ordovician, Silurian.* These mountains are wilder by far than in any part of England, and provided a formidable redoubt for the Welsh King Llewelyn to keep the Anglo-Saxons at bay. These rocks, too, were folded in part of the Caledonian chain, in the Wilson cycle before the Variscan: for cycle is piled upon cycle. From our high vantage point we can see how the rocks making high ground continue into the Lake District and further north again into Scotland.

* These subdivisions were worked out by a succession of pioneering nineteenth-century geologists, but it was many years before they were universally adopted. The derivation of Cambrian is obvious; Silures and Ordovices were tribes that inhabited the Welsh Borderland in Roman times.

Can the leisurely bite into the British coastline that makes the Solway Firth really mark where the great ocean Iapetus disappeared and two ancient continents conjoined? The nations of Scotland and England have been much at odds in the past, but would any Borderer have dreamt that the line of national schism was also set in stone at a time long before he could imagine? But there is more: on the coast of Antrim, in Northern Ireland, crops out black basalt, set in columns. From this height, the basalt's perfect polygons look like the lenses on a fly's eye. This is the Giant's Causeway, a sight once deemed so amazing that a special railway line was built to carry Victorian sightseers to admire its geometrical perfection, its countless hexagonal 'steps'. Now we can no longer fantasize that it is an ogre's staircase for we know it is a volcanic eruption connected with the latest Wilson cycle to leave its mark on the British Isles: the opening of the present Atlantic Ocean. This patterned basalt is the afterbirth of the creation of a new ocean, not so far from the line of old Iapetus. What giant could inspire more awe? The same eruptive events led to Fingal's Cave, on the island of Staffa, which inspired Felix Mendelssohn to some of his most delicate sound-painting, and William Wordsworth to three sonnets. Would they have written something fiercer had they pictured the cracking and parting of the two sides of the Atlantic Ocean, the beginnings of the world we know?

On Charles Lyell's own home islands, then, where much of the compass of geology as a science was defined, cycle after cycle belonging to the greater earth has left its mark; seas have advanced and retreated many times; volcanoes have had their day of fury and sunk into quiescence. If this small corner of the world boasts such complexity, we need not be surprised at the richness of the whole – an impossible concatenation of details, you might think. But as we move still further from the surface of the earth, the vision simplifies; distance loses many of the details but leaves the broader outlines clearer. See, there is the line of the Caledonian mountains continuing across the North Sea far beyond Scotland all along the western seaboard of Scandinavia. You can almost hear Professor Tornebohm's attempts to stuff the ancient nappes on to the still more ancient foreland of the Baltic Shield. See how the rivers drain from the heights that mark the boundary between Norway and Sweden, running eastwards through the birch and pine forests into the Gulf of Bothnia; and beyond the Gulf the lake-speckled, undulating wastes of Finland, where the exhumed remains of Wilson cycles far more ancient and arcane are interwoven between gneiss and granite and now support bogs of *Sphagnum*, cloudberries, and reindeer moss.

We are moving westwards, over the North Atlantic Ocean. The sea conceals its geological foundations. We have to remind ourselves that the continental shelves continue beyond the shorelines that we can pick out far below us. The true edges of the continents lie at the edges of the shelves, and there have been times when more of the shelves have been exposed, just as there have been other times when higher seas have drowned so much that is now dry land. Shores are just a temporary line on a shifting earth. Beyond the continental shelves: the deeps. For a moment, perhaps, looking at the endless unbroken blueness, we can empathize with Eduard Suess and his attempts to read global signals from concealed depths. We might for an instant imagine, even, that the oceans were the site of great subsided masses of the earth; that pieces in a global pattern might be missing because they had sunk to the abyss. From where we are, anything might be possible. Then, the sight of Iceland reminds us that the oceans really *are* different – that they are the realm of basalt and hold the genesis of the skin of the world. Why, we might even just make out the rift valley cutting southwards across the island, and those little cones that look like mounds left by solitary wasps – they must be the traces of volcanoes. As we pass by southern Iceland a larger cone is Maelifell on the edge of the Myrdalsjökull glacier, already transformed from primal black to green by the moss *Grimmia*. Now might be the moment to visualize again the slow creation of new crust at the mid-ocean ridges and recall that it is the surface expression of deeper things. Try to imagine a mantle plume rising from deep within the earth and spreading out beneath Iceland; try to imagine all those subtle changes in chemistry, in the way atoms are bonded together, including varied permutations in the silica frames, and understand that even a whole island – a whole ocean – can be written out in changes in molecular structure.

Westwards again, towards the coast of Laurentia. From this height it does not seem so far away from western Europe. Beyond us lies the frozen edge of Greenland. Here the oldest rocks on earth have stayed on the earthly carousel for turn after turn, escaping the recycling that has been the fate of almost every other scrap of rock on our second-hand world. An ice-cap obscures much of the huge island, and now it may not be so difficult to imagine much of the northern hemisphere encased in ice as thick or thicker just a few thousands years ago, the latest mighty scrape of erosion stripping away time to the depths of an ancient earth. Newfoundland now lies below us; we can see how Viking navigators might readily have found their way from Iceland to 'the Rock', with all its geology laid out upon its naked shores, like leaves from a crumpled book that must be restored before its text can be deciphered. We can see the grain of the land, the trend of almost every bay and promontory from the north-east to the south-west. Every pilot whale should be able to navigate it. We follow the trend southwards, past the Gulf of St Lawrence and into the deeply-forested Appalachians. There are breaks in relief – like shrugs in a green carpet – following ancient faults that might have been the San Andreases of 400 million years ago. Now is the time to admire Marcel Bertrand's insight in stitching together the Appalachians and the Caledonian mountains into a single system; the Atlantic Ocean then no more than an unexplained rent between the two halves. We can imagine the Caledonian to Appalachian belt rising and wasting away into James Hall's geosynclines. And there is molasse, too, in the Catskill Mountains, where peaks are formed from the rubble that torrents dragged and tumbled down from the elevated mountains at about the same time as higher plants were colonizing the land from the sea for the first time. Life evolved and changed and the face of the earth greened with it, but for mountains it was more a case of 'what goes around, comes around'. And there is an earlier Wilson cycle, too, a billion years old, entrapped alongside the Appalachians: the Grenville, which rises to the surface in Central Park, New York, to remind us that the human and urban is no more than foam on the sea of the past.

Across northern Canada, close to the boundary with the Arctic tundra, and the ground is sprinkled with a million lakes. They seem to be spattered over the surface as if they had been flicked from a paintbrush. The last ice age may have left behind these water-filled scrapings and scourings, but the land was reduced to a plain long, long before that. The Canadian Shield around the Great Slave Lake was ancient even when the Appalachians were young. From this height there are swirls and cracks to be made out upon its surface – like doodles almost, or the scribbled sketches of Paul Klee. These are the worn-out corpses of still older cycles, taking us back into the Archaean, thousands of millions of years ago, to the time when bacterial life alone spread over the face of the earth. 'Unimaginably old' the text books once described this period, as if the imagination were subject to the laws of time. All those scribblings might be the foliation of a rock metamorphosed deep in the earth, but they also write an invitation for us to try to understand. What lies below us is almost as impenetrable a territory now as it was when Bell made known its mysteries to the world. In Canada, to go back to the beginnings of things you have to start beyond the end of the road.

The Canadian Shield forms the ancient, triangular heart of North America, to which everything else was added round about the edges – like the work of a slapdash plasterer. There are ranges on the east, ranges on the west, and even an ancient mountain belt running across the north through the Canadian Arctic islands and North Greenland. Each was the product of one or more major tectonic events, and each added something on to the edge of Laurentia. Then former seas washed over on to the shield, leaving their sediments behind. Southwards of where we cross the continent, we might be able to make out the northern part of the Great Plains, where the ancient seas draped blanket after blanket of sedimentary rocks through more than 600 million years. From our great height, the view is much as it was after the Pleistocene: we are too far away to see whether there are buffalo on the plains, or, more likely, over-sized modern farm machinery perambulating up and down. West of the Plains, we have seen how the Colorado Plateau has been uplifted so that erosion over millions of years has cut down again through the sedimentary blankets to the ancient core beneath.

The Rocky Mountains contort the face of the earth from Alaska to Mexico, and west of them other ranges, the Cascades and Coastal Ranges, parallel the coastline in ruck after ruck. From our northerly vantage point we can see the Alaska Range reach out towards the tip of Asia. It is not difficult to imagine, when Pleistocene ice locked up much of the world's water and sea-levels were lowered, a land bridge connecting the Americas and Asia across which horses, bison, and humans could invade eastwards. The relatively recent withdrawal of the sea made much of America what it is today. It is more testing to imagine the mountainous land beneath us as a jigsaw puzzle of pieces shuffled and tethered together over many millions of years. It looks too solid and too unified. Nonetheless, a map published by the US Geological Survey in 1992 shows no less than two hundred terranes making up the Cordilleran Orogen. Just to list them with pertinent details would take up the rest of this book. The mountain chain has been put together in phase after phase, a litany of orogenies through time: in order, the Sonoma, Nevadan, Franciscan, Laramide, the whole stretching through 200 million years. What they share is accretion from the west as island arcs and other pieces of crust were plastered on the edge of the huge continent, and inward-dipping subduction zones developed at its edge. Naturally, the oldest events would be in the interior of the continent, and progressively younger ones outwards, range by range. Nor was it all push on push: from time to time stretching happened, which let down chunks of crust. Granites welled up, some of them huge. From where we are we can see snowy dissected peaks of the Columbia granodiorite, which Eduard Suess said 'is of unsurpassed magnificence', on average eighty kilometres broad, and in length 'almost fourteen degrees of latitude'. It is hard to think of a ready analogy for all this muddled-up tectonic complexity.* An approximation might be a mill-race, where a steady stream carries pieces of wood to bank up one by one against a grille when it plunges into the leat; from time to time a variation in current or eddy might pull the aggregation briefly apart or shuffle the pieces against their neighbours, but the overall onward pattern is inexorable. Today, the confrontation between the Pacific plate and its abutting continent continues, and what we have seen of the northward shift of the crust west of the San Andreas Fault is one consequence. Another is the periodic violent eruption of volcanoes; we can still see the scar left when Mount St Helens blew out one of its sides in 1980, flattening millions of trees and a few humans in an extraordinary pyroclastic surge. The perfectly circular Crater Lake to the south in Oregon was the site of an explosion eight thousand years ago that some geologists reckon to have been the equal of fifty Mount St Helens. My first schoolmaster was wont to instruct us, following the Book of Common Prayer to 'read, mark, learn, and inwardly digest'; but, as we soon discover, any fact about the earth involving amazingly large quantities is easy to read, learn, and mark, but impossible to digest. To underscore the point, before we leave the north-east of the North American continent we get a glimpse of the Snake River basalts: plateau basalts as black as my grandfather's bowler hat, 5000 metres thick and erupted 'only' three million years ago – they are a kind of postscript to the story of Laurentia. Yet they may be fifty times older than *Homo sapiens*, and a thousand times older than science, whilst the oldest rocks on Laurentia are more than three billion years old.

Out into the Pacific Ocean, and soon we are far enough away from the North American coast to look back and appreciate how the mountains run parallel to the shores of the continent we have left behind. The ocean below is calm and brilliantly blue, and apparently goes on forever. It is hard to believe that the ocean basin is actually shrinking. Yet to the north we can just make out the line of the

* Recent seismic research on deep structure indicates that the whole Cordilleran system may be under the control of a failure in the lower part of the crust – a so-called decollement.

Crater Lake in Oregon, a legacy of the volcanically active western coast of the USA and Canada. Mount St Helens was recent vigorous proof of the consequences of plate moving against plate.

Aleutian Islands continuing westwards from Alaska. What we *cannot* see from above is the deep ocean trench that exactly dogs the line of the island arc on its oceanward side, nor that the trench links in turn with the Kuril Trench, and thence to the Japan Trench: the long, thin line of the zone of subduction. Mountains in various stages of their evolution are consequent upon the activity of the northward-dipping subduction zones: they are to be found in Honshu, Hokkaido, and the Kuril Islands. Mount Fuji, which Lafcadio Hearn expatiated upon and Hokusai delineated delicately, is merely the most emblematic example of the associated volcanic activity.

Suess had already distinguished such a Pacific continental margin from one of Atlantic type. The borders of the Atlantic Ocean are as distinctive in their own way. What he called 'table-lands' of flat-lying sedimentary rocks commonly approached the coast – a good example would be the Karroo Series of South Africa – whereas in the Pacific type 'no table-land reaches the shores'. Mountain belts are truncated at the edge of the continents in the Atlantic type, as we saw in the Armorican chain running westwards across Europe. As usual, Suess had spotted important facts that subsequently became explicable in the light of plate tectonics: Atlantic coasts were 'passive margins' where severed continents were drifting apart: an ancient mountain belt might be 'cut', or a once-contiguous 'table-land' split in the process. Pacific coasts were active sites of subduction, where the parallel fringing mountain belts reflected the continuing processes of tectonic activity, as explicit in their way as sputtering volcanoes and frequent earthquakes, the twisted roads of Kobe, or the fiery wreckage of San Francisco. It is a paradox that Pacific coasts should be anything but pacific.

As we continue westwards we are able to make out one of the northern islands of the Hawaiian chain – one of the Midway Islands perhaps – and it comes as something of a shock to find the cerulean perfection of the great ocean disturbed at last by little white circles of foam where a sea-mount breaks the surface. We have to imagine a line of hidden, submarine mountains continuing northwards below us, each imprinted in turn by the same 'hot spot' that is forcing out gobs and lobes of lava on the Big Island even as this is being written: the blow-torch beneath the moving plate. We can imagine Polynesian sailors in insubstantial boats feeling their way from island to island – singing songs about Pele, whose volcanic power might be demonstrated only too dramatically upon a sudden whim. Perhaps we should follow their example, and head south-westwards now across Micronesia towards the Equator, an area where many more sea-mounts come to the surface. Almost every one was colonized. There below us are the Gilbert Islands, indelibly portrayed by Arthur Grimble in *A Pattern of Islands*. This is a place where the dead walk, and where shamanistic curses still count. When we reach the Mariana Islands – a classic island arc forming a beaded necklace of islands – we have already crossed the Mariana Trench, which includes the deepest hole on the planet at 36,198 feet (10,915 metres) below sea-level. We recall the *Challenger*'s half-bewildered plumbing of such depths, and the realization by ocean scientists that the surface of the world goes downwards further than it soars upwards. Westwards again lies one of the most complicated and tortuous bits of the planet, where several subduction zones have succeeded one another across the Philippines to the South China Seas. Somehow, you might guess its complexity from its appearance. There is the island of the Celebes beneath us, a place that looks all leggy and out of place. It is properly called Sulawesi today, but for some reason Celebes is the name that sticks in my mind, with its curiously classical sound, as if it were the name of some monster that ravaged Thebes instead of 197,000 square kilometres (76,260 square miles) of tectonics in the Far East. There are ten thousand islands in the Sulu and Celebes Seas, many without names. Pirates still lurk there. Furthermore, there are several tectonic plates: it's a place of mystery. As we continue westwards, we encounter a simple island arc – Indonesia – stretching through Sumatra, Java, and Bali and onwards towards the Banda Sea. The island of Komodo is part of the chain and is famous among zoologists as the home of the 'dragon' – the world's largest lizard, a creature that bites its prey and has saliva so foul it then hangs around to wait for its victim to die of infection. The conspicuous arc is fronted by the Java trench and active subduction along the junction is proved by the eruptions that regularly trouble the superstitious inhabitants of Indonesia. Oceanic crust meets continental crust directly along this line, and some of the resulting magma mixtures produce very violent explosions. On Mount Ijen, Sumatra, emaciated workmen carry on their backs great blocks of native sulphur scooped from the bowels of the volcano: hard labour in places that would reduce most of us to helpless tears.

The Java Trench is at the edge of the huge Indian–Antarctic plate, whilst the Mariana Trench to the north-east lies at the edge of the equally gargantuan Pacific plate. The mangled and complex area of South-east Asia in between – including Sulawesi's arachnoid silhouette – is the result of shuffling and adjustments between these two behemoths and the continent beyond, titanic jousting that has engendered short-lived basins, evanescent seas, and many successive tectonic events. The tremendous movements have continued for thirty million years and are still going on. Even the continental 'foreland' of Thailand, Vietnam, and China comprises separate, fault-bounded blocks that have shuffled about like dominoes on a tin tray. The curiously-shaped Malay Peninsula obviously follows the grain of the region. Its shape is rather like the thorax and abdomen of an ichneumon wasp, so narrow at one point that you can see the sea on both sides of the road that runs along its length through grove after grove of oil-palms before it bulges out into Malaysia. In a small boat I once dodged between limestone islands rising sheer from the Malaysian tropical seas in search of trilobite fossils, dining on crabs plucked fresh from the coral reefs and mangoes fresh from the tree. The shallow waters of South-east Asia are one of life's cornucopias, for its tectonic complexity has encouraged a thousand ecological niches under the beneficent gaze of the sun. The more varied the habitat, the more species it can support. Marine life, too, can 'read' a geological map, from the Grand Banks of Newfoundland to the complexities of Borneo and the South China Sea; the thousands of tiny fishing boats that dredge out tropical riches from this sea are ultimately in thrall to the adjustments of plates moving more slowly than limpets grow. From our high viewpoint we can see that the hills of the Malay Peninsula extend northwards into Burma, and thence curve westwards into the mountains that wrap around to the north of the Himalayas. They are just a part of a system that extends through the world as far as the Alps, draping over the irregular collection of continental fragments to the south like a dust sheet over the clutter in an attic.

But we will not pass that way yet. Instead, we will drift southwards and eastwards over New Guinea. A precipitous mountain range divides it lengthways, and we can just make out steep valleys cutting inwards. We begin to understand how this one island supports so many separate languages among the aboriginal peoples that live there. It is a Stone-Age version of the Alps: geology and philology acting in synergy. In the short distance from the Banda Sea we have passed over one of the great biological barriers on earth, and one that is completely invisible. This is 'Wallace's Line', its name celebrating Alfred Russel Wallace, who first recognized it. Wallace is mostly known today for his co-presentation with Charles Darwin of the theory of evolution by natural selection at the Linnean Society of London. He was also the founder of the discipline of bio-geography, stirred as he was by wonder at the variety of life he found on his

Alfred Russel Wallace (1823–1913) pioneer of biogeography.

travels through the Malay Archipelago and beyond. He saw that almost all nature changed abruptly across his 'line': westwards lay the Asian faunas and floras; southwards, almost everything spoke of Australia. It was as if an impalpable wall had been erected between the two. The root of it all – of course – is plate tectonics. Wallace's brilliant insight had identified the boundary between the Australian plate, and what lay to the north in the Philippines complex. Tectonically speaking, New Guinea *was* Australia. The Australian continent had formerly been further away from Asia, and during its long isolation since the break-up of the land of the Gonds evolved its own special flora and fauna – notably dozens of marsupial species and a varied endemic flora, including eucalyptus trees and bottle-brushes like *Banksia*. It is one of the world's biological treasure-houses. Northward movement of the Indo–Australian plate at last brought the hermetic continent into proximity with the rest of the world, and across the narrow gulf that now marks the line of contact a few daring species jumped – including humans. Most species, however, stayed where they were. Wallace himself was acutely aware of the aesthetic value of the rich fauna he studied. Describing the considerable difficulties in the way of collecting birds of paradise he wrote, in *The Malay Archipelago* (1869): 'It seems as if nature had taken precautions that her choicest treasures should not be made too common, and thus undervalued.' Several of the 'choicest' species of Paradisidae are now on the edge of extinction. Wallace would have been appalled.

Australia is so vastly brown. From a great height it seems to be a limitless, ochraceous to burnt-sienna expanse of almost nothing: stony semi-desert for the most part, dotted with eucalyptus and spinifex clumps that are unrecognizable from this altitude. The centre of the continent is nearly flat, or at least its gentle undulations hardly register from far above. It is possible to persuade yourself that you might be looking down on ancient Gondwana itself. In a sense, you are. Occasional ridges of rock break the monotony. Uluru, or Ayer's Rock, is the archetype of a piece of geology left behind when all around it has been removed by erosion. On the ground, it has the curious property of seeming both small and massive: something about the scale of the great interior expanse of Australia distorts the feeling for distance. Walking towards this small lump – which takes longer than you expected – you are taken by surprise to discover that it is actually enormous. Much of the western two-thirds of Australia is underlain by ancient Precambrian rocks, Archaean and Proterozoic in age, which emerge in battered hills in the interior. We have no time now to look at them in more detail. Australia has been around for a very long time, and it has been worn down over and over again by hundreds of millions of years of erosion. Its interior is dog-tired, out for the count, all passion spent. Over the last six or seven hundred million years the sea has made inroads onto it and sedimentary rocks overlie the ancient basement in many places. I was in the Toko Range in search of fossils of animals that lived during one of these episodes, 500 million years ago: you could readily imagine the ancient sea lapping over the already worn-down topography and leaving a legacy of sandstones – sandy shallows turned to stone. Other fossil occurrences are world-famous. In the Flinders Range are some of the most important fossils known anywhere, that record soft-bodied life forms in the latest Precambrian; and in Western Australia are found fossil bacteria that are among the oldest traces of life on the planet. As we continue drifting eastwards, we see the exception to the exhausted stretch of the interior: towards the eastern coastline the Great Dividing Range includes several areas of high relief, richly forested. It divides rivers that run fast to the coast from those that drain westwards and sometimes peter out in salt-pans in the desert. This is another ancient mountain range, which was folded at the end of the Palaeozoic and then deeply eroded; its present-day uplift is much younger. Even from high above it, the line of the Great Escarpment running through the Blue Mountains makes a gigantic step in the surface. I once sat in an Art-Deco hotel looking outwards from the top of this mighty vertical cliff; beyond the balcony lay ridge upon ridge of stately eucalyptus far below: even today, secret valleys are still being discovered in the hinterland. Who knows if fearsome Bunyips – the Bigfoot of the Antipodes – might lurk there? (Rather more prosaically, Australian scientists believe that a giant marsupial called *Diprotodon* is a possible origin of the Bunyip legend: it certainly overlapped in time with the colonization of Australia by those who made it across Wallace's divide.)

The fold belt at the Great Dividing Range makes sense when you fit Pangaea back together. Antarctica slots back adjacent to Australia, as neat as you like. In this altitude the marginal mountains of Australia run on into a similar belt adjacent to the Ross Sea in western Antarctica. It is rather like the Appalachian–Caledonian story over again: what time has ripped asunder, imagination can join together. Hence the eastern Australian fold belt was produced at a subduction zone that developed at the margin of the ancient supercontinent. The legacy of Pangaea lives on in forests of iron-bark and blue gums. Further along the north-eastern edge of Australia, the Queensland Plateau is a continuation of the continent out to sea, a platform that has provided a foundation allowing the Great Barrier Reef to flourish. From above, we observe a broken white line drawn by crashing waves marking its course along the Queensland coast: these ramparts of coral and algae support one of the most diverse habitats on earth.

Today there are distressing stories of coral die-back and bleaching on reefs. The death of these structures would be a unique tragedy.

Across the Tasman Sea to New Zealand, the furthest point on the globe from my desk in London. The two islands look as if the highest parts of the European Alps had somehow been excised and dropped bodily into the wide expanse of the Pacific Ocean, so steep are the mountains stretching along its unpolluted shores. Eduard Suess and Elie de Beaumont would have felt at home here – the latter, as previously mentioned, has a mountain named for him. New Zealand is a rival to Hawai'i for loneliness: it has been a place apart for so long. In the absence of voracious mammals, until humans arrived, flightless birds like moas, kiwis, and the kakapo proliferated there. Millions of sheep are now the commonest creatures, and from high over the North Island you see them scattered like a dusting of white pepper over the hillsides. The dark green line of rain forest fringing the west coast of the South Island is where tree ferns sprout in profligate profusion. It is a special place, no less than Hawai'i, and its origins go back to Gondwana and beyond. A sliver of Gondwana broke off from the disintegrating supercontinent to form the core of New Zealand. It carried with it an extraordinary primitive reptile, the tuatara, which survives only on New Zealand, a memory of Triassic times preserved against the odds. Subsequently, younger crust accreted to the growing island. At the present day, New Zealand sits astride two plates: the Australian plate to the west, and 10,000 kilometres of the Pacific plate to the east. The conflict between the movements of these plates generates mountains, earthquakes, volcanoes, and geysers alike: for the Australian plate is headed north and the Pacific plate westwards, at about forty millimetres a year. The result is a twisting of the crust, a rending of the fabric of the earth. We can see the surface effects of accommodation to this movement in the Alpine Fault in the South Island, which is a kind of antipodean San Andreas. Even in the 1940s the far-seeing geologist Harold Wellman had deduced that hundreds of kilometres of displacement must have accrued along the Alpine Fault over many millions of years, for the rocks to either side of it are so utterly different. With modern

GPS systems, comparable with those installed around the Bay of Naples, deformation can be continuously monitored to an accuracy of one or two millimetres over forty kilometres. They reveal that some parts of New Zealand are moving faster than others – Christchurch nearly forty millimetres a year, Auckland hardly at all. It is an irregularly fidgety bit of the crust.

So we continue eastwards across the southern hemisphere from New Zealand: beyond the Chatham Islands nothing breaks the waters of the Pacific Ocean. It is apparently the emptiest part of the world, an intensely blue continuum. We cross one of the truly arbitrary lines that humans have drawn on the face of the earth – the International Date Line. Tucked out of the way here, it will not cause trouble to those who have difficulties with Sunday suddenly changing to Monday. If we were able to see through 5000 metres (15,000 feet) of sea-water we would observe that the sea-floor is anything but featureless, for here is the ocean ridge that generates the Pacific and Nazca plates: the East Pacific Rise, running northwards to the Equator and beyond, but side-stepping at each transform fault, like the onward progress of a determined drunk. It leaves the surface of the sea untroubled, except for Easter Island, which is the merest pinhead from our vantage point. The people who called themselves Rapa Nui were the advance guard of all the Polynesian colonizers and may have reached this island about 1500 years ago. They celebrated its basalt geology in the most blatant way, hewing out from it huge and inscrutable heads, *Moai*, which now dot the island in heavy-featured profusion. We cannot read the meaning of their pursed and determined lips, nor their recessed and sightless eyes. But we know that the islanders ate themselves to extinction, over-population and isolation having done its worst: the original Great Ecological Disaster.

From where we are, we cannot quite make out the volcanic Galapagos archipelago further to the north. These islands were Charles Darwin's natural evolutionary laboratory, whose finches and tortoises figured prominently in *The Origin of Species*. They have consequently become a place of pilgrimage for modern biologists. Even here, the creative isolation afforded by the Pacific Ocean has been violated by our own species, and by the animals we brought with us. What geology has made over millions of years, humans, it appears, can undo in a century or so.

The coasts of Chile and Peru appear as relief (in both senses of the word) after the limitless seas. The Andes rise sheer from the coast – well, not quite sheer, because as we approach the shores of the southern continent we see that there is a narrow line of desert that borders the sea. Aridity rules in this rain-shadow of the great mountain range to the east. Below us, unseen, lies the ocean trench that follows the South American coast so closely. Here, the continent deflects the easterly ocean current of the southern Pacific so that it turns northwards along the Chilean coast as the Humboldt Current. This brings cool Antarctic waters to warmer climes, and supplies rich nutrients to a profusion of marine life. Anchovies abound – unless it is an El Niño year, when they suffer with the rest of the world. So on this part of our journey the most perniciously dry Atacama Desert and the most ebullient ocean life are found cheek by jowl. We can see rivers sprinting a few tens of kilometres to the sea from the high Andes; but those draining to the east from the far side of the range will have to wander 6000 kilometres to reach the Atlantic Ocean. From far above, the Andes do not seem that complicated. They comprise two mighty ranges running in parallel: at the point we are crossing these are called the Cordillera Occidental and Cordillera Real (or Oriental), west and east respectively, separated by a broad depression – but this still at a high altitude. A great belt of Cretaceous and Tertiary granites and other intrusive rocks runs along the Cordillera Occidental: they make some of the most inaccessible peaks, on which alpinists risk their lives. As we have seen in many other mountain belts, older rocks are caught up in the folded rocks of the present range. We have seen enough by now to recognize the median basin as a fault-bounded *graben,* as Suess would have called it. Conical volcanic cones line both sides, recalling Iceland or the Great African rift valley, however different their tectonic circumstances. The German explorer Friedrich Heinrich Alexander, Baron von Humboldt had already recognized this 'avenue of volcanoes' by the beginning of the nineteenth century. We pass over the Altiplano – literally, 'high and flat' – where the valley has been filled in with a succession of ashes and molasse: it is a dusty, brown, tough, cold place, to which llamas and alpacas are peculiarly adjusted. The indigenous people who live there probably have the blood of the Incas running in their veins. The last redoubts of this dead civilization were perched improbably high in the fierce terrain of the Cordillera, at Machu Picchu. Today's inhabitants still grow potatoes on Inca terraces. Lake Titicaca below us now is the highest great body of water on earth. No doubt, if we could swoop downwards and collect a fragment of rock from the side of a volcano, we would find it to be composed of andesite (what else?), a volcanic rock resulting from magma 'cooked up' by the interaction of subducting slab and continental margin. For this whole coast is the southerly continuation of the active margin of the eastern Pacific Ocean – trench, mountains, volcanoes and all – and perhaps rather simpler than the Californian story to the north, for there is no San Andreas fault here. The Andes are squashed and thickened against the edge of the stable, ancient South American shield to the east. The volcanic 'avenue' is interrupted only where the relatively thick Juan Fernandez and Nazca ocean ridges approach the subduction zone: they prove rather more to bite off than the tectonic mill can chew.

The eastern part of the Cordillera includes old terranes that accreted to a primitive South America long before the present Andean range – indeed before Pangaea had been assembled. I once went to visit one of these strange slabs of country near the town of San Juan, in western Argentina, where the country's wine is made. The theory has it that a chunk of Argentina now in the Precordillera had originally broken off Laurentia in the Ordovician and drifted across a vanished ocean to meld with South America. To reach the critical rocks our party had to go in a bus along a terrifying zig-zag road carved out of a mountain-side, so narrow that it had 'tidal flow' – you could go one way (upwards) for part of the day, and the other way (downwards) for the rest of it. From time to time I glanced downwards to see – hundreds of metres below among the cactus – the back ends of coaches past that had plummeted off the edge.

The thickened, light crust of the Andes is rising – and fast. Eduard Suess described it thus: 'Throughout Peru and Chili . . . signs of negative movement, and particularly terraces, present so striking an appearance that they have attracted the attention of observers for many years past.' Darwin had already connected such uplifted beaches with volcanic causes in a paper published in the *Transactions of the Geological Society of London* in 1840. Suess himself typically downplayed it – recall that he habitually attacked uplift as the cause of mountains. He went so far as to describe the habits of sea-birds lifting edible sea-shells to great heights to form 'kitchen middens' and tried to cast doubt on some of Darwin's allegedly elevated beds as no more than old dining-tables. But even he could not explain away the uplifted guano deposits in the Morro de Mejillones near Antofagasta, Chile, with shore-lines at around 500 metres and at various heights below, arranged like a series of steps.

We are lingering too long: we must press on. Our journey takes us onwards beyond the Andes, towards the Amazon Basin. The ancient core of the South American continent beneath us is floored by Precambrian granites and gneisses of similar ages to those in Africa, draped variously by younger sediments. We glimpse mountains to the north where the old basement rocks come to the surface. Those must be the sandstone cliffs of Mount Roiraima on the border of Venezuela and Brazil, a weird, isolated, cloud-covered plateau 3000 metres high with a unique biology, including endemic frogs and carnivorous plants, that is said to have inspired Sir Arthur Conan Doyle's novel *The Lost World*. The Amazon Basin itself is a sea of green forest below us that seems almost as vast as the blue Pacific. It has been the site of an inland sea at various times in the last hundred million years, but now every waterway drains ultimately into the mighty river: the Basin holds nearly two-thirds of the world's fresh water. The individual rivers and streams are beyond counting, adding up to a total of perhaps half a million miles of running water.

From above, we see the 'white-water' rivers draining from the Andes to the west – actually more coffee-coloured from suspended silt – meeting the Rio Negro from the north, which appears to us black as a stream of tar because of its dissolved tannin, produced by an abundance of partly-decomposed organic matter. The differently-coloured waters are reluctant to blend, running side by side for seven kilometres before combining into the true Amazon – *O Rio Mare*, the river sea, as the early explorers called it. The rain forest fills in all the space that is not river: it is a temple of biodiversity, whose congregation is composed of insects, plants, and birds that belong to so many species that they have yet to be numbered, or, in some cases, named.

The Amazon is no less than 200 miles wide at its mouth. More water passes through it in a day than does in a whole year through the River Thames, where our journey started. It is, to use a devalued word, awesome. Sediment brought in suspension by the brown Amazon river is then deposited over its wide delta, or carried far out to sea: the ultimate fate of the eastern Andes is to become mud at the bottom of the Atlantic Ocean. In 1500, a Spanish sea captain called Vincente Pinzon was sailing over open sea far from shore when he observed the sea changing colour from blue to a kind of bronze. The reddish water was quite fresh. The lighter, sediment-charged waters of the Amazon evidently 'floated' above the salt sea for some distance offshore. We can see it for ourselves: as we pass over the edge of the continent we can see the Amazonian efflux like a vast, brownish wraith gliding into the Atlantic beyond: a ghost of mountains reprocessed, one wisp displayed in the cycle of the earth.

As we continue eastwards, we cannot avoid the reflection that everything we have seen in South America is a consequence of plate structure. Were it not for the passive margin in the east, at the edge of the opening Atlantic, the Amazon could not debouch so freely into the Guiana Basin: we have to imagine an apron of sediment stretching out far, far beyond the last mangrove towards the deep

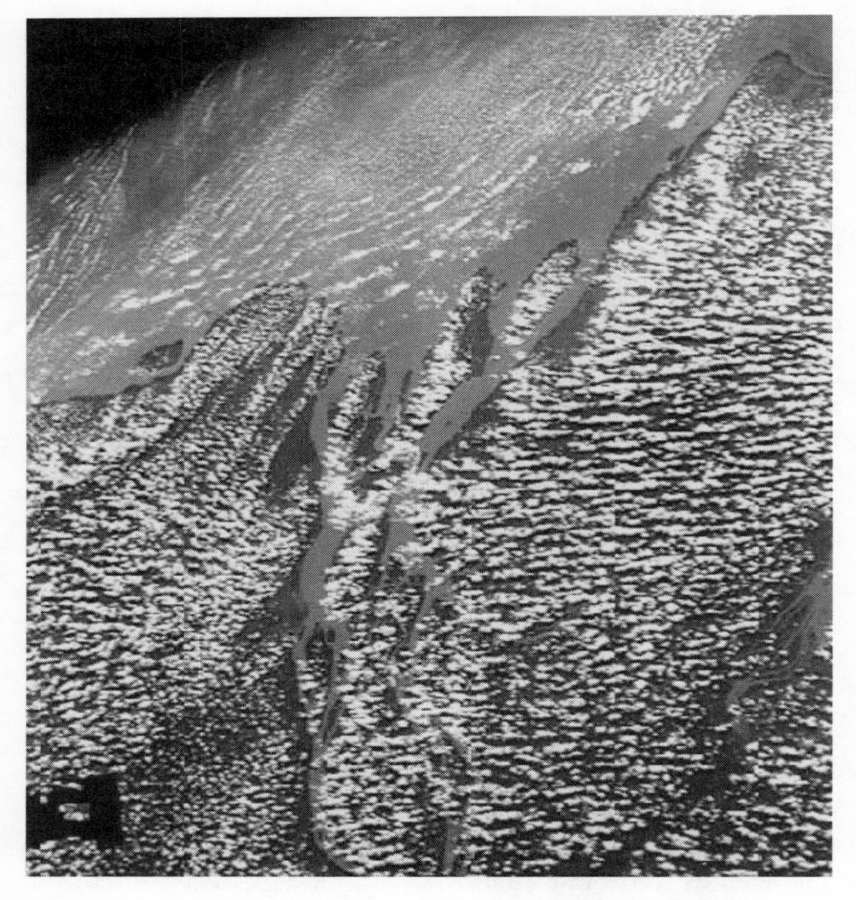

The greatest river on Earth: the Amazon carries sediment (and fresh water) far out into the Atlantic Ocean.

sea. The crust sags to accommodate the new load deposited upon it. Conversely, the western active margin guarantees the drainage pattern of the continent, so that the great rivers will continue to run eastwards until the Andes are brought low. But when will this be? For the inexorable operation of subduction along the Peru–Chile Trench equally guarantees that mountains will be reborn until the end of the current Wilson cycle. The world continually changes, but it changes according to rules. And one day – who knows? – the sedimentary pile dumped at the Atlantic edge will be revived as a mountain chain in some future cycle. No human being will witness it, that much is certain, for the whirligig of geological time moves too slowly for our ambition, our brief hegemony.

Passing urgently eastwards across the Atlantic Ocean there is little to remind us of the presence far beneath us of the Mid-Atlantic Ridge – no Iceland decked with recent cones – unless it is the solitary island of Ascension rising thousands of metres from the rugged sea-floor but appearing to us no more than a pimple breaking the surface of the waters. We have passed over the unseen rift that profoundly marks the change in spreading direction of the oceanic crust. The African coast lies beyond. You could argue that the Congo Basin is the eastern equivalent of the Amazon Basin, a distorted mirror image – populated by different species, surely, but ecologically similar and likewise spilling off a passive margin. Its dense, green endlessness looks familiar: somehow, we know that some African equivalent of the giant anaconda will lurk there beneath an inexhaustible canopy of trees.

Africa is the continent that the others left behind. India, South America, Antarctica, Australia, all drifted away from it when Pangaea split apart. Africa has passive continental margins, except in the north, where it engages with Europe – as we saw among the sweet chestnut trees in Italian Switzerland. Fully to understand the African continent, its scattered progeny must be restored to it, for it lay at the heart of Gondwana and its personality was shaped long, long ago. Beyond the Congo rain forest, rainfall is strongly seasonal and a vast savanna stretches out before us. It looks uniformly straw-coloured from above – an ocean of dry grass makes the background, while scattered dark dots are umbrella-shaped acacia trees spaced just so far apart as the annual precipitation will allow. This is grazing land, hunting land, herding land, and the cradle of humankind. Mounds, sometimes towers, of rock emerge from the general plain. Can that low hump, layered like a poorly-split onion, be all that remains of a granite? Can that low ridge covered in scrub be a Methuselah among gneisses? The resemblance of the scene below to that of Australia is no coincidence, for this, too, is land with an ancient core that was already old when Pangaea was young. The sea invaded over what is now Africa many times in its history, or ancient lakes and streams left a patchy cosmetic, a veneer of sediments, but which may be plastered on thickly in places. We have met the Karroo in South Africa, which Suess used to build his picture of Gondwana; I have studied sedimentary rocks 200 million years older again, in the shadow of Table Mountain, bearing trilobites and other extinct animals with jointed legs; and my colleagues have brought back much younger dinosaurs from the desert regions of the north-west. These fossil finds are all from rocks draped over an older geology, the Precambrian basement that passes into the core of South America and Australia: the heart of darkness of the ancient continent, the primeval layer, providing a vision of how things were even before the first fish, the first trilobite.

Combined with new fieldwork, the ability to date rocks in Africa was like suddenly being provided with a microscope after subsisting for years with a magnifying glass. So now we have a picture of the core of Africa (and the whole of Gondwana) as a series of truly ancient 'islands', or cratons, of Archaean age – greater than 2500 million years old – surrounded by, and interwoven with, younger Proterozoic fold belts. The latter mostly ignore the present boundary of Africa, which, after all, is just an arbitrary shape imposed by a later Wilson cycle, another slicing of the map of the world. Hence, with Gondwana restored, an ancient fold belt might well pass into Madagascar, or perhaps into Arabia and India, or Brazil. The youngest Precambrian events are so pervasive that they have been called Pan-African, 900–550 million years old: one such, the Mozambique Belt, runs along the eastern margin of Africa. When you put Gondwana back in place, a single shear zone runs from Africa through Madagascar to southernmost India. The Mozambique fold belt is interpreted today as a result of the *original* collision between two older continents comprising eastern and western Gondwana – a record of the coming-together of the ancient supercontinent that has figured so prominently in this book. Nothing is so massive on earth that it has not been created by stitching together smaller pieces of lithosphere.

Archaean memories are perhaps fresher in southern Africa than anywhere else in the world. There are cratons of greater than 3000 million years old, such as the Zimbabwe Craton and the Kaapval Craton around Johannesburg. Sedimentary and volcanic basins (such as those that are part of the Pongola Supergroup and Pretoria Series) formed around and upon these even more ancient nuclei – possibly in rifts – and these sediments survive to the present day. Imagine the lottery of these scraps surviving all earthly pot-shots of potential obliteration through 2900 million years. As D. H. Lawrence said of the tortoise, they are

> Fulfilled of the slow passion of pitching through immemorial ages
> Your little round house in the midst of chaos.

By now, we might be able to make some sense of the rocky mounds and small plateaux that rise out of the plains over which we are passing. Then the Great Rift Valley appears, sheer sided, let down as suddenly as a gutter: it comes as a surprise after all that near-horizontal emptiness, so definite are its lines scored across the wilderness. There is Lake Albert below us, pointing southwards to Lake Edward and Lake Tanganyika, clear as a signpost saying: 'This way, follow the geology.' Those obvious volcanic rocks at the edge of the rift may be as young as the Precambrian cratons are old, so here we have the primordial ends of the earth rubbing shoulders with what could be described as a geological afterthought. We think of our distant ancestors cowering as one of the volcanoes erupted – perhaps even the one we can see on the horizon. Now we can see this valley for what it is: an attempt to break up Africa one last time, just another episode in an old, old story. Another Wilson cycle struggling to be born. To the south, there is the shimmering sheet of Lake Victoria: no rift lake this, but a huge, shallow slop accumulated in a downwarp of the ancient African crust. And then out across the desert of Somalia to the Indian Ocean, where vast breakers draw a white line at the edge of the great continent, as if to mark out the boundary along which it was once dismembered, a memory of

NASA photograph of the Red Sea and the Gulf of Aden; it is easy from this image to imagine that this is a young ocean.

Gondwanan disruption now drawn out in dancing and ephemeral foam.

Onwards, onwards, we follow the coast to the Horn of Africa. From the advantage of our great height, we can see that the Red Sea and Gulf of Aden resemble a hinge that has opened. It is hard to look at this elbow of sea, this dog-leg of a crack between Africa and Arabia, without imagining a kind of creaking noise as the two continental blocks prise apart, like the opening of an old oak door in a haunted-house tale. Arabia, we can clearly see, is nothing more than part of the old African shield, and much of it was formed in the late Precambrian by the accretion of island arcs. The rocks that overlie and cover this deep foundation are the source of much of the world's oil, and no small measure of its problems. Oil is ultimately derived from the chemical transformation of the energy preserved in minute plant fossils, concentrated by natural geological processes into reserves. It just so happens that there is a disproportionate amount of both source and reserves in this desert appendage of Africa. But the truth is that there is nothing much to see from above except stretches of stony desert and fleets of dunes between bare scabs of rock, for we are skirting the edge of the *Rub al Khali*, the empty quarter. A dark and scrofulous-looking patch nearer the coast is a stretch of *sabkha* – a salt-flat of a special and unpleasant kind. It is the most treacherous place I have ever visited, a darkly crusty, boiling hot wasteland, sprouting gypsum crystals like perverse jewels. Wander off the track and the superficial crust can break, letting you and your vehicle bog down into a hot, noxious and embracing glue. Some bacteria thrive in this environment, I am told, which proves that bacteria can live just about anywhere. As for us, we shudder and pass on.

We speed across the Arabian Sea towards the north-west coast of India. We have no time to linger on the subcontinent, but we know now that much of what has been said about Africa applies here, too: it carries the same legacy of old Gondwana dressed in the newer clothes of younger sediments. In our mind's eye we can picture the triangular continent moving northwards from its starting position as part of Pangaea, eventually to engage with Asia. John Dewey and his colleagues have calculated and mapped its trajectory step-by-step through eighty-four million years, so that its passage looks like one of those photomontages of human movement with each frame frozen in time: India kicks the backside of Asia, in living motion. Had it not completed its journey, India would now be another Australia, isolated within a great ocean, and who knows what strange animals might have lived there? It would certainly not have been reached by the polyglot profusion of peoples that makes India such an exhilarating and confusing place. Look: below us there is a stepped plateau landscape that seems half familiar. We must be passing over the Deccan Traps: one of those caves decorated with a thousand human details lies beneath us. But from above, it is possible to imagine the whole area black and slick with fresh lava boiled out of the earth's interior, one layer after another, spilling out over on to another part of the old Precambrian core of Gondwana.

The great river system of the Ganges and its many tributaries lies before us; to the east, the Brahmaputra is nearly as great a waterway. We can see the infinitely complex, but infinitely repeated pattern of tiny farms, growing rice to feed the burgeoning millions on the subcontinent; in Bangladesh, there are even three different kinds of rice to be grown according to the season, and not a day wasted in the business of cultivation. During the monsoon season, floods are both a boon and a curse: what can fertilize one area can devastate another. Vast quantities of sediment are shifted then, hundreds of millions of tons every year, much of which finishes up as an apron of sediment blanketing the sea-floor of the Bay of Bengal. We can see that the Ganges drains the southern flank of the mighty Himalayan range: its tributaries cut back high into the mountains, and we can trace some of the headwaters to the glacier line. So the Himalayas are being wasted away, and ultimately ground down to silt that washes or slumps into the ocean. The Ganges Plain, flat and wide below us, is a basin that receives the debris from the tremendous range to the north, sinking to accommodate more and more sediment – ten kilometres of it: it is a molasse basin, and we might, for a moment, recall those reddish rocks that cropped out among the orchards on the flanks of the Rigi in Switzerland. The upper part of the Brahmaputra cuts through the *whole* Himalayan range, in a series of spectacular gorges. The river evidently antedated the rise of the mountains, working feverishly over millions of years to maintain its position and cut through what tectonics had raised aloft: the Via Mala raised to the *n*th degree. The mountains are still rising.

Vegetation cloaks the foothills: nothing to see from above except a green swathe tucked into rocky ridges. This is the natural habitat of the deodar and rhododendron species that make groves on the mountain-sides. The mountains rise so steeply in Nepal that they seem like a wall dividing the world. However we may remind ourselves that this is just the outcome of the way plates collide, there remains something obstinately purposeful about such a massive geographical and cultural barrier – no matter if geophysics tells us that the mountain front follows the Main Boundary Thrust, which can be traced to depth on seismic profiles. There are glaciers below us now, streaked and blue, and closely following valleys down from the heights, as if they had been coloured in by opaque crayon to cover up the brown rocks that surround them. The streaked lines on their surfaces are rocky waste – yet more erosional detritus. And there is Mount Everest itself, 8848 metres high on the 'roof of the world' – there is no avoiding the obvious phrase, and no way to know whether it is the highest mountain there has *ever* been. Was it topped in some other Wilson cycle long ago, in the Caledonides, perhaps, or the Hercynides? Any such peak will always remain Mount Invisible, for even its memory has been eroded away. It is unusual to get such a clear view of Mount Everest, for these altitudes are frequently wrapped in storms. The mountain was named for Sir George Everest, superintendent of the trigonometrical survey of India in 1823 and Surveyor General in 1830. He was also the first to prove by measurement* that the unexpectedly low gravitational attraction of the Himalayas showed that there had to be 'roots' of lighter rock beneath the great mountains – the first indication of the crustal thickening and

* He followed the example of Pierre Bouguer, leader of the Andes Expedition of 1735, who had noticed that the deflection of a plumb line towards the volcanic peak of Chimborazo was less than it should have been considering its size. The measurements of variations in the gravity field due to density variations in the subsurface are still called Bouguer anomalies.

shortening that had happened along the tectonic line where the two plates collided. The appropriate dip in the Mohorovičíc Discontinuity marking the base of the crust was subsequently recognized from seismic evidence.

As to the how and when: India moved northwards at a rate of about fifteen centimetres a year until it collided with Asia about forty-five million years ago – after which it still continued to move northwards at five centimetres annually. This was the 'big push', a heave that continued long into Tertiary times and spread its influence northwards into Asia. The Karakoram and the high plateau of Tibet, the 'celestial mountains' of Tien Shan, and the Altai Mountains – all these are a consequence of the persevering shove of one great continent against another. So the wrinkles on the face of the earth in Asia are not the furrowed frown of one confrontation, but phalanxes of massive corrugations spread across a thousand kilometres. The evolution of the Himalayan orogen was evidently long and complex. As push piled on push, a total of perhaps 1000 kilometres of crustal shortening was accumulated. As we have seen in the Appalachian–Caledonian chain – buried among the conifers of Newfoundland and halfway distant around the world – collision was not simply a question of continental 'crunch to crunch'. There were earlier 'dockings' of terranes that preceded the main continent-to-continent event. 'Pips' of ophiolites were squeezed out as nappes, to preserve fragments of vanished ocean floors high in the Himalayas: it is like the Oman Mountains promoted to the gods. Then came the confrontation of the prodigious protagonists: the Brobdingnagian broadside, the Titan's tussle, as the two continents, India and Asia, finally collided. A series of mighty thrusts directed broadly northwards mark the boundaries of parallel zones running all through the Himalayas. At depth, the crust of the Indian subcontinent dives beneath the Tibetan crust: the seismic profiles tell us so. In the face-off, the southerly giant ultimately cringed before its northern antagonist. Slices are piled atop this deep confrontation, each bounded by thrusts; granites were melted out and mobilized between twelve and twenty-three million years ago, ultimately to rise skywards. They make some of the most jagged peaks. Old geology was revivified, punched upwards, as deeper, ancient rocks were exhumed from their buried redoubts: there are even Ordovician fossils – old friends that I could recognize – on the summit of Mount Everest itself. Tethyan sediments were scrunched and metamorphosed, belt after belt. And these thrusts, as you would expect, are younging from north to south, as the Indian plate pushed onwards, onwards.

The mighty range might seem all too complicated for the human mind to grasp, and from our height we can see none of its details; but, at the end of the last nappe, it is only a compendium and concatenation of everything we have met before in this book: a combination of Newfoundland, the Andes, and the Alps, with a soupçon of South-east Asia thrown in for good measure. Sometimes it seems as if nothing is so complex on the face of the earth that it cannot be explained in Lyellian mode: match your mountain, fix your fault, gauge your geochemistry. Does the fact that Mount Everest can be rationally explained diminish its splendour? Would it be more impressive if we still believed it to be the outcome of battle royal among the gods? Quite the contrary, I believe. Our high prospect over the 'roof of the world' is enough to prove that the majesty of mountains endures even when its crags and folds have been rationalized. Far from whittling it away, understanding only increases our awe. As John Ruskin wrote in 1856: 'Mountains are the beginning and the end of all natural scenery.'

As we move northwards, we pass over the Tibetan Plateau, 'the loftiest of the world's plateau, with an average height of 16,000 feet,' as Arthur Holmes described it; and, he might have added, one of the toughest of human habitats – a cold brownish waste, a vaster version of the Altiplano, where morose yaks take the place of alpaca. There's little enough sign of human habitation from above. But what caused Tibet's elevation? Arthur Holmes seemed to have no trouble in believing that 'the ancestral Indian shield . . . instead of staging a head-on collision was drawn downwards to continue its unfinished journey beneath the area that has become Tibet', thus doubling the thickness of the light continental crust. 'The isostatic uplift was the simplest of the many tectonic consequences of this stupendous encounter,' he continued: it floated up, if you like. Tibet does, indeed, show crustal thickening, but here the problems begin. The rate of uplift of Tibet to its present height about eight million years ago was calculated as just too fast to be accountable to 'bouncing up': something else must be involved. That something else has proved controversial. One theory, evolved by Professors Platt and England (geologists at the universities of London and Oxford, respectively), has found favour recently. They proposed that at a critical stage in crustal thickening, a deep convection current in the asthenosphere removed, or polished away, part of the thickened, and relatively cool, continental 'root'. The cooler volume was thus replaced by hot asthenosphere, and this is what gave a thermal boost to the elevation, a helping hand to Tibet's ascent. It is all so deep and far away, how could you ever know? Some of the predictions of the effects on the basin far above, such as faults around its perimeter, proved consistent with the theory. If correct, it should change our understanding of certain ancient mountain belts, too, and I should be obliged to rewrite some of what lies above. Time's tapestry is, after all, woven to a common design.

As a postscript to the story of Tibet, it has recently been suggested that the elevation of the high plateau eight million years ago was responsible for modifying the climate. The atmospheric circulation was changed sufficiently to produce the current Indian Summer Monsoon. The knock-on effect was to increase the rate of erosion of the Himalayan flanks – and this is ultimately reflected in the Bengal Fan extending oceanwards 2500 kilometres from the subcontinent, where the mineralogy of the deep-sea sediments changed at exactly this time. Geological processes make mountains, and mountains make weather patterns. Weather patterns influence erosion. Erosion produces the rocks of the next Wilson cycle. Everything connects.

We have dallied too long. We must move northwards as fast as we can across the terrible Takla Makan desert. The Himalayas have stolen all the water that might have irrigated this arid region. As a

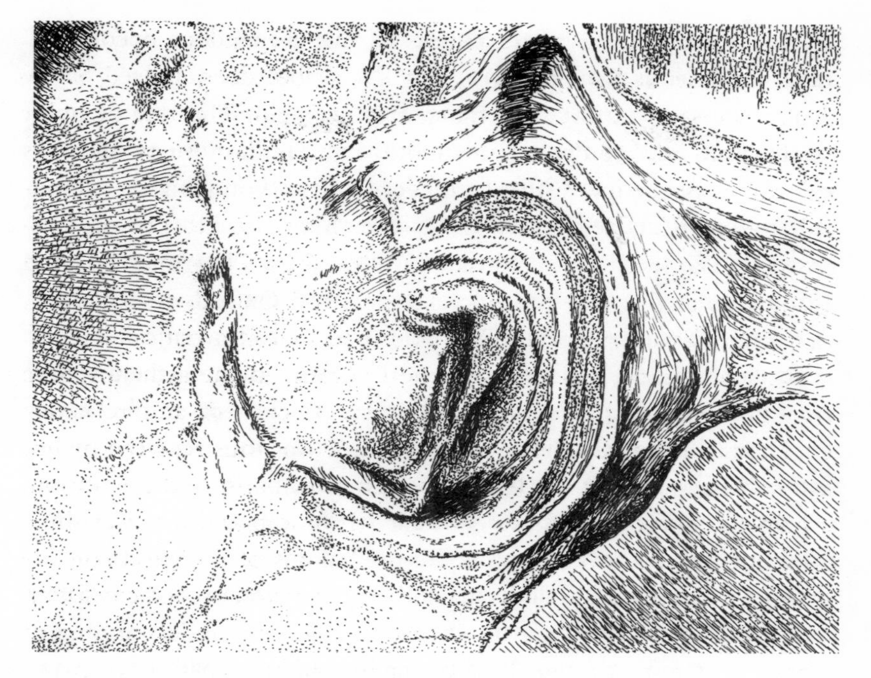

The 'Great Ear of China', Lop Nor, from above.

result, it is virtually lifeless. We can make out the 'Great Ear of China', Lop Nor, to the east: from above, this salt lake does indeed closely resemble an ear eighty kilometres (fifty miles) across. Its outlines are sculpted in ridges of crystallized salt and sand. The Chinese use this desolate place to test nuclear weapons. Further to the north lies another gigantic ridge, the Tien Shan range; below it is the Turfan depression, the second lowest place on Earth at 150 metres below sea-level. Cultivation of this remote area has been happening since the time of Christ, using water derived from the melting snows in the 'Celestial Mountains' beyond, streams that all too soon drain down into the subsurface. The local farmers tap into the aquifers using horizontal wells called *karez*. The Great Silk Road* ran along

* There were eventually three silk roads running from west to east, of which the one running by Turfan was the most important.

the north side of the Turfan Depression. Camel caravans once carried bales of precious stuff to Europe in the shadow of the Tien Shan: there was good money to be made in the middle of nowhere. A railway line follows the same route today. Marco Polo passed this way on his journey to China from Venice in 1271–5, flashing the seal of the Great Khan to ensure he would receive hospitality everywhere he went. We see that the fretted surface of Tien Shan spreads out into great alluvial fans both to the north and south as if its burden of rocky outcrop were too much for the range to bear and it wished to shrug off as much as possible. The Tien Shan range formed *within* the Asian plate as a series of mighty thrusts following an old line of weakness. These faults, like everything else, run east–west; they bring ancient Ordovician rocks to the surface, which even carry fossils of my own animals – trilobites. Ultimately, the range was yet another consequence of the continuing northward push of India, another spasm of the crust. What seems mighty on a human scale is but a shrug of the lithosphere, a tic in time.

We must turn westwards to follow the old Silk Road through the mountains of Tadjikistan and Uzbekistan. The geology of this area is immensely complicated: a collage of bits and pieces of geology sewn together over hundreds of millions of years. The geological map is a kaleidoscope of different colours, patterned like a tie-dye T-shirt. We pass above Samarkand, the 'Rome of the East', capital city of Tamerlane the Great (1336–1405) and where glazed tiles reach their geometrical apotheosis. Before we pass further westwards it is worth reflecting that the great warrior's grandson, Ulugbek, made Samarkand into one of the scientific centres of the Middle Ages, at a time when much western intellectual endeavour was still devoted to theological minutiae. Ulugbek himself taught mathematics. If it had not been for these Middle Eastern bridges between classical and Renaissance science, who knows if geology as a discipline would have been born at all?

Westwards again, and what might be an ocean basin appears to the north. The Caspian Sea is, in fact, the most extensive freshwater body in the world. It, too, owes its existence to the heave of tectonics, for it was once connected southwards to the ocean until the elevation of the land to the south landlocked it. Seals trapped there evolved into an endemic species and there are hundreds of species of crustaceans found nowhere else. Thus geology and biological evolution collaborated in adding richness to our planet. Everything connects. We can see where the Volga River empties into the north of the Caspian, clouding the clear water with sediment. One day, even the Caspian, mightiest of ponds, will silt up. And northwards again a glimpse of the end of the Ural chain comes almost as a shock after the transverse grain of the world we have followed ever since the Himalayas; for this range points north–south. It is the line marking a dead Wilson cycle, the coming-together of Eurasia prior to the full assembly of Pangaea. If Europe had a geological definition, this would mark the line of its eastern boundary, where a vanished ocean still leaves a legacy of copper mines and smashed remants of mid-ocean ridges 400 million years old. How different a journey around the world would have been that long ago, how unfamiliar the geography; only the motor of the plates would have worked in the same fashion.

By now, we have left the influence of India, only to fall under the sway of Arabia and Africa. There seems to be no end to the mountains. The northward movement of Africa – or its outriders – brings back memories of the Alps. We are now moving towards the shuffling and grinding edges of the plates that shaped Europe. As we cross in the shadow of the Caucasus between the Caspian and the Black Sea, Mount Ararat, or Agri Dagi (5165 metres), lies to the south. In the biblical account, the Ark came to shore here after the Flood, and we may remember how Eduard Suess spent so much of his great book providing a historical (and geological) explanation for the Flood as a massive incursion of the sea, garnering his evidence from the Epic of Gilgamesh. Only ten years ago, the remains of the Ark were supposed to have been discovered on Mount Ararat: to a geologist, however, the claimed 'Ark' was obviously a syncline composed of well-bedded sedimentary rocks. And now before us lies that most perverse of oceans, the Black Sea, which narrowly avoids being landlocked and whose shimmering surface belies its poisoned depths deprived of oxygen, so poor is its circulation. A much more recent explanation of the biblical Flood comes to mind – the breaching of the narrow entrance into the Black Sea that dramatically filled it with salt water, raising its surface level with that of the Mediterranean and drowning shores once rich with life. This is an intellectual territory as murky as the dark depths of the Black Sea itself, a place where history, mythology, and geology compete for the hearts and minds of humankind. To some, a cherished myth is still worth more than an unvarnished fact. Time has not yet delivered its judgement on the Black Sea flood, let alone whether it can really be identified with the Flood of Gilgamesh and the Bible. We know that there *were* catastrophes in the geological past that belie Charles Lyell's most extreme view of uniformity of process through geological time; equally, we know that sifting the evidence to understand the past requires rigour and experiment that are unquestionably Lyellian in spirit. Black Sea flood or not, we know only too well that great faults take up the stresses in the crust as it moves along the southern shore of the Black Sea; it is shifting in juddering, and sometimes catastrophic, steps eastwards relative to the rest of Turkey to the south.

Let us speed above the Dardanelles into the Mediterranean Sea and southwards through the Aegean. A pattern of islands set in a sparkling sea seems so intimate compared with what we have seen in the great ranges and wastes of the world, yet it was here that the adventurers of classical times faced monsters and tempests. Fossil bones became the limbs of giants: part of the appeal of mythic explanations lies in their proximity to our human concerns, our intimate history. It might seem to rob these islands of their individuality to learn that they are tipped blocks of limestone strata, which, in turn, are part of a response to north-dipping subduction along the Hellenic Arc lying to the south of Crete.* On the contrary, when you clamber along shore-lines shaped by the sea, looking down through the clear water at rocks that are bored by clams, like those that violated the

* In the jargon, a back-arc basin.

columns at the 'Temple' of Serapis, you rejoice in the intimate variations upon general geological processes. Geology may provide the foundations and the structure, but there are infinite possibilities for weather and vegetation to supply the decoration. Further to the east, we remember that Cyprus carries obducted ocean floor running along the length of the island; but does it not add to our enjoyment of the richness of the world to know that Mount Olympus itself is a mass of ultramafic rocks transported from the depths of the crust, that the home of the gods is truly a production of Hades?

As for the Mediterranean Sea itself, we know enough by now to be aware that the cradle of western civilization is really an unreliable, shifting nursery. Other seas have come and gone here, Suess' Tethys most notable among them, and one day the current sea will die. In a reverse of the Black Sea scenario, the Mediterranean almost dried out in the Miocene, when the narrow link to the Atlantic Ocean was temporarily sealed by tectonics. The sea evaporated under the fierce sun, throwing down huge quantities of salt, which still remain locked away under the current sea-floor. Imagine if we had taken our journey then: the Takla Makan desert would have been as nothing to the cracked and glistening wasteland beneath us, with patches of treacherous *sabkha* waiting to engulf any beast that dared to try its luck in crossing. The flood of floods would have happened when the dam broke, the force of a thousand Niagaras crashing through the Straits of Gibraltar, tumbling fish and mollusc willy-nilly into what would become their new home. Then the waters settled; what had been mountains not many months before took on a new life as islands; and the scene was laid for proud Odysseus and all the wrangling gods on their Olympian heights.

Nor can we see the two plates comprising the eastern part of the Mediterranean region – or microplates as they should be called, because they are so much smaller than the vast slabs in the Atlantic and Pacific Oceans. They are termed the Adriatic and Anatolian microplates, the Adriatic Sea being immediately west of Italy, and Anatolia comprising a large part of Asia Minor. Their current movements are still dictated by the northward movement of Africa towards

Europe, variously twisting and thinning the crust. The African plate continues northwards beyond its continental coastline, feeding into a subduction zone along the Cyprian and Hellenic arcs south of Turkey and Greece and the Calabrian arc south of Italy's 'sole'. The latter supplies magma to the active volcanoes in the Aeolian islands, which lie, where they should, above the subduction zone. Meanwhile, the Adriatic plate is rotating anticlockwise relative to the European plate and, as one consequence, Italy is still dangerously seismically active: frescos tumble, mudslides bury villages. The collision front between the Adriatic plate and 'Europe' lies under the eastern part of Italy, running along the length of the 'boot'. The relative movement between the Adriatic plate and Europe has also caused deep fault systems to migrate, which in turn has made the volcanoes related to them progressively appear to the south over the last five million years. It is a complicated piece of the world. You have to envisage masses of the earth jostling one another, twisting and sliding, as well as subducting; even in some places – like the Tyrrhenian Sea – locally stretching, and all within the crushing embrace of the great continents to north and south.

The time approaches to complete our Puckish aerial circumnavigation. So much there was to see, so much remains unseen. We turn northwards towards Calabria, the toe of Italy; the elongate triangle of the island of Sicily lies to our left. That plume of smoke streaming out like a wispy tress of dark hair must be emanating from Mount Etna – the first volcano actually in process of erupting that we have encountered on our long journey. Etna celebrated the new millennium by springing vigorously to life, something it has done with infuriating unpredictability since historical records began, and many millennia before that. In 1669, it destroyed the western part of the large town of Catania, whose castle was moated by erupting lava. In 1971, the volcano even destroyed the observatory built to predict its behaviour, an example of nature cocking a snook if ever there was one. During the 1992 eruption it was estimated that 240 million cubic metres of lava were spewed forth between the months of March and May. In 2001, it was the turn of the village of Sapienza. Fortunately,

Etna's lava moves slowly enough for sensible evacuation procedures to be observed and also allow attempts to divert it from its apparently inexorable course. In the midst of the latest eruption, an eyewitness recorded the smell of brimstone mixing with the aromatic whiff of burning pine resin, like a medical treatment from the time of Paracelsus.

Northwards along the Italian coast towards Naples, lower now, and to the east we see the wooded slopes of the Apennines, our last mountain chain. In spirit, we have almost come back to Glarus, for the spine of Italy is a mass of piled nappes, composed overwhelmingly of Mesozoic and Tertiary strata. The nappes came from what is now the west, while to the north-east the strata are comparatively undisturbed. Italy somehow seems out of place on the map of Europe – less a boot, more a sore thumb sticking out, away from the east–west trend of the Alps. How could this have happened as a result of an African–European *rapprochement*? Perhaps it is fitting to end with a puzzle. One theory promulgated by Italian geologists generates the orogen by swivelling a 'proto-Italy' outwards from a 'normal' Alpine position. You have to imagine the 'boot' starting adjacent to France, on a line with the Alpine chain, then swinging out at its 'knee' from this original position before the Oligocene, and finally, gradually, attaining its current position, all the while piling up nappes, with Corsica and Sardinia being left behind in the process. However it formed, the Italian peninsula is a scrambled mass of geology, and a rich resource. We think of churches floored with slabs of *ammonitico rosso* – a stone both warmly red and mottled with a subtlety no industrial process could duplicate, with every now and again the spiral ghost of the ammonite fossil that gave it its name. We think of marble- and limestone-clad side-chapels dedicated to the saint of choice; and, from Carrara in the north of the country, the white marble baked from the purest limestone from which Michelangelo made his unequalled sculptures: the progeny of tectonics transformed into art by the hand of genius.

* * *

See, there is Vesuvius below us now. The fug of Naples must have been blown clear away today. The wrecked courses of old lava flows can be seen tumbling and skulking among the trees. It is not difficult to imagine another one – perhaps a pyroclastic surge – wiping away urban man's impertinent roads and buildings. And there is Pompeii, looking from this height like some unfathomable board game, exhumed proof of our vulnerability. The duration of our present version of civilization, and all the versions that preceded it, is as one day in the life of the volcano, and the life of that volcano but a single breath in the life of the earth. Look, the Phlegrean Fields lie beyond the city (can you feel the magma rising deep beneath them?): that tranquil crater-lake was once the entrance to Hades. With what you now know, your mind's eye might follow Persephone downwards to the seat of the tectonic plates. And there is Baia at the end of the bay, where, Eduard Suess tells us, 'Nero attempted to drown his mother in a treacherous boat' and Pliny made the observations in AD 79 that marked the beginnings of geology and the death of his uncle. Earthwards now, and we can see the seafront at Pozzuoli. There are some local fishermen dining alfresco on *fusilli* dressed with tiny squid and such fish as the nets brought in. And beyond them is the 'Temple' of Serapis, where my story began. A few tourists wander about the ancient market-place: perhaps one or two of them may wonder about the pitted discoloration of the great columns that dominate the square. We have come a long way.

Life on a plate.

WORLD VIEW

We shall not cease from exploration
And the end of all our exploring
Will be to arrive where we started
And know the place for the first time.

T. S. Eliot *Little Gidding*

PICTURE CREDITS

The author and publishers gratefully acknowledge the following sources for permission to reproduce illustrations:

INTEGRATED ILLUSTRATIONS

p. 2 *Bay of Naples*, engraved by E. Benjamin from an original by G. Arnald, *c* 1830. *Mary Evans Picture Library.*

p. 10 Inside the cone of Vesuvius. Author's own collection.

p. 20 The 'Temple of Serapis' from the Frontispiece of Lyell's *Principles of Geology*, first edition, 1830.

p. 23 *'The Light of Science dispelling the darkness which covered the World.'* Drawn by Henry de la Beche.

p. 36 Plinian style of eruption of Vesuvius, in 1822. Drawn by George Scrope. Illustration from *De Re Metallica*, 1556, Georgius Agricola. *Mary Evans Picture Library.*

pp. 40–41 View of Honolulu, from Manley Hopkins, *Hawaii: The Past, Present and Future of its Island Kingdom* (London, 1862). *Bishop Museum, Honolulu, Hawai'i.*

p. 47 Sketch map of the Hawaiian chain. *Ray Burrows.*

p. 53 Frozen lava: Pele's tears, Pele's hair, resting on pumice. *Photo © Rob Francis.*

p. 81 HMS *Challenger*.

p. 100 The Lochseiten section. *Ray Burrows.*

p. 101 Pebbles elongated by Alpine deformation. *Ray Burrows.*

p. 103 Fossil fish from the flysch at Engi, as described by Louis Agassiz. *Photo courtesy of Peter Forey.*

p. 107 Albert Heim, with his mountain models, 1905. *Photo Image Archive of the ETH-Bibliothek, Zürich.*

p. 110 The Glarus nappe. Illustrated in *Principles of Physical Geology*, Arthur Holmes.

p. 250 Portrait of Georgius Agricola from *De Re Metallica* , 1556. *British Library/Heritage-Images.*

p. 251 Bringing ore from the mines. Illlustration from *De Re Metallica* , 1556. Mary Evans Picture Library.

p. 258 The Wollaston medal, Geological Society of London.

p. 267 Sluicing at Number 2 Claim at Anvil Creek, Nome, Alaska. *Photo by Hegg in* Souvenir of Nome.

p. 285 A granite cross in Cornwall. *Author's own collection.*

p. 292 The Varsican batholith, illustrated in *Principles of Physical Geology*, Arthur Holmes.

p. 300 Migmatites in Precambrian rocks. *Ray Burrows.*

p. 308 China clay workings. Author's own collection.

p. 312 San Andreas and associated faults. Author's own collection.

pp. 314–315 The aftermath of the San Francisco earthquake, 1906. *Courtesy National Information Service for Earthquake Engineering, University of California, Berkeley.*

p. 336 The Pony Express Trail, Great Basin, Nevada. *Author's own collection.*

p. 360 Fossil stromatolite from Precambrian rocks of eastern Siberia. *Photo © Natural History Museum, London.*

p. 367 Rodinia, late Precambrian supercontinent. Author's own collection.

p. 394 The Kolb family in Rust's cable car. Photo © Emery Kolb collection, Cline Library, North Arizona University.

p. 395 Hut designed by Mary Colter at the Phantom Ranch. *Ray Burrows.*

p. 403 The deep structure of the Earth. *Ray Burrows.*

p. 419 The atomic structure of perovskite. *Ray Burrows.*

p. 438 Cretaceous chalk, magnified. *Ray Burrows.*

p. 444 Crater Lake, Oregon. *Ray Burrows.*

p. 449 Alfred Russel Wallace.

p. 458 The Amazon © *NASA*

p. 462 The Red Sea © *NASA*

p. 467 The 'Great Ear of China', Lop Nor, from above. *Ray Burrows.*

p. 475 Life on a plate. *Ray Burrows.*

COLOUR PLATES

I

p. 1 Satellite view of the Bay of Naples © *NASA*.
Label showing View of Vesuvius from a Sorrento hotel. *Mary Evans Picture Library*.

p. 2 Limestone cliffs , Capri. *Author's own collection*.
Figures overwhelmed by the eruption of Vesuvius A.D. 79 at Pompeii. *Author's own collection*.
Mosaic floor at Pompeii, Casa del Fauno. *Photograph © AKG London/Eric Lessing*.

p. 3 Lake Agnano, Phlegrean Fields, from *Campi Phlegraei*, by William Hamilton, illustrated by Piero Fabris, 1776.
The Lyell Medal of the Geological Society of London.
Arthur Holmes. *Photo courtesy of the Geological Society of London*.
The earliest seismograph, designed by Ascanio Filomarino, from the old observatory on Vesuvius.

p. 4 Feathered cloak, probably belonging to King Kalani'opu'u, in the collection of the Bishop Museum, Honolulu, Hawai'i. *Photo Ben Patnoi*.
Pahoehoe lava, the Big Island, Hawai'i. *Photo © Rob Francis*.
The Lava Rock Café in Volcano, the Big Island, Hawai'i
A house engulfed by lava flows, the Big Island. *Photo © Rob Francis*.

p. 5 Crusty a'a lava by a roadside on the Big Island. *Author's own collection*.
Thurston Lava Tube, Volcanoes National Park, the Big Island. *Author's own collection*.

p. 6 Recent lava flows in Volcanoes National Park, the Big Island.
Black sand beach, with Hawaiian green turtles. Author's own collection.

p. 7 Na Pali cliffs on Kaua'i, Hawai'i. *Photo © Rob Francis*.
Waimea Canyon, Kaua'i. *Author's own collection*.

p. 8 Coral reef, Fiji. *Photo © Rob Francis*.
Carbonate chimney, Mid-Atlantic Ridge. *Photo © Mitch Elend/ University of Washington*.
The Blue Lagoon, Svartsengi, Iceland. *Photo © Rob Francis*.

II

p. 1 Weissbad, Canton of Appenzell, eastern Switzerland. *Photo Image Archive of the ETH-Bibliothek, Zürich.*
The base of the Glarus Nappe at the Lochseiten Section in Switzerland. *Author's own collection.*

p. 2 Slate quarry at Engi, near Elms, in the Sernft Valley, Switzerland. *Author's own collection.*
Bridge crossing the Insubric Line, near Pianazzo, Switzerland. *Author's own collection.*

p. 3 The Glarus 'Thrust', from Flimerstein. *Photo courtesy of Geoff Milnes.*
Summit of the old San Benardino Pass, Switzerland. *Author's own collection.*

p. 4 Satellite photo of the Jura Mountains. *Image courtesy of Earth Sciences and Image Analysis Laboratory, NASA Johnson Space Center (http://eol.jsc.nasa.gov)*

p. 5 The Oman ophiolite. *Photo courtesy of Mike Welland.*
South Wind, Clear Sky, from Thirty-six Views of Mount Fuji, Hokusai, *c.* 1830. *Photo: British Library/Heritage Images.*

p. 6 The Narrows, St John's Newfoundland
Almandine garnets. *Photo © Geoscience.*
Bell Island, Newfoundland. *Photo courtesy of Reg Durdle.*

p. 7 Western coast of Newfoundland. *Author's own collection.*
Rocks at Cow Head, western Newfoundland. *Photo courtesy of Robin Cocks.*

p. 8 The Blue Ridge Mountains, USA. *Photo © Jason Hawkes Library.*
An Ordovician trilobite fossil, *Pricyclopyge. Author's own collection.*

III

p. 1 View of Snowdon. *Photo © National Trust Photo Library/Joe Cornish.*
Belvedere Castle, Central Park, New York. *Photo © DK Images.*

p. 2 Silver thaler. *Photo © Kunsthistorisches Museum.*
Marie Curie in her laboratory. *Photo: Mary Evans Picture Library.*

p. 3 Uncut ruby. *Photo © GeoScience Features Picture Library/A.Fisher.*
Wollastonite crystals. *Photo © Natural History Museum, London.*
The Portland Vase. *Photo © Natural History Museum, London.*
The Wicklow Nugget. *Photo © Natural History Museum, London.*

p. 4 The Ajanta temples, the Deccan traps, India. *Photo © Rob Francis.*
Temple at Ellora, Deccan Traps, India. *Photo © Rob Francis.*
Sculpture at Ellora. *Photo © Rob Francis.*
Murals in the Ajanta caves. *Photo © Rob Francis.*
p. 5 Bowerman's Nose, Dartmoor. *Photo © National Trust Photo Library/David Dixon*
Polished Dartmoor granite. *Photo © John Moorby.*
p. 6 St Michael's Mount, Cornwall. *Photo © Caroline Jones.*
Lava lamp. *Photo © John Moorby.*
Wheal Coats, north Cornwall. *Author's own collection.*
p. 7 Mount Kinabalu, Indonesia. *Photo © Rob Francis.*
The collapsed Hanshin expressway, Kobe. *Photo © Topfoto.*
p. 8 San Andreas Fault, California. *Photo courtesy National Information Service for Earthquake Engineering, University of California, Berkeley.*

IV

p. 1 Death Valley, California. *Photo © Rob Francis.*
Eureka, Nevada. *Author's own collection.*
Basin and Range, Nevada. *Photo © Rob Francis.*
pp. 2–3 Great Rift Valley in Kenya. *Photo © Corbis.*
Lake Natron, African Rift Valley. *Photo © Rob Francis.*
p. 4 Scourie Dyke. *Photo courtesy Graham Park.*
Kinlochwe Thrust. *Photo courtesy Graham Park.*
Torridonian rocks, Liathach, northwest Scotland. *Photo courtesy Graham Park.*
p. 5 Crofter's cottage, South Harris. *Photo courtesy Graham Park.*
Lewisian Gneiss, south of Loch Tollie. *Photo courtesy Graham Park.*
Banded ironstone. *Photo © Geoscience Features Picture Library.*
p. 6 The Grand Canyon. *Photo © Rob Francis.*
Mules on Bright Angel Trail, The Grand Canyon. *Photo courtesy Jerry Ortner.*
Rock formations in the Grand Canyon. *Ray Burrows.*
p. 7 The Inner Canyon, showing the Colorado River. *Author's own collection.*
Winter at Phantom Ranch. *Author's own collection.*

High Coast World Heritage Site, Sweden. *Photo courtesy County Administration of Vasternorrland/Metriä.*

p. 8 Sulphur miner, Kawah Ijen volcano, Java. *Photo © Rob Francis.*
Blue Mountains, Australia. *Photo © Rob Francis.*
Mount Cook, New Zealand. *Photo © Rob Francis.*
Atacama Desert, Chile. *Photo © Rob Francis.*

FURTHER READING

Aubouin, J. *Geosynclines*. Elsevier (1995).

Bancroft, P. 'Gem and Mineral Treasures'. *Western Enterprises/Mineralogical Record* (1984).

Beus, S. S. and Morales, M. (eds) *Grand Canyon Geology*. 2nd edition. New York, Oxford University Press (2003).

Blundell, D. J. and Scott, A. C. (eds). 'Lyell: The Past is the Key to the Present'. Special Publications of the Geological Society of London 143 (1998).

Campbell, W. H. *Earth Magnetism: A Guided Tour through Magnetic Fields*. Academic Press (2000).

Craig, G. Y. and Hull, J. H. 'James Hutton – Present and Future'. Special paper of the Geological Society of London 150 (1999).

Condie, K. C. *Plate Tectonics and Crustal Evolution*. 4th edition. Heinemann (1997).

Dolnick, E. *Down the Great Unknown: John Wesley Powell's Journey of Discovery and Tragedy through the Grand Canyon*. HarperCollins (2002).

Drury, S. *Stepping Stones: The Making of our Home World*. Oxford University Press (1999).

Du Toit, A. L. *The Geology of South Africa*. 3rd Edition. Oliver and Boyd (1954).

Eide E. A. (ed.) *Batlas: Mid Norway Plate Reconstruction Atlas with Global and Atlantic Perspective*. Geological Survey of Norway (2002).

Ernst, W. G. (ed.) *Earth Systems: Processes and Issues*. Cambridge University Press (2000).

Fiero, W. *Geology of the Great Basin*. University of Nevada Press (1986).

Fisher, R. V., Hecken, G. *Volcanoes: Crucibles of Change*. Princeton University Press (1997).

Fortey, R. A. *Life: An Unauthorised Biography*. Flamingo (1998).

Glen. W. *Continental Drift and Plate Tectonics*. Merrill (1975).

Grayson, D. K. *The Desert's Past: A Natural Prehistory of the Great Basin*. Smithsonian Institution (1993).

Greene, M. T. *Geology in the Nineteenth Century*. Cornell University Press (1982).

Hallam, A. *Great Geological Controversies*. 2nd edition. Oxford University Press (1989).

Hallam, A. *A Revolution in the Earth Sciences: From Continental Drift to Plate Tectonics*. Oxford, Clarendon Press (1973).

Hazlett, R. W. and Hyndman, D. W. *Roadside Geology of Hawai'i*. Mountain Press (1996).

Hill, M. Gold: *A Californian Story*. University of California Press (1999).

Holmes, A. *Principles of Physical Geology*. 2nd edition. Nelson (1964).

Jacobs, J. A. *Deep Interior of the Earth*. Chapman and Hall (1992).

Keary, P. (ed.) *The Encyclopedia of the Solid Earth Sciences*. Blackwell (1993).

Keary, P. and Vine, F. J. *Global Tectonics*. 2nd edition. Blackwell (1996).

Kilburn, C. and McGuire, W. *Italian Volcanoes*. Terra (2001).

Koyi, H. A. and Mancktelow, N. S. (eds). 'Tectonic Modelling: A Volume in Honour of Hans Ramberg'. Memoir of the Geological Society of America 193 (2001).

Kunzig, R. *Mapping the Deep*. Sort of Books (2000).

Lewis, C. *The Dating Game: One Man's Search for the Age of the Earth*. Cambridge University Press (2000).

McDonald, G. A. *Volcanoes in the Sea: The Geology of Hawaii*. University of Hawaii Press (1979).

McGuire, W. and Kilburn, C. *Volcanoes of the World. Thunder Bay Press* (1997).

Menard, H. W. *Geology, Resources and Society*. W. H. Freeman (1974).

Mussett, A. E. and Khan, M. A. *Looking into the Earth*. Cambridge University Press (2000).

National Museum of Australia. *Gold and Civilisation*. National Museum of Australia Press (2000).

Nisbet, E. G. *The Young Earth: An Introduction to Archaean Geology*. Allen and Unwin (1987).
O'Donoghue, M. and Joyner, L. *Identification of Gemstones*. Butterworth-Heinemann (2002).
Oreskes, N. (ed.) *Plate Tectonics: An Insider's History of the Modern Theory of the Earth*. Westview Press, Boulder Col. (2001).
Penhallurick, R. D. *Tin in Antiquity*. Institute of Metals (1986).
Peltier, W. R. (ed.) *Mantle Convection: Plate Tectonics and Global Dynamics*. Gordon and Breach (1989).
Pfiffner, O. A. et al. (eds) *Deep Structure of the Swiss Alps*. Basel, Birkhauser (1995).
Sparks, R. S. J. et al. *Volcanic Plumes*. John Wiley & Sonbs (1997).
Powell, R. E., Weldon, R. J. and Matti, J. C. (eds). *The San Andreas Fault System*. Geological Society of America (1993).
Repchek, J. *The Man Who Found Time: James Hutton and the Discovery of the Earth's Antiquity*. Simon and Schuster (2003).
Suess, E. *The Face of the Earth*. Oxford, Clarendon Press (1904–24).
Walker, G. *Snowball Earth*. Bloomsbury (2003).
Windley, B. F. *The Evolving Continents*. 3rd edition. Wiley (1995).

INDEX

Page references in *italics* refers to illustrations

RGS GUILDFORD MALLISON
LIBRARY